E. M. FORSTER

E. M.
FORSTER

E.M. FORSTER

Where Angels Fear to Tread

The Longest Journey

A Room with a View

Howards End

A Passage to India

Heinemann/Octopus

Where Angels Fear to Tread first published in Great Britain in 1905 by
Edward Arnold Ltd.
The Longest Journey first published in Great Britain in 1907 by
Edward Arnold Ltd.
A Room with a View first published in Great Britain in 1908 by
Edward Arnold Ltd.
Howards End first published in Great Britain in 1910 by
Edward Arnold Ltd.
A Passage to India first published in Great Britain in 1924 by
Edward Arnold Ltd.

This edition first published in 1978 jointly by

William Heinemann Limited
15–16 Queen Street
London W1

Secker and Warburg Limited
14 Carlisle Street
London W1

and

Octopus Books Limited
59 Grosvenor Street
London W1

ISBN 0 905712 22 6

Inside photographs reproduced by kind permission of
the Library, Kings College Cambridge, the Italian State Tourist Office,
the Director of the India Office Library and Records
and Popperfoto Photographic Agency
Jacket – Mansell Collection

Printed in Great Britain by
Jarrold and Sons Ltd, Norwich

CONTENTS

Where Angels
Fear to Tread

Chapter One

They were all at Charing Cross to see Lilia off—Philip, Harriet, Irma, Mrs Herriton herself. Even Mrs Theobald, squired by Mr Kingcroft, had braved the journey from Yorkshire to bid her only daughter good-bye. Miss Abbott was likewise attended by numerous relatives, and the sight of so many people talking at once and saying such different things caused Lilia to break into ungovernable peals of laughter.

'Quite an ovation,' she cried, sprawling out of her first-class carriage. 'They'll take us for royalty. Oh, Mr Kingcroft, get us foot-warmers.'

The good-natured young man hurried away, and Philip, taking his place, flooded her with a final stream of advice and injunctions—where to stop, how to learn Italian, when to use mosquito-nets, what pictures to look at. 'Remember,' he concluded, 'that it is only by going off the track that you get to know the country. See the little towns—Gubbio, Pienza, Cortona, San Gimignano, Monteriano. And don't, let me beg you, go with that awful tourist idea that Italy's only a museum of antiquities and art. Love and understand the Italians, for the people are more marvellous than the land.'

'How I wish you were coming, Philip,' she said, flattered at the unwonted notice her brother-in-law was giving her.

'I wish I were.' He could have managed it without great difficulty, for his career at the Bar was not so intense as to prevent occasional holidays. But his family disliked his continual visits to the Continent, and he himself often found pleasure in the idea that he was too busy to leave town.

'Good-bye, dear every one. What a whirl!' She caught sight of her little daughter Irma, and felt that a touch of maternal solemnity was required. 'Good-bye, darling. Mind you're always good, and do what Granny tells you.'

She referred not to her own mother, but to her mother-in-law, Mrs Herriton, who hated the title of Granny.

Irma lifted a serious face to be kissed, and said cautiously, 'I'll do my best.'

'She is sure to be good,' said Mrs Herriton, who was standing pensively a little out of the hubbub. But Lilia was already calling to Miss Abbott, a tall, grave, rather nice-looking young lady who was conducting her adieus in a more decorous manner on the platform.

'Caroline, my Caroline! Jump in, or your chaperon will go off without you.'

And Philip, whom the idea of Italy always intoxicated, had started again, telling her of the supreme moments of her coming journey—the Campanile of Airolo, which would burst on her when she emerged from the St Gotthard tunnel, presaging the future; the view of the Ticino and Lago Maggiore as the train climbed the slopes of Monte Cenere; the view of Lugano, the view of Como—Italy gathering thick around her now—the arrival at her first resting-place, when, after long driving through dark and dirty streets, she should at last behold, amid the roar of trams and the glare of arc lamps, the buttresses of the cathedral of Milan.

'Handkerchiefs and collars,' screamed Harriet, 'in my inlaid box! I've lent you my inlaid box.'

'Good old Harry!' She kissed every one again, and there was a moment's silence. They all smiled steadily, excepting Philip, who was choking in the fog, and old Mrs Theobald, who had begun to cry. Miss Abbot got into the carriage. The guard himself shut the door, and told Lilia that she would be all right. Then the train moved, and they all moved with it a couple of steps, and waved their handkerchiefs, and uttered cheerful little cries. At that moment Mr Kingcroft reappeared, carrying a foot-warmer by both ends, as if it was a tea-tray. He was sorry that he was too late, and called out in a quavering voice, 'Good-bye, Mrs Charles. May you enjoy yourself, and may God bless you.'

Lilia smiled and nodded, and then the absurd position of the foot-warmer overcame her, and she began to laugh again.

'Oh, I am so sorry,' she cried back, 'but you do look so funny. Oh, you all look so funny waving! Oh, pray!' And laughing helplessly, she was carried out into the fog.

'High spirits to begin so long a journey,' said Mrs Theobald, dabbing her eyes.

Mr Kingcroft solemnly moved his head in token of agreement. 'I wish,' said he, 'that Mrs Charles had gotten the foot-warmer. These London porters won't take heed to a country chap.'

'But you did your best,' said Mrs Herriton. 'And I think it simply noble of you to have brought Mrs Theobald all the way here on such a day as this.' Then, rather hastily, she shook hands, and left him to take Mrs Theobald all the way back.

Sawston, her own home, was within easy reach of London, and they were not late for tea. Tea was in the dining-room, with an egg for Irma, to keep up the child's spirits. The house seemed strangely quiet after a fortnight's bustle, and their conversation was spasmodic and subdued. They wondered whether the travellers had got to Folkestone, whether it would be at all rough, and if so what would happen to poor Miss Abbott.

'And, Granny, when will the old ship get to Italy?' asked Irma.

'"Grandmother," dear; not "Granny,"' said Mrs Herriton, giving her a kiss. 'And we say "a boat" or "a steamer," not "a ship." Ships have sails. And mother won't go all the way by sea. You look at the map of Europe, and you'll see why. Harriet, take her. Go with Aunt Harriet, and she'll show you the map.'

'Right-o!' said the little girl, and dragged the reluctant Harriet into the library. Mrs Herriton and her son were left alone. There was immediately confidence between them.

'Here beginneth the New Life,' said Philip.

'Poor child, how vulgar!' murmured Mrs Herriton. 'It's surprising that she isn't worse. But she has got a look of poor Charles about her.'

'And—alas, alas!—a look of old Mrs Theobald. What appalling apparition was that? I did think the lady was bedridden as well as imbecile. Why ever did she come?'

'Mr Kingcroft made her. I am certain of it. He wanted to see Lilia again, and this was the only way.'

'I hope he is satisfied. I did not think my sister-in-law distinguished herself in her farewells.'

Mrs Herriton shuddered. 'I mind nothing, so long as she has gone—and gone with Miss Abbott. It is mortifying to think that a widow of thirty-three requires a girl ten years younger to look after her.'

'I pity Miss Abbott. Fortunately one admirer is chained to England. Mr Kingcroft cannot leave the crops or the climate or something. I don't think, either, he improved his chances to-day. He, as well as Lilia, has the knack of being absurd in public.'

Mrs Herriton replied, 'When a man is neither well-bred, nor well-connected, nor handsome, nor clever, nor rich, even Lilia may discard him in time.'

'No. I believe she would take anyone. Right up to the last, when her boxes were packed, she was "playing" the chinless curate. Both the curates are chinless, but hers had the dampest hands. I came on them in the Park. They were speaking of the Pentateuch.'

'My dear boy! If possible, she has got worse and worse. It was your idea of Italian travel that saved us!'

Philip brightened at the little compliment. 'The odd part is that she was quite eager—always asking me for information; and of course I was very glad to give it. I admit she is a Philistine, appallingly ignorant, and her taste in art is false. Still, to have any taste at all is something. And I do believe that Italy really purifies and ennobles all who visit her. She is the school as well as the playground of the world. It is really to Lilia's credit that she wants to go there.'

'She would go anywhere,' said his mother, who had heard enough of the praises of Italy. 'I and Caroline Abbot had the greatest difficulty in dissuading her from the Riviera.'

'No, mother; no. She was really keen on Italy. This travel is quite a crisis for her.' He found the situation full of whimsical romance: there was something half-attractive, half-repellent in the thought of this vulgar woman journeying to places he loved and revered. Why should she not be transfigured? The same had happened to the Goths.

Mrs Herriton did not believe in romance, nor in transfiguration, nor in parallels from history, nor in anything else that may disturb domestic life. She adroitly changed the subject before Philip got excited. Soon Harriet returned, having given her lesson in geography. Irma went to bed early, and was tucked up by her grandmother. Then the two ladies worked and played cards. Philip read a book. And so they all settled down to their quiet profitable existence, and continued it without interruption through the winter.

It was now nearly ten years since Charles had fallen in love with Lilia Theobald because she was pretty, and during that time Mrs Herriton had hardly known a moment's rest. For six months she schemed to prevent the match, and when it had taken place she turned to another task—the supervision of her daughter-in-law. Lilia must be pushed through life without bringing discredit on the family into which she had married. She was aided by Charles, by her daughter Harriet, and, as soon as he was old enough, by the clever one of the family, Philip. The birth of Irma made things still more difficult. But fortunately old Mrs Theobald, who had attempted interference, began to break up. It was an effort to her to leave Whitby, and Mrs Herriton discouraged the effort as far as possible. That curious duel which is fought over every baby was fought and decided early. Irma belonged to her father's family, not to her mother's.

Charles died, and the struggle recommenced. Lilia tried to assert herself, and said that she should go to take care of Mrs Theobald. It required all Mrs Herriton's kindness to prevent her. A house was finally taken for her at Sawston, and there for three years she lived with Irma, continually subject to the refining influences of her late husband's family.

During one of her rare Yorkshire visits trouble began again. Lilia confided to a friend that she liked a Mr Kingcroft extremely, but that she was not exactly engaged to him. The news came round to Mrs Herriton, who at once wrote, begging for information, and pointing out that Lilia must either be engaged or not, since no intermediate state existed. It was a good letter, and flurried Lilia extremely. She left Mr Kingcroft without even the pressure of a rescue-party. She cried a great deal on her return to Sawston, and said she was very sorry. Mrs Herriton took the opportunity of speaking more seriously about the duties of widowhood and motherhood than she had ever done before. But somehow things never went easily after. Lilia would not settle down in her place among Sawston matrons. She was a bad house-keeper, always in the throes of some domestic crisis, which Mrs Herriton, who kept her servants for years, had to step across and adjust. She let Irma stop away from school for insufficient reasons, and she allowed her to wear rings. She learnt to bicycle, for the purpose of waking the place up, and coasted down the High Street one Sunday evening, falling off at the turn by the church. If she had not been a relative, it would have been entertaining. But even Philip, who in theory loved outraging English conventions, rose to the occasion, and gave her a talking which she remembered to her dying day. It was just then, too, that they discovered that she still allowed Mr Kingcroft to write to her 'as a gentleman friend,' and to send presents to Irma.

Philip thought of Italy, and the situation was saved. Caroline, charming sober Caroline Abbott, who lived two turnings away, was seeking a companion for a year's travel. Lilia gave up her house, sold half her furniture, left the other half and Irma with Mrs Herriton, and had now departed, amid universal approval, for a change of scene.

She wrote to them frequently during the winter—more frequently than she wrote to her mother. Her letters were always prosperous. Florence she found perfectly sweet, Naples a dream, but very whiffy. In Rome one had simply to sit still and feel. Philip, however, declared that she was improving. He was particularly gratified when in the early spring she began to visit the smaller towns that he had recommended. 'In a place like this,' she wrote, 'one really does feel in the heart of things, and off the beaten track. Looking out of a Gothic window every morning, it seems impossible that the Middle Ages have passed away.' The letter was from Monteriano, and concluded with a not unsuccessful description of the wonderful little town.

'It is something that she is contented,' said Mrs Herriton. 'But no one could live three months with Caroline Abbott and not be the better for it.'

Just then Irma came in from school, and she read her mother's letter to her, carefully correcting any grammatical errors, for she was a loyal supporter of parental authority. Irma listened politely, but soon changed the subject to hockey, in which her whole being was absorbed. They were to vote for colours that afternoon—yellow and white or yellow and green. What did her grandmother think?

Of course Mrs Herriton had an opinion, which she sedately expounded, in spite of Harriet, who said that colours were unnecessary for children, and of Philip, who said that they were ugly. She was getting proud of Irma, who had certainly greatly improved, and could no longer be called that most appalling of things—a vulgar child. She was anxious to form her before her mother returned. So she had no objection to the leisurely movements of the travellers, and even suggested that they should overstay their year if it suited them.

Lilia's next letter was also from Monteriano, and Philip grew quite enthusiastic.

'They've stopped there over a week!' he cried. 'Why! I shouldn't have done as much myself. They must be really keen, for the hotel's none too comfortable.'

'I cannot understand people,' said Harriet. 'What can they be doing all day? And there is no church there, I suppose.'

'There is Santa Deodata, one of the most beautiful churches in Italy.'

'Of course I mean an English church,' said Harriet stiffly. 'Lilia promised me that she would always be in a large town on Sundays.'

'If she goes to a service at Santa Deodata's, she will find more beauty and sincerity than there is in all the Back Kitchens of Europe.'

The Back Kitchen was his nickname for St James's, a small and depressing edifice much patronised by his sister. She always resented any slight on it, and Mrs Herriton had to intervene.

'Now, dears, don't. Listen to Lilia's letter. "We love this place, and I do not know how I shall ever thank Philip for telling me it. It is not only so quaint, but one sees the Italians unspoiled in all their simplicity and charm here. The frescoes are wonderful. Caroline, who grows sweeter every day, is very busy sketching."'

'Every one to his taste!' said Harriet, who always delivered a platitude as if it was an epigram. She was curiously virulent about Italy, which she had never visited, her only experience of the Continent being an occasional six weeks in the Protestant parts of Switzerland.

'Oh, Harriet is a bad lot!' said Philip as soon as she left the room. His mother laughed, and told him not to be naughty; and the appearance of Irma, just off to school, prevented further discussion. Not only in Tracts is a child a peacemaker.

'One moment, Irma,' said her uncle. 'I'm going to the station. I'll give you the pleasure of my company.'

They started together. Irma was gratified; but conversation flagged, for Philip had not the art of talking to the young. Mrs Herriton sat a little longer at the breakfast-table, re-reading Lilia's letter. Then she helped the cook to clear, ordered dinner, and started the housemaid turning out the drawing-room, Tuesday being its day. The weather was lovely, and she thought she would do a little gardening, as it was quite early. She called Harriet, who had recovered from the insult to St James's, and together they went to the kitchen garden and began to sow some early vegetables.

'We will save the peas to the last; they are the greatest fun,' said Mrs Herriton, who had the gift of making work a treat. She and her elderly daughter always got on very well, though they had not a great deal in common. Harriet's education had been almost too successful. As Philip once said, she had 'bolted all the cardinal virtues and couldn't digest them.' Though pious and patriotic, and a great moral asset for the house, she lacked that pliancy and tact which her mother so much valued, and had expected her to pick up for herself. Harriet, if she had been allowed, would have driven Lilia to an open rupture, and, what was worse, she would have done the same to Philip two years before, when he returned full of passion for Italy, and ridiculing Sawston and its ways.

'It's a shame, mother!' she had cried. 'Philip laughs at everything—the Book Club, the Debating Society, the Progressive Whist, the bazaars. People won't like it. We have our reputation. A house divided against itself cannot stand.'

Mrs Herriton replied in the memorable words, 'Let Philip say what he likes, and he will let us do what we like.' And Harriet had acquiesced.

They sowed the duller vegetables first, and a pleasant feeling of righteous fatigue stole over them as they addressed themselves to the peas. Harriet stretched a string to guide the row straight, and Mrs Herriton scratched a furrow with a pointed stick. At the end of it she looked at her watch.

'It's twelve! The second post's in. Run and see if there are any letters.'

Harriet did not want to go. 'Let's finish the peas. There won't be any letters.'

'No, dear; please go. I'll sow the peas, but you shall cover them up—and mind the birds don't see 'em!'

Mrs Herriton was very careful to let those peas trickle evenly from her hand, and at the end of the row she was conscious that she had never sown better. They were expensive too.

'Actually old Mrs Theobald!' said Harriet, returning.

'Read me the letter. My hands are dirty. How intolerable the crested paper is.'

Harriet opened the envelope.

'I don't understand,' she said; 'it doesn't make sense.'

'Her letters never did.'

'But it must be sillier than usual,' said Harriet, and her voice began to quaver. 'Look here, read it, mother; I can't make head or tail.'

Mrs Herriton took the letter indulgently. 'What is the difficulty?' she said after a long pause. 'What is it that puzzles you in this letter?'

'The meaning—' faltered Harriet. The sparrows hopped nearer and began to eye the peas.

'The meaning is quite clear—Lilia is engaged to be married. Don't cry, dear; please me by not crying—don't talk at all. It's more than I could bear. She is going to marry some one she has met in an hotel. Take the letter and read for yourself.' Suddenly she broke down over what might seem a small point. 'How dare she not tell me direct! How dare she write first to Yorkshire! Pray, am I to hear through Mrs Theobald—a patronising, insolent letter like this? Have I no claim at all? Bear witness, dear'—she choked with passion—'bear witness that for this I'll never forgive her!'

'Oh, what is to be done?' moaned Harriet. 'What is to be done?'

'This first!' She tore the letter into little pieces and scattered it over the mould. 'Next a telegram for Lilia! No! a telegram for Miss Caroline Abbott. She, too, has something to explain.'

'Oh, what is to be done?' repeated Harriet, as she followed her mother to the house. She was helpless before such effrontery. What awful thing—what awful person had come to Lilia? 'Some one in the hotel.' The letter only said that. What kind of person? A gentleman? An Englishman? The letter did not say.

'Wire reason of stay at Monteriano. Strange rumours,' read Mrs Herriton, and addressed the telegram to Abbott, Stella d'Italia, Monteriano, Italy. 'If there is an office there,' she added, 'we might get an answer this evening. Since Philip is back at seven, and the eight-fifteen catches the midnight boat at Dover—Harriet, when you go with this, get £100 in £5 notes at the bank.'

'But why—what—'

'Go, dear, at once; do not talk. I see Irma coming back; go quickly. . . . Well, Irma dear, and whose team are you in this afternoon—Miss Edith's or Miss May's?'

But as soon as she had behaved as usual to her granddaughter, she went to the library and took out the large atlas, for she wanted to know about Monteriano. The name was in the smallest print, in the midst of a woolly-brown tangle of hills which were called the 'Sub-Apennines.' It was not so very far from Siena, which she had learnt at school. Past it there wandered a thin black line, notched at intervals like a saw, and she knew that this was a railway. But the map left a good deal to imagination, and she had not got any. She looked up the place in 'Childe Harold,' but Byron had not been there. Nor did Mark Twain visit it in the 'Tramp Abroad.' The resources of literature were exhausted: she must wait till Philip came home. And the thought of Philip made her try Philip's room, and there she found 'Central Italy,' by Baedeker, and opened it for the first time in her life and read in it as follows:

> *Monteriano* (pop. 4,800). Hotels: Stella d'Italia, moderate only; Globo, dirty. ★Caffè Garibaldi. Post and Telegraph office in Corso Vittorio Emmanuele, next to theatre. Photographs at Seghena's (cheaper in Florence). Diligence (1 lira) meets principal trains.
>
> Chief attractions (2–3 hours): Santa Deodata, Palazzo Pubblico, Sant' Agostino, Santa Caterina, Sant' Ambrogio, Palazzo Capocchi. Guide (2 lire) unnecessary. A walk round the Walls should on no account be omitted. The view from the Rocca (small gratuity) is finest at sunset.
>
> History: Monteriano, the Mons Rianus of Antiquity, whose Ghibelline tendencies are noted by Dante (Purg. xx.), definitely emancipated itself from Poggibonsi in 1261. Hence the distich, '*Poggibonizzi, fatti in là, che Monteriano si fa città!*' till recently inscribed over the Siena gate. It remained independent till 1530, when it was sacked by the Papal troops and became part of the Grand Duchy of Tuscany. It is now of small importance, and seat of the district prison. The inhabitants are still noted for their agreeable manners.
>
> The traveller will proceed direct from the Siena gate to the Collegiate Church of Santa Deodata, and inspect (5th chapel on right) the charming ★Frescoes. . . .

Mrs Herriton did not proceed. She was not one to detect the hidden charms of Baedeker. Some of the information seemed to her unnecessary, all of it was dull. Whereas Philip could never read 'The view from the Rocca (small gratuity) is finest at sunset' without a catching at the heart. Restoring the book to its place, she went downstairs, and looked up and down the asphalt paths for her daughter. She saw her at last, two turnings away, vainly trying to shake off Mr Abbott, Miss Caroline Abbott's father. Harriet was always unfortunate. At last she returned, hot, agitated, crackling with bank-notes, and Irma bounced to greet her, and trod heavily on her corn.

'Your feet grow larger every day,' said the agonised Harriet, and gave her niece a violent push. Then Irma cried, and Mrs Herriton was annoyed with Harriet for betraying irritation. Lunch was nasty; and during pudding news arrived that the cook, by sheer dexterity, had broken a very vital knob off the kitchen-range. 'It is too bad,' said Mrs Herriton. Irma said it was three bad, and was told not to be rude. After lunch Harriet would get out Baedeker, and read in injured tones about Monteriano, the Mons Rianus of Antiquity, till her mother stopped her.

'It's ridiculous to read, dear. She's not trying to marry any one in the place. Some tourist, obviously, who's stopping in the hotel. The place has nothing to do with it at all.'

'But what a place to go to! What nice person, too, do you meet in a hotel?'

'Nice or nasty, as I have told you several times before, is not the point. Lilia has insulted our family, and she shall suffer for it. And when you speak against hotels, I think you forget that I met your father at Chamonix. You can contribute nothing, dear, at present, and I think you had better hold your tongue. I am going to the kitchen, to speak about the range.'

She spoke just too much, and the cook said that if she could not give satisfaction she had better leave. A small thing at hand is greater than a great thing remote, and Lilia, misconducting herself upon a mountain in Central Italy, was immediately hidden. Mrs Herriton flew to a registry office, failed; flew to another, failed again; came home, was told by the housemaid that things seemed so unsettled that she had better leave as well; had tea, wrote six letters, was interrupted by cook and housemaid, both weeping, asking her pardon, and imploring to be taken back. In the flush of victory the doorbell rang, and there was the telegram: 'Lilia engaged to Italian nobility. Writing. Abbott.'

'No answer,' said Mrs Herriton. 'Get down Mr Philip's Gladstone from the attic.'

She would not allow herself to be frightened by the unknown. Indeed, she knew a little now. The man was not an Italian noble, otherwise the telegram would have said so. It must have been written by Lilia. None but she would have been guilty of the fatuous vulgarity of 'Italian nobility.' She recalled phrases of this morning's letter: 'We love this place—Caroline is sweeter than ever, and busy sketching—Italians full of simplicity and charm.' And the remark of Baedeker, 'The inhabitants are still noted for their agreeable manners,' had a baleful meaning now. If Mrs Herriton had no imagination, she had intuition, a more useful quality, and the picture she made to herself of Lilia's fiancé did not prove altogether wrong.

So Philip was received with the news that he must start in half an hour for Monteriano. He was in a painful position. For three years he had sung the praises of the Italians, but he had never contemplated having one as a relative. He tried to soften the thing down to his mother, but in his heart of hearts he agreed with her when she said, 'The man may be a duke or he may be an organ-grinder. That is not the point. If Lilia marries him she insults the memory of Charles, she insults Irma, she insults us. Therefore I forbid her, and if she disobeys we have done with her for ever.'

'I will do all I can,' said Philip in a low voice. It was the first time he had had anything to do. He kissed his mother and sister and puzzled Irma. The hall was warm and attractive as he looked back into it from the cold March night, and he departed for Italy reluctantly, as for something common-place and dull.

Before Mrs Herriton went to bed she wrote to Mrs Theobald, using plain language about Lilia's conduct, and hinting that it was a question on which every one must definitely choose sides. She added, as if it was an afterthought, that Mrs Theobald's letter had arrived that morning.

Just as she was going upstairs she remembered that she never covered up those peas. It upset her more than anything, and again and again she struck the banisters with vexation. Late as it was, she got a lantern from the tool-shed and went down the garden to rake the earth over them. The sparrows had taken every one. But countless fragments of the letter remained, disfiguring the tidy ground.

Chapter Two

When the bewildered tourist alights at the station of Monteriano, he finds himself in the middle of the country. There are a few houses round the railway, and many more dotted over the plain and the slopes of the hills, but of a town, mediæval or otherwise, not the slightest sign. He must take what is suitably termed a 'legno'–a piece of wood–and drive up eight miles of excellent road into the Middle Ages. For it is impossible, as well as sacrilegious, to be as quick as Baedeker.

It was three in the afternoon when Philip left the realms of common sense. He was so weary with travelling that he had fallen asleep in the train. His fellow-passengers had the usual Italian gift of divination, and when Monteriano came they knew he wanted to go there, and dropped him out. His feet sank into the hot asphalt of the platform, and in a dream he watched the train depart, while the porter who ought to have been carrying his bag ran up the line playing touch-you-last with the guard. Alas! he was in no humour for Italy. Bargaining for a legno bored him utterably. The man asked six lire; and though Philip knew that for eight miles it should scarcely be more than four, yet he was about to give what he was asked, and so make the man discontented and unhappy for the rest of the day. He was saved from this social blunder by loud shouts, and looking up the road saw one cracking his whip and waving his reins and driving two horses furiously, and behind him there appeared the swaying figure of a woman, holding star-fish fashion on to anything she could touch. It was Miss Abbott, who had just received his letter from Milan announcing the time of his arrival, and had hurried down to meet him.

He had known Miss Abbott for years, and had never had much opinion about her one way or the other. She was good, quiet, dull, and amiable, and young only because she was twenty-three: there was nothing in her appearance or manner to suggest the fire of youth. All her life had been spent at Sawston with a dull and amiable father, and her pleasant, pallid face, bent on some respectable charity, was a familiar object of the Sawston streets. Why she had ever wished to leave them was surprising; but as she truly said, 'I am John Bull to the backbone, yet I do want to see Italy, just once. Everybody says it is marvellous, and that one gets no idea of it from books at all.' The curate suggested that a year was a long time; and Miss Abbott, with decorous playfulness, answered him, 'Oh, but you must let me have my fling! I promise to have it once, and once only. It will give me things to think about and talk about for the rest of my life.' The curate had consented; so had Mr Abbott. And here she was in a legno, solitary, dusty, frightened, with as much to answer for as the most dashing adventuress could desire.

They shook hands without speaking. She made room for Philip and his luggage amidst the loud indignation of the unsuccessful driver, whom it required the combined eloquence of the station-master and the station beggar to confute. The silence was prolonged until they started. For three days he had been considering what he should do, and still more what he should say. He had invented a dozen imaginary conversations, in all of which his logic and eloquence procured him certain victory. But how to begin? He was in the enemy's country, and everything—the hot sun, the cold air behind the heat, the endless rows of olives, regular yet mysterious—seemed hostile to the placid atmosphere of Sawston in which his thoughts took birth. At the outset he made one great concession. If the match was really suitable, and Lilia were bent on it, he would give in, and trust to his influence with his mother to set things right. He would not have made the concession in England; but here in Italy, Lilia, however wilful and silly, was at all events growing to be a human being.

'Are we to talk it over now?' he asked.

'Certainly, please,' said Miss Abbott, in great agitation. 'If you will be so very kind.'

'Then how long has she been engaged?'

Her face was that of a perfect fool—a fool in terror.

'A short time—quite a short time,' she stammered, as if the shortness of the time would reassure him.

'I should like to know how long, if you can remember.'

She entered into elaborate calculations on her fingers. 'Exactly eleven days,' she said at last.

'How long have you been here?'

More calculations, while he tapped irritably with his foot. 'Close on three weeks.'

'Did you know him before you came?'

'No.'

'Oh! Who is he?'

'A native of the place.'

The second silence took place. They had left the plain now and were climbing up the outposts of the hills, the olive-trees still accompanying. The driver, a jolly fat man, had got out to ease the horses, and was walking by the side of the carriage.

'I understood they met at the hotel.'

'It was a mistake of Mrs Theobald's.'

'I also understand that he is a member of the Italian nobility.'

She did not reply.

'May I be told his name?'

Miss Abbott whispered 'Carella.' But the driver heard her, and a grin split over his face. The engagement must be known already.

'Carella? Conte or Marchese, or what?'

'Signor,' said Miss Abbott, and looked helplessly aside.

'Perhaps I bore you with these questions. If so, I will stop.'

'Oh no, please; not at all. I am here—my own idea—to give all information which you very naturally—and to see if somehow—please ask anything you like.'

'Then how old is he?'

'Oh, quite young. Twenty-one, I believe.'

There burst from Philip the exclamation, 'Good Lord!'

'One would never believe it,' said Miss Abbott, flushing. 'He looks much older.'

'And is he good-looking?' he asked, with gathering sarcasm.

She became decisive. 'Very good-looking. All his features are good, and he is well built—though I dare say English standards would find him too short.'

Philip, whose one physical advantage was his height, felt annoyed at her implied indifference to it.

'May I conclude that you like him?'

She replied decisively again, 'As far as I have seen him, I do.'

At that moment the carriage entered a little wood, which lay brown and sombre across the cultivated hill. The trees of the wood were small and leafless, but noticeable for this—that their stems stood in violets as rocks stand in the summer sea. There are such violets in England, but not so many. Nor are there so many in Art, for no painter has the courage. The cart-ruts were channels, the hollows lagoons; even the dry white margin of the road was splashed, like a causeway soon to be submerged under the advancing tide of spring. Philip paid no attention at the time: he was thinking what to say next. But his eyes had registered the beauty, and next March he did not forget that the road to Monteriano must traverse innumerable flowers.

'As far as I have seen him, I do like him,' repeated Miss Abbott, after a pause.

He thought she sounded a little defiant, and crushed her at once.

'What is he, please? You haven't told me that. What's his position?'

She opened her mouth to speak, and no sound came from it. Philip waited patiently. She tried to be audacious, and failed pitiably.

'No position at all. He is kicking his heels, as my father would say. You see, he has only just finished his military service.'

'As a private?'

'I suppose so. There is general conscription. He was in the Bersaglieri, I think. Isn't that the crack regiment?'

'The men in it must be short and broad. They must also be able to walk six miles an hour.'

She looked at him wildly, not understanding all that he said, but feeling that he was very clever. Then she continued her defence of Signor Carella.

'And now, like most young men, he is looking out for something to do.'

'Meanwhile?'

'Meanwhile, like most young men, he lives with his people—father, mother, two sisters, and a tiny tot of a brother.'

There was a grating sprightliness about her that drove him nearly mad. He determined to silence her at last.

'One more question, and only one more. What is his father?'

'His father,' said Miss Abbott. 'Well, I don't suppose you'll think it a good match. But that's not the point. I mean the point is not—I mean that social differences—love, after all—not but what—'

Philip ground his teeth together and said nothing.

'Gentlemen sometimes judge hardly. But I feel that you, and at all events your mother—so really good in every sense, so really unworldly—after all, love—marriages are made in heaven.'

'Yes, Miss Abbott, I know. But I am anxious to hear heaven's choice. You arouse my curiosity. Is my sister-in-law to marry an angel?'

'Mr Herriton, don't—please, Mr Herriton—a dentist. His father's a dentist.'

Philip gave a cry of personal disgust and pain. He shuddered all over, and edged away from his companion. A dentist! A dentist at Monteriano. A dentist in fairyland! False teeth and laughing gas and the tilting chair at a place which knew the Etruscan League, and the Pax Romana, and Alaric himself, and the Countess Matilda, and the Middle Ages, all fighting and holiness, and the Renaissance, all fighting and beauty! He thought of Lilia no longer. He was anxious for himself: he feared that Romance might die.

Romance only dies with life. No pair of pincers will ever pull it out of us. But there is a spurious sentiment which cannot resist the unexpected and the incongruous and the grotesque. A touch will loosen it, and the sooner it goes from us the better. It was going from Philip now, and therefore he gave the cry of pain.

'I cannot think what is in the air,' he began. 'If Lilia was determined to disgrace us, she might have found a less repulsive way. A boy of medium height with a pretty face, the son of a dentist at Monteriano. Have I put it correctly? May I surmise that he has not got one penny? May I also surmise that his social position is nil? Furthermore—'

'Stop! I'll tell you no more.'

'Really, Miss Abbott, it is a little late for reticence. You have equipped me admirably!'

'I'll tell you not another word!' she cried, with a spasm of terror. Then she got out her handkerchief, and seemed as if she would shed tears. After a silence, which he intended to symbolise to her the dropping of a curtain on the scene, he began to talk of other subjects.

They were among olives again, and the wood with its beauty and wildness had passed away. But as they climbed higher the country opened out, and there appeared, high on a hill to the right, Monteriano. The hazy green of the olives rose up to its walls, and it seemed to float in isolation between trees and sky, like some fantastic ship city of a dream. Its colour was brown, and it revealed not a single house—nothing but the narrow circle of the walls, and behind them seventeen towers—all that was left of the fifty-two that had filled the city in her prime. Some were only stumps, some were inclining stiffly to their fall, some were still erect, piercing like masts into the blue. It was impossible to praise it as beautiful, but it was also impossible to damn it as quaint.

Meanwhile Philip talked continually, thinking this to be great evidence of resource and tact. It showed Miss Abbott that he had probed her to the bottom, but was able to conquer his disgust, and by sheer force of intellect continue to be as agreeable and amusing as ever. He did not know that he talked a good deal of nonsense, and that the sheer force of his intellect was weakened by the sight of Monteriano, and by the thought of dentistry within those walls.

The town above them swung to the left, to the right, to the left again, as the road wound upward through the trees, and the towers began to glow in the descending sun. As they drew near, Philip saw the heads of people gathering black upon the walls, and he knew well what was happening—how the news was spreading that a stranger was in sight, and the beggars were aroused from their content and bid to adjust their deformities; how the alabaster man was running for his wares, and the Authorised Guide running for his peaked cap and his two cards of recommendation—one from Miss M'Gee, Maida Vale, the other, less valuable, from an Equerry to the Queen of Peru; how some one else was running to tell the landlady of the Stella d'Italia to put on her pearl necklace and brown boots and empty the slops from the spare bedroom; and how the landlady was running to tell Lilia and her boy that their fate was at hand.

Perhaps it was a pity Philip had talked so profusely. He had driven Miss Abbott half demented, but he had given himself no time to concert a plan. The end came so suddenly. They emerged from the trees on to the terrace before the walk, with the vision of half Tuscany radiant in the sun behind them, and then they turned in through the Siena gate, and their journey was over. The Dogana men admitted them with an air of gracious welcome, and they clattered up the narrow dark street, greeted by that mixture of curiosity and kindness which makes each Italian arrival so wonderful.

He was stunned and knew not what to do. At the hotel he received no ordinary reception. The landlady wrung him by the hand; one person snatched his umbrella, another his bag; people pushed each other out of his way. The entrance seemed blocked with a crowd. Dogs were barking, bladder whistles being blown, women waving their handkerchiefs, excited children screaming on the stairs, and at the top of the stairs was Lilia herself, very radiant, with her best blouse on.

'Welcome!' she cried. 'Welcome to Monteriano!' He greeted her, for he did not know what else to do, and a sympathetic murmur rose from the crowd below.

'You told me not to come here,' she continued, 'and I don't forget it. Let me introduce Signor Carella!'

Philip discerned in the corner behind her a young man who might eventually prove handsome and well-made, but certainly did not seem so then. He was half-enveloped in the drapery of a cold dirty curtain, and nervously stuck out a hand, which Philip took and found thick and damp. There were more murmurs of approval from the stairs.

'Well, din-din's nearly ready,' said Lilia. 'Your room's down the passage, Philip. You needn't go changing.'

He stumbled away to wash his hands, utterly crushed by her effrontery.

'Dear Caroline!' whispered Lilia as soon as he had gone. 'What an angel you've been to tell him! He takes it so well. But you must have had a *mauvais quart d'heure.*'

Miss Abbott's long terror suddenly turned into acidity. 'I've told nothing,' she snapped. 'It's all for you—and if it only takes a quarter of an hour you'll be lucky!'

Dinner was a nightmare. They had the smelly dining-room to themselves. Lilia, very smart and vociferous, was at the head of the table; Miss Abbott, also in her best, sat by Philip, looking, to his irritated nerves, more like the tragedy confidante every moment. That scion of the Italian nobility, Signor Carella, sat opposite. Behind him loomed a bowl of goldfish, who swam round and round, gaping at the guests.

The face of Signor Carella was twitching too much for Philip to study it. But he could see the hands, which were not particularly clean, and did not get cleaner by fidgeting amongst the shining slabs of hair. His starched cuffs were not clean either, and as for his suit, it had obviously been bought for the occasion as something really English—a gigantic check, which did not even fit. His handkerchief he had forgotten, but never missed it. Altogether, he was quite unpresentable, and very lucky to have a father who was a dentist in Monteriano. And why, even Lilia— But as soon as the meal began it furnished Philip with an explanation.

For the youth was hungry, and his lady filled his plate with spaghetti, and when those delicious slippery worms were flying down his throat, his face relaxed and became for a moment unconscious and calm. And Philip had seen that face before in Italy a hundred times—seen it and loved it, for it was not merely beautiful, but had the charm which is the rightful heritage of all who are born on that soil. But he did not want to see it opposite him at dinner. It was not the face of a gentleman.

Conversation, to give it that name, was carried on in a mixture of English and Italian. Lilia had picked up hardly any of the latter language, and Signor Carella had not yet learnt any of the former. Occasionally Miss Abbott had to act as interpreter between the lovers, and the situation became uncouth and revolting in the extreme. Yet Philip was too cowardly to break forth and denounce the engagement. He thought he should be more effective with Lilia if he had her alone, and pretended to himself that he must hear her defence before giving judgment.

Signor Carella, heartened by the spaghetti and the throat-rasping wine, attempted to talk, and, looking politely towards Philip, said, 'England is a great country. The Italians love England and the English.'

Philip, in no mood for international amenities, merely bowed.

'Italy too,' the other continued a little resentfully, 'is a great country. She has produced many famous men—for example, Garibaldi and Dante. The latter wrote the "Inferno," the "Purgatorio," the "Paradiso." The "Inferno" is the most beautiful.' And with the complacent tone of one who has received a solid education, he quoted the opening lines—

> *'Nel mezzo del cammin di nostra vita*
> *Mi ritrovai per una selva oscura,*
> *Chè la diritta via era smarrita'—*

a quotation which was more apt than he supposed.

Lilia glanced at Philip to see whether he noticed that she was marrying no ignoramus. Anxious to exhibit all the good qualities of her betrothed, she abruptly introduced the subject of Pallone, in which, it appeared, he was a proficient player. He suddenly became shy, and developed a conceited grin—the grin of the village yokel whose cricket score is mentioned before a stranger. Philip himself had loved to watch Pallone, that entrancing combination of lawn-tennis and fives. But he did not expect to love it quite so much again.

'Oh, look!' exclaimed Lilia, 'the poor wee fish!'

A starved cat had been worrying them all for pieces of the purple quivering beef they were trying to swallow. Signor Carella, with the brutality so common in Italians, had caught her by the paw and flung her away from him. Now she had climbed up to the bowl and was trying to hook out the fish. He got up, drove her off, and finding a large glass stopper by the bowl, entirely plugged up the aperture with it.

'But may not the fish die?' said Miss Abbott. 'They have no air.'

'Fish live on water, not on air,' he replied in a knowing voice, and sat down. Apparently he was at his ease again, for he took to spitting on the floor. Philip glanced at Lilia, but did not detect her wincing. She talked bravely till the end of the disgusting meal, and then got up saying, 'Well, Philip, I am sure you are ready for bye-bye. We shall meet at twelve o'clock lunch to-morrow, if we don't meet before. They give us *caffè latte* in our rooms.'

It was a little too impudent. Philip replied, 'I should like to see you now, please, in my room, as I have come all the way on business.' He heard Miss Abbott gasp. Signor Carella, who was lighting a rank cigar, had not understood.

It was as he expected. When he was alone with Lilia he lost all nervousness. The remembrance of his long intellectual supremacy strengthened him, and he began volubly—

'My dear Lilia, don't let's have a scene. Before I arrived I thought I might have to question you. It is unnecessary. I know everything. Miss Abbott has told me a certain amount, and the rest I see for myself.'

'See for yourself?' she exclaimed, and he remembered afterwards that she had flushed crimson.

'That he is probably a ruffian and certainly a cad.'

'There are no cads in Italy,' she said quickly.

He was taken aback. It was one of his own remarks. And she further upset him by adding, 'He is the son of a dentist. Why not?'

'Thank you for the information. I know everything, as I told you before. I am also aware of the social position of an Italian who pulls out teeth in a minute provincial town.'

He was not aware of it, but he ventured to conclude that it was pretty low. Nor did Lilia contradict him. But she was sharp enough to say, 'Indeed, Philip, you surprise me. I understood you went in for equality and so on.'

'And I understood that Signor Carella was a member of the Italian nobility.'

'Well, we put it like that in the telegram so as not to shock dear Mrs Herriton. But it is true. He is a younger branch. Of course families ramify—just as in yours there is your cousin Joseph.' She adroitly picked out the only undesirable member of the Herriton clan. 'Gino's father is courtesy itself, and rising rapidly in his profession. This very month he leaves Monteriano, and sets up at Poggibonsi. And for my own poor part, I think what people *are* is what matters, but I don't suppose you'll agree. And I should like you to know that Gino's uncle is a priest—the same as a clergyman at home.'

Philip was aware of the social position of an Italian priest, and said so much about it that Lilia interrupted him with, 'Well, his cousin's a lawyer at Rome.'

'What kind of "lawyer"?'

'Why, a lawyer just like you are—except that he has lots to do and can never get away.'

The remark hurt more than he cared to show. He changed his method, and in a gentle, conciliating tone delivered the following speech:

'The whole thing is like a bad dream—so bad that it cannot go on. If there was one redeeming feature about the man I might be uneasy. As it is I can trust to time. For the moment, Lilia, he has taken you in, but you will find him out soon. It is not possible that you, a lady, accustomed to ladies and gentlemen, will tolerate a man whose position is—well, not equal to the son of the servants' dentist in Coronation Place. I am not blaming you now. But I blame the glamour of Italy—I have felt it myself, you know—and I greatly blame Miss Abbott.'

'Caroline! why blame her? What's all this to do with Caroline?'

'Because we expected her to—' He saw that the answer would involve him in difficulties, and, waving his hand, continued, 'So I am confident, and you in your heart agree, that this engagement will not last. Think of your life at home—think of Irma! And I'll also say think of us; for you know, Lilia, that we count you more than a relation. I should feel I was losing my own sister if you did this, and my mother would lose a daughter.'

She seemed touched at last, for she turned away her face and said, 'I can't break it off now!'

'Poor Lilia,' said he, genuinely moved. 'I know it may be painful. But I have come to rescue you, and, book-worm though I may be, I am not frightened to stand up to a bully. He's merely an insolent boy. He thinks he can keep you to your word by threats. He will be different when he sees he has a man to deal with.'

What follows should be prefaced with some simile—the simile of a powder-mine, a thunder-bolt, an earthquake—for it blew Philip up in the air and flattened him on the ground and swallowed him up in the depths. Lilia turned on her gallant defender and said:

'For once in my life I'll thank you to leave me alone. I'll thank your mother too. For twelve years you've trained me and tortured me, and I'll stand it no more. Do you think I'm a fool? Do you think I never felt? Ah! when I came to your house a poor young bride, how you all looked me over—never a kind word—and discussed me, and thought I might just do; and your mother corrected me, and your sister snubbed me, and you said funny things about me to show how clever you were! And when Charles died I was still to run in strings for the honour of your beastly family, and I was to be cooped up at Sawston and learn to keep house, and all my chances spoilt of marrying again. No, thank you! No, thank you! "Bully"? "Insolent boy"? Who's that, pray, but you? But, thank goodness, I can stand up against the world now, for I've found Gino, and this time I marry for love!'

The coarseness and truth of her attack alike overwhelmed him. But her supreme insolence found him words, and he too burst forth.

'Yes! and I forbid you to do it! You despise me, perhaps, and think I'm feeble. But you're mistaken. You are ungrateful and impertinent and contemptible, but I will save you in order to save Irma and our name. There is going to be such a row in this town that you and he'll be sorry you came to it. I shall shrink from nothing, for my blood is up. It is unwise of you to laugh. I forbid you to marry Carella, and I shall tell him so now.'

'Do,' she cried. 'Tell him so now. Have it out with him. Gino! Gino! Come in! Avanti! Fra Filippo forbids the banns!'

Gino appeared so quickly that he must have been listening outside the door.

'Fra Filippo's blood's up. He shrinks from nothing. Oh, take care he doesn't hurt you!' She swayed about in vulgar imitation of Philip's walk, and then, with a proud glance at the square shoulders of her betrothed, flounced out of the room.

Did she intend them to fight? Philip had no intention of doing so; and no more, it seemed, had Gino, who stood nervously in the middle of the room with twitching lips and eyes.

'Please sit down, Signor Carella,' said Philip in Italian. 'Mrs Herriton is rather agitated, but there is no reason we should not be calm. Might I offer you a cigarette? Please sit down.'

He refused the cigarette and the chair, and remained standing in the full glare of the lamp. Philip, not averse to such assistance, got his own face into shadow.

For a long time he was silent. It might impress Gino, and it also gave him time to collect himself. He would not this time fall into the error of blustering, which he had caught so unaccountably from Lilia. He would make his power felt by restraint.

Why, when he looked up to begin, was Gino convulsed with silent laughter? It vanished immediately; but he became nervous, and was even more pompous than he intended.

'Signor Carella, I will be frank with you. I have come to prevent you marrying Mrs Herriton, because I see you will both be unhappy together. She is English, you are Italian; she is accustomed to one thing, you to another. And—pardon me if I say it—she is rich and you are poor.'

'I am not marrying her because she is rich,' was the sulky reply.

'I never suggested that for a moment,' said Philip courteously. 'You are honourable, I am sure; but are you wise? And let me remind you that we want her with us at home. Her little daughter will be motherless, our home will be broken up. If you grant my request you will earn our thanks—and you will not be without a reward for your disappointment.'

'Reward—what reward?' He bent over the back of a chair and looked earnestly at Philip. They were coming to terms pretty quickly. Poor Lilia!

Philip said slowly, 'What about a thousand lire?'

His soul went forth into one exclamation, and then he was silent, with gaping lips. Philip would have given double: he had expected a bargain.

'You can have them to-night.'

He found words, and said, 'It is too late.'

'But why?'

'Because—' His voice broke. Philip watched his face—a face without refinement, perhaps, but not without expression—watched it quiver and re-form and dissolve from emotion into emotion. There was avarice at one moment, and insolence, and politeness, and stupidity, and cunning—and let us hope that sometimes there was love. But gradually one emotion dominated, the most unexpected of all; for his chest began to heave and his eyes to wink and mouth to twitch, and suddenly he stood erect and roared forth his whole being in one tremendous laugh.

Philip sprang up, and Gino, who had flung wide his arms to let the glorious creature go, took him by the shoulders and shook him, and said, 'Because we are married—married—married as soon as I knew you were coming. There was no time to tell you. Oh, oh! You have come all the way for nothing. Oh! And oh, your generosity!' Suddenly he became grave, and said, 'Please pardon me; I am rude. I am no better than a peasant, and I—' Here he saw Philip's face, and it was too much for him. He gasped and exploded and crammed his hands into his mouth and spat them out in another explosion, and gave Philip an aimless push, which toppled him on to the bed. He uttered a horrified oh! and then gave up, and bolted away down the passage, shrieking like a child, to tell the joke to his wife.

For a time Philip lay on the bed, pretending to himself that he was hurt grievously. He could scarcely see for temper, and in the passage he ran against Miss Abbott, who promptly burst into tears.

'I sleep at the Globo,' he told her, 'and start for Sawston to-morrow morning early. He has assaulted me. I could prosecute him. But shall not.'

'I can't stop here,' she sobbed. 'I daren't stop here. You will have to take me with you!'

Chapter Three

Opposite the Volterra gate of Monteriano, outside the city, is a very respectable whitewashed mud wall, with a coping of red crinkled tiles to keep it from dissolution. It would suggest a gentleman's garden if there was not in its middle a large hole, which grows larger with every rainstorm. Through the hole is visible, firstly, the iron gate that is intended to close it; secondly, a square piece of ground which, though not quite mud, is at the same time not exactly grass; and finally, another wall, stone this time, which has a wooden door in the middle and two wooden-shuttered windows each side, and apparently forms the façade of a one-storey house.

This house is bigger than it looks, for it slides for two storeys down the hill behind, and the wooden door, which is always locked, really leads into the attic. The knowing person prefers to follow the precipitous mule-track round the turn of the mud wall till he can take the edifice in the rear. Then–being now on a level with the cellars–he lifts up his head and shouts. If his voice sounds like something light–a letter, for example, or some vegetables, or a bunch of flowers–a basket is let out of the first-floor windows by a string, into which he puts his burden and departs. But if he sounds like something heavy, such as a log of wood, or a piece of meat, or a visitor, he is interrogated, and then bidden or forbidden to ascend. The ground floor and the upper floor of that battered house are alike deserted, and the inmates keep to the central portion, just as in a dying body all life retires to the heart. There is a door at the top of the first flight of stairs, and if the visitor is admitted, he will find a welcome which is not necessarily cold. There are several rooms, some dark and mostly stuffy–a reception-room adorned with horse-hair chairs, wool-work stools, and a stove that is never lit–German bad taste without German domesticity broods over that room; also a living-room, which insensibly glides into a bedroom when the refining influence of hospitality is absent, and real bedrooms; and last, but not least, the loggia, where you can live day and night if you feel inclined, drinking vermouth and smoking cigarettes, with leagues of olive-trees and vineyards and blue-green hills to watch you.

It was in this house that the brief and inevitable tragedy of Lilia's married life took place. She made Gino buy it for her, because it was there she had first seen him sitting on the mud wall that faced the Volterra gate. She remembered how the evening sun had struck his hair, and how he had smiled down at her, and being both sentimental and unrefined, was determined to have the man and the place together. Things in Italy are cheap for an Italian, and, though he would have preferred a house in the piazza, or better still a house at Siena, or, bliss above bliss, a house at Leghorn, he did as she asked, thinking that perhaps she showed her good taste in preferring so retired an abode.

The house was far too big for them, and there was a general concourse of his relatives to fill it up. His father wished to make it a patriarchal concern, where all the family should have their rooms and meet together for meals, and was perfectly willing to give up the new practice at Poggibonsi and preside. Gino was quite willing too, for he was an affectionate youth who liked a large home-circle, and he told it as a pleasant bit of news to Lilia, who did not attempt to conceal her horror.

At once he was horrified too; saw that the idea was monstrous; abused himself to her for having suggested it; rushed off to tell his father that it was impossible. His father complained that prosperity was already corrupting him and making him unsympathetic and hard; his mother cried; his sisters accused him of blocking their social advance. He was apologetic, and even cringing, until they turned on Lilia. Then he turned on them, saying that they could not understand, much less associate with, the English lady who was his wife; that there should be one master in that house—himself.

Lilia praised and petted him on his return, calling him brave and a hero and other endearing epithets. But he was rather blue when his clan left Monteriano in much dignity—a dignity which was not at all impaired by the acceptance of a cheque. They took the cheque not to Poggibonsi, after all, but to Empoli—a lively, dusty town some twenty miles off. There they settled down in comfort; and the sisters said they had been driven to it by Gino.

The cheque was, of course, Lilia's, who was extremely generous, and was quite willing to know anybody so long as she had not to live with them, relations-in-law being on her nerves. She liked nothing better than finding out some obscure and distant connection—there were several of them—and acting the lady bountiful, leaving behind her bewilderment, and too often discontent. Gino wondered how it was that all his people, who had formerly seemed so pleasant, had suddenly become plaintive and disagreeable. He put it down to his lady-wife's magnificence, in comparison with which all seemed common. Her money flew apace, in spite of the cheap living. She was even richer than he expected; and he remembered with shame how he had once regretted his inability to accept the thousand lire that Philip Herriton offered him in exchange for her. It would have been a short-sighted bargain.

Lilia enjoyed settling into the house, with nothing to do except give orders to smiling workpeople, and a devoted husband as interpreter. She wrote a jaunty account of her happiness to Mrs Herriton, and Harriet answered the letter, saying (1) that all future communications should be addressed to the solicitors; (2) would Lilia return an inlaid box which Harriet had lent her—but not given—to keep handkerchiefs and collars in?

'Look what I am giving up to live with you!' she said to Gino, never omitting to lay stress on her condescension. He took her to mean the inlaid box, and said that she need not give it up at all.

'Silly fellow, no! I mean the life. Those Herritons are very well connected. They lead Sawston society. But what do I care, so long as I have my silly fellow!' She always treated him as a boy, which he was, and as a fool, which he was not, thinking herself so immeasurably superior to him that she neglected opportunity after opportunity of establishing her rule. He was good-looking and indolent; therefore he must be stupid. He was poor; therefore he would never dare to criticise his benefactress. He was passionately in love with her; therefore she could do exactly as she liked.

'It mayn't be heaven below,' she thought, 'but it's better than Charles.'

And all the time the boy was watching her, and growing up.

She was reminded of Charles by a disagreeable letter from the solicitors, bidding her disgorge a large sum of money for Irma, in accordance with her late husband's will. It was just like Charles's suspicious nature to have provided against a second marriage. Gino was equally indignant, and between them they composed a stinging reply, which had no effect. He then said that Irma had better come out and live with them. 'The air is good, so is the food; she will be happy here, and we shall not have to part with the money.' But Lilia had not the courage even to suggest this to the Herritons, and an unexpected terror seized her at the thought of Irma or any English child being educated at Monteriano.

Gino became terribly depressed over the solicitors' letter, more depressed than she thought necessary. There was no more to do in the house, and he spent whole days in the loggia leaning over the parapet or sitting astride it disconsolately.

'Oh, you idle boy!' she cried, pinching his muscles. 'Go and play pallone.'

'I am a married man,' he answered, without raising his head. 'I do not play games any more.'

'Go and see your friends then.'

'I have no friends now.'

'Silly, silly, silly! You can't stop indoors all day!'

'I want to see no one but you.' He spat on to an olive-tree.

'Now, Gino, don't be silly. Go and see your friends, and bring them to see me. We both of us like society.'

He looked puzzled, but allowed himself to be persuaded, went out, found that he was not as friendless as he supposed, and returned after several hours in altered spirits. Lilia congratulated herself on her good management.

'I'm ready, too, for people now,' she said. 'I mean to wake you all up, just as I woke up Sawston. Let's have plenty of men—and make them bring their womenkind. I mean to have real English tea-parties.'

'There is my aunt and her husband; but I thought you did not want to receive my relatives.'

'I never said such a—'

'But you would be right,' he said earnestly. 'They are not for you. Many of them are in trade, and even we are little more; you should have gentlefolk and nobility for your friends.'

'Poor fellow,' thought Lilia. 'It is sad for him to discover that his people are vulgar.' She began to tell him that she loved him just for his silly self, and he flushed and began tugging at his moustache.

'But besides your relatives I must have other people here. Your friends have wives and sisters, haven't they?'

'Oh yes; but of course I scarcely know them.'

'Not know your friends' people?'

'Why, no. If they are poor and have to work for their living I may see them—but not otherwise. Except—' He stopped. The chief exception was a young lady, to whom he had once been introduced for matrimonial purposes. But the dowry had proved inadequate, and the acquaintance terminated.

'How funny! But I mean to change all that. Bring your friends to see me, and I will make them bring their people.'

He looked at her rather hopelessly.

'Well, who are the principal people here? Who leads society?'

The governor of the prison, he supposed, and the officers who assisted him.

'Well, are they married?'

'Yes.'

'There we are. Do you know them?'

'Yes—in a way.'

'I see,' she exclaimed angrily. 'They look down on you, do they, poor boy? Wait!' He assented. 'Wait! I'll soon stop that. Now, who else is there?'

'The marchese, sometimes, and the canons of the Collegiate Church.'

'Married?'

'The canons—' he began with twinkling eyes.

'Oh, I forgot your horrid celibacy. In England they would be the centre of everything. But why shouldn't I know them? Would it make it easier if I called all round? Isn't that your foreign way?'

He did not think it would make it easier.

'But I must know some one! Who were the men you were talking to this afternoon?'

Low-class men. He could scarcely recollect their names.

'But, Gino dear, if they're low class, why did you talk to them? Don't you care about your position?'

All Gino cared about at present was idleness and pocket-money, and his way of expressing it was to exclaim, 'Ouf—pouf! How hot it is in here. No air; I sweat all over. I expire. I must cool myself, or I shall never get to sleep.' In his funny abrupt way he ran out on to the loggia, where he lay full length on the parapet, and began to smoke and spit under the silence of the stars.

Lilia gathered somehow from this conversation that Continental society was not the go-as-you-please thing she had expected. Indeed, she could not see where Continental society was. Italy is such a delightful place to live in if you happen to be a man. There one may enjoy that exquisite luxury of Socialism—that true Socialism which is based not on equality of income or character, but on the equality of manners. In the democracy of the *caffè* or the street the great question of our life has been solved, and the brotherhood of man is a reality. But it is accomplished at the expense of the sisterhood of women. Why should you not make friends with your neighbour at the theatre or in the train, when you know and he knows that feminine criticism and feminine insight and feminine prejudice will never come between you! Though you become as David and Jonathan, you need never enter his home, nor he yours. All your lives you will meet under the open air, the only roof-tree of the South, under which he will spit and swear, and you will drop your h's, and nobody will think the worse of either.

Meanwhile the women—they have, of course, their house and their church, with its admirable and frequent services, to which they are escorted by the maid. Otherwise they do not go out much, for it is not genteel to walk, and you are too poor to keep a carriage. Occasionally you will take them to the *caffè* or theatre, and immediately all your wonted acquaintance there desert you, except those few who are expecting and expected to marry into your family. It is all very sad. But one consolation emerges—life is very pleasant in Italy if you are a man.

Hitherto Gino had not interfered with Lilia. She was so much older than he was, and so much richer, that he regarded her as a superior being who answered to other laws. He was not wholly surprised, for strange rumours were always blowing over the Alps of lands where men and women had the same amusements and interests, and he had often met that privileged maniac, the lady tourist, on her solitary walks. Lilia took solitary walks, too, and only that week a tramp had grabbed at her watch—an episode which is supposed to be indigenous in Italy, though really less frequent there than in Bond Street. Now that he knew her better, he was inevitably losing his awe: no one could live with her and keep it, especially when she had been so silly as to lose a gold watch and chain. As he lay thoughtful along the parapet, he realised for the first time the responsibilities of married life. He must save her from dangers, physical and social, for after all she was a woman. 'And I,' he reflected, 'though I am young, am at all events a man, and know what is right.'

He found her still in the living-room, combing her hair, for she had something of the slattern in her nature, and there was no need to keep up appearances.

'You must not go out alone,' he said gently. 'It is not safe. If you want to walk, Perfetta shall accompany you.' Perfetta was a widowed cousin, too humble for social aspirations, who was living with them as factotum.

'Very well,' smiled Lilia, 'very well'—as if she were addressing a solicitous kitten. But for all that she never took a solitary walk again, with one exception, till the day of her death.

Days passed, and no one called except poor relatives. She began to feel dull. Didn't he know the Sindaco or the bank manager? Even the landlady of the Stella d'Italia would be better than no one. She, when she went into the town, was pleasantly received; but people naturally found a difficulty in getting on with a lady who could not learn their language. And the tea-party, under Gino's adroit management, receded ever and ever before her.

He had a good deal of anxiety over her welfare, for she did not settle down in the house at all. But he was comforted by a welcome and unexpected visitor. As he was going one afternoon for the letters—they were delivered at the door, but it took longer to get them at the office–some one humorously threw a cloak over his head, and when he disengaged himself he saw his very dear friend Spiridione Tesi of the custom-house at Chiasso, whom he had not met for two years. What joy! what salutations! so that all the passers-by smiled with approval on the amiable scene. Spiridione's brother was now station-master at Bologna, and thus he himself could spend his holiday travelling over Italy at the public expense. Hearing of Gino's marriage, he had come to see him on his way to Siena, where lived his own uncle, lately married too.

'They all do it,' he exclaimed, 'myself excepted.' He was not quite twenty-three. 'But tell me more. She is English. That is good, very good. An English wife is very good indeed. And she is rich?'

'Immensely rich.'

'Blonde or dark?'

'Blonde.'

'Is it possible!'

'It pleases me very much,' said Gino simply. 'If you remember, I always desired a blonde. Three or four men had collected, and were listening.

'We all desire one,' said Spiridione. 'But you, Gino, deserve your good fortune, for you are a good son, a brave man, and a true friend, and from the very first moment I saw you I wished you well.'

'No compliments, I beg,' said Gino, standing with his hands crossed on his chest and a smile of pleasure on his face.

Spiridione addressed the other men, none of whom he had ever seen before. 'Is it not true? Does not he deserve this wealthy blonde?'

'He does deserve her,' said all the men.

It is a marvellous land, whether you love it or hate it.

There were no letters, and of course they sat down at the Caffè Garibaldi, by the Collegiate Church–quite a good *caffè* that for so small a city. There were marble-topped tables, and pillars terra-cotta below and gold above, and on the ceiling was a fresco of the battle of Solferino. One could not have desired a prettier room. They had vermouth and little cakes with sugar on the top, which they chose gravely at the counter, pinching them first to be sure they were fresh. And though vermouth is barely alcoholic, Spiridione drenched his with soda-water to be sure that it should not get into his head.

They were in high spirits, and elaborate compliments alternated curiously with gentle horseplay. But soon they put up their legs on a pair of chairs and began to smoke.

'Tell me,' said Spiridione–'I forgot to ask–is she young?'

'Thirty-three.'

'Ah, well, we cannot have everything.'

'But you would be surprised. Had she told me twenty-eight, I should not have disbelieved her.'

'Is she simpatica?' (Nothing will translate that word.)

Gino dabbed at the sugar and said after a silence, 'Sufficiently so.'

'It is a most important thing.'

'She is rich, she is generous, she is affable, she addresses her inferiors with haughtiness.'

There was another silence. 'It is not sufficient,' said the other. 'One does not define it thus.' He lowered his voice to a whisper. 'Last month a German was smuggling cigars. The custom-house was dark. Yet I refused because I did not like him. The gift of such men do not bring happiness. Non era simpatico. He paid for every one, and the fine for deception besides.'

'Do you gain much beyond your pay?' asked Gino, diverted for an instant.

'I do not accept small sums now. It is not worth the risk. But the German was another matter. But listen, my Gino, for I am older than you and more full of experience. The person who understands us at first sight, who never irritates us, who never bores, to whom we can pour forth every thought and wish, not only in speech but in silence—that is what I mean by simpatico.'

'There are such men, I know,' said Gino. 'And I have heard it said of children. But where will you find such a woman?'

'That is true. Here you are wiser than I. Sono poco simpatiche le donne. And the time we waste over them is much.' He sighed dolefully, as if he found the nobility of his sex a burden.

'One I have seen who may be so. She spoke very little, but she was a young lady—different to most. She, too, was English, the companion of my wife here. But Fra Filippo, the brother-in-law, took her back with him. I saw them start. He was very angry.'

Then he spoke of his exciting and secret marriage, and they made fun of the unfortunate Philip, who had travelled over Europe to stop it.

'I regret though,' said Gino, when they had finished laughing, 'that I toppled him on to the bed. A great tall man! And when I am really amused I am often impolite.'

'You will never see him again,' said Spiridione, who carried plenty of philosophy about him. 'And by now the scene will have passed from his mind.'

'It sometimes happens that such things are recollected longest. I shall never see him again, of course; but it is no benefit to me that he should wish me ill. And even if he has forgotten, I am still sorry that I toppled him on to the bed.'

So their talk continued, at one moment full of childishness and tender wisdom, the next moment scandalously gross. The shadows of the terracotta pillars lengthened, and tourists, flying through the Palazzo Pubblico opposite, could observe how the Italians wasted time.

The sight of tourists reminded Gino of something he might say. 'I want to consult you since you are so kind as to take an interest in my affairs. My wife wishes to take solitary walks.'

Spiridione was shocked.

'But I have forbidden her.'

'Naturally.'

'She does not yet understand. She asked me to accompany her sometimes—to walk without object! You know, she would like me to be with her all day.'

'I see, I see.' He knitted his brows and tried to think how he could help his friend. 'She needs employment. Is she a Catholic?'

'No.'

'That is a pity. She must be persuaded. It will be a great solace to her when she is alone.'

'I am a Catholic, but of course I never go to church.'

'Of course not. Still, you might take her at first. That is what my brother has done with his wife at Bologna, and he has joined the Free Thinkers. He took her once or twice himself, and now she has acquired the habit and continues to go without him.'

'Most excellent advice, and I thank you for it. But she wishes to give tea-parties—men and women together whom she has never seen.'

'Oh, the English! they are always thinking of tea. They carry it by the kilogramme in their trunks, and they are so clumsy that they always pack it at the top. But it is absurd!'

'What am I to do about it?'

'Do nothing. Or ask me!'

'Come!' cried Gino, springing up. 'She will be quite pleased.'

The dashing young fellow coloured crimson. 'Of course I was only joking.'

'I know. But she wants me to take my friends. Come now! Waiter!'

'If I do come,' cried the other, 'and take tea with you, this bill must be my affair.'

'Certainly not; you are in my country!'

A long argument ensued, in which the waiter took part, suggesting various solutions. At last Gino triumphed. The bill came to eightpence-halfpenny, and a halfpenny for the waiter brought it up to ninepence. Then there was a shower of gratitude on one side and of deprecation on the other, and when courtesies were at their height they suddenly linked arms and swung down the street, tickling each other with lemonade straws as they went.

Lilia was delighted to see them, and became more animated than Gino had known her for a long time. The tea tasted of chopped hay, and they asked to be allowed to drink it out of a wineglass, and refused milk; but, as she repeatedly observed, this was something like. Spiridione's manners were very agreeable. He kissed her hand on introduction, and as his profession had taught him a little English, conversation did not flag.

'Do you like music?' she asked.

'Passionately,' he replied. 'I have not studied scientific music, but the music of the heart, yes.'

So she played on the humming piano very badly, and he sang, not so badly. Gino got out a guitar and sang too, sitting out on the loggia. It was a most agreeable visit.

Gino said he would just walk his friend back to his lodgings. As they went he said, without the least trace of malice or satire in his voice, 'I think you are quite right. I shall not bring people to the house any more. I do not see why an English wife should be treated differently. This is Italy.'

'You are very wise,' exclaimed the other; 'very wise indeed. The more precious a possession the more carefully it should be guarded.'

They had reached the lodging, but went on as far as the Caffè Garibaldi, where they spent a long and most delightful evening.

Chapter Four

The advance of regret can be so gradual that it is impossible to say 'yesterday I was happy, to-day I am not.' At no one moment did Lilia realise that her marriage was a failure; yet during the summer and autumn she became as unhappy as it was possible for her nature to be. She had no unkind treatment, and few unkind words, from her husband. He simply left her alone. In the morning he went out to do 'business,' which, as far as she could discover, meant sitting in the Farmacia. He usually returned to lunch, after which he retired to another room and slept. In the evening he grew vigorous again, and took the air on the ramparts, often having his dinner out, and seldom returning till midnight or later. There were, of course, the times when he was away altogether—at Empoli, Siena, Florence, Bologna—for he delighted in travel, and seemed to pick up friends all over the country. Lilia often heard what a favourite he was.

She began to see that she must assert herself, but she could not see how. Her self-confidence, which had overthrown Philip, had gradually oozed away. If she left the strange house there was the strange little town. If she were to disobey her husband and walk in the country, that would be stranger still—vast slopes of olives and vineyards, with chalk-white farms, and in the distance other slopes, with more olives and more farms, and more little towns outlined against the cloudless sky. 'I don't call this country,' she would say. 'Why, it's not as wild as Sawston Park!' And, indeed, there was scarcely a touch of wildness in it—some of those slopes had been under cultivation for two thousand years. But it was terrible and mysterious all the same, and its continued presence made Lilia so uncomfortable that she forgot her nature and began to reflect.

She reflected chiefly about her marriage. The ceremony had been hasty and expensive, and the rites, whatever they were, were not those of the Church of England. Lilia had no religion in her; but for hours at a time she would be seized with a vulgar fear that she was not 'married properly.' And that her social position in the next world might be as obscure as it was in this. It might be safer to do the thing thoroughly, and one day she took the advice of Spiridione and joined the Roman Catholic Church, or as she called it, 'Santa Deodata's.' Gino approved; he, too, thought it safer, and it was fun confessing, though the priest was a stupid old man, and the whole thing was a good slap in the face for the people at home.

The people at home took the slap very soberly; indeed, there were few left for her to give it to. The Herritons were out of the question; they would not even let her write to Irma, though Irma was occasionally allowed to write to her. Mrs Theobald was rapidly subsiding into dotage, and, as far as she could be definite about anything, had definitely sided with the Herritons. And Miss Abbott did likewise. Night after night did Lilia curse this false friend, who had agreed with her that the marriage would 'do,' and that the Herritons would come round to it, and then, at the first hint of opposition, had fled back to England shrieking and distraught. Miss Abbott headed the long list of those who should never be written to, and who should never be forgiven. Almost the only person who was not on that list was Mr Kingcroft, who had unexpectedly sent an affectionate and inquiring letter. He was quite sure never to cross the Channel, and Lilia drew freely on her fancy in the reply.

At first she had seen a few English people, for Monteriano was not the end of the earth. One or two inquisitive ladies, who had heard at home of her quarrel with the Herritons, came to call. She was very sprightly, and they thought her quite unconventional, and Gino a charming boy, so all that was to the good. But by May the season, such as it was, had finished, and there would be no one till next spring. As Mrs Herriton had often observed, Lilia had no resources. She did not like music, or reading, or work. Her one qualification for life was rather blowsy high spirits, which turned querulous or boisterous according to circumstances. She was not obedient, but she was cowardly, and in the most gentle way, which Mrs Herriton might have envied, Gino made her do what he wanted. At first it had been rather fun to let him get the upper hand. But it was galling to discover that he could not do otherwise. He had a good strong will when he chose to use it, and would not have had the least scruple in using bolts and locks to put it into effect. There was plenty of brutality deep down in him, and one day Lilia nearly touched it.

It was the old question of going out alone.

'I always do it in England.'

'This is Italy.'

'Yes, but I'm older than you, and I'll settle.'

'I am your husband,' he said smiling. They had finished their midday meal, and he wanted to go and sleep. Nothing would rouse him up, until at last Lilia, getting more and more angry, said, 'And I've got the money.'

He looked horrified.

Now was the moment to assert herself. She made the statement again. He got up from his chair.

'And you'd better mend your manners,' she continued, 'for you'd find it awkward if I stopped drawing cheques.'

She was no reader of character, but she quickly became alarmed. As she said to Perfetta afterwards, 'None of his clothes seemed to fit—too big in one place, too small in another.' His figure rather than his face altered, the shoulders falling forward till his coat wrinkled across the back and pulled away from the wrists. He seemed all arms. He edged round the table to where she was sitting, and she sprang away and held the chair between them, too frightened to speak or to move. He looked at her with round expressionless eyes, and slowly stretched out his left hand.

Perfetta was heard coming up from the kitchen. It seemed to wake him up, and he turned away and went to his room without a word.

'What has happened?' cried Lilia, nearly fainting. 'He is ill—ill.'

Perfetta looked suspicious when she heard the account. 'What did you say to him?' She crossed herself.

'Hardly anything,' said Lilia, and crossed herself also. Thus did the two women pay homage to their outraged male.

It was clear to Lilia at last that Gino had married her for money. But he had frightened her too much to leave any place for contempt. His return was terrifying, for he was frightened too, imploring her pardon, lying at her feet, embracing her, murmuring 'It was not I,' striving to define things which he did not understand. He stopped in the house for three days, positively ill with physical collapse. But for all his suffering he had tamed her, and she never threatened to cut off supplies again.

Perhaps he kept her even closer than convention demanded. But he was very young, and he could not bear it to be said of him that he did not know how to treat a lady—or to manage a wife. And his own social position was uncertain. Even in England a dentist is a troublesome creature, whom careful people find difficult to class. He hovers between the professions and the trades; he may be only a little lower than the doctors, or he may be down among the chemists, or even beneath them. The son of the Italian dentist felt this too. For himself nothing mattered; he made friends with the people he liked, for he was that glorious invariable creature, a man. But his wife should visit nowhere rather than visit wrongly: seclusion was both decent and safe. The social ideals of North and South had had their brief contention, and this time the South had won.

It would have been well if he had been as strict over his own behaviour as he was over hers. But the incongruity never occurred to him for a moment. His morality was that of the average Latin, and as he was suddenly placed in the position of a gentleman, he did not see why he should not behave as such. Of course, had Lilia been different—had she asserted herself and got a grip on his character—he might possibly—though not probably—have been made a better husband as well as a better man, and at all events he could have adopted the attitude of the Englishman, whose standard is higher even when his practice is the same. But had Lilia been different she might not have married him.

The discovery of his infidelity—which she made by accident—destroyed such remnants of self-satisfaction as her life might yet possess. She broke down utterly, and sobbed and cried in Perfetta's arms. Perfetta was kind and even sympathetic, but cautioned her on no account to speak to Gino, who would be furious if he was suspected. And Lilia agreed, partly because she was afraid of him, partly because it was, after all, the best and most dignified thing to do. She had given up everything for him—her daughter, her relatives, her friends, all the little comforts and luxuries of a civilised life—and even if she had the courage to break away, there was no one who would receive her now. The Herritons had been almost malignant in their efforts against her, and all her friends had one by one fallen off. So it was better to live on humbly, trying not to feel, endeavouring by a cheerful demeanour to put things right. 'Perhaps,' she thought, 'if I have a child he will be different. I know he wants a son.'

Lilia had achieved pathos despite herself, for there are some situations in which vulgarity counts no longer. Not Cordelia nor Imogen more deserve our tears.

She herself cried frequently, making herself look plain and old, which distressed her husband. He was particularly kind to her when he hardly ever saw her, and she accepted his kindness without resentment, even with gratitude, so docile had she become. She did not hate him, even as she had never loved him; with her it was only when she was excited that the semblance of either passion arose. People said she was headstrong, but really her weak brain left her cold.

Suffering, however, is more independent of temperament, and the wisest of women could hardly have suffered more.

As for Gino, he was quite as boyish as ever, and carried his iniquities like a feather. A favourite speech of his was, 'Ah, one ought to marry! Spiridione is wrong; I must persuade him. Not till marriage does one realise the pleasures and the possibilities of life.' So saying, he would take down his felt hat, strike it in the right place as infallibly as a German strikes his in the wrong place, and leave her.

One evening, when he had gone out thus, Lilia could stand it no longer. It was September. Sawston would be just filling up after the summer holidays. People would be running in and out of each other's houses all along the road. There were bicycle gymkhanas, and on the 30th Mrs Herriton would be holding the annual bazaar in her garden for the C.M.S. It seemed impossible that such a free, happy life could exist. She walked out on to the loggia. Moonlight and stars in a soft purple sky. The walls of Monteriano should be glorious on such a night as this. But the house faced away from them.

Perfetta was banging in the kitchen, and the stairs down led past the kitchen door. But the stairs up to the attic—the stairs no one ever used—opened out of the living-room, and by unlocking the door at the top one might slip out on to the square terrace above the house, and thus for ten minutes walk in freedom and peace.

The key was in the pocket of Gino's best suit—the English check—which he never wore. The stairs creaked and the keyhole screamed; but Perfetta was growing deaf. The walls were beautiful, but as they faced west they were in shadow. To see the light upon them she must walk round the town a little, till they were caught by the beams of the rising moon. She looked anxiously at the house, and started.

It was easy walking, for a little path ran all outside the ramparts. The few people she met wished her a civil good night, taking her, in her hatless condition, for a peasant. The walls trended round towards the moon; and presently she came into its light, and saw all the rough towers turn into pillars of silver and black, and the ramparts into cliffs of pearl. She had no great sense of beauty, but she was sentimental, and she began to cry; for here, where a great cypress interrupted the monotony of the girdle of olives, she had sat with Gino one afternoon in March, her head upon his shoulder, while Caroline was looking at the view and sketching. Round the corner was the Siena gate, from which the road to England started, and she could hear the rumble of the diligence which was going down to catch the night train to Empoli. The next moment it was upon her, for the high road came towards her a little before it began its long zigzag down the hill.

The driver slackened, and called to her to get in. He did not know who she was. He hoped she might be coming to the station.

'Non vengo!' she cried.

He wished her good night, and turned his horses down the corner. As the diligence came round she saw that it was empty.

'Vengo . . .'

Her voice was tremulous, and did not carry. The horses swung off.

'Vengo! Vengo!'

He had begun to sing, and heard nothing. She ran down the road screaming to him to stop—that she was coming; while the distance grew greater and the noise of the diligence increased. The man's back was black and square against the moon, and if he would but turn for an instant she would be saved. She tried to cut off the corner of the zigzag, stumbling over the great clods of earth, large and hard as rocks, which lay between the eternal olives. She was too late; for, just before she regained the road, the thing swept past her, thunderous, ploughing up choking clouds of moonlit dust.

She did not call any more, for she felt very ill, and fainted; and when she revived she was lying in the road, with dust in her eyes, and dust in her mouth, and dust down her ears. There is something very terrible in dust at night-time.

'What shall I do?' she moaned. 'He will be so angry.'

And without further effort she slowly climbed back to captivity, shaking her garments as she went.

Ill-luck pursued her to the end. It was one of the nights when Gino happened to come in. He was in the kitchen, swearing and smashing plates, while Perfetta, her apron over her head, was weeping violently. At the sight of Lilia he turned upon her and poured forth a flood of miscellaneous abuse. He was far more angry but much less alarming than he had been that day when he edged after her round the table. And Lilia gained more courage from her bad conscience than she ever had from her good one, for as he spoke she was seized with indignation and feared him no longer, and saw him for a cruel, worthless, hypocritical, dissolute upstart, and spoke in return.

Perfetta screamed, for she told him everything—all she knew and all she thought. He stood with open mouth, all the anger gone out of him, feeling ashamed, and an utter fool. He was fairly and rightfully cornered. When had husband so given himself away before? She finished; and he was dumb, for she had spoken truly. Then, alas! the absurdity of his own position grew upon him, and he laughed—as he would have laughed at the same situation on the stage.

'You laugh?' stammered Lilia.

'Ah!' he cried, 'who could help it? I, who thought you knew and saw nothing—I am tricked—I am conquered. I give in. Let us talk of it no more.'

He touched her on the shoulder like a good comrade, half-amused and half-penitent, and then, murmuring and smiling to himself, ran quietly out of the room.

Perfetta burst into congratulations. 'What courage you have!' she cried; 'and what good fortune! He is angry no longer! He has forgiven you!'

Neither Perfetta, nor Gino, nor Lilia herself knew the true reason of all the misery that followed. To the end he thought that kindness and a little attention would be enough to set things straight. His wife was a very ordinary woman, and why should her ideas differ from his own? No one realised that more than personalities were engaged; that the struggle was national; that generations of ancestors, good, bad, or indifferent, forbade the Latin man to be chivalrous to the northern woman, the northern woman to forgive the Latin man. All this might have been foreseen: Mrs Herriton foresaw it from the first.

Meanwhile Lilia prided herself on her high personal standard, and Gino simply wondered why she did not come round. He hated discomfort, and yearned for sympathy, but shrank from mentioning his difficulties in the town in case they were put down to his own incompetence. Spiridione was told, and replied in a philosophical but not very helpful letter. His other great friend, whom he trusted more, was still serving in Eretrea or some other desolate outpost. It would take too long to explain everything to him. And, besides, what was the good of letters? Friends cannot travel through the post.

Lilia, so similar to her husband in many ways, yearned for comfort and sympathy too. The night he laughed at her she wildly took up paper and pen and wrote page after page, analysing his character, enumerating his iniquities, reporting whole conversations, tracing all the causes and the growth of her misery. She was beside herself with passion, and though she could hardly think or see, she suddenly attained to magnificence and pathos which a practised stylist might have envied. It was written like a diary, and not till its conclusion did she realise for whom it was meant.

'Irma, darling Irma, this letter is for you. I almost forget I have a daughter. It will make you unhappy, but I want you to know everything, and you cannot learn things too soon. God bless you, my dearest, and save you. God bless your miserable mother.'

Fortunately Mrs Herriton was in when the letter arrived. She seized it and opened it in her bedroom. Another moment, and Irma's placid childhood would have been destroyed for ever.

Lilia received a brief note from Harriet, again forbidding direct communication between mother and daughter, and concluding with formal condolences. It nearly drove her mad.

'Gently! gently!' said her husband. They were sitting together on the loggia when the letter arrived. He often sat with her now, watching her for hours, puzzled and anxious, but not contrite.

'It's nothing.' She went in and tore it up, and then began to write—a very short letter, whose gist was 'Come and save me.'

It is not good to see your wife crying when she writes—especially if you are conscious that, on the whole, your treatment of her has been reasonable and kind. It is not good, when you accidentally look over her shoulder, to see that she is writing to a man. Nor should she shake her fist at you when she leaves the room, under the impression that you are engaged in lighting a cigar and cannot see her.

Lilia went to the post herself. But in Italy so many things can be arranged. The postman was a friend of Gino's and Mr Kingcroft never got his letter.

So she gave up hope, became ill, and all through the autumn lay in bed. Gino was distracted. She knew why: he wanted a son. He could talk and think of nothing else. His one desire was to become the father of a man like himself, and it held him with a grip he only partially understood, for it was the first great desire, the first great passion of his life. Falling in love was a mere physical triviality, like warm sun or cool water, beside this divine hope of immortality: 'I continue.' He gave candles to Santa Deodata, for he was always religious at a crisis, and sometimes he went to her himself and prayed the crude uncouth demands of the simple. Impetuously he summoned all his relatives back to bear him company in his time of need, and Lilia saw strange faces flitting past her in the darkened room.

'My love!' he would say, 'my dearest Lilia! Be calm. I have never loved anyone but you.'

She, knowing everything, would only smile gently, too broken by suffering to make sarcastic repartees.

Before the child was born he gave her a kiss, and said, 'I have prayed all night for a boy.'

Some strangely tender impulse moved her, and she said faintly, 'You are a boy yourself, Gino.'

He answered, 'Then we shall be brothers.'

He lay outside the room with his head against the door like a dog. When they came to tell him the glad news they found him half-unconscious, and his face was wet with tears.

As for Lilia, some one said to her, 'It is a beautiful boy!' But she had died in giving birth to him.

Chapter Five

At the time of Lilia's death Philip Herriton was just twenty-four years of age—indeed, the news reached Sawston on his birthday. He was a tall, weakly-built young man, whose clothes had to be judiciously padded on the shoulder in order to make him pass muster. His face was plain rather than not, and there was a curious mixture in it of good and bad. He had a fine forehead and a good large nose, and both observation and sympathy were in his eyes. But below the nose and eyes all was confusion, and those people who believe that destiny resides in the mouth and chin shook their heads when they looked at him.

Philip himself, as a boy, had been keenly conscious of these defects. Sometimes when he had been bullied or hustled about at school he would retire to his cubicle and examine his features in a looking-glass, and he would sigh and say, 'It is a weak face. I shall never carve a place for myself in the world.' But as years went on he became either less self-conscious or more self-satisfied. The world, he found, made a niche for him as it did for every one. Decision of character might come later—or he might have it without knowing. At all events he had got a sense of beauty and a sense of humour, two most desirable gifts. The sense of beauty developed first. It caused him at the age of twenty to wear parti-coloured ties and a squashy hat, to be late for dinner on account of the sunset, and to catch art from Burne-Jones to Praxiteles. At twenty-two he went to Italy with some cousins, and there he absorbed into one æsthetic whole olive-trees, blue sky, frescoes, country inns, saints, peasants, mosaics, statues, beggars. He came back with the air of a prophet who would either remodel Sawston or reject it. All the energies and enthusiasms of a rather friendless life had passed into the championship of beauty.

In a short time it was over. Nothing had happened either in Sawston or within himself. He had shocked half a dozen people, squabbled with his sister, and bickered with his mother. He concluded that nothing could happen, not knowing that human love and love of truth sometimes conquer where love of beauty fails.

A little disenchanted, a little tired, but æsthetically intact, he resumed his placid life, relying more and more on his second gift, the gift of humour. If he could not reform the world, he could at all events laugh at it, thus attaining at least an intellectual superiority. Laughter, he read and believed, was a sign of good moral health, and he laughed on contentedly, till Lilia's marriage toppled contentment down for ever. Italy, the land of beauty, was ruined for him. She had no power to change men and things who dwelt in her. She, too, could produce avarice, brutality, stupidity—and, what was worse, vulgarity. It was on her soil and through her influence that a silly woman had married a cad. He hated Gino, the betrayer of his life's ideal, and now that the sordid tragedy had come, it filled him with pangs, not of sympathy, but of final disillusion.

The disillusion was convenient for Mrs Herriton, who saw a trying little period ahead of her, and was glad to have her family united.

'Are we to go into mourning, do you think?' She always asked her children's advice where possible.

Harriet thought that they should. She had been detestable to Lilia while she lived, but she always felt that the dead deserve attention and sympathy. 'After all she has suffered. That letter kept me awake for nights. The whole thing is like one of those horrible modern plays where no one is in the right. But if we have mourning, it will mean telling Irma.'

'Of course we must tell Irma!' said Philip.

'Of course,' said his mother. 'But I think we can still not tell her about Lilia's marriage.'

'I don't think that. And she must have suspected something by now.'

'So one would have supposed. But she never cared for her mother, and little girls of nine don't reason clearly. She looks on it as a long visit. And it is important, most important, that she should not receive a shock. All a child's life depends on the ideal it has of its parents. Destroy that and everything goes—morals, behaviour, everything. Absolute trust in some one else is the essence of education. That is why I have been so careful about talking of poor Lilia before her.'

'But you forget this wretched baby. Waters and Adamson write that there is a baby.'

'Mrs Theobald must be told. But she doesn't count. She is breaking up very quickly. She doesn't even see Mr Kingcroft now. He, thank goodness, I hear, has at last consoled himself with some one else.'

'The child must know some time,' persisted Philip, who felt a little displeased, though he could not tell with what.

'The later the better. Every moment she is developing.'

'I must say it seems rather hard luck, doesn't it?'

'On Irma? Why?'

'On us, perhaps. We have morals and behaviour also, and I don't think this continual secrecy improves them.'

'There's no need to twist the thing round to that,' said Harriet, rather disturbed.

'Of course there isn't,' said her mother. 'Let's keep to the main issue. This baby's quite beside the point. Mrs Theobald will do nothing, and it's no concern of ours.'

'It will make a difference in the money, surely,' said he.

'No, dear; very little. Poor Charles provided for every kind of contingency in his will. The money will come to you and Harriet, as Irma's guardians.'

'Good. Does the Italian get anything?'

'He will get all hers. But you know what that is.'

'Good. So those are our tactics—to tell no one about the baby, not even Miss Abbott.'

'Most certainly this is the proper course,' said Mrs Herriton, preferring 'course' to 'tactics' for Harriet's sake. 'And whyever should we tell Caroline?'

'She was so mixed up in the affair.'

'Poor silly creature. The less she hears about it the better she will be pleased. I have come to be very sorry for Caroline. She, if anyone, has suffered and been penitent. She burst into tears when I told her a little, only a little, of that terrible letter. I never saw such genuine remorse. We must forgive her and forget. Let the dead bury their dead. We will not trouble her with them.'

Philip saw that his mother was scarcely logical. But there was no advantage in saying so. 'Here beginneth the New Life, then. Do you remember, mother, that was what we said when we saw Lilia off?'

'Yes, dear; but now it is really a New Life, because we are all at accord. Then you were still infatuated with Italy. It may be full of beautiful pictures and churches, but we cannot judge a country by anything but its men.'

'That is quite true,' he said sadly. And as the tactics were now settled, he went out and took an aimless and solitary walk.

By the time he came back two important things had happened. Irma had been told of her mother's death, and Miss Abbott, who had called for a subscription, had been told also.

Irma had wept loudly, had asked a few sensible questions and a good many silly ones, and had been content with evasive answers. Fortunately the school prizegiving was at hand, and that, together with the prospect of new black clothes, kept her from meditating on the fact that Lilia, who had been absent so long, would now be absent for ever.

'As for Caroline,' said Mrs Herriton, 'I was almost frightened. She broke down utterly. She cried even when she left the house. I comforted her as best I could, and I kissed her. It is something that the breach between her and ourselves is now entirely healed.'

'Did she ask no questions—as to the nature of Lilia's death, I mean?'

'She did. But she has a mind of extraordinary delicacy. She saw that I was reticent, and she did not press me. You see, Philip, I can say to you what I could not say before Harriet. Her ideas are so crude. Really we do not want it known in Sawston that there is a baby. All peace and comfort would be lost if people came inquiring after it.'

His mother knew how to manage him. He agreed enthusiastically. And a few days later, when he chanced to travel up to London with Miss Abbott, he had all the time the pleasant thrill of one who is better informed. Their last journey together had been from Monteriano back across Europe. It had been a ghastly journey, and Philip, from the force of association, rather expected something ghastly now.

He was surprised. Miss Abbott, between Sawston and Charing Cross, revealed qualities which he had never guessed her to possess. Without being exactly original, she did show a commendable intelligence, and though at times she was gauche and even uncourtly, he felt that here was a person whom it might be well to cultivate.

At first she annoyed him. They were talking, of course, about Lilia, when she broke the thread of vague commiseration and said abruptly, 'It is all so strange as well as so tragic. And what I did was as strange as anything.'

It was the first reference she had ever made to her contemptible behaviour. 'Never mind,' he said. 'It's all over now. Let the dead bury their dead. It's fallen out of our lives.'

'But that's why I can talk about it and tell you everything I have always wanted to. You thought me stupid and sentimental and wicked and mad, but you never really knew how much I was to blame.'

'Indeed, I never think about it now,' said Philip gently. He knew that her nature was in the main generous and upright: it was unnecessary of her to reveal her thoughts.

'The first evening we got to Monteriano,' she persisted, 'Lilia went out for a walk alone, saw that Italian in a picturesque position on a wall, and fell in love. He was shabbily dressed, and she did not even know he was the son of a dentist. I must tell you I was used to this sort of thing. Once or twice before I had had to send people about their business.'

'Yes; we counted on you,' said Philip, with sudden sharpness. After all, if she would reveal her thoughts, she must take the consequences.

'I know you did,' she retorted with equal sharpness. 'Lilia saw him several times again, and I knew I ought to interfere. I called her to my bedroom one night. She was very frightened, for she knew what it was about and how severe I could be. "Do you love this man?" I asked. "Yes or no?" She said "Yes." And I said, "Why don't you marry him if you think you'll be happy?"'

'Really—really,' exploded Philip, as exasperated as if the thing had happened yesterday. 'You knew Lilia all your life. Apart from everything else—as if she could choose what could make her happy!'

'Had you ever let her choose?' she flashed out. 'I'm afraid that's rude,' she added, trying to calm herself.

'Let us rather say unhappily expressed,' said Philip, who always adopted a dry satirical manner when he was puzzled.

'I want to finish. Next morning I found Signor Carella and said the same to him. He—well, he was willing. That's all.'

'And the telegram?' He looked scornfully out of the window.

Hitherto her voice had been hard, possibly in self-accusation, possibly in defiance. Now it became unmistakably sad. 'Ah, the telegram! That was wrong. Lilia there was more cowardly than I was. We should have told the truth. It lost me my nerve, at all events. I came to the station meaning to tell you everything then. But we had started with a lie, and I got frightened. And at the end, when you left, I got frightened again and came with you.'

'Did you really mean to stop?'

'For a time, at all events.'

'Would that have suited a newly married pair?'

'It would have suited them. Lilia needed me. And as for him—I can't help feeling I might have got influence over him.'

'I am ignorant of these matters,' said Philip; 'but I should have thought that would have increased the difficulty of the situation.'

The crisp remark was wasted on her. She looked hopelessly at the raw over-built country, and said, 'Well, I have explained.'

'But pardon me, Miss Abbott; of most of your conduct you have given a description rather than an explanation.'

He had fairly caught her, and expected that she would gape and collapse. To his surprise she answered with some spirit, 'An explanation may bore you, Mr Herriton: it drags in other topics.'

'Oh, never mind.'

'I hated Sawston, you see.'

He was delighted. 'So did and do I. That's splendid. Go on.'

'I hated the idleness, the stupidity, the respectability, the petty unselfishness.'

'Petty selfishness,' he corrected. Sawston psychology had long been his speciality.

'Petty unselfishness,' she repeated. 'I had got an idea that every one here spent their lives in making little sacrifices for objects they didn't care for, to please people they didn't love; that they never learnt to be sincere—and, what's as bad, never learnt how to enjoy themselves. That's what I thought—what I thought at Monteriano.'

'Why, Miss Abbott,' he cried, 'you should have told me this before! Think it still! I agree with lots of it. Magnificent!'

'Now Lilia,' she went on, 'though there were things about her I didn't like, had somehow kept the power of enjoying herself with sincerity. And Gino, I thought, was splendid, and young, and strong not only in body, and sincere as the day. If they wanted to marry, why shouldn't they do so? Why shouldn't she break with the deadening life where she had got into a groove, and would go on in it, getting more and more—worse than unhappy—apathetic till she died? Of course I was wrong. She only changed one groove for another—a worse groove. And as for him—well, you know more about him than I do. I can never trust myself to judge characters again. But I still feel he cannot have been quite bad when we first met him. Lilia—that I should dare to say it!—must have been cowardly. He was only a boy—just going to turn into something fine, I thought—and she must have mismanaged him. So that is the one time I have gone against what is proper, and there are the results. You have an explanation now.'

'And much of it has been most interesting, though I don't understand everything. Did you never think of the disparity of their social position?'

'We were mad—drunk with rebellion. We had no common sense. As soon as you came, you saw and foresaw everything.'

'Oh, I don't think that.' He was vaguely displeased at being credited with common sense. For a moment Miss Abbott had seemed to him more unconventional than himself.

'I hope you see,' she concluded, 'why I have troubled you with this long story. Women—I heard you say the other day—are never at ease till they tell their faults out loud. Lilia is dead and her husband gone to the bad—all through me. You see, Mr Herriton, it makes me specially unhappy; it's the only time I've ever gone into what my father calls "real life"—and look what I've made of it! All that winter I seemed to be waking up to beauty and splendour and I don't know what; and when the spring came, I wanted to fight against the things I hated—mediocrity and dullness and spitefulness and society. I actually hated society for a day or two at Monteriano. I didn't see that all these things are invincible, and that if we go against them they will break us to pieces. Thank you for listening to so much nonsense.'

'Oh, I quite sympathise with what you say,' said Philip encouragingly; 'it isn't nonsense, and a year or two ago I should have been saying it too. But I feel differently now, and I hope that you also will change. Society *is* invincible—to a certain degree. But your real life is your own, and nothing can touch it. There is no power on earth that can prevent your criticising and despising mediocrity—nothing that can stop you retreating into splendour and beauty—into the thoughts and beliefs that make the real life—the real you.'

'I have never had that experience yet. Surely I and my life must be where I live.'

Evidently she had the usual feminine incapacity for grasping philosophy. But she had developed quite a personality, and he must see more of her. 'There is another great consolation against invincible mediocrity,' he said—'the meeting a fellow-victim. I hope that this is only the first of many discussions that we shall have together.'

She made a suitable reply. The train reached Charing Cross, and they parted—he to go to a matinée, she to buy petticoats for the corpulent poor. Her thoughts wandered as she bought them: the gulf between herself and Mr Herriton, which she had always known to be great, now seemed to her immeasurable.

These events and conversations took place at Christmas-time. The New Life initiated by them lasted some seven months. Then a little incident—a mere little vexatious incident—brought it to its close.

Irma collected picture post cards, and Mrs Herriton or Harriet always glanced first at all that came, lest the child should get hold of something vulgar. On this occasion the subject seemed perfectly inoffensive—a lot of ruined factory chimneys—and Harriet was about to hand it to her niece when her eye was caught by the words on the margin. She gave a shriek and flung the card into the grate. Of course no fire was alight in July, and Irma only had to run and pick it out again.

'How dare you!' screamed her aunt. 'You wicked girl! Give it here!'

Unfortunately Mrs Herriton was out of the room. Irma, who was not in awe of Harriet, danced round the table, reading as she did so, 'View of the superb city of Monteriano—from your lital brother.'

Stupid Harriet caught her, boxed her ears, and tore the post card into fragments. Irma howled with pain, and began shouting indignantly, 'Who is my little brother? Why have I never heard of him before? Grandmamma! Grandmamma! Who is my little brother? Who is my—'

Mrs Herriton swept into the room, saying, 'Come with me, dear, and I will tell you. Now it is time for you to know.'

Irma returned from the interview sobbing, though, as a matter of fact, she had learnt very little. But that little took hold of her imagination. She had promised secrecy—she knew not why. But what harm in talking of the little brother to those who had heard of him already?

'Aunt Harriet!' she would say. 'Uncle Phil! Grandmamma! What do you suppose my little brother is doing now? Has he begun to play? Do Italian babies talk sooner than us, or would he be an English baby born abroad? Oh, I do long to see him, and be the first to teach him the Ten Commandments and the Catechism.'

The last remark always made Harriet look grave.

'Really,' exclaimed Mrs Herriton, 'Irma is getting too tiresome. She forgot poor Lilia soon enough.'

'A living brother is more to her than a dead mother,' said Philip dreamily. 'She can knit him socks.'

'I stopped that. She is bringing him in everywhere. It is most vexatious. The other night she asked if she might include him in the people she mentions specially in her prayers.'

'What did you say?'

'Of course I allowed her,' she replied coldly. 'She has a right to mention any one she chooses. But I was annoyed with her this morning, and I fear that I showed it.'

'And what happened this morning?'

'She asked if she could pray for her "new father"–for the Italian!'

'Did you let her?'

'I got up without saying anything.'

'You must have felt just as you did when I wanted to pray for the devil.'

'He is the devil,' cried Harriet.

'No, Harriet; he is too vulgar.'

'I will thank you not to scoff against religion!' was Harriet's retort. 'Think of that poor baby. Irma is right to pray for him. What an entrance into life for an English child!'

'My dear sister, I can reassure you. Firstly, the beastly baby is Italian. Secondly, it was promptly christened at Santa Deodata's, and a powerful combination of saints watch over—'

'Don't, dear. And, Harriet, don't be so serious–I mean not so serious when you are with Irma. She will be worse than ever if she thinks we have something to hide.'

Harriet's conscience could be quite as tiresome as Philip's uncon-ventionality. Mrs Herriton soon made it easy for her daughter to go for six weeks to the Tirol. Then she and Philip began to grapple with Irma alone.

Just as they had got things a little quiet the beastly baby sent another picture post card–a comic one, not particularly proper. Irma received it while they were out, and all the trouble began again.

'I cannot think,' said Mrs Herriton, 'what his motive is in sending them.'

Two years before, Philip would have said that the motive was to give pleasure. Now he, like his mother, tried to think of something sinister and subtle.

'Do you suppose that he guesses the situation–how anxious we are to hush the scandal up?'

'That is quite possible. He knows that Irma will worry us about the baby. Perhaps he hopes that we shall adopt it to quiet her.'

'Hopeful indeed.'

'At the same time he has the chance of corrupting the child's morals.' She unlocked a drawer, took out the post card, and regarded it gravely. 'He entreats her to send the baby one,' was her next remark.

'She might do it too!'

'I told her not to; but we must watch her carefully, without, of course, appearing to be suspicious.'

Philip was getting to enjoy his mother's diplomacy. He did not think of his own morals and behaviour any more.

'Who's to watch her at school, though? She may bubble out any moment.'

'We can but trust to our influence,' said Mrs Herriton.

Irma did bubble out, that very day. She was proof against a single post card, not against two. A new little brother is a valuable sentimental asset to a schoolgirl, and her school was then passing through an acute phase of baby-worship. Happy the girl who had her quiver full of them, who kissed them when she left home in the morning, who had the right to extricate them from mail-carts in the interval, who dangled them at tea ere they retired to rest! That one might sing the unwritten song of Miriam, blessed above all schoolgirls, who was allowed to hide her baby brother in a squashy place, where none but herself could find him!

How could Irma keep silent when pretentious girls spoke of baby cousins and baby visitors--she who had a baby brother, who wrote her post cards through his dear papa? She had promised not to tell about him—she knew not why—and she told. And one girl told another, and one girl told her mother, and the thing was out.

'Yes, it is all very sad,' Mrs Herriton kept saying. 'My daughter-in-law made a very unhappy marriage, as I dare say you know. I suppose that the child will be educated in Italy. Possibly his grandmother may be doing something, but I have not heard of it. I do not expect that she will have him over. She disapproves of the father. It is altogether a painful business for her.'

She was careful only to scold Irma for disobedience—that eighth deadly sin, so convenient to parents and guardians. Harriet would have plunged into needless explanations and abuse. The child was ashamed, and talked about the baby less. The end of the school year was at hand, and she hoped to get another prize. But she also had put her hand to the wheel.

It was several days before they saw Miss Abbott. Mrs Herriton had not come across her much since the kiss of reconciliation, nor Philip since the journey to London. She had, indeed, been rather a disappointment to him. Her creditable display of originality had never been repeated: he feared she was slipping back. Now she came about the Cottage Hospital—her life was devoted to dull acts of charity—and though she got money out of him and out of his mother, she still sat tight in her chair, looking graver and more wooden than ever.

'I dare say you have heard,' said Mrs Herriton, well knowing what the matter was.

'Yes, I have. I came to ask you; have any steps been taken?'

Philip was astonished. The question was impertinent in the extreme. He had a regard for Miss Abbott, and regretted that she had been guilty of it.

'About the baby?' asked Mrs Herriton pleasantly.

'Yes.'

'As far as I know, no steps. Mrs Theobald may have decided on something, but I have not heard of it.'

'I was meaning, had you decided on anything?'

'The child is no relation of ours,' said Philip. 'It is therefore scarcely for us to interfere.'

His mother glanced at him nervously. 'Poor Lilia was almost a daughter to me once. I know what Miss Abbott means. But now things have altered. Any initiative would naturally come from Mrs Theobald.'

'But does not Mrs Theobald always take any initiative from you?' asked Miss Abbott.

Mrs Herriton could not help colouring. 'I sometimes have given her advice in the past. I should not presume to do so now.'

'Then is nothing to be done for the child at all?'

'It is extraordinarily good of you to take this unexpected interest,' said Philip.

'The child came into the world through my negligence,' replied Miss Abbott. 'It is natural I should take an interest in it.'

'My dear Caroline,' said Mrs Herriton, 'you must not brood over the thing. Let bygones be bygones. The child should worry you even less than it worries us. We never even mention it. It belongs to another world.'

Miss Abbott got up without replying, and turned to go. Her extreme gravity made Mrs Herriton uneasy. 'Of course,' she added, 'if Mrs Theobald decides on any plan that seems at all practicable—I must say I don't see any such—I shall ask if I may join her in it, for Irma's sake, and share in any possible expenses.'

'Please would you let me know if she decides on anything. I should like to join as well.'

'My dear, how you throw about your money! We would never allow it.'

'And if she decides on nothing, please also let me know. Let me know in any case.'

Mrs Herriton made a point of kissing her.

'Is the young person mad?' burst out Philip as soon as she had departed. 'Never in my life have I seen such colossal impertinence. She ought to be well smacked, and sent back to Sunday-school.'

His mother said nothing.

'But don't you see—she is practically threatening us? You can't put her off with Mrs Theobald; she knows as well as we do that she is a nonentity. If we won't do anything she's going to raise a scandal—that we neglect our relatives, etc., which is, of course, a lie. Still, she'll say it. Oh dear, sweet, sober Caroline Abbott has a screw loose! We knew it at Monteriano. I had my suspicions last year one day in the train; and here it is again. The young person is mad.'

She still said nothing.

'Shall I go round at once and give it her well? I'd really enjoy it.'

In a low, serious voice—such a voice as she had not used to him for months—Mrs Herriton said, 'Caroline has been extremely impertinent. Yet there may be something in what she says after all. Ought the child to grow up in that place—and with that father?'

Philip started and shuddered. He saw that his mother was not sincere. Her insincerity to others had amused him, but it was disheartening when used against himself.

'Let us admit frankly,' she continued, 'that after all we may have responsibilities.'

'I don't understand you, mother. You are turning absolutely round. What are you up to?'

In one moment an impenetrable barrier had been erected between them. They were no longer in smiling confidence. Mrs Herriton was off on tactics of her own—tactics which might be beyond or beneath him.

His remark offended her. 'Up to? I am wondering whether I ought not to adopt the child. Is that sufficiently plain?'

'And this is the result of half a dozen idiocies of Miss Abbott?'

'It is. I repeat, she has been extremely impertinent. None the less she is showing me my duty. If I can rescue poor Lilia's baby from that horrible man, who will bring it up either as Papist or infidel—who will certainly bring it up to be vicious—I shall do it.'

'You talk like Harriet.'

'And why not?' said she, flushing at what she knew to be an insult. 'Say, if you choose, that I talk like Irma. That child has seen the thing more clearly than any of us. She longs for her little brother. She shall have him. I don't care if I am impulsive.'

He was sure that she was not impulsive, but did not dare to say so. Her ability frightened him. All his life he had been her puppet. She had let him worship Italy, and reform Sawston—just as she had let Harriet be Low Church. She had let him talk as much as he liked. But when she wanted a thing she always got it.

And though she was frightening him, she did not inspire him with reverence. Her life, he saw, was without meaning. To what purpose was her diplomacy, her insincerity, her continued repression of vigour? Did they make anyone better or happier? Did they even bring happiness to herself? Harriet with her gloomy peevish creed, Lilia with her clutches after pleasure, were after all more divine than this well-ordered, active, useless machine.

Now that his mother had wounded his vanity he could criticise her thus. But he could not rebel. To the end of his days he would probably go on doing what she wanted. He watched with a cold interest the duel between her and Miss Abbott. Mrs Herriton's policy only appeared gradually. It was to prevent Miss Abbott interfering with the child at all costs, and if possible to prevent her at a small cost. Pride was the only solid element in her disposition. She could not bear to seem less charitable than others.

'I am planning what can be done,' she would tell people, 'and that kind Caroline Abbott is helping me. It is no business of either of us, but we are getting to feel that the baby must not be left entirely to that horrible man. It would be unfair to little Irma; after all, he is her half-brother. No, we have come to nothing definite.'

Miss Abbott was equally civil, but not to be appeased by good intentions. The child's welfare was a sacred duty to her, not a matter of pride or even of sentiment. By it alone, she felt, could she undo a little of the evil that she had permitted to come into the world. To her imagination Monteriano had become a magic city of vice, beneath whose towers no person could grow up happy or pure. Sawston, with its semi-detached houses and snobby schools, its book teas and bazaars, was certainly petty and dull; at times she found it even contemptible. But it was not a place of sin, and at Sawston, either with the Herritons or with herself, the baby should grow up.

As soon as it was inevitable, Mrs Herriton wrote a letter for Waters and Adamson to send to Gino—the oddest letter; Philip saw a copy of it afterwards. Its ostensible purpose was to complain of the picture post cards. Right at the end, in a few nonchalant sentences, she offered to adopt the child, provided that Gino would undertake never to come near it, and would surrender some of Lilia's money for its education.

'What do you think of it?' she asked her son. 'It would not do to let him know that we are anxious for it.'

'Certainly he will never suppose that.'

'But what effect will the letter have on him?'

'When he gets it he will do a sum. If it is less expensive in the long run to part with a little money and to be clear of the baby, he will part with it. If he would lose, he will adopt the tone of the loving father.'

'Dear, you're shockingly cynical.' After a pause she added, 'How would the sum work out?'

'I don't know, I'm sure. But if you wanted to ensure the baby being posted by return, you should have sent a little sum to *him*. Oh, I'm not cynical—at least I only go by what I know of him. But I am weary of the whole show. Weary of Italy. Weary, weary, weary. Sawston's a kind, pitiful place, isn't it? I will go walk in it and seek comfort.'

He smiled as he spoke, for the sake of not appearing serious. When he had left her she began to smile also.

It was to the Abbotts' that he walked. Mr Abbott offered him tea, and Caroline, who was keeping up her Italian in the next room, came in to pour it out. He told them that his mother had written to Signor Carella, and they both uttered fervent wishes for her success.

'Very fine of Mrs Herriton, very fine indeed,' said Mr Abbott, who, like every one else, knew nothing of his daughter's exasperating behaviour. 'I'm afraid it will mean a lot of expense. She will get nothing out of Italy without paying.'

'There are sure to be incidental expenses,' said Philip cautiously. Then he turned to Miss Abbott and said, 'Do you suppose we shall have difficulty with the man?'

'It depends,' she replied, with equal caution.

'From what you saw of him, should you conclude that he would make an affectionate parent?'

'I don't go by what I saw of him, but by what I know of him.'

'Well, what do you conclude from that?'

'That he is a thoroughly wicked man.'

'Yet thoroughly wicked men have loved their children. Look at Rodrigo Borgia, for example.'

'I have also seen examples of that in my district.'

With this remark the admirable young woman rose, and returned to keep up her Italian. She puzzled Philip extremely. He could understand enthusiasm, but she did not seem the least enthusiastic. He could understand pure cussedness, but it did not seem to be that either. Apparently she was deriving neither amusement nor profit from the struggle. Why, then, had she undertaken it? Perhaps she was not sincere. Perhaps, on the whole, that was most likely. She must be professing one thing and aiming at another. What the other thing could be he did not stop to consider. Insincerity was becoming his stock explanation for anything unfamiliar, whether that thing was a kindly action or a high ideal.

'She fences well,' he said to his mother afterwards.

'What had you to fence about?' she said suavely. Her son might know her tactics, but she refused to admit that he knew. She still pretended to him that the baby was the one thing she wanted, and had always wanted, and that Miss Abbott was her valued ally.

And when, next week, the reply came from Italy, she showed him no face of triumph. 'Read the letters,' she said. 'We have failed.'

Gino wrote in his own language, but the solicitors had sent a laborious English translation, where 'Pregiatissima Signora' was rendered as 'Most Praiseworthy Madam,' and every delicate compliment and superlative—superlatives are delicate in Italian—would have felled an ox. For a moment Philip forgot the matter in the manner; this grotesque memorial of the land he had loved moved him almost to tears. He knew the originals of these lumbering phrases; he also had sent 'sincere auguries'; he also had addressed letters—who writes at home?—from the Caffè Garibaldi. 'I didn't know I was still such an ass,' he thought. 'Why can't I realise that it's merely tricks of expression? A bounder's a bounder, whether he lives in Sawston or Monteriano.'

'Isn't it disheartening?' said his mother.

He then read that Gino could not accept the generous offer. His paternal heart would not permit him to abandon this symbol of his deplored spouse. As for the picture post cards, it displeased him greatly that they had been obnoxious. He would send no more. Would Mrs Herriton, with her notorious kindness, explain this to Irma, and thank her for those which Irma (courteous Miss!) had sent to him?

'The sum works out against us,' said Philip. 'Or perhaps he is putting up the price.'

'No,' said Mrs Herriton decidedly. 'It is not that. For some perverse reason he will not part with the child. I must go and tell poor Caroline. She will be equally distressed.'

She returned from the visit in the most extraordinary condition. Her face was red, she panted for breath, there were dark circles round her eyes.

'The impudence!' she shouted. 'The cursed impudence! Oh, I'm swearing. I don't care. That beastly woman—how dare she interfere—I'll—Philip, dear, I'm sorry. It's no good. You must go.'

'Go where? Do sit down. What's happened?' This outburst of violence from his elegant ladylike mother pained him dreadfully. He had not known that it was in her.

'She won't accept—won't accept the letter as final. You must go to Monteriano!'

'I won't!' he shouted back. 'I've been and I've failed. I'll never see the place again. I hate Italy.'

'If you don't go, she will.'

'Abbott?'

'Yes. Going alone; would start this evening. I offered to write; she said it was "too late!" Too late! The child, if you please—Irma's brother—to live with her, to be brought up by her and her father at our very gates, to go to school like a gentleman, she paying. Oh, you're a man! It doesn't matter for you. You can laugh. But I know what people say; and that woman goes to Italy this evening.'

He seemed to be inspired. 'Then let her go! Let her mess with Italy by herself. She'll come to grief somehow. Italy's too dangerous, too—'

'Stop that nonsense, Philip. I will not be disgraced by her. I *will* have the child. Pay all we've got for it. I will have it.'

'Let her go to Italy!' he cried. 'Let her meddle with what she doesn't understand! Look at this letter! The man who wrote it will marry her, or murder her, or do for her somehow. He's a bounder, but he's not an English bounder. He's mysterious and terrible. He's got a country behind him that's upset people from the beginning of the world.'

'Harriet!' exclaimed his mother. 'Harriet shall go too. Harriet, now, will be invaluable!' And before Philip had stopped talking nonsense, she had planned the whole thing and was looking out the trains.

Chapter Six

Italy, Philip had always maintained, is only her true self in the height of the summer, when the tourists have left her, and her soul awakes under the beams of a vertical sun. He now had every opportunity of seeing her at her best, for it was nearly the middle of August before he went out to meet Harriet in the Tirol.

He found his sister in a dense cloud five thousand feet above the sea, chilled to the bone, overfed, bored, and not at all unwilling to be fetched away.

'It upsets one's plans terribly,' she remarked, as she squeezed out her sponges, 'but obviously it is my duty.'

'Did mother explain it all to you?' asked Philip.

'Yes, indeed! Mother has written me a really beautiful letter. She describes how it was that she gradually got to feel that we must rescue the poor baby from its terrible surroundings, how she has tried by letter, and it is no good—nothing but insincere compliments and hypocrisy came back. Then she says, "There is nothing like personal influence; you and Philip will succeed where I have failed." She says, too, that Caroline Abbott has been wonderful.'

Philip assented.

'Caroline feels it as keenly almost as us. That is because she knows the man. Oh, he must be loathsome! Goodness me! I've forgotten to pack the ammonia! . . . It has been a terrible lesson for Caroline, but I fancy it is her turning-point. I can't help liking to think that out of all this evil good will come.'

Philip saw no prospect of good, nor of beauty either. But the expedition promised to be highly comic. He was not averse to it any longer; he was simply indifferent to all in it except the humours. These would be wonderful. Harriet, worked by her mother; Mrs Herriton, worked by Miss Abbott; Gino, worked by a cheque;—what better entertainment could he desire? There was nothing to distract him this time; his sentimentality had died, so had his anxiety for the family honour. He might be a puppet's puppet, but he knew exactly the disposition of the strings.

They travelled for thirteen hours downhill, whilst the streams broadened and the mountains shrank, and the vegetation changed, and the people ceased being ugly and drinking beer, and began instead to drink wine and to be beautiful. And the train which had picked them at sunrise out of a waste of glaciers and hotels was waltzing at sunset round the walls of Verona.

'Absurd nonsense they talk about the heat,' said Philip, as they drove from the station. 'Supposing we were here for pleasure, what could be more pleasurable than this?'

'Did you hear, though, they are remarking on the cold?' said Harriet nervously. 'I should never have thought it cold.'

And on the second day the heat struck them, like a hand laid over the mouth, just as they were walking to see the tomb of Juliet. From that moment everything went wrong. They fled from Verona. Harriet's sketch-book was stolen, and the bottle of ammonia in her trunk burst over her prayer book, so that purple patches appeared on all her clothes. Then, as she was going through Mantua at four in the morning, Philip made her look out of the window because it was Virgil's birthplace, and a smut flew in her eye, and Harriet with a smut in her eye was notorious. At Bologna they stopped twenty-four hours to rest. It was a festa, and children blew bladder whistles night and day. 'What a religion!' said Harriet. The hotel smelt, two puppies were asleep on her bed, and her bedroom window looked into a belfry, which saluted her slumbering form every quarter of an hour. Philip left his walking-stick, his socks, and the Baedeker at Bologna; she only left her sponge-bag. Next day they crossed the Apennines with a train-sick child and a hot lady, who told them that never, never before had she sweated so profusely. 'Foreigners are a filthy nation,' said Harriet. 'I don't care if there are tunnels; open the windows.' He obeyed, and she got another smut in her eye. Nor did Florence improve matters. Eating, walking, even a cross word would bathe them both in boiling water. Philip, who was slighter of build, and less conscientious, suffered less. But Harriet had never been to Florence, and between the hours of eight and eleven she crawled like a wounded creature through the streets, and swooned before various masterpieces of art. It was an irritable couple who took tickets to Monteriano.

'Single or returns?' said he.

'A single for me,' said Harriet peevishly; 'I shall never get back alive.'

'Sweet creature!' said her brother, suddenly breaking down. 'How helpful you will be when we come to Signor Carella!'

'Do you suppose,' said Harriet, standing still among a whirl of porters— 'do you suppose I am going to enter that man's house?'

'Then what have you come for, pray? For ornament?'

'To see that you do your duty.'

'Oh, thanks!'

'So mother told me. For goodness' sake get the tickets; here comes that hot woman again! She has the impudence to bow.'

'Mother told you, did she?' said Philip wrathfully, as he went to struggle for tickets at a slit so narrow that they were handed to him edgeways. Italy was beastly, and Florence station is the centre of beastly Italy. But he had a strange feeling that he was to blame for it all; that a little influx into him of virtue would make the whole land not beastly but amusing. For there was enchantment, he was sure of that; solid enchantment, which lay behind the porters and the screaming and the dust. He could see it in the terrific blue sky beneath which they travelled, in the whitened plain which gripped life tighter than a frost, in the exhausted reaches of the Arno, in the ruins of brown castles which stood quivering upon the hills. He could see it, though his head ached and his skin was twitching, though he was here as a puppet, and though his sister knew how he was here. There was nothing pleasant in that journey to Monteriano station. But nothing—not even the discomfort— was common-place.

'But do people live inside?' asked Harriet. They had exchanged the railway carriage for the legno, and the legno had emerged from the withered trees, and had revealed to them their destination.

Philip, to be annoying, answered 'No.'

'What do they do there?' continued Harriet, with a frown.

'There is a caffè. A prison. A theatre. A church. Walls. A view.'

'Not for me, thank you,' said Harriet after a weighty pause.

'Nobody asked you, Miss, you see. Now Lilia was asked by such a nice young gentleman, with curls all over his forehead, and teeth just as white as father makes them.' Then his manner changed. 'But, Harriet, do you see nothing wonderful or attractive in that place—nothing at all?'

'Nothing at all. It's frightful.'

'I know it is. But it's old—awfully old.'

'Beauty is the only test,' said Harriet. 'At least so you told me when I sketched old buildings—for the sake, I suppose, of making yourself unpleasant.'

'Oh, I'm perfectly right. But at the same time—I don't know—so many things have happened here—people have lived so hard and so splendidly—I can't explain.'

'I shouldn't think you could. It doesn't seem the best moment to begin your Italy mania. I thought you were cured of it by now. Instead, will you kindly tell me what you are going to do when you arrive. I do beg you will not be taken unawares this time.'

'First, Harriet, I shall settle you at the Stella d'Italia, in the comfort that befits your sex and disposition. Then I shall make myself some tea. After tea I shall take a book into Santa Deodata's, and read there. It is always fresh and cool.'

The martyred Harriet exclaimed, 'I'm not clever, Philip. I don't go in for it, as you know. But I know what's rude. And I know what's wrong.'

'Meaning—?'

'You!' she shouted, bouncing on the cushions of the legno and startling all the fleas. 'What's the good of cleverness if a man's murdered a woman?'

'Harriet, I am hot. To whom do you refer?'

'He. Her. If you don't look out he'll murder you. I wish he would.'

'Tut, tut, tutlet! You'd find a corpse extraordinarily inconvenient.' Then he tried to be less aggravating. 'I heartily dislike the fellow, but we know he didn't murder her. In that letter, though she said a lot, she never said he was physically cruel.'

'He has murdered her. The things he did—things one can't even mention—'

'Things which one must mention if one's to talk at all. And things which one must keep in their proper place. Because he was unfaithful to his wife, it doesn't follow that in every way he's absolutely vile.' He looked at the city. It seemed to approve his remark.

'It's the supreme test. The man who is unchivalrous to a woman—'

'Oh, stow it! Take it to the Back Kitchen. It's no more a supreme test than anything else. The Italians never were chivalrous from the first. If you condemn him for that, you'll condemn the whole lot.'

'I condemn the whole lot.'

'And the French as well?'

'And the French as well.'

'Things aren't so jolly easy,' said Philip, more to himself than to her.

But for Harriet things were easy, though not jolly, and she turned upon her brother yet again. 'What about the baby, pray? You've said a lot of smart things and whittled away morality and religion and I don't know what; but what about the baby? You think me a fool, but I've been noticing you all to-day, and you haven't mentioned the baby once. You haven't thought about it, even. You don't care. Philip! I shall not speak to you. You are intolerable.'

She kept her promise, and never opened her lips all the rest of the way. But her eyes glowed with anger and resolution. For she was a straight, brave woman, as well as a peevish one.

Philip acknowledged her reproof to be true. He did not care about the baby one straw. Nevertheless, he meant to do his duty, and he was fairly confident of success. If Gino would have sold his wife for a thousand lire, for how much less would he not sell his child? It was just a commercial transaction. Why should it interfere with other things! His eyes were fixed on the towers again, just as they had been fixed when he drove with Miss Abbott. But this time his thoughts were pleasanter, for he had no such grave business on his mind. It was in the spirit of the cultivated tourist that he approached his destination.

One of the towers, rough as any other, was topped by a cross—the tower of the Collegiate Church of Santa Deodata. She was a holy maiden of the Dark Ages, the city's patron saint, and sweetness and barbarity mingle strangely in her story. So holy was she that all her life she lay upon her back in the house of her mother, refusing to eat, refusing to play, refusing to work. The devil, envious of such sanctity, tempted her in various ways. He dangled grapes above her, he showed her fascinating toys, he pushed soft pillows beneath her aching head. When all proved vain he tripped up the mother and flung her downstairs before her very eyes. But so holy was the saint that she never picked her mother up, but lay upon her back through all, and thus assured her throne in Paradise. She was only fifteen when she died, which shows how much is within the reach of any schoolgirl. Those who think her life was unpractical need only think of the victories upon Poggibonsi, San Gimignano, Volterra, Siena itself—all gained through the invocation of her name; they need only look at the church which rose over her grave. The grand schemes for a marble façade were never carried out, and it is brown unfinished stone until this day. But for the inside Giotto was summoned to decorate the walls of the nave. Giotto came—that is to say, he did not come, German research having decisively proved—but at all events the nave is covered with frescoes, and so are two chapels in the left transept, and the arch into the choir, and there are scraps in the choir itself. There the decoration stopped, till in the full spring of the Renaissance, a great painter came to pay a few weeks' visit to his friend the Lord of Monteriano. In the intervals between the banquets and the discussions on Latin etymology and the dancing, he would stroll over to the church, and there in the fifth chapel to the right he has painted two frescoes of the death and burial of Santa Deodata. That is why Baedeker gives the place a star.

Santa Deodata was better company than Harriet, and she kept Philip in a pleasant dream until the legno drew up at the hotel. Every one there was asleep, for it was still the hour when only idiots were moving. There were not even any beggars about. The cabman put their bags down in the passage—they had left heavy luggage at the station—and strolled about till he came on the landlady's room and woke her, and sent her to them.

Then Harriet pronounced the monosyllable 'Go!'

'Go where?' asked Philip, bowing to the landlady, who was swimming down the stairs.

'To the Italian. Go.'

'Buona sera, signora padrona. Si ritorna volontieri a Monteriano!' (Don't be a goose. I'm not going now. You're in the way, too.) 'Vorrei due camere—'

'Go. This instant. Now. I'll stand it no longer. Go!'

'I'm damned if I'll go. I want my tea.'

'Swear if you like!' she cried. 'Blaspheme! Abuse me! But understand, I'm in earnest.'

'Harriet, don't act. Or act better.'

'We've come here to get the baby back, and for nothing else. I'll not have this levity and slackness, and talk about pictures and churches. Think of mother; did she send you out for *them*?'

'Think of mother and don't straddle across the stairs. Let the cabman and the landlady come down, and let me go up and choose rooms.'

'I shan't.'

'Harriet, are you mad?'

'If you like. But you will not come up till you have seen the Italian.'

'La signorina si sente male,' said Philip. 'È il sole.'

'Poveretta!' cried the landlady and the cabman.

'Leave me alone!' said Harriet, snarling round at them. 'I don't care for the lot of you. I'm English, and neither you'll come down nor he up till he goes for the baby.'

'La prego—piano—piano—è un' altra signorina che dorme—'

'We shall probably be arrested for brawling, Harriet. Have you the very slightest sense of the ludicrous?'

Harriet had not; that was why she could be so powerful. She had concocted this scene in the carriage, and nothing should baulk her of it. To the abuse in front and the coaxing behind she was equally indifferent. How long she would have stood like a glorified Horatius, keeping the staircase at both ends, was never to be known. For the young lady, whose sleep they were disturbing, awoke and opened her bedroom door, and came out on to the landing. She was Miss Abbott.

Philip's first coherent feeling was one of indignation. To be run by his mother and hectored by his sister was as much as he could stand. The intervention of a third female drove him suddenly beyond politeness. He was about to say exactly what he thought about the thing from beginning to end. But before he could do so Harriet also had seen Miss Abbott. She uttered a shrill cry of joy.

'You, Caroline, here of all people!' And in spite of the heat she darted up the stairs and imprinted an affectionate kiss upon her friend.

Philip had an inspiration. 'You will have a lot to tell Miss Abbott, Harriet, and she may have as much to tell you. So I'll pay my call on Signor Carella, as you suggested, and see how things stand.'

Miss Abbott uttered some noise of greeting or alarm. He did not reply to it or approach nearer to her. Without even paying the cabman, he escaped into the street.

'Tear each other's eyes out!' he cried, gesticulating at the façade of the hotel. 'Give it her, Harriet! Teach her to leave us alone. Give it her, Caroline! Teach her to be grateful to you. Go it, ladies; go it!'

Such people as observed him were interested, but did not conclude that he was mad. This aftermath of conversation is not unknown in Italy.

He tried to think how amusing it was; but it would not do—Miss Abbott's presence affected him too personally. Either she suspected him of dishonesty, or else she was being dishonest herself. He preferred to suppose the latter. Perhaps she had seen Gino, and they had prepared some elaborate mortification for the Herritons. Perhaps Gino had sold the baby cheap to her for a joke: it was just the kind of joke that would appeal to him. Philip still remembered the laughter that had greeted his fruitless journey, and the uncouth push that had toppled him on to the bed. And whatever it might mean, Miss Abbott's presence spoilt the comedy: she would do nothing funny.

During this short meditation he had walked through the city, and was out on the other side. 'Where does Signor Carella live?' he asked the men at the Dogana.

'I'll show you!' cried a little girl, springing out of the ground as Italian children will.

'She will show you,' said the Dogana men, nodding reassuringly. 'Follow her always, always, and you will come to no harm. She is a trust-worthy guide. She is my { daughter.' { cousin.' { sister.'

Philip knew these relatives well: they ramify, if need be, all over the peninsula.

'Do you chance to know whether Signor Carella is in?' he asked her.

She had just seen him go in. Philip nodded. He was looking forward to the interview this time: it would be an intellectual duel with a man of no great intellect. What was Miss Abbott up to? That was one of the things he was going to discover. While she had it out with Harriet, he would have it out with Gino. He followed the Dogana's relative softly, like a diplomatist.

He did not follow her long, for this was the Volterra gate, and the house was exactly opposite to it. In half a minute they had scrambled down the mule-track and reached the only practicable entrance. Philip laughed, partly at the thought of Lilia in such a building, partly in the confidence of victory. Meanwhile the Dogana's relative lifted up her voice and gave a shout.

For an impressive interval there was no reply. Then the figure of a woman appeared high up on the loggia.

'That is Perfetta,' said the girl.

'I want to see Signor Carella,' cried Philip.

'Out!'

'Out,' echoed the girl complacently.

'Why on earth did you say he was in?' He could have strangled her for temper. He had been just ripe for an interview—just the right combination of indignation and acuteness: blood hot, brain cool. But nothing ever did go right in Monteriano. 'When will he be back?' he called to Perfetta. It really was too bad.

She did not know. He was away on business. He might be back this evening, he might not. He had gone to Poggibonsi.

At the sound of this word the little girl put her fingers to her nose and swept them at the plain. She sang as she did so, even as her foremothers had sung seven hundred years back—

> *'Poggibonizzi, fatti in là,*
> *Che Monteriano si fa città!'*

Then she asked Philip for a halfpenny. A German lady, friendly to the Past, had given her one that very spring.

'I shall have to leave a message,' he called.

'Now Perfetta has gone for her basket,' said the little girl. 'When she returns she will lower it—so. Then you will put your card into it. Then she will raise it—thus. By this means—'

When Perfetta returned, Philip remembered to ask after the baby. It took longer to find than the basket, and he stood perspiring in the evening sun, trying to avoid the smell of the drains and to prevent the little girl from singing against Poggibonsi. The olive-trees beside him were draped with the weekly—or more probably the monthly—wash. What a frightful spotty blouse! He could not think where he had seen it. Then he remembered that it was Lilia's. She had brought it 'to hack about in' at Sawston, and had taken it to Italy because 'in Italy anything does.' He had rebuked her for the sentiment.

'Beautiful as an angel!' bellowed Perfetta, holding out something which must be Lilia's baby. 'But who am I addressing?'

'Thank you—here is my card.' He had written on it a civil request to Gino for an interview next morning. But before he placed it in the basket and revealed his identity, he wished to find something out. 'Has a young lady happened to call here lately—a young English lady?'

Perfetta begged his pardon: she was a little deaf.

'A young lady—pale, large, tall.'

She did not quite catch.

'A YOUNG LADY!'

'Perfetta is deaf when she chooses,' said the Dogana's relative. At last Philip admitted the peculiarity and strode away. He paid off the detestable child at the Volterra gate. She got two nickel pieces and was not pleased, partly because it was too much, partly because he did not look pleased when he gave it to her. He caught her fathers and cousins winking at each other as he walked past them. Monteriano seemed in one conspiracy to make him look a fool. He felt tired and anxious and muddled, and not sure of anything except that his temper was lost. In this mood he returned to the Stella d'Italia, and there, as he was ascending the stairs, Miss Abbott popped out of the dining-room on the first floor and beckoned to him mysteriously.

'I was going to make myself some tea,' he said, with his hand still on the banisters.

'I should be grateful—'

So he followed her into the dining-room and shut the door.

'You see,' she began, 'Harriet knows nothing.'

'No more do I. He was out.'

'But what's that to do with it?'

He presented her with an unpleasant smile. She fenced well, as he had noticed before. 'He was out. You find me as ignorant as you have left Harriet.'

'What do you mean? Please, please, Mr Herriton, don't be mysterious: there isn't the time. Any moment Harriet may be down, and we shan't have decided how to behave to her. Sawston was different: we had to keep up appearances. But here we must speak out, and I think I can trust you to do it. Otherwise we'll never start clear.'

'Pray let us start clear,' said Philip, pacing up and down the room. 'Permit me to begin by asking you a question. In which capacity have you come to Monteriano—spy or traitor?'

'Spy!' she answered, without a moment's hesitation. She was standing by the little Gothic window as she spoke—the hotel had been a palace once—and with her finger she was following the curves of the moulding as if they might feel beautiful and strange. 'Spy,' she repeated, for Philip was bewildered at learning her guilt so easily, and could not answer a word. 'Your mother has behaved dishonourably all through. She never wanted the child: no harm in that; but she is too proud to let it come to me. She has done all she could to wreck things; she did not tell you everything; she has told Harriet nothing at all; she has lied or acted lies everywhere. I cannot trust your mother. So I have come here alone—all across Europe; no one knows it; my father thinks I am in Normandy—to spy on Mrs Herriton. Don't let's argue!' for he had begun, almost mechanically, to rebuke her for impertinence. 'If you are here to get the child, I will help you; if you are here to fail, I shall get it instead of you.'

'It is hopeless to expect you to believe me,' he stammered. 'But I can assert that we are here to get the child, even if it costs us all we've got. My mother has fixed no money limit whatever. I am here to carry out her instructions. I think that you will approve of them, as you have practically dictated them. I do not approve of them. They are absurd.'

She nodded carelessly. She did not mind what he said. All she wanted was to get the baby out of Monteriano.

'Harriet also carries out your instructions,' he continued. 'She, however, approves of them, and does not know that they proceed from you. I think, Miss Abbott, you had better take entire charge of the rescue party. I have asked for an interview with Signor Carella to-morrow morning. Do you acquiesce?'

She nodded again.

'Might I ask for details of your interview with him? They might be helpful to me.'

He had spoken at random. To his delight she suddenly collapsed. Her hand fell from the window. Her face was red with more than the reflection of evening.

'My interview—how do you know of it?'

'From Perfetta, if it interests you.'

'Whoever is Perfetta?'

'The woman who must have let you in.'

'In where?'

'Into Signor Carella's house.'

'Mr Herriton!' she exclaimed. 'How could you believe her? Do you suppose that I would have entered that man's house, knowing about him all that I do? I think you have very odd ideas of what is possible for a lady. I hear you wanted Harriet to go. Very properly she refused. Eighteen months ago I might have done such a thing. But I trust I have learnt how to behave by now.'

Philip began to see that there were two Miss Abbotts—the Miss Abbott who could travel alone to Monteriano, and the Miss Abbott who could not enter Gino's house when she got there. It was an amusing discovery. Which of them would respond to his next move?

'I suppose I misunderstood Perfetta. Where did you have your interview, then?'

'Not an interview—an accident—I am very sorry—I meant you to have the chance of seeing him first. Though it is your fault. You are a day late. You were due here yesterday. So I came yesterday, and, not finding you, went up to the Rocca—you know that kitchen-garden where they let you in, and there is a ladder up to a broken tower, where you can stand and see all the other towers below you and the plain and all the other hills?'

'Yes, yes. I know the Rocca: I told you of it.'

'So I went up in the evening for the sunset: I had nothing to do. He was in the garden: it belongs to a friend of his.'

'And you talked.'

'It was very awkward for me. But I had to talk: he seemed to make me. You see he thought I was here as a tourist; he thinks so still. He intended to be civil, and I judged it better to be civil also.'

'And of what did you talk?'

'The weather—there will be rain, he says, by to-morrow evening—the other towns, England, myself, about you a little, and he actually mentioned Lilia. He was perfectly disgusting; he pretended he loved her; he offered to show me her grave—the grave of the woman he has murdered!'

'My dear Miss Abbott, he is not a murderer. I have just been driving that into Harriet. And when you know the Italians as well as I do, you will realise that in all that he said to you he was perfectly sincere. The Italians are essentially dramatic: they look on death and love as spectacles. I don't doubt that he persuaded himself, for the moment, that he had behaved admirably, both as husband and widower.'

'You may be right,' said Miss Abbott, impressed for the first time. 'When I tried to pave the way, so to speak—to hint that he had not behaved as he ought—well, it was no good at all. He couldn't or wouldn't understand.'

There was something very humorous in the idea of Miss Abbott approaching Gino, on the Rocca, in the spirit of a district visitor. Philip, whose temper was returning, laughed.

'Harriet would say he has no sense of sin.'

'Harriet may be right, I am afraid.'

'If so, perhaps he isn't sinful!'

Miss Abbott was not one to encourage levity. 'I know what he has done,' she said. 'What he says and what he thinks is of very little importance.'

Philip smiled at her crudity. 'I should like to hear, though, what he said about me. Is he preparing a warm reception?'

'Oh no, not that. I never told him that you and Harriet were coming. You could have taken him by surprise if you liked. He only asked for you, and wished he hadn't been so rude to you eighteen months ago.'

'What a memory the fellow has for little things!' He turned away as he spoke, for he did not want her to see his face. It was suffused with pleasure. For an apology, which would have been intolerable eighteen months ago, was gracious and agreeable now.

She would not let this pass. 'You did not think it a little thing at the time. You told me he had assaulted you.'

'I lost my temper,' said Philip lightly. His vanity had been appeased, and he knew it. This tiny piece of civility had changed his mood. 'Did he really—what exactly did he say?'

'He said he was sorry—pleasantly, as Italians do say such things. But he never mentioned the baby once.'

What did the baby matter when the world was suddenly right way up? Philip smiled, and was shocked at himself for smiling, and smiled again. For romance had come back to Italy; there were no cads in her; she was beautiful, courteous, lovable, as of old. And Miss Abbott—she, too, was beautiful in her way, for all her gaucheness and conventionality. She really cared about life, and tried to live it properly. And Harriet—even Harriet tried.

This admirable change in Philip proceeds from nothing admirable, and may therefore provoke the gibes of the cynical. But angels and other practical people will accept it reverently, and write it down as good.

'The view from the Rocca (small gratuity) is finest at sunset,' he murmured, more to himself than to her.

'And he never mentioned the baby once,' Miss Abbott repeated. But she had returned to the window, and again her finger pursued the delicate curves. He watched her in silence, and was more attracted to her than he had ever been before. She really was the strangest mixture.

'The view from the Rocca—wasn't it fine?'

'What isn't fine here?' she answered gently, and then added, 'I wish I was Harriet,' throwing an extraordinary meaning into the words.

'Because Harriet—?'

She would not go further, but he believed that she had paid homage to the complexity of life. For her, at all events, the expedition was neither easy nor jolly. Beauty, evil, charm, vulgarity, mystery—she also acknowledged this tangle, in spite of herself. And her voice thrilled him when she broke silence with 'Mr Herriton—come here—look at this!'

She removed a pile of plates from the Gothic window, and they leant out of it. Close opposite, wedged between mean houses, there rose up one of the great towers. It is your tower: you stretch a barricade between it and the hotel, and the traffic is blocked in a moment. Farther up, where the street empties out by the church, your connections, the Merli and the Capocchi, do likewise. They command the Piazza, you the Siena gate. No one can move in either but he shall be instantly slain, either by bows or by cross-bows, or by Greek fire. Beware, however, of the back bedroom windows. For they are menaced by the tower of the Aldobrandeschi, and before now arrows have stuck quivering over the washstand. Guard these windows well, lest there be a repetition of the events of February 1338, when the hotel was surprised from the rear, and your dearest friend—you could just make out that it was he—was thrown at you over the stairs.

'It reaches up to heaven,' said Philip, 'and down to the other place.' The summit of the tower was radiant in the sun, while its base was in shadow and pasted over with advertisements. 'Is it to be a symbol of the town?'

She gave no hint that she understood him. But they remained together at the window because it was a little cooler and so pleasant. Philip found a certain grace and lightness in his companion which he had never noticed in England. She was appallingly narrow, but her consciousness of wider things gave to her narrowness a pathetic charm. He did not suspect that he was more graceful too. For our vanity is such that we hold our own characters immutable, and we are slow to acknowledge that they have changed, even for the better.

Citizens came out for a little stroll before dinner. Some of them stood and gazed at the advertisements on the tower.

'Surely that isn't an opera-bill?' said Miss Abbott.

Philip put on his pince-nez. '"Lucia di Lammermoor. By the Master Donizetti. Unique representation. This evening."'

'But is there an opera? Right up here?'

'Why, yes. These people know how to live. They would sooner have a thing bad than not have it at all. That is why they have got to have so much that is good. However bad the performance is to-night, it will be alive. Italians don't love music silently, like the beastly Germans. The audience takes its share—sometimes more.'

'Can't we go?'

He turned on her, but not unkindly. 'But we're here to rescue a child!'

He cursed himself for the remark. All the pleasure and the light went out of her face, and she became again Miss Abbott of Sawston—good, oh, most undoubtedly good, but most appallingly dull. Dull and remorseful: it is a deadly combination, and he strove against it in vain till he was interrupted by the opening of the dining-room door.

They started as guiltily as if they had been flirting. Their interview had taken such an unexpected course. Anger, cynicism, stubborn morality—all had ended in a feeling of good-will towards each other and towards the city which had received them. And now Harriet was here—acrid, indissoluble, large; the same in Italy as in England—changing her disposition never, and her atmosphere under protest.

Yet even Harriet was human, and the better for a little tea. She did not scold Philip for finding Gino out, as she might reasonably have done. She showered civilities on Miss Abbott, exclaiming again and again that

Caroline's visit was one of the most fortunate coincidences in the world. Caroline did not contradict her.

'You see him to-morrow at ten, Philip. Well, don't forget the blank cheque. Say an hour for the business. No, Italians are so slow; say two. twelve o'clock. Lunch. Well—then it's no good going till the evening train. I can manage the baby as far as Florence—'

'My dear sister, you can't run on like that. You don't buy a pair of gloves in two hours, much less a baby.'

'Three hours, then, or four; or make him learn English ways. At Florence we get a nurse—'

'But, Harriet,' said Miss Abbott, 'what if at first he was to refuse?'

'I don't know the meaning of the word,' said Harriet impressively. 'I've told the landlady that Philip and I only want our rooms one night, and we shall keep to it.'

'I dare say it will be all right. But, as I told you, I thought the man I met on the Rocca a strange, difficult man.'

'He's insolent to ladies, we know. But my brother can be trusted to bring him to his senses. That woman, Philip, whom you saw will carry the baby to the hotel. Of course you must tip her for it. And try, if you can, to get poor Lilia's silver bangles. They were nice quiet things, and will do for Irma. And there is an inlaid box I lent her—lent, not gave—to keep her handkerchiefs in. It's of no real value; but this is our only chance. Don't ask for it; but if you see it lying about, just say—'

'No, Harriet; I'll try for the baby, but for nothing else. I promise to do that to-morrow, and to do it in the way you wish. But to-night, as we're all tired, we want a change of topic. We want relaxation. We want to go to the theatre.'

'Theatres here? And at such a moment?'

'We should hardly enjoy it, with the great interview impending,' said Miss Abbott, with an anxious glance at Philip.

He did not betray her, but said, 'Don't you think it's better than sitting in all the evening and getting nervous?'

His sister shook her head. 'Mother wouldn't like it. It would be most unsuitable—almost irreverent. Besides all that, foreign theatres are notorious. Don't you remember those letters in the "Church Family Newspaper"?'

'But this is an opera—"Lucia di Lammermoor"—Sir Walter Scott—classical, you know.'

Harriet's face grew resigned. 'Certainly one has so few opportunities of hearing music. It is sure to be very bad. But it might be better than sitting idle all the evening. We have no book, and I lost my crochet at Florence.'

'Good. Miss Abbott, you are coming too?'

'It is very kind of you, Mr Herriton. In some ways I should enjoy it; but—excuse the suggestion—I don't think we ought to go to cheap seats.'

'Good gracious me!' cried Harriet, 'I should never have thought of that. As likely as not, we should have tried to save money and sat among the most awful people. One keeps on forgetting this is Italy.'

'Unfortunately I have no evening dress; and if the seats—'

'Oh, that'll be all right,' said Philip, smiling at his timorous, scrupulous women-kind. 'We'll go as we are, and buy the best we can get. Monteriano is not formal.'

So this strenuous day of resolutions, plans, alarms, battles, victories, defeats, truces, ended at the opera. Miss Abbott and Harriet were both a little shamefaced. They thought of their friends at Sawston, who were supposing them to be now tilting against the powers of evil. What would Mrs Herriton, or Irma, or the curates at the Back Kitchen say if they could see the rescue party at a place of amusement on the very first day of its mission? Philip, too, marvelled at his wish to go. He began to see that he was enjoying his time in Monteriano, in spite of the tiresomeness of his companions and the occasional contrariness of himself.

He had been to this theatre many years before, on the occasion of a performance of 'La Zia di Carlo.' Since then it had been thoroughly done up, in the tints of the beetroot and the tomato, and was in many other ways a credit to the little town. The orchestra had been enlarged, some of the boxes had terra-cotta draperies, and over each box was now suspended an enormous tablet, neatly framed, bearing upon it the number of that box. There was also a drop-scene, representing a pink and purple landscape, wherein sported many a lady lightly clad, and two more ladies lay along the top of the proscenium to steady a large and pallid clock. So rich and so appalling was the effect, that Philip could scarcely suppress a cry. There is something majestic in the bad taste of Italy; it is not the bad taste of a country which knows no better; it has not the nervous vulgarity of England, or the blinded vulgarity of Germany. It observes beauty, and chooses to pass it by. But it attains to beauty's confidence. This tiny theatre of Monteriano spraddled and swaggered with the best of them, and these ladies with their clock would have nodded to the young men on the ceiling of the Sistine.

Philip had tried for a box, but all the best were taken: it was rather a grand performance, and he had to be content with stalls. Harriet was fretful and insular. Miss Abbott was pleasant, and insisted on praising everything: her only regret was that she had no pretty clothes with her.

'We do all right,' said Philip, amused at her unwonted vanity.

'Yes, I know; but pretty things pack as easily as ugly ones. We had no need to come to Italy like guys.'

This time he did not reply 'But we're here to rescue a baby.' For he saw a charming picture, as charming a picture as he had seen for years—the hot red theatre; outside the theatre, towers and dark gates and mediæval walls; beyond the walls olive-trees in the starlight and white winding roads and fireflies and untroubled dust; and here in the middle of it all, Miss Abbott, wishing she had not come looking like a guy. She had made the right remark. Most undoubtedly she had made the right remark. This stiff suburban woman was unbending before the shrine.

'Don't you like it at all?' he asked her.

'Most awfully.' And by this bald interchange they convinced each other that Romance was here.

Harriet, meanwhile, had been coughing ominously at the drop-scene,

which presently rose on the grounds of Ravenswood, and the chorus of
Scotch retainers burst into cry. The audience accompanied with tappings
and drummings, swaying in the melody like corn in the wind. Harriet,
though she did not care for music, knew how to listen to it. She uttered an
acid 'Shish!'

'Shut it,' whispered her brother.

'We must make a stand from the beginning. They're talking.'

'It is tiresome,' murmured Miss Abbott; 'but perhaps it isn't for us to
interfere.'

Harriet shook her head and shished again. The people were quiet, not
because it is wrong to talk during a chorus, but because it is natural to be civil
to a visitor. For a little time she kept the whole house in order, and could
smile at her brother complacently.

Her success annoyed him. He had grasped the principle of opera in
Italy—it aims not at illusion but at entertainment—and he did not want this
great evening-party to turn into a prayer-meeting. But soon the boxes began
to fill, and Harriet's power was over. Families greeted each other across the
auditorium. People in the pit hailed their brothers and sons in the chorus,
and told them how well they were singing. When Lucia appeared by the
fountain there was loud applause, and cries of 'Welcome to Monteriano!'

'Ridiculous babies!' said Harriet, settling down in her stall.

'Why, it is the famous hot lady of the Apennines,' cried Philip; 'the one
who had never, never before—'

'Ugh! Don't. She will be very vulgar. And I'm sure it's even worse here
than in the tunnel. I wish we'd never—'

Lucia began to sing, and there was a moment's silence. She was stout and
ugly; but her voice was still beautiful, and as she sang the theatre murmured
like a hive of happy bees. All through the coloratura she was accompanied by
sighs, and its top note was drowned in a shout of universal joy.

So the opera proceeded. The singers drew inspiration from the audience,
and the two great sextetts were rendered not unworthily. Miss Abbott fell
into the spirit of the thing. She, too, chatted and laughed and applauded and
encored, and rejoiced in the existence of beauty. As for Philip, he forgot
himself as well as his mission. He was not even an enthusiastic visitor. For he
had been in this place always. It was his home.

Harriet, like M. Bovary on a more famous occasion, was trying to follow
the plot. Occasionally she nudged her companions, and asked them what
had become of Walter Scott. She looked round grimly. The audience
sounded drunk, and even Caroline, who never took a drop, was swaying
oddly. Violent waves of excitement, all arising from very little, went
sweeping round the theatre. The climax was reached in the mad scene. Lucia
clad in white, as befitted her malady, suddenly gathered up her streaming
hair and bowed her acknowledgments to the audience. Then from the back
of the stage—she feigned not to see it—there advanced a kind of bamboo
clothes-horse, stuck all over with bouquets. It was very ugly, and most of the
flowers in it were false. Lucia knew this, and so did the audience; and they all
knew that the clothes-horse was a piece of stage property, brought in to make

the performance go year after year. None the less did it unloose the great
deeps. With a scream of amazement and joy she embraced the animal, pulled
out one or two practicable blossoms, pressed them to her lips, and flung
them into her admirers. They flung them back, with loud melodious cries,
and a little boy in one of the stage-boxes snatched up his sister's carnations
and offered them. 'Che carino!' exclaimed the singer. She darted at the little
boy and kissed him. Now the noise became tremendous. 'Silence! silence!'
shouted many old gentlemen behind. 'Let the divine creature continue!' But
the young men in the adjacent box were imploring Lucia to extend her
civility to them. She refused, with a humorous expressive gesture. One of
them hurled a bouquet at her. She spurned it with her foot. Then,
encouraged by the roars of the audience, she picked it up and tossed it to
them. Harriet was always unfortunate. The bouquet struck her full in the
chest, and a little *billet-doux* fell out of it into her lap.

'Call this classical?' she cried, rising from her seat. 'It's not even
respectable! Philip! take me out at once.'

'Whose is it?' shouted her brother, holding up the bouquet in one hand
and the *billet-doux* in the other. 'Whose is it?'

The house exploded, and one of the boxes was violently agitated, as if
some one was being hauled to the front. Harriet moved down the gangway,
and compelled Miss Abbott to follow her. Philip, still laughing and calling
'Whose is it?' brought up the rear. He was drunk with excitement. The heat,
the fatigue, and the enjoyment had mounted into his head.

'To the left!' the people cried. 'The innamorato is to the left.'

He deserted his ladies and plunged towards the box. A young man was
flung stomach downwards across the balustrade. Philip handed him up the
bouquet and the note. Then his own hands were seized affectionately. It all
seemed quite natural.

'Why have you not written?' cried the young man. 'Why do you take me
by surprise?'

'Oh, I've written,' said Philip hilariously. 'I left a note this afternoon.'

'Silence! silence!' cried the audience, who were beginning to have enough.
'Let the divine creature continue.' Miss Abbott and Harriet had
disappeared.

'No! no!' cried the young man. 'You don't escape me now.' For Philip was
trying feebly to disengage his hands. Amiable youths bent out of the box and
invited him to enter it.

'Gino's friends are ours—'

'Friends?' cried Gino. 'A relative! A brother! Fra Filippo, who has come
all the way from England and never written.'

'I left a message.'

The audience began to hiss.

'Come in to us.'

'Thank you—ladies—there is not time—'

The next moment he was swinging by his arms. The moment after he shot
over the balustrade into the box. Then the conductor, seeing that the
incident was over, raised his baton. The house was hushed, and Lucia di

Lammermoor resumed her song of madness and death.

Philip had whispered introductions to the pleasant people who had pulled him in—tradesmen's sons perhaps they were, or medical students, or solicitors' clerks, or sons of other dentists. There is no knowing who is who in Italy. The guest of the evening was a private soldier. He shared the honour now with Philip. The two had to stand side by side in the front, and exchange compliments, whilst Gino presided, courteous, but delightfully familiar. Philip would have a spasm of horror at the muddle he had made. But the spasm would pass, and again he would be enchanted by the kind, cheerful voices, the laughter that was never vapid, and the light caress of the arm across his back.

He could not get away till the play was nearly finished, and Edgardo was singing amongst the tombs of his ancestors. His new friends hoped to see him at the Garibaldi to-morrow evening. He promised; then he remembered that if they kept to Harriet's plan he would have left Monteriano. 'At ten o'clock, then,' he said to Gino. 'I want to speak to you alone. At ten.'

'Certainly!' laughed the other.

Miss Abbott was sitting up for him when he got back. Harriet, it seemed, had gone straight to bed.

'That was he, wasn't it?' she asked.

'Yes, rather.'

'I suppose you didn't settle anything?'

'Why, no; how could I? The fact is—well, I got taken by surprise, but after all, what does it matter? There's no earthly reason why we shouldn't do the business pleasantly. He's a perfectly charming person, and so are his friends. I'm his friend now—his long-lost brother. What's the harm? I tell you, Miss Abbott, it's one thing for England and another for Italy. There we plan and get on high moral horses. Here we find what asses we are, for things go off quite easily, all by themselves. My hat, what a night! Did you ever see a really purple sky and really silver stars before? Well, as I was saying, it's absurd to worry; he's not a porky father. He wants that baby as little as I do. He's been ragging my dear mother—just as he ragged me eighteen months ago, and I've forgiven him. Oh, but he has a sense of humour!'

Miss Abbott, too, had a wonderful evening, nor did she ever remember such stars or such a sky. Her head, too, was full of music, and that night when she opened the window her room was filled with warm sweet air. She was bathed in beauty within and without; she could not go to bed for happiness. Had she ever been so happy before? Yes, once before, and here, a night in March, the night Gino and Lilia had told her of their love—the night whose evil she had come now to undo.

She gave a sudden cry of shame. 'This time—the same place—the same thing,'—and she began to beat down her happiness, knowing it to be sinful. She was here to fight against this place, to rescue a little soul who was innocent as yet. She was here to champion morality and purity, and the holy life of an English home. In the spring she had sinned through ignorance; she was not ignorant now. 'Help me!' she cried, and shut the window as if there was magic in the encircling air. But the tunes would not go out of her head, and all night long she was troubled by torrents of music, and by applause and laughter, and angry young men who shouted the distich out of Baedeker:

'Poggibonizzi fatti in là,
Che Monteriano si fa città!'

Poggibonsi was revealed to her as they sang—a joyless, straggling place, full of people who pretended. When she woke up she knew that it had been Sawston.

Chapter Seven

At about nine o'clock next morning Perfetta went out on to the loggia, not to look at the view, but to throw some dirty water at it. 'Scuse tante!' she wailed, for the water spattered a tall young lady who had for some time been tapping at the lower door.

'Is Signor Carella in?' the young lady asked. It was no business of Perfetta's to be shocked, and the style of the visitor seemed to demand the reception-room. Accordingly she opened its shutters, dusted a round patch on one of the horse-hair chairs, and bade the lady do herself the inconvenience of sitting down. Then she ran into Monteriano and shouted up and down its streets until such time as her young master should hear her.

The reception-room was sacred to the dead wife. Her shiny portrait hung upon the wall—similar, doubtless, in all respects to the one which would be pasted on her tombstone. A little piece of black drapery had been tacked above the frame to lend a dignity to woe. But two of the tacks had fallen out, and the effect was now rakish, as of a drunkard's bonnet. A coon song lay open on the piano, and of the two tables one supported Baedeker's 'Central Italy,' the other Harriet's inlaid box. And over everything there lay a deposit of heavy white dust, which was only blown off one memento to thicken on another. It is well to be remembered with love. It is not so very dreadful to be forgotten entirely. But if we shall resent anything on earth at all, we shall resent the consecration of a deserted room.

Miss Abbott did not sit down, partly because the antimacassars might harbour fleas, partly because she had suddenly felt faint, and was glad to cling on to the funnel of the stove. She struggled with herself, for she had need to be very calm; only if she was very calm might her behaviour be justified. She had broken faith with Philip and Harriet: she was going to try for the baby before they did. If she failed she could scarcely look them in the face again.

'Harriet and her brother,' she reasoned, 'don't realise what is before them. She would bluster and be rude; he would be pleasant and take it as a joke. Both of them—even if they offered money—would fail. But I begin to understand the man's nature: he does not love the child, but he will be touchy about it—and that is quite as bad for us. He's charming, but he's no fool; he conquered me last year; he conquered Mr Herriton yesterday, and if I am not careful he will conquer us all to-day, and the baby will grow up in Monteriano. He is terribly strong; Lilia found that out, but only I remember it now.'

This attempt, and this justification of it, were the results of the long and restless night. Miss Abbott had come to believe that she alone could do battle with Gino, because she alone understood him; and she had put this, as nicely as she could, in a note which she had left for Philip. It distressed her to write such a note, partly because her education inclined her to reverence the male, partly because she had got to like Philip a good deal after their last strange interview. His pettiness would be dispersed, and as for his 'unconventionality,' which was so much gossiped about at Sawston, she began to see that it did not differ greatly from certain familiar notions of her own. If only he would forgive her for what she was doing now, there might perhaps be before them a long and profitable friendship. But she must succeed. No one would forgive her if she did not succeed. She prepared to do battle with the powers of evil.

The voice of her adversary was heard at last, singing fearlessly from his expanded lungs, like a professional. Herein he differed from Englishmen, who always have a little feeling against music, and sing only from the throat, apologetically. He padded upstairs, and looked in at the open door of the reception-room without seeing her. Her heart leapt and her throat was dry when he turned away and passed, still singing, into the room opposite. It is alarming not to be seen.

He had left the door of this room open, and she could see into it, right across the landing. It was in a shocking mess. Food, bedclothes, patent-leather boots, dirty plates, and knives lay strewn over a large table and on the floor. But it was the mess that comes of life, not of desolation. It was preferable to the charnel-chamber in which she was standing now, and the light in it was soft and large, as from some gracious noble opening.

He stopped singing, and cried, 'Where is Perfetta?'

His back was turned, and he was lighting a cigar. He was not speaking to Miss Abbott. He could not even be expecting her. The vista of the landing and the two open doors made him both remote and significant, like an actor on the stage, intimate and unapproachable at the same time. She could no more call out to him than if he was Hamlet.

'You know!' he continued, 'but you will not tell me. Exactly like you.' He reclined on the table and blew a fat smoke-ring. 'And why won't you tell me the numbers? I have dreamt of a red hen—that is two hundred and five, and a friend unexpected—he means eighty-two. But I try for the Terno this week. So tell me another number.'

Miss Abbott did not know of the Tombola. His speech terrified her. She felt those subtle restrictions which come upon us in fatigue. Had she slept well she would have greeted him as soon as she saw him. Now it was impossible. He had got into another world.

She watched his smoke-ring. The air had carried it slowly away from him, and brought it out intact upon the landing.

'Two hundred and five—eighty-two. In any case I shall put them on Bari, not on Florence. I cannot tell you why; I have a feeling this week for Bari.' Again she tried to speak. But the ring mesmerised her. It had become vast and elliptical, and floated in at the reception-room door.

'Ah! you don't care if you get the profits. You won't even say "Thank you, Gino." Say it, or I'll drop hot, red-hot ashes on you. "Thank you, Gino—"'

The ring had extended its pale blue coils towards her. She lost self-control. It enveloped her. As if it was a breath from the pit, she screamed.

There he was, wanting to know what had frightened her, how she had got here, why she had never spoken. He made her sit down. He brought her wine, which she refused. She had not one word to say to him.

'What is it?' he repeated. 'What has frightened you?'

He, too, was frightened, and perspiration came starting through the tan. For it is a serious thing to have been watched. We all radiate something curiously intimate when we believe ourselves to be alone.

'Business—' she said at last.

'Business with me?'

'Most important business.' She was lying, white and limp, in the dusty chair.

'Before business you must get well; this is the best wine.'

She refused it feebly. He poured out a glass. She drank it. As she did so she became self-conscious. However important the business, it was not proper of her to have called on him, or to accept his hospitality.

'Perhaps you are engaged,' she said. 'And as I am not very well—'

'You are not well enough to go back. And I am not engaged.'

She looked nervously at the other room.

'Ah, now I understand,' he exclaimed. 'Now I see what frightened you. But why did you never speak?' And taking her into the room where he lived, he pointed to—the baby.

She had thought so much about this baby, of its welfare, its soul, its morals, its probable defects. But, like most unmarried people, she had only thought of it as a word—just as the healthy man only thinks of the word death, not of death itself. The real thing, lying asleep on a dirty rug, disconcerted her. It did not stand for a principle any longer. It was so much flesh and blood, so many inches and ounces of life—a glorious, unquestionable fact, which a man and another woman had given to the world. You could talk to it; in time it would answer you; in time it would not answer you unless it chose, but would secrete, within the compass of its body, thoughts and wonderful passions of its own. And this was the machine on which she and Mrs Herriton and Philip and Harriet had for the last month been exercising their various ideals—had determined that in time it should move this way or that way, should accomplish this and not that. It was to be Low Church, it was to be high-principled, it was to be tactful, gentlemanly, artistic—excellent things all. Yet now that she saw this baby, lying asleep on a dirty rug, she had a great disposition not to dictate one of them, and to exert no more influence than there may be in a kiss or in the vaguest of the heartfelt prayers.

But she had practised self-discipline, and her thoughts and actions were not yet to correspond. To recover her self-esteem she tried to imagine that she was in her district, and to behave accordingly.

'What a fine child, Signor Carella. And how nice of you to talk to it. Though I see that the ungrateful little fellow is asleep! Seven months? No, eight; of course eight. Still, he is a remarkably fine child for his age.'

Italian is a bad medium for condescension. The patronising words came out gracious and sincere, and he smiled with pleasure.

'You must not stand. Let us sit on the loggia, where it is cool. I am afraid the room is very untidy,' he added, with the air of a hostess who apologises for a stray thread on the drawing-room carpet. Miss Abbott picked her way to the chair. He sat near her, astride the parapet, with one foot in the loggia and the other dangling into the view. His face was in profile, and its beautiful contours drove artfully against the misty green of the opposing hills. 'Posing!' said Miss Abbott to herself. 'A born artist's model.'

'Mr Herriton called yesterday,' she began, 'but you were out.'

He started an elaborate and graceful explanation. He had gone for the day to Poggibonsi. Why had the Herritons not written to him, so that he could have received them properly? Poggibonsi would have done any day; not but what his business there was fairly important. What did she suppose that it was?

Naturally she was not greatly interested. She had not come from Sawston to guess why he had been to Poggibonsi. She answered politely that she had no idea, and returned to her mission.

'But guess!' he persisted, clapping the balustrade between his hands.

She suggested, with gentle sarcasm, that perhaps he had gone to Poggibonsi to find something to do.

He intimated that it was not as important as all that. Something to do–an almost hopeless quest! 'É manca questo!' He rubbed his thumb and forefinger together, to indicate that he had no money. Then he sighed, and blew another smoke-ring. Miss Abbott took heart and turned diplomatic.

'This house,' she said, 'is a large house.'

'Exactly,' was his gloomy reply. 'And when my poor wife died—' He got up, went in, and walked across the landing to the reception-room door, which he closed reverently. Then he shut the door of the living-room with his foot, returned briskly to his seat, and continued his sentence. 'When my poor wife died I thought of having my relatives to live here. My father wished to give up his practice at Empoli; my mother and sisters and two aunts were also willing. But it was impossible. They have their ways of doing things, and when I was younger I was content with them. But now I am a man. I have my own ways. Do you understand?'

'Yes, I do,' said Miss Abbott, thinking of her own dear father, whose tricks and habits, after twenty-five years spent in their company, were beginning to get on her nerves. She remembered, though, that she was not here to sympathise with Gino–at all events, not to show that she

sympathised. She also reminded herself that he was not worthy of sympathy.
'It is a large house,' she repeated.

'Immense; and the taxes! But it will be better when— Ah! but you have
never guessed why I went to Poggibonsi—why it was that I was out when he
called.'

'I cannot guess, Signor Carella. I am here on business.'

'But try.'

'I cannot; I hardly know you.'

'But we are old friends,' he said, 'and your approval will be grateful to me.
You gave it me once before. Will you give it now?'

'I have not come as a friend this time,' she answered stiffly. 'I am not
likely, Signor Carella, to approve of anything you do.'

'Oh, Signorina!' He laughed, as if he found her piquante and amusing.
'Surely you approve of marriage?'

'Where there is love,' said Miss Abbott, looking at him hard. His face had
altered in the last year, but not for the worse, which was baffling.

'Where there is love,' said he, politely echoing the English view. Then he
smiled on her, expecting congratulations.

'Do I understand that you are proposing to marry again?'

He nodded.

'I forbid you, then!'

He looked puzzled, but took it for some foreign banter, and laughed.

'I forbid you!' repeated Miss Abbott, and all the indignation of her sex
and her nationality went thrilling through the words.

'But why?' He jumped up frowning. His voice was squeaky and petulant,
like that of a child who is suddenly forbidden a toy.

'You have ruined one woman; I forbid you to ruin another. It is not a year
since Lilia died. You pretended to me the other day that you loved her. It is a
lie. You wanted her money. Has this woman money too?'

'Why, yes!' he said irritably. 'A little.'

'And I suppose you will say that you love her.'

'I shall not say it. It will be untrue. Now my poor wife—' He stopped,
seeing that the comparison would involve him in difficulties. And indeed he
had often found Lilia as agreeable as anyone else.

Miss Abbott was furious at this final insult to her dead acquaintance. She
was glad that after all she could be so angry with the boy. She glowed and
throbbed; her tongue moved nimbly. At the finish, if the real business of the
day had been completed, she could have swept majestically from the house.
But the baby still remained, asleep on a dirty rug.

Gino was thoughtful, and stood scratching his head. He respected Miss
Abbott. He wished that she would respect him. 'So you do not advise me?'
he said dolefully. 'But why should it be a failure?'

Miss Abbott tried to remember that he was really a child still—a child with
the strength and the passions of a disreputable man. 'How can it succeed,'
she said solemnly, 'where there is no love?'

'But she does love me! I forgot to tell you that.'

'Indeed.'

'Passionately.' He laid his hand upon his own heart.

'Then God help her!'

He stamped impatiently. 'Whatever I say displeases you, Signorina. God help you, for you are most unfair. You say that I ill-treated my dear wife. It is not so. I have never ill-treated anyone. You complain that there is no love in this marriage. I prove that there is, and you become still more angry. What do you want? Do you suppose she will not be contented? Glad enough she is to get me, and she will do her duty well.'

'Her duty!' cried Miss Abbott, with all the bitterness of which she was capable.

'Why, of course. She knows why I am marrying her.'

'To succeed where Lilia failed! To be your housekeeper, your slave, your—' The words she would like to have said were too violent for her.

'To look after the baby, certainly,' said he.

'The baby—?' She had forgotten it.

'It is an English marriage,' he said proudly. 'I do not care about the money. I am having her for my son. Did you not understand that?'

'No,' said Miss Abbott, utterly bewildered. Then, for a moment, she saw light. 'It is not necessary, Signor Carella. Since you are tired of the baby—'

Ever after she remembered it to her credit that she saw her mistake at once. 'I don't mean that,' she added quickly.

'I know,' was his courteous response. 'Ah, in a foreign language (and how perfectly you speak Italian) one is certain to make slips.'

She looked at his face. It was apparently innocent of satire.

'You meant that we could not always be together yet, he and I. You are right. What is to be done? I cannot afford a nurse, and Perfetta is too rough. When he was ill I dare not let her touch him. When he has to be washed, which happens now and then, who does it?—I. I feed him, or settle what he shall have. I sleep with him and comfort him when he is unhappy in the night. No one talks, no one may sing to him but I. Do not be unfair this time; I like to do these things. But nevertheless' (his voice became pathetic) 'they take up a great deal of time, and are not all suitable for a young man.'

'Not at all suitable,' said Miss Abbott, and closed her eyes wearily. Each moment her difficulties were increasing. She wished that she was not so tired, so open to contradictory impressions. She longed for Harriet's burly obtuseness or for the soulless diplomacy of Mrs Herriton.

'A little more wine?' asked Gino kindly.

'Oh no, thank you! But marriage, Signor Carella, is a very serious step. Could you not manage more simply? Your relative, for example—'

'Empoli! I would as soon have him in England!'

'England, then—'

He laughed.

'He has a grandmother there, you know—Mrs Theobald.'

'He has a grandmother here. No, he is troublesome, but I must have him with me. I will not even have my father and mother too. For they would separate us,' he added.

'How?'

'They would separate our thoughts.'

She was silent. This cruel, vicious fellow knew of strange refinements. The horrible truth, that wicked people are capable of love, stood naked before her, and her moral being was abashed. It was her duty to rescue the baby, to save it from contagion, and she still meant to do her duty. But the comfortable sense of virtue left her. She was in the presence of something greater than right or wrong.

Forgetting that this was an interview, he had strolled back into the room, driven by the instinct she had aroused in him. 'Wake up!' he cried to his baby, as if it was some grown-up friend. Then he lifted his foot and trod lightly on its stomach.

Miss Abbott cried, 'Oh, take care!' She was unaccustomed to this method of wakening the young.

'He is not much longer than my boot, is he? Can you believe that in time his own boots will be as large? And that he also—'

'But ought you to treat him like that?'

He stood with one foot resting on the little body, suddenly musing, filled with the desire that his son should be like him, and should have sons like him, to people the earth. It is the strongest desire that can come to a man—if it comes to him at all—stronger even than love or the desire for personal immortality. All men vaunt it, and declare that it is theirs; but the hearts of most are set elsewhere. It is the exception who comprehends that physical and spiritual life may stream out of him for ever. Miss Abbott, for all her goodness, could not comprehend it, though such a thing is more within the comprehension of women. And when Gino pointed first to himself and then to his baby and said 'Father—son,' she still took it as a piece of nursery prattle, and smiled mechanically.

The child, the firstfruits, woke up and glared at her. Gino did not greet it, but continued the exposition of his policy.

'This woman will do exactly what I tell her. She is fond of children. She is clean; she has a pleasant voice. She is not beautiful; I cannot pretend that to you for a moment. But she is what I require.'

The baby gave a piercing yell.

'Oh, do take care!' begged Miss Abbott. 'You are squeezing it.'

'It is nothing. If he cries silently then you may be frightened. He thinks I am going to wash him, and he is quite right.'

'Wash him!' she cried. 'You? Here?' The homely piece of news seemed to shatter all her plans. She had spent a long half-hour in elaborate approaches, in high moral attacks; she had neither frightened her enemy nor made him angry, nor interfered with the least detail of his domestic life.

'I had gone to the Farmacia,' he continued, 'and was sitting there comfortably, when suddenly I remembered that Perfetta had heated water an hour ago—over there, look, covered with a cushion. You must excuse me. I can put it off no longer.'

'I have wasted your time,' she said feebly.

He walked sternly to the loggia and drew from it a large earthenware bowl. It was dirty inside; he dusted it with a tablecloth. Then he fetched the hot water, which was in a copper pot. He poured it out. He added cold. He felt in his pocket and brought out a piece of soap. Then he took up the baby, and, holding his cigar between his teeth, began to unwrap it. Miss Abbott turned to go.

'But why are you going? Excuse me if I wash him while we talk.'

'I have nothing more to say,' said Miss Abbott. All she could do now was to find Philip, confess her miserable defeat, and bid him go in her stead and prosper better. She cursed her feebleness: she longed to expose it, with apologies or tears.

'Oh, but stop a moment!' he cried. 'You have not seen him yet.'

'I have seen as much as I want, thank you.'

The last wrapping slid off. He held out to her in his two hands a little kicking image of bronze.

'Take him!'

She would not touch the child.

'I must go at once,' she cried; for the tears—the wrong tears—were hurrying to her eyes.

'Who would have believed his mother was blonde? For he is brown all over—brown every inch of him. Ah, but how beautiful he is! And he is mine; mine for ever. Even if he hates me he will be mine. He cannot help it; he is made out of me; I am his father.'

It was too late to go. She could not tell why, but it was too late. She turned away her head when Gino lifted his son to his lips. This was something too remote from the prettiness of the nursery. The man was majestic; he was a part of Nature; in no ordinary love scene could he ever be so great. For a wonderful physical tie binds the parents to the children; and—by some sad, strange irony—it does not bind us children to our parents. For if it did, if we could answer their love not with gratitude but with equal love, life would lose much of its pathos and much of its squalor, and we might be wonderfully happy. Gino passionately embracing, Miss Abbott reverently averting her eyes—both of them had parents whom they did not love so very much.

'May I help you to wash him?' she asked humbly.

He gave her his son without speaking, and they knelt side by side, tucking up their sleeves. The child had stopped crying, and his arms and legs were agitated by some overpowering joy. Miss Abbott had a woman's pleasure in cleaning anything—more especially when the thing was human. She understood little babies from long experience in a district, and Gino soon ceased to give her directions, and only gave her thanks.

'It is very kind of you,' he murmured, 'especially in your beautiful dress. He is nearly clean already. Why, I take the whole morning! There is so much more of a baby than one expects. And Perfetta washes him just as she washes clothes. Then he screams for hours. My wife is to have a light hand. Ah, how he kicks! Has he splashed you! I am very sorry.'

'I am ready for a soft towel now,' said Miss Abbott, who was strangely exalted by the service.

'Certainly! certainly!' He strode in a knowing way to a cupboard. But he had no idea where the soft towel was. Generally he dabbed the baby on the first dry thing he found.

'And if you had any powder.'

He struck his forehead despairingly. Apparently the stock of powder was just exhausted.

She sacrificed her own clean handkerchief. He put a chair for her on the loggia, which faced westward, and was still pleasant and cool. There she sat, with twenty miles of view behind her, and he placed the dripping baby on her knee. It shone now with health and beauty; it seemed to reflect light, like a copper vessel. Just such a baby Bellini sets languid on his mother's lap, or Signorelli flings wriggling on pavements of marble, or Lorenzo di Credi, more reverent but less divine, lays carefully among flowers, with his head upon a wisp of golden straw. For a time Gino contemplated them standing. Then, to get a better view, he knelt by the side of the chair, with his hands clasped before him.

So they were when Philip entered, and saw, to all intents and purposes, the Virgin and Child, with Donor.

'Hallo!' he exclaimed; for he was glad to find things in such cheerful trim.

She did not greet him, but rose up unsteadily and handed the baby to his father.

'No, do stop!' whispered Philip. 'I got your note. I'm not offended; you're quite right. I really want you; I could never have done it alone.'

No words came from her, but she raised her hands to her mouth, like one who is in sudden agony.

'Signorina, do stop a little–after all your kindness.'

She burst into tears.

'What is it?' said Philip kindly.

She tried to speak, and then went away, weeping bitterly.

The two men stared at each other. By a common impulse they ran on to the loggia. They were just in time to see Miss Abbott disappear among the trees.

'What is it?' asked Philip again. There was no answer, and somehow he did not want an answer. Some strange thing had happened which he could not presume to understand. He would find out from Miss Abbott, if ever he found out at all.

'Well, your business,' said Gino, after a puzzled sigh.

'Our business–Miss Abbott has told you of that.'

'No.'

'But surely—'

'She came for business. But she forgot about it; so did I.'

Perfetta, who had a genius for missing people, now returned, loudly complaining of the size of Monteriano and the intricacies of its streets. Gino told her to watch the baby. Then he offered Philip a cigar, and they proceeded to the business.

Chapter Eight

'Mad!' screamed Harriet—'absolutely stark, staring, raving mad!'

Philip judged it better not to contradict her.

'What's she here for? Answer me that. What's she doing in Monteriano in August? Why isn't she in Normandy? Answer that. She won't. I can: she's come to thwart us; she's betrayed us—got hold of mother's plans. Oh, goodness, my head!'

He was unwise enough to reply, 'You mustn't accuse her of that. Though she is exasperating, she hasn't come here to betray us.'

'Then why has she come here? Answer me that.'

He made no answer. But fortunately his sister was too much agitated to wait for one. 'Bursting in on me—crying and looking a disgusting sight—and says she has been to see the Italian. Couldn't even talk properly; pretended she had changed her opinions. What are her opinions to us? I was very calm. I said: "Miss Abbott, I think there is a little misapprehension in this matter. My mother, Mrs Herriton—" Oh, goodness, my head! Of course you've failed—don't trouble to answer—I know you've failed. Where's the baby, pray? Of course you haven't got it. Dear sweet Caroline won't let you. Oh yes, and we're to go away at once and trouble the father no more. Those are her commands. Commands! COMMANDS!' And Harriet also burst into tears.

Philip governed his temper. His sister was annoying, but quite reasonable in her indignation. Moreover, Miss Abbott had behaved even worse than she supposed.

'I've not got the baby, Harriet, but at the same time I haven't exactly failed. I and Signor Carella are to have another interview this afternoon, at the Caffè Garibaldi. He is perfectly reasonable and pleasant. Should you be disposed to come with me, you would find him quite willing to discuss things. He is desperately in want of money, and has no prospect of getting any. I discovered that. At the same time, he has a certain affection for the child.' For Philip's insight, or perhaps his opportunities, had not been equal to Miss Abbott's.

Harriet would only sob, and accuse her brother of insulting her; how could a lady speak to such a horrible man? That, and nothing else, was enough to stamp Caroline. Oh, poor Lilia!

Philip drummed on the bedroom window-sill. He saw no escape from the deadlock. For though he spoke cheerfully about his second interview with Gino, he felt at the bottom of his heart that it would fail. Gino was too courteous: he would not break off negotiations by sharp denial; he loved this civil, half-humorous bargaining. And he loved fooling his opponent, and did it so nicely that his opponent did not mind being fooled.

'Miss Abbott has behaved extraordinarily,' he said at last; 'but at the same time—'

His sister would not hear him. She burst forth again on the madness, the interference, the intolerable duplicity of Caroline.

'Harriet, you must listen. My dear, you must stop crying. I have something quite important to say.'

'I shall not stop crying,' said she. But in time, finding that he would not speak to her, she did stop.

'Remember that Miss Abbott has done us no harm. She said nothing to him about the matter. He assumes that she is working with us: I gathered that.'

'Well, she isn't.'

'Yes; but if you're careful she may be. I interpret her behaviour thus: she went to see him, honestly intending to get the child away. In the note she left me she says so, and I don't believe she'd lie.'

'I do.'

'When she got there, there was some pretty domestic scene between him and the baby, and she has got swept off in a gush of sentimentalism. Before very long, if I know anything about psychology, there will be a reaction. She'll be swept back.'

'I don't understand your long words. Say plainly—'

'When she's swept back, she'll be invaluable. For she has made quite an impression on him. He thinks her so nice with the baby. You know, she washed it for him.'

'Disgusting!'

Harriet's ejaculations were more aggravating than the rest of her. But Philip was averse to losing his temper. The access of joy that had come to him yesterday in the theatre promised to be permanent. He was more anxious than heretofore to be charitable towards the world.

'If you want to carry off the baby, keep your peace with Miss Abbott. For if she chooses, she can help you better than I can.'

'There can be no peace between me and her,' said Harriet gloomily.

'Did you—'

'Oh, not all I wanted. She went away before I had finished speaking—just like those cowardly people!—into the church.'

'Into Santa Deodata's?'

'Yes; I'm sure she needs it. Anything more unchristian—'

In time Philip went to the church also, leaving his sister a little calmer and a little disposed to think over his advice. What had come over Miss Abbott? He had always thought her both stable and sincere. That conversation he had had with her last Christmas in the train to Charing Cross—that alone furnished him with a parallel. For the second time, Monteriano must have turned her head. He was not angry with her, for he was quite indifferent to the outcome of their expedition. He was only extremely interested.

It was now nearly midday, and the streets were clearing. But the intense heat had broken, and there was a pleasant suggestion of rain. The Piazza, with its three great attractions–the Palazzo Pubblico, the Collegiate Church, and the Caffè Garibaldi: the intellect, the soul, and the body–had never looked more charming. For a moment Philip stood in its centre, much inclined to be dreamy, and thinking how wonderful it must feel to belong to a city, however mean. He was here, however, as an emissary of civilisation and as a student of character, and, after a sigh, he entered Santa Deodata's to continue his mission.

There had been a festa two days before, and the church still smelt of incense and of garlic. The little son of the sacristan was sweeping the nave, more for amusement than for cleanliness, sending great clouds of dust over the frescoes and the scattered worshippers. The sacristan himself had propped a ladder in the centre of the Deluge–which fills one of the nave spandrels–and was freeing a column from its wealth of scarlet calico. Much scarlet calico also lay upon the floor–for the church can look as fine as any theatre–and the sacristan's little daughter was trying to fold it up. She was wearing a tinsel crown. The crown really belonged to St Augustine. But it had been cut too big: it fell down over his cheeks like a collar–you never saw anything so absurd. One of the canons had unhooked it just before the festa began, and had given it to the sacristan's daughter.

'Please,' cried Philip, 'is there an English lady here?'

The man's mouth was full of tin-tacks, but he nodded cheerfully towards a kneeling figure. In the midst of this confusion Miss Abbott was praying.

He was not much surprised: a spiritual breakdown was quite to be expected. For though he was growing more charitable towards mankind, he was still a little jaunty, and too apt to stake out beforehand the course that will be pursued by the wounded soul. It did surprise him, however, that she should greet him naturally, with none of the sour self-consciousness of a person who had just risen from her knees. This was indeed the spirit of Santa Deodata's, where a prayer to God is thought none the worse of because it comes next to a pleasant word to a neighbour. 'I am sure that I need it,' said she; and he, who had expected her to be ashamed, became confused, and knew not what to reply.

'I've nothing to tell you,' she continued. 'I have simply changed straight round. If I had planned the whole thing out, I could not have treated you worse. I can talk it over now; but please believe that I have been crying.'

'And please believe that I have not come to scold you,' said Philip. 'I know what has happened.'

'What?' asked Miss Abbott. Instinctively she led the way to the famous chapel, the fifth chapel on the right, wherein Giovanni da Empoli has painted the death and burial of the saint. Here they could sit out of the dust and the noise, and proceed with a discussion which promised to be important.

'What might have happened to me–he has made you believe that he loves the child.'

'Oh yes; he has. He will never give it up.'

'At present it is still unsettled.'

'It will never be settled.'

'Perhaps not. Well, as I said, I know what has happened, and I am not here to scold you. But I must ask you to withdraw from the thing for the present. Harriet is furious. But she will calm down when she realises that you have done us no harm, and will do none.'

'I can do no more,' she said. 'But I tell you plainly I have changed sides.'

'If you do no more, that is all we want. You promise not to prejudice our cause by speaking to Signor Carella?'

'Oh, certainly. I don't want to speak to him again; I shan't ever see him again.'

'Quite nice, wasn't he?'

'Quite.'

'Well, that's all I wanted to know. I'll go and tell Harriet of your promise, and I think things'll quiet down now.'

But he did not move, for it was an increasing pleasure to him to be near her, and her charm was at its strongest to-day. He thought less of psychology and feminine reaction. The gush of sentimentalism which had carried her away had only made her more alluring. He was content to observe her beauty and to profit by the tenderness and the wisdom that dwelt within her.

'Why aren't you angry with me?' she asked, after a pause.

'Because I understand you—all sides, I think—Harriet, Signor Carella, even my mother.'

'You do understand wonderfully. You are the only one of us who has a general view of the muddle.'

He smiled with pleasure. It was the first time she had ever praised him. His eyes rested agreeably on Santa Deodata, who was dying in full sanctity, upon her back. There was a window open behind her, revealing just such a view as he had seen that morning, and on her widowed mother's dresser there stood just such another copper pot. The saint looked neither at the view nor at the pot, and at her widowed mother still less. For lo! she had a vision: the head and shoulders of St Augustine were sliding like some miraculous enamel along the roughcast wall. It is a gentle saint who is content with half another saint to see her die. In her death, as in her life, Santa Deodata did not accomplish much.

'So what are you going to do?' said Miss Abbott.

Philip started, not so much at the words as at the sudden change in the voice. 'Do?' he echoed, rather dismayed. 'This afternoon I have another interview.'

'It will come to nothing. Well?'

'Then another. If that fails I shall wire home for instructions. I dare say we may fail altogether, but we shall fail honourably.'

She had often been decided. But now behind her decision there was a note of passion. She struck him not as different, but as more important, and he minded it very much when she said—

'That's not doing anything! You would be doing something if you kidnapped the baby, or if you went straight away. But that! To fail honourably! To come out of the thing as well as you can! Is that all you are after?'

'Why, yes,' he stammered. 'Since we talk openly, that is all I am after just now. What else is there? If I can persuade Signor Carella to give in, so much the better. If he won't, I must report the failure to my mother, and then go home. Why, Miss Abbott, you can't expect me to follow you through all these turns—'

'I don't! But I do expect you to settle what is right and to follow that. Do you want the child to stop with his father, who loves him and will bring him up badly, or do you want him to come to Sawston, where no one loves him, but where he will be brought up well? There is the question put dispassionately enough even for you. Settle it. Settle which side you'll fight on. But don't go talking about an "honourable failure," which means simply not thinking and not acting at all.'

'Because I understand the position of Signor Carella and of you, it's no reason that—'

'None at all. Fight as if you think us wrong. Oh, what's the use of your fairmindedness if you never decide for yourself? Anyone gets hold of you and makes you do what they want. And you see through them and laugh at them—and do it. It's not enough to see clearly; I'm muddle-headed and stupid, and not worth a quarter of you, but I have tried to do what seemed right at the time. And you—your brain and your insight are splendid. But when you see what's right you're too idle to do it. You told me once that we shall be judged by our intentions, not by our accomplishments. I thought it a grand remark. But we must intend to accomplish—not sit intending on a chair.'

'You are wonderful!' he said gravely.

'Oh, you appreciate me!' she burst out again. 'I wish you didn't. You appreciate us all—see good in all of us. And all the time you are dead—dead—dead. Look, why aren't you angry?' She came up to him, and then her mood suddenly changed, and she took hold of both his hands. 'You are so splendid, Mr Herriton, that I can't bear to see you wasted. I can't bear—she has not been good to you—your mother.'

'Miss Abbott, don't worry over me. Some people are born not to do things. I'm one of them; I never did anything at school or at the Bar. I came out to stop Lilia's marriage, and it was too late. I came out intending to get the baby, and I shall return an "honourable failure." I never expect anything to happen now, and so I am never disappointed. You would be surprised to know what my great events are. Going to the theatre yesterday, talking to you now—I don't suppose I shall ever meet anything greater. I seem fated to pass through the world without colliding with it or moving it—and I'm sure I can't tell you whether the fate's good or evil. I don't die—I don't fall in love. And if other people die or fall in love they always do it when I'm just not there. You are quite right; life to me is just a spectacle, which—thank God, and thank Italy, and thank you—is now more beautiful and heartening than it has ever been before.'

She said solemnly, 'I wish something would happen to you, my dear friend; I wish something would happen to you.'

'But why?' he asked, smiling. 'Prove to me why I don't do as I am.'

She also smiled, very gravely. She could not prove it. No argument existed. Their discourse, splendid as it had been, resulted in nothing, and their respective opinions and policies were exactly the same when they left the church as when they had entered it.

Harriet was rude at lunch. She called Miss Abbott a turncoat and a coward to her face. Miss Abbott resented neither epithet, feeling that one was justified and the other not unreasonable. She tried to avoid even the suspicion of satire in her replies. But Harriet was sure that she was satirical because she was so calm. She got more and more violent, and Philip at one time feared that she would come to blows.

'Look here!' he cried, with something of the old manner, 'it's too hot for this. We've been talking and interviewing each other all the morning, and I have another interview this afternoon. I do stipulate for silence. Let each lady retire to her bedroom with a book.'

'I retire to pack,' said Harriet. 'Please remind Signor Carella, Philip, that the baby is to be here by half-past eight this evening.'

'Oh, certainly, Harriet. I shall make a point of reminding him.'

'And order a carriage to take us to the evening train.'

'And please,' said Miss Abbott, 'would you order a carriage for me too?'

'You going?' he exclaimed.

'Of course,' she replied, suddenly flushing. 'Why not?'

'Why, of course you would be going. Two carriages, then. Two carriages for the evening train.' He looked at his sister hopelessly. 'Harriet, whatever are you up to? We shall never be ready.'

'Order my carriage for the evening train,' said Harriet, and departed.

'Well, I suppose I shall. And I shall also have my interview with Signor Carella.'

Miss Abbott gave a little sigh.

'But why should you mind? Do you suppose that I shall have the slightest influence over him?'

'No. But—I can't repeat all that I said in the church. You ought never to see him again. You ought to bundle Harriet into a carriage, not this evening, but now, and drive her straight away.'

'Perhaps I ought. But it isn't a very big "ought." Whatever Harriet and I do the issue is the same. Why, I can see the splendour of it—even the humour. Gino sitting up here on the mountain-top with his cub. We come and ask for it. He welcomes us. We ask for it again. He is equally pleasant. I'm agreeable to spend the whole week bargaining with him. But I know that at the end of it I shall descend empty-handed to the plains. It might be finer of me to make up my mind. But I'm not a fine character. And nothing hangs on it.'

'Perhaps I am extreme,' she said humbly. 'I've been trying to run you, just like your mother. I feel you ought to fight it out with Harriet. Every little trifle, for some reason, does seem incalculably important to-day, and when you say of a thing that "nothing hangs on it," it sounds like blasphemy. There's never any knowing—(how am I to put it?)—which of our actions, which of our idleness won't have things hanging on it for ever.'

He assented, but her remark had only an æsthetic value. He was not prepared to take it to his heart. All the afternoon he rested—worried, but not exactly despondent. The thing would jog out somehow. Probably Miss Abbott was right. The baby had better stop where it was loved. And that, probably, was what the fates had decreed. He felt little interest in the matter, and he was sure that he had no influence.

It was not surprising, therefore, that the interview at the Caffè Garibaldi came to nothing. Neither of them took it very seriously. And before long Gino had discovered how things lay, and was ragging his companion hopelessly. Philip tried to look offended, but in the end he had to laugh. 'Well, you are right,' he said. 'The affair *is* being managed by the ladies.'

'Ah, the ladies—the ladies!' cried the other, and then he roared like a millionaire for two cups of black coffee, and insisted on treating his friend, as a sign that their strife was over.

'Well, I have done my best,' said Philip, dipping a long slice of sugar into his cup, and watching the brown liquid ascend into it. 'I shall face my mother with a good conscience. Will you bear me witness that I've done my best?'

'My poor fellow, I will!' He laid a sympathetic hand on Philip's knee.

'And that I have—' The sugar was now impregnated with coffee, and he bent forward to swallow it. As he did so his eyes swept the opposite side of the Piazza, and he saw there, watching them, Harriet. 'Mia sorella!' he exclaimed. Gino, much amused, laid his hand upon the little table, and beat the marble humorously with his fists. Harriet turned away and began gloomily to inspect the Palazzo Pubblico.

'Poor Harriet!' said Philip, swallowing the sugar. 'One more wrench and it will all be over for her; we are leaving this evening.'

Gino was sorry for this. 'Then you will not be here this evening as you promised us. All three leaving?'

'All three,' said Philip, who had not revealed the secession of Miss Abbott; 'by the night train; at least, that is my sister's plan. So I'm afraid I shan't be here.'

They watched the departing figure of Harriet, and then entered upon the final civilities. They shook each other warmly by both hands. Philip was to come again next year, and to write beforehand. He was to be introduced to Gino's wife, for he was told of the marriage now. He was to be godfather to his next baby. As for Gino, he would remember some time that Philip liked vermouth. He begged him to give his love to Irma. Mrs Herriton—should he send her his sympathetic regards? No; perhaps that would hardly do.

So the two young men parted with a good deal of genuine affection. For the barrier of language is sometimes a blessed barrier, which only lets pass what is good. Or—to put the thing less cynically—we may be better in new clean words, which have never been tainted by our pettiness or vice. Philip, at all events, lived more graciously in Italian, the very phrases of which entice one to be happy and kind. It was horrible to think of the English of Harriet, whose every word would be as hard, as distinct, and as unfinished as a lump of coal.

Harriet, however, talked little. She had seen enough to know that her brother had failed again, and with unwonted dignity she accepted the situation. She did her packing, she wrote up her diary, she made a brown paper cover for the new Baedeker. Philip, finding her so amenable, tried to discuss their future plans. But she only said that they would sleep in Florence, and told him to telegraph for rooms. They had supper alone. Miss Abbott did not come down. The landlady told them that Signor Carella had called on Miss Abbott to say good-bye, but she, though in, had not been able to see him. She also told them that it had begun to rain. Harriet sighed, but indicated to her brother that he was not responsible.

The carriages came round at a quarter past eight. It was not raining much, but the night was extraordinarily dark, and one of the drivers wanted to go slowly to the station. Miss Abbott came down and said that she was ready, and would start at once.

'Yes, do,' said Philip, who was standing in the hall. 'Now that we have quarrelled we scarcely want to travel in procession all the way down the hill. Well, good-bye; it's all over at last; another scene in my pageant has shifted.'

'Good-bye; it's been a great pleasure to see you. I hope that won't shift, at all events.' She gripped his hand.

'You sound despondent,' he said, laughing. 'Don't forget that you return victorious.'

'I suppose I do,' she replied, more despondently than ever, and got into the carriage. He concluded that she was thinking of her reception at Sawston, whither her fame would doubtless precede her. Whatever would Mrs Herriton do? She could make things quite unpleasant when she thought it right. She might think it right to be silent, but then there was Harriet. Who would bridle Harriet's tongue? Between the two of them Miss Abbott was bound to have a bad time. Her reputation, both for consistency and for moral enthusiasm, would be lost for ever.

'It's hard luck on her,' he thought. 'She is a good person. I must do for her anything I can.' Their intimacy had been very rapid, but he too hoped that it would not shift. He believed that he understood her, and that she, by now, had seen the worst of him. What if after a long time—if after all—he flushed like a boy as he looked after her carriage.

He went into the dining-room to look for Harriet. Harriet was not to be found. Her bedroom, too, was empty. All that was left of her was the purple prayer-book which lay open on the bed. Philip took it up aimlessly, and saw—'Blessed be the Lord my God who teacheth my hands to war and my fingers to fight.' He put the book in his pocket, and began to brood over more profitable themes.

Santa Deodata gave out half-past eight. All the luggage was on, and still Harriet had not appeared. 'Depend upon it,' said the landlady, 'she has gone to Signor Carella's to say good-bye to her little nephew.' Philip did not think it likely. They shouted all over the house and still there was no Harriet. He began to be uneasy. He was helpless without Miss Abbott; her grave kind face had cheered him wonderfully, even when it looked displeased. Monteriano was sad without her; the rain was thickening; the scraps of

Donizetti floated tunelessly out of the wineshops, and of the great tower opposite he could only see the base, fresh papered with the advertisements of quacks.

A man came up the street with a note. Philip read, 'Start at once. Pick me up outside the gate. Pay the bearer. H.H.'

'Did the lady give you this note?' he cried.

The man was unintelligible.

'Speak up!' exclaimed Philip. 'Who gave it you—and where?'

Nothing but horrible sighings and bubblings came out of the man.

'Be patient with him,' said the driver, turning round on the box. 'It is the poor idiot.' And the landlady came out of the hotel and echoed 'The poor idiot. He cannot speak. He takes messages for us all.'

Philip then saw that the messenger was a ghastly creature, quite bald, with trickling eyes and grey twitching nose. In another country he would have been shut up; here he was accepted as a public institution, and part of Nature's scheme.

'Ugh!' shuddered the Englishman. 'Signora padrona, find out from him; this note is from my sister. What does it mean? Where did he see her?'

'It is no good,' said the landlady. 'He understands everything, but he can explain nothing.'

'He has visions of the saints,' said the man who drove the cab.

'But my sister—where has she gone? How has she met him?'

'She has gone for a walk,' asserted the landlady. It was a nasty evening, but she was beginning to understand the English. 'She has gone for a walk—perhaps to wish good-bye to her little nephew. Preferring to come back another way, she has sent you this note by the poor idiot and is waiting for you outside the Siena gate. Many of my guests do this.'

There was nothing to do but to obey the message. He shook hands with the landlady, gave the messenger a nickel piece, and drove away. After a dozen yards the carriage stopped. The poor idiot was running and whimpering behind.

'Go on,' cried Philip. 'I have paid him plenty.'

A horrible hand pushed three soldi into his lap. It was part of the idiot's malady only to receive what was just for his services. This was the change out of the nickel piece.

'Go on!' shouted Philip, and flung the money into the road. He was frightened at the episode; the whole of life had become unreal. It was a relief to be out of the Siena gate. They drew up for a moment on the terrace. But there was no sign of Harriet. The driver called to the Dogana men. But they had seen no English lady pass.

'What am I to do?' he cried; 'it is not like the lady to be late. We shall miss the train.'

'Let us drive slowly,' said the driver, 'and you shall call her by name as we go.'

So they started down into the night, Philip calling 'Harriet! Harriet! Harriet!' And there she was, waiting for them in the wet, at the first turn of the zigzag.

'Harriet, why don't you answer?'

'I heard you coming,' said she, and got quickly in. Not till then did he see that she carried a bundle.

'What's that?'

'Hush—'

'Whatever is that?'

'Hush—sleeping.'

Harriet had succeeded where Miss Abbott and Philip had failed. It was the baby.

She would not let him talk. The baby, she repeated, was asleep, and she put up an umbrella to shield it and her from the rain. He should hear all later, so he had to conjecture the course of the wonderful interview—an interview between the South Pole and the North. It was quite easy to conjecture: Gino crumpling up suddenly before the intense conviction of Harriet; being told, perhaps, to his face that he was a villain; yielding his only son perhaps for money, perhaps for nothing. 'Poor Gino,' he thought. 'He's no greater than I am, after all.'

Then he thought of Miss Abbott, whose carriage must be descending the darkness some mile or two below them, and his easy self-accusation failed. She, too, had conviction; he had felt its force; he would feel it again when she knew this day's sombre and unexpected close.

'You have been pretty secret,' he said; 'you might tell me a little now. What do we pay for him? All we've got?'

'Hush!' answered Harriet, and dandled the bundle laboriously, like some bony prophetess—Judith, or Deborah, or Jael. He had last seen the baby sprawling on the knees of Miss Abbott, shining and naked, with twenty miles of view behind him, and his father kneeling by his feet. And that remembrance, together with Harriet, and the darkness, and the poor idiot, and the silent rain, filled him with sorrow and with the expectation of sorrow to come.

Monteriano had long disappeared, and he could see nothing but the occasional wet stem of an olive, which their lamp illumined as they passed it. They travelled quickly, for this driver did not care how fast he went to the station, and would dash down each incline and scuttle perilously round the curves.

'Look here, Harriet,' he said at last, 'I feel bad; I want to see the baby.'

'Hush!'

'I don't mind if I do wake him up. I want to see him. I've as much right in him as you.'

Harriet gave in. But it was too dark for him to see the child's face. 'Wait a minute,' he whispered, and before she could stop him he had lit a match under the shelter of her umbrella. 'But he's awake!' he exclaimed. The match went out.

'Good ickle quiet boysey, then.'

Philip winced. 'His face, do you know, struck me as all wrong.'

'All wrong?'

'All puckered queerly.'

'Of course–with the shadows–you couldn't see him.'

'Well, hold him up again.' She did so. He lit another match. It went out quickly, but not before he had seen that the baby was crying.

'Nonsense,' said Harriet sharply. 'We should hear him if he cried.'

'No, he's crying hard; I thought so before, and I'm certain now.'

Harriet touched the child's face. It was bathed in tears. 'Oh, the night air, I suppose,' she said, 'or perhaps the wet of the rain.'

'I say, you haven't hurt it, or held it the wrong way, or anything; it is too uncanny–crying and no noise. Why didn't you get Perfetta to carry it to the hotel instead of muddling with the messenger? It's a marvel he understood about the note.'

'Oh, he understands.' And he could feel her shudder. 'He tried to carry the baby—'

'But why not Gino or Perfetta?'

'Philip, don't talk. Must I say it again? Don't talk. The baby wants to sleep.' She crooned harshly as they descended, and now and then she wiped up the tears which welled inexhaustibly from the little eyes. Philip looked away, winking at times himself. It was as if they were travelling with the whole world's sorrow, as if all the mystery, all the persistency of woe were gathered to a single fount. The roads were now coated with mud, and the carriage went more quietly but not less swiftly, sliding by long zigzags into the night. He knew the landmarks pretty well: here was the cross-road to Poggibonsi; and the last view of Monteriano, if they had light, would be from here. Soon they ought to come to that little wood where violets were so plentiful in spring. He wished the weather had not changed; it was not cold, but the air was extraordinarily damp. It could not be good for the child.

'I suppose he breathes, and all that sort of thing?' he said.

'Of course,' said Harriet, in an angry whisper. 'You've started him again. I'm certain he was asleep. I do wish you wouldn't talk; it makes me so nervous.'

'I'm nervous too. I wish he'd scream. It's too uncanny. Poor Gino! I'm terribly sorry for Gino.'

'Are you?'

'Because he's weak–like most of us. He doesn't know what he wants. He doesn't grip on to life. But I like that man, and I'm sorry for him.'

Naturally enough she made no answer.

'You despise him, Harriet, and you despise me. But you do us no good by it. We fools want some one to set us on our feet. Suppose a really decent woman had set up Gino–I believe Caroline Abbott might have done it–mightn't he have been another man?'

'Philip,' she interrupted, with an attempt at nonchalance, 'do you happen to have those matches handy? We might as well look at the baby again if you have.'

The first match blew out immediately. So did the second. He suggested that they should stop the carriage and borrow the lamp from the driver.

'Oh, I don't want all that bother. Try again.'

They entered the little wood as he tried to strike the third match. At last it caught. Harriet poised the umbrella rightly, and for a full quarter-minute they contemplated the face that trembled in the light of the trembling flame. Then there was a shout and a crash. They were lying in the mud in darkness. The carriage had overturned.

Philip was a good deal hurt. He sat up and rocked himself to and fro, holding his arm. He could just make out the outline of the carriage above him, and the outlines of the carriage cushions and of their luggage upon the grey road. The accident had taken place in the wood, where it was even darker than in the open.

'Are you all right?' he managed to say. Harriet was screaming, the horse was kicking, the driver was cursing some other man.

Harriet's screams became coherent. 'The baby–the baby–it slipped–it's gone from my arms! I stole it!'

'God help me!' said Philip. A cold circle came round his mouth, and he fainted.

When he recovered it was still the same confusion. The horse was kicking, the baby had not been found, and Harriet still screamed like a maniac, 'I stole it! I stole it! I stole it! It slipped out of my arms!'

'Keep still!' he commanded the driver. 'Let no one move. We may tread on it. Keep still.'

For a moment they all obeyed him. He began to crawl through the mud, touching first this, then that, grasping the cushions by mistake, listening for the faintest whisper that might guide him. He tried to light a match, holding the box in his teeth and striking at it with the uninjured hand. At last he succeeded, and the light fell upon the bundle which he was seeking.

It had rolled off the road into the wood a little way, and had fallen across a great rut. So tiny it was that had it fallen lengthways it would have disappeared, and he might never have found it.

'I stole it! I and the idiot–no one was there.' She burst out laughing.

He sat down and laid it on his knee. Then he tried to cleanse the face from the mud and the rain and the tears. His arm, he supposed, was broken, but he could still move it a little, and for the moment he forgot all pain. He was listening–not for a cry, but for the tick of a heart or the slightest tremor of breath.

'Where are you?' called a voice. It was Miss Abbott, against whose carriage they had collided. She had re-lit one of the lamps, and was picking her way towards him.

'Silence!' he called again, and again they obeyed. He shook the bundle; he breathed into it; he opened his coat and pressed it against him. Then he listened, and heard nothing but the rain and the panting horses, and Harriet, who was somewhere chuckling to herself in the dark.

Miss Abbott approached, and took it gently from him. The face was already chilly, but thanks to Philip it was no longer wet. Nor would it again be wetted by any tear.

Chapter Nine

The details of Harriet's crime were never known. In her illness she spoke more of the inlaid box that she had lent to Lilia—lent, not given—than of recent troubles. It was clear that she had gone prepared for an interview with Gino, and finding him out, she had yielded to a grotesque temptation. But how far this was the result of ill-temper, to what extent she had been fortified by her religion, when and how she had met the poor idiot—these questions were never answered, nor did they interest Philip greatly. Detection was certain: they would have been arrested by the police of Florence or Milan, or at the frontier. As it was, they had been stopped in a simpler manner a few miles out of the town.

As yet he could scarcely survey the thing. It was too great. Round the Italian baby who had died in the mud there centred deep passions and high hopes. People have been wicked or wrong in the matter; no one save himself had been trivial. Now the baby had gone, but there remained this vast apparatus of pride and pity and love. For the dead, who seem to take away so much, really take with them nothing that is ours. The passion they have aroused lives after them, easy to transmute or to transfer, but well-nigh impossible to destroy. And Philip knew that he was still voyaging on the same magnificent, perilous sea, with the sun or the clouds above him, and the tides below.

The course of the moment—that, at all events, was certain. He and no one else must take the news to Gino. It was easy to talk of Harriet's crime—easy also to blame the negligent Perfetta or Mrs Herriton at home. Every one had contributed—even Miss Abbott and Irma. If one chose, one might consider the catastrophe composite or the work of fate. But Philip did not so choose. It was his own fault, due to acknowledged weakness in his own character. Therefore he, and no one else, must take the news of it to Gino.

Nothing prevented him. Miss Abbott was engaged with Harriet, and people had sprung out of the darkness and were conducting them towards some cottage. Philip had only to get into the uninjured carriage and order the driver to return. He was back at Monteriano after a two hours' absence. Perfetta was in the house now, and greeted him cheerfully. Pain, physical and mental, had made him stupid. It was some time before he realised that she had never missed the child.

Gino was still out. The woman took him to the reception-room, just as she had taken Miss Abbott in the morning, and dusted a circle for him on one of the horse-hair chairs. But it was dark now, so she left the guest a little lamp.

'I will be as quick as I can,' she told him. 'But there are many streets in Monteriano; he is sometimes difficult to find. I could not find him this morning.'

'Go first to the Caffè Garibaldi,' said Philip, remembering that this was the hour appointed by his friends of yesterday.

He occupied the time he was left alone not in thinking—there was nothing to think about; he simply had to tell a few facts—but in trying to make a sling for his broken arm. The trouble was in the elbow-joint, and as long as he kept this motionless he could go on as usual. But inflammation was beginning, and the slightest jar gave him agony. The sling was not fitted before Gino leapt up the stairs, crying—

'So you are back! How glad I am! We are all waiting—'

Philip had seen too much to be nervous. In low, even tones, he told what had happened; and the other, also perfectly calm, heard him to the end. In the silence Perfetta called up that she had forgotten the baby's evening milk; she must fetch it. When she had gone Gino took up the lamp without a word, and they went into the other room.

'My sister is ill,' said Philip, 'and Miss Abbott is guiltless. I should be glad if you did not have to trouble them.'

Gino had stooped down by the way, and was feeling the place where his son had lain. Now and then he frowned a little and glanced at Philip.

'It is through me,' he continued. 'It happened because I was cowardly and idle. I have come to know what you will do.'

Gino had left the rug, and began to pat the table from the end, as if he was blind. The action was so uncanny that Philip was driven to intervene.

'Gently, man, gently; he is not here.'

He went up and touched him on the shoulder.

He twitched away, and began to pass his hands over things more rapidly—over the table, the chairs, the entire floor, the walls as high as he could reach them. Philip had not presumed to comfort him. But now the tension was too great—he tried.

'Break down, Gino; you must break down. Scream and curse and give in for a little; you must break down.'

There was no reply, and no cessation of the sweeping hands.

'It is time to be unhappy. Break down or you will be ill like my sister. You will go—'

The tour of the room was over. He had touched everything in it except Philip. Now he approached him. His face was that of a man who has lost his old reason for life and seeks a new one.

'Gino!'

He stopped for a moment; then he came nearer. Philip stood his ground.

'You are to do what you like with me, Gino. Your son is dead, Gino. He died in my arms, remember. It does not excuse me; but he did die in my arms.'

The left hand came forward, slowly this time. It hovered before Philip like an insect. Then it descended and gripped him by his broken elbow.

Philip struck out with all the strength of his other arm. Gino fell to the blow without a cry or a word.

'You brute!' exclaimed the Englishman. 'Kill me if you like! But just you leave my broken arm alone.'

Then he was seized with remorse, and knelt beside his adversary and tried to revive him. He managed to raise him up, and propped his body against his own. He passed his arm round him. Again he was filled with pity and tenderness. He awaited the revival without fear, sure that both of them were safe at last.

Gino recovered suddenly. His lips moved. For one blessed moment it seemed that he was going to speak. But he scrambled up in silence, remembering everything, and he made not towards Philip, but towards the lamp.

'Do what you like; but think first—'

The lamp was tossed across the room, out through the loggia. It broke against one of the trees below. Philip began to cry out in the dark.

Gino approached from behind and gave him a sharp pinch. Philip spun round with a yell. He had only been pinched on the back, but he knew what was in store for him. He struck out, exhorting the devil to fight him, to kill him, to do anything but this. Then he stumbled to the door. It was open. He lost his head and, instead of turning down the stairs, he ran across the landing into the room opposite. There he lay down on the floor between the stove and the skirting-board.

His senses grew sharper. He could hear Gino coming in on tiptoe. He even knew what was passing in his mind, how now he was at fault, now he was hopeful, now he was wondering whether after all the victim had not escaped down the stairs. There was a quick swoop above him, and then a low growl like a dog's. Gino had broken his finger-nails against the stove.

Physical pain is almost too terrible to bear. We can just bear it when it comes by accident or for our good—as it generally does in modern life— except at school. But when it is caused by the malignity of a man, full grown, fashioned like ourselves, all our control disappears. Philip's one thought was to get away from that room at whatever sacrifice of nobility or pride.

Gino was now at the farther end of the room, groping by the little tables. Suddenly the instinct came to him. He crawled quickly to where Philip lay and had him clean by the elbow.

The whole arm seemed red-hot, and the broken bone grated in the joint sending out shoots of the essence of pain. His other arm was pinioned against the wall, and Gino had trampled in behind the stove and was kneeling on his legs. For the space of a minute he yelled and yelled with all the force of his lungs. Then this solace was denied him. The other hand, moist and strong, began to close round his throat.

At first he was glad, for here, he thought, was death at last. But it was only a new torture; perhaps Gino inherited the skill of his ancestors—the childlike ruffians who flung each other from the towers. Just as the windpipe closed the hand fell off, and Philip was revived by the motion of his arm. And just as he was about to faint and gain at last one moment of oblivion, the motion stopped, and he would struggle instead against the pressure on this throat.

Vivid pictures were dancing through the pain—Lilia dying some months back in this very house, Miss Abbott bending over the baby, his mother at home, now reading evening prayers to the servants. He felt that he was growing weaker; his brain wandered; the agony did not seem so great. Not all Gino's care could indefinitely postpone the end. His yells and gurgles became mechanical—functions of the tortured flesh rather than true notes of indignation and despair. He was conscious of a horrid tumbling. Then his arm was pulled a little too roughly, and everything was quiet at last.

'But your son is dead, Gino. Your son is dead, dear Gino. Your son is dead.'

The room was full of light, and Miss Abbott had Gino by the shoulders, holding him down in a chair. She was exhausted with the struggle, and her arms were trembling.

'What is the good of another death? What is the good of more pain?'

He too began to tremble. Then he turned and looked curiously at Philip, whose face, covered with dust and foam, was visible by the stove. Miss Abbott allowed him to get up, though she still held him firmly. He gave a loud and curious cry—a cry of interrogation it might be called. Below there was the noise of Perfetta returning with the baby's milk.

'Go to him,' said Miss Abbott, indicating Philip. 'Pick him up. Treat him kindly.'

She released him, and he approached Philip slowly. His eyes were filling with trouble. He bent down, as if he would gently raise him up.

'Help! Help!' moaned Philip. His body had suffered too much from Gino. It could not bear to be touched by him.

Gino seemed to understand. He stopped, crouched above him. Miss Abbott herself came forward and lifted her friend in her arms.

'Oh, the foul devil!' he murmured. 'Kill him! Kill him for me.'

Miss Abbott laid him tenderly on the couch and wiped his face. Then she said gravely to them both, 'This thing stops here.'

'Latte! latte!' cried Perfetta, hilariously ascending the stairs.

'Remember,' she continued, 'there is to be no revenge. I will have no more intentional evil. We are not to fight with each other any more.'

'I shall never forgive him,' sighed Philip.

'Latte! latte freschissimo! bianco come neve!' Perfetta came in with another lamp and a little jug.

Gino spoke for the first time. 'Put the milk on the table,' he said. 'It will not be wanted in the other room.' The peril was over at last. A great sob shook the whole body, another followed, and then he gave a piercing cry of woe, and stumbled towards Miss Abbott like a child and clung to her.

All through the day Miss Abbott had seemed to Philip like a goddess, and more than ever did she seem so now. Many people look younger and more intimate during great emotion. But some there are who look older, and remote, and he could not think that there was little difference in years, and none in composition, between her and the man whose head was laid upon her breast. Her eyes were open, full of infinite pity and full of majesty, as if they discerned the boundaries of sorrow, and saw unimaginable tracts beyond. Such eyes he had seen in great pictures but never in a mortal. Her hands were folded round the sufferer, stroking him lightly, for even a goddess can do no more than that. And it seemed fitting, too, that she should bend her head and touch his forehead with her lips.

Philip looked away, as he sometimes looked away from the great pictures where visible forms suddenly became inadequate for the things they have shown to us. He was happy; he was assured that there was greatness in the world. There came to him an earnest desire to be good through the example of this good woman. He would try henceforward to be worthy of the things she had revealed. Quietly, without hysterical prayers or banging of drums, he underwent conversion. He was saved.

'That milk,' said she, 'need not be wasted. Take it, Signor Carella, and persuade Mr Herriton to drink.'

Gino obeyed her, and carried the child's milk to Philip. And Philip obeyed also and drank.

'Is there any left?'

'A little,' answered Gino.

'Then finish it.' For she was determined to use such remnants as lie about the world.

'Will you not have some?'

'I do not care for milk; finish it all.'

'Philip, have you had enough milk?'

'Yes, thank you, Gino; finish it all.'

He drank the milk, and then, either by accident or in some spasm of pain, broke the jug to pieces. Perfetta exclaimed in bewilderment. 'It does not matter,' he told her. 'It does not matter. It will never be wanted any more.'

Chapter Ten

'He will have to marry her,' said Philip. 'I heard from him this morning, just as we left Milan. He finds he has gone too far to back out. It would be expensive. I don't know how much he minds–not as much as we suppose, I think. At all events there's not a word of blame in the letter. I don't believe he even feels angry. I never was so completely forgiven. Ever since you stopped him killing me, it has been a vision of perfect friendship. He nursed me, he lied for me at the inquest, and at the funeral, though he was crying, you would have thought it was my own son who had died. Certainly I was the only person he had to be kind to; he was so distressed not to make Harriet's acquaintance, and that he scarcely saw anything of you. In his letter he says so again.'

'Thank him, please, when you write,' said Miss Abbott, 'and give him my kindest regards.'

'Indeed I will.' He was surprised that she could slide away from the man so easily. For his own part, he was bound by ties of almost alarming intimacy. Gino had the southern knack of friendship. In the intervals of business he would pull out Philip's life, turn it inside out, remodel it, and advise him how to use it for the best. The sensation was pleasant, for he was a kind as well as a skilful operator. But Philip came away feeling that he had not a secret corner left. In that very letter Gino had again implored him, as a refuge from domestic difficulties, 'to marry Miss Abbott, even if her dowry is small.' And how Miss Abbott herself, after such tragic intercourse, could resume the conventions and send calm messages of esteem, was more than he could understand.

'When will you see him again?' she asked. They were standing together in the corridor of the train, slowly ascending out of Italy towards the San Gotthard tunnel.

'I hope next spring. Perhaps we shall paint Siena red for a day or two with some of the new wife's money. It was one of the arguments for marrying her.'

'He has no heart,' she said severely. 'He does not really mind about the child at all.'

'No; you're wrong. He does. He is unhappy, like the rest of us. But he doesn't try to keep up appearances as we do. He knows that the things that have made him happy once will probably make him happy again.'

'He said he would never be happy again.'

'In his passion. Not when he was calm. We English say it when we are calm—when we do not really believe it any longer. Gino is not ashamed of inconsistency. It is one of the many things I like him for.'

'Yes; I was wrong. That is so.'

'He's much more honest with himself than I am,' continued Philip, 'and he is honest without an effort and without pride. But you, Miss Abbott, what about you? Will you be in Italy next spring?'

'No.'

'I'm sorry. When will you come back, do you think?'

'I think never.'

'For whatever reason?' He stared at her as if she were some monstrosity.

'Because I understand the place. There is no need.'

'Understand Italy!' he exclaimed.

'Perfectly.'

'Well, I don't. And I don't understand you,' he murmured to himself, as he paced away from her up the corridor. By this time he loved her very much, and he could not bear to be puzzled. He had reached love by the spiritual path: her thoughts and her goodness and her nobility had moved him first, and now her whole body and all its gestures had become transfigured by them. The beauties that are called obvious—the beauties of her hair and her voice and her limbs—he had noticed these last; Gino, who never traversed any path at all, had commended them dispassionately to his friend.

Why was she so puzzling? He had known so much about her once—what she thought, how she felt, the reasons for her actions. And now he only knew that he loved her, and all the other knowledge seemed passing from him just as he needed it most. Why would she never come to Italy again? Why had she avoided himself and Gino ever since the evening that she had saved their lives? The train was nearly empty. Harriet slumbered in a compartment by herself. He must ask her these questions now, and he returned quickly to her down the corridor.

She greeted him with a question of her own. 'Are your plans decided?'

'Yes. I can't live at Sawston.'

'Have you told Mrs Herriton?'

'I wrote from Monteriano. I tried to explain things; but she will never understand me. Her view will be that the affair is settled–sadly settled since the baby is dead. Still it's over; our family circle need be vexed no more. She won't even be angry with you. You see, you have done us no harm in the long run. Unless, of course, you talk about Harriet and make a scandal. So that is my plan–London and work. What is yours?'

'Poor Harriet!' said Miss Abbott. 'As if I dare judge Harriet! Or anybody.' And without replying to Philip's question she left him to visit the other invalid.

Philip gazed after her mournfully, and then he looked mournfully out of the window at the decreasing streams. All the excitement was over–the inquest, Harriet's short illness, his own visit to the surgeon. He was convalescent, both in body and spirit, but convalescence brought no joy. In the looking-glass at the end of the corridor he saw his face haggard, and his shoulders pulled forward by the weight of the sling. Life was greater than he had supposed, but it was even less complete. He had seen the need for strenuous work and for righteousness. And now he saw what a very little way those things would go.

'Is Harriet going to be all right?' he asked. Miss Abbott had come back to him.

'She will soon be her old self,' was the reply. For Harriet, after a sharp paroxysm of illness and remorse, was quickly returning to her normal state. She had been 'thoroughly upset,' as she phrased it, but she soon ceased to realise that anything was wrong beyond the death of a poor little child. Already she spoke of 'this unlucky accident,' and 'the mysterious frustration of one's attempts to make things better.' Miss Abbott had seen that she was comfortable, and had given her a kind kiss. But she returned feeling that Harriet, like her mother, considered the affair as settled.

'I'm clear enough about Harriet's future, and about parts of my own. But I ask again, What about yours?'

'Sawston and work,' said Miss Abbott.

'No.'

'Why not?' she asked, smiling.

'You've seen too much. You've seen as much and done more than I have.'

'But it's so different. Of course I shall go to Sawston. You forget my father; and even if he wasn't there, I've a hundred ties: my district–I'm neglecting it shamefully–my evening classes, the St James'—'

'Silly nonsense!' he exploded, suddenly moved to have the whole thing out with her. 'You're too good–about a thousand times better than I am. You can't live in that hole; you must go among people who can hope to understand you. I mind for myself: I want to see you often—again and again.'

'Of course we shall meet whenever you come down; and I hope that it will mean often.'

'It's not enough; it'll only be in the old horrible way, each with a dozen relatives round us. No, Miss Abbott; it's not good enough.'

'We can write at all events.'

'You will write?' he cried, with a flush of pleasure. At times his hopes seemed so solid.

'I will indeed.'

'But I say it's not enough—you can't go back to the old life if you wanted to. Too much has happened.'

'I know that,' she said sadly.

'Not only pain and sorrow, but wonderful things: that tower in the sunlight—do you remember it, and all you said to me? The theatre, even. And the next day—in the church; and our times with Gino.'

'All the wonderful things are over,' she said. 'That is just where it is.'

'I don't believe it. At all events not for me. The most wonderful things may be to come—'

'The wonderful things are over,' she repeated, and looked at him so mournfully that he dare not contradict her. The train was crawling up the last ascent towards the Campanile of Airolo and the entrance of the tunnel.

'Miss Abbott,' he murmured, speaking quickly, as if their free intercourse might soon be ended, 'what is the matter with you? I thought I understood you, and I don't. All those two great first days at Monteriano I read you as clearly as you read me still. I saw why you had come, and why you changed sides, and afterwards I saw your wonderful courage and pity. And now you're frank with me one moment, as you used to be, and the next moment you shut me up. You see I owe too much to you—my life, and I don't know what besides. I won't stand it. You've gone too far to turn mysterious. I'll quote what you said to me: "Don't be mysterious; there isn't the time." I'll quote something else: "I and my life must be where I live." You can't live at Sawston.'

He had moved her at last. She whispered to herself hurriedly. 'It is tempting—' And those three words threw him into a tumult of joy. What was tempting to her? After all was the greatest of things possible? Perhaps, after long estrangement, after much tragedy, the South had brought them together in the end. That laughter in the theatre, those silver stars in the purple sky, even the violets of a departed spring, all had helped, and sorrow had helped also, and so had tenderness to others.

'It is tempting,' she repeated, 'not to be mysterious. I've wanted often to tell you, and then been afraid. I could never tell anyone else, certainly no woman, and I think you're the one man who might understand and not be disgusted.'

'Are you lonely?' he whispered. 'Is it anything like that?'

'Yes.' The train seemed to shake him towards her. He was resolved that though a dozen people were looking, he would yet take her in his arms. 'I'm terribly lonely, or I wouldn't speak. I think you must know already.' Their faces were crimson, as if the same thought was surging through them both.

'Perhaps I do.' He came close to her. 'Perhaps I could speak instead. But if you will say the word plainly you'll never be sorry; I will thank you for it all my life.'

She said plainly 'That I love him.' Then she broke down. Her body was shaken with sobs, and lest there should be any doubt she cried between the sobs for Gino! Gino! Gino!

He heard himself remark 'Rather! I love him too! When I can forget how he hurt me that evening. Though whenever we shake hands—' One of them must have moved a step or two, for when she spoke again she was already a little way apart.

'You've upset me.' She stifled something that was perilously near hysterics. 'I thought I was past all this. You're taking it wrongly. I'm in love with Gino—don't pass it off—I mean it crudely—you know what I mean. So laugh at me.'

'Laugh at love?' asked Philip.

'Yes. Pull it to pieces. Tell me I'm a fool or worse—that he's a cad. Say all you said when Lilia fell in love with him. That's the help I want. I dare tell you this because I like you—and because you're without passion; you look on life as a spectacle; you don't enter it; you only find it funny or beautiful. So I can trust you to cure me. Mr Herriton, isn't it funny?' She tried to laugh herself, but became frightened and had to stop. 'He's not a gentleman, nor a Christian, nor good in any way. He's never flattered me nor honoured me. But because he's handsome, that's been enough. The son of an Italian dentist, with a pretty face.' She repeated the phrase as if it was a charm against passion. 'Oh, Mr Herriton, isn't it funny!' Then, to his relief, she began to cry. 'I love him, and I'm not ashamed of it. I love him, and I'm going to Sawston, and if I mayn't speak about him to you sometimes, I shall die.'

In that terrible discovery Philip managed to think not of himself but of her. He did not lament. He did not even speak to her kindly, for he saw that she could not stand it. A flippant reply was what she asked and needed—something flippant and a little cynical. And indeed it was the only reply he could trust himself to make.

'Perhaps it is what the books call "a passing fancy"?'

She shook her head. Even this question was too pathetic. For as far as she knew anything about herself, she knew that her passions, once aroused, were sure. 'If I saw him often,' she said, 'I might remember what he is like. Or he might grow old. But I dare not risk it, so nothing can alter me now.'

'Well, if the fancy does pass, let me know.' After all, he could say what he wanted.

'Oh, you shall know quick enough.'

'But before you retire to Sawston—are you so mighty sure?'

'What of?' She had stopped crying. He was treating her exactly as she had hoped.

'That you and he—' He smiled bitterly at the thought of them together. Here was the cruel antique malice of the gods, such as they once sent forth against Pasiphae. Centuries of aspiration and culture—and the world could not escape it. 'I was going to say—whatever have you got in common?'

'Nothing except the times we have seen each other.' Again her face was crimson. He turned his own face away.

'Which—which times?'

'The time I thought you weak and heedless, and went instead of you to get the baby. That began it, as far as I know the beginning. Or it may have begun when you took us to the theatre, and I saw him mixed up with music and light. But I didn't understand till the morning. Then you opened the door—and I knew why I had been so happy. Afterwards, in the church, I prayed for us all; not for anything new, but that we might just be as we were—he with the child he loved, you and I and Harriet safe out of the place—and that I might never see him or speak to him again. I could have pulled through then—the thing was only coming near, like a wreath of smoke; it hadn't wrapped me round.'

'But through my fault,' said Philip solemnly, 'he is parted from the child he loves. And because my life was in danger you came and saw him and spoke to him again.' For the thing was even greater than she imagined. Nobody but himself would ever see round it now. And to see round it he was standing at an immense distance. He could even be glad that she had once held the beloved in her arms.

'Don't talk of "faults." You're my friend for ever, Mr Herriton, I think. Only don't be charitable and shift or take the blame. Get over supposing I'm refined. That's what puzzles you. Get over that.'

As she spoke she seemed to be transfigured, and to have indeed no part with refinement or unrefinement any longer. Out of this wreck there was revealed to him something indestructible—something which she, who had given it, could never take away.

'I say again, don't be charitable. If he had asked me, I might have given myself body and soul. That would have been the end of my rescue party. But all through he took me for a superior being—a goddess. I who was worshipping every inch of him, and every word he spoke. And that saved me.'

Philip's eyes were fixed on the Campanile of Airolo. But he saw instead the fair myth of Endymion. This woman was a goddess to the end. For her no love could be degrading; she stood outside all degradation. This episode, which she thought so sordid, and which was so tragic for him, remained supremely beautiful. To such a height was he lifted, that without regret he could now have told her that he was her worshipper too. But what was the use of telling her? For all the wonderful things had happened.

'Thank you,' was all that he permitted himself. 'Thank you for everything.'

She looked at him with great friendliness, for he had made her life endurable. At that moment the train entered the San Gotthard tunnel. They hurried back to the carriage to close the windows lest the smuts should get into Harriet's eyes.

THE END

The
Longest Journey

THE LONGEST JOURNEY

FRATRIBUS

Cambridge

Chapter One

'The cow is there,' said Ansell, lighting a match and holding it out over the carpet. No one spoke. He waited till the end of the match fell off. Then he said again, 'She is there, the cow. There, now.'

'You have not proved it,' said a voice.

'I have proved it to myself.'

'I have proved to myself that she isn't,' said the voice. 'The cow is *not* there.' Ansell frowned and lit another match.

'She's there for me,' he declared. 'I don't care whether she's there for you or not. Whether I'm in Cambridge or Iceland or dead, the cow will be there.'

It was philosophy. They were discussing the existence of objects. Do they exist only when there is some one to look at them? or have they a real existence of their own? It is all very interesting, but at the same time it is difficult. Hence the cow. She seemed to make things easier. She was so familiar, so solid, that surely the truths that she illustrated would in time become familiar and solid also. Is the cow there or not? This was better than deciding between objectivity and subjectivity. So at Oxford, just at the same time, one was asking, 'What do our rooms look like in the vac.?'

'Look here, Ansell. I'm there—in the meadow—the cow's there. You're there—the cow's there. Do you agree so far?'

'Well?'

'Well, if you go, the cow stops; but if I go, the cow goes. Then what will happen if you stop and I go?'

Several voices cried out that this was quibbling.

'I know it is,' said the speaker brightly, and silence descended again, while they tried honestly to think the matter out.

Rickie, on whose carpet the matches were being dropped, did not like to join in the discussion. It was too difficult for him. He could not even quibble. If he spoke, he should simply make himself a fool. He preferred to listen, and to watch the tobacco-smoke stealing out past the window-seat into the tranquil October air. He could see the court too, and the college cat teasing the college tortoise, and the kitchen-men with supper-trays upon their heads. Hot food for one—that must be for the geographical don, who never came in for Hall; cold food for three, apparently at half-a-crown a head, for some one he did not know; hot food, *à la carte*—obviously for the ladies haunting the next staircase; cold food for two, at two shillings—going to Ansell's rooms for himself and Ansell, and as it passed under the lamp he saw that it was meringues again. Then the bedmakers began to arrive, chatting to each other pleasantly, and he could hear Ansell's bedmaker say, 'Oh dang!' when she found she had to lay Ansell's tablecloth; for there was not a breath stirring. The great elms were motionless, and seemed still in the glory of midsummer, for the darkness hid the yellow blotches on their leaves, and their outlines were still rounded against the tender sky. Those elms were Dryads—so Rickie believed or pretended, and the line between the two is subtler than we admit. At all events they were lady trees, and had for generations fooled the college statutes by their residence in the haunts of youth.

But what about the cow? He returned to her with a start, for this would never do. He also would try to think the matter out. Was she there or not? The cow. There or not. He strained his eyes into the night.

Either way it was attractive. If she was there, other cows were there too. The darkness of Europe was dotted with them, and in the far East their flanks were shining in the rising sun. Great herds of them stood browsing in pastures where no man came nor need ever come, or plashed knee-deep by the brink of impassable rivers. And this, moreover, was the view of Ansell. Yet Tilliard's view had a good deal in it. One might do worse than follow Tilliard, and suppose the cow not to be there unless oneself was there to see her. A cowless world, then, stretched round him on every side. Yet he had only to peep into a field, and, click! it would at once become radiant with bovine life.

Suddenly he realized that this, again, would never do. As usual, he had missed the whole point, and was overlaying philosophy with gross and senseless details. For if the cow was not there, the world and the fields were not there either. And what would Ansell care about sunlit flanks or impassable streams? Rickie rebuked his own grovelling soul, and turned his eyes away from the night, which had led him to such absurd conclusions.

The fire was dancing, and the shadow of Ansell, who stood close up to it, seemed to dominate the little room. He was still talking, or rather jerking, and he was still lighting matches and dropping their ends upon the carpet. Now and then he would make a motion with his feet as if he were running quickly backward upstairs, and would tread on the edge of the fender, so that the fire-irons went flying and the buttered-bun dishes crashed against each other in the hearth. The other philosophers were crouched in odd shapes on the sofa and table and chairs, and one, who was a little bored, had crawled to the piano and was timidly trying the Prelude to Rhinegold with his knee upon the soft pedal. The air was heavy with good tobacco-smoke and the pleasant warmth of tea, and as Rickie became more sleepy the events of the day seemed to float one by one before his acquiescent eyes. In the morning he had read Theocritus, whom he believed to be the greatest of Greek poets; he had lunched with a merry don and had tasted Zwieback biscuits; then he had walked with people he liked, and had walked just long enough; and now his room was full of other people whom he liked, and when they left he would go and have supper with Ansell, whom he liked as well as any one. A year ago he had known none of these joys. He had crept cold and friendless and ignorant out of a great public school, preparing for a silent and solitary journey, and praying as a highest favour that he might be left alone. Cambridge had not answered his prayer. She had taken and soothed him, and warmed him, and had laughed at him a little, saying that he must not be so tragic yet awhile, for his boyhood had been but a dusty corridor that led to the spacious halls of youth. In one year he had made many friends and learnt much, and he might learn even more if he could but concentrate his attention on that cow.

The fire had died down, and in the gloom the man by the piano ventured to ask what would happen if an objective cow had a subjective calf. Ansell gave an angry sigh, and at that moment there was a tap on the door.

'Come in!' said Rickie.

The door opened. A tall young woman stood framed in the light that fell from the passage.

'Ladies!' whispered every one in great agitation.

'Yes?' he said nervously, limping towards the door (he was rather lame). 'Yes? Please come in. Can I be any good—'

'Wicked boy!' exclaimed the young lady, advancing a gloved finger into the room. 'Wicked, wicked boy!'

He clasped his head with his hands.

'Agnes! Oh how perfectly awful!'

'Wicked, intolerable boy!' She turned on the electric light. The philosophers were revealed with unpleasing suddenness. 'My goodness, a tea-party! Oh really, Rickie, you are too bad! I say again: wicked, abominable, intolerable boy! I'll have you horsewhipped. If you please'–she turned to the symposium, which had now risen to its feet–'If you please, he asks me and my brother for the week-end. We accept. At the station, no Rickie. We drive to where his old lodgings were–Trumpery Road or some such name–and he's left them. I'm furious, and before I can stop my brother, he's paid off the cab and there we are stranded. I've walked–walked for miles. Pray can you tell me what is to be done with Rickie?'

'He must indeed be horsewhipped,' said Tilliard pleasantly. Then he made a bolt for the door.

'Tilliard–do stop–let me introduce Miss Pembroke–don't all go!' For his friends were flying from his visitor like mists before the sun. 'Oh, Agnes, I am so sorry; I've nothing to say. I simply forgot you were coming, and everything about you.'

'Thank you, thank you! And how soon will you remember to ask where Herbert is?'

'Where is he, then?'

'I shall not tell you.'

'But didn't he walk with you?'

'I shall not tell, Rickie. It's part of your punishment. You are not really sorry yet. I shall punish you again later.'

She was quite right. Rickie was not as much upset as he ought to have been. He was sorry that he had forgotten, and that he had caused his visitors inconvenience. But he did not feel profoundly degraded, as a young man should who has acted discourteously to a young lady. Had he acted discourteously to his bedmaker or his gyp, he would have minded just as much, which was not polite of him.

'First, I'll go and get food. Do sit down and rest. Oh, let me introduce—'

Ansell was now the sole remnant of the discussion party. He still stood on the heathrug with a burnt match in his hand. Miss Pembroke's arrival had never disturbed him.

'Let me introduce Mr Ansell—Miss Pembroke.'

There came an awful moment—a moment when he almost regretted that he had a clever friend. Ansell remained absolutely motionless, moving neither hand nor head. Such behaviour is so unknown that Miss Pembroke did not realize what had happened, and kept her own hand stretched out longer than is maidenly.

'Coming to supper?' asked Ansell in low, grave tones.

'I don't think so,' said Rickie helplessly.

Ansell departed without another word.

'Don't mind us,' said Miss Pembroke pleasantly. 'Why shouldn't you keep your engagement with your friend? Herbert's finding lodgings—that's why he's not here—and they're sure to be able to give us some dinner. What jolly rooms you've got!'

'Oh no—not a bit. I say, I am sorry. I am sorry. I am most awfully sorry.'

'What about?'

'Ansell—' Then he burst forth. 'Ansell isn't a gentleman. His father's a draper. His uncles are farmers. He's here because he's so clever—just on account of his brains. Now, sit down. He isn't a gentleman at all.' And he hurried off to order some dinner.

'What a snob the boy is getting!' thought Agnes, a good deal mollified. It never struck her that those could be the words of affection—that Rickie would never have spoken them about a person whom he disliked. Nor did it strike her that Ansell's humble birth scarcely explained the quality of his rudeness. She was willing to find life full of trivialities. Six months ago and she might have minded; but now—she cared not what men might do unto her, for she had her own splendid lover, who could have knocked all these unhealthy undergraduates into a cocked-hat. She dared not tell Gerald a word of what had happened: he might have come up from wherever he was and half killed Ansell. And she determined not to tell her brother either, for her nature was kindly, and it pleased her to pass things over.

She took off her gloves, and then she took off her ear-rings and began to admire them. These ear-rings were a freak of hers—her only freak. She had always wanted some, and the day Gerald asked her to marry him she went to a shop and had her ears pierced. In some wonderful way she knew that it was right. And he had given her the rings—little gold knobs, copied, the jeweller told them, from something prehistoric—and he had kissed the spots of blood on her handkerchief. Herbert, as usual, had been shocked.

'I can't help it,' she cried, springing up. 'I'm not like other girls.' She began to pace about Rickie's room, for she hated to keep quiet. There was nothing much to see in it. The pictures were not attractive, nor did they attract her—school groups, Watts' 'Sir Percival,' a dog running after a rabbit, a man running after a maid, a cheap brown Madonna in a cheap green frame—in short, a collection where one mediocrity was generally cancelled by another. Over the door there hung a long photograph of a city with waterways, which Agnes, who had never been to Venice, took to be Venice, but which people who had been to Stockholm knew to be Stockholm. Rickie's mother, looking rather sweet, was standing on the mantelpiece. Some more pictures had just arrived from the framers and were leaning with their faces to the wall, but she did not bother to turn them round. On the table were dirty teacups, a flat chocolate cake, and Omar Khayyam, with an Oswego biscuit between his pages. Also a vase filled with the crimson leaves of autumn. This made her smile.

Then she saw her host's shoes: he had left them lying on the sofa. Rickie was slightly deformed, and so the shoes were not the same size, and one of them had a thick heel to help him towards an even walk. 'Ugh!' she exclaimed, and removed them gingerly to the bedroom. There she saw other shoes and boots and pumps, a whole row of them, all deformed. 'Ugh! Poor boy! It is too bad. Why shouldn't he be like other people? This hereditary business is too awful.' She shut the door with a sigh. Then she recalled the perfect form of Gerald, his athletic walk, the poise of his shoulders, his arms stretched forward to receive her. Gradually she was comforted.

'I beg your pardon, miss, but might I ask how many to lay?' It was the bedmaker, Mrs Aberdeen.

'Three, I think,' said Agnes, smiling pleasantly. 'Mr Elliot 'll be back in a minute. He has gone to order dinner.'

'Thank you, miss.'

'Plenty of teacups to wash up!'

'But teacups is easy washing, particularly Mr Elliot's.'

'Why are his so easy?'

'Because no nasty corners in them to hold the dirt. Mr Anderson—he's below—has crinkly noctagons, and one wouldn't believe the difference. It was I bought these for Mr Elliot. His one thought is to save one trouble. I never seed such a thoughtful gentleman. The world, I say, will be the better for him.' She took the teacups into the gyp room, and then returned with the tablecloth, and added, 'if he's spared.'

'I'm afraid he isn't strong,' said Agnes.

'Oh, miss, his nose! I don't know what he'd say if he knew I mentioned his nose, but really I must speak to some one, and he has neither father nor mother. His nose! It poured twice with blood in the Long.'

'Yes?'

'It's a thing that ought to be known. I assure you, that little room! . . . And in any case, Mr Elliot's a gentleman that can ill afford to lose it. Luckily his friends were up; and I always say they're more like brothers than anything else.'

'Nice for him. He has no real brothers.'

'Oh, Mr Hornblower, he is a merry gentleman, and Mr Tilliard too! And Mr Elliot himself likes his romp at times. Why, it's the merriest staircase in the buildings! Last night the bedmaker from W said to me, "What are you doing to my gentlemen? Here's Mr Ansell come back 'ot with his collar flopping." I said, "And a good thing." Some bedders keep their gentlemen just so; but surely, miss, the world being what it is, the longer one is able to laugh in it the better.'

Bedmakers have to be comic and dishonest. It is expected of them. In a picture of university life it is their only function. So when we meet one who has the face of a lady, and feelings of which a lady might be proud, we pass her by.

'Yes?' said Miss Pembroke, and then their talk was stopped by the arrival of her brother.

'It is too bad!' he exclaimed. 'It is really too bad.'

'Now, Bertie boy, Bertie boy! I'll have no peevishness.'

'I am not peevish, Agnes, but I have a full right to be. Pray, why did he not meet us? Why did he not provide rooms? And pray, why did you leave me to do all the settling? All the lodgings I knew are full, and our bedrooms look into a mews. I cannot help it. And then—look here! It really is too bad.' He held up his foot like a wounded dog. It was dripping with water.

'Oho! This explains the peevishness. Off with it at once. It'll be another of your colds.'

'I really think I had better.' He sat down by the fire and daintily unlaced his boot. 'I notice a great change in university tone. I can never remember swaggering three abreast along the pavement and charging inoffensive visitors into a gutter when I was an undergraduate. One of the men, too, wore an Eton tie. But the others, I should say, came from very queer schools, if they came from any schools at all.'

Mr Pembroke was nearly twenty years older than his sister, and had never been as handsome. But he was not at all the person to knock into a gutter, for though not in orders, he had the air of being on the verge of them, and his features, as well as his clothes, had the clerical cut. In his presence conversation became pure and colourless and full of under statements, and—just as if he was a real clergyman—neither men nor boys ever forgot that he was there. He had observed this, and it pleased him very much. His conscience permitted him to enter the Church whenever his profession, which was the scholastic, should demand it.

'No gutter in the world's as wet as this,' said Agnes, who had peeled off her brother's sock, and was now toasting it at the embers on a pair of tongs.

'Surely you know the running water by the edge of the Trumpington road? It's turned on occasionally to clear away the refuse—a most primitive idea. When I was up we had a joke about it, and called it the "Pem."'

'How complimentary!'

'You foolish girl—not after me, of course. We called it the "Pem" because it is close to Pembroke College. I remember—' He smiled a little, and twiddled his toes. Then he remembered the bedmaker, and said, 'My sock is now dry. My sock, please.'

'Your sock is sopping. No, you don't!' She twitched the tongs away from him. Mrs Aberdeen, without speaking, fetched a pair of Rickie's socks and a pair of Rickie's shoes.

'Thank you; ah, thank you. I am sure Mr Elliot would allow it.' Then he said in French to his sister, 'Has there been the slightest sign of Frederick?'

'Now, do call him Rickie, and talk English. I found him here. He had forgotten about us, and was very sorry. Now he's gone to get some dinner, and I can't think why he isn't back.'

Mrs Aberdeen left them.

'He wants pulling up sharply. There is nothing original in absent-mindedness. True originality lies elsewhere. Really, the lower classes have no *nous*. However can I wear such deformities?' For he had been madly trying to cram a right-hand foot into a left-hand shoe.

'Don't!' said Agnes hastily. 'Don't touch the poor fellow's things.' The sight of the smart, stubby patent leather made her almost feel faint. She had known Rickie for many years, but it seemed so dreadful and so different now that he was a man. It was her first great contact with the abnormal, and unknown fibres of her being rose in revolt against it. She frowned when she heard his uneven tread upon the stairs.

'Agnes—before he arrives—you ought never to have left me and gone to his rooms alone. A most elementary transgression. Imagine the unpleasantness if you had found him with friends. If Gerald—'

Rickie by now had got into a fluster. At the kitchens he had lost his head, and when his turn came—he had had to wait—he had yielded his place to those behind, saying that he didn't matter. And he had wasted more precious time buying bananas, though he knew that the Pembrokes were not partial to fruit. Amid much tardy and chaotic hospitality the meal got under way. All the spoons and forks were anyhow, for Mrs Aberdeen's virtues were not practical. The fish seemed never to have been alive, the meat had no kick, and the cork of the college claret slid forth silently, as if ashamed of the contents. Agnes was particularly pleasant. But her brother could not recover himself. He still remembered their desolate arrival, and he could feel the waters of the Pem eating into his instep.

'Rickie,' cried the lady, 'are you aware that you haven't congratulated me on my engagement?'

Rickie laughed nervously, and said, 'Why no! No more I have.'

'Say something pretty, then.'

'I hope you'll be very happy,' he mumbled. 'But I don't know anything about marriage.'

'Oh, you awful boy! Herbert, isn't he just the same? But you do know something about Gerald, so don't be so chilly and cautious. I've just realized, looking at those groups, that you must have been at school together. Did you come much across him?'

'Very little,' he answered, and sounded shy. He got up hastily, and began to muddle with the coffee.

'But he was in the same house. Surely that's a house group?'

'He was a prefect.' He made his coffee on the simple system. One had a brown pot, into which the boiling stuff was poured. Just before serving one put in a drop of cold water, and the idea was that the grounds fell to the bottom.

'Wasn't he a kind of athletic marvel? Couldn't he knock any boy or master down?'

'Yes.'

'If he had wanted to,' said Mr Pembroke, who had not spoken for some time.

'If he had wanted to,' echoed Rickie. 'I do hope, Agnes, you'll be most awfully happy. I don't know anything about the army, but I should think it must be most awfully interesting.'

Mr Pembroke laughed faintly.

'Yes, Rickie. The army is a most interesting profession–the profession of Wellington and Marlborough and Lord Roberts; a most interesting profession, as you observe. A profession that may mean death–death, rather than dishonour.'

'That's nice,' said Rickie, speaking to himself. 'Any profession may mean dishonour, but one isn't allowed to die instead. The army's different. If a soldier makes a mess, it's thought rather decent of him, isn't it, if he blows out his brains? In the other professions it somehow seems cowardly.'

'I am not competent to pronounce,' said Mr Pembroke, who was not accustomed to have his schoolroom satire commented on. 'I merely know that the army is the finest profession in the world. Which reminds me, Rickie–have you been thinking about yours?'

'No.'

'Not at all?'

'No.'

'Now, Herbert, don't bother him. Have another meringue.'

'But, Rickie, my dear boy, you're twenty. It's time you thought. The Tripos is the beginning of life, not the end. In less than two years you will have got your B.A. What are you going to do with it?'

'I don't know.'

'You're M.A., aren't you?' asked Agnes; but her brother proceeded–

'I have seen so many promising, brilliant lives wrecked simply on account of this–*not selling soon enough*. My dear boy, you must think. Consult your tastes if possible–but think. You have not a moment to lose. The Bar, like your father?'

'Oh, I wouldn't like that at all.'

'I don't mention the Church.'

'Oh, Rickie, do be a clergyman!' said Miss Pembroke. 'You'd be simply killing in a wide-awake.'

He looked at his guests hopelessly. Their kindness and competence overwhelmed him. 'I wish I could talk to them as I talk to myself,' he thought. 'I'm not such an ass when I talk to myself. I don't believe, for instance, that quite all I thought about the cow was rot.' Aloud he said, 'I've sometimes wondered about writing.'

'Writing?' said Mr Pembroke, with the tone of one who gives everything its trial. 'Well, what about writing? What kind of writing?'

'I rather like'—he suppressed something in his throat—'I rather like trying to write little stories.'

'Why, I made sure it was poetry!' said Agnes. 'You're just the boy for poetry.'

'I had no idea you wrote. Would you let me see something? Then I could judge.'

The author shook his head. 'I don't show it to any one. It isn't anything. I just try because it amuses me.'

'What is it about?'

'Silly nonsense.'

'Are you ever going to show it to any one?'

'I don't think so.'

Mr Pembroke did not reply, firstly, because the meringue he was eating was, after all, Rickie's; secondly, because it was gluey and stuck his jaws together. Agnes observed that the writing was really a very good idea: there was Rickie's aunt—she could push him.

'Aunt Emily never pushes any one; she says they always rebound and crush her.'

'I only had the pleasure of seeing your aunt once. I should have thought her a quite uncrushable person. But she would be sure to help you.'

'I couldn't show her anything. She'd think them even sillier than they are.'

'Always running yourself down! There speaks the artist!'

'I'm not modest,' he said anxiously. 'I just know they're bad.'

Mr Pembroke's teeth were clear of meringue, and he could refrain no longer. 'My dear Rickie, your father and mother are dead, and you often say your aunt takes no interest in you. Therefore your life depends on yourself. Think it over carefully, but settle, and having once settled, stick. If you think that this writing is practicable, and that you could make your living by it—that you could, if needs be, support a wife—then by all means write. But you must work. Work and drudge. Begin at the bottom of the ladder and work upwards.'

Rickie's head drooped. Any metaphor silenced him. He never thought of replying that art is not a ladder—with a curate, as it were, on the first rung, a rector on the second, and a bishop, still nearer heaven, at the top. He never retorted that the artist is not a bricklayer at all, but a horseman, whose business it is to catch Pegasus at once, not to practise for him by mounting tamer colts. This is hard, hot, and generally ungraceful work, but it is not drudgery. For drudgery is not art, and cannot lead to it.

'Of course I don't really think about writing,' he said, as he poured the cold water into the coffee. 'Even if my things ever were decent, I don't think the magazines would take them, and the magazines are one's only chance. I read somewhere, too, that Marie Corelli's about the only person who makes a thing out of literature. I'm certain it wouldn't pay me.'

'I never mentioned the word "pay,"' said Mr Pembroke uneasily. 'You must not consider money. There are ideals too.'

'I have no ideals.'

'Rickie!' she exclaimed. 'Horrible boy!'

'No, Agnes, I have no ideals.' Then he got very red, for it was a phrase he had caught from Ansell, and he could not remember what came next.

'The person who has no ideals,' she exclaimed, 'is to be pitied.'

'I think so too,' said Mr Pembroke, sipping his coffee. 'Life without an ideal would be like the sky without the sun.'

Rickie looked towards the night, wherein there now twinkled innumerable stars–gods and heroes, virgins and brides, to whom the Greeks have given their names.

'Life without an ideal—' repeated Mr Pembroke, and then stopped, for his mouth was full of coffee grounds. The same affliction had overtaken Agnes. After a little jocose laughter they departed to their lodgings, and Rickie, having seen them as far as the porter's lodge, hurried, singing as he went, to Ansell's room, burst open the door, and said, 'Look here! Whatever do you mean by it?'

'By what?' Ansell was sitting alone with a piece of paper in front of him. On it was a diagram–a circle inside a square, inside which was again a square.

'By being so rude. You're no gentleman, and I told her so.' He slammed him on the head with a sofa-cushion. 'I'm certain one ought to be polite, even to people who aren't saved.' ('Not saved' was a phrase they applied just then to those whom they did not like or intimately know.) 'And I believe she is saved. I never knew any one so always good-tempered and kind. She's been kind to me ever since I knew her. I wish you'd heard her trying to stop her brother: you'd have certainly come round. Not but what he was only being nice as well. But she is really nice. And I thought she came into the room so beautifully. Do you know–oh, of course, you despise music–but Anderson was playing Wagner, and he'd just got to the part where they sing

> *Rheingold!*
> *Rheingold!*

and the sun strikes into the waters, and the music, which up to then has so often been in E flat—'

'Goes into D sharp. I have not understood a single word, partly because you talk as if your mouth was full of plums, partly because I don't know whom you're talking about.'

'Miss Pembroke–whom you saw.'

'I saw no one.'

'Who came in?'

'No one came in.'

'You're an ass!' shrieked Rickie. 'She came in. You saw her come in. She and her brother have been to dinner.'

'You only think so. They were not really there.'

'But they stop till Monday.'

'You only think that they are stopping.'

'But – oh, look here, shut up! The girl like an empress—'

'I saw no empress, nor any girl, nor have you seen them.'

'Ansell, don't rag.'

'Elliot, I never rag, and you know it. She was not really there.'

There was a moment's silence. Then Rickie exclaimed, 'I've got you. You say—or was it Tilliard?—no, *you* say that the cow's there. Well—there these people are, then. Got you. Yah!'

'Did it never strike you that phenomena may be of two kinds: *one*, those which have a real existence, such as the cow; *two*, those which are the subjective product of a diseased imagination, and which, to our destruction, we invest with the semblance of reality? If this never struck you, let it strike you now.'

Rickie spoke again, but received no answer. He paced a little up and down the sombre room. Then he sat on the edge of the table and watched his clever friend draw within the square a circle, and within the circle a square, and inside that another circle, and inside that another square.

'Why will you do that?'

No answer.

'Are they real?'

'The inside one is—the one in the middle of everything, that there's never room enough to draw.'

Chapter Two

A little this side of Madingley, to the left of the road, there is a secluded dell, paved with grass and planted with fir-trees. It could not have been worth a visit twenty years ago, for then it was only a scar of chalk, and it is not worth a visit at the present day, for the trees have grown too thick and choked it. But when Rickie was up, it chanced to be the brief season of its romance, a season as brief for a chalk-pit as a man—its divine interval between the bareness of boyhood and the stuffiness of age. Rickie had discovered it in his second term, when the January snows had melted and left fiords and lagoons of clearest water between the inequalities of the floor. The place looked as big as Switzerland or Norway—as indeed for the moment it was—and he came upon it at a time when his life too was beginning to expand. Accordingly the dell became for him a kind of church—a church where indeed you could do anything you liked, but where anything you did would be transfigured. Like the ancient Greeks, he could even laugh at his holy place and leave it no less holy. He chatted gaily about it, and about the pleasant thoughts with which it inspired him; he took his friends there; he even took people whom he did not like. *'Procul este, profani!'* exclaimed a delighted æsthete on being introduced to it. But this was never to be the attitude of Rickie. He did not love the vulgar herd, but he knew that his own vulgarity would be greater if he forbade it ingress, and that it was not by preciosity that he would attain to the intimate spirit of the dell. Indeed, if he had agreed with the æsthete, he would possibly not have introduced him. If the dell was to bear any inscription, he would have liked it to be 'This way to Heaven,' painted on a sign-post by the high-road, and he did not realize till later years that the number of visitors would not thereby have sensibly increased.

On the blessed Monday that the Pembrokes left, he walked out here with three friends. It was a day when the sky seemed enormous. One cloud, as large as a continent, was voyaging near the sun, whilst other clouds seemed anchored to the horizon, too lazy or too happy to move. The sky itself was of the palest blue, paling to white where it approached the earth; and the earth, brown, wet and odorous, was engaged beneath it on its yearly duty of decay. Rickie was open to the complexities of autumn; he felt extremely tiny—extremely tiny and extremely important; and perhaps the combination is as fair as any that exists. He hoped that all his life he would never be peevish or unkind.

'Elliot is in a dangerous state,' said Ansell. They had reached the dell, and had stood for some time in silence, each leaning against a tree. It was too wet to sit down.

'How's that?' asked Rickie who had not known he was in any state at all. He shut up Keats, whom he thought he had been reading, and slipped him back into his coat-pocket. Scarcely ever was he without a book.

'He's trying to like people.'

'Then he's done for,' said Widdrington. 'He's dead.'

'He's trying to like Hornblower.'

The others gave shrill agonized cries.

'He wants to bind the college together. He wants to link us to the beefy set.'

'I do like Hornblower,' he protested. 'I don't try.'

'And Hornblower tries to like you.'

'That part doesn't matter.'

'But he does try to like you. He tries not to despise you. It is altogether a most public-spirited affair.'

'Tilliard started them,' said Widdrington. 'Tilliard thinks it such a pity the college should be split into sets.'

'Oh, Tilliard!' said Ansell, with much irritation. 'But what can you expect from a person who's eternally beautiful? The other night we had been discussing a long time, and suddenly the light was turned on. Every one else looked a sight, as they ought. But there was Tilliard, sitting neatly on a little chair, like an undersized god, with not a curl crooked. I should say he will get into the Foreign Office.'

'Why are most of us so ugly?' laughed Rickie.

'It's merely a sign of our salvation—merely another sign that the college is split.'

'The college isn't split,' cried Rickie, who got excited on this subject with unfailing regularity. 'The college is, and has been, and always will be, one. What you call the beefy set aren't a set at all. They're just the rowing people, and naturally they chiefly see each other; but they're always nice to me or to any one. Of course, they think us rather asses, but it's quite in a pleasant way.'

'That's my whole objection,' said Ansell. 'What right have they to think us asses in a pleasant way? Why don't they hate us? What right has Hornblower to smack me on the back when I've been rude to him?'

'Well, what right have you to be rude to him?'

'Because I hate him. You think it is so splendid to hate no one. I tell you it is a crime. You want to love every one equally, and that's worse than impossible—it's wrong. When you denounce sets, you're really trying to destroy friendship.'

'I maintain,' said Rickie—it was a verb he clung to, in the hope that it would lend stability to what followed—'I maintain that one can like many more people than one supposes.'

'And I maintain that you hate many more people than you pretend.'

'I hate no one,' he exclaimed with extraordinary vehemence, and the dell re-echoed that it hated no one.

'We are obliged to believe you,' said Widdrington, smiling a little; 'but we are sorry about it.'

'Not even your father?' asked Ansell.

Rickie was silent.

'Not even your father?'

The cloud above extended a great promontory across the sun. It only lay there for a moment, yet that was enough to summon the lurking coldness from the earth.

'Does he hate his father?' said Widdrington, who had not known. 'Oh, good!'

'But his father's dead. He will say it doesn't count.'

'Still, it's something. Do you hate yours?'

Ansell did not reply. Rickie said: 'I say, I wonder whether one ought to talk like this?'

'About hating dead people?'

'Yes—'

'Did you hate your mother?' asked Widdrington.

Rickie turned crimson.

'I don't see Hornblower's such a rotter,' remarked the other man, whose name was James.

'James, you are diplomatic,' said Ansell. 'You are trying to tide over an awkward moment. You can go.'

Widdrington was crimson too. In his wish to be sprightly he had used words without thinking of their meanings. Suddenly he realized that 'father' and 'mother' really meant father and mother—people whom he had himself at home. He was very uncomfortable, and thought Rickie had been rather queer. He too tried to revert to Hornblower, but Ansell would not let him. The sun came out, and struck on the white ramparts of the dell. Rickie looked straight at it. Then he said abruptly—

'I think I want to talk.'

'I think you do,' replied Ansell.

'Shouldn't I be rather a fool if I went through Cambridge without talking? It's said never to come so easy again. All the people are dead too. I can't see why I shouldn't tell you most things about my birth and parentage and education.'

'Talk away. If you bore us, we have books.'

With this invitation Rickie began to relate his history. The reader who has no book will be obliged to listen to it.

Some people spend their lives in a suburb, and not for any urgent reason. This had been the fate of Rickie. He had opened his eyes to filmy heavens, and taken his first walk on asphalt. He had seen civilization as a row of semi-detached villas, and society as a state in which men do not know the men who live next door. He had himself become part of the grey monotony that surrounds all cities. There was no necessity for this—it was only rather convenient to his father.

Mr Elliot was a barrister. In appearance he resembled his son, being weakly and lame, with hollow little cheeks, a broad white band of forehead, and stiff impoverished hair. His voice, which he did not transmit, was very suave, with a fine command of cynical intonation. By altering it ever so little he could make people wince, especially if they were simple or poor. Nor did he transmit his eyes. Their peculiar flatness, as if the soul looked through dirty window-panes, the unkindness of them, the cowardice, the fear in them, were to trouble the world no longer.

He married a girl whose voice was beautiful. There was no caress in it, yet all who heard it were soothed, as though the world held some unexpected blessing. She called to her dogs one night over invisible water, and he, a tourist up on the bridge, thought 'that is extraordinarily adequate.' In time he discovered that her figure, face, and thoughts were adequate also, and as she was not impossible socially, he married her. 'I have taken a plunge,' he told his family. The family, hostile at first, had not a word to say when the woman was introduced to them; and his sister declared that the plunge had been taken from the opposite bank.

Things only went right for a little time. Though beautiful without and within, Mrs Elliot had not the gift of making her home beautiful; and one day, when she bought a carpet for the dining-room that clashed, he laughed gently, said he 'really couldn't,' and departed. Departure is perhaps too strong a word. In Mrs Elliot's mouth it became, 'My husband has to sleep more in town.' He often came down to see them, nearly always unexpectedly, and occasionally they went to see him. 'Father's house,' as Rickie called it, only had three rooms, but these were full of books and pictures and flowers; and the flowers, instead of being squashed down into the vases as they were in mummy's house, rose gracefully from frames of lead which lay coiled at the bottom, as doubtless the sea serpent has to lie, coiled at the bottom of the sea. Once he was let to lift a frame out—only once, for he dropped some water on a creton. 'I think he's going to have taste,' said Mr Elliot languidly. 'It is quite possible,' his wife replied. She had not taken off her hat and gloves, nor even pulled up her veil. Mr Elliot laughed, and soon afterwards another lady came in, and they went away.

'Why does father always laugh?' asked Rickie in the evening when he and his mother were sitting in the nursery.

'It is a way of your father's.'

'Why does he always laugh at me? Am I so funny?' Then after a pause, 'You have no sense of humour, have you, mummy?'

Mrs Elliot, who was raising a thread of cotton to her lips, held it suspended in amazement.

'You told him so this afternoon. But I have seen you laugh.' He nodded wisely. 'I have seen you laugh ever so often. One day you were laughing alone all down in the sweet peas.'

'Was I?'

'Yes. Were you laughing at me?'

'I was not thinking about you. Cotton, please—a reel of No. 50 white from my chest of drawers. Left-hand drawer. Now which is your left hand?'

'The side my pocket is.'

'And if you had no pocket?'

'The side my bad foot is.'

'I meant you to say, "the side my heart is,"' said Mrs Elliot, holding up the duster between them. 'Most of us—I mean all of us—can feel on one side a little watch, that never stops ticking. So even if you had no bad foot you would still know which is the left. No. 50 white, please. No; I'll get it myself.' For she had remembered that the dark passage frightened him.

These were the outlines. Rickie filled them in with the slowness and the accuracy of a child. He was never told anything, but he discovered for himself that his father and mother did not love each other, and that his mother was lovable. He discovered that Mr Elliot had dubbed him Rickie because he was rickety, that he took pleasure in alluding to his son's deformity, and was sorry that it was not more serious than his own. Mr Elliot had not one scrap of genius. He gathered the pictures and the books and the flower-supports mechanically, not in any impulse of love. He passed for a cultured man because he knew how to select, and he passed for an unconventional man because he did not select quite like other people. In reality he never did or said or thought one single thing that had the slightest beauty or value. And in time Rickie discovered this as well.

The boy grew up in great loneliness. He worshipped his mother, and she was fond of him. But she was dignified and reticent, and pathos, like tattle, was disgusting to her. She was afraid of intimacy, in case it led to confidences and tears, and so all her life she held her son at a little distance. Her kindness and unselfishness knew no limits, but if he tried to be dramatic and thank her, she told him not to be a little goose. And so the only person he came to know at all was himself. He would play Halma against himself. He would conduct solitary conversations, in which one part of him asked and another part answered. It was an exciting game, and concluded with the formula: 'Good-bye. Thank you. I am glad to have met you. I hope before long we shall enjoy another chat.' And then perhaps he would sob for loneliness, for he would see real people—real brothers, real friends—doing in warm life the things he had pretended. 'Shall I ever have a friend?' he demanded at the age of twelve. 'I don't see how. They walk too fast. And a brother I shall never have.'

('No loss,' interrupted Widdrington.

'But I shall never have one, and so I quite want one, even now.')

When he was thirteen Mr Elliot entered on his illness. The pretty rooms in town would not do for an invalid, and so he came back to his home. One of the first consequences was that Rickie was sent to a public school. Mrs Elliot did what she could, but she had no hold whatever over her husband.

'He worries me,' he declared. 'He's a joke of which I have got tired.'

'Would it be possible to send him to a private tutor's?'

'No,' said Mr Elliot, who had all the money. 'Coddling.'

'I agree that boys ought to rough it; but when a boy is lame and very delicate, he roughs it sufficiently if he leaves home. Rickie can't play games. He doesn't make friends. He isn't brilliant. Thinking it over, I feel that as it's like this, we can't ever hope to give him the ordinary education. Perhaps you could think it over too.'

'No.'

'I am sure that things are best for him as they are. The day-school knocks quite as many corners off him as he can stand. He hates it, but it is good for him. A public school will not be good for him. It is too rough. Instead of getting manly and hard, he will—'

'My head, please.'

Rickie departed in a state of bewildered misery, which was scarcely ever to grow clearer.

Each holiday he found his father more irritable, and a little weaker. Mrs Elliot was quickly growing old. She had to manage the servants, to hush the neighbouring children, to answer the correspondence, to paper and re-paper the rooms—and all for the sake of a man whom she did not like, and who did not conceal his dislike for her. One day she found Rickie tearful, and said rather crossly, 'Well, what is it this time?'

He replied, 'Oh, mummy, I've seen your wrinkles—your grey hair—I'm unhappy.'

Sudden tenderness overcame her, and she cried, 'My darling, what does it matter? Whatever does it matter now?'

He had never known her so emotional. Yet even better did he remember another incident. Hearing high voices from his father's room, he went upstairs in the hope that the sound of his tread might stop them. Mrs Elliot burst open the door, and seeing him, exclaimed, 'My dear! If you please, he's hit me.' She tried to laugh it off, but a few hours later he saw the bruise which the stick of the invalid had raised upon his mother's hand.

God alone knows how far we are in the grip of our bodies. He alone can judge how far the cruelty of Mr Elliot was the outcome of extenuating circumstances. But Mrs Elliot could accurately judge of its extent.

At last he died. Rickie was now fifteen, and got off a whole week's school for the funeral. His mother was rather strange. She was much happier, she looked younger, and her mourning was as unobtrusive as convention permitted. All this he had expected. But she seemed to be watching him, and to be extremely anxious for his opinion on any subject—more especially on his father. Why? At last he saw that she was trying to establish confidence between them. But confidence cannot be established in a moment. They were both shy. The habit of years was upon them, and they alluded to the death of Mr Elliot as an irreparable loss.

'Now that your father has gone, things will be very different.'

'Shall we be poorer, mother?'

'No.'

'Oh!'

'But naturally things will be very different.'

'Yes, naturally.'

'For instance, your poor father liked being near London, but I almost think we might move. Would you like that?'

'Of course, mummy.' He looked down at the ground. He was not accustomed to being consulted, and it bewildered him.

'Perhaps you might like quite a different life better?'

He giggled.

'It's a little difficult for me,' said Mrs Elliot, pacing vigorously up and down the room, and more and more did her black dress seem a mockery. 'In some ways you ought to be consulted: nearly all the money is left to you, as you must hear some time or other. But in other ways you're only a boy. What am I to do?'

'I don't know,' he replied, appearing more helpless and unhelpful than he really was.

'For instance, would you like me to arrange things exactly as I like?'

'Oh, do!' he exclaimed, thinking this a most brilliant suggestion. 'The very nicest thing of all.' And he added, in his half-pedantic, half-pleasing way, 'I shall be as wax in your hands, mamma.'

She smiled. 'Very well, darling. You shall be.' And she pressed him lovingly, as though she would mould him into something beautiful.

For the next few days great preparations were in the air. She went to see his father's sister, the gifted and vivacious Aunt Emily. They were to live in the country—somewhere right in the country, with grass and trees up to the door, and birds singing everywhere, and a tutor. For he was not to go back to school. Unbelievable! He was never to go back to school, and the headmaster had written saying that he regretted the step, but that possibly it was a wise one.

It was raw weather, and Mrs Elliot watched over him with ceaseless tenderness. It seemed as if she could not do too much to shield him and to draw him nearer to her.

'Put on your greatcoat, dearest,' she said to him.

'I don't think I want it,' answered Rickie, remembering that he was now fifteen.

'The wind is bitter. You ought to put it on.'

'But it's so heavy.'

'Do put it on, dear.'

He was not very often irritable or rude, but he answered, 'Oh, I shan't catch cold. I do wish you wouldn't keep on bothering.'

He did not catch cold, but while he was out his mother died. She only survived her husband eleven days, a coincidence which was recorded on their tombstone.

Such, in substance, was the story which Rickie told his friends as they stood together in the shelter of the dell. The green bank at the entrance hid the road and the world, and now, as in spring, they could see nothing but snow-white ramparts and the evergreen foliage of the firs. Only from time to time would a beech leaf flutter in from the woods above, to comment on the waning year, and the warmth and radiance of the sun would vanish behind a passing cloud.

About the greatcoat he did not tell them, for he could not have spoken of it without tears.

Chapter Three

Mr Ansell, a provincial draper of moderate prosperity, ought by rights to have been classed not with the cow, but with those phenomena that are not really there. But his son, with pardonable illogicality, excepted him. He never suspected that his father might be the subjective product of a diseased imagination. From his earliest years he had taken him for granted, as a most undeniable and lovable fact. To be born one thing and grow up another—Ansell had accomplished this without weakening one of the ties that bound him to his home. The rooms above the shop still seemed as comfortable, the garden behind it as gracious, as they had seemed fifteen years before, when he would sit behind Miss Appleblossom's central throne, and she, like some allegorical figure, would send the change and receipted bills spinning away from her in little boxwood balls. At first the young man had attributed these happy relations to his own tact. But in time he perceived that the tact was all on the side of his father. Mr Ansell was not merely a man of some education; he had what no education can bring—the power of detecting what is important. Like many fathers, he had spared no expense over his boy—he had borrowed money to start him at a rapacious and fashionable private school; he had sent him to tutors; he had sent him to Cambridge. But he knew that all this was not the important thing. The important thing was freedom. The boy must use his education as he chose, and if he paid his father back it would certainly not be in his own coin. So when Stewart said, 'At Cambridge, can I read for the Moral Science Tripos?' Mr Ansell had only replied, 'This philosophy—do you say that it lies behind everything?'

'Yes, I think so. It tries to discover what is good and true.'

'Then, my boy, you had better read as much of it as you can.'

And a year later: 'I'd like to take up this philosophy seriously, but I don't feel justified.'

'Why not?'

'Because it brings in no return. I think I'm a great philosopher, but then all philosophers think that, though they don't dare to say so. But, however great I am, I shan't earn money. Perhaps I shan't ever be able to keep myself. I shan't even get a good social position. You've only to say one word, and I'll work for the Civil Service. I'm good enough to get in high.'

Mr Ansell liked money and social position. But he knew that there is a more important thing, and replied, 'You must take up this philosophy seriously, I think.'

'Another thing—there are the girls.'

'There is enough money now to get Mary and Maud as good husbands as they deserve.' And Mary and Maud took the same view.

It was in this plebeian household that Rickie spent part of the Christmas vacation. His own home, such as it was, was with the Silts, needy cousins of his father's, and combined to a peculiar degree the restrictions of hospitality with the discomforts of a boarding-house. Such pleasure as he had outside Cambridge was in the homes of his friends, and it was a particular joy and honour to visit Ansell, who, though as free from social snobbishness as most of us will ever manage to be, was rather careful whom he drove up to the *façade* of his shop.

'I like our new lettering,' he said thoughtfully. The words 'Stewart Ansell' were repeated again and again along the High Street—curly gold letters that seemed to float in tanks of glazed chocolate.

'Rather!' said Rickie. But he wondered whether one of the bonds that kept the Ansell family united might not be their complete absence of taste—a surer bond by far than the identity of it. And he wondered this again when he sat at tea opposite a long row of crayons—Stewart as a baby, Stewart as a small boy with large feet, Stewart as a larger boy with smaller feet, Mary reading a book whose leaves were as thick as eider-downs. And yet again did he wonder it when he woke with a gasp in the night to find a harp in luminous paint throbbing and glowering at him from the adjacent wall. 'Watch and pray' was written on the harp, and until Rickie hung a towel over it the exhortation was partially successful.

It was a very happy visit. Miss Appleblossom—who now acted as housekeeper—had met him before, during her never-forgotten expedition to

Cambridge, and her admiration of University life was as shrill and as genuine now as it had been then. The girls at first were a little aggressive, for on his arrival he had been tired, and Maud had taken it for haughtiness, and said he was looking down on them. But this passed. They did not fall in love with him, nor he with them, but a morning was spent very pleasantly in snowballing in the back garden. Ansell was rather different to what he was in Cambridge, but to Rickie not less attractive. And there was a curious charm in the hum of the shop, which swelled into a roar if one opened the partition door on a market-day.

'Listen to your money!' said Rickie. 'I wish I could hear mine. I wish my money was alive.'

'I don't understand.'

'Mine's dead money. It's come to me through about six dead people—silently.'

'Getting a little smaller and a little more respectable each time, on account of the death-duties.'

'It needed to get respectable.'

'Why? Did your people, too, once keep a shop?'

'Oh, not as bad as that! They only swindled. About a hundred years ago an Elliot did something shady and founded the fortunes of our house.'

'I never knew any one so relentless to his ancestors. You make up for your soapiness towards the living.'

'You'd be relentless if you'd heard the Silts, as I have, talk about "a fortune, small perhaps, but unsoiled by trade!" Of course Aunt Emily is rather different. Oh, goodness me! I've forgotten my aunt. She lives not so far. I shall have to call on her.'

Accordingly he wrote to Mrs Failing, and said he should like to pay his respects. He told her about the Ansells, and so worded the letter that she might reasonably have sent an invitation to his friend.

She replied that she was looking forward to their *tête-à-tête*.

'You mustn't go round by the trains,' said Mr Ansell. 'It means changing at Salisbury. By the road it's no great way. Stewart shall drive you over Salisbury Plain, and fetch you too.'

'There's too much snow,' said Ansell.

'Then the girls shall take you in their sledge.'

'That I will,' said Maud, who was not unwilling to see the inside of Cadover. But Rickie went round by the trains.

'We have all missed you,' said Ansell, when he returned. 'There is a general feeling that you are no nuisance, and had better stop till the end of the vac.'

This he could not do. He was bound for Christmas to the Silts—'as a *real* guest,' Mrs Silt had written, underlining the word 'real' twice. And after Christmas he must go to the Pembrokes.

'These are no reasons. The only real reason for doing a thing is because you want to do it. I think the talk about "engagements" is cant.'

'I think perhaps it is,' said Rickie. But he went. Never had the turkey been so athletic, or the plum-pudding tied into its cloth so tightly. Yet he knew that both these symbols of hilarity had cost money, and it went to his heart when Mr Silt said in a hungry voice, 'Have you thought at all of what you want to be? No? Well, why should you? You have no need to be anything.' And at dessert: 'I wonder who Cadover goes to? I expect money will follow money. It always does.' It was with a guilty feeling of relief that he left for the Pembrokes.

The Pembrokes lived in an adjacent suburb, or rather 'sububurb,'—the tract called Sawston, celebrated for its public school. Their style of life, however, was not particularly suburban. Their house was small and its name was Shelthorpe, but it had an air about it which suggested a certain amount of money and a certain amount of taste. There were decent water-colours in the drawing-room. Madonnas of acknowledged merit hung upon the stairs. A replica of the Hermes of Praxiteles—of course only the bust—stood in the hall with a real palm behind it. Agnes, in her slap-dash way, was a good housekeeper, and kept the pretty things well dusted. It was she who insisted on the strip of brown holland that led diagonally from the front door to the door of Herbert's study: boys' grubby feet should not go treading on her Indian square. It was she who always cleaned the picture-frames and washed the bust and the leaves of the palm. In short, if a house could speak—and sometimes it does speak more clearly than the people who live in it—the house of the Pembrokes would have said, 'I am not quite like other houses, yet I am perfectly comfortable. I contain works of art and a microscope and books. But I do not live for any of these things or suffer them to disarrange me. I live for myself and for the greater houses that shall come after me. Yet in me neither the cry of money nor the cry for money shall ever be heard.'

Mr Pembroke was at the station. He did better as a host than as a guest, and welcomed the young man with real friendliness.

'We were all coming, but Gerald has strained his ankle slightly, and wants to keep quiet, as he is playing next week in a match. And, needless to say, that explains the absence of my sister.'

'Gerald Dawes?'

'Yes; he's with us. I'm so glad you'll meet again.'

'So am I,' said Rickie with extreme awkwardness. 'Does he remember me?'

'Vividly.'

Vivid also was Rickie's remembrance of him.

'A splendid fellow,' asserted Mr Pembroke.

'I hope that Agnes is well.'

'Thank you, yes; she is well. And I think you're looking more like other people yourself.'

'I've been having a very good time with a friend.'

'Indeed. That's right. Who was that?'

Rickie had a young man's reticence. He generally spoke of 'a friend,' 'a person I know,' 'a place I was at.' When the book of life is opening, our readings are secret, and we are unwilling to give chapter and verse. Mr Pembroke, who was half-way through the volume, and had skipped or forgotten the earlier pages, could not understand Rickie's hesitation, nor why with such awkwardness he should pronounce the harmless dissyllable 'Ansell.'

'Ansell? Wasn't that the pleasant fellow who asked us to lunch?'

'No. That was Anderson, who keeps below. You didn't see Ansell. The ones who came to breakfast were Tilliard and Hornblower.'

'Of course. And since then you have been with the Silts. How are they?'

'Very well, thank you. They want to be remembered to you.'

The Pembrokes had formerly lived near the Elliots, and had shown great kindness to Rickie when his parents died. They were thus rather in the position of family friends.

'Please remember us when you write.' He added, almost roguishly, 'The Silts are kindness itself. All the same, it must be just a little—dull, we thought, and we thought that you might like a change. And of course we are delighted to have you besides. That goes without saying.'

'It's very good of you,' said Rickie, who had accepted the invitation because he felt he ought to.

'Not a bit. And you mustn't expect us to be otherwise than quiet in the holidays. There is a library of a sort, as you know, and you will find Gerald a splendid fellow.'

'Will they be married soon?'

'Oh no!' whispered Mr Pembroke, shutting his eyes, as if Rickie had made some terrible *faux pas*. 'It will be a very long engagement. He must make his way first. I have seen such endless misery result from people marrying before they have made their way.'

'Yes. That is so,' said Rickie despondently, thinking of the Silts.

'It's a sad unpalatable truth,' said Mr Pembroke, thinking that the despondency might be personal, 'but one must accept it. My sister and Gerald, I am thankful to say, have accepted it, though naturally it has been a little pill.'

Their cab lurched round the corner as he spoke, and the two patients came in sight. Agnes was leaning over the creosoted garden-gate, and behind her there stood a young man who had the figure of a Greek athlete and the face of an English one. He was fair and clean-shaven, and his colourless hair was cut rather short. The sun was in his eyes, and they, like his mouth, seemed scarcely more than slits in his healthy skin. Just where he began to be beautiful the clothes started. Round his neck went an up-and-down collar and a mauve-and-gold tie, and the rest of his limbs were hidden by a grey lounge suit, carefully creased in the right places.

'Lovely! lovely!' cried Agnes, banging on the gate. 'Your train must have been to the minute.'

'Hullo!' said the athlete, and vomited with the greeting a cloud of tobacco-smoke. It must have been imprisoned in his mouth some time, for no pipe was visible.

'Hullo!' returned Rickie, laughing violently. They shook hands.

'Where are you going, Rickie?' asked Agnes. 'You aren't grubby. Why don't you stop? Gerald, get the large wicker-chair. Herbert has letters, but we can sit here till lunch. It's like spring.'

The garden of Shelthorpe was nearly all in front—an unusual and pleasant arrangement. The front gate and the servants' entrance were both at the side, and in the remaining space the gardener had contrived a little lawn where one could sit concealed from the road by a fence, from the neighbour by a fence, from the house by a tree, and from the path by a bush.

'This is the lovers' bower,' observed Agnes, sitting down on the bench. Rickie stood by her till the chair arrived.

'Are you smoking before lunch?' asked Mr Dawes.

'No, thank you. I hardly ever smoke.'

'No vices. Aren't you at Cambridge now?'

'Yes.'

'What's your college?'

Rickie told him.

'Do you know Carruthers?'

'Rather!'

'I mean A. P. Carruthers, who got his socker blue.'

'Rather! He's secretary to the college musical society.'

'A. P. Carruthers?'

'Yes.'

Mr Dawes seemed offended. He tapped on his teeth, and remarked that the weather had no business to be so warm in winter.

'But it was fiendish before Christmas,' said Agnes.

He frowned, and asked, 'Do you know a man called Gerrish?'

'No.'

'Ah.'

'Do you know James?'

'Never heard of him.'

'He's my year too. He got a blue for hockey his second term.'

'I know nothing about the 'Varsity.'

Rickie winced at the abbreviation ''Varsity.' It was at that time the proper thing to speak of 'the University.'

'I haven't the time,' pursued Mr Dawes.

'No, no,' said Rickie politely.

'I had the chance of being an Undergrad. myself, and, by Jove, I'm thankful I didn't!'

'Why?' asked Agnes, for there was a pause.

'Puts you back in your profession. Men who go there first, before the Army, start hopelessly behind. The same with the Stock Exchange or Painting. I know men in both, and they've never caught up the time they lost in the 'Varsity—unless, of course, you turn parson.'

'I love Cambridge,' said she. 'All those glorious buildings, and every one so happy and running in and out of each other's rooms all day long.'

'That might make an Undergrad. happy, but I beg leave to state it wouldn't me. I haven't four years to throw away for the sake of being called a 'Varsity man and hobnobbing with lords.'

Rickie was prepared to find his old schoolfellow ungrammatical and bumptious, but he was not prepared to find him peevish. Athletes, he believed, were simple, straightforward people, cruel and brutal if you like, but never petty. They knocked you down and hurt you, and then went on their way rejoicing. For this, Rickie thought, there is something to be said: he had escaped the sin of despising the physically strong–a sin against which the physically weak must guard. But here was Dawes returning again and again to the subject of the University, full of transparent jealousy and petty spite, nagging, nagging, nagging, like a maiden lady who has not been invited to a tea-party. Rickie wondered whether, after all, Ansell and the extremists might not be right, and bodily beauty and strength be signs of the soul's damnation.

He glanced at Agnes. She was writing down some orderings for the tradespeople on a piece of paper. Her handsome face was intent on the work. The bench on which she and Gerald were sitting had no back, but she sat as straight as a dart. He, though strong enough to sit straight, did not take the trouble.

'Why don't they talk to each other?' thought Rickie.

'Gerald, give this paper to the cook.'

'I can give it to the other slavey, can't I?'

'She'll be dressing.'

'Well, there's Herbert.'

'He's busy. Oh, you know where the kitchen is. Take it to the cook.'

He disappeared slowly behind the tree.

'What do you think of him?' she immediately asked.

He murmured civilly.

'Has he changed since he was a schoolboy?'

'In a way.'

'Do tell me all about him. Why won't you?'

She might have seen a flash of horror pass over Rickie's face. The horror disappeared, for, thank God, he was now a man, whom civilization protects. But he and Gerald had met, as it were, behind the scenes, before our decorous drama opens, and there the elder boy had done things to him–absurd things, not worth chronicling separately. An apple-pie bed is nothing; pinches, kicks, boxed ears, twisted arms, pulled hair, ghosts at night, inky books, befouled photographs, amount to very little by themselves. But let them be united and continuous, and you have a hell that no grown-up devil can devise. Between Rickie and Gerald there lay a shadow that darkens life more often than we suppose. The bully and his victim never quite forget their first relations. They meet in clubs and country houses, and clap one another on the back; but in both the memory is green of a more strenuous day, when they were boys together.

He tried to say, 'He was the right kind of boy, and I was the wrong kind.' But Cambridge would not let him smooth the situation over by self-belittlement. If he had been the wrong kind of boy, Gerald had been a worse kind. He murmured, 'We are different, very,' and Miss Pembroke, perhaps suspecting something, asked no more. But she kept to the subject of Mr Dawes, humorously depreciating her lover and discussing him without reverence. Rickie laughed, but felt uncomfortable. When people were engaged, he felt that they should be outside criticism. Yet here he was criticizing. He could not help it. He was dragged in.

'I hope his ankle is better.'

'Never was bad. He's always fussing over something.'

'He plays next week in a match, I think Herbert says.'

'I dare say he does.'

'Shall we be going?'

'Pray go if you like. I shall stop at home. I've had enough of cold feet.'

It was all very colourless and odd.

Gerald returned, saying, 'I can't stand your cook. What's she want to ask me questions for? I can't stand talking to servants. I say, "If I speak to you, well and good"–and it's another thing besides if she were pretty.'

'Well, I hope our ugly cook will have lunch ready in a minute,' said Agnes. 'We're frightfully unpunctual this morning, and I daren't say anything, because it was the same yesterday, and if I complain again they might leave. Poor Rickie must be starved.'

'Why, the Silts gave me all these sandwiches and I've never eaten them. They always stuff one.'

'And you thought you'd better, eh?' said Mr Dawes, 'in case you weren't stuffed here.'

Miss Pembroke, who house-kept somewhat economically, looked annoyed.

The voice of Mr Pembroke was now heard calling from the house, 'Frederick! Frederick! My dear boy, pardon me. It was an important letter about the Church Defence, otherwise— Come in and see your room.'

He was glad to quit the little lawn. He had learnt too much there. It was dreadful: they did not love each other. More dreadful even than the case of his father and mother, for they, until they married, had got on pretty well. But this man was already rude and brutal and cold: he was still the school bully who twisted up the arms of little boys, and ran pins into them at chapel, and struck them in the stomach when they were swinging on the horizontal bar. Poor Agnes; why ever had she done it? Ought not somebody to interfere?

He had forgotten his sandwiches, and went back to get them.

Gerald and Agnes were locked in each other's arms.

He only looked for a moment, but the sight burnt into his brain. The man's grip was the stronger. He had drawn the woman on to his knee, was pressing her, with all his strength, against him. Already her hands slipped off him, and she whispered, 'Don't–you hurt—' Her face had no expression. It stared at the intruder and never saw him. Then her lover kissed it, and immediately it shone with mysterious beauty, like some star.

Rickie limped away without the sandwiches, crimson and afraid. He thought, 'Do such things actually happen?' and he seemed to be looking down coloured valleys. Brighter they glowed, till gods of pure flame were born in them, and then he was looking at pinnacles of virgin snow. While Mr Pembroke talked, the riot of fair images increased. They invaded his being and lit lamps at unsuspected shrines. Their orchestra commenced in that suburban house, where he had to stand aside for the maid to carry in the luncheon. Music flowed past him like a river. He stood at the springs of creation and heard the primeval monotony. Then an obscure instrument gave out a little phrase. The river continued unheeding. The phrase was repeated, and a listener might know it was a fragment of the Tune of tunes. Nobler instruments accepted it, the clarionet protected, the brass encouraged, and it rose to the surface to the whisper of violins. In full unison was Love born, flame of the flame, flushing the dark river beneath him and the virgin snows above. His wings were infinite, his youth eternal; the sun was a jewel on his finger as he passed it in benediction over the world. Creation, no longer monotonous, acclaimed him, in widening melody, in brighter radiances. Was Love a column of fire? Was he a torrent of song? Was he greater than either–the touch of a man on a woman?

It was the merest accident that Rickie had not been disgusted. But this he could not know.

Mr Pembroke, when he called the two dawdlers into lunch, was aware of a hand on his arm and a voice that murmured, 'Don't–they may be happy.'

He stared, and struck the gong. To its music they approached, priest and high priestess.

'Rickie, can I give these sandwiches to the boot boy?' said the one. 'He would love them.'

'The gong! Be quick! The gong!'

'Are you smoking before lunch?' said the other.

But they had got into heaven, and nothing could get them out of it. Others might think them surly or prosaic. He knew. He could remember every word they spoke. He would treasure every motion, every glance of either, and so in time to come when the gates of heaven had shut, some faint radiance, some echo of wisdom might remain with him outside.

As a matter of fact, he saw them very little during his visit. He checked himself because he was unworthy. What right had he to pry, even in the spirit, upon their bliss? It was no crime to have seen them on the lawn. It would be a crime to go to it again. He tried to keep himself and his thoughts away, not because he was ascetic, but because they would not like it if they knew. This behaviour of his suited them admirably. And when any gracious little thing occurred to them–any little thing that his sympathy had contrived and allowed–they put it down to chance or to each other.

So the lovers fall into the background. They are part of the distant sunrise, and only the mountains speak to them. Rickie talks to Mr Pembroke, amidst the unlit valleys of our over-habitable world.

Chapter Four

Sawston School had been founded by a tradesman in the seventeenth century. It was then a tiny grammar-school in a tiny town, and the City Company who governed it had to drive half a day through the woods and heath on the occasion of their annual visit. In the twentieth century they still drove, but only from the railway station; and found themselves not in a tiny town, nor yet in a large one, but amongst innumerable residences, detached and semi-detached, which had gathered round the school. For the intentions of the founder had been altered, or at all events amplified, and instead of educating the 'poore of my home,' he now educated the upper middle classes of England. The change had taken place not so very far back. Till the nineteenth century the grammar-school was still composed of day scholars from the neighbourhood. Then two things happened. Firstly, the school's property rose in value, and it became rich. Secondly, for no obvious reason, it suddenly emitted a quantity of bishops. The bishops, like the stars from a Roman candle, were of all colours, and flew in all directions, some high, some low, some to distant colonies, one into the Church of Rome. But many a father traced their course in the papers; many a mother wondered whether her son, if properly ignited, might not burn as bright; many a family moved to the place where living and education were so cheap, where day-boys were not looked down upon, and where the orthodox and the up-to-date were said to be combined. The school doubled its numbers. It built new class-rooms, laboratories, and a gymnasium. It dropped the prefix 'Grammar.' It coaxed the sons of the local tradesmen into a new foundation, the 'Commercial School,' built a couple of miles away. And it started boarding-houses. It had not the gracious antiquity of Eton or Winchester, nor, on the other hand, had it a conscious policy like Lancing, Wellington, and other purely modern foundations. Where traditions served, it clung to them. Where new departures seemed desirable, they were made. It aimed at producing the average Englishman, and, to a very great extent, it succeeded.

Here Mr Pembroke passed his happy and industrious life. His technical position was that of master to a form low down on the Modern Side. But his work lay elsewhere. He organized. If no organization existed, he would create one. If one did exist, he would modify it. 'An organization,' he would say, 'is after all not an end in itself. It must contribute to a movement.' When one good custom seemed likely to corrupt the school, he was ready with another; he believed that without innumerable customs there was no safety, either for boys or men. Perhaps he is right, and always will be right. Perhaps each of us would go to ruin if for one short hour we acted as we thought fit, and attempted the service of perfect freedom. The school caps, with their elaborate symbolism, were his; his the many-tinted bathing-drawers, that showed how far a boy could swim; his the hierarchy of jerseys and blazers. It was he who instituted Bounds, and Call, and the two sorts of exercise-paper, and the three sorts of caning, and 'The Sawstonian,' a bi-terminal magazine. His plump finger was in every pie. The dome of his skull, mild but impressive, shone at every masters' meeting. He was generally acknowledged to be the coming man.

His last achievement had been the organization of the day-boys. They had been left too much to themselves, and were weak in *esprit de corps*; they were apt to regard home, not school, as the most important thing in their lives. Moreover, they got out of their parents' hands; they did their preparation any time and sometimes anyhow. They shirked games, they were out at all hours, they ate what they should not, they smoked, they bicycled on the asphalt. Now all was over. Like the boarders, they were to be in at 7.15 p.m., and were not allowed out after unless with a written order from their parent or guardian; they, too, must work at fixed hours in the evening, and before breakfast next morning from 7 to 8. Games were compulsory. They must not go to parties in term time. They must keep to bounds. Of course the reform was not complete. It was impossible to control the dieting, though, on a printed circular, day-parents were implored to provide simple food. And it is also believed that some mothers disobeyed the rule about preparation, and allowed their sons to do all the work overnight and have a longer sleep in the morning. But the gulf between day-boys and boarders was considerably lessened, and grew still narrower when the day-boys too were organized into a House with house-master and colours of their own. 'Through the House,' said Mr Pembroke, 'one learns patriotism for the school, just as through the school one learns patriotism for the country. Our only course, therefore, is to organize the day-boys into a House.' The headmaster agreed, as he often did, and the new community was formed. Mr Pembroke, to avoid the tongues of malice, had refused the post of house-master for himself, saying to Mr Jackson, who taught the sixth, 'You keep too much in the background. Here is a chance for you.' But this was a failure. Mr Jackson, a scholar and a student, neither felt nor conveyed any enthusiasm, and when confronted with his House, would say, 'Well, I don't know what we're all here for. Now I should think you'd better go home to your mothers.' He returned to his background, and next term Mr Pembroke was to take his place.

Such were the themes on which Mr Pembroke discoursed to Rickie's civil ear. He showed him the school, and the library, and the subterranean hall where the day-boys might leave their coats and caps, and where, on festal occasions, they supped. He showed him Mr Jackson's pretty house, and whispered, 'Were it not for his brilliant intellect, it would be a case of Quick-march!' He showed him the racquet-court, happily completed, and the chapel, unhappily still in need of funds. Rickie was impressed, but then he was impressed by everything. Of course a House of day-boys seemed a little shadowy after Agnes and Gerald, but he imparted some reality even to that.

'The racquet-court,' said Mr Pembroke, 'is most gratifying. We never expected to manage it this year. But before the Easter holidays every boy received a subscription card, and was given to understand that he must collect thirty shillings. You will scarcely believed me, but they nearly all responded. Next term there was a dinner in the great school, and all who had collected, not thirty shillings, but as much as a pound, were invited to it—for naturally one was not precise for a few shillings, the response being the really valuable thing. Practically the whole school had to come.'

'They must enjoy the court tremendously.'

'Ah, it isn't very much. Racquets, as I daresay you know, is rather an expensive game. Only the wealthier boys play—and I'm sorry to say that it is not of our wealthier boys that we are always proudest. But the point is that no public school can be called first-class until it has one. They are building them right and left.'

'And now you must finish the chapel?'

'Now we must complete the chapel.' He paused reverently, and said, 'And here is a fragment of the original building.'

Rickie at once had a rush of sympathy. He, too, looked with reverence at the morsel of Jacobean brickwork, ruddy and beautiful amidst the machine-squared stones of the modern apse. The two men, who had so little in common, were thrilled with patriotism. They rejoiced that their country was great, noble, and old.

'Thank God I'm English,' said Rickie suddenly.

'Thank Him indeed,' said Mr Pembroke, laying a hand on his back.

'We've been nearly as great as the Greeks, I do believe. Greater, I'm sure, than the Italians, though they did get closer to beauty. Greater than the French, though we do take all their ideas. I can't help thinking that England is immense. English literature certainly.'

Mr Pembroke removed his hand. He found such patriotism somewhat craven. Genuine patriotism comes only from the heart. It knows no parleying with reason. English ladies will declare abroad that there are no fogs in London, and Mr Pembroke, though he would not go to this, was only restrained by the certainty of being found out. On this occasion he remarked that the Greeks lacked spiritual insight, and had a low conception of woman.

'As to women—oh! there they were dreadful,' said Rickie, leaning his hand on the chapel. 'I realize that more and more. But as to spiritual insight, I don't quite like to say; and I find Plato too difficult, but I know men who don't, and I fancy they mightn't agree with you.'

'Far be it from me to disparage Plato. And for philosophy as a whole I have the greatest respect. But it is the crown of a man's education, not the foundation. Myself, I read it with the utmost profit, but I have known endless trouble result from boys who attempted it too soon, before they were set.'

'But if those boys had died first,' cried Rickie with sudden vehemence, 'without knowing what there is to know—'

'Or isn't to know!' said Mr Pembroke sarcastically.

'Or what there isn't to know. Exactly. That's it.'

'My dear Rickie, what do you mean? If an old friend may be frank, you are talking great rubbish.' And, with a few well-worn formulæ, he propped up the young man's orthodoxy. The props were unnecessary. Rickie had his own equilibrium. Neither the Revivalism that assails a boy at about the age of fifteen, nor the scepticism that meets him five years later, could sway him from his allegiance to the church into which he had been born. But his equilibrium was personal, and the secret of it useless to others. He desired that each man should find his own.

'What does philosophy do?' the propper continued. 'Does it make a man happier in life? Does it make him die more peacefully? I fancy that in the long-run Herbert Spencer will get no further than the rest of us. Ah, Rickie! I wish you could move among schoolboys, and see their healthy contempt for all that they cannot touch!' Here he was going too far, and had to add, 'Their spiritual capacities, of course, are another matter.' Then he remembered the Greeks, and said, 'Which proves my original statement.'

Submissive signs, as of one propped, appeared in Rickie's face. Mr Pembroke then questioned him about the men who found Plato not difficult. But here he kept silence, patting the school chapel gently, and presently the conversation turned to topics with which they were both more competent to deal.

'Does Agnes take much interest in the school?'

'Not as much as she did. It is the result of her engagement. If our naughty soldier had not carried her off, she might have made an ideal schoolmaster's wife. I often chaff him about it, for he a little despises the intellectual professions. Natural, perfectly natural. How can a man who faces death feel as we do towards *mensa* or *tupto*?'

'Perfectly true. Absolutely true.'

Mr Pembroke remarked to himself that Frederick was improving.

'If a man shoots straight and hits straight and speaks straight, if his heart is in the right place, if he has the instincts of a Christian and a gentleman—then I, at all events, ask no better husband for my sister.'

'How could you get a better?' he cried. 'Do you remember the thing in "The Clouds"?' And he quoted, as well as he could, from the invitation of the Dikaios Logos, the description of the young Athenian, perfect in body, placid in mind, who neglects his work at the Bar and trains all day among the woods and meadows, with a garland on his head and a friend to set the pace; the scent of new leaves is upon them; they rejoice in the freshness of spring; over their heads the plane-tree whispers to the elm—perhaps the most glorious invitation to the brainless life that has ever been given.

'Yes, yes,' said Mr Pembroke, who did not want a brother-in-law out of Aristophanes. Nor had he got one, for Mr Dawes would not have bothered over the garland or noticed the spring, and would have complained that the friend ran too slowly or too fast.

'And as for her—!' But he could think of no classical parallel for Agnes. She slipped between examples. A kindly Medea, a Cleopatra with a sense of duty—these suggested her a little. She was not born in Greece, but came overseas to it—a dark, intelligent princess. With all her splendour, there were hints of splendour still hidden—hints of an older, richer, and more mysterious land. He smiled at the idea of her being 'not there.' Ansell, clever as he was, had made a bad blunder. She had more reality than any other woman in the world.

Mr Pembroke looked pleased at this boyish enthusiasm. He was fond of his sister, though he knew her to be full of faults. 'Yes, I envy her,' he said. 'She has found a worthy helpmeet for life's journey, I do believe. And though they chafe at the long engagement, it is a blessing in disguise. They learn to know each other thoroughly before contracting more intimate ties.'

Rickie did not assent. The length of the engagement seemed to him unspeakably cruel. Here were two people who loved each other, and they could not marry for years because they had no beastly money. Not all Herbert's pious skill could make this out a blessing. It was bad enough being 'so rich' at the Silts; here he was more ashamed of it than ever. In a few weeks he would come of age and his money be his own. What a pity things were so crookedly arranged. He did not want money, or at all events he did not want so much.

'Suppose,' he meditated, for he became much worried over this—'suppose I had a hundred pounds a year less than I shall have. Well, I should still have enough. I don't want anything but food, lodging, clothes, and now and then a railway fare. I haven't any tastes. I don't collect anything or play games. Books are nice to have, but after all there is Mudie's, or if it comes to that, the Free Library. Oh, my profession! I forgot I shall have a profession. Well, that will leave me with more to spare than ever.' And he supposed away till he lost touch with the world and with what it permits, and committed an unpardonable sin.

It happened towards the end of his visit—another airless day of that mild January. Mr Dawes was playing against a scratch team of cads, and had to go down to the ground in the morning to settle something. Rickie proposed to come too.

Hitherto he had been no nuisance. 'You will be frightfully bored,' said Agnes, observing the cloud on her lover's face. 'And Gerald walks like a maniac.'

'I had a little thought of the Museum this morning,' said Mr Pembroke. 'It is very strong in flint arrowheads.'

'Ah, that's your line, Rickie. I do envy you and Herbert the way you enjoy the past.'

'I almost think I'll go with Dawes, if he'll have me. I can walk quite fast just to the ground and back. Arrowheads are wonderful, but I don't really enjoy them yet, though I hope I shall in time.'

Mr Pembroke was offended, but Rickie held firm.

In a quarter of an hour he was back at the house alone, nearly crying.

'Oh, did the wretch go too fast?' called Miss Pembroke from her bedroom window.

'I went too fast for him.' He spoke quite sharply, and before he had time to say he was sorry and didn't mean exactly that, the window had shut.

'They've quarrelled,' she thought. 'Whatever about?'

She soon heard. Gerald returned in a cold stormy temper. Rickie had offered him money.

'My dear fellow, don't be so cross. The child's mad.'

'If it was, I'd forgive that. But I can't stand unhealthiness.'

'Now, Gerald, that's where I hate you. You don't know what it is to pity the weak.'

'Woman's job. So you wish I'd taken a hundred pounds a year from him. Did you ever hear such blasted cheek? Marry us—he, you, and me—a hundred pounds down and as much annual—he, of course, to pry into all we did, and we to kowtow and eat dirt-pie to him. If that's Mr Rickety Elliot's idea of a soldier and an Englishman, it isn't mine, and I wish I'd had a horse-whip.'

She was roaring with laughter. 'You're babies, a pair of you, and you're the worst. Why couldn't you let the little silly down gently? There he was puffing and sniffing under my window, and I thought he'd insulted you. Why didn't you accept?'

'Accept?' he thundered.

'It would have taken the nonsense out of him for ever. Why, he was only talking out of a book.'

'More fool he.'

'Well, don't be angry with a fool. He means no harm. He muddles all day with poetry and old dead people, and then tries to bring it into life. It's too funny for words.'

Gerald repeated that he could not stand unhealthiness.

'I don't call that exactly unhealthy.'

'I do. And why he could give the money's worse.'

'What do you mean?'

He became shy. 'I hadn't meant to tell you. It's not quite for a lady.' For, like most men who are rather animal, he was intellectually a prude. 'He says he can't ever marry, owing to his foot. It wouldn't be fair to posterity. His grandfather was crocked, his father too, and he's as bad. He thinks that it's hereditary, and may get worse next generation. He's discussed it all over with other Undergrads. A bright lot they must be. He daren't risk having any children. Hence the hundred quid.'

She stopped laughing. 'Oh, little beast, if he said all that!'

He was encouraged to proceed. Hitherto he had not talked about their school days. Now he told her everything—the 'barley-sugar,' as he called it, the pins in chapel, and how one afternoon he had tied him head downward on to a tree-trunk and then ran away—of course only for a moment.

For this she scolded him well. But she had a thrill of joy when she thought of the weak boy in the clutches of the strong one.

Chapter Five

Gerald died that afternoon. He was broken up in the football match. Rickie and Mr Pembroke were on the ground when the accident took place. It was no good torturing him by a drive to the hospital, and he was merely carried to the little pavilion and laid upon the floor. A doctor came, and so did a clergyman, but it seemed better to leave him for the last few minutes with Agnes, who had ridden down on her bicycle.

It was a strange lamentable interview. The girl was so accustomed to health, that for a time she could not understand. It must be a joke that he chose to lie there in the dust, with a rug over him, and his knees bent up towards his chin. His arms were as she knew them, and their admirable muscles showed clear and clean beneath the jersey. The face, too, though a little flushed, was uninjured: it must be some curious joke.

'Gerald, what have you been doing?'

He replied, 'I can't see you. It's too dark.'

'Oh, I'll soon alter that,' she said in her old brisk way. She opened the pavilion door. The people who were standing by it moved aside. She saw a deserted meadow, steaming and grey, and beyond it slate-roofed cottages, row beside row, climbing a shapeless hill. Towards London the sky was yellow. 'There. That's better.' She sat down by him again, and drew his hand into her own. 'Now we are all right, aren't we?'

'Where are you?'

This time she could not reply.

'What is it? Where am I going?'

'Wasn't the rector here?' said she after a silence.

'He explained heaven, and thinks that I—but—I couldn't tell a parson; but I don't seem to have any use for any of the things there.'

'We are Christians,' said Agnes shyly. 'Dear love, we don't talk about these things, but we believe them. I think that you will get well and be as strong again as ever; but, in any case, there is a spiritual life, and we know that some day you and I—'

'I shan't do as a spirit,' he interrupted, sighing pitifully. 'I want you as I am, and it cannot be managed. The rector had to say so. I want—I don't want to talk. I can't see you. Shut that door.'

She obeyed, and crept into his arms. Only this time her grasp was the stronger. Her heart beat louder and louder as the sound of his grew more faint. He was crying like a little frightened child, and her lips were wet with his tears. 'Bear it bravely,' she told him.

'I can't,' he whispered. 'It isn't to be done. I can't see you,' and passed from her trembling, with open eyes.

She rode home on her bicycle, leaving the others to follow. Some ladies who did not know what had happened bowed and smiled as she passed, and she returned their salute.

'Oh, miss, is it true?' cried the cook, her face streaming with tears.

Agnes nodded. Presumably it was true. Letters had just arrived: one was for Gerald from his mother. Life, which had given them no warning, seemed to make no comment now. The incident was outside nature, and would surely pass away like a dream. She felt slightly irritable, and the grief of the servants annoyed her.

They sobbed. 'Ah, look at his marks! Ah, little he thought–little he thought!' In the brown holland strip by the front door a heavy football boot had left its impress. They had not liked Gerald, but he was a man, they were women, he had died. Their mistress ordered them to leave her.

For many minutes she sat at the foot of the stairs, rubbing her eyes. An obscure spiritual crisis was going on. Should she weep like the servants? or should she bear up and trust in the consoler Time? Was the death of a man so terrible after all? As she invited herself to apathy there were steps on the gravel, and Rickie Elliot burst in. He was splashed with mud, his breath was gone, and his hair fell wildly over his meagre face. She thought, 'These are the people who are left alive!' From the bottom of her soul she hated him.

'I came to see what you're doing,' he cried.

'Resting.'

He knelt beside her, and she said, 'Would you please go away?'

'Yes, dear Agnes, of course; but I must see first that you mind.'

Her breath caught. Her eyes moved to the treads, going outwards, so firmly, so irretrievably.

He panted, 'It's the worst thing that can ever happen to you in all your life, and you've got to mind it–you've got to mind it. They'll come saying, "Bear up–trust to time." No, no; they're wrong. Mind it.'

Through all her misery she knew that this boy was greater than they supposed. He rose to his feet, and with intense conviction cried: 'But I know–I understand. It's your death as well as his. He's gone, Agnes, and his arms will never hold you again. In God's name, mind such a thing, and don't sit fencing with your soul. Don't stop being great; that's the one crime he'll never forgive you.'

She faltered, 'Who–who forgives?'

'Gerald.'

At the sound of his name she slid forward, and all her dishonesty left her. She acknowledged that life's meaning had vanished. Bending down, she kissed the footprint. 'How can he forgive me?' she sobbed. 'Where has he gone to? You never could dream such an awful thing. He couldn't see me though I opened the door–wide–plenty of light; and then he could not remember the things that should comfort him. He wasn't a–he wasn't ever a great reader, and he couldn't remember the things. The rector tried, and he couldn't–I came, and I couldn't—' She could not speak for tears. Rickie did not check her. He let her accuse herself, and fate, and Herbert, who had postponed their marriage. She might have been a wife six months; but Herbert had spoken of self-control and of all life before them. He let her kiss the footprints till their marks gave way to the marks of her lips. She moaned, 'He is gone—where is he?' and then he replied quite quietly, 'He is in heaven.'

She begged him not to comfort her; she could not bear it.

'I did not come to comfort you. I came to see that you mind. He is in heaven, Agnes. The greatest thing is over.'

Her hatred was lulled. She murmured, 'Dear Rickie!' and held up her hand to him. Through her tears his meagre face showed as a seraph's who spoke the truth and forbade her to juggle with her soul. 'Dear Rickie—but for the rest of my life what am I to do?'

'Anything—if you remember that the greatest thing is over.'

'I don't know you,' she said tremulously. 'You have grown up in a moment. You never talked to us, and yet you understand it all. Tell me again—I can only trust you—where is he.'

'He is in heaven.'

'You are sure?'

It puzzled her that Rickie, who could scarcely tell you the time without a saving clause, should be so certain about immortality.

Chapter Six

He did not stop for the funeral. Mr Pembroke thought that he had a bad effect on Agnes, and prevented her from acquiescing in the tragedy as rapidly as she might have done. As he expressed it, 'one must not court sorrow,' and he hinted to the young man that they desired to be alone. Rickie went back to the Silts.

He was only there a few days. As soon as term opened he returned to Cambridge, for which he longed passionately. The journey thither was now familiar to him, and he took pleasure in each landmark. The fair valley of Tewin Water, the cutting into Hitchin where the train traverses the chalk, Baldock Church, Royston with its promise of downs, were nothing in themselves, but dear as stages in his pilgrimage towards the abode of peace. On the platform he met friends. They had all had pleasant vacations: it was a happy world. The atmosphere alters.

Cambridge, according to her custom, welcomed her sons with open drains. Pettycury was up, so was Trinity Street, and navvies peeped out of King's Parade. Here it was gas, there electric light, but everywhere something, and always a smell. It was also the day that the wheels fell off the station tram, and Rickie, who was naturally inside, was among the passengers who 'sustained no injury but a shock, and had as hearty a laugh over the mishap afterwards as any one.'

Tilliard fled into a hansom, cursing himself for having tried to do the thing cheaply. Hornblower also swept past yelling derisively, with his luggage neatly piled above his head. 'Let's get out and walk,' muttered Ansell. But Rickie was succouring a distressed female—Mrs Aberdeen. 'Oh, Mrs Aberdeen, I never saw you; I am so glad to see you—I am so very glad.' Mrs Aberdeen was cold. She did not like being spoken to outside the college, and was also distrait about her basket. Hitherto no genteel eye had ever seen inside it, but in the collision its little calico veil fell off, and there was revealed—nothing. The basket was empty, and never would hold anything illegal. All the same she was distrait, and 'We shall meet later, sir, I dessy,' was all the greeting Rickie got from her.

'Now what kind of life has Mrs Aberdeen?' he exclaimed, as he and Ansell pursued the Station Road. 'Here these bedders come and make us comfortable. We owe an enormous amount to them, their wages are absurd, and we know nothing about them. Off they go to Barnwell, and then their lives are hidden. I just know that Mrs Aberdeen has a husband, but that's all. She never will talk about him. Now I do so want to fill in her life. I see one-half of it. What's the other half? She may have a real jolly house in good taste, with a little garden, and books, and pictures. Or, again, she mayn't. But in any case one ought to know. I know she'd dislike it, but she oughtn't to dislike. After all, bedders are to blame for the present lamentable state of things, just as much as gentlefolk. She ought to want me to come. She ought to introduce me to her husband.'

They had reached the corner of Hills Road. Ansell spoke for the first time. He said, 'Ugh!'

'Drains?'

'Yes. A spiritual cesspool.'

Rickie laughed.

'I expected it from your letter.'

'The one you never answered?'

'I answer none of your letters. You are quite hopeless by now. You can go to the bad. But I refuse to accompany you. I refuse to believe that every human being is a moving wonder of supreme interest and tragedy and beauty—which was what the letter in question amounted to. You'll find plenty who will believe it. It's a very popular view among people who are too idle to think; it saves them the trouble of detecting the beautiful from the ugly, the interesting from the dull, the tragic from the melodramatic. You had just come from Sawston, and were apparently carried away by the fact that Miss Pembroke had the usual amount of arms and legs.'

Rickie was silent. He had told his friend how he felt, but not what had happened. Ansell could discuss love and death admirably, but somehow he would not understand lovers or a dying man, and in the letter there had been scant allusion to these concrete facts. Would Cambridge understand them either? He watched some dons who were peeping into an excavation, and throwing up their hands with humorous gestures of despair. These men would lecture next week on Catiline's conspiracy, on Luther, on Evolution, on Catullus. They dealt with so much and they had experienced so little.

Was it possible he would ever come to think Cambridge narrow? In his short life Rickie had known two sudden deaths, and that is enough to disarrange any placid outlook on the world. He knew once for all that we are all of us bubbles on an extremely rough sea. Into this sea humanity has built, as it were, some little breakwaters–scientific knowledge, civilized restraint–so that the bubbles do not break so frequently or so soon. But the sea has not altered, and it was only a chance that he, Ansell, Tilliard, and Mrs Aberdeen had not all been killed in the tram.

They waited for the other tram by the Roman Catholic Church, whose florid bulk was already receding into twilight. It is the first big building that the incoming visitor sees. 'Oh, here come the colleges!' cries the Protestant parent, and then learns that it was built by a Papist who made a fortune out of movable eyes for dolls. 'Built out of dolls' eyes to contain idols'–that, at all events, is the legend and the joke. It watches over the apostate city, taller by many a yard than anything within, and asserting, however wildly, that here is eternity, stability, and bubbles unbreakable upon a windless sea.

A costly hymn tune announced five o'clock, and in the distance the more lovable note of St Mary's could be heard, speaking from the heart of the town. Then the tram arrived–the slow stuffy tram that plies every twenty minutes between the unknown and the market-place–and took them past the desecrated grounds of Downing, past Addenbrooke's Hospital, girt like any Venetian palace with a mantling canal, past the Fitz William, towering upon immense substructions like any Roman temple, right up to the gates of one's own college, which looked like nothing else in the world. The porters were glad to see them, but wished it had been a hansom. 'Our luggage,' explained Rickie, 'comes in the hotel omnibus, if you would kindly pay a shilling for mine.' Ansell turned aside to some large lighted windows, the abode of a hospitable don, and from other windows there floated familiar voices and the familiar mistakes in a Beethoven sonata. The college, though small, was civilized, and proud of its civilization. It was not sufficient glory to be a Blue there, nor an additional glory to get drunk. Many a maiden lady who had read that Cambridge men were sad dogs, was surprised and perhaps a little disappointed at the reasonable life which greeted her. Miss Appleblossom in particular had had a tremendous shock. The sight of young fellows making tea and drinking water had made her wonder whether this was Cambridge College at all. 'It is so,' she exclaimed afterwards. 'It is just as I say; and what's more, I wouldn't have it otherwise. Stewart says it's as easy as easy to get into the swim, and not at all expensive.' The direction of the swim was determined a little by the genius of the place–for places have a genius, though the less we talk about it the better–and a good deal by the tutors and resident fellows, who treated with rare dexterity the products that came up yearly from the public schools. They taught the perky boy that he was not everything, and the limp boy that he might be something. They even welcomed those boys who were neither limp nor perky, but odd–those boys who had never been at a public school at all, and such do not find a welcome everywhere. And they did everything with ease–one might almost say with nonchalance–so that the boys noticed nothing, and received education, often for the first time in their lives.

But Rickie turned to none of these friends, for just then he loved his rooms better than any person. They were all he really possessed in the world, the only place he could call his own. Over the door was his name, and through the paint, like a grey ghost, he could still read the name of his predecessor. With a sigh of joy he entered the perishable home that was his for a couple of years. There was a beautiful fire, and the kettle boiled at once. He made tea on the hearth-rug and ate the biscuits which Mrs Aberdeen had brought for him up from Anderson's. 'Gentlemen,' she said, 'must learn to give and take.' He sighed again and again, like one who has escaped from danger. With his head on the fender and all his limbs relaxed, he felt almost as safe as he felt once when his mother killed a ghost in the passage by carrying him through it in her arms. There was no ghost now; he was frightened at reality; he was frightened at the splendours and horrors of the world.

A letter from Miss Pembroke was on the table. He did not hurry to open it, for she, and all that she did, was overwhelming. She wrote like the Sibyl; her sorrowful face moved over the stars and shattered their harmonies; last night he saw her with the eyes of Blake, a virgin widow, tall, veiled, consecrated, with her hands stretched out against an everlasting wind. Why would she write? Her letters were not for the likes of him, nor to be read in rooms like his.

'We are not leaving Sawston,' she wrote. 'I saw how selfish it was of me to risk spoiling Herbert's career. I shall get used to any place. Now that he is gone, nothing of that sort can matter. Every one has been most kind, but you have comforted me most, though you did not mean to. I cannot think how you did it, or understood so much. I still think of you as a little boy with a lame leg—I know you will let me say this—and yet when it came to the point you knew more than people who have been all their lives with sorrow and death.'

Rickie burnt this letter, which he ought not to have done, for it was one of the few tributes Miss Pembroke ever paid to imagination. But he felt that it did not belong to him: words so sincere should be for Gerald alone. The smoke rushed up the chimney, and he indulged in a vision. He saw it reach the outer air and beat against the low ceiling of clouds. The clouds were too strong for it: but in them was one chink, revealing one star, and through this the smoke escaped into the light of stars innumerable. Then—but then the vision failed, and the voice of science whispered that all smoke remains on earth in the form of smuts, and is troublesome to Mrs Aberdeen.

'I am jolly unpractical,' he mused. 'And what is the point of it when real things are so wonderful? Who wants visions in a world that has Agnes and Gerald?' He turned on the electric light and pulled open the table-drawer. There, among spoons and corks and string, he found a fragment of a little story that he had tried to write last term. It was called 'The Bay of the Fifteen Islets,' and the action took place on St John's Eve off the coast of Sicily. A party of tourists land on one of the islands. Suddenly the boatmen become uneasy, and say that the island is not generally there. It is an extra one, and they had better have tea on one of the ordinaries. 'Pooh, volcanic!' says the leading tourist, and the ladies say how interesting. The island begins to rock, and so do the minds of its visitors. They start and quarrel and jabber. Fingers burst up through the sand–black fingers of sea devils. The island tilts. The tourists go mad. But just before the catastrophe one man, *integer vitæ scelerisque purus*, sees the truth. Here are no devils. Other muscles, other minds, are pulling the island to its subterranean home. Through the advancing wall of waters he sees no grisly faces, no ghastly medieval limbs, but— But what nonsense! When real things are so wonderful, what is the point of pretending?

And so Rickie deflected his enthusiasms. Hitherto they had played on gods and heroes, on the infinite and the impossible, on virtue and beauty and strength. Now, with a steadier radiance, they transfigured a man who was dead and a woman who was still alive.

Chapter Seven

Love, say orderly people, can be fallen into by two methods: (1) through the desires, (2) through the imagination. And if the orderly people are English, they add that (1) is the inferior method, and characteristic of the South. It is inferior. Yet those who pursue it at all events know what they want; they are not puzzling to themselves or ludicrous to others; they do not take the wings of the morning and fly into the uttermost parts of the sea before walking to the registry office; they cannot breed a tragedy quite like Rickie's.

He is, of course, absurdly young–not twenty-one–and he will be engaged to be married at twenty-three. He has no knowledge of the world; for example, he thinks that if you do not want money you can give it to friends who do. He believes in humanity because he knows a dozen decent people. He believes in women because he has loved his mother. And his friends are as young and as ignorant as himself. They are full of the wine of life. But they have not tasted the cup–let us call it the teacup–of experience, which has made men of Mr Pembroke's type what they are. Oh, that teacup! To be taken at prayers, at friendship, at love, till we are quite sane, quite efficient, quite experienced, and quite useless to God or man. We must drink it, or we shall die. But we need not drink it always. Here is our problem and our salvation. There comes a moment–God knows when–at which we can say, 'I will experience no longer. I will create. I will be an experience.' But to do this we must be both acute and heroic. For it is not easy, after accepting six cups of tea, to throw the seventh in the face of the hostess. And to Rickie this moment has not, as yet, been offered.

Ansell, at the end of his third year, got a first in the Moral Science Tripos. Being a scholar, he kept his rooms in college, and at once began to work for a Fellowship. Rickie got a creditable second in the Classical Tripos, Part I, and retired to sallow lodgings in Mill Lane, carrying with him the degree of

B.A. and a small exhibition, which was quite as much as he deserved. For Part II he read Greek Archæology, and got a second. All this means that Ansell was much cleverer than Rickie. As for the cow, she was still going strong, though turning a little academic as the years passed over her.

'We are bound to get narrow,' sighed Rickie. He and his friend were lying in a meadow during their last summer term. In his incurable love for flowers he had plaited two garlands of buttercups and cow-parsley, and Ansell's lean Jewish face was framed in one of them. 'Cambridge is wonderful, but–but it's so tiny. You have no idea–at least, I think you have no idea–how the great world looks down on it.'

'I read the letters in the paper.'

'It's a bad look-out.'

'How?'

'Cambridge has lost touch with the times.'

'Was she ever intended to touch them?'

'She satisfies,' said Rickie mysteriously, 'neither the professions, nor the public schools, nor the great thinking mass of men and women. There is a general feeling that her day is over, and naturally one feels pretty sick.'

'Do you still write short stories?'

'Why?'

'Because your English has gone to the devil. You think and talk in Journalese. Define a great thinking mass.'

Rickie sat up and adjusted his floral crown.

'Estimate the worth of a general feeling.'

Silence.

'And thirdly, where is the great world?'

'Oh, that—!'

'Yes. That,' exclaimed Ansell, rising from his couch in violent excitement. 'Where is it? How do you set about finding it? How long does it take to get there? What does it think? What does it do? What does it want? Oblige me with specimens of its art and literature.' Silence. 'Till you do, my opinions will be as follows: There is no great world at all, only a little earth, for ever isolated from the rest of the little solar system. The little earth is full of tiny societies, and Cambridge is one of them. All the societies are narrow, but some are good and some are bad–just as one house is beautiful inside and another ugly. Observe the metaphor of the houses: I am coming back to it. The good societies say, "I tell you to do this because I am Cambridge." The bad ones say, "I tell you to do that because I am the great world"–not because I am "Peckham," or "Billingsgate," or "Park Lane," but "because I am the great world." They lie. And fools like you listen to them, and believe that they are a thing which does not exist and never has existed, and confuse "great," which has no meaning whatever, with "good," which means salvation. Look at this great wreath: it'll be dead to-morrow. Look at that good flower: it'll come up again next year. Now for the other metaphor. To compare the world to Cambridge is like comparing the outsides of houses with the inside of a house. No intellectual effort is needed, no moral result is attained. You only have to say, "Oh, what a difference! Oh, what a difference!'' and then come indoors again and exhibit your broadened mind.'

'I shall never come indoors again.' said Rickie. 'That's the whole point.' And his voice began to quiver. 'It's well enough for those who'll get a Fellowship, but in a few weeks I shall go down. In a few years it'll be as if I've never been up. It matters very much to me what the world is like. I can't answer your questions about it; and that's no loss to you, but so much the worse for me. And then you've got a house—not a metaphorical one, but a house with father and sisters. I haven't, and never shall have. There'll never again be a home for me like Cambridge. I shall only look at the outsides of homes. According to your metaphor, I shall live in the street, and it matters very much to me what I find there.'

'You'll live in another house right enough,' said Ansell, rather uneasily. 'Only take care you pick out a decent one. I can't think why you flop about so helplessly, like a bit of sea-weed. In four years you've taken as much root as any one.'

'Where?'

'I should say you've been fortunate in your friends.'

'Oh—that!' But he was not cynical—or cynical in a very tender way. He was thinking of the irony of friendship—so strong it is, and so fragile. We fly together, like straws in an eddy, to part in the open stream. Nature has no use for us; she has cut her stuff differently. Dutiful sons, loving husbands, responsible fathers—these are what she wants, and if we are friends it must be in our spare time. Abram and Sarai were sorrowful, yet their seed became as sand of the sea, and distracts the politics of Europe at this moment. But a few verses of poetry is all that survives of David and Jonathan.

'I wish we were labelled,' said Rickie. He wished that all the confidence and mutual knowledge that is born in such a place as Cambridge could be organized. People went down into the world saying, 'We know and like each other; we shan't forget.' But they did forget, for man is so made that he cannot remember long without a symbol; he wished there was a society, a kind of friendship office, where the marriage of true minds could be registered.

'Why labels?'

'To know each other again.'

'I have taught you pessimism splendidly.' He looked at his watch.

'What time?'

'Not twelve.'

Rickie got up.

'Why go?' He stretched out his hand and caught hold of Rickie's ankle.

'I've got that Miss Pembroke to lunch—that girl whom you say never's there.'

'Then why go? All this week you have pretended Miss Pembroke awaited you. Wednesday—Miss Pembroke to lunch. Thursday—Miss Pembroke to tea. Now again—and you didn't even invite her.'

'To Cambridge, no. But the Hall man they're stopping with has so many engagements that she and her friend can often come to me, I'm glad to say. I don't think I ever told you much, but over two years ago the man she was going to marry was killed at football. She nearly died of grief. This visit to Cambridge is almost the first amusement she has felt up to taking. Oh, they go back to-morrow! Give me breakfast to-morrow.'

'All right.'

'But I shall see you this evening. I shall be round at your paper on Schopenhauer. Lemme go.'

'Don't go,' he said idly. 'It's much better for you to talk to me.'

'Lemme go, Stewart.'

'It's amusing that you're so feeble. You—simply—can't—get—away. I wish I wanted to bully you.'

Rickie laughed, and suddenly overbalanced into the grass. Ansell, with unusual playfulness, held him prisoner. They lay there for a few minutes, talking and ragging aimlessly. Then Rickie seized his opportunity and jerked away.

'Go, go!' yawned the other. But he was a little vexed, for he was a young man with great capacity for pleasure, and it pleased him that morning to be with his friend. The thought of two ladies waiting lunch did not deter him; stupid women, why shouldn't they wait? Why should they interfere with their betters? With his ear on the ground he listened to Rickie's departing steps, and thought, 'He wastes a lot of time keeping engagements. Why will he be pleasant to fools?' And then he thought, 'Why has he turned so unhappy? It isn't as if he's a philosopher, or tries to solve the riddle of existence. And he's got money of his own.' Thus thinking, he fell asleep.

Meanwhile Rickie hurried away from him, and slackened and stopped, and hurried again. He was due at the Union in ten minutes, but he could not bring himself there. He dared not meet Miss Pembroke: he loved her.

The devil must have planned it. They had started so gloriously; she had been a goddess both in joy and sorrow. She was a goddess still. But he had dethroned the god whom once he had glorified equally. Slowly, slowly, the image of Gerald had faded. That was the first step. Rickie had thought, 'No matter. He will be bright again. Just now all the radiance chances to be in her.' And on her he had fixed his eyes. He thought of her awake. He entertained her willingly in dreams. He found her in poetry and music and in the sunset. She made him kind and strong. She made him clever. Through her he kept Cambridge in its proper place, and lived as a citizen of the great world. But one night he dreamt that she lay in his arms. This displeased him. He determined to think a little about Gerald instead. Then the fabric collapsed.

It was hard on Rickie thus to meet the devil. He did not deserve it, for he was comparatively civilized, and knew that there was nothing shameful in love. But to love this woman! If only it had been any one else! Love in return—that he could expect from no one, being too ugly and too unattractive. But the love he offered would not then have been vile. The insult to Miss Pembroke, who was consecrated, and whom he had consecrated, who could still see Gerald, and always would see him, shining on his everlasting throne—this was the crime from the devil, the crime that no penance would ever purge. She knew nothing. She never would know. But the crime was registered in heaven.

He had been tempted to confide in Ansell. But to what purpose? He would say, 'I love Miss Pembroke.' and Stewart would reply, 'You ass.' And then, 'I'm never going to tell her.' 'You ass,' again. After all, it was not a practical question; Agnes would never hear of his fall. If his friend had been, as he expressed it, 'labelled'; if he had been a father, or still better a brother, one might tell him of the discreditable passion. But why irritate him for no reason? Thinking 'I am always angling for sympathy; I must stop myself.' he hurried onward to the Union.

He found his guests half-way up the stairs, reading the advertisements of coaches for the Long Vacation. He heard Mrs Lewin say, 'I wonder what he'll end by doing.' A little over-acting his part, he apologized nonchalantly for his lateness.

'It's always the same,' cried Agnes. 'Last time he forgot I was coming altogether.' She wore a flowered muslin—something indescribably liquid and cool. It reminded him a little of those swift piercing streams, neither blue nor green, that gush out of the dolomites. Her face was clear and brown, like the face of a mountaineer; her hair was so plentiful that it seemed banked up above it; and her little toque, though it answered the note of the dress, was almost ludicrous, poised on so much natural glory. When she moved, the sunlight flashed on her ear-rings.

He led them up to the luncheon-room. By now he was conscious of his limitations as a host, and never attempted to entertain ladies in his lodgings. Moreover, the Union seemed less intimate. It had a faint flavour of a London club; it marked the undergraduate's nearest approach to the great world. Amid its waiters and serviettes one felt impersonal, and able to conceal the private emotions. Rickie felt that if Miss Pembroke knew one thing about him, she knew everything. During this visit he took her to no place that he greatly loved.

'Sit down, ladies. Fall to. I'm sorry. I was out towards Coton with a dreadful friend.'

Mrs Lewin pushed up her veil. She was a typical May-term chaperon, always pleasant, always hungry, and always tired. Year after year she came up to Cambridge in a tight silk dress, and year after year she nearly died of it. Her feet hurt, her limbs were cramped in a canoe, black spots danced before her eyes from eating too much mayonnaise. But still she came, if not as a mother as an aunt, if not as an aunt as a friend. Still she ascended the roof of King's, still she counted the balls of Clare, still she was on the point of grasping the organization of the May races. 'And who is your friend?' she asked.

'His name is Ansell.'

'Well, now, did I see him two years ago—as a bedmaker in something they did at the Foot Lights? Oh, how I roared.'

'You didn't see Mr Ansell at the Foot Lights,' said Agnes, smiling.

'How do you know?' asked Rickie.

'He'd scarcely be so frivolous.'

'Do you remember seeing him?'

'For a moment.'

What a memory she had! And how splendidly during that moment she had behaved!

'Isn't he marvellously clever?'

'I believe so.'

'Oh, give me clever people!' cried Mrs Lewin. 'They are kindness itself at the Hall, but I assure you I am depressed at times. One cannot talk bumprowing for ever.'

'I never hear about him, Rickie; but isn't he really your greatest friend?'

'I don't go in for greatest friends.'

'Do you mean you like us all equally?'

'All differently, those of you I like.'

'Ah, you've caught it!' cried Mrs Lewin. 'Mr Elliot gave it you there well.'

Agnes laughed, and, her elbows on the table, regarded them both through her fingers—a habit of hers. Then she said, 'Can't we see the great Mr Ansell?'

'Oh, let's. Or would he frighten me?'

'He would frighten you,' said Rickie. 'He's a trifle weird.'

'My good Rickie, if you knew the deathly dullness of Sawston—every one saying the proper thing at the proper time, I so proper, Herbert so proper! Why, weirdness is the one thing I long for! Do arrange something.'

'I'm afraid there's no opportunity. Ansell goes some vast bicycle ride this afternoon; this evening you're tied up at the Hall; and to-morrow you go.'

'But there's breakfast to-morrow,' said Agnes. 'Look here, Rickie, bring Mr Ansell to breakfast with us at Buol's.'

Mrs Lewin seconded the invitation.

'Bad luck again,' said Rickie boldly; 'I'm already fixed up for breakfast. I'll tell him of your very kind intention.'

'Let's have him alone,' murmured Agnes.

'My dear girl, I should die through the floor! Oh, it'll be all right about breakfast. I rather think we shall get asked this evening by that shy man who has the pretty rooms in Trinity.'

'Oh, very well. Where is it you breakfast, Rickie?'

He faltered. 'To Ansell's, it is—' It seemed as if he was making some great admission. So self-conscious was he, that he thought the two women exchanged glances. Had Agnes already explored that part of him that did not belong to her? Would another chance step reveal the part that did? He asked them abruptly what they would like to do after lunch.

'Anything,' said Mrs Lewin—'anything in the world.'

A walk? A boat? Ely? A drive? Some objection was raised to each. 'To tell the truth,' she said at last, 'I do feel a wee bit tired, and what occurs to me is this. You and Agnes shall leave me here and have no more bother. I shall be perfectly happy snoozling in one of these delightful drawing-room chairs. Do what you like, and then pick me up after it.'

'Alas! it's against regulations,' said Rickie. 'The Union won't trust lady visitors on its premises alone.'

'But who's to know I'm alone? With a lot of men in the drawing-room, how's each to know that I'm not with the others?'

'That would shock Rickie,' said Agnes, laughing. 'He's frightfully high-principled.'

'No, I'm not,' said Rickie, thinking of his recent shiftiness over breakfast.

'Then come for a walk with me. I want exercise. Some connection of ours was once rector of Madingley. I shall walk out and see the church.'

Mrs Lewin was accordingly left in the Union.

'This is jolly!' Agnes exclaimed as she strode along the somewhat depressing road that leads out of Cambridge past the observatory. 'Do I go too fast?'

'No, thank you. I get stronger every year. If it wasn't for the look of the thing, I should be quite happy.'

'But you don't care for the look of the thing. It's only ignorant people who do that, surely.'

'Perhaps. I care. I like people who are well-made and beautiful. They are of some use in the world. I understand why they are there. I cannot understand why the ugly and crippled are there, however healthy they may feel inside. Don't you know how Turner spoils his pictures by introducing a man like a bolster in the foreground? Well, in actual life every landscape is spoilt by men of worse shapes still.'

'You sound like a bolster with the stuffing out.' They laughed. She always blew his cobwebs away like this, with a puff of humorous mountain air. Just now—the associations he attached to her were various—she reminded him of a heroine of Meredith's—but a heroine at the end of the book. All had been written about her. She had played her mighty part, and knew that it was over. He and he alone was not content, and wrote for her daily a trivial and impossible sequel.

Last time they had talked about Gerald. But that was some six months ago, when things felt easier. To-day Gerald was the faintest blur. Fortunately the conversation turned to Mr Pembroke and to education. Did women lose a lot by not knowing Greek? 'A heap,' said Rickie, roughly. But modern languages? Thus they got to Germany, which he had visited last Easter with Ansell; and thence to the German Emperor, and what a to-do he made; and from him to our own king (still Prince of Wales), who had lived while an undergraduate at Madingley Hall. Here it was. And all the time he thought, 'It is hard on her. She has no right to be walking with me. She would be ill with disgust if she knew. It is hard on her to be loved.'

They looked at the Hall, and went inside the pretty little church. Some Arundel prints hung upon the pillars, and Agnes expressed the opinion that pictures inside a place of worship were a pity. Rickie did not agree with this. He said again that nothing beautiful was ever to be regretted.

'You're cracked on beauty,' she whispered—they were still inside the church. 'Do hurry up and write something.'

'Something beautiful?'

'I believe you can. I'm going to lecture you seriously all the way home. Take care that you don't waste your life.'

They continued the conversation outside. 'But I've got to hate my own writing. I believe that most people come to that stage—not so early though. What I write is too silly. It can't happen. For instance, a stupid vulgar man is engaged to a lovely young lady. He wants her to live in the towns, but she only cares for woods. She shocks him this way and that, but gradually he tames her, and makes her nearly as dull as he is. One day she has a last explosion—over the snobby wedding-presents—and flies out of the drawing-room window, shouting, "Freedom and truth!" Near the house is a little dell full of fir-trees, and she runs into it. He comes there the next moment. But she's gone.'

'Awfully exciting. Where?'

'Oh Lord, she's a Dryad!' cried Rickie, in great disgust. 'She's turned into a tree.'

'Rickie, it's very good indeed. That kind of thing has something in it. Of course you get it all through Greek and Latin. How upset the man must be when he sees the girl turn.'

'He doesn't see her. He never guesses. Such a man could never see a Dryad.'

'So you describe how she turns just before he comes up?'

'No. Indeed I don't ever say that she does turn. I don't use the word "Dryad" once.'

'I think you ought to put that part plainly. Otherwise, with such an original story, people might miss the point. Have you had any luck with it?'

'Magazines? I haven't tried. I know what the stuff's worth. You see, a year or two ago I had a great idea of getting into touch with Nature, just as the Greeks were in touch; and seeing England so beautiful, I used to pretend that her trees and coppices and summer fields of parsley were alive. It's funny enough now, but it wasn't funny then, for I got in such a state that I believed, actually believed, that Fauns lived in a certain double hedgerow near the Gog Magogs, and one evening I walked round a mile sooner than go through it alone.'

'Good gracious!' She laid her hand on his shoulder.

He moved to the other side of the road. 'It's all right now. I've changed those follies for others. But while I had them I began to write, and even now I keep on writing, though I know better. I've got quite a pile of little stories, all harping on this ridiculous idea of getting into touch with Nature.'

'I wish you weren't so modest. It's simply splendid as an idea. Though—but tell me about the Dryad who was engaged to be married. What was she like?'

'I can show you the dell in which the young person disappeared. We pass it on the right in a moment.'

'It does seem a pity that you don't make something of your talents. It seems such a waste to write little stories and never publish them. You must have enough for a book. Life is so full in our days that short stories are the very thing; they get read by people who'd never tackle a novel. For example, at our Dorcas we tried to read out a long affair by Henry James—Herbert saw it recommended in "The Times." There was no doubt it was very good, but one simply couldn't remember from one week to another what had happened. So now our aim is to get something that just lasts the hour. I take you seriously, Rickie, and that is why I am so offensive. You are too modest. People who think they can do nothing so often do nothing. I want you to plunge.'

It thrilled him like a trumpet-blast. She took him seriously. Could he but thank her for her divine affability! But the words would stick in his throat, or worse still, would bring other words along with them. His breath came quickly, for he seldom spoke of his writing, and no one, not even Ansell, had advised him to plunge.

'But do you really think that I could take up literature?'

'Why not? You can try. Even if you fail, you can try. Of course we think you tremendously clever; and I met one of your dons at tea, and he said that your degree was not in the least a proof of your abilities: he said that you knocked up and got flurried in examinations. Oh!'—her cheek flushed—'I wish I was a man. The whole world lies before them. They can do anything. They aren't cooped up with servants and tea-parties and twaddle. But where's this dell where the Dryad disappeared?'

'We've passed it.' He had meant to pass it. It was too beautiful. All he had read, all he had hoped, all he had loved, seemed to quiver in its enchanted air. It was perilous. He dared not enter it with such a woman.

'How long ago?' She turned back. 'I don't want to miss the dell. Here it must be,' she added after a few moments, and sprang up the green bank that hid the entrance from the road. 'Oh, what a jolly place!'

'Go right in if you want to see it,' said Rickie, and did not offer to go with her. She stood for a moment looking at the view, for a few steps will increase a view in Cambridgeshire. The wind blew her dress against her. Then, like a cataract again, she vanished pure and cool into the dell.

The young man thought of her feelings no longer. His heart throbbed louder and louder, and seemed to shake him to pieces.

'Rickie!'

She was calling from the dell. For an answer he sat down where he was, on the dust-bespattered margin. She could call as loud as she liked. The devil had done much, but he should not take him to her.

'Rickie!'—and it came with the tones of an angel. He drove his fingers into his ears, and invoked the name of Gerald. But there was no sign, neither angry motion in the air nor hint of January mist. June—fields of June, sky of June, songs of June. Grass of June beneath him, grass of June over the tragedy he had deemed immortal. A bird called out of the dell: 'Rickie!'

A bird flew into the dell.

'Did you take me for the Dryad?' she asked. She was sitting down with his head on her lap. He had laid it there for a moment before he went out to die, and she had not let him take it away.

'I prayed you might not be a woman,' he whispered.

'Darling, I am very much a woman. I do not vanish into groves and trees. I thought you would never come to me.'

'Did you expect—?'

'I hoped. I called hoping.'

Inside the dell it was neither June nor January. The chalk walls barred out the seasons, and the fir-trees did not seem to feel their passage. Only from time to time the odours of summer slipped in from the wood above, to comment on the waxing year. She bent down to touch him with her lips.

He started, and cried passionately, 'Never forget that your greatest thing is over. I have forgotten: I am too weak. You shall never forget. What I said to you then is greater than what I say to you now. What he gave you then is greater than anything you will get from me.'

She was frightened. Again she had the sense of something abnormal. Then she said, 'What is all this nonsense?' and folded him in her arms.

Chapter Eight

Ansell stood looking at his breakfast-table, which was laid for four instead of for two. His bedmaker, equally peevish, explained how it had happened. Last night, at one in the morning, the porter had been awoke with a note for the kitchens, and in that note Mr Elliot said that all these things were to be sent to Mr Ansell's.

'The fools have sent the original order as well. Here's the lemon-sole for two. I can't move for food.'

'The note being ambigerous, the Kitchens judged best to send it all.' She spoke of the kitchens in a half-respectful, half-pitying way, much as one speaks of Parliament.

'Who's to pay for it?' He peeped into the new dishes. Kidneys entombed in an omelette, hot roast chicken in watery gravy, a glazed but pallid pie.

'And who's to wash it up?' said the bedmaker to her help outside.

Ansell had disputed late last night concerning Schopenhauer, and was a little cross and tired. He bounced over to Tilliard, who kept opposite. Tilliard was eating gooseberry jam.

'Did Elliot ask you to breakfast with me?'

'No,' said Tilliard mildly.

'Well, you'd better come, and bring every one you know.'

So Tilliard came, bearing himself a little formally, for he was not very intimate with his neighbour. Out of the window they called to Widdrington. But he laid his hand on his stomach, thus indicating it was too late.

'Who's to pay for it?' repeated Ansell, as a man appeared from the Buttery carrying coffee on a bright tin tray.

'College coffee! How nice!' remarked Tilliard, who was cutting the pie. 'But before term ends you must come and try my new machine. My sister gave it me. There is a bulb at the top, and as the water boils—'

'He might have counter-ordered the lemon-sole. That's Rickie all over.

Violently economical, and then loses his head, and all the things go bad.'

'Give them to the bedder while they're hot.' This was done. She accepted them dispassionately, with the air of one who lives without nourishment. Tilliard continued to describe his sister's coffee machine.

'What's that?' They could hear panting and rustling on the stairs.

'It sounds like a lady,' said Tilliard fearfully. He slipped the piece of pie back. It fell into position like a brick.

'Is it here? And I right? Is it here?' The door opened and in came Mrs Lewin. 'Oh horrors! I've made a mistake.'

'That's all right,' said Ansell awkwardly.

'I wanted Mr Elliot. Where are they?'

'We expect Mr Elliot every moment,' said Tilliard.

'Don't tell me I'm right,' cried Mrs Lewin, 'and that you're the terrifying Mr Ansell.' And, with obvious relief, she wrung Tilliard warmly by the hand.

'I'm Ansell,' said Ansell, looking very uncouth and grim.

'How stupid of me not to know it,' she gasped, and would have gone on to I know not what, but the door opened again. It was Rickie.

'Here's Miss Pembroke,' he said. 'I am going to marry her.'

There was a profound silence.

'We oughtn't to have done things like this,' said Agnes, turning to Mrs Lewin. 'We have no right to take Mr Ansell by surprise. It is Rickie's fault. He was that obstinate. He would bring us. He ought to be horse-whipped.'

'He ought indeed,' said Tilliard pleasantly, and bolted. Not till he gained his room did he realize that he had been less apt than usual. As for Ansell, the first thing he said was, 'Why didn't you counter-order the lemon-sole?'

In such a situation Mrs Lewin was of priceless value. She led the way to the table, observing, 'I quite agree with Miss Pembroke. I loathe surprises. Never shall I forget my horror when the knife-boy painted the dove's cage with the dove inside. He did it as a surprise. Poor Parsival nearly died. His feathers were bright green!'

'Well, give me the lemon-soles,' said Rickie. 'I like them.'

'The bedder's got them.'

'Well, there you are! What's there to be annoyed about?'

'And while the cage was drying we put him among the bantams. They had been the greatest allies. But I suppose they took him for a parrot or a hawk, or something that bantams hate; for while his cage was drying they picked out his feathers, and *picked* out his feathers, and *Picked* out his feathers, till he was perfectly bald. "Hugo, look," said I. "This is the end of Parsival. Let me have no more surprises." He burst into tears.'

Thus did Mrs Lewin create an atmosphere. At first it seemed unreal, but gradually they got used to it, and breathed scarcely anything else throughout the meal. In such an atmosphere everything seemed of small and equal value, and the engagement of Rickie and Agnes, like the feathers of Parsival, fluttered lightly to the ground. Ansell was generally silent. He was no match for these two quiet clever women. Only once was there a hitch.

They had been talking gaily enough about the betrothal when Ansell suddenly interrupted with, 'When is the marriage?'

'Mr Ansell,' said Agnes, blushing, 'I wish you hadn't asked that. That part's dreadful. Not for years, as far as we can see.'

But Rickie had not seen as far. He had not talked to her of this at all. Last night they had spoken only of love. He exclaimed, 'Oh, Agnes–don't!' Mrs Lewin laughed roguishly.

'Why this delay?' asked Ansell.

Agnes looked at Rickie, who replied, 'I must get money, worse luck.'

'I thought you'd got money.'

He hesitated, and then said, 'I must get my foot on the ladder, then.'

Ansell began with, 'On which ladder?' but Mrs Lewin, using the privilege of her sex, exclaimed, 'Not another word. If there's a thing I abominate, it is plans. My head goes whirling at once.' What she really abominated was questions, and she saw that Ansell was turning serious. To appease him, she put on her clever manner and asked him about Germany. How had it impressed him? Were we so totally unfitted to repel invasion? Was not German scholarship overestimated? He replied discourteously, but he did reply; and if she could have stopped him thinking, her triumph would have been complete.

When they rose to go, Agnes held Ansell's hand for a moment in her own.

'Good-bye,' she said. 'It was very unconventional of us to come as we did, but I don't think any of us are conventional people.'

He only replied, 'Good-bye.' The ladies started off. Rickie lingered behind to whisper, 'I would have it so. I would have you begin square together. I can't talk yet–I've loved her for years–I can't think what she's done it for. I'm going to write short stories. I shall start this afternoon. She declares there may be something in me.'

As soon as he had left, Tilliard burst in, white with agitation, and crying, 'Did you see my awful *faux pas*–about the horsewhip? What shall I do? I must call on Elliot. Or had I better write?'

'Miss Pembroke will not mind,' said Ansell gravely. 'She is unconventional.' He knelt in an arm-chair and hid his face in the back.

'It was like a bomb,' said Tilliard.

'It was meant to be.'

'I do feel a fool. What must she think?'

'Never mind, Tilliard. You've not been as big a fool as myself. At all events, you told her he must be horsewhipped.'

Tilliard hummed a little tune. He hated anything nasty, and there was nastiness in Ansell. 'What did *you* tell her?' he asked.

'Nothing.'

'What do you think of it?'

'I think: Damn those women.'

'Ah, yes. One hates one's friends to get engaged. It makes one feel so old: I think that is one of the reasons. The brother just above me has lately married, and my sister was quite sick about it, though the thing was suitable in every way.'

'Damn *these* women, then,' said Ansell, bouncing round in the chair. 'Damn these particular women.'

'They looked and spoke like ladies.'

'Exactly. Their diplomacy was ladylike. Their lies were ladylike. They've caught Elliot in a most ladylike way. I saw it all during the one moment we were natural. Generally we were clattering after the married one, whom–like a fool–I took for a fool. But for one moment we were natural, and during that moment Miss Pembroke told a lie, and made Rickie believe it was the truth.'

'What did she say?'

'She said "we see" instead of "I see."'

Tilliard burst into laughter. This jaundiced young philosopher, with his kinky view of life, was too much for him.

'She said "we see,"' repeated Ansell, 'instead of "I see," and she made him believe that it was the truth. She caught him and makes him believe that he caught her. She came to see me and makes him think that it is his idea. That is what I mean when I say that she is a lady.'

'You are too subtle for me. My dull eyes could only see two happy people.'

'I never said they weren't happy.'

'Then, my dear Ansell, why are you so cut up? It's beastly when a friend marries–and I grant he's rather young–but I should say it's the best thing for him. A decent woman–and you have proved not one thing against her–a decent woman will keep him up to the mark and stop him getting slack. She'll make him responsible and manly, for much as I like Rickie, I always think him a little effeminate. And, really,'–his voice grew sharper, for he was irritated by Ansell's conceit,–'and, really, you talk as if you were mixed up in the affair. They pay a civil visit to your rooms, and you see nothing but dark plots and challenges to war.'

'War!' cried Ansell, crashing his fists together. 'It's war, then!'

'Oh, what a lot of tommy-rot,' said Tilliard. 'Can't a man and woman get engaged? My dear boy–excuse me talking like this–what on earth is it to do with us? We're his friends, and I hope we always shall be, but we shan't keep his friendship by fighting. We're bound to fall into the background. Wife first, friends some way after. You may resent the order, but it is ordained by nature.'

'The point is, not what's ordained by nature or any other fool, but what's right.'

'You are hopelessly unpractical,' said Tilliard, turning away. 'And let me remind you that you've already given away your case by acknowledging that they're happy.'

'She is happy because she has conquered; he is happy because he has at last hung all the world's beauty on to a single peg. He was always trying to do it. He used to call the peg humanity. Will either of these happinesses last? His can't. Hers only for a time. I fight this woman not only because she fights me, but because I foresee the most appalling catastrophe. She wants Rickie, partly to replace another man whom she lost two years ago, partly to make something out of him. He is to write. In time she will get sick of this. He won't get famous. She will only see how thin he is and how lame. She will long for a jollier husband, and I don't blame her. And, having made him thoroughly miserable and degraded, she will bolt—if she can do it like a lady.'

Such were the opinions of Stewart Ansell.

Chapter Nine

Seven letters written in June:

Cambridge

Dear Rickie—I would rather write, and you can guess what kind of letter this is when I say it is a fair copy: I have been making rough drafts all the morning. When I talk I get angry, and also at times try to be clever—two reasons why I fail to get attention paid to me. This is a letter of the prudent sort. If it makes you break off the engagement, its work is done. You are not a person who ought to marry at all. You are unfitted in body: that we once discussed. You are also unfitted in soul: you want and you need to like many people, and a man of that sort ought not to marry. 'You never were attached to that great sect' who can like one person only, and if you try to enter it you will find destruction. I have read in books—and I cannot afford to despise books, they are all that I have to go by—that men and women desire different things. Man wants to love mankind; woman wants to love one man. When she has him her work is over. She is the emissary of Nature, and Nature's bidding has been fulfilled. But man does not care a damn for Nature—or at least only a very little damn. He cares for a hundred things besides, and the more civilized he is the more he will care for these other hundred things, and demand not only a wife and children, but also friends, and work, and spiritual freedom.

I believe you to be extraordinarily civilized.—Yours ever,

S.A.

Shelthorpe, 9 Sawston Park Road, Sawston

Dear Ansell—But I'm in love—a detail you've forgotten. I can't listen to English Essays. The wretched Agnes may be an 'emissary of Nature,' but I only grinned when I read it. I may be extraordinarily civilized, but I don't feel so; I'm in love, and I've found a woman to love me, and I mean to have the hundred other things as well. She wants me to have them—friends, and work, and spiritual freedom, and everything. You and your books miss this, because your books are too sedate. Read poetry—not only Shelley. Understand Beatrice, and Clara Middleton, and Brunhilde in the first scene of Götterdämmerung. Understand Goethe when he says 'the eternal feminine leads us on,' and don't write another English Essay.–Yours ever affectionately,

R. E.

Cambridge

Dear Rickie–What am I to say? 'Understand Xanthippe and Mrs Bennett, and Elsa in the question scene of Lohengrin'? 'Understand Euripides when he says the eternal feminine leads us a pretty dance'? I shall say nothing of the sort. The allusions in this English Essay shall not be literary. My personal objections to Miss Pembroke are as follows:

(1) She is not serious.
(2) She is not truthful.

Shelthorpe, 9 Sawston Park Road, Sawston

My Dear Stewart–You couldn't know. I didn't know for a moment. But this letter of yours is the most wonderful thing that has ever happened to me yet–more wonderful (I don't exaggerate) than the moment when Agnes promised to marry me. I always knew you liked me, but I never knew how much until this letter. Up to now I think we have been too much like the strong heroes in books who feel so much and say so little, and feel all the more for saying so little. Now that's over and we shall never be that kind of an ass again. We've hit–by accident–upon something permanent. You've written to me, 'I hate the woman who will be your wife,' and I write back, 'Hate her. Can't I love you both?' She will never come between us, Stewart (she wouldn't wish to, but that's by the way), because our friendship has now passed beyond intervention. No third person could break it. We couldn't ourselves, I fancy. We may quarrel and argue till one of us dies, but the thing is registered. I only wish, dear man, you could be happier. For me, it's as if a light was suddenly held behind the world.

R. E.

Shelthorpe, 9 Sawston Park Road, Sawston

Dear Mrs Lewin–The time goes flying, but I am getting to learn my wonderful boy. We speak a great deal about his work. He has just finished a curious thing called "Nemi"–about a Roman ship that is actually sunk in some lake. I cannot think how he describes the things, when he has never seen them. If, as I hope, he goes to Italy next year, he should turn out something really good. Meanwhile we are hunting for a publisher. Herbert believes that a collection of short stories is hard to get published. It is, after all, better to write one long one.

But you must not think we only talk books. What we say on other topics cannot so easily be repeated! Oh, Mrs Lewin, he is a dear, and dearer than ever now that we have him at Sawston. Herbert, in a quiet way, has been making enquiries about those Cambridge friends of his. Nothing against them, but they seem to be terribly eccentric. None of them are good at games, and they spend all their spare time thinking and discussing. They discuss what one knows and what one never will know and what one had much better not know. Herbert says it is because they have not got enough to do.–Ever your grateful and affectionate friend,

Agnes Pembroke

Shelthorpe, 9 Sawston Park Road, Sawston

Dear Mr Silt–Thank you for the congratulations, which I have handed over to the delighted Rickie.* I am sorry that the rumour reached you that I was not pleased. Anything pleases me that promises my sister's happiness, and I have known your cousin nearly as long as you have. It will be a very long engagement, for he must make his way first. The dear boy is not nearly as wealthy as he supposed; having no tastes, and hardly any expenses, he used to talk as if he was a millionaire. He must at least double his income before they can dream of more intimate ties. This has been a bitter pill, but I am glad to say that they have accepted it bravely.

Hoping that you and Mrs Silt will profit by your week at Margate.–I remain, yours very sincerely,

Herbert Pembroke

Cadover, Wilts.

Dear $\left\{ \begin{array}{l} \text{Miss Pembroke,} \\ \text{Agnes,} \end{array} \right\}$ –I hear that you are going to marry my nephew. I have no idea what he is like, and wonder whether you would bring him that I may find out. Isn't September rather a nice month? You might have to go to Stone Henge, but with that exception would be left unmolested. I do hope you will manage to visit. We met once at Mrs Lewin's, and I have a very clear recollection of you.–Believe me, yours sincerely,

Emily Failing

Chapter Ten

The rain tilted a little from the south-west. For the most part it fell from a grey cloud silently, but now and then the tilt increased, and a kind of sigh passed over the country as the drops lashed the walls, trees, shepherds, and other motionless objects that stood in their slanting career. At times the cloud would descend and visibly embrace the earth, to which it had only sent messages; and the earth itself would bring forth clouds–clouds of a whiter

---

* The congratulations were really addressed to Agnes–a social blunder which Mr Pembroke deftly corrects.

breed—which formed in the shallow valleys and followed the courses of the streams. It seemed the beginning of life. Again God said, 'Shall we divide the waters from the land or not? Was not the firmament labour and glory sufficient?' At all events it was the beginning of life pastoral, behind which imagination cannot travel.

Yet complicated people were getting wet—not only the shepherds. For instance, the piano-tuner was sopping. So was the vicar's wife. So were the lieutenant and the peevish damsels in his Battleston car. Gallantry, charity, and art pursued their various missions, perspiring and muddy, while out on the slopes beyond them stood the eternal man and the eternal dog, guarding eternal sheep until the world is vegetarian.

Inside an arbour—which faced east, and thus avoided the bad weather—there sat a complicated person who was dry. She looked at the drenched world with a pleased expression, and would smile when a cloud lay down on the village, or when the rain sighed louder than usual against her solid shelter. Ink, paper-clips, and foolscap paper were on a table before her, and she could also reach an umbrella, a waterproof, a walking-stick, and an electric bell. Her age was between elderly and old, and her forehead was wrinkled with an expression of slight but perpetual pain. But the lines round her mouth indicated that she had laughed a great deal during her life, just as the clean tight skin round her eyes perhaps indicated that she had not often cried. She was dressed in brown silk. A brown silk shawl lay most becomingly over her beautiful hair.

After long thought she wrote on the paper in front of her, 'The subject of this memoir first saw the light at Wolverhampton on May the 14th, 1842.' She laid down her pen and said 'Ugh!' A robin hopped in and she welcomed him. A sparrow followed and she stamped her foot. She watched some thick white water which was sliding like a snake down the gutter of the gravel path. It had just appeared. It must have escaped from a hollow in the chalk up behind. The earth could absorb no longer. The lady did not think of all this, for she hated questions of whence and wherefore, and the ways of the earth ('our dull stepmother') bored her unspeakably. But the water, just the snake of water was amusing, and she flung her golosh at it to dam it up. Then she wrote feverishly, 'The subject of this memoir first saw the light in the middle of the night. It was twenty to eleven. His pa was a parson, but he was not his pa's son, and never went to heaven.' There was the sound of a train, and presently white smoke appeared, rising laboriously through the heavy air. It distracted her, and for about a quarter of an hour she sat perfectly still, doing nothing. At last she pushed the spoilt paper aside, took a fresh piece, and was beginning to write, 'On May the 14th, 1842,' when there was a crunch on the gravel, and a furious voice said, 'I am sorry for Flea Thompson.'

'I daresay I am sorry for him too,' said the lady: her voice was languid and pleasant. 'Who is he?'

'Flea's a liar, and next time we meet he'll be a football.' Off slipped a sodden ulster. He hung it up angrily upon a peg: the arbour provided several.

'But who is he, and why has he that disastrous name?'

'Flea? Fleance. All the Thompsons are named out of Shakespeare. He grazes the Rings.'

'Ah, I see. A pet lamb.'

'Lamb! Shepherd!'

'One of my shepherds?'

'The last time I go with his sheep. But not the last time he sees me. I am sorry for him. He dodged me to-day.'

'Do you mean to say'–she became animated–'that you have been out in the wet keeping the sheep of Flea Thompson?'

'I had to.' He blew on his fingers and took off his cap. Water trickled over his unshaven cheeks. His hair was so wet that it seemed worked upon his scalp in bronze.

'Get away, bad dog!' screamed the lady, for he had given himself a shake and spattered her dress with water. He was a powerful boy of twenty, admirably muscular, but rather too broad for his height. People called him 'Podge' until they were dissuaded. Then they called him 'Stephen' or 'Mr Wonham.' Then he said, 'You can call me Podge if you like.'

'As for Flea—!' he began tempestuously. He sat down by her, and with much heavy breathing told the story–'Flea has a girl at Wintersbridge, and I had to go with his sheep while he went to see her. Two hours. We agreed, Half an hour to go, an hour to kiss his girl, and half an hour back–and he had my bike. Four hours! Four hours and seven minutes I was on the Rings, with a fool of a dog, and sheep doing all they knew to get the turnips.'

'My farm is a mystery to me,' said the lady, stroking her fingers. 'Some day you must really take me to see it. It must be like a Gilbert and Sullivan opera, with a chorus of agitated employers. How is it that I have escaped? Why have I never been summoned to milk the cows, or flay the pigs, or drive the young bullocks to the pasture?'

He looked at her with astonishingly blue eyes–the only dry things he had about him. He could not see into her: she would have puzzled an older and a cleverer man. He may have seen round her.

'A thing of beauty you are not. But I sometimes think you are a joy for ever.'

'I beg your pardon?'

'Oh, you understand right enough,' she exclaimed irritably, and then smiled, for he was conceited, and did not like being told that he was not a thing of beauty. 'Large and steady feet,' she continued, 'have this disadvantage–you can knock down a man, but you will never knock down a woman.'

'I don't know what you mean. I'm not likely—'

'Oh, never mind–never, never mind. I was being funny. I repent. Tell me about the sheep. Why did you go with them?'

'I did tell you. I had to.'

'But why?'

'He had to see his girl.'

'But why?'

His eyes shot past her again. It was so obvious that the man had to see his girl. For two hours though—not for four hours seven minutes.

'Did you have any lunch?'

'I don't hold with regular meals.'

'Did you have a book?'

'I don't hold with books in the open. None of the older men read.'

'Did you commune with yourself, or don't you hold with that?'

'Oh Lord, don't ask me!'

'You distress me. You rob the Pastoral of its lingering romance. Is there no poetry and no thought in England? Is there no one, in all these downs, who warbles with eager thought the Doric lay?'

'Chaps sing to themselves at times, if you mean that.'

'I dream of Arcady. I open my eyes: Wiltshire. Of Amaryllis: Flea Thompson's girl. Of the pensive shepherd, twitching his mantle blue: you in an ulster. Aren't you sorry for me?'

'May I put in a pipe?'

'By all means put a pipe in. In return, tell me of what you were thinking for the four hours and the seven minutes.'

He laughed shyly. 'You do ask a man such questions.'

'Do you simply waste the time?'

'I suppose so.'

'I thought that Colonel Robert Ingersoll says you must be strenuous.'

At the sound of this name he whisked open a little cupboard, and declaring, 'I haven't a moment to spare,' took out of it a pile of 'Clarion' and other reprints, adorned as to their covers with bald or bearded apostles of humanity. Selecting a bald one, he began at once to read, occasionally exclaiming, 'That's got them,' 'That's knocked Genesis,' with similar ejaculations of an aspiring mind. She glanced at the pile. Renan, minus the style. Darwin, minus the modesty. A comic edition of the book of Job, by 'Excelsior,' Pittsburg, Pa. 'The Beginning of Life,' with diagrams. 'Angel or Ape?' by Mrs Julia P. Chunk. She was amused, and wondered idly what was passing within his narrow but not uninteresting brain. Did he suppose that he was going to 'find out'? She had tried once herself, but had since subsided into a sprightly orthodoxy. Why didn't he read poetry, instead of wasting his time between books like these and country like that?

The cloud parted, and the increase of light made her look up. Over the valley she saw a grave sullen down, and on its flanks a little brown smudge—her sheep, together with her shepherd, Fleance Thompson, returned to his duties at last. A trickle of water came through the arbour roof. She shrieked in dismay.

'That's all right,' said her companion, moving her chair, but still keeping his place in his book.

She dried up the spot on the manuscript. Then she wrote: 'Anthony Eustace Failing, the subject of this memoir, was born at Wolverhampton.' But she wrote no more. She was fidgety. Another drop fell from the roof.

Likewise an earwig. She wished she had not been so playful in flinging her golosh into the path. The boy who was overthrowing religion breathed somewhat heavily as he did so. Another earwig. She touched the electric bell.

'I'm going in,' she observed. 'It's far too wet.' Again the cloud parted and caused her to add, 'Weren't you rather kind to Flea?' But he was deep in the book. He read like a poor person, with lips apart and a finger that followed the print. At times he scratched his ear, or ran his tongue along a straggling blonde moustache. His face had after all a certain beauty: at all events the colouring was regal—a steady crimson from throat to forehead: the sun and the winds had worked on him daily ever since he was born. 'The face of a strong man,' thought the lady. 'Let him thank his stars he isn't a silent strong man, or I'd turn him into the gutter.' Suddenly it struck her that he was like an Irish terrier. He worried infinitely as if it was a bone. Gnashing his teeth, he tried to carry the eternal subtleties by violence. As a man he often bored her, for he was always saying and doing the same things. But as a philosopher he really was a joy for ever, an inexhaustible buffoon. Taking up her pen, she began to caricature him. She drew a rabbit-warren where rabbits were at play in four dimensions. Before she had introduced the principal figure, she was interrupted by the footman. He had come up from the house to answer the bell. On seeing her he uttered a respectful cry.

'Madame! Are you here? I am very sorry. I looked for you everywhere. Mr Elliot and Miss Pembroke arrived nearly an hour ago.'

'Oh dear, oh dear!' exclaimed Mrs Failing. 'Take these papers. Where's the umbrella? Mr Stephen will hold it over me. You hurry back and apologize. Are they happy?'

'Miss Pembroke inquired after you, madam.'

'Have they had tea?'

'Yes, madam.'

'Leighton!'

'Yes, sir.'

'I believe you knew she was here all the time. You didn't want to wet your pretty skin.'

'You must not call me "she" to the servants,' said Mrs Failing as they walked away, she limping with a stick, he holding a great umbrella over her. 'I will not have it.' Then more pleasantly, 'And don't tell him he lies. We all lie. I knew quite well they were coming by the four six train. I saw it pass.'

'That reminds me. Another child run over at the Roman crossing. Whish—bang—dead.'

'Oh my foot! Oh my foot, my foot!' said Mrs Failing, and paused to take breath.

'Bad?' he asked callously.

Leighton, with bowed head, passed them with the manuscript and disappeared among the laurels. The twinge of pain, which had been slight, passed away, and they proceeded, descending a green airless corridor which opened into the gravel drive.

'Isn't it odd,' said Mrs Failing, 'that the Greeks should be enthusiastic about laurels—that Apollo should pursue any one who could possibly turn into such a frightful plant? What do you make of Rickie?'

'Oh, I don't know.'

'Shall I lend you his story to read?'

He made no reply.

'Don't you think, Stephen, that a person in your precarious position ought to be civil to my relatives?'

'Sorry, Mrs Failing. I meant to be civil. I only hadn't anything to say.'

She laughed. 'Are you a dear boy? I sometimes wonder; or are you a brute?'

Again he had nothing to say. Then she laughed more mischievously, and said—

'How can you be either, when you are a philosopher? Would you mind telling me—I am so anxious to learn—what happens to people when they die?'

'Don't ask *me*.' He knew by bitter experience that she was making fun of him.

'Oh, but I do ask you. Those paper books of yours are so up-to-date. For instance, what has happened to the child you say was killed on the line?'

The rain increased. The drops pattered hard on the leaves, and outside the corridor men and women were struggling, however stupidly, with the facts of life. Inside it they wrangled. She teased the boy, and laughed at his theories, and proved that no man can be an agnostic who has a sense of humour. Suddenly she stopped, not through any skill of his, but because she had remembered some words of Bacon: 'The true atheist is he whose hands are cauterized by holy things.' She thought of her distant youth. The world was not so humorous then, but it had been more important. For a moment she respected her companion, and determined to vex him no more.

They left the shelter of the laurels, crossed the broad drive, and were inside the house at last. She had got quite wet, for the weather would not let her play the simple life with impunity. As for him, he seemed a piece of the wet.

'Look here,' she cried, as he hurried up to his attic, 'don't shave!'

He was delighted with the permission.

'I have an idea that Miss Pembroke is of the type that pretends to be unconventional and really isn't. I want to see how she takes it. Don't shave.'

In the drawing-room she could hear the guests conversing in the subdued tones of those who have not been welcomed. Having changed her dress and glanced at the poems of Milton, she went to them, with uplifted hands of apology and horror.

'But I must have tea,' she announced, when they had assured her that they understood. 'Otherwise I shall start by being cross. Agnes, stop me. Give me tea.'

Agnes, looking pleased, moved to the table and served her hostess. Rickie followed with a pagoda of sandwiches and little cakes.

'I feel twenty-seven years younger. Rickie, you are so like your father. I feel it is twenty-seven years ago, and that he is bringing your mother to see me for the first time. It is curious—almost terrible—to see history repeating itself.'

The remark was not tactful.

'I remember that visit well,' she continued thoughtfully. 'I suppose it was a wonderful visit, though we none of us knew it at the time. We all fell in love with your mother. I wish she would have fallen in love with us. She couldn't bear me, could she?'

'I never heard her say so, Aunt Emily.'

'No; she wouldn't. I am sure your father said so, though. My dear boy, don't look so shocked. Your father and I hated each other. He said so, I said so, I say so; say so too. Then we shall start fair. – Just a coconut cake. – Agnes, don't you agree that it's always best to speak out?'

'Oh, rather, Mrs Failing. But I'm shockingly straightforward.'

'So am I,' said the lady. 'I like to get down to the bed-rock – Hullo! Slippers? Slippers in the drawing-room?'

A young man had come in silently. Agnes observed with a feeling of regret that he had not shaved. Rickie, after a moment's hesitation, remembered who it was, and shook hands with him.

'You've grown since I saw you last.'

He showed his teeth amiably.

'How long ago was that?' asked Mrs Failing.

'Three years, wasn't it? Came over from the Ansells – friends.'

'How disgraceful, Rickie! Why don't you come and see me oftener?'

He could not retort that she never asked him.

'Agnes will make you come. Oh, let me introduce – Mr Wonham – Miss Pembroke.'

'I am deputy hostess,' said Agnes. 'May I give you some tea?'

'Thank you, but I have had a little beer.'

'It is one of the shepherds,' said Mrs Failing, in low tones. Agnes smiled rather wildly. Mrs Lewin had warned her that Cadover was an extraordinary place, and that one must never be astonished at anything. A shepherd in the drawing-room! No harm. Still one ought to know whether it was a shepherd or not. At all events he was in gentleman's clothing. She was anxious not to start with a blunder, and therefore did not talk to the young fellow, but tried to gather what he was from the demeanour of Rickie.

'I am sure, Mrs Failing, that you need not talk of "making" people come to Cadover. There will be no difficulty, I should say.'

'Thank you, my dear. Do you know who once said those exact words to me?'

'Who?'

'Rickie's mother.'

'Did she really?'

'My sister-in-law was a dear. You will have heard Rickie's praises, but now you must hear mine. I never knew a woman who was so unselfish and yet had such capacities for life.'

'Does one generally exclude the other?' asked Rickie.

'Unselfish people, as a rule, are deathly dull. They have no colour. They think of other people because it is easier. They give money because they are too stupid or too idle to spend it properly on themselves. That was the beauty of your mother – she gave away, but she also spent on herself, or tried to.'

The light faded out of the drawing-room, in spite of it being September and only half-past six. From her low chair Agnes could see the trees by the drive, black against a blackening sky. That drive was half a mile long, and she was praising its gravelled surface when Rickie called in a voice of alarm, 'I say, when did our train arrive?'

'Four-six.'

'I said so.'

'It arrived at four-six on the time-table,' said Mr Wonham. 'I want to know when it got to the station?'

'I tell you again it was punctual. I tell you I looked at my watch. I can do no more.'

Agnes was amazed. Was Rickie mad? A minute ago and they were boring each other over dogs. What had happened?

'Now, now! Quarrelling already?' asked Mrs Failing. The footman, bringing a lamp, lit up two angry faces.

'He says—'

'He says—'

'He says we ran over a child.'

'So you did. You ran over a child in the village at four-seven by my watch. Your train was late. You couldn't have got to the station till four-ten.'

'I don't believe it. We had passed the village by four-seven. Agnes, hadn't we passed the village? It must have been an express that ran over the child.'

'Now is it likely'—he appealed to the practical world—'is it likely that the company would run a stopping train and then an express three minutes after it?'

'A child—' said Rickie. 'I can't believe that the train killed a child.' He thought of their journey. They were alone in the carriage. As the train slackened speed he had caught her for a moment in his arms. The rain beat on the windows, but they were in heaven.

'You've got to believe it,' said the other, and proceeded to 'rub it in'. His healthy, irritable face drew close to Rickie's. 'Two children were kicking and screaming on the Roman crossing. Your train, being late, came down on them. One of them was pulled off the line, but the other was caught. How will you get out of that?'

'And how will you get out of it?' cried Mrs Failing, turning the tables on him. 'Where's the child now? What has happened to its soul? You must know, Agnes, that this young gentleman is a philosopher.'

'Oh, drop all that,' said Mr Wonham, suddenly collapsing.

'Drop it? Where? On my nice carpet?'

'I hate philosophy,' remarked Agnes, trying to turn the subject, for she saw that it made Rickie unhappy.

'So do I. But I daren't say so before Stephen. He despises us women.'

'No, I don't,' said the victim, swaying to and fro on the window-sill, whither he had retreated.

'Yes, he does. He won't even trouble to answer us.

Stephen! Podge! Answer me. What has happened to the child's soul?'

He flung open the window and leant from them into the dusk. They heard him mutter something about a bridge.

'What did I tell you? He won't answer my question.' The delightful moment was approaching when the boy would lose his temper: she knew it by a certain tremor in his heels.

'There wants a bridge,' he exploded. 'A bridge instead of all this rotten talk and the level-crossing. It wouldn't break you to build a two-arch bridge. Then the child's soul, as you call it—well, nothing would have happened to the child at all.'

A gust of night air entered, accompanied by rain. The flowers in the vases rustled, and the flame of the lamp shot up and smoked the glass. Slightly irritated, she ordered him to close the window.

Chapter Eleven

Cadover was not a large house. But it is the largest house with which this story has dealings, and must always be thought of with a respect. It was built about the year 1800, and favoured the architecture of ancient Rome—chiefly by means of five lank pilasters, which stretched from the top of it to the bottom. Between the pilasters was the glass front door, to the right of them the drawing-room windows, to the left of them the windows of the dining-room, above them a triangular area, which the better-class servants knew as a 'pendiment,' and which had in its middle a small round hole, according to the usage of Palladio. The classical note was also sustained by eight grey steps which led from the building down into the drive, and by an attempt at a formal garden on the adjoining lawn. The lawn ended in a Ha-ha ('Ha! ha! who shall regard it?'), and thence the bare land sloped down into the village. The main garden (walled) was to the left as one faced the house, while to the right was that laurel avenue, leading up to Mrs Failing's arbour.

It was a comfortable but not very attractive place, and, to a certain type of mind, its situation was not attractive either. From the distance it showed as a grey box, huddled against evergreens. There was no mystery about it. You saw it for miles. Its hill had none of the beetling romance of Devonshire, none of the subtle contours that prelude a cottage in Kent, but proffered its burden crudely, on a huge bare palm. 'There's Cadover,' visitors would say. 'How small it still looks. We shall be late for lunch.' And the view from the windows, though extensive, would have not been accepted by the Royal Academy. A valley, containing a stream, a road, a railway; over the valley fields of barley and wurzel, divided by no pretty hedges, and passing into a great and formless down—this was the outlook, desolate at all times, and almost terrifying beneath a cloudy sky. The down was called 'Cadbury Rings' ('Cocoa Squares' if you were young and funny), because high upon it—one cannot say 'on the top,' there being scarcely any tops in Wiltshire—because high upon it there stood a double circle of entrenchments. A bank of grass enclosed a ring of turnips, which enclosed a second bank of grass, which enclosed more turnips, and in the middle of the pattern grew one small tree. British? Roman? Saxon? Danish? The competent reader will decide. The Thompson family knew it to be far older than the Franco-German war. It was the property of Government. It was full of gold and dead soldiers who had fought with the soldiers on Castle Rings and been beaten. The road to Londinium, having forded the stream and crossed the valley road and the railway, passed up by these entrenchments. The road to London lay half a mile to the right of them.

To complete this survey one must mention the church and the farm, both of which lay over the stream, in Cadford. Between them they ruled the village, one claiming the souls of the labourers, the other their bodies. If a man desired other religion or other employment he must leave. The church lay up by the railway, the farm was down by the water meadows. The vicar, a gentle charitable man, scarcely realized his power, and never tried to abuse it. Mr Wilbraham, the agent, was of another mould. He knew his place, and kept others to theirs: all society seemed spread before him like a map. The line between the county and the local, the line between the labourer and the artisan—he knew them all, and strengthened them with no uncertain touch. Everything with him was graduated—carefully graduated civility towards his superiors, towards his inferiors carefully graduated incivility. So—for he was a thoughtful person—so alone, declared he, could things be kept together.

Perhaps the Comic Muse, to whom so much is now attributed, had caused this estate to be left to Mr Failing. Mr Failing was the author of some brilliant books on socialism—that was why his wife married him—and for twenty-five years he reigned up at Cadover and tried to put his theories into practice. He believed that things could be kept together by accenting the similarities, not the differences of men. 'We are all much more alike than we confess,' was one of his favourite speeches. As a speech it sounded very well, and his wife had applauded; but when it resulted in hard work, evenings in the reading-room, mixed parties, and long unobtrusive talks with dull people, she got bored. In her piquant way she declared that she was not going to love her husband, and succeeded. He took it quietly, but his brilliancy decreased. His health grew worse, and he knew that when he died there was no one to carry on his work. He felt, besides, that he had done very little. Toil as he would, he had not a practical mind, and could never dispense with Mr Wilbraham. For all his tact, he would often stretch out the hand of brotherhood too soon, or withhold it when it would have been accepted. Most people misunderstood him, or only understood him when he was dead. In after years his reign became a golden age; but he counted a few disciples in his lifetime, a few young labourers and tenant farmers, who swore tempestuously that he was not really a fool. This, he told himself, was as much as he deserved.

Cadover was inherited by his widow. She tried to sell it; she tried to let it; but she asked too much, and as it was neither a pretty place nor fertile, it was left on her hands. With many a groan she settled down to banishment. Wiltshire people, she declared, were the stupidest in England. She told them so to their faces, which made them no brighter. And their county was worthy of them: no distinction in it—no style—simply land.

But her wrath passed, or remained only as a graceful fretfulness. She made the house comfortable, and abandoned the farm to Mr Wilbraham. With a good deal of care she selected a small circle of acquaintants, and had them to stop in the summer months. In the winter she would go to town and frequent the *salons* of the literary. As her lameness increased she moved about less, and at the time of her nephew's visit seldom left the place that had been forced upon her as a home. Just now she was busy. A prominent politician had quoted her husband. The young generation asked, 'Who is this Mr Failing?' and the publishers wrote, 'Now is the time.' She was collecting some essays and penning an introductory memoir.

Rickie admired his aunt, but did not care for her. She reminded him too much of his father. She had the same affliction, the same heartlessness, the same habit of taking life with a laugh—as if life is a pill! He also felt that she had neglected him. He would not have asked much: as for 'prospects,' they never entered his head; but she was his only near relative, and a little kindness and hospitality during the lonely years would have made incalculable difference. Now that he was happier and could bring her Agnes, she had asked him to stop at once. The sun as it rose next morning spoke to him of a new life. He too had a purpose and a value in the world at last. Leaning out of the window, he gazed at the earth washed clean and heard through the pure air the distant noises of the farm.

But that day nothing was to remain divine but the weather. His aunt, for reasons of her own, decreed that he should go for a ride with the Wonham boy. They were to look at Old Sarum, proceed thence to Salisbury, lunch there, see the sights, call on a certain canon for tea, and return to Cadover in the evening. The arrangement suited no one. He did not want to ride, but to be with Agnes; nor did Agnes want to be parted from him, nor Stephen to go with him. But the clearer the wishes of her guests became, the more determined was Mrs Failing to disregard them. She smoothed away every difficulty, she converted every objection into a reason, and she ordered the horses for half-past nine.

'It is a bore,' he grumbled as he sat in their little private sitting-room, breaking his finger-nails upon the coachman's gaiters. 'I can't ride. I shall fall off. We should have been so happy here. It's just like Aunt Emily. Can't you imagine her saying afterwards, "Lovers are absurd. I made a point of keeping them apart," and then everybody laughing.'

With a pretty foretaste of the future, Agnes knelt before him and did the gaiters up. 'Who is this Mr Wonham, by the bye?'

'I don't know. Some connection of Mr Failing's, I think.'

'Does he live here?'

'He used to be at school or something. He seems to have grown into a tiresome person.'

'I suppose that Mrs Failing has adopted him?'

'I suppose so. I believe that she has been quite kind. I do hope that she'll be kind to you this morning. I hate leaving you with her.'

'Why, you say she likes me.'

'Yes, but that wouldn't prevent—you see she doesn't mind what she says or what she repeats if it amuses her. If she thought it really funny, for instance, to break off our engagement, she'd try.'

'Dear boy, what a frightful remark! But it would be funnier for us to see her trying. Whatever could she do?'

He kissed the hands that were still busy with the fastenings. 'Nothing. I can't see one thing. We simply lie open to each other, you and I. There isn't one new corner in either of us that she could reveal. It's only that I always have in this house the most awful feeling of insecurity.'

'Why?'

'If any one says or does a foolish thing it's always here. All the family breezes have started here. It's a kind of focus for aimed and aimless scandal. You know, when my father and mother had their special quarrel, my aunt was mixed up in it—I never knew how or how much—but you may be sure that she didn't calm things down, unless she found things more entertaining calm.'

'Rickie! Rickie!' cried the lady from the garden, 'your riding-master's impatient.'

'We really oughtn't to talk of her like this here,' whispered Agnes. 'It's a horrible habit.'

'The habit of the country, Agnes. Ugh, this gossip!' Suddenly he flung his arms over her. 'Dear—dear—let's beware of I don't know what—of nothing at all perhaps.'

'Oh, buck up!' yelled the irritable Stephen. 'Which am I to shorten—left stirrup or right?'

'Left!' shouted Agnes.

'How many holes?'

They hurried down. On the way she said: 'I'm glad of the warning. Now I'm prepared. Your aunt will get nothing out of me.'

Her betrothed tried to mount with the wrong foot, according to his invariable custom. She also had to pick up his whip. At last they started, the boy showing off pretty consistently, and she was left alone with her hostess.

'Dido is quiet as a lamb,' said Mrs Failing, 'and Stephen is a good fielder. What a blessing it is to have cleared out the men. What shall you and I do this heavenly morning?'

'I'm game for anything.'

'Have you quite unpacked?'

'Yes.'

'Any letters to write?'

'No.'

'Then let's go to my arbour. No, we won't. It gets the morning sun, and it'll be too hot to-day.' Already she regretted clearing out the men. On such a morning she would have liked to drive, but her third animal had gone lame. She feared, too, that Miss Pembroke was going to bore her. However, they did go to the arbour. In languid tones she pointed out the various objects of interest.

'There's the Cad, which goes into the something, which goes into the Avon. Cadbury Rings opposite, Cadchurch to the extreme left: you can't see it. You were there last night. It is famous for the drunken parson and the railway-station. Then Cad Dauntsey. Then Cadford, that side of the stream, connected with Cadover, this. Observe the fertility of the Wiltshire mind.'

'A terrible lot of Cads,' said Agnes brightly.

Mrs Failing divided her guests into those who made this joke and those who did not. The latter class was very small.

'The vicar of Cadford—not the nice drunkard—declares the name is really "Chadford," and he worried on till I put up a window to St Chad in our church. His wife pronounces it "Hyadford." I could smack them both. How do you like Podge? Ah! you jump; I meant you to. How do you like Podge Wonham?'

'Very nice,' said Agnes, laughing.

'Nice! He is a hero.'

There was a long interval of silence. Each lady looked, without much interest, at the view. Mrs Failing's attitude towards Nature was severely æsthetic—an attitude more sterile than the severely practical. She applied the test of beauty to shadow and odour and sound; they never filled her with reverence or excitement; she never knew them as a resistless trinity that may intoxicate the worshipper with joy. If she liked a ploughed field, it was only as a spot of colour—not also as a hint of the endless strength of the earth. And to-day she could approve of one cloud, but object to its fellow. As for Miss Pembroke, she was not approving or objecting at all. 'A hero?' she questioned, when the interval had passed. Her voice was indifferent, as if she had been thinking of other things.

'A hero? Yes. Didn't you notice how heroic he was?'

'I don't think I did.'

'Not at dinner? Ah, Agnes, always look out for heroism at dinner. It is their great time. They live up to the stiffness of their shirt fronts. Do you mean to say that you never noticed how he sat down Rickie?'

'Oh, that about poetry!' said Agnes, laughing. 'Rickie would not mind it for a moment. But why do you single out that as heroic?'

'To snub people! to set them down! to be rude to them! to make them feel small! Surely that's the life-work of a hero?'

'I shouldn't have said that. And as a matter of fact Mr Wonham was wrong over the poetry. I made Rickie look it up afterwards.'

'But of course. A hero always is wrong.'

'To me,' she persisted, rather gently, 'a hero has always been a strong wonderful being, who champions—'

'Ah, wait till you are the dragon! I have been a dragon most of my life, I think. A dragon that wants nothing but a peaceful cave. Then in comes the strong, wonderful, delightful being, and gains a princess by piercing my hide. No, seriously, my dear Agnes, the chief characteristics of a hero are infinite disregard for the feelings of others, plus general inability to understand them.'

'But surely Mr Wonham—'

'Yes; aren't we being unkind to the poor boy. Ought we to go on talking?'

Agnes waited, remembering the warnings of Rickie, and thinking that anything she said might perhaps be repeated.

'Though even if he was here he wouldn't understand what we are saying.'

'Wouldn't understand?'

Mrs Failing gave the least flicker of an eye towards her companion. 'Did you take him for clever?'

'I don't think I took him for anything.' She smiled. 'I have been thinking of other things, and of another boy.'

'But do think for a moment of Stephen. I will describe how he spent yesterday. He rose at eight. From eight to eleven he sang. The song was called, "Father's boots will soon fit Willie." He stopped once to say to the footman, "She'll never finish her book. She idles." "She" being I. At eleven he went out, and stood in the rain till four, but had the luck to see a child run over at the level-crossing. By half-past four he had knocked the bottom out of Christianity.'

Agnes looked bewildered.

'Aren't you impressed? I was. I told him that he was on no account to unsettle the vicar. Open that cupboard. One of those sixpenny books tells Podge that he's made of hard little black things, another that he's made of brown things, larger and squashy. There seems a discrepancy, but anything is better for a thoughtful youth than to be made in the Garden of Eden. Let us eliminate the poetic, at whatever cost to the probable.' Then for a moment she spoke more gravely. 'Here he is at twenty, with nothing to hold on by. I don't know what's to be done. I suppose it's my fault. But I've never had any bother over the Church of England; have you?'

'Of course I go with my Church,' said Miss Pembroke, who hated this style of conversation. 'I don't know, I'm sure. I think you should consult a man.'

'Would Rickie help me?'

'Rickie would do anything he can.' And Mrs Failing noted the half official way in which she vouched for her lover. 'But of course Rickie is a little—complicated. I doubt whether Mr Wonham would understand him. He wants—doesn't he?—some one who's a little more assertive and more accustomed to boys. Some one more like my brother.'

'Agnes!' she seized her by the arm. 'Do you suppose that Mr Pembroke would undertake my Podge?'

She shook her head. 'His time is so filled up. He gets a boarding-house next term. Besides—after all I don't know what Herbert would do.'

'Morality. He would teach him morality. The Thirty-Nine Articles may come of themselves, but if you have no morals you come to grief. Morality is all I demand from Mr Herbert Pembroke. He shall be excused the use of the globes. You know, of course, that Stephen was expelled from a public school? He stole.'

The school was not a public one, and the expulsion, or rather request for removal, had taken place when Stephen was fourteen. A violent spasm of dishonesty—such as often heralds the approach of manhood—had overcome him. He stole everything, especially what was difficult to steal, and hid the plunder beneath a loose plank in the passage. He was betrayed by the inclusion of a ham. This was the crisis of his career. His benefactress was just then rather bored with him. He had stopped being a pretty boy, and she rather doubted whether she would see him through. But she was so enraged with the letters of the schoolmaster, and so delighted with those of the criminal, that she had him back and gave him a prize.

'No,' said Agnes, 'I didn't know. I should be happy to speak to Herbert, but, as I said, his time will be very full. But I know he has friends who make a speciality of weakly or–or unusual boys.'

'My dear, I've tried it. Stephen kicked the weakly boys and robbed apples with the unusual ones. He was expelled again.'

Agnes began to find Mrs Failing rather tiresome. Wherever you trod on her, she seemed to slip away from beneath your feet. Agnes liked to know where she was and where other people were as well. She said: 'My brother thinks a great deal of home life. I daresay he'd think that Mr Wonham is best where he is–with you. You have been so kind to him. You'–she paused–'have been to him both father and mother.'

'I'm too hot,' was Mrs Failing's reply. It seemed that Miss Pembroke had at last touched a topic on which she was reticent. She rang the electric bell–it was only to tell the footman to take the reprints to Mr Wonham's room–and then murmuring something about work, proceeded herself to the house.

'Mrs Failing—' said Agnes, who had not expected such a speedy end to their chat.

'Call me Aunt Emily. My dear?'

'Aunt Emily, what did you think of that story Rickie sent you?'

'It is bad,' said Mrs Failing. 'But. But. But.' Then she escaped, having told the truth, and yet leaving a pleasurable impression behind her.

Chapter Twelve

The excursion to Salisbury was but a poor business–in fact, Rickie never got there. They were not out of the drive before Mr Wonham began doing acrobatics. He showed Rickie how very quickly he could turn round in his saddle and sit with his face to Æneas's tail. 'I see,' said Rickie coldly, and became almost cross when they arrived in this condition at the gate behind the house, for he had to open it, and was afraid of falling. As usual, he anchored just beyond the fastenings, and then had to turn Dido, who seemed as long as a battleship. To his relief a man came forward and murmuring, 'Worst gate in the parish,' pushed it wide and held it respectfully. 'Thank you,' cried Rickie; 'many thanks.' But Stephen, who was riding into the world back first, said majestically, 'No, no; it doesn't count. You needn't think it. You make it worse by touching your hat. Four hours and seven minutes! You'll see me again.' The man answered nothing.

'Eh, but I'll hurt him,' he chanted, as he swung into position. 'That was Flea. Eh, but he's forgotten my fists; eh, but I'll hurt him.'

'Why?' ventured Rickie. Last night, over cigarettes, he had been bored to death by the story of Flea. The boy had a little reminded him of Gerald—the Gerald of history, not the Gerald of romance. He was more genial, but there was the same brutality, the same peevish insistence on the pound of flesh.

'Hurt him till he learns.'

'Learns what?'

'Learns, of course,' retorted Stephen. Neither of them was very civil. They did not dislike each other, but they each wanted to be somewhere else—exactly the situation that Mrs Failing had expected.

'He behaved badly,' said Rickie, 'because he is poorer than we are, and more ignorant. Less money has been spent on teaching him to behave.'

'Well, I'll teach him for nothing.'

'Perhaps his fists are stronger than yours!'

'They aren't. I looked.'

After this conversation flagged. Rickie glanced back at Cadover, and thought of the insipid day that lay before him. Generally he was attracted by fresh people, and Stephen was almost fresh: they had been to him symbols of the unknown, and all that they did was interesting. But now he cared for the unknown no longer. He knew.

Mr Wilbraham passed them in his dog-cart, and lifted his hat to his employer's nephew. Stephen he ignored: he could not find him on the map.

'Good morning,' said Rickie. 'What a lovely morning!'

'I say,' called the other, 'another child dead!' Mr Wilbraham, who had seemed inclined to chat, whipped up his horse and left them.

'There goes an out and outer,' said Stephen; and then, as if introducing an entirely new subject—'Don't you think Flea Thompson treated me disgracefully?'

'I suppose he did. But I'm scarcely the person to sympathize.' The allusion fell flat, and he had to explain it. 'I should have done the same myself—promised to be away two hours, and stopped four.'

'Stopped—oh—oh, I understand. You being in love, you mean?'

He smiled and nodded.

'Oh, I've no objection to Flea loving. He says he can't help it. But as long as my fists are stronger, he's got to keep it in line.'

'In line?'

'A man like that, when he's got a girl, thinks the rest can go to the devil. He goes cutting his work and breaking his word. Wilbraham ought to sack him. I promise you when I've a girl I'll keep her in line, and if she turns nasty, I'll get another.'

Rickie smiled and said no more. But he was sorry that any one should start life with such a creed—all the more sorry because the creed caricatured his own. He too believed that life should be in a line—a line of enormous length, full of countless interests and countless figures, all well beloved. But woman was not to be 'kept' to this line. Rather did she advance it continually, like some triumphant general, making each unit still more interesting, still more lovable, than it had been before. He loved Agnes, not only for herself, but because she was lighting up the human world. But he could scarcely explain this to an inexperienced animal, nor did he make the attempt.

For a long time they proceeded in silence. The hill behind Cadover was in harvest, and the horses moved regretfully between the sheaves. Stephen had picked a grass leaf, and was blowing cat-calls upon it. He blew very well, and this morning all his soul went into the wail. For he was ill. He was tortured with the feeling that he could not get away and do—do something, instead of being civil to this anæmic prig. Four hours in the rain was better than this: he had not wanted to fidget in the rain. But now the air was like wine, and the stubble was smelling of wet, and over his head white clouds trundled more slowly and more seldom through broadening tracts of blue. There never had been such a morning, and he shut up his eyes and called to it. And whenever he called, Rickie shut up his eyes and winced.

At last the blade broke. 'We don't go quick, do we?' he remarked, and looked on the weedy track for another.

'I wish you wouldn't let me keep you. If you were alone you would be galloping or something of that sort.'

'I was told I must go your pace,' he said mournfully. 'And you promised Miss Pembroke not to hurry.'

'Well, I'll disobey.' But he could not rise above a gentle trot, and even that nearly jerked him out of the saddle.

'Sit like *this*', said Stephen. 'Can't you see—like *this*?' Rickie lurched forward, and broke his thumb-nail on the horse's neck. It bled a little, and had to be bound up.

'Thank you—awfully kind—no tighter, please—I'm simply spoiling your day.'

'I can't think how a man can help riding. You've only to leave it to the horse so!—so!—just as you leave it to the water in swimming.'

Rickie left it to Dido, who stopped immediately.

'I said *leave* it.' His voice rose irritably. 'I didn't say "die." Of course she stops if you die. First you sit her as if you're Sandow exercising, and then you sit like a corpse. Can't you tell her you're alive? That's all she wants.'

In trying to convey the information, Rickie dropped his whip. Stephen picked it up and rammed it into the belt of his own Norfolk jacket. He was scarcely a fashionable horseman. He was not even graceful. But he rode as a living man, though Rickie was too much bored to notice it. Not a muscle in him was idle, not a muscle working hard. When he returned from a gallop his limbs were still unsatisfied and his manners still irritable. He did not know that he was ill: he knew nothing about himself at all.

'Like a howdah in the Zoo,' he grumbled. 'Mother Failing will buy elephants.' And he proceeded to criticize his benefactress. Rickie, keenly alive to bad taste, tried to stop him, and gained instead a criticism of religion. Stephen overthrew the Mosaic cosmogony. He pointed out the discrepancies in the Gospels. He levelled his wit against the most beautiful spire in the world, now rising against the southern sky. Between whiles he went for a gallop. After a time Rickie stopped listening, and simply went his way. For Dido was a perfect mount, and as indifferent to the motions of Æneas as if she was strolling in the Elysian fields. He had had a bad night, and the strong air made him sleepy. The wind blew from the Plain. Cadover and its valley had disappeared, and though they had not climbed much and could not see far, there was a sense of infinite space. The fields were enormous, like fields on the Continent, and the brilliant sun showed up their colours well. The green of the turnips, the gold of the harvest, and the brown of the newly turned clods, were each contrasted with morsels of grey down. But the general effect was pale, or rather silvery, for Wiltshire is not a county of heavy tints. Beneath these colours lurked the unconquerable chalk, and wherever the soil was poor it emerged. The grassy track, so gay with scabious and bed-straw, was snow-white at the bottom of its ruts. A dazzling amphitheatre gleamed in the flank of a distant hill, cut for some Olympian audience. And here and there, whatever the surface crop, the earth broke into little embankments, little ditches, little mounds: there had been no lack of drama to solace the gods.

In Cadover, the perilous house, Agnes had already parted from Mrs Failing. His thoughts returned to her. Was she, the soul of truth, in safety? Was her purity vexed by the lies and selfishness? Would she elude the caprice which had, he vaguely knew, caused suffering before? Ah, the frailty of joy! Ah, the myriads of longings that pass without fruition, and the turf grows over them! Better men, women as noble—they had died up here and their dust had been mingled, but only their dust. These are morbid thoughts, but who dare contradict them? There is much good luck in the world, but it is luck. We are none of us safe. We are children, playing or quarrelling on the line, and some of us have Rickie's temperament, or his experiences, and admit it.

So he mused, that anxious little speck, and all the land seemed to comment on his fears and on his love.

Their path lay upward, over a great bald skull, half grass, half stubble. It seemed each moment there would be a splendid view. The view never came, for none of the inclines were sharp enough, and they moved over the skull for many minutes, scarcely shifting a landmark or altering the blue fringe of the distance. The spire of Salisbury did alter, but very slightly, rising and falling like the mercury in a thermometer. At the most it would be half hidden; at the least the tip would show behind the swelling barrier of earth. They passed two elder-trees—a great event. The bare patch, said Stephen, was owing to the gallows. Rickie nodded. He had lost all sense of incident. In this great solitude—more solitary than any Alpine range—he and Agnes were floating alone and for ever, between the shapeless earth and the shapeless clouds. An immense silence seemed to move towards them. A lark stopped singing, and they were glad of it. They were approaching the Throne of God. The silence touched them; the earth and all danger dissolved, but ere they quite vanished Rickie heard himself saying, 'Is it exactly what we intended?'

'Yes,' said a man's voice; 'it's the old plan.' They were in another valley. Its sides were thick with trees. Down it ran another stream and another road:

it, too, sheltered a string of villages. But all was richer, larger, and more beautiful—the valley of the Avon below Amesbury.

'I've been asleep!' said Rickie, in awestruck tones.

'Never!' said the other facetiously. 'Pleasant dreams?'

'Perhaps—I'm really tired of apologizing to you. How long have you been holding me on?'

'All in the day's work.' He gave him back the reins.

'Where's that round hill?'

'Gone where the good niggers go. I want a drink.'

This is Nature's joke in Wiltshire—her one joke. You toil on windy slopes, and feel very primeval. You are miles from your fellows, and lo! a little valley full of elms and cottages. Before Rickie had waked up to it, they had stopped by a thatched public-house, and Stephen was yelling like a maniac for beer.

There was no occasion to yell. He was not very thirsty, and they were quite ready to serve him. Nor need he have drunk in the saddle, with the air of a warrior who carries important despatches and has not the time to dismount. A real soldier, bound on a similar errand, rode up to the inn, and Stephen at first feared that he would yell louder, and was hostile. But they made friends and treated each other, and slanged the proprietor and ragged the pretty girls; while Rickie, as each wave of vulgarity burst over him, sunk his head lower and lower and wished that the earth would swallow him up. He was only used to Cambridge, and to a very small corner of that. He and his friends there believed in free speech. But they spoke freely about generalities. They were scientific and philosophic. They would have shrunk from the empirical freedom that results from a little beer.

That was what annoyed him as he rode down the new valley with two chattering companions. He was more skilled than they were in the principles of human existence, but he was not so indecently familiar with the examples. A sordid village scandal—such as Stephen described as a huge joke—sprang from certain defects in human nature, with which he was theoretically acquainted. But the example! He blushed at it like a maiden lady, in spite of its having a parallel in a beautiful idyll of Theocritus. Was experience going to be such a splendid thing after all? Were the outside of houses so very beautiful?

'That's spicy!' the soldier was saying. 'Got any more like that?'

'I'se got a pome,' said Stephen, and drew a piece of paper from his pocket. The valley had broadened. Old Sarum rose before them, ugly and majestic.

'Write this yourself?' he asked, chuckling.

'Rather,' said Stephen, lowering his head and kissing Æneas between the ears.

'But who's old Em'ly?' Rickie winced and frowned.

'Now you're asking.

> *"Old Em'ly she limps,*
> *And as—"* '

'I am so tired,' said Rickie. Why should he stand it any longer? He would go home to the woman he loved. 'Do you mind if I give up Salisbury?'

'But we've seen nothing!' cried Stephen.

'I shouldn't enjoy anything, I am so absurdly tired.'

'Left turn, then—all in the day's work.' He bit at his moustache angrily.

'Good gracious me, man!—of course I'm going back alone. I'm not going to spoil your day. How could you think it of me?'

Stephen gave a loud sigh of relief. 'If you do want to go home, here's your whip. Don't fall off. Say to her *you* wanted it, or there might be ructions.'

'Certainly. Thank you for your kind care of me.'

> *'Old Em'ly she limps,*
> *And as—'*

Soon he was out of earshot. Soon they were lost to view. Soon they were out of his thoughts. He forgot the coarseness and the drinking and the ingratitude. A few months ago he would not have forgotten so quickly, and he might also have detected something else. But a lover is dogmatic. To him the world shall be beautiful and pure. When it is not, he ignores it.

'He's not tired,' said Stephen to the soldier; 'he wants his girl.' And they winked at each other, and cracked jokes over the eternal comedy of love. They asked each other if they'd let a girl spoil a morning's ride. They both exhibited a profound cynicism. Stephen, who was quite without ballast, described the household at Cadover: he should say that Rickie would find Miss Pembroke kissing the footman.

'I say the footman's kissing old Em'ly.'

'Jolly day,' said Stephen. His voice was suddenly constrained. He was not sure whether he liked the soldier after all, nor whether he had been wise in showing him his compositions.

> *'Old Em'ly she limps,*
> *And as I—'*

'All right, Thomas. That'll do.'

> *'Old Em'ly—'*

'I wish you'd dry up, like a good fellow. This is the lady's horse, you know, hang it, after all.'

'In-deed!'

'Don't you see—when a fellow's on a horse, he can't let another fellow—kind of—don't you know?'

The man did know. 'There's sense in that,' he said approvingly. Peace was restored, and they would have reached Salisbury if they had not had some more beer. It unloosed the soldier's fancies, and again he spoke of old Em'ly and recited the poem, with Aristophanic variations.

'Jolly day,' repeated Stephen, with a straightening of the eyebrows and a quick glance at the other's body. He then warned him against the variations.

In consequence he was accused of being a member of the Y.M.C.A. His blood boiled at this. He refuted the charge, and became great friends with the soldier, for the third time.

'Any objection to "Sorcy Mr and Mrs Tackleton"?'

'Rather not.'

The soldier sang 'Saucy Mr and Mrs Tackleton.' It is really a work for two voices, most of the sauciness disappearing when taken as a solo. Nor is Mrs Tackleton's name Em'ly.

'I call it a jolly rotten song,' said Stephen crossly. 'I won't stand being got at.'

'P'r'aps y'like therold songs. Lishen.

> *"Of all the gulls that arsshmart,*
> *There's none like pretty—Em'ly;*
> *For she's the darling of merart—" '*

'Now, that's wrong.' He rode up close to the singer.

'Shright.'

''Tisn't.'

'It's as my mother taught me.'

'I don't care.'

'I'll not alter from my mother's way.'

Stephen was baffled. Then he said, 'How does your mother make it rhyme?'

'Wot?'

'Squat. You're an ass, and I'm not. Poems want rhymes. "Alley" comes next line.'

He said 'alley' was—welcome to come if it liked.

'It can't. You want Sally. Sally—alley. Em'ly—alley doesn't do.'

'Emily—femily!' cried the soldier, with an inspiration that was not his when sober. 'My mother taught me femily.

> *"For she's the darling of merart,*
> *And she lives in my femily." '*

'Well, you'd best be careful, Thomas, and your mother too.'

'*Your* mother's no better than she should be,' said Thomas vaguely.

'Do you think I haven't heard that before?' retorted the boy.

The other concluded he might now say anything. So he might—the name of old Emily excepted. Stephen cared little about his benefactress's honour, but a great deal about his own. He had made Mrs Failing into a test. For the moment he would die for her, as a knight would die for a glove. He is not to be distinguished from a hero.

Old Sarum was passed. They approached the most beautiful spire in the world. 'Lord! another of these large churches!' said the soldier. Unfriendly to Gothic, he lifted both hands to his nose, and declared that old Em'ly was buried there. He lay in the mud. His horse trotted back towards Amesbury.

Stephen had twisted him out of the saddle.

'I've done him!' he yelled, though no one was there to hear. He rose up in his stirrups and shouted with joy. He flung his arms round Æneas's neck. The elderly horse understood, capered, and bolted. It was a centaur that dashed into Salisbury and scattered the people. In the stable he would not dismount. 'I've done him!' he yelled to the ostlers–apathetic men. Stretching upwards, he clung to a beam. Æneas moved on and he was left hanging. Greatly did he incommode them by his exercises. He pulled up, he circled, he kicked the other customers. At last he fell to the earth, deliciously fatigued. His body worried him no longer.

He went, like the baby he was, to buy a white linen hat. There were soldiers about, and he thought it would disguise him. Then he had a little lunch to steady the beer. This day had turned out admirably. All the money that should have fed Rickie he could spend on himself. Instead of toiling over the Cathedral and seeing the stuffed penguins, he could stop the whole time in the cattle market. There he met and made some friends. He watched the cheap-jacks and saw how necessary it was to have a confident manner. He spoke confidently himself about lambs, and people listened. He spoke confidently about pigs, and they roared with laughter. He must learn more about pigs. He witnessed a performance–not too namby-pamby–of Punch and Judy. 'Hullo, Podge!' cried a naughty little girl. He tried to catch her, and failed. She was one of the Cadford children. For Salisbury on market day, though it is not picturesque, is certainly representative, and you read the names of half the Wiltshire villages upon the carriers' carts. He found, in Penny Farthing Street, the cart from Wintersbridge. It would not start for several hours, but the passengers always used it as a club, and sat in it every now and then during the day. No less than three ladies were there now, staring at the shafts. One of them was Flea Thompson's girl. He asked her, quite politely, why her lover had broken faith with him in the rain. She was silent. He warned her of approaching vengeance. She was still silent, but another woman hoped that a gentleman would not be hard on a poor person. Something in this annoyed him; it wasn't a question of gentility and poverty–it was a question of two men. He determined to go back by Cadbury Rings, where the shepherd would now be.

He did. But this part must be treated lightly. He rode up to the culprit with the air of a Saint George, spoke a few stern words from the saddle, tethered his steed to a hurdle, and took off his coat. 'Are you ready?' he asked.

'Yes, sir,' said Flea, and flung him on his back.

'That's not fair,' he protested.

The other did not reply, but flung him on his head.

'How on earth did you learn that?'

'By trying often,' said Flea.

Stephen sat on the ground, picking mud out of his forehead. 'I meant it to be fists,' he said gloomily.

'I know, sir.'

'It's jolly smart though, and–and I beg your pardon all round.' It cost him a great deal to say this, but he was sure that it was the right thing to say. He must acknowledge the better man. Whereas most people, if they provoke a fight and are flung, say, 'You cannot rob me of my moral victory.'

There was nothing further to be done. He mounted again, not exactly depressed, but feeling that this delightful world is extraordinary unreliable. He had never expected to fling the soldier or to be flung by Flea. 'One nips or is nipped,' he thought, 'and never knows beforehand. I should not be surprised if many people had more in them than I suppose, while others were just the other way round. I haven't seen that sort of thing in Ingersoll, but it's quite important.' Then his thoughts turned to a curious incident of long ago, when he had been 'nipped'—as a little boy. He was trespassing in those woods, when he met in a narrow glade a flock of sheep. They had neither dog nor shepherd, and advanced towards him silently. He was accustomed to sheep, but had never happened to meet them in a wood before, and disliked it. He retired, slowly at first, then fast; and the flock, in a dense mass, pressed after him. His terror increased. He turned and screamed at their long white faces; and still they came on, all stuck together like some horrible jelly. If once he got into them! Bellowing and screeching, he rushed into the undergrowth, tore himself all over, and reached home in convulsions. Mr Failing, his only grown-up friend, was sympathetic, but quite stupid. 'Pan ovium custos,' he remarked as he pulled out the thorns. 'Why not?' 'Pan ovium custos.' Stephen learnt the meaning of the phrase at school, 'A pan of eggs for custard.' He still remembered how the other boys looked as he peeped at them between his legs, awaiting the descending cane.

So he returned, full of pleasant disconnected thoughts. He had had a rare good time. He liked every one—even that poor little Elliot—and yet no one mattered. They were all out. On the landing he saw the new housemaid. He felt skittish and irresistible. Should he slip his arm round her waist? Perhaps better not; she might box his ears. And he wanted to smoke on the roof before dinner. So he only said, 'Please will you stop the boy blacking my brown boots,' and she, with downcast eyes, answered, 'Yes, sir; I will indeed.'

His room was in the pediment. Classical architecture, like all things in this world that attempt serenity, is bound to have its lapses into the undignified, and Cadover lapsed hopelessly when it came to Stephen's room. It gave him one round window, to see through which he must lie upon his stomach, one trap-door opening upon the leads, three iron girders, three beams, six buttresses, no ceiling, unless you count the walls, no walls unless you count the ceiling, and in its embarrassment presented him with the gurgly cistern that supplied the bath water. Here he lived, absolutely happy, and unaware that Mrs Failing had poked him up here on purpose, to prevent him from growing too bumptious. Here he worked and sang and practised on the ocharoon. Here, in the crannies, he had constructed shelves and cupboards and useless little drawers. He had only one picture—the Demeter of Cnidus—and she hung straight from the roof like a joint of meat. Once she was in the drawing-room; but Mrs Failing had got tired of her, and decreed her removal and this degradation. Now she faced the sunrise; and when the moon rose its light also fell on her, and trembled, like light upon the sea. For she was never still, and if the draught increased she would twist on her string, and would sway and tap upon the rafters until Stephen woke up and said what he thought of her. 'Want your nose?' he would murmur. 'Don't you wish you may get it.' Then he drew the clothes over his ears, while above him, in the wind and the darkness, the goddess continued her motions.

To-day, as he entered, he trod on the pile of sixpenny reprints. Leighton had brought them up. He looked at the portraits on their covers, and began to think that these people were not everything. What a fate, to look like Colonel Ingersoll, or to marry Mrs Julia P. Chunk! The Demeter turned towards him as he bathed, and in the cold water he sang—

> '*They aren't beautiful, they aren't modest;*
> *I'd just as soon follow an old stone goddess*'—

and sprang upward through the skylight on to the roof.

Years ago, when a nurse was washing him, he had slipped from her soapy hands and got up here. She implored him to remember that he was a little gentleman; but he forgot the fact—if it was a fact—and not even the butler could get him down. Mr Failing, who was sitting alone in the garden too ill to read, heard a shout, 'Am I an acro-terium?' He looked up and saw a naked child poised on the summit of Cadover. 'Yes,' he replied; 'but they are unfashionable. Go in,' and the vision had remained with him as something peculiarly gracious. He felt that nonsense and beauty have close connections—closer connections than Art will allow—and that both would remain when his own heaviness and his own ugliness had perished. Mrs Failing found in his remains a sentence that puzzled her. 'I see the respectable mansion. I see the smug fortress of culture. The doors are shut. The windows are shut. But on the roof the children go dancing for ever.'

Stephen was a child no longer. He never stood on the pediment now, except for a bet. He never, or scarcely ever, poured water down the chimneys. When he caught the cat, he seldom dropped her into the housekeeper's bedroom. But still, when the weather was fair, he liked to come up after bathing, and get dry in the sun. To-day he brought with him a towel, a pipe of tobacco, and Rickie's story. He must get it done some time, and he was tired of the sixpenny reprints. The sloping gable was warm, and he lay back on it with closed eyes, gasping for pleasure. Starlings criticized him, soots fell on his clean body, and over him a little cloud was tinged with the colours of evening. 'Good! good!' he whispered. 'Good, oh good!' and opened the manuscript reluctantly.

What a production! Who was this girl? Where did she go to? Why so much talk about trees? 'I take it he wrote it when feeling bad,' he murmured, and let it fall into the gutter. It fell face downwards, and on the back he saw a neat little *résumé* in Miss Pembroke's handwriting, intended for such as him. 'Allegory. Man=modern civilization (in bad sense). Girl=getting into touch with Nature.'

In touch with Nature! The girl was a tree! He lit his pipe and gazed at the radiant earth. The foreground was hidden, but there was the village with its elms, and the Roman Road, and Cadbury Rings. There, too, were those woods, and little beech copses, crowning a waste of down. Not to mention the air, or the sun, or water. Good, oh good!

In touch with Nature! What cant would the books think of next? His eyes closed. He was sleepy. Good, oh good! Sighing into his pipe, he fell asleep.

Chapter Thirteen

Glad as Agnes was when her lover returned for lunch, she was at the same time rather dismayed: she knew that Mrs Failing would not like her plans altered. And her dismay was justified. Their hostess was a little stiff, and asked whether Stephen had been obnoxious.

'Indeed he hasn't. He spent the whole time looking after me.'

'From which I conclude he was more obnoxious than usual.'

Rickie praised him diligently. But his candid nature showed everything through. His aunt soon saw that they had not got on. She had expected this—almost planned it. Nevertheless she resented it, and her resentment was to fall on him.

The storm gathered slowly, and many other things went to swell it. Weakly people, if they are not careful, hate one another, and when the weakness is hereditary the temptation increases. Elliots had never got on among themselves. They talked of 'The Family,' but they always turned outwards to the health and beauty that lie so promiscuously about the world. Rickie's father had turned, for a time at all events, to his mother. Rickie himself was turning to Agnes. And Mrs Failing now was irritable, and unfair to the nephew who was lame like her horrible brother and like herself. She thought him invertebrate and conventional. She was envious of his happiness. She did not trouble to understand his art. She longed to shatter him, but knowing as she did that the human thunderbolt often rebounds and strikes the wielder, she held her hand.

Agnes watched the approaching clouds. Rickie had warned her; now she began to warn him. As the visit wore away she urged him to be pleasant to his aunt, and so convert it into a success.

He replied, 'Why need it be a success?'—a reply in the manner of Ansell.

She laughed. 'Oh, that's so like you men—all theory! What about your great theory of hating no one? As soon as it comes in useful you drop it.'

'I don't hate Aunt Emily. Honestly. But certainly I don't want to be near her or think about her. Don't you think there are two great things in life that we ought to aim at—truth and kindness? Let's have both if we can, but let's be sure of having one or the other. My aunt gives up both for the sake of being funny.'

'And Stephen Wonham,' pursued Agnes. 'There's another person you hate—or don't think about, if you prefer it put like that.'

'The truth is, I'm changing. I'm beginning to see that the world has many people in it who don't matter. I had time for them once. Not now.' There was only one gate to the kingdom of heaven now.

Agnes surprised him by saying, 'But the Wonham boy is evidently a part of your aunt's life. She laughs at him, but she is fond of him.'

'What's that to do with it?'

'You ought to be pleasant to him on account of it.'

'Why on earth?'

She flushed a little. 'I'm old-fashioned. One ought to consider one's hostess, and fall in with her life. After we leave it's another thing. But while we take her hospitality I think it's our duty.'

Her good sense triumphed. Henceforth he tried to fall in with Aunt Emily's life. Aunt Emily watched him trying. The storm broke, as storms sometimes do, on Sunday.

Sunday church was a function at Cadover, though a strange one. The pompous landau rolled up to the house at a quarter to eleven. Then Mrs Failing said, 'Why am I being hurried?' and after an interval descended the steps in her ordinary clothes. She regarded the church as a sort of sitting-room, and refused even to wear a bonnet there. The village was shocked, but at the same time a little proud; it would point out the carriage to strangers and gossip about the pale smiling lady who sat in it, always alone, always late, her hair always draped in an expensive shawl.

This Sunday, though late as usual, she was not alone. Miss Pembroke, *en grande toilette*, sat by her side. Rickie, looking plain and devout, perched opposite. And Stephen actually came too, murmuring that it would be the Benedicite, which he had never minded. There was also the Litany, which drove him into the air again, much to Mrs Failing's delight. She enjoyed this sort of thing. It amused her when her *protégé* left the pew, looking bored, athletic, and dishevelled, and groping most obviously for his pipe. She liked to keep a thoroughbred pagan to shock people. 'He's gone to worship Nature,' she whispered. Rickie did not look up. 'Don't you think he's charming?' He made no reply. 'Charming,' whispered Agnes over his head.

During the sermon she analysed her guests. Miss Pembroke—undistinguished, unimaginative, tolerable. Rickie—intolerable. 'And how pedantic!' she mused. 'He smells of the University library. If he was stupid in the right way he would be a don.' She looked round the tiny church; at the whitewashed pillars, the humble pavement, the window full of magenta saints. There was the vicar's wife. And Mrs Wilbraham's bonnet. Ugh! The rest of the congregation were poor women, with flat, hopeless faces—she saw them Sunday after Sunday, but did not know their names—diversified with a few reluctant ploughboys, and the vile little school children, row upon row. 'Ugh! what a hole,' thought Mrs Failing, whose Christianity was of the type best described as 'cathedral.' 'What a hole for a cultured woman! I don't think it has blunted my sensations, though; I still see its squalor as clearly as ever. And my nephew pretends he is worshipping. Pah! the hypocrite.' Above her the vicar spoke of the danger of hurrying from one dissipation to another. She treasured his words, and continued: 'I cannot stand smugness. It is the one, the unpardonable sin. Fresh air! The fresh air that has made Stephen Wonham fresh and companionable and strong. Even if it kills, I will let in the fresh air.'

Thus reasoned Mrs Failing, in the facile vein of Ibsenism. She imagined herself to be a cold-eyed Scandinavian heroine. Really she was an English old lady, who did not mind giving other people a chill provided it was not infectious.

Agnes, on the way back, noted that her hostess was a little snappish. But one is so hungry after morning service, and either so hot or so cold, that he would be a saint indeed who becomes a saint at once. Mrs Failing, after asserting vindictively that it was impossible to make a living out of literature, was courteously left alone. Roast-beef and moselle might yet work miracles, and Agnes still hoped for the introductions—the introductions to certain editors and publishers—on which her whole diplomacy was bent. Rickie would not push himself. It was his besetting sin. Well for him that he would have a wife, and a loving wife, who knew the value of enterprise.

Unfortunately lunch was a quarter of an hour late, and during that quarter of an hour the aunt and the nephew quarrelled. She had been inveighing against the morning service, and he quietly and deliberately replied, 'If organized religion is anything—and it is something to me—it will not be wrecked by a harmonium and a dull sermon.'

Mrs Failing frowned. 'I envy you. It is a great thing to have no sense of beauty.'

'I think I have a sense of beauty, which leads me astray if I am not careful.'

'But this is a great relief to me. I thought the present-day young man was an agnostic! Isn't agnosticism all the thing at Cambridge?'

'Nothing is the "thing" at Cambridge. If a few men are agnostic there, it is for some grave reason, not because they are irritated with the way the parson says his vowels.'

Agnes intervened. 'Well, I side with Aunt Emily. I believe in ritual.'

'Don't, my dear, side with me. He will only say you have no sense of religion either.'

'Excuse me,' said Rickie—perhaps he too was a little hungry—'I never suggested such a thing. I never would suggest such a thing. Why cannot you understand my position? I almost feel it is that you won't.'

'I try to understand your position night and day, dear—what you mean, what you like, why you came to Cadover, and why you stop here when my presence is so obviously unpleasing to you.'

'Luncheon is served,' said Leighton, but he said it too late. They discussed the beef and the moselle in silence. The air was heavy and ominous. Even the Wonham boy was affected by it, shivered at times, choked once, and hastened anew into the sun. He could not understand clever people.

Agnes, in a brief anxious interview, advised the culprit to take a solitary walk. She would stop near Aunt Emily, and pave the way for an apology.

'Don't worry too much. It doesn't really matter.'

'I suppose not, dear. But it seems a pity, considering we are so near the end of our visit.'

'Rudeness and crossness matter, and I've shown both, and already I'm sorry, and hope she'll let me apologize. But from the selfish point of view it doesn't matter a straw. She's no more to us than the Wonham boy or the boot boy.'

'Which way will you walk?'

'I think to that entrenchment. Look at it.' They were sitting on the steps. He stretched out his hand to Cadbury Rings, and then let it rest for a moment on her shoulder. 'You're changing me,' he said gently. 'God bless you for it.'

He enjoyed his walk. Cadford was a charming village, and for a time he hung over the bridge by the mill. So clear was the stream that it seemed not water at all, but some invisible quintessence in which the happy minnows and the weeds were vibrating. And he paused again at the Roman crossing, and thought for a moment of the unknown child. The line curved suddenly: certainly it was dangerous. Then he lifted his eyes to the down. The entrenchment showed like the rim of a saucer, and over its narrow line peeped the summit of the central tree. It looked interesting. He hurried forward, with the wind behind him.

The Rings were curious rather than impressive. Neither embankment was over twelve feet high, and the grass on them had not the exquisite green of Old Sarum, but was grey and wiry. But Nature (if she arranges anything) had arranged that from them, at all events, there should be a view. The whole system of the country lay spread before Rickie, and he gained an idea of it that he never got in his elaborate ride. He saw how all the water converges at Salisbury; how Salisbury lies in a shallow basin, just at the change of the soil. He saw to the north the Plain, and the stream of the Cad flowing down from it, with a tributary that broke out suddenly, as the chalk streams do: one village had clustered round the source and clothed itself with trees. He saw Old Sarum, and hints of the Avon valley, and the land above Stonehenge. And behind him he saw the great wood beginning unobtrusively, as if the down too needed shaving; and into it the road to London slipped, covering the bushes with white dust. Chalk made the dust white, chalk made the water clear, chalk made the clean rolling outlines of the land, and favoured the grass and the distant coronals of trees. Here is the heart of our island: the Chilterns, the North Downs, the South Downs radiate hence. The fibres of England unite in Wiltshire, and did we condescend to worship her, here we should erect our national shrine.

People at that time were trying to think imperially. Rickie wondered how they did it, for he could not imagine a place larger than England. And other people talked of Italy, the spiritual fatherland of us all. Perhaps Italy would prove marvellous. But at present he conceived it as something exotic, to be admired and reverenced, but not to be loved like these unostentatious fields. He drew out a book—it was natural for him to read when he was happy, and to read out loud—and for a little time his voice disturbed the silence of that glorious afternoon. The book was Shelley, and it opened at a passage that he had cherished greatly two years before, and marked as 'very good.'

I never was attached to that great sect
Whose doctrine is that each one should select
Out of the world a mistress or a friend,
And all the rest, though fair and wise, commend
To cold oblivion—though it is the code
Of modern morals, and the beaten road
Which those poor slaves with weary footsteps tread
Who travel to their home among the dead
By the broad highway of the world—and so
With one sad friend, perhaps a jealous foe,
The dreariest and the longest journey go.

It was 'very good'—fine poetry, and, in a sense, true. Yet he was surprised that he had ever selected it so vehemently. This afternoon it seemed a little inhuman. Half a mile off two lovers were keeping company where all the villagers could see them. They cared for no one else; they felt only the pressure of each other, and so progressed, silent and oblivious, across the land. He felt them to be nearer the truth than Shelley. Even if they suffered or quarrelled, they would have been nearer the truth. He wondered whether they were Henry Adams and Jessica Thompson, both of his parish, whose banns had been asked, for the second time, in the church this morning. Why could he not marry on fifteen shillings a week? And he looked at them with respect, and wished that he was not a cumbersome gentleman.

Presently he saw something less pleasant—his aunt's pony carriage. It had crossed the railway, and was advancing up the Roman road along by the straw sacks. His impulse was to retreat, but some one waved to him. It was Agnes. She waved continually, as much as to say, 'Wait for us.' Mrs Failing herself raised the whip in a nonchalant way. Stephen Wonham was following on foot, some way behind. He put the Shelley back into his pocket and waited for them. When the carriage stopped by some hurdles he went down from the embankment and helped them to dismount. He felt rather nervous.

His aunt gave him one of her disquieting smiles, but said pleasantly enough, 'Aren't the Rings a little immense? Agnes and I came here because we wanted an antidote to the morning service.'

'Pang!' said the church bell suddenly; 'pang! pang!' It sounded petty and ludicrous. They all laughed. Rickie blushed, and Agnes, with a glance that said 'apologize,' darted away to the entrenchment, as though unable to restrain her curiosity.

'The pony won't move,' said Mrs Failing. 'Leave him for Stephen to tie up. Will you walk me to the tree in the middle? Booh! I'm tired. Give me your arm—unless you're tired as well.'

'No. I came out partly in the hope of helping you.'

'How sweet of you.' She contrasted his blatant unselfishness with the hardness of Stephen. Stephen never came out to help you. But if you got hold of him he was some good. He didn't wobble and bend at the critical moment. Her fancy compared Rickie to the cracked church bell sending

forth its message of 'Pang! pang!' to the countryside, and Stephen to the
young pagans who were said to lie under this field guarding their pagan gold.

'This place is full of ghosties,' she remarked; 'have you seen any yet?'

'I've kept on the outer rim so far.'

'Let's go to the tree in the centre.'

'Here's the path. The bank of grass where he had sat was broken by a gap,
through which chariots had entered, and farm carts entered now. The track,
following the ancient track, led straight through turnips to a similar gap in
the second circle and thence continued, through more turnips, to the central
tree.

'Pang!' said the bell, as they paused at the entrance.

'You needn't unharness,' shouted Mrs Failing, for Stephen was
approaching the carriage.

'Yes, I will,' he retorted.

'You will, will you?' she murmured with a smile. 'I wish your brother
wasn't quite so uppish. Let's get on. Doesn't that church distract you?'

'It's so faint here,' said Rickie. And it sounded fainter inside, though the
earthwork was neither thick nor tall; and the view, though not hidden, was
greatly diminished. He was reminded for a moment of that chalk pit near
Madingley, whose ramparts excluded the familiar world. Agnes was here, as
she had once been there. She stood on the farther barrier, waiting to receive
them when they had traversed the heart of the camp.

'Admire my mangel-wurzels,' said Mrs Failing. 'They are said to grow so
splendidly on account of the dead soldiers, Isn't it a sweet thought? Need I
say it is your brother's?'

'Wonham's—?' he suggested. It was the second time that she had made
the little slip. She nodded, and he asked her what kind of ghosties haunted
this curious field.

'The D.,' was her prompt reply. 'He leans against the tree in the middle,
especially on Sunday afternoons, and all his worshippers rise through the
turnips and dance round him.'

'Oh, these were decent people,' he replied, looking downwards–'soldiers
and shepherds. They have no ghosts. They worshipped Mars or Pan–Erda
perhaps; not the devil.'

'Pang!' went the church, and was silent, for the afternoon service had
begun. They entered the second entrenchment, which was in height,
breadth, and composition similar to the first, and excluded still more of the
view. His aunt continued friendly. Agnes stood watching them.

'Soldiers may seem decent in the past,' she continued, 'but wait till they
turn into Tommies from Bulford Camp, who rob the chickens.'

'I don't mind Bulford Camp,' said Rickie, looking, though in vain, for
signs of its snowy tents. 'The men there are the sons of the men here, and
have come back to the old country. War's horrible, yet one loves all
continuity. And no one could mind a shepherd.'

'Indeed! What about your brother–a shepherd if ever there was? Look
how he bores you! Don't be so sentimental.'

'But–oh, you mean—'

'Your brother Stephen.'

He glanced at her nervously. He had never known her so queer before. Perhaps it was some literary allusion that he had not caught; but her face did not at that moment suggest literature. In the deferential tones that one uses to an old and infirm person he said, 'Stephen Wonham isn't my brother, Aunt Emily.'

'My dear, you're that precise. One can't say "half-brother" every time.'

They approached the central tree.

'How you do puzzle me,' he said, dropping her arm and beginning to laugh. 'How could I have a half-brother?'

She made no answer.

Then a horror leapt straight at him, and he beat it back and said, 'I will not be frightened.' The tree in the centre revolved, the tree disappeared, and he saw a room—the room where his father had lived in town. 'Gently,' he told himself, 'gently.'

Still laughing, he said, 'I, with a brother—younger—it's not possible.' The horror leapt again, and he exclaimed, 'It's a foul lie!'

'My dear, my dear!'

'It's a foul lie! He wasn't—I won't stand—'

'My dear, before you say several noble things remember that it's worse for him than for you—worse for your brother, for your half-brother, for your younger brother.'

But he heard her no longer. He was gazing at the past, which he had praised so recently, which gaped ever wider, like an unhallowed grave. Turn where he would, it encircled him. It took visible form: it was this double entrenchment of the Rings. His mouth went cold, and he knew that he was going to faint among the dead. He started running, missed the exit, stumbled on the inner barrier, fell into darkness—

'Get his head down,' said a voice. 'Get the blood back into him. That's all he wants. Leave him to me. Elliot!'—the blood was returning—'Elliot, wake up!'

He woke up. The earth he had dreaded lay close to his eyes, and seemed beautiful. He saw the structure of the clods. A tiny beetle swung on the grass blade. On his own neck a human hand pressed, guiding the blood back to his brain.

There broke from him a cry, not of horror but of acceptance. For one short moment he understood. 'Stephen—' he began, and then he heard his own name called: 'Rickie! Rickie!' Agnes had hurried from her post on the margin, and, as if understanding also, caught him to her breast.

Stephen offered to help them further, but finding that he made things worse, he stepped aside to let them pass and then sauntered inwards. The whole field, with its concentric circles, was visible, and the broad leaves of the turnips rustled in the gathering wind. Miss Pembroke and Elliot were moving towards the Cadover entrance. Mrs Failing stood watching in her turn on the opposite bank. He was not an inquisitive boy; but as he leant against the tree he wondered what it was all about, and whether he would ever know.

Chapter Fourteen

On the way back—at that very level-crossing where he had paused on his upward route—Rickie stopped suddenly and told the girl why he had fainted. Hitherto she had asked him in vain. His tone had gone from him, and he told her harshly and brutally, so that she started away with a horrified cry. Then his manner altered, and he exclaimed: 'Will you mind? Are you going to mind?'

'Of course I mind,' she whispered. She turned from him, and saw up on the sky-line two figures that seemed to be of enormous size.

'They're watching us. They stand on the edge watching us. This country's so open—you—you can't—they watch us wherever we go. Of course you mind.'

They heard the rumble of the train, and she pulled herself together. 'Come, dearest, we shall be run over next. We're saying things that have no sense.' But on the way back he repeated: 'They can still see us. They can see every inch of this road. They watch us for ever.' And when they arrived at the steps, there, sure enough, were still the two figures gazing from the outer circle of the Rings.

She made him go to his room at once: he was almost hysterical. Leighton brought out some tea for her, and she sat drinking it on the little terrace. Of course she minded. Again she was menaced by the abnormal. All had seemed so fair and so simple, so in accordance with her ideas; and then, like a corpse, this horror rose up to the surface. She saw the two figures descend and pause while one of them harnessed the pony; she saw them drive downward, and knew that before long she must face them and the world. She glanced at her engagement ring.

When the carriage drove up Mrs Failing dismounted, but did not speak. It was Stephen who inquired after Rickie. She, scarcely knowing the sound of her own voice, replied that he was a little tired.

'Go and put up the pony,' said Mrs Failing rather sharply. 'Agnes, give me some tea.'

'It is rather strong,' said Agnes as the carriage drove off and left them alone. The she noticed that Mrs Failing herself was agitated. Her lips were trembling, and she saw the boy depart with manifest relief.

'Do you know,' she said hurriedly, as if talking against time—'do you know what upset Rickie?'

'I do indeed know.'

'He has told any one else?'

'I believe not.'

'Agnes—have I been a fool?'

'You have been very unkind,' said the girl, and her eyes filled with tears.

For a moment Mrs Failing was annoyed. 'Unkind? I do not see that at all. I believe in looking facts in the face. Rickie must know his ghosts in time. Why not this afternoon?'

She rose with quiet dignity, but her tears came faster. 'That is not so. You told him to hurt him. I cannot think what you did it for. I suppose because he was rude to you after church. It is a mean, cowardly revenge.'

'What—what if it's a lie?'

'Then, Mrs Failing, it is sickening of you. There is no other word. Sickening. I am sorry—a nobody like myself—to speak like this. How *could* you, oh, how could you demean yourself? Why, not even a poor person—' Her indignation was fine and genuine. But her tears fell no longer. Nothing menaced her if they were not really brothers.

'It is not a lie, my dear; sit down. I will swear so much solemnly. It is not a lie, but—'

Agnes waited.

'—we can call it a lie if we choose.'

'I am not so childish. You have said it, and we must all suffer. You have had your fun: I conclude you did it for fun. You cannot go back. He—' She pointed towards the stables, and could not finish her sentence.

'I have not been a fool twice.'

Agnes did not understand.

'My dense lady, can't you follow? I have not told Stephen one single word, neither before nor now.'

There was a long silence.

Indeed, Mrs Failing was in an awkward position. Rickie had irritated her, and, in her desire to shock him, she had imperilled her own peace. She had felt so unconventional upon the hillside, when she loosed the horror against him; but now it was darting at her as well. Suppose the scandal out. Stephen, who was absolutely without delicacy, would tell it to people as soon as tell them the time. His paganism would be too assertive; it might even be in bad taste. After all, she had a prominent position in the neighbourhood; she was talked about, respected, looked up to. After all, she was growing old. And therefore, though she had no true regard for Rickie, nor for Agnes, nor for Stephen, nor for Stephen's parents, in whose tragedy she had assisted, yet she did feel that if the scandal revived it would disturb the harmony of Cadover, and therefore tried to retrace her steps. It is easy to say shocking things: it is so different to be connected with anything shocking. Life and death were not involved, but comfort and discomfort were.

The silence was broken by the sound of feet on the gravel. Agnes said hastily, 'Is that really true—that he knows nothing?'

'You, Rickie, and I are the only people alive that know. He realizes what he is—with a precision that is sometimes alarming. Who he is, he doesn't know and doesn't care. I suppose he would know when I'm dead. There are papers.'

'Aunt Emily, before he comes, may I say to you I'm sorry I was so rude?'

Mrs Failing had not disliked her courage. 'My dear, you may. We're all off our hinges this Sunday. Sit down by me again.'

Agnes obeyed, and they awaited the arrival of Stephen. They were clever enough to understand each other. The thing must be hushed up. The matron must repair the consequences of her petulance. The girl must hide the stain in her future husband's family. Why not? Who was injured? What does a grown-up man want with a grown-up brother? Rickie upstairs, how grateful he would be to them for saving him.

'Stephen!'

'Yes.'

'I'm tired of you. Go and bathe in the sea.'

'All right.'

And the whole thing was settled. She liked no fuss, and so did he. He sat down on the step to tighten his boot-laces. Then he would be ready. Mrs Failing laid two or three sovereigns on the step above him. Agnes tried to make conversation, and said, with averted eyes, that the sea was a long way off.

'The sea's downhill. That's all I know about it.' He swept up the money with a word of pleasure: he was kept like a baby in such things. Then he started off, but slowly, for he meant to walk till the morning.

'He will be gone days,' said Mrs Failing. 'The comedy is finished. Let us come in.'

She went to her room. The storm that she had raised had shattered her. Yet, because it was stilled for a moment, she resumed her old emancipated manner, and spoke of it as a comedy.

As for Miss Pembroke, she pretended to be emancipated no longer. People like 'Stephen Wonham' were social thunderbolts, to be shunned at all costs, or at almost all costs. Her joy was now unfeigned, and she hurried upstairs to impart it to Rickie.

'I don't think we are rewarded if we do right, but we are punished if we lie. It's the fashion to laugh at poetic justice, but I do believe in half of it. Cast bitter bread upon the waters, and after many days it really will come back to you.' These were the words of Mr Failing. They were also the opinions of Stewart Ansell, another unpractical person. Rickie was trying to write to him when she entered with the good news.

'Dear, we're saved! He doesn't know, and he never is to know. I can't tell you how glad I am. All the time we saw them standing together up there, she wasn't telling him at all. She was keeping him out of the way, in case you let it out. Oh, I like her! She may be unwise, but she is nice, really. She said, "I've been a fool, but I haven't been a fool twice." You must forgive her, Rickie. I've forgiven her, and she me; for at first I was so angry with her. Oh, my darling boy, I am so glad!'

He was shivering all over, and could not reply. At last he said, 'Why hasn't she told him?'

'Because she has come to her senses.'

'But she can't behave to people like that. She must tell him.'

'Why?'

'Because he must be told such a real thing.'

'Such a real thing?' the girl echoed, screwing up her forehead. 'But—but you don't mean you're glad about it?'

His head bowed over the letter. 'My God—no! But it's a real thing. She must tell him. I nearly told him myself—up there—when he made me look at the ground, but you happened to prevent me.'

How Providence had watched over them!

'She won't tell him. I know that much.'

'Then, Agnes, darling'—he drew her to the table—'we must talk together a little. If she won't, then we ought to.'

'*We* tell him?' cried the girl, white with horror. 'Tell him now, when everything has been comfortably arranged?'

'You see, darling'—he took hold of her hand—'what one must do is to think the thing out and settle what's right. I'm still all trembling and stupid. I see it mixed up with other things. I want you to help me. It seems to me that here and there in life we meet with a person or incident that is symbolical. It's nothing in itself, yet for the moment it stands for some eternal principle. We accept it, at whatever cost, and we have accepted life. But if we are frightened and reject it, the moment, so to speak, passes; the symbol is never offered again. Is this nonsense? Once before a symbol was offered to me—I shall not tell you how; but I did accept it, and cherished it through much anxiety and repulsion. And in the end I am rewarded. There will be no reward this time, I think, from such a man—the son of such a man. But I want to do what is right.'

'Because doing right is its own reward,' said Agnes anxiously.

'I do not think that. I have seen few examples of it. Doing right is simply doing right.'

'I think that all you say is wonderfully clever; but since you ask me, it *is* nonsense, dear Rickie, absolutely.'

'Thank you,' he said humbly, and began to stroke her hand. 'But all my disgust; my indignation with my father, my love for—' He broke off; he could not bear to mention the name of his mother. 'I was trying to say, I oughtn't to follow these impulses too much. There are other things. Truth. Our duty to acknowledge each man accurately, however vile he is. And apart from ideals' (here she had won the battle)—'and leaving ideals aside, I couldn't meet him and keep silent. It isn't in me. I should blurt it out.'

'But you won't meet him!' she cried. 'It's all been arranged. We've sent him to the sea. Isn't it splendid? He's gone. My own boy won't be fantastic, will he?' Then she fought the fantasy on its own ground. 'And, by the bye, what you call the "symbolic moment" is over. You had it up by the Rings. You tried to tell him. I interrupted you. It's not your fault. You did all you could.'

She thought this excellent logic, and was surprised that he looked so gloomy. 'So he's gone to the sea. For the present that does settle it. Has Aunt Emily talked about him yet?'

'No. Ask her to-morrow if you wish to know. Ask her kindly. It would be so dreadful if you did not part friends, and—'

'What's that?'

It was Stephen calling up from the drive. He had come back. Agnes threw out her hand in despair.

'Elliot!' the voice called.

They were facing each other, silent and motionless. Then Rickie advanced to the window. The girl darted in front of him. He thought he had never seen her so beautiful. She was stopping his advance quite frankly with widespread arms.

'Elliot!'

He moved forward–into what? He pretended to himself he would rather see his brother before he answered; that it was easier to acknowledge him thus. But at the back of his soul he knew that the woman had conquered, and that he was moving forward to acknowledge her. 'If he calls me again—' he thought.

'Elliot!'

'Well, if he calls me once again, I will answer him, vile as he is.'

He did not call again.

Stephen had really come back for some tobacco, but as he passed under the windows he thought of the poor fellow who had been 'nipped' (nothing serious, said Mrs Failing), and determined to shout good-bye to him. And once or twice, as he followed the river into darkness, he wondered what it was like to be so weak–not to ride, not to swim, not to care for anything but books and a girl.

They embraced passionately. The danger had brought them very near to each other. They both needed a home to confront the menacing tumultuous world. And what weary years of work, of waiting, lay between them and that home! Still holding her fast, he said, 'I was writing to Ansell when you came in.'

'Do you owe him a letter?'

'No.' He paused. 'I was writing to tell him about this. He would help us. He always picks out the important point.'

'Darling, I don't like to say anything, and I know that Mr Ansell would keep a secret, but haven't we picked out the important point for ourselves?'

He released her and tore the letter up.

Chapter Fifteen

The sense of purity is a puzzling, and at times a fearful thing. It seems so noble, and it starts at one with morality. But it is a dangerous guide, and can lead us away not only from what is gracious, but also from what is good. Agnes, in this tangle, had followed it blindly, partly because she was a woman, and it meant more to her than it can ever mean to a man; partly because, though dangerous, it is also obvious, and makes no demand upon the intellect. She could not feel that Stephen had full human rights. He was illicit, abnormal, worse than a man diseased. And Rickie, remembering whose son he was, gradually adopted her opinion. He, too, came to be glad that his brother had passd from him untried, that the symbolic moment had been rejected. Stephen was the fruit of sin; therefore he was sinful. He, too, became a sexual snob.

And now he must hear the unsavoury details. That evening they sat in the walled garden. Agnes, according to arrangement, left him alone with his aunt. He asked her, and was not answered.

'You are shocked,' she said in a hard, mocking voice. 'It is very nice of you to be shocked, and I do not wish to grieve you further. We will not allude to it again. Let us all go on just as we are. The comedy is finished.'

He could not tolerate this. His nerves were shattered, and all that was good in him revolted as well. To the horror of Agnes, who was within earshot, he replied, 'You used to puzzle me, Aunt Emily, but I understand you at last. You have forgotten what other people are like. Continual selfishness leads to that. I am sure of it. I see now how you look at the world. "Nice of me to be shocked!" I want to go to-morrow, if I may.'

'Certainly, dear. The morning trains are the best.' And so the disastrous visit ended.

As he walked back to the house he met a certain poor woman, whose child Stephen had rescued at the level-crossing, and who had decided, after some delay, that she must thank the kind gentleman in person. 'He has got some brute courage,' thought Rickie, 'and it was decent of him not to boast about it.' But he had labelled the boy as 'Bad,' and it was convenient to revert to his good qualities as seldom as possible. He preferred to brood over his coarseness, his caddish ingratitude, his irreligion. Out of these he constructed a repulsive figure, forgetting how slovenly his own perceptions had been during the past week, how dogmatic and intolerant his attitude to all that was not Love.

During the packing he was obliged to go up to the attic to find the Dryad manuscript, which had never been returned. Leighton came too, and for about half an hour they hunted in the flickering light of a candle. It was a strange ghostly place, and Rickie was quite startled when a picture swung towards him, and he saw the Demeter of Cnidus, shimmering and grey. Leighton suggested the roof: Mr Stepehen sometimes left things on the roof. So they climbed out of the skylight—the night was perfectly still—and continued the search among the gables. Enormous stars hung overhead, and the roof was bounded by chasms, impenetrable and black. 'It doesn't matter,' said Rickie, suddenly convinced of the futility of all that he did. 'Oh, let us look properly,' said Leighton, a kindly, pliable man, who had tried to shirk coming, but who was genuinely sympathetic now that he had come. They were rewarded: the manuscript lay in a gutter, charred and smudged.

The rest of the year was spent by Rickie partly in bed—he had a curious breakdown—partly in the attempt to get his little stories published. He had written eight or nine, and hoped they would make up a book, and that the book might be called "Pan Pipes." He was very energetic over this; he liked to work, for some imperceptible bloom had passed from the world, and he no longer found such acute pleasure in people. Mr Failing's old publishers, to whom the book was submitted, replied that, greatly as they found themselves interested, they did not see their way to making an offer at present. They were very polite, and singled out for special praise "Andante Pastorale," which Rickie had thought too sentimental, but which Agnes had persuaded him to include. The stories were sent to another publisher, who considered them for six weeks, and then returned them. A fragment of red cotton, placed by Agnes between the leaves, had not shifted its position.

'Can't you try something longer, Rickie?' she said; 'I believe we're on the wrong track. Try an out-and-out love-story.'

'My notion just now,' he replied, 'is to leave the passions on the fringe.' She nodded, and tapped for the waiter: they had met in a London restaurant. 'I can't soar; I can only indicate. That's where the musicians have the pull, for music has wings, and when she says "Tristan" and he says "Isolde," you are on the heights at once. What do people mean when they call love music artificial?'

'I know what they mean, though I can't exactly explain. Or couldn't you make your stories more obvious? I don't see any harm in that. Uncle Willie floundered hopelessly. He doesn't read much, and he got muddled. I had to explain, and then he was delighted. Of course, to write down to the public would be quite another thing and horrible. You have certain ideas, and you must express them. But couldn't you express them more clearly?'

'You see—' He got no further than 'you see.'

'The soul and the body. The soul's what matters,' said Agnes, and tapped for the waiter again. He looked at her admiringly, but felt that she was not a perfect critic. Perhaps she was too perfect to be a critic. Actual life might seem to her so real that she could not detect the union of shadow and adamant that men call poetry. He would even go further and acknowledge that she was not as clever as himself—and he was stupid enough! She did not like discussing anything or reading solid books, and she was a little angry with such women as did. It pleased him to make these concessions, for they touched nothing in her that he valued. He looked round the restaurant, which was in Soho, and decided that she was incomparable.

'At half-past two I call on the editor of the "Holborn." He's got a stray story to look at, and he's written about it.'

'Oh, Rickie! Rickie! Why didn't you put on a boiled shirt!'

He laughed, and teased her. 'The soul's what matters. We literary people don't care about dress.'

'Well, you ought to care. And I believe you do. Can't you change?'

'Too far.' He had rooms in South Kensington. 'And I've forgot my card-case. There's for you!'

She shook her head. 'Naughty, naughty boy! Whatever will you do?'

'Send in my name, or ask for a bit of paper and write it. Hullo! That's Tilliard!'

Tilliard blushed, partly on account of the *faux pas* he had made last June, partly on account of the restaurant. He explained how he came to be pigging in Soho: it was so frightfully convenient and so frightfully cheap.

'Just why Rickie brings me,' said Miss Pembroke.

'And I suppose you're here to study life?' said Tilliard, sitting down.

'I don't know,' said Rickie, gazing round at the waiters and the guests. 'Doesn't one want to see a good deal of life for writing? There's life of a sort in Soho—*Un peu de faisan, s'il vous plaît.*'

Agnes also grabbed at the waiter, and paid. She always did the paying, Rickie muddled so with his purse.

'I'm cramming,' pursued Tilliard, 'and so naturally I come into contact with very little at present. But later on I hope to see things.' He blushed a little, for he was talking for Rickie's edification. 'It is most frightfully important not to get a narrow or academic outlook, don't you think? A person like Ansell, who goes from Cambridge, home—home, Cambridge—it must tell on him in time.'

'But Mr Ansell is a philosopher.'

'A very kinky one,' said Tilliard abruptly. 'Not my idea of a philosopher. How goes his dissertation?'

'He never answers my letters,' replied Rickie. 'He never would. I've heard nothing since June.'

'It's a pity he sends in this year. There are so many good people in. He'd have a far better chance if he waited.'

'So I said, but he wouldn't wait. He's so keen about this particular subject.'

'What is it?' asked Agnes.

'About things being real, wasn't it, Tilliard?'

'That's near enough.'

'Well, good luck to him!' said the girl. 'And good luck to you, Mr Tilliard! Later on, I hope, we'll meet again.'

They parted. Tilliard liked her, though he did not feel that she was quite in his *couche sociale*. His sister, for instance, would never have been lured into a Soho restaurant—except for the experience of the thing. Tilliard's *couche sociale* permitted experiences. Provided his heart did not go out to the poor and the unorthodox, he might stare at them as much as he liked. It was seeing life.

Agnes put her lover safely into an omnibus at Cambridge Circus. She shouted after him that his tie was rising over his collar, but he did not hear her. For a moment she felt depressed, and pictured quite accurately the effect that his appearance would have on the editor. The editor was a tall neat man of forty, slow of speech, slow of soul, and extraordinarily kind. He and Rickie sat over a fire, with an enormous table behind them, whereon stood many books waiting to be reviewed.

'I'm sorry,' he said, and paused.

Rickie smiled feebly.

'Your story does not convince.' He tapped it. 'I have read it—with very great pleasure. It convinces in parts, but it does not convince as a whole; and stories, don't you think, ought to convince as a whole?'

'They ought indeed,' said Rickie, and plunged into self-depreciation. But the editor checked him.

'No–no. Please don't talk like that. I can't bear to hear any one talk against imagination. There are countless openings for imagination–for the mysterious, for the supernatural, for all the things you are trying to do, and which, I hope, you will succeed in doing. I'm not *objecting* to imagination; on the contrary, I'd advise you to cultivate it, to accent it. Write a really good ghost story and we'd take it at once. Or'–he suggested it as an alternative to imagination–'or you might get inside life. It's worth doing.'

'Life?' echoed Rickie anxiously. He looked round the pleasant room, as if life might be fluttering there, like an imprisoned bird. Then he looked at the editor; perhaps he was sitting inside life at this very moment.

'See life, Mr Elliot, and then send us another story.' He held out his hand. 'I am sorry I have had to say "No, thank you"; it's so much nicer to say, "Yes, please."' He laid his hand on the young man's sleeve, and added, 'Well, the interview's not been so alarming after all, has it?'

'I don't think that either of us is a very alarming person,' was not Rickie's reply. It was what he thought out afterwards in the omnibus. His reply was 'Ow,' delivered with a slight giggle.

As he rumbled westward, his face was drawn, and his eyes moved quickly to the right and left, as if he would discover something in the squalid fashionable streets–some bird on the wing, some radiant archway, the face of some god beneath a beaver hat. He loved, he was loved, he had seen death and other things; but the heart of all things was hidden. There was a password and he could not learn it, nor could the kind editor of the 'Holborn' teach him. He sighed, and then sighed more piteously. For had he not known the password once–known it and forgotten it already?

But at this point his fortunes became intimately connected with those of Mr Pembroke.

Sawston

Chapter Sixteen

In three years Mr Pembroke had done much to solidify the day-boys at
Sawston School. If they were not solid, they were at all events curdling, and
his activities might reasonably turn elsewhere. He had served the school for
many years, and it was really time he should be entrusted with a boarding-
house. The headmaster, an impulsive man who darted about like a minnow
and gave his mother a great deal of trouble, agreed with him, and also agreed
with Mrs Jackson when she said that Mr Jackson had served the school for
many years and that it was really time he should be entrusted with a
boarding-house. Consequently, when Dunwood House fell vacant, the
headmaster found himself in rather a difficult position.

Dunwood House was the largest and most lucrative of the boarding-
houses. It stood almost opposite the school buildings. Originally it had been
a villa residence—a red-brick villa, covered with creepers and crowned with
terra-cotta dragons. Mr Annison, founder of its glory, had lived here, and
had had one or two boys to live with him. Times changed. The fame of the
bishops blazed brighter, the school increased, the one or two boys became a
dozen, and an addition was made to Dunwood House that more than
doubled its size. A huge new building, replete with every convenience, was
stuck on to its right flank. Dormitories, cubicles, studies, a preparation-
room, a dining-room, parquet floors, hot-air pipes—no expense was spared,
and the twelve boys roamed over it like princes. Baize doors communicated
on every floor with Mr Annison's part, and he, an anxious gentle man, would
stroll backwards and forwards, a little depressed at the hygienic splendours,
and conscious of some vanished intimacy. Somehow he had known his boys
better when they had all muddled together as one family, and algebras lay
strewn upon the drawing-room chairs. As the house filled, his interest in it
decreased. When he retired—which he did the same summer that Rickie left

Cambridge—it had already passed the summit of excellence and was beginning to decline. Its numbers were still satisfactory, and for a little time it would subsist on its past reputation. But that mysterious asset the tone had lowered, and it was therefore of great importance that Mr Annison's successor should be a first-class man. Mr Coates, who came next in seniority, was passed over, and rightly. The choice lay between Mr Pembroke and Mr Jackson, the one an organizer, the other a humanist. Mr Jackson was master of the Sixth, and—with the exception of the headmaster, who was too busy to impart knowledge—the only first-class intellect in the school. But he could not, or rather would not, keep order. He told his form that if it chose to listen to him it would learn; if it didn't, it wouldn't. One half listened. The other half made paper frogs, and bored holes in the raised map of Italy with their penknives. When the penknives gritted he punished them with undue severity, and then forgot to make them show the punishments up. Yet out of this chaos two facts emerged. Half the boys got scholarships at the University, and some of them—including several of the paper-frog sort—remained friends with him throughout their lives. Moreover, he was rich, and had a competent wife. His claim to Dunwood House was stronger than one would have supposed.

The qualifications of Mr Pembroke have already been indicated. They prevailed—but under conditions. If things went wrong, he must promise to resign.

'In the first place,' said the headmaster, 'you are doing so splendidly with the day-boys. Your attitude towards the parents is magnificent. I don't know how to replace you there. Whereas, of course, the parents of a boarder—'

'Of course,' said Mr Pembroke.

The parent of a boarder, who only had to remove his son if he was discontented with the school, was naturally in a more independent position than the parent who had brought all his goods and chattels to Sawston, and was renting a house there.

'Now the parents of boarders—this is my second point—practically demand that the house-master should have a wife.'

'A most unreasonable demand,' said Mr Pembroke.

'To my mind also a bright motherly matron is quite sufficient. But that is what they demand. And that is why—do you see?—we *have* to regard your appointment as experimental. Possibly Miss Pembroke will be able to help you. Or I don't know whether if ever—' He left the sentence unfinished. Two days later Mr Pembroke proposed to Mrs Orr.

He had always intended to marry when he could afford it; and once he had been in love, violently in love, but had laid the passion aside, and told it to wait till a more convenient season. This was, of course, the proper thing to do, and prudence should have been rewarded. But when, after the lapse of fifteen years, he went, as it were, to his spiritual larder and took down Love from the top shelf to offer him to Mrs Orr, he was rather dismayed. Something had happened. Perhaps the god had flown; perhaps he had been eaten by the rats. At all events, he was not there.

Mr Pembroke was conscientious and romantic, and knew that marriage

without love is intolerable. On the other hand, he could not admit that love
had vanished from him. To admit this would argue that he had deteriorated.
Whereas he knew for a fact that he improved, year by year. Each year he
grew more moral, more efficient, more learned, more genial. So how could
he fail to be more loving? He did not speak to himself as follows, because he
never spoke to himself; but the following notions moved in the recesses of his
mind: 'It is not the fire of youth. But I am not sure that I approve of the fire of
youth. Look at my sister! Once she has suffered, twice she has been most
imprudent, and put me to great inconvenience besides, for if she was
stopping with me she would have done the housekeeping. I rather suspect
that it is a nobler, riper emotion that I am laying at the feet of Mrs Orr.' It
never took him long to get muddled, or to reverse cause and effect. In a short
time he believed that he had been pining for years, and only waiting for this
good fortune to ask the lady to share it with him.

Mrs Orr was quiet, clever, kindly, capable, and amusing, and they were
old acquaintances. Altogether it was not surprising that he should ask her to
be his wife, nor very surprising that she should refuse. But she refused with a
violence that alarmed them both. He left her house declaring that he had
been insulted, and she, as soon as he left, passed from disgust into tears.

He was much annoyed. There was a certain Miss Herriton who, though
far inferior to Mrs Orr, would have done instead of her. But now it was
impossible. He could not go offering himself about Sawston. Having
engaged a matron who had a reputation for being bright and motherly, he
moved into Dunwood House and opened the Michaelmas term. Everything
went wrong. The cook left; the boys had a disease called roseola; Agnes, who
was still drunk with her engagement, was of no assistance, but kept flying up
to London to push Rickie's fortunes; and, to crown everything, the matron
was too bright and not motherly enough: she neglected the little boys and
was over-attentive to the big ones. She left abruptly, and the voice of Mrs
Jackson arose, prophesying disaster.

Should he avert it by taking orders? Parents do not demand that a house-
master should be a clergyman, yet it reassures them when he is. And he
would have to take orders some time, if he hoped for a school of his own. His
religious convictions were ready to hand, but he spent several uncomfortable days hunting up his religious enthusiasms. It was not unlike his attempt
to marry Mrs Orr. But his piety was more genuine, and this time he never
came to the point. His sense of decency forbade him hurrying into a Church
that he reverenced. Moreover, he thought of another solution: Agnes must
marry Rickie in the Christmas holidays, and they must come, both of them,
to Sawston, she as housekeeper, he as assistant-master. The girl was a good
worker when once she was settled down; and as for Rickie, he could easily be
fitted in somewhere in the school. He was not a good classic, but good
enough to take the Lower Fifth. He was no athlete, but boys might
profitably note that he was a perfect gentleman all the same. He had no
experience, but he would gain it. He had no decision, but he could simulate
it. 'Above all,' thought Mr Pembroke, 'it will be something regular for him
to do.' Of course this was not 'above all.' Dunwood House held that position.

But Mr Pembroke soon came to think that it was, and believed that he was planning for Rickie, just as he had believed that he was pining for Mrs Orr.

Agnes, when she got back from the lunch in Soho, was told of the plan. She refused to give any opinoin until she had seen her lover. A telegram was sent to him, and next morning he arrived. He was very susceptible to the weather, and perhaps it was unfortunate that the morning was foggy. His train had been stopped outside Sawston Station, and there he had sat for half an hour, listening to the unreal noises that came from the line, and watching the shadowy figures that worked there. The gas was alight in the great drawing-room, and in its depressing rays he and Agnes greeted each other, and discussed the most momentous question of their lives. They wanted to be married: there was no doubt of that. They wanted it, both of them, dreadfully. But should they marry on these terms?

'I'd never thought of such a thing, you see. When the scholastic agencies sent me circulars after the Tripos, I tore them up at once.'

'There are the holidays,' said Agnes. 'You would have three months in the year to yourself and could do your writing then.'

'But who'll read what I've written?' and he told her about the editor of the 'Holborn.'

She became extremely grave. At the bottom of her heart she had always mistrusted the little stories, and now people who knew agreed with her. How could Rickie, or any one, make a living by pretending that Greek gods were alive, or that young ladies could vanish into trees? A sparkling society tale, full of verve and pathos, would have been another thing, and the editor might have been convinced by it.

'But what does he *mean*?' Rickie was saying. 'What does he *mean* by life?'

'I know what he means, but I can't exactly explain. You ought to see life, Rickie. I think he's right there. And Mr Tilliard was right when he said one oughtn't to be academic.'

He stood in the twilight that fell from the window, she in the twilight of the gas. 'I wonder what Ansell would say,' he murmured.

'Oh, poor Mr Ansell!'

He was somewhat surprised. Why was Ansell poor? It was the first time the epithet had been applied to him.

'But to change the conversation,' said Agnes. 'If we did marry, we might get to Italy at Easter and escape this horrible fog.'

'Yes. Perhaps there—' Perhaps life would be there. He thought of Renan, who declares that on the Acropolis at Athens beauty and wisdom do exist, really exist, as external powers. He did not aspire to beauty or wisdom, but he prayed to be delivered from the shadow of unreality that had begun to darken the world. For it was as if some power had pronounced against him—as if, by some heedless action, he had offended an Olympian god. Like many another, he wondered whether the god might be appeased by work—hard uncongenial work. Perhaps he had not worked hard enough, or had enjoyed his work too much, and for that reason the shadow was falling.

'—And above all, a schoolmaster has wonderful opportunities of doing good; one mustn't forget that.'

To do good! For what other reason are we here? Let us give up our refined sensations, and our comforts, and our art, if thereby we can make other people happier and better. The woman he loved had urged him to do good! With a vehemence that surprised her, he exclaimed, 'I'll do it.'

'Think it over,' she cautioned, though she was greatly pleased.

'No; I think over things too much.'

The room grew brighter. A boy's laughter floated in, and it seemed to him that people were as important and vivid as they had been six months before. Then he was at Cambridge, idling in the parsley meadows, and weaving perishable garlands out of flowers. Now he was at Sawston, preparing to work a beneficent machine. No man works for nothing, and Rickie trusted that to him also benefits might accrue; that his wound might heal as he laboured, and his eyes recapture the Holy Grail.

Chapter Seventeen

In practical matters Mr Pembroke was often a generous man. He offered Rickie a good salary, and insisted on paying Agnes as well. And as he housed them for nothing, and as Rickie would also have a salary from the school, the money question disappeared—if not for ever, at all events for the present.

'I can work you in,' he said. 'Leave all that to me, and in a few days you shall hear from the headmaster. He shall create a vacancy. And once in, we stand or fall together. I am resolved on that.'

Rickie did not like the idea of being 'worked in,' but he was determined to raise no difficulties. It is so easy to be refined and high-minded when we have nothing to do. But the active, useful man cannot be equally particular. Rickie's programme involved a change in values as well as a change of occupation.

'Adopt a frankly intellectual attitude,' Mr Pembroke continued. 'I do not advise you at present even to profess any interest in athletics or organization. When the headmaster writes, he will probably ask whether you are an all-round man. Boldly say no. A bold 'no' is at times the best. Take your stand upon classics and general culture.'

Classics! A second in the Tripos. General culture! A smattering of English Literature, and less than a smattering of French.

'That is how we begin. Then we get you a little post—say that of librarian. And so on, until you are indispensable.'

Rickie laughed; the headmaster wrote, the reply was satisfactory, and in due course the new life began.

Sawston was already familiar to him. But he knew it as an amateur, and under an official gaze it grouped itself afresh. The school, a bland Gothic building, now showed as a fortress of learning, whose outworks were the boarding-houses. Those straggling roads were full of the houses of the parents of the day-boys. These shops were in bounds, those out. How often had he passed Dunwood House! He had once confused it with its rival, Cedar View. Now he was to live there–perhaps for many years. On the left of the entrance a large saffron drawing-room, full of cosy corners and dumpy chairs: here the parents would be received. On the right of the entrance a study, which he shared with Herbert: here the boys would be caned–he hoped not often. In the hall a framed certificate praising the drains, the bust of Hermes, and a carved teak monkey holding out a salver. Some of the furniture had come from Shelthorpe, some had been bought from Mr Annison, some of it was new. But throughout he recognized a certain decision of arrangement. Nothing in the house was accidental, or there merely for its own sake. He contrasted it with his room at Cambridge, which had been a jumble of things that he loved dearly and of things that he did not love at all. Now these also had come to Dunwood House, and had been distributed where each was seemly–Sir Percival to the drawing-room, the photograph of Stockholm to the passage, his chair, his inkpot, and the portrait of his mother to the study. And then he contrasted it with the Ansells' house, to which their resolute ill-taste had given unity. He was extremely sensitive to the inside of a house, holding it an organism that expressed the thoughts, conscious and subconscious, of its inmates. He was equally sensitive to places. He would compare Cambridge with Sawston, and either with a third type of existence, to which, for want of a better name, he gave the name of 'Wiltshire.'

It must not be thought that he is going to waste his time. These contrasts and comparisons never took him long, and he never indulged in them until the serious business of the day was over. And, as time passed, he never indulged in them at all.

The school returned at the end of January, before he had been settled in a week. His health had improved, but not greatly, and he was nervous at the prospect of confronting the assembled house. All day long cabs had been driving up, full of boys in bowler hats too big for them; and Agnes had been superintending the numbering of the said hats, and the placing of them in cupboards, since they would not be wanted till the end of the term. Each boy had, or should have had, a bag so that he need not unpack his box till the morrow. One boy had only a brown-paper parcel, tied with hairy string, and Rickie heard the firm pleasant voice say, 'But you'll bring a bag next term,' and the submissive, 'Yes, Mrs Elliot,' of the reply. In the passage he ran against the head boy, who was alarmingly like an undergraduate. They looked at each other suspiciously, and parted. Two minutes later he ran into another boy, and then into another, and began to wonder whether they were doing it on purpose, and if so, whether he ought to mind. As the day wore on, the noises grew louder–trampings of feet, breakdowns, jolly little squawks–and the cubicles were assigned, and the bags unpacked, and the bathing arrangements posted up, and Herbert kept on saying, 'All this is informal–all this is informal. We shall meet the house at eight fifteen.'

And so, at eight ten, Rickie put on his cap and gown–hitherto symbols of pupilage, now to be symbols of dignity–the very cap and gown that

Widdrington had so recently hung upon the college fountain. Herbert, similarly attired, was waiting for him in their private dining-room, where also sat Agnes, ravenously devouring scrambled eggs. 'But you'll wear your hoods,' she cried. Herbert considered, and then said she was quite right. He fetched his white silk, Rickie the fragment of rabbits' wool that marks the degree of B.A. Thus attired, they proceeded through the baize door. They were a little late, and the boys, who were marshalled in the preparation-room, were getting uproarious. One, forgetting how far his voice carried, shouted, 'Cave! Here comes the Whelk.' And another young devil yelled, 'The Whelk's brought a limpet with him!'

'You mustn't mind,' said Herbert kindly. 'We masters make a point of never minding nicknames—unless, of course, they are applied openly, in which case a thousand lines is not too much.' Rickie assented, and they entered the preparation-room just as the prefects had established order.

Here Herbert took his seat on a high-legged chair, while Rickie, like a queen-consort, sat near him on a chair with somewhat shorter legs. Each chair had a desk attached to it, and Herbert flung up the lid of his, and then looked round the preparation-room with a quick frown, as if the contents had surprised him. So impressed was Rickie that he peeped sideways, but could only see a little blotting-paper in the desk. Then he noticed that the boys were impressed too. Their chatter ceased. They attended.

The room was almost full. The prefects, instead of lolling disdainfully in the back row, were ranged like councillors beneath the central throne. This was an innovation of Mr Pembroke's. Carruthers, the head boy, sat in the middle, with his arm round Lloyd. It was Lloyd who had made the matron too bright: he nearly lost his colours in consequence. These two were very grown up. Beside them sat Tewson, a saintly child in spectacles, who had risen to this height by reason of his immense learning. He, like the others, was a school prefect. The house prefects, an inferior brand, were beyond, and behind came the indistinguishable many. The faces all looked alike as yet—except the face of one boy, who was inclined to cry.

'School,' said Mr Pembroke, slowly closing the lid of the desk—'school is the world in miniature.' Then he paused, as a man well may who has made such a remark. It is not, however, the intention of this work to quote an opening address. Rickie, at all events, refused to be critical: Herbert's experience was far greater than his, and he must take his tone from him. Nor could any one criticize the exhortations to be patriotic, athletic, learned, and religious, that flowed like a four-part fugue from Mr Pembroke's mouth. He was a practised speaker—that is to say, he held his audience's attention. He told them that this term, the second of his reign, was *the* term for Dunwood House; that it behoved every boy to labour during it for his house's honour, and, through the house, for the honour of the school. Taking a wider range, he spoke of England, or rather of Great Britain, and of her continental foes. Portraits of empire-builders hung on the wall, and he pointed to them. He quoted imperial poets. He showed how patriotism has broadened since the days of Shakespeare, who, for all his genius, could only write of his country as—

This fortress built by Nature for herself
Against infection and the hand of war,
This happy breed of men, this little world,
This precious stone set in the silver sea.

And it seemed that only a short ladder lay between the preparation-room and the Anglo-Saxon hegemony of the globe. Then he paused, and in the silence came 'sob, sob, sob,' from a little boy, who was regretting a villa in Guildford and his mother's half acre of garden.

The proceeding terminated with the broader patriotism of the school anthem, recently composed by the organist. Words and tune were still a matter for taste, and it was Mr Pembroke (and he only because he had the music) who gave the right intonation to

Perish each laggard! Let it not be said
That Sawston such within her walls hath bred.

'Come, come,' he said pleasantly, as they ended with harmonies in the style of Richard Strauss. 'This will never do. We must grapple with the anthem this term. You're as tuneful as—as day-boys!' Hearty laughter, and then the whole house filed past them and shook hands.

'But how did it impress you?' Herbert asked, as soon as they were back in their own part. Agnes had provided them with a tray of food: the meals were still anyhow, and she had to fly at once to see after the boys.

'I liked the look of them.'

'I meant rather, how did the house impress you as a house?'

'I don't think I thought,' said Rickie rather nervously. 'It is not easy to catch the spirit of a thing at once. I only saw a room full of boys.'

'My dear Rickie, don't be so diffident. You are prefectly right. You only did see a roomful of boys. As yet there's nothing else to see. The house, like the school, lacks tradition. Look at the traditional rivalry between Eton and Harrow. Tradition is of incalculable importance, if a school is to have any status. Why should Sawston be without?'

'Yes. Tradition is of incalculable value. And I envy those schools that have a natural connection with the past. Of course Sawston has a past, though not of the kind that you quite want. The sons of poor tradesmen went to it at first. So wouldn't its traditions be more likely to linger in the Commercial School?' he concluded nervously.

'You have a great deal to learn—a very great deal. Listen to me. Why has Sawston no traditions?' His round, rather foolish, face assumed the expression of a conspirator. Bending over the mutton, he whispered, 'I can tell you why. Owing to the day-boys. How can traditions flourish in such soil? Picture the day-boy's life—at home for meals, at home for preparation, at home for sleep, running home with every fancied wrong. There are day-boys in your class, and, mark my words, they will give you ten times as much trouble as the boarders—late, slovenly, stopping away at the slightest pretext. And then the letters from the parents! 'Why has my boy not been moved this term?' 'Why has my boy been moved this term?' 'I am a dissenter, and do not wish my boy to subscribe to the school mission.' 'Can you let my boy off early to water the garden?' Remember that I have been a day-boy house-master, and tried to infuse some *esprit de corps* into them. It is practically impossible. They come as units, and units they remain. Worse. They infect the boarders. Their pestilential, critical, discontented attitude is spreading over the school. If I had my own way—'

He stopped somewhat abruptly.

'Was that why you laughed at their singing?'

'Not at all. Not at all. It is not my habit to set one section of the school against the other.'

After a little they went the rounds. The boys were in bed now. 'Good night!' called Herbert, standing in the corridor of the cubicles, and from behind each of the green curtains came the sound of a voice replying, 'Good night, sir!' 'Good night,' he observed into each dormitory. Then he went to the switch in the passage and plunged the whole house into darkness. Rickie lingered behind him, strangely impressed. In the morning those boys had been scattered over England, leading their own lives. Now, for three months, they must change everything—see new faces, accept new ideals. They, like himself, must enter a beneficent machine, and learn the value of *esprit de corps*. Good luck attend them—good luck and a happy release. For his heart would have them not in these cubicles and dormitories, but each in his own dear home, amongst faces and things that he knew.

Next morning, after chapel, he made the acquaintance of his class. Towards that he felt very differently. *Esprit de corps* was not expected of it. It was simply two dozen boys who were gathered together for the purpose of learning Latin. His duties and difficulties would not lie here. He was not required to provide it with an atmosphere. The scheme of work was already mapped out, and he started gaily upon familiar words—

> *Pan ovium custos, tua si tibi Mænala curæ,*
> *Adsis, O Tegæe, favens.*

'Do you think that beautiful?' he asked, and received the honest answer, 'No, sir; I don't think I do.' He met Herbert in high spirits in the quadrangle during the interval. But Herbert thought his enthusiasm rather amateurish, and cautioned him.

'You must take care they don't get out of hand. I approve of a lively teacher, but discipline must be established first.'

'I felt myself a learner, not a teacher. If I'm wrong over a point, or don't know, I mean to tell them at once.'

Herbert shook his head.

'It's different if I was really a scholar. But I can't pose as one, can I? I know much more than the boys, but I know very little. Surely the honest thing is to be myself to them. Let them accept or refuse me as that. That's the only attitude we shall any of us profit by in the end.'

Mr Pembroke was silent. Then he observed, 'There is, as you say, a higher attitude and a lower attitude. Yet here, as so often, cannot we find a golden mean between them?'

'What's that?' said a dreamy voice. They turned and saw a tall, spectacled man, who greeted the newcomer kindly and took hold of his arm. 'What's that about the golden mean?'

'Mr Jackson—Mr Elliot: Mr Elliot—Mr Jackson,' said Herbert, who did not seem quite pleased. 'Rickie, have you a moment to spare me?'

But the humanist spoke to the young man about the golden mean and the pinchbeck mean, adding, 'You know the Greeks aren't broad church clergymen. They really aren't, in spite of much conflicting evidence. Boys will regard Sophocles as a kind of enlightened bishop, and something tells me that they are wrong.'

'Mr Jackson is a classical enthusiast,' said Herbert. 'He makes the past live. I want to talk to you about the humdrum present.'

'And I am warning him against the humdrum past. That's another point, Mr Elliot. Impress on your class that many Greeks and most Romans were frightfully stupid, and if they disbelieve you, read Ctesiphon with them, or Valerius Flaccus. Whatever is that noise?'

'It comes from your class-room, I think,' snapped the other master.

'So it does. Ah, yes. I expect they are putting your little Tewson into the waste-paper basket.'

'I always lock my class-room in the interval—'

'Yes?'

'—and carry the key in my pocket.'

'Ah. But, Mr Elliot, I am a cousin of Widdrington's. He wrote to me about you. I am so glad. Will you, first of all, come to supper next Sunday?'

'I am afraid,' put in Herbert, 'that we poor house-masters must deny ourselves festivities in term time.'

'But mayn't he come once, just once?'

'May, my dear Jackson! My brother-in-law is not a baby. He decides for himself.'

Rickie naturally refused. As soon as they were out of hearing, Herbert said, 'This is a little unfortunate. Who is Mr Widdrington?'

'I knew him at Cambridge.'

'Let me explain how we stand,' he continued, after a pause. 'Jackson is the worst of the reactionaries here, while I—why should I conceal it?—have thrown in my lot with the party of progress. You will see how we suffer from him at the masters' meetings. He has no talent for organization, and yet he is always inflicting his ideas on others. It was like his impertinence to dictate to you what authors you should read, and meanwhile the sixth-form room like a bear-garden, and a school prefect being put into the waste-paper basket. My good Rickie, there's nothing to smile at. How is the school to go on with a man like that? It would be a case of "quick march," if it was not for his brilliant intellect. That's why I say it's a little unfortunate. You will have very little in common, you and he.'

Rickie did not answer. He was very fond of Widdrington, who was a quaint, sensitive person. And he could not help being attracted by Mr

Jackson, whose welcome contrasted pleasantly with the official breeziness of his other colleagues. He wondered, too, whether it is so very reactionary to contemplate the antique.

'It is true that I vote Conservative,' pursued Mr Pembroke, apparently confronting some objector. 'But why? Because the Conservatives, rather than the Liberals, stand for progress. One must not be misled by catch-words.'

'Didn't you want to ask me something?'

'Ah, yes. You found a boy in your form called Varden?'

'Varden? Yes; there is.'

'Drop on him heavily. He has broken the statutes of the school. He is attending as a day-boy. The statutes provide that a boy must reside with his parents or guardians. He does neither. It must be stopped. You must tell the headmaster.'

'Where does the boy live?'

'At a certain Mrs Orr's, who has no connection with the school of any kind. It must be stopped. He must either enter a boarding-house or go.'

'But why should I tell?' said Rickie. He remembered the boy, an unattractive person with protruding ears. 'It is the business of his house-master.'

'House-master—exactly. Here we come back again. Who is now the day-boys' house-master? Jackson once again—as if anything was Jackson's business! I handed the house back last term in a most flourishing condition. It has already gone to rack and ruin for the second time. To return to Varden. I have unearthed a put-up job. Mrs Jackson and Mrs Orr are friends. Do you see? It all works round.'

'I see. It does—or might.'

'The headmaster will never sanction it when it's put to him plainly.'

'But why should I put it?' said Rickie, twisting the ribbons of his gown round his fingers.

'Because you're the boy's form-master.'

'Is that a reason?'

'Of course it is.'

'I only wondered whether—' He did not like to say that he wondered whether he need do it his first morning.

'By some means or other you must find out—of course you know already, but you must find out from the boy. I know—I have it! Where's his health certificate?'

'He had forgotten it.'

'Just like them. Well, when he brings it, it will be signed by Mrs Orr, and you must look at it and say, "Orr—Orr—Mrs Orr?" or something to that effect, and then the whole thing will come naturally out.'

The bell rang, and they went in for the hour of school that concluded the morning. Varden brought his health certificate—a pompous document asserting that he had not suffered from roseola or kindred ailments in the holidays—and for a long time Rickie sat with it before him, spread open upon his desk. He did not quite like the job. It suggested intrigue, and he had come to Sawston not to intrigue but to labour. Doubtless Herbert was right, and Mr Jackson and Mrs Orr were wrong. But why could they not have it out among themselves? Then he thought, 'I am a coward, and that's why I'm raising these objections,' called the boy up to him, and it did all come out naturally, more or less. Hitherto Varden had lived with his mother; but she had left Sawston at Christmas, and now he would live with Mrs Orr. 'Mr Jackson, sir, said it would be all right.'

'Yes, yes,' said Rickie; 'quite so.' He remembered Herbert's dictum: 'Masters must present a united front. If they do not—the deluge.' He sent the boy back to his seat, and after school took the compromising health certificate to the headmaster. The headmaster was at that time easily excited by a breach of the constitution. 'Parents or guardians,' he repeated—'parents or guardians,' and flew with those words on his lips to Mr Jackson.

To say that Rickie was a cat's-paw is to put it too strongly. Herbert was strictly honourable, and never pushed him into an illegal or really dangerous position; but there is no doubt that on this and on many other occasions he had to do things that he would not otherwise have done. There was always some diplomatic corner that had to be turned, always something that he had to say or not to say. As the term wore on he lost his independence—almost without knowing it. He had much to learn about boys, and he learnt not by direct observation—for which he believed he was unfitted—but by sedulous imitation of the more experienced masters. Originally he had intended to be friends with his pupils, and Mr Pembroke commended the intention highly; but you cannot be friends either with boy or man unless you give yourself away in the process, and Mr Pembroke did not commend this. He, for 'personal intercourse,' substituted the safer 'personal influence,' and gave his junior hints on the setting of kindly traps, in which the boy does give himself away and reveals his shy delicate thoughts, while the master, intact, commends or corrects them. Originally Rickie had meant to help boys in the anxieties that they undergo when changing into men: at Cambridge he had numbered this among life's duties. But here is a subject in which we must inevitably speak as one human being to another, not as one who has authority or the shadow of authority, and for this reason the elder schoolmaster could suggest nothing but a few formulæ. Formulæ, like kindly traps, were not in Rickie's line, so he abandoned these subjects altogether and confined himself to working hard at what was easy. In the house he did as Herbert did, and referred all doubtful subjects to him. In his form, oddly enough, he became a martinet. It is so much simpler to be severe. He grasped the school regulations, and insisted on prompt obedience to them. He adopted the doctrine of collective responsibility. When one boy was late, he punished the whole form. 'I can't help it,' he would say, as if he was a power of nature. As a teacher he was rather dull. He curbed his own enthusiasms, finding that they distracted his attention, and that while he throbbed to the music of Virgil the boys in the back row were getting unruly. But on the whole he liked his form work: he knew why he was there, and Herbert did not overshadow him so completely.

What was amiss with Herbert? He had known that something was amiss, and had entered into partnership with open eyes. The man was kind and unselfish; more than that, he was truly charitable, and it was a real pleasure to him to give pleasure to others. Certainly he might talk too much about it afterwards; but it was the doing, not the talking, that he really valued, and benefactors of this sort are not too common. He was, moreover, diligent and conscientious: his heart was in his work, and his adherence to the Church of England no mere matter of form. He was capable of affection: he was usually courteous and tolerant. Then what was amiss? Why, in spite of all these qualities, should Rickie feel that there was something wrong with him—nay, that he was wrong as a whole, and that if the Spirit of Humanity should ever hold a judgment he would assuredly be classed among the goats? The answer at first sight appeared a graceless one—it was that Herbert was stupid. Not stupid in the ordinary sense—he had a business-like brain, and acquired knowledge easily—but stupid in the important sense: his whole life was coloured by a contempt of the intellect. That he had a tolerable intellect of his own was not the point: it is in what we value, not in what we have, that the test of us resides. Now, Rickie's intellect was not remarkable. He came to his worthier results rather by imagination and instinct than by logic. An argument confused him, and he could with difficulty follow it even on paper. But he saw in this no reason for satisfaction, and tried to make such use of his brain as he could, just as a weak athlete might lovingly exercise his body. Like a weak athlete, too, he loved to watch the exploits, or rather the efforts, of others—their efforts not so much to acquire knowledge as to dispel a little of the darkness by which we and all our acquisitions are surrounded. Cambridge had taught him this, and he knew, if for no other reason, that his time there had not been vain. And Herbert's contempt for such efforts revolted him. He saw that for all his fine talk about a spiritual life he had but one test for things—success: success for the body in this life or for the soul in the life to come. And for this reason Humanity, and perhaps such other tribunals as there may be, would assuredly reject him.

Chapter Eighteen

Meanwhile he was a husband. Perhaps his union should have been emphasized before. The crown of life had been attained, the vague yearnings, the misread impulses, had found accomplishment at last. Never again must he feel lonely, or as one who stands out of the broad highway of the world and fears, like poor Shelley, to undertake the longest journey. So he reasoned, and at first took the accomplishment for granted. But as the term passed he knew that behind the yearning there remained a yearning, behind the drawn veil a veil that he could not draw. His wedding had been no mighty landmark: he would often wonder whether such and such a speech or incident came after it or before. Since that meeting in the Soho restaurant there had been so much to do—clothes to buy, presents to thank for, a brief visit to a Training College, a honeymoon as brief. In such a bustle, what spiritual union could take place? Surely the dust would settle soon: in Italy, at Easter, he might perceive the infinities of love. But love had shown him its infinities already. Neither by marriage nor by any other device can men ensure themselves a vision; and Rickie's had been granted him three years before, when he had seen his wife and a dead man clasped in each other's arms. She was never to be so real to him again.

She ran about the house looking handsomer than ever. Her cheerful voice gave orders to the servants. As he sat in the study correcting compositions, she would dart in and give him a kiss. 'Dear girl—' he would murmur, with a glance at the rings on her hand. The tone of their marriage life was soon set. It was to be a frank good-fellowship, and before long he found it difficult to speak in a deeper key.

One evening he made the effort. There had been more beauty than was usual at Sawston. The air was pure and quiet. To-morrow the fog might be here, but to-day one said, 'It is like the country.' Arm in arm they strolled in the side-garden, stopping at times to notice the crocuses, or to wonder when the daffodils would flower. Suddenly he tightened his pressure, and said, 'Darling, why don't you still wear ear-rings?'

'Ear-rings?' She laughed. 'May taste has improved, perhaps.'

So after all they never mentioned Gerald's name. But he hoped it was still dear to her. He did not want her to forget the greatest moment in her life. His love desired not ownership but confidence, and to a love so pure it does not seem terrible to come second.

He valued emotion—not for itself, but because it is the only final path to intimacy. She, ever robust and practical, always discouraged him. She was not cold; she would willingly embrace him. But she hated being upset, and would laugh or thrust him off when his voice grew serious. In this she reminded him of his mother. But his mother—he had never concealed it from himself—had glories to which his wife would never attain; glories that had unfolded against a life of horror—a life even more horrible than he had guessed. He thought of her often during these earlier months. Did she bless his union, so different to her own? Did she love his wife? He tried to speak of her to Agnes, but again she was reluctant. And perhaps it was this aversion to acknowledge the dead, whose images alone have immortality, that made her own image somewhat transient, so that when he left her no mystic influence remained, and only by an effort could he realize that God had united them for ever.

They conversed and differed healthily upon other topics. A rifle corps was to be formed: she hoped that the boys would have proper uniforms, instead of shooting in their old clothes, as Mr Jackson had suggested. There was Tewson; could nothing be done about him? He would slink away from the other prefects and go with boys of his own age. There was Lloyd: he would not learn the school anthem, saying that it hurt his throat. And above all there was Varden, who, to Rickie's bewilderment, was now a member of Dunwood House.

'He had to go somewhere,' said Agnes. 'Lucky for his mother that we had a vacancy.'

'Yes—but when I meet Mrs Orr—I can't help feeling ashamed.'

'Oh, Mrs Orr! Who cares for her? Her teeth are drawn. If she chooses to insinuate that we planned it, let her. Hers was rank dishonesty. She attempted to set up a boarding-house.'

Mrs Orr, who was quite rich, had attempted no such thing. She had taken the boy out of charity, and without a thought of being unconstitutional. But in had come this officious 'Limpet' and upset the headmaster, and she was scolded, and Mrs Varden was scolded, and Mr Jackson was scolded, and the boy was scolded and placed with Mr Pembroke, whom she revered less than any man in the world. Naturally enough, she considered it a further attempt of the authorities to snub the day-boys, for whose advantage the school had been founded. She and Mrs Jackson discussed the subject at their tea-parties, and the latter lady was sure that no good, no good of any kind, would come to Dunwood House from such ill-gotten plunder.

'We say, "Let them talk,"' persisted Rickie, 'but I never did like letting people talk. We are right and they are wrong, but I wish the thing could have been done more quietly. The headmaster does get so excited. He has given a gang of foolish people their opportunity. I don't like being branded as the "day-boy's foe," when I think how much I would have given to be a day-boy myself. My father found me a nuisance, and put me through the mill, and I can never forget it—particularly the evenings.'

'There's very little bullying here,' said Agnes.

'There was very little bullying at my school. There was simply the atmosphere of unkindness, which no discipline can dispel. It's not what people do to you, but what they mean, that hurts.'

'I don't understand.'

'Physical pain doesn't hurt—at least not what I call hurt—if a man hits you by accident or in play. But just a little tap, when you know it comes from hatred, is too terrible. Boys do hate each other: I remember it, and see it again. They can make strong isolated friendships, but of general good-fellowship they haven't a notion.'

'All I know is there's very little bullying here.'

'You see, the notion of good-fellowship develops late: you can just see its beginning here among the prefects: up at Cambridge it flourishes amazingly. That's why I pity people who don't go up to Cambridge: not because a University is smart, but because those are the magic years, and—with luck—you see up there what you couldn't see before and mayn't ever see again.'

'Aren't these the magic years?' the lady demanded.

He laughed and hit at her. 'I'm getting somewhat involved. But hear me, O Agnes, for I am practical. I approve of our public schools. Long may they flourish. But I do not approve of the boarding-house system. It isn't an inevitable adjunct—'

'Good gracious me!' she shrieked. 'Have you gone mad?'

'Silence, madam. Don't betray me to Herbert, or he'll give us the sack.

But seriously, what is the good of throwing boys so much together? Isn't it building their lives on a wrong basis? They don't understand each other. I wish they did, but they don't. They don't realize that human beings are simply marvellous. When they do, the whole of life changes, and you get the true thing. But don't pretend you've got it before you have. Patriotism and *esprit de corps* are all very well, but masters a little forget that they must grow from a sentiment. They cannot create one. Cannot—cannot—cannot. I never cared a straw for England until I cared for Englishmen, and boys can't love the school when they hate each other. Ladies and gentlemen, I will now conclude my address. And most of it is copied out of Mr Ansell.'

The truth is, he was suddenly ashamed. He had been carried away on a flood of his old emotions. Cambridge and all that it meant had stood before him passionately clear, and beside it stood his mother and the sweet family life which nurses up a boy until he can salute his equals. He was ashamed, for he remembered his new resolution—to work without criticizing, to throw himself vigorously into the machine, not to mind if he was pinched now and then by the elaborate wheels.

'Mr Ansell!' cried his wife, laughing somewhat shrilly. 'Aha! Now I understand. It's just the kind of thing poor Mr Ansell would say. Well, I'm brutal. I believe it *does* Varden *good* to have his ears pulled now and then, and I don't care whether they pull them in play or not. Boys ought to rough it, or they never grow up into men, and your mother would have agreed with me. Oh yes; and you're all wrong about patriotism. It can, can, can create a sentiment.'

She was unusually precise, and had followed his thoughts with an attention that was also unusual. He wondered whether she was not right, and regretted that she proceeded to say, 'My dear boy, you mustn't talk these heresies inside Dunwood House! You sound just like one of that reactionary Jackson set, who want to fling the school back a hundred years and have nothing but day-boys all dressed anyhow.'

'The Jackson set have their points.'

'You'd better join it.'

'The Dunwood House set has its points.' For Rickie suffered from the Primal Curse, which is not—as the Authorized Version suggests—the knowledge of good and evil, but the knowledge of good-and-evil.

'Then stick to the Dunwood House set.'

'I do, and shall.' Again he was ashamed. Why would he see the other side of things? He rebuked his soul, not unsuccessfully, and then they returned to the subject of Varden.

'I'm certain he suffers,' said he, for she would do nothing but laugh. 'Each boy who passes pulls his ears—very funny, no doubt; but every day they stick out more and get redder, and this afternoon, when he didn't know he was being watched, he was holding his head and moaning. I hate the look about his eyes.'

'I hate the whole boy. Nasty weedy thing.'

'Well, I'm a nasty weedy thing, if it comes to that.'

'No, you aren't,' she cried, kissing him. But he led her back to the subject.

Could nothing be suggested? He drew up some new rules–alterations in the times of going to bed, and so on–the effect of which would be to provide few opportunities for the pulling of Varden's ears. The rules were submitted to Herbert, who sympathized with weakliness more than did his sister, and gave them his careful consideration. But unfortunately they collided with other rules, and on a closer examination he found that they also ran contrary to the fundamentals on which the government of Dunwood House was based. So nothing was done. Agnes was rather pleased, and took to teasing her husband about Varden. At last he asked her to stop. He felt uneasy about the boy–almost superstitious. His first morning's work had brought sixty pounds a-year to their hotel.

Chapter Nineteen

They did not get to Italy at Easter. Herbert had the offer of some private pupils, and needed Rickie's help. It seemed unreasonable to leave England when money was to be made in it, so they went to Ilfracombe instead. They spent three weeks among the natural advantages and unnatural disadvantages of that resort. It was out of the season, and they encamped in a huge hotel, which took them at a reduction. By a disastrous chance the Jacksons were down there too, and a good deal of constrained civility had to pass between the two families. Constrained it was not in Mr Jackson's case. At all times he was ready to talk, and as long as they kept off the school it was pleasant enough. But he was very indiscreet and feminine tact had often to intervene. 'Go away, dear ladies,' he would then observe. 'You think you see life because you see the chasms in it. Yet all the chasms are full of female skeletons.' The ladies smiled anxiously. To Rickie he was friendly and even intimate. They had long talks on the deserted Capstone, while their wives sat reading in the Winter Garden and Mr Pembroke kept an eye upon the tutored youths. 'Once I had tutored youths,' said Mr Jackson, 'but I lost them all by letting them paddle with my nieces. It is so impossible to remember what is proper.' And sooner or later their talk gravitated towards his central passion–the Fragments of Sophocles. Some day ('never,' said Herbert) he would edit them. At present they were merely in his blood. With the zeal of a scholar and the imagination of a poet he reconstructed lost dramas–Niobe, Phædra, Philoctetes against Troy, whose names, but for an accident, would have thrilled the world. 'Is it worth it?' he cried. 'Had we better be planting potatoes?' And then: 'We had; but this is the second best.'

Agnes did not approve of these colloquies. Mr Jackson was not a buffoon, but he behaved like one, which is what matters; and from the Winter Garden she could see people laughing at him, and at her husband, who got excited too. She hinted once or twice, but no notice was taken, and at last she said rather sharply, 'Now, you're not to, Rickie. I won't have it.'

'He's a type that suits me. He knows people I know, or would like to have
known. He was a friend of Tony Failing's. It is so hard to realize that a man
connected with one was great. Uncle Tony seems to have been. He loved
poetry and music and pictures, and everthing tempted him to live in a kind of
cultured paradise, with the door shut upon a squalor. But to have more
decent people in the world—he sacrificed everything to that. He would have
"smashed the whole beauty-shop" if it would help him. I really couldn't go
as far as that. I don't think one need go as far—pictures might have to be
smashed, but not music or poetry; surely they help—and Jackson doesn't
think so either.'

'Well, I won't have it, and that's enough.' She laughed, for her voice had a
little been that of the professional scold. 'You see we must hang together.
He's in the reactionary camp.'

'He doesn't know it. He doesn't know that he is in any camp at all.'

'His wife is, which comes to the same.'

'Still, it's the holidays—' He and Mr Jackson had drifted apart in the
term, chiefly owing to the affair of Varden. 'We were to have the holidays to
ourselves, you know.' And following some line of thought, he continued,
'He cheers one up. He does believe in poetry. Smart, sentimental books do
seem absolutely absurd to him, and gods and fairies far nearer to reality. He
tries to express all modern life in the terms of Greek mythology, because the
Greeks looked very straight at things, and Demeter or Aphrodite are thinner
veils than "The survival of the fittest," or "A marriage has been arranged,"
and other draperies of modern journalese.'

'And do you know what that means?'

'It means that poetry, not prose, lies at the core.'

'No. I can tell you what it means—balderdash.'

His mouth fell. She was sweeping away the cobwebs with a vengeance. 'I
hope you're wrong,' he replied, 'for those are the lines on which I've been
writing, however badly, for the last two years.'

'But you write stories, not poems.'

He looked at his watch. 'Lessons again. One never has a moment's
peace.'

'Poor Rickie! You shall have a real holiday in the summer.' And she called
after him to say, 'Remember, dear, about Mr Jackson. Don't go talking so
much to him.'

Rather arbitrary. Her tone had been a little arbitrary of late. But what did
it matter? Mr Jackson was not a friend, and he must risk the chance of
offending Widdrington. After the lesson he wrote to Ansell, whom he had
not seen since June, asking him to come down to Ilfracombe, if only for a
day. On reading the letter over, its tone displeased him. It was quite
pathetic: it sounded like a cry from prison. 'I can't send him such nonsense,'
he thought, and wrote again. But phrase it as he would, the letter always
suggested that he was unhappy. 'What's wrong?' he wondered. 'I could
write anything I wanted to him once.' So he scrawled 'Come!' on a post-
card. But even this seemed too serious. The post-card followed the letters,
and Agnes found them all in the waste-paper basket.

Then she said, 'I've been thinking–oughtn't you to ask Mr Ansell over? A breath of sea air would do the poor thing good.'

There was no difficulty now. He wrote at once, 'My dear Stewart–We both so much wish you could come over.' But the invitation was refused. A little uneasy, he wrote again, using the dialect of their past intimacy. The effect of this letter was not pathetic but jaunty, and he felt a keen regret as soon as it slipped into the box. It was a relief to receive no reply.

He brooded a good deal over this painful yet intangible episode. Was the pain all of his own creating? or had it been produced by something external? And he got the answer that brooding always gives–it was both. He was morbid, and had been so since his visit to Cadover–quicker to register discomfort than joy. But, none the less, Ansell was definitely brutal, and Agnes definitely jealous. Brutality he could understand, alien as it was to himself. Jealousy, equally alien, was a harder matter. Let husband and wife be as sun and moon, or as moon and sun. Shall they therefore not give greeting to the stars? He was willing to grant that the love that inspired her might be higher than his own. Yet did it not exclude them both from much that is gracious? That dream of his when he rode on the Wiltshire expanses–a curious dream: the lark silent, the earth dissolving. And he awoke from it into a valley full of men.

She was jealous in many ways–sometimes in an open humorous fashion, sometimes more subtly, never content till 'we' had extended our patronage and, if possible, our pity. She began to patronize and pity Ansell, and most sincerely trusted that he would get his fellowship. Otherwise what was the poor fellow to do? Ridiculous as it may seem, she was even jealous of Nature. One day her husband escaped from Ilfracombe to Morthoe, and came back ecstatic over its fangs of slate, piercing an oily sea. 'Sounds like an hippopotamus,' she said peevishly. And when they returned to Sawston through the Virgilian counties, she disliked him looking out of the window, for all the world as if Nature was some dangerous woman.

He resumed his duties with a feeling that he had never left them. Again he confronted the assembled house. This term was again *the* term; school still the world in miniature. The music of the four-part fugue entered into him more deeply, and he began to hum its little phrases. The same routine, the same diplomacies, the same old sense of only half knowing boys or men–he returned to it all; and all that changed was the cloud of unreality, which ever brooded a little more densely than before. He spoke to his wife about this–he spoke to her about everything–and she was alarmed, and wanted him to see a doctor. But he explained that it was nothing of any practical importance, nothing that interfered with his work or his appetite, nothing more than a feeling that the cow was not really there. She laughed, and 'How is the cow to-day?' soon passed into a domestic joke.

Chapter Twenty

Ansell was in his favourite haunt—the reading-room of the British Museum. In that book-encircled space he always could find peace. He loved to see the volumes rising tier above tier into the misty dome. He loved the chairs that glide so noiselessly, and the radiating desks, and the central area, where the catalogue shelves curve round the superintendent's throne. There he knew that his life was not ignoble. It was worth while to grow old and dusty seeking for truth though truth is unattainable, restating questions that have been stated at the beginning of the world. Failure would await him, but not disillusionment. It was worth while reading books, and writing a book or two which few would read, and no one, perhaps, endorse. He was not a hero, and he knew it. His father and sisters, by their steady goodness, had made this life possible. But, all the same, it was not the life of a spoilt child.

In the next chair to him sat Widdrington, engaged in his historical research. His desk was edged with enormous volumes, and every few moments an assistant brought him more. They rose like a wall against Ansell. Towards the end of the morning a gap was made, and through it they held the following conversation.

'I've been stopping with my cousin at Sawston.'

'M'm.'

'It was quite exciting. The air rang with battle. About two-thirds of the masters have lost their heads, and are trying to produce a gimcrack copy of Eton. Last term, you know, with a great deal of puffing and blowing, they fixed the numbers of the school. This term they want to create a new boarding-house.'

'They are very welcome.'

'But the more boarding-houses they create, the less room they leave for day-boys. The local mothers are frantic, and so is my queer cousin. I never knew him so excited over sub-Hellenic things. There was an indignation meeting at his house. He is supposed to look after the day-boys' interests, but no one thought he would—least of all the people who gave him the post. The speeches were most eloquent. They argued that the school was founded for day-boys, and that it's intolerable to handicap them. One poor lady cried, "Here's my Harold in the school, and my Toddie coming on. As likely as not I shall be told there is no vacancy for him. Then what am I to do? If I go, what's to become of Harold; and if I stop, what's to become of Toddie?" I must say I was touched. Family life is more real than national life—at least I've ordered all these books to prove it is—and I fancy that the bust of

Euripides agreed with me, and was sorry for the hot-faced mothers. Jackson will do what he can. He didn't quite like to state the naked truth—which is, that boarding-houses pay. He explained it to me afterwards: they are the only future open to a stupid master. It's easy enough to be a beak when you're young and athletic, and can offer the latest University smattering. The difficulty is to keep your place when you get old and stiff, and younger smatterers are pushing up behind you. Crawl into a boarding-house and you're safe. A master's life is frightfully tragic. Jackson's fairly right himself, because he has got a first-class intellect. But I met a poor brute who was hired as an athlete. He has missed his shot at a boarding-house, and there's nothing in the world for him to do but to trundle down the hill.'

Ansell yawned.

'I saw Rickie too. Once I dined there.'

Another yawn.

'My cousin thinks Mrs Elliot one of the most horrible women he has ever seen. He calls her "Medusa in Arcady." She's so pleasant, too. But certainly it was a very stony meal.'

'What kind of stoniness?'

'No one stopped talking for a moment.'

'That's the real kind,' said Ansell moodily, 'The only kind.'

'Well, I,' he continued, 'am inclined to compare her to an electric light. Click! she's on. Click! she's off. No waste. No flicker.'

'I wish she'd fuse.'

'She'll never fuse—unless anything was to happen at the main.'

'What do you mean by the main?' said Ansell, who always pursued a metaphor relentlessly.

Widdrington did not know what he meant, and suggested that Ansell should visit Sawston to see whether one could know.

'It is no good me going. I should not find Mrs Elliot: she has no real existence.'

'Rickie has.'

'I very much doubt it. I had two letters from Ilfracombe last April, and I very much doubt that the man who wrote them can exist.' Bending downwards, he began to adorn the manuscript of his dissertation with a square, and inside that a circle, and inside that another square. It was his second dissertation: the first had failed.

'I think he exists: he is so unhappy.'

Ansell nodded, 'How did you know he was unhappy?'

'Because he was always talking.' After a pause he added, 'What clever young men we are!'

'Aren't we? I expect we shall get asked in marriage soon. I say, Widdrington, shall we—?'

'Accept? Of course. It is not young-manly to say no.'

'I meant shall we ever do a more tremendous thing—fuse Mrs Elliot.'

'No,' said Widdrington promptly. 'We shall never do that all our lives.' He added, 'I think you might go down to Sawston, though.'

'I have already refused or ignored three invitations.'

'So I gathered.'

'What's the good of it?' said Ansell through his teeth. 'I will not put up with little things. I would rather be rude than listen to twaddle from a man I've known.'

'You might go down to Sawston, just for a night, to see him.'

'I saw him last month—at least, so Tilliard informs me. He says that we all three lunched together, that Rickie paid, and that the conversation was most interesting.'

'Well, I contend that he does exist, and that if you go—oh, I can't be clever any longer. You really must go, man. I'm certain he's miserable and lonely. Dunwood House reeks of commerce and snobbery and all the things he hated most. He doesn't do any writing. He doesn't make any friends. He is so odd, too. In this day-boy row that has just started he's gone for my cousin. Would you believe it? Quite spitefully. It made quite a difficulty when I wanted to dine. It isn't like him—either the sentiments or the behaviour. I'm sure he's not himself. Pembroke used to look after the day-boys, and so he can't very well take the lead against them, and perhaps Rickie's doing his dirty work—and has overdone it, as decent people generally do. He's even altering to talk to. Yet he's not been married a year. Pembroke and that wife simply run him. I don't see why they should, and no more do you; and that's why I want you to go to Sawston, if only for one night.'

Ansell shook his head, and looked up at the dome as other men look at the sky. In it the great arc lamps spluttered and flared, for the month was again November. Then he lowered his eyes from the cold violet radiance to the books.

'No, Widdrington; no. We don't go to see people because they are happy or unhappy. We go when we can talk to them. I cannot talk to Rickie, therefore I will not waste my time at Sawston.'

'I think you're right,' said Widdrington softly. 'But we are bloodless brutes. I wonder whether—if we were different people—something might be done to save him. That is the curse of being a little intellectual. You and our sort have always seen too clearly. We stand aside—and meanwhile he turns into stone. Two philosophic youths repining in the British Museum! What have we done? What shall we ever do? Just drift and criticize, while people who know what they want snatch it away from us and laugh.'

'Perhaps you are that sort. I'm not. When the moment comes I shall hit out like any ploughboy. Don't believe those lies about intellectual people. They're only written to soothe the majority. Do you suppose, with the world as it is, that it's an easy matter to keep quiet? Do you suppose that I didn't want to rescue him from that ghastly woman? Action! Nothing's easier than action; as fools testify. But I want to act rightly.'

'The superintendent is looking at us. I must get back to my work.'

'You think this all nonsense,' said Ansell, detaining him. 'Please remember that if I do act, you are bound to help me.'

Widdrington looked a little grave. He was no anarchist. A few plaintive cries against Mrs Elliot were all that he was prepared to emit.

'There's no mystery,' continued Ansell. 'I haven't the shadow of a plan in

my head. I know not only Rickie but the whole of his history: you remember
the day near Madingley. Nothing in either helps me: I'm just watching.'

'But what for?'

'For the Spirit of Life.'

Widdrington was surprised. It was a phrase unknown to their philosophy.
They had trespassed into poetry.

'You can't fight Medusa with anything else. If you ask me what the Spirit
of Life is, or to what it is attached, I can't tell you. I only tell you, watch for it.
Myself I've found it in books. Some people find it out of doors or in each
other. Never mind. It's the same spirit, and I trust myself to know it
anywhere, and to use it rightly.'

But at this point the superintendent sent a message.

Widdrington then suggested a stroll in the galleries. It was foggy: they
needed fresh air. He loved and admired his friend, but to-day he could not
grasp him. The world as Ansell saw it seemed such a fantastic place,
governed by brand-new laws. What more could one do than to see Rickie as
often as possible, to invite his confidence to offer him spiritual support? And
Mrs Elliot—what power could 'fuse' a respectable woman?

Ansell consented to the stroll, but, as usual, only breathed depression.
The comfort of books deserted him among those marble goddesses and
gods. The eye of an artist finds pleasure in texture and poise, but he could
only think of the vanished incense and deserted temples beside an
unfurrowed sea.

'Let us go,' he said. 'I do not like carved stones.'

'You are too particular,' said Widdrington. 'You are always expecting to
meet living people. One never does. I am content with the Parthenon frieze.'
And he moved along a few yards of it, while Ansell followed, conscious only
of its pathos.

'There's Tilliard,' he observed. 'Shall we kill him?'

'Please,' said Widdrington, and as he spoke Tilliard joined them. He
brought them news. That morning he had heard from Rickie: Mrs Elliot was
expecting a child.

'A child?' said Ansell, suddenly bewildered.

'Oh, I forgot,' interposed Widdrington. 'My cousin did tell me.'

'You forgot! Well, after all, I forgot that it might be. We are indeed young
men.' He leant against the pedestal of Ilissus and remembered their talk
about the Spirit of Life. In his ignorance of what a child means, he wondered
whether the opportunity he sought lay here.

'I am very glad,' said Tilliard, not without intention. 'A child will draw
them even closer together. I like to see young people wrapped up in their
child.'

'I suppose I must be getting back to my dissertation,' said Ansell. He left
the Parthenon to pass by the monuments of our more reticent beliefs—the
temple of the Ephesian Artemis, the statue of the Cnidian Demeter. Honest,
he knew that here were powers he could not cope with, nor, as yet,
understand.

Chapter Twenty-one

The mists that had gathered round Rickie seemed to be breaking. He had found light neither in work for which he was unfitted nor in a woman who had ceased to respect him, and whom he was ceasing to love. Though he called himself fickle and took all the blame of their marriage on his own shoulders, there remained in Agnes certain terrible faults of heart and head, and no self-reproach would diminish them. The glamour of wedlock had faded; indeed, he saw now that it had faded even before wedlock, and that during the final months he had shut his eyes and pretended it was still there. But now the mists were breaking.

That November the supreme event approached. He saw it with Nature's eyes. It dawned on him, as on Ansell, that personal love and marriage only cover one side of the shield, and that on the other is graven the epic of birth. In the midst of lessons he would grow dreamy, as one who spies a new symbol for the universe, a fresh circle within the square. Within the square shall be a circle, within the circle another square, until the visual eye is baffled. Here is meaning of a kind. His mother had forgotten herself in him. He would forget himself in his son.

He was at his duties when the news arrived—taking preparation. Boys are marvellous creatures. Perhaps they will sink below the brutes; perhaps they will attain to a woman's tenderness. Though they despised Rickie, and had suffered under Agnes's meanness, their one thought this term was to be gentle and to give no trouble.

'Rickie—one moment—'

His face grew ashen. He followed Herbert into the passage, closing the door of the preparation-room behind him. 'Oh, is she safe?' he whispered.

'Yes, yes,' said Herbert; but there sounded in his answer a sombre hostile note.

'Our boy?'

'Girl—a girl, dear Rickie; a little daughter. She—she is in many ways a healthy child. She will live—oh yes.' A flash of horror passed over his face. He hurried into the preparation-room, lifted the lid of his desk, glanced mechanically at the boys, and came out again.

Mrs Lewin appeared through the door that led into their own part of the house.

'Both going on well!' she cried; but her voice also was grave, exasperated.

'What is it?' he gasped. 'It's something you daren't tell me.'

'Only this—' stuttered Herbert. 'You mustn't mind when you see—she's lame.'

Mrs Lewin disappeared.

'Lame! but not as lame as I am?'

'Oh, my dear boy, worse. Don't—oh, be a man in this. Come away from the preparation-room. Remember she'll live—in many ways healthy—only just this one defect.'

The horror of that week never passed away from him. To the end of his life, he remembered the excuses—the consolations that the child would live; suffered very little, if at all; would walk with crutches; would certainly live. God was more merciful. A window was opened too wide on a draughty day. After a short, painless illness his daughter died. But the lesson he had learnt so glibly at Cambridge should be heeded now; no child should ever be born to him again.

Chapter Twenty-two

That same term there took place at Dunwood House another event. With their private tragedy it seemed to have no connection; but in time Rickie perceived it as a bitter comment. Its developments were unforeseen and lasting. It was perhaps the most terrible thing he had to bear.

Varden had now been a boarder for ten months. His health had broken in the previous term—partly, it is to be feared, as the result of the indifferent food—and during the summer holidays he was attacked by a series of agonizing earaches. His mother, a feeble person, wished to keep him at home, but Herbert dissuaded her. Soon after the death of the child there arose at Dunwood House one of those waves of hostility of which no boy knows the origin nor any master can calculate the course. Varden had never been popular—there was no reason why he should be—but he had never been seriously bullied hitherto. One evening nearly the whole house set on him. The prefects absented themselves, the bigger boys stood round, and the lesser boys, to whom power was delegated, flung him down, and rubbed his face under the desks, and wrenched at his ears. The noise penetrated the baize doors, and Herbert swept through and punished the whole house, including Varden, whom it would not do to leave out. The poor man was horrified. He approved of a little healthy roughness, but this was pure brutality. What had come over his boys? Were they not gentlemen's sons? He would not admit that if you herd together human beings before they can understand each other the great god Pan is angry, and will in the end evade your regulations and drive them mad. That night the victim was screaming with pain, and the doctor next day spoke of an operation. The suspense lasted a whole week. Comment was made in the local papers, and the reputation not only of the house but of the school was imperilled. 'If only I had known,' repeated Herbert—'if only I had known I would have arranged it all differently. He should have had a cubicle.' The boy did not die, but he left Sawston, never to return.

The day before his departure Rickie sat with him some time, and tried to talk in a way that was not pedantic. In his own sorrow, which he could share with no one, least of all with his wife, he was still alive to the sorrows of others. He still fought against apathy, though he was losing the battle.

'Don't lose heart,' he told him. 'The world isn't all going to be like this. There are temptations and trials, of course, but nothing at all of the kind you have had here.'

'But school is the world in miniature, is it not, sir?' asked the boy, hoping to please one master by echoing what had been told him by another. He was always on the look-out for sympathy: it was one of the things that had contributed to his downfall.

'I never noticed that myself. I was unhappy at school, and in the world people can be very happy.'

Varden sighed and rolled about his eyes. 'Are the fellows sorry for what they did to me?' he asked in an affected voice. 'I am sure I forgive them from the bottom of my heart. We ought to forgive our enemies, oughtn't we, sir?'

'But they aren't your enemies. If you meet in five years' time you may find each other splendid fellows.'

The boy would not admit this. He had been reading some revivalistic literature. 'We ought to forgive our enemies,' he repeated; 'and however wicked they are, we ought not to wish them evil. When I was ill, and death seemed nearest, I had many kind letters on this subject.'

Rickie knew about these 'many kind letters.' Varden had induced the silly nurse to write to people—people of all sorts, people that he scarcely knew or did not know at all—detailing his misfortune, and asking for spiritual aid and sympathy.

'I am sorry for them,' he pursued. 'I would not like to be like them.'

Rickie sighed. He saw that a year at Dunwood House had produced a sanctimonious prig. 'Don't think about them, Varden. Think about anything beautiful—say, music. You like music. Be happy. It's your duty. You can't be good until you've had a little happiness. Then perhaps you will think less about forgiving people and more about loving them.'

'I love them already, sir.' And Rickie, in desperation, asked if he might look at the many kind letters.

Permission was gladly given. A neat bundle was produced, and for about twenty minutes the master perused it, while the invalid kept watch on his face. Rooks cawed out in the playing-fields, and close under the window there was the sound of delightful, good-tempered laughter. A boy is no devil, whatever boys may be. The letters were chilly productions, somewhat clerical in tone, by whomsoever written. Varden, because he was ill at the time, had been taken seriously. The writers declared that his illness was fulfilling some mysterious purpose: suffering engendered spiritual growth: he was showing signs of this already. They consented to pray for him, some majestically, others shyly. But they all consented with one exception, who worded his refusal as follows:

> Dear A. C. Varden—I ought to say that I never remember seeing you. I am sorry that you are ill, and hope you are wrong about it. Why did you not write before, for I could have helped you then. When they pulled your ear, you ought to have gone like this (here was a rough sketch). I could not undertake praying, but would think of you instead, if that would do. I am twenty-two in April, built rather heavy, ordinary broad face, with eyes, &c. I write all this because you have mixed me with some one else, for I am not married, and do not want to be. I cannot think of you always, but will promise a quarter of an hour daily (say 7.0–7.15 a.m.), and might come to see you when you are better—that is, if you are a kid, and you read like one. I have been otter-hunting.—Yours sincerely,
>
> Stephen Wonham

Chapter Twenty-three

Rickie went straight from Varden to his wife, who lay on the sofa in her bedroom. There was now a wide gulf between them. She, like the world she had created for him, was unreal.

'Agnes, darling,' he began, stroking her hand, 'such an awkward little thing has happened.'

'What is it, dear? Just wait, till I've added up this book.'

She had got over the tragedy: she got over everything.

When she was at leisure he told her. Hitherto they had seldom mentioned Stephen. He was classed among the unprofitable dead.

She was more sympathetic than he expected. 'Dear Rickie,' she murmured with averted eyes. 'How tiresome for you.'

'I wish that Varden had stopped with Mrs Orr.'

'Well, he leaves us for good to-morrow.'

'Yes, yes. And I made him answer the letter and apologize. They had never met. It was some confusion with a man in the Church Army, living at a place called Codford. I asked the nurse. It is all explained.'

'There the matter ends.'

'I suppose so—if matters ever end.'

'If, by ill-luck, the person does call, I will just see him and say that the boy has gone.'

'You, or I. I have got over all nonsense by this time. He's absolutely nothing to me now.' He took up the tradesman's book and played with it idly. On its crimson cover was stamped a grotesque sheep. How stale and stupid their life had become!

'Don't talk like that, though,' she said uneasily. 'Think how disastrous it would be if you made a slip in speaking to him.'

'Would it? It would have been disastrous once. But I expect, as a matter of fact, that Aunt Emily has made the slip already.'

His wife was displeased. 'You need not talk in that cynical way. I credit Aunt Emily with better feeling. When I was there she did mention the matter, but only once. She, and I, and all who have any sense of decency, know better than to make slips, or to think of making them.'

Agnes kept up what she called 'the family connection.' She had been once alone to Cadover, and also corresponded with Mrs Failing. She had never told Rickie anything about her visit, nor had he ever asked her. But, from this moment, the whole subject was reopened.

'Most certainly he knows nothing,' she continued. 'Why, he does not even realize that Varden lives in our house! We are perfectly safe—unless Aunt Emily were to die. Perhaps then—but we are perfectly safe for the present.'

'When she did mention the matter, what did she say?'

'We had a long talk,' said Agnes quietly. 'She told me nothing new—nothing new about the past, I mean. But we had a long talk about the present. I think'—and her voice grew displeased again—'that you have been both wrong and foolish in refusing to make up your quarrel with Aunt Emily.'

'Wrong and wise, I should say.'

'It isn't to be expected that she—so much older and so sensitive—can make the first step. But I know she'd be glad to see you.'

'As far as I can remember that final scene in the garden, I accused her of "forgetting what other people were like." She'll never pardon me for saying that.'

Agnes was silent. To her the phrase was meaningless. Yet Rickie was correct: Mrs Failing had resented it more than anything.

'At all events,' she suggested, 'you might go and see her.'

'No, dear. Thank you, no.'

'She is, after all—' She was going to say 'your father's sister,' but the expression was scarcely a happy one, and she turned it into, 'She is, after all, growing old and lonely.'

'So are we all!' he cried, with a lapse of tone that was now characteristic in him.

'She oughtn't to be so isolated from her proper relatives.'

There was a moment's silence. Still playing with the book, he remarked, 'You forget, she's got her favourite nephew.'

A bright red flush spread over her cheeks. 'What is the matter with you this afternoon?' she asked. 'I should think you'd better go for a walk.'

'Before I go, tell me what is the matter with you.' He also flushed. 'Why do you want me to make it up with my aunt?'

'Because it's right and proper.'

'So? Or because she is old?'

'I don't understand,' she retorted. But her eyes dropped. His sudden suspicion was true: she was legacy-hunting.

'Agnes, dear Agnes,' he began with passing tenderness, 'how can you think of such things? You behave like a poor person. We don't want any money from Aunt Emily, or from any one else. It isn't virtue that makes me say it: we are not tempted in that way: we have as much as we want already.'

'For the present,' she answered, still looking aside.

'There isn't any future,' he cried in a gust of despair.

'Rickie, what do you mean?'

What did he mean? He meant that the relations between them were fixed—that there would never be an influx of interest, nor even of passion. To the end of life they would go on beating time, and this was enough for her. She was content with the daily round, the common task, performed indifferently. But he had dreamt of another helpmate, and of other things.

'We don't want money—why, we don't even spend any on travelling. I've invested all my salary and more. As far as human foresight goes, we shall never want money.' And his thoughts went out to the tiny grave. 'You spoke of "right and proper," but the right and proper thing for my aunt to do is to leave every penny she's got to Stephen.'

Her lip quivered, and for one moment he thought that she was going to cry. 'What am I to do with you?' she said. 'You talk like a person in poetry.'

'I'll put it in prose. He's lived with her for twenty years, and he ought to be paid for it.'

Poor Agnes! Indeed, what was she to do? The first moment she set foot in Cadover she had thought, 'Oh, here is money. We must try and get it.' Being a lady, she never mentioned the thought to her husband, but she concluded that it would occur to him too. And now, though it had occurred to him at last, he would not even write his aunt a little note.

He was to try her yet further. While they argued this point he flashed out with, 'I ought to have told him that day when he called up to our room. There's where I went wrong first.'

'Rickie!'

'In those days I was sentimental. I minded. For two pins I'd write to him this afternoon. Why shouldn't he know he's my brother? What's all this ridiculous mystery?'

She became incoherent.

'But *why* not? A reason why he shouldn't know.'

'A reason why he *should* know,' she retorted. 'I never heard such rubbish! Give me a reason why he should know.'

'Because the lie we acted has ruined our lives.'

She looked in bewilderment at the well-appointed room.

'It's been like a poison we won't acknowledge. How many times have you thought of my brother? I've thought of him every day—not in love; don't misunderstand; only as a medicine I shirked. Down in what they call the subconscious self he has been hurting me.' His voice broke. 'Oh, my darling, we acted a lie then, and this letter reminds us of it and gives us one more chance. I have to say "we" lied. I should be lying again if I took quite all the blame. Let us ask God's forgiveness together. Then let us write, as coldly as you please, to Stephen, and tell him he is my father's son.'

Her reply need not be quoted. It was the last time he attempted intimacy. And the remainder of their conversation, though long and stormy, is also best forgotten.

Thus the first effect of Varden's letter was to make them quarrel. They had not openly disagreed before. In the evening he kissed her and said, 'How absurd I was to get angry about things that happened last year. I will certainly not write to the person.' She returned the kiss. But he knew that they had destroyed the habit of reverence, and would quarrel again.

On his rounds he looked in at Varden and asked non-chalantly for the letter. He carried it off to his room. It was unwise of him, for his nerves were already unstrung, and the man he had tried to bury was stirring ominously. In the silence he examined the handwriting till he felt that a living creature was with him, whereas he, because his child had died, was dead. He perceived more clearly the cruelty of Nature, to whom our refinement and piety are but as bubbles, hurrying downwards on the turbid waters. They break, and the stream continues. His father, as a final insult, had brought into the world a man unlike all the rest of them—a man dowered with coarse kindliness, and rustic strength, a kind of cynical ploughboy, against whom their own misery and weakness might stand more vividly relieved. 'Born an Elliot—born a gentleman.' So the vile phrase ran. But here was an Elliot whose badness was not even gentlemanly. For that Stephen was bad inherently he never doubted for a moment. And he would have children: he, not Rickie, would contribute to the stream; he, through his remote posterity, might be mingled with the unknown sea.

Thus musing he lay down to sleep, feeling diseased in body and soul. It was no wonder that the night was the most terrible he had ever known. He revisited Cambridge, and his name was a grey ghost over the door. Then there recurred the voice of a gentle shadowy woman, Mrs Aberdeen, 'It doesn't seem hardly right.' Those had been her words, her only complaint against the mysteries of change and death. She bowed her head and laboured to make her 'gentlemen' comfortable. She was labouring still. As he lay in bed he asked God to grant him her wisdom; that he might keep sorrow within due bounds; that he might abstain from extreme hatred and envy of Stephen. It was seldom that he prayed so definitely, or ventured to obtrude his private wishes. Religion was to him a service, a mystic communion with good; not a means of getting what he wanted on the earth. But to-night, through suffering, he was humbled, and became like Mrs Aberdeen.

Hour after hour he awaited sleep and tried to endure the faces that frothed in the gloom—his aunt's, his father's, and, worst of all, the triumphant face of his brother. Once he struck at it, and awoke, having hurt his hand on the wall. Then he prayed hysterically for pardon and rest.

Yet again did he awake, and from a more mysterious dream. He heard his mother crying. She was crying quite distinctly in the darkened room. He whispered, 'Never mind, my darling, never mind,' and a voice echoed, 'Never mind—come away—let them die out—let them die out.' He lit a candle, and the room was empty. Then, hurrying to the window, he saw above mean houses the frosty glories of Orion.

Henceforward he deteriorates. Let those who censure him suggest what he should do. He has lost the work that he loved, his friends, and his child. He remained conscientious and decent, but the spiritual part of him proceeded towards ruin.

Chapter Twenty-four

The coming months, though full of degradation and anxiety, were to bring him nothing so terrible as that night. It was the crisis of his agony. He was an outcast and a failure. But he was not again forced to contemplate these facts so clearly. Varden left in the morning, carrying the fatal letter with him. The whole house was relieved. The good angel was with the boys again, or else (as Herbert preferred to think) they had learnt a lesson, and were more humane in consequence. At all events, the disastrous term concluded quietly.

In the Christmas holidays the two masters made an abortive attempt to visit Italy, and at Easter there was talk of a cruise in the Ægean. Herbert actually went, and enjoyed Athens and Delphi. The Elliots paid a few visits together in England. They returned to Sawston about ten days before school opened, to find that Widdrington was again stopping with the Jacksons. Intercourse was painful, for the two families were scarcely on speaking terms; nor did the triumphant scaffoldings of the new boarding-house make things easier. (The party of progress had carried the day.) Widdrington was by nature touchy, but on this occasion he refused to take offence, and often dropped in to see them. His manner was friendly but critical. They agreed he was a nuisance. Then Agnes left, very abruptly, to see Mrs Failing, and while she was away Rickie had a little stealthy intercourse.

Her absence, convenient as it was, puzzled him. Mrs Silt, half goose, half stormy-petrel, had recently paid a flying visit to Cadover, and thence had flown, without an invitation, to Sawston. Generally, she was not a welcome guest. On this occasion Agnes had welcomed her, and—so Rickie thought—had made her promise not to tell him something that she knew. The ladies had talked mysteriously. 'Mr Silt would be one with you there,' said Mrs Silt. Could there be any connection between the two visits?

Agnes's letters told him nothing: they never did. She was too clumsy or too cautious to express herself on paper. A drive to Stonehenge; an anthem in the Cathedral; Aunt Emily's love. And when he met her at Waterloo he learnt nothing (if there was anything to learn) from her face.

'How did you enjoy yourself?'

'Thoroughly.'

'Were you and she alone?'

'Sometimes. Sometimes other people.'

'Will Uncle Tony's Essays be published?'

Here she was more communicative. The book was at last in proof. Aunt

Emily had written a charming introduction; but she was so idle, she never finished things off.

They got into an omnibus for the Army and Navy Stores; she wanted to do some shopping before going down to Sawston.

'Did you read any of the Essays?'

'Every one. Delightful. Couldn't put them down. Now and then he spoilt them by statistics–but you should read his descriptions of Nature. He agrees with you: says the hills and trees are alive! Aunt Emily called you his spiritual heir, which I thought nice of her. We both so lamented that you have stopped writing.' She quoted fragments of the Essays as they went up in the Stores' lift.

'What else did you talk about?'

'I've told you all my news. Now for yours. Let's have tea first.'

They sat down in the corridor amid ladies in every stage of fatigue–haggard ladies, scarlet ladies, ladies with parcels that twisted from every finger like joints of meat. Gentlemen were scarcer, but all were of the sub-fashionable type, to which Rickie himself now belonged.

'I haven't done anything,' he said feebly. 'Ate, read, been rude to tradespeople, talked to Widdrington. Herbert arrived this morning. He has brought a most beautiful photograph of the Parthenon.'

'Mr Widdrington?'

'Yes.'

'What did you talk about?'

She might have heard every word. It was only the feeling of pleasure that he wished to conceal. Even when we love people, we desire to keep some corner secret from them, however small: it is a human right: it is personality. She began to cross-question him, but they were interrupted. A young lady at an adjacent table suddenly rose and cried, 'Yes, it is you. I thought so from your walk.' It was Maud Ansell.

'Oh, do come and join us!' he cried. 'Let me introduce my wife.'

Maud bowed quite stiffly, but Agnes, taking it for ill-breeding, was not offended.

'That I will come!' she continued in shrill, pleasant tones, adroitly poising her tea things on either hand, and transferring them to the Elliots' table. 'Why haven't you ever come to us, pray?'

'I think you didn't ask me!'

'You weren't to be asked.' She sprawled forward with a wagging finger. But her eyes had the honesty of her brother's. 'Don't you remember the day you left us? Father said, "Now, Mr Elliot—" Or did he call you "Elliot"? How one does forget. Anyhow, father said you weren't to wait for an invitation, and you said, "No; I won't." Ours is a fair-sized house,'–she turned somewhat haughtily to Agnes–'and the second spare room, which we call the "harp room" on account of a harp that hangs on the wall, is always reserved for Stewart's friends.'

'How is Mr Ansell, your brother?'

Maud's face fell. 'Hadn't you heard?' she said in awestruck tones.

'No.'

'He hasn't got his fellowship. It's the second time he's failed. That means he will never get one. He will never be a don, nor live in Cambridge and that, as we had hoped.'

'Oh, poor, poor fellow!' said Mrs Elliot with a remorse that was sincere, though her congratulations would not have been. 'I am so very sorry.'

But Maud turned to Rickie. 'Mr Elliot, you might know. Tell me. What is wrong with Stewart's philosophy? What ought he to put in, or to alter, so as to succeed?'

Agnes, who knew better than this, smiled.

'I don't know,' said Rickie sadly. They were none of them so clever, after all.'

'Hegel,' she continued vindictively. 'They say he's read too much Hegel. But they never tell him what to read instead. Their own stuffy books, I suppose. Look here—no, that's the "Windsor."' After a little groping she produced a copy of "Mind," and handed it round as if it was a geological specimen. 'Inside that there's a paragraph written about something Stewart's written about before, and there it says he's read too much Hegel, and it seems now that that's been the trouble all along.' Her voice trembled. 'I call it most unfair, and the fellowship's gone to a man who has counted the petals on an anemone.'

Rickie had no inclination to smile.

'I wish Stewart had tried Oxford instead.'

'I don't wish it!'

'You say that,' she continued hotly, 'and then you never come to see him, though you knew you were not to wait for an invitation.'

'If it comes to that, Miss Ansell,' retorted Rickie, in the laughing tones that one adopts on such occasions, 'Stewart won't come to me, though he *has* had an invitation.'

'Yes,' chimed in Agnes, 'we ask Mr Ansell again and again, and he will have none of us.'

Maud looked at her with a flashing eye. 'My brother is a very peculiar person, and we ladies can't understand him. But I know one thing, and that's that he has a reason all round for what he does. Look here, I must be getting on. Waiter! Wai-ai-aiter! Bill, please. Separately, of course. Call the Army and Navy cheap! I know better!'

'How does the drapery department compare?' said Agnes sweetly.

The girl gave a sharp choking sound, gathered up her parcels, and left them. Rickie was too much disgusted with his wife to speak.

'Appalling person!' she gasped. 'It was naughty of me, but I couldn't help it. What a dreadful fate for a clever man! To fail in life completely, and then to be thrown back on a family like that!'

'Maud is a snob and a Philistine. But, in her case, something emerges.'

She glanced at him, but proceeded in her suavest tones, 'Do let us make one great united attempt to get Mr Ansell to Sawston.'

'No.'

'What a changeable friend you are! When we were engaged you were always talking about him.'

'Would you finish your tea, and then we will buy the linoleum for the cubicles.'

But she returned to the subject again, not only on that day but throughout the term. Could nothing be done for poor Mr Ansell? It seemed that she could not rest until all that he had once held dear was humiliated. In this she strayed outside her nature; she was unpractical. And those who stray outside their nature invite disaster. Rickie, goaded by her, wrote to his friend again. The letter was in all ways unlike his old self. Ansell did not answer it. But he did write to Mr Jackson, with whom he was not acquainted.

> Dear Mr Jackson—I understand from Widdrington that you have a large house. I would like to tell you how convenient it would be for me to come and stop in it. June suits me best.—Yours truly,
>
> Stewart Ansell

To which Mr Jackson replied that not only in June but during the whole year his house was at the disposal of Mr Ansell and of any one who resembled him.

But Agnes continued her life, cheerfully beating time. She, too, knew that her marriage was a failure, and in her spare moments regretted it. She wished that her husband was handsomer, more successful, more dictatorial. But she would think, 'No, no; one mustn't grumble. It can't be helped.' Ansell was wrong in supposing she might ever leave Rickie. Spiritual apathy prevented her. Nor would she ever be tempted by a jollier man. Here criticism would willingly alter its tone. For Agnes also has her tragedy. She belonged to the type—not necessarily an elevated one—that loves once and once only. Her love for Gerald had not been a noble passion: no imagination transfigured it. But such as it was, it sprang to embrace him, and he carried it away with him when he died. *Les amours qui suivent sont moins involuntaires*: by an effort of the will she had warned herself for Rickie.

She is not conscious of her tragedy, and therefore only the gods need weep at it. But it is fair to remember that hitherto she moves as one from whom the inner life has been withdrawn.

Chapter Twenty-five

'I am afraid,' said Agnes, unfolding a letter that she had received in the morning, 'that things go far from satisfactory at Cadover.'

The three were alone at supper. It was the June of Rickie's second year at Sawston.

'Indeed?' said Herbert, who took a friendly interest. 'In what way?'

'Do you remember us talking of Stephen—Stephen Wonham, who by an odd coincidence—'

'Yes. Who wrote last year to that miserable failure Varden. I do.'

'It is about him.'

'I did not like the tone of his letter.'

Agnes had made her first move. She waited for her husband to reply to it. But he, though full of a painful curiosity, would not speak. She moved again.

'I don't think, Herbert, that Aunt Emily, much as I like her, is the kind of person to bring a young man up. At all events the results have been disastrous this time.'

'What has happened?'

'A tangle of things.' She lowered her voice. 'Drink.'

'Dear! Really! Was Mrs Failing fond of him?'

'She used to be. She let him live at Cadover ever since he was a little boy. Naturally that cannot continue.'

Rickie never spoke.

'And now he has taken to be violent and rude,' she went on.

'In short, a beggar on horseback. Who is he? Has he no relatives?'

'She has always been both father and mother to him. Now is must all come to an end. I blame her—and she blames herself—for not being severe enough. He has grown up without fixed principles. He has always followed his inclinations, and one knows the result of that.'

Herbert assented. 'To me Mrs Failing's course is perfectly plain. She has a certain responsibility. She must pay the youth's passage to one of the colonies, start him handsomely in some business, and then break off all communications.'

'How funny! It is exactly what she is going to do.'

'I shall then consider that she has behaved in a thoroughly honourable manner.' He held out his plate for gooseberries. 'His letter to Varden was neither helpful nor sympathetic, and, if written at all, it ought to have been both. I am not in the least surprised to learn that he has turned out badly. When you write next, would you tell her how sorry I am?'

'Indeed I will. Two years ago, when she was already a little anxious, she did so wish you could undertake him.'

'I could not alter a grown man.' But in his heart he thought he could, and smiled at his sister amiably. 'Terrible, isn't it?' he remarked to Rickie. Rickie, who was trying not to mind anything, assented. And an onlooker would have supposed them a dispassionate trio, who were sorry both for Mrs Failing and for the beggar who would bestride her horses' backs no longer. A new topic was introduced by the arrival of the evening post.

Herbert took up all the letters, as he often did.

'Jackson?' he exclaimed. 'What does the fellow want?' He read, and his tone was mollified, '"Dear Mr Pembroke—Could you, Mrs Elliot, and Mr Elliot come to supper with us on Saturday next? I should not merely be pleased, I should be grateful. My wife is writing formally to Mrs Elliot"—(Here, Agnes, take your letter)—"but I venture to write as well, and to add my more uncouth entreaties."—An olive-branch. It is time! But (ridiculous person!) does he think that we can leave the House deserted and all go out pleasuring in term time?—Rickie, a letter for you.'

'Mine's the formal invitation,' said Agnes. 'How very odd! Mr Ansell will be there. Surely we asked him here! Did you know he knew the Jacksons?'

'This makes refusal very difficult,' said Herbert, who was anxious to accept. 'At all events, Rickie ought to go.'

'I do not want to go,' said Rickie, slowly opening his own letter. 'As Agnes says, Ansell has refused to come to us. I cannot put myself out for him.'

'Who's yours from?' she demanded.

'Mrs Silt,' replied Herbert, who had seen the handwriting.

'I trust she does not want to pay us a visit this term, with the examinations impending and all the machinery at full pressure. Though, Rickie, you will have to accept the Jacksons' invitation.'

'I cannot possibly go. I have been too rude; with Widdrington we always meet here. I'll stop with the boys—' His voice caught suddenly. He had opened Mrs Silt's letter.

'The Silts are not ill, I hope?'

'No. But, I say,'—he looked at his wife—'I do think this is going too far. Really, Agnes—'

'What has happened?'

'It is going too far,' he repeated. He was nerving himself for another battle. 'I cannot stand this sort of thing. There are limits.'

He laid the letter down. It was Herbert who picked it up, and read: 'Aunt Emily has just written to us. We are so glad that her troubles are over, in spite of the expense. It never does to live apart from one's own relatives so much as she has done up to now. He goes next Saturday to Canada. What you told her about him just turned the scale. She has asked us—'

'No, it's too much,' he interrupted. 'What I told her—told her about him—no, I will have it out at last. Agnes!'

'Yes?' said his wife, raising her eyes from Mrs Jackson's formal invitation.

'It's you—it's you. I never mentioned him to her. Why, I've never seen her or written to her since. I accuse you.'

Then Herbert overbore him, and he collapsed. He was asked what he meant. Why was he so excited? Of what did he accuse his wife? Each time he spoke more feebly, and before long the brother and sister were laughing at him. He felt bewildered, like a boy who knows that he is right but cannot put his case correctly. He repeated, 'I've never mentioned him to her. It's a libel. Never in my life.' And they cried, 'My dear Rickie, what an absurd fuss!' Then his brain cleared. His eye fell on the letter that his wife had received from his aunt, and he reopened the battle.

'Agnes, give me that letter if you please.'

'Mrs Jackson's?'

'My aunt's.'

She put her hand on it, and looked at him doubtfully. She saw that she had failed to bully him.

'My aunt's letter,' he repeated, rising to his feet and bending over the table towards her.

'Why, dear?'

'Yes, why indeed?' echoed Herbert. He too had bullied Rickie, but from a purer motive: he had tried to stamp out a dissension between husband and wife. It was not the first time he had intervened.

'The letter. For this reason: it will show me what you have done. I believe you have ruined Stephen. You have worked at it for two years. You have put words into my mouth to "turn the scale" against him. He goes to Canada—and all the world thinks it is owing to me. As I said before—I advise you to stop smiling—you have gone a little too far.'

They were all on their feet now, standing round the little table. Agnes said nothing, but the fingers of her delicate hand tightened upon the letter. When her husband snatched at it she resisted, and with the effect of a harlequinade everything went on the floor—lamb, mint sauce, gooseberries, lemonade, whisky. At once they were swamped in domesticities. She rang the bell for the servant, cries arose, dusters were brought, broken crockery (a wedding present) picked up from the carpet; while he stood wrathfully at the window, regarding the obscured sun's decline.

'I *must* see her letter,' he repeated, when the agitation was over. He was too angry to be diverted from his purpose. Only slight emotions are thwarted by an interlude of farce.

'I've had enough of this quarrelling,' she retorted. 'You know that the Silts are inaccurate. I think you might have given me the benefit of the doubt. If you will know—have you forgotten that ride you took with him?'

'I—' he was again bewildered. 'The ride where I dreamt—'

'The ride where you turned back because you could not listen to a disgraceful poem?'

'I don't understand.'

'The poem was Aunt Emily. He read it to you and a stray soldier. Afterwards you told me. You said, "Really it is shocking, his ingratitude. She ought to know about it." She does know, and I should be glad of an apology.'

He had said something of the sort in a fit of irritation. Mrs Silt was right—he had helped to turn the scale.

'Whatever I said, you knew what I meant. You knew I'd sooner cut my tongue out than have it used against him. Even then.' He sighed. Had he ruined his brother? A curious tenderness came over him, and passed when he remembered his own dead child. '*We* have ruined him, then. Have you any objection to "we"? *We* have disinherited him.'

'I decide against you,' interposed Herbert. 'I have now heard both sides of this deplorable affair. You are talking most criminal nonsense. "Disinherit!" Sentimental twaddle. It's been clear to me from the first that Mrs Failing has been imposed upon by the Wonham man, a person with no legal claim on her, and any one who exposes him performs a public duty—'

'—And gets money.'

'Money?' He was always uneasy at the word. 'Who mentioned money?'

'Just understand me, Herbert, and of what it is that I accuse my wife.' Tears came into his eyes. 'It is not that I like the Wonham man, or think that he isn't a drunkard and worse. He's too awful in every way. But he ought to have my aunt's money, because he's lived all his life with her, and is her nephew as much as I am. You see, my father went wrong.' He stopped, amazed at himself. How easy it had been to say! He was withering up: the power to care about this stupid secret had died.

When Herbert understood, his first thought was for Dunwood House. 'Why have I never been told?' was his first remark.

'We settled to tell no one.' said Agnes. 'Rickie, in his anxiety to prove me a liar, has broken his promise.'

'I ought to have been told,' said Herbert, his anger increasing. 'Had I known, I could have averted this deplorable scene.'

'Let me conclude it,' said Rickie, again collapsing and leaving the dining-room. His impulse was to go straight to Cadover and make a business-like statement of the position to Stephen. Then the man would be armed, and perhaps fight the two women successfully. But he resisted the impulse. Why should he help one power of evil against another? Let them go intertwined to destruction. To enrich his brother would be as bad as enriching himself. If their aunt's money ever did come to him, he would refuse to accept it. That was the easiest and most dignified course. He troubled himself no longer with justice or pity, and the next day he asked his wife's pardon for his behaviour.

In the dining-room the conversation continued. Agnes, without much difficulty, gained her brother as an ally. She acknowledged that she had been wrong in not telling him, and he then declared that she had been right on every other point. She slurred a little over the incident of her treachery, for Herbert was sometimes clear-sighted over details, though easily muddled in a general survey. Mrs Failing had had plenty of direct causes of complaint, and she dwelt on these. She dwelt, too, on the very handsome way in which the young man, 'though he knew nothing, and had never asked to know,' was being treated by his aunt.

'"Handsome" is the word,' said Herbert. 'I hope not indulgently. He does not deserve indulgence.'

And she knew that he, like herself, could remember money, and that it lent an acknowledged halo to her cause.

'It is not a savoury subject,' he continued, with sudden stiffness. 'I understand why Rickie is so hysterical. My impulse'—he laid his hand on her shoulder—'is to abandon it at once. But if I am to be of any use to you, I must hear it all. There are moments when we must look facts in the face.'

She did not shrink from the subject as much as he thought, as much as she herself could have wished. Two years before, it had filled her with a physical loathing. But by now she had accustomed herself to it.

'I am afraid, Bertie boy, there is nothing else to hear. I have tried to find out again and again, but Aunt Emily will not tell me. I suppose it is natural. She wants to shield the Elliot name. She only told us in a fit of temper; then we all agreed to keep it to ourselves; then Rickie again mismanaged her, and ever since she has refused to let us know any details.'

'A most unsatisfactory position.'

'So I feel.' She sat down again with a sigh. Mrs Failing had been a great trial to her orderly mind. 'She is an odd woman. She is always laughing. She actually finds it amusing that we know no more.'

'They are an odd family.'

'They are indeed.'

Herbert, with unusual sweetness, bent down and kissed her.

She thanked him.

Their tenderness soon passed. They exchanged it with averted eyes. It embarrassed them. There are moments for all of us when we seem obliged to speak in a new unprofitable tongue. One might fancy a seraph, vexed with our normal language, who touches the pious to blasphemy, the blasphemous to piety. The seraph passes, and we proceed unaltered–conscious, however, that we have not been ourselves, and that we may fail in this function yet again. So Agnes and Herbert, as they proceeded to discuss the Jacksons' supper-party, had an uneasy memory of spiritual deserts, spiritual streams.

Chapter Twenty-six

Poor Mr Ansell was actually sitting in the garden of Dunwood House. It was Sunday morning. The air was full of roasting beef. The sound of a manly hymn, taken very fast, floated over the road from the school chapel. He frowned, for he was reading a book, the Essays of Anthony Eustace Failing.

He was here on account of this book–at least so he told himself. It had just been published, and the Jacksons were sure that Mr Elliot would have a copy. For a book one may go anywhere. It would not have been logical to enter Dunwood House for the purpose of seeing Rickie, when Rickie had not come to supper yesterday to see him. He was at Sawston to assure himself of his friend's grave. With quiet eyes he had intended to view the sods, with unfaltering fingers to inscribe the epitaph. Love remained. But in high matters he was practical. He knew that it would be useless to reveal it.

'Morning!' said a voice behind him.

He saw no reason to reply to this superfluous statement, and went on with his reading.

'Morning!' said the voice again.

As for the Essays, the thought was somewhat old-fashioned, and he picked many holes in it; nor was he anything but bored by the prospect of the brotherhood of man. However, Mr Failing stuck to his guns, such as they were, and fired from them several good remarks. Very notable was his distinction between coarseness and vulgarity (coarseness, revealing something; vulgarity, concealing something), and his avowed preference for coarseness. Vulgarity, to him, had been the primal curse, the shoddy reticence that prevents man opening his heart to man, the power that makes against equality. From it sprang all the things he hated–class shibboleths, ladies, lidies, the game laws, the Conservative party–all the things that accent the divergencies rather than the similarities in human nature. Whereas coarseness— But at this point Herbert Pembroke had scrawled with a blue pencil: 'Childish. One reads no further.'

'Morning!' repeated the voice.

Ansell read further, for here was the book of a man who had tried, however unsuccessfully, to practise what he preached. Mrs Failing, in her Introduction, described with delicate irony his difficulties as a landlord; but she did not record the love in which his name was held. Nor could her irony touch him when he cried: 'Attain the practical through the unpractical. There is no other road.' Ansell was inclined to think that the unpractical is its own reward, but he respected those who attempted to journey beyond it. We must all of us go over the mountains. There is certainly no other road.

'Nice morning!' said the voice.

It was not a nice morning, so Ansell felt bound to speak. He answered: 'No. Why?' A clod of earth immediately struck him on the back. He turned round indignantly, for he hated physical rudeness. A square man of ruddy aspect was pacing the gravel path, his hands deep in his pockets. He was very angry. Then he saw that the clod of earth nourished a blue lobelia, and that a wound of corresponding size appeared on the pie-shaped bed. He was not so angry. 'I expect they will mind it,' he reflected. Last night, at the Jacksons', Agnes had displayed a brisk pity that made him wish to wring her neck. Maud had not exaggerated. Mr Pembroke had patronized through a sorrowful voice and large round eyes. Till he met these people he had never been told that his career was a failure. Apparently it was. They would never have been civil to him if it had been a success, if they or theirs had anything to fear from him.

In many ways Ansell was a conceited man; but he was never proud of being right. He had foreseen Rickie's catastrophe from the first, but derived from this no consolation. In many ways he was pedantic; but his pedantry lay close to the vineyards of life—far closer than the fetich Experience of the innumerable teacups. He had a great many facts to learn, and before he died he learnt a suitable quantity. But he never forgot that the holiness of the heart's imagination can alone classify these facts—can alone decide which is an exception, which an example. 'How unpractical it all is!' That was his comment on Dunwood House. 'How unbusiness-like! They live together without love. They work without conviction. They seek money without requiring it. They die, and nothing will have happened, either for themselves or for others.' It is a comment that the academic mind will often make when first confronted with the world.

But he was becoming illogical. The clod of earth had disturbed him. Brushing the dirt off his back, he returned to the book. What a curious affair was the essay on 'Gaps'! Solitude, star-crowned, pacing the fields of England, has a dialogue with Seclusion. He, poor little man, lives in the choicest scenery—among rocks, forests, emerald lawns, azure lakes. To keep people out he has built round his domain a high wall, on which is graven his motto—'Procul este profani.' But he cannot enjoy himself. His only pleasure is in mocking the absent Profane. They are in his mind night and day. Their blemishes and stupidities form the subject of his great poem, 'In the Heart of Nature.' Then Solitude tells him that so it always will be until he makes a gap in the wall, and permits his seclusion to be the sport of circumstance. He obeys. The Profane invade him; but for short intervals they wander elsewhere, and during those intervals the heart of Nature is revealed to him.

This dialogue had really been suggested to Mr Failing by a talk with his brother-in-law. It also touched Ansell. He looked at the man who had thrown the clod, and was now pacing with obvious youth and impudence upon the lawn. 'Shall I improve my soul at his expense?' he thought. 'I suppose I had better.' In friendly tones he remarked, 'Were you waiting for Mr Pembroke?'

'No,' said the young man. 'Why?'

Ansell, after a moment's admiration, flung the Essays at him. They hit him in the back. The next moment he lay on his own back in the lobelia pie.

'But it hurts!' he gasped, in the tones of a puzzled civilization. 'What you do hurts!' For the young man was nicking him over the shins with the rim of the book cover. 'Little brute—*ee—ow*!'

'Then say Pax!'

Something revolted in Ansell. Why should he say Pax? Freeing his hand, he caught the little brute under the chin, and was again knocked into the lobelias by a blow on the mouth.

'Say Pax!' he repeated, pressing the philosopher's skull into the mould; and he added, with an anxiety that was somehow not offensive, 'I do advise you. You'd really better.'

Ansell swallowed a little blood. He tried to move, and he could not. He looked carefully into the young man's eyes and into the palm of his right hand, which at present swung unclenched, and he said 'Pax!'

'Shake hands!' said the other, helping him up. There was nothing Ansell loathed so much as the hearty Britisher; but he shook hands, and they stared at each other awkwardly. With civil murmurs they picked the little blue flowers off each other's clothes. Ansell was trying to remember why they had quarrelled, and the young man was wondering why he had not guarded his chin properly. In the distance a hymn swung off—

Fight the good . Fight with . All thy . Might.

They would be across from chapel soon.

'Your book, sir?'

'Thank you, sir—yes.'

'Why!' cried the young man—'why, it's "What We Want"! At least the binding's exactly the same.'

'It's called "Essays,"' said Ansell.

'Then that's it. Mrs Failing, you see, she wouldn't call it that, because three W's, you see, in a row, she said, are vulgar, and sound like Tolstoy, if you've heard of him.'

Ansell confessed to an acquaintance, and then said, 'Do you think "What We Want" vulgar?' He was not at all interested, but he desired to escape from the atmosphere of pugilistic courtesy, more painful to him than blows themselves.

'It *is* the same book,' said the other—'same title, same binding.' He weighed it like a brick in his muddy hands.

'Open it to see if the inside corresponds,' said Ansell, swallowing a laugh and a little more blood with it.

With a liberal allowance of thumb-marks, he turned the pages over and read, '"—the rural silence that is not a poet's luxury but a practical need for all men." Yes, it *is* the same book.' Smiling pleasantly over the discovery, he handed it back to the owner.

'And is it true?'

'I beg your pardon?'

'Is it true that rural silence is a practical need?'

'Don't ask me!'

'Have you ever tried it?'

'What?'

'Rural silence.'

'A field with no noise in it, I suppose you mean. I don't understand.'

Ansell smiled, but a slight fire in the man's eye checked him. After all, this was a person who could knock one down. Moreover, there was no reason why he should be teased. He had it in him to retort 'No. Why?' He was not stupid in essentials. He was irritable—in Ansell's eyes a frequent sign of grace. Sitting down on the upturned seat, he remarked, 'I like the book in many ways. I don't think "What We Want" would have been a vulgar title. But I don't intend to spoil myself on the chance of mending the world, which is what the creed amounts to. Nor am I keen on rural silences.'

'Curse!' he said thoughtfully, sucking at an empty pipe.

'Tobacco?'

'Please.'

'Rickie's is invariably filthy.'

'Who says I know Rickie?'

'Well, you know his aunt. It's a possible link. Be gentle with Rickie. Don't knock him down if he doesn't think it's a nice morning.'

The other was silent.

'Do you know him well?'

'Kind of.' He was not inclined to talk. The wish to smoke was very violent in him, and Ansell noticed how he gazed at the wreaths that ascended from bowl and stem, and how, when the stem was in his mouth, he bit it. He gave the idea of an animal with just enough soul to contemplate its own bliss. United with refinement, such a type was common in Greece. It is not common to-day, and Ansell was surprised to find it in a friend of Rickie's. Rickie, if he could even 'kind of know' such a creature, must be stirring in his grave.

'Do you know his wife too?'

'Oh, yes. In a way I know Agnes. But thank you for this tobacco. Last night I nearly died. I have no money.'

'Take the whole pouch—do.'

After a moment's hesitation he did. 'Fight the good' had scarcely ended, so quickly had their intimacy grown.

'I suppose you're a friend of Rickie's?'

Ansell was tempted to reply, 'I don't know him at all.' But it seemed no moment for the severer truths, so he said, 'I knew him well at Cambridge, but I have seen very little of him since.'

'Is it true that his baby was lame?'

'I believe so.'

His teeth closed on his pipe. Chapel was over. The organist was prancing through the voluntary, and the first ripple of boys had already reached Dunwood House. In a few minutes the masters would be here too, and Ansell, who was becoming interested, hurried the conversation forward.

'Have you come far?'

'From Wiltshire. Do you know Wiltshire?' And for the first time there came into his face the shadow of a sentiment, the passing tribute to some mystery. 'It's a good country. I live in one of the finest valleys out of Salisbury Plain. I mean, I lived.'

'Have you been dismissed from Cadover, without a penny in your pocket?'

He was alarmed at this. Such knowledge seemed simply diabolical. Ansell explained that if his boots were chalky, if his clothes had obviously been slept in, if he knew Mrs Failing, if he knew Wiltshire, and if he could buy no tobacco—then the deduction was possible. 'You do just attend,' he murmured.

The house was filling with boys, and Ansell saw, to his regret, the head of Agnes over the thuya hedge that separated the small front garden from the side lawn where he was sitting. After a few minutes it was followed by the heads of Rickie and Mr Pembroke. All the heads were turned the other way. But they would find his card in the hall, and if the man had left any message they would find that too. 'What are you?' he demanded. 'Who are you—your name—I don't care about that. But it interests me to class people, and up to now I have failed with you.'

'I—' He stopped. Ansell reflected that there are worse answers. 'I really don't know what I am. Used to think I was something special, but strikes me now I feel much like other chaps. Used to look down on the labourers. Used to take for granted I was a gentleman, but really I don't know where I do belong.'

'One belongs to the place one sleeps in and to the people one eats with.'

'As often as not I sleep out of doors and eat by myself, so that doesn't get you any further.'

A silence, akin to poetry, invaded Ansell. Was it only a pose to like this man, or was he really wonderful? He was not romantic, for Romance is a figure with outstretched hands, yearning for the unattainable. Certain figures of the Greeks, to whom we continually return, suggested him a little. One expected nothing of him—no purity of phrase nor swift-edged thought. Yet the conviction grew that he had been back somewhere—back to some table of the gods, spread in a field where there is no noise, and that he belonged for ever to the guests with whom he had eaten.

Meanwhile he was simple and frank, and what he could tell he would tell to any one. He had not the suburban reticence. Ansell asked him, 'Why did

Mrs Failing turn you out of Cadover? I should like to hear that too.'

'Because she was tired of me. Because, again, I couldn't keep quiet over the farm hands. I ask you, is it right?' He became incoherent. Ansell caught, 'And they grow old—they don't play games—it ends they can't play.' An illustration emerged. 'Take a kitten—if you fool about with her, she goes on playing well into a cat.'

'But Mrs Failing minded no mice being caught.'

'Mice?' said the young man blankly. 'What I was going to say is, that some one was jealous of my being at Cadover. I'll mention no names, but I fancy it was Mrs Silt. I'm sorry for her if it was. Anyhow, she set Mrs Failing against me. It came on the top of other things—and out I went.'

'What did Mrs Silt, whose name I don't mention, say?'

He looked guilty. 'I don't know. Easy enough to find something to say. The point is that she said something. You know, Mr—I don't know your name, mine's Wonham, but I'm more grateful than I can put it over this tobacco. I mean, you ought to know there *is* another side to this quarrel. It's wrong, but it's there.'

Ansell told him not to be uneasy: he had already guessed that there might be another side. But he could not make out why Mr Wonham should have come straight from the aunt to the nephew. They were now sitting on the upturned seat. 'What We Want,' a good deal shattered, lay between them.

'On account of above-mentioned reasons, there was a row. I don't know—you can guess the style of thing. She wanted to treat me to the colonies, and had up the parson to talk soft-sawder and make out that a boundless continent was the place for a lad like me. I said, "I can't run up to the Rings without getting tired, nor gallop a horse out of this view without tiring it, so what is the point of a boundless continent?" Then I saw that she was frightened of me, and bluffed a bit more, and in the end I was nipped. She caught me—just like her—when I had nothing on but flannels, and was coming into the house, having licked the Cadchurch team. She stood up in the doorway between those stone pilasters and said, "No! Never again!" and behind her was Wilbraham, whom I tried to turn out, and the gardener, and poor old Leighton, who hates being hurt. She said, "There's a hundred pounds for you at the London bank, and as much more in December. Go!" I said, "Keep your—money, and tell me whose son I am." I didn't care really. I only said it on the off-chance of hurting her. Sure enough, she caught on to the door-handle (being lame) and said, "I can't—I promised—I don't really want to," and Wilbraham did stare. Then—she's very queer—she burst out laughing, and went for the packet after all, and we heard her laugh through the window as she got it. She rolled it at me down the steps, and she says, "A leaf out of the eternal comedy for you, Stephen," or something of that sort. I opened it as I walked down the drive, she laughing always and catching on to the handle of the front door. Of course it wasn't comic at all. But down in the village there were both cricket teams, already a little tight, and the mad plumber shouting "Rights of Man!" They knew I was turned out. We did have a row, and kept it up too. They daren't touch Wilbraham's windows, but there isn't much glass left up at Cadover. When you start, it's worth going on, but in the end I had to cut. They subscribed a bob here and bob there, and these are Flea Thompson's Sundays. I sent a line to Leighton not to forward my own things: I don't fancy them. They aren't really mine.' He did not mention his great symbolic act, performed, it is to be feared, when he was rather drunk and the friendly policeman was looking the other way. He had cast all his flannels into the little mill-pond, and then waded himself through the dark cold water to the new clothes on the other side. Some one had flung his pipe and his packet after him. The packet had fallen short. For this reason it was wet when he handed it to Ansell, and ink that had been dry for twenty-three years had begun to run again.

'I wonder if you're right about the hundred pounds.' said Ansell gravely. 'It is pleasant to be proud, but it is unpleasant to die in the night through not having any tobacco.'

'But I'm not proud. Look how I've taken your pouch! The hundred pounds was—well, can't you see yourself, it was quite different? It was, so to speak, *inconvenient* for me to take the hundred pounds. Or look again how I took a shilling from a boy who earns nine bob a week! Proves pretty conclusively I'm not proud.'

Ansell saw it was useless to argue. He perceived, beneath the slatternly use of words, the man—buttoned up in them, just as his body was buttoned up in a shoddy suit—and he wondered more than ever that such a man should know the Elliots. He looked at the face, which was frank, proud, and beautiful, if truth is beauty. Of mercy or tact such a face knew little. It might be coarse, but it had in it nothing vulgar or wantonly cruel. 'May I read these papers?' he said.

'Of course. Oh yes; didn't I say? I'm Rickie's half-brother, come here to tell him the news. He doesn't know. There it is, put shortly for you. I was saying, though, that I bolted in the dark, slept in the rifle-butts above Salisbury—the sheds where they keep the cardboard men, you know, never locked up as they ought to be. I turned the whole place upside down to teach them.'

'Here is your packet again,' said Ansell. 'Thank you. How interesting!' He rose from the seat and turned towards Dunwood House. He looked at the bow-windows, the cheap picturesque gables, the terra-cotta dragons clawing a dirty sky. He listened to the clink of plates and to the voice of Mr Pembroke taking one of his innumerable roll-calls. He looked at the bed of lobelias. How interesting! What else was there to say?

'One must be the son of some one,' remarked Stephen. And that was all he had to say. To him those names on the moistened paper were mere antiquities. He was neither proud of them nor ashamed. A man must have parents, or he cannot enter the delightful world. A man, if he has a brother, may reasonably visit him, for they may have interests in common. He continued his narrative—how in the night he had heard the clocks, how at daybreak, instead of entering the city, he had struck eastward to save money—while Ansell still looked at the house and found that all his imagination and knowledge could lead him no farther than this: how interesting!

'—And what do you think of that for a holy horror?'

'For a what?' said Ansell, his thoughts far away.

'This man I am telling you about, who gave me a lift towards Andover, who said I was a blot on God's earth.'

One o'clock struck. It was strange that neither of them had had any summons from the house.

'He said I ought to be ashamed of myself. He said, "*I*'ll not be the means of bringing shame to an honest gentleman and lady." I told him not to be a fool. I said I knew what I was about. Rickie and Agnes are properly educated, which leads people to look at things straight, and not go screaming about blots. A man like me, with just a little reading at odd hours—I've got so far, and Rickie has been through Cambridge.'

'And Mrs Elliot?'

'Oh, she won't mind, and I told the man so; but he kept on saying, "*I*'ll not be the means of bringing shame to an honest gentleman and lady," until I got out of his rotten cart.' His eye watched the man, a Nonconformist, driving away over God's earth. 'I caught the train by running. I got to Waterloo at—'

Here the parlourmaid fluttered towards them. Would Mr Wonham come in? Mrs Elliot would be glad to see him now.

'Mrs Elliot?' cried Ansell. 'Not Mr Elliot?'

'It's all the same,' said Stephen, and moved towards the house. 'You see, I only left my name. They don't know why I've come.'

'Perhaps Mr Elliot sees me meanwhile?'

The parlourmaid looked blank. Mr Elliot had not said so. He had been with Mrs Elliot and Mr Pembroke in the study. Now the gentlemen had gone upstairs.

'All right, I can wait.' After all, Rickie was treating him as he had treated Rickie, as one in the grave, to whom it is futile to make any loving motion. Gone upstairs—to brush his hair for dinner! The irony of the situation appealed to him strongly. It reminded him of the Greek Drama, where the actors know so little and the spectators so much.

'But, by the bye,' he called after Stephen, 'I think I ought to tell you—don't—'

'What is it?'

'Don't—' Then he was silent. He had been tempted to explain everything, to tell the fellow how things stood—that he must avoid this if he wanted to attain that; that he must break the news to Rickie gently; that he must have at least one battle royal with Agnes. But it was contrary to his own spirit to coach people: he held the human soul to be a very delicate thing, which can receive eternal damage from a little patronage. Stephen must go into the house simply as himself, for thus alone would he remain there.

'I ought to knock my pipe out? Was that it?'

'By no means. Go in, your pipe and you.'

He hesitated, torn between propriety and desire. Then he followed the parlourmaid into the house smoking. As he entered the dinner-bell rang, and there was the sound of rushing feet, which died away into shuffling and silence. Through the window of the boys' dining-hall came the colourless voice of Rickie—

'*Benedictus benedicat.*'

Ansell prepared himself to witness the second act of the drama; forgetting that all this world, and not part of it, is a stage.

Chapter Twenty-seven

The parlourmaid took Mr Wonham to the study. He had been in the drawing-room before, but had got bored, and so had strolled out into the garden. Now he was in better spirits, as a man ought to be who has knocked down a man. As he passed through the hall he sparred at the teak monkey, and hung his cap on the bust of Hermes. And he greeted Mrs Elliot with a pleasant clap of laughter. 'Oh, I've come with the most tremendous news!' he cried.

She bowed, but did not shake hands, which rather surprised him. But he never troubled over 'details.' He seldom watched people, and never thought that they were watching him. Nor could he guess how much it meant to her that he should enter her presence smoking. Had she not said once at Cadover, 'Oh, *please* smoke; I love the smell of a pipe'?

'Would you sit down? Exactly there, please.' She placed him at a large table, opposite an inkpot and a pad of blotting-paper. 'Will you tell your "tremendous news" to me? My brother and my husband are giving the boys their dinner.'

'Ah!' said Stephen, who had had neither time nor money for breakfast in London.

'I told them not to wait for me.'

So he came to the point at once. He trusted this handsome woman. His strength and his youth called to hers, expecting no prudish response. 'It's very odd. It is that I'm Rickie's brother. I've just found out. I've come to tell you all.'

'Yes?'

He felt in his pocket for the papers. 'Half-brother I ought to have said.'

'Yes?'

'I'm illegitimate. Legally speaking, that is, I've been turned out of Cadover. I haven't a penny. I—'

'There is no occasion to inflict the details.' Her face, which had been an even brown, began to flush slowly in the centre of the cheeks. The colour spread till all that he saw of her was suffused, and she turned away. He thought he had shocked her, and so did she. Neither knew that the body can be insincere and express not the emotions we feel but those that we should like to feel. In reality she was quite calm, and her dislike of him had nothing emotional in it as yet.

'You see—' he began. He was determined to tell the fidgety story, for the sooner it was over the sooner they would have something to eat. Delicacy he lacked, and his sympathies were limited. But such as they were, they rang true: he put no decorous phantom between him and his desires.

'I do see. I have seen for two years.' She sat down at the head of the table, where there was another inkpot. Into this she dipped a pen. 'I have seen everything, Mr Wonham—who you are, how you have behaved at Cadover, how you must have treated Mrs Failing yesterday; and now'—her voice became very grave—'I see why you have come here, penniless. Before you speak, we know what you will say.'

His mouth fell open, and he laughed so merrily that it might have given her a warning. But she was thinking how to follow up her first success. 'And I thought I was bringing tremendous news!' he cried. 'I only twisted it out of Mrs Failing last night. And Rickie knows too?'

'We have known for two years.'

'But come, by the bye, if you've known for two years, how is it you didn't—' The laugh died out of his eyes. 'You aren't ashamed?' he asked, half rising from his chair. 'You aren't like the man towards Andover?'

'Please, please sit down,' said Agnes, in the even tones she used when speaking to the servants; 'let us not discuss side issues. I am a horribly direct person, Mr Wonham. I go always straight to the point.' She opened a cheque-book. 'I am afraid I shall shock you. For how much?'

He was not attending.

'There is the paper we suggest you shall sign.' She pushed towards him a pseudo-legal document, just composed by Herbert.

> 'In consideration of the sum of.............., I agree to perpetual silence—to restrain from libellous . . . never to molest the said Frederick Elliot by intruding—'

His brain was not quick. He read the document over twice, and he could still say, 'But what's that cheque for?'

'It is my husband's. He signed for you as soon as we heard you were here. We guessed you had come to be silenced. Here is his signature. But he has left the filling in for me. For how much? I will cross it, shall I? You will just have started a banking account, if I understand Mrs Failing rightly. It is not quite accurate to say you are penniless; I heard from her just before you returned from your cricket. She allows you two hundred a year, I think. But this additional sum—shall I date the cheque Saturday or for to-morrow?'

At last he found words. Knocking his pipe out on the table, he said slowly, 'Here's a very bad mistake.'

'It is quite possible,' retorted Agnes. She was glad she had taken the offensive, instead of waiting till he began his blackmailing, as had been the advice of Rickie. Aunt Emily had said that very spring, 'One's only hope with Stephen is to start bullying first.' Here he was, quite bewildered, smearing the pipe-ashes with his thumb. He asked to read the document again. 'A stamp and all!' he remarked.

They had anticipated that his claim would exceed two pounds.

'I see. All right. It takes a fool a minute. Never mind. I've made a bad mistake.'

'You refuse?' she exclaimed, for he was standing at the door. 'Then do your worst! We defy you!'

'That's all right, Mrs Elliot,' he said roughly. 'I don't want a scene with you, nor yet with your husband. We'll say no more about it. It's all right. I meant no harm.'

'But your signature then! You must sign–you—'

He pushed past her, and said as he reached for his cap, 'There, that's all right. It's my mistake. I'm sorry.' He spoke like a farmer who has failed to sell a sheep. His manner was utterly prosaic, and up to the last she thought he had not understood her. 'But it's money we offer you,' she informed him, and then darted back to the study, believing for one terrible moment that he had picked up the blank cheque. When she returned to the hall he had gone. He was walking down the road rather quickly. At the corner he cleared his throat, spat into the gutter, and disappeared.

'There's an odd finish,' she thought. She was puzzled, and determined to recast the interview a little when she related it to Rickie. She had not succeeded, for the paper was still unsigned. But she had so cowed Stephen that he would probably rest content with his two hundred a year, and never come troubling them again. Clever management, for one knew him to be rapacious: she had heard tales of him lending to the poor and exacting repayment to the uttermost farthing. He had also stolen at school. Moderately triumphant, she hurried into the side-garden: she had just remembered Ansell: she, not Rickie, had received his card.

'Oh, Mr Ansell!' she exclaimed, awaking him from some day-dream. 'Haven't either Rickie or Herbert been out to you? Now, do come into dinner, to show you aren't offended. You will find all of us assembled in the boys' dining-hall.'

To her annoyance he accepted.

'That is, if the Jacksons are not expecting you.'

The Jacksons did not matter. If he might brush his clothes and bathe his lip, he would like to come.

'Oh, what has happened to you? And oh, my pretty lobelias!'

He replied, 'A momentary contact with reality,' and she, who did not look for sense in his remarks, hurried away to the dining-hall to announce him.

The dining-hall was not unlike the preparation-room. There was the same parquet floor, and dado of shiny pitch-pine. On its walls also were imperial portraits, and over the harmonium to which they sang the evening hymns was spread the Union Jack. Sunday dinner, the most pompous meal of the week, was in progress. Her brother sat at the head of the high table, her husband at the head of the second. To each she gave a reassuring nod and went to her own seat, which was among the junior boys. The beef was being carried out; she stopped it. 'Mr Ansell is coming,' she called. 'Herbert, there

is more room by you; sit up straight, boys.' The boys sat up straight, and a
respectful hush spread over the room.

'Here he is!' called Rickie cheerfully, taking his cue from his wife. 'Oh,
this is splendid!' Ansell came in. 'I'm so glad you managed this. I couldn't
leave these wretches last night!' The boys tittered suitably. The atmosphere
seemed normal. Even Herbert, though longing to hear what had happened
to the blackmailer, gave adequate greeting to their guest: 'Come in, Mr
Ansell; come here. Take us as you find us!'

'I understood,' said Stewart, 'that I should find you all. Mrs Elliot told me
I should. On that understanding I came.'

It was at once evident that something had gone wrong.

Ansell looked round the room carefully. Then clearing his throat and
ruffling his hair, he began—

'I cannot see the man with whom I have talked, intimately, for an hour, in
your garden.'

The worst of it was they were all so far from him and from each other, each
at the end of a tableful of inquisitive boys. The two masters looked at Agnes
for information, for her reassuring nod had not told them much. She looked
hopelessly back.

'I cannot see this man,' repeated Ansell, who remained by the harmonium
in the midst of astonished waitresses. 'Is he to be given no lunch?'

Herbert broke the silence by fresh greetings. Rickie knew that the contest
was lost, and that his friend had sided with the enemy. It was the kind of
thing he would do. One must face the catastrophe quietly and with dignity.
Perhaps Ansell would have turned on his heel, and left behind him only
vague suspicions, if Mrs Elliot had not tried to talk him down. 'Man,' she
cried—'what man? Oh, I know—terrible bore! Did he get hold of you?'—thus
committing their first blunder, and causing Ansell to say to Rickie, 'Have
you seen your brother?'

'I have not.'

'Have you been told he was here?'

Rickie's answer was inaudible.

'Have you been told you have a brother?'

'Let us continue this conversation later.'

'Continue it? My dear man, how can we until you know what I'm talking
about? You must think me mad; but I tell you solemnly that you have a
brother of whom you've never heard, and that he was in this house ten
minutes ago.' He paused impressively. 'Your wife has happened to see him
first. Being neither serious nor truthful, she is keeping you apart, telling him
some lie and not telling you a word.'

There was a murmur of alarm. One of the prefects rose, and Ansell set his
back to the wall, quite ready for a battle. For two years he had waited for his
opportunity. He would hit out at Mrs Elliot like any ploughboy now that it
had come. Rickie said: 'There is a slight misunderstanding. I, like my wife,
have known what there is to know for two years'—a dignified rebuff, but their
second blunder.

'Exactly,' said Agnes. 'Now I think Mr Ansell had better go.'

'Go?' exploded Ansell. 'I've everything to say yet. I beg your pardon, Mrs Elliot, I am concerned with you no longer. This man'—he turned to the avenue of faces—'this man who teaches you has a brother. He has known of him two years and been ashamed. He has—oh—oh—how it fits together! Rickie, it's you, not Mrs Silt, who must have sent tales of him to your aunt. It's you who've turned him out of Cadover. It's you who've ordered him to be ruined to-day. Mrs Elliot, I beg your pardon.'

Now Herbert arose. 'Out of my sight, sir! But have it from me first that Rickie and his aunt have both behaved most generously. No, no, Agnes, I will not be interrupted. Garbled versions must not get about. If the Wonham man is not satisfied now, he must be insatiable. He cannot levy blackmail on us for ever. Sir, I give you two minutes; then you will be expelled by force.'

'Two minutes!' sang Ansell. 'I can say a great deal in that.' He put one foot on a chair and held his arms over the quivering room. He seemed transfigured into a Hebrew prophet passionate for satire and the truth. 'Oh, keep quiet for two minutes,' he cried, 'and I'll tell you something you'll be glad to hear. You're a little afraid Stephen may come back. Don't be afraid. I bring good news. You'll never see him nor any one like him again. I must speak very plainly, for you are all three fools. I don't want you to say afterwards, "Poor Mr Ansell tried to be clever." Generally I don't mind, but I should mind to-day. Please listen. Stephen is a bully; he drinks; he knocks one down; but he would sooner die than take money from people he did not love. Perhaps he will die, for he has nothing but a few pence that the poor gave him and some tobacco which, to my eternal glory, he accepted from me. Please listen again. Why did he come here? Because he thought you would love him, and was ready to love you. But I tell you, don't be afraid. He would sooner die now than say you were his brother. Perhaps he will die, for he has nothing but a few pence that the poor gave him and some tobacco which, to my eternal glory, he accepted from me. Please listen again—'

'Now, Stewart, don't go on like that,' said Rickie bitterly. 'It's easy enough to preach when you are an outsider. You would be more charitable if such a thing had happened to yourself. Easy enough to be unconventional when you haven't suffered and know nothing of the facts. You love anything out of the way, anything queer, that doesn't often happen, and so you get excited over this. It's useless, my dear man; you have hurt me, but you will never upset me. As soon as you stop this ridiculous scene we will finish our dinner. Spread this scandal; add to it. I'm too old to mind such nonsense. I cannot help my father's disgrace, on the one hand; nor, on the other, will I have anything to do with his blackguard of a son.'

So the secret was given to the world. Agnes might colour at his speech; Herbert might calculate the effect of it on the entries for Dunwood House; but he cared for none of these things. Thank God! he was withered up at last.

'Please listen again,' resumed Ansell. 'Please correct two slight mistakes: firstly, Stephen is one of the greatest people I have ever met; secondly, he's not your father's son. He's the son of your mother.'

It was Rickie, not Ansell, who was carried from the hall, and it was Herbert who pronounced the blessing—

Benedicto benedicatur.

A profound stillness succeeded the storm, and the boys, slipping away from their meal, told the news to the rest of the school, or put it in the letters they were writing home.

Chapter Twenty-eight

The soul has her own currency. She mints her spiritual coinage and stamps it with the image of some beloved face. With it she pays her debts, with it she reckons, saying, 'This man has worth, this man is worthless.' And in time she forgets its origin; it seems to her to be a thing unalterable, divine. But the soul can also have her bankruptcies.

Perhaps she will be the richer in the end. In her agony she learns to reckon clearly. Fair as the coin may have been, it was not accurate; and though she knew it not, there were treasures that it could not buy. The face, however beloved, was mortal, and as liable as the soul herself to err. We do but shift responsibility by making a standard of the dead.

There is, indeed, another coinage that bears on it not man's image but God's. It is incorruptible, and the soul may trust it safely; it will serve her beyond the stars. But it cannot give us friends, or the embrace of a lover, or the touch of children, for with our fellow-mortals it has no concern. It cannot even give the joys we call trivial—fine weather, the pleasures of meat and drink, bathing and the hot sand afterwards, running, dreamless sleep. Have we learnt the true discipline of a bankruptcy if we turn to such coinage as this? Will it really profit us so much if we save our souls and lose the whole world?

Wiltshire

Chapter Twenty-nine

Robert—there is no occasion to mention his surname: he was a young farmer of some education who tried to coax the aged soil of Wiltshire scientifically—came to Cadover on business and fell in love with Mrs Elliot. She was there on her bridal visit, and he, an obscure nobody, was received by Mrs Failing into the house and treated as her social equal. He was good-looking in a bucolic way, and people sometimes mistook him for a gentleman until they saw his hands. He discovered this, and one of the slow, gentle jokes he played on society was to talk upon some cultured subject with his hands behind his back and then suddenly reveal them. 'Do you go in for boating?' the lady would ask; and then he explained that those particular weals are made by the handles of the plough. Upon which she became extremely interested, but found an early opportunity of talking to some one else.

He played this joke on Mrs Elliot the first evening, not knowing that she observed him as he entered the room. He walked heavily, lifting his feet as if the carpet was furrowed, and he had no evening clothes. Every one tried to put him at his ease, but she rather suspected that he was there already, and envied him. They were introduced, and spoke of Byron, who was still fashionable. Out came his hands—the only rough hands in the drawing-room, the only hands that had ever worked. She was filled with some strange approval, and liked him.

After dinner they met again, to speak not of Byron but of manure. The other people were so clever and so amusing that it relieved her to listen to a man who told her three times not to buy artificial manure ready made, but, if she would use it, to make it herself at the last moment. Because the ammonia evaporated. Here were two packets of powder. Did they smell? No. Mix them together and pour some coffee— An appalling smell at once burst forth, and every one began to cough and cry. This was good for the earth when she felt sour, for he knew when the earth was ill. He knew, too, when she was hungry: he spoke of her tantrums—the strange unscientific element in her that will baffle the scientist to the end of time. 'Study away, Mrs Elliot,' he told her; 'read all the books you can get hold of; but when it comes to the point, stroll out with a pipe in your mouth and do a bit of guessing.' As he talked, the earth became a living being—or rather a being with a living skin—and manure no longer dirty stuff, but a symbol of regeneration and of the birth of life from life. 'So it goes on for ever!' she cried excitedly. He replied: 'Not for ever. In time the fire at the centre will cool, and nothing can go on then.'

He advanced into love with open eyes, slowly, heavily, just as he had advanced across the drawing-room carpet. But this time the bride did not observe his tread. She was listening to her husband, and trying not to be so stupid. When he was close to her—so close that it was difficult not to take her in his arms—he spoke to Mr Failing, and was at once turned out of Cadover.

'I'm sorry,' said Mr Failing, as he walked down the drive with his hand on his guest's shoulder. 'I had no notion you were that sort. Any one who behaves like that has to stop at the farm.'

'Any one?'

'Anyone.' He sighed heavily, not for any personal grievance, but because he saw how unruly, how barbaric, is the soul of man. After all, this man was more civilized than most.

'Are you angry with me, sir?' He called him 'sir,' not because he was richer or cleverer or smarter, not because he had helped to educate him and had lent him money, but for a reason more profound—for the reason that there are gradations in heaven.

'I did think you—that a man like you wouldn't risk making people unhappy. My sister-in-law—I don't say this to stop you loving her; something else must do that—my sister-in-law, as far as I know, doesn't care for you one little bit. If you had said anything, if she had guessed that a chance person was in this fearful state, you would simply have opened hell. A woman of her sort would have lost all—'

'I knew that.'

Mr Failing removed his hand. He was displeased.

'But something here,' said Robert incoherently. 'This here.' He struck himself heavily on the heart. 'This here, doing something so unusual, makes it not matter what she loses—I—' After a silence, he asked, 'Have I quite followed you, sir, in that business of the brotherhood of man?'

'How do you mean?'

'I thought love was to bring it about.'

'Love of another man's wife? Sensual love? You have understood nothing—nothing.' Then he was ashamed, and cried, 'I understand nothing myself.' For he remembered that sensual and spiritual are not easy words to use; that there are, perhaps, not two Aphrodites, but one Aphrodite with a Janus face. 'I only understand that you must try to forget her.'

'I will not try.'

'Promise me just this, then—not to do anything crooked.'

'I'm straight. No boasting, but I couldn't do a crooked thing—no, not if I tried.'

And so appallingly straight was he in after years, that Mr Failing wished that he had phrased the promise differently.

Robert simply waited. He told himself that it was hopeless; but something deeper than himself declared that there was hope. He gave up drink, and kept himself in all ways clean, for he wanted to be worthy of her when the time came. Women seemed fond of him, and caused him to reflect with pleasure, 'They do run after me. There must be something in me. Good. I'd be done for if there wasn't.' For six years he turned up the earth of Wiltshire, and read books for the sake of his mind, and talked to gentlemen for the sake of their patois, and each year he rode to Cadover to take off his hat to Mrs Elliot, and, perhaps, to speak to her about the crops. Mr Failing was generally present, and it struck neither man that those dull little visits were so many words out of which a lonely woman might build sentences. Then Robert went to London on business. He chanced to see Mr Elliot with a strange lady. The time had come.

He became diplomatic, and called at Mr Elliot's rooms to find things out. For if Mrs Elliot was happier than he could ever make her, he would withdraw, and love her in renunciation. But if he could make her happier, he would love her in fulfilment. Mr Elliot admitted him as a friend of his brother-in-law's, and felt very broad-minded as he did so. Robert, however, was a success. The youngish men there found him interesting, and liked to shock him with tales of naughty London and naughtier Paris. They spoke of 'experience' and 'sensations' and 'seeing life,' and when a smile ploughed over his face, concluded that his prudery was vanquished. He saw that they were much less vicious than they supposed: one boy had obviously read his sensations in a book. But he could pardon vice. What he could not pardon was triviality, and he hoped that no decent woman would pardon it either. There grew up in him a cold, steady anger against these silly people who thought it advanced to be shocking, and who described, as something particularly choice and educational, things that he had understood and fought against for years. He inquired after Mrs Elliot, and a boy tittered. It seemed that she 'did not know' that she lived in a remote suburb, taking care of a skinny baby. 'I shall call some time or other,' said Robert. 'Do,' said Mr Elliot, smiling. And next time he saw his wife he congratulated her on her rustic admirer.

She had suffered terribly. She had asked for bread, and had been given not even a stone. People talk of hungering for the ideal, but there is another hunger, quite as divine, for facts. She had asked for facts and had been given 'views,' 'emotional standpoints,' 'attitudes towards life.' To a women who believed that facts are beautiful, that the living world is beautiful beyond the laws of beauty, that manure is neither gross nor ludicrous, that a fire, not eternal, glows at the heart of the earth, it was intolerable to be put off with what the Elliots called 'philosophy,' and, if she refused, to be told that she had no sense of humour. 'Marrying into the Elliot family.' It had sounded so splendid, for she was a penniless child with nothing to offer, and the Elliots held their heads high. For what reason? What had they ever done, except say sarcastic things, and limp, and be refined? Mr Failing suffered too, but she suffered more, inasmuch as Frederick was more impossible than Emily. He did not like her, he practically lived apart, he was not even faithful or polite. These were grave faults, but they were human ones: she could even imagine them in a man she loved. What she could never love was a dilettante.

Robert brought her an armful of sweet-peas. He laid it on the table, put his hands behind his back, and kept them there till the end of the visit. She knew quite well why he had come, and though she also knew that he would fail, she loved him too much to snub him or to stare in virtuous indignation. 'Why have you come?' she asked gravely, 'and why have you brought me so many flowers?'

'My garden is full of them,' he answered. 'Sweet-peas need picking down. And, generally speaking, flowers are plentiful in July.'

She broke his present into bunches—so much for the drawing-room, so much for the nursery, so much for the kitchen and her husband's room: he would be down for the night. The most beautiful she would keep for herself. Presently he said, 'Your husband is no good. I've watched him for a week. I'm thirty, and not what you call hasty, as I used to be, or thinking that nothing matters like the French. No. I'm a plain Britisher, yet—I—I've begun wrong end, Mrs Elliot; I should have said that I've thought chiefly of you for six years, and that though I talk here so respectfully, if I once unhooked my hands—'

There was a pause. Then she said with great sweetness, 'Thank you; I am glad you love me,' and rang the bell.

'What have you done that for?' he cried.

'Because you must now leave the house, and never enter it again.'

'I don't go alone,' and he began to get furious.

Her voice was still sweet, but strength lay in it too, as she said, 'You either go now with my thanks and my blessing, or else you go with the police. I am Mrs Elliot. We need not discuss Mr Elliot. I am Mrs Elliot, and if you make one step towards me I give you in charge.'

But the maid answered the bell not of the drawing-room, but of the front door. They were joined by Mr Elliot, who held out his hand with much urbanity. It was not taken. He looked quickly at his wife, and said, 'Am I *de trop*?' There was a long silence. At last she said, 'Frederick, turn this man out.'

'My love, why?'

Robert said that he loved her.

'Then I am *de trop*,' said Mr Elliot, smoothing out his gloves. He would give these sodden barbarians a lesson. 'My hansom is waiting at the door. Pray make use of it.'

'Don't!' she cried, almost affectionately. 'Dear Frederick, it isn't a play. Just tell this man to go, or send for the police.'

'On the contrary; it is French comedy of the best type. Don't you agree, sir, that the police would be an inartistic error?' He was perfectly calm and collected, whereas they were in a pitiable state.

'Turn him out at once!' she cried. 'He has insulted your wife. Save me, save me!' She clung to her husband and wept. 'He was going—I had managed him—he would never have known—' Mr Elliot repulsed her.

'If you don't feel inclined to start at once,' he said, with easy civility, 'let us have a little tea. My dear sir, do forgive me for not shooting you. *Nous avons changé tout cela*. Please don't look so nervous. Please unclasp your hands—'

He was alone.

'That's all right,' he exclaimed, and strolled to the door. The hansom was disappearing round the corner. 'That's all right,' he repeated in more quavering tones as he returned to the drawing-room and saw that it was littered with sweet-peas. Their colour got on his nerves—magenta, crimson; magenta, crimson. He tried to pick them up, and they escaped. He trod them underfoot, and they multiplied and danced in the triumph of summer like a thousand butterflies. The train had left when he got to the station. He followed on to London, and there he lost all traces. At midnight he began to realize that his wife could never belong to him again.

Mr Failing had a letter from Stockholm. It was never known what impulse sent them there. 'I am sorry about it all, but it was the only way.' The letter censured the law of England, 'which obliges us to behave like this, or else we should never get married. I shall come back to face things: she will not come back till she is my wife. He must bring an action soon, or else we shall try one against him. It seems all very unconventional, but it is not really. It is only a difficult start. We are not like you or your wife: we want to be just ordinary people, and make the farm pay, and not be noticed all our lives.'

And they were capable of living as they wanted. The class difference, which so intrigued Mrs Failing, meant very little to them. It was there, but so were other things. They both cared for work and living in the open, and for not speaking unless they had got something to say. Their love of beauty, like their love for each other, was not dependent on detail: it grew not from the nerves but from the soul.

> *I believe a leaf of grass is no less than the journey work of the stars,*
> *And the pismire is equally perfect, and a grain of sand, and the egg of the*
> *wren,*
> *And the tree toad is a chef-d'œuvre for the highest,*
> *And the running blackberry would adorn the parlours of heaven.*

They had never read these lines, and would have thought them nonsense if they had. They did not dissect—indeed they could not. But she, at all events, divined that more than perfect health and perfect weather, more than personal love, had gone to the making of those seventeen days.

'Ordinary people!' cried Mrs Failing on hearing the letter. At that time she was young and daring. 'Why, they're divine! They're forces of Nature! They're as ordinary as volcanoes. We all knew my brother was disgusting, and wanted him to be blown to pieces, but we never thought it would happen. Do look at the thing bravely, and say, as I do, that they are guiltless in the sight of God.'

'I think they are,' replied her husband. 'But they are not guiltless in the sight of man.'

'You conventional!' she exclaimed in disgust.

'What they have done means misery not only for themselves but for others. For your brother, though you will not think of him. For the little boy—did you think of him? And perhaps for another child, who will have the whole world against him if it knows. They have sinned against society, and you do not diminish the misery by proving that society is as bad or foolish. It is the saddest truth I have yet perceived that the Beloved Republic'—here she took up a book—'of which Swinburne speaks'—she put the book down—'will not be brought about by love alone. It will approach with no flourish of trumpets, and have no declaration of independence. Self-sacrifice and—worse still—self-mutilation are the things that sometimes help it most, and that is why we should start for Stockholm this evening.' He waited for her indignation to subside, and then continued. 'I don't know whether it can be hushed up. I don't yet know whether it ought to be hushed up. But we ought to provide the opportunity. There is no scandal yet. If we go, it is just possible there never will be any. We must talk over the whole thing and—'

'—And lie!' interrupted Mrs Failing, who hated travel.

'—And see how to avoid the greatest unhappiness.'

There was to be no scandal. By the time they arrived Robert had been drowned. Mrs Elliot described how they had gone swimming, and how, 'since he always lived inland,' the great waves had tired him. They had raced for the open sea.

'What are your plans?' he asked. 'I bring you a message from Frederick.'

'I heard him call,' she continued, 'but I thought he was laughing. When I turned, it was too late. He put his hands behind his back and sank. For he would only have drowned me with him. I should have done the same.'

Mrs Failing was thrilled, and kissed her. But Mr Failing knew that life does not continue heroic for long, and he gave her the message from her husband: Would she come back to him?

To his intense astonishment—at first to his regret—she replied, 'I will think about it. If I loved him the very least bit I should say no. If I had anything to do with my life I should say no. But it is simply a question of beating time till I die. Nothing that is coming matters. I may as well sit in his drawing-room and dust his furniture, since he has suggested it.'

And Mr Elliot, though he made certain stipulations, was positively glad to see her. People had begun to laugh at him, and to say that his wife had run away. She had not. She had been with his sister in Sweden. In a half miraculous way the matter was hushed up. Even the Silts only scented 'something strange.' When Stephen was born, it was abroad. When he came to England, it was as the child of a friend of Mr Failing's. Mrs Elliot returned unsuspected to her husband.

But though things can be hushed up, there is no such thing as beating time; and as the years passed she realized her terrible mistake. When her lover sank, eluding her last embrace, she thought, as Agnes was to think after her, that her soul had sunk with him, and that never again should she be capable of earthly love. Nothing mattered. She might as well go and be useful to her husband and to the little boy who looked exactly like him, and who, she thought, was exactly like him in disposition. Then Stephen was born, and altered her life. She could still love people passionately; she still drew strength from the heroic past. Yet, to keep to her bond, she must see this son only as a stranger. She was protected by the conventions, and must pay them their fee. And a curious thing happened. Her second child drew her towards her first, She began to love Rickie also, and to be more than useful to him. And as her love revived, so did her capacity for suffering. Life, more important, grew more bitter. She minded her husband more, not less; and when as last he died, and she saw a glorious autumn, beautiful with the voices of boys who should call her mother, the end came for her as well, before she could remember the grave in the alien north and the dust that would never return to the dear fields that had given it.

Chapter Thirty

Stephen, the son of these people, had one instinct that troubled him. At night—especially out of doors—it seemed rather strange that he was alive. The dry grass pricked his cheek, the fields were invisible and mute, and here was he, throwing stones at the darkness or smoking a pipe. The stones vanished, the pipe would burn out. But he would be here in the morning when the sun rose, and he would bathe, and run in the mist. He was proud of his good circulation, and in the morning it seemed quite natural. But at night, why should there be this difference between him and the acres of land that cooled all round him until the sun returned? What lucky chance had heated him up, and sent him, warm and lovable, into a passive world? He had other instincts, but these gave him no trouble. He simply gratified each as it occurred, provided he could do so without grave injury to his fellows. But the instinct to wonder at the night was not to be thus appeased.

At first he had lived under the care of Mr Failing—the only person to whom his mother spoke freely, the only person who had treated her neither as a criminal nor as a pioneer. In their rare but intimate conversations she had asked him to educate her son. 'I will teach him Latin,' he answered. 'The rest such a boy must remember.' Latin, at all events, was a failure: who could attend to Virgil when the sound of the thresher arose, and you knew that the stack was decreasing and that rats rushed more plentifully each moment to their doom. But he was fond of Mr Failing, and cried when he died. Mrs Elliot, a pleasant woman, died soon after.

There was something fatal in the order of these deaths. Mr Failing had made no provision for the boy in his will: his wife had promised to see to this.

Then came Mr Elliot's death, and, before the new home was created, the sudden death of Mrs Elliot. She also left Stephen no money: she had none to leave. Chance threw him into the power of Mrs Failing. 'Let things go on as they are,' she thought. 'I will take care of this pretty little boy, and the ugly little boy can live with the Silts. After my death, well, the papers will be found after my death, and they can meet then. I like the idea of their mutual ignorance. It is amusing.'

He was then twelve. With a few brief intervals of school, he lived in Wiltshire until he was driven out. Life had two distinct sides—the drawing-room and the other. In the drawing-room people talked a good deal, laughing as they talked. Being clever, they did not care for animals: one man had never seen a hedgehog. In the other life people talked and laughed separately, or even did neither. On the whole, in spite of the wet and gamekeepers, this life was preferable. He knew where he was. He glanced at the boy, or later at the man, and behaved accordingly. There was no law—the policeman was negligible. Nothing bound him but his own word, and he gave that sparingly.

It is impossible to be romantic when you have your heart's desire, and such a boy disappointed Mrs Failing greatly. His parents had met for one brief embrace, had found one little interval between the power of the rulers of this world and the power of death. He was the child of poetry and of rebellion, and poetry should run in his veins. But he lived too near to the things he loved to seem poetical. Parted from them, he might yet satisfy her, and stretch out his hands with a pagan's yearning. As it was, he only rode her horses, and trespassed, and bathed, and worked, for no obvious reason, upon her fields. Affection she did not believe in, and made no attempt to mould him; and he, for his part, was very content to harden untouched into a man. His parents had given him excellent gifts—health, sturdy limbs, and a face not ugly—gifts that his habits confirmed. They had also given him a cloudless spirit—the spirit of the seventeen days in which he was created. But they had not given him the spirit of their six years of waiting, and love for one person was never to be the greatest thing he knew.

'Philosophy' had postponed the quarrel between them. Incurious about his personal origin, he had a certain interest in our eternal problems. The interest never became a passion: it sprang out of his physical growth, and was soon merged in it again. Or, as he put it himself, 'I must get fixed up before starting.' He was soon fixed up as a materialist. Then he tore up the sixpenny reprints, and never amused Mrs Failing so much again.

About the time he fixed himself up, he took to drink. He knew of no reason against it. The instinct was in him, and it hurt nobody. Here, as elsewhere, his motions were decided, and he passed at once from roaring jollity to silence. For those who live on the fuddled borderland, who crawl home by the railings and maunder repentance in the morning, he had a biting contempt. A man must take his tumble and his headache. He was, in fact, as little disgusting as is conceivable; and hitherto he had not strained his constitution or his will. Nor did he get drunk as often as Agnes suggested. The real quarrel gathered elsewhere.

Presentable people have run wild in their youth. But the hour comes when they turn from their boorish company to higher things. This hour never came for Stephen. Somewhat a bully by nature, he kept where his powers would tell, and continued to quarrel and play with the men he had known as boys. He prolonged their youth unduly. 'They won't settle down,' said Mr Wilbraham to his wife. 'They're wanting things. It's the germ of a Trades Union. I shall get rid of a few of the worst.' Then Stephen rushed up to Mrs Failing and worried her. 'It wasn't fair. So-and-so was a good sort. He did his work. Keen about it? No. Why should he be? Why should he be keen about somebody else's land? But keen enough. And very keen on football.' She laughed, and said a word about So-and-so to Mr Wilbraham. Mr Wilbraham blazed up. 'How could the farm go on without discipline? How could there be discipline if Mr Stephen interfered? Mr Stephen liked power. He spoke to the men like one of themselves, and pretended it was all equality, but he took care to come out top. Natural, of course, that, being a gentleman, he should. But not natural for a gentleman to loiter all day with poor people and learn their work, and put wrong notions into their heads, and carry their new-fangled grievances to Mrs Failing. Which partly accounted for the deficit on the past year.' She rebuked Stephen. Then he lost his temper, was rude to her, and insulted Mr Wilbraham.

The worst days of Mr Failing's rule seemed to be returning. And Stephen had a practical experience, and also a taste for battle, that her husband had never possessed. He drew up a list of grievances, some absurd, others fundamental. No newspapers in the reading-room, you could put a plate under the Thompsons' door, no level cricket-pitch, no allotments, and no time to work in them, Mrs Wilbraham's knife-boy underpaid. 'Aren't you a little unwise?' she asked coldly. 'I am more bored than you think over the farm.' She was wanting to correct the proofs of the book and re-write the prefatory memoir. In her irritation she wrote to Agnes. Agnes replied sympathetically, and Mrs Failing, clever as she was, fell into the power of the younger woman. They discussed him at first as a wretch of a boy; then he got drunk and somehow it seemed more criminal. All that she needed now was a personal grievance, which Agnes casually supplied. Though vindictive, she was determined to treat him well, and thought with satisfaction of our distant colonies. But he burst into an odd passion: he would sooner starve than leave England. 'Why?' she asked. 'Are you in love?' He picked up a lump of the chalk—they were by the arbour—and made no answer. The vicar murmured, 'It is not like going abroad—Greater Britain—blood is thicker than water—' A lump of chalk broke her drawing-room window on the Saturday.

Thus Stephen left Wiltshire, half-blackguard, half-martyr. Do not brand him as a socialist. He had no quarrel with society, nor any particular belief in people because they are poor. He only held the creed of 'here am I and there are you,' and therefore class distinctions were trivial things to him, and life no decorous scheme, but a personal combat or a personal truce. For the same reason ancestry also was trivial, and a man not the dearer because the same woman was mother to them both. Yet it seemed worth while to go to

Sawston with the news. Perhaps nothing would come of it; perhaps friendly intercourse, and a home while he looked around.

When they wronged him he walked quietly away. He never thought of allotting the blame nor of appealing to Ansell, who still sat brooding in the side-garden. He only knew that educated people could be horrible, and that a clean liver must never enter Dunwood House again. The air seemed stuffy. He spat in the gutter. Was it yesterday he had lain in the rifle-butts over Salisbury? Slightly aggrieved, he wondered why he was not back there now. 'I ought to have written first,' he reflected. 'Here is my money gone. I cannot move. The Elliots have, as it were, practically robbed me.' That was the only grudge he retained against them. Their suspicions and insults were to him as the curses of a tramp whom he passed by the wayside. They were dirty people, not his sort. He summed up the complicated tragedy as a 'take in.'

While Rickie was being carried upstairs, and while Ansell (had he known it) was dashing about the streets for him, he lay under a railway arch trying to settle his plans. He must pay back the friends who had given him shillings and clothes. He thought of Flea, whose Sundays he was spoiling—poor Flea, who ought to be in them now, shining before his girl. 'I daresay he'll be ashamed and not go to see her, and then she'll take the other man.' He was also very hungry. That worm Mrs Elliot would be through her lunch by now. Tying his braces round him and tearing up those old wet documents, he stepped forth to make money. A villainous young brute he looked: his clothes were dirty, and he had lost the spring of the morning. Touching the walls, frowning, talking to himself at times, he slouched disconsolately northwards; no wonder that some tawdry girls screamed at him, or that matrons averted their eyes as they hurried to afternoon church. He wandered from one suburb to another, till he was among people more villainous than himself, who bought his tobacco from him and sold him food. Again the neighbourhood 'went up,' and families, instead of sitting on their doorsteps, would sit behind thick muslin curtains. Again it would 'go down' into a more avowed despair. Far into the night he wandered, until he came to a solemn river majestic as a stream in hell. Therein were gathered the waters of Central England—those that flow off Hindhead, off the Chilterns, off Wiltshire north of the Plain. Therein they were made intolerable ere they reached the sea. But the waters he had known escaped. Their course lay southward into the Avon by forests and beautiful fields, even swift, even pure, until they mirrored the tower of Christchurch and greeted the ramparts of the Isle of Wight. Of these he thought for a moment as he crossed the black river and entered the heart of the modern world.

Here he found employment. He was not hampered by genteel traditions, and, as it was near quarter-day, managed to get taken on at a furniture warehouse. He moved people from the suburbs to London, from London to the suburbs, from one suburb to another. His companions were hurried and querulous. In particular, he loathed the foreman, a pious humbug who allowed no swearing, but indulged in something far more degraded—the Cockney repartee. The London intellect, so pert and shallow, like a stream that never reaches the ocean, disgusted him almost as much as the London physique, which for all its dexterity is not permanent, and seldom continues into the third generation. His father, had he known it, had felt the same; for between Mr Elliot and the foreman the gulf was social, not spiritual: both spent their lives in trying to be clever. And Tony Failing had once put the thing into words: 'There's no such thing as a Londoner. He's only a country man on the road to sterility.'

At the end of ten days he had saved scarcely anything. Once he passed the bank where a hundred pounds lay ready for him, but it was still inconvenient for him to take them. Then duty sent him to a suburb not very far from Sawston. In the evening a man who was driving a trap asked him to hold it, and by mistake tipped him a sovereign. Stephen called after him; but the man had a woman with him and wanted to show off, and though he had meant to tip a shilling, and could not afford that, he shouted back that his sovereign was as good as any one's, and that if Stephen did not think so he could do various things and go to various places. On the action of this man much depends. Stephen changed the sovereign into a postal order, and sent it off to the people at Cadford. It did not pay them back, but it paid them something, and he felt that his soul was free.

A few shillings remained in his pocket. They would have paid his fare towards Wiltshire, a good county; but what should he do there? Who would employ him? To-day the journey did not seem worth while. 'To-morrow, perhaps,' he thought, and determined to spend the money on pleasure of another kind. Twopence went for a ride on an electric tram. From the top he saw the sun descend–a disc with a dark red edge. The same sun was descending over Salisbury intolerably bright. Out of the golden haze the spire would be piercing, like a purple needle; then mists arose from the Avon and the other streams. Lamps flickered, but in the outer purity the villages were already slumbering. Salisbury is only a Gothic upstart beside these. For generations they have come down to her to buy or to worship, and have found in her the reasonable crisis of their lives; but generations before she was built they were clinging to the soil, and renewing it with sheep and dogs and men, who found the crisis of their lives upon Stonehenge. The blood of these men ran in Stephen; the vigour they had won for him was as yet untarnished; out on those downs they had united with rough women to make the thing he spoke of as 'himself'; the last of them had rescued a woman of a different kind from streets and houses such as these. As the sun descended he got off the tram with a smile of expectation. A public-house lay opposite, and a boy in a dirty uniform was already lighting its enormous lamp. His lips parted, and he went in.

Two hours later, when Rickie and Herbert were going the rounds, a brick came crashing at the study window. Herbert peered into the garden, and a hooligan slipped by him into the house, wrecked the hall, lurched up the stairs, fell against the banisters, balanced for a moment on his spine, and slid over. Herbert called for the police. Rickie, who was upon the landing, caught the man by the knees and saved his life.

'What is it?' cried Agnes, emerging.

'It's Stephen come back,' was the answer 'Hullo, Stephen!'

Chapter Thirty-one

Hither had Rickie moved in ten days–from disgust to penitence, from penitence to longing, from a life of horror to a new life, in which he still surprised himself by unexpected words. Hullo, Stephen! For the son of his mother had come back, to forgive him, as she would have done, to live with him, as she had planned.

'He's drunk this time,' said Agnes wearily. She too had altered: the scandal was ageing her, and Ansell came to the house daily.

'Hullo, Stephen!'

But Stephen was now insensible.

'Stephen, you live here—'

'Good gracious me!' interposed Herbert. 'My advice is, that we all go to bed. The less said the better while our nerves are in this state. Very well, Rickie. Of course, Wonham sleeps the night if you wish.' They carried the drunken mass into the spare room. A mass of scandal it seemed to one of them, a symbol of redemption to the other. Neither acknowledged it a man, who would answer them back after a few hours' rest.

'Ansell thought he would never forgive me,' said Rickie. 'For once he's wrong.'

'Come to bed now, I think.' And as Rickie laid his hand on the sleeper's hair, he added, 'You won't do anything foolish, will you? You are still in a morbid state. Your poor mother— Pardon me, dear boy; it is my turn to speak out. You thought it was your father, and minded. It is your mother. Surely you ought to mind more?'

'I have been too far back,' said Rickie gently. 'Ansell took me a journey that was even new to him. We got behind right and wrong, to a place where only one thing matters–that the Beloved should rise from the dead.'

'But you won't do anything rash?'

'Why should I?'

'Remember poor Agnes,' he stammered. 'I–I am the first to acknowledge that we might have pursued a different policy. But we are committed to it now. It makes no difference whose son he is. I mean, he is the same person. You and I and my sister stand or fall together. It was our agreement from the first. I hope–No more of these distressing scenes with her, there's a dear fellow. I assure you they make my heart bleed.'

'Things will quiet down now.'

'To bed now; I insist upon that much.'

'Very well,' said Rickie, and when they were in the passage, locked the door from the outside. 'We want no more muddles,' he explained.

Mr Pembroke was left examining the hall. The bust of Hermes was broken. So was the pot of the palm. He could not go to bed without once more sounding Rickie. 'You'll do nothing rash,' he called. 'The notion of him living here was, of course, a passing impulse. We three have adopted a common policy.'

'Now, you go away!' called a voice that was almost flippant. 'I never did belong to that great sect whose doctrine is that each one should select—at least, I'm not going to belong to it any longer. Go away to bed.'

'A good night's rest is what you need,' threatened Herbert, and retired, not to find one for himself.

But Rickie slept. The guilt of months and the remorse of the last ten days had alike departed. He had thought that his life was poisoned, and lo! it was purified. He had cursed his mother, and Ansell had replied, 'You may be right, but you stand too near to settle. Step backwards. Pretend that it happened to me. Do you want me to curse my mother? Now, step forward and see whether anything has changed.' Something had changed. He had journeyed—as on rare occasions a man must—till he stood behind right and wrong. On the banks of the grey torrent of life, love is the only flower. A little way up the stream and a little way down had Rickie glanced, and he knew that she whom he loved had risen from the dead, and might rise again. 'Come away—let them die out—let them die out.' Surely that dream was a vision! To-night also he hurried to the window—to remember, with a smile, that Orion is not among the stars of June.

'Let me die out. She will continue,' he murmured, and in making plans for Stephen's happiness, fell asleep.

Next morning after breakfast he announced that his brother must live at Dunwood House. They were awed by the very moderation of his tone. 'There's nothing else to be done. Cadover's hopeless, and a boy of those tendencies can't go drifting. There is also the question of a profession for him, and his allowance.'

'We have to thank Mr Ansell for this,' was all that Agnes could say; and 'I foresee disaster,' was the contribution of Herbert.

'There's plenty of money about,' Rickie continued. 'Quite a man's-worth too much. It has been one of our absurdities. Don't look so sad, Herbert. I'm sorry for you people, but he's sure to let us down easy.' For his experience of drunkards and of Stephen was small. He supposed that he had come without malice to renew the offer of ten days ago.

'It is the end of Dunwood House.'

Rickie nodded, and hoped not. Agnes, who was not looking well, began to cry. 'Oh, it is too bad,' she complained, 'when I've saved you from him all these years.' But he could not pity her, nor even sympathize with her wounded delicacy. The time for such nonsense was over. He would take his share of the blame: it was cant to assume it all.

Perhaps he was over-hard. He did not realize how large his share was, nor how his very virtues were to blame for her deterioration. 'If I had a girl, I'd keep her in line,' is not the remark of a fool nor of a cad. Rickie had not kept his wife in line. He had shown her all the workings of his soul, mistaking this for love; and in consequence she was the worse woman after two years of marriage, and he, on this morning of freedom, was harder upon her than he need have been.

The spare room bell rang. Herbert had a painful struggle between curiosity and duty, for the bell for chapel was ringing also, and he must go through the drizzle to school. He promised to come up in the interval. Rickie, who had rapped his head that Sunday on the edge of the table, was still forbidden to work. Before him a quiet morning lay. Secure of his victory, he took the portrait of their mother in his hand and walked leisurely upstairs. The bell continued to ring.

'See about his breakfast,' he called to Agnes, who replied, 'Very well.' The handle of the spare room door was moving slowly. 'I'm coming,' he cried. The handle was still. He unlocked and entered, his heart full of charity. But within stood a man who probably owned the world.

Rickie scarcely knew him; last night he had seemed so colourless, so negligible. In a few hours he had recaptured motion and passion and the imprint of the sunlight and the wind. He stood, not consciously heroic, with arms that dangled from broad stooping shoulders, and feet that played with a hassock on the carpet. But his hair was beautiful against the grey sky, and his eyes, recalling the sky unclouded, shot past the intruder as if to some worthier vision. So intent was their gaze that Rickie himself glanced backwards, only to see the neat passage and the banisters at the top of the stairs. Then the lips beat together twice, and out burst a torrent of amazing words.

'Add it all up, and let me know how much. I'd sooner have died. It never took me that way before. I must have broken pounds' worth. If you'll not tell the police, I promise you shan't lose, Mr Elliot, I swear. But it may be months before I send it. Everything is to be new. You've not to be a penny out of pocket, do you see? Do let me go, this once again.'

'What's the trouble?' asked Rickie, as if they had been friends for years. 'My dear man, we've other things to talk about. Gracious me, what a fuss! If you'd smashed the whole house I wouldn't mind, so long as you came back.'

'I'd sooner have died,' gulped Stephen.

'You did nearly! It was I who caught you. Never mind yesterday's rag. What can you manage for breakfast.'

The face grew more angry and more puzzled. 'Yesterday wasn't a rag,' he said without focussing his eyes. 'I was drunk, but naturally meant it.'

'Meant what?'

'To smash you. Bad liquor did what Mrs Elliot couldn't. I've put myself in the wrong. You've got me.'

It was a poor beginning.

'As I have got you,' said Rickie, controlling himself, 'I want to have a talk with you. There has been a ghastly mistake.'

But Stephen, with a countryman's persistency, continued on his own line. He meant to be civil, but Rickie went cold round the mouth. For he had not even been angry with them. Until he was drunk, they had been dirty people—not his sort. Then the trivial injury recurred, and he had reeled to smash them as he passed. 'And I will pay for everything,' was his refrain, with which the sighing of raindrops mingled. 'You shan't lose a penny, if only you let me free.'

'You'll pay for my coffin if you talk like that any longer! Will you, one, forgive my frightful behaviour; two, live with me?' For his only hope was in a cheerful precision.

Stephen grew more agitated. He thought it was some trick.

'I was saying I made an unspeakable mistake. Ansell put me right, but it was too late to find you. Don't think I got off easily. Ansell doesn't spare one. And you've got to forgive me, to share my life, to share my money–I've brought you this photograph–I want it to be the first thing you accept from me–you have the greater right–I know all the story now. You know who it is?'

'Oh yes; but I don't want to drag all that in.'

'It is only her wish if we live together. She was planning it when she died.'

'I can't follow–because–to share your life? Did you know I called here last Sunday week?'

'Yes. But then I only knew half. I thought you were my father's son.'

Stephen's anger and bewilderment were increasing. He stuttered. 'What–what's the odds if you did?'

'I hated my father,' said Rickie. 'I loved my mother.' And never had the phrases seemed so destitute of meaning.

'Last Sunday week,' interrupted Stephen, his voice suddenly rising, 'I came to call on you. Not as this or that's son. Not to fall on your neck. Nor to live here. Nor–damn your dirty little mind! I meant to say I didn't come for money. Sorry. Sorry. I simply came as I was, and I haven't altered since.'

'Yes–yet our mother–for me she has risen from the dead since then–I know I was wrong–'

'And where do I come in?' He kicked the hassock. '*I* haven't risen from the dead. *I* haven't altered since last Sunday week. I'm—' He stuttered again. He could not quite explain what he was. 'The man towards Andover–after all, he was having principles. But you've—' His voice broke. 'I mind it–I'm–*I* don't alter–blackguard one week–live here the next–I keep to one or the other–you've hurt something most badly in me that I didn't know was there.'

'Don't let us talk,' said Rickie. 'It gets worse every minute. Simply say you forgive me; shake hands, and have done with it.'

'That I won't. That I couldn't. In fact, I don't know what you mean.'

Then Rickie began a new appeal–not to pity, for now he was in no mood to whimper. For all its pathos, there was something heroic in this meeting. 'I warn you to stop here with me, Stephen. No one else in the world will look after you. As far as I know, you have never been really unhappy yet or suffered, as you should do, from your faults. Last night you nearly killed yourself with drink. Never mind why I'm willing to cure you. I am willing, and I warn you to give me the chance. Forgive me or not, as you choose. I care for other things more.'

Stephen looked at him at last, faintly approving. The offer was ridiculous, but it did treat him as a man.

'Let me tell you of a fault of mine, and how I was punished for it,' continued Rickie. 'Two years ago I behaved badly to you, up at the Rings. No, even a few days before that. We went for a ride, and I thought too much of other matters, and did not try to understand you. Then came the Rings, and in the evening, when you called up to me most kindly, I never answered. But the ride was the beginning. Ever since then I have taken the world at second-hand. I have bothered less and less to look it in the face—until not only you, but every one else has turned unreal. Never Ansell: he kept away, and somehow saved himself. But every one else. Do you remember in one of Tony Failing's books, "Cast bitter bread upon the waters, and after many days it really does come back to you"? This has been true of my life; it will be equally true of a drunkard's, and I warn you to stop with me.'

'I can't stop after that cheque,' said Stephen more gently. 'But I do remember the ride. I was a bit bored myself.'

Agnes, who had not been seeing to the breakfast, chose this moment to call from the passage. 'Of course he can't stop,' she exclaimed. 'For better or worse, it's settled. We've none of us altered since last Sunday week.'

'There you're right, Mrs Elliot!' he shouted, starting out of the temperate past. 'We haven't altered.' With a rare flash of insight he turned on Rickie. 'I see your game. You don't care about *me* drinking, or to shake *my* hand. It's some one else you want to cure—as it were, that old photograph. You talk to me, but all the time you look at the photograph. He snatched it up. 'I've my own idea of good manners, and to look friends between the eyes is one of them; and this'—he tore the photograph across—'and this'—he tore it again—'and these—' He flung the pieces at the man, who had sunk into a chair. 'For my part, I'm off.'

Then Rickie was heroic no longer. Turning round in his chair, he covered his face. The man was right. He did not love him, even as he had never hated him. In either passion he had degraded him to be a symbol for the vanished past. The man was right, and would have been lovable. He longed to be back riding over those windy fields, to be back in those mystic circles, beneath pure sky. Then they could have watched and helped and taught each other, until the word was a reality, and the past not a torn photograph, but Demeter the goddess rejoicing in the spring. Ah, if he had seized those high opportunities! For they led to the highest of all, the symbolic moment, which, if a man accepts, he has accepted life.

The voice of Agnes, which had lured him then ('For my sake,' she had whispered), pealed over him now in triumph. Abruptly it broke into sobs that had the effect of rain. He started up. The anger had died out of Stephen's face, not for a subtle reason but because here was a woman, near him, and unhappy.

She tried to apologize, and brought on a fresh burst of tears. Something had upset her. They heard her locking the door of her room. From that moment their intercourse was changed.

'Why does she keep crying to-day?' mused Rickie, as if he spoke to some mutual friend.

'I can make a guess,' said Stephen, and his heavy face flushed.

'Did you insult her?' he asked feebly.

'But who's Gerald?'

Rickie raised his hand to his mouth.

'She looked at me as if she knew me, and then gasps "Gerald," and started crying.'

'Gerald is the name of some one she once knew.'

'So I thought.' There was a long silence, in which they could hear a piteous gulping cough. 'Where is he now?' asked Stephen.

'Dead.'

'And then you—?'

Rickie nodded.

'Bad, this sort of thing.'

'I didn't know of this particular thing. She acted as if she had forgotten him. Perhaps she had, and you woke him up. There are queer tricks in the world. She is overstrained. She has probably been plotting ever since you burst in last night.'

'Against me?'

'Yes.'

Stephen stood irresolute. 'I suppose you and she pulled together?' he said at last.

'Get away from us, man! I mind losing you. Yet it's as well you don't stop.'

'Oh, *that's* out of the question,' said Stephen, brushing his cap.

'If you've guessed anything, I'd be obliged if you didn't mention it. I've no right to ask, but I'd be obliged.'

He nodded and walked slowly along the landing and down the stairs. Rickie accompanied him, and even opened the front door. It was as if Agnes had absorbed the passion out of both of them. The suburb was now wrapped in a cloud, not of its own making. Sigh after sigh passed along its streets to break against dripping walls. The school, the houses were hidden, and all civilization seemed in abeyance. Only the simplest sounds, the simplest desires emerged. They agreed that this weather was strange after such a sunset.

'That's a collie,' said Stephen, listening.

'I wish you'd have some breakfast before starting.'

'No food, thanks. But you know—' He paused. 'It's all been a muddle, and I've no objection to your coming along with me.'

The cloud descended lower.

'Come with me as a man,' said Stephen, already out in the mist. 'Not as a brother; who cares what people did years back? We're alive together, and the rest is cant. Here am I, Rickie, and there are you, a fair wreck. They've no use for you here—never had any, if the truth was known—and they've only made you beastly. This house, so to speak, has the rot. It's common sense that you should come.'

'Stephen, wait a minute. What do you mean?'

'Wait's what we won't do,' said Stephen at the gate.

'I must ask—'

He did wait for a minute, and sobs were heard, faint, hopeless, vindictive. Then he trudged away, and Rickie soon lost his colour and his form. But a voice persisted, saying, 'Come, I do mean it. Come; I will take care of you, I can manage you.'

The words were kind; yet it was not for their sake that Rickie plunged into the impalpable cloud. In the voice he had found a surer guarantee. Habits and sex may change with the new generation, features may alter with the play of a private passion, but a voice is apart from these. It lies nearer to the racial essence and perhaps to the divine; it can, at all events, overleap one grave.

Chapter Thirty-two

Mr Pembroke did not receive a clear account of what had happened when he returned for the interval. His sister—he told her frankly—was concealing something from him. She could make no reply. Had she gone mad, she wondered. Hitherto she had pretended to love her husband. Why choose such a moment for the truth?

'But I understand Rickie's position,' he told her. 'It is an unbalanced position, yet I understand it; I noted its approach while he was ill. He imagines himself his brother's keeper. Therefore we must make concessions. We must negotiate.' The negotiations were still progressing in November, the month during which this story draws to its close.

'I understand his position,' he then told her. 'It is both weak and defiant. He is still with those Ansells. Read this letter, which thanks me for his little stories. We sent them last month, you remember—such of them as we could find. It seems that he fills up his time by writing: he has already written a book.'

She only gave him half her attention, for a beautiful wreath had just arrived from the florist's. She was taking it up to the cemetery: to-day her child had been dead a year.

'On the other hand, he has altered his will. Fortunately, he cannot alter much. But I fear that what is not settled on you, will go. Should I read what I wrote on this point, and also my minutes of the interview with old Mr Ansell, and the copy of my correspondence with Stephen Wonham?'

But her fly was announced. While he put the wreath in for her, she ran for a moment upstairs. A few tears had come to her eyes. A scandalous divorce would have been more bearable than this withdrawal. People asked, 'Why did her husband leave her?' and the answer came, 'Oh, nothing particular; he only couldn't stand her; she lied and taught him to lie; she kept him from the work that suited him, from his friends, from his brother—in a word, she tried to run him, which a man won't pardon.' A few tears; not many. To her, life never showed itself as a classic drama, in which, by trying to advance our fortunes, we shatter them. She had turned Stephen out of Wiltshire, and he fell like a thunderbolt on Sawston and on herself. In trying to gain Mrs Failing's money she had probably lost money which would have been her own. But irony is a subtle teacher, and she was not the woman to learn from such lessons as these. Her suffering was more direct. Three men had wronged her; therefore she hated them, and, if she could, would do them harm.

'These negotiations are quite useless,' she told Herbert when she came downstairs. 'We had much better bide our time. Tell me just about Stephen Wonham, though.'

He drew her into the study again. 'Wonham is or was in Scotland, learning to farm with connections of the Ansells: I believe the money is to go towards setting him up. Apparently he is a hard worker. He also drinks!'

She nodded and smiled. 'More than he did?'

'My informant, Mr Tilliard—oh, I ought not to have mentioned his name. He is one of the better sort of Rickie's Cambridge friends, and has been dreadfully grieved at the collapse, but he does not want to be mixed up in it. This autumn he was up in the Lowlands, close by, and very kindly made a few unobtrusive inquiries, for me. The man is becoming an habitual drunkard.'

She smiled again. Stephen had evoked her secret, and she hated him more for that than for anything else that he had done. The poise of his shoulders that morning—it was no more—had recalled Gerald. If only she had not been so tired! He had reminded her of the greatest thing she had known, and to her cloudy mind this seemed degradation. She had turned to him as to her lover; with a look, which a man of his type understood, she had asked for his pity; for one terrible moment she had desired to be held in his arms. Even Herbert was surprised when she said, 'I'm glad he drinks. I hope he'll kill himself. A man like that ought never to have been born.'

'Perhaps the sins of the parents are visited on the children,' said Herbert, taking her to the carriage. 'Yet it is not for us to decide.'

'I feel sure he will be punished. What right has he—' She broke off. What right had he to our common humanity? It was a hard lesson for any one to learn. For Agnes it was impossible. Stephen was illicit, abnormal, worse than a man diseased. Yet she had turned to him: he had drawn out the truth.

'My dear, don't cry,' said her brother, drawing up the windows. 'I have great hopes of Mr Tilliard—the Silts have written—Mrs Failing will do what she can—'

As she drove to the cemetery, her bitterness turned against Ansell, who had kept her husband alive in the days after Stephen's expulsion. If he had not been there, Rickie would have renounced his mother and his brother and all the outer world, troubling no one. The mystic, inherent in him, would have prevailed. So Ansell himself had told her. And Ansell, too, had sheltered the fugitives and given them money, and saved them from the ludicrous checks that so often stop young men. But when she reached the cemetery, and stood beside the tiny grave, all her bitterness, all her hatred were turned against Rickie.

'But he'll come back in the end,' she thought. 'A wife has only to wait. What are his friends beside me? They too will marry. I have only to wait. His book, like all that he has done, will fail. His brother is drinking himself away. Poor aimless Rickie! I have only to keep civil. He will come back in the end.'

She had moved, and found herself close to the grave of Gerald. The flowers she had planted after his death were dead, and she had not liked to renew them. There lay the athlete, and his dust was as the little child's whom she had brought into the world with such hope, with such pain.

Chapter Thirty-three

That same day Rickie, feeling neither poor nor aimless, left the Ansells' for a night's visit to Cadover. His aunt had invited him—why, he could not think, nor could he think why he should refuse the invitation. She could not annoy him now, and he was not vindictive. In the dell near Madingley he had cried, 'I hate no one,' in his ignorance. Now, with full knowledge, he hated no one again. The weather was pleasant, the country attractive, and he was ready for a little change.

Maud and Stewart saw him off. Stephen, who was down for a holiday, had been left with his chin on the luncheon-table. He had wanted to come to Cadover also. Rickie pointed out that you cannot visit where you have broken the windows. There was an argument—there generally was—and now the young man had turned sulky.

'Let him do what he likes,' said Ansell. 'He knows more than we do. He knows everything.'

'Is he to get drunk?' Rickie asked.

'Most certainly.'

'And to go where he isn't asked?'

Maud, though liking a little spirit in a man, declared this to be impossible.

'Well, I wish you joy!' Rickie called, as the train moved away. 'He means mischief this evening. He told me piously that he felt it beating up. Goodbye!'

'But we'll wait for you to pass,' they cried. For the Salisbury train always backed out of the station and then returned, and the Ansell family, including Stewart, took an incredible pleasure in seeing it do this.

The carriage was empty. Rickie settled himself down for his little journey. First he looked at the coloured photographs. Then he read the directions for obtaining luncheon-baskets, and felt the texture of the cushions. Through the windows a signal-box interested him. Then he saw the ugly little town that was now his home, and up its chief street the Ansells' memorable façade. The spirit of a genial comedy dwelt there. It was so absurd, so kindly. The house was divided against itself and yet stood. Metaphysics, commerce, social aspirations—all lived together in harmony. Mr Ansell had done much, but one was tempted to believe in a more capricious power—the power that abstains from 'nipping.' 'One nips or is nipped, and never knows beforehand,' quoted Rickie, and opened the poems of Shelley, a man less foolish than you supposed. How pleasant it was to read! If business worried him, if Stephen was noisy or Ansell perverse there still remained this paradise of books. It seemed as if he had read nothing for two years.

Then the train stopped for the shunting, and he heard protests from minor officials who were working on the line. They complained that some one who didn't ought to, had mounted on the footboard of the carriage. Stephen's face appeared, convulsed with laughter. With the action of a swimmer he dived in through the open window, and fell comfortably on Rickie's luggage and Rickie. He declared it was the finest joke ever known. Rickie was not so sure. 'You'll be run over next,' he said. 'What did you do that for?'

'I'm coming with you,' he giggled, rolling all that he could on to the dusty floor.

'Now, Stephen, this is too bad. Get up. We went into the whole question yesterday.'

'I know; and I settled we wouldn't go into it again, spoiling my holiday.'

'Well, it's execrable taste.'

Now he was waving to the Ansells, and showing them a piece of soap: it was all his luggage, and even that he abandoned, for he flung it at Stewart's lofty brow.

'I can't think what you've done it for. You know how strongly I felt.'

Stephen replied that he should stop in the village; meet Rickie at the lodge gates; that kind of thing.

'It's execrable taste,' he repeated, trying to keep grave.

'Well, you did all you could,' he exclaimed with sudden sympathy. 'Leaving me talking to old Ansell, you might have thought you'd got your way. I've as much taste as most chaps, but, hang it! your aunt isn't the German Emperor. She doesn't own Wiltshire.'

'You ass!' sputtered Rickie, who had taken to laugh at nonsense again.

'No, she isn't,' he repeated, blowing a kiss out of the window to maidens. 'Why, we started for Wiltshire on the wet morning!'

'When Stewart found us at Sawston railway station?' He smiled happily. 'I never thought we should pull through.'

'Well, we *didn't*. We never did what we meant. It's nonsense that I couldn't have managed you alone. I've a notion. Slip out after your dinner this evening, and we'll get thundering tight together.'

'I've a notion I won't.'

'It'd do you no end of good. You'll get to know people—shepherds, carters—' He waved his arms vaguely, indicating democracy. 'Then you'll sing.'

'And then?'

'Plop.'

'Precisely.'

'But I'll catch you,' promised Stephen. 'We shall carry you up the hill to bed. In the morning you wake, have your row with old Em'ly, she kicks you out, we meet—we'll meet at the Rings!' He danced up and down the carriage. Some one in the next carriage punched at the partition, and when this happens, all lads of mettle know that they must punch the partition back.

'Thank you. I've a notion I won't,' said Rickie when the noise subsided—subsided for a moment only, for the following conversation took place to an accompaniment of dust and bangs. 'Except as regards the Rings. We will meet there.'

'Then I'll get tight by myself.'

'No, you won't.'

'Yes, I will. I swore to do something special this evening. I feel like it.'

'In that case, I get out at the next station.' He was laughing, but quite determined. Stephen had grown too dictatorial of late. The Ansells spoilt him. 'It's bad enough having you there at all. Having you there drunk is impossible. I'd sooner not visit my aunt than think, when I sat with her, that you're down in the village teaching her labourers to be as beastly as yourself. Go if you will. But not with me.'

'Why shouldn't I have a good time while I'm young, if I don't harm any one?' said Stephen defiantly.

'Need we discuss it again? Because you harm yourself.'

'Oh, I can stop myself any minute I choose. I just say "I won't" to you or any other fool, and I don't.'

Rickie knew that the boast was true. He continued, 'There is also a thing call Morality. You may learn in the Bible, and also from the Greeks, that your body is a temple.'

'So you said in your longest letter.'

'Probably I wrote like a prig, for the reason that I have never been tempted in this way; but surely it is wrong that your body should escape you.'

'I don't follow,' he retorted, punching.

'It isn't right, even for a little time, to forget that you exist.'

'I suppose you've never been tempted to go to sleep?'

Just then the train passed through a coppice in which the grey undergrowth looked no more alive than firewood. Yet every twig in it was waiting for the spring. Rickie knew that the analogy was false, but argument confused him, and he gave up this line of attack also.

'Do be more careful over life. If your body escapes you in one thing, why not in more? A man will have other temptations.'

'You mean women,' said Stephen quietly, pausing for a moment in his game. 'But that's absolutely different. That would be harming some one else.'

'Is that the only thing that keeps you straight?'

'What else should?' And he looked not into Rickie, but past him, with the wondering eyes of a child. Rickie nodded, and referred himself to the window.

He observed that the country was smoother and more plastic. The woods had gone, and under a pale-blue sky long contours of earth were flowing, merging, rising a little to bear some coronal of beeches, parting a little to disclose some green valley, where cottages stood under elms or beside translucent waters. It was Wiltshire at last. The train had entered the chalk. At last it slackened at a wayside platform. Without speaking he opened the door.

'What's that for?'

'To go back.'

Stephen had forgotten the threat. He said that this was not playing the game.

'Surely!'

'I can't have you going back.'

'Promise to behave decently then.'

He was seized and pulled away from the door.

'We change at Salisbury,' he remarked. 'There is an hour to wait. You will find me troublesome.'

'It isn't fair,' exploded Stephen. 'It's a low-down trick. How can I let you go back?'

'Promise, then.'

'Oh, yes, yes, yes. Y.M.C.A. But for this occasion only.'

'No, no. For the rest of your holiday.'

'Yes, yes. Very well. I promise.'

'For the rest of your life?'

Somehow it pleased him that Stephen should bang him crossly with his elbow and say, 'No. Get out. You've gone too far.' So had the train. The porter at the end of the wayside platform slammed the door, and they proceeded towards Salisbury through the slowly modulating downs. Rickie pretended to read. Over the book he watched his brother's face, and wondered how bad temper could be consistent with a mind so radiant. In spite of his obstinacy and conceit, Stephen was an easy person to live with. He never fidgeted or nursed hidden grievances, or indulged in a shoddy pride. Though he spent Rickie's money as slowly as he could, he asked for it without apology: 'You must put it down against me,' he would say. In time—it was still very vague—he would rent or purchase a farm. There is no formula in which we may sum up decent people. So Ansell had preached, and had of course proceeded to offer a formula: 'They must be serious, they must be truthful.' Serious not in the sense of glum; but they must be convinced that our life is a state of some importance, and our earth not a place to beat time on. Of so much Stephen was convinced: he showed it in his work, in his play, in his self-respect, and above all—though the fact is hard to face—in his sacred passion for alcohol. Drink, to-day, is an unlovely thing. Between us and the heights of Cithæron the river of sin now flows. Yet the cries still call from the mountain, and granted a man has responded to them, it is better he respond with the candour of the Greek.

'I shall stop at the Thompsons' now,' said the disappointed reveller. 'Prayers.'

Rickie did not press his triumph, but it was a happy moment, partly because of the triumph, partly because he was sure that his brother must care for him. Stephen was too selfish to give up any pleasure without grave reasons. He was certain that he had been right to disentangle himself from Sawston, and to ignore the threats and tears that still tempted him to return. Here there was real work for him to do. Moreover, though he sought no reward, it had come. His health was better, his brain sound, his life washed clean, not by the waters of sentiment, but by the efforts of a fellow-man. Stephen was man first, brother afterwards. Herein lay his brutality and also his virtue. 'Look me in the face. Don't hang on me clothes that don't belong—as you did on your wife, giving her saint's robes, whereas she was simply a woman of her own sort, who needed careful watching. Tear up the photographs. Here am I, and there are you. The rest is cant.' The rest was not cant, and perhaps Stephen would confess as much in time. But Rickie needed a tonic, and a man, not a brother, must hold it to his lips.

'I see the old spire,' he called, and then added, 'I don't mind seeing it again.'

'No one does, as far as I know. People have come from the other side of the world to see it again.'

'Pious people. But I don't hold with bishops.' He was young enough to be uneasy. The cathedral, a fount of superstition, must find no place in his life. At the age of twenty he had settled things. 'I've got my own philosophy,' he once told Ansell, 'and I don't care a straw about yours.' Ansell's mirth had annoyed him not a little. And it was strange that one so settled should feel his heart leap up at the sight of an old spire. 'I regard it as a public building,' he told Rickie, who agreed. 'It's useful, too, as a landmark.' His attitude to-day was defensive. It was part of a subtle change that Rickie had noted in him since his return from Scotland. His face gave hints of a new maturity. 'You can see the old spire from the Ridgeway,' he said, suddenly laying a hand on Rickie's knee, 'before rain as clearly as any telegraph post.'

'How far is the Ridgeway?'

'Seventeen miles.'

'Which direction?'

'North, naturally. North again from that you see Devizes, the vale of Pewsey, and the other downs. Also towards Bath. It is something of a view. You ought to get on the Ridgeway.'

'I shouldn't have time for that.'

'Or Beacon Hill. Or let's do Stonehenge.'

'If it's fine, I suggest the Rings.'

'It will be fine.' Then he murmured the names of villages.

'I wish you could live here,' said Rickie kindly. 'I believe you love these particular acres more than the whole world.'

Stephen replied that this was not the case: he was only used to them. He wished they were driving out, instead of waiting for the Cadchurch train.

They had advanced into Salisbury, and the cathedral, a public building, was grey against a tender sky. Rickie suggested that, while waiting for the train, they should visit it. He spoke of the incomparable north porch.

'I've never been inside it, and I never will. Sorry to shock you, Rickie, but

I must tell you plainly. I'm an atheist. I don't believe in anything.'

'I do,' said Rickie.

'When a man dies, it's as if he's never been,' he asserted. The train drew up in Salisbury station. Here a little incident took place which caused them to alter their plans.

They found outside the station a trap driven by a small boy, who had come in from Cadford to fetch some wire-netting. 'That'll do us,' said Stephen, and called to the boy, 'If I pay your railway-ticket back, and if I give you sixpence as well, will you let us drive back in the trap?' The boy said no. 'It will be all right,' said Rickie. 'I am Mrs Failing's nephew.' The boy shook his head. 'And you know Mr Wonham?' The boy couldn't say he didn't. 'Then what's your objection? Why? What is it? Why not?' But Stephen leant against the time-tables and spoke of other matters.

Presently the boy said, 'Did you say you'd pay my railway-ticket back, Mr Wonham?'

'Yes,' said a bystander. 'Didn't you hear him?'

'I heard him right enough.'

Now Stephen laid his hand on the splash-board, saying, 'What I want, though, is this trap here of yours, see, to drive in back myself'; and as he spoke the bystander followed him in canon, 'What he wants, though, is that there trap of yours, see, to drive hisself back in.'

'*I've* no objection,' said the boy, as if deeply offended. For a time he sat motionless, and then got down, remarking, 'I won't rob you of your sixpence.'

'Silly little fool,' snapped Rickie, as they drove through the town.

Stephen looked surprised. 'What's wrong with the boy? He had to think it over. No one had asked him to do such a thing before. Next time he'd let us have the trap quick enough.'

'Not if he had driven in for a cabbage instead of wire-netting.'

'He never would drive in for a cabbage.'

Rickie shuffled his feet. But his irritation passed. He saw that the little incident had been a quiet challenge to the civilization that he had known. 'Organize,' 'Systematize,' 'Fill up every moment,' 'Induce *esprit de corps*.' He reviewed the watchwords of the last two years, and found that they ignored personal contest, personal truces, personal love. By following them Sawston School had lost its quiet usefulness and become a frothy sea, wherein plunged Dunwood House, that unnecessary ship. Humbled, he turned to Stephen and said, 'No, you're right. Nothing is wrong with the boy. He was honestly thinking it out.' But Stephen had forgotten the incident, or else he was not inclined to talk about it. His assertive fit was over.

The direct road from Salisbury to Cadover is extremely dull. The city—which God intended to keep by the river; did she not move there, being thirsty, in the reign of William Rufus?—the city has strayed out of her own plain, climbed up her slopes, and tumbled over them in ugly cataracts of brick. The cataracts are still short, and doubtless they meet or create some commercial need. But instead of looking towards the cathedral, as all the city should, they look outwards at a pagan entrenchment, as the city should not.

They neglect the poise of the earth, and the sentiments she has decreed. They are the modern spirit.

Through them the road descends into an unobtrusive country where, nevertheless, the power of the earth grows stronger. Streams do divide. Distances do still exist. It is easier to know the men in your valley than those who live in the next, across a waste of down. It is easier to know men well. The country is not paradise, and can show the vices that grieve a good man everywhere. But there is room in it, and leisure.

'I suppose,' said Rickie as the twilight fell, 'this kind of thing is going on all over England.' Perhaps he meant that towns are after all excrescences, grey fluxions, where men, hurrying to find one another, have lost themselves. But he got no response, and expected none. Turning round in his seat, he watched the winter sun slide out of a quiet sky. The horizon was primrose, and the earth against it gave momentary hints of purple. All faded: no pageant would conclude the gracious day, and when he turned eastward the night was already established.

'Those verlands—' said Stephen, scarcely above his breath.

'What are verlands?'

He pointed at the dusk, and said, 'Our name for a kind of field.' Then he drove his whip into its socket, and seemed to swallow something. Rickie, straining his eyes for verlands, could only see a tumbling wilderness of brown.

'Are there many local words?'

'There have been.'

'I suppose they die out.'

The conversation turned curiously. In the tone of one who replies, he said, 'I expect that some time or other I shall marry.'

'I expect you will,' said Rickie, and wondered a little why the reply seemed not abrupt. 'Would we see the Rings in the daytime from here?'

'(We do see them.) But Mrs Failing once said no decent woman would have me.'

'Did you agree to that?'

'Drive a little, will you?'

The horse went slowly forward into the wilderness, that turned from brown to black. Then a luminous glimmer surrounded them, and the air grew cooler: the road was descending between parapets of chalk.

'But, Rickie, mightn't I find a girl—naturally not refined—and be happy with her in my own way? I would tell her straight I was nothing much—faithful, of course, but that she should never have all my thoughts. Out of no disrespect to her, but because all one's thoughts can't belong to any single person.'

While he spoke even the road vanished, and invisible water came gurgling through the wheel-spokes. The horse had chosen the ford.

'You can't own people. At least a fellow can't. It may be different for a poet. (Let the horse drink.) And I want to marry some one, and don't yet know who she is, which a poet again will tell you is disgusting. Does it disgust you? Being nothing much, surely I'd better go gently. For it's something rather outside that makes one marry, if you follow me: not exactly oneself. (Don't hurry the horse.) We want to marry, and yet—I can't explain. I fancy I'll go wading: this is our stream.'

Romantic love is greater than this. There are men and women—we know it from history—who have been born into the world for each other, and for no one else, who have accomplished the longest journey locked in each other's arms. But romantic love is also the code of modern morals, and, for this reason, popular. Eternal union, eternal ownership—these are tempting baits for the average man. He swallows them, will not confess his mistake, and—perhaps to cover it—cries 'dirty cynic' at such a man as Stephen.

Rickie watched the black earth unite to the black sky. But the sky overhead grew clearer, and in it twinkled the Plough and the central stars. He thought of his brother's future and of his own past, and of how much truth might lie in that antithesis of Ansell's: 'A man wants to love mankind, a woman wants to love one man.' At all events, he and his wife had illustrated it, and perhaps the conflict, so tragic in their own case, was elsewhere the salt of the world. Meanwhile Stephen called from the water for matches: there was some trick with paper which Mr Failing had showed him, and which he would show Rickie now, instead of talking nonsense. Bending down, he illumined the dimpled surface of the ford, 'Quite a current,' he said, and his face flickered out in the darkness. 'Yes, give me the loose paper, quick! Crumple it into a ball.'

Rickie obeyed, though intent on the transfigured face. He believed that a new spirit dwelt there, expelling the crudities of youth. He saw steadier eyes, and the sign of manhood set like a bar of gold upon steadier lips. Some faces are knit by beauty, or by intellect, or by a great passion: had Stephen's waited for the touch of the years?

But they played as boys who continued the nonsense of the railway carriage. The paper caught fire from the match, and spread into a rose of flame. 'Now gently with me,' said Stephen, and they laid it flower-like on the stream. Gravel and tremulous weeds leapt into sight, and then the flower sailed into deep water, and up leapt the two arches of a bridge. 'It'll strike!' they cried; 'no, it won't; it's chosen the left,' and one arch became a fairy tunnel, dropping diamonds. Then it vanished for Rickie; but Stephen, who knelt in the water, declared that it was still afloat, far through the arch, burning as if it would burn for ever.

Chapter Thirty-four

The carriage that Mrs Failing had sent to meet her nephew returned from Cadchurch station empty. She was preparing for a solitary dinner when he somehow arrived, full of apologies, but more sedate than she had expected. She cut his explanations short. 'Never mind how you got here. You are here, and I am quite pleased to see you.' He changed his clothes and they proceeded to the dining-room.

There was a bright fire, but the curtains were not drawn. Mr Failing had believed that windows with the night behind are more beautiful than any pictures, and his widow had kept to the custom. It was brave of her to persevere, lumps of chalk having come out of the night last June. For some obscure reason—not so obscure to Rickie—she had preserved them as mementoes of an episode. Seeing them in a row on the mantlepiece, he expected that their first topic would be Stephen. But they never mentioned him, though he was latent in all that they said.

It was of Mr Failing that they spoke. The Essays had been a success. She was really pleased. The book was brought in at her request, and between the courses she read it aloud to her nephew, in her soft yet unsympathetic voice. Then she sent for the Press notices—after all no one despises them—and read their comments on her introduction. She wielded a graceful pen, was apt, adequate, suggestive, indispensable, unnecessary. So the meal passed pleasantly away, for no one could so well combine the formal with the unconventional, and it only seemed charming when papers littered her stately table.

'My man wrote very nicely,' she observed. 'Now, you read me something out of him that you like. Read "The True Patriot."'

He took the book and found: 'Let us love one another. Let our children, physical and spiritual, love one another. It is all that we can do. Perhaps the earth will neglect our love. Perhaps she will confirm it, and suffer some rallying-point, spire, mound, for the new generations to cherish.'

'He wrote that when he was young. Later on he doubted whether we had better love one another, or whether the earth will confirm anything. He died a most unhappy man.'

He could not help saying, 'Not knowing that the earth had confirmed him.'

'Has she? It is quite possible. We meet so seldom in these days, she and I. Do you see much of the earth?'

'A little.'

'Do you expect that she will confirm you?'

'It is quite possible.'

'Beware of her, Rickie, I think.'

'I think not.'

'Beware of her, surely. Going back to her really is going back—throwing away the artificiality which (though you young people won't confess it) is the only good thing in life. Don't pretend you are simple. Once I pretended. Don't pretend that you care for anything but for clever talk such as this, and for books.'

'The talk,' said Leighton afterwards, 'certainly was clever. But it meant something all the same.' He heard no more, for his mistress told him to retire.

'And my nephew, this being so, make up your quarrel with your wife.' She stretched out her hand to him with real feeling. 'It is easier now than it will

be later. Poor lady, she has written to me foolishly and often, but, on the
whole, I side with her against you. She would grant you all that you fought
for—all the people, all the theories. I have it, in her writing, that she will
never interfere with your life again.'

'She cannot help interfering,' said Rickie, with his eyes on the black
windows. 'She despises me. Besides, I do not love her.'

'I know, my dear. Nor she you. I am not being sentimental. I say once
more, beware of the earth. We are conventional people, and conventions—if
you will but see it—are majestic in their way, and will claim us in the end. We
do not live for great passions or for great memories or for anything great.'

He threw up his head. 'We do.'

'Now listen to me. I am serious and friendly to-night, as you must have
observed. I have asked you here partly to amuse myself—you belong to my
March Past—but also to give you good advice. There has been a volcano—a
phenomenon which I too once greatly admired. The erruption is over. Let
the conventions do their work now, and clear the rubbish away. My age is
fifty-nine, and I tell you solemnly that the important things in life are little
things, and that people are not important at all. Go back to your wife.'

He looked at her, and was filled with pity. He knew that he would never be
frightened of her again. Only because she was serious and friendly did he
trouble himself to reply. 'There is one little fact I should like to tell you, as
confuting your theory. The idea of a story—a long story—had been in my
head for a year. As a dream to amuse myself—the kind of amusement you
would recommend for the future. I should have had time to write it, but the
people round me coloured my life, and so it never seemed worth while. For
the story is not likely to pay. Then came the volcano. A few days after it was
over I lay in bed looking out upon the world of rubbish. Two men I
know—one intellectual, the other very much the reverse—burst into the
room. They said, "What happened to your short stories? They weren't
good, but where are they? Why have you stopped writing? Why haven't you
been to Italy? You *must* write. You *must* go. Because to write, to go, is you."
Well, I have written, and yesterday we sent the long story out on its rounds.
The men do not like it, for different reasons. But it mattered very much to
them that I should write it, and so it got written. As I told you, this is only
one fact; other facts, I trust, have happened in the last five months. But I
mention it to prove that people are important, and therefore, however much
it inconveniences my wife, I will not go back to her.'

'And Italy?' asked Mrs Failing.

This question he avoided. Italy must wait. Now that he had the time, he
had not the money.

'Or what is the long story about, then?'

'About a man and a woman who meet and are happy.'

'Somewhat of a *tour de force*, I conclude.'

He frowned. 'In literature we needn't intrude our own limitations. I'm
not so silly as to think that all marriages turn out like mine. My character is to
blame for our catastrophe, not marriage.'

'My dear, I too have married; marriage is to blame.'

But here again he seemed to know better.

'Well,' she said, leaving the table and moving with her dessert to the mantelpiece, 'so you are abandoning marriage and taking to literature. And are happy.'

'Yes.'

'Why?'

'Because, as we used to say at Cambridge, the cow is there. The world is real again. This is a room, that a window, outside is the night—'

'Go on.'

He pointed to the floor. 'The day is straight below, shining through other windows into other rooms.'

'You are very odd,' she said after a pause, 'and I do not like you at all. There you sit, eating my biscuits, and all the time you know that the earth is round. Who taught you? I am going to bed now, and all the night, you tell me, you and I and the biscuits go plunging eastwards, until we reach the sun. But breakfast will be at nine as usual. Good night.'

She rang the bell twice, and her maid came with her candle and her walking-stick: it was her habit of late to go to her room as soon as dinner was over, for she had no one to sit up with. Rickie was impressed by her loneliness, and also by the mixture in her of insight and obtuseness. She was so quick, so clear-headed, so imaginative even. But all the same, she had forgotten what people were like. Finding life dull, she had dropped lies into it, as a chemist drops a new element into a solution, hoping that life would thereby sparkle or turn some beautiful colour. She loved to mislead others, and in the end her private view of false and true was obscured, and she misled herself. How she must have enjoyed their errors over Stephen! But her own error had been greater, inasmuch as it was spiritual entirely.

Leighton came in with some coffee. Feeling it unnecessary to light the drawing-room lamp for one small young man, he persuaded Rickie to say he preferred the dining-room. So Rickie sat down by the fire playing with one of the lumps of chalk. His thoughts went back to the ford, from which they had scarcely wandered. Still he heard the horse in the dark drinking, still he saw the mystic rose, and the tunnel dropping diamonds. He had driven away alone, believing the earth had confirmed him. He stood behind things at last, and knew that conventions are not majestic, and that they will not claim us in the end.

As he mused, the chalk slipped from his fingers, and fell on the coffee-cup, which broke. The china, said Leighton, was expensive. He believed it was impossible to match it now. Each cup was different. It was a harlequin set. The saucer, without the cup, was therefore useless. Would Mr Elliot please explain to Mrs Failing how it happened.

Rickie promised he would explain.

He had left Stephen preparing to bathe, and had heard him working up-stream like an animal, splashing in the shallows, breathing heavily as he swam the pools; at times reeds snapped, or clods of earth were pulled in. By the fire he remembered it was again November. 'Should you like a walk?' he asked Leighton, and told him who stopped in the village to-night. Leighton was pleased. At nine o'clock the two young men left the house, under a sky that was still only bright in the zenith. 'It will rain to-morrow,' Leighton said.

'My brother says, fine to-morrow.'

'Fine to-morrow,' Leighton echoed.

'Now which do you mean?' asked Rickie, laughing.

Since the plumes of the fir-trees touched over the drive, only a very little light penetrated. It was clearer outside the lodge gate, and bubbles of air, which seemed to have travelled from an immense distance, broke gently and separately on his face. They paused on the bridge. He asked whether the little fish and the bright green weeds were here now as well as in the summer. The footman had not noticed. Over the bridge they came to the cross-roads, of which one led to Salisbury and the other up through the string of villages to the railway station. The road in front was only the Roman road, the one that went on to the downs. Turning to the left, they were in Cadover.

'He will be with the Thompsons,' said Rickie, looking up at dark eaves. 'Perhaps he's in bed already.'

'Perhaps he will be at The Antelope.'

'No. To-night he is with the Thompsons.'

'With the Thompsons.' After a dozen paces he said, 'The Thompsons have gone away.'

'Where? Why?'

'They were turned out by Mr Wilbraham on account of our broken windows.'

'Are you sure?'

'Five families were turned out.'

'That's bad for Stephen,' said Rickie, after a pause. 'He was looking forward—oh, it's monstrous in any case!'

'But the Thompsons have gone to London,' said Leighton. 'Why, that family—they say it's been in the valley hundreds of years, and never got beyond shepherding. To various parts of London.'

'Let us try The Antelope then.'

'Let us try The Antelope.'

The inn lay up in the village. Rickie hastened his pace. This tyranny was monstrous. Some men of the age of undergraduates had broken windows, and therefore they and their families were to be ruined. The fools who govern us find it easier to be severe. It saves them trouble to say, 'The innocent must suffer with the guilty.' It even gives them a thrill of pride. Against all this wicked nonsense, against the Wilbrahams and Pembrokes who try to rule our world Stephen would fight till he died. Stephen was a hero. He was a law to himself, and rightly. He was great enough to despise our small moralities. He was attaining love. This evening Rickie caught Ansell's enthusiasm, and felt it worth while to sacrifice everything for such a man.

'The Antelope,' said Leighton. 'Those lights under the greatest elm.'

'Would you please ask if he's there, and if he'd come for a turn with me. I don't think I'll go in.'

Leighton opened the door. They saw a little room, blue with tobacco-smoke. Flanking the fire were deep settles, hiding all but the legs of the men who lounged in them. Between the settles stood a table, covered with mugs and glasses. The scene was picturesque—fairer than the cut-glass palaces of the town.

'Oh yes, he's there,' he called, and after a moment's hesitation came out. 'Would he come?'

'No. I shouldn't say so,' replied Leighton, with a furtive glance. He knew that Rickie was a milksop. 'First night, you know sir, among old friends.'

'Yes, I know,' said Rickie. 'But he might like a turn down the village. It looks stuffy inside there, and poor fun probably to watch others drinking.'

Leighton shut the door.

'What was that he called after you?'

'Oh, nothing. A man when he's drunk—he says the worst he's ever heard. At least, so they say.'

'A man when he's drunk?'

'Yes, sir.'

'But Stephen isn't drinking?'

'No, no.'

'He couldn't be. If he broke a promise—I don't pretend he's a saint. I don't want him one. But it isn't in him to break a promise.'

'Yes, sir; I understand.'

'In the train he promised me not to drink—nothing theatrical: just a promise for these few days.'

'No, sir.'

'"No, sir,"' stamped Rickie. '"Yes! no! yes!" Can't you speak out? Is he drunk or isn't he?'

Leighton, justly exasperated, cried, 'He can't stand, and I've told you so again and again.'

'Stephen!' shouted Rickie, darting up the steps. Heat and the smell of beer awaited him, and he spoke more furiously than he had intended. 'Is there any one here who's sober?' he cried. The landlord looked over the bar angrily, and asked him what he meant. He pointed to the deep settles. 'Inside there he's drunk. Tell him he's broken his word, and I will not go with him to the Rings.'

'Very well. You won't go with him to the Rings,' said the landlord, stepping forward and slamming the door in his face.

In the room he was only angry, but out in the cool air he remembered that Stephen was a law to himself. He had chosen to break his word, and would break it again. Nothing else bound him. To yield to temptation is not fatal for most of us. But it was the end of everything for a hero.

'He's suddenly ruined!' he cried, not yet remembering himself. For a little he stood by the elm-tree, clutching the ridges of its bark. Even so would he wrestle to-morrow, and Stephen, imperturbable, reply, 'My body is my own.' Or worse still, he might wrestle with a pliant Stephen who promised him glibly again. While he prayed for a miracle to convert his brother, it struck him that he must pray for himself. For he, too, was ruined.

'Why, what's the matter?' asked Leighton. 'Stephen's only being with friends. Mr Elliot, sir, don't break down. Nothing's happened bad. No one's died yet, or even hurt themselves.' Ever kind, he took hold of Rickie's arm, and, pitying such a nervous fellow, set out with him for home. The shoulders of Orion rose behind them over the topmost boughs of the elm. From the bridge the whole constellation was visible and Rickie said, 'May God receive me and pardon me for trusting the earth.'

'But, Mr Elliot, what have you done that's wrong?'

'Gone bankrupt, Leighton, for the second time. Pretended again that people were real. May God have mercy on me!'

Leighton dropped his arm. Though he did not understand, a chill of disgust passed over him, and he said, 'I will go back to The Antelope. I will help them put Stephen to bed.'

'Do. I will wait for you here.' Then he leant against the parapet and prayed passionately, for he knew that the conventions would claim him soon. God was beyond them, but ah, how far beyond, and to be reached after what degradation! At the end of this childish detour his wife awaited him, not less surely because she was only his wife in name. He was too weak. Books and friends were not enough. Little by little she would claim him and corrupt him and make him what he had been; and the woman he loved would die out, in drunkenness, in debauchery, and her strength would be dissipated by a man, her beauty defiled in a man. She would not continue. That mystic rose and the face it illumined meant nothing. The stream—he was above it now—meant nothing, though it burst from the pure turf and ran for ever to the sea. The bather, the shoulders of Orion—they all meant nothing, and were going nowhere. The whole affair was a ridiculous dream.

Leighton returned, saying, 'Haven't you seen Stephen? They say he followed us: he can still walk: I told you he wasn't so bad.'

'I don't think he passed me. Ought one to look?' He wandered a little along the Roman road. Again nothing mattered. At the level-crossing he leant on the gate to watch a slow goods train pass. In the glare of the engine he saw that his brother had come this way, perhaps through some sodden memory of the Rings, and now lay drunk over the rails. Wearily he did a man's duty. There was time to raise him up and push him into safety. It is also a man's duty to save his own life, and therefore he tried. The train went over his knees. He died up in Cadover, whispering. 'You have been right,' to Mrs Failing.

She wrote of him to Mrs Lewin afterwards as 'one who has failed in all he undertook; one of the thousands whose dust returns to the dust, accomplishing nothing in the interval. Agnes and I buried him to the sound of our cracked bell, and pretended that he had once been alive. The other, who was always honest, kept away.'

Chapter Thirty-five

From the window they looked over a sober valley, whose sides were not too sloping to be ploughed, and whose trend was followed by a grass-grown track. It was late on Saturday afternoon, and the valley was deserted except for one labourer, who was coasting slowly downward on a rusty bicycle. The air was very quiet. A jay screamed up in the woods behind, but the ring-doves, who roost early, were already silent. Since the window opened westward, the room was flooded with light, and Stephen, finding it hot, was working in his shirt-sleeves.

'You guarantee they'll sell?' he asked, with a pen between his teeth. He was tidying up a pile of manuscripts.

'I guarantee that the world will be the gainer,' said Mr Pembroke, now a clergyman, who sat beside him at the table with an expression of refined disapproval on his face.

'I'd got the idea that the long story had its points, but that these shorter things didn't—what's the word?'

'"Convince" is probably the word you want. But that type of criticism is quite a thing of the past. Have you seen the illustrated American edition?'

'I don't remember.'

'Might I send you a copy? I think you ought to possess one.'

'Thank you.' His eye wandered. The bicycle had disappeared into some trees, and thither, through a cloudless sky, the sun was also descending.

'Is all quite plain?' said Mr Pembroke. 'Submit these ten stories to the magazines, and make your own terms with the editors. Then—I have your word for it—you will join forces with me; and the four stories in my possession, together with yours, should make up a volume, which we might well call "Pan Pipes."'

'Are you sure "Pan Pipes" haven't been used up already?'

Mr Pembroke clenched his teeth. He had been bearing with this sort of thing for nearly an hour. 'If that is the case, we can select another. A title is easy to come by. But that is the idea it must suggest. The stories, as I have twice explained to you, all centre round a Nature theme. Pan, being the god of—'

'I know that,' said Stephen impatiently.

'—Being the god of—'

'All right. Let's get furrard. I've learnt that.'

It was years since the schoolmaster had been interrupted, and he could not stand it. 'Very well,' he said. 'I bow to your superior knowledge of the classics. Let us proceed.'

'Oh yes—the introduction. There must be one. It was the introduction with all those wrong details that sold the other book.'

'You overwhelm me. I never penned the memoir with that intention.'

'If you won't do one, Mrs Keynes must!'

'My sister leads a busy life. I could not ask her. I will do it myself since you insist.'

'And the binding?'

'The binding,' said Mr Pembroke coldly, 'must really be left to the discretion of the publisher. We cannot be concerned with such details. Our task is purely literary.' His attention wandered. He began to fidget, and finally bent down and looked under the table. 'What have we here?' he asked.

Stephen looked also, and for a moment they smiled at each other over the prostrate figure of a child, who was cuddling Mr Pembroke's boots. 'She's after the blacking,' he explained. 'If we left her there, she'd lick them brown.'

'Indeed. Is that so very safe?'

'It never did me any harm. Come up! Your tongue's dirty.'

'Can I—' She was understood to ask whether she could clean her tongue on a lollie.

'No, no!' said Mr Pembroke. 'Lollipops don't clean little girls' tongues.'

'Yes, they do,' he retorted. 'But she won't get one.' He lifted her on his knee, and rasped her tongue with his handkerchief.

'Dear little thing,' said the visitor perfunctorily. The child began to squall, and kicked her father in the stomach. Stephen regarded her quietly. 'You tried to hurt me,' he said. 'Hurting doesn't count. Trying to hurt counts. Go and clean your tongue yourself. Get off my knee.' Tears of another sort came into her eyes, but she obeyed him. 'How's the great Bertie?' he asked.

'Thank you. My nephew is perfectly well. How came you to hear of his existence?'

'Through the Silts, of course. It isn't five miles to Cadover.'

Mr Pembroke raised his eyes mournfully. 'I cannot conceive how the poor Silts go on in that great house. Whatever she intended, it could not have been that. The house, the farm, the money—everything down to the personal articles that belong to Mr Failing, and should have reverted to his family—!'

'It's legal. Intestate succession.'

'I do not dispute it. But it is a lesson to one to make a will. Mrs Keynes and myself were electrified.'

'They'll do there. They offered me the agency, but—' He looked down the cultivated slopes. His manners were growing rough, for he saw few gentlemen now, and he was either incoherent or else alarmingly direct. 'However, if Lawrie Silt's a Cockney like his father, and if my next is a boy and like me—' A shy beautiful look came into his eyes, and passed unnoticed. 'They'll do,' he repeated. 'They've turned out Wilbraham and built new cottages, and bridged the railway, and made other necessary alterations.' There was a moment's silence.

Mr Pembroke took out his watch. 'I wonder if I might have the trap? I mustn't miss my train, must I? It is good of you to have granted me an interview. It is all quite plain?'

'Yes.'

'A case of half and half–division of profits.'

'Half and half?' said the young farmer slowly. 'What do you take me for? Half and half when I provide ten of the stories and you only four?'

'I–I—' stammered Mr Pembroke.

'I consider you did me over the long story, and I'm damned if you do me over the short ones!'

'Hush! if you please, hush!–if only for your little girl's sake.' He lifted a clerical palm.

'You did me,' his voice drove, 'and all the Thirty-nine Articles won't stop me saying so. That long story was meant to be mine. I got it written. You've done me out of every penny it fetched. It's dedicated to me–flat out–and you even crossed out the dedication and tidied me out of the introduction. Listen to me, Pembroke. You've done people all your life–I think without knowing it, but that won't comfort us. A wretched devil at your school once wrote to me, and he'd been done. Sham food, sham religion, sham straigh talks–and when he broke down, you said it was the world in miniature.' He snatched at him roughly. 'But I'll show you the world.' He twisted him round like a baby, and through the open door they saw only the quiet valley, but in it a rivulet that would in time bring its waters to the sea. 'Look even at that–and up behind where the Plain begins and you get on the solid chalk–think of us riding some night when you're ordering your hot bottle–that's the world, and there's no miniature world. There's one world, Pembroke, and you can't tidy men out of it. They answer you back–do you hear?–they answer back if you do them. If you tell a man this way that four sheep equal ten, he answers back you're a liar.'

Mr Pembroke was speechless, and–such is human nature–he chiefly resented the allusion to the hot bottle; an unmanly luxury in which he never indulged; contenting himself with night-socks. 'Enough–there is no witness present–as you had doubtless observed.' But there was. For a little voice cried, 'Oh, mummy, they're fighting–such fun—' and feet went pattering up the stairs. 'Enough. You talk of "doing," but what about the money out of which you "did" my sister? What about this picture'–he pointed to a faded photograph of Stockholm–'which you caused to be filched from the walls of my house? What about–enough! Let us conclude this disheartening scene. You object to my terms. Name yours. I shall accept them. It is futile to reason with one who is the worse for drink.'

Stephen was quiet at once. 'Steady on!' he said gently. 'Steady on in that direction. Take one-third for your four stories and the introduction, and I will keep two thirds for myself.' Then he went to harness the horse, while Mr Pembroke, watching his broad back, desired to bury a knife in it. The desire passed, partly because it was unclerical, partly because he had no knife, and partly because he soon blurred over what had happened. To him all criticism was 'rudeness': he never heeded it, for he never needed it: he was never wrong. All his life he had ordered little human beings about, and now he was equally magisterial to big ones: Stephen was a fifth-form lout whom, owing to some flaw in the regulations, he could not send up to the headmaster to be caned.

This attitude makes for tranquillity. Before long he felt merely an injured martyr. His brain cleared. He stood deep in thought before the only other picture that the bare room boasted–the Demeter of Cnidus. Outside the sun was sinking, and its last rays fell upon the immortal features and the shattered knees. Sweet-peas offered their fragrance, and with it there entered those more mysterious scents that come from no one flower or clod of earth, but from the whole bosom of evening. He tried not to be cynical. But in his heart he could not regret that tragedy, already half-forgotten, conventionalized, indistinct. Of course death is a terrible thing. Yet death is merciful when it weeds out a failure. If we look deep enough it is all for the best. He stared at the picture and nodded.

Stephen, who had met his visitor at the station, had intended to drive him back there. But after their spurt of temper he sent him with the boy. He remained in the doorway, glad that he was going to make money, glad that he had been angry; while the glow of the clear sky deepened and the silence was perfected, and the scents of the night grew stronger. Old vagrances awoke, and he resolved that, dearly as he loved his house, he would not enter it again till dawn. 'Good night!' he called, and then the child came running, and he whispered, 'Quick, then! Bring me a rug. Good night,' he repeated, and a pleasant voice called through an upper window, 'Why good night?' He did not answer till the child was wrapped up in his arms.

'It is time that she learnt to sleep out,' he cried. 'If you want me, we're on the hillside, where I used to be.'

The voice protested, saying this and that.

'Stewart's in the house,' said the man, 'and it cannot matter, and I am going anyway.'

'Stephen, I wish you wouldn't. I wish you wouldn't take her. Promise you won't say foolish things to her. Don't–I wish you'd come up for a minute—'

The child, whose face was laid against his, felt the muscles in it harden.

'Don't tell her foolish things about yourself–things that aren't any longer true. Don't worry her with old dead dreadfulnesses. To please me–don't.'

'Just to-night I won't, then.'

'Stevie, dear, please me more–don't take her with you.'

At this he laughed impertinently. 'I suppose I'm being kept in line,' she called, and, though he could not see her, she stretched her arms towards him. For a time he stood motionless, under her window, musing on his happy tangible life. Then his breath quickened, and he wondered why he was here, and why he should hold a warm child in his arms. 'It's time we were starting,' he whispered, and showed the sky, whose orange was already fading into green. 'Wish everything good night.'

'Good night, dear mummy,' she said sleepily. 'Good night, dear house.

Good night, you pictures—long picture—stone lady. I see you through the window—your faces are pink.'

The twilight descended. He rested his lips on her hair, and carried her, without speaking, until he reached the open down. He had often slept here himself, alone, and on his wedding-night, and he knew that the turf was dry, and that if you laid your face to it you would smell the thyme. For a moment the earth aroused her, and she began to chatter. 'My prayers—' she said anxiously. He gave her one hand, and she was asleep before her fingers had nestled in its palm. Their touch made him pensive, and again he marvelled why he, the accident, was here. He was alive and had created life. By whose authority? Though he could not phrase it, he believed that he guided the future of our race, and that, century after century, his thoughts and his passions would triumph in England. The dead who had evoked him, the unborn whom he would evoke—he governed the paths between them. By whose authority?

Out in the west lay Cadover and the fields of his earlier youth, and over them descended the crescent moon. His eyes followed her decline, and against her final radiance he saw, or thought he saw, the outline of the Rings. He had always been grateful, as people who understood him knew. But this evening his gratitude seemed a gift of small account. The ear was deaf, and what thanks of his could reach it? The body was dust, and in what ecstasy of his could it share? The spirit had fled, in agony and loneliness, never to know that it bequeathed him salvation.

He filled his pipe, and then sat pressing the unlit tobacco with his thumb. 'What am I to do?' he thought. 'Can he notice the things he gave me? A parson would know. But what's a man like me to do, who works all his life out of doors?' As he wondered, the silence of the night was broken. The whistle of Mr Pembroke's train came faintly, and a lurid spot passed over the land—passed, and the silence returned. One thing remained that a man of his sort might do. He bent down reverently and saluted the child; to whom he had given the name of their mother.

THE END

A Room
with a View

A ROOM WITH A VIEW

To H.O.M.

Chapter One

The Bertolini

'The Signora had no business to do it,' said Miss Bartlett, 'no business at all. She promised us south rooms with a view close together, instead of which here are north rooms, here are north rooms, looking into a courtyard, and a long way apart. Oh, Lucy!'

'And a Cockney, besides!' said Lucy, who had been further saddened by the Signora's unexpected accent. 'It might be London.' She looked at the two rows of English people who were sitting at the table; at the row of white bottles of water and red bottles of wine that ran between the English people; at the portraits of the late Queen and the late Poet Laureate that hung behind the English people, heavily framed; at the notice of the English church (Rev. Cuthbert Eager, M.A. Oxon), that was the only other decoration of the wall. 'Charlotte, don't you feel, too, that we might be in London? I can hardly believe that all kinds of other things are just outside. I suppose it is one's being so tired.'

'This meat has surely been used for soup,' said Miss Bartlett, laying down her fork.

'I wanted so to see the Arno. The rooms the Signora promised us in her letter would have looked over the Arno. The Signora had no business to do it at all. Oh, it is a shame!'

'Any nook does for me,' Miss Bartlett continued; 'but it does seem hard that you shouldn't have a view.'

Lucy felt that she had been selfish. 'Charlotte, you mustn't spoil me: of course, you must look over the Arno, too. I meant that. The first vacant room in the front—'

'You must have it,' said Miss Bartlett, part of whose travelling expenses were paid by Lucy's mother–a piece of generosity to which she made many a tactful allusion.

'No, no. You must have it.'

'I insist on it. Your mother would never forgive me, Lucy.'

'She would never forgive *me*.'

The ladies' voices grew animated, and–if the sad truth be owned–a little peevish. They were tired, and under the guise of unselfishness they wrangled. Some of their neighbours interchanged glances, and one of them–one of the ill-bred people whom one does meet abroad–leant forward over the table and actually intruded into their argument. He said:

'I have a view, I have a view.'

Miss Bartlett was startled. Generally at a pension people looked them over for a day or two before speaking, and often did not find out that they would 'do' till they had gone. She knew that the intruder was ill-bred, even before she glanced at him. He was an old man, of heavy build, with a fair, shaven face and large eyes. There was something childish in those eyes, though it was not the childishness of senility. What exactly it was Miss Bartlett did not stop to consider, for her glance passed on to his clothes. These did not attract her. He was probably trying to become acquainted with them before they got into the swim. So she assumed a dazed expression when he spoke to her, and then said: 'A view? Oh, a view! How delightful a view is!'

'This is my son,' said the old man; 'his name's George. He has a view, too.'

'Ah,' said Miss Bartlett, repressing Lucy, who was about to speak.

'What I mean,' he continued, 'is that you can have our rooms, and we'll have yours. We'll change.'

The better class of tourist was shocked at this, and sympathized with the new-comers. Miss Bartlett, in reply, opened her mouth as little as possible, and said:

'Thank you very much indeed: that is out of the question.'

'Why?' said the old man, with both fists on the table.

'Because it is quite out of the question, thank you.'

'You see, we don't like to take—' began Lucy.

Her cousin again repressed her.

'But why?' he persisted. 'Women like looking at a view; men don't.' And he thumped with his fists like a naughty child, and turned to his son, saying, 'George, persuade them!'

'It's so obvious they should have the rooms,' said the son. 'There's nothing else to say.'

He did not look at the ladies as he spoke, but his voice was perplexed and sorrowful. Lucy, too, was perplexed; but she saw that they were in for what is known as 'quite a scene,' and she had an odd feeling that whenever these ill-bred tourists spoke the contest widened and deepened till it dealt, not with rooms and views, but with–well, with something quite different, whose existence she had not realized before. Now the old man attacked Miss Bartlett almost violently: Why should she not change? What possible objection had she? They would clear out in half an hour.

Miss Bartlett, though skilled in the delicacies of conversation, was powerless in the presence of brutality. It was impossible to snub anyone so gross. Her face reddened with displeasure. She looked around as much as to say, 'Are you all like this?' And two little old ladies, who were sitting farther up the table, with shawls hanging over the backs of the chairs, looked back, clearly indicating 'We are not; we are genteel.'

'Eat your dinner, dear,' she said to Lucy, and began to toy again with the meat that she had once censured.

Lucy mumbled that those seemed very odd people opposite.

'Eat your dinner, dear. This pension is a failure. To-morrow we will make a change.'

Hardly had she announced this fell decision when she reversed it. The curtains at the end of the room parted, and revealed a clergyman, stout but attractive, who hurried forward to take his place at the table, cheerfully apologizing for his lateness. Lucy, who had not yet acquired decency, at once rose to her feet, exclaiming: 'Oh, oh! Why, it's Mr Beebe! Oh, how perfectly lovely! Oh, Charlotte, we must stop now, however bad the rooms are. Oh!'

Miss Bartlett said, with more restraint:

'How do you do, Mr Beebe? I expect that you have forgotten us: Miss Bartlett and Miss Honeychurch, who were at Tunbridge Wells when you helped the vicar of St Peter's that very cold Easter.'

The clergyman, who had the air of one on a holiday, did not remember the ladies quite as clearly as they remembered him. But he came forward pleasantly enough and accepted the chair into which he was beckoned by Lucy.

'I *am* so glad to see you,' said the girl, who was in a state of spiritual starvation, and would have been glad to see the waiter if her cousin had permitted it. 'Just fancy how small the world is. Summer Street, too, makes it so specially funny.'

'Miss Honeychurch lives in the parish of Summer Street,' said Miss Bartlett, filling up the gap, 'and she happened to tell me in the course of conversation that you have just accepted the living—'

'Yes, I heard from mother so last week. She didn't know that I knew you at Tunbridge Wells; but I wrote back at once, and I said: "Mr Beebe is—"'

'Quite right,' said the clergyman. 'I move into the Rectory at Summer Street next June. I am lucky to be appointed to such a charming neighbourhood.'

'Oh, how glad I am! The name of our house is Windy Corner.'

Mr Beebe bowed.

'There is mother and me generally, and my brother, though it's not often we get him to ch— The church is rather far off, I mean.'

'Lucy dearest, let Mr Beebe eat his dinner.'

'I am eating it, thank you, and enjoying it.'

He preferred to talk to Lucy, whose playing he remembered, rather than to Miss Bartlett, who probably remembered his sermons. He asked the girl whether she knew Florence well, and was informed at some length that she had never been there before. It is delightful to advise a new-comer, and he was first in the field.

'Don't neglect the country round,' his advice concluded. 'The first fine afternoon drive up to Fiesole, and round by Settignano, or something of that sort.'

'No!' cried a voice from the top of the table. 'Mr Beebe, you are wrong. The first fine afternoon your ladies must go to Prato.'

'That lady looks so clever,' whispered Miss Bartlett to her cousin. 'We are in luck.'

And, indeed, a perfect torrent of information burst on them. People told them what to see, when to see it, how to stop the electric trams, how to get rid of the beggars, how much to give for a vellum blotter, how much the place would grow upon them. The Pension Bertolini had decided, almost enthusiastically, that they would do. Whichever way they looked, kind ladies smiled and shouted at them. And above all rose the voice of the clever lady, crying: 'Prato! They must go to Prato. That place is too sweetly squalid for words. I love it; I revel in shaking off the trammels of respectability as you know.'

The young man named George glanced at the clever lady, and then returned moodily to his plate. Obviously he and his father did not do. Lucy, in the midst of her success, found time to wish they did. It gave her no extra pleasure that anyone should be left in the cold; and when she rose to go, she turned back and gave the two outsiders a nervous little bow.

The father did not see it; the son acknowledged it, not by another bow, but by raising his eyebrows and smiling; he seemed to be smiling across something.

She hastened after her cousin, who had already disappeared through the curtains—curtains which smote one in the face, and seemed heavy with more than cloth. Beyond them stood the unreliable Signora, bowing good-evening to her guests, and supported by 'Enery, her little boy, and Victorier, her daughter. It made a curious little scene, this attempt of the Cockney to convey the grace and geniality of the South. And even more curious was the drawing-room, which attempted to rival the solid comfort of a Bloomsbury boarding-house. Was this really Italy?

Miss Bartlett was already seated on a tightly stuffed arm-chair, which had the colour and the contours of a tomato. She was talking to Mr Beebe, and as she spoke, her long narrow head drove backwards and forwards, slowly, regularly, as though she were demolishing some invisible obstacle. 'We are most grateful to you,' she was saying. 'The first evening means so much. When you arrived we were in for a peculiarly *mauvais quart d'heure*.'

He expressed his regret.

'Do you, by any chance, know the name of an old man who sat opposite us at dinner?'

'Emerson.'

'Is he a friend of yours?'

'We are friendly—as one is in pensions.'

'Then I will say no more.'

He pressed her very slightly, and she said more.

'I am, as it were,' she concluded, 'the chaperon of my young cousin, Lucy, and it would be a serious thing if I put her under an obligation to people of whom we knew nothing. His manner was somewhat unfortunate. I hope I acted for the best.'

'You acted very naturally,' said he. He seemed thoughtful, and after a few moments added: 'All the same, I don't think much harm would have come of accepting.'

'No *harm*, of course. But we could not be under an obligation.'

'He is rather a peculiar man.' Again he hesitated, and then said gently: 'I think he would not take advantage of your acceptance, nor expect you to show gratitude. He has the merit—if it is one—of saying exactly what he means. He has rooms he does not value, and he thinks you would value them. He no more thought of putting you under an obligation than he thought of being polite. It is so difficult—at least, I find it difficult—to understand people who speak the truth.'

Lucy was pleased, and said: 'I was hoping that he was nice; I do so always hope that people will be nice.'

'I think he is; nice and tiresome. I differ from him on almost every point of any importance, and so, I expect—I may say I hope—you will differ. But his is a type one disagrees with rather than deplores. When he first came here he not unnaturally put people's backs up. He has no tact and no manners—I don't mean by that that he has bad manners—and he will not keep his opinions to himself. We nearly complained about him to our depressing Signora, but I am glad to say we thought better of it.'

'Am I to conclude,' said Miss Bartlett, 'that he is a Socialist?'

Mr Beebe accepted the convenient word, not without a slight twitching of the lips.

'And presumably he has brought up his son to be a Socialist, too?'

'I hardly know George, for he hasn't learnt to talk yet. He seems a nice creature, and I think he has brains. Of course, he has all his father's mannerisms, and it is quite possible that he, too, may be a Socialist.'

'Oh, you relieve me,' said Miss Bartlett. 'So you think I ought to have accepted their offer? You feel I have been narrow-minded and suspicious?'

'Not at all,' he answered; 'I never suggested that.'

'But ought I not to apologize, at all events, for my apparent rudeness?'

He replied, with some irritation, that it would be quite unnecessary, and got up from his seat to go to the smoking-room.

'Was I a bore?' said Miss Bartlett, as soon as he had disappeared. 'Why didn't you talk, Lucy? He prefers young people, I'm sure. I do hope I haven't monopolized him. I hoped you would have him all the evening, as well as all dinner-time.'

'He is nice,' exclaimed Lucy. 'Just what I remember. He seems to see good in every one. No one would take him for a clergyman.'

'My dear Lucia—'

'Well, you know what I mean. And you know how clergymen generally laugh; Mr Beebe laughs just like an ordinary man.'

'Funny girl! How you remind me of your mother. I wonder if she will approve of Mr Beebe.'

'I'm sure she will; and so will Freddy.'

'I think every one at Windy Corner will approve; it is the fashionable world. I am used to Tunbridge Wells, where we are all hopelessly behind the times.'

'Yes,' said Lucy despondently.

There was a haze of disapproval in the air, but whether the disapproval was of herself, or of Mr Beebe, or of the fashionable world at Windy Corner, or of the narrow world at Tunbridge Wells, she could not determine. She tried to locate it, but as usual she blundered. Miss Bartlett sedulously denied disapproving of anyone, and added: 'I am afraid you are finding me a very depressing companion.'

And the girl again thought: 'I must have been selfish or unkind; I must be more careful. It is so dreadful for Charlotte, being poor.'

Fortunately one of the little old ladies, who for some time had been smiling very benignly, now approached and asked if she might be allowed to sit where Mr Beebe had sat. Permission granted, she began to chatter gently about Italy, the plunge it had been to come there, the gratifying success of the plunge, the improvement in her sister's health, the necessity of closing the bedroom windows at night, and of thoroughly emptying the water-bottles in the morning. She handled her subjects agreeably, and they were, perhaps, more worthy of attention than the high discourse upon Guelfs and Ghibellines which was proceeding tempestuously at the other end of the room. It was a real catastrophe, not a mere episode, that evening of hers at Venice, when she had found in her bedroom something that is one worse than a flea, though one better than something else.

'But here you are as safe as in England; Signora Bertolini is so English.'

'Yet our rooms smell,' said poor Lucy. 'We dread going to bed.'

'Ah, then you look into the court.' She sighed. 'If only Mr Emerson was more tactful! We were so sorry for you at dinner.'

'I think he was meaning to be kind.'

'Undoubtedly he was,' said Miss Bartlett. 'Mr Beebe has just been scolding me for my suspicious nature. Of course, I was holding back on my cousin's account.'

'Of course,' said the little old lady; and they murmured that one could not be too careful with a young girl.

Lucy tried to look demure, but could not help feeling a great fool. No one was careful with her at home; or, at all events, she had not noticed it.

'About old Mr Emerson—I hardly know. No, he is not tactful; yet, have you ever noticed that there are people who do things which are most indelicate, and yet at the same time—beautiful?'

'Beautiful?' said Miss Bartlett, puzzled at the word. 'Are not beauty and delicacy the same?'

'So one would have thought,' said the other helplessly. 'But things are so difficult, I sometimes think.'

She proceeded no further into things, for Mr Beebe reappeared, looking extremely pleasant.

'Miss Bartlett,' he cried, 'it's all right about the rooms. I'm so glad. Mr Emerson was talking about it in the smoking-room, and, knowing what I did, I encouraged him to make the offer again. He has let me come and ask you. He would be so pleased.'

'Oh, Charlotte,' cried Lucy to her cousin, 'we must have the rooms now. The old man is just as nice and kind as he can be.'

Miss Bartlett was silent.

'I fear,' said Mr Beebe, after a pause, 'that I have been officious. I must apologize for my interference.'

Gravely displeased, he turned to go. Not till then did Miss Bartlett reply: 'My own wishes, dearest Lucy, are unimportant in comparison with yours. It would be hard indeed if I stopped you doing as you liked at Florence, when I am only here through your kindness. If you wish me to turn these gentlemen out of their rooms, I will do it. Would you then, Mr Beebe, kindly tell Mr Emerson that I accept his kind offer, and then conduct him to me, in order that I may thank him personally?'

She raised her voice as she spoke; it was heard all over the drawing-room, and silenced the Guelfs and the Ghibellines. The clergyman, inwardly cursing the female sex, bowed and departed with her message.

'Remember, Lucy, I alone am implicated in this. I do not wish the acceptance to come from you. Grant me that, at all events.'

Mr Beebe was back, saying rather nervously:

'Mr Emerson is engaged, but here is his son instead.'

The young man gazed down on the three ladies, who felt seated on the floor, so low were their chairs.

'My father,' he said, 'is in his bath, so you cannot thank him personally. But any message given by you to me will be given by me to him as soon as he comes out.'

Miss Bartlett was unequal to the bath. All her barbed civilities came forth wrong end first. Young Mr Emerson scored a notable triumph to the delight of Mr Beebe and to the secret delight of Lucy.

'Poor young man!' said Miss Bartlett, as soon as he had gone. 'How angry he is with his father about the rooms! It is all he can do to keep polite.'

'In half an hour or so your rooms will be ready,' said Mr Beebe. Then, looking rather thoughtfully at the two cousins, he retired to his own room, to write up his philosophic diary.

'Oh dear!' breathed the little old lady, and shuddered as if all the winds of heaven had entered the apartment. 'Gentlemen sometimes do not realize—' Her voice faded away, but Miss Bartlett seemed to understand, and a conversation developed, in which gentlemen who did not thoroughly realize played a principal part. Lucy, not realizing either, was reduced to literature. Taking up Baedeker's 'Handbook to Northern Italy,' she committed to memory the most important dates of Florentine History. For she was determined to enjoy herself on the morrow. Thus the half-hour crept profitably away, and at last Miss Bartlett rose with a sigh, and said:

'I think one might venture now. No, Lucy, do not stir. I will superintend the move.'

'How you do do everything,' said Lucy.

'Naturally, dear. It is my affair.'

'But I would like to help you.'

'No, dear.'

Charlotte's energy! And her unselfishness! She had been thus all her life, but really, on this Italian tour, she was surpassing herself. So Lucy felt, or strove to feel. And yet—there was a rebellious spirit in her which wondered whether the acceptance might not have been less delicate and more beautiful. At all events, she entered her own room without any feeling of joy.

'I want to explain,' said Miss Bartlett, 'why it is that I have taken the largest room. Naturally, of course, I should have given it to you; but I happen to know that it belongs to the young man, and I was sure your mother would not like it.'

Lucy was bewildered.

'If you are to accept a favour, it is more suitable you should be under an obligation to his father than to him. I am a woman of the world, in my small way, and I know where things lead to. However, Mr Beebe is a guarantee of a sort that they will not presume on this.'

'Mother wouldn't mind, I'm sure,' said Lucy, but again had the sense of larger and unsuspected issues.

Miss Bartlett only sighed, and enveloped her in a protecting embrace as she wished her good-night. It gave Lucy the sensation of a fog, and when she reached her own room she opened the window and breathed the clean night air, thinking of the kind old man who had enabled her to see the lights dancing in the Arno and the cypresses of San Miniato, and the foot-hills of the Apennines, black against the rising moon.

Miss Bartlett, in her room, fastened the window-shutters and locked the door, and then made a tour of the apartment to see where the cupboards led, and whether there were any oubliettes or secret entrances. It was then that she saw, pinned up over the wash-stand, a sheet of paper on which was scrawled an enormous note of interrogation. Nothing more.

'What does it mean?' she thought, and she examined it carefully by the light of a candle. Meaningless at first, it gradually became menacing, obnoxious, portentous with evil. She was seized with an impulse to destroy it, but fortunately remembered that she had no right to do so, since it must be the property of young Mr Emerson. So she unpinned it carefully, and put it between two pieces of blotting-paper to keep it clean for him. Then she completed her inspection of the room, sighed heavily according to her habit, and went to bed.

Chapter Two

In Santa Croce with no Baedeker

It was pleasant to wake up in Florence, to open the eyes upon a bright bare room, with a floor of red tiles which look clean though they are not; with a painted ceiling whereon pink griffins and blue amorini sport in a forest of yellow violins and bassoons. It was pleasant, too, to fling wide the windows, pinching the fingers in unfamiliar fastenings, to lean out into sunshine with beautiful hills and trees and marble churches opposite, and, close below, the Arno, gurgling against the embankment of the road.

Over the river men were at work with spades and sieves on the sandy foreshore, and on the river was a boat, also diligently employed for some mysterious end. An electric tram came rushing underneath the window. No one was inside it, except one tourist; but its platforms were overflowing with Italians, who preferred to stand. Children tried to hang on behind, and the conductor, with no malice, spat in their faces to make them let go. Then soldiers appeared–good-looking, under-sized men–wearing each a knap-sack covered with mangy fur, and a great-coat which had been cut for some larger soldier. Beside them walked officers, looking foolish and fierce, and before them went little boys, turning somersaults in time with the band. The tramcar became entangled in their ranks, and moved on painfully, like a caterpillar in a swarm of ants. One of the little boys fell down, and some white bullocks came out of an archway. Indeed, if it had not been for the good advice of an old man who was selling button-hooks, the road might never have got clear.

Over such trivialities as these many a valuable hour may slip away, and the traveller who has gone to Italy to study the tactile values of Giotto, or the corruption of the Papacy, may return remembering nothing but the blue sky and the men and women who live under it. So it was as well that Miss Bartlett should tap and come in, and having commented on Lucy's leaving the door unlocked, and on her leaning out of the window before she was fully dressed, should urge her to hasten herself, or the best of the day would be gone. By the time Lucy was ready her cousin had done her breakfast, and was listening to the clever lady among the crumbs.

A conversation then ensued, on not unfamiliar lines. Miss Bartlett was, after all, a wee bit tired, and thought they had better spend the morning settling in; unless Lucy would at all like to go out? Lucy would rather like to go out, as it was her first day in Florence, but, of course, she could go alone. Miss Bartlett could not allow this. Of course she would accompany Lucy everywhere. Oh, certainly not; Lucy would stop with her cousin. Oh no! that would never do! Oh yes!

At this point the clever lady broke in.

'If it is Mrs Grundy who is troubling you, I do assure you that you can neglect the good person. Being English, Miss Honeychurch will be perfectly safe. Italians understand. A dear friend of mine, Contessa Baroncelli, has two daughters, and when she cannot send a maid to school with them, she lets them go in sailor-hats instead. Every one takes them for English, you see, especially if their hair is strained tightly behind.'

Miss Bartlett was unconvinced by the safety of Contessa Baroncelli's daughters. She was determined to take Lucy herself, her head not being so very bad. The clever lady then said that she was going to spend a long morning in Santa Croce, and if Lucy would come too, she would be delighted.

'I will take you by a dear dirty back way, Miss Honeychurch, and if you bring me luck, we shall have an adventure.'

Lucy said that this was most kind, and at once opened the Baedeker, to see where Santa Croce was.

'Tut, tut! Miss Lucy! I hope we shall soon emancipate you from Baedeker.

He does but touch the surface of things. As to the true Italy—he does not even dream of it. The true Italy is only to be found by patient observation.'

This sounded very interesting, and Lucy hurried over her breakfast, and started with her new friend in high spirits. Italy was coming at last. The Cockney Signora and her works had vanished like a bad dream.

Miss Lavish—for that was the clever lady's name—turned to the right along the sunny Lung' Arno. How delightfully warm! But a wind down the side streets that cut like a knife, didn't it? Ponte alle Grazie—particularly interesting, mentioned by Dante. San Miniato—beautiful as well as interesting; the crucifix that kissed a murderer—Miss Honeychurch would remember the story. The men on the river were fishing. (Untrue; but then, so is most information.) Then Miss Lavish darted under the archway of the white bullocks, and she stopped, and she cried:

'A smell! a true Florentine smell! Every city, let me teach you, has its own smell.'

'Is it a very nice smell?' said Lucy, who had inherited from her mother a distaste to dirt.

'One doesn't come to Italy for niceness,' was the retort; 'one comes for life. Buon giorno! Buon giorno!' bowing right and left. 'Look at that adorable wine-cart! How the driver stares at us, dear, simple soul!'

So Miss Lavish proceeded through the streets of the city of Florence, short, fidgety, and playful as a kitten, though without a kitten's grace. It was a treat for the girl to be with anyone so clever and so cheerful; and a blue military cloak, such as an Italian officer wears, only increased the sense of festivity.

'Buon giorno! Take the word of an old woman, Miss Lucy: you will never repent of a little civility to your inferiors. *That* is the true democracy. Though I am a real Radical as well. There, now you're shocked.'

'Indeed, I'm not!' exclaimed Lucy. 'We are Radicals, too, out and out. My father always voted for Mr Gladstone, until he was so dreadful about Ireland.'

'I see, I see. And now you have gone over to the enemy.'

'Oh, please—! If my father was alive, I am sure he would vote Radical again now that Ireland is all right. And as it is, the glass over our front-door was broken last election, and Freddy is sure it was the Tories; but mother says nonsense, a tramp.'

'Shameful! A manufacturing district, I suppose?'

'No—in the Surrey hills. About five miles from Dorking, looking over the Weald.'

Miss Lavish seemed interested, and slackened her trot.

'What a delightful part; I know it so well. It is full of the very nicest people. Do you know Sir Harry Otway—a Radical if ever there was?'

'Very well indeed.'

'And old Mrs Butterworth the philanthropist?'

'Why, she rents a field of us! How funny!'

Miss Lavish looked at the narrow ribbon of sky, and murmured:

'Oh, you have property in Surrey?'

'Hardly any,' said Lucy, fearful of being thought a snob. 'Only thirty acres—just the garden, all downhill, and some fields.'

Miss Lavish was not disgusted, and said it was just the size of her aunt's Suffolk estate. Italy receded. They tried to remember the last name of Lady Louisa someone, who had taken a house near Summer Street the other year, but she had not liked it, which was odd of her. And just as Miss Lavish had got the name she broke off and exclaimed:

'Bless us! Bless us and save us! We've lost the way.'

Certainly they had seemed a long time in reaching Santa Croce, the tower of which had been plainly visible from the landing window. But Miss Lavish had said so much about knowing her Florence by heart, that Lucy had followed her with no misgivings.

'Lost! lost! My dear Miss Lucy, during our political diatribes we have taken a wrong turning. How those horrid Conservatives would jeer at us! What are we to do? Two lone females in an unknown town. Now, this is what *I* call an adventure.'

Lucy, who wanted to see Santa Croce, suggested, as a possible solution, that they should ask the way there.

'Oh, but that is the word of a craven! And no, you are not, not, *not* to look at your Baedeker. Give it to me; I shan't let you carry it. We will simply drift.'

Accordingly they drifted through a series of those grey-brown streets, neither commodious nor picturesque, in which the eastern quarter of the city abounds. Lucy soon lost interest in the discontent of Lady Louisa, and became discontented herself. For one ravishing moment Italy appeared. She stood in the Square of the Annunziata and saw in the living terra-cotta those divine babies whom no cheap reproduction can ever stale. There they stood, with their shining limbs bursting from the garments of charity, and their strong white arms extended against circlets of heaven. Lucy thought she had never seen anything more beautiful; but Miss Lavish, with a shriek of dismay, dragged her forward, declaring that they were out of their path now by at least a mile.

The hour was approaching at which the continental breakfast begins, or rather ceases, to tell, and the ladies bought some hot chestnut paste out of a little shop, because it looked so typical. It tasted partly of the paper in which it was wrapped, partly of hair-oil, partly of the great unknown. But it gave them strength to drift into another Piazza, large and dusty, on the farther side of which rose a black-and-white façade of surpassing ugliness. Miss Lavish spoke to it dramatically. It was Santa Croce. The adventure was over.

'Stop a minute; let those two people go on, or I shall have to speak to them. I do detest conventional intercourse. Nasty! they are going into the church, too. Oh, the Britisher abroad!'

'We sat opposite them at dinner last night. They have given us their rooms. They were so very kind.'

'Look at their figures!' laughed Miss Lavish. 'They walk through my Italy like a pair of cows. It's very naughty of me, but I would like to set an examination paper at Dover, and turn back every tourist who couldn't pass it.'

'What would you ask us?'

Miss Lavish laid her hand pleasantly on Lucy's arm, as if to suggest that she, at all events, would get full marks. In this exalted mood they reached the steps of the great church, and were about to enter it when Miss Lavish stopped, squeaked, flung up her arms, and cried:

'There goes my local-colour box! I must have a word with him!'

And in a moment she was away over the Piazza, her military cloak flapping in the wind; nor did she slacken speed till she caught up an old man with white whiskers, and nipped him playfully upon the arm.

Lucy waited for nearly ten minutes. Then she began to get tired. The beggars worried her, the dust blew in her eyes, and she remembered that a young girl ought not to loiter in public places. She descended slowly into the Piazza with the intention of rejoining Miss Lavish, who was really almost too original. But at that moment Miss Lavish and her local-colour box moved also, and disappeared down a side street, both gesticulating largely.

Tears of indignation came to Lucy's eyes—partly because Miss Lavish had jilted her, partly because she had taken her Baedeker. How could she find her way home? How could she find her way about in Santa Croce? Her first morning was ruined, and she might never be in Florence again. A few minutes ago she had been all high spirits, talking as a woman of culture, and half-persuading herself that she was full of originality. Now she entered the church depressed and humiliated, not even able to remember whether it was built by the Franciscans or the Dominicans.

Of course, it must be a wonderful building. But how like a barn! And how very cold! Of course, it contained frescoes by Giotto, in the presence of whose tactile values she was capable of feeling what was proper. But who was to tell her which they were? She walked about disdainfully, unwilling to be enthusiastic over monuments of uncertain authorship or date. There was no one even to tell her which, of all the sepulchral slabs that paved the nave and transepts, was the one that was really beautiful, the one that had been most praised by Mr Ruskin.

Then the pernicious charm of Italy worked on her, and, instead of acquiring information, she began to be happy. She puzzled out the Italian notices—the notice that forbade people to introduce dogs into the church—the notice that prayed people, in the interests of health and out of respect to the sacred edifice in which they found themselves, not to spit. She watched the tourists; their noses were as red as their Baedekers, so cold was Santa Croce. She beheld the horrible fate that overtook three Papists—two he-babies and a she-baby—who began their career by sousing each other with the Holy Water, and then proceeded to the Machiavelli memorial, dripping, but hallowed. Advancing towards it very slowly and from immense distances, they touched the stone with their fingers, with their handkerchiefs, with their heads, and then retreated. What could this mean? They did it again and again. Then Lucy realized that they had mistaken Machiavelli for some saint, and by continual contact with his shrine were hoping to acquire virtue. Punishment followed quickly. The smallest he-baby stumbled over one of the sepulchral slabs so much admired by Mr Ruskin, and entangled his feet in the features of a recumbent bishop.

Protestant as she was, Lucy darted forward. She was too late. He fell heavily upon the prelate's upturned toes.

'Hateful bishop!' exclaimed the voice of Old Mr Emerson, who had darted forward also. 'Hard in life, hard in death. Go out into the sunshine, little boy, and kiss your hand to the sun, for that is where you ought to be. Intolerable bishop!'

The child screamed frantically at these words, and at these dreadful people who picked him up, dusted him, rubbed his bruises, and told him not to be superstitious.

'Look at him!' said Mr Emerson to Lucy. 'Here's a mess: a baby hurt, cold, and frightened! But what else can you expect from a church?'

The child's legs had become as melting wax. Each time that old Mr Emerson and Lucy set it erect it collapsed with a roar. Fortunately an Italian lady, who ought to have been saying her prayers, came to the rescue. By some mysterious virtue, which mothers alone possess, she stiffened the little boy's backbone and imparted strength to his knees. He stood. Still gibbering with agitation, he walked away.

'You are a clever woman,' said Mr Emerson. 'You have done more than all the relics in the world. I am not of your creed, but I do believe in those who make their fellow-creatures happy. There is no scheme of the universe—'

He paused for a phrase.

'Niente,' said the Italian lady, and returned to her prayers.

'I'm not sure she understands English,' suggested Lucy.

In her chastened mood she no longer despised the Emersons. She was determined to be gracious to them, beautiful rather than delicate, and, if possible, to erase Miss Bartlett's civility by some gracious reference to the pleasant rooms.

'That woman understands everything,' was Mr Emerson's reply. 'But what are you doing here? Are you doing the church? Are you through with the church?'

'No,' cried Lucy, remembering her grievance. 'I came here with Miss Lavish, who was to explain everything; and just by the door—it is too bad!—she simply ran away, and after waiting quite a time, I had to come in by myself.'

'Why shouldn't you?' said Mr Emerson.

'Yes, why shouldn't you come by yourself?' said the son, addressing the young lady for the first time.

'But Miss Lavish has even taken away Baedeker.'

'Baedeker?' said Mr Emerson. 'I'm glad it's *that* that you minded. It's worth minding, the loss of a Baedeker. *That's* worth minding.'

Lucy was puzzled. She was again conscious of some new idea, and was not sure whither it would lead her.

'If you've no Baedeker,' said the son, 'you'd better join us.'

Was this where the idea would lead? She took refuge in her dignity.

'Thank you very much, but I could not think of that. I hope you do not suppose that I came to join on to you. I really came to help with the child, and to thank you for so kindly giving us your rooms last night. I hope that you have not been put to any great inconvenience.'

'My dear,' said the old man gently, 'I think that you are repeating what you have heard older people say. You are pretending to be touchy; but you are not really. Stop being so tiresome, and tell me instead what part of the church you want to see. To take you to it will be a real pleasure.'

Now, this was abominably impertinent, and she ought to have been furious. But it is sometimes as difficult to lose one's temper as it is difficult at other times to keep it. Lucy could not get cross. Mr Emerson was an old man, and surely a girl might humour him. On the other hand, his son was a young man, and she felt that a girl ought to be offended with him, or at all events be offended before him. It was at him that she gazed before replying.

'I am not touchy, I hope. It is the Giottos that I want to see, if you will kindly tell me which they are.'

The son nodded. With a look of sombre satisfaction, he led the way to the Peruzzi Chapel. There was a hint of the teacher about him. She felt like a child in school who had answered a question rightly.

The chapel was already filled with an earnest congregation, and out of them rose the voice of a lecturer, directing them how to worship Giotto, not by tactile valuations, but by the standards of the spirit.

'Remember,' he was saying, 'the facts about this church of Santa Croce; how it was built by faith in the full fervour of medievalism, before any taint of the Renaissance had appeared. Observe how Giotto in these frescoes—now, unhappily, ruined by restoration—is untroubled by the snares of anatomy and perspective. Could anything be more majestic, more pathetic, beautiful, true? How little, we feel, avails knowledge and technical cleverness against a man who truly feels!'

'No!' exclaimed Mr Emerson, in much too loud a voice for church. 'Remember nothing of the sort! Built by faith indeed! That simply means the workmen weren't paid properly. And as for the frescoes, I see no truth in them. Look at that fat man in blue! He must weigh as much as I do, and he is shooting into the sky like an air-balloon.'

He was referring to the fresco of the Ascension of St John. Inside, the lecturer's voice faltered, as well it might. The audience shifted uneasily, and so did Lucy. She was sure that she ought not to be with these men; but they had cast a spell over her. They were so serious and so strange that she could not remember how to behave.

'Now, did this happen, or didn't it? Yes or no?'

George replied.

'It happened like this, if it happened at all. I would rather go up to heaven by myself than be pushed by cherubs; and if I got there I should like my friends to lean out of it, just as they do here.'

'You will never go up,' said his father. 'You and I, dear boy, will lie at peace in the earth that bore us, and our names will disappear as surely as our work survives.'

'Some of the people can only see the empty grave, not the saint, whoever he is, going up. It did happen like that, if it happened at all.'

'Pardon me,' said a frigid voice. 'The chapel is somewhat small for two parties. We will incommode you no longer.'

The lecturer was a clergyman, and his audience must be also his flock, for they held Prayer Books as well as guide-books in their hands. They filed out of the chapel in silence. Amongst them were the two little old ladies of the Pension Bertolini–Miss Teresa and Miss Catharine Alan.

'Stop!' cried Mr Emerson. 'There's plenty of room for us all. Stop!'

The procession disappeared without a word. Soon the lecturer could be heard in the next chapel, describing the life of St Francis.

'George, I do believe that clergyman is the Brixton curate.'

George went into the next chapel and returned, saying, 'Perhaps he is. I don't remember.'

'Then I had better speak to him and remind him who I am. It's that Mr Eager. Why did he go? Did we talk too loud? How vexatious! I shall go and say we are sorry. Hadn't I better? Then perhaps he will come back.'

'He will not come back,' said George.

But Mr Emerson, contrite and unhappy, hurried away to apologize to the Rev. Cuthbert Eager. Lucy, apparently absorbed in a lunette, could hear the lecture again interrupted, the anxious, aggressive voice of the old man, the curt, injured replies of his opponent. The son, who took every little contretemps as if it were a tragedy, was listening also.

'My father has that effect on nearly every one,' he informed her. 'He will try to be kind.'

'I hope we all try,' said she, smiling nervously.

'Because we think it improves our characters. But he is kind to people because he loves them; and they find him out, and are offended, or frightened.'

'How silly of them!' said Lucy, though in her heart she sympathized; 'I think that a kind action done tactfully—'

'Tact!'

He threw up his head in disdain. Apparently she had given the wrong answer. She watched the singular creature pace up and down the chapel. For a young man his face was rugged, and–until the shadows fell upon it–hard. Enshadowed, it sprang into tenderness. She saw him once again at Rome, on the ceiling of the Sistine Chapel, carrying a burden of acorns. Healthy and muscular, he yet gave her the feeling of greyness, of tragedy that might only find solution in the night. The feeling soon passed; it was unlike her to have entertained anything so subtle. Born of silence and of unknown emotion, it passed when Mr Emerson returned, and she could re-enter the world of rapid talk, which was alone familiar to her.

'Were you snubbed?' asked his son tranquilly.

'But we have spoilt the pleasure of I don't know how many people. They won't come back.'

'. . . full of innate sympathy . . . quickness to perceive good in others . . . vision of the brotherhood of man . . .' Scraps of the lecture on St Francis came floating round the partition wall.

'Don't let us spoil yours,' he continued to Lucy. 'Have you looked at those saints?'

'Yes,' said Lucy. 'They are lovely. Do you know which is the tombstone that is praised in Ruskin?'

He did not know, and suggested that they should try to guess it. George, rather to her relief, refused to move, and she and the old man wandered not unpleasantly about Santa Croce, which, though it is like a barn, has harvested many beautiful things inside its walls. There were also beggars to avoid, and guides to dodge round the pillars, and an old lady with her dog, and here and there was a priest modestly edging to his Mass through the groups of tourists. But Mr Emerson was only half-interested. He watched the lecturer, whose success he believed that he had impaired, and then he anxiously watched his son.

'Why will he look at that fresco?' he said uneasily. 'I saw nothing in it.'

'I like Giotto,' she replied. 'It is so wonderful what they say about his tactile values. Though I like things like the Della Robbia babies better.'

'So you ought. A baby is worth a dozen saints. And my baby's worth the whole of Paradise, and as far as I can see he lives in Hell.'

Lucy again felt that this did not do.

'In Hell,' he repeated. 'He's unhappy.'

'Oh dear!' said Lucy.

'How can he be unhappy when he is strong and alive? What more is one to give him? And think how he has been brought up—free from all the superstition and ignorance that lead men to hate one another in the name of God. With such an education as that, I thought he was bound to grow up happy.'

She was no theologian, but she felt that here was a very foolish old man, as well as a very irreligious one. She also felt that her mother might not like her talking to that kind of person, and that Charlotte would object most strongly.

'What are we to do with him?' he asked. 'He comes out for his holiday to Italy, and behaves—like that; like the little child who ought to have been playing, and who hurt himself upon the tombstone. Eh? What did you say?'

Lucy had made no suggestion. Suddenly he said:

'Now don't be stupid over this. I don't require you to fall in love with my boy, but I do think you might try and understand him. You are nearer his age, and if you let yourself go I am sure you are sensible. You might help me. He has known so few women, and you have the time. You stop here several weeks, I suppose? But let yourself go. You are inclined to get muddled, if I may judge from last night. Let yourself go. Pull out from the depths those thoughts that you do not understand, and spread them out in the sunlight and know the meaning of them. By understanding George you may learn to understand yourself. It will be good for both of you.'

To this extraordinary speech Lucy found no answer.

'I only know what it is that's wrong with him; not why it is.'

'And what is it?' asked Lucy fearfully, expecting some harrowing tale.

'The old trouble; things won't fit.'

'What things?'

'The things of the universe. It is quite true. They don't.'

'Oh, Mr Emerson, whatever do you mean?'

In his ordinary voice, so that she scarcely realized he was quoting poetry, he said:

> 'From far, from eve and morning,
> And yon twelve-winded sky,
> The stuff of life to knit me
> Blew hither: here am I.

George and I both know this, but why does it distress him? We know that we come from the winds, and that we shall return to them; that all life is perhaps a knot, a tangle, a blemish in the eternal smoothness. But why should this make us unhappy? Let us rather love one another, and work and rejoice. I don't believe in this world sorrow.'

Miss Honeychurch assented.

'Then make my boy think like us. Make him realize that by the side of the everlasting Why there is a Yes—a transitory Yes if you like, but a Yes.'

Suddenly she laughed; surely one ought to laugh. A young man melancholy because the universe wouldn't fit, because life was a tangle or a wind, or a Yes, or something!

'I'm very sorry,' she cried. 'You'll think me unfeeling, but—but—' Then she became matronly. 'Oh, but your son wants employment. Has he no particular hobby? Why, I myself have worries, but I can generally forget them at the piano; and collecting stamps did no end of good for my brother. Perhaps Italy bores him; you ought to try the Alps or the Lakes.'

The old man's face saddened, and he touched her gently with his hand. This did not alarm her; she thought that her advice had impressed him, and that he was thanking her for it. Indeed, he no longer alarmed her at all; she regarded him as a kind thing, but quite silly. Her feelings were as inflated spiritually as they had been an hour ago æsthetically, before she lost Baedeker. The dear George, now striding towards them over the tomb-stones, seemed both pitiable and absurd. He approached, his face in the shadow. He said:

'Miss Bartlett.'

'Oh, good gracious me!' said Lucy, suddenly collapsing and again seeing the whole of life in a new perspective. 'Where? Where?'

'In the nave.'

'I see. Those gossiping little old Miss Alans must have—' She checked herself.

'Poor girl!' exploded old Mr Emerson. 'Poor girl!'

She could not let this pass, for it was just what she was feeling herself.

'Poor girl? I fail to understand the point of that remark. I think myself a very fortunate girl, I assure you. I'm thoroughly happy, and having a splendid time. Pray don't waste time mourning over *me*. There's enough sorrow in the world, isn't there, without trying to invent it. Good-bye. Thank you both so much for all your kindness. Ah yes! there does come my cousin. A delightful morning! Santa Croce is a wonderful church.'

She rejoined her cousin.

Chapter Three

Music, Violets, and the Letter S

It so happened that Lucy, who found daily life rather chaotic, entered a more solid world when she opened the piano. She was then no longer either deferential or patronizing; no longer either a rebel or a slave. The kingdom of music is not the kingdom of this world; it will accept those whom breeding and intellect and culture have alike rejected. The commonplace person begins to play, and shoots into the empyrean without effort, whilst we look up, marvelling how he has escaped us, and thinking how we could worship him and love him, would he but translate his visions into human words, and his experiences into human actions. Perhaps he cannot; certainly he does not, or does so very seldom. Lucy had done so never.

She was no dazzling *exécutante*; her runs were not at all like strings of pearls, and she struck no more right notes than was suitable for one of her age and situation. Nor was she the passionate young lady, who performs so tragically on a summer's evening with the window open. Passion was there, but it could not be easily labelled; it slipped between love and hatred and jealousy, and all the furniture of the pictorial style. And she was tragical only in the sense that she was great, for she loved to play on the side of Victory. Victory of what and over what—that is more than the words of daily life can tell us. But that some sonatas of Beethoven are written tragic no one can gainsay; yet they can triumph or despair as the player decides, and Lucy had decided that they should triumph.

A very wet afternoon at the Bertolini permitted her to do the thing she really liked, and after lunch she opened the little draped piano. A few people lingered round and praised her playing, but finding that she made no reply, dispersed to their rooms to write up their diaries or to sleep. She took no notice of Mr Emerson looking for his son, nor of Miss Bartlett looking for Miss Lavish, nor of Miss Lavish looking for her cigarette-case. Like every true performer, she was intoxicated by the mere feel of the notes: they were fingers caressing her own; and by touch, not by sound alone, did she come to her desire.

Mr Beebe, sitting unnoticed in the window, pondered over this illogical element in Miss Honeychurch, and recalled the occasion at Tunbridge Wells when he had discovered it. It was at one of those entertainments where the upper classes entertain the lower. The seats were filled with a respectful audience, and the ladies and gentlemen of the parish, under the auspices of their vicar, sang, or recited, or imitated the drawing of a champagne cork. Among the promised items was 'Miss Honeychurch. Piano. Beethoven,' and Mr Beebe was wondering whether it would be 'Adelaida,' or the march of 'The Ruins of Athens,' when his composure was disturbed by the opening bars of Opus III. He was in suspense all through the introduction, for not until the pace quickens does one know what the performer intends. With the roar of the opening theme he knew that things were going extraordinarily; in the chords that herald the conclusion he heard the hammer strokes of victory. He was glad that she only played the first movement, for he could have paid no attention to the winding intricacies of the measure of nine-sixteen. The audience clapped, no less respectful. It was Mr Beebe who started the stamping; it was all that one could do.

'Who is she?' he asked the vicar afterwards.

'Cousin of one of my parishioners. I do not consider her choice of a piece happy. Beethoven is so usually simple and direct in his appeal that it is sheer perversity to choose a thing like that, which, if anything, disturbs.'

'Introduce me.'

'She will be delighted. She and Miss Bartlett are full of the praises of your sermon.'

'My sermon?' cried Mr Beebe. 'Why ever did she listen to it?'

When he was introduced he understood why, for Miss Honeychurch, disjoined from her music-stool, was only a young lady with a quantity of dark hair and a very pretty, pale, undeveloped face. She loved going to concerts, she loved stopping with her cousin, she loved iced coffee and meringues. He did not doubt that she loved his sermon also. But before he left Tunbridge Wells he made a remark to the vicar, which he now made to Lucy herself when she closed the little piano and moved dreamily towards him.

'If Miss Honeychurch ever takes to live as she plays, it will be very exciting–both for us and for her.'

Lucy at once re-entered daily life.

'Oh, what a funny thing! Some one said just the same to mother, and she said she trusted I should never live a duet.'

'Doesn't Mrs Honeychurch like music?'

'She doesn't mind it. But she doesn't like one to get excited over anything; she thinks I am silly about it. She thinks–I can't make out. Once, you know, I said that I liked my own playing better than anyone's. She has never got over it. Of course, I didn't mean that I played well; I only meant—'

'Of course,' said he, wondering why she bothered to explain.

'Music—' said Lucy, as if attempting some generality. She could not complete it, and looked out absently upon Italy in the wet. The whole life of the South was disorganized, and the most graceful nation in Europe had turned into formless lumps of clothes. The street and the river were dirty yellow, the bridge was dirty grey, and the hills were dirty purple. Somewhere in their folds were concealed Miss Lavish, and Miss Bartlett, who had chosen this afternoon to visit the Torre del Gallo.

'What about music?' said Mr Beebe.

'Poor Charlotte will be sopped,' was Lucy's reply.

The expedition was typical of Miss Bartlett, who would return cold, tired, hungry, and angelic, with a ruined skirt, a pulpy Baedeker, and a tickling cough in her throat. On another day, when the whole world was singing and the air ran into the mouth like wine, she would refuse to stir from the drawing-room, saying that she was an old thing, and no fit companion for a hearty girl.

'Miss Lavish has led your cousin astray. She hopes to find the true Italy in the wet, I believe.'

'Miss Lavish is so original,' murmured Lucy. This was the stock remark, the supreme achievement of the Pension Bertolini in the way of definition. Miss Lavish was so original. Mr Beebe had his doubts, but they would have been put down to clerical narrowness. For that, and for other reasons, he held his peace.

'Is it true,' continued Lucy in awe-struck tones, 'that Miss Lavish is writing a book?'

'They do say so.'

'What is it about?'

'It will be a novel,' replied Mr Beebe, 'dealing with modern Italy. Let me refer you for an account to Miss Catharine Alan, who uses words herself more admirably than anyone I know.'

'I wish Miss Lavish would tell me herself. We started such friends. But I don't think she ought to have run away with Baedeker that morning in Santa Croce. Charlotte was most annoyed at finding me practically alone, and so I couldn't help being a little annoyed with Miss Lavish.'

'The two ladies, at all events, have made it up.'

He was interested in the sudden friendship between women so apparently dissimilar as Miss Bartlett and Miss Lavish. They were always in each other's company, with Lucy a slighted third. Miss Lavish he believed he understood, but Miss Bartlett might reveal unknown depths of strangeness, though not, perhaps, of meaning. Was Italy deflecting her from the path of prim chaperon, which he had assigned to her at Tunbridge Wells? All his life he had loved to study maiden ladies; they were his speciality, and his profession had provided him with ample opportunities for the work. Girls like Lucy were charming to look at, but Mr Beebe was, from rather profound reasons, somewhat chilly in his attitude towards the other sex, and preferred to be interested rather than enthralled.

Lucy, for the third time, said that poor Charlotte would be sopped. The Arno was rising in flood, washing away the traces of the little carts upon the foreshore. But in the south-west there had appeared a dull haze of yellow, which might mean better weather if it did not mean worse. She opened the window to inspect, and a cold blast entered the room, drawing a plaintive cry from Miss Catharine Alan, who entered at the same moment by the door.

'Oh, dear Miss Honeychurch, you will catch a chill! And Mr Beebe here besides. Who would suppose this is Italy? There is my sister actually nursing the hot-water can: no comforts or proper provisions.'

She sidled towards them and sat down, self-conscious as she always was on entering a room which contained one man, or a man and one woman.

'I could hear your beautiful playing, Miss Honeychurch, though I was in my room with the door shut. Doors shut; indeed, most necessary. No one has the least idea of privacy in this country. And one person catches it from another.'

Lucy answered suitably. Mr Beebe was not able to tell the ladies of his adventure at Modena, where the chambermaid burst in upon him in his bath, exclaiming cheerfully, 'Fa niente, sono vecchia.' He contented himself with saying: 'I quite agree with you, Miss Alan. The Italians are a most unpleasant people. They pry everywhere, they see everything, and they know what we want before we know it ourselves. We are at their mercy. They read our thoughts, they foretell our desires. From the cab-driver down to—to Giotto, they turn us inside out, and I resent it. Yet in their heart of hearts they are—how superficial! They have no conception of the intellectual life. How right is Signora Bertolini, who exclaimed to me the other day: "Ho, Mr Beebe, if you knew what I suffer over the children's edjucaishion! *Hi* won't 'ave my little Victorier taught by a hignorant Italian what can't explain nothink!"'

Miss Alan did not follow, but gathered that she was being mocked in an agreeable way. Her sister was a little disappointed in Mr Beebe, having expected better things from a clergyman whose head was bald and who wore a pair of russet whiskers. Indeed, who would have supposed that tolerance, sympathy, and a sense of humour would inhabit that militant form?

In the midst of her satisfaction she continued to sidle, and at last the cause was disclosed. From the chair beneath her she extracted a gun-metal cigarette case, on which were powdered in turquoise the initials 'E. L.'

'That belongs to Lavish,' said the clergyman. 'A good fellow, Lavish, but I wish she'd start a pipe.'

'Oh, Mr Beebe,' said Miss Alan, divided between awe and mirth. 'Indeed, though it is dreadful of her to smoke, it is not quite as dreadful as you suppose. She took to it, practically in despair, after her life's work was carried away in a landslip. Surely that makes it more excusable.'

'What was that?' asked Lucy.

Mr Beebe sat back complacently, and Miss Alan began as follows:

'It was a novel—and I am afraid, from what I can gather, not a very nice novel. It is so sad when people who have abilities misuse them, and I must say they nearly always do. Anyhow, she left it almost finished in the Grotto of the Calvary at the Capuccini Hotel at Amalfi while she went for a little ink. She said: "Can I have a little ink, please?" But you know what Italians are, and meanwhile the Grotto fell roaring on to the beach, and the saddest thing of all is that she cannot remember what she has written. The poor thing was very ill after it, and so got tempted into cigarettes. It is a great secret, but I am glad to say that she is writing another novel. She told Teresa and Miss Pole the other day that she had got up all the local colour—this novel is to be about modern Italy; the other was historical—but that she could not start till she had an idea. First she tried Perugia for an inspiration, then she came here—this must on no account get round. And so cheerful through it all! I cannot help thinking that there is something to admire in every one, even if you do not approve of them.'

Miss Alan was always thus being charitable against her better judgment.

A delicate pathos perfumed her disconnected remarks, giving them unexpected beauty, just as in the decaying autumn woods there sometimes rise odours reminiscent of spring. She felt she had made almost too many allowances, and apologized hurriedly for her toleration.

'All the same, she is a little too—I hardly like to say unwomanly, but she behaved most strangely when the Emersons arrived.'

Mr Beebe smiled as Miss Alan plunged into an anecdote which he knew she would be unable to finish in the presence of a gentleman.

'I don't know, Miss Honeychurch, if you have noticed that Miss Pole, the lady who has so much rather yellow hair, takes lemonade. That old Mr Emerson, who puts things very strangely—'

Her jaw dropped. She was silent. Mr Beebe, whose social resources were endless, went out to order some tea, and she continued to Lucy in a hasty whisper:

'Stomach. He warned Miss Pole of her stomach—acidity, he called it—and he may have meant to be kind. I must say I forgot myself and laughed; it was so sudden. As Teresa truly said, it was no laughing matter. But the point is that Miss Lavish was positively *attracted* by his mentioning S., and said that she liked plain speaking, and meeting different grades of thought. She thought they were commercial travellers—"drummers" was the word she used—and all through dinner she tried to prove that England, our great and beloved country, rests on nothing but commerce. Teresa was very much annoyed, and left the table before the cheese, saying as she did so: "There, Miss Lavish, is one who can confute you better than I," and pointed to that beautiful picture of Lord Tennyson. Then Miss Lavish said: "Tut! The early Victorians." Just imagine! "Tut! The early Victorians." My sister had gone, and I felt bound to speak. I said: "Miss Lavish, *I* am an early Victorian; at least, that is to say, I will hear no breath of censure against our dear Queen." It was horrible speaking. I reminded her how the Queen had been to Ireland when she did not want to go, and I must say she was dumbfounded, and made no reply. But, unluckily, Mr Emerson overheard this part, and called in his deep voice: "Quite so, quite so! I honour the woman for her Irish visit." The woman! I tell things so badly; but you see what a tangle we were in by this time, all on account of S. having been mentioned in the first place. But that was not all. After dinner Miss Lavish actually came up and said: "Miss Alan, I am going into the smoking-room to talk to those two nice men. Come, too." Needless to say, I refused such an unsuitable invitation, and she had the impertinence to tell me that it would broaden my ideas, and said that she had four brothers, all University men, except one who was in the army, who always made a point of talking to commercial travellers.'

'Let me finish the story,' said Mr Beebe, who had returned. 'Miss Lavish tried Miss Pole, myself, every one, and finally said: "I shall go alone." She went. At the end of five minutes she returned unobtrusively with a green baize board, and began playing patience.'

'Whatever happened?' cried Lucy.

'No one knows. No one will ever know. Miss Lavish will never dare to tell, and Mr Emerson does not think it worth telling.'

'Mr Beebe—old Mr Emerson, is he nice or not nice? I do so want to know.'

Mr Beebe laughed and suggested that she should settle the question for herself.

'No; but it is so difficult. Sometimes he is so silly, and then I do not mind him. Miss Alan, what do you think? Is he nice?'

The little old lady shook her head, and sighed disapprovingly. Mr Beebe, whom the conversation amused, stirred her up by saying:

'I consider that you are bound to class him as nice, Miss Alan, after that business of the violets.'

'Violets? Oh dear! Who told you about the violets? How do things get round? A pension is a sad place for gossips. No, I cannot forget how they behaved at Mr Eager's lecture at Santa Croce. Oh, poor Miss Honeychurch! It really was too bad! No, I have quite changed. I do *not* like the Emersons. They are *not* nice.'

Mr Beebe smiled nonchalantly. He had made a gentle effort to introduce the Emersons into Bertolini society, and the effort had failed. He was almost the only person who remained friendly to them. Miss Lavish, who represented intellect, was avowedly hostile, and now the Miss Alans, who stood for good breeding, were following her. Miss Bartlett, smarting under an obligation, would scarcely be civil. The case of Lucy was different. She had given him a hazy account of her adventures in Santa Croce, and he gathered that the two men had made a curious and possibly concerted attempt to annex her, to show her the world from their own strange standpoint, to interest her in their private sorrows and joys. This was impertinent; he did not wish their cause to be championed by a young girl: he would rather it should fail. After all, he knew nothing about them, and pension joys, pension sorrows, are flimsy things; whereas Lucy would be his parishioner.

Lucy, with one eye upon the weather, finally said that she thought the Emersons were nice; not that she saw anything of them now. Even their seats at dinner had been moved.

'But aren't they always waylaying you to go out with them, dear?' said the little lady inquisitively.

'Only once. Charlotte didn't like it, and said something—quite politely, of course.'

'Most right of her. They don't understand our ways. They must find their level.'

Mr Beebe rather felt that they had gone under. They had given up their attempt—if it was one—to conquer society, and now the father was almost as silent as the son. He wondered whether he would not plan a pleasant day for these folk before they left—some expedition, perhaps, with Lucy well chaperoned to be nice to them. It was one of Mr Beebe's chief pleasures to provide people with happy memories.

Evening approached while they chatted; the air became brighter; the colours on the trees and hills were purified, and the Arno lost its muddy solidity and began to twinkle. There were a few streaks of bluish-green among the clouds, a few patches of watery light upon the earth, and then the dripping façade of San Miniato shone brilliantly in the declining sun.

'Too late to go out,' said Miss Alan in a voice of relief. 'All the galleries are shut.'

'I think I shall go out,' said Lucy. 'I want to go round the town in the circular tram—on the platform by the driver.'

Her two companions looked grave. Mr Beebe, who felt responsible for her in the absence of Miss Bartlett, ventured to say:

'I wish we could. Unluckily I have letters. If you do want to go out alone, won't you be better on your feet?'

'Italians, dear, you know,' said Miss Alan.

'Perhaps I shall meet some one who reads me through and through!'

But they still looked disapproval, and she so far conceded to Mr Beebe as to say that she would only go for a little walk, and keep to the streets frequented by tourists.

'She oughtn't really to go at all,' said Mr Beebe, as they watched her from the window, 'and she knows it. I put it down to too much Beethoven.'

Chapter Four

Fourth Chapter

Mr Beebe was right. Lucy never knew her desires so clearly as after music. She had not really appreciated the clergyman's wit, nor the suggestive twitterings of Miss Alan. Conversation was tedious; she wanted something big, and she believed that it would have come to her on the wind-swept platform of an electric tram.

This she might not attempt. It was unladylike. Why? Why were most big things unladylike? Charlotte had once explained to her why. It was not that ladies were inferior to men; it was that they were different. Their mission was to inspire others to achievement rather than to achieve themselves. Indirectly, by means of tact and a spotless name, a lady could accomplish much. But if she rushed into the fray herself she would be first censured, then despised, and finally ignored. Poems had been written to illustrate this point.

There is much that is immortal in this medieval lady. The dragons have gone, and so have the knights, but still she lingers in our midst. She reigned in many an early Victorian castle, and was Queen of much early Victorian song. It is sweet to protect her in the intervals of business, sweet to pay her honour when she has cooked our dinner well. But alas! the creature grows degenerate. In her heart also there are springing up strange desires. She too is enamoured of heavy winds, and vast panoramas, and green expanses of the sea. She has marked the kingdom of this world, how full it is of wealth, and beauty, and war–a radiant crust, built around the central fires, spinning towards the receding heavens. Men, declaring that she inspires them to it, move joyfully over the surface, having the most delightful meetings with other men, happy, not because they are masculine, but because they are alive. Before the show breaks up she would like to drop the august title of the Eternal Woman, and go there as her transitory self.

Lucy does not stand for the medieval lady, who was rather an ideal to which she was bidden to lift her eyes when feeling serious. Nor has she any system of revolt. Here and there a restriction annoyed her particularly, and she would transgress it, and perhaps be sorry that she had done so. This afternoon she was peculiarly restive. She would really like to do something of which her well-wishers disapproved. As she might not go on the electric tram, she went to Alinari's shop.

There she bought a photograph of Botticelli's 'Birth of Venus.' Venus, being a pity, spoilt the picture, otherwise so charming, and Miss Bartlett had persuaded her to do without it. (A pity in art of course signified the nude.) Giorgione's 'Tempestà,' the 'Idolino,' some of the Sistine frescoes and the Apoxyomenos, were added to it. She felt a little calmer then, and bought Fra Angelico's 'Coronation,' Giotto's 'Ascension of St John,' some Della Robbia babies, and some Guido Reni Madonnas. For her taste was catholic, and she extended uncritical approval to every well-known name.

But though she spent nearly seven lire, the gates of liberty seemed still unopened. She was conscious of her discontent; it was new to her to be conscious of it. 'The world,' she thought, 'is certainly full of beautiful things, if only I could come across them.' It was not surprising that Mrs Honeychurch disapproved of music, declaring that it always left her daughter peevish, unpractical, and touchy.

'Nothing ever happens to me,' she reflected, as she entered the Piazza Signoria and looked nonchalantly at its marvels, now fairly familiar to her. The great square was in shadow; the sunshine had come too late to strike it. Neptune was already unsubstantial in the twilight, half god, half ghost, and his fountain plashed dreamily to the men and satyrs who idled together on its marge. The Loggia showed as the triple entrance of a cave, wherein dwelt many a deity, shadowy, but immortal, looking forth upon the arrivals and departures of mankind. It was the hour of unreality–the hour, that is, when unfamiliar things are real. An older person at such an hour and in such a place might think that sufficient was happening to him, and rest content. Lucy desired more.

She fixed her eyes wistfully on the tower of the palace, which rose out of the lower darkness like a pillar of roughened gold. It seemed no longer a tower, no longer supported by earth, but some unattainable treasure throbbing in the tranquil sky. Its brightness mesmerized her, still dancing before her eyes when she bent them to the ground and started towards home.

Then something did happen.

Two Italians by the Loggia had been bickering about a debt. 'Cinque lire,' they had cried, 'cinque lire!' They sparred at each other, and one of them was hit lightly upon the chest. He frowned; he bent towards Lucy with a look of interest, as if he had an important message for her. He opened his lips to deliver it, and a stream of red came out between them and trickled down his unshaven chin.

That was all. A crowd rose out of the dusk. It hid this extraordinary man from her, and bore him away to the fountain. Mr George Emerson happened to be a few paces away, looking at her across the spot where the man had been. How very odd! Across something. Even as she caught sight of him he grew dim; the palace itself grew dim, swayed above her, fell on to her softly, slowly, noiselessly, and the sky fell with it.

She thought: 'Oh, what have I done?'

'Oh, what have I done?' she murmured, and opened her eyes.

George Emerson still looked at her, but not across anything. She had complained of dullness, and lo! one man was stabbed, and another held her in his arms.

They were sitting on some steps in the Uffizi Arcade. He must have carried her. He rose when she spoke, and began to dust his knees. She repeated:

'Oh, what have I done?'

'You fainted.'

'I–I am very sorry.'

'How are you now?'

'Perfectly well–absolutely well.' And she began to nod and smile.

'Then let us come home. There's no point in our stopping.'

He held out his hand to pull her up. She pretended not to see it. The cries from the fountain–they had never ceased–rang emptily. The whole world seemed pale and void of its original meaning.

'How very kind you have been! I might have hurt myself falling. But now I am well. I can go alone, thank you.'

His hand was still extended.

'Oh, my photographs!' she exclaimed suddenly.

'What photographs?'

'I bought some photographs at Alinari's. I must have dropped them out there in the square.' She looked at him cautiously. 'Would you add to your kindness by fetching them?'

He added to his kindness. As soon as he had turned his back, Lucy arose with the cunning of a maniac and stole down the arcade towards the Arno.

'Miss Honeychurch!'

She stopped with her hand on her heart.

'You sit still; you aren't fit to go home alone.'

'Yes, I am, thank you so very much.'

'No, you aren't. You'd go openly if you were.'

'But I had rather—'

'Then I don't fetch your photographs.'

'I had rather be alone.'

He said imperiously: 'The man is dead–the man is probably dead; sit down till you are rested.' She was bewildered, and obeyed him. 'And don't move till I come back.'

In the distance she saw creatures with black hoods, such as appear in dreams. The palace tower had lost the reflection of the declining day, and joined itself to earth. How should she talk to Mr Emerson when he returned from the shadowy square? Again the thought occurred to her, 'Oh, what have I done?'–the thought that she, as well as the dying man, had crossed some spiritual boundary.

He returned, and she talked of the murder. Oddly enough, it was an easy topic. She spoke of the Italian character; she became almost garrulous over the incident that had made her faint five minutes before. Being strong physically, she soon overcame the horror of blood. She rose without his assistance, and though wings seemed to flutter inside her, she walked firmly enough towards the Arno. There a cabman signalled to them; they refused him.

'And the murderer tried to kiss him, you say–how very odd Italians are!–and gave himself up to the police! Mr Beebe was saying that Italians know everything, but I think they are rather childish. When my cousin and I were at the Pitti yesterday— What was that?'

He had thrown something into the stream.

'What did you throw in?'

'Things I didn't want,' he said crossly.

'Mr Emerson!'

'Well?'

'Where are the photographs?'

He was silent.

'I believe it was my photographs that you threw away.'

'I didn't know what to do with them,' he cried, and his voice was that of an anxious boy. Her heart warmed towards him for the first time. 'They were covered with blood. There! I'm glad I've told you; and all the time we were making conversation I was wondering what to do with them.' He pointed downstream. 'They've gone.' The river swirled under the bridge. 'I did mind them so, and one is so foolish, it seemed better that they should go out to the sea–I don't know; I may just mean that they frightened me.' Then the boy verged into a man. 'For something tremendous has happened; I must face it without getting muddled. It isn't exactly that a man has died.'

Something warned Lucy that she must stop him.

'It has happened,' he repeated, 'and I mean to find out what it is.'

'Mr Emerson—'

He turned towards her frowning, as if she had disturbed him in some abstract quest.

'I want to ask you something before we go in.'

They were close to their pension. She stopped and leant her elbows against the parapet of the embankment. He did likewise. There is at times a magic in identity of position; it is one of the things that have suggested to us eternal comradeship. She moved her elbows before saying:

'I have behaved ridiculously.'

He was following his own thoughts.

'I was never so much ashamed of myself in my life; I cannot think what came over me.'

'I nearly fainted myself,' he said; but she felt that her attitude repelled him.

'Well, I owe you a thousand apologies.'

'Oh, all right.'

'And–this is the real point–you know how silly people are gossiping–ladies especially, I am afraid–you understand what I mean?'

'I'm afraid I don't.'

'I mean, would you not mention it to anyone, my foolish behaviour?'

'Your behaviour? Oh yes, all right–all right.'

'Thank you so much. And would you—'

She could not carry her request any further. The river was gushing below them, almost black in the advancing night. He had thrown her photographs into it, and then he had told her the reason. It struck her that it was hopeless to look for chivalry in such a man. He would do her no harm by idle gossip; he was trustworthy, intelligent, and even kind; he might even have a high opinion of her. But he lacked chivalry; his thoughts, like his behaviour, would not be modified by awe. It was useless to say to him, 'And would you—' and hope that he would complete the sentence for himself, averting his eyes from her nakedness like the knight in that beautiful picture. She had been in his arms, and he remembered it, just as he remembered the blood on the photographs that she had bought in Alinari's shop. It was not exactly that a man had died; something had happened to the living: they had come to a situation where character tells, and where Childhood enters upon the branching paths of Youth.

'Well, thank you so much,' she repeated. 'How quickly these accidents do happen, and then one returns to the old life!'

'I don't.'

Anxiety moved her to question him.

His answer was puzzling: 'I shall probably want to live.'

'But why, Mr Emerson? What do you mean?'

'I shall want to live, I say.'

Leaning her elbows on the parapet, she contemplated the River Arno, whose roar was suggesting some unexpected melody to her ears.

Chapter Five

Possibilities of a Pleasant Outing

It was a family saying that 'you never knew which way Charlotte Bartlett would turn.' She was perfectly pleasant and sensible over Lucy's adventure, found the abridged account of it quite adequate, and paid suitable tribute to the courtesy of Mr George Emerson. She and Miss Lavish had had an adventure also. They had been stopped at the Dazio coming back, and the young officials there, who seemed impudent and *désœuvré*, had tried to search their reticules for provisions. It might have been most unpleasant. Fortunately, Miss Lavish was a match for anyone.

For good or for evil, Lucy was left to face her problem alone. None of her friends had seen her, either in the Piazza or, later on, by the embankment. Mr Beebe, indeed, noticing her startled eyes at dinner-time, had again passed to himself the remark of 'Too much Beethoven.' But he only supposed that she was ready for an adventure, not that she had encountered it. This solitude oppressed her; she was accustomed to have her thoughts confirmed by others or, at all events, contradicted; it was too dreadful not to know whether she was thinking right or wrong.

At breakfast next morning she took decisive action. There were two plans between which she had to choose. Mr Beebe was walking up to the Torre del Gallo with the Emersons and some American ladies. Would Miss Bartlett and Miss Honeychurch join the party? Charlotte declined for herself; she had been there in the rain the previous afternoon. But she thought it an admirable idea for Lucy, who hated shopping, changing money, fetching letters, and other irksome duties—all of which Miss Bartlett must accomplish this morning, and could easily accomplish alone.

'No, Charlotte!' cried the girl, with real warmth. 'It's very kind of Mr Beebe, but I am certainly coming with you. I had much rather.'

'Very well, dear,' said Miss Bartlett, with a faint flush of pleasure that called forth a deep flush of shame on the cheeks of Lucy. How abominably she behaved to Charlotte, now as always! But now she should alter. All the morning she would be really nice to her.

She slipped her arm into her cousin's, and they started off along the Lung' Arno. The river was a lion that morning in strength, voice, and colour. Miss Bartlett insisted on leaning over the parapet to look at it. She then made her usual remark, which was:

'How I do wish Freddy and your mother could see this, too!'

Lucy fidgeted; it was tiresome of Charlotte to have stopped exactly where she did.

'Look, Lucia! Oh, you are watching for the Torre del Gallo party. I feared you would repent you of your choice.'

Serious as the choice had been, Lucy did not repent. Yesterday had been a muddle—queer and odd, the kind of thing one could not write down easily on paper—but she had a feeling that Charlotte and her shopping were preferable to George Emerson and the summit of the Torre del Gallo. Since she could not unravel the tangle, she must take care not to re-enter it. She could protest sincerely against Miss Bartlett's insinuations.

But though she had avoided the chief actor, the scenery unfortunately remained. Charlotte, with the complacency of fate, led her from the river to the Piazza Signoria. She could not have believed that stones, a Loggia, a fountain, a palace tower, would have such significance. For a moment she understood the nature of ghosts.

The exact site of the murder was occupied, not by a ghost, but by Miss

Lavish, who had the morning newspaper in her hand. She hailed them briskly. The dreadful catastrophe of the previous day had given her an idea which she thought would work up into a book.

'Oh, let me congratulate you!' said Miss Bartlett. 'After your despair of yesterday! What a fortunate thing!'

'Aha! Miss Honeychurch, come you here! I am in luck. Now, you are to tell me absolutely everything that you saw from the beginning.'

Lucy poked at the ground with her parasol.

'But perhaps you would rather not?'

'I'm sorry—if you could manage without it, I think I would rather not.'

The elder ladies exchanged glances, not of disapproval; it is suitable that a girl should feel deeply.

'It is I who am sorry,' said Miss Lavish. 'We literary hacks are shameless creatures. I believe there's no secret of the human heart into which we wouldn't pry.'

She marched cheerfully to the fountain and back, and did a few calculations in realism. Then she said that she had been in the Piazza since eight o'clock collecting material. A good deal of it was unsuitable, but of course one always had to adapt. The two men had quarrelled over a five-franc note. For the five-franc note she should substitute a young lady, which would raise the tone of the tragedy, and at the same time furnish an excellent plot.

'What is the heroine's name?' asked Miss Bartlett.

'Leonora,' said Miss Lavish; her own name was Eleanor.

'I do hope she's nice.'

That desideratum would not be omitted.

'And what is the plot?'

Love, murder, abduction, revenge, was the plot. Out it all came while the fountain plashed to the satyrs in the morning sun.

'I hope you will excuse me for boring on like this,' Miss Lavish concluded. 'It is so tempting to talk to really sympathetic people. Of course, this is the barest outline. There will be a deal of local colouring, descriptions of Florence and the neighbourhood, and I shall also introduce some humorous characters. And let me give you all fair warning: I intend to be unmerciful to the British tourist.'

'Oh, you wicked woman!' cried Miss Bartlett. 'I am sure you are thinking of the Emersons.'

Miss Lavish gave a Machiavellian smile.

'I confess that in Italy my sympathies are not with my own countrymen. It is the neglected Italians who attract me, and whose lives I am going to paint so far as I can. For I repeat and I insist, and I have always held most strongly, that a tragedy such as yesterday's is not the less tragic because it happened in humble life.'

There was a fitting silence when Miss Lavish had concluded. Then the cousins wished success to her labours, and walked slowly away across the square.

'She is my idea of a really clever woman,' said Miss Bartlett. 'That last remark struck me as so particularly true. It should be a most pathetic novel.'

Lucy assented. At present her great aim was not to get put into it. Her perceptions this morning were curiously keen, and she believed that Miss Lavish had her on trial for an *ingénue*.

'She is emancipated, but only in the very best sense of the word,' continued Miss Bartlett slowly. 'None but the superficial would be shocked at her. We had a long talk yesterday. She believes in justice and truth and human interest. She told me also that she has a high opinion of the destiny of woman—Mr Eager! Why, how nice! What a pleasant surprise!'

'Ah, not for me,' said the chaplain blandly, 'for I have been watching you and Miss Honeychurch for quite a little time.'

'We were chatting to Miss Lavish.'

His brow contracted.

'So I saw. Were you indeed? Andate via! sono occupato!' The last remark was made to a vendor of panoramic photographs who was approaching with a courteous smile. 'I am about to venture a suggestion. Would you and Miss Honeychurch be disposed to join me in a drive some day this week–a drive in the hills? We might go up by Fiesole and back by Settignano. There is a point on that road where we could get down and have an hour's ramble on the hill-side. The view thence of Florence is most beautiful–far better than the hackneyed view from Fiesole. It is the view that Alessio Baldovinetti is fond of introducing into his pictures. That man had a decided feeling for landscape. Decidedly. But who looks at it to-day? Ah, the world is too much with us.'

Miss Bartlett had not heard of Alessio Baldovinetti, but she knew that Mr Eager was no commonplace chaplain. He was a member of the residential colony who had made Florence their home. He knew the people who never walked about with Baedekers, who had learnt to take a siesta after lunch, who took drives the pension tourists had never heard of, and saw by private influence galleries which were closed to them. Living in delicate seclusion, some in furnished flats, others in Renaissance villas on Fiesole's slope, they read, wrote, studied, and exchanged ideas, thus attaining to that intimate knowledge, or rather perception, of Florence which is denied to all who carry in their pockets the coupons of Cook.

Therefore an invitation from the chaplain was something to be proud of. Between the two sections of his flock he was often the only link, and it was his avowed custom to select those of his migratory sheep who seemed worthy, and give them a few hours in the pastures of the permanent. Tea at a Renaissance villa? Nothing had been said about it yet. But if it did come to that–how Lucy would enjoy it!

A few days ago and Lucy would have felt the same. But the joys of life were grouping themselves anew. A drive in the hills with Mr Eager and Miss Bartlett–even if culminating in a residential tea-party–was no longer the greatest of them. She echoed the raptures of Charlotte somewhat faintly. Only when she heard that Mr Beebe was also coming did her thanks become more sincere.

'So we shall be a *partée carrée*,' said the chaplain. 'In these days of toil and

tumult one has great needs of the country and its message of purity. Andate
via! andate presto, presto! Ah, the town! Beautiful as it is, it is the town.'

They assented.

'This very square—so I am told—witnessed yesterday the most sordid of
tragedies. To one who loves the Florence of Dante and Savonarola there is
something portentous in such desecration—portentous and humiliating.'

'Humiliating indeed,' said Miss Bartlett. 'Miss Honeychurch happened
to be passing through as it happened. She can hardly bear to speak of it.' She
glanced at Lucy proudly.

'And how came we to have you here?' asked the chaplain paternally.

Miss Bartlett's recent liberalism oozed away at the question.

'Do not blame her, please, Mr Eager. The fault is mine: I left her
unchaperoned.'

'So you were here alone, Miss Honeychurch?' His voice suggested
sympathetic reproof, but at the same time indicated that a few harrowing
details would not be unacceptable. His dark, handsome face drooped
mournfully towards her to catch her reply.

'Practically.'

'One of our pension acquaintances kindly brought her home,' said Miss
Bartlett, adroitly concealing the sex of the preserver.

'For her also it must have been a terrible experience. I trust that neither of
you were at all—that it was not in your immediate proximity.'

Of the many things Lucy was noticing to-day, not the least remarkable
was this: the ghoulish fashion in which respectable people will nibble after
blood. George Emerson had kept the subject strangely pure.

'He died by the fountain, I believe,' was her reply.

'And you and your friend—'

'Were over at the Loggia.'

'That must have saved you much. You have not, of course, seen the
disgraceful illustrations which the gutter Press— This man is a public
nuisance; he knows that I am a resident perfectly well, and yet he goes on
worrying me to buy his vulgar views.'

Surely the vendor of photographs was in league with Lucy—in the eternal
league of Italy with youth. He had suddenly extended his book before Miss
Bartlett and Mr Eager, binding their hands together by a long glossy ribbon
of churches, pictures, and views.

'This is too much!' cried the chaplain, striking petulantly at one of Fra
Angelico's angels. She tore. A shrill cry arose from the vendor. The book, it
seemed, was more valuable than one would have supposed.

'Willingly would I purchase—' began Miss Bartlett.

'Ignore him,' said Mr Eager sharply, and they all walked rapidly away
from the square.

But an Italian can never be ignored, least of all when he has a grievance.
His mysterious persecution of Mr Eager became relentless; the air rang with
his threats and lamentations. He appealed to Lucy; would not she intercede?
He was poor—he sheltered a family—the tax on bread. He waited, he gib-
bered, he was recompensed, he was dissatisfied, he did not leave them until

he had swept their minds clean of all thoughts, whether pleasant or unpleasant.

Shopping was the topic that now ensued. Under the chaplain's guidance they selected many hideous presents and mementoes–florid little picture-frames that seemed fashioned in gilded pastry; other little frames, more severe, that stood on little easels, and were carven out of oak; a blotting book of vellum; a Dante of the same material; cheap mosaic brooches, which the maids, next Christmas, would never tell from real; pins, pots, heraldic saucers, brown art-photographs; Eros and Psyche in alabaster; St Peter to match–all of which would have cost less in London.

This successful morning left no pleasant impressions on Lucy. She had been a little frightened, both by Miss Lavish and by Mr Eager, she knew not why. And as they frightened her, she had, strangely enough, ceased to respect them. She doubted that Miss Lavish was a great artist. She doubted that Mr Eager was as full of spirituality and culture as she had been led to suppose. They were tried by some new test, and they were found wanting. As for Charlotte–as for Charlotte she was exactly the same. It might be possible to be nice to her; it was impossible to love her.

'The son of a labourer; I happen to know if for a fact. A mechanic of some sort himself when he was young; then he took to writing for the Socialistic Press. I came across him at Brixton.'

They were talking about the Emersons.

'How wonderfully people rise in these days!' sighed Miss Bartlett, fingering a model of the Leaning Tower of Pisa.

'Generally,' replied Mr Eager, 'one has only sympathy with their success. The desire for education and for social advance–in these things there is something not wholly vile. There are some working men whom one would be very willing to see out here in Florence–little as they would make of it.'

'Is he a journalist now?' Miss Bartlett asked.

'He is not; he made an advantageous marriage.'

He uttered this remark with a voice full of meaning, and ended it with a sigh.

'Oh, so he has a wife.'

'Dead, Miss Bartlett, dead. I wonder–yes, I wonder how he has the effrontery to look me in the face, to dare to claim acquaintance with me. He was in my London parish long ago. The other day in Santa Croce, when he was with Miss Honeychurch, I snubbed him. Let him beware that he does not get more than a snub.'

'What?' cried Lucy, flushing.

'Exposure!' hissed Mr Eager.

He tried to change the subject; but in scoring a dramatic point he had interested his audience more than he had intended. Miss Bartlett was full of very natural curiosity. Lucy, though she wished never to see the Emersons again, was not disposed to condemn them on a single word.

'Do you mean,' she asked, 'that he is an irreligious man? We know that already.'

'Lucy dear—' said Miss Bartlett, gently reproving her cousin's penetration.

'I should be astonished if you knew all. The boy–an innocent child at the time–I will exclude. God knows what his education and his inherited qualities may have made him.'

'Perhaps,' said Miss Bartlett, 'it is something that we had better not hear.'

'To speak plainly,' said Mr Eager, 'it is. I will say no more.'

For the first time Lucy's rebellious thoughts swept out in words–for the first time in her life.

'You have said very little.'

'It was my intention to say very little,' was his frigid reply.

He gazed indignantly at the girl, who met him with equal indignation. She turned towards him from the shop counter; her breast heaved quickly. He observed her brow, and the sudden strength of her lips. It was intolerable that she should disbelieve him.

'Murder, if you want to know,' he cried angrily. 'That man murdered his wife!'

'How?' she retorted.

'To all intents and purposes he murdered her. That day in Santa Croce–did they say anything against me?'

'Not a word, Mr Eager–not a single word.'

'Oh, I thought they had been libelling me to you. But I suppose it is only their personal charms that make you defend them.'

'I'm not defending them,' said Lucy, losing her courage, and relapsing into the old chaotic methods. 'They're nothing to me.'

'How could you think she was defending them?' said Miss Bartlett, much discomfited by the unpleasant scene. The shopman was possibly listening.

'She will find it difficult. For that man has murdered his wife in the sight of God.'

The addition of God was striking. But the chaplain was really trying to qualify a rash remark. A silence followed which might have been impressive, but was merely awkward. Then Miss Bartlett hastily purchased the Leaning Tower, and led the way into the street.

'I must be going,' said he, shutting his eyes and taking out his watch.

Miss Bartlett thanked him for his kindness, and spoke with enthusiasm of the approaching drive.

'Drive? Oh, is our drive to come off?'

Lucy was recalled to her manners, and after a little exertion the complacency of Mr Eager was restored.

'Bother the drive!' exclaimed the girl, as soon as he had departed. 'It is just the drive we had arranged with Mr Beebe without any fuss at all. Why should he invite us in that absurd manner? We might as well invite him. We are each paying for ourselves.'

Miss Bartlett, who had intended to lament over the Emersons, was launched by this remark into unexpected thoughts.

'If that is so, dear–if the drive we and Mr Beebe are going with Mr Eager is really the same as the one we were going with Mr Beebe, then I foresee a sad kettle of fish.'

'How?'

'Because Mr Beebe has asked Eleanor Lavish to come, too.'

'That will mean another carriage.'

'Far worse. Mr Eager does not like Eleanor. She knows it herself. The truth must be told; she is too unconventional for him.'

They were now in the newspaper-room at the English bank. Lucy stood by the central table, heedless of 'Punch' and the 'Graphic,' trying to answer, or at all events to formulate the questions rioting in her brain. The well-known world had broken up, and there emerged Florence, a magic city where people thought and did the most extraordinary things. Murder, accusations of murder, a lady clinging to one man and being rude to another—were these the daily incidents of her streets? Was there more in her frank beauty than met the eye—the power, perhaps, to evoke passions, good and bad, and to bring them speedily to a fulfilment?

Happy Charlotte, who, though greatly troubled over things that did not matter, seemed oblivious to things that did; who could conjecture with admirable delicacy 'where things might lead to,' but apparently lost sight of the goal as she approached it! Now she was crouching in the corner trying to extract a circular note from a kind of linen nose-bag which hung in chaste concealment round her neck. She had been told that his was the only safe way to carry money in Italy; it must only be broached within the walls of the English bank. As she groped she murmured: 'Whether it is Mr Beebe who forgot to tell Mr Eager, or Mr Eager who forgot when he told us, or whether they have decided to leave Eleanor out altogether—which they could scarcely do—but in any case we must be prepared. It is you they really want; I am only asked for appearances. You shall go with the two gentlemen, and I and Eleanor will follow behind. A one-horse carriage would do for us. Yet how difficult it is!'

'It is indeed,' replied the girl, with a gravity that sounded sympathetic.

'What do you think about it?' asked Miss Bartlett, flushed from the struggle, and buttoning up her dress.

'I don't know what I think, nor what I want.'

'Oh dear, Lucy! I do hope Florence isn't boring you. Speak the word, and, as you know, I would take you to the ends of the earth to-morrow.'

'Thank you, Charlotte,' said Lucy, and pondered over the offer.

There were letters for her at the bureau—one from her brother, full of athletics and biology; one from her mother, delightful as only her mother's letters could be. She read in it of the crocuses which had been bought for yellow and were coming up puce, of the new parlour-maid, who had watered the ferns with essence of lemonade, of the semi-detached cottages which were ruining Summer Street, and breaking the heart of Sir Harry Otway. She recalled the free, pleasant life of her home, where she was allowed to do everything, and where nothing ever happened to her. The road up through the pine-woods, the clean drawing-room, the view over the Sussex Weald—all hung before her bright and distinct, but pathetic as the pictures in a gallery to which, after much experience, a traveller returns.

'And the news?' asked Miss Bartlett.

'Mrs Vyse and her son have gone to Rome,' said Lucy, giving the news that interested her least. 'Do you know the Vyses?'

'Oh, not that way back. We can never have too much of the dear Piazza Signoria.'

'They're nice people, the Vyses. So clever—my idea of what's really clever. Don't you long to be in Rome?'

'I die for it!'

The Piazza Signoria is too stony to be brilliant. It has no grass, no flowers, no frescoes, no glittering walls of marble or comforting patches of ruddy brick. By an odd chance—unless we believe in a presiding genius of places—the statues that relieve its severity suggest, not the innocence of childhood, nor the glorious bewilderment of youth, but the conscious achievements of maturity. Perseus and Judith, Hercules and Thusnelda, they have done or suffered something, and though they are immortal, immortality has come to them after experience, not before. Here, not only in the solitude of Nature, might a hero meet a goddess, or a heroine a god.

'Charlotte!' cried the girl suddenly. 'Here's an idea. What if we popped off to Rome to-morrow—straight—to the Vyses' hotel? For I do know what I want. I'm sick of Florence. Now, you said you'd go to the ends of the earth! Do! Do!'

Miss Bartlett, with equal vivacity, replied:

'Oh, you droll person! Pray, what would become of your drive in the hills?'

They passed together through the gaunt beauty of the square, laughing over the unpractical suggestion.

Chapter Six

The Reverend Arthur Beebe, the Reverend Cuthbert Eager,
Mr Emerson, Mr George Emerson, Miss Eleanor Lavish,
Miss Charlotte Bartlett, and Miss Lucy Honeychurch,
Drive out in Carriages to see a View: Italians Drive them

It was Phaethon who drove them to Fiesole that memorable day, a youth all irresponsibility and fire, recklessly urging his master's horses up the stony hill. Mr Beebe recognized him at once. Neither the Ages of Faith nor the Age of Doubt had touched him; he was Phaethon in Tuscany driving a cab. And it was Persephone whom he asked leave to pick up on the way, saying that she was his sister—Persephone, tall and slender and pale, returning with the spring to her mother's cottage, and still shading her eyes from the unaccustomed light. To her Mr Eager objected, saying that here was the thin edge of the wedge, and one must guard against imposition. But the ladies interceded, and when it had been made clear that it was a very great favour, the goddess was allowed to mount beside the god.

Phaethon at once slipped the left rein over her head, thus enabling himself to drive with his arm round her waist. She did not mind. Mr Eager, who sat with his back to the horses, saw nothing of the indecorous proceeding, and continued his conversation with Lucy. The other two occupants of the carriage were old Mr Emerson and Miss Lavish. For a dreadful thing had happened: Mr Beebe, without consulting Mr Eager, had doubled the size of the party. And though Miss Bartlett and Miss Lavish had planned all the morning how people were to sit, at the critical moment when the carriages came round they lost their heads, and Miss Lavish got in with Lucy, while Miss Bartlett, with George Emerson and Mr Beebe, followed on behind.

It was hard on the poor chaplain to have his *partie carrée* thus transformed. Tea at a Renaissance villa, if he had ever meditated it, was now impossible. Lucy and Miss Bartlett had a certain style about them, and Mr Beebe, though unreliable, was a man of parts. But a shoddy lady writer and a journalist who had murdered his wife in the sight of God—they should enter no villa at his introduction.

Lucy, elegantly dressed in white, sat erect and nervous amid these explosive ingredients, attentive to Mr Eager, repressive towards Miss Lavish, watchful of old Mr Emerson—hitherto fortunately asleep, thanks to a heavy lunch and the drowsy atmosphere of spring. She looked on the expedition as the work of Fate. But for it she would have avoided George Emerson successfully. In an open manner he had shown that he wished to continue their intimacy. She had refused, not because she disliked him, but because she did not know what had happened, and suspected that he did know. And this frightened her.

For the real event—whatever it was—had taken place, not in the Loggia, but by the river. To behave wildly at the sight of death is pardonable. But to discuss it afterwards, to pass from discussion into silence, and through silence into sympathy, that is an error, not of a startled emotion, but of the whole fabric. There was really something blameworthy (she thought) in their joint contemplation of the shadowy stream, in the common impulse which had turned them to the house without the passing of a look or word. This sense of wickedness had been slight at first. She had nearly joined the party to the Torre del Gallo. But each time that she avoided George it became more imperative that she should avoid him again. And now celestial irony, working through her cousin and two clergymen, did not suffer her to leave Florence till she had made this expedition with him through the hills.

Meanwhile Mr Eager held her in civil converse; their little tiff was over.

'So, Miss Honeychurch, you are travelling? As a student of art?'

'Oh dear me, no—oh no!'

'Perhaps as a student of human nature,' interposed Miss Lavish, 'like myself?'

'Oh no. I am here as a tourist.'

'Oh, indeed,' said Mr Eager. 'Are you indeed? If you will not think me rude, we residents sometimes pity you poor tourists not a little—handed about like a parcel of goods from Venice to Florence, from Florence to

Rome, living herded together in pensions or hotels, quite unconscious of
anything that is outside Baedeker, their one anxiety to get "done" or
"through" and go on somewhere else. The result is, they mix up towns,
rivers, palaces in one inextricable whirl. You know the American girl in
"Punch" who says: "Say, poppa, what did we see at Rome?" And the father
replies: "Why, guess Rome was the place where we saw the yaller dog."
There's travelling for you. Ha! ha! ha!'

'I quite agree,' said Miss Lavish, who had several times tried to interrupt
his mordant wit. 'The narrowness and superficiality of the Anglo-Saxon
tourist is nothing less than a menace.'

'Quite so. Now, the English colony at Florence, Miss Honeychurch—and
it is of considerable size, though, of course, not all equally—a few are here for
trade, for example. But the greater part are students. Lady Helen
Laverstock is at present busy over Fra Angelico. I mention her name
because we are passing her villa on the left. No, you can only see it if you
stand—no, do not stand; you will fall. She is very proud of that thick hedge.
Inside, perfect seclusion. One might have gone back six hundred years.
Some critics believe that her garden was the scene of "The Decameron,"
which lends it an additional interest, does it not?'

'It does indeed!' cried Miss Lavish. 'Tell me, where do they place the
scene of that wonderful seventh day?'

But Mr Eager proceeded to tell Miss Honeychurch that on the right lived
Mr Someone Something, an American of the best type—so rare!—and that
the Somebody Elses were farther down the hill. 'Doubtless you know her
monographs in the series of "Mediæval Byways"? He is working at
"Gemistus Pletho." Sometimes as I take tea in their beautiful grounds I
hear, over the wall, the electric tram squealing up the new road with its load
of hot, dusty, unintelligent tourists who are going to "do" Fiesole in an hour
in order that they may say they have been there, and I think—I think—I think
how little they think what lies so near them.'

During this speech the two figures on the box were sporting with each
other disgracefully. Lucy had a spasm of envy. Granted that they wished to
misbehave, it was pleasant for them to be able to do so. They were probably
the only people enjoying the expedition. The carriage swept with agonizing
jolts up through the Piazza of Fiesole and into the Settignano road.

'Piano! piano!' said Mr Eager, elegantly waving his hand over his head.

'Va bene, signore, va bene, va bene,' crooned the driver, and whipped his
horses up again.

Now Mr Eager and Miss Lavish began to talk against each other on the
subject of Alessio Baldovinetti. Was he a cause of the Renaissance, or was he
one of its manifestations? The other carriage was left behind. As the pace
increased to a gallop the large, slumbering form of Mr Emerson was thrown
against the chaplain with the regularity of a machine.

'Piano! piano!' said he, with a martyred look at Lucy.

An extra lurch made him turn angrily in his seat. Phaethon, who for some
time had been endeavouring to kiss Persephone, had just succeeded.

A little scene ensued, which, as Miss Bartlett said afterwards, was most unpleasant. The horses were stopped, the lovers were ordered to disentangle themselves, the boy was to lose his *pourboire*, the girl was immediately to get down.

'She is my sister,' said he, turning round on them with piteous eyes.

Mr Eager took the trouble to tell him that he was a liar. Phaethon hung down his head, not at the matter of the accusation, but at its manner. At this point Mr Emerson, whom the shock of stopping had awoken, declared that the lovers must on no account be separated, and patted them on the back to signify his approval. And Miss Lavish, though unwilling to ally with him, felt bound to support the cause of Bohemianism.

'Most certainly I would let them be,' she cried. 'But I dare say I shall receive scant support. I have always flown in the face of the conventions all my life. This is what *I* call an adventure.'

'We must not submit,' said Mr Eager. 'I knew he was trying it on. He is treating us as if we were a party of Cook's tourists.'

'Surely no!' said Miss Lavish, her ardour visibly decreasing.

The other carriage had drawn up behind, and sensible Mr Beebe called out that after this warning the couple would be sure to behave themselves properly.

'Leave them alone,' Mr Emerson begged the chaplain, of whom he stood in no awe. 'Do we find happiness so often that we should turn it off the box when it happens to sit there? To be driven by lovers— A king might envy us, and if we part them it's more like sacrilege than anything I know.'

Here the voice of Miss Bartlett was heard saying that a crowd had begun to collect.

Mr Eager, who suffered from an over-fluent tongue rather than a resolute will, was determined to make himself heard. He addressed the driver again. Italian in the mouth of Italians is a deep-voiced stream, with unexpected cataracts and boulders to preserve it from monotony. In Mr Eager's mouth it resembled nothing so much as an acid whistling fountain which played ever higher and higher, and quicker and quicker, and more and more shrilly, till abruptly it was turned off with a click.

'Signorina!' said the man to Lucy, when the display had ceased. Why should he appeal to Lucy?

'Signorina!' echoed Persephone in her glorious contralto. She pointed at the other carriage. Why?

For a moment the two girls looked at each other. Then Persephone got down from the box.

'Victory at last!' said Mr Eager, smiting his hands together as the carriages started again.

'It is not victory,' said Mr Emerson. 'It is defeat. You have parted two people who were happy.'

Mr Eager shut his eyes. He was obliged to sit next to Mr Emerson, but he would not speak to him. The old man was refreshed by sleep, and took up the matter warmly. He commanded Lucy to agree with him; he shouted for support to his son.

'We have tried to buy what cannot be bought with money. He has bargained to drive us, and he is doing it. We have no rights over his soul.'

Miss Lavish frowned. It is hard when a person you have classed as typically British speaks out of his character.

'He was not driving us well,' she said. 'He jolted us.'

'That I deny. It was as restful as sleeping. Aha! he is jolting us now. Can you wonder? He would like to throw us out, and most certainly he is justified. And if I were superstitious I'd be frightened of the girl, too. It doesn't do to injure young people. Have you ever heard of Lorenzo de Medici?'

Miss Lavish bristled.

'Most certainly I have. Do you refer to Lorenzo il Magnifico, or to Lorenzo, Duke of Urbino, or to Lorenzo surnamed Lorenzino on account of his diminutive stature?'

'The Lord knows. Possibly he does know, for I refer to Lorenzo the poet. He wrote a line—so I heard yesterday—which runs like this: "Don't go fighting against the Spring."'

Mr Eager could not resist the opportunity for erudition.

'Non fate guerra al Maggio,' he murmured. '"War not with the May" would render a correct meaning.'

'The point is, we have warred with it. Look.' He pointed to the Val d' Arno, which was visible far below them, through the budding trees. 'Fifty miles of spring, and we've come up to admire them. Do you suppose there's any difference between spring in nature and spring in man? But there we go, praising the one and condemning the other as improper, ashamed that the same laws work eternally through both.'

No one encouraged him to talk. Presently Mr Eager gave a signal for the carriages to stop, and marshalled the party for their ramble on the hill. A hollow like a great amphitheatre, full of terraced steps and misty olives, now lay between them and the heights of Fiesole, and the road, still following its curve, was about to sweep on to a promontory which stood out into the plain. It was this promontory, uncultivated, wet, covered with bushes and occasional trees, which had caught the fancy of Alessio Baldovinetti nearly five hundred years before. He had ascended it, that diligent and rather obscure master, possibly with an eye to business, possibly for the joy of ascending. Standing, there he had seen that view of the Val d' Arno and distant Florence, which he afterwards had introduced not very effectively into his work. But where exactly had he stood? That was the question which Mr Eager hoped to solve now. And Miss Lavish, whose nature was attracted by anything problematical, had become equally enthusiastic.

But it is not easy to carry the pictures of Alessio Baldovinetti in your head, even if you have remembered to look at them before starting. And the haze in the valley increased the difficulty of the quest. The party sprang about from tuft to tuft of grass, their anxiety to keep together being only equalled by their desire to go in different directions. Finally they split into groups. Lucy clung to Miss Bartlett and Miss Lavish; the Emersons returned to hold laborious converse with the drivers; while the two clergymen, who were expected to have topics in common, were left to each other.

The two elder ladies soon threw off the mask. In the audible whisper that was now so familiar to Lucy they began to discuss, not Alessio Baldovinetti, but the drive. Miss Bartlett had asked Mr George Emerson what his profession was, and he had answered 'the railway.' She was very sorry that she had asked him. She had no idea that it would be such a dreadful answer, or she would not have asked him. Mr Beebe had turned the conversation so cleverly, and she hoped that the young man was not very much hurt at her asking him.

'The railway!' gasped Miss Lavish. 'Oh, but I shall die! Of course it was the railway!' She could not control her mirth. 'He is the image of a porter—on, on the South-Eastern.'

'Eleanor, be quiet,' plucking at her vivacious companion. 'Hush! They'll hear—the Emersons—'

'I can't stop. Let me go my wicked way. A porter—'

'Eleanor!'

'I'm sure it's all right,' put in Lucy. 'The Emersons won't hear, and they wouldn't mind if they did.'

Miss Lavish did not seem pleased at this.

'Miss Honeychurch listening!' she said rather crossly. 'Pouf! wouf! You naughty girl! Go away!'

'Oh, Lucy, you ought to be with Mr Eager, I'm sure.'

'I can't find them now, and I don't want to either.'

'Mr Eager will be offended. It is your party.'

'Please, I'd rather stop here with you.'

'No, I agree,' said Miss Lavish. 'It's like a school feast; the boys have got separated from the girls. Miss Lucy, you are to go. We wish to converse on high topics unsuited for your ear.'

The girl was stubborn. As her time at Florence drew to its close she was only at ease amongst those to whom she felt indifferent. Such a one was Miss Lavish, and such for the moment was Charlotte. She wished she had not called attention to herself; they were both annoyed at her remark and seemed determined to get rid of her.

'How tired one gets,' said Miss Bartlett. 'Oh, I do wish Freddy and your mother could be here.'

Unselfishness with Miss Bartlett had entirely usurped the functions of enthusiasm. Lucy did not look at the view either. She would not enjoy anything till she was safe at Rome.

'Then sit you down,' said Miss Lavish. 'Observe my foresight.'

With many a smile she produced two of those mackintosh squares that protect the frame of the tourist from damp grass or cold marble steps. She sat on one; who was to sit on the other?

'Lucy; without a moment's doubt, Lucy. The ground will do for me. Really I have not had rheumatism for years. If I do feel it coming on I shall stand. Imagine your mother's feelings if I let you sit in the wet in your white linen.' She sat down heavily where the ground looked particularly moist. 'Here we are, all settled delightfully. Even if my dress is thinner it will not show so much, being brown. Sit down, dear; you are too unselfish; you don't assert yourself enough.' She cleared her throat. 'Now don't be alarmed; this isn't a cold. It's the tiniest cough, and I have had it three days. It's nothing to do with sitting here at all.'

There was only one way of treating the situation. At the end of five minutes Lucy departed in search of Mr Beebe and Mr Eager, vanquished by the makintosh square.

She addressed herself to the drivers, who were sprawling in the carriages, perfuming the cushions with cigars. The miscreant, a bony young man scorched black by the sun, rose to greet her with the courtesy of a host and the assurance of a relative.

'Dove?' said Lucy, after much anxious thought.

His face lit up. Of course he knew where. Not so far either. His arm swept three-fourths of the horizon. He should just think he did know where. He pressed his finger-tips to his forehead and then pushed them towards her, as if oozing with visible extract of knowledge.

More seemed necessary. What was the Italian for 'clergymen'?

'Dove buoni uomini?' said she at last.

Good? Scarcely the adjective for those noble beings! He showed her his cigar.

'Uno–piu–piccolo,' was her next remark, implying 'Has the cigar been given to you by Mr Beebe, the smaller of the two good men?'

She was correct as usual. He tied the horse to a tree, kicked it to make it stay quiet, dusted the carriage, arranged his hair, remoulded his hat, encouraged his moustache, and in rather less than a quarter of a minute was ready to conduct her. Italians are born knowing the way. It would seem that the whole earth lay before them, not as a map, but as a chessboard, whereon they continually behold the changing pieces as well as the squares. Anyone can find places, but the finding of people is a gift from God.

He only stopped once, to pick her some great blue violets. She thanked him with real pleasure. In the company of this common man the world was beautiful and direct. For the first time she felt the influence of spring. His arm swept the horizon gracefully; violets, like other things, existed in great profusion there; would she like to see them?

'Ma buoni uomini.'

He bowed. Certainly. Good men first, violets afterwards. They proceeded briskly through the undergrowth, which became thicker and thicker. They were nearing the edge of the promontory, and the view was stealing round them, but the brown network of the bushes shattered it into countless pieces. He was occupied in his cigar, and in holding back the pliant boughs. She was rejoicing in her escape from dullness. Not a step, not a twig, was unimportant to her.

'What is that?'

There was a voice in the wood, in the distance behind them. The voice of Mr Eager? He shrugged his shoulders. An Italian's ignorance is sometimes more remarkable than his knowledge. She could not make him understand that perhaps they had missed the clergymen. The view was forming at last; she could discern the river, the golden plain, other hills.

'Eccolo!' he exclaimed.

At the same moment the ground gave way, and with a cry she fell out of the wood. Light and beauty enveloped her. She had fallen on to a little open terrace, which was covered with violets from end to end.

'Courage!' cried her companion, now standing some six feet above. 'Courage and love.'

She did not answer. From her feet the ground sloped sharply into the view, and violets ran down in rivulets and streams and cataracts, irrigating the hill-side with blue, eddying round the tree stems, collecting into pools in the hollows, covering the grass with spots of azure foam. But never again were they in such profusion; this terrace was the well-head, the primal source whence beauty gushed out to water the earth.

Standing at its brink, like a swimmer who prepares, was the good man. But he was not the good man that she had expected, and he was alone.

George had turned at the sound of her arrival. For a moment he contemplated her, as one who had fallen out of heaven. He saw radiant joy in her face, he saw the flowers beat against her dress in blue waves. The bushes above them closed. He stepped quickly forward and kissed her.

Before she could speak, almost before she could feel, a voice called, 'Lucy! Lucy! Lucy!' The silence of life had been broken by Miss Bartlett, who stood brown against the view.

Chapter Seven

They Return

Some complicated game had been playing up and down the hill-side all the afternoon. What it was and exactly how the players had sided, Lucy was slow to discover. Mr Eager had met them with a questioning eye. Charlotte had repulsed him with much small talk. Mr Emerson, seeking his son, was told whereabouts to find him. Mr Beebe, who wore the heated aspect of a neutral, was bidden to collect the factions for the return home. There was a general sense of groping and bewilderment. Pan had been amongst them—not the great god Pan, who has been buried these two thousand years, but the little god Pan, who presides over social contretemps and unsuccessful picnics. Mr Beebe had lost every one, and had consumed in solitude the tea-basket which he had brought up as a pleasant surprise. Miss Lavish had lost Miss Bartlett. Lucy had lost Mr Eager. Mr Emerson had lost George. Miss Bartlett had lost a mackintosh square. Phaethon had lost the game.

That last fact was undeniable. He climbed on to the box shivering, with his collar up, prophesying the swift approach of bad weather.

'Let us go immediately,' he told them. 'The signorino will walk.'

'All the way? He will be hours,' said Mr Beebe.

'Apparently. I told him it was unwise.' He would look no one in the face; perhaps defeat was particularly mortifying for him. He alone had played skilfully, using the whole of his instinct, while the others had used scraps of their intelligence. He alone had divined what things were, and what he wished them to be. He alone had interpreted the message that Lucy had received five days before from the lips of a dying man. Persephone, who spends half her life in the grave—she could interpret it also. Not so these English. They gain knowledge slowly, and perhaps too late.

The thoughts of a cab-driver, however just, seldom affect the lives of his employers. He was the most competent of Miss Bartlett's opponents, but infinitely the least dangerous. Once back in the town, he and his insight and his knowledge would trouble English ladies no more. Of course, it was most unpleasant; she had seen his black head in the bushes; he might make a tavern story out of it. But after all, what have we to do with taverns? Real menace belongs to the drawing-room. It was of drawing-room people that Miss Bartlett thought as she journeyed downwards towards the fading sun. Lucy sat beside her; Mr Eager sat opposite, trying to catch her eye: he was vaguely suspicious. They spoke of Alessio Baldovinetti.

Rain and darkness came on together. The two ladies huddled together under an inadequate parasol. There was a lightning flash, and Miss Lavish, who was nervous, screamed from the carriage in front. At the next flash, Lucy screamed also. Mr Eager addressed her professionally.

'Courage, Miss Honeychurch, courage and faith, If I might say so, there is something almost blasphemous in this horror of the elements. Are we seriously to suppose that all these clouds, all this immense electrical display, is simply called into existence to extinguish you or me?'

'No—of course—'

'Even from the scientific standpoint the chances against our being struck are enormous. The steel knives, the only articles which might attract the current, are in the other carriage. And, in any case, we are infinitely safer than if we were walking. Courage—courage and faith.'

Under the rug, Lucy felt the kindly pressure of her cousin's hand. At times our need for a sympathetic gesture is so great that we care not what exactly it signifies or how much we may have to pay for it afterwards. Miss Bartlett, by this timely exercise of her muscles, gained more than she would have got in hours of preaching or cross-examination.

She renewed it when the two carriages stopped, half into Florence.

'Mr Eager!' called Mr Beebe. 'We want your assistance. Will you interpret for us?'

'George!' cried Mr Emerson. 'Ask your driver which way George went. The boy may lose his way. He may be killed.'

'Go, Mr Eager,' said Miss Bartlett. 'No, don't ask our driver; our driver is no help. Go and support poor Mr Beebe; he is nearly demented.'

'He may be killed!' cried the old man. 'He may be killed!'

'Typical behaviour,' said the chaplain, as he quitted the carriage. 'In the presence of reality that kind of person invariably breaks down.'

'What does he know?' whispered Lucy as soon as they were alone.

'Charlotte, how much does Mr Eager know?'

'Nothing, dearest; he knows nothing. But'–she pointed at the driver–'*he* knows everything. Dearest, had we better? Shall I?' She took out her purse. 'It is dreadful to be entangled with low-class people. He saw it all.' Tapping Phaethon's back with her guide-book, she said, 'Silenzio!' and offered him a franc.

'Va bene,' he replied, and accepted it. As well this ending to his day as any. But Lucy, a mortal maid, was disappointed in him.

There was an explosion up the road. The storm had struck the overhead wire of the tramline, and one of the great supports had fallen. If they had not stopped perhaps they might have been hurt. They chose to regard it as a miraculous preservation, and the floods of love and sincerity, which might fructify every hour of life, burst forth in tumult. They descended from the carriages; they embraced each other. It was as joyful to be forgiven past unworthinesses as to forgive them. For a moment they realized vast possibilities of good.

The older people recovered quickly. In the very height of their emotion they knew it to be unmanly or unladylike. Miss Lavish calculated that, even if they had continued, they would not have been caught in the accident. Mr Eager mumbled a temperate prayer. But the drivers, through miles of dark squalid road, poured out their souls to the dryads and the saints, and Lucy poured out hers to her cousin.

'Charlotte, dear Charlotte, kiss me. Kiss me again. Only you can understand me. You warned me to be careful. And I–I thought I was developing.'

'Do not cry, dearest. Take your time.'

'I have been obstinate and silly–worse than you know, far worse. Once by the river— Oh, but he isn't killed–he wouldn't be killed, would he!'

The thought disturbed her repentance. As a matter of fact, the storm was worst along the road; but she had been near danger, and so she thought it must be near to every one.

'I trust not. One would always pray against that.'

'He is really–I think he was taken by surprise, just as I was before. But this time I'm not to blame; I do want you to believe that. I simply slipped into those violets. No, I want to be really truthful. I am a little to blame. I had silly thoughts. The sky, you know, was gold, and the ground all blue, and for a moment he looked like some one in a book.'

'In a book?'

'Heroes–gods–the nonsense of schoolgirls.'

'And then?'

'But, Charlotte, you know what happened then.'

Miss Bartlett was silent. Indeed, she had little more to learn. With a certain amount of insight she drew her young cousin affectionately to her. All the way back Lucy's body was shaken by deep sighs, which nothing could repress.

'I want to be truthful,' she whispered. 'It is so hard to be absolutely truthful.'

'Don't be troubled, dearest. Wait till you are calmer. We will talk it over before bed-time in my room.'

So they re-entered the city with hands clasped. It was a shock to the girl to find how far emotion had ebbed in others. The storm had ceased, and Mr Emerson was easier about his son. Mr Beebe had regained good humour, and Mr Eager was already snubbing Miss Lavish. Charlotte alone she was sure of—Charlotte, whose exterior concealed so much insight and love.

The luxury of self-exposure kept her almost happy through the long evening. She thought not so much of what had happened as of how she should describe it. All her sensations, her spasms of courage, her moments of unreasonable joy, her mysterious discontent, should be carefully laid before her cousin. And together in divine confidence they would disentangle and interpret them all.

'At last,' thought she, ' I shall understand myself. I shan't again be troubled by things that come out of nothing, and mean I don't know what.'

Miss Alan asked her to play. She refused vehemently. Music seemed to her the employment of a child. She sat close to her cousin, who, with commendable patience, was listening to a long story about lost luggage. When it was over she capped it by a story of her own. Lucy became rather hysterical with the delay. In vain she tried to check, or at all events to accelerate, the tale. It was not till a late hour that Miss Bartlett had recovered her luggage and could say in her usual tone of gentle reproach: 'Well, dear, I at all events am ready for Bedfordshire. Come into my room, and I will give a good brush to your hair.'

With some solemnity the door was shut, and a cane chair placed for the girl. Then Miss Bartlett said:

'So what is to be done?'

She was unprepared for the question. It had not occurred to her that she would have to do anything. A detailed exhibition of her emotions was all that she had counted upon.

'What is to be done? A point, dearest, which you alone can settle.'

The rain was streaming down the black windows, and the great room felt damp and chilly. One candle burnt trembling on the chest of drawers close to Miss Bartlett's toque, which cast monstrous and fantastic shadows on the bolted door. A tram roared by in the dark, and Lucy felt unaccountably sad, though she had long since dried her eyes. She lifted them to the ceiling, where the griffins and bassoons were colourless and vague, the very ghosts of joy.

'It has been raining for nearly four hours,' she said at last.

Miss Bartlett ignored the remark.

'How do you propose to silence him?'

'The driver?'

'My dear girl, no; Mr George Emerson.'

Lucy began to pace up and down the room.

'I don't understand,' she said at last.

She understood very well, but she no longer wished to be absolutely truthful.

'How are you going to stop him talking about it?'

'I have a feeling that talk is a thing he will never do.'

'I, too, intend to judge him charitably. But unfortunately I have met the type before. They seldom keep their exploits to themselves.'

'Exploits?' cried Lucy, wincing under the horrible plural.

'My poor dear, did you suppose that this was his first? Come here and listen to me. I am only gathering it from his own remarks. Do you remember that day at lunch when he argued with Miss Alan that liking one person is an extra reason for liking another?'

'Yes,' said Lucy, whom at the time the argument had pleased.

'Well, I am no prude. There is no need to call him a wicked young man, but obviously he is thoroughly unrefined. Let us put it down to his deplorable antecedents and education, if you wish. But we are no further on with our question. What do you propose to do?'

An idea rushed across Lucy's brain, which, had she thought of it sooner and made it part of her, might have proved victorious.

'I propose to speak to him,' said she.

Miss Bartlett uttered a cry of genuine alarm.

'You see, Charlotte, your kindness—I shall never forget it. But—as you said—it is my affair. Mine and his.'

And you are going to *implore* him, to *beg* him to keep silence?'

'Certainly not. There would be no difficulty. Whatever you ask him he answers, yes or no; then it is over. I have been frightened of him. But now I am not one little bit.'

'But we fear him for you, dear. You are so young and inexperienced, you have lived among such nice people, that you cannot realize what men can be—how they can take a brutal pleasure in insulting a woman whom her sex does not protect and rally round. This afternoon, for example, if I had not arrived, what would have happened?'

'I can't think,' said Lucy gravely.

Something in her voice made Miss Bartlett repeat her question, intoning it more vigorously.

'What would have happened if I hadn't arrived?'

'I can't think,' said Lucy again.

'When he insulted you, how would you have replied?'

'I hadn't time to think. You came.'

'Yes, but won't you tell me now what you would have done?'

'I should have—' She checked herself, and broke the sentence off. She went up to the dripping window and strained her eyes into the darkness. She could not think what she would have done.

'Come away from the window, dear,' said Miss Bartlett. 'You will be seen from the road.'

Lucy obeyed. She was in her cousin's power. She could not modulate out of the key of self-abasement in which she had started. Neither of them referred again to her suggestion that she should speak to George and settle the matter, whatever it was, with him.

Miss Bartlett became plaintive.

'Oh, for a real man! We are only two women, you and I. Mr Beebe is hopeless. There is Mr Eager, but you do not trust him. Oh, for your brother! He is young, but I know that his sister's insult would rouse in him a very lion. Thank God, chivalry is not yet dead. There are still left some men who can reverence woman.

As she spoke, she pulled off her rings, of which she wore several, and ranged them upon the pin-cushion. Then she blew into her gloves and said:

'It will be a push to catch the morning train, but we must try.'

'What train?'

'The train to Rome.' She looked at her gloves critically.

The girl received the announcement as easily as it had been given.

'When does the train to Rome go?'

'At eight.'

'Signora Bertolini would be upset.'

'We must face that,' said Miss Bartlett, not liking to say that she had given notice already.

'She will make us pay for a whole week's pension.'

'I expect she will. However, we shall be much more comfortable at the Vyses' hotel. Isn't afternoon tea given there for nothing?'

'Yes, but they pay extra for wine.'

After this remark she remained motionless and silent. To her tired eyes Charlotte throbbed and swelled like a ghostly figure in a dream.

They began to sort their clothes for packing, for there was no time to lose, if they were to catch the train to Rome. Lucy, when admonished, began to move to and fro between the rooms, more conscious of the discomforts of packing by candle-light than of a subtler ill. Charlotte, who was practical without ability, knelt by the side of an empty trunk, vainly endeavouring to pave it with books of varying thickness and size. She gave two or three sighs, for the stooping posture hurt her back, and, for all her diplomacy, she felt that she was growing old. The girl heard her as she entered the room, and was seized with one of those emotional impulses to which she could never attribute a cause. She only felt that the candle would burn better, the packing go easier, the world be happier, if she could give and receive some human love. The impulse had come before to-day, but never so strongly. She knelt down by her cousin's side and took her in her arms.

Miss Bartlett returned the embrace with tenderness and warmth. But she was not a stupid woman, and she knew perfectly well that Lucy did not love her, but needed her to love. For it was in ominous tones that she said, after a long pause:

'Dearest Lucy, how will you ever forgive me?'

Lucy was on her guard at once, knowing by bitter experience what forgiving Miss Bartlett meant. Her emotion relaxed; she modified her embrace a little, and she said:

'Charlotte dear, what to you mean? As if I have anything to forgive!'

'You have a great deal, and I have a very great deal to forgive myself, too. I know well how much I vex you at every turn.'

'But no—'

Miss Bartlett assumed her favourite rôle, that of the prematurely aged martyr.

'Ah, but yes! I feel that our tour together is hardly the success I had hoped. I might have known it would not do. You want some one younger and stronger and more in sympathy with you. I am too uninteresting and old-fashioned—only fit to pack and unpack your things.'

'Please—'

'My only consolation was that you found people more to your taste, and were often able to leave me at home. I had my own poor ideas of what a lady ought to do, but I hope I did not inflict them on you more than was necessary. You had your own way about these rooms, at all events.'

'You mustn't say these things,' said Lucy softly.

She still clung to the hope that she and Charlotte loved each other, heart and soul. They continued to pack in silence.

'I have been a failure,' said Miss Bartlett, as she struggled with the straps of Lucy's trunk instead of strapping her own. 'Failed to make you happy; failed in my duty to your mother. She has been so generous to me; I shall never face her again after this disaster.'

'But mother will understand. It is not your fault, this trouble, and it isn't a disaster either.'

'It is my fault, it is a disaster. She will never forgive me, and rightly. For instance, what right had I to make friends with Miss Lavish?'

'Every right.'

'When I was here for your sake? If I have vexed you it is equally true that I have neglected you. Your mother will see this as clearly as I do, when you tell her.'

Lucy, from a cowardly wish to improve the situation, said:

'Why need mother hear of it?'

'But you tell her everything?'

'I suppose I do generally.'

'I dare not break your confidence. There is something sacred in it. Unless you feel that it is a thing you could not tell her.'

The girl would not be degraded to this.

'Naturally I should have told her. But in case she should blame you in any way, I promise I will not. I am very willing not to. I will never speak of it either to her or to anyone.'

Her promise brought the long-drawn interview to a sudden close. Miss Bartlett pecked her smartly on both cheeks, wished her good-night, and sent her to her own room.

For a moment the original trouble was in the background. George would seem to have behaved like a cad throughout; perhaps that was the view which one would take eventually. At present she neither acquitted nor condemned him; she did not pass judgment. At the moment when she was about to judge him her cousin's voice had intervened, and, ever since, it was Miss Bartlett who had dominated; Miss Bartlett who, even now, could be heard sighing into a crack in the partition wall; Miss Bartlett, who had really been neither pliable nor humble nor inconsistent. She had worked like a great artist; for a time—indeed, for years—she had been meaningless, but at the end there was presented to the girl the complete picture of a cheerless, loveless world in which the young rush to destruction until they learn better—a shame-faced world of precautions and barriers which may avert evil, but which do not seem to bring good, if we may judge from those who have used them most.

Lucy was suffering from the most grievous wrong which this world has yet discovered: diplomatic advantage had been taken of her sincerity, of her craving for sympathy and love. Such a wrong is not easily forgotten. Never again did she expose herself without due consideration and precaution against rebuff. And such a wrong may react disastrously upon the soul.

The door-bell rang, and she started to the shutters. Before she reached them she hesitated, turned, and blew out the candle. Thus it was that, though she saw some one standing in the wet below, he, though he looked up, did not see her.

To reach his room he had to go by hers. She was still dressed. It struck her that she might slip into the passage and just say that she would be gone before he was up, and that their extraordinary intercourse was over.

Whether she would have dared to do this was never proved. At the critical moment Miss Bartlett opened her own door, and her voice said:

'I wish one word with you in the drawing-room, Mr Emerson, please.'

Soon their footsteps returned, and Miss Bartlett said: 'Good night, Mr Emerson.'

His heavy, tired breathing was the only reply; the chaperon had done her work.

Lucy cried aloud: 'It isn't true. It can't all be true. I want not to be muddled. I want to grow older quickly.'

Miss Bartlett tapped on the wall.

'Go to bed at once, dear. You need all the rest you can get.'

In the morning they left for Rome.

Chapter Eight

Medieval

The drawing-room curtains at Windy Corner had been pulled to meet, for the carpet was new and deserved protection from the August sun. They were heavy curtains, reaching almost to the ground, and the light that filtered through them was subdued and varied. A poet–none was present–might have quoted, 'Life like a dome of many coloured glass,' or might have compared the curtains to sluice-gates, lowered against the intolerable tides of heaven. Without was poured a sea of radiance; within, the glory, though visible, was tempered to the capacities of man.

Two pleasant people sat in the room. One–a boy of nineteen–was studying a small manual of anatomy, and peering occasionally at a bone which lay upon the piano. From time to time he bounced in his chair and puffed, and groaned, for the day was hot and the print small, and the human frame fearfully made; and his mother, who was writing a letter, did continually read out to him what she had written. And continually did she rise from her seat and part the curtains so that a rivulet of light fell across the carpet, and make the remark that they were still there.

'Where aren't they?' said the boy, who was Freddy, Lucy's brother. 'I tell you I'm getting fairly sick.'

'For goodness' sake go out of my drawing-room, then!' cried Mrs Honeychurch, who hoped to cure her children of slang by taking it literally.

Freddy did not move or reply.

'I think things are coming to a head,' she observed, rather wanting her son's opinion on the situation if she could obtain it without undue supplication.

'Time they did.'

'I am glad that Cecil is asking her this once more.'

'It's his third go, isn't it?'

'Freddy, I do call the way you talk unkind.'

'I didn't mean to be unkind.' Then he added: 'But I do think Lucy might have got this off her chest in Italy. I don't know how girls manage things, but she can't have said "No" properly before, or she wouldn't have to say it again now. Over the whole thing–I can't explain–I do feel so uncomfortable.'

'Do you indeed, dear? How interesting!'

'I feel—never mind.'

He returned to his work.

'Just listen to what I have written to Mrs Vyse. I said: "Dear Mrs Vyse"—'

'Yes, mother, you told me. A jolly good letter.'

'I said: "Dear Mrs Vyse—Cecil has just asked my permission about it, and I should be delighted, if Lucy wishes it. But—"' She stopped reading. 'I was rather amused at Cecil asking my permission at all. He has always gone in for unconventionality, and parents nowhere, and so forth. When it comes to the point, he can't get on without me.'

'Nor me.'

'You?'

Freddy nodded.

'What do you mean?'

'He asked me for my permission also.'

She exclaimed: 'How very odd of him!'

'Why so?' asked the son and heir. 'Why shouldn't my permission be asked?'

'What do you know about Lucy or girls or anything? Whatever did you say?'

'I said to Cecil, "Take her or leave her; it's no business of mine!"'

'What a helpful answer!' But her own answer, though more normal in its wording, had been to the same effect.

'The bother is this,' began Freddy.

Then he took up his work again, too shy to say what the bother was. Mrs Honeychurch went back to the window.

'Freddy, you must come. There they still are!'

'I don't see you ought to go peeping like that.'

'Peeping like that! Can't I look out of my own window?'

But she returned to the writing-table, observing, as she passed her son, 'Still page 322?' Freddy snorted, and turned over two leaves. For a brief space they were silent. Close by, beyond the curtains, the gentle murmur of a long conversation had never ceased.

'The bother is this: I have put my foot in it with Cecil most awfully.' He gave a nervous gulp. 'Not content with "permission," which I did give—that is to say, I said, "I don't mind"—well, not content with that, he wanted to know whether I wasn't off my head with joy. He practically put it like this: Wasn't it a splendid thing for Lucy and for Windy Corner generally if he married her? And he would have an answer—he said it would strengthen his hand.'

'I hope you gave a careful answer, dear.'

'I answered "No,"' said the boy, grinding his teeth. 'There! Fly into a stew! I can't help it—I had to say it. I had to say no. He ought never to have asked me.'

'Ridiculous child!' cried his mother. 'You think you're so holy and truthful, but really it's only abominable conceit. Do you suppose that a man like Cecil would take the slightest notice of anything you say? I hope he boxed your ears. How dare you say no?'

'Oh, do keep quiet, mother! I had to say no when I couldn't say yes. I tried to laugh as if I didn't mean what I said, and, as Cecil laughed too, and went away, it may be all right. But I feel my foot's in it. Oh, do keep quiet, though, and let a man do some work.'

'No,' said Mrs Honeychurch, with the air of one who had considered the subject. 'I shall not keep quiet. You know all that has passed between them in Rome; you know why he is down here, and yet you deliberately insult him, and try to turn him out of my house.'

'Not a bit!' he pleaded. 'I only let out I didn't like him. I don't hate him, but I don't like him. What I mind is that he'll tell Lucy.'

He glanced at the curtains dismally.

'Well, *I* like him,' said Mrs Honeychurch. 'I know his mother; he's good, he's clever, he's rich, he's well connected— Oh, you needn't kick the piano! He's well connected— I'll say it again if you like: he's well connected.' She paused, as if rehearsing her eulogy, but her face remained dissatisfied. She added: 'And he has beautiful manners.'

'I liked him till just now. I suppose it's having him spoiling Lucy's first week at home; and it's also something that Mr Beebe said, not knowing.'

'Mr Beebe?' said his mother, trying to conceal her interest. 'I don't see how Mr Beebe comes in.'

'You know Mr Beebe's funny way, when you never quite know what he means. He said: "Mr Vyse is an ideal bachelor." I was very cute. I asked him what he meant. He said: "Oh, he's like me–better detached." I couldn't make him say any more, but it set me thinking. Since Cecil has come after Lucy he hasn't been so pleasant, at least–I can't explain.'

'You never can, dear. But I can. You are jealous of Cecil because he may stop Lucy knitting you silk ties.'

The explanation seemed plausible, and Freddy tried to accept it. But at the back of his brain there lurked a dim mistrust. Cecil praised one too much for being athletic. Was that it? Cecil made one talk in his way, instead of letting one talk in one's own way. This tired one. Was that it? And Cecil was the kind of fellow who would never wear another fellow's cap. Unaware of his own profundity, Freddy checked himself. He must be jealous, or he would not dislike a man for such foolish reasons.

'Will this do?' called his mother. '"Dear Mrs Vyse–Cecil has just asked my permission about it, and I should be delighted if Lucy wishes it." Then I put in at the top, "and I have told Lucy so." I must write the letter out again–"and I have told Lucy so. But Lucy seems very uncertain, and in these days young people must decide for themselves." I said that because I didn't want Mrs Vyse to think us old-fashioned. She goes in for lectures and improving her mind, and all the time a thick layer of flue under the beds, and the maids' dirty thumb-marks where you turn on the electric light. She keeps that flat abominably—'

'Suppose Lucy marries Cecil, would she live in a flat, or in the country?'

'Don't interrupt so foolishly. Where was I? Oh yes–"Young people must decide for themselves. I know that Lucy likes your son, because she tells me everything, and she wrote to me from Rome when he asked her first." No,

I'll cross that last bit out–it looks patronizing. I'll stop at "because she tells me everything." Or shall I cross that out, too?'

'Cross it out, too,' said Freddy.

Mrs Honeychurch left it in.

'Then the whole thing runs: "Dear Mrs Vyse–Cecil has just asked my permission about it, and I should be delighted if Lucy wishes it, and I have told Lucy so. But Lucy seems very uncertain, and in these days young people must decide for themselves. I know that Lucy likes your son, because she tells me everything. But I do not know—"'

'Look out!' cried Freddy.

The curtains parted.

Cecil's first movement was one of irritation. He couldn't bear the Honeychurch habit of sitting in the dark to save the furniture. Instinctively he gave the curtains a twitch, and sent them swinging down their poles. Light entered. There was revealed a terrace, such as is owned by many villas, with trees each side of it, and on it a little rustic seat, and two flower-beds. But it was transfigured by the view beyond, for Windy Corner was built on the range that overlooks the Sussex Weald. Lucy, who was in the little seat, seemed on the edge of a green magic carpet which hovered in the air above the tremulous world.

Cecil entered.

Appearing thus late in the story, Cecil must be at once described. He was medieval. Like a Gothic statue. Tall and refined, with shoulders that seemed braced square by an effort of the will, and a head that was tilted a little higher than the usual level of vision, he resembled those fastidious saints who guard the portals of a French cathedral. Well educated, well endowed, and not deficient physically, he remained in the grip of a certain devil whom the modern world knows as self-consciousness, and whom the medieval, with dimmer vision, worshipped as asceticism. A Gothic statue implies celibacy, just as a Greek statue implies fruition, and perhaps this was what Mr Beebe meant. And Freddy, who ignored history and art, perhaps meant the same when he failed to imagine Cecil wearing another fellow's cap.

Mrs Honeychurch left her letter on the writing-table and moved towards her young acquaintance.

'Oh, Cecil!' she exclaimed–'oh, Cecil, do tell me!'

'I promessi sposi,' said he.

They stared at him anxiously.

'She has accepted me,' he said, and the sound of the thing in English made him flush and smile with pleasure, and look more human.

'I am so glad,' said Mrs Honeychurch, while Freddy proffered a hand that was yellow with chemicals. They wished that they also knew Italian, for our phrases of approval and of amazement are so connected with little occasions that we fear to use them on great ones. We are obliged to become vaguely poetic, or to take refuge in Scriptural reminiscences.

'Welcome as one of the family!' said Mrs Honeychurch, waving her hand at the furniture. 'This is indeed a joyous day! I feel sure that you will make dear Lucy happy.'

'I hope so,' replied the young man, shifting his eyes to the ceiling.

'We mothers—' simpered Mrs Honeychurch, and then realized that she was affected, sentimental, bombastic—all the things she hated most. Why could she not be as Freddy, who stood stiff in the middle of the room, looking very cross and almost handsome?

'I say, Lucy!' called Cecil, for conversation seemed to flag.

Lucy rose from the seat. She moved across the lawn and smiled in at them, just as if she was going to ask them to play tennis. Then she saw her brother's face. Her lips parted, and she took him in her arms. He said, 'Steady on!'

'Not a kiss for me?' asked her mother.

Lucy kissed her also.

'Would you take them into the garden and tell Mrs Honeychurch all about it?' Cecil suggested. 'And I'd stop here and tell my mother.'

'We go with Lucy?' said Freddy, as if taking orders.

'Yes, you go with Lucy.'

They passed into the sunlight. Cecil watched them cross the terrace, and descend out of sight by the steps. They would descend—he knew their ways—past the shrubbery, and past the tennis-lawn and the dahlia-bed, until the reached the kitchen-garden, and there, in the presence of the potatoes and the peas, the great event would be discussed.

Smiling indulgently, he lit a cigarette, and rehearsed the events that had led to such a happy conclusion.

He had known Lucy for several years, but only as a commonplace girl who happened to be musical. He could still remember his depression that afternoon at Rome, when she and her terrible cousin fell on him out of the blue, and demanded to be taken to St Peter's. That day she had seemed a typical tourist—shrill, crude, and gaunt with travel. But Italy worked some marvel in her. It gave her light, and—which he held more precious—it gave her shadow. Soon he detected in her a wonderful reticence. She was like a woman of Leonardo da Vinci's, whom we love not so much for herself as for the things that she will not tell us. The things are assuredly not of this life; no woman of Leonardo's could have anything so vulgar as a 'story.' She did develop most wonderfully day by day.

So it happened that from patronizing civility he had slowly passed, if not to passion, at least to a profound uneasiness. Already at Rome he had hinted to her that they might be suitable for each other. It had touched him greatly that she had not broken away at the suggestion. Her refusal had been clear and gentle; after it—as the horrid phrase went—she had been exactly the same to him as before. Three months later, on the margin of Italy, among the flower-clad Alps, he had asked her again in bald, traditional language. She reminded him of a Leonardo more than ever; her sunburnt features were shadowed by fantastic rocks; at his words she had turned and stood between him and the light with immeasurable plains behind her. He walked home with her unashamed, feeling not at all like a rejected suitor. The things that really mattered were unshaken.

So now he had asked her once more, and, clear and gentle as ever, she had accepted him, giving no coy reasons for her delay, but simply saying that she loved him and would do her best to make him happy. His mother, too, would be pleased; she had counselled the step; he must write her a long account.

Glancing at his hand, in case any of Freddy's chemicals had come off on it, he moved to the writing-table. There he saw 'Dear Mrs Vyse,' followed by many erasures. He recoiled without reading any more, and after a little hesitation sat down elsewhere, and pencilled a note on his knee.

Then he lit another cigarette, which did not seem quite as divine as the first, and considered what might be done to make the Windy Corner drawing-room more distinctive. With that outlook it should have been a successful room, but the trail of Tottenham Court Road was upon it; he could almost visualize the motor-vans of Messrs Shoolbred and Messrs Maple arriving at the door and depositing this chair, those varnished book-cases, that writing-table. The table recalled Mrs Honeychurch's letter. He did not want to read that letter—his temptations never lay in that direction; but he worried about it none the less. It was his own fault that she was discussing him with his mother; he had wanted her support in his third attempt to win Lucy; he wanted to feel that others, no matter who they were, agreed with him, and so he had asked their permission. Mrs Honeychurch had been civil, but obtuse in essentials, while as for Freddy—

'He is only a boy,' he reflected. 'I represent all that he despises. Why should he want me for a brother-in-law?'

The Honeychurches were a worthy family, but he began to realize that Lucy was of another clay; and perhaps—he did not put it very definitely—he ought to introduce her into more congenial circles as soon as possible.

'Mr Beebe!' said the maid, and the new rector of Summer Street was shown in; he had at once started on friendly relations, owing to Lucy's praise of him in her letters from Florence.

Cecil greeted him rather critically.

'I've come for tea, Mr Vyse. Do you suppose that I shall get it?'

'I should say so. Food is the thing one does get here— Don't sit in that chair; young Honeychurch has left a bone in it.'

'Pfui!'

'I know,' said Cecil, 'I know. I can't think why Mrs Honeychurch allows it.'

For Cecil considered the bone and the Maple's furniture separately; he did not realize that, taken together, they kindled the room into the life that he desired.

'I've come for tea and for gossip. Isn't this news?'

'News? I don't understand you,' said Cecil. 'News?'

Mr Beebe, whose news was of a very different nature, prattled forward.

'I met Sir Harry Otway as I came up; I have every reason to hope that I am first in the field. He has bought Cissie and Albert from Mr Flack!'

'Has he indeed?' said Cecil, trying to recover himself. Into what a grotesque mistake had he fallen! Was it likely that a clergyman and a gentleman would refer to his engagement in a manner so flippant? But his stiffness remained, and, though he asked who Cissie and Albert might be, he still thought Mr Beebe rather a bounder.

'Unpardonable question! To have stopped a week at Windy Corner and not to have met Cissie and Albert, the semi-detached villas that have been run up opposite the church! I'll set Mrs Honeychurch after you.'

'I'm shockingly stupid over local affairs,' said the young man languidly. 'I can't even remember the difference between a Parish Council and a Local Government Board. Perhaps there is no difference, or perhaps those aren't the right names. I only go into the country to see my friends and to enjoy the scenery. It is very remiss of me. Italy and London are the only places where I don't feel to exist on sufferance.'

Mr Beebe, distressed at this heavy reception of Cissie and Albert, determined to shift the subject.

'Let me see, Mr Vyse—I forget—what is your profession?'

'I have no profession,' said Cecil. 'It is another example of my decadence. My attitude—quite an indefensible one—is that so long as I am no trouble to anyone I have a right to do as I like. I know I ought to be getting money out of people, or devoting myself to things I don't care a straw about, but somehow, I've not been able to begin.'

'You are very fortunate,' said Mr Beebe. 'It is a wonderful opportunity, the possession of leisure.'

His voice was rather parochial, but he did not quite see his way to answering naturally. He felt, as all who have regular occupation must feel, that others should have it also.

'I am glad that you approve. I daren't face the healthy person—for example, Freddy Honeychurch.'

'Oh, Freddy's a good sort, isn't he?'

'Admirable. The sort who has made England what she is.'

Cecil wondered at himself. Why, on this day of all others, was he so hopelessly contrary? He tried to get right by inquiring effusively after Mr Beebe's mother, an old lady for whom he had no particular regard. Then he flattered the clergyman, praised his liberal-mindedness, his enlightened attitude towards philosophy and science.

'Where are the others?' said Mr Beebe at last. 'I insist on extracting tea before evening service.'

'I suppose Anne never told them you were here. In this house one is so coached in the servants the day one arrives. The fault of Anne is that she begs your pardon when she hears you perfectly, and kicks the chair-legs with her feet. The faults of Mary—I forget the faults of Mary, but they are very grave. Shall we look in the garden?'

'I know the faults of Mary. She leaves the dust-pans standing on the stairs.'

'The fault of Euphemia is that she will not, simply will not, chop the suet sufficiently small.'

They both laughed, and things began to go better.

'The faults of Freddy—' Cecil continued.

'Ah, he has too many. No one but his mother can remember the faults of Freddy. Try the faults of Miss Honeychurch; they are not innumerable.'

'She has none,' said the young man, with grave sincerity.

'I quite agree. At present she has none.'

'At present?'

'I'm not cynical. I'm only thinking of my pet theory about Miss Honeychurch. Does it seem reasonable that she should play so wonderfully, and live so quietly? I suspect that one day she will be wonderful in both. The water-tight compartments in her will break down, and music and life will mingle. Then we shall have her heroically good, heroically bad—too heroic, perhaps, to be good or bad.'

Cecil found his companion interesting.

'And at present you think her not wonderful as far as life goes?'

'Well, I must say I've only seen her at Tunbridge Wells, where she was not wonderful, and at Florence. Since I came to Summer Street she has been away. You saw her, didn't you, at Rome and in the Alps. Oh, I forgot; of course, you knew her before. No, she wasn't wonderful in Florence either, but I kept on expecting that she would be.'

'In what way?'

Conversation had become agreeable to them, and they were pacing up and down the terrace.

'I could as easily tell you what tune she'll play next. There was simply the sense that she had found wings, and meant to use them. I can show you a beautiful picture in my Italian diary: Miss Honeychurch as a kite, Miss Bartlett holding the string. Picture number two: the string breaks.'

The sketch was in his diary, but it had been made afterwards, when he viewed things artistically. At the time he had given surreptitious tugs to the string himself.

'But the string never broke?'

'No. I mightn't have seen Miss Honeychurch rise, but I should certainly have heard Miss Bartlett fall.'

'It has broken now,' said the young man in low, vibrating tones.

Immediately he realized that of all the conceited, ludicrous, contemptible ways of announcing an engagement this was the worst. He cursed his love of metaphor; had he suggested that he was a star and that Lucy was soaring up to reach him?

'Broken? What do you mean?'

'I meant,' said Cecil stiffly, 'that she is going to marry me.'

The clergyman was conscious of some bitter disappointment which he could not keep out of his voice.

'I am sorry; I must apologize. I had no idea you were intimate with her, or I should never have talked in this flippant, superficial way. Mr Vyse, you ought to have stopped me.' And down the garden he saw Lucy herself; yes, he was disappointed.

Cecil, who naturally preferred congratulations to apologies, drew down his mouth at the corners. Was this the reception his action would get from the world? Of course, he despised the world as a whole; every thoughtful man should; it is almost a test of refinement. But he was sensitive to the successive particles of it which he encountered.

Occasionally he could be quite crude.

'I am sorry I have given you a shock,' he said dryly. 'I fear that Lucy's choice does not meet with your approval.'

'Not that. But you ought to have stopped me. I know Miss Honeychurch only a little as time goes. Perhaps I oughtn't to have discussed her so freely with anyone; certainly not with you.'

'You are conscious of having said something indiscreet?'

Mr Beebe pulled himself together. Really, Mr Vyse had the art of placing one in the most tiresome positions. He was driven to use the prerogatives of his profession.

'No, I have said nothing indiscreet. I foresaw at Florence that her quiet, uneventful childhood must end, and it has ended. I realized dimly enough that she might take some momentous step. She has taken it. She has learnt—you will let me talk freely, as I have begun freely—she has learnt what it is to love: the greatest lesson, some people will tell you, that our earthly life provides.' It was now time for him to wave his hat at the approaching trio. He did not omit to do so. 'She has learnt through you,' and if his voice was still clerical, it was now also sincere; 'let it be your care that her knowledge is profitable to her.'

'Grazie tante!' said Cecil, who did not like parsons.

'Have you heard?' shouted Mrs Honeychurch as she toiled up the sloping garden. 'Oh, Mr Beebe, have you heard the news?'

Freddy, now full of geniality, whistled the wedding march. Youth seldom criticizes the accomplished fact.

'Indeed I have!' he cried. He looked at Lucy. In her presence he could not act the parson any longer—at all events not without apology. 'Mrs Honeychurch, I'm going to do what I am always supposed to do, but generally I'm too shy. I want to invoke every kind of blessing on them, grave and gay, great and small. I want them all their lives to be supremely good and supremely happy as husband and wife, as father and mother. And now I want my tea.'

'You only asked for it just in time,' the lady retorted. 'How dare you be serious at Windy Corner?'

He took his tone from her. There was no more heavy beneficence, no more attempts to dignify the situation with poetry or the Scriptures. None of them dared or was able to be serious any more.

An engagement is so potent a thing that sooner or later it reduces all who speak of it to this state of cheerful awe. Away from it, in the solitude of their rooms, Mr Beebe, and even Freddy, might again be critical. But in its presence and in the presence of each other they were sincerely hilarious. It has a strange power, for it compels not only the lips, but the very heart. The chief parallel—to compare one great thing with another—is the power over us of a temple of some alien creed. Standing outside, we deride or oppose it, or at the most feel sentimental. Inside, though the saints and gods are not ours, we become true believers, in case any true believer should be present.

So it was that after the gropings and the misgivings of the afternoon they pulled themselves together and settled down to a very pleasant tea-party. If they were hypocrites they did not know it, and their hypocrisy had every chance of setting and of becoming true. Anne, putting down each plate as if it were a wedding present, stimulated them greatly. They could not lag behind that smile of hers which she gave them ere she kicked the drawing-room door. Mr Beebe chirruped. Freddy was at his wittiest, referring to Cecil as the 'Fiasco'—family honoured pun on fiancé. Mrs Honeychurch, amusing and portly, promised well as a mother-in-law. As for Lucy and Cecil, for whom the temple had been built, they also joined in the merry ritual, but waited, as earnest worshippers should, for the disclosure of some holier shrine of joy.

Chapter Nine

Lucy as a Work of Art

A few days after the engagement was announced Mrs Honeychurch made Lucy and her Fiasco come to a little garden-party in the neighbourhood, for naturally she wanted to show people that her daughter was marrying a presentable man.

Cecil was more than presentable; he looked distinguished, and it was very pleasant to see his slim figure keeping step with Lucy, and his long, fair face responding when Lucy spoke to him, People congratulated Mrs Honeychurch, which is, I believe, a social blunder, but it pleased her, and she introduced Cecil rather indiscriminately to some stuffy dowagers.

At tea a misfortune took place: a cup of coffee was upset over Lucy's figured silk, and though Lucy feigned indifference, her mother feigned nothing of the sort, but dragged her indoors to have the frock treated by a sympathetic maid. They were gone some time, and Cecil was left with the dowagers. When they returned he was not as pleasant as he had been.

'Do you go to much of this sort of thing?' he asked when they were driving home.

'Oh, now and then,' said Lucy, who had rather enjoyed herself.

'Is it typical of county society?'

'I suppose so. Mother, would it be?'

'Plenty of society,' said Mrs Honeychurch, who was trying to remember the hang of one of the dresses.

Seeing that her thoughts were elsewhere, Cecil bent towards Lucy and said:

'To me it seemed perfectly appalling, disastrous, portentous.'

'I am so sorry that you were stranded.'

'Not that, but the congratulations. It is so disgusting, the way an engagement is regarded as public property—a kind of waste place where every outsider may shoot his vulgar sentiment. All those old women smirking!'

'One has to go through it, I suppose. They won't notice us so much next time.'

'But my point is that their whole attitude is wrong. An engagement—horrid word in the first place—is a private matter, and should be treated as such.'

Yet the smirking old women, however wrong individually, were racially correct. The spirit of the generations had smiled through them, rejoicing in the engagement of Cecil and Lucy because it promised the continuance of life on earth. To Cecil and Lucy it promised something quite different—personal love. Hence Cecil's irritation and Lucy's belief that his irritation was just.

'How tiresome!' she said. 'Couldn't you have escaped to tennis?'

'I don't play tennis—at least, not in public. The neighbourhood is deprived of the romance of me being athletic. Such romance as I have is that of the Inglese Italianato.'

'Inglese Italianato?'

'E un diavolo incarnato! You know the proverb?'

She did not. Nor did it seem applicable to a young man who had spent a quiet winter in Rome with his mother. But Cecil, since his engagement, had taken to affect a cosmopolitan naughtiness which he was far from possessing.

'Well,' said he, 'I cannot help it if they do disapprove of me. There are certain irremovable barriers between myself and them, and I must accept them.'

'We all have our limitations, I suppose,' said wise Lucy.

'Sometimes they are forced on us, though,' said Cecil, who saw from her remark that she did not quite understand his position.

'How?'

'It makes a difference, doesn't it, whether we fence ourselves in, or whether we are fenced out by the barriers of others?'

She thought a moment, and agreed that it did make a difference.

'Difference?' cried Mrs Honeychurch, suddenly alert. 'I don't see any difference. Fences are fences, especially when they are in the same place.'

'We were speaking of motives,' said Cecil, on whom the interruption jarred.

'My dear Cecil, look here.' She spread out her knees and perched her card-case on her lap. 'This is me. That's Windy Corner. The rest of the pattern is the other people. Motives are all very well, but the fence comes here.'

'We weren't talking of real fences,' said Lucy, laughing.

'Oh, I see, dear—poetry.'

She leant placidly back. Cecil wondered why Lucy had been amused.

'I tell you who has no "fences," as you call them,' she said, 'and that's Mr Beebe.'

'A parson fenceless would mean a parson defenceless.'

Lucy was slow to follow what people said, but quick enough to detect what they meant. She missed Cecil's epigram, but grasped the feeling that prompted it.

'Don't you like Mr Beebe?' she asked thoughtfully.

'I never said so!' he cried. 'I consider him far above the average. I only denied—' And he swept off on the subject of fences again, and was brilliant.

'Now, a clergyman that I do hate,' said she, wanting to say something sympathetic, 'a clergyman that does have fences, and the most dreadful ones, is Mr Eager, the English chaplain at Florence. He was truly insincere—not merely the manner unfortunate. He was a snob, and so conceited, and he did say such unkind things.'

'What sort of things?'

'There was an old man at the Bertolini whom he said had murdered his wife.'

'Perhaps he had.'

'Why, no.'

'Why "no"?'

'He was such a nice old man, I'm sure.'

Cecil laughed at her feminine inconsequence.

'Well, I did try to sift the thing. Mr Eager would never come to the point. He prefers it vague—said the old man had "practically" murdered his wife—had murdered her in the sight of God.'

'Hush, dear!' said Mrs Honeychurch absently.

'But isn't it intolerable that a person whom we're told to imitate should go round spreading slander? It was, I believe, chiefly owing to him that the old man was dropped. People pretended he was vulgar, but he certainly wasn't that.'

'Poor old man! What was his name?'

'Harris,' said Lucy glibly.

'Let's hope that Mrs Harris there warn't no sich person,' said her mother. Cecil nodded intelligently.

'Isn't Mr Eager a parson of the cultured type?' he asked.

'I don't know. I hate him. I've heard him lecture on Giotto. I hate him. Nothing can hide a petty nature. I *hate* him!'

'My goodness gracious me, child!' said Mrs Honeychurch. 'You'll blow my head off! Whatever is there to shout over? I forbid you and Cecil to hate any more clergymen.'

He smiled. There was indeed something rather incongruous in Lucy's moral outburst over Mr Eager. It was as if one should see the Leonardo on the ceiling of the Sistine. He longed to hint to her that not here lay her vocation; that a woman's power and charm reside in mystery, not in muscular rant. But possibly rant is a sign of vitality: it mars the beautiful creature, but shows that she is alive. After a moment, he contemplated her flushed face and excited gestures with a certain approval. He forebore to repress the sources of youth.

Nature—simplest of topics, he thought—lay around them. He praised the pine-woods, the deep lakes of bracken, the crimson leaves that spotted the hurt-bushes, the serviceable beauty of the turnpike road. The outdoor world was not very familiar to him, and occasionally he went wrong in a question of fact. Mrs Honeychurch's mouth twitched when he spoke of the perpetual green of the larch.

'I count myself a lucky person,' he concluded. 'When I'm in London I feel I could never live out of it. When I'm in the country I feel the same about the country. After all, I do believe that birds and trees and the sky are the most wonderful things in life, and that the people who live amongst them must be the best. It's true that in nine cases out of ten they don't seem to notice anything. The country gentleman and the country labourer are each in their way the most depressing of companions. Yet they may have a tacit sympathy with the workings of Nature which is denied to us of the town. Do you feel that, Mrs Honeychurch?'

Mrs Honeychurch started and smiled. She had not been attending. Cecil, who was rather crushed on the front seat of the victoria, felt irritable, and determined not to say anything interesting again.

Lucy had not attended either. Her brow was wrinkled, and she still looked furiously cross—the result, he conluded, of too much moral gymnastics. It was sad to see her thus blind to the beauties of an August wood.

'"Come down, O maid, from yonder mountain height,"' he quoted, and touched her knee with his own.

She flushed again and said: 'What height?'

> 'Come down, O maid, from yonder mountain height,
> What pleasure lives in height (the shepherd sang),
> In height and in the splendour of the hills?

Let us take Mrs Honeychurch's advice and hate clergymen no more. What's this place?'

'Summer Street, of course,' said Lucy, and roused herself.

The woods had opened to leave space for a sloping triangular meadow. Pretty cottages lined it on two sides, and the upper and third side was occupied by a new stone church, expensively simple, with a charming shingled spire. Mr Beebe's house was near the church. In height it scarcely exceeded the cottages. Some great mansions were at hand, but they were hidden in the trees. The scene suggested a Swiss Alp rather than the shrine and centre of a leisured world, and was only marred by two ugly little villas—the villas that had competed with Cecil's engagement, having been acquired by Sir Harry Otway the very afternoon that Lucy had been acquired by him.

'Cissie' was the name of one of these villas, 'Albert' of the other. These titles were not only picked out in shaded Gothic on the garden gates, but appeared a second time on the porches, where they followed the semicircular curve of the entrance arch in block capitals. Albert was inhabited. His tortured garden was bright with geraniums and lobelias and polished shells. His little windows were chastely swathed in Nottingham lace. Cissie was to let. Three notice-boards, belonging to Dorking agents, lolled on her fence and announced the not surprising fact. Her paths were already weedy; her pocket-handkerchief of a lawn was yellow with dandelions.

'The place is ruined!' said the ladies mechanically. 'Summer Street will never be the same again.'

As the carriage passed, Cissie's door opened, and a gentleman came out of her.

'Stop!' cried Mrs Honeychurch, touching the coachman with her parasol. 'Here's Sir Harry. Now we shall know. Sir Harry, pull those things down at once!'

Sir Harry Otway—who need not be described—came to the carriage and said:

'Mrs Honeychurch, I meant to. I can't, I really can't turn out Miss Flack.'

'Am I not always right? She ought to have gone before the contract was signed. Does she still live rent free, as she did in her nephew's time?'

'But what can I do?' He lowered his voice. 'An old lady, so very vulgar, and almost bedridden.'

'Turn her out,' said Cecil bravely.

Sir Harry sighed, and looked at the villas mournfully. He had had full warning of Mr Flack's intentions, and might have bought the plot before building commenced; but he was apathetic and dilatory. He had known Summer Street for so many years that he could not imagine it being spoilt. Not till Mrs Flack had laid the foundation stone, and the apparition of red and cream brick began to rise, did he take alarm. He called on Mr Flack, the local builder—a most reasonable and respectful man—who agreed that tiles would have made a more artistic roof, but pointed out that slates were cheaper. He ventured to differ, however, about the Corinthian columns which were to cling like leeches to the frames of the bow-windows, saying that, for his part, he liked to relieve the façade by a bit of decoration. Sir Harry hinted that a column, if possible, should be structural as well as decorative. Mr Flack replied that all the columns had been ordered, adding, 'and all the capitals different—one with dragons in the foliage, another approaching to the Ionian style, another introducing Mrs Flack's initials—every one different.' For he had read his Ruskin. He built his villas according to his desire; and not till he had inserted an immovable aunt into one of them did Sir Harry buy.

This futile and unprofitable transaction filled the knight with sadness as he leant on Mrs Honeychurch's carriage. He had failed in his duties to the country-side, and the country-side was laughing at him as well. He had spent money, and yet Summer Street was spoilt as much as ever. All he could do now was to find a desirable tenant for Cissie—some one really desirable.

'The rent is absurdly low,' he told them, 'and perhaps I am an easy landlord. But it is such an awkward size. It is too large for the peasant class, and too small for anyone the least like ourselves.'

Cecil had been hesitating whether he should despise the villas or despise Sir Harry for despising them. The latter impulse seemed the more fruitful.

'You ought to find a tenant at once,' he said maliciously. 'It would be a perfect paradise for a bank clerk.'

'Exactly!' said Sir Harry excitedly. 'That is exactly what I fear, Mr Vyse. It will attract the wrong type of people. The train service has improved—a fatal improvement, to my mind. And what are five miles from a station in these days of bicycles?'

'Rather a strenuous clerk it would be,' said Lucy.

Cecil, who had his full share of medieval mischievousness, replied that the physique of the lower middle classes was improving at a most appalling rate. She saw that he was laughing at their harmless neighbour, and roused herself to stop him.

'Sir Harry!' she exclaimed, 'I have an idea. How would you like spinsters?'

'My dear Lucy, it would be splendid. Do you know any such?'

'Yes; I met them abroad.'

'Gentlewomen?' he asked tentatively.

'Yes, indeed, and at the present moment homeless. I heard from them last week. Miss Teresa and Miss Catharine Alan. I'm really not joking. They are quite the right people. Mr Beebe knows them, too. May I tell them to write to you?'

'Indeed you may!' he cried. 'Here we are with the difficulty solved already. How delightful it is! Extra facilities—please tell them they shall have extra facilities, for I shall have no agents' fees. Oh, the agents! The appalling people they have sent me! One woman, when I wrote—a tactful letter, you know—asking her to explain her social position to me, replied that she would pay the rent in advance. As if one cares about that! And several references I took up were most unsatisfactory—people swindlers, or not respectable. And oh, the deceit! I have seen a good deal of the seamy side this last week. The deceit of the most promising people! My dear Lucy, the deceit!'

She nodded.

'My advice,' put in Mrs Honeychurch, 'is to have nothing to do with Lucy and her decayed gentlewomen at all. I know the type. Preserve me from people who have seen better days, and bring heirlooms with them that make the house smell stuffy. It's a sad thing, but I'd far rather let to some one who is going up in the world than to some one who has come down.'

'I think I follow you,' said Sir Harry; 'but it is, as you say, a very sad thing.'

'The Miss Alans aren't that!' cried Lucy.

'Yes, they are!' said Cecil. 'I haven't met them, but I should say they were a highly unsuitable addition to the neighbourhood.'

'Don't listen to him, Sir Harry—he's tiresome.'

'It's I who am tiresome,' he replied. 'I oughtn't to come with my troubles to young people. But really I am so worried, and Lady Otway will only say that I cannot be too careful, which is quite true, but no real help.'

'Then may I write to my Miss Alans?'

'Please!' he cried.

But his eye wavered when Mrs Honeychurch exclaimed:

'Beware! They are certain to have canaries. Sir Harry, beware of canaries: they spit the seed out through the bars of the cages, and then the mice come. Beware of women altogether. Only let to a man.'

'Really—' he murmured gallantly, though he saw the wisdom of her remark.

'Men don't gossip over tea-cups. If they get drunk, there's an end of them—they lie down comfortably, and sleep it off. If they're vulgar, they somehow keep it to themselves. It doesn't spread so. Give me a man—of course, provided he's clean.'

Sir Harry blushed. Neither he nor Cecil enjoyed these open compliments to their sex. Even the exclusion of the dirty did not leave them much distinction. He suggested that Mrs Honeychurch, if she had time, should descend from the carriage and inspect Cissie for herself. She was delighted. Nature had intended her to be poor and to live in such a house. Domestic arrangements always attracted her, especially when they were on a small scale.

Cecil pulled Lucy back as she followed her mother.

'Mrs Honeychurch,' he said, 'what if we two walk home and leave you?'

'Certainly!' was her cordial reply.

Sir Harry likewise seemed almost too glad to get rid of them. He beamed at them knowingly, said, 'Aha! young people, young people, young people!' and then hastened to unlock the house.

'Hopeless vulgarian!' exclaimed Cecil, almost before they were out of earshot.

'Oh, Cecil!'

'I can't help it. It would be wrong not to loathe that man.'

'He isn't clever, but really he is nice.'

'No, Lucy; he stands for all that is bad in country life. In London he would keep his place. He would belong to a brainless club, and his wife would give brainless dinner-parties. But down here he acts the little god with his gentility, and his patronage, and his sham æsthetics, and every one—even your mother—is taken in.'

'All that you say is quite true,' said Lucy, though she felt discouraged. 'I wonder whether—whether it matters so very much.'

'It matters supremely. Sir Harry is the essence of that garden-party. Oh, goodness, how cross I feel! How I do hope he'll get some vulgar tenant in that villa—some woman so really vulgar that he'll notice it. *Gentlefolks!* Ugh! with his bald head and retreating chin! But let's forget him.'

This Lucy was glad enough to do. If Cecil disliked Sir Harry Otway and Mr Beebe, what guarantee was there that the people who really mattered to her would escape? For instance, Freddy. Freddy was neither clever, nor subtle, nor beautiful, and what prevented Cecil from saying, any minute, 'It would be wrong not to loathe Freddy'? And what would she reply? Further than Freddy she did not go, but he gave her anxiety enough. She could only assure herself that Cecil had known Freddy some time, and that they had always got on pleasantly, except, perhaps, during the last few days, which was an accident, perhaps.

'Which way shall we go?' she asked him.

Nature—simplest of topics, she thought—was around them. Summer Street lay deep in the woods, and she had stopped where a footpath diverged from the highroad.

'Are there two ways?'

'Perhaps the road is more sensible, as we're got up smart.'

'I'd rather go through the wood,' said Cecil, with that subdued irritation that she had noticed in him all the afternoon. 'Why is it, Lucy, that you always say the road? Do you know that you have never once been with me in the fields or the wood since we were engaged?'

'Haven't I? The wood, then,' said Lucy, startled at his queerness, but pretty sure that he would explain later; it was not his habit to leave her in doubt as to his meaning.

She led the way into the whispering pines, and sure enough he did explain before they had gone a dozen yards.

'I had got an idea—I dare say wrongly—that you feel more at home with me in a room.'

'A room?' she echoed, hopelessly bewildered.

'Yes. Or, at the most, in a garden, or on a road. Never in the real country like this.'

'Oh, Cecil, whatever do you mean? I have never felt anything of the sort. You talk as if I was a kind of poetess sort of person.'

'I don't know that you aren't. I connect you with a view—a certain type of view. Why shouldn't you connect me with a room?'

She reflected a moment, and then said, laughing:

'Do you know that you're right? I do. I must be a poetess after all. When I think of you it's always as in a room. How funny!'

To her surprise, he seemed annoyed.

'A drawing-room, pray? With no view?'

'Yes, with no view, I fancy. Why not?'

'I'd rather,' he said reproachfully, 'that you connected me with the open air.'

She said again, 'Oh, Cecil, whatever do you mean?'

As no explanation was forthcoming, she shook off the subject as too difficult for a girl, and led him farther into the wood, pausing every now and then at some particularly beautiful or familiar combination of the trees. She had known the wood between Summer Street and Windy Corner ever since she could walk alone; she had played at losing Freddy in it, when Freddy was a purple-faced baby; and though she had now been to Italy, it had lost none of its charm.

Presently they came to a little clearing among the pines—another tiny green alp, solitary this time, and holding in its bosom a shallow pool.

She exclaimed, 'The Sacred Lake!'

'Why do you call it that?'

'I can't remember why. I suppose it comes out of some book. It's only a puddle now, but you see that stream going through it? Well, a good deal of water comes down after heavy rains, and can't get away at once, and the pool becomes quite large and beautiful. Then Freddy used to bathe there. He is very fond of it.'

'And you?'

He meant, 'Are you fond of it?' But she answered dreamily, 'I bathed here, too, till I was found out. Then there was a row.'

At another time he might have been shocked, for he had depths of prudishness within him. But now, with his momentary cult of the fresh air,

he was delighted at her admirable simplicity. He looked at her as she stood
by the pool's edge. She was got up smart, as she phrased it, and she reminded
him of some brilliant flower that has no leaves of its own, but blooms
abruptly out of a world of green.

'Who found you out?'

'Charlotte,' she murmured. 'She was stopping with us. Charlotte
—Charlotte.'

'Poor girl!'

She smiled gravely. A certain scheme, from which hitherto he had shrank,
now appeared practical.

'Lucy!'

'Yes, I suppose we ought to be going,' was her reply.

'Lucy, I want to ask something of you that I have never asked before.'

At the serious note in his voice she stepped frankly and kindly towards
him.

'What, Cecil?'

'Hitherto never—not even that day on the lawn when you agreed to marry
me—'

He became self-conscious and kept glancing round to see if they were
observed. His courage had gone.

'Yes?'

'Up to now I have never kissed you.'

She was as scarlet as if he had put the thing most indelicately.

'No—more you have,' she stammered.

'Then I ask you—may I now?'

'Of course you may, Cecil. You might before. I can't run at you, you
know.'

At that supreme moment he was conscious of nothing but absurdities. Her
reply was inadequate. She gave such a business-like lift to her veil. As he
approached her he found time to wish that he could recoil. As he touched
her, his gold pince-nez became dislodged and was flattened between them.

Such was the embrace. He considered, with truth, that it had been a
failure. Passion should believe itself irresistible. It should forget civility and
consideration and all the other curses of a refined nature. Above all, it should
never ask for leave where there is a right of way. Why could he not do as any
labourer or navvy—nay, as any young man behind the counter would have
done? He recast the scene. Lucy was standing flower-like by the water; he
rushed up and took her in his arms; she rebuked him, permitted him, and
revered him ever after for his manliness. For he believed that woman revere
men for their manliness.

They left the pool in silence, after this one salutation. He waited for her to
make some remark which should show him her inmost thoughts. At last she
spoke, and with fitting gravity.

'Emerson the name was, not Harris.'

'What name?'

'The old man's.'

'What old man?'

'That old man I told you about. The one Mr Eager was so unkind to.'

He could not know that this was the most intimate conversation they had ever had.

Chapter Ten

Cecil as a Humorist

The society out of which Cecil proposed to rescue Lucy was perhaps no very splendid affair, yet it was more splendid than her antecedents entitled her to. Her father, a prosperous local solicitor, had built Windy Corner as a speculation at the time the district was opening up, and, falling in love with his own creation, had ended by living there himself. Soon after his marriage, the social atmosphere began to alter. Other houses were built on the brow of that steep southern slope, and others, again, among the pine-trees behind, and northward on the chalk barrier of the downs. Most of these houses were larger than Windy Corner, and were filled by people who came, not from the district, but from London, and who mistook the Honeychurches for the remnants of an indigenous aristocracy. He was inclined to be frightened, but his wife accepted the situation without either pride or humility. 'I cannot think what people are doing,' she would say, 'but it is extremely fortunate for the children.' She called everywhere; her calls were returned with enthusiasm, and by the time people found out that she was not exactly of their *milieu*, they liked her, and it did not seem to matter. When Mr Honeychurch died, he had the satisfaction—which few honest solicitors despise—of leaving his family rooted in the best society obtainable.

The best obtainable. Certainly many of the immigrants were rather dull, and Lucy realized this more vividly since her return from Italy. Hitherto she had accepted their ideals without questioning—their kindly affluence, their inexplosive religion, their dislike of paper-bags, orange-peel, and broken bottles. A Radical out and out, she learnt to speak with horror of Suburbia. Life, so far as she troubled to conceive it, was a circle of rich, pleasant people, with identical interests and identical foes. In this circle one thought, married, and died. Outside, it were poverty and vulgarity, for ever trying to enter, just as the London fog tries to enter the pine-woods, pouring through the gaps in the northern hills. But in Italy, where anyone who chooses may warm himself in equality, as in the sun, this conception of life vanished. Her senses expanded; she felt that there was no one whom she might not get to like, that social barriers were irremovable, doubtless, but not particularly high. You jump over them just as you jump into a peasant's olive-yard in the Apennines, and he is glad to see you. She returned with new eyes.

So did Cecil; but Italy had quickened Cecil, not to tolerance, but to irritation. He saw that the local society was narrow, but, instead of saying. 'Does this very much matter?' he rebelled, and tried to substitute for it the society he called broad. He did not realize that Lucy had consecrated her environment by the thousand little civilities that create a tenderness in time, and that though her eyes saw its defects, her heart refused to despise it entirely. Nor did he realize a more important point—that if she was too great for this society, she was too great for all society, and had reached the stage where personal intercourse would alone satisfy her. A rebel she was, but not of the kind he understood—a rebel who desired, not a wider dwelling-room, but equality beside the man she loved. For Italy was offering her the most priceless of all possessions—her own soul.

Playing bumble-puppy with Minnie Beebe, niece to the rector, and aged thirteen—an ancient and most honourable game, which consists in striking tennis-balls high into the air, so that they fall over the net and immoderately bounce; some hit Mrs Honeychurch; others are lost. The sentence is confused, but the better illustrates Lucy's state of mind, for she was trying to talk to Mr Beebe at the same time.

'Oh, it has been such a nuisance—first he, then they—no one knowing what they wanted, and every one so tiresome.'

'But they really are coming now,' said Mr Beebe. 'I wrote to Miss Teresa a few days ago—she was wondering how often the butcher called, and my reply of once a month must have impressed her favourably. They are coming. I heard from them this morning.'

'I shall hate those Miss Alans!' Mrs Honeychurch cried. 'Just because they're old and silly one's expected to say, "How sweet!" I hate their "if"-ing and "but"-ing and "and"-ing. And poor Lucy—serve her right—worn to a shadow.'

Mr Beebe watched the shadow springing and shouting over the tennis-court. Cecil was absent—one did not play bumble-puppy when he was there.

'Well, if they are coming— No, Minnie, not Saturn.' Saturn was a tennis-ball whose skin was partially unsown. When in motion his orb was encircled by a ring. 'If they are coming, Sir Harry will let them move in before the twenty-ninth, and he will cross out the clause about whitewashing the ceilings, because it made them nervous, and put in the fair wear and tear one.—That doesn't count. I told you not Saturn.'

'Saturn's all right for bumble-puppy,' cried Freddy, joining them. 'Minnie, don't you listen to her.'

'Saturn doesn't bounce.'

'Saturn bounces enough.'

'No, he doesn't.'

'Well, he bounces better than the Beautiful White Devil.'

'Hush, dear,' said Mrs Honeychurch.

'But look at Lucy—complaining of Saturn, and all the time's got the Beautiful White Devil in her hand, ready to plug it in. That's right, Minnie, go for her—get her over the shins with the racquet—get her over the shins!'

Lucy fell; the Beautiful White Devil rolled from her hand.

Mr Beebe picked it up, and said: 'The name of this ball is Vittoria

Corombona, please.' But his correction passed unheeded.

Freddy possessed to a high degree the power of lashing little girls to fury, and in half a minute he had transformed Minnie from a well-mannered child into a howling wilderness. Up in the house Cecil heard them, and, though he was full of entertaining news, he did not come down to impart it, in case he got hurt. He was not a coward, and bore necessary pain as well as any man. But he hated the physical violence of the young. How right it was! Sure enough it ended in a cry.

'I wish the Miss Alans could see this,' observed Mr Beebe, just as Lucy, who was nursing the injured Minnie, was in turn lifted off her feet by her brother.

'Who are the Miss Alans?' Freddy panted.

'They have taken Cissie Villa.'

'That wasn't the name—'

Here his foot slipped, and they all fell most agreeably on to the grass. An interval elapses.

'Wasn't what name?' asked Lucy, with her brother's head in her lap.

'Alan wasn't. The name of the people Sir Harry's let to.'

'Nonsense, Freddy! You know nothing about it.'

'Nonsense yourself! I've this minute seen him. He said to me: "Ahem! Honeychurch"'–Freddy was an indifferent mimic–'"ahem! ahem! I have at last procured really dee-sire-rebel tenants." I said, "Hooray, old boy!" and slapped him on the back.'

'Exactly. The Miss Alans?'

'Rather not. More like Anderson.'

'Oh, good gracious, there isn't going to be another muddle!' Mrs Honeychurch exclaimed. 'Do you notice, Lucy, I'm always right? I *said* don't interfere with Cissie Villa. I'm always right. I'm quite uneasy at being always right so often.'

'It's only another muddle of Freddy's. Freddy doesn't even know the name of the people he pretends have taken it instead.'

'Yes, I do. I've got it. Emerson.'

'What name?'

'Emerson. I'll bet you anything you like.'

'What a weathercock Sir Harry is,' said Lucy quietly. 'I wish I had never bothered over it at all.'

Then she lay on her back and gazed at the cloudless sky. Mr Beebe, whose opinion of her rose daily, whispered to his niece that *that* was the proper way to behave if any little thing went wrong.

Meanwhile the name of the new tenants had diverted Mrs Honeychurch from the contemplation of her own abilities.

'Emerson, Freddy? Do you know what Emersons they are?'

'I don't know whether they're any Emersons,' retorted Freddy, who was democratic. Like his sister, and like most young people, he was naturally attracted by the idea of equality, and the undeniable fact that there are different kinds of Emersons annoyed him beyond due measure.

'I trust they are the right sort of person. All right, Lucy'–she was sitting up again–'I see you looking down your nose and thinking your mother's a snob. But there *is* a right sort and a wrong sort, and it's affectation to pretend there isn't.'

'Emerson's a common enough name,' Lucy remarked.

She was gazing sideways. Seated on a promontory herself, she could see the pine-clad promontories descending one beyond another into the Weald. The farther one descended the garden, the more glorious was this lateral view.

'I was merely going to remark, Freddy, that I trusted they were no relations of Emerson the philosopher, a most trying man. Pray, does that satisfy you?'

'Oh yes,' he grumbled. 'And you will be satisfied too, for they're friends of Cecil; so'–with elaborate irony–'you and the other county families will be able to call in perfect safety.'

'*Cecil?*' exclaimed Lucy.

'Don't be rude, dear,' said his mother placidly. 'Lucy, don't screech. It's a new bad habit you're getting into.'

'But has Cecil—'

'Friends of Cecil's,' he repeated, '"and so really dee-sire-rebel. Ahem! Honeychurch, I have just telegraphed to them."'

She got up from the grass.

It was hard on Lucy. Mr Beebe sympathized with her very much. While she believed that her snub about the Miss Alans came from Sir Harry Otway, she had borne it like a good girl. She might well 'screech' when she heard that it came partly from her lover. Mr Vyse was a tease–something worse than a tease: he took a malicious pleasure in thwarting people. The clergyman, knowing this, looked at Miss Honeychurch with more than his usual kindness.

When she exclaimed, 'But Cecil's Emersons–they can't possibly be the same ones–there is that—' he did not consider that the exclamation was strange, but saw in it an opportunity of diverting the conversation while she recovered her composure. He diverted it as follows:

'The Emersons who were at Florence, do you mean? No, I don't suppose it will prove to be them. It is probably a long cry from them to friends of Mr Vyse's. Oh, Mrs Honeychurch, the oddest people! The queerest people! For our part we liked them, didn't we?' He appealed to Lucy. 'There was a great scene over some violets. They picked violets and filled all the vases in the room of these very Miss Alans who have failed to come to Cissie Villa. Poor little ladies! So shocked and so pleased. It used to be one of Miss Catharine's great stories. "My dear sister loves flowers," it began. They found the whole room a mass of blue–vases and jugs–and the story ends with "So ungentlemanly and yet so beautiful. It is all very difficult." Yes, I always connect those Florentine Emersons with violets.'

'Fiasco's done you this time,' remarked Freddy, not seeing that his sister's face was very red. She could not recover herself. Mr Beebe saw it, and continued to divert the conversation.

'These particular Emersons consisted of a father and a son–the son a goodly, if not a good young man; not a fool, I fancy, but very immature—pessimism, et cetera. Our special joy was the father—such a sentimental darling, and people declared he had murdered his wife.'

In his normal state Mr Beebe would never have repeated such gossip, but he was trying to shelter Lucy in her little trouble. He repeated any rubbish that came into his head.

'Murdered his wife?' said Mrs Honeychurch. 'Lucy, don't desert us—go on playing bumble-puppy. Really, the Pension Bertolini must have been the oddest place. That's the second murderer I've heard of as being there. Whatever was Charlotte doing to stop? By the by, we really must ask Charlotte here some time.'

Mr Beebe could recall no second murderer. He suggested that his hostess was mistaken. At the hint of opposition she warmed. She was perfectly sure that there had been a second tourist of whom the same story had been told. The name escaped her. What was the name? Oh, what was the name? She clasped her knees for the name. Something in Thackeray. She struck her matronly forehead.

Lucy asked her brother whether Cecil was in.

'Oh, don't go!' he cried, and tried to catch her by the ankles.

'I must go,' she said gravely. 'Don't be silly. You always overdo it when you play.'

As she left them her mother's shout of 'Harris!' shivered the tranquil air, and reminded her that she had told a lie and had never put it right. Such a senseless lie, too, yet it shattered her nerves, and made her connect these Emersons, friends of Cecil's, with a pair of nondescript tourists. Hitherto truth had come to her naturally. She saw that for the future she must be more vigilant, and be—absolutely truthful? Well, at all events, she must not tell lies. She hurried up the garden, still flushed with shame. A word from Cecil would soothe her, she was sure.

'Cecil!'

'Hullo!' he called, and leant out of the smoking-room window. He seemed in high spirits. 'I was hoping you'd come. I heard you all bear-gardening, but there's better fun up here. I, even I, have won a great victory for the Comic Muse. George Meredith's right—the cause of Comedy and the cause of Truth are really the same; and I, even I, have found tenants for the distressful Cissie Villa. Don't be angry! Don't be angry! You'll forgive me when you hear it all.'

He looked very attractive when his face was bright, and he dispelled her ridiculous forebodings at once.

'I have heard,' she said. 'Freddy has told us. Naughty Cecil! I suppose I must forgive you. Just think of all the trouble I took for nothing! Certainly the Miss Alans are a little tiresome, and I'd rather have nice friends of yours. But you oughtn't to tease one so.'

'Friends of mine?' he laughed. 'But, Lucy, the whole joke is to come! Come here.' But she remained standing where she was. 'Do you know where I met these desirable tenants? In the National Gallery, when I was up to see my mother last week.'

'What an odd place to meet people!' she said nervously. 'I don't quite understand.'

'In the Umbrian Room. Absolute strangers. They were admiring Luca Signorelli–of course, quite stupidly. However, we got talking, and they refreshed me not a little. They had been to Italy.'

'But, Cecil—'

He proceeded hilariously.

'In the course of conversation they said that they wanted a country cottage–the father to live there, the son to run down for week-ends. I thought, "What a chance of scoring off Sir Harry!" and I took their address and a London reference, found they weren't actual blackguards–it was great sport–and wrote to him, making out—'

'Cecil! No, it's not fair. I've probably met them before—'

He bore her down.

'Perfectly fair. Anything is fair that punishes a snob. That old man will do the neighbourhood a world of good. Sir Harry is too disgusting with his "decayed gentlewomen." I meant to read him a lesson some time. No, Lucy, the classes ought to mix, and before long you'll agree with me. There ought to be intermarriage–all sorts of things. I believe in democracy—'

'No, you don't,' she snapped. 'You don't know what the word means.'

He stared at her, and felt again that she had failed to be Leonardesque. 'No, you don't?' Her face was inartistic–that of a peevish virago.

'It isn't fair, Cecil. I blame you–I blame you very much indeed. You had no business to undo my work about the Miss Alans, and make me look ridiculous. You call it scoring off Sir Harry, but do you realize that it is all at my expense? I consider it most disloyal of you.'

She left him.

'Temper!' he thought, raising his eyebrows.

No, it was worse than temper–snobbishness. As long as Lucy thought that his own smart friends were supplanting the Miss Alans, she had not minded. He perceived that these new tenants might be of value educationally. He would tolerate the father and draw out the son, who was silent. In the interests of the Comic Muse and of Truth, he would bring them to Windy Corner.

Chapter Eleven

In Mrs Vyse's well-appointed Flat

The Comic Muse, though able to look after her own interests, did not disdain the assistance of Mr Vyse. His idea of bringing the Emersons to Windy Corner struck her as decidedly good, and she carried through the negotiations without a hitch. Sir Harry Otway signed the agreement, met Mr Emerson, and was duly disillusioned. The Miss Alans were duly offended, and wrote a dignified letter to Lucy, whom they held responsible for the failure. Mr Beebe planned pleasant moments for the new-comers, and told Mrs Honeychurch that Freddy must call on them as soon as they arrived. Indeed, so ample was the Muse's equipment that she permitted Mr Harris, never a very robust criminal, to droop his head, to be forgotten, and to die.

Lucy—to descend from bright heaven to earth, whereon there are shadows because there are hills—Lucy was at first plunged into despair, but settled after a little thought that it did not matter in the very least. Now that she was engaged, the Emersons would scarcely insult her, and were welcome to come into the neighbourhood. And Cecil was welcome to bring whom he would into the neighbourhood. Therefore Cecil was welcome to bring the Emersons into the neighbourhood. But, as I say, this took a little thinking, and—so illogical are girls—the event remained rather greater and rather more dreadful than it should have done. She was glad that a visit to Mrs Vyse now fell due; the tenants moved into Cissie Villa while she was safe in the London flat.

'Cecil—Cecil darling,' she whispered the evening she arrived, and crept into his arms.

Cecil, too, became demonstrative. He saw that the needful fire had been kindled in Lucy. At last she longed for attention, as a woman should, and looked up to him because he was a man.

'So you do love me, little thing?' he murmured.

'Oh, Cecil, I do, I do! I don't know what I should do without you.'

Several days passed. Then she had a letter from Miss Bartlett.

A coolness had sprung up between the two cousins, and they had not corresponded since they parted in August. The coolness dated from what Charlotte would call 'the flight to Rome,' and in Rome it had increased amazingly. For the companion who is merely uncongenial in the medieval world becomes exasperating in the classical. Charlotte, unselfish in the Forum, would have tried a sweeter temper than Lucy's, and once, in the Baths of Caracalla, they had doubted whether they could continue their tour. Lucy had said she would join the Vyses—Mrs Vyse was an acquaintance of her mother, so there was no impropriety in the plan—and Miss Bartlett had replied that she was quite used to being abandoned suddenly. Finally nothing happened; but the coolness remained, and, for Lucy, was even increased when she opened the letter and read as follows. It had been forwarded from Windy Corner.

Tunbridge Wells
September

Dearest Lucia,

I have news of you at last! Miss Lavish has been bicycling in your parts, but was not sure whether a call would be welcome. Puncturing her tyre near Summer Street, and it being mended while she sat very woebegone in that pretty churchyard, she saw, to her astonishment, a door open opposite and the younger Emerson man come out. He said his father had just taken the house. He *said* he did not know that you lived in the neighbourhood (?). He never suggested giving Eleanor a cup of tea. Dear Lucy, I am much worried, and I advise you to make a clean breast of his past behaviour to your mother, Freddy and Mr Vyse, who will forbid him to enter the house, etc. That was a great misfortune, and I dare say you have told them already. Mr Vyse is so sensitive. I remember how I used to get on his nerves at Rome. I am very sorry about it all, and should not feel easy unless I warned you.

Believe me,

Your anxious and loving cousin,

Charlotte.

Lucy was much annoyed, and replied as follows:

Beauchamp Mansions, S.W.

Dear Charlotte,

Many thanks for your warning. When Mr Emerson forgot himself on the mountain, you made me promise not to tell mother, because you said she would blame you for not being always with me. I have kept that promise, and cannot possibly tell her now. I have said both to her and to Cecil that I met the Emersons at Florence, and that they are respectable people—which I *do* think—and the reason that he offered Miss Lavish no tea was probably that he had none himself. She should have tried at the Rectory. I cannot begin making a fuss at this stage. You must see that it would be too absurd. If the Emersons heard I had complained of them, they would think themselves of importance, which is exactly what they are not. I like the old father, and look forward to seeing him again. As for the son, I am sorry for *him* when we meet, rather than for myself. They are known to Cecil, who is very well, and spoke of you the other day. We expect to be married in January.

Miss Lavish cannot have told you much about me, for I am not at Windy Corner at all, but here. Please do not put 'Private' outside your envelope again. No one opens my letters.

Yours affectionately,

L. M. Honeychurch.

Secrecy has this disadvantage: we lose the sense of proportion; we cannot tell whether our secret is important or not. Were Lucy and her cousin closeted with a great thing which would destroy Cecil's life if he discovered it, or with a little thing which he would laugh at? Miss Bartlett suggested the former. Perhaps she was right. It had become a great thing now. Left to herself, Lucy would have told her mother and her lover ingenuously, and it would have remained a little thing. 'Emerson, not Harris': it was only that a few weeks ago. She tried to tell Cecil even now when they were laughing about some beautiful lady who had smitten his heart at school. But her body behaved so ridiculously that she stopped.

She and her secret stayed ten days longer in the deserted Metropolis visiting the scenes they were to know so well later on. It did her no harm, Cecil thought, to learn the framework of society, while society itself was absent on the golf-links or the moors. The weather was cool, and it did her no harm. In spite of the season, Mrs Vyse managed to scrape together a dinner-party consisting entirely of the grandchildren of famous people. The food was poor, but the talk had a witty weariness that impressed the girl. One was tired of everything, it seemed. One launched into enthusiasms only to collapse gracefully, and pick oneself up amid sympathetic laughter. In this atmosphere the Pension Bertolini and Windy Corner appeared equally crude, and Lucy saw that her London career would estrange her a little from all that she had loved in the past.

The grandchildren asked her to play the piano. She played Schumann. 'Now some Beethoven,' called Cecil, when the querulous beauty of the music had died. She shook her head and played Schumann again. The melody rose, unprofitably magical. It broke; it was resumed broken, not marching once from the cradle to the grave. The sadness of the incomplete–the sadness that is often Life, but should never be Art–throbbed in its disjected phrases, and made the nerves of the audience throb. Not thus had she played on the little draped piano at the Bertolini, and 'Too much Schumann' was not the remark that Mr Beebe had passed to himself when she returned.

When the guests were gone, and Lucy had gone to bed, Mrs Vyse paced up and down the drawing-room, discussing her little party with her son. Mrs Vyse was a nice woman, but her personality, like many another's, had been swamped by London, for it needs a strong head to live among many people. The too vast orb of her fate had crushed her; she had seen too many seasons, too many cities, too many men for her abilities, and even with Cecil she was mechanical, and behaved as if he was not one son, but, so to speak, a filial crowd.

'Make Lucy one of us,' she said, looking round intelligently at the end of each sentence, and straining her lips apart until she spoke again. 'Lucy is becoming wonderful–wonderful.'

'Her music always was wonderful.'

'Yes, but she is purging off the Honeychurch taint–most excellent Honeychurches, but you know what I mean. She is not always quoting servants, or asking one how the pudding is made.'

'Italy has done it.'

'Perhaps,' she murmured, thinking of the museum that represented Italy to her. 'It is just possible. Cecil, mind you marry her next January. She is one of us already.'

'But her music!' he exclaimed. 'The style of her! How she kept to Schumann when, like an idiot, I wanted Beethoven. Schumann was right for this evening. Schumann was the thing. Do you know, mother, I shall have our children educated just like Lucy. Bring them up among honest country folk for freshness, send them to Italy for subtlety, and then–not till then–let them come to London. I don't believe in these London educations—' He broke off, remembering that he had had one himself, and concluded, 'At all events, not for women.'

'Make her one of us,' repeated Mrs Vyse, and processed to bed.

As she was dozing off, a cry–the cry of nightmare–rang from Lucy's room. Lucy could ring for the maid if she liked, but Mrs Vyse thought it kind to go herself. She found the girl sitting upright with her hand on her cheek.

'I am so sorry, Mrs Vyse–it is these dreams.'

'Bad dreams?'

'Just dreams.'

The elder lady smiled and kissed her, saying very distinctly: 'You should have heard us talking about you, dear. He admires you more than ever. Dream of that.'

Lucy returned the kiss, still covering one cheek with her hand. Mrs Vyse recessed to bed. Cecil, whome the cry had not awoke, snored. Darkness enveloped the flat.

Chapter Twelve

Twelfth Chapter

It was a Saturday afternoon, gay and brilliant after abundant rains, and the spirit of youth dwelt in it, though the season was now autumn. All that was gracious triumphed. As the motor-cars passed through Summer Street they raised only a little dust, and their stench was soon dispersed by the wind and replaced by the scent of the wet birches or of the pines. Mr Beebe, at leisure for life's amenities, leant over his rectory gate. Freddy leant by him, smoking a pendant pipe.

'Suppose we go and hinder those new people opposite for a little.'

'M'm.'

'They might amuse you.'

Freddy, whom his fellow-creatures never amused, suggested that the new people might be feeling a bit busy, and so on, since they had only just moved in.

'I suggested we should hinder them,' said Mr Beebe. 'They are worth it.' Unlatching the gate, he sauntered over the triangular green to Cissie Villa. 'Hullo!' he called, shouting in at the open door, through which much squalor was visible.

A grave voice replied, 'Hullo!'

'I've brought some one to see you.'

'I'll be down in a minute.'

The passage was blocked by a wardrobe, which the removal men had failed to carry up the stairs. Mr Beebe edged round it with difficulty. The sitting-room itself was blocked with books.

'Are these people great readers?' Freddy whispered. 'Are they that sort?'

'I fancy they know how to read—a rare accomplishment. What have they got? Byron. Exactly. "A Shropshire Lad." Never heard of it. "The Way of all Flesh." Never heard of it. Gibbon. Hullo! dear George reads German. Um—um—Schopenhauer, Nietzsche, and so we go on. Well, I suppose your generation knows its own business, Honeychurch.'

'Mr Beebe, look at that,' said Freddy in awestruck tones.

On the cornice of the wardrobe the hand of an amateur had painted this inscription: 'Mistrust all enterprises that require new clothes.'

'I know. Isn't it jolly? I like that. I'm certain that's the old man's doing.'

'How very odd of him!'

'Surely you agree?'

But Freddy was his mother's son, and felt that one ought not to go spoiling the furniture.

'Pictures!' the clergyman continued, scrambling about the room. 'Giotto–they got that at Florence, I'll be bound.'

'The same as Lucy's got.'

'Oh, by the by, did Miss Honeychurch enjoy London?'

'She came back yesterday.'

'I suppose she had a good time?'

'Yes, very,' said Freddy, taking up a book. 'She and Cecil are thicker than ever.'

'That's good hearing.'

'I wish I wasn't such a fool, Mr Beebe.'

Mr Beebe ignored the remark.

'Lucy used to be nearly as stupid as I am, but it'll be very different now, mother thinks. She will read all kinds of books.'

'So will you.'

'Only medical books. Not books that you can talk about afterwards. Cecil is teaching Lucy Italian, and he says her playing is wonderful. There are all kinds of things in it that we have never noticed. Cecil says—'

'What on earth are those people doing upstairs? Emerson–we think we'll come another time.'

George ran downstairs and pushed them into the room without speaking.

'Let me introduce Mr Honeychurch, a neighbour.'

Then Freddy hurled one of the thunderbolts of youth. Perhaps he was shy, perhaps he was friendly, or perhaps he thought that George's face wanted washing. At all events, he greeted him with, 'How d'ye do? Come and have a bathe.'

'Oh, all right,' said George, impassive.

Mr Beebe was highly entertained.

'"How d'ye do? how d'ye do? Come and have a bathe,"' he chuckled. 'That's the best conversational opening I've ever heard. But I'm afraid it will only act between men. Can you picture a lady who has been introduced to another lady by a third lady opening civilities with "How do you do? Come and have a bathe"? And yet you will tell me that the sexes are equal.'

'I tell you that they shall be,' said Mr Emerson, who had been slowly descending the stairs. 'Good afternoon, Mr Beebe. I tell you they shall be comrades, and George thinks the same.'

'We are to raise ladies to our level?' the clergyman inquired.

'The Garden of Eden,' pursued Mr Emerson, still descending, 'which you place in the past, is really yet to come. We shall enter it when we no longer despise our bodies.'

Mr Beebe disclaimed placing the Garden of Eden anywhere.

'In this—not in other things—we men are ahead. We despise the body less than women do. But not until we are comrades shall we enter the garden.'

'I say, what about this bathe?' murmured Freddy, appalled at the mass of philosophy that was approaching him.

'I believed in a return to Nature once. But how can we return to Nature when we have never been with her? To-day, I believe that we must discover Nature. After many conquests we shall attain simplicity. It is our heritage.'

'Let me introduce Mr Honeychurch, whose sister you will remember at Florence.'

'How do you do? Very glad to see you, and that you are taking George for a bathe. Very glad to hear that your sister is going to marry. Marriage is a duty. I am sure that she will be happy, for we know Mr Vyse, too. He has been most kind. He met us by chance in the National Gallery, and arranged everything about this delightful house. Though I hope I have not vexed Sir Harry Otway. I have met so few Liberal landowners, and I was anxious to compare his attitude towards the game laws with the Conservative attitude. Ah, this wind! You do well to bathe. Yours is a glorious country, Honeychurch!'

'Not a bit!' mumbled Freddy. 'I must—that is to say, I have to—have the pleasure of calling on you later on, my mother says, I hope.'

'*Call*, my lad? Who taught us that drawing-room twaddle? Call on your grandmother! Listen to the wind among the pines! Yours is a glorious country.'

Mr Beebe came to the rescue.

'Mr Emerson, he will call, I shall call; you or your son will return our calls before ten days have elapsed. I trust that you have realized about the ten days' interval. It does not count that I helped you with the stair-eyes yesterday. It does not count that they are going to bathe this afternoon.'

'Yes, go and bathe, George. Why do you dawdle talking? Bring them back to tea. Bring back some milk, cakes, honey. The change will do you good. George has been working very hard at his office. I can't believe he's well.'

George bowed his head, dusty and sombre, exhaling the peculiar smell of one who has handled furniture.

'Do you really want this bathe?' Freddy asked him. 'It is only a pond, don't you know. I dare say you are used to something much better.'

'Yes—I have said "Yes" already.'

Mr Beebe felt bound to assist his young friend, and led the way out of the house into the pinewoods. How glorious it was! For a little time the voice of old Mr Emerson pursued them, dispensing good wishes and philosophy. It ceased, and they only heard the fair wind blowing the bracken and the trees.

Mr Beebe, who could be silent, but who could not bear silence, was compelled to chatter, since the expedition looked like a failure, and neither of his companions would utter a word. He spoke of Florence. George attended gravely, assenting or dissenting with slight but determined gestures that were as inexplicable as the motions of the tree-tops above their heads.

'And what a coincidence that you should meet Mr Vyse! Did you realize that you would find all the Pension Bertolini down here?'

'I did not. Miss Lavish told me.'

'When I was a young man I always meant to write a "History of Coincidence."'

No enthusiasm.

'Though, as a matter of fact, coincidences are much rare than we suppose. For example, it isn't pure coincidentality that you are here now, when one comes to reflect.'

To his relief, George began to talk.

'It is. I have reflected. It is Fate. Everything is Fate. We are flung together by Fate, drawn apart by Fate—flung together, drawn apart. The twelve winds blow us—we settle nothing—'

'You have not reflected at all,' rapped the clergyman. 'Let me give you a useful tip, Emerson: attribute nothing to Fate. Don't say, "I didn't do this," for you did it, ten to one. Now I'll cross-question you. Where did you first meet Miss Honeychurch and myself?'

'Italy.'

'And where did you meet Mr Vyse, who is going to marry Miss Honeychurch?'

'National Gallery.'

'Looking at Italian art. There you are, and yet you talk of coincidence and Fate! You naturally seek out things Italian, and so do we and our friends. This narrows the field immeasurably, and we meet again in it.'

'It is Fate that I am here,' persisted George. 'But you can call it Italy if it makes you less unhappy.'

Mr Beebe slid away from such heavy treatment of the subject. But he was infinitely tolerant of the young, and had no desire to snub George.

'And so for this and for other reasons my "History of Coincidence" is still to write.'

Silence.

Wishing to round off the episode, he added:

'We are all so glad that you have come.'

Silence.

'Here we are!' called Freddy.

'Oh, good!' exclaimed Mr Beebe, mopping his brow.

'In there's the pond. I wish it was bigger,' he added apologetically.

They climbed down a slippery bank of pine-needles. There lay the pond, set in its little alp of green—only a pond, but large enough to contain the human body, and pure enough to reflect the sky. On account of the rains, the waters had flooded the surrounding grass, which showed like a beautiful emerald path, tempting the feet towards the central pool.

'It's distinctly successful, as ponds go,' said Mr Beebe. 'No apologies are necessary for the pond.'

George sat down where the ground was dry, and drearily unlaced his boots.

'Aren't those masses of willow-herb splendid? I love willow-herb in seed. What's the name of this aromatic plant?'

No one knew, or seemed to care.

'These abrupt changes of vegetation—this little spongeous tract of water-plants, and on either side of it all the growths are tough or brittle—heather, bracken, hurts, pines. Very charming, very charming.'

'Mr Beebe, aren't you bathing?' called Freddy, as he stripped himself.

Mr Beebe thought he was not.

'Water's wonderful!' cried Freddy, prancing in.

'Water's water,' murmured George. Wetting his hair first—a sure sign of apathy—he followed Freddy into the divine, as indifferent as if he were a statue and the pond a pail of soapsuds. It was necessary to use his muscles. It was necessary to keep clean. Mr Beebe watched them, and watched the seeds of the willow-herb dance chorically above their heads.

'Apooshoo, apooshoo, apooshoo,' went Freddy, swimming for two strokes in either direction, and then becoming involved in reeds or mud.

'It is worth it?' asked the other, Michelangelesque on the flooded margin.

The bank broke away, and he fell into the pool before he had weighted the question properly.

'Hee—poof—I've swallowed a polly-wog. Mr Beebe, water's wonderful, water's simply ripping.'

'Water's not so bad,' said George, reappearing from his plunge, and sputtering at the sun.

'Water's wonderful. Mr Beebe, do.'

'Apooshoo, kouf.'

Mr Beebe, who was hot, and who always acquiesced where possible, looked around him. He could detect no parishioners except the pine-trees, rising up steeply on all sides, and gesturing to each other against the blue. How glorious it was! The world of motor-cars and Rural Deans receded illimitably. Water, sky, evergreens, a wind—these things not even the seasons can touch, and surely they lie beyond the intrusion of man?

'I may as well wash too'; and soon his garments made a third little pile on the sward, and he too asserted the wonder of the water.

It was ordinary water, nor was there very much of it, and, as Freddy said, it reminded one of swimming in a salad. The three gentlemen rotated in the pool breast high, after the fashion of the nymphs in Götterdämmerung. But either because the rains had given a freshness, or because the sun was shedding a most glorious heat, or because two of the gentlemen were young in years and the third young in the spirit—for some reason or other a change came over them, and they forgot Italy and Botany and Fate. They began to play. Mr Beebe and Freddy splashed each other. A little deferentially, they splashed George. He was quiet: they feared they had offended him. Then all the forces of youth burst out. He smiled, flung himself at them, splashed them, ducked them, kicked them, muddied them, and drove them out of the pool.

'Race you round it, then,' cried Freddy, and they raced in the sunshine, and George took a short cut and dirtied his shins, and had to bathe a second time. Then Mr Beebe consented to run—a memorable sight.

They ran to get dry, they bathed to get cool, they played at being Indians in the willow-herbs and in the bracken, they bathed to get clean. And all the time three little bundles lay discreetly on the sward, proclaiming:

'No. We are what matters. Without us shall no enterprise begin. To us shall all flesh turn in the end.'

'A try! A try!' yelled Freddy, snatching up George's bundle and placing it beside an imaginary goal-post.

'Socker rules,' George retorted, scattering Freddy's bundle with a kick. 'Goal!'

'Goal!'

'Pass!'

'Take care my watch!' cried Mr Beebe.

Clothes flew in all directions.

'Take care my hat! No, that's enough, Freddy. Dress now. No, I say!'

But the two young men were delirious. Away they twinkled into the trees, Freddy with a clerical waistcoat under his arm, George with a wideawake hat on his dripping hair.

'That'll do!' shouted Mr Beebe, remembering that after all he was in his own parish. Then his voice changed as if every pine-tree was a Rural Dean. 'Hi! Steady on! I see people coming, you fellows!'

Yells, and widening circles over the dappled earth.

'Hi! hi! *Ladies!*'

Neither George nor Freddy was truly refined. Still, they did not hear Mr Beebe's last warning or they would have avoided Mrs Honeychurch, Cecil, and Lucy, who were walking down to call on old Mrs Butterworth. Freddy dropped the waistcoat at their feet, and dashed into some bracken. George whooped in their faces, turned, and scudded away down the path to the pond, still clad in Mr Beebe's hat.

'Gracious alive!' cried Mrs Honeychurch. 'Whoever were those unfortunate people? Oh, dears, look away! And poor Mr Beebe, too! Whatever has happened?'

'Come this way immediately,' commanded Cecil, who always felt that he must lead women, though he knew not whither, and protect them, though he knew not against what. He led them now towards the bracken where Freddy sat concealed.

'Oh, poor Mr Beebe! Was that his waistcoat we left in the path? Cecil, Mr Beebe's waistcoat—'

'No business of ours,' said Cecil, glancing at Lucy, who was all parasol and evidently 'minded.'

'I fancy Mr Beebe jumped back into the pond.'

'This way, please, Mrs Honeychurch, this way.'

They followed him up the bank, attempting the tense yet nonchalant expression that is suitable for ladies on such occasions.

'Well, *I* can't help it,' said a voice close ahead, and Freddy reared a freckled face and a pair of snowy shoulders out of the fronds. 'I can't be trodden on, can I?'

'Good gracious me, dear; so it's you! What miserable management! Why not have a comfortable bath at home, with hot and cold laid on?'

'Look here, mother: a fellow must wash, and a fellow's got to dry, and if another fellow—'

'Dear, no doubt you're right as usual, but you are in no position to argue. Come, Lucy,' They turned. 'Oh, look–don't look! Oh, poor Mr Beebe! How unfortunate again—'

For Mr Beebe was just crawling out of the pond, on whose surface garments of an intimate nature did float; while George, the world-weary George, shouted to Freddy that he had hooked a fish.

'And me, I've swallowed one, answered he of the bracken. 'I've swallowed a polly-wog. It wriggleth in my tummy. I shall die–Emerson, you beast, you've got on my bags.'

'Hush, dears,' said Mrs Honeychurch, who found it impossible to remain shocked. 'And do be sure you dry yourselves thoroughly first. All these colds come of not drying thoroughly.'

'Mother, do come away,' said Lucy. 'Oh, for goodness' sake, do come.'

'Hullo!' cried George, so that again the ladies stopped.

He regarded himself as dressed. Barefoot, bare-chested, radiant and personable against the shadowy woods, he called:

'Hullo, Miss Honeychurch! Hullo!'

'Bow, Lucy; better bow. Whoever is it? I shall bow.'

Miss Honeychurch bowed.

That evening and all that night the water ran away. On the morrow the pool had shrunk to its old size and lost its glory. It had been a call to the blood and to the relaxed will, a passing benediction whose influence did not pass, a holiness, a spell, a momentary chalice for youth.

Chapter Thirteen

How Miss Bartlett's Boiler was so Tiresome

How often had Lucy rehearsed this bow, this interview! But she had always rehearsed them indoors, and with certain accessories, which surely we have a right to assume. Who could foretell that she and George would meet in the rout of a civilization, amidst an army of coats and collars and boots that lay wounded over the sunlit earth? She had imagined a young Mr Emerson, who might be shy or morbid or indifferent or furtively impudent. She was prepared for all of these. But she had never imagined one who would be happy and greet her with the shout of the morning star.

Indoors herself, partaking of tea with old Mrs Butterworth, she reflected that it is impossible to foretell the future with any degree of accuracy, that it is impossible to rehearse life. A fault in the scenery, a face in the audience, an irruption of the audience on to the stage, and all our carefully planned gestures mean nothing, or mean too much. 'I will bow,' she had thought. 'I will not shake hands with him. That will be just the proper thing.' She had bowed–but to whom? To gods, to heroes, to the nonsense of schoolgirls! She had bowed across the rubbish that cumbers the world.

So ran her thoughts, while her faculties were busy with Cecil. It was another of those dreadful engagement calls. Mrs Butterworth had wanted to see him, and he did not want to be seen. He did not want to hear about hydrangeas, why they change their colour at the seaside. He did not want to join the C.O.S. When cross he was always elaborate, and made long, clever answers where 'Yes' or 'No' would have done. Lucy soothed him and tinkered at the conversation in a way that promised well for their married peace. No one is perfect, and surely it is wiser to discover the imperfections before wedlock. Miss Bartlett, in deed, though not in word, had taught the girl that this our life contains nothing satisfactory. Lucy, though she disliked the teacher, regarded the teaching as profound, and applied it to her lover.

'Lucy,' said her mother, when they got home, 'is anything the matter with Cecil?'

The question was ominous: up till now Mrs Honeychurch had behaved with charity and restraint.

'No, I don't think so, mother; Cecil's all right.'

'Perhaps he's tired.'

Lucy compromised: perhaps Cecil was a little tired.

'Because otherwise'–she pulled out her bonnet-pins with gathering displeasure–'because otherwise I cannot account for him.'

'I do think Mrs Butterworth is rather tiresome, if you mean that.'

'Cecil has told you to think so. You were devoted to her as a little girl, and nothing will describe her goodness to you through the typhoid fever. No–it is just the same thing everywhere.'

'Let me just put your bonnet away, may I?'

'Surely he could answer her civilly for one half-hour?'

'Cecil has a very high standard for people,' faltered Lucy, seeing trouble ahead. 'It's part of his ideals–it is really that that makes him sometimes seem—'

'Oh, rubbish! If high ideals make a young man rude, the sooner he gets rid of them the better,' said Mrs Honeychurch, handing her the bonnet.

'Now mother! I've seen you cross with Mrs Butterworth yourself!'

'Not in that way. At times I could wring her neck. But not in that way. No. It is the same with Cecil all over.'

'By the by–I never told you. I had a letter from Charlotte while I was away in London.'

This attempt to divert the conversation was too puerile, and Mrs Honeychurch resented it.

'Since Cecil came back from London, nothing appears to please him. Whenever I speak he winces;–I see him, Lucy; it is useless to contradict me. No doubt I am neither artistic nor literary nor intellectual nor musical, but I cannot help the drawing-room furniture: your father bought it and we must put up with it, will Cecil kindly remember.'

'I—I see what you mean, and certainly Cecil oughtn't to. But he does not mean to be uncivil—he once explained—it is the *things* that upset him—he is easily upset by ugly things—he is not uncivil to *people*.'

'Is it a thing or a person when Freddy sings?'

'You can't expect a really musical person to enjoy comic songs as we do.'

'Then why didn't he leave the room? Why sit wriggling and sneering and spoiling every one's pleasure?'

'We mustn't be unjust to people,' faltered Lucy. Something had enfeebled her, and the case for Cecil, which she had mastered so perfectly in London, would not come forth in an effective form. The two civilizations had clashed—Cecil had hinted that they might—and she was dazzled and bewildered, as though the radiance that lies behind all civilization had blinded her eyes. Good taste and bad taste were only catch-words, garments of diverse cut; and music itself dissolved to a whisper through pine-trees, where the song is not distinguishable from the comic song.

She remained in much embarrassment, while Mrs Honeychurch changed her frock for dinner; and every now and then she said a word, and made things no better. There was no concealing the fact—Cecil had meant to be supercilious, and he had succeeded. And Lucy—she knew not why—wished that the trouble could have come at any other time.

'Go and dress, dear; you'll be late.'

'All right, mother—'

'Don't say "All right" and stop. Go.'

She obeyed, but loitered disconsolately at the landing window. It faced north, so there was little view, and now view of the sky. Now, as in the winter, the pine-trees hung close to her eyes. One connected the landing window with depression. No definite problem menaced her, but she sighed to herself, 'Oh dear, what shall I do, what shall I do?' It seemed to her that every one else was behaving very badly. And she ought not to have mentioned Miss Bartlett's letter. She must be more careful: her mother was rather inquisitive, and might have asked what it was about. Oh dear, what should she do?—and then Freddy came bounding upstairs, and joined the ranks of the ill-behaved.

'I say, those are topping people.'

'My dear baby, how tiresome you've been! You had no business to take them bathing in the Sacred Lake: it's much too public. It was all right for you, but most awkward for every one else. Do be more careful. You forget the place is growing half suburban.'

'I say, is anything on to-morrow week?'

'Not that I know of.'

'Then I want to ask the Emersons up to Sunday tennis.'

'Oh, I wouldn't do that, Freddy, I wouldn't do that with all this muddle.'

'What's wrong with the court? They won't mind a bump or two, and I've ordered new balls.'

'I meant *it's* better not. I really mean it.'

He seized her by the elbows and humorously danced her up and down the passage. She pretended not to mind, but she could have screamed with temper. Cecil glanced at them as he proceeded to his toilet and they impeded Mary with her brood of hot-water cans. Then Mrs Honeychurch opened her door and said: 'Lucy, what a noise you're making! I have something to say to you. Did you say you had had a letter from Charlotte?' and Freddy ran away.

'Yes. I really can't stop. I must dress too.'

'How's Charlotte?'

'All right.'

'Lucy!'

The unfortunate girl returned.

'You've a bad habit of hurrying away in the middle of one's sentences. Did Charlotte mention her boiler?'

'Her *what*?'

'Don't you remember that her boiler was to be had out in October, and her bath cistern cleaned out, and all kinds of terrible to-doing?'

'I can't remember all Charlotte's worries,' said Lucy bitterly. 'I shall have enough of my own, now that you are not pleased with Cecil.'

Mrs Honeychurch might have flamed out. She did not. She said: 'Come here, old lady—thank you for putting away my bonnet—kiss me.' And, though nothing is perfect, Lucy felt for the moment that her mother and Windy Corner and the Weald in the declining sun were perfect.

So the grittiness went out of life. It generally did at Windy Corner. At the last minute, when the social machine was clogged hopelessly, one member or other of the family poured in a drop of oil. Cecil despised their methods—perhaps rightly. At all events, they were not his own.

Dinner was at half-past seven. Freddy gabbled a grace, and they drew up their heavy chairs and fell to. Fortunately, the men were hungry. Nothing untoward occurred until the pudding. Then Freddy said:

'Lucy, what's Emerson like?'

'I saw him in Florence,' said Lucy, hoping that this would pass for a reply.

'Is he the clever sort, or is he a decent chap?'

'Ask Cecil; it is Cecil who brought him here.'

'He is the clever sort, like myself,' said Cecil.

Freddy looked at him doubtfully.

'How well did you know them at the Bertolini?' asked Mrs Honeychurch.

'Oh, very slightly. I mean, Charlotte knew them even less than I did.'

'Oh, that reminds me—you never told me what Charlotte said in her letter.'

'One thing and another,' said Lucy, wondering whether she would get through the meal without a lie. 'Among other things, that an awful friend of hers had been bicycling through Summer Street, wondered if she'd come up and see us, and mercifully didn't.'

'Lucy, I do call the way you talk unkind.'

'She was a novelist,' said Lucy craftily. The remark was a happy one, for nothing roused Mrs Honeychurch so much as literature in the hands of females. She would abandon every topic to inveigh against those women who (instead of minding their houses and their children) seek notoriety by print. Her attitude was: 'If books must be written, let them be written by men'; and she developed it at great length, while Cecil yawned and Freddy played at "This year, next year, now, never," with his plumstones, and Lucy artfully fed the flames of her mother's wrath. But soon the conflagration died down, and the ghosts began to gather in the darkness. There were too many ghosts about. The original ghost—that touch of lips on her cheek—had surely been laid long ago; it could be nothing to her that a man had kissed her on a mountain once. But it had begotten a spectral family—Mr Harris, Miss Bartlett's letter, Mr Beebe's memories of violets—and one or other of these was bound to haunt her before Cecil's very eyes. It was Miss Bartlett who returned now, and with appalling vividness.

'I have been thinking, Lucy, of that letter of Charlotte's. How is she?'

'I tore the thing up.'

'Didn't she say how she was? How does she sound? Cheerful?'

'Oh yes, I suppose so—no—not very cheerful, I suppose.'

'Then, depend upon it, it *is* the boiler. I know myself how water preys upon one's mind. I would rather anything else—even a misfortune with the Meat.'

Cecil laid his hand over his eyes.

'So would I,' asserted Freddy, backing his mother up—backing up the spirit of her remark rather than its substance.

'And I have been thinking,' she added rather nervously, 'surely we could squeeze Charlotte in here next week, and give her a nice holiday while the plumbers at Tunbridge Wells finish. I have not seen poor Charlotte for so long.'

It was more than her nerves could stand. And yet she could not protest violently after her mother's goodness to her upstairs.

'Mother, no!' she pleaded. 'It's impossible. We can't have Charlotte on the top of the other things; we're squeezed to death as it is. Freddy's got a friend coming Tuesday, there's Cecil, and you've promised to take in Minnie Beebe because of the diphtheria scare. It simply can't be done.'

'Nonsense! It can.'

'If Minnie sleeps in the bath. Not otherwise.'

'Minnie can sleep with you.'

'I won't have her.'

'Then, if you're so selfish, Mr Floyd must share a room with Freddy.'

'Miss Bartlett, Miss Bartlett, Miss Bartlett,' moaned Cecil, again laying his hand over his eyes.

'It's impossible,' repeated Lucy. 'I don't want to make difficulties, but it really isn't fair on the maids to fill up the house so.'

Alas!

'The truth is, dear, you don't like Charlotte.'

'No, I don't. And no more does Cecil. She gets on our nerves. You haven't seen her lately, and don't realize how tiresome she can be, though so good. So please, mother, don't worry us this last summer; but spoil us by not asking her to come.'

'Hear, hear!' said Cecil.

Mrs Honeychurch, with more gravity than usual, and with more feeling than she usually permitted herself replied: 'This isn't very kind of you two. You have each other and all these woods to walk in, so full of beautiful things; and poor Charlotte has only the water turned off and plumbers. You are young, dears, and however clever young people are, and however many books they read, they will never guess what it feels like to grow old.'

Cecil crumbled his bread.

'I must say Cousin Charlotte was very kind to me that year I called on my bike,' put in Freddy. 'She thanked me for coming till I felt like such a fool, and fussed round no end to get an egg boiled for my tea just right.'

'I know, dear. She is kind to every one, and yet Lucy makes this difficulty when we try to give her some little return.'

But Lucy hardened her heart. It was no good being kind to Miss Bartlett. She had tried herself too often and too recently. One might lay up treasure in heaven by the attempt, but one enriched neither Miss Bartlett nor anyone else upon earth. She was reduced to saying: 'I can't help it, mother. I don't like Charlotte. I admit it's horrid of me.'

'From your own account, you told her as much.'

'Well, she would leave Florence so stupidly. She flurried—'

The ghosts were returning; they filled Italy, they were even usurping the places she had known as a child. The Sacred Lake would never be the same again, and, on Sunday week, something would even happen to Windy Corner. How would she fight against ghosts? For a moment the visible world faded away, and memories and emotions alone seemed real.

'I suppose Miss Bartlett must come, since she boils eggs so well,' said Cecil, who was in rather a happier frame of mind, thanks to the admirable cooking.

'I didn't mean the egg was *well* boiled,' corrected Freddy, 'because in point of fact she forgot to take it off, and as a matter of fact I don't care for eggs. I only meant how jolly kind she seemed.'

Cecil frowned again. Oh, these Honeychurches! Eggs, boilers, hydrangeas, maids—of such were their lives compact. 'May me and Lucy get down from our chairs?' he asked, with scarcely veiled insolence. 'We don't want no dessert.'

Chapter Fourteen

How Lucy Faced the External Situation Bravely

Of course Miss Bartlett accepted. And, equally of course, she felt sure that she would prove a nuisance, and begged to be given an inferior spare room—something with no view, anything. Her love to Lucy. And, equally of course, George Emerson could come to tennis on the Sunday week.

Lucy faced the situation bravely, though, like most of us, she only faced the situation that encompassed her. She never gazed inwards. If at times strange images rose from the depths, she put them down to nerves. When Cecil brought the Emersons to Summer Street, it had upset her nerves. Charlotte would burnish up past foolishness, and this might upset her nerves. She was nervous at night. When she talked to George—they met again almost immediately at the Rectory—his voice moved her deeply, and she wished to remain near him. How dreadful if she really wished to remain near him! Of course, the wish was due to nerves, which love to play such perverse tricks upon us. Once she had suffered from 'things that came out of nothing and meant she didn't know what.' Now Cecil had explained psychology to her one wet afternoon, and all the troubles of youth in an unknown world could be dismissed.

It is obvious enough for the reader to conclude, 'She loves young Emerson.' A reader in Lucy's place would not find it obvious. Life is easy to chronicle, but bewildering to practise, and we welcome 'nerves' or any other shibboleth that will cloak our personal desire. She loved Cecil; George made her nervous; will the reader explain to her that the phrases should have been reversed?

But the external situation—she will face that bravely.

The meeting at the Rectory had passed off well enough. Standing between Mr Beebe and Cecil, she had made a few temperate allusions to Italy, and George had replied. She was anxious to show that she was not shy, and was glad that he did not seem shy either.

'A nice fellow,' said Mr Beebe afterwards. 'He will work off his crudities in time. I rather mistrust young men who slip into life gracefully.'

Lucy said, 'He seems in better spirits. He laughs more.'

'Yes,' replied the clergyman. 'He is waking up.

That was all. But, as the week wore on, more of her defences fell, and she entertained an image that had physical beauty.

In spite of the clearest directions, Miss Bartlett contrived to bungle her arrival. She was due at the South-Eastern station at Dorking, whither Mrs Honeychurch drove to meet her. She arrived at the London and Brighton station, and had to hire a cab up. No one was at home except Freddy and his friend, who had to stop their tennis and to entertain her for a solid hour. Cecil and Lucy turned up at four o'clock, and these, with little Minnie Beebe, made a somewhat lugubrious sextette upon the upper lawn for tea.

'I shall never forgive myself,' said Miss Bartlett, who kept on rising from her seat, and had to be begged by the united company to remain. 'I have upset everything. Bursting in on young people! But I insist on paying for my cab up. Grant me that, at any rate.'

'Our visitors never do such a dreadful thing,' said Lucy, while her brother, in whose memory the boiled egg had already grown unsubstantial, exclaimed in irritable tones: 'Just what I've been trying to convince Cousin Charlotte of, Lucy, for the last half-hour.'

'I do not feel myself an ordinary visitor,' said Miss Bartlett, and looked at her frayed gloves.

'All right, if you'd really rather. Five shillings, and I gave a bob to the driver.'

Miss Bartlett looked in her purse. Only sovereigns and pennies. Could anyone give her change? Freddy had half a quid and his friend had four half-crowns. Miss Bartlett accepted their moneys and then said: 'But who am I to give the sovereign to?'

'Let's leave it all till mother comes back,' suggested Lucy.

'No, dear; your mother may take quite a long drive now that she is not hampered with me. We all have our little foibles, and mine is the promptly settling of accounts.'

Here Freddy's friend, Mr Floyd, made the one remark of his that need be quoted: he offered to toss Freddy for Miss Bartlett's quid. A solution seemed in sight, and even Cecil, who had been ostentatiously drinking his tea at the view, felt the eternal attraction of Chance, and turned round.

But this did not do, either.

'Please—please—I know I am a sad spoil-sport, but it would make me wretched. I should practically be robbing the one who lost.'

'Freddy owes me fifteen shillings,' interposed Cecil. 'So it will work out right if you give the pound to me.'

'Fifteen shillings,' said Miss Bartlett dubiously. 'How is that, Mr Vyse?'

'Because, don't you see, Freddy paid your cab. Give me the pound, and we shall avoid this deplorable gambling.'

Miss Bartlett, who was poor at figures, became bewildered and rendered up the sovereign, amidst the suppressed gurgles of the other youths. For a moment Cecil was happy. He was playing at nonsense among his peers. Then he glanced at Lucy, in whose face petty anxieties had marred the smiles. In January he would rescue his Leonardo from this stupefying twaddle.

'But I don't see that!' exclaimed Minnie Beebe, who had narrowly watched the iniquitous transaction. 'I don't see why Mr Vyse is to have the quid.'

'Because of the fifteen shillings and the five,' they said solemnly. 'Fifteen shillings and five shillings make one pound, you see.'

'But I don't see—'

They tried to stifle her with cake.

'No, thank you. I'm done. I don't see why— Freddy, don't poke me. Miss Honeychurch, your brother's hurting me. Ow! What about Mr Floyd's ten shillings? Ow! No, I don't see and I never shall see why Miss What's-her-name shouldn't pay that bob for the driver.'

'I had forgotten the driver,' said Miss Bartlett, reddening. 'Thank you, dear, for reminding me. A shilling was it? Can anyone give me change for half a crown?'

'I'll get it,' said the young hostess, rising with decision. 'Cecil, give me that sovereign. No—give me up that sovereign. I'll get Euphemia to change it, and we'll start the whole thing again from the beginning.'

'Lucy—Lucy—what a nuisance I am!' protested Miss Bartlett, and followed her across the lawn. Lucy tripped ahead, simulating hilarity. When they were out of earshot, Miss Bartlett stopped her wails and said quite briskly: 'Have you told him about him yet?'

'No, I haven't,' replied Lucy, and then could have bitten her tongue for understanding so quickly what her cousin meant. 'Let me see—a sovereign's worth of silver.'

She escaped into the kitchen. Miss Bartlett's sudden transitions were too uncanny. It sometimes seemed as if she planned every word she spoke or caused to be spoken; as if all this worry about cabs and change had been a ruse to surprise the soul.

'No, I haven't told Cecil or anyone,' she remarked, when she returned. 'I promised you I shouldn't. Here is your money—all shillings, except two half-crowns. Would you count it? You can settle your debt nicely now.'

Miss Bartlett was in the drawing-room, gazing at the photograph of St John ascending, who had been framed.

'How dreadful!' she murmured, 'how more than dreadful, if Mr Vyse should come to hear of it from some other source.'

'Oh no, Charlotte,' said the girl, entering the battle, 'George Emerson is all right, and what other source is there?'

Miss Bartlett considered. 'For instance, the driver. I saw him looking through the bushes at you. I remember he had a violet between his teeth.'

Lucy shuddered a little. 'We shall get the silly affair on our nerves if we aren't careful. How could a Florentine cab-driver ever get hold of Cecil?'

'We must think of every possibility.'

'Oh, it's all right.'

'Or perhaps old Mr Emerson knows. In fact, he is certain to know.'

'I don't care if he does. I was grateful to you for your letter, but even if the news does get round, I think I can trust Cecil to laugh at it.'

'To contradict it?'

'No, to laugh at it.' But she knew in her heart that she could not trust him, for he desired her untouched.

'Very well, dear, you know best. Perhaps gentlemen are different to what they were when I was young. Ladies are certainly different.'

'Now, Charlotte!' She struck at her playfully. 'You kind, anxious thing! What *would* you have me do? First you say, "Don't tell"; and then you say, "Tell." Which is it to be? Quick!'

Miss Bartlett sighed. 'I am no match for you in conversation, dearest. I blush when I think how I interfered at Florence, and you so well able to look after yourself, and so much cleverer in all ways than I am. You will never forgive me.'

'Shall we go out, then? They will smash all the china if we don't.'

For the air rang with the shrieks of Minnie, who was being scalped with a teaspoon.

'Dear, one moment—we may not have this chance for a chat again. Have you seen the young one yet?'

'Yes, I have.'

'What happened?'

'We met at the Rectory.'

'What line is he taking up?'

'No line. He talked about Italy, like any other person. It is really all right. What advantage would he get from being a cad, to put it bluntly? I do wish I could make you see it my way. He really won't be any nuisance, Charlotte.'

'Once a cad, always a cad. That is my poor opinion.'

Lucy paused. 'Cecil said one day—and I thought it so profound—that there are two kinds of cads—the conscious and the subconscious.' She paused again, to be sure of doing justice to Cecil's profundity. Through the window she saw Cecil himself, turning over the pages of a novel. It was a new one from Smith's library. Her mother must have returned from the station.

'Once a cad, always a cad,' droned Miss Bartlett.

'What I mean by subconscious is that Mr Emerson lost his head. I fell into all those violets, and he was silly and surprised. I don't think we ought to blame him very much. It makes such a difference when you see a person with beautiful things behind him unexpectedly. It really does; it makes an enormous difference, and he lost his head: he doesn't admire me, or any of that nonsense, one straw. Freddy rather likes him, and has asked him up here on Sunday, so you can judge for yourself. He has improved: he doesn't always look as if he is going to burst into tears. He is a clerk in the General Manager's office at one of the big railways—not a porter! and runs down to his father for week-ends. Papa was to do with journalism, but is rheumatic and has retired. There! Now for the garden.' She took hold of her guest by the arm. 'Suppose we don't talk about this silly Italian business any more. We want you to have a nice restful visit at Windy Corner, with no worriting.'

Lucy thought this rather a good speech. The reader may have detected an unfortunate slip in it. Whether Miss Bartlett detected the slip one cannot say, for it is impossible to penetrate into the minds of elderly people. She might have spoken further, but they were interrupted by the entrance of her hostess. Explanations took place, and in the midst of them Lucy escaped, the images throbbing a little more vividly in her brain.

Chapter Fifteen

The Disaster Within

The Sunday after Miss Bartlett's arrival was a glorious day, like most of the days of that year. In the Weald, autumn approached, breaking up the green monotony of summer, touching the parks with the grey bloom of mist, the beech-trees with russet, the oak-trees with gold. Up on the heights, battalions of black pines witnessed the change, themselves unchangeable.

Either country was spanned by a cloudless sky, and in either arose the tinkle
of church bells.

The garden of Windy Corner was deserted except for a red book, which
lay sunning itself upon the gravel path. From the house came incoherent
sounds, as of females preparing for worship. 'The men say they won't
go'–'Well, I don't blame them'–'Minnie says, need she go?'–'Tell her, no
nonsense'–'Anne! Mary! Hook me behind!'–'Dearest Lucia, may I trespass
upon you for a pin?' For Miss Bartlett had announced that she at all events
was one for church.

The sun rose higher on its journey, guided, not by Phaethon, but by
Apollo, competent, unswerving, divine. Its rays fell on the ladies whenever
they advanced towards the bedroom windows; on Mr Beebe down at
Summer Street as he smiled over a letter from Miss Catharine Alan; on
George Emerson cleaning his father's boots; and lastly, to complete the
catalogue of memorable things, on the red book mentioned above. The
ladies move, Mr Beebe moves, George moves, and movement may engender
shadow. But this book lies motionless, to be caressed all the morning by the
sun and to raise its covers slightly, as though acknowledging the caress.

Presently Lucy steps out of the drawing-room window. Her new cerise
dress has been a failure, and makes her look tawdry and wan. At her throat is
a garnet brooch, on her finger a ring set with rubies–an engagement ring.
Her eyes are bent to the Weald. She frowns a little–not in anger, but as a
brave child frowns when he is trying not to cry. In all that expanse no human
eye is looking at her, and she may frown unrebuked and measure the spaces
that yet survive between Apollo and the western hills.

'Lucy! Lucy! What's that book? Who's been taking a book out of the shelf
and leaving it about to spoil?'

'It's only the library book that Cecil's been reading.'

'But pick it up, and don't stand idling there like a flamingo.'

Lucy picked up the book and glanced at the title listlessly, 'Under a
Loggia.' She no longer read novels herself, devoting all her spare time to
solid literature in the hope of catching Cecil up. It was dreadful how little
she knew, and even when she thought she knew a thing, like the Italian
painters, she found she had forgotten it. Only this morning she had confused
Francesco Francia with Piero della Francesca, and Cecil had said, 'What!
you aren't forgetting your Italy already?' And this too had lent anxiety to her
eyes when she saluted the dear view and the dear garden in the foreground,
and above them, scarce conceivable elsewhere, the dear sun.

'Lucy–have you a sixpence for Minnie and a shilling for yourself?'

She hastened in to her mother, who was rapidly working herself into a
Sunday fluster.

'It's a special collection–I forget what for. I do beg, no vulgar clinking in
the plate with halfpennies; see that Minnie has a nice bright sixpence. Where
is the child? Minnie! That book's all warped' (Gracious, how plain you
look!) Put it under the Atlas to press. Minnie!'

'Oh, Mrs Honeychurch—' from the upper regions.

'Minnie, don't be late. Here comes the horse'–it was always the horse, never the carriage. 'Where's Charlotte? Run up and hurry her. Why is she so long? She had nothing to do. She never brings anything but blouses. Poor Charlotte—How I do detest blouses! Minnie!'

Paganism is infectious—more infectious than diphtheria or piety—and the Rector's niece was taken to church protesting. As usual, she didn't see why. Why shouldn't she sit in the sun with the young men? The young men, who had now appeared, mocked her with ungenerous words. Mrs Honeychurch defended orthodoxy, and in the midst of the confusion Miss Bartlett, dressed in the very height of the fashion, came strolling down the stairs.

'Dear Marian, I am very sorry, but I have no small change—nothing but sovereigns and half-crowns. Could anyone give me—'

'Yes, easily. Jump in. Gracious me, how smart you look. What a lovely frock! You put us all to shame.'

'If I did not wear my best rags and tatters now, when should I wear them?' said Miss Bartlett reproachfully. She got into the victoria and placed herself with her back to the horse. The necessary uproar ensued, and then they drove off.

'Goodbye! Be good!' called out Cecil.

Lucy bit her lip, for the tone was sneering. On the subject of 'church and so on' they had had rather an unsatisfactory conversation. He had said that people ought to overhaul themselves, and she did not want to overhaul herself: she did not know how it was done. Honest orthodoxy Cecil respected, but he always assumed that honesty is the result of a spiritual crisis: he could not imagine it as a natural birthright, that might grow heavenward like the flowers. All that he said on this subject pained her, though he exuded tolerance from every pore; somehow the Emersons were different.

She saw the Emersons after church. There was a line of carriages down the road, and the Honeychurch vehicle happened to be opposite Cissie Villa. To save time, they walked over the green to it, and found father and son smoking in the garden.

'Introduce me,' said her mother. 'Unless the young man considers that he knows me already.'

He probably did; but Lucy ignored the Sacred Lake and introduced them formally. Old Mr. Emerson claimed her with much warmth, and said how glad he was that she was going to be married. She said yes, she was glad too; and then, as Miss Bartlett and Minnie were lingering behind with Mr Beebe, she turned the conversation to a less disturbing topic, and asked him how he liked his new house.

'Very much,' he replied, but there was a note of offence in his voice: she had never known him offended before. He added: 'We find, though, that the Miss Alans were coming, and that we have turned them out. Women mind such a thing. I am very much upset about it.'

'I believe that there was some misunderstanding,' said Mrs Honeychurch uneasily.

'Our landlord was told that we should be a different type of person,' said George, who seemed disposed to carry the matter further. 'He thought we should be artistic. He is disappointed.'

'And I wonder whether we ought to write to the Miss Alans and offer to give it up. What do you think?' He appealed to Lucy.

'Oh, stop now you have come,' said Lucy lightly. She must avoid censuring Cecil. For it was on Cecil that the little episode turned, though his name was never mentioned.

'So George says. He says that the Miss Alans must go to the wall. Yet it does seem so unkind.'

'There is only a certain amount of kindness in the world,' said George, watching the sunlight flash on the panels of the passing carriages.

'Yes!' exclaimed Mrs Honeychurch. 'That's exactly what I say. Why all this twiddling and twaddling over two Miss Alans?'

'There is a certain amount of kindness, just as there is a certain amount of light,' he continued in measured tones. 'We cast a shadow on something wherever we stand, and it is no good moving from place to place to save things; because the shadow always follows. Choose a place where you won't do harm—yes, choose a place where you won't do very much harm, and stand in it for all you are worth, facing the sunshine.'

'Oh, Mr Emerson, I see you're clever!'

'Eh—?'

'I see you're going to be clever. I hope you didn't go behaving like that to poor Freddy.'

George's eyes laughed, and Lucy suspected that he and her mother would get on rather well.

'No, I didn't,' he said. 'He behaved that way to me. It is his philosophy. Only he starts life with it; and I have tried the Note of Interrogation first.'

'What *do* you mean? No, never mind what you mean. Don't explain. He looks forward to seeing you this afternoon. Do you play tennis? Do you mind tennis on Sunday—?'

'George mind tennis on Sunday! George, after his education, distinguish between Sunday—'

'Very well, George doesn't mind tennis on Sunday. No more do I. That's settled. Mr Emerson, if you could come with your son we should be so pleased.'

He thanked her, but the walk sounded rather far: he could only potter about in these days.

She turned to George: 'And then he wants to give up his house to the Miss Alans.'

'I know,' said George, and put his arm round his father's neck. The kindness that Mr Beebe and Lucy had always known to exist in him came out suddenly, like sunlight touching a vast landscape—a touch of the morning sun? She remembered that in all his perversities he had never spoken against affection.

Miss Bartlett approached.

'You know our cousin, Miss Bartlett,' said Mrs Honeychurch pleasantly. 'You met her with my daughter in Florence.'

'Yes, indeed!' said the old man, and made as if he would come out of the garden to greet the lady. Miss Bartlett promptly got into the victoria. Thus entrenched, she emitted a formal bow. It was the Pension Bertolini again, the dining-table with the decanters of water and wine. It was the old, old battle of the room with the view.

George did not respond to the bow. Like any boy, he blushed and was ashamed: he knew that the chaperon remembered. He said: 'I–I'll come up to tennis if I can manage it,' and went into the house. Perhaps anything that he did would have pleased Lucy, but his awkwardness went straight to her heart: men were not gods after all, but as human and as clumsy as girls; even men might suffer from unexplained desires, and need help. To one of her upbringing, and of her destination, the weakness of men was a truth unfamiliar, but she had surmised it at Florence, when George threw her photographs into the River Arno.

'George, don't go,' cried his father, who thought it a great treat for people if his son would talk to them. 'George has been in such good spirits to-day, and I am sure he will end by coming up this afternoon.'

Lucy caught her cousin's eye. Something in its mute appeal made her reckless. 'Yes,' she said, raising her voice, 'I do hope he will.' Then she went to the carriage and murmured, 'The old man hasn't been told; I knew it was all right.' Mrs Honeychurch followed her, and they drove away.

Satisfactory that Mr Emerson had not been told of the Florence escapade; yet Lucy's spirits should not have leapt up as if she had sighted the ramparts of heaven. Satisfactory; yet surely she greeted it with disproportionate joy. All the way home the horses' hoofs sang a tune to her: 'He has not told, he has not told.' Her brain expanded the melody: 'He has not told his father–to whom he tells all things. It was not an exploit. He did not laugh at me when I had gone.' She raised her hand to her cheek. 'He does not love me. No. How terrible if he did! But he has not told. He will not tell.'

She longed to shout the words: 'It is all right. It's a secret between us two for ever. Cecil will never hear.' She was even glad that Miss Bartlett had made her promise secrecy, that last dark evening at Florence, when they had knelt packing in his room. The secret, big or little, was guarded. Only three English people knew of it in the world.

Thus she interpreted her joy. She greeted Cecil with unusual radiance, because she felt so safe. As he helped her out of the carriage, she said:

'The Emersons have been so nice. George Emerson has improved enormously.'

'Oh, how are my protégés?' asked Cecil, who took no real interest in them, and had long since forgotten his resolution to bring them to Windy Corner for educational purposes.

'Protégés!' she exclaimed with some warmth.

For the only relationship which Cecil conceived was feudal: that of protector and protected. He had no glimpse of the comradeship after which the girl's soul yearned.

'You shall see for youself how your protégés are. George Emerson is coming up this afternoon. He is a most interesting man to talk to. Only don't—' She nearly said, 'Don't protect him.' But the bell was ringing for luch, and, as often happened, Cecil had paid no great attention to her remarks. Charm, not argument, was to be her forte.

Lunch was a cheerful meal. Generally Lucy was depressed at meals. Some one had to be soothed–either Cecil or Miss Bartlett or a Being not visible to the mortal eye–a Being who whispered to her soul: 'It will not last, this cheerfulness. In January you must go to London to entertain the grandchildren of celebrated men.' But to-day she felt she had received a guarantee. Her mother would always sit there, her brother here. The sun, though it had moved a little since the morning, would never be hidden behind the western hills. After luncheon they asked her to play. She had seen Gluck's 'Armide' that year, and played from memory the music of the enchanted garden–the music to which Renaud approaches, beneath the light of an eternal dawn, the music that never gains, never wanes, but ripples for ever like the tideless seas of fairyland. Such music is not for the piano, and her audience began to get restive, and Cecil, sharing the discontent, called out: 'Now play us the other garden–the one in "Parsifal."'

She closed the instrument.

'Not very dutiful,' said her mother's voice.

Fearing that she had offended Cecil, she turned quickly round. There George was. He had crept in without interrupting her.

'Oh, I had no idea?' she exclaimed, getting very red; and then, without a word of greeting, she reopened the piano. Cecil should have the 'Parsifal,' and anything else that he liked.

'Our performer has changed her mind,' said Miss Bartlett, perhaps implying, 'she will play the music to Mr Emerson. Lucy did not know what to do, nor even what she wanted to do. She played a few bars of the Flower Maidens' song very badly, and then she stopped.

'I vote tennis,' said Freddy, disgusted at the scrappy entertainment.

'Yes, so do I.' Once more she closed the unfortunate piano. 'I vote you have a men's four.'

'All right.'

'Not for me, thank you,' said Cecil. 'I will not spoil the set.' He never realized that it may be an act of kindness in a bad player to make up a fourth.

'Oh, come along, Cecil. I'm bad, Floyd's rotten, and so I dare say's Emerson.'

George corrected him: 'I am not bad.'

One looked down one's nose at this. 'Then certainly I won't play,' said Cecil, while Miss Bartlett, under the impression that she was snubbing George, added: 'I agree with you, Mr Vyse. You had much better not play. Much better not.'

Minnie, rushing in where Cecil feared to tread, announced that she would play. 'I shall miss every ball anyway, so what does it matter?' But Sunday intervened and stamped heavily upon the kind suggestion.

'Then it will have to be Lucy,' said Mrs Honeychurch; 'you must fall back on Lucy. There is no other way out of it. Lucy, go and change your frock.'

Lucy's Sabbath was generally of this amphibious nature. She kept it without hypocrisy in the morning, and broke it without reluctance in the afternoon. As she changed her frock, she wondered whether Cecil was sneering at her: really she must overhaul herself and settle everything up before she married him.

Mr Floyd was her partner. She liked music, but how much better tennis seemed. How much better to run about in comfortable clothes than to sit at the piano and feel girt under the arms. Once more music appeared to her the employment of a child. George served, and surprised her by his anxiety to win. She remembered how he had sighed among the tombs at Santa Croce because things wouldn't fit; how after the death of that obscure Italian he had leant over the parapet by the Arno and said to her: 'I shall want to live, I tell you.' He wanted to live now, to win at tennis, to stand for all he was worth in the sun—in the sun which had begun to decline and was shining in her eyes; and he did win.

Ah, how beautiful the Weald looked! The hills stood out above its radiance, as Fiesole stands above the Tuscan Plain, and the South Downs, if one chose, were the mountains of Carrara. She might be forgetting her Italy, but she was noticing more things in her England. One could play a new game with the view, and try to find in its innumerable folds some town or village that would do for Florence. Ah, how beautiful the Weald looked!

But now Cecil claimed her. He chanced to be in a lucid critical mood, and would not sympathize with exaltation. He had been rather a nuisance all through the tennis, for the novel that he was reading was so bad that he was obliged to read it aloud to others. He would stroll round the precincts of the court and call out: 'I say, listen to this, Lucy. Three split infinitives.' 'Dreadful!' said Lucy, and missed her stroke. When they had finished their set, he still went on reading; there was some murder scene, and really every one must listen to it. Freddy and Mr Floyd were obliged to hunt for a lost ball in the laurels, but the other two acquiesced.

'The scene is laid in Florence.'

'What fun, Cecil! Read away. Come, Mr Emerson, sit down after all your energy.' She had 'forgiven' George, as she put it, and she made a point of being pleasant to him.

He jumped over the net and sat down at her feet, asking: 'You—and are you tired?'

'Of course I'm not!'

'Do you mind being beaten?'

She was going to answer 'No,' when it struck her that she did mind, so she answered 'Yes.' She added merrily, 'I don't see *you're* such a splendid player, though. The light was behind you, and it was in my eyes.'

'I never said I was.'

'Why, you did!'

'You didn't attend.'

'You said—oh, don't go in for accuracy at this house. We all exaggerate, and we get very angry with people who don't.'

'The scene is laid in Florence,' repeated Cecil, with an upward note.

Lucy recollected herself.

'"Sunset. Leonora was speeding—"'

Lucy interrupted. 'Leonora? Is Leonora the heroine? Who's the book by?'

'Joseph Emery Prank. "Sunset. Leonora was speeding across the square. Pray the saints she might not arrive too late. Sunset—the sunset of Italy. Under Orcagna's Loggia—the Loggia de' Lanzi, as we sometimes call it now—"'

Lucy burst into laughter. '"Joseph Emery Prank" indeed! Why, it's Miss Lavish! It's Miss Lavish's novel, and she's publishing it under somebody else's name.'

'Who may Miss Lavish be?'

'Oh, a dreadful person—Mr Emerson, you remember Miss Lavish?' Excited by her pleasant afternoon, she clapped her hands.

George looked up. 'Of course I do. I saw her the day I arrived at Summer Street. It was she who told me that you lived here.'

'Weren't you pleased?' She meant—'to see Miss Lavish,' but when he bent down to the grass without replying, it struck her that she could mean something else. She watched his head, which was almost resting against her knee, and she thought that the ears were reddening. 'No wonder the novel's bad,' she added. 'I never liked Miss Lavish. But I suppose one ought to read it as one's met her.'

'All modern books are bad,' said Cecil, who was annoyed at her inattention, and vented his annoyance on literature. 'Every one writes for money in these days.'

'Oh, Cecil—!'

'It is so. I will inflict Joseph Emery Prank on you no longer.'

Cecil, this afternoon, seemed such a twittering sparrow. The ups and downs in his voice were noticeable, but they did not affect her. She had dwelt amongst melody and movement, and her nerves refused to answer to the clang of his. Leaving him to be annoyed, she gazed at the black head again. She did not want to stroke it, but she saw herself wanting to stroke it: the sensation was curious.

'How do you like this view of ours, Mr Emerson?'

'I never notice much difference in views.'

'What do you mean?'

'Because they are all alike. Because all that matters in them is distance and air.'

'H'm!' said Cecil, uncertain whether the remark was striking or not.

'My father'—he looked up at her (and he was a little flushed)—'says that there is only one perfect view—the view of the sky straight over our heads, and that all these views on earth are but bungled copies of it.'

'I expect your father has been reading Dante,' said Cecil, fingering the novel, which alone permitted him to lead the conversation.

'He told us another day that views are really crowds – crowds of trees and houses and hills—and are bound to resemble each other, like human crowds—and that the power they have over us is something supernatural, for the same reason.'

Lucy's lips parted.

'For a crowd is more than the people who make it up. Something gets added to it—no one knows how—just as something has got added to those hills.'

He pointed with his racquet to the South Downs.

'What a splendid idea!' she murmured. 'I shall enjoy hearing your father talk again. I'm so sorry he's not so well.'

'No, he isn't well.'

'There's an absurd account of a view in this book,' said Cecil.

'Also that men fall into two classes—those who forget views and those who remember them, even in small rooms.'

'Mr Emerson, have you any brothers or sisters?'

'None. Why?'

'You spoke of "us."'

'My mother, I was meaning.'

Cecil closed the novel with a bang.

'Oh, Cecil—how you make me jump!'

'I will inflict Joseph Emery Prank on you no longer.'

'I can just remember us all three going into the country for the day and seeing as far as Hindhead. It is the first thing that I remember.'

Cecil got up: the man was ill-bred—he hadn't put on his coat after tennis—he didn't do. He would have strolled away if Lucy had not stopped him.

'Cecil, do read the thing about the view.'

'Not while Mr Emerson is here to entertain us.'

'No—read away. I think nothing's funnier than to hear silly things read out loud. If Mr Emerson thinks us frivolous he can go.'

This struck Cecil as subtle, and pleased him. It put their visitor in the position of a prig. Somewhat mollified, he sat down again.

'Mr Emerson, go and find tennis balls.' She opened the book. Cecil must have his reading and anything else that he liked. But her attention wandered to George's mother, who—according to Mr Eager—had been murdered in the sight of God and – according to her son—had seen as far as Hindhead.

'Am I really to go?' asked George.

'No, of course, not really,' she answered.

'Chapter two,' said Cecil, yawning. 'Find me chapter two, if it isn't bothering you.'

Chapter two was found, and she glanced at its opening sentences.

She thought she had gone mad.

'Here—hand me the book.'

She heard her voice saying: 'It isn't worth reading—it's too silly to read—I never saw such rubbish – it oughtn't to be allowed to be printed.'

He took the book from her.

'"Leonora,"' he read, '"sat pensive and alone. Before her lay the rich champaign of Tuscany, dotted over with many a smiling village. The season was spring."'

Miss Lavish knew, somehow, and had printed the past in draggled prose, for Cecil to read and for George to hear.

'"A golden haze,"' he read. He read: '"Afar off the towers of Florence, while the bank on which she sat was carpeted with violets. All unobserved, Antonio stole up behind her—"'

Lest Cecil should see her face she turned to George, and she saw his face.

He read: "'There came from his lips no wordy protestation such as formal lovers use. No eloquence was his, nor did he suffer from the lack of it. He simply enfolded her in his manly arms.'"

There was a silence.

'This isn't the passage I wanted,' he informed them. 'There is another much funnier, further on.' He turned over the leaves.

'Should we go in to tea?' said Lucy, whose voice remained steady.

She led the way up the garden, Cecil following her, George last. She thought a disaster was averted. But when they entered the shrubbery it came. The book, as if it had not worked mischief enough, had been forgotten, and Cecil must go back for it; and George, who loved passionately, must blunder against her in the narrow path.

'No—' she gasped, and, for the second time, was kissed by him.

As if no more was possible, he slipped back; Cecil rejoined her; they reached the upper lawn alone.

Chapter Sixteen

Lying to George

But Lucy had developed since the spring. That is to say, she was now better able to stifle the emotions of which the conventions and the world disapprove. Though the danger was greater, she was not shaken by deep sobs. She said to Cecil, 'I am not coming in to tea—tell mother—I must write some letters,' and went up to her room. There she prepared for action. Love felt and returned, love which our bodies exact and our hearts have transfigured, love which is the most real thing that we shall ever meet, reappeared now as the world's enemy, and she must stifle it.

She sent for Miss Bartlett.

The contest lay not between love and duty. Perhaps there never is such a contest. It lay between the real and the pretended, and Lucy's first aim was to defeat herself. As her brain clouded over, as the memory of the views grew dim and the words of the book died away, she returned to her old shibboleth of nerves. She 'conquered her breakdown'. Tampering with the truth, she forgot that the truth had ever been. Remembering that she was engaged to Cecil, she compelled herself to confused remembrances of George; he was nothing to her: he never had been anything: he had behaved abominably; she had never encouraged him. The armour of falsehood is subtly wrought out of darkness, and hides a man not only from others, but from his own soul. In a few moments Lucy was equipped for battle.

'Something too awful has happened,' she began, as soon as her cousin arrived. 'Do you know anything about Miss Lavish's novel?'

Miss Bartlett looked surprised, and said that she had not read the book, nor known that it was published; Eleanor was a reticent woman at heart.

'There is a scene in it. The hero and heroine make love. Do you know about that?'

'Dear—?'

'Do you know about it, please?' she repeated. 'They are on a hill-side, and Florence is in the distance.'

'My good Lucia, I am all at sea. I know nothing about it whatever.'

'There are violets. I cannot believe it is a coincidence. Charlotte, Charlotte, how *could* you have told her? I have thought before speaking: it *must* be you.'

'Told her what?' she asked, with growing agitation.

'About that dreadful afternoon in February.'

Miss Bartlett was genuinely moved. 'Oh, Lucy, dearest girl—she hasn't put that in her book?'

Lucy nodded.

'Not so that one could recognize it?'

'Yes.'

'Then never—never—never more shall Eleanor Lavish be friend of mine.'

'So you did tell?'

'I did just happen—when I had tea with her at Rome—in the course of conversation—'

'But, Charlotte—what about the promise you gave me when we were packing? Why did you tell Miss Lavish, when you wouldn't even let me tell mother?'

'I will never forgive Eleanor. She has betrayed my confidence.'

'Why did you tell her, though? This is a most serious thing.'

Why does anyone tell anything? The question is eternal, and it was not surprising that Miss Bartlett should only sigh faintly in response. She had done wrong—she admitted it; she only hoped that she had not done harm; she had told Eleanor in the strictest confidence.

Lucy stamped with irritation.

'Cecil happened to read out the passage aloud to me and to Mr Emerson; it upset Mr Emerson, and he insulted me again. Behind Cecil's back. Ugh! Is it possible that men are such brutes? Behind Cecil's back as we were walking up the garden.'

Miss Bartlett burst into self-accusations and regrets.

'What is to be done now? Can you tell me?'

'Oh, Lucy—I shall never forgive myself, never to my dying day. Fancy if your prospects—'

'I know,' said Lucy, wincing at the word. 'I see now why you wanted me to tell Cecil, and what you meant by "some other source". You knew that you had told Miss Lavish, and that she was not reliable.'

It was Miss Bartlett's turn to wince.

'However,' said the girl, despising her cousin's shiftiness, 'what's done's done. You have put me in a most awkward position. How am I to get out of it?'

Miss Bartlett could not think. The days of her energy were over. She was a visitor, not a chaperon, and a discredited visitor at that. She stood with clasped hands while the girl worked herself into the necessary rage.

'He must—that man must have such a setting down that he won't forget. And who's to give it him? I can't tell mother now—owing to you. Nor Cecil, Charlotte, owing to you. I am caught up every way. I think I shall go mad. I have no one to help me. That's why I've sent for you. What's wanted is a man with a whip.'

Miss Bartlett agreed: one wanted a man with a whip.

'Yes—but it's no good agreeing. What's to be *done*? We women go maundering on. What *does* a girl do when she comes across a cad?'

'I always said he was a cad, dear. Give me credit for that, at all events. From the very first moment—when he said his father was having a bath.'

'Oh, bother the credit and who's been right or wrong! We've both made a muddle of it. George Emerson is still down the garden there, and is he to be left unpunished, or isn't he? I want to know.'

Miss Bartlett was absolutely helpless. Her own exposure had unnerved her, and thoughts were colliding painfully in her brain. She moved feebly to the window, and tried to detect the cad's white flannels among the laurels.

'You were ready enough at the Bertolini when you rushed me off to Rome. Can't you speak again to him now?'

'Willingly would I move heaven and earth—'

'I want something more definite,' said Lucy contemptuously. 'Will you speak to him? It is the least you can do, surely, considering it all happened because you broke your word.'

'Never again shall Eleanor Lavish be friend of mine.'

Really, Charlotte was outdoing herself.

'Yes or no, please: yes or no.'

'It is the kind of thing that only a gentleman can settle.'

George Emerson was coming up the garden with a tennis ball in his hand.

'Very well,' said Lucy, with an angry gesture. 'No one will help me. I will speak to him myself.' And immediately she realized that this was what her cousin had intended all along.

'Hullo, Emerson!' called Freddy from below. 'Found the lost ball? Good man! Want any tea?' And there was an irruption from the house on to the terrace.

'Oh, Lucy, but that is brave of you! I admire you—'

They had gathered round George, who beckoned, she felt, over the rubbish, the sloppy thoughts, the furtive yearnings that were beginning to cumber her soul. Her anger faded at the sight of him. Ah! the Emersons were fine people in their way. She had to subdue a rush in her blood before saying:

'Freddy has taken him into the dining-room. The others are going down the garden. Come. Let us get this over quickly. Come. I want you in the room, of course.'

'Lucy, do you mind doing it?'

'How can you ask such a ridiculous question?'

'Poor Lucy—' She stretched out her hand. 'I seem to bring nothing but misfortune wherever I go.' Lucy nodded. She remembered their last evening at Florence–the packing, the candle, the shadow of Miss Bartlett's toque on the door. She was not to be trapped by pathos a second time. Eluding her cousin's caress, she led the way downstairs.

'Try the jam,' Freddy was saying. 'The jam's jolly good.'

George, looking big and dishevelled, was pacing up and down the dining-room. As she entered he stopped, and said:

'No–nothing to eat.'

'You go down to the others,' said Lucy; 'Charlotte and I will give Mr Emerson all he wants. Where's mother?'

'She's started on her Sunday writing. She's in the drawing-room.'

'That's all right. You go away.'

He went off singing.

Lucy sat down at the table. Miss Bartlett, who was thoroughly frightened, took up a book and pretended to read.

She would not be drawn into an elaborate speech. She just said: 'I can't have it, Mr Emerson. I cannot even talk to you. Go out of this house, and never come into it again as long as I live here'–flushing as she spoke and pointing to the door. 'I hate a row. Go, please.'

'What—'

'No discussion.'

'But I can't—'

She shook her head. 'Go, please. I do not want to call in Mr Vyse.'

'You don't mean,' he said, absolutely ignoring Miss Bartlett–'you don't mean that you are going to marry that man?'

The line was unexpected.

She shrugged her shoulders, as if his vulgarity wearied her. 'You are merely ridiculous,' she said quietly.

Then his words rose gravely over hers: 'You cannot live with Vyse. He's only for an acquaintance. He is for society and cultivated talk. He should know no one intimately, least of all a woman.'

It was a new light on Cecil's character.

'Have you ever talked to Vyse without feeling tired?'

'I can scarcely discuss—'

'No, but have you ever? He is the sort who are all right so long as they keep to things–books, pictures–but kill when they come to people. That's why I'll speak out through all this muddle even now. It's shocking enough to lose you in any case, but generally a man must deny himself joy, and I would have held back if your Cecil had been a different person. I would never have let myself go. But I saw him first in the National Gallery, when he winced because my father mispronounced the names of great painters. Then he brings us here, and we find it is to play some silly trick on a kind neighbour. That is the man all over–playing tricks on people, on the most sacred form of life that he can find. Next, I meet you together, and find him protecting and teaching you and your mother to be shocked, when it was for *you* to settle whether you were shocked or no. Cecil all over again. He daren't let a woman decide. He's the type who's kept Europe back for a thousand years. Every moment of his life he's forming you, telling you what's charming or amusing or ladylike, telling you what a man thinks womanly; and you, you of all women, listen to his voice instead of your own. So it was at the Rectory, when I met you both again; so it has been the whole of this afternoon. Therefore—not "therefore I kissed you," because the book made me do that, and I wish to goodness I had more self-control. I'm not ashamed. I don't apologize. But it has frightened you, and you may not have noticed that I love you. Or would you have told me to go, and dealt with a tremendous thing so lightly? But therefore—therefore I settled to fight him.'

Lucy thought of a very good remark.

'You say Mr Vyse wants me to listen to him, Mr Emerson. Pardon me for suggesting that you have caught the habit.'

And he took the shoddy reproof and touched it into immortality. He said:

'Yes, I have,' and sank down as if suddenly weary. 'I'm the same kind of brute at bottom. This desire to govern a woman—it lies very deep, and men and women must fight it together before they shall enter the garden. But I do love you—surely in a better way than he does.' He thought. 'Yes—really in a better way. I want you to have your own thoughts even when I hold you in my arms.' He stretched them towards her. 'Lucy, be quick—there's no time for us to talk now—come to me as you came in the spring, and afterwards I will be gentle and explain. I have cared for you since that man died. I cannot live without you. "No, good," I thought: "she is marrying some one else"; but I meet you again when all the world is glorious water and sun. As you came through the wood I saw that nothing else mattered. I called. I wanted to live and have my chance of joy.'

'And Mr Vyse?' said Lucy, who kept commendably calm. 'Does he not matter? That I love Cecil and shall be his wife shortly? A detail of no importance, I suppose?'

But he stretched his arms over the table towards her.

'May I ask what you intend to gain by this exhibition?'

He said: 'It is our last chance. I shall do all that I can.' And as if he had done all else, he turned to Miss Bartlett, who sat like some portent against the skies of evening. 'You wouldn't stop us this second time if you understood,' he said. 'I have been into the dark, and I am going back into it, unless you will try to understand.'

Her long, narrow head drove backwards and forwards, as though demolishing some invisible obstacle. She did not answer.

'It is being young,' he said quietly, picking up his racquet from the floor and preparing to go. 'It is being certain that Lucy cares for me really. It is that love and youth matter intellectually.'

In silence the two women watched him. His last remark, they knew, was nonsense, but was he going after it or not? Would not he, the cad, the charlatan, attempt a more dramatic finish? No. He was apparently content. He left them, carefully closing the front door; and when they looked through the hall window, they saw him go up the drive and begin to climb the slopes of withered fern behind the house. Their tongues were loosed, and they burst into stealthy rejoicings.

'Oh, Lucia–come back here–oh, what an awful man!'

Lucy had no reaction–at least, not yet. 'Well, he amuses me,' she said. 'Either I'm mad, or else he is, and I'm inclined to think it's the latter. One more fuss through with you, Charlotte. Many thanks. I think, though, that this is the last. My admirer will hardly trouble me again.'

And Miss Bartlett, too, essayed the roguish:

'Well, it isn't every one who could boast such a conquest, dearest, is it? Oh, one oughtn't to laugh, really. It might have been very serious. But you were so sensible and brave–so unlike the girls of my day.'

'Let's go down to them.'

But, once in the open air, she paused. Some emotion–pity, terror, love, but the emotion was strong–seized her, and she was aware of autumn. Summer was ending, and the evening brought her odours of decay, the more pathetic because they were reminiscent of spring. That something or other mattered intellectually? A leaf, violently agitated, danced past her, while other leaves lay motionless. That the earth was hastening to re-enter darkness, and the shadows of those trees to creep over Windy Corner?

'Hullo, Lucy! There's still light enough for another set, if you two'll hurry.'

'Mr Emerson has had to go.'

'What a nuisance! That spoils the four. I say, Cecil, do play, do, there's a good chap. It's Floyd's last day. Do play tennis with us, just this once.'

Cecil's voice came: 'My dear Freddy, I am no athlete. As you well remarked this very morning, "There are some chaps who are no good for anything but books"; I plead guilty to being such a chap, and will not inflict myself on you.'

The scales fell from Lucy's eyes. How had she stood Cecil for a moment? He was absolutely intolerable, and the same evening she broke her engagement off.

Chapter Seventeen

Lying to Cecil

He was bewildered. He had nothing to say. He was not even angry, but stood, with a glass of whisky between his hands, trying to think what had led her to such a conclusion.

She had chosen the moment before bed, when, in accordance with their bourgeois habit, she always dispensed drinks to the men. Freddy and Mr Floyd were sure to retire with their glasses, while Cecil invariably lingered, sipping at his while she locked up the sideboard.

'I am very sorry about it,' she said; 'I have carefully thought things over. We are too different. I must ask you to release me, and try to forget that there ever was such a foolish girl.'

It was a suitable speech, but she was more angry than sorry, and her voice showed it.

'Different—how—how—'

'I haven't had a really good education, for one thing,' she continued, still on her knees by the sideboard. 'My Italian trip came too late, and I am forgetting all that I learnt there. I shall never be able to talk to your friends, or behave as a wife of yours should.'

'I don't understand you. You aren't like yourself. You're tired, Lucy.'

'Tired!' she retorted, kindling at once. 'That is exactly like you. You always think women don't mean what they say.'

'Well, you sound tired, as if something has worried you.'

'What if I do? It doesn't prevent me from realizing the truth. I can't marry you, and you will thank me for saying so some day.'

'You had that bad headache yesterday— All right'–for she had exclaimed indignantly–'I see it's much more than headaches. But give me a moment's time.' He closed his eyes. 'You must excuse me if I say stupid things, but my brain has gone to pieces. Part of it lives three minutes back, when I was sure that you loved me, and the other part–I find it difficult–I am likely to say the wrong thing.'

It struck her that he was not behaving so badly, and her irritation increased. She again desired a struggle, not a discussion. To bring on the crisis, she said:

'There are days when one sees clearly, and this is one of them. Things must come to a breaking-point some time, and it happens to be to-day. If you want to know, quite a little thing decided me to speak to you–when you wouldn't play tennis with Freddy.'

'I never do play tennis,' said Cecil, painfully bewildered; 'I never could play. I don't understand a word you say.'

'You can play well enough to make up a four. I thought it abominably selfish of you.'

'No, I can't–well, never mind the tennis. Why couldn't you–couldn't you have warned me if you felt anything wrong? You talked of our wedding at lunch–at least, you let me talk.'

'I knew you wouldn't understand,' said Lucy quite crossly. 'I might have known there would have been these dreadful explanations. Of course, it isn't the tennis–that was only the last straw to all I have been feeling for weeks. Surely it was better not to speak till I felt certain.' She developed this position. 'Often before I have wondered if I was fitted for your wife–for instance, in London; and are you fitted to be my husband? I don't think so. You don't like Freddy, nor my mother. There was always a lot against our engagement, Cecil, but all our relations seemed pleased, and we met so often, and it was no good mentioning it until–well, until all things came to a point. They have to-day. I see clearly. I must speak. That's all.'

'I cannot think you were right,' said Cecil gently. 'I cannot tell why, but though all that you say sounds true, I feel that you are not treating me fairly. It's all too horrible.'

'What's the good of a scene?'

'No good. But surely I have a right to hear a little more.'

He put down his glass and opened the window. From where she knelt, jangling her keys, she could see a slit of darkness, and, peering into it, as if it would tell him that 'little more,' his long, thoughtful face.

'Don't open the window; and you'd better draw the curtain, too; Freddy or anyone might be outside.' He obeyed. 'I really think we had better to go bed, if you don't mind. I shall only say things that will make me unhappy afterwards. As you say, it is all too horrible, and it is no good talking.'

But to Cecil, now that he was about to lose her, she seemed each moment more desirable. He looked at her, instead of through her, for the first time since they were engaged. From a Leonardo she had become a living woman, with mysteries and forces of her own, with qualities that even eluded art. His brain recovered from the shock, and in a burst of genuine devotion, he cried: 'But I love you, and I did think you loved me!'

'I did not,' she said. 'I thought I did at first. I am sorry, and ought to have refused you this last time, too.'

He began to walk up and down the room, and she grew more and more vexed at his dignified behaviour. She had counted on his being petty. It would have made things easier for her. By a cruel irony she was drawing out all that was finest in his disposition.

'You don't love me, evidently. I dare say you are right not to. But it would hurt a little less if I knew why.'

'Because'—a phrase came to her, and she accepted it—'you're the sort who can't know anyone intimately.'

A horrified look came into his eyes.

'I don't mean exactly that. But you will question me, though I beg you not to, and I must say something. It is that, more or less. When we were only acquaintances, you let me be myself, but now you're always protecting me.' Her voice swelled. 'I won't be protected. I will choose for myself what is ladylike and right. To shield me is an insult. Can't I be trusted to face the truth but I must get it second-hand through you? A woman's place! You despise my mother—I know you do—because she's conventional and bothers over puddings; but, oh goodness!'—she rose to her feet—'conventional, Cecil, you're that, for you may understand beautiful things, but you don't know how to use them; and you wrap yourself up in art and books and music, and would try to wrap up me. I won't be stifled, not by the most glorious music, for people are more glorious, and you hide them from me. That's why I break off my engagement. You were all right as long as you kept to things, but when you came to people—' She stopped.

There was a pause. Then Cecil said with great emotion:

'It is true.'

'True on the whole,' she corrected, full of some vague shame.

'True, every word. It is a revelation. It is—I.'

'Anyhow, those are my reasons for not being your wife.'

He repeated: '"The sort that can know no one intimately." It is true. I fell to pieces the very first day we were engaged. I behaved like a cad to Beebe and to your brother. You are even greater than I thought.' She withdrew a step. 'I'm not going to worry you. You are far too good to me. I shall never forget your insight; and, dear, I only blame you for this: you might have warned me in the early stages, before you felt you wouldn't marry me, and so have given me a chance to improve. I have never known you till this evening. I have just used you as a peg for my silly notions of what a woman should be. But this evening you are a different person: new thoughts—even a new voice—'

'What do you mean by a new voice?' she asked, seized with incontrollable anger.

'I mean that a new person seems speaking through you,' said he.

Then she lost her balance. She cried: 'If you think I am in love with some one else, you are very much mistaken.'

'Of course I don't think that. You are not that kind, Lucy.'

'Oh yes, you do think it. It's your old idea, the idea that has kept Europe back—I mean the idea that women are always thinking of men. If a girl breaks off her engagement, every one says: "Oh, she had some one else in her mind; she hopes to get some one else." It's disgusting, brutal! As if a girl can't break it off for the sake of freedom.'

He answered reverently: 'I may have said that in the past. I shall never say it again. You have taught me better.'

She began to redden, and pretended to examine the windows again.

'Of course, there is no question of "some one else" in this, no "jilting" or any such nauseous stupidity. I beg your pardon most humbly if my words suggested that there was. I only meant that there was a force in you that I hadn't known of up till now.'

'All right, Cecil, that will do. Don't apologize to me. It was my mistake.'

'It is a question between ideals, yours and mine—pure abstract ideals, and yours are the nobler. I was bound up in the old vicious notions, and all the time you were splendid and new.' His voice broke. 'I must actually thank you for what you have done—for showing me what I really am. Solemnly, I thank you for showing me a true woman. Will you shake hands?'

'Of course I will,' said Lucy, twisting up her other hand in the curtains. 'Good night, Cecil. Good-bye. That's all right. I'm sorry about it. Thank you very much for your gentleness.'

'Let me light your candle, shall I?'

They went into the hall.

'Thank you. Good night again. God bless you, Lucy!'

'Good-bye, Cecil.'

She watched him steal upstairs, while the shadows from the banisters passed over her face like the beat of wings. On the landing he paused, strong in his renunciation, and gave her a look of memorable beauty. For all his culture, Cecil was an ascetic at heart, and nothing in his love became him like the leaving of it.

She could never marry. In the tumult of her soul, that stood firm. Cecil believed in her; she must some day believe in herself. She must be one of the women whom she had praised so eloquently, who care for liberty and not for men; she must forget that George loved her, that George had been thinking through her and gained her this honourable release, that George had gone away into—what was it?—the darkness.

She put out the lamp.

It did not do to think, nor, for the matter of that, to feel. She gave up trying to understand herself, and joined the vast armies of the benighted, who follow neither the heart nor the brain, and march to their destiny by catch-words. The armies are full of pleasant and pious folk. But they have yielded to the only enemy that matters—the enemy within. They have sinned against passion and truth, and vain will be their strife after virtue. As the years pass, they are censured. Their pleasantry and their piety show cracks, their wit becomes cynicism, their unselfishness hypocrisy; they feel and produce discomfort wherever they go. They have sinned against Eros and against Pallas Athene, and not by any heavenly intervention, but by the ordinary course of nature, those allied deities will be avenged.

Lucy entered this army when she pretended to George that she did not love him, and pretended to Cecil that she loved no one. The night received her, as it had received Miss Bartlett thirty years before.

Chapter Eighteen

Lying to Mr Beebe, Mrs Honeychurch, Freddy, and the Servants

Windy Corner lay, not on the summit of the ridge, but a few hundred feet down the southern slope, at the springing of one of the great buttresses that supported the hill. On either side of it was a shallow ravine, filled with ferns and pine-trees, and down the ravine on the left ran the highway into the Weald.

Whenever Mr Beebe crossed the ridge and caught sight of these noble dispositions of the earth, and, poised in the middle of them, Windy Corner—he laughed. The situation was so glorious, the house so commonplace, not to say impertinent. The late Mr Honeychurch had affected the cube, because it gave him the most accommodation for his money, and the only addition made by his widow had been a small turret, shaped like a rhinoceros' horn, where she could sit in wet weather and watch the carts going up and down the road. So impertinent—and yet the house 'did,' for it was the home of people who loved their surroundings honestly. Other houses in the neighbourhood had been built by expensive architects, over others their inmates had fidgeted sedulously, yet all these suggested the accidental, the temporary; while Windy Corner seemed as inevitable as an ugliness of Nature's own creation. One might laugh at the house, but one never shuddered.

Mr Beebe was bicycling over this Monday afternoon with a little piece of gossip. He had heard from the Miss Alans. These admirable ladies, since they could not go to Cissie Villa, had changed their plans. They were going to Greece instead.

'Since Florence did my poor sister so much good,' wrote Miss Catherine, 'we do not see why we should not try Athens this winter. Of course, Athens is a plunge, and the doctor has ordered her special digestive bread; but, after all, we can take that with us, and it is only getting first into a steamer and then into a train. But is there an English Church?' And the letter went on to say: 'I do not expect we shall go any farther than Athens, but if you knew of a really comfortable pension at Constantinople, we should be so grateful.'

Lucy would enjoy this letter, and the smile with which Mr Beebe greeted Windy Corner was partly for her. She would see the fun of it, and some of its beauty, for she must see some beauty. Though she was hopeless about pictures, and though she dressed so unevenly–oh, that cerise frock yesterday at church!–she must see some beauty in life, or she could not play the piano as she did. He had a theory that musicians are incredibly complex, and know far less than other artists what they want and what they are; that they puzzle themselves as well as their friends; that their psychology is a modern development, and has not yet been understood. This theory, had he known it, had possibly just been illustrated by facts. Ignorant of the events of yesterday, he was only riding over to get some tea, to see his niece, and to observe whether Miss Honeychurch saw anything beautiful in the desire of two old ladies to visit Athens.

A carriage was drawn up outside Windy Corner, and just as he caught sight of the house it started, bowled up the drive, and stopped abruptly when it reached the main road. Therefore it must be the horse, who always expected people to walk up the hill in case they tired him. The door opened obediently, and two men emerged, whom Mr Beebe recognized as Cecil and Freddy. They were an odd couple to go driving; but he saw a trunk beside the coachman's legs. Cecil, who wore a bowler, must be going away, while Freddy–(a cap)–was seeing him to the station. They walked rapidly, taking the short cuts, and reached the summit while the carriage was still pursuing the windings of the road.

They shook hands with the clergyman, but did not speak.

'So you're off for a minute, Mr Vyse?' he asked.

Cecil said 'Yes,' while Freddy edged away.

'I was coming to show you this delightful letter from those friends of Miss Honeychurch's.' He quoted from it. 'Isn't it wonderful? Isn't it romance? Most certainly they will go to Constantinople. They are taken in a snare that cannot fail. They will end by going round the world.'

Cecil listened civilly, and said he was sure that Lucy would be amused and interested.

'Isn't Romance capricious! I never notice it in you young people; you do nothing but play lawn tennis, and say that Romance is dead, while the Miss Alans are struggling with all the weapons of propriety against the terrible thing. "A really comfortable pension at Constantinople!" So they call it out of decency, but in their hearts they want a pension with magic windows opening on the foam of perilous seas in fairylands forlorn! No ordinary view will content the Miss Alans. They want the Pension Keats.'

'I'm awfully sorry to interrupt, Mr Beebe,' said Freddy, 'but have you any matches?'

'I have,' said Cecil, and it did not escape Mr Beebe's notice that he spoke to the boy more kindly.

'You have never met these Miss Alans, have you, Mr Vyse?'

'Never.'

'Then you don't see the wonder of this Greek visit. I haven't been to Greece myself, and don't mean to go, and I can't imagine any of my friends going. It is altogether too big for our little lot. Don't you think so? Italy is just about as much as we can manage. Italy is heroic, but Greece is godlike or devilish—I am not sure which, and in either case absolutely out of our suburban focus. All right, Freddy—I am not being clever, upon my word I am not—I took the idea from another fellow; and give me those matches when you've done with them.' He lit a cigarette, and went on talking to the two young men. 'I was saying, if our poor little Cockney lives must have a background, let it be Italian. Big enough in all conscience. The ceiling of the Sistine Chapel for me. There the contrast is just as much as I can realize. But not the Parthenon, not the frieze of Phidias at any price; and here comes the victoria.'

'You're quite right,' said Cecil. 'Greece is not for our little lot'; and he got in. Freddy followed, nodding to the clergyman, whom he trusted not to be pulling one's leg, really. And before they had gone a dozen yards he jumped out, and came running back for Vyse's match-box, which had not been returned. As he took it, he said: 'I am so glad you only talked about books. Cecil's hard hit. Lucy won't marry him. If you'd gone on about her, as you did about them, he might have broken down.'

'But when—'

'Late last night. I must go.'

'Perhaps they won't want me down there.'

'No—go on. Good-bye.'

'Thank goodness!' exclaimed Mr Beebe to himself, and struck the saddle of his bicycle approvingly. 'It was the one foolish thing she ever did. Oh, what a glorious riddance!' And, after a little thought, he negotiated the slope into Windy Corner, light of heart. The house was again as it ought to be—cut off for ever from Cecil's pretentious world.

He would find Miss Minnie down the garden.

In the drawing-room Lucy was tinkling at a Mozart Sonata. He hesitated a moment, but went down the garden as requested. There he found a mournful company. It was a blustering day, and the wind had taken and broken the dahlias. Mrs Honeychurch, who looked cross, was tying them up, while Miss Bartlett, unsuitably dressed, impeded her with offers of assistance. At a little distance stood Minnie and the 'garden-child,' a minute importation, each holding either end of a long piece of bass.

'Oh, how do you do, Mr Beebe? Gracious, what a mess everything is! Look at my scarlet pompoms, and the wind blowing your skirts about, and the ground so hard that not a prop will stick in, and then the carriage having to go out, when I had counted on having Powell, who—give every one their due—does tie up dahlias properly.'

Evidently Mrs Honeychurch was shattered.

'How do you do?' said Miss Bartlett, with a meaning glance, as though conveying that more than dahlias had been broken off by the autumn gales.

'Here, Lennie, the bass,' cried Mrs Honeychurch. The garden-child, who did not know what bass was, stood rooted to the path with horror. Minnie slipped to her uncle and whispered that every one was very disagreeable to-day, and that it was not her fault if dahlia-strings would tear longways instead of across.

'Come for a walk with me,' he told her. 'You have worried them as much as they can stand. Mrs Honeychurch, I only called in aimlessly. I shall take her up to tea at the Beehive Tavern, if I may.'

'Oh, must you? Yes, do.—Not the scissors, thank you, Charlotte, when both my hands are full already—I'm perfectly certain that the orange cactus will go before I can get to it.'

Mr Beebe, who was an adept at relieving situations, invited Miss Bartlett to accompany them to this mild festivity.

'Yes, Charlotte, I don't want you—do go; there's nothing to stop about for, either in the house or out of it.'

Miss Bartlett said that her duty lay in the dahlia-bed, but when she had exasperated every one, except Minnie, by a refusal, she turned round and exasperated Minnie by an acceptance. As they walked up the garden, the orange cactus fell, and Mr Beebe's last vision was of the garden-child clasping it like a lover, his dark head buried in a wealth of blossom.

'It is terrible, this havoc among the flowers,' he remarked.

'It is always terrible when the promise of months is destroyed in a moment,' enunciated Miss Bartlett.

'Perhaps we ought to send Miss Honeychurch down to her mother. Or will she come with us?'

'I think we had better leave Lucy to herself, and to her own pursuits.'

'They're angry with Miss Honeychurch, because she was late for breakfast,' whispered Minnie, 'and Mr Floyd has gone, and Mr Vyse has gone, and Freddy won't play with me. In fact, Uncle Arthur, the house is not *at all* what it was yesterday.'

'Don't be a prig,' said her Uncle Arthur. 'Go and put on your boots.'

He stepped into the drawing-room, where Lucy was still attentively pursuing the Sonatas of Mozart. She stopped when he entered.

'How do you do? Miss Bartlett and Minnie are coming with me to tea at the Beehive. Would you come too?'

'I don't think I will, thank you.'

'No, I didn't suppose you would care to much.'

Lucy turned to the piano and struck a few chords.

'How delicate those Sonatas are!' said Mr Beebe, though, at the bottom of his heart, he thought them silly little things.

Lucy passed into Schumann.

'Miss Honeychurch!'

'Yes.'

'I met them on the hill. Your brother told me.'

'Oh, did he?' She sounded annoyed. Mr Beebe felt hurt, for he had thought that she would like him to be told.

'I needn't say that it will go no further.'

'Mother, Charlotte, Cecil, Freddy, you,' said Lucy, playing a note for each person who knew, and then playing a sixth note.

'If you'll let me say so, I am very glad, and I am certain that you have done the right thing.'

'So I hoped other people would think, but they don't seem to.'

'I could see that Miss Bartlett thought it unwise.'

'So does mother. Mother minds dreadfully.'

'I am very sorry for that,' said Mr Beebe with feeling.

Mrs Honeychurch, who hated all changes, did mind, but not nearly as much as her daughter pretended, and only for the minute. It was really a ruse of Lucy's to justify her despondency—a ruse of which she was not herself conscious, for she was marching in the armies of darkness.

'And Freddy minds.'

'Still Freddy never hit it off with Vyse much, did he? I gathered that he disliked the engagement, and felt it might separate him from you.'

'Boys are so odd.'

Minnie could be heard arguing with Miss Bartlett through the floor. Tea at the Beehive appparently involved a complete change of apparel. Mr Beebe saw that Lucy—very properly—did not wish to discuss her action, so after a sincere expression of sympathy, he said, 'I have had an absurd letter from Miss Alan. That was really what brought me over. I thought it might amuse you all.'

'How delightful!' said Lucy, in a dull voice.

For the sake of something do do, he began to read her the letter. After a few words her eyes grew alert, and soon she interrupted him with—'Going abroad? When do they start?'

'Next week, I gather.'

'Did Freddy say whether he was driving straight back?'

'No, he didn't.'

'Because I do hope he won't go gossiping.'

So she did want to talk about her broken engagement. Always complaisant, he put the letter away. But she at once exclaimed in a high voice, 'Oh, do tell me more about the Miss Alans! How perfectly splendid of them to go abroad!'

'I want them to start from Venice, and go in a cargo steamer down the Illyrian coast!'

She laughed heartily. 'Oh, delightful! I wish they'd take me.'

'Has Italy filled you with the fever of travel? Perhaps George Emerson is right. He says that "Italy is only an euphuism for Fate."'

'Oh, not Italy, but Constantinople. I have always longed to go to Constantinople. Constantinople is practically Asia, isn't it?'

Mr Beebe reminded her that Constantinople was still unlikely, and that the Miss Alans only aimed at Athens, 'with Delphi, perhaps, if the roads are safe.' But this made no difference to her enthusiasm. She had always longed to go to Greece even more, it seemed. He saw, to his surprise, that she was apparently serious.

'I didn't realize that you and the Miss Alans were still such friends, after Cissie Villa.'

'Oh, that's nothing; I assure you Cissie Villa's nothing to me; I would give anything to go with them.'

'Would your mother spare you again so soon? You have scarcely been home three months.'

'She *must* spare me!' cried Lucy, in growing excitement. 'I simply *must* go away. I have to.' She ran her fingers hysterically through her hair. 'Don't you see that I *have* to go away? I didn't realize at the time—and of course I want to see Constantinople so particularly.'

'You mean that since you have broken off your engagement you feel—'

'Yes, yes. I knew you would understand.'

Mr Beebe did not quite understand. Why could not Miss Honeychurch repose in the bosom of her family? Cecil had evidently taken up the dignified line, and was not going to annoy her. Then it struck him that her family itself might be annoying. He hinted this to her, and she accepted the hint eagerly.

'Yes, of course; to go to Constantinople until they are used to the idea and everything has calmed down.'

'I am afraid it has been a bothersome business,' he said gently.

'No, not at all. Cecil was very kind indeed; only—I had better tell you the whole truth, since you have heard a little—it was that he is so masterful. I found that he wouldn't let me go my own way. He would improve me in places where I can't be improved. Cecil won't let a woman decide for herself—in fact, he daren't. What nonsense I do talk! but that is the kind of thing.'

'It is what I gathered from my own observation of Mr Vyse; it is what I gather from all that I have known of you. I do sympathize and agree most profoundly. I agree so much that you must let me make one little criticism: Is it worth while rushing off to Greece?'

'But I must go somewhere!' she cried. 'I have been worrying all the morning, and here comes the very thing.' She struck her knees with clenched fists, and repeated: 'I must! And the time I shall have with mother, and all the money she spent on me last spring. You all think much too highly of me. I wish you weren't so kind.' At this moment Miss Bartlett entered, and her nervousness increased. 'I must get away, ever so far. I must know my own mind and where I want to go.'

'Come along; tea, tea, tea,' said Mr Beebe, and hustled his guests out of the front door. He hustled them so quickly that he forgot his hat. When he returned for it he heard, to his relief and surprise, the tinkling of a Mozart Sonata.

'She is playing again,' he said to Miss Bartlett.

'Lucy can always play,' was the acid reply.

'One is very thankful that she has such a resource. She is evidently much worried, as, of course, she ought to be. I know all about it. The marriage was so near that it must have been a hard struggle before she could wind herself up to speak.'

Miss Bartlett gave a kind of wriggle, and he prepared for a discussion. He had never fathomed Miss Bartlett. As he had put it to himself at Florence, 'she might yet reveal depths of strangeness, if not of meaning.' But she was so unsympathetic that she must be reliable. He assumed that much, and he had no hesitation in discussing Lucy with her. Minnie was fortunately collecting ferns.

She opened the discussion with: 'We had much better let the matter drop.'

'I wonder.'

'It is of the highest importance that there should be no gossip in Summer Street. It would be *death* to gossip about Mr Vyse's dismissal at the present moment.'

Mr Beebe raised his eyebrows. Death is a strong word–surely too strong. There was no question of tragedy. He said: 'Of course, Miss Honeychurch will make the fact public in her own way, and when she chooses. Freddy only told me because he knew she would not mind.'

'I know,' said Miss Bartlett civilly. 'Yet Freddy ought not to have told even you. One cannot be too careful.'

'Quite so.'

'I do implore absolute secrecy. A chance word to a chattering friend, and—'

'Exactly.' He was used to these nervous old maids and to the exaggerated importance that they attach to words. A rector lives in a web of petty secrets, and confidences, and warnings, and the wiser he is the less he will regard them. He will change the subject, as did Mr Beebe, saying cheerfully: 'Have you heard from any Bertolini people lately? I believe you keep up with Miss Lavish. It is odd how we of that pension, who seemed such a fortuitous collection, have been working into one another's lives. Two, three, four, six of us–no, eight; I had forgotten the Emersons–have kept more or less in touch. We must really give the Signora a testimonial.'

And, Miss Bartlett not favouring the scheme, they walked up the hill in a silence which was only broken by the rector naming some fern. On the summit they paused. They sky had grown wilder since he stood there last hour, giving to the land a tragic greatness that is rare in Surrey. Grey clouds were charging across tissues of white, which stretched and shredded and tore slowly, until through their final layers there gleamed a hint of the disappearing blue. Summer was retreating. The wind roared, the trees groaned, yet the noise seemed insufficient for those vast operations in heaven. The weather was breaking up, breaking, broken, and it is a sense of the fit rather than of the supernatural that equips such crises with the salvos of angelic artillery. Mr Beebe's eyes rested on Windy Corner, where Lucy sat, practising Mozart. No smile came to his lips, and, changing the subject again, he said: 'We shan't have rain, but we shall have darkness, so let us hurry on. The darkness last night was appalling.'

They reached the Beehive Tavern at about five o'clock. That amiable hostelry possesses a verandah, in which the young and the unwise do dearly love to sit, while guests of more mature years seek a pleasant sanded room, and have tea at a table comfortably. Mr Beebe saw that Miss Bartlett would be cold if she sat out, and that Minnie would be dull if she sat in, so he proposed a division of forces. They would hand the child her food through the window. Thus he was incidentally enabled to discuss the fortunes of Lucy.

'I have been thinking, Miss Bartlett,' he said, 'and, unless you very much object, I would like to reopen that discussion.' She bowed. 'Nothing about the past. I know little and care less about that; I am absolutely certain that it is to your cousin's credit. She has acted loftily and rightly, and it is like her gentle modesty to say that we think too highly of her. But the future. Seriously, what do you think of this Greek plan?' He pulled out the letter again. 'I don't know whether you overheard, but she wants to join the Miss Alans in their mad career. It's all—I can't explain—it's wrong.'

Miss Bartlett read the letter in silence, laid it down, seemed to hesitate, and then read it again.

'I can't see the point of it myself.'

To his astonishment, she replied: 'There I cannot agree with you. In it I spy Lucy's salvation.'

'Really. Now, why?'

'She wanted to leave Windy Corner.'

'I know—but it seems so odd, so unlike her, so—I was going to say—selfish.'

'It is natural, surely—after such painful scenes—that she should desire a change.'

Here, apparently, was one of those points that the male intellect misses. Mr Beebe exclaimed: 'So she says herself, and since another lady agrees with her, I must own that I am partially convinced. Perhaps she must have a change. I have no sisters or—and I don't understand these things. But why need she go as far as Greece?'

'You may well ask that,' replied Miss Bartlett, who was evidently interested, and had almost dropped her evasive manner. 'Why Greece? (What is it, Minnie dear—jam?) Why not Tunbridge Wells? Oh, Mr Beebe! I had a long and most unsatisfactory interview with dear Lucy this morning. I cannot help her. I will say no more. Perhaps I have already said too much. I am not to talk—a point on which she is almost bitter. I am not to talk. I wanted her to spend six months with me at Tunbridge Wells, and she refused.'

Mr Beebe poked at a crumb with his knife.

'But my feelings are of no importance. I know too well that I get on Lucy's nerves. Our tour was a failure. She wanted to leave Florence, and when we got to Rome she did not want to be in Rome, and all the time I felt that I was spending her mother's money—'

'Let us keep to the future, though,' interrupted Mr Beebe. 'I want your advice.'

'Very well,' said Charlotte, with a choky abruptness that was new to him, though familiar to Lucy. 'I for one will help her to go to Greece. Will you?'

Mr Beebe considered.

'It is absolutely necessary,' she continued, lowering her veil and whispered through it with a passion, an intensity, that surprised him. 'I know—I *know.*' The darkness was coming on, and he felt that this odd woman really did know. 'She must not stop here a moment, and we must keep quiet till she goes. I trust that the servants know nothing. Afterwards—but I may have said too much already. Only, Lucy and I are helpless against Mrs Honeychurch alone. If you help, we may succeed. Otherwise—'

'Otherwise—?'

'Otherwise,' she repeated, as if the word held finality.

'Yes, I will help her,' said the clergyman, setting his jaw firm. 'Come, let us go back now, and settle the whole thing up.'

Miss Bartlett burst into florid gratitude. The tavern sign—a beehive trimmed evenly with bees—creaked in the wind outside as she thanked him. Mr Beebe did not quite understand the situation; but then, he did not desire to understand it, nor to jump to the conclusion of "another man" that would have attracted a grosser mind. He only felt that Miss Bartlett knew of some vague influence from which the girl desired to be delivered, and which might well be clothed in the fleshly form. Its very vagueness spurred him into knight-errantry. His belief in celibacy, so reticent, so carefully concealed beneath his tolerance and culture, now came to the surface and expanded like some delicate flower. "They that marry do well, but they that refrain do better." So ran his belief, and he never heard that an engagement was broken off but with a slight feeling of pleasure. In the case of Lucy, the feeling was intensified through dislike of Cecil; and he was willing to go further—to place her out of danger until she could confirm her resolution of virginity. The feeling was very subtle and quite undogmatic, and he never imparted it to any other of the characters in this entanglement. Yet it existed, and it alone explains his action subsequently, and his influence on the action of others. The compact that he made with Miss Bartlett in the tavern was to help not only Lucy, but religion also.

They hurried home through a world of black and grey. He conversed on indifferent topics: the Emersons' need of a housekeeper; servants; Italian servants; novels about Italy; novels with a purpose; could literature influence life? Windy Corner glimmered. In the garden, Mrs Honeychurch, now helped by Freddy, still wrestled with the lives of her flowers.

'It gets too dark,' she said hopelessly. 'This comes of putting off. We might have known the weather would break up soon; and now Lucy wants to go to Greece. I don't know what the world's coming to.'

'Mrs Honeychurch,' he said, 'go to Greece she must. Come up to the house and let's talk it over. Do you, in the first place, mind her breaking with Vyse?'

'Mr Beebe, I'm thankful—simply thankful.'

'So am I,' said Freddy.

'Good. Now come up to the house.'

They conferred in the dining-room for half and hour.

Lucy would never have carried the Greek scheme alone. It was expensive and dramatic—both qualities that her mother loathed. Nor would Charlotte have succeeded. The honours of the day rested with Mr Beebe. By his tact and common sense, and by his influence as a clergyman—for a clergyman who was not a fool influenced Mrs Honeychurch greatly—he bent her to their purpose.

'I don't see why Greece is necessary,' she said; 'but as you do, I suppose it is all right. It must be something I can't understand. Lucy! Let's tell her. Lucy!'

'She is playing the piano,' Mr Beebe said. He opened the door, and heard the words of a song:

Look not thou on beauty's charming.

'I didn't know that Miss Honeychurch sang, too.'

> *Sit thou still when kings are arming,*
> *Taste not when the wine-cup glistens—*

'It's a song that Cecil gave her. How odd girls are!'

'What's that?' called Lucy, stopping short.

'All right, dear,' said Mrs Honeychurch kindly. She went into the drawing-room, and Mr Beebe heard her kiss Lucy and say: 'I am sorry I was so cross about Greece, but it came on the top of the dahlias.'

Rather a hard voice said: 'Thank you, mother; that doesn't matter a bit.'

'And you are right, too—Greece will be all right; you can go if the Miss Alans will have you.'

'Oh, splendid! Oh, thank you!'

Mr Beebe followed. Lucy still sat at the piano with her hands over the keys. She was glad, but he had expected greater gladness. Her mother bent over her. Freddy, to whom she had been singing, reclined on the floor with his head against her, and an unlit pipe between his lips. Oddly enough, the group was beautiful. Mr Beebe, who loved the art of the past, was reminded of a favourite theme, the *Santa Conversazione*, in which people who care for one another are painted chatting together about noble things—a theme neither sensual nor sensational, and therefore ignored by the art of to-day. Why should Lucy want either to marry or to travel when she had such friends at home?

> *Taste not when the wine-cup glistens,*
> *Speak not when the people listens.*

she continued.

'Here's Mr Beebe.'

'Mr Beebe knows my rude ways.'

'It's a beautiful song and a wise one,' said he. 'Go on.'

'It isn't very good,' she said listlessly. 'I forget why–harmony or something.'

'I suspected it was unscholarly. It's so beautiful.'

'The tune's right enough,' said Freddy, 'but the words are rotten. Why throw up the sponge?'

'How stupidly you talk!' said his sister. The *Santa Conversazione* was broken up. After all, there was no reason that Lucy should talk about Greece or thank him for persuading her mother, so he said good-bye.

Freddy lit his bicycle-lamp for him in the porch, and with his usual felicity of phrase, said: 'This has been a day and a half.'

> *Stop thine ear against the singer—*

'Wait a minute; she is finishing.'

> *From the red gold keep thy finger;*
> *Vacant heart and hand and eye*
> *Easy live and quiet die.*

'I love weather like this,' said Freddy.

Mr Beebe passed into it.

The two main facts were clear. She had behaved splendidly, and he had helped her. He could not expect to master the details of so big a change in a girl's life. If here and there he was dissatisfied or puzzled, he must acquiesce: she was choosing the better part.

> *Vacant heart and hand and eye—*

Perhaps the song stated 'the better part' rather too strongly. He half fancied that the soaring accompaniment–which he did not lose in the shout of the gale–really agreed with Freddy, and was gently criticizing the words that it adorned:

> *Vacant heart and hand and eye*
> *Easy live and quiet die.*

However. For the fourth time Windy Corner lay poised below him–now as a beacon in the roaring tides of darkness.

Chapter Nineteen

Lying to Mr Emerson

The Miss Alans were found in their beloved temperance hotel near Bloomsbury—a clean, airless establishment much patronized by provincial England. They always perched there before crossing the great seas, and for a week or two would fidget gently over clothes, guide-books, mackintosh squares, digestive bread, and other Continental necessaries. That there are shops abroad, even in Athens, never occurred to them, for they regarded travel as a species of warfare, only to be undertaken by those who have been fully armed at the Haymarket Stores. Miss Honeychurch, they trusted, would take care to equip herself duly. Quinine could now be obtained in tabloids; paper soap was a great help towards freshening up one's face in the train. Lucy promised, a little depressed.

'But, of course, you know all about these things, and you have Mr Vyse to help you. A gentleman is such a stand-by.'

Mrs Honeychurch, who had come up to town with her daughter, began to drum nervously upon her cardcase.

'We think it so good of Mr Vyse to spare you,' Miss Catharine continued. 'It is not every young man who would be so unselfish. But perhaps he will come out and join you later on.'

'Or does his work keep him in London?' said Miss Teresa, the more acute and less kindly of the two sisters.

'However, we shall see him when he sees you off. I do so long to see him.'

'No one will see Lucy off,' interposed Mrs Honeychurch. 'She doesn't like it.'

'No, I hate seeings-off,' said Lucy.

'Really? How funny! I should have thought that in this case—'

'Oh, Mrs Honeychurch, you aren't going? It is such a pleasure to have met you!'

They escaped, and Lucy said with relief: 'That's all right. We just got through that time.'

But her mother was annoyed. 'I shall be told, dear, that I am unsympathetic. But I cannot see why you didn't tell your friends about Cecil and be done with it. There all the time we had to sit fencing, and almost telling lies, and be seen through, too, I dare say, which is most unpleasant.'

Lucy had plenty to say in reply. She described the Miss Alans' character: they were such gossips, and if one told them, the news would be everywhere in no time.

'But why shouldn't it be everywhere in no time?'

'Because I settled with Cecil not to announce it until I left England. I shall tell them then. It's much pleasanter. How wet it is! Let's turn in here.'

'Here' was the British Museum. Mrs Honeychurch refused. If they must take shelter, let it be in a shop. Lucy felt contemptuous, for she was on the tack of caring for Greek sculpture, and had already borrowed a mythological dictionary from Mr Beebe to get up the names of the goddesses and gods.

'Oh, well, let it be a shop, then. Let's go to Mudie's. I'll buy a guide-book.'

'You know, Lucy, you and Charlotte and Mr Beebe all tell me I'm so stupid, so I suppose I am, but I shall never understand this hole-and-corner work. You've got rid of Cecil—well and good, and I'm thankful he's gone, though I did feel angry for the minute. But why not announce it? Why this hushing up and tip-toeing?'

'It's only for a few days.'

'But why at all?'

Lucy was silent. She was drifting away from her mother. It was quite easy to say, 'Because George Emerson has been bothering me, and if he hears I've given up Cecil may begin again'—quite easy, and it had the incidental advantage of being true. But she could not say it. She disliked confidences, for they might lead to self-knowledge and to that king of terrors—Light. Ever since that last evening at Florence she had deemed it unwise to reveal her soul.

Mrs Honeychurch, too, was silent. She was thinking, 'My daughter won't answer me; she would rather be with those inquisitive old maids than with Freddy and me. Any rag, tag and bobtail apparently does if she can leave her home.' And as in her case thoughts never remained unspoken long, she burst out with: 'You're tired of Windy Corner.'

This was perfectly true. Lucy had hoped to return to Windy Corner when she escaped from Cecil, but she discovered that her home existed no longer. It might exist for Freddy, who still lived and thought straight, but not for one who had deliberately warped the brain. She did not acknowledge that her brain was warped, for the brain itself must assist in that acknowledgment, and she was disordering the very instruments of life. She only felt, 'I do not love George; I broke off my engagement because I did not love George; I must go to Greece because I do not love George; it is more important that I should look up gods in the dictionary than that I should help my mother; every one else is behaving very badly.' She only felt irritable and petulant, and anxious to do what she was not expected to do, and in this spirit she proceeded with the conversation.

'Oh, mother, what rubbish you talk! Of course I'm not tired of Windy Corner.'

'Then why not say so at once, instead of considering half an hour first?'

She laughed faintly, 'Half a *minute* would be nearer.'

'Perhaps you would like to stay away from your home altogether?'

'Hush, mother! People will hear you'; for they had entered Mudie's. She bought Baedeker, and then continued: 'Of course I want to live at home; but as we are talking about it, I may as well say that I shall want to be away in the future more than I have been. You see, I come into my money next year.'

Tears came into her mother's eyes.

Driven by nameless bewilderment, by what is in older people termed 'eccentricity,' Lucy determined to make this point clear. 'I've seen the world so little—I felt so out of things in Italy. I have seen so little of life; one ought to come up to London more—not a cheap ticket like to-day, but to stop. I might even share a flat for a little with some other girl.'

'And mess with typewriters and latch-keys,' exploded Mrs Honeychurch. 'And agitate and scream, and be carried off kicking by the police. And call it a Mission—when no one wants you! And call it Duty—when it means that you can't stand your own home! And call it Work—when thousands of men are starving with the competition as it is! And then to prepare yourself, find two doddering old ladies, and go abroad with them.'

'I want more independence,' said Lucy lamely; she knew that she wanted something, and independence is a useful cry: we can always say that we have not got it. She tried to remember her emotions in Florence: those had been sincere and passionate, and had suggested beauty rather than short skirts and latch-keys. But independence was certainly her cue.

'Very well. Take your independence and be gone. Rush up and down and round the world, and come back as thin as a lath with the bad food. Despise the house that your father built and the garden that he planted, and our dear view—and then share a flat with another girl.'

Lucy screwed up her mouth and said: 'Perhaps I spoke hastily.'

'Oh, goodness!' her mother flashed. 'How you do remind me of Charlotte Bartlett!'

'*Charlotte?*' flashed Lucy in her turn, pierced at last by a vivid pain.

'More every moment.'

'I don't know what you mean, mother; Charlotte and I are not the very least alike.'

'Well, I see the likeness. The same eternal worrying, the same taking back of words. You and Charlotte trying to divide two apples among three people last night might be sisters.'

'What rubbish! And if you dislike Charlotte so, it's rather a pity you asked her to stop. I warned you about her; I begged you, implored you not to, but of course I was not listened to.'

'There you go.'

'I beg your pardon?'

'Charlotte again, my dear; that's all; her very words.'

Lucy clenched her teeth. 'My point is that you oughtn't to have asked Charlotte to stop. I wish you would keep to the point.' And the conversation dies off into a wrangle.

She and her mother shopped in silence, spoke little in the train, little again in the carriage, which met them at Dorking Station. It had poured all day, and as they ascended through the deep Surrey lanes showers of water fell from the overhanging beech-trees and rattled on the hood. Lucy complained that the hood was stuffy. Leaning forward, she looked out into the steaming dusk, and watched the carriage-lamp pass like a search-light over mud and leaves, and reveal nothing beautiful. 'The crush when Charlotte gets in will be abominable,' she remarked. For they were to pick up Miss Bartlett at Summer Street, where she had been dropped as the carriage went down, to pay a call on Mr. Beebe's old mother. 'We shall have to sit three a side, because the trees drop, and yet it isn't raining. Oh for a little air!' Then she listened to the horse's hoofs – 'He has not told – he has not told.' That melody was blurred by the soft road. '*Can't* we have the hood down?' she demanded, and her mother, with sudden tenderness, said: 'Very well, old lady, stop the horse.' And the horse was stopped, and Lucy and Powell wrestled with the hood, and squirted water down Mrs Honeychurch's neck. But now that the hood was down, she did see something that she would have missed – there were no lights in the windows of Cissie Villa, and round the garden gate she fancied she saw a padlock.

'Is that house to let again, Powell?' she called.

'Yes, miss,' he replied.

'Have they gone?'

'It is too far out of town for the young gentleman, and his father's rheumatism has come on, so he can't stop on alone, so they are trying to let furnished,' was the answer.

'They have gone, then?'

'Yes, miss, they have gone.'

Lucy sank back. The carriage stopped at the Rectory. She got out to call for Miss Bartlett. So the Emersons had gone, and all this bother about Greece had been unnecessary. Waste! That word seemed to sum up the whole of life. Wasted plans, wasted money, wasted love, and she had wounded her mother. Was it possible that she had muddled things away? Quite possible. Other people had. When the maid opened the door, she was unable to speak, and stared stupidly into the hall.

Miss Bartlett at once came forward, and after a long preamble asked a great favour: might she go to church? Mr Beebe and his mother had already gone, but she had refused to start until she obtained her hostess's full sanction, for it would mean keeping the horse waiting a good ten minutes more.

'Certainly,' said the hostess wearily. 'I forgot it was Friday. Let's all go. Powell can go round to the stables.'

'Lucy dearest—'

'No church for me, thank you.'

A sigh, and they departed. The church was invisible, but up in the darkness to the left there was a hint of colour. This was a stained window, through which some feeble light was shining, and when the door opened Lucy heard Mr Beebe's voice running through the litany to a minute congregation. Even their church, built upon the slope of the hill so artfully, with its beautiful raised transept and its spire of silvery shingle – even their church had lost its charm; and the thing one never talked about – religion – was fading like all the other things.

She followed the maid into the Rectory.

Would she object to sitting in Mr Beebe's study? There was only that one fire.

She would not object.

Some one was there already, for Lucy heard the words 'A lady to wait, sir.'

Old Mr Emerson was sitting by the fire, with his foot upon a gout-stool.

'Oh, Miss Honeychurch, that you should come!' he quavered; and Lucy saw an alteration in him since last Sunday.

Not a word would come to her lips. George she had faced, and could have faced again, but she had forgotten how to treat his father.

'Miss Honeychurch, dear, we are so sorry! George is so sorry! He thought he had a right to try. I cannot blame my boy, and yet I wish he had told me first. He ought not to have tried. I knew nothing about it at all.'

If only she could remember how to behave!

He held up his hand. 'But you must not scold him.'

Lucy turned her back, and began to look at Mr Beebe's books.

'I taught him,' he quavered, 'to trust in love. I said: "When love comes, that is reality." I said: "Passion does not blind. No. Passion is sanity, and the woman you love, she is the only person you will ever really understand."' He sighed: 'True, everlastingly true, though my day is over, and though there is the result. Poor boy! He is so sorry! He said he knew it was madness when you brought your cousin in; that whatever you felt you did not mean. Yet'—his voice gathered strength; he spoke out to make certain—'Miss Honeychurch, do you remember Italy?'

Lucy selected a book—a volume of Old Testament commentaries. Holding it up to her eyes, she said: 'I have no wish to discuss Italy or any subject connected with your son.'

'But you do remember it?'

'He has misbehaved himself from the first.'

'I only was told that he loved you last Sunday. I never could judge behaviour. I—I—suppose he has.'

Feeling a little steadier, she put the book back and turned round to him. His face was drooping and swollen, but his eyes, though they were sunken deep, gleamed with a child's courage.

'Why, he has behaved abominably,' she said. 'I am glad he is sorry. Do you know what he did?'

'Not "abominably,"' was the gentle correction. 'He only tried when he should not have tried. You have all you want, Miss Honeychurch: you are going to marry the man you love. Do not go out of George's life saying he is abominable.'

'No, of course,' said Lucy, ashamed at the reference to Cecil. '"Abominable" is much too strong. I am sorry I used it about your son. I think I will go to church, after all. My mother and my cousin have gone. I shall not be so very late—'

'Especially as he has gone under,' he said quietly.

'What was that?'

'Gone under naturally.' He beat his palms together in silence; his head fell on his chest.

'I don't understand.'

'As his mother did.'

'But, Mr Emerson—*Mr Emerson*—what are you talking about?'

'When I wouldn't have George baptized,' said he.

Lucy was frightened.

'And she agreed that baptism was nothing, but he caught that fever when he was twelve, and she turned round. She thought it a judgment.' He shuddered. 'Oh, horrible, when we had given up that sort of thing and broken away from her parents. Oh, horrible—worst of all—worse than death, when you have made a little clearing in the wilderness, planted your little garden, let in your sunlight, and then the weeds creep in again! A judgment! And our boy had typhoid because no clergyman had dropped water on him in church! Is it possible, Miss Honeychurch? Shall we slip back into the darkness for ever?'

'I don't know,' gasped Lucy. 'I don't understand this sort of thing. I was not meant to understand it.'

'But Mr Eager—he came when I was out, and acted according to his principles. I don't blame him or anyone . . . but by the time George was well she was ill. He made her think about sin, and she went under thinking about it.'

It was thus that Mr Emerson had murdered his wife in the sight of God.

'Oh, how terrible!' said Lucy, forgetting her own affairs at last.

'He was not baptized,' said the old man. 'I did hold firm.' And he looked with unwavering eyes at the rows of books, as if—at what cost!—he had won a victory over them. 'My boy shall go back to the earth untouched.'

She asked whether young Mr Emerson was ill.

'Oh—last Sunday.' He started into the present. 'George last Sunday—no, not ill: just gone under. He is never ill. But he is his mother's son. Her eyes were his, and she had that forehead that I think so beautiful, and he will not think it worth while to live. It was always touch and go. He will live; but he will not think it worth while to live. He will never think anything worth while. You remember that church at Florence?'

Lucy did remember, and how she had suggested that George should collect postage-stamps.

'After you left Florence—horrible. Then we take the house here, and he goes bathing with your brother, and became better. You saw him bathing?'

'I am so sorry, but it is no good discussing this affair. I am really deeply sorry about it.'

'Then there came something about a novel. I didn't follow it all; I had to hear so much, and he minded telling me; he finds me too old. Ah, well, one must have failures. George comes down to-morrow, and takes me up to his London rooms. He can't bear to be about here, and I must be where he is.'

'Mr Emerson,' cried the girl, 'don't leave—at least, not on my account. I am going to Greece. Don't leave your comfortable house.'

It was the first time her voice had been kind, and he smiled. 'How good every one is! And look at Mr Beebe housing me—came over this morning and heard I was going! Here I am so comfortable with a fire.'

'Yes, but you won't go back to London. It's absurd.'

'I must be with George; I must make him care to live, and down here he can't. He says the thought of seeing you and of hearing about you— I am not justifying him: I am only saying what has happened.'

'Oh, Mr Emerson'–she took hold of his hand–'you mustn't. I've been bother enough to the world by now. I can't have you moving out of your house when you like it, and perhaps losing money through it–all on my account. You must stop! I am just going to Greece.'

'All the way to Greece?'

Her manner altered.

'To Greece?'

'So you must stop. You won't talk about this business, I know. I can trust you both.'

'Certainly you can. We either have you in our lives, or leave you to the life that you have chosen.'

'I shouldn't want—'

'I suppose Mr. Vyse is very angry with George? No, it was wrong of George to try. We have pushed our beliefs too far. I fancy that we deserve sorrow.'

She looked at the books again–black, brown, and that acrid, theological blue. They surrounded the visitors on every side; they were piled on the tables, they pressed against the very ceiling. To Lucy–who could not see that Mr Emerson was profoundly religious, and differed from Mr Beebe chiefly by his acknowledgment of passion–it seemed dreadful that the old man should crawl into such a sanctum, when he was unhappy, and be dependent on the bounty of a clergyman.

More certain than ever that she was tired, he offered her his chair.

'No, please sit still. I think I will sit in the carriage.'

'Miss Honeychurch, you do sound tired.'

'Not a bit,' said Lucy, with trembling lips.

'But you are, and there's a look of George about you. And what were you saying about going abroad?'

She was silent.

'Greece'–and she saw that he was thinking the word over–'Greece'; but you were to be married this year, I thought.'

'Not till January, it wasn't,' said Lucy, clasping her hands. Would she tell an actual lie when it came to the point?

'I suppose that Mr. Vyse is going with you. I hope–it isn't because George spoke that you are both going?'

'No.'

'I hope that you will enjoy Greece with Mr Vyse.'

'Thank you.'

At that moment Mr Beebe came back from church. His cassock was covered with rain. 'That's all right,' he said kindly. 'I counted on you two keeping each other company. It's pouring again. The entire congregation, which consists of your cousin, your mother, and my mother, stands waiting in the church till the carriage fetches it. Did Powell go round?'

'I think so; I'll see.'

'No–of course, I'll see. How are the Miss Alans?'

'Very well, thank you.'

'Did you tell Mr Emerson about Greece?'

'I–I did.'

'Don't you think it very plucky of her, Mr Emerson, to undertake the two Miss Alans? Now, Miss Honeychurch, go back–keep warm. I think three is such a courageous number to go travelling.' And he hurried off to the stables.

'He is not going,' she said hoarsely. 'I made a slip. Mr Vyse does stop behind in England.' Somehow it was impossible to cheat this old man. To George, to Cecil, she would have lied again; but he seemed so near the end of things, so dignified in his approach to the gulf, of which he gave one account, and the books that surrounded him another, so mild to the rough paths that he had traversed, that the true chivalry–not the worn-out chivalry of sex, but the true chivalry that all the young may show to all the old–awoke in her, and, at whatever risk, she told him that Cecil was not her companion to Greece. And she spoke so seriously that the risk became a certainty and he, lifting his eyes, said: 'You are leaving him? You are leaving the man you love?'

'I–I had to.'

'Why, Miss Honeychurch, why?'

Terror came over her, and she lied again. She made the long, convincing speech that she had made to Mr Beebe, and intended to make to the world when she announced that her engagement was no more. He heard her in silence, and then said: 'My dear, I am worried about you. It seems to me'–dreamily; she was not alarmed–'that you are in a muddle.'

She shook her head.

'Take an old man's word: there's nothing worse than a muddle in all the world. It is easy to face Death and Fate, and the things that sound so dreadful. It is on my muddles that I look back with horror–on the things that I might have avoided. We can help one another but little. I used to think I could teach young people the whole of life, but I know better now, and all my teaching of George has come down to this: beware of muddle. Do you remember in that church, when you pretended to be annoyed with me and weren't? Do you remember before, when you refused the room with the view? Those were muddles–little, but ominous–and I am fearing that you are in one now.' She was silent. 'Do trust me, Miss Honeychurch. Though life is very glorious, it is difficult.' She was still silent. '"Life", wrote a friend of mine, "is a public performance on the violin, in which you must learn the instrument as you go along." I think he puts it well. Man has to pick up the use of his functions as he goes along–especially the function of Love.' Then he burst out excitedly: 'That's it; that's what I mean. You love George!' And after his long preamble, the three words burst against Lucy like waves from the open sea.

'But you do,' he went on, not waiting for contradiction. 'You love the boy body and soul, plainly, directly, as he loves you, and no other word expresses it. You won't marry the other man for his sake.'

'How dare you!' gasped Lucy, with the roaring of waters in her ears. 'Oh, how like a man!–I mean, to suppose that a woman is always thinking about a man.'

'But you are.'

She summoned physical disgust.

'You're shocked, but I mean to shock you. It's the only hope at times. I can reach you no other way. You must marry, or your life will be wasted. You have gone too far to retreat. I have no time for the tenderness, and the comradeship, and the poetry, and the things that really matter, and *for which* you marry. I know that, with George, you will find them, and that you love him. Then be his wife. He is already part of you. Though you fly to Greece, and never see him again, or forget his very name, George will work in your thoughts till you die. It isn't possible to love and to part. You will wish that it was. You can transmute love, ignore it, muddle it, but you can never pull it out of you. I know by experience that the poets are right: love is eternal.'

Lucy began to cry with anger, and though her anger passed away soon, her tears remained.

'I only wish poets would say this, too: that love is of the body; not the body, but of the body. Ah! the misery that would be saved if we confessed that! Ah for a little directness to liberate the soul! Your soul, dear Lucy! I hate the word now, because of all the cant with which superstition has wrapped it round. But we have souls. I cannot say how they came nor whither they go, but we have them, and I see you ruining yours. I cannot bear it. It is again the darkness creeping in; it is hell.' Then he checked himself. 'What nonsense I have talked–how abstract and remote! And I have made you cry! Dear girl, forgive my prosiness; marry my boy. When I think what life is, and how seldom love is answered by love— Marry him; it is one of the moments for which the world was made.'

She could not understand him: the words were indeed remote. Yet as he spoke the darkness was withdrawn, veil after veil, and she saw to the bottom of her soul.

'Then, Lucy—'

'You've frightened me,' she moaned. 'Cecil–Mr Beebe–the ticket's bought–everything.' She fell sobbing into the chair. 'I'm caught in the tangle. I must suffer and grow old away from him. I cannot break the whole of life for his sake. They trusted me.'

A carriage drew up at the front door.

'Give George my love–once only. Tell him "muddle."' Then she arranged her veil, while the tears poured over her cheeks inside.

'Lucy—'

'No–they are in the hall–oh, please not, Mr Emerson–they trust me—'

'But why should they, when you have deceived them?'

Mr Beebe opened the door, saying: 'Here's my mother.'

'You're not worthy of their trust.'

'What's that?' said Mr Beebe sharply.

'I was saying, why should you trust her when she deceived you?'

'One minute, mother.' He came in and shut the door.

'I don't follow you, Mr Emerson. To whom do you refer? Trust whom?'

'I mean, she has pretended to you that she did not love George. They have loved one another all along.'

Mr Beebe looked at the sobbing girl. He was very quiet, and his white face, with its ruddy whiskers, seemed suddenly inhuman. A long black column, he stood and awaited her reply.

'I shall never marry him,' quavered Lucy.

A look of contempt came over him, and he said, 'Why not?'

'Mr Beebe—I have misled you—I have misled myself—'

'Oh, rubbish, Miss Honeychurch!'

'It is not rubbish!' said the old man hotly. 'It's the part of people that you don't understand.'

Mr Beebe laid his hand on his shoulder pleasantly.

'Lucy! Lucy!' called voices from the carriage.

'Mr Beebe, could you help me?'

He looked amazed at the request, and said in a low, stern voice: 'I am more grieved than I can possibly express. It is lamentable, lamentable—incredible.'

'What's wrong with the boy?' fired up the other again.

'Nothing, Mr Emerson, except that he no longer interests me. Marry George, Miss Honeychurch. He will do admirably.'

He walked out and left them. They heard him guiding his mother upstairs.

'Lucy!' the voices called.

She turned to Mr Emerson in despair. But his face revived her. It was the face of a saint who understood.

'Now it is all dark. Now Beauty and Passion seem never to have existed. I know. But remember the mountains over Florence and the view. Ah, dear, if I were George, and gave you one kiss, it would make you brave. You have to go cold into a battle that needs warmth, out into the muddle that you have made yourself; and your mother and all your friends will despise you, oh my darling, and rightly, if it is ever right to despise. George still dark, all the tussle and the misery without a word from him. Am I justified?' Into his own eyes tears came. 'Yes, for we fight for more than Love or Pleasure: there is Truth. Truth counts, Truth does count.'

'You kiss me,' said the girl. 'You kiss me. I will try.'

He gave her a sense of deities reconciled, a feeling that, in gaining the man she loved, she would gain something for the whole world. Throughout the squalor of her homeward drive—she spoke at once—his salutation remained. He had robbed the body of its taint, the world's taunts of their sting; he had shown her the holiness of direct desire. She 'never exactly understood,' she would say in after years, 'how he managed to strengthen her. It was as if he had made her see the whole of everything at once.'

Chapter Twenty

The End of the Middle Ages

The Miss Alans did go to Greece, but they went by themselves. They alone of this little company will double Malea and plough the waters of the Saronic gulf. They alone will visit Athens and Delphi, and either shrine of intellectual song—that upon the Acropolis, encircled by blue seas; that under Parnassus, where the eagles build and the bronze charioteer drives undismayed towards infinity. Trembling, anxious, cumbered with much digestive bread, they did proceed to Constantinople, they did go round the world. The rest of us must be contented with a fair, but a less arduous, goal. Italiam petimus: we return to the Pension Bertolini.

George said it was his old room.

'No, it isn't,' said Lucy; 'because it is the room I had, and I had your father's room. I forget why; Charlotte made me, for some reason.'

He knelt on the tiled floor, and laid his face in her lap.

'George, you baby, get up.'

'Why shouldn't I be a baby?' murmured George.

Unable to answer this question, she put down his sock, which she was trying to mend, and gazed out through the window. It was evening and again the spring.

'Oh, bother Charlotte,' she said thoughtfully. 'What can such people be made of?'

'Same stuff as parsons are made of.'

'Nonsense!'

'Quite right. It is nonsense.'

'Now you get up off the cold floor, or you'll be starting rheumatism next, and you stop laughing and being so silly.'

'Why shouldn't I laugh?' he asked, pinning her with his elbows, and advancing his face to hers. 'What's there to cry at? Kiss me here.' He indicated the spot where a kiss would be welcome.

He was a boy, after all. When it came to the point, it was she who remembered the past, she into whose soul the iron had entered, she who knew whose this room had been last year. It endeared him to her strangely that he should be sometimes wrong.

'Any letters?' he asked.

'Just a line from Freddy.'

'Now kiss me here; then here.'

Then, threatened again with rheumatism, he strolled to the window, opened it (as the English will), and leant out. There was the parapet, there the river, there to the left the beginnings of the hills. The cab-driver, who at once saluted him with the hiss of a serpent, might be that very Phaethon who had set this happiness in motion twelve months ago. A passion of gratitude–all feelings grow to passions in the South–came over the husband, and he blessed the people and the things who had taken so much trouble about a young fool. He had helped himself, it is true, but how stupidly! All the fighting that mattered had been done by others–by Italy, by his father, by his wife.

'Lucy, you come and look at the cypresses; and the church, whatever its name is, still shows.'

'San Miniato. I'll just finish your sock.'

'Signorino, domani faremo uno giro,' called the cabman, with engaging certainty.

George told him that he was mistaken; they had no money to throw away on driving.

And the people who had not meant to help–the Miss Lavishes, the Cecils, the Miss Bartletts! Ever prone to magnify Fate, George counted up the forces that had swept him into this contentment.

'Anything good in Freddy's letter?'

'Not yet.'

His own content was absolute, but hers held bitterness: the Honeychurches had not forgiven them; they were disgusted at her past hypocrisy; she had alienated Windy Corner, perhaps for ever.

'What does he say?'

'Silly boy! He thinks he's being dignified. He knew we should go off in the spring–he has known it for six months–that if mother wouldn't give her consent we should take the thing into our own hands. They had fair warning, and now he calls it an elopement. Ridiculous boy—'

'Signorino, domani faremo uno giro—'

'But it will all come right in the end. He has to build us both up from the beginning again. I wish, though, that Cecil had not turned so cynical about women. He has, for the second time, quite altered. Why will men have theories about women? I haven't any about men. I wish, too, that Mr Beebe—'

'You may well wish that.'

'He will never forgive us–I mean, he will never be interested in us again. I wish that he did not influence them so much at Windy Corner. I wish he hadn't— But if we act the truth, the people who really love us are sure to come back to us in the long-run.'

'Perhaps.' Then he said more gently: 'Well, I acted the truth–the only thing I did do–and you came back to me. So possibly you know.' He turned back into the room. 'Nonsense with that sock.' He carried her to the window, so that she, too, saw all the view. They sank upon their knees invisible from the road, they hoped, and began to whisper one another's names. Ah! it was worth while; it was the great joy that they had expected, and countless little joys of which they had never dreamt. They were silent.

'Signorino, domani faremo—'

'Oh, bother that man!'

But Lucy remembered the vendor of photographs and said, 'No, don't be rude to him.' Then, with a catching of her breath, she murmured: 'Mr Eager and Charlotte, dreadful frozen Charlotte! How cruel she would be to a man like that!'

'Look at the lights going over the bridge.'

'But this room reminds me of Charlotte. How horrible to grow old in Charlotte's way! To think that evening at the Rectory that she shouldn't have heard your father was in the house. For she would have stopped me going in, and he was the only person alive who could have made me see sense. You couldn't have made me. When I am very happy'–she kissed him–'I remember on how little it all hangs. If Charlotte had only known, she would have stopped me going in, and I should have gone to silly Greece, and become different for ever.'

'But she did know,' said George; 'she did see my father, surely. He said so.'

'Oh no, she didn't see him. She was upstairs with old Mrs Beebe, don't you remember, and then went straight to the church. She said so.'

George was obstinate again. 'My father,' said he, 'saw her, and I prefer his word. He was dozing by the study fire, and he opened his eyes, and there was Miss Bartlett. A few minutes before you came in. She was turning to go as he woke up. He didn't speak to her.'

Then they spoke of other things–the desultory talk of those who have been fighting to reach one another, and whose reward is to rest quietly in each other's arms. It was long ere they returned to Miss Bartlett, but when they did her behaviour seemed more interesting. George, who disliked any darkness, said: 'It's clear that she knew. Then, why did she risk the meeting? She knew he was there, and yet she went to church.'

They tried to piece the thing together.

As they talked, an incredible solution came into Lucy's mind. She rejected it, and said: 'How like Charlotte to undo her work by a feeble muddle at the last moment.' But something in the dying evening, in the roar of the river, in their very embrace, warned them that her words fell short of life, and George whispered: 'Or did she mean it?'

'Mean what?'

'Signorino, domani faremo uno giro—'

Lucy bent forward and said with gentleness: 'Lascia, prego, lascia. Siamo sposati.'

'Scusi tanto, signora,' he replied, in tones as gentle, and whipped up his horse.

'Buona sera–e grazie.'

'Niente.'

The cabman drove away singing.

'Mean what, George?'

He whispered: 'Is it this? Is this possible? I'll put a marvel to you. That your cousin has always hoped. That from the very first moment we met, she hoped, far down in her mind, that we should be like this–of course, very far down. That she fought us on the surface, and yet she hoped. I can't explain her any other way. Can you? Look how she kept me alive in you all the summer; how she gave you no peace; how month after month she became more eccentric and unreliable. The sight of us haunted her – or she couldn't have described us as she did to her friend. There are details–it burnt. I read the book afterwards. She is not frozen, Lucy, she is not withered up all through. She tore us apart twice, but in the Rectory that evening she was given one more chance to make us happy. We can never make friends with her or thank her. But I do believe that, far down in her heart, far below all speech and behaviour, she is glad.'

'It is impossible,' murmured Lucy, and then, remembering the experiences of her own heart, she said: 'No–it is just possible.'

Youth enwrapped them; the song of Phaethon announced passion requited, love attained. But they were conscious of a love more mysterious than this. The song died away; they heard the river, bearing down the snows of winter into the Mediterranean.

THE END

Howards
End

HOWARDS END

'Only connect . . .'

Chapter One

One may as well begin with Helen's letters to her sister.

Howards End
Tuesday

Dearest Meg,

It isn't going to be what we expected. It is old and little, and altogether delightful—red brick. We can scarcely pack in as it is, and the dear knows what will happen when Paul (younger son) arrives to-morrow. From hall you go right or left into dining-room or drawing-room. Hall itself is practically a room. You open another door in it, and there are the stairs going up in a sort of tunnel to the first-floor. Three bedrooms in a row there, and three attics in a row above. That isn't all the house really, but it's all that one notices—nine windows as you look up from the front garden.

Then there's a very big wych-elm—to the left as you look up—leaning a little over the house, and standing on the boundary between the garden and meadow. I quite love that tree already. Also ordinary elms, oaks—no nastier than ordinary oaks—pear-trees, apple-trees, and a vine. No silver birches, though. However, I must get on to my host and hostess. I only wanted to show that it isn't the least what we expected. Why did we settle that their house would be all gables and wiggles, and their garden all gamboge-coloured paths? I believe simply because we associate them with expensive hotels—Mrs Wilcox trailing in beautiful dresses down long corridors, Mr Wilcox bullying porters, etc. We females are that unjust.

I shall be back Saturday; will let you know train later. They are as angry as I am that you did not come too; really Tibby is too tiresome, he starts a new mortal disease every month. How could he have got hay fever in London? and even if he could, it seems hard that you should give up a visit to hear a schoolboy sneeze. Tell him that Charles Wilcox (the son who is here) has hay fever too, but he's brave, and gets quite cross when we inquire after it. Men like the Wilcoxes would do Tibby a power of good. But you won't agree, and I'd better change the subject.

This long letter is because I'm writing before breakfast. Oh, the beautiful vine leaves! The house is covered with a vine. I looked out earlier, and Mrs Wilcox was already in the garden. She evidently loves it. No wonder she sometimes looks tired. She was watching the large red poppies come out. Then she walked off the lawn to the meadow, whose corner to the right I can just see. Trail, trail, went her long dress over the sopping grass, and she came back with her hands full of the hay that was cut yesterday—I suppose for rabbits or something, as she kept on smelling it. The air here is delicious. Later on I heard the noise of croquet balls, and looked out again, and it was Charles Wilcox practising; they are keen on all games. Presently he started sneezing and had to stop. Then I hear more clicketing, and it is Mr Wilcox practising, and then, 'a-tissue, a-tissue': he has to stop too. Then Evie comes out, and does some calisthenic exercises on a machine that is tacked on to a greengage-tree—they put everything to use—and then she says 'a-tissue,' and in she goes. And finally Mrs Wilcox reappears, trail, trail, still smelling hay and looking at the flowers. I inflict all this on you because once you said that life is sometimes life and sometimes only a drama, and one must learn to distinguish tother from which, and up to now I have always put that down as 'Meg's clever nonsense.' But this morning, it really does seem not life but a play, and it did amuse me enormously to watch the W's. Now Mrs Wilcox has come in.

I am going to wear [omission]. Last night Mrs Wilcox wore an [omission], and Evie [omission]. So it isn't exactly a go-as-you-please place, and if you shut your eyes it still seems the wiggly hotel that we expected. Not if you open them. The dog-roses are too sweet. There is a great hedge of them over the lawn—magnificently tall, so that they fall down in garlands, and nice and thin at the bottom, so that you can see ducks through it and a cow. These belong to the farm, which is the only house near us. There goes the breakfast gong. Much love. Modified love to Tibby. Love to Aunt Juley; how good of her to come and keep you company, but what a bore. Burn this. Will write again Thursday.

Helen

Howards End
Friday

Dearest Meg,

I am having a glorious time. I like them all. Mrs Wilcox, if quieter than in Germany, is sweeter than ever, and I never saw anything like her steady unselfishness, and the best of it is that the others do not take advantage of her. They are the very happiest, jolliest family that you can imagine. I do really feel that we are making friends. The fun of it is that they think me a noodle, and say so—at least, Mr Wilcox does—and when that happens, and one doesn't mind, it's a pretty sure test, isn't it? He says the most horrid things about women's suffrage so nicely, and when I said I believed in equality he just folded his arms and gave me such a setting down as I've never heard. Meg, shall we ever learn to talk less? I never felt so ashamed of myself in my life. I couldn't point to a time when men had been equal, nor even to a time when the wish to be equal had made them happier in other ways. I couldn't say a word. I had just picked up the notion that equality is good from some book—probably from poetry, or you. Anyhow, it's been knocked into pieces, and, like all people who are really strong, Mr Wilcox did it without hurting me. On the other hand, I laugh at them for catching hay fever. We live like fighting-cocks, and Charles takes us out every day in the motor—a tomb with trees in it, a hermit's house, a wonderful road that was made by the Kings of Mercia—tennis—a cricket match—bridge—and at night we squeeze up in this lovely house. The whole clan's here now—it's like a rabbit warren. Evie is a dear. They want me to stop over Sunday—I suppose it won't matter if I do. Marvellous weather and the views marvellous—views westward to the high ground. Thank you for your letter. Burn this.

Your affectionate
Helen

Howards End
Sunday

Dearest dearest Meg,

I do not know what you will say: Paul and I are in love—the younger son who only came here Wednesday.

Chapter Two

Margaret glanced at her sister's note and pushed it over the breakfast-table to her aunt. There was a moment's hush, and then the flood-gates opened.

'I can tell you nothing, Aunt Juley. I know no more than you do. We met—we only met the father and mother abroad last spring. I know so little that I didn't even know their son's name. It's all so—' She waved her hand and laughed a little.

'In that case it is far too sudden.'

'Who knows, Aunt Juley, who knows?'

'But, Margaret dear, I mean, we mustn't be unpractical now that we've come to facts. It is too sudden, surely.'

'Who knows!'

'But Margaret dear—'

·'I'll go for her other letters,' said Margaret. 'No, I won't, I'll finish my breakfast. In fact, I haven't them. We met the Wilcoxes on an awful expedition that we made from Heidelberg to Speyer. Helen and I had got it into our heads that there was a grand old cathedral at Speyer—the Archbishop of Speyer was one of the seven electors—you know—"Speyer, Maintz, and Köln." Those three sees once commanded the Rhine Valley and got it the name of Priest Street.'

'I still feel quite uneasy about this business, Margaret.'

'The train crossed by a bridge of boats, and at first sight it looked quite fine. But oh, in five minutes we had seen the whole thing. The cathedral had been ruined, absolutely ruined, by restoration; not an inch left of the original structure. We wasted a whole day, and came across the Wilcoxes as we were eating our sandwiches in the public gardens. They too, poor things, had been taken in—they were actually stopping at Speyer—and they rather liked Helen insisting that they must fly with us to Heidelberg. As a matter of fact, they did come on next day. We all took some drives together. They knew us well enough to ask Helen to come and see them—at least, I was asked too, but Tibby's illness prevented me, so last Monday she went alone. That's all. You know as much as I do now. It's a young man out the unknown. She was to have come back Saturday, but put off till Monday, perhaps on account of—I don't know.'

She broke off, and listened to the sounds of a London morning. Their house was in Wickham Place, and fairly quiet, for a lofty promontory of buildings separated it from the main thoroughfare. One had the sense of a backwater, or rather of an estuary, whose waters flowed in from the invisible sea, and ebbed into a profound silence while the waves without were still beating. Though the promontory consisted of flats—expensive, with cavernous entrance halls, full of concierges and palms—it fulfilled its purpose, and gained for the older houses opposite a certain measure of peace. These, too, would be swept away in time, and another promontory would arise upon their site, as humanity piled itself higher and higher on the precious soil of London.

Mrs Munt had her own method of interpreting her nieces. She decided that Margaret was a little hysterical, and was trying to gain time by a torrent of talk. Feeling very diplomatic, she lamented the fate of Speyer, and declared that never, never should she be so misguided as to visit it, and added of her own accord that the principles of restoration were ill understood in Germany. 'The Germans,' she said, 'are too thorough, and this is all very well sometimes, but at other times it does not do.'

'Exactly,' said Margaret; 'Germans are too thorough.' And her eyes began to shine.

'Of course I regard you Schlegels as English,' said Mrs Munt hastily—'English to the backbone.'

Margaret leaned forward and stroked her hand.

'And that reminds me—Helen's letter—'

'Oh yes, Aunt Juley, I am thinking all right about Helen's letter. I know—I must go down and see her. I am thinking about her all right. I am meaning to go down.'

'But go with some plan,' said Mrs Munt, admitting into her kindly voice a note of exasperation. 'Margaret, if I may interfere, don't be taken by surprise. What do you think of the Wilcoxes? Are they our sort? Are they likely people? Could they appreciate Helen, who is to my mind a very special sort of person? Do they care about Literature and Art? That is most important when you come to think of it. Literature and Art. Most important. How old would the son be? She says "younger son." Would he be in a position to marry? Is he likely to make Helen happy? Did you gather—'

'I gathered nothing.'

They began to talk at once.

'Then in that case—'

'In that case I can make no plans, don't you see.'

'On the contrary—'

'I hate plans. I hate lines of action. Helen isn't a baby.'

'Then in that case, my dear, why go down?'

Margaret was silent. If her aunt could not see why she must go down, she was not going to tell her. She was not going to say 'I love my dear sister; I must be near her at this crisis of her life.' The affections are more reticent than the passions, and their expression more subtle. If she herself should ever fall in love with a man, she, like Helen, would proclaim it from the house-tops, but as she only loved a sister she used the voiceless language of sympathy.

'I consider you odd girls,' continued Mrs Munt, 'and very wonderful girls, and in many ways far older than your years. But—you won't be offended?—frankly, I feel you are not up to this business. It requires an older person. Dear, I have nothing to call me back to Swanage.' She spread out her plump arms. 'I am all at your disposal. Let me go down to this house whose name I forget instead of you.'

'Aunt Juley'—she jumped up and kissed her—'I must, must go to Howards End myself. You don't exactly understand, though I can never thank you properly for offering.'

'I do understand,' retorted Mrs Munt, with immense confidence. 'I go down in no spirit of interference, but to make inquiries. Inquiries are necessary. Now, I am going to be rude. You would say the wrong thing; to a certainty you would. In your anxiety for Helen's happiness you would offend the whole of these Wilcoxes by asking one of your impetuous questions—not that one minds offending them.'

'I shall ask no questions. I have it in Helen's writing that she and a man are in love. There is no question to ask as long as she keeps to that. All the rest isn't worth a straw. A long engagement if you like, but inquiries, questions, plans, lines of action—no, Aunt Juley, no.'

Away she hurried, not beautiful, not supremely brilliant, but filled with something that took the place of both qualities—something best described as a profound vivacity, a continual and sincere response to all that she encountered in her path through life.

'If Helen had written the same to me about a shop-assistant or a penniless clerk—'

'Dear Margaret, do come into the library and shut the door. Your good maids are dusting the banisters.'

'—or if she had wanted to marry the man who calls for Carter Paterson, I should have said the same.' Then, with one of those turns that convinced her aunt that she was not mad really, and convinced observers of another type that she was not a barren theorist, she added: 'Though in the case of Carter Paterson I should want it to be a very long engagement indeed, I must say.'

'I should think so,' said Mrs Munt; 'and, indeed, I can scarcely follow you. Now, just imagine if you said anything of that sort to the Wilcoxes. I understand it, but most good people would think you mad. Imagine how disconcerting for Helen! What is wanted is a person who will go slowly, slowly in this business, and see how things are and where they are likely to lead to.'

Margaret was down on this.

'But you implied just now that the engagement must be broken off.'

'I think probably it must; but slowly.'

'Can you break an engagement off slowly?' Her eyes lit up. 'What's an engagement made of, do you suppose? I think it's made of some hard stuff, that may snap, but can't break. It is different to the other ties of life. They stretch or bend. They admit of degree. They're different.'

'Exactly so. But won't you let me just run down to Howards House, and save you all the discomfort? I will really not interfere, but I do so thoroughly understand the kind of thing you Schlegels want that one quiet look round will be enough for me.'

Margaret again thanked her, again kissed her, and then ran upstairs to see her brother.

He was not so well.

The hay fever had worried him a good deal all night. His head ached, his eyes were wet, his mucous membrane, he informed her, in a most unsatisfactory condition. The only thing that made life worth living was the thought of Walter Savage Landor, from whose 'Imaginary Conversations' she had promised to read at frequent intervals during the day.

It was rather difficult. Something must be done about Helen. She must be assured that it is not a criminal offence to love at first sight. A telegram to this effect would be cold and cryptic, a personal visit seemed each moment more impossible. Now the doctor arrived, and said that Tibby was quite bad. Might it really be best to accept Aunt Juley's kind offer, and to send her down to Howards End with a note?

Certainly Margaret was impulsive. She did swing rapidly from one decision to another. Running downstairs into the library, she cried: 'Yes, I have changed my mind; I do wish that you would go.'

There was a train from King's Cross at eleven. At half-past ten Tibby, with rare self-effacement, fell asleep, and Margaret was able to drive her aunt to the station.

'You will remember, Aunt Juley, not to be drawn into discussing the engagement. Give my letter to Helen, and say whatever you feel yourself, but do keep clear of the relatives. We have scarcely got their names straight yet, and, besides, that sort of thing is so uncivilized and wrong.'

'So uncivilized?' queried Mrs Munt, fearing that she was losing the point of some brilliant remark.

'Oh, I used an affected word. I only meant would you please only talk the thing over with Helen.'

'Only with Helen.'

'Because—' But it was no moment to expound the personal nature of love. Even Margaret shrank from it, and contented herself with stroking her good aunt's hand, and with meditating, half sensibly and half poetically, on the journey that was about to begin from King's Cross.

Like many others who have lived long in a great capital, she had strong feelings about the various railway termini. They are our gates to the glorious and the unknown. Through them we pass out into adventure and sunshine, to them, alas! we return. In Paddington all Cornwall is latent and the remoter west; down the inclines of Liverpool Street lie fenlands and the illimitable Broads; Scotland is through the pylons of Euston; Wessex behind the poised chaos of Waterloo. Italians realize this, as is natural; those of them who are so unfortunate as to serve as waiters in Berlin call the Anhalt Bahnhof the Stazione d'Italia, because by it they must return to their homes. And he is a chilly Londoner who does not endow his stations with some personality, and extend to them, however shyly, the emotions of fear and love.

To Margaret—I hope that it will not set the reader against her—the station of King's Cross had always suggested Infinity. Its very situation—withdrawn a little behind the facile splendours of St Pancras—implied a comment on the materialism of life. Those two great arches, colourless, indifferent, shouldering between them an unlovely clock, were fit portals for some eternal adventure, whose issue might be prosperous, but would certainly not be expressed in the ordinary language of prosperity. If you think this ridiculous, remember that it is not Margaret who is telling you about it; and let me hasten to add that they were in plenty of time for the train; that Mrs Munt secured a comfortable seat, facing the engine, but not too near it; and that Margaret, on her return to Wickham Place, was confronted with the following telegram

'ALL OVER. WISH I HAD NEVER WRITTEN. TELL NO ONE.—HELEN.'

But Aunt Juley was gone—gone irrevocably, and no power on earth could stop her.

Chapter Three

Most complacently did Mrs Munt rehearse her mission. Her nieces were independent young women, and it was not often that she was able to help them. Emily's daughters had never been quite like other girls. They had been left motherless when Tibby was born, when Helen was five and Margaret herself but thirteen. It was before the passing of the Deceased Wife's Sister Bill, so Mrs Munt could without impropriety offer to go and keep house at Wickham Place. But her brother-in-law, who was peculiar and a German, had referred the question to Margaret, who with the crudity of youth had answered, 'No, they could manage much better alone.' Five years later Mr Schlegel had died too, and Mrs Munt had repeated her offer. Margaret, crude no longer, had been grateful and extremely nice, but the substance of her answer had been the same. 'I must not interfere a third time,' thought Mrs Munt. However, of course she did. She learnt, to her horror, that Margaret, now of age, was taking her money out of the old safe investments and putting it into Foreign Things, which always smash. Silence would have been criminal. Her own fortune was invested in Home Rails, and most ardently did she beg her niece to imitate her. 'Then we should be together, dear.' Margaret, out of politeness, invested a few hundreds in the Nottingham and Derby Railway, and though the Foreign Things did admirably and the Nottingham and Derby declined with the steady dignity of which only Home Rails are capable, Mrs Munt never ceased to rejoice, and to say, 'I did manage that, at all events. When the smash comes poor Margaret will have a nest-egg to fall back upon.' This year Helen came of age, and exactly the same thing happened in Helen's case; she also would shift her money out of Consols, but she, too, almost without being pressed, consecrated a fraction of it to the Nottingham and Derby Railway. So far so good, but in social matters their aunt had accomplished nothing. Sooner or later the girls would enter on the process known as throwing themselves away, and if they had delayed hitherto, it was only that they might throw themselves more vehemently in the future. They saw too many people at Wickham Place—unshaven musicians, an actress even, German cousins (one knows what foreigners are), acquaintances picked up at Continental hotels (one knows what they are too). It was interesting, and down at Swanage no one appreciated culture more than Mrs Munt; but it was dangerous, and disaster was bound to come. How right she was, and how lucky to be on the spot when the disaster came!

The train sped northward, under innumerable tunnels. It was only an hour's journey, but Mrs Munt had to raise and lower the window again and again. She passed through the South Welwyn Tunnel, saw light for a moment, and entered the North Welwyn Tunnel, of tragic fame. She traversed the immense viaduct, whose arches span untroubled meadows and the dreamy flow of Tewin Water. She skirted the parks of politicians. At times the Great North Road accompanied her, more suggestive of infinity than any railway, awakening, after a nap of a hundred years, to such life as is conferred by the stench of motor-cars, and to such culture as is implied by the advertisements of antibilious pills. To history, to tragedy, to the past, to the future, Mrs Munt remained equally indifferent; hers but to concentrate on the end of her journey, and to rescue poor Helen from this dreadful mess.

The station for Howards End was at Hilton, one of the large villages that are strung so frequently along the North Road, and that owe their size to the traffic of coaching and pre-coaching days. Being near London, it had not shared in the rural decay, and its long High Street had budded out right and left into residential estates. For about a mile a series of tiled and slated houses passed before Mrs Munt's inattentive eyes, a series broken at one point by six Danish tumuli that stood shoulder to shoulder along the highroad, tombs of soldiers. Beyond these tumuli habitations thickened, and the train came to a standstill in a tangle that was almost a town.

The station, like the scenery, like Helen's letters, struck an indeterminate note. Into which country will it lead, England or Suburbia? It was new, it had island platforms and a subway, and the superficial comfort exacted by business men. But it held hints of local life, personal intercourse, as even Mrs Munt was to discover.

'I want a house,' she confided to the ticket boy. 'Its name is Howards Lodge. Do you know where it is?'

'Mr Wilcox!' the boy called.

A young man in front of them turned round.

'She's wanting Howards End.'

There was nothing for it but to go forward, though Mrs Munt was too much agitated even to stare at the stranger. But remembering that there were two brothers, she had the sense to say to him, 'Excuse me asking, but are you the younger Mr Wilcox or the elder?'

'The younger. Can I do anything for you?'

'Oh, well'—she controlled herself with difficulty. 'Really. Are you? I—' She moved away from the ticket boy and lowered her voice. 'I am Miss Schlegel's aunt. I ought to introduce myself, oughtn't I? My name is Mrs Munt.'

She was conscious that he raised his cap and said quite coolly, 'Oh, rather; Miss Schlegel is stopping with us. Did you want to see her?'

'Possibly—'

'I'll call you a cab. No; wait a mo.' He thought. 'Our motor's here. I'll run you up in it.'

'That is very kind—'

'Not at all, if you'll just wait till they bring out a parcel from the office. This way.'

'My niece is not with you by any chance?'

'No; I came over with my father. He has gone on north in your train. You'll see Miss Schlegel at lunch. You're coming up to lunch, I hope?'

'I should like to come *up*,' said Mrs Munt, not committing herself to nourishment until she had studied Helen's lover a little more. He seemed a gentleman, but had so rattled her round that her powers of observation were numbed. She glanced at him stealthily. To a feminine eye there was nothing amiss in the sharp depressions at the corners of his mouth, nor in the rather box-like construction of his forehead. He was dark, clean-shaven, and seemed accustomed to command.

'In front or behind? Which do you prefer? It may be windy in front.'

'In front if I may; then we can talk.'

'But excuse me one moment—I can't think what they're doing with that parcel.' He strode into the booking-office, and called with a new voice: 'Hi! hi, you there! Are you going to keep me waiting all day? Parcel for Wilcox, Howards End. Just look sharp!' Emerging, he said in quieter tones: 'This station's abominably organized; if I had my way, the whole lot of 'em should get the sack. May I help you in?'

'This is very good of you,' said Mrs Munt, as she settled herself into a luxurious cavern of red leather, and suffered her person to be padded with rugs and shawls. She was more civil than she had intended, but really this young man was very kind. Moreover, she was a little afraid of him: his self-possession was extraordinary. 'Very good indeed,' she repeated, adding: 'It is just what I should have wished.'

'Very good of you to say so,' he replied, with a slight look of surprise, which, like most slight looks, escaped Mrs Munt's attention. 'I was just tooling my father over to catch the down train.'

'You see, we heard from Helen this morning.'

Young Wilcox was pouring in petrol, starting his engine, and performing other actions with which this story has no concern. The great car began to rock, and the form of Mrs Munt, trying to explain things, sprang agreeably up and down among the red cushions. 'The mater will be very glad to see you,' he mumbled. 'Hi! I say. Parcel. Parcel for Howards End. Bring it out. Hi!'

A bearded porter emerged with the parcel in one hand and an entry book in the other. With the gathering whir of the motor these ejaculations mingled: 'Sign, must I? Why the —— should I sign after all this bother? Not even got a pencil on you? Remember next time I report you to the station-master. My time's of value, though yours mayn't be. Here'–here being a tip.

'Extremely sorry, Mrs Munt.'

'Not at all, Mr Wilcox.'

'And do you object to going through the village? It is rather a longer spin, but I have one or two commissions.'

'I should love going through the village. Naturally I am very anxious to talk things over with you.'

As she said this she felt ashamed, for she was disobeying Margaret's instructions. Only disobeying them in the letter, surely. Margaret had only warned her against discussing the incident with outsiders. Surely it was not 'uncivilized or wrong' to discuss it with the young man himself, since chance had thrown them together.

A reticent fellow, he made no reply. Mounting by her side, he put on gloves and spectacles, and off they drove, the bearded porter–life is a mysterious business–looking after them with admiration.

The wind was in their faces down the station road, blowing the dust into Mrs Munt's eyes. But as soon as they turned into the Great North Road she opened fire. 'You can well imagine,' she said, 'that the news was a great shock to us.'

'What news?'

'Mr Wilcox,' she said frankly, 'Margaret has told me everything–everything. I have seen Helen's letter.'

He could not look her in the face, as his eyes were fixed on his work; he was travelling as quickly as he dared down the High Street. But he inclined his head in her direction, and said, 'I beg your pardon; I didn't catch.'

'About Helen. Helen, of course. Helen is a very exceptional person–I am sure you will let me say this, feeling towards her as you do–indeed, all the Schlegels are exceptional. I come in no spirit of interference, but it was a great shock.'

They drew up opposite a draper's. Without replying, he turned round in his seat, and contemplated the cloud of dust that they had raised in their passage through the village. It was settling again, but not all into the road from which he had taken it. Some of it had percolated through the open windows, some had whitened the roses and gooseberries of the wayside gardens, while a certain proportion had entered the lungs of the villagers. 'I wonder when they'll learn wisdom and tar the roads,' was his comment. Then a man ran out of the draper's with a roll of oilcloth, and off they went again.

'Margaret could not come herself, on account of poor Tibby, so I am here to represent her and to have a good talk.'

'I'm sorry to be so dense,' said the young man, again drawing up outside a shop. 'But I still haven't quite understood.'

'Helen, Mr Wilcox—my niece and you.'

He pushed up his goggles and gazed at her, absolutely bewildered. Horror smote her to the heart, for even she began to suspect that they were at cross-purposes, and that she had commenced her mission by some hideous blunder.

'Miss Schlegel and myself?' he asked, compressing his lips.

'I trust there has been no misunderstanding,' quavered Mrs Munt. 'Her letter certainly read that way.'

'What way?'

'That you and she—' She paused, then drooped her eyelids.

'I think I catch your meaning,' he said stickily. 'What an extraordinary mistake!'

'Then you didn't the least—' she stammered, getting blood-red in the face, and wishing she had never been born.

'Scarcely, as I am already engaged to another lady.' There was a moment's silence, and then he caught his breath and exploded with, 'Oh, good God! Don't tell me it's some silliness of Paul's.'

'But you are Paul.'

'I'm not.'

'Then why did you say so at the station?'

'I said nothing of the sort.'

'I beg your pardon, you did.'

'I beg your pardon, I did not. My name is Charles.'

'Younger' may mean son as opposed to father, or second brother as opposed to first. There is much to be said for either view, and later on they said it. But they had other questions before them now.

'Do you mean to tell me that Paul—'

But she did not like his voice. He sounded as if he was talking to a porter, and, certain that he had deceived her at the station, she too grew angry.

'Do you mean to tell me that Paul and your niece—'

Mrs Munt—such is human nature—determined that she would champion the lovers. She was not going to be bullied by a severe young man. 'Yes, they care for one another very much indeed,' she said. 'I dare say they will tell you about it by-and-by. We heard this morning.'

And Charles clenched his fist and cried, 'The idiot, the idiot, the little fool!'

Mrs Munt tried to divest herself of her rugs. 'If that is your attitude, Mr Wilcox, I prefer to walk.'

'I beg you will do no such thing. I take you up this moment to the house. Let me tell you the thing's impossible, and must be stopped.'

Mrs Munt did not often lose her temper, and when she did it was only to protect those whom she loved. On this occasion she blazed out. 'I quite agree, sir. The thing is impossible, and I will come up and stop it. My niece is a very exceptional person, and I am not inclined to sit still while she throws herself away on those who will not appreciate her.'

Charles worked his jaws.

'Considering she has only known your brother since Wednesday, and only met your father and mother at a stray hotel—'

'Could you possibly lower your voice? The shopman will overhear.'

'Esprit de classe'–if one may coin the phrase–was strong in Mrs Munt. She sat quivering while a member of the lower orders deposited a metal funnel, a saucepan, and a garden squirt beside the roll of oilcloth.

'Right behind?'

'Yes, sir.' And the lower orders vanished in a cloud of dust.

'I warn you: Paul hasn't a penny, it's useless.'

'No need to warn us, Mr Wilcox, I assure you. The warning is all the other way. My niece has been very foolish, and I shall give her a good scolding and take her back to London with me.'

'He has to make his way out in Nigeria. He couldn't think of marrying for years, and when he does it must be a woman who can stand the climate, and is in other ways— Why hasn't he told us? Of course he's ashamed. He knows he's been a fool. And so he has–a damned fool.'

She grew furious.

'Whereas Miss Schlegel has lost no time in publishing the news.'

'If I were a man, Mr Wilcox, for the last remark I'd box your ears. You're not fit to clean my niece's boots, to sit in the same room with her, and you dare–you actually dare— I decline to argue with such a person.'

'All I know is, she's spread the thing and he hasn't, and my father's away and I—'

'And all that I know is—'

'Might I finish my sentence, please?'

'No.'

Charles clenched his teeth and sent the motor swerving all over the lane. She screamed.

So they played the game of Capping Families, a round of which is always played when love would unite two members of our race. But they played it with unusual vigour, stating in so many words that Schlegels were better than Wilcoxes, Wilcoxes better than Schlegels. They flung decency aside. The man was young, the woman deeply stirred; in both a vein of coarseness was latent. Their quarrel was no more surprising than are most quarrels–inevitable at the time, incredible afterwards. But it was more than usually futile. A few minutes, and they were enlightened. The motor drew up at Howards End, and Helen, looking very pale, ran out to meet her aunt.

'Aunt Juley, I have just had a telegram from Margaret; I–I meant to stop your coming. It isn't–it's over.'

The climax was too much for Mrs Munt. She burst into tears.

'Aunt Juley dear, don't. Don't let them know I've been so silly. It wasn't anything. Do bear up for my sake.'

'Paul,' cried Charles Wilcox, pulling his gloves off.

'Don't let them know. They are never to know.'

'Oh, my darling Helen—'

'Paul! Paul!'

A very young man came out of the house.

'Paul, is there any truth in this?'

'I didn't–I don't—'

'Yes or no, man; plain question, plain answer. Did or didn't Miss Schlegel—'

'Charles dear,' said a voice from the garden. 'Charles, dear Charles, one doesn't ask plain questions. There aren't such things.'

They were all silent. It was Mrs Wilcox.

She approached just as Helen's letter had described her, trailing noiselessly over the lawn, and there was actually a wisp of hay in her hands. She seemed to belong not to the young people and their motor, but to the house, and to the tree that overshadowed it. One knew that she worshipped the past, and that the instinctive wisdom the past can alone bestow had descended upon her–that wisdom to which we give the clumsy name of aristocracy. High born she might not be. But assuredly she cared about her ancestors, and let them help her. When she saw Charles angry, Paul frightened, and Mrs Munt in tears, she heard her ancestors say, 'Separate those human beings who will hurt each other most. The rest can wait.' So she did not ask questions. Still less did she pretend that nothing had happened, as a competent society hostess would have done. She said, 'Miss Schlegel, would you take your aunt up to your room or to my room, whichever you think best. Paul, do find Evie, and tell her lunch for six, but I'm not sure whether we shall all be downstairs for it.' And when they had obeyed her, she turned to her elder son, who still stood in the throbbing, stinking car, and smiled at him with tenderness, and without saying a word, turned away from him towards her flowers.

'Mother,' he called, 'are you aware that Paul has been playing the fool again?'

'It is all right, dear. They have broken off the engagement.'

'Engagement—!'

'They do not love any longer, if you prefer it put that way,' said Mrs Wilcox, stooping down to smell a rose.

Chapter Four

Helen and her aunt returned to Wickham Place in a state of collapse, and for a little time Margaret had three invalids on her hands. Mrs Munt soon recovered. She possessed to a remarkable degree the power of distorting the past, and before many days were over she had forgotten the part played by her own imprudence in the catastrophe. Even at the crisis she had cried, 'Thank goodness, poor Margaret is saved this!' which during the journey to London evolved into, 'It had to be gone through by someone,' which in its turn ripened into the permanent form of 'The one time I really did help Emily's girls was over the Wilcox business.' But Helen was a more serious patient. New ideas had burst upon her like a thunder clap, and by them and by their reverberations she had been stunned.

The truth was that she had fallen in love, not with an individual, but with a family.

Before Paul arrived she had, as it were, been tuned up into his key. The energy of the Wilcoxes had fascinated her, had created new images of beauty in her responsive mind. To be all day with them in the open air, to sleep at night under their roof, had seemed the supreme joy of life, and had led to that abandonment of personality that is a possible prelude to love. She had liked giving in to Mr Wilcox, or Evie, or Charles; she had liked being told that her notions of life were sheltered or academic; that Equality was nonsense, Votes for Women nonsense, Socialism nonsense, Art and Literature, except when conducive to strengthening the character, nonsense. One by one the Schlegel fetiches had been overthrown, and, though professing to defend them, she had rejoiced. When Mr Wilcox said that one sound man of business did more good to the world than a dozen of your social reformers, she had swallowed the curious assertion without a gasp, and had leant back luxuriously among the cushions of his motor-car. When Charles said, 'Why be so polite to servants? they don't understand it,' she had not given the Schlegel retort of, 'If they don't understand it, I do.' No; she had vowed to be less polite to servants in the future. 'I am swathed in cant,' she thought, 'and it is good for me to be stripped of it.' And all that she thought or did or breathed was a quiet preparation for Paul. Paul was inevitable. Charles was taken up with another girl, Mr Wilcox was so old, Evie so young, Mrs Wilcox so different. Round the absent brother she began to throw the halo of Romance, to irradiate him with all the splendour of those happy days, to feel that in him she should draw nearest to the robust ideal. He and she were about the same age, Evie said. Most people thought

Paul handsomer than his brother. He was certainly a better shot, though not so good at golf. And when Paul appeared, flushed with the triumph of getting through an examination, and ready to flirt with any pretty girl, Helen met him halfway, or more than halfway, and turned towards him on the Sunday evening.

He had been talking of his approaching exile in Nigeria, and he should have continued to talk of it, and allowed their guest to recover. But the heave of her bosom flattered him. Passion was possible, and he became passionate. Deep down in him something whispered, 'This girl would let you kiss her; you might not have such a chance again.'

That was 'how it happened,' or, rather, how Helen described it to her sister, using words even more unsympathetic than my own. But the poetry of that kiss, the wonder of it, the magic that there was in life for hours after it—who can describe that? It is so easy for an Englishman to sneer at these chance collisions of human beings. To the insular cynic and the insular moralist they offer an equal opportunity. It is so easy to talk of 'passing emotion,' and to forget how vivid the emotion was ere it passed. Our impulse to sneer, to forget, is at root a good one. We recognize that emotion is not enough, and that men and women are personalities capable of sustained relations, not mere opportunities for an electrical discharge. Yet we rate the impulse too highly. We do not admit that by collisions of this trivial sort the doors of heaven may be shaken open. To Helen, at all events, her life was to bring nothing more intense than the embrace of this boy who played no part in it. He had drawn her out of the house, where there was danger of surprise and light; he had led her by a path he knew, until they stood under the column of the vast wych-elm. A man in the darkness, he had whispered 'I love you' when she was desiring love. In time his slender personality faded, the scene that he had evoked endured. In all the variable years that followed she never saw the like of it again.

'I understand,' said Margaret—'at least, I understand as much as ever is understood of these things. Tell me now what happened on the Monday morning.'

'It was over at once.'

'How, Helen?'

'I was still happy while I dressed, but as I came downstairs I got nervous, and when I went into the dining-room I knew it was no good. There was Evie—I can't explain—managing the tea-urn, and Mr Wilcox reading the "Times."'

'Was Paul there?'

'Yes; and Charles was talking to him about Stocks and Shares, and he looked frightened.'

By slight indications the sisters could convey much to each other. Margaret saw horror latent in the scene, and Helen's next remark did not surprise her.

'Somehow, when that kind of man looks frightened it is too awful. It is all right for us to be frightened, or for men of another sort—father, for instance; but for men like that! When I saw all the others so placid, and Paul mad with

terror in case I said the wrong thing, I felt for a moment that the whole
Wilcox family was a fraud, just a wall of newspapers and motor-cars and
golf-clubs, and that if it fell I should find nothing behind it but panic and
emptiness.'

'I don't think that. The Wilcoxes struck me as being genuine people,
particularly the wife.'

'No, I don't really think that. But Paul was so broad-shouldered; all kinds
of extraordinary things made it worse, and I knew that it would never
do—never. I said to him after breakfast, when the others were practising
strokes, "We rather lost our heads," and he looked better at once, though
frightfully ashamed. He began a speech about having no money to marry on,
but it hurt him to make it, and I stopped him. Then he said, "I must beg
your pardon over this, Miss Schlegel; I can't think what came over me last
night." And I said, "Nor what over me; never mind." And then we
parted—at least, until I remembered that I had written straight off to tell you
the night before, and that frightened him again. I asked him to send a
telegram for me, for he knew you would be coming or something; and he
tried to get hold of the motor, but Charles and Mr Wilcox wanted it to go to
the station; and Charles offered to send the telegram for me, and then I had
to say that the telegram was of no consequence, for Paul said Charles might
read it, and though I wrote it out several times, he always said people would
suspect something. He took it himself at last, pretending that he must walk
down to get cartridges, and, what with one thing and the other, it was not
handed in at the Post Office until too late. It was the most terrible morning.
Paul disliked me more and more, and Evie talked cricket averages till I
nearly screamed. I cannot think how I stood her all the other days. At last
Charles and his father started for the station, and then came your telegram
warning me that Aunt Juley was coming by that train, and Paul—oh, rather
horrible—said that I had muddled it. But Mrs Wilcox knew.'

'Knew what?'

'Everything; though we neither of us told her a word, and had known all
along, I think.'

'Oh, she must have overheard you.'

'I suppose so, but it seemed wonderful. When Charles and Aunt Juley
drove up, calling each other names, Mrs Wilcox stepped in from the garden
and made everything less terrible. Ugh! but it has been a disgusting
business. To think that—' She sighed.

'To think that because you and a young man meet for a moment, there
must be all these telegrams and anger,' supplied Margaret.

Helen nodded.

'I've often thought about it, Helen. It's one of the most interesting things
in the world. The truth is that there is a great outer life that you and I
have never touched—a life in which telegrams and anger count. Personal
relations, that we think supreme, are not supreme there. There love means
marriage settlements, death, death duties. So far I'm clear. But here my
difficulty. This outer life, though obviously horrid, often seems the real
one—there's grit in it. It does breed character. Do personal relations lead

to sloppiness in the end?'

'Oh, Meg, that's what I felt, only not so clearly, when the Wilcoxes were so competent, and seemed to have their hands on all the ropes.'

'Don't you feel it now?'

'I remember Paul at breakfast,' said Helen quietly. 'I shall never forget him. He had nothing to fall back upon. I know that personal relations are the real life, for ever and ever.'

'Amen!'

So the Wilcox episode fell into the background, leaving behind it memories of sweetness and horror that mingled, and the sisters pursued the life that Helen had commended. They talked to each other and to other people, they filled the tall thin house at Wickham Place with those whom they liked or could befriend. They even attended public meetings. In their own fashion they cared deeply about politics, though not as politicians would have us care; they desired that public life should mirror whatever is good in the life within. Temperance, tolerance, and sexual equality were intelligible cries to them; whereas they did not follow our Forward Policy in Thibet with the keen attention that it merits, and would at times dismiss the whole British Empire with a puzzled, if reverent, sigh. Not out of them are the shows of history erected: the world would be a grey, bloodless place were it entirely composed of Miss Schlegels. But the world being what it is, perhaps they shine out in it like stars.

A word on their origin. They were not 'English to the backbone,' as their aunt had piously asserted. But, on the other hand, they were not 'Germans of the dreadful sort.' Their father had belonged to a type that was more prominent in Germany fifty years ago than now. He was not the aggressive German, so dear to the English journalist, nor the domestic German, so dear to the English wit. If one classed him at all it would be as the countryman of Hegel and Kant, as the idealist, inclined to be dreamy, whose Imperialism was the Imperialism of the air. Not that his life had been inactive. He had fought like blazes against Denmark, Austria, France. But he had fought without visualizing the results of victory. A hint of the truth broke on him after Sedan, when he saw the dyed moustaches of Napoleon going grey; another when he entered Paris, and saw the smashed windows of the Tuileries. Peace came—it was all very immense, one had turned into an Empire—but he knew that some quality had vanished for which not all Alsace-Lorraine could compensate him. Germany a commercial Power, Germany a naval Power, Germany with colonies here and a Forward Policy there, and legitimate aspirations in the other place, might appeal to others, and be fitly served by them; for his own part, he abstained from the fruits of victory, and naturalized himself in England. The more earnest members of his family never forgave him, and knew that his children, though scarcely English of the dreadful sort, would never be German to the backbone. He had obtained work in one of our provincial Universities, and there married Poor Emily (or Die Engländerin as the case may be), and as she had money, they proceeded to London, and came to know a good many people. But his gaze was always fixed beyond the sea. It was his hope that the clouds of materialism obscuring the Fatherland would part in time, and the mild intellectual light re-emerge. 'Do you imply that we Germans are stupid, Uncle Ernst?' exclaimed a haughty and magnificent nephew. Uncle Ernst replied, 'To my mind. You use the intellect, but you no longer care about it. That I call stupidity.' As the haughty nephew did not follow, he continued, 'You only care about the things that you can use, and therefore arrange them in the following order: Money, supremely useful; intellect, rather useful; imagination, of no use at all. No'—for the other had protested—'your Pan-Germanism is no more imaginative than is our Imperialism over here. It is the vice of a vulgar mind to be thrilled by bigness, to think that a thousand square miles are a thousand times more wonderful than one square mile, and that a million square miles are almost the same as heaven. That is not imagination. No, it kills it. When their poets over here try to celebrate bigness they are dead at once, and naturally. Your poets too are dying, your philosophers, your musicians, to whom Europe has listened for two hundred years. Gone. Gone with the little courts that nurtured them—gone with Esterhaz and Weimar. What? What's that? Your Universities? Oh yes, you have learned men, who collect more facts than do the learned men of England. They collect facts, and facts, and empires of facts. But which of them will rekindle the light within?'

To all this Margaret listened, sitting on the haughty nephew's knee.

It was a unique education for the little girls. The haughty nephew would be at Wickham Place one day, bringing with him an even haughtier wife, both convinced that Germany was appointed by God to govern the world. Aunt Juley would come the next day, convinced that Great Britain had been appointed to the same post by the same authority. Were both these loud-voiced parties right? On one occasion they had met, and Margaret with clasped hands had implored them to argue the subject out in her presence. Whereat they blushed, and began to talk about the weather. 'Papa,' she cried—she was a most offensive child—'why will they not discuss this most clear question?' Her father, surveying the parties grimly, replied that he did not know. Putting her head on one side, Margaret then remarked, 'To me one of two things is very clear; either God does not know his own mind about England and Germany, or else these do not know the mind of God.' A hateful little girl, but at thirteen she had grasped a dilemma that most people travel through life without perceiving. Her brain darted up and down; it grew pliant and strong. Her conclusion was, that any human being lies nearer to the unseen than any organization, and from this she never varied.

Helen advanced along the same lines, though with a more irresponsible tread. In character she resembled her sister, but she was pretty, and so apt to have a more amusing time. People gathered round her more readily, especially when they were new acquaintances, and she did enjoy a little homage very much. When their father died and they ruled alone at Wickham Place, she often absorbed the whole of the company, while Margaret—both were tremendous talkers—fell flat. Neither sister bothered about this. Helen never apologized afterwards, Margaret did not feel the slightest rancour. But looks have their influence upon character. The sisters were alike as little girls, but at the time of the Wilcox episode their methods were beginning to diverge; the younger was rather apt to entice people, and, in enticing them, to be herself enticed; the elder went straight ahead, and accepted an occasional failure as part of the game.

Little need be premised about Tibby. He was now an intelligent man of sixteen, but dyspeptic and difficile.

Chapter Five

It will be generally admitted that Beethoven's Fifth Symphony is the most sublime noise that has ever penetrated into the ear of man. All sorts and conditions are satisfied by it. Whether you are like Mrs Munt, and tap surreptitiously when the tunes come—of course, not so as to disturb the others—or like Helen, who can see heroes and shipwrecks in the music's flood; or like Margaret, who can only see the music; or like Tibby, who is profoundly versed in counterpoint, and holds the full score open on his knee; or like their cousin, Fräulein Mosebach, who remembers all the time that Beethoven is 'echt Deutsch'; or like Fräulein Mosebach's young man, who can remember nothing but Fräulein Mosebach: in any case, the passion of your life becomes more vivid, and you are bound to admit that such a noise is cheap at two shillings. It is cheap, even if you hear it in the Queen's Hall, dreariest music-room in London, though not as dreary as the Free Trade Hall, Manchester; and even if you sit on the extreme left of that hall, so that the brass bumps at you before the rest of the orchestra arrives, it is still cheap.

'Who is Margaret talking to?' said Mrs Munt, at the conclusion of the first movement. She was again in London on a visit to Wickham Place.

Helen looked down the long line of their party, and said that she did not know.

'Would it be some young man or other whom she takes an interest in?'

'I expect so,' Helen replied. Music enwrapped her, and she could not enter into the distinction that divides young men whom one takes an interest in from young men whom one knows.

'You girls are so wonderful in always having— Oh dear! one mustn't talk.'

For the Andante had begun—very beautiful, but bearing a family likeness to all the other beautiful Andantes that Beethoven had written, and, to Helen's mind, rather disconnecting the heroes and shipwrecks of the first movement from the heroes and goblins of the third. She heard the tune through once, and then her attention wandered, and she gazed at the audience, or the organ, or the architecture. Much did she censure the attenuated Cupids who encircle the ceiling of the Queen's Hall, inclining each to each with vapid gesture, and clad in sallow pantaloons, on which the October sunlight struck. 'How awful to marry a man like those Cupids!'

thought Helen. Here Beethoven started decorating his tune, so she heard him through once more, and then she smiled at her cousin Frieda. But Frieda, listening to Classical Music, could not respond. Herr Liesecke, too, looked as if wild horses could not make him inattentive; there were lines across his forehead, his lips were parted, his pince-nez at right angles to his nose, and he had laid a thick, white hand on either knee. And next to her was Aunt Juley, so British, and wanting to tap. How interesting that row of people was! What diverse influences had gone to the making! Here Beethoven, after humming and hawing with great sweetness, said 'Heigho,' and the Andante came to an end. Applause, and a round of 'wunderschön-ing' and 'pract' volleying from the German contingent. Margaret started talking to her new young man; Helen said to her aunt: 'Now comes the wonderful movement: first of all the goblins, and then a trio of elephants dancing;' and Tibby implored the company generally to look out for the transitional passage on the drum.

'On the what, dear?'

'On the *drum*, Aunt Juley.'

'No; look out for the part where you think you have done with the goblins and they come back,' breathed Helen, as the music started with a goblin walking quietly over the universe, from end to end. Others followed him. They were not aggressive creatures; it was that that made them so terrible to Helen. They merely observed in passing that there was no such thing as splendour or heroism in the world. After the interlude of elephants dancing, they returned and made the observation for the second time. Helen could not contradict them, for, once at all events, she had felt the same, and had seen the reliable walls of youth collapse. Panic and emptiness! Panic and emptiness! The goblins were right.

Her brother raised his finger: it was the transitional passage on the drum.

For, as if things were going too far, Beethoven took hold of the goblins and made them do what he wanted. He appeared in person. He gave them a little push, and they began to walk in major key instead of in a minor, and then—he blew with his mouth and they were scattered! Gusts of splendour, gods and demi-gods contending with vast swords, colour and fragrance broadcast on the field of battle, magnificent victory, magnificent death! Oh, it all burst before the girl, and she even stretched out her gloved hands as if it was tangible. Any fate was titanic; any contest desirable; conqueror and conquered would alike be applauded by the angels of the utmost stars.

And the goblins—they had not really been there at all? They were only the phantoms of cowardice and unbelief? One healthy human impulse would dispel them? Men like the Wilcoxes, or President Roosevelt, would say yes. Beethoven knew better. The goblins really had been there. They might return—and they did. It was as if the splendour of life might boil over and waste to steam and froth. In its dissolution one heard the terrible, ominous note, and a goblin, with increased malignity, walked quietly over the universe from end to end. Panic and emptiness! Panic and emptiness! Even the flaming ramparts of the world might fall.

Beethoven chose to make all right in the end. He built the ramparts up. He blew with his mouth for the second time, and again the goblins were scattered. He brought back the gusts of splendour, the heroism, the youth, the magnificence of life and of death, and, amid vast roarings of a superhuman joy, he led his Fifth Symphony to its conclusion. But the goblins were there. They could return. He had said so bravely, and that is why one can trust Beethoven when he says other things.

Helen pushed her way out during the applause. She desired to be alone. The music had summed up to her all that had happened or could happen in her career. She read it as a tangible statement, which could never be superseded. The notes meant this and that to her, and they could have no other meaning, and life could have no other meaning. She pushed right out of the building, and walked slowly down the outside staircase, breathing the autumnal air, and then she strolled home.

'Margaret,' called Mrs Munt, 'is Helen all right?'

'Oh yes.'

'She is always going away in the middle of a programme,' said Tibby.

'The music had evidently moved her deeply,' said Fräulein Mosebach.

'Excuse me,' said Margaret's young man, who had for some time been preparing a sentence, 'but that lady has, quite inadvertently, taken my umbrella.'

'Oh, good gracious me!—I am so sorry. Tibby, run after Helen.'

'I shall miss the Four Serious Songs if I do.'

'Tibby love, you must go.'

'It isn't of any consequence,' said the young man, in truth a little uneasy about his umbrella.

'But of course it is. Tibby! Tibby!'

Tibby rose to his feet, and wilfully caught his person on the backs of the chairs. By the time he had tipped up the seat and had found his hat, and had deposited his full score in safety, it was 'too late' to go after Helen. The Four Serious Songs had begun, and one could not move during their performance.

'My sister is so careless,' whispered Margaret.

'Not at all,' replied the young man; but his voice was dead and cold.

'If you would give me your address—'

'Oh, not at all, not at all;' and he wrapped his greatcoat over his knees.

Then the Four Serious Songs rang shallow in Margaret's ears. Brahms, for all his grumbling and grizzling, had never guessed what it felt like to be suspected of stealing an umbrella. For this fool of a young man thought that she and Helen and Tibby had been playing the confidence trick on him, and that if he gave his address they would break into his rooms some midnight or other and steal his walking-stick too. Most ladies would have laughed, but Margaret really minded, for it gave her a glimpse into squalor. To trust people is a luxury in which only the wealthy can indulge; the poor cannot afford it. As soon as Brahms had grunted himself out, she gave him her card and said, 'That is where we live; if you preferred, you could call for the umbrella after the concert, but I didn't like to trouble you when it has all been our fault.'

His face brightened a little when he saw that Wickham Place was W. It was sad to see him corroded with suspicion, and yet not daring to be impolite, in case these well-dressed people were honest after all. She took it as a good sign that he said to her, 'It's a fine programme this afternoon, is it not?' for this was the remark with which he had originally opened, before the umbrella intervened.

'The Beethoven's fine,' said Margaret, who was not a female of the encouraging type. 'I don't like the Brahms, though, nor the Mendelssohn that came first—and ugh! I don't like this Elgar that's coming.'

'What, what?' called Herr Liesecke, overhearing. 'The "Pomp and Circumstance" will not be fine?'

'Oh, Margaret, you tiresome girl!' cried her aunt. 'Here have I been persuading Herr Liesecke to stop for "Pomp and Circumstance," and you are undoing all my work. I am so anxious for him to hear what *we* are doing in music. Oh, you mustn't run down our English composers, Margaret.'

'For my part, I have heard the composition at Stettin,' said Fräulein Mosebach. 'On two occasions. It is dramatic, a little.'

'Frieda, you despise English music. You know you do. And English art. And English literature, except Shakespeare and he's a German. Very well, Frieda, you may go.'

The lovers laughed and glanced at each other. Moved by a common impulse, they rose to their feet and fled from 'Pomp and Circumstance.'

'We have this call to pay in Finsbury Circus, it is true,' said Herr Liesecke, as he edged past her and reached the gangway just as the music started.

'Margaret—' loudly whispered by Aunt Juley. 'Margaret, Margaret! Fräulein Mosebach has left her beautiful little bag behind her on the seat.'

Sure enough, there was Frieda's reticule, containing her address book, her pocket dictionary, her map of London, and her money.

'Oh, what a bother—what a family we are! Fr-frieda!'

'Hush!' said all those who thought the music fine.

'But it's the number they want in Finsbury Circus—'

'Might I—couldn't I—' said the suspicious young man, and got very red.

'Oh, I would be so grateful.'

He took the bag—money clinking inside it—and slipped up the gangway with it. He was just in time to catch them at the swing-door, and he received a pretty smile from the German girl and a fine bow from her cavalier. He returned to his seat upsides with the world. The trust that they had reposed in him was trivial, but he felt that it cancelled his mistrust for them, and that probably he would not be 'had' over his umbrella. This young man had been 'had' in the past—badly, perhaps overwhelmingly—and now most of his energies went in defending himself against the unknown. But this afternoon—perhaps on account of music—he perceived that one must slack off occasionally, or what is the good of being alive? Wickham Place, W., though a risk, was as safe as most things, and he would risk it.

So when the concert was over and Margaret said, 'We live quite near; I am going there now. Could you walk round with me, and we'll find your umbrella?' he said, 'Thank you,' peaceably, and followed her out of the

Queen's Hall. She wished that he was not so anxious to hand a lady downstairs, or to carry a lady's programme for her—his class was near enough her own for its manners to vex her. But she found him interesting on the whole—everyone interested the Schlegels on the whole at that time—and while her lips talked culture, her heart was planning to invite him to tea.

'How tired one gets after music!' she began.

'Do you find the atmosphere of Queen's Hall oppressive?'

'Yes, horribly.'

'But surely the atmosphere of Covent Garden is even more oppressive.'

'Do you go there much?'

'When my work permits, I attend the gallery for the Royal Opera.'

Helen would have exclaimed, 'So do I. I love the gallery,' and thus have endeared herself to the young man. Helen could do these things. But Margaret had an almost morbid horror of 'drawing people out,' of 'making things go.' She had been to the gallery at Covent Garden, but she did not 'attend' it, preferring the more expensive seats; still less did she love it. So she made no reply.

'This year I have been three times—to "Faust," "Tosca," and—' Was it 'Tannhouser' or 'Tannhoyser'? Better not risk the word.

Margaret disliked 'Tosca' and 'Faust.' And so, for one reason and another, they walked on in silence, chaperoned by the voice of Mrs Munt, who was getting into difficulties with her nephew.

'I do in a *way* remember the passage, Tibby, but when every instrument is so beautiful, it is difficult to pick out one thing rather than another. I am sure that you and Helen take me to the very nicest concerts. Not a dull note from beginning to end. I only wish that our German friends would have stayed till it finished.'

'But surely you haven't forgotten the drum steadily beating on the low C, Aunt Juley?' came Tibby's voice. 'No one could. It's unmistakable.'

'A specially loud part?' hazarded Mrs Munt. 'Of course I do not go in for being musical,' she added, the shot failing. 'I only care for music—a very different thing. But still I will say this for myself—I do know when I like a thing and when I don't. Some people are the same about pictures. They can go into a picture gallery—Miss Conder can—and say straight off what they feel, all round the wall. I never could do that. But music is so different to pictures, to my mind. When it comes to music I am as safe as houses, and I assure you, Tibby, I am by no means pleased by everything. There was a thing—something about a faun in French—which Helen went into ecstasies over, but I thought it most tinkling and superficial, and said so, and I held to my opinion too.'

'Do you agree?' asked Margaret. 'Do you think music is so different to pictures?'

'I—I should have thought so, kind of,' he said.

'So should I. Now, my sister declares they're just the same. We have great arguments over it. She says I'm dense; I say she's sloppy.' Getting under way, she cried: 'Now, doesn't it seem absurd to you? What *is* the good of the Arts if they're interchangeable? What *is* the good of the ear if it tells you the same as the eye? Helen's one aim is to translate tunes into the language of painting, and pictures into the language of music. It's very ingenious, and she says several pretty things in the process, but what's gained, I'd like to know? Oh, it's all rubbish, radically false. If Monet's really Debussy, and Debussy's really Monet, neither gentleman is worth his salt—that's my opinion.'

Evidently these sisters quarrelled.

'Now, this very symphony that we've just been having—she won't let it alone. She labels it with meanings from start to finish; turns it into literature. I wonder if the day will ever return when music will be treated as music. Yet I don't know. There's my brother—behind us. He treats music as music, and oh, my goodness! He makes me angrier than anyone, simply furious. With him I daren't even argue.'

An unhappy family, if talented.

'But, of course, the real villain is Wagner. He had done more than any man in the nineteenth century towards the muddling of the arts. I do feel that music is in a very serious state just now, though extraordinarily interesting. Every now and then in history there do come these terrible geniuses, like Wagner, who stir up all the wells of thought at once. For a moment it's splendid. Such a splash as never was. But afterwards—such a lot of mud; and the wells—as it were, they communicate with each other too easily now, and not one of them will run quite clear. That's what Wagner's done.'

Her speeches fluttered away from the young man like birds. If only he could talk like this, he would have caught the world. Oh to acquire culture! Oh, to pronounce foreign names correctly! Oh, to be well informed, discoursing at ease on every subject that a lady started! But it would take one years. With an hour at lunch and a few shattered hours in the evening, how was it possible to catch up with leisured women, who had been reading steadily from childhood? His brain might be full of names, he might have even heard of Monet and Debussy; the trouble was that he could not string them together into a sentence, he could not make them 'tell,' he could not quite forget about his stolen umbrella. Yes, the umbrella was the real trouble. Behind Monet and Debussy the umbrella persisted, with the steady beat of a drum. 'I suppose my umbrella will be all right,' he was thinking. 'I don't really mind about it. I will think about music instead. I suppose my umbrella will be all right.' Earlier in the afternoon he had worried about seats. Ought he to have paid as much as two shillings? Earlier still he had wondered, 'Shall I try to do without a programme?' There had always been something to worry him ever since he could remember, always something that distracted him in the pursuit of beauty. For he did pursue beauty, and, therefore, Margaret's speeches did flutter away from him like birds.

Margaret talked ahead, occasionally saying, 'Don't you think so? don't you feel the same?' And once she stopped, and said, 'Oh, do interrupt me!' which terrified him. She did not attract him, though she filled him with awe. Her figure was meagre, her face seemed all teeth and eyes, her references to her sister and brother were uncharitable. For all her cleverness and culture, she was probably one of those soulless, atheistical women who have been so shown up by Miss Corelli. It was surprising (and alarming) that she should suddenly say, 'I do hope that you'll come in and have some tea.'

'I do hope that you'll come in and have some tea. We should be so glad. I have dragged you so far out of your way.'

They had arrived at Wickham Place. The sun had set, and the backwater, in deep shadow, was filling with a gentle haze. To the right the fantastic sky-line of the flats towered black against the hues of evening; to the left of the older houses raised a square-cut, irregular parapet against the grey. Margaret fumbled for her latchkey. Of course she had forgotten it. So, grasping her umbrella by its ferrule, she leant over the area and tapped at the dining-room window.

'Helen! Let us in!'

'All right,' said a voice.

'You've been taking this gentleman's umbrella.'

'Taken a what?' said Helen, opening the door. 'Oh, what's that? Do come in! How do you do?'

'Helen, you must not be so ramshackly. You took this gentleman's umbrella away from Queen's Hall, and he has had the trouble of coming round for it.'

'Oh, I am so sorry!' cried Helen, all her hair flying. She had pulled off her hat as soon as she returned, and had flung herself into the big dining-room chair. 'I do nothing but steal umbrellas. I am so very sorry! Do come in and choose one. Is yours a hooky or a nobbly? Mine's a nobbly—at least, I *think* it is.'

The light was turned on, and they began to search the hall, Helen, who had abruptly parted with the Fifth Symphony, commenting with shrill little cries.

'Don't you talk, Meg! You stole an old gentleman's silk top-hat. Yes, she did, Aunt Juley. It is a positive fact. She thought it was a muff. Oh, heavens! I've knocked the In and Out card down. Where's Frieda? Tibby, why don't you ever— No, I can't remember what I was going to say. That wasn't it, but do tell the maids to hurry tea up. What about this umbrella?' She opened it. 'No, it's all gone along the seams. It's an appalling umbrella. It must be mine.'

But it was not.

He took it from her, murmured a few words of thanks, and then fled, with the lilting step of the clerk.

'But if you will stop—' cried Margaret. 'Now, Helen, how stupid you've been!'

'Whatever have I done?'

'Don't you see that you've frightened him away? I meant him to stop to tea. You oughtn't to talk about stealing or holes in an umbrella. I saw his nice eyes getting so miserable. No, it's not a bit of good now.' For Helen had darted out into the street, shouting. 'Oh, do stop!'

'I dare say it is all for the best,' opined Mrs Munt. 'We know nothing about the young man, Margaret, and your drawing-room is full of very tempting little things.'

But Helen cried: 'Aunt Juley, how can you! You make me more and more ashamed. I'd rather he *had* been a thief and taken all the apostle spoons than that I— Well, I must shut the front-door, I suppose. One more failure for Helen.'

'Yes, I think the apostle spoons could have gone as rent,' said Margaret. Seeing that her aunt did not understand, she added: 'You remember "rent"? It was one of father's words–Rent to the ideal, to his own faith in human nature. You remember how he would trust strangers, and if they fooled him he would say, "It's better to be fooled than to be suspicious"–that the confidence trick is the work of man, but the want-of-confidence-trick is the work of the devil.'

'I remember something of the sort now,' said Mrs Munt, rather tartly, for she longed to add, 'It was lucky that your father married a wife with money.' But this was unkind, and she contended herself with, 'Why, he might have stolen the little Ricketts picture as well.'

'Better that he had,' said Helen stoutly.

'No, I agree with Aunt Juley,' said Margaret. 'I'd rather mistrust people than lose my little Ricketts. There are limits.'

Their brother, finding the incident commonplace, had stolen upstairs to see whether there were scones for tea. He warmed the teapot–almost too deftly–rejected the Orange Pekoe that the parlour-maid had provided, poured in five spoonfuls of a superior blend, filled up with really boiling water, and now called to the ladies to be quick or they would lose the aroma.

'All right, Auntie Tibby,' called Helen, while Margaret, thoughtful again, said: 'In a way, I wish we had a real boy in the house–the kind of boy who cares for men. It would make entertaining so much easier.'

'So do I,' said her sister. 'Tibby only cares for cultured females singing Brahms.' And when they joined him she said rather sharply: 'Why didn't you make that young man welcome, Tibby? You must do the host a little, you know. You ought to have taken his hat and coaxed him into stopping, instead of letting him be swamped by screaming women.'

Tibby sighed, and drew a long strand of hair over his forehead.

'Oh, it's no good looking superior. I mean what I say.'

'Leave Tibby alone!' said Margaret, who could not bear her brother to be scolded.

'Here's the house a regular hen-coop!' grumbled Helen.

'Oh, my dear!' protested Mrs Munt. 'How can you say such dreadful things! The number of men you get here has always astonished me. If there is any danger it's the other way round.'

'Yes, but it's the wrong sort of men, Helen means.'

'No, I don't,' corrected Helen. 'We get the right sort of man, but the wrong side of him, and I say that's Tibby's fault. There ought to be a something about the house–an–I don't know what.'

'A touch of the W.'s, perhaps?'

Helen put out her tongue.

'Who are the W.'s?' asked Tibby.

'The W.'s are things I and Meg and Aunt Juley know about and you don't, so there!'

'I suppose that ours is a female house,' said Margaret, 'and one must just accept it. No, Aunt Juley, I don't mean that this house is full of women. I am trying to say something much more clever. I mean that it was irrevocably feminine, even in father's time. Now I'm sure you understand! Well, I'll give you another example. It'll shock you, but I don't care. Suppose Queen Victoria gave a dinner-party, and that the guests had been Leighton, Millais, Swinburne, Rossetti, Meredith, Fitzgerald, etc. Do you suppose that the atmosphere of that dinner would have been artistic? Heavens, no! The very chairs on which they sat would have seen to that. So with our house—it must be feminine, and all we can do is to see that it isn't effeminate. Just as another house that I can mention, but won't, sounded irrevocably masculine, and all its inmates can do is to see that it isn't brutal.'

'That house being the W.'s house, I presume,' said Tibby.

'You're not going to be told about the W.'s, my child,' Helen cried, 'so don't you think it. And on the other hand, I don't the least mind if you find out, so don't you think you've done anything clever, in either case. Give me a cigarette.'

'You do what you can for the house,' said Margaret. 'The drawing-room reeks of smoke.'

'If you smoked too, the house might suddenly turn masculine. Atmosphere is probably a question of touch and go. Even at Queen Victoria's dinner-party—if something had been just a little different—perhaps if she'd worn a clinging Liberty tea-gown instead of a magenta satin—'

'With an Indian shawl over her shoulders—'

'Fastened at the bosom with a Cairngorm-pin—'

Bursts of disloyal laughter—you must remember that they are half German—greeted these suggestions, and Margaret said pensively, 'How inconceivable it would be if the Royal Family cared about Art.' And the conversation drifted away and away, and Helen's cigarette turned to a spot in the darkness, and the great flats opposite were sown with lighted windows, which vanished and were relit again, and vanished incessantly. Beyond them the thoroughfare roared gently—a tide that could never be quiet, while in the east, invisible behind the smokes of Wapping, the moon was rising.

'That reminds me, Margaret. We might have taken that young man into the dining-room, at all events. Only the majolica plate—and that is so firmly set in the wall. I am really distressed that he had no tea.'

For that little incident had impressed the three women more than might be supposed. It remained as a goblin footfall, as a hint that all is not for the best in the best of all possible worlds, and that beneath these superstructures of wealth and art there wanders an ill-fed boy, who has recovered his umbrella indeed, but who has left no address behind him, and no name.

Chapter Six

We are not concerned with the very poor. They are unthinkable, and only to be approached by the statistician or the poet. This story deals with gentlefolk, or with those who are obliged to pretend that they are gentlefolk.

The boy, Leonard Bast, stood at the extreme verge of gentility. He was not in the abyss, but he could see it, and at times people whom he knew had dropped in, and counted no more. He knew that he was poor, and would admit it: he would have died sooner than confess any inferiority to the rich. This may be splendid of him. But he was inferior to most rich people, there is not the least doubt of it. He was not as courteous as the average rich man, nor as intelligent, nor as healthy, nor as lovable. His mind and his body had been alike underfed, because he was poor, and because he was modern they were always craving better food. Had he lived some centuries ago, in the brightly coloured civilizations of the past, he would have had a definite status, his rank and his income would have corresponded. But in his day the angel of Democracy had arisen, enshadowing the classes with leathern wings, and proclaiming, 'All men are equal—all men, that is to say, who possess umbrellas,' and so he was obliged to assert gentility, lest he slipped into the abyss where nothing counts, and the statements of Democracy are inaudible.

As he walked away from Wickham Place, his first care was to prove that he was as good as the Miss Schlegels. Obscurely wounded in his pride, he tried to wound them in return. They were probably not ladies. Would real ladies have asked him to tea? They were certainly ill-natured and cold. At each step his feeling of superiority increased. Would a real lady have talked about stealing an umbrella? Perhaps they were thieves after all, and if he had gone into the house they would have clapped a chloroformed handkerchief over his face. He walked on complacently as far as the Houses of Parliament. There an empty stomach asserted itself, and told him that he was a fool.

'Evening, Mr Bast.'

'Evening, Mr Dealtry.'

'Nice evening.'

'Evening.'

Mr Dealtry, a fellow clerk, passed on, and Leonard stood wondering whether he would take the tram as far as a penny would take him, or whether he would walk. He decided to walk—it is no good giving in, and he had spent money enough at Queen's Hall—and he walked over Westminster Bridge, in front of St Thomas's Hospital and through the immense tunnel that passes under the South-Western main line at Vauxhall. In the tunnel he paused and listened to the roar of the trains. A sharp pain darted through his head, and he was conscious of the exact form of his eye sockets. He pushed on for another mile, and did not slacken speed until he stood at the entrance of a road called Camelia Road, which was at present his home.

Here he stopped again, and glanced suspiciously to right and left, like a rabbit that is going to bolt into its hole. A block of flats, constructed with extreme cheapness, towered on either hand. Farther down the road two more blocks were being built, and beyond these an old house was being demolished to accommodate another pair. It was the kind of scene that may be observed all over London, whatever the locality—bricks and mortar rising and falling with the restlessness of the water in a fountain, as the city receives more and more men upon her soil. Camelia Road would soon stand out like a fortress, and command, for a little, an extensive view. Only for a little. Plans were out for the erection of flats in Magnolia Road also. And again a few years, and all the flats in either road might be pulled down, and new buildings, a vastness at present unimaginable, might arise where they had fallen.

'Evening, Mr Bast.'

'Evening, Mr Cunningham.

'Very serious thing this decline of the birth-rate in Manchester.'

'I beg your pardon?'

'Very serious thing this decline of the birth-rate in Manchester,' repeated Mr Cunningham, tapping the Sunday paper, in which the calamity in question had just been announced to him.

'Ah, yes,' said Leonard, who was not going to let on that he had not bought a Sunday paper.

'If this kind of thing goes on the population of England will be stationary in 1960.'

'You don't say so.'

'I call it a very serious thing, eh?'

'Good-evening, Mr Cunningham.'

'Good-evening, Mr Bast.'

Then Leonard entered Block B of the flats, and turned, not upstairs, but down, into what is known to house agents as a semi-basement, and to other men as a cellar. He opened the door, and cried 'Hullo!' with the pseudo-geniality of the Cockney. There was no reply. 'Hullo!' he repeated. The sitting-room was empty, though the electric light had been left burning. A look of relief came over his face, and he flung himself into the armchair.

The sitting-room contained, besides the armchair, two other chairs, a piano, a three-legged table, and a cosy corner. Of the walls, one was occupied by a window, the other by a draped mantelshelf bristling with Cupids. Opposite the window was the door, and beside the door a bookcase, while over the piano there extended one of the masterpieces of Maud Goodman. It was an amorous and not unpleasant little hole when the curtains were drawn, and the lights turned on, and the gas-stove unlit. But it struck that shallow makeshift note that is so often heard in the modern dwelling-place. It had been too easily gained, and could be relinquished too easily.

As Leonard was kicking off his boots he jarred the three-legged table, and a photograph frame, honourably poised upon it, slid sideways, fell off into the fireplace, and smashed. He swore in a colourless sort of way, and picked the photograph up. It represented a young lady called Jacky, and had been taken at the time when young ladies called Jacky were often photographed with their mouths open. Teeth of dazzling whiteness extended along either of Jacky's jaws, and positively weighed her head sideways, so large were they and so numerous. Take my word for it, that smile was simply stunning, and it is only you and I who will be fastidious, and complain that true joy begins in the eyes, and that the eyes of Jacky did not accord with her smile, but were anxious and hungry.

Leonard tried to pull out the fragments of glass, and cut his fingers and swore again. A drop of blood fell on the frame, another followed, spilling over on to the exposed photograph. He swore more vigorously, and dashed into the kitchen, where he bathed his hands. The kitchen was the same size as the sitting-room: through it was a bedroom. This completed his home. He was renting the flat furnished: of all the objects that encumbered it none were his own except the photograph frame, the Cupids, and the books.

'Damn, damn, damnation!' he murmured, together with such other words as he had learnt from older men. Then he raised his hand to his forehead and said, 'Oh, damn it all—' which meant something different. He pulled himself together. He drank a little tea, black and silent, that still survived upon an upper shelf. He swallowed some dusty crumbs of a cake. Then he went back to the sitting-room, settled himself anew, and began to read a volume of Ruskin.

'Seven miles to the north of Venice—'

How perfectly the famous chapter opens! How supreme its command of admonition and of poetry! The rich man is speaking to us from his gondola.

'Seven miles to the north of Venice the banks of sand which nearer the city rise little above low-water mark attain by degrees a higher level, and knit themselves at last into fields of salt morass, raised here and there into shapeless mounds, and intercepted by narrow creeks of sea.'

Leonard was trying to form his style on Ruskin: he understood him to be the greatest master of English Prose. He read forward steadily, occasionally making a few notes.

'Let us consider a little each of these characters in succession, and first (for of the shafts enough has been said already), what is very peculiar to this church—its luminousness.'

Was there anything to be learnt from this fine sentence? Could he adapt it to the needs of daily life? Could he introduce it, with modifications, when he next wrote a letter to his brother, the lay-reader? For example—

'Let us consider a little each of these characters in succession, and first (for of the absence of ventilation enough has been said already), what is very peculiar to this flat—its obscurity.'

Something told him that the modifications would not do; and that something, had he known it, was the spirit of English Prose. 'My flat is dark as well as stuffy.' Those were the words for him.

And the voice in the gondola rolled on, piping melodiously of Effort and Self-Sacrifice, full of high purpose, full of beauty, full even of sympathy and the love of men, yet somehow eluding all that was actual and insistent in Leonard's life. For it was the voice of one who had never been dirty or hungry, and had not guessed successfully what dirt and hunger are.

Leonard listened to it with reverence. He felt that he was being done good to, and that if he kept on with Ruskin, and the Queen's Hall Concerts, and some pictures by Watts, he would one day push his head out of the grey waters and see the universe. He believed in sudden conversion, a belief which may be right, but which is peculiarly attractive to a half-baked mind. It is the basis of much popular religion: in the domain of business it dominates the Stock Exchange, and becomes that 'bit of luck' by which all successes and failures are explained. 'If only I had a bit of luck, the whole thing would come straight. . . . He's got a most magnificent place down at Streatham and a 20 h.p. Fiat, but then, mind you, he's had luck. . . . I'm sorry the wife's so late, but she never has any luck over catching trains.' Leonard was superior to these people; he did believe in effort and in a steady preparation for the change that he desired. But of a heritage that may expand gradually, he had no conception: he hoped to come to Culture suddenly, much as the Revivalist hopes to come to Jesus. Those Miss Schlegels had come to it; they had done the trick; their hands were upon the ropes, once and for all. And meanwhile, his flat was dark, as well as stuffy.

Presently there was a noise on the staircase. He shut up Margaret's card in the pages of Ruskin, and opened the door. A woman entered, of whom it is simplest to say that she was not respectable. Her appearance was awesome. She seemed all strings and bell-pulls—ribbons, chains, bead necklaces that clinked and caught—and a boa of azure feathers hung round her neck, with the ends uneven. Her throat was bare, wound with a double row of pearls, her arms were bare to the elbows, and might again be detected at the shoulder, through cheap lace. Her hat, which was flowery, resembled those punnets covered with flannel, which we sowed with mustard and cress in our childhood, and which germinated here yes, and there no. She wore it on the back of her head. As for her hair, or rather hairs, they are too complicated to describe, but one system went down her back, lying in a thick pad there, while another, created for a lighter destiny, rippled around her forehead. The face—the face does not signify. It was the face of the photograph, but older, and the teeth were not so numerous as the photographer had suggested, and certainly not so white. Yes, Jacky was past her prime, whatever that prime may have been. She was descending quicker than most women into the colourless years, and the look in her eyes confessed it.

'What ho!' said Leonard, greeting the apparition with much spirit, and helping it off with its boa.

Jacky, in husky tones, replied. 'What ho?'

'Been out?' he asked. The question sounds superfluous, but it cannot have been really, for the lady answered, 'No,' adding, 'Oh, I am so tired.'

'You tired?'

'Eh?'

'I'm tired,' said he, hanging the boa up.

'Oh, Len, I am so tired.'

'I've been to that classical concert I told you about,' said Leonard.

'What's that?'

'I came back as soon as it was over.'

'Anyone been round to our place?' asked Jacky.

'Not that I've seen. I met Mr Cunningham outside, and we passed a few remarks.'

'What, not Mr Cunningham?'

'Yes.'

'Oh, you mean Mr Cunningham.'

'Yes. Mr Cunningham.'

'I've been out to tea at a lady friend's.'

Her secret being at last given to the world, and the name of the lady-friend being even adumbrated, Jacky made no further experiments in the difficult and tiring art of conversation. She never had been a great talker. Even in her photographic days she had relied upon her smile and her figure to attract, and now that she was—

> *On the shelf,*
> *On the shelf,*
> *Boys, boys, I'm on the shelf,*

she was not likely to find her tongue. Occasional bursts of song (of which the above is an example) still issued from her lips, but the spoken word was rare.

She sat down on Leonard's knee, and began to fondle him. She was now a massive woman of thirty-three, and her weight hurt him, but he could not very well say anything. Then she said, 'Is that a book you're reading?' and he said, 'That's a book,' and drew it from her unreluctant grasp. Margaret's card fell out of it. It fell face downwards, and he murmured, 'Book-marker.'

'Len—'

'What is it?' he asked, a little wearily, for she only had one topic of conversation when she sat upon his knee.

'You do love me?'

'Jacky, you know that I do. How can you ask such questions?'

'But you do love me, Len, don't you?'

'Of course I do.'

A pause. The other remark was still due.

'Len—'

'Well? What is it?'

'Len, you will make it all right?'

'I can't have you ask me that again,' said the boy, flaring up into a sudden passion. 'I've promised to marry you when I'm of age, and that's enough. My word's my word. I've promised to marry you as soon as ever I'm twenty-one, and I can't keep on being worried. I've worries enough. It isn't likely I'd throw you over, let alone my word, when I've spent all this money. Besides, I'm an Englishman, and I never go back on my word. Jacky, do be reasonable. Of course I'll marry you. Only do stop badgering me.

'When's your birthday, Len?'

'I've told you again and again, the eleventh of November next. Now get off my knee a bit; someone must get supper, I suppose.'

Jacky went through to the bedroom, and began to see to her hat. This meant blowing at it with short sharp puffs. Leonard tidied up the sitting-room, and began to prepare their evening meal. He put a penny into the slot of the gas-meter, and soon the flat was reeking with metallic fumes. Somehow he could not recover his temper, and all the time he was cooking he continued to complain bitterly.

'It really is too bad when a fellow isn't trusted. It makes one feel so wild, when I've pretended to the people here that you're my wife—all right, all right, you *shall* be my wife—and I've bought you the ring to wear, and I've taken this flat furnished, and it's far more than I can afford, and yet you aren't content, and I've also not told the truth when I've written home.' He lowered his voice. 'He'd stop it.' In a tone of horror, that was a little luxurious, he repeated: 'My brother'd stop it I'm going against the whole world, Jacky.

'That's what I am, Jacky. I don't take any heed of what anyone says. I just go straight forward, I do. That's always been my way. I'm not one of your weak knock-kneed chaps. If a woman's in trouble, I don't leave her in the lurch. That's not my street. No, thank you.

'I'll tell you another thing too. I care a good deal about improving myself by means of Literature and Art, and so getting a wider outlook. For instance, when you came in I was reading Ruskin's "Stones of Venice." I don't say this to boast, but just to show you the kind of man I am. I can tell you, I enjoyed that classical concert this afternoon.'

To all his moods Jacky remained equally indifferent. When supper was ready—and not before—she emerged from the bedroom, saying: 'But you do love me, don't you?'

They began with a soup square, which Leonard had just dissolved in some hot water. It was followed by the tongue—a freckled cylinder of meat, with a little jelly at the top, and a great deal of yellow fat at the bottom—ending with another square dissolved in water (jelly: pineapple), which Leonard had prepared earlier in the day. Jacky ate contentedly enough, occasionally looking at her man with those anxious eyes, to which nothing else in her appearance corresponded, and which yet seemed to mirror her soul. And Leonard managed to convince his stomach that it was having a nourishing meal.

After supper they smoked cigarettes and exchanged a few statements. She observed that her 'likeness' had been broken. He found occasion to remark, for the second time, that he had come straight back home after the concert at Queen's Hall. Presently she sat upon his knee. The inhabitants of Camelia Road tramped to and fro outside the window, just on a level with their heads, and the family in the flat on the ground-floor began to sing, 'Hark, my soul, it is the Lord.'

'That tune fairly gives me the hump,' said Leonard.

Jacky followed this, and said that, for her part, she thought it a lovely tune.

'No; I'll play you something lovely. Get up, dear, for a minute.'

He went to the piano and jingled out a little Grieg. He played badly and vulgarly, but the performance was not without its effect, for Jacky said she thought she'd be going to bed. As she receded, a new set of interests possessed the boy, and he began to think of what had been said about music by that odd Miss Schlegel—the one that twisted her face about so when she spoke. Then the thoughts grew sad and envious. There was the girl named Helen, who had pinched his umbrella, and the German girl who had smiled at him pleasantly, and Herr someone, and Aunt someone, and the brother—all, all with their hands on the ropes. They had all passed up that narrow, rich staircase at Wickham Place, to some ample room, whither he could never follow them, not if he read for ten hours a day. Oh, it was no good, this continual aspiration. Some are born cultured; the rest had better go in for whatever comes easy. To see life steadily and to see it whole was not for the likes of him.

From the darkness beyond the kitchen a voice called, 'Len?'

'You in bed?' he asked, his forehead twitching.

'M'm.'

'All right.'

Presently she called him again.

'I must clean my boots ready for the morning,' he answered.

Presently she called him again.

'I rather want to get this chapter done.'

'What?'

He closed his ears against her.

'What's that?'

'All right, Jacky, nothing; I'm reading a book.'

'What?'

'What?' he answered, catching her degraded deafness.

Presently she called him again.

Ruskin had visited Torcello by this time, and was ordering his gondoliers to take him to Murano. It occurred to him, as he glided over the whispering lagoons, that the power of Nature could not be shortened by the folly, nor her beauty altogether saddened by the misery, of such as Leonard.

Chapter Seven

'Oh, Margaret,' cried her aunt next morning, 'such a most unfortunate thing has happened. I could not get you alone.'

The most unfortunate thing was not very serious. One of the flats in the ornate block opposite had been taken furnished by the Wilcox family, 'coming up, no doubt, in the hope of getting into London society.' That Mrs

Munt should be the first to discover the misfortune was not remarkable, for she was so interested in the flats, that she watched their every mutation with unwearying care. In theory she despised them–they took away that old-world look–they cut off the sun–flats house a flashy type of person. But if the truth had been known, she found her visits to Wickham Place twice as amusing since Wickham Mansions had arisen, and would in a couple of days learn more about them than her nieces in a couple of months, or her nephew in a couple of years. She would stroll across and make friends with the porters, and inquire what the rents were, exclaiming for example: 'What! a hundred and twenty for a basement? You'll never get it!' And they would answer: 'One can but try, madam.' The passenger lifts, the provision lifts, the arrangement for coals (a great temptation for a dishonest porter), were all familiar matters to her, and perhaps a relief from the politico-economical-æsthetic atmosphere that reigned at the Schlegels'.

Margaret received the information calmly, and did not agree that it would throw a cloud over poor Helen's life.

'Oh, but Helen isn't a girl with no interests,' she explained. 'She has plenty of other things and other people to think about. She made a false start with the Wilcoxes, and she'll be as willing as we are to have nothing more to do with them.'

'For a clever girl, dear, how very oddly you do talk. Helen'll *have* to have something more to do with them, now that they're all opposite. She may meet that Paul in the street. She cannot very well not bow.'

'Of course she must bow. But look here; let's do the flowers. I was going to say, the will to be interested in him has died, and what else matters? I look on that disastrous episode (over which you were so kind) as the killing of a nerve in Helen. It's dead, and she'll never be troubled with it again. The only things that matter are the things that interest one. Bowing, even calling and leaving cards, even a dinner-party–we can do all those things to the Wilcoxes, if they find it agreeable; but the other thing, the one important thing–never again. Don't you see?'

Mrs. Munt did not see, and indeed Margaret was making a most questionable statement–that any emotion, any interest once vividly aroused, can wholly die.

'I also have the honour to inform you that the Wilcoxes are bored with us. I didn't tell you at the time–it might have made you angry, and you had enough to worry you–but I wrote a letter to Mrs W., and apologized for the trouble that Helen had given them. She didn't answer it.'

'How very rude!'

'I wonder. Or was it sensible?'

'No, Margaret, most rude.'

'In either case one can class it as reassuring.'

Mrs Munt sighed. She was going back to Swanage on the morrow, just as her nieces were wanting her most. Other regrets crowded upon her: for instance, how magnificently she would have cut Charles if she had met him face to face. She had already seen him, giving an order to the porter–and very common he looked in a tall hat. But unfortunately his back was turned to her, and though she had cut his back, she could not regard this as a telling snub.

'But you will be careful, won't you?' she exhorted.

'Oh, certainly. Fiendishly careful.'

'And Helen must be careful, too.'

'Careful over what?' cried Helen, at that moment coming into the room with her cousin.

'Nothing,' said Margaret, seized with a momentary awkwardness.

'Careful over what, Aunt Juley?'

Mrs Munt assumed a cryptic air. 'It is only that a certain family, whom we know by name but do not mention, as you said yourself last night after the concert, have taken the flat opposite from the Mathesons—where the plants are in the balcony.'

Helen began some laughing reply, and then disconcerted them all by blushing. Mrs Munt was so disconcerted that she exclaimed, 'What, Helen, you don't mind them coming, do you?' and deepened the blush to crimson.

'Of course I don't mind,' said Helen a little crossly. 'It is that you and Meg are both so absurdly grave about it, when there's nothing to be grave about at all.'

'I'm not grave,' protested Margaret, a little cross in her turn.

'Well, you look grave; doesn't she, Frieda?'

'I don't feel grave, that's all I can say; you're going quite on the wrong tack.'

'No, she does not feel grave,' echoed Mrs Munt. 'I can bear witness to that. She disagrees—'

'Hark!' interrupted Fräulein Mosebach. 'I hear Bruno entering the hall.'

For Herr Liesecke was due at Wickham Place to call for the two younger girls. He was not entering the hall—in fact, he did not enter it for quite five minutes. But Frieda detected a delicate situation, and said that she and Helen had much better wait for Bruno down below, and leave Margaret and Mrs Munt to finish arranging the flowers. Helen acquiesced. But, as if to prove that the situation was not delicate really, she stopped in the doorway and said:

'Did you say the Mathesons' flat, Aunt Juley? How wonderful you are! *I* never knew that the woman who laced too tightly's name was Matheson.'

'Come, Helen,' said her cousin.

'Go, Helen,' said her aunt; and continued to Margaret almost in the same breath: 'Helen cannot deceive me. She does mind.'

'Oh, hush!' breathed Margaret. 'Frieda'll hear you, and she can be so tiresome.'

'She minds,' persisted Mrs Munt, moving thoughtfully about the room, and pulling the dead chrysanthemums out of the vases. 'I knew she'd mind—and I'm sure a girl ought to! Such an experience! Such awful coarse-grained people! I know more about them than you do, which you forget, and if Charles had taken you that motor drive—well, you'd have reached the house a perfect wreck. Oh, Margaret, you don't know what you are in for. They're all bottled up against the drawing-room window. There's Mrs

Wilcox—I've seen her. There's Paul. There's Evie, who is a minx. There's Charles—I saw him to start with. And who would an elderly man with a moustache and a copper-coloured face be?'

'Mr Wilcox, possibly.'

'I knew it. And there's Mr Wilcox.'

'It's a shame to call his face copper colour,' complained Margaret. 'He has a remarkably good complexion for a man of his age.'

Mrs Munt, triumphant elsewhere, could afford to concede Mr Wilcox his complexion. She passed on from it to the plan of campaign that her nieces should pursue in the future. Margaret tried to stop her.

'Helen did not take the news quite as I expected, but the Wilcox nerve is dead in her really, so there's no need for plans.'

'It's as well to be prepared.'

'No—it's as well not to be prepared.'

'Why?'

'Because—'

Her thought drew being from the obscure borderland. She could not explain in so many words, but she felt that those who prepare for all the emergencies of life beforehand may equip themselves at the expense of joy. It is necessary to prepare for an examination, or a dinner-party, or a possible fall in the price of stock: those who attempt human relations must adopt another method, or fail. 'Because I'd sooner risk it,' was her lame conclusion.

'But imagine the evenings,' exclaimed her aunt, pointing to the Mansions with the spout of the watering-can. 'Turn the electric light on here and there, and it's almost the same room. One evening they may forget to draw their blinds down, and you'll see them; and the next, you yours, and they'll see you. Impossible to sit out on the balconies. Impossible to water the plants, or even speak. Imagine going out of the front-door, and they come out opposite at the same moment. And yet you tell me that plans are unnecessary, and you'd rather risk it.'

'I hope to risk things all my life.'

'Oh, Margaret, most dangerous.'

'But after all,' she continued with a smile, 'there's never any great risk as long as you have money.'

'Oh, shame! What a shocking speech!'

'Money pads the edges of things,' said Miss Schlegel. 'God help those who have none.'

'But this is something quite new!' said Mrs Munt, who collected new ideas as a squirrel collects nuts, and was especially attracted by those that are portable.

'New for me; sensible people have acknowledged it for years. You and I and the Wilcoxes stand upon money as upon islands. It is so firm beneath our feet that we forget its very existence. It's only when we see someone near us tottering that we realize all that an independent income means. Last night, when we were talking up here round the fire, I began to think that the very soul of the world is economic, and that the lowest abyss is not the absence of love, but the absence of coin.'

'I call that rather cynical.'

'So do I. But Helen and I, we ought to remember, when we are tempted to criticize others, that we are standing on these islands, and that most of the others are down below the surface of the sea. The poor cannot always reach those whom they want to love, and they can hardly ever escape from those whom they love no longer. We rich can. Imagine the tragedy last June if Helen and Paul Wilcox had been poor people, and couldn't invoke railways and motor-cars to part them.'

'That's more like Socialism,' said Mrs Munt suspiciously.

'Call it what you like. I call it going through life with one's hand spread open on the table. I'm tired of these rich people who pretend to be poor, and think it shows a nice mind to ignore the piles of money that keep their feet above the waves. I stand each year upon six hundred pounds, and Helen upon the same, and Tibby will stand upon eight, and as fast as our pounds crumble away into the sea they are renewed—from the sea, yes, from the sea. And all our thoughts are the thoughts of six-hundred-pounders, and all our speeches; and because we don't want to steal umbrellas ourselves, we forget that below the sea people do want to steal them, and do steal them sometimes, and that what's a joke up here is down there reality—'

'There they go—there goes Fräulein Mosebach. Really, for a German she does dress charmingly. Oh—!'

'What is it?'

'Helen was looking up at the Wilcoxes' flat.'

'Why shouldn't she?'

'I beg your pardon, I interrupted you. What was it you were saying about reality?'

'I had worked round to myself, as usual,' answered Margaret in tones that were suddenly preoccupied.

'Do tell me this, at all events. Are you for the rich or for the poor?'

'Too difficult. Ask me another. Am I for poverty or for riches? For riches. Hurrah for riches!'

'For riches!' echoed Mrs Munt, having, as it were, at last secured her nut.

'Yes. For riches. Money for ever!'

'So am I, and so, I am afraid, are most of my acquaintances at Swanage, but I am surprised that you agree with us.'

'Thank you so much, Aunt Juley. While I have talked theories, you have done the flowers.'

'Not at all, dear. I wish you would let me help you in more important things.'

'Well, would you be very kind? Would you come round with me to the registry office? There's a housemaid who won't say yes but doesn't say no.'

On their way thither they too looked up at the Wilcoxes' flat. Evie was in the balcony, 'staring most rudely,' according to Mrs Munt. Oh yes, it was a nuisance, there was no doubt of it. Helen was proof against a passing encounter, but— Margaret began to lose confidence. Might it reawake the dying nerve if the family were living close against her eyes? And Frieda

Mosebach was stopping with them for another fortnight, and Frieda was sharp, abominably sharp, and quite capable of remarking, 'You love one of the young gentlemen opposite, yes?' The remark would be untrue, but of the kind which, if started often enough, may become true; just as the remark, 'England and Germany are bound to fight,' renders war a little more likely each time that it is made, and is therefore made the more readily by the gutter press of either nation. Have the private emotions also their gutter press? Margaret thought so, and feared that good Aunt Juley and Frieda were typical specimens of it. They might, by continual chatter, lead Helen into a repetition of the desires of June. Into a repetition–they could not do more; they could not lead her into lasting love. They were–she saw it clearly–Journalism; her father, with all his defects and wrong-headedness, had been Literature, and had he lived, he would have persuaded his daughter rightly.

The registry office was holding its morning reception. A string of carriages filled the street. Miss Schlegel waited her turn, and finally had to be content with an insidious 'temporary,' being rejected by genuine housemaids on the ground of her numerous stairs. Her failure depressed her, and though she forgot the failure, the depression remained. On her way home she again glanced up at the Wilcoxes' flat, and took the rather matronly step of speaking about the matter to Helen.

'Helen, you must tell me whether this thing worries you.'

'If what?' said Helen, who was washing her hands for lunch.

'The W.s' coming.'

'No, of course not.'

'Really?'

'Really.' Then she admitted that she was a little worried on Mrs Wilcox's account; she implied that Mrs Wilcox might reach backward into deep feelings, and be pained by things that never touched the other members of that clan. 'I shan't mind if Paul points at our house and says, "There lives the girl who tried to catch me." But she might.'

'If even that worries you, we could arrange something. There's no reason we should be near people who displease us or whom we displease, thanks to our money. We might even go away for a little.'

'Well, I am going away. Frieda's just asked me to Stettin, and I shan't be back till after the New Year. Will that do? Or must I fly the country altogether? Really, Meg, what has come over you to make such a fuss?'

'Oh, I'm getting an old maid, I suppose. I thought I minded nothing, but really I–I should be bored if you fell in love with the same man twice and'–she cleared her throat–'you did go red, you know, when Aunt Juley attacked you this morning. I shouldn't have referred to it otherwise.'

But Helen's laugh rang true, as she raised a soapy hand to heaven and swore that never, nowhere and nohow, would she again fall in love with any of the Wilcox family, down to its remotest collaterals.

Chapter Eight

The friendship between Margaret and Mrs Wilcox, which was to develop so quickly and with such strange results, may perhaps have had its beginnings at Speyer, in the spring. Perhaps the elder lady, as she gazed at the vulgar, ruddy cathedral, and listened to the talk of Helen and her husband, may have detected in the other and less charming of the sisters a deeper sympathy, a sounder judgment. She was capable of detecting such things. Perhaps it was she who had desired the Miss Schlegels to be invited to Howards End, and Margaret whose presence she had particularly desired. All this is speculation: Mrs Wilcox has left few clear indications behind her. It is certain that she came to call at Wickham Place a fortnight later, the very day that Helen was going with her cousin to Stettin.

'Helen!' cried Fräulein Mosebach in awestruck tones (she was now in her cousin's confidence)–'his mother has forgiven you!' And then, remembering that in England the new-comer ought not to call before she is called upon, she changed her tone from awe to disapproval, and opined that Mrs Wilcox was 'keine Dame.'

'Bother the whole family!' snapped Margaret. 'Helen, stop giggling and pirouetting, and go and finish your packing. Why can't the woman leave us alone?'

'I don't know what I shall do with Meg,' Helen retorted, collapsing upon the stairs. She's got Wilcox and Box upon the brain. Meg, Meg, I don't love the young gentleman; I don't love the young genterman, Meg, Meg. Can a body speak plainer?'

'Most certainly her love has died.' asserted Fräulein Mosebach.

'Most certainly it has, Frieda, but that will not prevent me from being bored with the Wilcoxes if I return the call.'

Then Helen simulated tears, and Fräulein Mosebach, who thought her extremely amusing, did the same. 'Oh, boo hoo! boo hoo hoo! Meg's going to return the call, and I can't. 'Cos why? 'Cos I'm going to German-eye.'

'If you are going to Germany, go and pack; if you aren't, go and call on the Wilcoxes instead of me.'

'But, Meg, Meg, I don't love the young gentleman; I don't love the young– O lud, who's that coming down the stairs? I vow 'tis my brother. O crimini!'

A male–even such a male as Tibby–was enough to stop the foolery. The barrier of sex, though decreasing among the civilized, is still high, and higher on the side of women. Helen could tell her sister all, and her cousin much about Paul; she told her brother nothing. It was not prudishness, for she now spoke of 'the Wilcox ideal' with laughter, and even with a growing brutality. Nor was it precaution, for Tibby seldom repeated any news that did not concern himself. It was rather the feeling that she betrayed a secret into the camp of men, and that, however trivial it was on this side of the barrier, it would become important on that. So she stopped, or rather began to fool on other subjects, until her long-suffering relatives drove her upstairs. Fräulein Mosebach followed her, but lingered to say heavily over the banisters to Margaret, 'It is all right—she does not love the young man—he has not been worthy of her.'

'Yes, I know; thanks very much.'

'I thought I did right to tell you.'

'Ever so many thanks.'

'What's that?' asked Tibby. No one told him, and he proceeded into the dining-room, to eat Elvas plums.

That evening Margaret took decisive action. The house was very quiet, and the fog—we are in November now—pressed against the windows like an excluded ghost. Frieda and Helen and all their luggages had gone. Tibby, who was not feeling well, lay stretched on a sofa by the fire. Margaret sat by him, thinking. Her mind darted from impulse to impulse, and finally marshalled them all in review. The practical person, who knows what he wants at once, and generally knows nothing else, will excuse her of indecision. But this was the way her mind worked. And when she did act, no one could accuse her of indecision then. She hit out as lustily as if she had not considered the matter at all. The letter that she wrote Mrs Wilcox glowed with the native hue of resolution. The pale cast of thought was with her a breath rather than a tarnish, a breath that leaves the colours all the more vivid when it has been wiped away.

Dear Mrs Wilcox,
   I have to write something discourteous. It would be better if we did not meet. Both my sister and my aunt have given displeasure to your family, and, in my sister's case, the grounds for displeasure might recur. As far as I know, she no longer occupies her thoughts with your son. But it would not be fair, either to her or to you, if they met, and it is therefore right that our acquaintance, which began so pleasantly, should end.
   I fear that you will not agree with this; indeed, I know that you will not, since you have been good enough to call on us. It is only an instinct on my part, and no doubt the instinct is wrong. My sister would, undoubtedly, say that it is wrong. I write without her knowledge, and I hope that you will not associate her with my discourtesy.

Believe me,
Yours truly,
M. J. Schlegel.

Margaret sent this letter round by the post. Next morning she received the following reply by hand:

Dear Miss Schlegel,
   You should not have written me such a letter. I called to tell you that Paul has gone abroad.

Ruth Wilcox.

Margaret's cheeks burnt. She could not finish her breakfast. She was on fire with shame. Helen had told her that the youth was leaving England, but other things had seemed more important, and she had forgotten. All her absurd anxieties fell to the ground, and in their place arose the certainty that she had been rude to Mrs Wilcox. Rudeness affected Margaret like a bitter taste in the mouth. It poisoned life. At times it is necessary, but woe to those who employ it without due need. She flung on a hat and shawl, just like a poor woman, and plunged into the fog, which still continued. Her lips were compressed, the letter remained in her hand, and in this state she crossed the street, entered the marble vestibule of the flats, eluded the concierges, and ran up the stairs till she reached the second-floor.

She sent in her name, and to her surprise was shown straight into Mrs Wilcox's bedroom.

'Oh, Mrs Wilcox, I have made the baddest blunder. I am more, more ashamed and sorry than I can say.'

Mrs Wilcox bowed gravely. She was offended, and did not pretend to the contrary. She was sitting up in bed, writing letters on an invalid table that spanned her knees. A breakfast tray was on another table beside her. The light of the fire, the light from the window, and the light of a candle-lamp, which threw a quivering halo round her hands, combined to create a strange atmosphere of dissolution.

'I knew he was going to India in November, but I forgot.'

'He sailed on the 17th for Nigeria, in Africa.'

'I knew—I know. I have been too absurd all through. I am very much ashamed.'

Mrs Wilcox did not answer.

'I am more sorry than I can say, and I hope that you will forgive me.'

'It doesn't matter, Miss Schlegel. It is good of you to have come round so promptly.'

'It does matter,' cried Margaret. 'I have been rude to you; and my sister is not even at home, so there was not even that excuse.'

'Indeed?'

'She has just gone to Germany.'

'She gone as well,' murmured the other. 'Yes, certainly, it is quite safe—safe, absolutely, now.'

'You've been worrying too!' exclaimed Margaret, getting more and more excited, and taking a chair without invitation. 'How perfectly extraordinary! I can see that you have. You felt as I do; Helen mustn't meet him again.'

'I did think it best.'

'Now why?'

'That's a most difficult question,' said Mrs Wilcox, smiling, and a little losing her expression of annoyance. 'I think you put it best in your letter—it was an instinct, which may be wrong.'

'It wasn't that your son still—'

'Oh no; he often—my Paul is very young, you see.'

'Then what was it?'

She repeated: 'An instinct which may be wrong.'

'In other words, they belong to types that can fall in love, but couldn't live together. That's dreadfully probable. I'm afraid that in nine cases out of ten Nature pulls one way and human nature another.'

'These are indeed "other words,"' said Mrs Wilcox. 'I had nothing so coherent in my head. I was merely alarmed when I knew that my boy cared for your sister.'

'Ah, I have always been wanting to ask you. How *did* you know? Helen was so surprised when our aunt drove up, and you stepped forward and arranged things. Did Paul tell you?'

'There is nothing to be gained by discussing that,' said Mrs Wilcox after a moment's pause.

'Mrs Wilcox, were you very angry with us last June? I wrote you a letter and you didn't answer it.'

'I was certainly against taking Mrs Matheson's flat. I knew it was opposite your house.'

'But it's all right now?'

'I think so.'

'You only think? You aren't sure? I do love these little muddles tidied up?'

'Oh yes, I'm sure,' said Mrs Wilcox, moving with uneasiness beneath the clothes. 'I always sound uncertain over things. It is my way of speaking.'

'That's all right, and I'm sure too.'

Here the maid came in to remove the breakfast-tray. They were interrupted, and when they resumed conversation it was on more normal lines.

'I must say good-bye now—you will be getting up.'

'No—please stop a little longer—I am taking a day in bed. Now and then I do.'

'I thought of you as one of the early risers.'

'At Howards End—yes; there is nothing to get up for in London.'

'Nothing to get up for?' cried the scandalized Margaret. 'When there are all the autumn exhibitions, and Ysaye playing in the afternoon! Not to mention people.'

'The truth is, I am a little tired. First came the wedding, and then Paul went off, and, instead of resting yesterday, I paid a round of calls.'

'A wedding?'

'Yes; Charles, my elder son, is married.'

'Indeed!'

'We took the flat chiefly on that account, and also that Paul could get his African outfit. The flat belongs to a cousin of my husband's, and she most kindly offered it to us. So before the day came we were able to make the acquaintance of Dolly's people, which we had not yet done.'

Margaret asked who Dolly's people were.

'Fussell. The father is in the Indian army—retired; the brother is in the army. The mother is dead.'

So perhaps these were the 'chinless sunburnt men' whom Helen had espied one afternoon through the window. Margaret felt mildly interested in the fortunes of the Wilcox family. She had acquired the habit on Helen's account, and it still clung to her. She asked for more information about Miss Dolly Fussell that was, and was given it in even, unemotional tones. Mrs Wilcox's voice, though sweet and compelling, had little range of expression. It suggested that pictures, concerts, and people are all of small and equal value. Only once had it quickened–when speaking of Howards End.

'Charles and Albert Fussell have known one another some time. They belong to the same club, and are both devoted to golf. Dolly plays golf too, though I believe not so well, and they first met in a mixed foursome. We all like her, and are very much pleased. They were married on the 11th, a few days before Paul sailed. Charles was very anxious to have his brother as best man, so he made a great point of having it on the 11th. The Fussells would have preferred it after Christmas, but they were very nice about it. There is Dolly's photograph–in that double frame.'

'Are you quite certain that I'm not interrupting, Mrs Wilcox?'

'Yes, quite.'

'Then I will stay. I'm enjoying this.'

Dolly's photograph was now examined. It was signed 'For dear Mims,' which Mrs Wilcox interpreted as 'the name she and Charles had settled that she should call me.' Dolly looked silly, and had one of those triangular faces that so often prove attractive to a robust man. She was very pretty. From her Margaret passed to Charles, whose features prevailed opposite. She speculated on the forces that had drawn the two together till God parted them. She found time to hope that they would be happy.

'They have gone to Naples for their honeymoon.'

'Lucky people!'

'I can hardly imagine Charles in Italy.'

'Doesn't he care for travelling?'

'He likes travel, but he does see through foreigners so. What he enjoys most is a motor tour in England, and I think that would have carried the day if the weather had not been so abominable. His father gave him a car of his own for a wedding present, which for the present is being stored at Howards End.'

'I suppose you have a garage there?'

'Yes. My husband built a little one only last month, to the west of the house, not far from the wych-elm, in what used to be the paddock for the pony.'

The last words had an indescribable ring about them.

'Where's the pony gone?' asked Margaret after a pause.

'The pony? Oh, dead, ever so long ago.'

'The wych-elm I remember. Helen spoke of it as a very splendid tree.'

'It is the finest wych-elm in Hertfordshire. Did your sister tell you about the teeth?'

'No.'

'Oh, it might interest you. There are pigs' teeth stuck into the trunk, about four feet from the ground. The country people put them in long ago, and they think that if they chew a piece of the bark, it will cure the toothache. The teeth are almost grown over now, and no one comes to the tree.'

'I should. I love folklore and all festering superstitions.'

'Do you think that the tree really did cure toothache, if one believed in it?'

'Of course it did. It would cure anything—once.'

'Certainly I remember cases—you see I lived at Howards End long, long before Mr Wilcox knew it. I was born there.'

The conversation again shifted. At the time it seemed little more than aimless chatter. She was interested when her hostess explained that Howards End was her own property. She was bored when too minute an account was given of the Fussell family, of the anxieties of Charles concerning Naples, of the movements of Mr Wilcox and Evie, who were motoring in Yorkshire. Margaret could not bear being bored. She grew inattentive, played with the photograph frame, dropped it, smashed Dolly's glass, apologized, was pardoned, cut her finger thereon, was pitied, and finally said she must be going—there was all the housekeeping to do, and she had to interview Tibby's riding-master.

Then the curious note was struck again.

'Good-bye, Miss Schlegel, good-bye. Thank you for coming. You have cheered me up.'

'I'm so glad!'

'I—I wonder whether you ever think about yourself?'

'I think of nothing else,' said Margaret, blushing, but letting her hand remain in that of the invalid.

'I wonder. I wondered at Heidelberg.'

'*I'm* sure!'

'I almost think—'

'Yes?' asked Margaret, for there was a long pause—a pause that was somehow akin to the flicker of the fire, the quiver of the reading-lamp upon their hands, the white blur from the window; a pause of shifting and eternal shadows.

'I almost think you forget you're a girl.'

Margaret was startled and a little annoyed. 'I'm twenty-nine,' she remarked. 'That's not so wildly girlish.'

Mrs Wilcox smiled.

'What makes you say that? Do you mean that I have been gauche and rude?'

A shake of the head. 'I only meant that I am fifty-one, and that to me, both of you— Read it all in some book or other; I cannot put things clearly.'

'Oh, I've got it—inexperience. I'm no better than Helen, you mean, and yet I presume to advise her.'

'Yes. You have got it. Inexperience is the word.'

'Inexperience,' repeated Margaret, in serious yet buoyant tones. 'Of course, I have everything to learn—absolutely everything—just as much as Helen. Life's very difficult and full of surprises. At all events, I've got as far as that. To be humble and kind, to go straight ahead, to love people rather than pity them, to remember the submerged—well, one can't do all these things at once, worse luck, because they're so contradictory. It's then that proportion comes in—to live by proportion. Don't *begin* with proportion. Only prigs do that. Let proportion come in as a last resource, when the better things have failed, and a deadlock— Gracious me, I've started preaching!'

'Indeed, you put the difficulties of life splendidly,' said Mrs Wilcox, withdrawing her hand into the deeper shadows. 'It is just what I should have liked to say about them myself.'

Chapter Nine

Mrs Wilcox cannot be accused of giving Margaret much information about life. And Margaret, on the other hand, has made a fair show of modesty, and has pretended to an inexperience that she certainly did not feel. She had kept house for over ten years; she had entertained, almost with distinction; she had brought up a charming sister, and was bringing up a brother. Surely, if experience is attainable, she had attained it.

Yet the little luncheon-party that she gave in Mrs Wilcox's honour was not a success. The new friend did not blend with the 'one or two delightful people' who had been asked to meet her, and the atmosphere was one of polite bewilderment. Her tastes were simple, her knowledge of culture slight, and she was not interested in the New English Art Club, nor in the dividing-line between Journalism and Literature, which was started as a conversational hare. The delightful people darted after it with cries of joy, Margaret leading them, and not till the meal was half over did they realize that the principal guest had taken no part in the chase. There was no common topic. Mrs Wilcox, whose life had been spent in the service of husband and sons, had little to say to strangers who had never shared it, and whose age was half her own. Clever talk alarmed her, and withered her delicate imaginings; it was the social counterpart of a motor-car, all jerks, and she was a wisp of hay, a flower. Twice she deplored the weather, twice criticized the train service on the Great Northern Railway. They vigorously assented, and rushed on, and when she inquired whether there was any news of Helen, her hostess was too much occupied in placing Rothenstein to answer. The question was repeated: 'I hope that your sister is safe in Germany by now.' Margaret checked herself and said 'Yes, thank you; I heard on Tuesday.' But the demon of vociferation was in her, and the next moment she was off again.

'Only on Tuesday, for they live right away at Stettin. Did you ever know anyone living at Stettin?'

'Never,' said Mrs Wilcox gravely, while her neighbour, a young man low down in the Education Office, began to discuss what people who lived at Stettin ought to look like. Was there such a thing as Stettininity? Margaret swept on.

'People at Stettin drop things into boats out of overhanging warehouses. At least, our cousins do, but aren't particularly rich. The town isn't interesting, except for a clock that rolls its eyes, and the view of the Oder, which truly is something special. Oh, Mrs Wilcox, you would love the Oder! The river, or rather rivers—there seem to be dozens of them—are intense blue, and the plain they run through an intensest green.'

'Indeed! That sounds like a most beautiful view, Miss Schlegel.'

'So I say, but Helen, who will muddle things, says no, it's like music. The course of the Oder is to be like music. It's obliged to remind her of a symphonic poem. The part by the landing-stage is in B minor, if I remember rightly, but lower down things get extremely mixed. There is a slodgy theme in several keys at once, meaning mud-banks, and another for the navigable canal, and the exit into the Baltic is in C sharp major, pianissimo.'

'What do the overhanging warehouses make of that?' asked the man, laughing.

'They make a great deal of it,' replied Margaret, unexpectedly rushing off on a new track. 'I think it's affectation to compare the Oder to music, and so do you, but the overhanging warehouses of Stettin take beauty seriously, which we don't, and the average Englishman doesn't, and despises all who do. Now don't say "Germans have no taste," or I shall scream. They haven't. But—but—such a tremendous but!—they take poetry seriously. They do take poetry seriously.'

'Is anything gained by that?'

'Yes, yes. The German is always on the lookout for beauty. He may miss it through stupidity, or misinterpret it, but he is always asking beauty to enter his life, and I believe that in the end it will come. At Heidelberg I met a fat veterinary surgeon whose voice broke with sobs as he repeated some mawkish poetry. So easy for me to laugh—I, who never repeat poetry, good or bad, and cannot remember one fragment of verse to thrill myself with. My blood boils—well, I'm half German, so put it down to patriotism—when I listen to the tasteful contempt of the average islander for things Teutonic, whether they're Böcklin or my veterinary surgeon. "Oh, Böcklin," they say; "he strains after beauty, he peoples Nature with gods too consciously." Of course Böcklin strains, because he wants something—beauty and all the other intangible gifts that are floating about the world. So his landscapes don't come off, and Leader's do.'

'I am not sure that I agree. Do you?' said he, turning to Mrs Wilcox.

She replied: 'I think Miss Schlegel puts everything splendidly'; and a chill fell on the conversation.

'Oh, Mrs Wilcox, say something nicer than that. It's such a snub to be told you put things splendidly.'

'I do not mean it as a snub. Your last speech interested me so much. Generally people do not seem quite to like Germany. I have long wanted to hear what is said on the other side.'

'The other side? Then you do disagree. Oh, good! Give us your side.'

'I have no side. But my husband'—her voice softened, the chill increased—'has very little faith in the Continent, and our children have all taken after him.'

'On what grounds? Do they feel that the Continent is in bad form?'

Mrs Wilcox had no idea; she paid little attention to grounds. She was not intellectual, nor even alert, and it was odd that, all the same, she should give the idea of greatness. Margaret, zig-zagging with her friends over Thought and Art, was conscious of a personality that transcended their own and dwarfed their activities. There was no bitterness in Mrs Wilcox; there was not even criticism; she was lovable, and no ungracious or uncharitable word had passed her lips. Yet she and daily life were out of focus: one or the other must show blurred. And at lunch she seemed more out of focus than usual, and nearer the line that divides daily life from a life that may be of greater importance.

'You will admit, though, that the Continent—it seems silly to speak of "the Continent," but really it is all more like itself than any part of it is like England. England is unique. Do have another jelly first. I was going to say that the Continent, for good or for evil, is interested in ideas. Its Literature and Art have what one might call the kink of the unseen about them, and this persists even through decadence and affectation. There is more liberty of action in England, but for liberty of thought go to bureaucratic Prussia. People will there discuss with humility vital questions that we here think ourselves too good to touch with tongs.

'I do not want to go to Prussia,' said Mrs Wilcox—'not even to see that interesting view that you were describing. And for discussing with humility I am too old. We never discuss anything at Howards End.'

'Then you ought to!' said Margaret. 'Discussion keeps a house alive. It cannot stand by bricks and mortar alone.'

'It cannot stand without them,' said Mrs Wilcox, unexpectedly catching on to the thought, and rousing, for the first and last time, a faint hope in the breasts of the delightful people. 'It cannot stand without them, and I sometimes think— But I cannot expect your generation to agree, for even my daughter disagrees with me here.'

'Never mind us or her. Do say!'

'I sometimes think that it is wiser to leave action and discussion to men.'

There was a little silence.

'One admits that the arguments against the suffrage *are* extraordinarily strong,' said a girl opposite, leaning forward and crumbling her bread.

'Are they? I never follow any arguments. I am only too thankful not to have a vote myself.'

'We didn't mean the vote, though, did we?' supplied Margaret. 'Aren't we differing on something much wider, Mrs Wilcox? Whether women are to remain what they have been since the dawn of history; or whether, since men have moved forward so far, they too may move forward a little now. I say they may. I would even admit a biological change.'

'I don't know, I don't know.'

'I must be getting back to my overhanging warehouse,' said the man. 'They've turned disgracefully strict.'

Mrs Wilcox also rose.

'Oh, but come upstairs for a little. Miss Quested plays. Do you like MacDowell? Do you mind him only having two noises? If you must really go, I'll see you out. Won't you even have coffee?'

They left the dining-room, closing the door behind them, and as Mrs Wilcox buttoned up her jacket, she said: 'What an interesting life you all lead in London!'

'No, we don't,' said Margaret, with a sudden revulsion. 'We lead the lives of gibbering monkeys. Mrs Wilcox—really—— We have something quiet and stable at the bottom. We really have. All my friends have. Don't pretend you enjoyed lunch, for you loathed it, but forgive me by coming again, alone, or by asking me to you.'

'I am used to young people,' said Mrs Wilcox, and with each word she spoke the outlines of known things grew dim. 'I hear a great deal of chatter at home, for we, like you, entertain a great deal. With us it is more sport and politics, but—I enjoyed my lunch very much, Miss Schlegel, dear, and am not pretending, and only wish I could have joined in more. For one thing, I'm not particularly well just to-day. For another, you younger people move so quickly that it dazes me. Charles is the same, Dolly the same. But we are all in the same boat, old and young. I never forget that.'

They were silent for a moment. Then, with a newborn emotion, they shook hands. The conversation ceased suddenly when Margaret re-entered the dining-room: her friends had been talking over her new friend, and had dismissed her as uninteresting.

Chapter Ten

Several days passed.

Was Mrs Wilcox one of the unsatisfactory people—there are many of them—who dangle intimacy and then withdraw it? They evoke our interests and affections, and keep the life of the spirit dawdling round them. Then they withdraw. When physical passion is involved, there is a definite name for such behaviour—flirting—and if carried far enough it is punishable by law. But no law—not public opinion even—punishes those who coquette with friendship, though the dull ache that they inflict, the sense of misdirected effort and exhaustion, may be as intolerable. Was she one of these?

Margaret feared so at first, for, with a Londoner's impatience, she wanted everything to be settled up immediately. She mistrusted the periods of quiet that are essential to true growth. Desiring to book Mrs Wilcox as a friend, she pressed on the ceremony, pencil, as it were, in hand, pressing the more because the rest of the family were away, and the opportunity seemed favourable. But the elder woman would not be hurried. She refused to fit in with the Wickham Place set, or to reopen discussion of Helen and Paul, whom Margaret would have utilized as a short-cut. She took her time, or perhaps let time take her, and when the crisis did come all was ready.

The crisis opened with a message: would Miss Schlegel come shopping? Christmas was nearing, and Mrs Wilcox felt behind-hand with the presents.

She had taken some more days in bed, and must make up for lost time. Margaret accepted, and at eleven o'clock one cheerless morning they started out in a brougham.

'First of all,' began Margaret, 'we must make a list and tick off the people's names. My aunt always does, and this fog may thicken up any moment. Have you any ideas?'

'I thought we would go to Harrod's or the Haymarket Stores,' said Mrs Wilcox rather hopelessly. 'Everything is sure to be there. I am not a good shopper. The din is so confusing, and your aunt is quite right—one ought to make a list. Take my note-book, then, and write your own name at the top of the page.'

'Oh, hooray!' said Margaret, writing it. 'How very kind of you to start with me!' But she did not want to receive anything expensive. Their acquaintance was singular rather than intimate, and she divined that the Wilcox clan would resent any expenditure on outsiders; the more compact families do. She did not want to be thought a second Helen, who would snatch presents since she could not snatch young men, nor to be exposed, like a second Aunt Juley, to the insults of Charles. A certain austerity of demeanour was best, and she added: 'I don't really want a Yuletide gift, though. In fact, I'd rather not.'

'Why?'

'Because I've odd ideas about Christmas. Because I have all that money can buy. I want more people, but no more things.'

'I should like to give you something worth your acquaintance, Miss Schlegel, in memory of your kindness to me during my lonely fortnight. It has so happened that I have been left alone, and you have stopped me from brooding. I am too apt to brood.'

'If that is so,' said Margaret, 'if I have happened to be of use to you, which I didn't know, you cannot pay me back with anything tangible.'

'I suppose not, but one would like to. Perhaps I shall think of something as we go about.'

Her name remained at the head of the list, but nothing was written opposite it. They drove from shop to shop. The air was white, and when they alighted it tasted like cold pennies. At times they passed through a clot of grey. Mrs Wilcox's vitality was low that morning, and it was Margaret who decided on a horse for this little girl, a golliwog for that, for the rector's wife a copper warming-tray. 'We always give the servants money.' 'Yes, do you, yes, much easier,' replied Margaret, but felt the grotesque impact of the unseen upon the seen, and saw issuing from a forgotten manger at Bethlehem this torrent of coins and toys. Vulgarity reigned. Public-houses, besides their usual exhortation against temperance reform, invited men to 'Join our Christmas goose club'—one bottle of gin, etc., or two, according to subscription. A poster of a woman in tights heralded the Christmas pantomime, and little red devils, who had come in again that year, were prevalent upon the Christmas-cards. Margaret was no morbid idealist. She did not wish this spate of business and self-advertisement checked. It was only the occasion of it that struck her with amazement annually. How many of these vacillating shoppers and tired shop-assistants realized that it was a divine event that drew them together? She realized it, though standing outside in the matter. She was not a Christian in the accepted sense; she did not believe that God had ever worked among us as a young artisan. These people, or most of them, believed it, and if pressed, would affirm it in words. But the visible signs of their belief were Regent Street or Drury Lane, a little mud displaced, a little money spent, a little food cooked, eaten, and forgotten. Inadequate. But in public who shall express the unseen adequately? It is private life that holds out the mirror to infinity; personal intercourse, and that alone, that ever hints at a personality beyond our daily vision.

'No, I do like Christmas on the whole,' she announced. 'In its clumsy way, it does approach Peace and Goodwill. But oh, it is clumsier every year.'

'Is it? I am only used to country Christmases.'

'We are usually in London, and play the game with vigour—carols at the Abbey, clumsy midday meal, clumsy dinner for the maids, followed by Christmas-tree and dancing of poor children, with songs from Helen. The drawing-room does very well for that. We put the tree in the powder-closet, and draw a curtain when the candles are lighted, and with the looking-glass behind it looks quite pretty. I wish we might have a powder-closet in our next house. Of course, the tree has to be very small, and the presents don't hang on it. No; the presents reside in a sort of rocky landscape made of crumpled brown paper.'

'You spoke of your "next house," Miss Schlegel. Then are you leaving Wickham Place?'

'Yes, in two or three years, when the lease expires. We must.'

'Have you been there long?'

'All our lives.'

'You will be very sorry to leave it.'

'I suppose so. We scarcely realize it yet. My father— She broke off, for they had reached the stationery department of the Haymarket Stores, and Mrs Wilcox wanted to order some private greeting cards.

'If possible, something distinctive,' she sighed. At the counter she found a friend, bent on the same errand, and conversed with her insipidly, wasting much time. 'My husband and our daughter are motoring.' 'Bertha too? Oh, fancy, what a coincidence!' Margaret, though not practical, could shine in such company as this. While they talked, she went through a volume of specimen cards, and submitted one for Mrs Wilcox's inspection. Mrs Wilcox was delighted—so original, words so sweet; she would order a hundred like that, and could never be sufficiently grateful. Then, just as the assistant was booking the order, she said: 'Do you know, I'll wait. On second thoughts, I'll wait. There's plenty of time still, isn't there, and I shall be able to get Evie's opinion.'

They returned to the carriage by devious paths; when they were in, she said, 'But couldn't you get it renewed?'

'I beg your pardon?' asked Margaret.

'The lease, I mean.'

'Oh, the lease! Have you been thinking of that all the time? How very kind of you!'

'Surely something could be done.'

'No; values have risen too enormously. They mean to pull down Wickham Place, and build flats like yours.'

'But how horrible!'

'Landlords are horrible.'

Then she said vehemently: 'It is monstrous, Miss Schlegel; it isn't right. I had no idea that this was hanging over you. I do pity you from the bottom of my heart. To be parted from your house, your father's house—it oughtn't to be allowed. It is worse than dying. I would rather die than— Oh, poor girls! Can what they call civilization be right, if people mayn't die in the room where they were born? My dear, I am so sorry—'

Margaret did not know what to say. Mrs Wilcox had been overtired by the shopping, and was inclined to hysteria.

'Howards End was nearly pulled down once. It would have killed me.'

'Howards End must be a very different house to ours. We are fond of ours, but there is nothing distinctive about it. As you saw, it is an ordinary London house. We shall easily find another.'

'So you think.'

'Again my lack of experience, I suppose!' said Margaret, easing away from the subject. 'I can't say anything when you take up that line, Mrs Wilcox. I wish I could see myself as you see me—foreshortened into a backfisch. Quite the ingénue. Very charming—wonderfully well read for my age, but incapable—'

Mrs Wilcox would not be deterred. 'Come down with me to Howards End now,' she said, more vehemently than ever. 'I want you to see it. You have never seen it. I want to hear what you say about it, for you do put things so wonderfully.'

Margaret glanced at the pitiless air and then at the tired face of her companion. 'Later on I should love it,' she continued, 'but it's hardly the weather for such an expedition, and we ought to start when we're fresh. Isn't the house shut up, too?'

She received no answer. Mrs Wilcox appeared to be annoyed.

'Might I come some other day?'

Mrs Wilcox bent forward and tapped the glass. 'Back to Wickham Place, please!' was her order to the coachman. Margaret had been snubbed.

'A thousand thanks, Miss Schlegel, for all your help.'

'Not at all.'

'It is such a comfort to get the presents off my mind—the Christmas-cards especially. I do admire your choice.'

It was her turn to receive no answer. In her turn Margaret became annoyed.

'My husband and Evie will be back the day after to-morrow. That is why I dragged you out shopping to-day. I stayed in town chiefly to shop, but got through nothing, and now he writes that they must cut their tour short, the weather is so bad, and the police-traps have been so bad—nearly as bad as in

Surrey. Ours is such a careful chauffeur, and my husband feels it particularly hard that they should be treated like road-hogs.'

'Why?'

'Well, naturally he–he isn't a road-hog.'

'He was exceeding the speed-limit, I conclude. He must expect to suffer with the lower animals.'

Mrs Wilcox was silenced. In growing discomfort they drove homewards. The city seemed Satanic, the narrower streets oppressing like the galleries of a mine. No harm was done by the fog to trade, for it lay high, and the lighted windows of the shops were thronged with customers. It was rather a darkening of the spirit which fell back upon itself, to find a more grievous darkness within. Margaret nearly spoke a dozen times, but something throttled her. She felt petty and awkward, and her meditations on Christmas grew more cynical. Peace? It may bring other gifts, but is there a single Londoner to whom Christmas is peaceful? The craving for excitement and for elaboration has ruined that blessing. Goodwill? Had she seen any example of it in the hordes of purchasers? Or in herself? She had failed to respond to this investigation merely because it was a little queer and imaginative–she, whose birthright it was to nourish imagination! Better to have accepted, to have tired themselves a little by the journey, than coldly to reply, 'Might I come some other day?' Her cynicism left her. There would be no other day. This shadowy woman would never ask her again.

They parted at the Mansions. Mrs Wilcox went in after due civilities, and Margaret watched the tall, lonely figure sweep up the hall to the lift. As the glass doors closed on it she had the sense of an imprisonment. The beautiful head disappeared first, still buried in the muff; the long trailing skirt followed. A woman of undefinable rarity was going up heavenward, like a specimen in a bottle. And into what a heaven–a vault as of hell, sooty black, from which soots descended!

At lunch her brother, seeing her inclined for silence, insisted on talking. Tibby was not ill-natured, but from babyhood something drove him to do the unwelcome and the unexpected. Now he gave her a long account of the day-school that he sometimes patronized. The account was interesting, and she had often pressed him for it before, but she could not attend now, for her mind was focussed on the invisible. She discerned that Mrs Wilcox, though a loving wife and mother, had only one passion in life–her house–and that the moment was solemn when she invited a friend to share this passion with her. To answer 'another day' was to answer as a fool. 'Another day' will do for brick and mortar, but not for the Holy of Holies into which Howards End had been transfigured. Her own curiosity was slight. She had heard more than enough about it in the summer. The nine windows, the vine, and the wych-elm had no pleasant connections for her, and she would have preferred to spend the afternoon at a concert. But imagination triumphed. While her brother held forth she determined to go, at whatever cost, and to compel Mrs Wilcox to go, too. When lunch was over she stepped over to the flats.

Mrs Wilcox had just gone away for the night.

Margaret said that it was of no consequence, hurried downstairs, and took a hansom to King's Cross. She was convinced that the escapade was important, though it would have puzzled her to say why. There was question of imprisonment and escape, and though she did not know the time of the train, she strained her eyes for St Pancras' clock.

Then the clock of King's Cross swung into sight, a second moon in that infernal sky, and her cab drew up at the station. There was a train for Hilton in five minutes. She took a ticket, asking in her agitation for a single. As she did so, a grave and happy voice saluted her and thanked her.

'I will come if I still may,' said Margaret, laughing nervously.

'You are coming to sleep, dear, too. It is in the morning that my house is most beautiful. You are coming to stop. I cannot show you my meadow properly except at sunrise. These fogs'–she pointed at the station roof–'never spread far. I dare say they are sitting in the sun in Hertfordshire, and you will never repent joining them.'

'I shall never repent joining you.'

'It is the same.'

They began the walk up the long platform. Far at its end stood the train, breasting the darkness without. They never reached it. Before imagination could triumph, there were cries of 'Mother! mother!' and a heavy-browed girl darted out of the cloak-room and seized Mrs Wilcox by the arm.

'Evie!' she gasped–'Evie, my pet—'

The girl called, 'Father! I say! look who's here.'

'Evie, dearest girl, why aren't you in Yorkshire?'

'No–motor smash–changed plans–father's coming.'

'Why, Ruth!' cried Mr Wilcox, joining them. 'What in the name of all that's wonderful are you doing here, Ruth?'

Mrs Wilcox had recovered herself.

'Oh, Henry dear!–here's a lovely surprise–but let me introduce–but I think you know Miss Schlegel.'

'Oh yes,' he replied, not greatly interested. 'But how's yourself, Ruth?'

'Fit as a fiddle,' she answered gaily.

'So are we, and so was our car, which ran A1 as far as Ripon, but there a wretched horse and cart which a fool of a driver—'

'Miss Schlegel, our little outing must be for another day.'

'I was saying that this fool of a driver, as the policeman himself admits—'

'Another day, Mrs Wilcox. Of course.'

'—But as we've insured against third party risks, it won't so much matter—'

'—Cart and car being practically at right angles—'

The voice of the happy family rose high. Margaret was left alone. No one wanted her. Mrs Wilcox walked out of King's Cross between her husband and her daughter, listening to both of them.

Chapter Eleven

The funeral was over. The carriages had rolled away through the soft mud, and only the poor remained. They approached to the newly-dug shaft and looked their last at the coffin, now almost hidden beneath the spadefuls of clay. It was their moment. Most of them were women from the dead woman's district, to whom black garments had been served out by Mr Wilcox's orders. Pure curiosity had brought others. They thrilled with the excitement of a death, and of a rapid death, and stood in groups or moved between the graves, like drops of ink. The son of one of them, a wood-cutter, was perched high above their heads, pollarding one of the churchyard elms. From where he sat he could see the village of Hilton, strung upon the North Road, with its accreting suburbs; the sunset beyond, scarlet and orange, winking at him beneath brows of grey; the church; the plantations; and behind him an unspoilt country of fields and farms. But he, too, was rolling the event luxuriously in his mouth. He tried to tell his mother down below all that he had felt when he saw the coffin approaching: how he could not leave his work, and yet did not like to go on with it; how he had almost slipped out of the tree, he was so upset; the rooks had cawed, and no wonder—it was as if rooks knew too. His mother claimed the prophetic power herself—she had seen a strange look about Mrs Wilcox for some time. London had done the mischief, said others. She had been a kind lady; her grandmother had been kind, too—a plainer person, but very kind. Ah, the old sort was dying out! Mr Wilcox, he was a kind gentleman. They advanced to the topic again and again, dully, but with exaltation. The funeral of a rich person was to them what the funeral of Alcestis or Ophelia is to the educated. It was Art; though remote from life, it enhanced life's values, and they witnessed it avidly.

The grave-diggers, who had kept up an undercurrent of disapproval—they disliked Charles; it was not a moment to speak of such things, but they did not like Charles Wilcox—the grave-diggers finished their work and piled up the wreaths and crosses above it. The sun set over Hilton: the grey brows of the evening flushed a little, and were cleft with one scarlet frown. Chattering sadly to each other, the mourners passed through the lych-gate and traversed the chestnut avenues that led down to the village. The young wood-cutter stayed a little longer, poised above the silence and swaying rhythmically. At last the bough fell beneath his saw. With a grunt, he descended, his thoughts dwelling no longer on death, but on love, for he was mating. He stopped as he passed the new grave; a sheaf of tawny chrysanthemums had caught his eye. 'They didn't ought to have coloured flowers at buryings,' he reflected. Trudging on a few steps, he stopped again, looked furtively at the dusk, turned back, wrenched a chrysanthemum from the sheaf, and hid it in his pocket.

After him came silence absolute. The cottage that abutted on the churchyard was empty, and no other house stood near. Hour after hour the scene of the interment remained without an eye to witness it. Clouds drifted over it from the west; or the church may have been a ship, high-prowed, steering with all its company towards infinity. Towards morning the air grew colder, the sky clearer, the surface of the earth hard and sparkling above the prostrate dead. The wood-cutter, returning after a night of joy, reflected: 'They lilies, they chrysants; it's a pity I didn't take them all.'

Up at Howards End they were attempting breakfast. Charles and Evie sat in the dining-room, with Mrs Charles. Their father, who could not bear to see a face, breakfasted upstairs. He suffered acutely. Pain came over him in spasms, as if it was physical, and even while he was about to eat, his eyes would fill with tears, and he would lay down the morsel untasted.

He remembered his wife's even goodness during thirty years. Not anything in detail—not courtship or early raptures—but just the unvarying virtue, that seemed to him a woman's noblest quality. So many women are capricious, breaking into odd flaws of passion or frivolity. Not so his wife. Year after year, summer and winter, as bride and mother, she had been the same, he had always trusted her. Her tenderness! Her innocence! The wonderful innocence that was hers by the gift of God. Ruth knew no more of worldly wickedness and wisdom than did the flowers in her garden, or the grass in her field. Her idea of business—'Henry, why do people who have enough money try to get more money?' Her idea of politics—'I am sure that if the mothers of various nations could meet, there would be no more wars.' Her idea of religion—ah, this had been a cloud, but a cloud that passed. She came of Quaker stock, and he and his family, formerly Dissenters, were now members of the Church of England. The rector's sermons had at first repelled her, and she had expressed a desire for 'a more inward light,' adding, 'not so much for myself as for baby' (Charles). Inward light must have been granted, for he heard no complaints in later years. They brought up their three children without dispute. They had never disputed.

She lay under the earth now. She had gone, and as if to make her going the more bitter, had gone with a touch of mystery that was all unlike her. 'Why didn't you tell me you knew of it?' he had moaned, and her faint voice had answered: 'I didn't want to, Henry—I might have been wrong—and everyone hates illnesses.' He had been told of the horror by a strange doctor, whom she had consulted during his absence from town. Was this altogether just? Without fully explaining, she had died. It was a fault on her part, and – tears rushed into his eyes—what a little fault! It was the only time she had deceived him in those thirty years.

He rose to his feet and looked out of the window, for Evie had come in with the letters, and he could meet no one's eye. Ah yes—she had been a good woman—she had been steady. He chose the word deliberately. To him steadiness included all praise.

He himself, gazing at the wintry garden, is in appearance a steady man. His face was not as square as his son's, and, indeed, the chin, though firm enough in outline, retreated a little, and the lips, ambiguous, were curtained by a moustache. But there was no external hint of weakness. The eyes, if capable of kindness and good-fellowship, if ruddy for the moment with tears, were the eyes of one who could not be driven. The forehead, too, was like Charles's. High and straight, brown and polished, merging abruptly into temples and skull, it had the effect of a bastion that protected his head from the world. At times it had the effect of a blank wall. He had dwelt behind it, intact and happy, for fifty years.

'The post's come, father,' said Evie awkwardly.

'Thanks. Put it down.'

'Has the breakfast been all right?'

'Yes, thanks.'

The girl glanced at him and at it with constraint. She did not know what to do.

'Charles says do you want the "Times"?'

'No, I'll read it later.'

'Ring if you want anything, father, won't you?'

'I've all I want.'

Having sorted the letters from the circulars, she went back to the dining-room.

'Father's eaten nothing,' she announced, sitting down with wrinkled brows behind the tea-urn.

Charles did not answer, but after a moment he ran quickly upstairs, opened the door, and said: 'Look here, father, you must eat, you know;' and having paused for a reply that did not come, stole down again. 'He's going to read his letters first, I think,' he said evasively; 'I dare say he will go on with his breakfast afterwards.' Then he took up the 'Times,' and for some time there was no sound except the clink of cup against saucer and of knife on plate.

Poor Mrs Charles sat between her silent companions, terrified at the course of events, and a little bored. She was a rubbishy little creature, and she knew it. A telegram had dragged her from Naples to the death-bed of a woman whom she had scarcely known. A word from her husband had plunged her into mourning. She desired to mourn inwardly as well, but she wished that Mrs Wilcox, since fated to die, could have died before the marriage, for then less would have been expected of her. Crumbling her toast, and too nervous to ask for the butter, she remained almost motionless, thankful only for this, that her father-in-law was having his breakfast upstairs.

At last Charles spoke. 'They had no business to be pollarding those elms yesterday,' he said to his sister.

'No indeed.'

'I must make a note of that,' he continued. 'I am surprised that the rector allowed it.'

'Perhaps it may not be the rector's affair.'

'Whose else could it be?'

'The lord of the manor.'

'Impossible.'

'Butter, Dolly?'

'Thank you, Evie dear. Charles—'

'Yes, dear?'

'I didn't know one could pollard elms. I thought one only pollarded willows.'

'Oh no, one can pollard elms.'

'Then why oughtn't the elms in the churchyard to be pollarded?' Charles frowned a little, and turned again to his sister.

'Another point. I must speak to Chalkeley.'

'Yes, rather; you must complain to Chalkeley.'

'It's no good him saying he is not responsible for those men. He is responsible.'

'Yes, rather.'

Brother and sister were not callous. They spoke thus, partly because they desired to keep Chalkeley up to the mark—a healthy desire in its way—partly because they avoided the personal note in life. All Wilcoxes did. It did not seem to them of supreme importance. Or it may be as Helen supposed: they realized its importance, but were afraid of it. Panic and emptiness, could one glance behind. They were not callous, and they left the breakfast-table with aching hearts. Their mother never had come in to breakfast. It was in the other rooms, and especially in the garden, that they felt her loss most. As Charles went out to the garage, he was reminded at every step of the woman who had loved him and whom he could never replace. What battles he had fought against her gentle conservatism! How she had disliked improvements, yet how loyally she had accepted them when made! He and his father—what trouble they had had to get this very garage! With what difficulty had they persuaded her to yield them the paddock for it—the paddock that she loved more dearly than the garden itself! The vine—she had got her way about the vine. It still encumbered the south wall with its unproductive branches. And so with Evie, as she stood talking to the cook. Though she could take up her mother's work inside the house, just as the man could take it up without, she felt that something unique had fallen out of her life. Their grief, though less poignant than their father's, grew from deeper roots, for a wife may be replaced; a mother never.

Charles would go back to the office. There was little to do at Howards End. The contents of his mother's will had been long known to them. There were no legacies, no annuities, none of the posthumous bustle with which some of the dead prolong their activities. Trusting her husband, she had left him everything without reserve. She was quite a poor woman—the house had been all her dowry, and the house would come to Charles in time. Her watercolours Mr Wilcox intended to reserve for Paul, while Evie would take the jewellery and lace. How easily she slipped out of life! Charles thought the habit laudable, though he did not intend to adopt it himself, whereas

Margaret would have seen in it an almost culpable indifference to earthly fame. Cynicism—not the superficial cynicism that snarls and sneers, but the cynicism that can go with courtesy and tenderness—that was the note of Mrs Wilcox's will. She wanted not to vex people. That accomplished, the earth might freeze over her for ever.

No, there was nothing for Charles to wait for. He could not go on with his honeymoon, so he would go up to London and work—he felt too miserable hanging about. He and Dolly would have the furnished flat while his father rested quietly in the country with Evie. He could also keep an eye on his own little house, which was being painted and decorated for him in one of the Surrey suburbs, and in which he hoped to instal himself soon after Christmas. Yes, he would go up after lunch in his new motor, and the town servants, who had come down for the funeral, would go up by train.

He found his father's chauffeur in the garage, said 'Morning' without looking at the man's face, and, bending over the car, continued: 'Hullo! my new car's been driven!'

'Has it, sir?'

'Yes,' said Charles, getting rather red; 'and whoever's driven it hasn't cleaned it properly, for there's mud on the axle. Take it off.'

The man went for the cloths without a word. He was a chauffeur as ugly as sin—not that this did him disservice with Charles, who thought charm in a man rather rot, and had soon got rid of the little Italian beast with whom they had started.

'Charles—' His bride was tripping after him over the hoar-frost, a dainty black column, her little face and elaborate mourning hat forming the capital thereof.

'One minute, I'm busy. Well, Crane, who's been driving it, do you suppose?'

'Don't know, I'm sure, sir. No one's driven it since I've been back, but, of course, there's the fortnight I've been away with the other car in Yorkshire.'

The mud came off easily.

'Charles, your father's down. Something's happened. He wants you in the house at once. Oh, Charles!'

'Wait, dear, wait a minute. Who had the key of the garage while you were away, Crane?'

'The gardener, sir.'

'Do you mean to tell me that old Penny can drive a motor?'

'No, sir; no one's had the motor out, sir.'

'Then how do you account for the mud on the axle?'

'I can't, of course, say for the time I've been in Yorkshire. No more mud now, sir.'

Charles was vexed. The man was treating him as a fool, and if his heart had not been so heavy he would have reported him to his father. But it was not a morning for complaints. Ordering the motor to be round after lunch, he joined his wife, who had all the while been pouring out some incoherent story about a letter and a Miss Schlegel.

'Now, Dolly, I can attend to you. Miss Schlegel? What does she want?'

When people wrote a letter Charles always asked what they wanted. Want
was to him the only cause of action. And the question in this case was correct,
for his wife replied, 'She wants Howards End.'

'Howards End? Now, Crane, just don't forget to put on the Stepney
wheel.'

'No, sir.'

'Now, mind you don't forget, for I— Come, little woman.' When they
were out of the chauffeur's sight he put his arm round her waist and pressed
her against him. All his affection and half his attention—it was what he
granted her throughout their happy married life.

'But you haven't listened, Charles—'

'What's wrong?'

'I keep on telling you—Howards End. Miss Schlegel's got it.'

'Got what?' said Charles, unclasping her. 'What the dickens are you
talking about?'

'Now, Charles, you promised not to say those naughty—'

'Look here, I'm in no mood for foolery. It's no morning for it either.'

'I tell you—I keep on telling you—Miss Schlegel—she's got it—your
mother's left it to her—and you've all got to move out!'

'*Howards End?*'

'*Howards End!*' she screamed, mimicking him, and as she did so Evie
came dashing out of the shrubbery.

'Dolly, go back at once! My father's much annoyed with you.
Charles'—she hit herself wildly—'come in at once to father. He's had a letter
that's too awful.'

Charles began to run, but checked himself, and stepped heavily across the
gravel path. There the house was—the nine windows, the unprolific vine. He
exclaimed, 'Schlegels again!' and as if to complete chaos, Dolly said, 'Oh no,
the matron of the nursing home has written instead of her.'

'Come in, all three of you!' cried his father, no longer inert. 'Dolly, why
have you disobeyed me?'

'Oh, Mr Wilcox—'

'I told you not to go out to the garage. I've heard you all shouting in the
garden. I won't have it. Come in.'

He stood in the porch, transformed, letters in his hand.

'Into the dining-room, every one of you. We can't discuss private matters
in the middle of all the servants. Here, Charles, here; read these. See what
you make.'

Charles took two letters, and read them as he followed the procession. The
first was a covering note from the matron. Mrs Wilcox had desired her, when
the funeral should be over to forward the enclosed. The enclosed—it was
from his mother herself. She had written: 'To my husband: I should like
Miss Schlegel (Margaret) to have Howards End.'

'I suppose we're going to have a talk about this?' he remarked, ominously
calm.

'Certainly. I was coming out to you when Dolly—'

'Well, let's sit down.'

'Come, Evie, don't waste time, sit down.'

In silence they drew up to the breakfast-table. The events of yesterday—indeed, of this morning—suddenly receded into a past so remote that they seemed scarcely to have lived in it. Heavy breathings were heard. They were calming themselves. Charles, to steady them further, read the enclosure out loud: 'A note in my mother's handwriting, in an envelope addressed to my father, sealed. Inside: "I should like Miss Schlegel (Margaret) to have Howards End." No date, no signature. Forwarded through the matron of that nursing home. Now, the question is—'

Dolly interrupted him. 'But I say that note isn't legal. Houses ought to be done by a lawyer, Charles, surely.'

Her husband worked his jaw severely. Little lumps appeared in front of either ear—a sympton that she had not yet learnt to respect, and she asked whether she might see the note. Charles looked at his father for permission, who said abstractedly, 'Give it her.' She seized it, and at once exclaimed: 'Why, it's only in pencil! I said so. Pencil never counts.'

'We know that it is not legally binding, Dolly,' said Mr Wilcox, speaking from out of his fortress. 'We are aware of that. Legally, I should be justified in tearing it up and throwing it into the fire. Of course, my dear, we consider you as one of the family, but it will be better if you do not interfere with what you do not understand.'

Charles, vexed both with his father and his wife, then repeated: 'The question is—' He had cleared a space of the breakfast-table from plates and knives, so that he could draw patterns on the tablecloth. 'The question is whether Miss Schlegel, during the fortnight we were all away, whether she unduly—' He stopped.

'I don't think that,' said his father, whose nature was nobler than his son's.

'Don't think what?'

'That she would have—that it is a case of undue influence. No, to my mind the question is the—the invalid's condition at the time she wrote.'

'My dear father, consult an expert if you like, but I don't admit it is my mother's writing.'

'Why, you just said it was!' cried Dolly.

'Never mind if I did,' he blazed out; 'and hold your tongue.'

The poor little wife coloured at this, and, drawing her handkerchief from her pocket, shed a few tears. No one noticed her. Evie was scowling like an angry boy. The two men were gradually assuming the manner of the committee-room. They were both at their best when serving on committees. They did not make the mistake of handling human affairs in the bulk, but disposed of them item by item, sharply. Caligraphy was the item before them now, and on it they turned their well-trained brains. Charles, after a little demur, accepted the writing as genuine, and they passed on to the next point. It is the best—perhaps the only—way of dodging emotion. They were the average human article, and had they considered the note as a whole it would have driven them miserable or mad. Considered item by item, the emotional content was minimized, and all went forward smoothly. The clock ticked, the coals blazed higher, and contended with the white radiance that poured in through the windows. Unnoticed, the sun occupied his sky, and the shadows of the tree stems, extraordinarily solid, fell like trenches of purple across the frosted lawn. It was a glorious winter morning. Evie's fox terrier, who had passed for white, was only a dirty grey dog now, so intense was the purity that surrounded him. He was discredited, but the blackbirds that he was chasing glowed with Arabian darkness, for all the conventional colouring of life had been altered. Inside, the clock struck ten with a rich and confident note. Other clocks confirmed it, and the discussion moved towards its close.

To follow it is unnecessary. It is rather a moment when the commentator should step forward. Ought the Wilcoxes to have offered their home to Margaret? I think not. The appeal was too flimsy. It was not legal; it had been written in illness, and under the spell of a sudden friendship; it was contrary to the dead woman's intentions in the past, contrary to her very nature, so far as that nature was understood by them. To them Howards End was a house: they could not know that to her it had been a spirit, for which she sought a spiritual heir. And—pushing one step farther in these mists—may they not have decided even better than they supposed? Is it credible that the possessions of the spirit can be bequeathed at all? Has the soul offspring? A wych-elm tree, a vine, a wisp of hay with dew on it—can passion for such things be transmitted where there is no bond of blood? No; the Wilcoxes are not to be blamed. The problem is too terrific, and they could not even perceive a problem. No; it is natural and fitting that after due debate they should tear the note up and throw it on to their dining-room fire. The practical moralist may acquit them absolutely. He who strives to look deeper may acquit them—almost. For one hard fact remains. They did neglect a personal appeal. The woman who had died did say to them, 'Do this,' and they answered, 'We will not.'

The incident made a most painful impression on them. Grief mounted into the brain and worked there disquietingly. Yesterday they had lamented: 'She was a dear mother, a true wife: in our absence she neglected her health and died.' To-day they thought: 'She was not as true, as dear, as we supposed.' The desire for a more inward light had found expression at last, the unseen had impacted on the seen, and all that they could say was 'Treachery.' Mrs Wilcox had been treacherous to the family, to the laws of property, to her own written word. How did she expect Howards End to be conveyed to Miss Schlegel? Was her husband, to whom it legally belonged, to make it over to her as a free gift? Was the said Miss Schlegel to have a life interest in it, or to own it absolutely? Was there to be no compensation for the garage and other improvements that they had made under the assumption that all would be theirs some day? Treacherous! treacherous and absurd! When we think the dead both treacherous and absurd, we have gone far towards reconciling ourselves to their departure. That note, scribbled in pencil, sent through the matron, was unbusinesslike as well as cruel, and decreased at once the value of the woman who had written it.

'Ah, well!' said Mr Wilcox, rising from the table. 'I shouldn't have thought it possible.'

'Mother couldn't have meant it,' said Evie, still frowning.

'No, my girl, of course not.'

'Mother believed so in ancestors too—it isn't like her to leave anything to an outsider, who'd never appreciate.'

'The whole thing is unlike her,' he announced. 'If Miss Schlegel had been poor, if she had wanted a house, I could understand it a little. But she has a house of her own. Why should she want another? She wouldn't have any use for Howards End.'

'That time may prove,' murmured Charles.

'How?' asked his sister.

'Presumably she knows—mother will have told her. She got twice or three times into the nursing home. Presumably she is awaiting developments.'

'What a horrid woman!' And Dolly, who had recovered, cried, 'Why, she may be coming down to turn us out now!'

Charles put her right. 'I wish she would,' he said ominously. 'I could then deal with her.'

'So could I,' echoed his father, who was feeling rather in the cold. Charles had been kind in undertaking the funeral arrangements and in telling him to eat his breakfast, but the boy as he grew up was a little dictatorial, and assumed the post of chairman too readily. 'I could deal with her, if she comes, but she won't come. You're all a bit hard on Miss Schlegel.'

'That Paul business was pretty scandalous, though.'

'I want no more of the Paul business, Charles, as I said at the time, and besides, it is quite apart from this business. Margaret Schlegel has been officious and tiresome during this terrible week, and we have all suffered under her, but upon my soul she's honest. She's *not* in collusion with the matron. I'm absolutely certain of it. Nor was she with the doctor, I'm equally certain of that. She did not hide anything from us, for up to that very afternoon she was as ignorant as we are. She, like ourselves, was a dupe—' He stopped for a moment. 'You see, Charles, in her terrible pain your poor mother put us all in false positions. Paul would not have left England, you would not have gone to Italy, nor Evie and I into Yorkshire, if only we had known. Well, Miss Schlegel's position has been equally false. Take all in all, she has not come out of it badly.'

Evie said: 'But those chrysanthemums—'

'Or coming down to the funeral at all—' echoed Dolly.

'Why shouldn't she come down? She had the right to, and she stood far back among the Hilton women. The flowers—certainly we should not have sent such flowers, but they may have seemed the right thing to her, Evie, and for all you know they may be the custom in Germany.'

'Oh, I forget she isn't really English,' cried Evie. 'That would explain a lot.'

'She's a cosmopolitan,' said Charles, looking at his watch. 'I admit I'm rather down on cosmopolitans. My fault, doubtless. I cannot stand them, and a German cosmopolitan is the limit. I think that's about all, isn't it? I want to run down and see Chalkeley. A bicycle will do. And, by the way, I wish you'd speak to Crane some time. I'm certain he's had my new car out.'

'Has he done it any harm?'

'No.'

'In that case I shall let it pass. It's not worth while having a row.'

Charles and his father sometimes disagreed. But they always parted with an increased regard for one another, and each desired no doughtier comrade when it was necessary to voyage for a little past the emotions. So the sailors of Ulysses voyaged past the Sirens, having first stopped one another's ears with wool.

Chapter Twelve

Charles need not have been anxious. Miss Schlegel had never heard of his mother's strange request. She was to hear of it in after years, when she had built up her life differently, and it was to fit into position as the headstone of the corner. Her mind was bent on other questions now, and by her also it would have been rejected as the fantasy of an invalid.

She was parting from these Wilcoxes for the second time. Paul and his mother, ripple and great wave, had flowed into her life and ebbed out of it for ever. The ripple had left no traces behind: the wave had strewn at her feet fragments torn from the unknown. A curious seeker, she stood for a while at the verge of the sea that tells so little, but tells a little, and watched the outgoing of this last tremendous tide. Her friend had vanished in agony, but not, she believed, in degradation. Her withdrawal had hinted at other things besides disease and pain. Some leave our life with tears, others with an insane frigidity; Mrs Wilcox had taken the middle course, which only rarer natures can pursue. She had kept proportion. She had told a little of her grim secret to her friends, but not too much; she had shut up her heart—almost, but not entirely. It is thus, if there is any rule, that we ought to die—neither as victim nor as fanatic, but as the seafarer who can greet with an equal eye the deep that he is entering, and the shore that he must leave.

The last word—whatever it would be—had certainly not been said in Hilton churchyard. She had not died there. A funeral is not death, any more than baptism is birth or marriage union. All three are the clumsy devices, coming now too late, now too early, by which Society would register the quick motions of man. In Margaret's eyes Mrs Wilcox had escaped registration. She had gone out of life vividly, her own way, and no dust was so truly dust as the contents of that heavy coffin, lowered with ceremonial until it rested on the dust of the earth, no flowers so utterly wasted as the chrysanthemums that the frost must have withered before morning. Margaret had once said she 'loved superstition.' It was not true. Few women had tried more earnestly to pierce the accretions in which body and soul are enwrapped. The death of Mrs Wilcox had helped her in her work. She saw a little more clearly than hitherto what a human being is, and to what he may aspire. Truer relationships gleamed. Perhaps the last word would be hope—hope even on this side of the grave.

Meanwhile, she could take an interest in the survivors. In spite of her Christmas duties, in spite of her brother, the Wilcoxes continued to play a considerable part in her thoughts. She had seen so much of them in the final week. They were not 'her sort,' they were often suspicious and stupid, and deficient where she excelled; but collision with them stimulated her, and she felt an interest that verged into liking, even for Charles. She desired to protect them, and often felt that they could protect her, excelling where she was deficient. Once past the rocks of emotion, they knew so well what to do, whom to send for; their hands were on all the ropes, they had grit as well as grittiness, and she valued grit enormously. They led a life that she could not attain to—the outer life of 'telegrams and anger,' which had detonated when Helen and Paul had touched in June, and had detonated again the other week. To Margaret this life was to remain a real force. She could not despise it, as Helen and Tibby affected to do. It fostered such virtues as neatness, decision, and obedience, virtues of the second rank, no doubt, but they have formed our civilization. They form character, too; Margaret could not doubt it: they keep the soul from becoming sloppy. How dare Schlegels despise Wilcoxes, when it takes all sorts to make a world?

'Don't brood too much,' she wrote to Helen, 'on the superiority of the unseen to the seen. It's true, but to brood on it is medieval. Our business is not to contrast the two, but to reconcile them.'

Helen replied that she had no intention of brooding on such a dull subject. What did her sister take her for? The weather was magnificent. She and the Mosebachs had gone tobogganing on the only hill that Pomerania boasted. It was fun, but over-crowded, for the rest of Pomerania had gone there too. Helen loved the country, and her letter glowed with physical exercise and poetry. She spoke of the scenery, quiet, yet august; of the snow-clad fields, with their scampering herds of deer; of the river and its quaint entrance into the Baltic Sea; of the Oderberge, only three hundred feet high, from which one slid all too quickly back into the Pomeranian plains, and yet these Oderberge were real mountains, with pine-forests, streams, and views complete. 'It isn't size that counts so much as the way things are arranged.' In another paragraph she referred to Mrs Wilcox sympathetically, but the news had not bitten into her. She had not realized the accessories of death, which are in a sense more memorable than death itself. The atmosphere of precautions and recriminations, and in the midst a human body growing more vivid because it was in pain; the end of that body in Hilton churchyard; the survival of something that suggested hope, vivid in its turn against life's workaday cheerfulness;—all these were lost to Helen, who only felt that a pleasant lady could now be pleasant no longer. She returned to Wickham Place full of her own affairs—she had had another proposal—and Margaret, after a moment's hesitation, was content that this should be so.

The proposal had not been a serious matter. It was the work of Fräulein Mosebach, who had conceived the large and patriotic notion of winning back her cousins to the Fatherland by matrimony. England had played Paul

Wilcox, and lost; Germany played Herr Förstmeister someone—Helen could not remember his name. Herr Förstmeister lived in a wood, and, standing on the summit of the Oderberge, he had pointed out his house to Helen, or rather, had pointed out the wedge of pines in which it lay. She had exclaimed, 'Oh, how lovely! That's the place for me!' and in the evening Frieda appeared in her bedroom. 'I have a message, dear Helen,' etc., and so she had, but had been very nice when Helen laughed; quite understood—a forest too solitary and damp—quite agreed, but Herr Förstmeister believed he had assurance to the contrary. Germany had lost, but with good-humour; holding the manhood of the world, she felt bound to win. 'And there will even be someone for Tibby,' concluded Helen. 'There now, Tibby, think of that; Frieda is saving up a little girl for you, in pig-tails and white worsted stockings, but the feet of the stockings are pink, as if the little girl had trodden in strawberries. I've talked too much. My head aches. Now you talk.'

Tibby consented to talk. He too was full of his own affairs, for he had just been up to try for a scholarship at Oxford. The men were down, and the candidates had been housed in various colleges, and had dined in hall. Tibby was sensitive to beauty, the experience was new, and he gave a description of his visit that was almost glowing. The august and mellow University, soaked with the richness of the western counties that it has served for a thousand years, appealed at once to the boy's taste: it was the kind of thing he could understand, and he understood it all the better because it was empty. Oxford is—Oxford: not a mere receptacle for youth, like Cambridge. Perhaps it wants its inmates to love it rather than to love one another: such at all events was to be its effect on Tibby. His sisters sent him there that he might make friends, for they knew that his education had been cranky, and had severed him from other boys and men. He made no friends. His Oxford remained Oxford empty, and he took into life with him, not the memory of a radiance, but the memory of a colour scheme.

It pleased Margaret to hear her brother and sister talking. They did not get on overwell as a rule. For a few moments she listened to them, feeling elderly and benign. Then something occurred to her, and she interrupted:

'Helen, I told you about poor Mrs Wilcox; that sad business?'

'Yes.'

'I have had a correspondence with her son. He was winding up the estate, and wrote to ask me whether his mother had wanted me to have anything. I thought it good of him, considering I knew her for so little. I said that she had once spoken of giving me a Christmas present, but we both forgot about it afterwards.'

'I hope Charles took the hint.'

'Yes—that is to say, her husband wrote later on, and thanked me for being a little kind to her, and actually gave me her silver vinaigrette. Don't you think that is extraordinarily generous? It has made me like him very much. He hopes that this will not be the end of our acquaintance, but that you and I will go and stop with Evie some time in the future. I like Mr Wilcox. He is taking up his work—rubber—it is a big business. I gather he is launching out rather. Charles is in it, too. Charles is married—a pretty little creature, but she doesn't seem wise. They took on the flat, but now they have gone off to a house of their own.'

Helen, after a decent pause, continued her account of Stettin. How quickly a situation changes! In June she had been in a crisis; even in November she could blush and be unnatural; now it was January, and the whole affair lay forgotten. Looking back on the past six months, Margaret realized the chaotic nature of our daily life, and its difference from the orderly sequence that has been fabricated by historians. Actual life is full of false clues and sign-posts that lead nowhere. With infinite effort we nerve ourselves for a crisis that never comes. The most successful career must show a waste of strength that might have removed mountains, and the most unsuccessful is not that of the man who is taken unprepared, but of him who has prepared and is never taken. On a tragedy of that kind our national morality is duly silent. It assumes that preparation against danger is in itself a good, and that men, like nations, are the better for staggering through life fully armed. The tragedy of preparedness has scarcely been handled, save by the Greeks. Life is indeed dangerous, but not in the way morality would have us believe. It is indeed unmanageable, but the essence of it is not a battle. It is unmanageable because it is a romance, and its essence is romantic beauty.

Margaret hoped that for the future she would be less cautious, not more cautious, than she had been in the past.

Chapter Thirteen

Over two years passed, and the Schlegel household continued to lead its life of cultured but not ignoble ease, still swimming gracefully on the grey tides of London. Concerts and plays swept past them, money had been spent and renewed, reputations won and lost, and the city herself, emblematic of their lives, rose and fell in a continual flux, while her shallows washed more widely against the hills of Surrey and over the fields of Hertfordshire. This famous building had arisen, that was doomed. To-day Whitehall had been transformed: it would be the turn of Regent Street to-morrow. And month by month the roads smelt more strongly of petrol, and were more difficult to cross, and human beings heard each other speak with greater difficulty, breathed less of the air, and saw less of the sky. Nature withdrew: the leaves were falling by midsummer; the sun shone through dirt with an admired obscurity.

To speak against London is no longer fashionable. The Earth as an artistic cult has had its day, and the literature of the near future will probably ignore the country and seek inspiration from the town. One can understand the reaction. Of Pan and the elemental forces, the public has heard a little too

,much—they seem Victorian, while London is Georgian—and those who care for the earth with sincerity may wait long ere the pendulum swings back to her again. Certainly London fascinates. One visualizes it as a tract of quivering grey, intelligent without purpose, and excitable without love; as a spirit that has altered before it can be chronicled; as a heart that certainly beats, but with no pulsation of humanity. It lies beyond everything: Nature, with all her cruelty, comes nearer to us than do these crowds of men. A friend explains himself: the earth is explicable—from her we came, and we must return to her. But who can explain Westminster Bridge Road or Liverpool Street in the morning—the city inhaling—or the same thoroughfares in the evening—the city exhaling her exhausted air? We reach in desperation beyond the fog, beyond the very stars, the voids of the universe are ransacked to justify the monster, and stamped with a human face. London is religion's opportunity—not the decorous religion of theologians, but anthropomorphic, crude. Yes, the continuous flow would be tolerable if a man of our own sort—not anyone pompous or tearful—were caring for us up in the sky.

The Londoner seldom understands his city until it sweeps him, too, away from his moorings, and Margaret's eyes were not opened until the lease of Wickham Place expired. She had always known that it must expire, but the knowledge only became vivid about nine months before the event. Then the house was suddenly ringed with pathos. It had seen so much happiness. Why had it to be swept away? In the streets of the city she noted for the first time the architecture of hurry, and heard the language of hurry on the mouths of its inhabitants—clipped words, formless sentences, potted expressions of approval or disgust. Month by month things were stepping livelier, but to what goal? The population still rose, but what was the quality of the men born? The particular millionaire who owned the freehold of Wickham Place, and desired to erect Babylonian flats upon it—what right had he to stir so large a portion of the quivering jelly? He was not a fool—she had heard him expose Socialism—but true insight began just where his intelligence ended, and one gathered that this was the case with most millionaires. What right had such men— But Margaret checked herself. That way lies madness. Thank goodness she, too, had some money, and could purchase a new home.

Tibby, now in his second year at Oxford, was down for the Easter vacation, and Margaret took the opportunity of having a serious talk with him. Did he at all know where he wanted to live? Tibby didn't know that he did know. Did he at all know what he wanted to do? He was equally uncertain, but when pressed remarked that he should prefer to be quite free of any profession. Margaret was not shocked, but went on sewing for a few minutes before she replied:

'I was thinking of Mr Vyse. He never strikes me as particularly happy.'

'Ye-es,' said Tibby, and then held his mouth open in a curious quiver, as if he, too, had thought of Mr Vyse, had seen round, through, over, and beyond Mr Vyse, had weighed Mr Vyse, grouped him, and finally dismissed him as having no possible bearing on the subject under discussion. That bleat of

Tibby's infuriated Helen. But Helen was now down in the dining-room preparing a speech about political economy. At times her voice could be heard declaiming through the floor.

'But Mr Vyse is rather a wretched, weedy man, don't you think? Then there's Guy. That was a pitiful business. Besides'–shifting to the general–'everyone is the better for some regular work.'

Groans.

'I shall stick to it,' she continued, smiling. 'I am not saying it to educate you; it is what I really think. I believe that in the last century men have developed the desire for work, and they must not starve it. It's a new desire. It goes with a great deal that's bad, but in itself it's good, and I hope that for women, too, "not to work" will soon become as shocking as "not to be married" was a hundred years ago.'

'I have no experience of this profound desire to which you allude,' enunciated Tibby.

'Then we'll leave the subject till you do. I'm not going to rattle you round. Take your time. Only do think over the lives of the men you like most, and see how they've arranged them.'

'I like Guy and Mr Vyse most,' said Tibby faintly, and leant so far back in his chair that he extended in a horizontal line from knees to throat.

'And don't think I'm not serious because I don't use the traditional arguments–making money, a sphere awaiting you, and so on–all of which are, for various reasons, cant.' She sewed on. 'I'm only your sister. I haven't any authority over you, and I don't want to have any. Just to put before you what I think the truth. You see'–she shook off the pince-nez to which she had recently taken–'in a few years we shall be the same age practically, and I shall want you to help me. Men are so much nicer than women.'

'Labouring under such a delusion, why do you not marry?'

'I sometimes jolly well think I would if I got the chance.'

'Has no body arst you?'

'Only ninnies.'

'Do people ask Helen?'

'Plentifully.'

'Tell me about them.'

'No.'

'Tell me about your ninnies, then.'

'They were men who had nothing better to do,' said his sister, feeling that she was entitled to score this point. 'So take warning: you must work, or else you must pretend to work, which is what I do. Work, work, work if you'd save your soul and your body. It is honestly a necessity, dear boy. Look at the Wilcoxes, look at Mr Pembroke. With all their defects of temper and understanding, such men give me more pleasure than many who are better equipped, and I think it is because they have worked regularly and honestly.'

'Spare me the Wilcoxes,' he moaned.

'I shall not. They are the right sort.'

'Oh, goodness me, Meg!' he protested, suddenly sitting up, alert and angry. Tibby, for all his defects, had a genuine personality.

'Well, they're as near the right sort as you can imagine.'

'No, no–oh, no!'

'I was thinking of the younger son, whom I once classed as a ninny, but who came back so ill from Nigeria. He's gone out there again, Evie Wilcox tells me–out to his duty.'

'Duty' always elicited a groan.

'He doesn't want the money, it is work he wants, though it is beastly work–dull country, dishonest natives, an eternal fidget over fresh water and food. A nation who can produce men of that sort may well be proud. No wonder England has become an Empire.'

'*Empire!*'

'I can't bother over results,' said Margaret, a little sadly. 'They are too difficult for me. I can only look at the men. An Empire bores me, so far, but I can appreciate the heroism that builds it up. London bores me, but what thousands of splendid people are labouring to make London—'

'What it is,' he sneered.

'What it is, worse luck. I want activity without civilization. How paradoxical! Yet I expect that is what we shall find in heaven.'

'And I,' said Tibby, 'want civilization without activity, which, I expect, is what we shall find in the other place.'

'You needn't go as far as the other place, Tibbikins, if you want that. You can find it at Oxford.'

'Stupid—'

'If I'm stupid, get me back to the house-hunting. I'll even live in Oxford if you like–North Oxford. I'll live anywhere except Bournemouth, Torquay, and Cheltenham. Oh yes, or Ilfracombe and Swanage and Tunbridge Wells and Surbiton and Bedford. There on no account.'

'London, then.'

'I agree, but Helen rather wants to get away from London. However, there's no reason we shouldn't have a house in the country and also a flat in town, provided we all stick together and contribute. Though of course—Oh, how one does maunder on, and to think, to think of the people who are really poor. How do they live? Not to move about the world would kill me.'

As she spoke, the door was flung open, and Helen burst in in a state of extreme excitement.

'Oh, my dears, what do you think? You'll never guess. A woman's been here asking me for her husband. Her *what?*' (Helen was fond of supplying her own surprise.) 'Yes, for her husband, and it really is so.'

'Not anything to do with Bracknell?' cried Margaret, who had lately taken on an unemployed of that name to clean the knives and boots.

'I offered Bracknell, and he was rejected. So was Tibby. (Cheer up, Tibby!) It's no one we know. I said, "Hunt, my good woman; have a good look round, hunt under the tables, poke up the chimney, shake out the antimacassars. Husband? husband?' Oh, and she so magnificently dressed and tinkling like a chandelier.'

'Now, Helen, what did happen really?'

'What I say. I was, as it were, orating my speech. Annie opens the door like a fool, and shows a female straight in on me, with my mouth open. Then we began—very civilly. "I want my husband, what I have reason to believe is here." No—how unjust one is. She said "whom," not "what." She got it perfectly. So I said, "Name, please?" and she said, "Lan, Miss," and there we were.'

'Lan?'

'Lan or Len. We were not nice about our vowels. Lanoline.'

'But what an extraordinary—'

'I said, "My good Mrs Lanoline, we have some grave misunderstanding here. Beautiful as I am, my modesty is even more remarkable than my beauty, and never, never has Mr Lanoline rested his eyes on mine.'

'I hope you were pleased,' said Tibby.

'Of course,' Helen squeaked. 'A perfectly delightful experience. Oh, Mrs Lanoline's a dear—she asked for a husband as if he was an umbrella. She mislaid him Saturday afternoon—and for a long time suffered no inconvenience. But all night, and all this morning her apprehensions grew. Breakfast didn't seem the same—no, no more did lunch, and so she strolled up to 2, Wickham Place as being the most likely place for the missing article.'

'But how on earth—'

'Don't begin how on earthing. "I know what I know," she kept repeating, not uncivilly, but with extreme gloom. In vain I asked her what she did know. Some knew what others knew, and others didn't, and if they didn't, then others again had better be careful. Oh dear, she was incompetent! She had a face like a silkworm, and the dining-room reeks of orris-root. We chatted pleasantly a little about husbands, and I wondered where hers was too, and advised her to go to the police. She thanked me. We agreed that Mr Lanoline's a notty, notty man, and hasn't no business to go on the lardy-da. But I think she suspected me up to the last. Bags I writing to Aunt Juley about this. Now, Meg, remember—bags I.'

'Bag it by all means,' murmured Margaret, putting down her work. 'I'm not sure that this is so funny, Helen. It means some horrible volcano smoking somewhere, doesn't it?'

'I don't think so—she doesn't really mind. The admirable creature isn't capable of tragedy.'

'Her husband may be, though,' said Margaret, moving to the window.

'Oh no, not likely. No one capable of tragedy could have married Mrs Lanoline.'

'Was she pretty?'

'Her figure may have been good once.'

The flats, their only outlook, hung like an ornate curtain between Margaret and the welter of London. Her thoughts turned sadly to house-hunting. Wickham Place had been so safe. She feared, fantastically, that her own little flock might be moving into turmoil and squalor, into nearer contact with such episodes as these.

'Tibby and I have again been wondering where we'll live next September,' she said at last.

'Tibby had better first wonder what he'll do,' retorted Helen; and that topic was resumed, but with acrimony. Then tea came, and after tea Helen went on preparing her speech, and Margaret prepared one, too, for they were going out to a discussion society on the morrow. But her thoughts were poisoned. Mrs Lanoline had risen out of the abyss, like a faint smell, a goblin footfall, telling of a life where love and hatred had both decayed.

Chapter Fourteen

The mystery, like so many mysteries, was explained. Next day, just as they were dressed to go out to dinner, a Mr Bast called. He was a clerk in the employment of the Porphyrion Fire Insurance Company. Thus much from his card. He had come 'about the lady yesterday.' Thus much from Annie, who had shown him into the dining-room.

'Cheers, children!' cried Helen. 'It's Mrs Lanoline.'

Tibby was interested. The three hurried downstairs, to find, not the gay dog they expected, but a young man, colourless, toneless, who had already the mournful eyes above a drooping moustache that are so common in London, and that haunt some streets of the city like accusing presences. One guessed him as the third generation, grandson to the shepherd or ploughboy whom civilization had sucked into the town; as one of the thousands who have lost the life of the body and failed to reach the life of the spirit. Hints of robustness survived in him, more than a hint of primitive good looks, and Margaret, noting the spine that might have been straight, and the chest that might have broadened, wondered whether it paid to give up the glory of the animal for a tail coat and a couple of ideas. Culture had worked in her own case, but during the last few weeks she had doubted whether it humanized the majority, so wide and so widening is the gulf that stretches between the natural and the philosophic man, so many the good chaps who are wrecked in trying to cross it. She knew this type very well—the vague aspirations, the mental dishonesty, the familiarity with the outsides of books. She knew the tones in which he would address her. She was only unprepared for an example of her own visiting-card.

'You wouldn't remember giving me this, Miss Schlegel?' said he, uneasily familiar.

'No; I can't say I do.'

'Well, that was how it happened, you see.'

'Where did we meet, Mr Bast? For the minute I don't remember.'

'It was a concert at the Queen's Hall. I think you will recollect,' he added pretentiously, 'when I tell you that it included a performance of the Fifth Symphony of Beethoven.'

'We hear the Fifth practically every time it's done, so I'm not sure—do you remember, Helen?'

'Was it the time the sandy cat walked round the balustrade?'

He thought not.

'Then I don't remember. That's the only Beethoven I ever remember specially.'

'And you, if I may say so, took away my umbrella, inadvertently of course.'

'Likely enough,' Helen laughed, 'for I steal umbrellas even oftener than I hear Beethoven. Did you get it back?'

'Yes, thank you, Miss Schlegel.'

'The mistake arose out of my card, did it?' interposed Margaret.

'Yes, the mistake arose—it was a mistake.'

'The lady who called here yesterday thought that you were calling too, and that she could find you?' she continued, pushing him forward, for, though he had promised an explanation, he seemed unable to give one.

'That's so, calling too—a mistake.'

'Then why—?' began Helen, but Margaret laid a hand on her arm.

'I said to my wife,' he continued more rapidly—'I said to Mrs Bast, "I have to pay a call on some friends," and Mrs Bast said to me, "Do go." While I was gone, however, she wanted me on important business, and thought I had come here, owing to the card, and so came after me, and I beg to tender my apologies, and hers as well, for any inconvenience we may have inadvertently caused you.'

'No inconvenience,' said Helen; 'but I still don't understand.'

An air of evasion characterized Mr Bast. He explained again, but was obviously lying, and Helen didn't see why he should get off. She had the cruelty of youth. Neglecting her sister's pressure, she said, 'I still don't understand. When did you say you paid this call?'

'Call? What call?' said he, staring as if her question had been a foolish one, a favourite device of those in mid-stream.

'This afternoon call.'

'In the afternoon, of course!' he replied, and looked at Tibby to see how the repartee went. But Tibby, himself a repartee, was unsympathetic, and said, 'Saturday afternoon or Sunday afternoon?'

'S—Saturday.'

'Really!' said Helen; 'and you were still calling on Sunday, when your wife came here. A long visit.'

'I don't call that fair,' said Mr Bast, going scarlet and handsome. There was fight in his eyes. 'I know what you mean, and it isn't so.'

'Oh, don't let us mind,' said Margaret, distressed again by odours from the abyss.

'It was something else,' he asserted, his elaborate manner breaking down. 'I was somewhere else to what you think, so there!'

'It was good of you to come and explain,' she said. 'The rest is naturally no concern of ours.'

'Yes, but I want—I wanted—have you ever read "The Ordeal of Richard Feverel"?'

Margaret nodded.

'It's a beautiful book. I wanted to get back to the Earth, don't you see, like

Richard does in the end. Or have you ever read Stevenson's "Prince Otto"?'

Helen and Tibby groaned gently.

'That's another beautiful book. You get back to the Earth in that. I wanted—' He mouthed affectedly. Then through the mists of his culture came a hard fact, hard as a pebble. 'I walked all the Saturday night,' said Leonard. 'I walked.' A thrill of approval ran through the sisters. But culture closed in again. He asked whether they had ever read E. V. Lucas's 'Open Road.'

Said Helen, 'No doubt it's another beautiful book, but I'd rather hear about your road.'

'Oh, I walked.'

'How far?'

'I don't know, nor for how long. It got too dark to see my watch.'

'Were you walking alone, may I ask?'

'Yes,' he said, straightening himself; 'but we'd been talking it over at the office. There's been a lot of talk at the office lately about these things. The fellows there said one steers by the Pole Star, and I looked it up in the celestial atlas, but once out of doors everything gets so mixed—'

'Don't talk to me about the Pole Star,' interrupted Helen, who was becoming interested. 'I know its little ways. It goes round and round, and you go round after it.'

'Well, I lost it entirely. First of all the street lamps, then the trees, and towards morning it got cloudy.'

Tibby, who preferred his comedy undiluted, slipped from the room. He knew that this fellow would never attain to poetry, and did not want to hear him trying. Margaret and Helen remained. Their brother influenced them more than they knew: in his absence they were stirred to enthusiasm more easily.

'Where did you start from?' cried Margaret. 'Do tell us more.'

'I took the Underground to Wimbledon. As I came out of the office I said to myself, "I must have a walk once in a way. If I don't take this walk now, I shall never take it." I had a bit of dinner at Wimbledon, and then—'

'But not good country there, is it?'

'It was gas-lamps for hours. Still, I had all the night, and being out was the great thing. I did get into woods, too, presently.'

'Yes, go on,' said Helen.

'You've no idea how difficult uneven ground is when it's dark.'

'Did you actually go off the roads?'

'Oh yes. I always meant to go off the roads, but the worst of it is that it's more difficult to find one's way.'

'Mr Bast, you're a born adventurer,' laughed Margaret. 'No professional athlete would have attempted what you've done. It's a wonder your walk didn't end in a broken neck. Whatever did your wife say?'

'Professional athletes never move without lanterns and compasses,' said Helen. 'Besides, they can't walk. It tires them. Go on.'

'I felt like R. L. S. You probably remember how in "Virginibus—"'

'Yes, but the wood. This 'ere wood. How did you get out of it?'

'I managed one wood, and found a road the other side which went a good bit uphill. I rather fancy it was those North Downs, for the road went off into grass, and I got into another wood. That was awful, with gorse bushes. I did wish I'd never come, but suddenly it got light—just while I seemed going under one tree. Then I found a road down to a station, and took the first train I could back to London.'

'But was the dawn wonderful?' asked Helen.

With unforgettable sincerity he replied, 'No.' The word flew again like a pebble from the sling. Down toppled all that had seemed ignoble or literary in his talk, down toppled tiresome R. L. S. and the 'love of the earth' and his silk top-hat. In the presence of these women Leonard had arrived, and he spoke with a flow, an exultation, that he had seldom known.

'The dawn was only grey, it was nothing to mention—'

'Just a grey evening turned upside down. I know.'

'—and I was too tired to lift up my head to look at it, and so cold too. I'm glad I did it, and yet at the time it bored me more than I can say. And besides—you can believe me or not as you choose—I was very hungry. That dinner at Wimbledon—I meant it to last me all night like other dinners. I never thought that walking would make such a difference. Why, when you're walking you want, as it were, a breakfast and luncheon and tea during the night as well, and I'd nothing but a packet of Woodbines. Lord, I did feel bad! Looking back, it wasn't what you may call enjoyment. It was more a case of sticking to it. I did stick. I—I was determined. Oh, hang it all! what's the good—I mean, the good of living in a room for ever? There one goes on day after day, same old game, same up and down to town, until you forget there is any other game. You ought to see once in a way what's going on outside, if it's only nothing particular after all.'

'I should just think you ought,' said Helen, sitting on the edge of the table.

The sound of a lady's voice recalled him from sincerity, and he said: 'Curious it should all come about from reading something of Richard Jefferies.'

'Excuse me, Mr Bast, but you're wrong there. It didn't. It came from something far greater.'

But she could not stop him. Borrow was imminent after Jefferies—Borrow, Thoreau, and sorrow. R. L. S. brought up the rear, and the outburst ended in a swamp of books. No disrespect to these great names. The fault is ours, not theirs. They mean us to use them for sign-posts, and are not to blame if, in our weakness, we mistake the sign-post for the destination. And Leonard had reached the destination. He had visited the county of Surrey when darkness covered its amenities, and its cosy villas had re-entered ancient night. Every twelve hours this miracle happens, but he had troubled to go and see for himself. Within his cramped little mind dwelt something that was greater than Jefferies' books—the spirit that led Jefferies to write them; and his dawn, though revealing nothing but monotones, was part of the eternal sunrise that shows George Borrow Stonehenge.

'Then you don't think I was foolish?' he asked, becoming again the naïve and sweet-tempered boy for whom Nature had intended him.

'Heavens, no!' replied Margaret.

'Heaven help us if we do!' replied Helen.

'I'm very glad you say that. Now, my wife would never understand—not if I explained for days.'

'No, it wasn't foolish!' cried Helen, her eyes aflame. 'You've pushed back the boundaries; I think it splendid of you.'

'You've not been content to dream as we have—'

'Though we have walked, too—'

'I must show you a picture upstairs—'

Here the door-bell rang. The hansom had come to take them to their evening party.

'Oh, bother, not to say dash—I had forgotten we were dining out; but do, do, come round again and have a talk.'

'Yes, you must—do,' echoed Margaret.

Leonard, with extreme sentiment, replied: 'No, I shall not. It's better like this.'

'Why better?' asked Margaret.

'No, it is better not to risk a second interview. I shall always look back on this talk with you as one of the finest things in my life. Really. I mean this. We can never repeat. It has done me real good, and there we had better leave it.'

'That's rather a sad view of life, surely.'

'Things so often get spoiled.'

'I know,' flashed Helen, 'but people don't.'

He could not understand this. He continued in a vein which mingled true imagination and false. What he said wasn't wrong, but it wasn't right, and a false note jarred. One little twist, they felt, and the instrument might be in tune. One little strain, and it might be silent for ever. He thanked the ladies very much, but he would not call again. There was a moment's awkwardness, and then Helen said: 'Go, then; perhaps you know best; but never forget you're better than Jefferies.' And he went. Their hansom caught him up at the corner, passed with a waving of hands, and vanished with its accomplished load into the evening.

London was beginning to illuminate herself against the night. Electric lights sizzled and jagged in the main thoroughfares, gas-lamps in the side streets glimmered a canary gold or green. The sky was a crimson battlefield of spring, but London was not afraid. Her smoke mitigated the splendour, and the clouds down Oxford Street were a delicately painted ceiling, which adorned while it did not distract. She has never known the clear-cut armies of the purer air. Leonard hurried through her tinted wonders, very much part of the picture. His was a grey life, and to brighten it he had ruled off a few corners for romance. The Miss Schlegels—or, to speak more accurately, his interview with them—were to fill such a corner, nor was it by any means the first time that he had talked intimately to strangers. The habit was analogous to a debauch, an outlet, though the worst of outlets, for instincts that would not be denied. Terrifying him, it would beat down his suspicions and prudence until he was confiding secrets to people whom he had scarcely seen. It brought him many fears and some pleasant memories. Perhaps the keenest happiness he had ever known was during a railway journey to Cambridge, where a decent-mannered undergraduate had spoken to him. They had got into conversation, and gradually Leonard flung reticence aside, told some of his domestic troubles, and hinted at the rest. The undergraduate, supposing they could start a friendship, asked him to 'coffee after hall,' which he accepted, but afterwards grew shy, and took care not to stir from the commercial hotel where he lodged. He did not want Romance to collide with the Porphyrion, still less with Jacky, and people with fuller, happier lives are slow to understand this. To the Schlegels, as to the undergraduate, he was an interesting creature, of whom they wanted to see more. But they to him were denizens of Romance, who must keep to the corner he had assigned them, pictures that must not walk out of their frames.

His behaviour over Margaret's visiting-card had been typical. His had scarcely been a tragic marriage. Where there is no money and no inclination to violence tragedy cannot be generated. He could not leave his wife, and he did not want to hit her. Petulance and squalor was enough. Here 'that card' had come in. Leonard, though furtive, was untidy, and left it lying about. Jacky found it, and then began, 'What's that card, eh?' 'Yes, don't you wish you knew what that card was?' 'Len, who's Miss Schlegel?' etc. Months passed, and the card, now as a joke, now as a grievance, was handed about, getting dirtier and dirtier. It followed them when they moved from Camelia Road to Tulse Hill. It was submitted to third parties. A few inches of pasteboard, it became the battlefield on which the souls of Leonard and his wife contended. Why did he not say, 'A lady took my umbrella, another gave me this that I might call for my umbrella'? Because Jacky would have disbelieved him? Partly, but chiefly because he was sentimental. No affection gathered round the card, but it symbolized the life of culture, that Jacky should never spoil. At night he would say to himself, 'Well, at all events, she doesn't know about that card. Yah! done her there.'

Poor Jacky! she was not a bad sort, and had a great deal to bear. She drew her own conclusion—she was only capable of drawing one conclusion—and in the fulness of time she acted upon it. All the Friday Leonard had refused to speak to her, and had spent the evening observing the stars. On the Saturday he went up, as usual, to town, but he came not back Saturday night, nor Sunday morning, nor Sunday afternoon. The inconvenience grew intolerable, and though she was now of a retiring habit, and shy of women, she went up to Wickham Place. Leonard returned in her absence. The card, the fatal card, was gone from the pages of Ruskin, and he guessed what had happened.

'Well?' he had exclaimed, greeting her with peals of laughter. 'I know where you've been, but you don't know where I've been.'

Jacky sighed, said, 'Len, I do think you might explain,' and resumed domesticity.

Explanations were difficult at this stage, and Leonard was too silly—or it is tempting to write, too sound a chap to attempt them. His reticence was not

entirely the shoddy article that a business life promotes, the reticence that
pretends that nothing is something, and hides behind the 'Daily Telegraph.'
The adventurer, also, is reticent, and it is an adventure for a clerk to walk for
a few hours in darkness. You may laugh at him, you who have slept nights
out on the veldt, with your rifle beside you and all the atmosphere of
adventure pat. And you also may laugh who think adventures silly. But do
not be surprised if Leonard is shy whenever he meets you, and if the
Schlegels rather than Jacky hear about the dawn.

That the Schlegels had not thought him foolish became a permanent joy.
He was at his best when he thought of them. It buoyed him as he journeyed
home beneath fading heavens. Somehow the barriers of wealth had fallen,
and there had been—he could not phrase it—a general assertion of the wonder
of the world. 'My conviction,' says the mystic, 'gains infinitely the moment
another soul will believe in it,' and they had agreed that there was something
beyond life's daily grey. He took off his top-hat and smoothed it
thoughtfully. He had hitherto supposed the unknown to be books,
literature, clever conversation, culture. One raised oneself by study, and got
upsides with the world. But in that quick interchange a new light dawned.
Was that 'something' walking in the dark among the suburban hills?

He discovered that he was going bareheaded down Regent Street. London
came back with a rush. Few were about at this hour, but all whom he passed
looked at him with a hostility that was the more impressive because it was
unconscious. He put his hat on. It was too big; his head disappeared like a
pudding into a basin, the ears bending outwards at the touch of the curly
brim. He wore it a little backwards, and its effect was greatly to elongate the
face and to bring out the distance between the eyes and the moustache. Thus
equipped, he escaped criticism. No one felt uneasy as he titupped along the
pavements, the heart of a man ticking fast in his chest.

Chapter Fifteen

The sisters went out to dinner full of their adventure, and when they were
both full of the same subject, there were few dinner-parties that could stand
up against them. This particular one, which was all ladies, had more kick in
it than most, but succumbed after a struggle. Helen at one part of the table,
Margaret at the other, would talk of Mr Bast and of no one else, and
somewhere about the entrée their monologues collided, fell ruining, and
became common property. Nor was this all. The dinner-party was really an
informal discussion club; there was a paper after it, read amid coffee-cups
and laughter in the drawing-room, but dealing more or less thoughtfully
with some topic of general interest. After the paper came a debate, and in this
debate Mr Bast also figured, appearing now as a bright spot in civilization,
now as a dark spot, according to the temperament of the speaker. The

subject of the paper had been, 'How ought I to dispose of my money?' the reader professing to be a millionaire on the point of death, inclined to bequeath her fortune for the foundation of local art galleries, but open to conviction from other sources. The various parts had been assigned beforehand, and some of the speeches were amusing. The hostess assumed the ungrateful rôle of 'the millionaire's eldest son,' and implored her expiring parent not to dislocate Society by allowing such vast sums to pass out of the family. Money was the fruit of self-denial, and the second generation had a right to profit by the self-denial of the first. What right had 'Mr Bast' to profit? The National Gallery was good enough for the likes of him. After property had had its say—a saying that is necessarily ungracious—the various philanthropists stepped forward. Something must be done for 'Mr Bast'; his conditions must be improved without impairing his independence; he must have a free library, or free tennis-courts; his rent must be paid in such a way that he did not know it was being paid; it must be made worth his while to join the Territorials; he must be forcibly parted from his uninspiring wife, the money going to her as compensation; he must be assigned a Twin Star, some member of the leisured classes who would watch over him ceaselessly (groans from Helen); he must be given food but no clothes, clothes but no food, a third-return ticket to Venice, without either food or clothes when he arrived there. In short, he might be given anything and everything so long as it was not the money itself.

And here Margaret interrupted.

'Order, order, Miss Schlegel!' said the reader of the paper. 'You are here, I understand, to advise me in the interest of the Society for the Preservation of Places of Historic Interest or Natural Beauty. I cannot have you speaking out of your rôle. It makes my poor head go round, and I think you forget that I am very ill.'

'Your head won't go round if only you'll listen to my argument,' said Margaret. 'Why not give him the money itself? You're supposed to have about thirty thousand a year.'

'Have I? I thought I had a million.'

'Wasn't a million your capital? Dear me! we ought to have settled that. Still, it doesn't matter. Whatever you've got, I order you to give as many poor men as you can three hundred a year each.'

'But that would be pauperizing them,' said an earnest girl, who liked the Schlegels, but thought them a little unspiritual at times.

'Not if you gave them so much. A big windfall would not pauperize a man. It is these little driblets, distributed among too many, that do the harm. Money's educational. It's far more educational than the things it buys.' There was a protest. 'In a sense,' added Margaret, but the protest continued. 'Well, isn't the most civilized thing going, the man who has learnt to wear his income properly?'

'Exactly what your Mr Basts won't do.'

'Give them a chance. Give them money. Don't dole them out poetry-books and railway-tickets like babies. Give them the wherewithal to buy these things. When your Socialism comes it may be different, and we may think in terms of commodities instead of cash. Till it comes give people cash, for it is the warp of civilization, whatever the woof may be. The imagination ought to play upon money and realize it vividly, for it's the–the second most important thing in the world. It is so slurred over and hushed up, there is so little clear thinking–oh, political economy, of course, but so few of us think clearly about our own private incomes, and admit that independent thoughts are in nine cases out of ten the result of independent means. Money: give Mr Bast money, and don't bother about his ideals. He'll pick up those for himself.'

She leant back while the more earnest members of the club began to misconstrue her. The female mind, though cruelly practical in daily life, cannot bear to hear ideals belittled in conversation, and Miss Schlegel was asked however she could say such dreadful things, and what it would profit Mr Bast if he gained the whole world and lost his own soul. She answered, 'Nothing, but he would not gain his soul until he had gained a little of the world.' Then they said, 'No, they did not believe it,' and she admitted that an overworked clerk may save his soul in the superterrestrial sense, where the effort will be taken for the deed, but she denied that he will ever explore the spiritual resources of this world, will ever know the rarer joys of the body, or attain to clear and passionate intercourse with his fellows. Others had attacked the fabric of Society–Property, Interest, etc.; she only fixed her eyes on a few human beings, to see how, under present conditions, they could be made happier. Doing good to humanity was useless: the many-coloured efforts thereto spreading over the vast area like films and resulting in an universal grey. To do good to one, or, as in this case, to a few, was the utmost she dare hope for.

Between the idealists, and the political economists, Margaret had a bad time. Disagreeing elsewhere, they agreed in disowning her, and in keeping the administration of the millionaire's money in their own hands. The earnest girl brought forward a scheme of 'personal supervision and mutual help,' the effect of which was to alter poor people until they became exactly like people who were not so poor. The hostess pertinently remarked that she, as eldest son, might surely rank among the millionaire's legatees. Margaret weakly admitted the claim, and another claim was at once set up by Helen, who declared that she had been the millionaire's housemaid for over forty years, overfed and underpaid; was nothing to be done for her, so corpulent and poor? The millionaire then read out her last will and testament, in which she left the whole of her fortune to the Chancellor of the Exchequer. Then she died. The serious parts of the discussion had been of higher merit than the playful–in a men's debate is the reverse more general?–but the meeting broke up hilariously enough, and a dozen happy ladies dispersed to their homes.

Helen and Margaret walked the earnest girl as far as Battersea Bridge Station, arguing copiously all the way. When she had gone they were conscious of an alleviation, and of the great beauty of the evening. They turned back towards Oakley Street. The lamps and the plane-trees, following the line of the embankment, struck a note of dignity that is rare in

English cities. The seats, almost deserted, were here and there occupied by gentlefolk in evening dress, who had strolled out from the houses behind to enjoy fresh air and the whisper of the rising tide. There is something continental about Chelsea Embankment. It is an open space used rightly, a blessing more frequent in Germany than here. As Margaret and Helen sat down, the city behind them seemed to be a vast theatre, an opera-house in which some endless trilogy was performing, and they themselves a pair of satisfied subscribers, who did not mind losing a little of the second act.

'Cold?'

'No.'

'Tired?'

'Doesn't matter.'

The earnest girl's train rumbled away over the bridge.

'I say, Helen—'

'Well?'

'Are we really going to follow up Mr Bast?'

'I don't know.'

'I think we won't.'

'As you like.'

'It's no good, I think, unless you really mean to know people. The discussion brought that home to me. We got on well enough with him in a spirit of excitement, but think of rational intercourse. We mustn't play at friendship. No, it's no good.'

'There's Mrs Lanoline, too,' Helen yawned. 'So dull.'

'Just so, and possibly worse than dull.'

'I should like to know how he got hold of your card.'

'But he said—something about a concert and an umbrella—'

'Then did the card see the wife—'

'Helen, come to bed.'

'No, just a little longer, it is so beautiful. Tell me; oh yes; did you say money is the warp of the world?'

'Yes.'

'Then what's the woof?'

'Very much what one chooses,' said Margaret. 'It's something that isn't money—one can't say more.'

'Walking at night?'

'Probably.'

'For Tibby, Oxford?'

'It seems so.'

'For you?'

'Now that we have to leave Wickham Place, I begin to think it's that. For Mrs Wilcox it was certainly Howards End.'

One's own name will carry immense distances. Mr Wilcox, who was sitting with friends many seats away, heard his, rose to his feet, and strolled along towards the speakers.

'It is sad to suppose that places may ever be more important than people,' continued Margaret.

'Why, Meg? They're so much nicer generally. I'd rather think of that forester's house in Pomerania than of the fat Herr Förstmeister who lived in it.'

'I believe we shall come to care about people less and less, Helen. The more people one knows the easier it becomes to replace them. It's one of the curses of London. I quite expect to end my life caring most for a place.'

Here Mr Wilcox reached them. It was several weeks since they had met.

'How do you do?' he cried. 'I thought I recognized your voices. Whatever are you both doing down here?'

His tones were protective. He implied that one ought not to sit out on Chelsea Embankment without a male escort. Helen resented this, but Margaret accepted it as part of the good man's equipment.

'What an age it is since I've seen you, Mr Wilcox. I met Evie in the Tube, though, lately. I hope you have good news of your son.'

'Paul?' said Mr Wilcox, extinguishing his cigarette, and sitting down between them. 'Oh, Paul's all right. We had a line from Madeira. He'll be at work again by now.'

'Ugh—' said Helen, shuddering from complex causes.

'I beg your pardon?'

'Isn't the climate of Nigeria too horrible?'

'Someone's got to go,' he said simply. 'England will never keep her trade overseas unless she is prepared to make sacrifices. Unless we get firm in West Africa, Ger— untold complications my follow. Now tell me all your news.'

'Oh, we've had a splendid evening,' cried Helen, who always woke up at the advent of a visitor. 'We belong to a kind of club that reads papers, Margaret and I—all women, but there is a discussion after. This evening it was on how one ought to leave one's money—whether to one's family, or to the poor, and if so how—oh, most interesting.'

The man of business smiled. Since his wife's death he had almost doubled his income. He was an important figure at last, a reassuring name on company prospectuses, and life had treated him very well. The world seemed in his grasp as he listened to the River Thames, which still flowed inland from the sea. So wonderful to the girls, it held no mysteries for him. He had helped to shorten its long tidal trough by taking shares in the lock at Teddington, and if he and other capitalists thought good, some day it could be shortened again. With a good dinner inside him and an amiable but academic woman on either flank, he felt that his hands were on all the ropes of life, and that what he did not know could not be worth knowing.

'Sounds a most original entertainment!' he exclaimed, and laughed in his pleasant way. 'I wish Evie would go to that sort of thing. But she hasn't the time. She's taken to breed Aberdeen terriers—jolly little dogs.'

'I expect we'd better be doing the same, really.'

'We pretend we're improving ourselves, you see,' said Helen a little sharply, for the Wilcox glamour is not of the kind that returns, and she had bitter memories of the days when a speech such as he had just made would have impressed her favourably. 'We suppose it a good thing to waste an evening once a fortnight over a debate, but, as my sister says, it may be better to breed dogs.'

'Not at all. I don't agree with your sister. There's nothing like a debate to teach one quickness. I often wish I had gone in for them when I was a youngster. It would have helped me no end.'

'Quickness—?'

'Yes. Quickness in argument. Time after time I've missed scoring a point because the other man has had the gift of the gab and I haven't. Oh, I believe in these discussions.'

The patronizing tone, thought Margaret, came well enough from a man who was old enough to be their father. She had always maintained that Mr Wilcox had a charm. In times of sorrow or emotion his inadequacy had pained her, but it was pleasant to listen to him now, and to watch his thick brown moustache and high forehead confronting the stars. But Helen was nettled. The aim of *their* debates she implied was Truth.

'Oh yes, it doesn't much matter what subject you take,' said he.

Margaret laughed and said, 'But this is going to be far better than the debate itself.' Helen recovered herself and laughed too. 'No, I won't go on,' she declared. 'I'll just put our special case to Mr Wilcox.'

'About Mr Bast? Yes, do. He'll be more lenient to a special case.'

'But, Mr Wilcox, do first light another cigarette. It's this. We've just come across a young fellow, who's evidently very poor, and who seems interest—'

'What's his profession?'

'Clerk.'

'What in?'

'Do you remember, Margaret?'

'Porphyrion Fire Insurance Company.'

'Oh yes; the nice people who gave Aunt Juley a new hearth-rug. He seems interesting, in some ways very, and one wishes one could help him. He is married to a wife whom he doesn't seem to care for much. He likes books, and what one may roughly call adventure, and if he had a chance— But he is so poor. He lives a life where all the money is apt to go on nonsense and clothes. One is so afraid that circumstances will be too strong for him and that he will sink. Well, he got mixed up in our debate. He wasn't the subject of it, but it seemed to bear on his point. Suppose a millionaire died, and desired to leave money to help such a man. How should he be helped? Should he be given three hundred pounds a year direct, which was Margaret's plan? Most of them thought this would pauperize him. Should he and those like him be given free libraries? I said "No!" He doesn't want more books to read, but to read books rightly. My suggestion was he should be given something every year towards a summer holiday, but then there is his wife, and they said she would have to go too. Nothing seemed quite right! Now what do you think? Imagine that you were a millionaire, and wanted to help the poor. What would you do?'

Mr Wilcox, whose fortune was not so very far below the standard indicated, laughed exuberantly. 'My dear Miss Schlegel, I will not rush in where your sex has been unable to tread. I will not add another plan to the

numerous excellent ones that have been already suggested. My only
contribution is this: let your young friend clear out of the Porphyrion Fire
Insurance Company with all possible speed.'

'Why?' said Margaret.

He lowered his voice. 'This is between friends. It'll be in the Receiver's
hands before Christmas. It'll smash,' he added, thinking that she had not
understood.

'Dear me, Helen, listen to that. And he'll have to get another place!'

'*Will* have? Let him leave the ship before it sinks. Let him get one now.'

'Rather than wait, to make sure?'

'Decidedly.'

'Why's that?'

Again the Olympian laugh, and the lowered voice. 'Naturally the man
who's in a situation when he applies stands a better chance, is in a stronger
position, than the man who isn't. It looks as if he's worth something. I know
by myself–(this is letting you into the State secrets)–it affects an employer
greatly. Human nature, I'm afraid.'

'I hadn't thought of that,' murmured Margaret, while Helen said, 'Our
human nature appears to be the other way round. We employ people because
they're unemployed. The boot man, for instance:'

'And how does he clean the boots?'

'Not well,' confessed Margaret.

'There you are!'

'Then do you really advise us to tell this youth—?'

'I advise nothing,' he interrupted, glancing up and down the
Embankment, in case his indiscretion had been overhead. 'I oughtn't to
have spoken–but I happen to know, being more or less behind the scenes.
The Porphyrion's a bad, bad concern— Now, don't say I said so. It's outside the Tariff Ring.'

'Certainly I won't say. In fact, I don't know what that means.'

'I thought an insurance company never smashed,' was Helen's
contribution. 'Don't the others always run in and save them?'

'You're thinking of reinsurance,' said Mr Wilcox mildly. 'It is exactly
there that the Porphyrion is weak. It has tried to undercut, has been badly
hit by a long series of small fires, and it hasn't been able to reinsure. I'm
afraid that public companies don't save one another for love.'

'"Human nature," I suppose,' quoted Helen, and he laughed and agreed
that it was. When Margaret said that she supposed that clerks, like everyone
else, found it extremely difficult to get situations in these days, he replied,
'Yes, extremely,' and rose to rejoin his friends. He knew by his own
office–seldom a vacant post, and hundreds of applicants for it; at present no
vacant post.

'And how's Howards End looking?' said Margaret, wishing to change the
subject before they parted. Mr Wilcox was a little apt to think one wanted to
get something out of him.

'It's let.'

'Really. And you wandering homeless in long-haired Chelsea? How strange are the ways of Fate!'

'No; it's let unfurnished. We've moved.'

'Why, I thought of you both as anchored there for ever. Evie never told me.'

'I dare say when you met Evie the thing wasn't settled. We only moved a week ago. Paul has rather a feeling for the old place, and we held on for him to have his holiday there; but, really, it is impossibly small. Endless drawbacks. I forget whether you've been up to it?'

'As far as the house, never.'

'Well, Howards End is one of those converted farms. They don't really do, spend what you will on them. We messed away with a garage all among the wych-elm roots, and last year we enclosed a bit of the meadow and attempted a rockery. Evie got rather keen on Alpine plants. But it didn't do—no, it didn't do. You remember, or your sister will remember, the farm with those abominable guinea-fowls, and the hedge that the old woman never would cut properly, so that it all went thin at the bottom. And, inside the house, the beams—and the staircase through a door—picturesque enough, but not a place to live in.' He glanced over the parapet cheerfully. 'Full tide. And the position wasn't right either. The neighbourhood's getting suburban. Either be in London or out of it, I say; so we've taken a house in Ducie Street, close to Sloane Street, and a place right down in Shropshire—Oniton Grange. Ever heard of Oniton? Do come and see us—right away from everywhere, up towards Wales.'

'What a change!' said Margaret. But the change was in her own voice, which had become most sad. 'I can't imagine Howards End or Hilton without you.'

'Hilton isn't without us,' he replied. 'Charles is there still.'

'Still?' said Margaret, who had not kept up with the Charles'. 'But I thought he was still at Epsom. They were furnishing that Christmas—one Christmas. How everything alters! I used to admire Mrs Charles from our windows very often. Wasn't it Epsom?'

'Yes, but they moved eighteen months ago. Charles, the good chap'—his voice dropped—'thought I should be lonely. I didn't want him to move, but he would, and took a house at the other end of Hilton, down by the Six Hills. He had a motor, too. There they all are, a very jolly party—he and she and the two grandchildren.'

'I manage other people's affairs so much better than they manage them themselves,' said Margaret as they shook hands. 'When you moved out of Howards End, I should have moved Mr Charles Wilcox into it. I should have kept so remarkable a place in the family.'

'So it is,' he replied. 'I haven't sold it, and don't mean to.'

'No; but none of you are there.'

'Oh, we've got a splendid tenant—Hamar Bryce, an invalid. If Charles ever wanted it—but he won't. Dolly is so dependent on modern conveniences. No, we have all decided against Howards End. We like it in a way, but now we feel that it is neither one thing nor the other. One must have one thing or the other.'

'And some people are lucky enough to have both. You're doing yourself proud, Mr Wilcox. My congratulations.'

'And mine,' said Helen.

'Do remind Evie to come and see us—two, Wickham Place. We shan't be there very long, either.'

'You, too, on the move?'

'Next September,' Margaret sighed.

'Everyone moving! Good-bye.'

The tide had begun to ebb. Margaret leant over the parapet and watched it sadly. Mr Wilcox had forgotten his wife, Helen her lover; she herself was probably forgetting. Everyone moving. Is it worth while attempting the past when there is this continual flux even in the hearts of men?

Helen roused her by saying: 'What a prosperous vulgarian Mr Wilcox has grown! I have very little use for him in these days. However, he did tell us about the Porphyrion. Let us write to Mr Bast as soon as ever we get home, and tell him to clear out of it at once.'

'Do; yes, that's worth doing. Let us.'

'Let's ask him to tea.'

Chapter Sixteen

Leonard accepted the invitation to tea next Saturday. But he was right; the visit proved a conspicuous failure.

'Sugar?' said Margaret.

'Cake?' said Helen. 'The big cake or the little deadlies? I'm afraid you thought my letter rather odd, but we'll explain—we aren't cold, really—nor affected, really. We're over-expressive: that's all.'

As a lady's lap-dog Leonard did not excel. He was not an Italian, still less a Frenchman, in whose blood there runs the very spirit of persiflage and of gracious repartee. His wit was the Cockney's; it opened no doors into imagination, and Helen was drawn up short by 'The more a lady has to say, the better,' administered waggishly.

'Oh yes,' she said.

'Ladies brighten—'

'Yes, I know. The darlings are regular sunbeams. Let me give you a plate.'

'How do you like your work?' interposed Margaret.

He, too, was drawn up short. He would not have these women prying into his work. They were Romance, and so was the room to which he had at last penetrated, with the queer sketches of people bathing upon its walls, and so were the very tea-cups, with their delicate borders of wild strawberries. But he would not let Romance interfere with his life. There is the devil to pay then.

'Oh, well enough,' he answered.

'Your company is the Porphyrion, isn't it?'

'Yes, that's so'—becoming rather offended. 'It's funny how things get round.'

'Why funny?' asked Helen, who did not follow the workings of his mind. 'It was written as large as life on your card, and considering we wrote to you there, and that you replied on the stamped paper—'

'Would you call the Porphyrion one of the big Insurance Companies?' pursued Margaret.

'It depends what you call big.'

'I mean by big, a solid, well-established concern, that offers a reasonably good career to its employés.'

' I couldn't say—some would tell you one thing and others another,' said the employé uneasily. 'For my own part'—he shook his head—'I only believe half I hear. Not that even; it's safer. Those clever ones come to the worse grief, I've often noticed. Ah, you can't be too careful.'

He drank, and wiped his moustache, which was going to be one of those moustaches that always droop into tea-cups—more bother than they're worth, surely, and not fashionable either.

'I quite agree, and that's why I was curious to know: is it a solid, well-established concern?'

Leonard had no idea. He understood his own corner of the machine, but nothing beyond it. He desired to confess neither knowledge nor ignorance, and under these circumstances, another motion of the head seemed safest. To him, as to the British public, the Porphyrion was the Porphyrion of the advertisement—a giant, in the classical style, but draped sufficiently, who held in one hand a burning torch, and pointed with the other to St Paul's and Windsor Castle. A large sum of money was inscribed below, and you drew your own conclusions. This giant caused Leonard to do arithmetic and write letters, to explain the regulations to new clients, and re-explain them to old ones. A giant was of an impulsive morality—one knew that much. He would pay for Mrs Munt's hearth-rug with ostentatious haste, a large claim he would repudiate quietly, and fight court by court. But his true fighting weight, his antecedents, his amours with other members of the commercial Pantheon—all these were as uncertain to ordinary mortals as were the escapades of Zeus. While the gods are powerful, we learn little about them. It is only in the days of their decadence that a strong light beats into heaven.

'We were told the Porphyrion's no go,' blurted Helen. 'We wanted to tell you; that's why we wrote.'

'A friend of ours did think that it is insufficiently reinsured,' said Margaret.

Now Leonard had his clue. He must praise the Porphyrion. 'You can tell your friend,' he said, 'that he's quite wrong.'

'Oh, good!'

The young man coloured a little. In his circle to be wrong was fatal. The Miss Schlegels did not mind being wrong. They were genuinely glad that they had been misinformed. To them nothing was fatal but evil.

'Wrong, so to speak,' he added.

'How "so to speak"?'

'I mean I wouldn't say he's right altogether.'

But this was a blunder. 'Then he is right partly,' said the elder woman, quick as lightening.

Leonard replied that everyone was right partly, if it came to that.

'Mr Bast, I don't understand business, and I dare say my questions are stupid, but can you tell me what makes a concern "right" or "wrong"?'

Leonard sat back with a sigh.

'Our friend, who is also a business man, was so positive. He said before Christmas—'

'And advised you to clear out of it,' concluded Helen. 'But I don't see why he should know better than you do.'

Leonard rubbed his hands. He was tempted to say that he knew nothing about the thing at all. But a commercial training was too strong for him. Nor could he say it was a bad thing, for this would be giving it away; not yet that it was good, for this would be giving it away equally. He attempted to suggest that it was something between the two, with vast possibilities in either direction, but broke down under the gaze of four sincere eyes. And yet he scarcely distinguished between the two sisters. One was more beautiful and more lively, but 'the Miss Schlegels' still remained a composite Indian god, whose waving arms and contradictory speeches were the product of a single mind.

'One can but see,' he remarked, adding, 'as Ibsen says, "things happen."' He was itching to talk about books and make the most of his romantic hour. Minute after minute slipped away, while the ladies, with imperfect skill, discussed the subject of reinsurance or praised their anonymous friend. Leonard grew annoyed—perhaps rightly. He made vague remarks about not being one of those who minded their affairs being talked over by others, but they did not take the hint. Men might have shown more tact. Women, however tactful elsewhere, are heavy-handed here. They cannot see why we should shroud our incomes and our prospects in a veil. 'How much exactly have you, and how much do you expect to have next June?' And these were women with a theory, who held that reticence about money matters is absurd, and that life would be truer if each would state the exact size of the golden island upon which he stands, the exact stretch of warp over which he throws the woof that is not money. How can we do justice to the pattern otherwise?

And the precious minutes slipped away, and Jacky and squalor came nearer. At last he could bear it no longer, and broke in, reciting the names of books feverishly. There was a moment of piercing joy when Margaret said, 'So *you* like Carlyle,' and then the door opened, and 'Mr Wilcox, Miss Wilcox' entered, preceded by two prancing puppies.

'Oh, the dears! Oh, Evie, how too impossibly sweet!' screamed Helen, falling on her hands and knees.

'We brought the little fellows round,' said Mr Wilcox.

'I bred 'em myself.'

'Oh, really! Mr Bast, come and play with puppies.'

'I've got to be going now,' said Leonard sourly.

'But play with puppies a little first.'

'This is Ahab, that's Jezebel,' said Evie, who was one of those who name animals after the less successful characters of Old Testament history.

'I've got to be going.'

Helen was too much occupied with puppies to notice him.

'Mr Wilcox, Mr Ba— Must you be really? Good-bye!'

'Come again,' said Helen from the floor.

Then Leonard's gorge arose. Why should he come again? What was the good of it? He said roundly: 'No, I shan't; I knew it would be a failure.'

Most people would have let him go. 'A little mistake. We tried knowing another class–impossible.' But the Schlegels had never played with life. They had attempted friendship, and they would take the consequences. Helen retorted, 'I call that a very rude remark. What do you want to turn on me like that for?' and suddenly the drawing-room re-echoed to a vulgar row.

'You ask me why I turn on you?'

'Yes.'

'What do you want to have me here for?'

'To help you, you silly boy!' cried Helen. 'And don't shout.'

'*I* don't want your patronage. *I* don't want your tea. I was quite happy. What do you want to unsettle me for?' He turned to Mr Wilcox. 'I put it to this gentleman. I ask you, sir, am I to have my brain picked?'

Mr Wilcox turned to Margaret with the air of humorous strength that he could so well command. 'Are we intruding, Miss Schlegel? Can we be of any use, or shall we go?'

But Margaret ignored him.

'I'm connected with a leading insurance company, sir. I receive what I take to be an invitation from these–ladies' (he drawled the word). 'I come, and it's to have my brain picked. I ask you, is it fair?'

'Highly unfair,' said Mr Wilcox, drawing a gasp from Evie, who knew that her father was becoming dangerous.

'There, you hear that? Most unfair, the gentleman says. There! Not content with'–pointing at Margaret–'you can't deny it.' His voice rose: he was falling into the rhythm of a scene with Jacky. 'But as soon as I'm useful it's a very different thing. "Oh yes, send for him. Cross-question him. Pick his brains." Oh yes. Now, take me on the whole, I'm a quiet fellow: I'm law-abiding, I don't wish any unpleasantness; but I–I—'

'You,' said Margaret–'you–you—'

Laughter from Evie, as at a repartee.

'You are the man who tried to walk by the Pole star.'

More laughter.

'You saw the sunrise.'

Laughter.

'You tried to get away from the fogs that are stifling us all–away past books and houses to the truth. You were looking for a real home.'

'I fail to see the connection,' said Leonard, hot with stupid anger.

'So do I.' There was a pause. 'You were that last Sunday–you are this today. Mr Bast! I and my sister have talked you over. We wanted to help you; we also supposed you might help us. We did not have you here out of charity—which bores us—but because we hoped there would be a connection between last Sunday and other days. What is the good of your stars and trees, your sunrise and the wind, if they do not enter into our daily lives? They have never entered into mine, but into yours, we thought— Haven't we all to struggle against life's daily greyness, against pettiness, against mechanical cheerfulness, against suspicion? I struggle by remembering my friends; others I have known by remembering some place—some beloved place or tree—we thought you one of these.'

'Of course, if there's been any misunderstanding,' mumbled Leonard, 'all I can do is to go. But I beg to state—' He paused. Ahab and Jezebel danced at his boots and made him look ridiculous. 'You were picking my brain for official information—I can prove it—I—' He blew his nose and left them.

'Can I help you now?' said Mr Wilcox, turning to Margaret. 'May I have one quiet word with him in the hall?'

'Helen, go after him—do anything—*anything*—to make the noodle understand.'

Helen hesitated.

'But really—' said their visitor. 'Ought she to?'

At once she went.

He resumed. 'I would have chimed in, but I felt that you could polish him off for yourselves—I didn't interfere. You were splendid, Miss Schlegel—absolutely splendid. You can take my word for it, but there are very few women who could have managed him.'

'Oh yes,' said Margaret distractedly.

'Bowling him over with those long sentences was what fetched me,' cried Evie.

'Yes, indeed,' chuckled her father; 'all that part about "mechanical cheerfulness"—oh, fine!'

'I'm very sorry,' said Margaret, collecting herself. 'He's a nice creature really. I cannot think what set him off. It has been most unpleasant for you.'

'Oh, *I* didn't mind.' Then he changed his mood. He asked if he might speak as an old friend, and, permission given, said: 'Oughtn't you really to be more careful?'

Margaret laughed, though her thoughts still strayed after Helen. 'Do you realize that it's all your fault?' she said. 'You're responsible.'

'I?'

'This is the young man whom we were to warn against the Porphyrion. We warn him, and—look!'

Mr Wilcox was annoyed. 'I hardly consider that a fair deduction,' he said.

'Obviously unfair,' said Margaret. 'I was only thinking how tangled things are. It's our fault mostly—neither yours nor his.'

'Not his?'

'No.'

'Miss Schlegel, you are too kind.'

'Yes, indeed,' nodded Evie, a little contemptuously.

'You behave much too well to people, and then they impose on you. I know the world and that type of man, and as soon as I entered the room I saw you had not been treating him properly. You must keep that type at a distance. Otherwise they forget themselves. Sad, but true. They aren't our sort, and one must face the fact.'

'Ye-es.'

'Do admit that we should never have had the outburst if he was a gentleman.'

'I admit it willingly,' said Margaret, who was pacing up and down the room. 'A gentleman would have kept his suspicions to himself.'

Mr Wilcox watched her with a vague uneasiness.

'What did he suspect you of?'

'Of wanting to make money out of him.'

'Intolerable brute! But how were you to benefit?'

'Exactly. How indeed! Just horrible, corroding suspicion. One touch of thought or of goodwill would have brushed it away. Just the senseless fear that does make men intolerable brutes.'

'I come back to my original point. You ought to be more careful, Miss Schlegel. Your servants ought to have orders not to let such people in.'

She turned to him frankly. 'Let me explain exactly why we like this man, and want to see him again.'

'That's your clever way of talking. I shall never believe you like him.'

'I do. Firstly, because he cares for physical adventure, just as you do. Yes, you go motoring and shooting; he would like to go camping out. Secondly, he cares for something special *in* adventure. It is quickest to call that special something poetry—'

'Oh, he's one of that writer sort.'

'No—oh no! I mean he may be, but it would be loathsome stuff. His brain is filled with the husks of books, culture—horrible; we want him to wash out his brain and go to the real thing. We want to show him how he may get upsides with life. As I said, either friends or the country, some'—she hesitated—'either some very dear person or some very dear place seems necessary to relieve life's daily grey, and to show that it is grey. If possible, one should have both.'

Some of her words ran past Mr Wilcox. He let them run past. Others he caught and criticized with admirable lucidity.

'Your mistake is this, and it is a very common mistake. This young bounder has a life of his own. What right have you to conclude it is an unsuccessful life, or, as you call it, "grey"?'

'Because—'

'One minute. You know nothing about him. He probably has his own joys and interests—wife, children, snug little home. That's where we practical fellows'—he smiled—'are more tolerant than you intellectuals. We live and let live, and assume that things are jogging on fairly well elsewhere, and that the ordinary plain man may be trusted to look after his own affairs. I quite grant—I look at the faces of the clerks in my own office, and observe them to be dull, but I don't know what's going on beneath. So, by the way, with

London. I have heard you rail against London, Miss Schlegel, and it seems a funny thing to say but I was very angry with you. What do you know about London? You only see civilization from the outside. I don't say in your case, but in too many cases that attitude leads to morbidity, discontent, and Socialism.'

She admitted the strength of his position, though it undermined imagination. As he spoke, some outposts of poetry and perhaps of sympathy fell ruining, and she retreated to what she called her 'second line'—to the special facts of the case.

'His wife is an old bore,' she said simply. 'He never came home last Saturday night because he wanted to be alone, and she thought he was with us.'

'With *you*?'

'Yes.' Evie tittered. 'He hasn't got the cosy home that you assumed. He needs outside interests.

'Naughty young man!' cried the girl.

'Naughty?' said Margaret, who hated naughtiness more than sin. 'When you're married, Miss Wilcox, won't you want outside interests?'

'He has apparently got them,' put in Mr Wilcox slyly.

'Yes, indeed, father.'

'He was tramping in Surrey, if you mean that,' said Margaret, pacing away rather crossly.

'Oh, I dare say!'

'Miss Wilcox, he was!'

'M-m-m-m!' from Mr Wilcox, who thought the episode amusing, if risqué. With most ladies he would not have discussed it, but he was trading on Margaret's reputation as an emancipated woman.

'He said so, and about such a thing he wouldn't lie.'

They both began to laugh.

'That's where I differ from you. Men lie about their positions and prospects, but not about a thing of that sort.'

He shook his head. 'Miss Schlegel, excuse me, but I know the type.'

'I said before—he isn't a type. He cares about adventures rightly. He's certain that our smug existence isn't all. He's vulgar and hysterical and bookish, but don't think that sums him up. There's manhood in him as well. Yes, that's what I'm trying to say. He's a real man.'

As she spoke their eyes met, and it was as if Mr Wilcox's defences fell. She saw back to the real man in him. Unwittingly she had touched his emotions. A woman and two men—they had formed the magic triangle of sex, and the male was thrilled to jealousy, in case the female was attracted by another male. Love, say the ascetics, reveals our shameful kinship with the beasts. Be it so: one can bear that; jealousy is the real shame. It is jealousy, not love, that connects us with the farmyard intolerably, and calls up visions of two angry cocks and a complacent hen. Margaret crushed complacency down because she was civilized. Mr Wilcox, uncivilized, continued to feel anger long after he had rebuilt his defences, and was again presenting a bastion to the world.

'Miss Schlegel, you're a pair of dear creatures, but you really *must* be careful in this uncharitable world. What does your brother say?'

'I forget.'

'Surely he has some opinion?'

'He laughs, if I remember correctly.'

'He's very clever, isn't he?' said Evie, who had met and detested Tibby at Oxford.

'Yes, pretty well–but I wonder what Helen's doing.'

'She is very young to undertake this sort of thing,' said Mr Wilcox.

Margaret went out into the landing. She heard no sound, and Mr Bast's topper was missing from the hall.

'Helen!' she called.

'Yes!' replied a voice from the library.

'You in there?'

'Yes–he's gone some time.'

Margaret went to her. 'Why, you're all alone,' she said.

'Yes–it's all right, Meg. Poor, poor creature—'

'Come back to the Wilcoxes and tell me later–Mr W. much concerned, and slightly titillated.'

'Oh, I've no patience with him. I hate him. Poor dear Mr Bast! he wanted to talk literature, and we would talk business. Such a muddle of a man, and yet so worth pulling through. I like him extraordinarily.'

'Well done,' said Margaret, kissing her, 'but come into the drawing-room now, and don't talk about him to the Wilcoxes. Make light of the whole thing.'

Helen came and behaved with a cheerfulness that reassured their visitor–this hen at all events was fancy-free.

'He's gone with my blessing,' she cried, 'and now for puppies.'

As they drove away, Mr Wilcox said to his daughter:

'I am really concerned at the way those girls go on. They are as clever as you make 'em, but unpractical–God bless me! One of these days they'll go too far. Girls like that oughtn't to live alone in London. Until they marry, they ought to have someone to look after them. We must look in more often–we're better than no one. You like them, don't you, Evie?'

Evie replied: 'Helen's right enough, but I can't stand the toothy one. And I shouldn't have called either of them girls.'

Evie had grown up handsome. Dark-eyed, with the glow of youth under sunburn, built firmly and firm-lipped, she was the best the Wilcoxes could do in the way of feminine beauty. For the present, puppies and her father were the only things she loved, but the net of matrimony was being prepared for her, and a few days later she was attracted to a Mr Percy Cahill, an uncle of Mrs Charles', and he was attracted to her.

Chapter Seventeen

The Age of Property holds bitter moments even for a proprietor. When a move is imminent, furniture becomes ridiculous, and Margaret now lay awake at nights wondering where, where on earth they and all their belongings would be deposited in September next. Chairs, tables, pictures, books, that had rumbled down to them through the generations, must rumble forward again like a slide of rubbish to which she longed to give the final push, and send toppling into the sea. But there were all their father's books—they never read them, but they were their father's and must be kept. There was the marble-topped cheffonier—their mother had set store by it, they could not remember why. Round every knob and cushion in the house sentiment gathered, a sentiment that was at times personal, but more often a faint piety to the dead, a prolongation of rites that might have ended at the grave.

It was absurd, if you came to think of it; Helen and Tibby came to think of it: Margaret was too busy with the house-agents. The feudal ownership of land did bring dignity, whereas the modern ownership of movables is reducing us again to a nomadic horde. We are reverting to the civilization of luggage, and historians of the future will note how the middle classes accreted possessions without taking root in the earth, and may find in this the secret of their imaginative poverty. The Schlegels were certainly the poorer for the loss of Wickham Place. It had helped to balance their lives, and almost to counsel them. Nor is their ground-landlord spiritually the richer. He has built flats on its site, his motor-cars grow swifter, his exposures of Socialism more trenchant. But he has spilt the precious distillation of the years, and no chemistry of his can give it back to society again.

Margaret grew depressed; she was anxious to settle on a house before they left town to pay their annual visit to Mrs Munt. She enjoyed this visit, and wanted to have her mind at ease for it. Swanage, though dull, was stable, and this year she longed more than usual for its fresh air and for the magnificent downs that guard it on the north. But London thwarted her; in its atmosphere she could not concentrate. London only stimulates, it cannot sustain; and Margaret, hurrying over its surface for a house without knowing what sort of a house she wanted, was paying for many a thrilling sensation in the past. She could not even break loose from culture, and her time was wasted by concerts which it would be a sin to miss, and invitations which it would never do to refuse. At last she grew desperate; she resolved that she would go nowhere and be at home to no one until she found a house, and broke the resolution in half an hour.

Once she had humorously lamented that she had never been to Simpson's restaurant in the Strand. Now a note arrived from Miss Wilcox, asking her to lunch there. Mr Cahill was coming, and the three would have such a jolly chat, and perhaps end up at the Hippodrome. Margaret had no strong regard for Evie, and no desire to meet her fiancé, and she was surprised that Helen, who had been far funnier about Simpson's, had not been asked instead. But the invitation touched her by its intimate tone. She must know Evie Wilcox better than she supposed, and declaring that she 'simply must,' she accepted.

But when she saw Evie at the entrance of the restaurant, staring fiercely at nothing after the fashion of athletic women, her heart failed her anew. Miss Wilcox had changed perceptibly since her engagement. Her voice was gruffer, her manner more downright, and she was inclined to patronize the more foolish virgin. Margaret was silly enough to be pained at this. Depressed at her isolation, she saw not only houses and furniture, but the vessel of life itself slipping past her, with people like Evie and Mr Cahill on board.

There are moments when virtue and wisdom fail us, and one of them came to her at Simpson's in the Strand. As she trod the staircase, narrow, but carpeted thickly, as she entered the eating-room, where saddles of mutton were being trundled up to expectant clergymen, she had a strong, if erroneous, conviction of her own futility, and wished she had never come out of her backwater, where nothing happened except art and literature, and where no one ever got married or succeeded in remaining engaged. Then came a little surprise. 'Father might be of the party—yes, father was.' With a smile of pleasure she moved forward to greet him, and her feeling of loneliness vanished.

'I thought I'd get round if I could,' said he. 'Evie told me of her little plan, so I just slipped in and secured a table. Always secure a table first. Evie, don't pretend you want to sit by your old father, because you don't. Miss Schlegel, come in my side, out of pity. My goodness, but you look tired! Been worrying round after your young clerks?'

'No, after houses,' said Margaret, edging past him into the box. 'I'm hungry, not tired; I want to eat heaps.'

'That's good. What'll you have?'

'Fish pie,' said she, with a glance at the menu.

'Fish pie! Fancy coming for fish pie to Simpson's. It's not a bit the thing to go for here.'

'Go for something for me, then,' said Margaret, pulling off her gloves. Her spirits were rising, and his reference to Leonard Bast had warmed her curiously.

'Saddle of mutton,' said he after profound reflection; 'and cider to drink. That's the type of thing. I like this place, for a joke, once in a way. It is so thoroughly Old English. Don't you agree?'

'Yes,' said Margaret, who didn't. The order was given, the joint rolled up, and the carver, under Mr Wilcox's direction, cut the meat where it was succulent, and piled their plates high. Mr Cahill insisted on sirloin, but admitted that he had made a mistake later on. He and Evie soon fell into a conversation of the 'No I didn't; yes, you did' type–conversation which, though fascinating to those who are engaged in it, neither desires nor deserves the attention of others.

'It's a golden rule to tip the carver. Tip everywhere's my motto.'

'Perhaps it does make life more human.'

'Then the fellows know one again. Especially in the East, if you tip, they remember you from year's end to year's end.'

'Have you been in the East?'

'Oh, Greece and the Levant. I used to go out for sport and business to Cyprus; some military society of a sort there. A few piastres, properly distributed, help to keep one's memory green. But you, of course, think this shockingly cynical. How's your discussion society getting on? Any new Utopias lately?'

'No, I'm house-hunting, Mr Wilcox, as I've already told you once. Do you know of any houses?'

'Afraid I don't.'

'Well, what's the point of being practical if you can't find two distressed females a house? We merely want a small house with large rooms, and plenty of them.'

'Evie, I like that! Miss Schlegel expects me to turn house agent for her!'

'What's that, father!'

'I want a new home in September, and someone must find it. I can't.'

'Percy, do you know of anything?'

'I can't say I do,' said Mr Cahill.

'How like you! You're never any good.'

'Never any good. Just listen to her! Never any good. Oh, come!'

'Well, you aren't. Miss Schlegel, is he?'

The torrent of their love, having splashed these drops at Margaret, swept away on its habitual course. She sympathized with it now, for a little comfort had restored her geniality. Speech and silence pleased her equally, and while Mr Wilcox made some preliminary inquiries about cheese, her eyes surveyed the restaurant, and admired its well-calculated tributes to the solidity of our past. Though no more Old English than the works of Kipling, it had selected its reminiscences so adroitly that her criticism was lulled, and the guests whom it was nourishing for imperial purposes bore the outer semblance of Parson Adams or Tom Jones. Scraps of their talk jarred oddly on the ear. 'Right you are! I'll cable out to Uganda this evening,' came from the table behind. 'Their Emperor wants war; well, let him have it,' was the opinion of a clergyman. She smiled at such incongruities. 'Next time,' she said to Mr Wilcox, 'you shall come to lunch with me at Mr Eustace Miles's.'

'With pleasure.'

'No, you'd hate it,' she said, pushing her glass towards him for some more cider. 'It's all proteids and body buildings, and people come up to you and beg your pardon, but you have such a beautiful aura.'

'A what?'

'Never heard of an aura? Oh, happy, happy man! I scrub at mine for hours. Nor of an astral plane?'

He had heard of astral planes, and censured them.

'Just so. Luckily it was Helen's aura, not mine, and she had to chaperone it and do the politeness. I just sat with my handkerchief in my mouth till the man went.'

'Funny experiences seem to come to you two girls. No one's ever asked me about my–what d'ye call it? Perhaps I've not got one.'

'You're bound to have one, but it may be such a terrible colour that no one dares mention it.'

'Tell me, though, Miss Schlegel, do you really believe in the supernatural and all that?'

'Too difficult a question.'

'Why's that? Gruyère or Stilton?'

'Gruyère, please.'

'Better have Stilton.'

'Stilton. Because, though I don't believe in auras, and think Theosophy's only a halfway-house—'

'—Yet there may be something in it all the same,' he concluded, with a frown.

'Not even that. It may be halfway in the wrong direction. I can't explain. I don't believe in all these fads, and yet I don't like saying that I don't believe in them.'

He seemed unsatisfied, and said: 'So you wouldn't give me your word that you *don't* hold with astral bodies and all the rest of it?'

'I could,' said Margaret, surprised that the point was of any importance to him. 'Indeed, I will. When I talked about scrubbing my aura, I was only trying to be funny. But why do you want this settled?'

'I don't know.'

'Now, Mr Wilcox, you do know.'

'Yes, I am,' 'No, you're not,' burst from the lovers opposite. Margaret was silent for a moment, and then changed the subject.

'How's your house?'

'Much the same as when you honoured it last week.'

'I don't mean Ducie Street. Howards End, of course.'

'Why "of course"?'

'Can't you turn out your tenant and let it to us? We're nearly demented.'

'Let me think. I wish I could help you. But I thought you wanted to be in town. One bit of advice: fix your district, then fix your price, and then don't budge. That's how I got both Ducie Street and Oniton. I said to myself, 'I mean to be exactly here,' and I was, and Oniton's a place in a thousand.'

'But I do budge. Gentlemen seem to mesmerize houses–cow them with an eye, and up they come, trembling. Ladies can't. It's the houses that are mesmerizing me. I've no control over the saucy things. Houses are alive. No?'

'I'm out of my depth,' he said, and added: 'Didn't you talk rather like that to your office boy?'

'Did I—I mean I did, more or less. I talk the same way to everyone—or try to.'

'Yes, I know. And how much do you suppose that he understood of it?'

'That's his lookout. I don't believe in suiting my conversation to my company. One can doubtless hit upon some medium of exchange that seems to do well enough, but it's no more like the real thing than money is like food. 'There's no nourishment in it. You pass it to the lower classes, and they pass it back to you, and this you call 'social intercourse' or 'mutual endeavour,' when it's mutual priggishness if it's anything. Our friends at Chelsea don't see this. They say one ought to be at all costs intelligible, and sacrifice—'

'Lower classes,' interrupted Mr Wilcox, as it were thrusting his hand into her speech. 'Well, you do admit that there are rich and poor. That's something.'

Margaret could not reply. Was he incredibly stupid, or did he understand her better than she understood herself?

'You do admit that, if wealth was divided up equally, in a few years there would be rich and poor again just the same. The hard-working man would come to the top, the wastrel sink to the bottom.'

'Everyone admits that.'

'Your Socialists don't.'

'My Socialists do. Yours mayn't; but I strongly suspect yours of being not Socialists, but ninepins, which you have constructed for your own amusement. I can't imagine any living creature who would bowl over quite so easily.'

He would have resented this had she not been a woman. But women may say anything—it was one of his holiest beliefs—and he only retorted, with a gay smile: 'I don't care. You've made two damaging admissions, and I'm heartily with you in both.'

In time they finished lunch, and Margaret, who had excused herself from the Hippodrome, took her leave. Evie had scarcely addressed her, and she suspected that the entertainment had been planned by the father. He and she were advancing out of their respective families towards a more intimate acquaintance. It had begun long ago. She had been his wife's friend, and, as such, he had given her that silver vinaigrette as a memento. It was pretty of him to have given that vinaigrette, and he had always preferred her to Helen—unlike most men. But the advance had been astonishing lately. They had done more in a week than in two years, and were really beginning to know each other.

She did not forget his promise to sample Eustace Miles, and asked him as soon as she could secure Tibby as his chaperon. He came, and partook of body-building dishes with humility.

Next morning the Schlegels left for Swanage. They had not succeeded in finding a new home.

Chapter Eighteen

As they were seated at Aunt Juley's breakfast-table at The Bays, parrying her excessive hospitality and enjoying the view of the bay, a letter came for Margaret and threw her into perturbation. It was from Mr Wilcox. It announced an 'important change' in his plans. Owing to Evie's marriage, he had decided to give up his house in Ducie Street, and was willing to let it on a yearly tenancy. It was a businesslike letter, and stated frankly what he would do for them and what he would not do. Also the rent. If they approved, Margaret was to come up *at once*—the words were underlined, as is necessary when dealing with women—and to go over the house with him. If they disapproved, a wire would oblige, as he should put it into the hands of an agent.

The letter perturbed, because she was not sure what it meant. If he liked her, if he had manœuvred to get her to Simpson's, might this be a manœuvre to get her to London, and result in an offer of marriage? She put it to herself as indelicately as possible, in the hope that her brain would cry, 'Rubbish, you're a self-conscious fool!' But her brain only tingled a little and was silent, and for a time she sat gazing at the mincing waves, and wondering whether the news would seem strange to the others.

As soon as she began speaking, the sound of her own voice reassured her. There could be nothing in it. The replies also were typical, and in the burr of conversation her fears vanished.

'You needn't go though—' began her hostess.

'I needn't, but hadn't I better? It's really getting rather serious. We let chance after chance slip, and the end of it is we shall be bundled out bag and baggage into the street. We don't know what we *want*, that's the mischief with us—'

'No, we have no real ties,' said Helen, helping herself to toast.

'Shan't I go up to town to-day, take the house if it's the least possible, and then come down by the afternoon train to-morrow, and start enjoying myself. I shall be no fun to myself or to others until this business is off my mind.'

'But you won't do anything rash, Margaret?'

'There's nothing rash to do.'

'Who *are* the Wilcoxes?' said Tibby, a question that sounds silly, but was really extremely subtle, as his aunt found to her cost when she tried to answer it. 'I don't *manage* the Wilcoxes; I don't see where they come *in*.'

'No more do I,' agreed Helen. 'It's funny that we just don't lose sight of them. Out of all our hotel acquaintances, Mr Wilcox is the only one who has stuck. It is now over three years, and we have drifted away from far more interesting people in that time.'

'Interesting people don't get one houses.'

'Meg, if you start in your honest-English vein, I shall throw the treacle at you.'

'It's a better vein than the cosmopolitan,' said Margaret, getting up. 'Now, children, which is it to be? You know the Ducie Street house. Shall I say yes or shall I say no? Tibby love—which? I'm specially anxious to pin you both.'

'It all depends what meaning you attach to the word "possi—"'

'It depends on nothing of the sort. Say "yes."'

'Say "no."'

Then Margaret spoke rather seriously. 'I think,' she said, 'that our race is degenerating. We cannot settle even this little thing; what will it be like when we have to settle a big one?'

'It will be as easy as eating,' returned Helen.

'I was thinking of father. How could he settle to leave Germany as he did, when he had fought for it as a young man, and all his feelings and friends were Prussian? How could he break loose with Patriotism and begin aiming at something else? It would have killed me. When he was nearly forty he could change countries and ideals—and we, at our age, can't change houses. It's humiliating.'

'Your father may have been able to change countries,' said Mrs Munt with asperity, 'and that may or may not be a good thing. But he could change houses no better than you can, in fact, much worse. Never shall I forget what poor Emily suffered in the move from Manchester.'

'I knew it,' cried Helen. 'I told you so. It is the little things one bungles at. The big, real ones are nothing when they come.'

'Bungle, my dear! You are too little to recollect—in fact, you weren't there. But the furniture was actually in the vans and on the move before the lease for Wickham Place was signed, and Emily took train with baby—who was Margaret then—and the smaller luggage for London, without so much as knowing where her new home would be. Getting away from that house may be hard, but it is nothing to the misery that we all went through getting you into it.'

Helen, with her mouth full, cried:

'And that's the man who beat the Austrians, and the Danes, and the French, and who beat the Germans that were inside himself. And we're like him.'

'Speak for yourself,' said Tibby. 'Remember that I am cosmopolitan, please.'

'Helen may be right.'

'Of course she's right,' said Helen.

Helen might be right, but she did not go up to London. Margaret did that. An interrupted holiday is the worst of the minor worries, and one may be pardoned for feeling morbid when a business letter snatches one away from the sea and friends. She could not believe that her father had ever felt the same. Her eyes had been troubling her lately, so that she could not read in the train, and it bored her to look at the landscape, which she had seen but yesterday. At Southampton she 'waved' to Frieda: Frieda was on her way down to join them at Swanage, and Mrs Munt had calculated that their trains would cross. But Frieda was looking the other way, and Margaret travelled on to town feeling solitary and old-maidish. How like an old maid to fancy that Mr Wilcox was courting her! She had once visited a spinster—poor, silly, and unattractive—whose mania it was that every man who approached her fell in love. How Margaret's heart had bled for the deluded thing! How she had lectured, reasoned, and in despair acquiesced! 'I may have been deceived by the curate, my dear, but the young fellow who brings the midday post really is fond of me, and has, as a matter fact—' It had always seemed to her the most hideous corner of old age, yet she might be driven into it herself by the mere pressure of virginity.

Mr Wilcox met her at Waterloo himself. She felt certain that he was not the same as usual; for one thing, he took offence at everything she said.

'This is awfully kind of you,' she began, 'but I'm afraid it's not going to do. The house has not been built that suits the Schlegel family.'

'What! Have you come up determined not to deal?'

'Not exactly.'

'Not exactly? In that case let's be starting.'

She lingered to admire the motor, which was new, and a fairer creature than the vermilion giant that had borne Aunt Juley to her doom three years before.

'Presumably it's very beautiful,' she said. 'How do you like it, Crane?'

'Come, let's be starting,' repeated her host. 'How on earth did you know that my chauffeur was called Crane?'

'Why, I know Crane: I've been for a drive with Evie once. I know that you've got a parlourmaid called Milton. I know all sorts of things.'

'Evie!' he echoed in injured tones. 'You won't see her. She's gone out with Cahill. It's no fun, I can tell you, being left so much alone. I've got my work all day—indeed, a great deal too much of it—but when I come home in the evening, I tell you, I can't stand the house.'

'In my absurd way, I'm lonely too,' Margaret replied. 'It's heart-breaking to leave one's old home. I scarcely remember anything before Wickham Place, and Helen and Tibby were born there. Helen says—'

'You, too, feel lonely?'

'Horribly. Hullo, Parliament's back!'

Mr Wilcox glanced at Parliament contemptuously. The more important ropes of life lay elsewhere. 'Yes, they are talking again,' said he. 'But you were going to say—'

'Only some rubbish about furniture. Helen says it alone endures while men and houses perish, and that in the end the world will be a desert of chairs and sofas—just imagine it!—rolling through infinity with no one to sit upon them.'

'Your sister always likes her little joke.'

'She says "Yes," my brother says "No," to Ducie Street. It's' no fun helping us, Mr Wilcox, I assure you.'

'You are not as unpractical as you pretend. I shall never believe it.'

Margaret laughed. But she was–quite as unpractical. She could not concentrate on details. Parliament, the Thames, the irresponsive chauffeur, would flash into the field of house-hunting, and all demand some comment or response. It is impossible to see modern life steadily and see it whole, and she had chosen to see it whole. Mr Wilcox saw steadily. He never bothered over the mysterious or the private. The Thames might run inland from the sea, the chauffeur might conceal all passion and philosophy beneath his unhealthy skin. They knew their own business, and he knew his.

Yet she liked being with him. He was not a rebuke, but a stimulus, and banished morbidity. Some twenty years her senior, he preserved a gift that she supposed herself to have already lost – not youth's creative power, but its self-confidence and optimism. He was so sure that it was a very pleasant world. His complexion was robust, his hair had receded but not thinned, the thick moustache and the eyes that Helen had compared to brandy-balls had an agreeable menace in them, whether they were turned towards the slums or towards the stars. Some day–in the millennium–there may be no need for his type. At present, homage is due to it from those who think themselves superior, and who possibly are.

'At all events you responded to my telegram promptly,' he remarked.

'Oh, even I know a good thing when I see it.'

'I'm glad you don't despise the goods of this world.'

'Heavens, no! Only idiots and prigs do that.'

'I am glad, very glad,' he repeated, suddenly softening and turning to her, as if the remark had pleased him. 'There is so much cant talked in would-be intellectual circles. I am glad you don't share it. Self-denial is all very well as a means of strengthening the character. But I can't stand those people who run down comforts. They have usually some axe to grind. Can you?'

'Comforts are of two kinds,' said Margaret, who was keeping herself in hand–'those we can share with others, like fire, weather, or music; and those we can't–food, for instance. It depends.'

'I mean reasonable comforts, of course. I shouldn't like to think that you—' He bent nearer; the sentence died unfinished. Margaret's head turned very stupid, and the inside of it seemed to revolve like the beacon in a lighthouse. He did not kiss her, for the hour was half-past twelve, and the car was passing by the stables of Buckingham Palace. But the atmosphere was so charged with emotion that people only seemed to exist on her account, and she was surprised that Crane did not realize this, and turn round. Idiot though she might be, surely Mr Wilcox was more – how should one put it? – more psychological than usual. Always a good judge of character for business purposes, he seemed this afternoon to enlarge his field, and to note qualities outside neatness, obedience, and decision.

'I want to go over the whole house,' she announced when they arrived. 'As soon as I get back to Swanage, which will be to-morrow afternoon, I'll talk it over once more with Helen and Tibby, and wire you "yes" or "no."''

'Right. The dining-room.' And they began their survey.

The dining-room was big, but over-furnished. Chelsea would have moaned aloud. Mr Wilcox had eschewed those decorative schemes that wince, and relent, and refrain, and achieve beauty by sacrificing comfort and pluck. After so much self-colour and self-denial, Margaret viewed with relief the sumptuous dado, the frieze, the gilded wall-paper, amid whose foliage parrots sang. It would never do with her own furniture, but those heavy chairs, that immense sideboard loaded with presentation plate, stood up against its pressure like men. The room suggested men, and Margaret, keen to derive the modern capitalist from the warriors and hunters of the past, saw it as an ancient guest-hall, where the lord sat at meat among his thanes. Even the Bible—the Dutch Bible that Charles had brought back from the Boer War—fell into position. Such a room admitted loot.

'Now the entrance-hall.'

The entrance-hall was paved.

'Here we fellows smoke.'

We fellows smoked in chairs of maroon leather. It was as if a motor-car had spawned. 'Oh, jolly!' said Margaret, sinking into one of them.

'You do like it?' he said, fixing his eyes on her upturned face, and surely betraying an almost intimate note. 'It's all rubbish not making oneself comfortable. Isn't it?'

'Ye-es. Semi-rubbish. Are those Cruikshanks?'

'Gillrays. Shall we go on upstairs?'

'Does all this furniture come from Howards End?'

'The Howards End furniture has all gone to Oniton.'

'Does— However, I'm concerned with the house, not the furniture. How big is this smoking-room?'

'Thirty by fifteen. No, wait a minute. Fifteen and a half.'

'Ah, well. Mr Wilcox, aren't you ever amused at the solemnity with which we middle classes approach the subject of houses?'

They proceeded to the drawing-room. Chelsea managed better here. It was sallow and ineffective. One could visualize the ladies withdrawing to it, while their lords discussed life's realities below, to the accompaniment of cigars. Had Mrs Wilcox's drawing-room looked thus at Howards End? Just as this thought entered Margaret's brain, Mr Wilcox did ask her to be his wife, and the knowledge that she had been right so overcame her that she nearly fainted.

But the proposal was not to rank among the world's great love scenes.

'Miss Schlegel'—his voice was firm—'I have had you up on false pretences. I want to speak about a much more serious matter than a house.'

Margaret almost answered: 'I know—'

'Could you be induced to share my—is it probable—'

'Oh, Mr Wilcox!' she interrupted, holding the piano and averting her eyes. 'I see, I see. I will write to you afterwards if I may.'

He began to stammer. 'Miss Schlegel—Margaret—you don't understand.'

'Oh yes! Indeed, yes!' said Margaret.

'I am asking you to be my wife.'

So deep already was her sympathy, that when he said, 'I am asking you to be my wife,' she made herself give a little start. She must show surprise if he expected it. An immense joy came over her. It was indescribable. It had nothing to do with humanity, and most resembled the all-pervading happiness of fine weather. Fine weather is due to the sun, but Margaret could think of no central radiance here. She stood in his drawing-room happy, and longing to give happiness. On leaving him she realized that the central radiance had been love.

'You aren't offended, Miss Schlegel?'

'How could I be offended?'

There was a moment's pause. He was anxious to get rid of her, and she knew it. She had too much intuition to look at him as he struggled for possessions that money cannot buy. He desired comradeship and affection, but he feared them, and she, who had taught herself only to desire, and could have clothed the struggle with beauty, held back, and hesitated with him.

'Good-bye,' she continued. 'You will have a letter from me–I am going back to Swanage to-morrow.'

'Thank you.'

'Good-bye, and it's you I thank.'

'I may order the motor round, mayn't I?'

'That would be most kind.'

'I wish I had written instead. Ought I to have written?'

'Not at all.'

'There's just one question—'

She shook her head. He looked a little bewildered, and they parted.

They parted without shaking hands: she had kept the interview, for his sake, in tints of the quietest grey. Yet she thrilled with happiness ere she reached her own house. Others had loved her in the past, if one may apply to their brief desires so grave a word, but those others had been 'ninnies'–young men who had nothing to do, old men who could find nobody better. And she had often 'loved,' too, but only so far as the facts of sex demanded: mere yearnings for the masculine, to be dismissed for what they were worth, with a smile. Never before had her personality been touched. She was not young or very rich, and it amazed her that a man of any standing should take her seriously. As she sat trying to do accounts in her empty house, amidst beautiful pictures and noble books, waves of emotion broke, as if a tide of passion was flowing through the night air. She shook her head, tried to concentrate her attention, and failed. In vain did she repeat: 'But I've been through this sort of thing before.' She had never been through it; the big machinery, as opposed to the little, had been set in motion, and the idea that Mr Wilcox loved, obsessed her before she came to love him in return.

She would come to no decision yet. 'Oh, sir, this is so sudden'–that prudish phrase exactly expressed her when her time came. Premonitions are not preparation. She must examine more closely her own nature and his; she must talk it over judicially with Helen. It has been a strange love-scene–the central radiance unacknowledged from first to last. She, in his place, would have said 'Ich liebe dich,' but perhaps it was not his habit to open the heart. He might have done it if she had pressed him—as a matter of duty, perhaps; England expects every man to open his heart once; but the effort would have jarred him, and never, if she could avoid it, should he lose those defences that he had chosen to raise against the world. He must never be bothered with emotional talk, or with a display of sympathy. He was an elderly man now, and it would be futile and impudent to correct him.

Mrs Wilcox strayed in and out, ever a welcome ghost; surveying the scene, thought Margaret, without one hint of bitterness.

Chapter Nineteen

If one wanted to show a foreigner England, perhaps the wisest course would be to take him to the final section of the Purbeck Hills, and stand him on their summit, a few miles to the east of Corfe. Then system after system of our island would roll together under his feet. Beneath him is the valley of the Frome, and all the wild lands that come tossing down from Dorchester, black and gold, to mirror their gorse in the expanses of Poole. The valley of the Stour is beyond, unaccountable stream, dirty at Blandford, pure at Wimborne—the Stour, sliding out of fat fields, to marry the Avon beneath the tower of Christchurch. The valley of the Avon—invisible, but far to the north the trained eye may see Clearbury Ring that guards it, and the imagination may leap beyond that on to Salisbury Plain itself, and beyond the Plain to all the glorious downs of Central England. Nor is Suburbia absent. Bournemouth's ignoble coast cowers to the right, heralding the pine-trees that mean, for all their beauty, red houses, and the Stock Exchange, and extend to the gates of London itself. So tremendous is the City's trail! But the cliffs of Freshwater it shall never touch, and the island will guard the Island's purity till the end of time. Seen from the west, the Wight is beautiful beyond all laws of beauty. It is as if a fragment of England floated forward to greet the foreigner—chalk of our chalk, turf of our turf, epitome of what will follow. And behind the fragment lies Southampton, hostess to the nations, and Portsmouth, a latent fire, and all around it, with double and treble collision of tides, swirls the sea. How many villages appear in this view! How many castles! How many churches, vanished or triumphant! How many ships, railways, and roads! What incredible variety of men working beneath that lucent sky to what final end! The reason fails, like a wave on the Swanage beach; the imagination swells, spreads, and deepens, until it becomes geographic and encircles England.

So Frieda Mosebach, now Frau Architect Liesecke, and mother to her husband's baby, was brought up to these heights to be impressed, and, after a prolonged gaze, she said that the hills were more swelling here than in Pomerania, which was true, but did not seem to Mrs Munt apposite. Poole

Harbour was dry, which led her to praise the absence of muddy foreshore at Friedrich Wilhelms Bad, Rügen, where beech-trees hang over the tideless Baltic, and cows may contemplate the brine. Rather unhealthy Mrs Munt thought his would be, water being safer when it moved about.

'And your English lakes—Vindermere, Grasmere—are they, then, unhealthy?'

'No, Frau Liesecke; but that is because they are fresh water, and different. Salt water ought to have tides, and go up and down a great deal, or else it smells. Look, for instance, at an aquarium.'

'An aquarium! Oh, *Meesis* Munt, you mean to tell me that fresh aquariums stink less than salt? Why, when Victor, my brother-in-law, collected many tadpoles—'

'You are not to say "stink,"' interrupted Helen; 'at least, you may say it, but you must pretend you are being funny while you say it.'

'Then "smell." And the mud of your Pool down there—does it not smell, or may I say "stink, ha, ha"?'

'There always has been mud in Poole Harbour,' said Mrs Munt, with a slight frown. 'The rivers bring it down, and a most valuable oyster-fishery depends upon it.'

'Yes, that is so,' conceded Frieda; and another international incident was closed.

'"Bournemouth is,"' resumed their hostess, quoting a local rhyme to which she was much attached—'"Bournemouth is, Poole was, and Swanage is to be the most important town of all and biggest of the three." Now, Frau Liesecke, I have shown you Bournemouth, and I have shown you Poole, so let us walk backward a little, and look down again at Swanage.'

'Aunt Juley, wouldn't that be Meg's train?'

A tiny puff of smoke had been circling the harbour, and now was bearing southwards towards them over the black and the gold.

'Oh, dearest Margaret, I do hope she won't be overtired.'

'Oh, I do wonder—I do wonder whether she's taken the house.'

'I hope she hasn't been hasty.'

'So do I—oh, *so* do I.'

'Will it be as beautiful as Wickham Place?' Frieda asked.

'I should think it would. Trust Mr Wilcox for doing himself proud. All those Ducie Street houses are beautiful in their modern way, and I can't think why he doesn't keep on with it. But it's really for Evie that he went there, and now that Evie's going to be married—'

'Ah?'

'You've never seen Miss Wilcox, Frieda. How absurdly matrimonial you are!'

'But sister to that Paul?'

'Yes.'

'And to that Charles,' said Mrs Munt with feeling. 'Oh, Helen, Helen, what a time that was!'

Helen laughed. 'Meg and I haven't got such tender hearts. If there's a chance of a cheap house, we go for it.'

'Now look, Frau Liesecke, at my niece's train. You see, it is coming towards us—coming, coming; and, when it gets to Corfe, it will actually go *through* the downs, on which we are standing, so that, if we walk over, as I suggested, and look down on Swanage, we shall see it coming on the other side. Shall we?'

Frieda assented, and in a few minutes they had crossed the ridge and exchanged the greater view for the lesser. Rather a dull valley lay below, backed by the slope of the coastward downs. They were looking across the Isle of Purbeck and on to Swanage, soon to be the most important town of all, and ugliest of the three. Margaret's train reappeared as promised, and was greeted with approval by her aunt. It came to a standstill in the middle distance, and there it had been planned that Tibby should meet her, and drive her, and a tea-basket, up to join them.

'You see,' continued Helen to her cousin, 'the Wilcoxes collect houses as your Victor collects tadpoles. They have, one, Ducie Street; two, Howards End, where my great rumpus was; three, a country seat in Shropshire; four, Charles has a house in Hilton; and five, another near Epsom; and six, Evie will have a house when she marries, and probably a pied-à-terre in the country—which makes seven. Oh yes, and Paul a hut in Africa makes eight. I wish we could get Howards End. That was something like a dear little house! Didn't you think so, Aunt Juley?'

'I had too much to do, dear, to look at it,' said Mrs Munt, with a gracious dignity. 'I had everything to settle and explain, and Charles Wilcox to keep in his place besides. It isn't likely I should remember much. I just remember having lunch in your bedroom.'

'Yes, so do I. But, oh dear, dear, how dead it all seems! And in the autumn there began that anti-Pauline movement—you, and Frieda, and Meg, and Mrs Wilcox, all obsessed with the idea that I might yet marry Paul.'

'You yet may,' said Frieda despondently.

Helen shook her head. 'The Great Wilcox Peril will never return. If I'm certain of anything it's of that.'

'One is certain of nothing but the truth of one's own emotions.'

The remark fell damply on the conversation. But Helen slipped her arm round her cousin, somehow liking her the better for making it. It was not an original remark, nor had Frieda appropriated it passionately, for she had a patriotic rather than a philosophic mind. Yet it betrayed that interest in the universal which the average Teuton possesses and the average Englishman does not. It was, however illogically, the good, the beautiful, the true, as opposed to the respectable, the pretty, the adequate. It was a landscape of Böcklin's beside a landscape of Leader's, strident and ill-considered, but quivering into supernatural life. It sharpened idealism, stirred the soul. It may have been a bad preparation for what followed.

'Look!' cried Aunt Juley, hurrying away from generalities over the narrow summit of the down. 'Stand where I stand, and you will see the pony-cart coming. I see the pony-cart coming.'

They stood and saw the pony-cart coming. Margaret and Tibby were presently seen coming in it. Leaving the outskirts of Swanage, it drove for a little through the budding lanes, and then began the ascent.

'Have you got the house?' they shouted, long before she could possibly hear.

Helen ran down to meet her. The highroad passed over a saddle, and a track went thence at right angles along the ridge of the down.

'Have you got the house?'

Margaret shook her head.

'Oh, what a nuisance! So we're as we were?'

'Not exactly.'

She got out, looking tired.

'Some mystery,' said Tibby. 'We are to be enlightened presently.'

Margaret came close up to her and whispered that she had had a proposal of marriage from Mr Wilcox.

Helen was amused. She opened the gate on to the downs so that her brother might lead the pony through. 'It's just like a widower,' she remarked. 'They've cheek enough for anything, and invariably select one of their first wife's friends.'

Margaret's face flashed despair.

'That type—' She broke off with a cry. 'Meg, not anything wrong with you?'

'Wait one minute,' said Margaret, whispering always.

'But you've never conceivably–you've never—' She pulled herself together. 'Tibby, hurry up through; I can't hold this gate indefinitely. Aunt Juley! I say, Aunt Juley, make the tea, will you, and Frieda; we've got to talk houses, and 'll come on afterwards.' And then, turning her face to her sister's, she burst into tears.

Margaret was stupefied. She heard herself saying, 'Oh, really—' She felt herself touched with a hand that trembled.

'Don't,' sobbed Helen, 'don't, don't, Meg, don't!' She seemed incapable of saying any other word. Margaret, trembling herself, led her forward up the road, till they strayed through another gate on to the down.

'Don't, don't do such a thing! I tell you not to–don't! I know–don't!'

'What do you know?'

'Panic and emptiness,' sobbed Helen. 'Don't!'

Then Margaret thought, 'Helen is a little selfish. I have never behaved like this when there has seemed a chance of her marrying.' She said: 'But we would still see each other very often, and you—'

'It's not a thing like that,' sobbed Helen. And she broke right away and wandered distractedly upwards, stretching her hands towards the view and crying.

'What's happened to you?' called Margaret, following through the wind that gathers at sundown on the northern slopes of hills. 'But it's stupid!' And suddenly stupidity seized her, and the immense landscape was blurred. But Helen turned back.

'Meg—'

'I don't know what's happened to either of us,' said Margaret, wiping her eyes. 'We must both have gone mad.' Then Helen wiped hers, and they even laughed a little.

'Look here, sit down.'

'All right; I'll sit down if you'll sit down.'

'There. (One kiss.) Now, whatever, whatever is the matter?'

'I do mean what I said. Don't; it wouldn't do.'

'Oh, Helen, stop saying "don't"! It's ignorant. It's as if your head wasn't out of the slime. "Don't" is probably what Mrs Bast says all the day to Mr Bast.'

Helen was silent.

'Well?'

'Tell me about it first, and meanwhile perhaps I'll have got my head out of the slime.'

'That's better. Well, where shall I begin? When I arrived at Waterloo—no, I'll go back before that, because I'm anxious you should know everything from the first. The "first" was about ten days ago. It was the day Mr Bast came to tea and lost his temper. I was defending him, and Mr Wilcox became jealous about me, however slightly. I thought it was the involuntary thing, which men can't help any more than we can. You know—at least, I know in my own case—when a man has said to me, "So-and-so's a pretty girl," I am seized with a momentary sourness against So-and-so, and long to tweak her ear. It's a tiresome feeling, but not an important one, and one easily manages it. But it wasn't only this in Mr Wilcox's case, I gather now.'

'Then you love him?'

Margaret considered. 'It is wonderful knowing that a real man cares for you,' she said. 'The mere fact of that grows more tremendous. Remember, I've known and liked him steadily for nearly three years.'

'But loved him?'

Margaret peered into her past. It is pleasant to analyze feelings while they are still only feelings, and unembodied in the social fabric. With her arm round Helen, and her eyes shifting over the view, as if this county or that could reveal the secret of her own heart, she meditated honestly, and said, 'No.'

'But you will?'

'Yes,' said Margaret, 'of that I'm pretty sure. Indeed, I began the moment he spoke to me.'

'And have settled to marry him?'

'I had, but am wanting a long talk about it now. What *is* it against him, Helen? You must try and say.'

Helen, in her turn, looked outwards. 'It is ever since Paul,' she said finally.

'But what has Mr Wilcox to do with Paul?'

'But he was there, they were all there that morning when I came down to breakfast, and saw that Paul was frightened—the man who loved me frightened and all his paraphernalia fallen, so that I knew it was impossible, because personal relations are the important thing for ever and ever, and not this outer life of telegrams and anger.'

She poured the sentence forth in one breath, but her sister understood it, because it touched on thoughts that were familiar between them.

'That's foolish. In the first place, I disagree about the outer life. Well, we've often argued that. The real point is that there is the widest gulf

between my love-making and yours. Yours was romance; mine will be prose.
I'm not running it down—a very good kind of prose, but well considered,
well thought out. For instance, I know all Mr Wilcox's faults. He's afraid of
emotion. He cares too much about success, too little about the past. His
sympathy lacks poetry, and so isn't sympathy really. I'd even say'—she
looked at the shining lagoons—'that, spiritually, he's not as honest as I am.
Doesn't that satisfy you?'

'No, it doesn't,' said Helen. 'It makes me feel worse and worse. You must
be mad.'

Margaret made a movement of irritation.

'I don't intend him, or any man or any woman, to be all my life—good
heavens, no! There are heaps of things in me that he doesn't, and shall never,
understand.'

Thus she spoke before the wedding ceremony and the physical union,
before the astonishing glass shade had fallen that interposes between
married couples and the world. She was to keep her independence more than
do most women as yet. Marriage was to alter her fortunes rather than her
character, and she was not far wrong in boasting that she understood her
future husband. Yet he did alter her character—a little. There was an
unforeseen surprise, a cessation of the winds and odours of life, a social
pressure that would have her think conjugally.

'So with him,' she continued. 'There are heaps of things in him—more
especially things that he does—that will always be hidden from me. He has all
those public qualities which you so despise and enable all this—' She waved
her hand at the landscape, which confirmed anything. 'If Wilcoxes hadn't
worked and died in England for thousands of years, you and I couldn't sit
here without having our throats cut. There would be no trains, no ships to
carry us literary people about in, no fields even. Just savagery. No—perhaps
not even that. Without their spirit life might never have moved out of
protoplasm. More and more do I refuse to draw my income and sneer at
those who guarantee it. There are times when it seems to me—'

'And to me, and to all women. So one kissed Paul.'

'That's brutal,' said Margaret. 'Mine is an absolutely different case. I've
thought things out.'

'It makes no difference thinking things out. They come to the same.'

'Rubbish!'

There was a long silence, during which the tide returned into Poole
Harbour. 'One would lose something,' murmured Helen, apparently to
herself. The water crept over the mud-flats towards the gorse and the
blackened heather. Branksea Island lost its immense foreshores, and became
a sombre episode of trees. Frome was forced inward towards Dorchester,
Stour against Wimborne, Avon towards Salisbury, and over the immense
displacement the sun presided, leading it to triumph ere he sank to rest.
England was alive, throbbing through all her estuaries, crying for joy
through the mouths of all her gulls, and the north wind, with contrary
motion, blew stronger against her rising seas. What did it mean? For what
end are her fair complexities, her changes of soil, her sinuous coast? Does she

belong to those who have moulded her and made her feared by other lands, or to those who have added nothing to her power, but have somehow seen her, seen the whole island at once, lying as a jewel in a silver sea, sailing as a ship of souls, with all the brave world's fleet accompanying her towards eternity?

Chapter Twenty

Margaret had often wondered at the disturbance that takes place in the world's waters, when Love, who seems so tiny a pebble, slips in. Whom does Love concern beyond the beloved and the lover? Yet his impact deluges a hundred shores. No doubt the disturbance is really the spirit of the generations, welcoming the new generation, and chafing against the ultimate Fate, who holds all the seas in the palm of her hand. But Love cannot understand this. He cannot comprehend another's infinity; he is conscious only of his own—flying sunbeam, falling rose, pebble that asks for one quiet plunge below the fretting interplay of space and time. He knows that he will survive at the end of things, and be gathered by Fate as a jewel from the slime, and be handed with admiration round the assembly of the gods. 'Men did produce this,' they will say, and, saying, they will give men immortality. But meanwhile—what agitations meanwhile! The foundations of Property and Propriety are laid bare, twin rocks; Family Pride flounders to the surface, puffing and blowing, and refusing to be comforted; Theology, vaguely ascetic, gets up a nasty ground swell. Then the lawyers are aroused—cold brood—and creep out of their holes. They do what they can; they tidy up Property and Propriety, reassure Theology and Family Pride. Half-guineas are poured on the troubled waters, the lawyers creep back, and, if all has gone well, Love joins one man and woman together in Matrimony.

Margaret had expected the disturbance, and was not irritated by it. For a sensitive woman she had steady nerves, and could bear with the incongruous and the grotesque; and, besides, there was nothing excessive about her love-affair. Good-humour was the dominant note of her relations with Mr Wilcox, or, as I must now call him, Henry. Henry did not encourage romance, and she was no girl to fidget for it. An acquaintance had become a lover, might become a husband, but would retain all that she had noted in the acquaintance; and love must confirm an old relation rather than reveal a new one.

In this spirit she promised to marry him.

He was in Swanage on the morrow, bearing the engagement-ring. They greeted one another with a hearty cordiality that impressed Aunt Juley. Henry dined at The Bays, but had engaged a bedroom in the principal hotel: he was one of those men who know the principal hotel by instinct. After dinner he asked Margaret if she wouldn't care for a turn on the Parade. She accepted, and could not repress a little tremor; it would be her first real love scene. But as she put on her hat she burst out laughing. Love was so unlike the article served up in books: the joy, though genuine, was different; the mystery an unexpected mystery. For one thing, Mr Wilcox still seemed a stranger.'

For a time they talked about the ring; then she said:

'Do you remember the Embankment at Chelsea? It can't be ten days ago.'

'Yes,' he said, laughing. 'And you and your sister were head and ears deep in some Quixotic scheme. Ah well!'

'I little thought then, certainly. Did you?'

'I don't know about that; I shouldn't like to say.'

'Why, was it earlier?' she cried. 'Did you think of me this way earlier! How extraordinarily interesting, Henry! Tell me.'

But Henry had no intention of telling. Perhaps he could not have told, for his mental states became obscure as soon as he had passed through them. He misliked the very word 'interesting,' connoting it with wasted energy and even with morbidity. Hard facts were enough for him.

'I didn't think of it,' she pursued. 'No; when you spoke to me in the drawing-room, that was practically the first. It was all so different from what it's supposed to be. On the stage or in books, a proposal is—how shall I put it?—a full-blown affair, a kind of bouquet; it loses its literal meaning. But in life a proposal really is a proposal—'

'By the way—'

'—a suggestion, a seed,' she concluded; and the thought flew away into darkness.

'I was thinking, if you didn't mind, that we ought to spend this evening in a business talk; there will be so much to settle.'

'I think so too. Tell me, in the first place, how did you get on with Tibby?'

'With your brother?'

'Yes, during cigarettes.'

'Oh, very well.'

'I am so glad,' she answered, a little surprised. 'What did you talk about? Me, presumably.'

'About Greece too.'

'Greece was a very good card, Henry. Tibby's only a boy still, and one has to pick and choose subjects a little. Well done.'

'I was telling him I have shares in a currant-farm near Calamata.'

'What a delightful thing to have shares in! Can't we go there for our honeymoon?'

'What to do?'

'To eat the currants. And isn't there marvellous scenery?'

'Moderately, but it's not the kind of place one could possibly go to with a lady.'

'Why not?'

'No hotels.'

'Some ladies do without hotels. Are you aware that Helen and I have walked alone over the Apennines, with our luggage on our backs?'

'I wasn't aware, and, if I can manage it, you will never do such a thing again.'

She said more gravely: 'You haven't found time for a talk with Helen yet, I suppose?'

'No.'

'Do, before you go. I am so anxious you two should be friends.'

'Your sister and I have always hit it off,' he said negligently. 'But we're drifting away from our business. Let me begin at the beginning. You know that Evie is going to marry Percy Cahill.'

'Dolly's uncle.'

'Exactly. The girl's madly in love with him. A very good sort of fellow, but he demands—and rightly—a suitable provision with her. And in the second place, you will naturally understand, there is Charles. Before leaving town, I wrote Charles a very careful letter. You see, he has an increasing family and increasing expenses, and the I. and W.A. is nothing particular just now, though capable of development.'

'Poor fellow!' murmured Margaret, looking out to sea, and not understanding.

'Charles being the elder son, some day Charles will have Howards End; but I am anxious, in my own happiness, not to be unjust to others.'

'Of course not,' she began, and then gave a little cry. 'You mean money. How stupid I am! Of course not!'

Oddly enough, he winced a little at the word. 'Yes. Money, since you put it so frankly. I am determined to be just to all—just to you, just to them. I am determined that my children shall have no case against me.'

'Be generous to them,' she said sharply. 'Bother justice!'

'I am determined—and have already written to Charles to that effect—'

'But how much have you got?'

'What?'

'How much have you a year? I've six hundred.'

'My income?'

'Yes. We must begin with how much you have, before we can settle how much you can give Charles. Justice, and even generosity, depend on that.'

'I must say you're a downright young woman,' he observed, patting her arm and laughing a little. 'What a question to spring on a fellow!'

'Don't you know your income? Or don't you want to tell it me?'

'I—'

'That's all right'—now she patted him—'don't tell me. I don't want to know. I can do the sum just as well by proportion. Divide your income into ten parts. How many parts would you give to Evie, how many to Charles, how many to Paul?'

'The fact is, my dear, I hadn't any intention of bothering you with details. I only wanted to let you know that—well, that something must be done for the others, and you've understood me perfectly, so let's pass on to the next point.'

'Yes, we've settled that,' said Margaret, undisturbed by his strategic blunderings. 'Go ahead; give away all you can, bearing in mind I've a clear six hundred. What a mercy it is to have all this money about one!'

'We've none too much, I assure you; you're marrying a poor man.'

'Helen wouldn't agree with me here,' she continued. 'Helen daren't slang the rich, being rich herself, but she would like to. There's an odd notion, that I haven't yet got hold of, running about at the back of her brain, that poverty is somehow "real." She dislikes all organization, and probably confuses wealth with the technique of wealth. Sovereigns in a stocking wouldn't bother her; cheques do. Helen is too relentless. One can't deal in her high-handed manner with the world.'

'There's this other point, and then I must go back to my hotel and write some letters. What's to be done now about the house in Ducie Street?'

'Keep it on—at least, it depends. When do you want to marry me?'

She raised her voice, as too often, and some youths, who were also taking the evening air, overheard her. 'Getting a bit hot, eh?' said one. Mr Wilcox turned on them, and said sharply, 'I say!' There was silence. 'Take care I don't report you to the police.' They moved away quietly enough, but were only biding their time, and the rest of the conversation was punctuated by peals of ungovernable laughter.

Lowering his voice and infusing a hint of reproof into it, he said: 'Evie will probably be married in September. We could scarcely think of anything before then.'

'The earlier the nicer, Henry. Females are not supposed to say such things, but the earlier the nicer.'

'How about September for us too?' he asked, rather dryly.

'Right. Shall we go into Ducie Street ourselves in September? Or shall we try to bounce Helen and Tibby into it? That's rather an idea. They are so unbusinesslike, we could make them do anything by judicious management. Look here—yes. We'll do that. And we ourselves could live at Howards End or Shropshire.'

He blew out his cheeks. 'Heavens! how you women do fly round! My head's in a whirl. Point by point, Margaret. Howards End's impossible. I let it to Hamar Bryce on a three years' agreement last March. Don't you remember? Oniton. Well, that is much, much too far away to rely on entirely. You will be able to be down there entertaining a certain amount, but we must have a house within easy reach of Town. Only Ducie Street has huge drawbacks. There's a mews behind.'

Margaret could not help laughing. It was the first she had heard of the mews behind Ducie Street. When she was a possible tenant it had suppressed itself, not consciously, but automatically. The breezy Wilcox manner, though genuine, lacked the clearness of vision that is imperative for truth. When Henry lived in Ducie Street he remembered the mews; when he tried to let he forgot it; and if anyone had remarked that the mews must be either there or not, he would have felt annoyed, and afterwards have found some opportunity of stigmatizing the speaker as academic. So does my grocer stigmatize me when I complain of the quality of his sultanas, and he answers in one breath that they are the best sultanas, and how can I expect the best sultanas at that price? It is a flaw inherent in the business mind, and Margaret may do well to be tender to it, considering all that the business mind has done for England.

'Yes, in summer especially, the mews is a serious nuisance. The smoking-room, too, is an abominable little den. The house opposite has been taken by operatic people. Ducie Street's going down, it's my private opinion.'

'How sad! It's only a few years since they built those pretty houses.'

'Shows things are moving. Good for trade.'

'I hate this continual flux in London. It is an epitome of us at our worst—eternal formlessness; all the qualities, good, bad, and indifferent, streaming away—streaming, streaming for ever. That's why I dread it so. I mistrust rivers, even in scenery. Now, the sea—'

'High tide, yes.'

'Hoy toid'—from the promenading youths.

'And these are the men to whom we give the vote,' observed Mr Wilcox, omitting to add that they were also the men to whom he gave work as clerks—work that scarcely encouraged them to grow into other men. 'However, they have their own lives and interests. Let's get on.'

He turned as he spoke, and prepared to see her back to The Bays. The business was over. His hotel was in the opposite direction, and if he accompanied her his letters would be late for the post. She implored him not to come, but he was obdurate.

'A nice beginning, if your aunt saw you slip in alone!'

'But I always do go about alone. Considering I've walked over the Apennines, it's common sense. You will make me so angry. I don't the least take it as a compliment.'

He laughed, and lit a cigar. 'It isn't meant as a compliment, my dear. I just won't have you going about in the dark. Such people about too! It's dangerous.'

'Can't I look after myself? I do wish—'

'Come along, Margaret; no wheedling.'

A younger woman might have resented his masterly ways, but Margaret had too firm a grip of life to make a fuss. She was, in her own way, as masterly. If he was a fortress she was a mountain peak, whom all might tread, but whom the snows made nightly virginal. Disdaining the heroic outfit, excitable in her methods, garrulous, episodical, shrill, she misled her lover much as she had misled her aunt. He mistook her fertility for weakness. He supposed her 'as clever as they make 'em,' but no more, not realizing that she was penetrating to the depths of his soul, and approving of what she found there.

And if insight were sufficient, if the inner life were the whole of life, their happiness had been assured.

They walked ahead briskly. The parade and the road after it were well lighted, but it was darker in Aunt Juley's garden. As they were going up by the side-paths, through some rhododendrons, Mr Wilcox, who was in front, said 'Margaret' rather huskily, turned, dropped his cigar, and took her in his arms.

She was startled, and nearly screamed, but recovered herself at once, and kissed with genuine love the lips that were pressed against her own. It was their first kiss, and when it was over he saw her safely to the door and rang the bell for her, but disappeared into the night before the maid answered it. On looking back, the incident displeased her. It was so isolated. Nothing in their previous conversation had heralded it, and, worse still, no tenderness had ensued. If a man cannot lead up to passion he can at all events lead down from it, and she had hoped, after her complaisance, for some interchange of gentle words. But he had hurried away as if ashamed, and for an instant she was reminded of Helen and Paul.

Chapter Twenty-one

Charles had just been scolding his Dolly. She deserved the scolding, and had bent before it, but her head, though bloody, was unsubdued, and her chirrupings began to mingle with his retreating thunder.

'You've woken the baby. I knew you would. (Rum-ti-foo, Rackety-tackety-Tompkin!) I'm not responsible for what Uncle Percy does, nor for anybody else or anything, so there!'

'Who asked him while I was away! Who asked my sister down to meet him! Who sent them out in the motor day after day?'

'Charles, that reminds me of some poem.'

'Does it indeed? We shall all be dancing to a very different music presently. Miss Schlegel has fairly got us on toast.'

'I could simply scratch that woman's eyes out, and to say it's my fault is most unfair.'

'It's your fault, and five months ago you admitted it.'

'I didn't.'

'You did.'

'Tootle, tootle, playing on the pootle!' exclaimed Dolly, suddenly devoting herself to the child.

'It's all very well to turn the conversation, but father would never have dreamt of marrying as long as Evie was there to make him comfortable. But you must needs start match-making. Besides, Cahill's too old.'

'Of course, if you're going to be rude to Uncle Percy—'

'Miss Schlegel always meant to get hold of Howards End, and, thanks to you, she's got it.'

'I call the way you twist things round and make them hang together most unfair. You couldn't have been nastier if you'd caught me flirting. Could he, diddums?'

'We're in a bad hole, and must make the best of it. I shall answer the pater's letter civilly. He's evidently anxious to do the decent thing. But I do not intend to forget these Schlegels in a hurry. As long as they're on their best behaviour—Dolly, are you listening?—we'll behave, too. But if I find them giving themselves airs, or monopolizing my father, or at all ill-treating him, or worrying him with their artistic beastliness, I intend to put my foot down, yes, firmly. Taking my mother's place! Heaven knows what poor old Paul will say when the news reaches him.'

The interlude closes. It has taken place in Charles's garden at Hilton. He and Dolly are sitting in deck-chairs, and their motor is regarding them placidly from its garage across the lawn. A short-frocked edition of Charles also regards them placidly; a perambulator edition is squeaking; a third edition is expected shortly. Nature is turning out Wilcoxes in this peaceful abode, so that they may inherit the earth.

Chapter Twenty-two

Margaret greeted her lord with peculiar tenderness on the morrow. Mature as he was, she might yet be able to help him to the building of the rainbow bridge that should connect the prose in us with the passion. Without it we are meaningless fragments, half monks, half beasts, unconnected arches that have never joined into a man. With it love is born, and alights on the highest curve, glowing against the grey, sober against the fire. Happy the man who sees from either aspect the glory of these outspread wings. The roads of his soul lie clear, and he and his friends shall find easy-going.

It was hard-going in the roads of Mr Wilcox's soul. From boyhood he had neglected them. 'I am not a fellow who bothers about my own inside.' Outwardly he was cheerful, reliable, and brave; but within, all had reverted to chaos, ruled, so far as it was ruled at all, by an incomplete asceticism. Whether as boy, husband, or widower, he had always the sneaking belief that bodily passion is bad, a belief that is desirable only when held passionately. Religion had confirmed him. The words that were read aloud on Sunday to him and to other respectable men were the words that had once kindled the souls of St Catharine and St Francis into a white-hot hatred of the carnal. He could not be as the saints and love the Infinite with a seraphic ardour, but he could be a little ashamed of loving a wife. 'Amabat, amare timebat.' And it was here that Margaret hoped to help him.

It did not seem so difficult. She need trouble him with no gift of her own. She would only point out the salvation that was latent in his own soul, and in the soul of every man. Only connect! That was the whole of her sermon. Only connect the prose and the passion, and both will be exalted, and human love will be seen at its height. Live in fragments no longer. Only connect, and the beast and the monk, robbed of the isolation that is life to either, will die.

Nor was the message difficult to give. It need not take the form of a good 'talking.' By quiet indications the bridge would be built and span their lives with beauty.

But she failed. For there was one quality in Henry for which she was never prepared, however much she reminded herself of it: his obtuseness. He simply did not notice things, and there was no more to be said. He never noticed that Helen and Frieda were hostile, or that Tibby was not interested in currant plantations; he never noticed the lights and shades that exist in the greyest conversation, the finger-posts, the milestones, the collisions, the illimitable views. Once—on another occasion—she scolded him about it. He was puzzled, but replied with a laugh: 'My motto is Concentrate. I've no intention of frittering away my strength on that sort of thing.' 'It isn't frittering away the strength,' she protested. 'It's enlarging the space in which you may be strong.' He answered: 'You're a clever little woman, but my motto's Concentrate.' And this morning he concentrated with a vengeance.

They met in the rhododendrons of yesterday. In the daylight the bushes were inconsiderable and the path was bright in the morning sun. She was with Helen, who had been ominously quiet since the affair was settled. 'Here we all are!' she cried, and took him by one hand, retaining her sister's in the other.

'Here we are. Good-morning, Helen.'

Helen replied, 'Good-morning, Mr Wilcox.'

'Henry, she has had such a nice letter from the queer, cross boy. Do you remember him? He had a sad moustache, but the back of his head was young.'

'I have had a letter too. Not a nice one—I want to talk it over with you:' for Leonard Bast was nothing to him now that she had given him her word; the triangle of sex was broken for ever.

'Thanks to your hint, he's clearing out of the Porphyrion.'

'Not a bad business that Porphyrion,' he said absently, as he took his own letter out of his pocket.

'Not a *bad*—' she exclaimed, dropping his hand. 'Surely, on Chelsea Embankment—'

'Here's our hostess. Good-morning, Mrs Munt. Fine rhododendrons. Good-morning, Frau Liesecke; we manage to grow flowers in England, don't we?'

'Not a *bad* business?'

'No. My letter's about Howards End. Bryce has been ordered abroad, and wants to sublet it. I am far from sure that I shall give him permission. There was no clause in the agreement. In my opinion, subletting is a mistake. If he can find me another tenant, whom I consider suitable, I may cancel the agreement. Morning, Schlegel. Don't you think that's better than subletting?'

Helen had dropped her hand now, and he had steered her past the whole party to the seaward side of the house. Beneath them was the bourgeois little bay, which must have yearned all through the centuries for just such a watering-place as Swanage to be built on its margin. The waves were colourless, and the Bournemouth steamer gave a further touch of insipidity, drawn up against the pier and hooting wildly for excursionists.

'When there is a sublet I find that damage—'

'Do excuse me, but about the Porphyrion. I don't feel easy–might I just bother you, Henry?'

Her manner was so serious that he stopped, and asked her a little sharply what she wanted.

'You said on Chelsea Embankment, surely, that it was a bad concern, so we advised this clerk to clear out. He writes this morning that he's taken our advice, and now you say it's not a bad concern.'

'A clerk who clears out of any concern, good or bad, without securing a berth somewhere else first, is a fool, and I've no pity for him.'

'He has not done that. He's going into a bank in Camden Town, he says. The salary's much lower, but he hopes to manage–a branch of Dempster's Bank. Is that all right?'

'Dempster! My goodness me, yes.'

'More than that the Porphyrion?'

'Yes, yes, yes; safe as houses–safer.'

'Very many thanks. I'm sorry–if you sublet—?'

'If he sublets, I shan't have the same control. In theory there should be no more damage done at Howards End; in practice there will be. Things may be done for which no money can compensate. For instance, I shouldn't want that fine wych-elm spoilt. It hangs— Margaret, we must go and see the old place some time. It's pretty in its way. We'll motor down and have lunch with Charles.'

'I should enjoy that,' said Margaret bravely.

'What about next Wednesday?'

'Wednesday? No, I couldn't well do that. Aunt Juley expects us to stop here another week at least.'

'But you can give that up now.'

'Er–no,' said Margaret, after a moment's thought.

'Oh, that'll be all right. I'll speak to her.'

'This visit is a high solemnity. My aunt counts on it year after year. She turns the house upside down for us; she invites our special friends–she scarcely knows Frieda, and we can't leave her on her hands. I missed one day, and she would be so hurt if I didn't stay the full ten.'

'But I'll say a word to her. Don't you bother.'

'Henry, I won't go. Don't bully me.'

'You want to see the house, though?'

'Very much–I've heard so much about it, one way or the other. Aren't there pigs' teeth in the wych-elm?'

'*Pig's teeth?*'

'And you chew the bark for toothache.'

'What a rum notion! Of course not!'

'Perhaps I have confused it with some other tree. There are still a great number of sacred trees in England, it seems.'

But he left her to intercept Mrs Munt, whose voice could be heard in the distance: to be intercepted himself by Helen.

'Oh, Mr Wilcox, about the Porphyrion—' she began, and went scarlet all over her face.

'It's all right,' called Margaret, catching them up. 'Dempster's Bank's better.'

'But I think you told us the Porphyrion was bad, and would smash before Christmas.'

'Did I? It was still outside the Tariff Ring, and had to take rotten policies. Lately it came in—safe as houses now.'

'In other words, Mr Bast need never have left it.'

'No, the fellow needn't.'

'—and needn't have started life elsewhere at a greatly reduced salary.'

'He only says "reduced,"' corrected Margaret, seeing trouble ahead.

'With a man so poor, every reduction must be great. I consider it a deplorable misfortune.'

Mr Wilcox, intent on his business with Mrs Munt, was going steadily on, but the last remark made him say: 'What? What's that? Do you mean that I'm responsible?'

'You're ridiculous, Helen.'

'You seem to think—' He looked at his watch. 'Let me explain the point to you. It is like this. You seem to assume, when a business concern is conducting a delicate negotiation, it ought to keep the public informed stage by stage. The Porphyrion, according to you, was bound to say, "I am trying all I can to get into the Tariff Ring. I am not sure that I shall succeed, but it is the only thing that will save me from insolvency, and I am trying." My dear Helen—'

'Is that your point? A man who had little money has less—that's mine.'

'I am grieved for your clerk. But it is all in the day's work. It's part of the battle of life.'

'A man who had little money,' she repeated, 'has less, owing to us. Under these circumstances I do not consider "the battle of life" a happy expression.'

'Oh come, come!' he protested pleasantly. 'You're not to blame. No one's to blame.'

'Is no one to blame for anything?'

'I wouldn't say that, but you're taking it far too seriously. Who is this fellow?'

'We have told you about the fellow twice already,' said Helen. 'You have even met the fellow. He is very poor and his wife is an extravagant imbecile. He is capable of better things. We—we, the upper classes—thought we would help him from the height of our superior knowledge—and here's the result!'

He raised his finger. 'Now, a word of advice.'

'I require no more advice.'

'A word of advice. Don't take up that sentimental attitude over the poor. See that she doesn't, Margaret. The poor are poor, and one's sorry for them, but there it is. As civilization moves forward, the shoe is bound to pinch in places, and it's absurd to pretend that anyone is responsible personally. Neither you, nor I, nor my informant, nor the man who informed him, nor the directors of the Porphyrion, are to blame for this clerk's loss of salary.'

It's just the shoe pinching—no one can help it; and it might easily have been worse.'

Helen quivered with indignation.

'By all means subscribe to charities—subscribe to them largely—but don't get carried away by absurd schemes of Social Reform. I see a good deal behind the scenes, and you can take it from me that there is no Social Question—except for a few journalists who try to get a living out of the phrase. There are just rich and poor, as there always have been and always will be. Point me out a time when men have been equal—'

'I didn't say—'

'Point me out a time when desire for equality has made them happier. No, no. You can't. There always have been rich and poor. I'm no fatalist. Heaven forbid! But our civilization is moulded by great impersonal forces' (his voice grew complacent; it always did when he eliminated the personal), 'and there always will be rich and poor. You can't deny it' (and now it was a respectful voice)—'and you can't deny that, in spite of all, the tendency of civilization has on the whole been upward.'

'Owing to God, I suppose,' flashed Helen.

He stared at her.

'You grab the dollars. God does the rest.'

It was no good instructing the girl if she was going to talk about God in that neurotic modern way. Fraternal to the last, he left her for the quieter company of Mrs Munt. He thought, 'She rather reminds me of Dolly.'

Helen looked out at the sea.

'Don't ever discuss political economy with Henry,' advised her sister. 'It'll only end in a cry.'

'But he must be one of those men who have reconciled science with religion,' said Helen slowly. 'I don't like those men. They are scientific themselves, and talk of the survival of the fittest, and cut down the salaries of their clerks, and stunt the independence of all who may menace their comfort, but yet they believe that somehow good—it is always that sloppy "somehow"—will be the outcome, and that in some mystical way the Mr Basts of the future will benefit because the Mr Basts of to-day are in pain.'

'He is such a man in theory. But oh, Helen, in theory!'

'But oh, Meg, what a theory!'

'Why should you put things so bitterly, dearie?'

'Because I'm an old maid,' said Helen, biting her lip. 'I can't think why I go on like this myself.' She shook off her sister's hand and went into the house. Margaret, distressed at the day's beginning, followed the Bournemouth steamer with her eyes. She saw that Helen's nerves were exasperated by the unlucky Bast business beyond the bounds of politeness. There might at any minute be a real explosion, which even Henry would notice. Henry must be removed.

'Margaret!' her aunt called. 'Magsy! It isn't true, surely, what Mr Wilcox says, that you want to go away early next week?'

'Not "want,"' was Margaret's prompt reply; 'but there is so much to be settled, and I do want to see the Charles'.'

'But going away without taking the Weymouth trip, or even the Lulworth?' said Mrs Munt, coming nearer. 'Without going once more up Nine Barrows Down?'

'I'm afraid so.'

Mr Wilcox rejoined her with, 'Good! I did the breaking of the ice.'

A wave of tenderness came over her. She put a hand on either shoulder, and looked deeply into the black, bright eyes. What was behind their competent stare? She knew, but was not disquieted.

Chapter Twenty-three

Margaret had no intention of letting things slide, and the evening before she left Swanage she gave her sister a thorough scolding. She censured her, not for disapproving of the engagement, but for throwing over her disapproval a veil of mystery. Helen was equally frank. 'Yes,' she said, with the air of one looking inwards, 'there is a mystery. I can't help it. It's not my fault. It's the way life has been made.' Helen in those days was over-interested in the subconscious self. She exaggerated the Punch and Judy aspect of life, and spoke of mankind as puppets, whom an invisible showman twitches into love and war. Margaret pointed out that if she dwelt on this she, too, would eliminate the personal. Helen was silent for a minute, and then burst into a queer speech, which cleared the air. 'Go on and marry him. I think you're splendid; and if anyone can pull it off, you will.' Margaret denied that there was anything to 'pull off,' but she continued: 'Yes, there is, and I wasn't up to it with Paul. I can only do what's easy. I can only entice and be enticed. I can't, and won't, attempt difficult relations. If I marry, it will either be a man who's strong enough to boss me or whom I'm strong enough to boss. So I shan't ever marry, for there aren't such men. And Heaven help anyone whom I do marry, for I shall certainly run away from him before you can say "Jack Robinson." There! Because I'm uneducated. But you, you're different; you're a heroine.'

'Oh, Helen! Am I? Will it be as dreadful for poor Henry as all that?'

'You mean to keep proportion, and that's heroic, it's Greek, and I don't see why it shouldn't succeed with you. Go on and fight with him and help him. Don't ask *me* for help, or even for sympathy. Henceforward I'm going my own way. I mean to be thorough, because thoroughness is easy. I mean to dislike your husband, and to tell him so. I mean to make no concessions to Tibby. If Tibby wants to live with me, he must lump me. I mean to love *you* more than ever. Yes, I do. You and I have built up something real, because it is purely spiritual. There's no veil of mystery over us. Unreality and mystery begin as soon as one touches the body. The popular view is, as usual, exactly the wrong one. Our bothers are over tangible things—money, husbands, house-hunting. But Heaven will work of itself.'

Margaret was grateful for this expression of affection, and answered, 'Perhaps.' All vistas close in the unseen—no one doubts it—but Helen closed them rather too quickly for her taste. At every turn of speech one was confronted with reality and the absolute. Perhaps Margaret grew too old for metaphysics, perhaps Henry was weaning her from them, but she felt that there was something a little unbalanced in the mind that so readily shreds the visible. The business man who assumes that this life is everything, and the mystic who asserts that it is nothing, fail, on this side and on that, to hit the truth. 'Yes, I see, dear; it's about halfway between,' Aunt Juley had hazarded in earlier years. No; truth, being alive, was not halfway between anything. It was only to be found by continuous excursions into either realm, and though proportion is the final secret, to espouse it at the outset is to insure sterility.

Helen, agreeing here, disagreeing there, would have talked till midnight, but Margaret, with her packing to do, focussed the conversation on Henry. She might abuse Henry behind his back, but please would she always be civil to him in company? 'I definitely dislike him, but I'll do what I can,' promised Helen. 'Do what you can with my friends in return.'

This conversation made Margaret easier. Their inner life was so safe that they could bargain over externals in a way that would have been incredible to Aunt Juley, and impossible for Tibby or Charles. There are moments when the inner life actually 'pays,' when years of self-scrutiny, conducted for no ulterior motive, are suddenly of practical use. Such moments are still rare in the West; that they come at all promises a fairer future. Margaret, though unable to understand her sister, was assured against estrangement, and returned to London with a more peaceful mind.

The following morning, at eleven o'clock, she presented herself at the offices of the Imperial and West African Rubber Company. She was glad to go there, for Henry had implied his business rather than described it, and the formlessness and vagueness that one associates with Africa itself had hitherto brooded over the main sources of his wealth. Not that a visit to the office cleared things up. There was just the ordinary surface scum of ledgers and polished counters and brass bars that began and stopped for no possible reason, of electric-light globes blossoming in triplets, of little rabbit-hutches faced with glass or wire, of little rabbits. And even when she penetrated to the inner depths, she found only the ordinary table and Turkey carpet, and though the map over the fireplace did depict a helping of West Africa, it was a very ordinary map. Another map hung opposite, on which the whole continent appeared, looking like a whale marked out for a blubber, and by its side was a door, shut, but Henry's voice came through it, dictating a 'strong' letter. She might have been at the Porphyrion, or Dempster's Bank, or her own wine-merchant's. Everything seems just alike in these days. But perhaps she was seeing the Imperial side of the company rather than its West African, the Imperialism always had been one of her difficulties.

'One minute!' called Mr Wilcox on receiving her name. He touched a bell, the effect of which was to produce Charles.

Charles had written his father an adequate letter—more adequate than

Evie's, through which a girlish indignation throbbed. And he greeted his future stepmother with propriety.

'I hope that my wife—how do you do?—will give you a decent lunch,' was his opening. 'I left instructions, but we live in a rough-and-ready way. She expects you back to tea, too, after you have had a look at Howards End. I wonder what you'll think of the place. I wouldn't touch it with tongs myself. Do sit down! It's a measly little place.'

'I shall enjoy seeing it,' said Margaret, feeling, for the first time, shy.

'You'll see it at its worst, for Bryce decamped abroad last Monday without even arranging for a charwoman to clear up after him. I never saw such a disgraceful mess. It's unbelievable. He wasn't in the house a month.'

'I've more than a little bone to pick with Bryce,' called Henry from the inner chamber.

'Why did he go so suddenly?'

'Invalid type; couldn't sleep.'

'Poor fellow!'

'Poor fiddlesticks!' said Mr Wilcox, joining them. 'He had the impudence to put up notice-boards without as much as saying with your leave or by your leave. Charles flung them down.'

'Yes, I flung them down,' said Charles modestly.

'I've sent a telegram after him, and a pretty sharp one, too. He, and he in person, is responsible for the upkeep of that house for the next three years.'

'The keys are at the farm; we wouldn't have the keys.'

'Quite right.'

'Dolly would have taken them, but I was in, fortunately.'

'What's Mr Bryce like?' asked Margaret.

But nobody cared. Mr Bryce was the tenant, who had no right to sublet; to have defined him further was a waste of time. On his misdeeds they descanted profusely, until the girl who had been typing the strong letter came out with it. Mr Wilcox added his signature. 'Now we'll be off,' said he.

A motor-drive, a form of felicity detested by Margaret, awaited her. Charles saw them in, civil to the last, and in a moment the offices of the Imperial and West African Rubber Company faded away. But it was not an impressive drive. Perhaps the weather was to blame, being grey and banked high with weary clouds. Perhaps Hertfordshire is scarcely intended for motorists. Did not a gentleman once motor so quickly through Westmoreland that he missed it? and if Westmoreland can be missed, it will fare ill with a county whose delicate structure particularly needs the attentive eye. Hertfordshire is England at its quietest, with little emphasis of river and hill; it is England meditative. If Drayton were with us again to write a new edition of his incomparable poem, he would sing the nymphs of Hertfordshire as indeterminate of feature, with hair obfuscated by the London smoke. Their eyes would be sad, and averted from their fate towards the Northern flats, their leader not Isis or Sabrina, but the slowly flowing Lea. No glory of raiment would be theirs, no urgency of dance; but they would be real nymphs.

The chauffeur could not travel as quickly as he had hoped, for the Great

North Road was full of Easter traffic. But we went quite quick enough for Margaret, a poor-spirited creature, who had chickens and children on the brain.

'They're all right,' said Mr Wilcox. 'They'll learn—like the swallows and the telegraph-wires.'

'Yes, but, while they're learning—'

'The motor's come to stay,' he answered. 'One must get about. There's a pretty church—oh, you aren't sharp enough. Well, look, out, if the road worries you—right outward at the scenery.'

She looked at the scenery. It heaved and merged like porridge. Presently it congealed. They had arrived.

Charles's house on the left; on the right the swelling forms of the Six Hills. Their appearance in such a neighbourhood surprised her. They interrupted the stream of residences that was thickening up towards Hilton. Beyond them she saw meadows and a wood, and beneath them she settled that soldiers of the best kind lay buried. She hated war and liked soldiers—it was one of her amiable inconsistencies.

But here was Dolly, dressed up to the nines, standing at the door to greet them, and here were the first drops of the rain. They ran in gaily and, after a long wait in the drawing-room, sat down to the rough-and-ready lunch, every dish in which concealed or exuded cream. Mr Bryce was the chief topic of conversation. Dolly described his visit with the key, while her father-in-law gave satisfaction by chaffing her and contradicting all she said. It was evidently the custom to laugh at Dolly. He chaffed Margaret, too, and Margaret, roused from a grave meditation, was pleased, and chaffed him back. Dolly seemed surprised, and eyed her curiously. After lunch the two children came down. Margaret disliked babies, but hit it off better with the two-year-old, and sent Dolly into fits of laughter by talking sense to him. 'Kiss then now, and come away,' said Mr Wilcox. She came, but refused to kiss them: it was such hard luck on the little things, she said, and though Dolly proffered Chorly-worly and Porgly-woggles in turn, she was obdurate.

By this time it was raining steadily. The car came round with the hood up, and again she lost all sense of space. In a few minutes they stopped, and Crane opened the door of the car.

'What's happened?' asked Margaret.

'What do you suppose?' said Henry.

A little porch was close up against her face.

'Are we there already?'

'We are.'

'Well, I never! In years ago it seemed so far away.'

Smiling, but somehow disillusioned, she jumped out, and her impetus carried her to the front-door. She was about to open it, when Henry said: 'That's no good; it's locked. Who's got the key?'

As he had himself forgotten to call for the key at the farm, no one replied. He also wanted to know who had left the front gate open, since a cow had strayed in from the road, and was spoiling the croquet lawn. Then he said rather crossly: 'Margaret, you wait in the dry. I'll go down for the key. It isn't a hundred yards.'

'Mayn't I come too?'

'No; I shall be back before I'm gone.'

Then the car turned away, and it was as if a curtain had risen. For the second time that day she saw the appearance of the earth.

There were the greengage-trees that Helen had once described, there the tennis lawn, there the hedge that would be glorious with dog-roses in June, but the vision now was of black and palest green. Down by the dell-hole more vivid colours were awakening, and Lent lilies stood sentinel on its margin, or advanced in battalions over the grass. Tulips were a tray of jewels. She could not see the wych-elm tree, but a branch of the celebrated vine, studded with velvet knobs, had covered the porch. She was struck by the fertility of the soil; she had seldom been in a garden where the flowers looked so well, and even the weeds she was idly plucking out of the porch were intensely green. Why had poor Mr Bryce fled from all this beauty? For she had already decided that the place was beautiful.

'Naughty cow! Go away!' cried Margaret to the cow, but without indignation.

Harder came the rain, pouring out of a windless sky, and spattering up from the notice-boards of the house-agents, which lay in a row on the lawn where Charles had hurled them. She must have interviewed Charles in another world—where one did have interviews. How Helen would revel in such a notion! Charles dead, all people dead, nothing alive but houses and gardens. The obvious dead, the intangible alive, and—no connection at all between them! Margaret smiled. Would that her own fancies were as clear-cut! Would that she could deal as high-handedly with the world! Smiling and sighing, she laid her hand upon the door. It opened. The house was not locked up at all.

She hesitated. Ought she to wait for Henry? He felt strongly about property, and might prefer to show her over himself. On the other hand, he had told her to keep in the dry, and the porch was beginning to drip. So she went in, and the draught from inside slammed the door behind.

Desolation greeted her. Dirty finger-prints were on the hall-windows, flue and rubbish on its unwashed boards. The civilization of luggage had been here for a month, and then decamped. Dining-room and drawing-room—right and left—were guessed only by their wall-papers. They were just rooms where one could shelter from the rain. Across the ceiling of each ran a great beam. The dining-room and hall revealed theirs openly, but the drawing-room's was match-boarded—because the facts of life must be concealed from ladies? Drawing-room, dining-room, and hall—how petty the names sounded! Here were simply three rooms where children could play and friends shelter from the rain. Yes, and they were beautiful.

Then she opened one of the doors opposite—there were two—and exchanged wall-papers for whitewash. It was the servants' part, though she scarcely realized that: just rooms again, where friends might shelter. The garden at the back was full of flowering cherries and plums. Farther on were hints of the meadow and a black cliff of pines. Yes, the meadow was beautiful.

Penned in by the desolate weather, she recaptured the sense of space which the motor had tried to rob from her. She remembered again that ten square miles are not ten times as wonderful as one square mile, that a thousand square miles are not practically the same as heaven. The phantom of bigness, which London encourages, was laid for ever when she paced from the hall at Howards End to its kitchen and heard the rains run this way and that where the watershed of the roof divided them.

Now Helen came to her mind, scrutinizing half Wessex from the ridge of the Purbeck Downs, and saying: 'You will have to lose something.' She was not so sure. For instance, she would double her kingdom by opening the door that concealed the stairs.

Now she thought of the map of Africa; of empires; of her father; of the two supreme nations, streams of whose life warmed her blood, but, mingling, had cooled her brain. She paced back into the hall, and as she did so the house reverberated.

'Is that you, Henry?' she called.

There was no answer, but the house reverberated again.

'Henry, have you got in?'

But it was the heart of the house beating, faintly at first, then loudly, martially. It dominated the rain.

It is the starved imagination, not the well-nourished, that is afraid. Margaret flung open the doors to the stairs. A noise as of drums seemed to deafen her. A woman, an old woman, was descending, with figure erect, with face impassive, with lips that parted and said dryly:

'Oh! Well, I took you for Ruth Wilcox.'

Margaret stammered: 'I— Mrs Wilcox—I?'

'In fancy, of course—in fancy. You had her way of walking. Good-day.' And the old woman passed out into the rain.

Chapter Twenty-four

'It gave her quite a turn,' said Mr Wilcox, when retailing the incident to Dolly at tea-time. 'None of you girls have any nerves, really. Of course, a word from me put it all right, but silly old Miss Avery—she frightened you, didn't she, Margaret? There you stood clutching a bunch of weeds. She might have said something, instead of coming down the stairs with that alarming bonnet on. I passed her as I came in. Enough to make the car shy. I believe Miss Avery goes in for being a character; some old maids do.' He lit a cigarette. 'It is their last resource. Heaven knows what she was doing in the place; but that's Bryce's business, not mine.'

'I wasn't as foolish as you suggest,' said Margaret. 'She only startled me, for the house had been silent so long.'

'Did you take her for a spook?' asked Dolly, for whom 'spooks' and 'going to church' summarized the unseen.

'Not exactly.'

'She really did frighten you,' said Henry, who was far from discouraging timidity in females. 'Poor Margaret! And very naturally. Uneducated classes are so stupid.'

'Is Miss Avery uneducated classes?' Margaret asked, and found herself looking at the decoration scheme of Dolly's drawing-room.

'She's just one of the crew at the farm. People like that always assume things. She assumed you'd know who she was. She left all the Howards End keys in the front lobby, and assumed that you'd seen them as you came in, that you'd lock up the house when you'd gone, and would bring them down to her. And there was her niece hunting for them down at the farm. Lack of education makes people very casual. Hilton was full of woman like Miss Avery once.'

'I shouldn't have disliked it, perhaps.'

'Or Miss Avery giving me a wedding present,' said Dolly.

Which was illogical but interesting. Through Dolly, Margaret was destined to learn a good deal.

'But Charles said I must try not to mind, because she had known his grandmother.'

'As usual, you've got the story wrong, my good Dorothea.'

'I meant great-grandmother—the one who left Mrs Wilcox the house. Weren't both of them and Miss Avery friends when Howards End, too, was a farm?'

Her father-in-law blew out a shaft of smoke. His attitude to his dead wife was curious. He would allude to her, and hear her discussed, but never mentioned her by name. Nor was he interested in the dim, bucolic past. Dolly was—for the following reason.

'Then hadn't Mrs Wilcox a brother—or was it an uncle? Anyhow, he popped the question, and Miss Avery, she said "No." Just imagine, if she'd said "Yes," she would have been Charles's aunt. (Oh, I say, that's rather good! "Charlie's Aunt"! I must chaff him about that this evening.) And the man went out and was killed. Yes, I'm certain I've got it right now. Tom Howard—he was the last of them.'

'I believe so,' said Mr Wilcox negligently.

'I say! Howards End—Howards Ended!' cried Dolly. 'I'm rather on the spot this evening, eh?'

'I wish you'd ask whether Crane's ended.'

'Oh, Mr Wilcox, how *can* you?'

'Because, if he has had enough tea, we ought to go.—Dolly's a good little woman,' he continued, 'but a little of her goes a long way. I couldn't live near her if you paid me.'

Margaret smiled. Though presenting a firm front to outsiders, no Wilcox could live near, or near the possessions of, any other Wilcox. They had the colonial spirit, and were always making for some spot where the white man might carry his burden unobserved. Of course, Howards End was impossible, so long as the younger couple were established in Hilton. His objections to the house were plain as daylight now.

Crane had had enough tea, and was sent to the garage, where their car had been trickling muddy water over Charles's. The downpour had surely penetrated the Six Hills by now, bringing news of our restless civilization. 'Curious mounds,' said Henry, 'but in with you now; another time.' He had to be up in London by seven–if possible, by six-thirty. Once more she lost the sense of space; once more trees, houses, people, animals, hills, merged and heaved into one dirtiness, and she was at Wickham Place.

Her evening was pleasant. The sense of flux which had haunted her all the year disappeared for a time. She forgot the luggage and the motor-cars, and the hurrying men who know so much and connect so little. She recaptured the sense of space, which is the basis of all earthly beauty, and, starting from Howards End, she attempted to realize England. She failed–visions do not come when we try, though they may come through trying. But an unexpected love of the island awoke in her, connecting on this side with the joys of the flesh, on that with the inconceivable. Helen and her father had known this love, poor Leonard Bast was groping after it, but it had been hidden from Margaret till this afternoon. It had certainly come through the house and old Miss Avery. Through them: the notion of 'through' persisted; her mind trembled towards a conclusion which only the unwise have put into words. Then, veering back into warmth, it dwelt on ruddy bricks, flowering plum-trees, and all the tangible joys of spring.

Henry, after allaying her agitation, had taken her over his property, and had explained to her the use and dimensions of the various rooms. He had sketched the history of the little estate. 'It is so unlucky,' ran the monologue, 'that money wasn't put into it about fifty years ago. Then it had four–five–times the land–thirty acres at least. One could have made something out of it then–a small park, or at all events shrubberies, and rebuilt the house farther away from the road. What's the good of taking it in hand now? Nothing but the meadow left, and even that was heavily mortgaged when I first had to do with things–yes, and the house too. Oh, it was no joke.' She saw two women as he spoke, one old, the other young, watching their inheritance melt away. She saw them greet him as a deliverer. 'Mismanagement did it–besides, the days for small farms are over. It doesn't pay–except with intensive cultivation. Small holdings, back to the land–ah! philanthropic bunkum. Take it as a rule that nothing pays on a small scale. Most of the land you see (they were standing at an upper window, the only one which faced west) belongs to the people at the Park–they made their pile over copper–good chaps. Avery's Farm, Sishe's–what they call the Common, where you see that ruined oak–one after the other fell in, and so did this, as near as is no matter.' But Henry had saved it; without fine feelings or deep insight, but he had saved it, and she loved him for the deed. 'When I had more control I did what I could: sold off the two and a half animals, and the mangy pony, and the superannuated tools; pulled down the outhouses; drained; thinned out I don't know how many guelder-roses and elder-trees; and inside the house I turned the old kitchen into a hall, and made a kitchen behind where the dairy was. Garage and so on came later. But one could still tell it's been an old farm. And yet it isn't the place that would fetch one of your artistic crew.' No, it wasn't; and if he did not quite understand it, the artistic crew would still less: it was English, and the wych-elm that she saw from the window was an English tree. No report had prepared her for its peculiar glory. It was neither warrior, nor lover, nor god; in none of these rôles do the English excel. It was a comrade, bending over the house, strength and adventure in its roots, but in its utmost fingers tenderness, and the girth, that a dozen men could not have spanned, became in the end evanescent, till pale bud clusters seemed to float in the air. It was a comrade. House and tree transcended any similes of sex. Margaret thought of them now, and was to think of them through many a windy night and London day, but to compare either to man, to woman, always dwarfed the vision. Yet they kept within limits of the human. Their message was not of eternity, but of hope on this side of the grave. As she stood in the one, gazing at the other, truer relationship had gleamed.

Another touch, and the account of her day is finished. They entered the garden for a minute, and to Mr Wilcox's surprise she was right. Teeth, pigs' teeth, could be seen in the bark of the wych-elm tree—just the white tips of them showing. 'Extraordinary!' he cried. 'Who told you?'

'I heard of it one winter in London,' was her answer, for she, too, avoided mentioning Mrs Wilcox by name.

Chapter Twenty-five

Evie heard of her father's engagement when she was in for a tennis tournament, and her play went simply to pot. That she should marry and leave him had seemed natural enough; that he, left alone, should do the same was deceitful; and now Charles and Dolly said that it was all her fault. 'But I never dreamt of such a thing,' she grumbled. 'Dad took me to call now and then, and made me ask her to Simpson's. Well, I'm altogether off dad.' It was also an insult to their mother's memory; there they were agreed, and Evie had the idea of returning Mrs Wilcox's lace and jewellery 'as a protest.' Against what it would protest she was not clear; but being only eighteen, the idea of renunciation appealed to her, the more as she did not care for jewellery or lace. Dolly then suggested that she and Uncle Percy should pretend to break off their engagement, and then perhaps Mr Wilcox would quarrel with Miss Schlegel, and break off his; or Paul might be cabled for. But at this point Charles told them not to talk nonsense. So Evie settled to marry as soon as possible; it was no good hanging about with these Schlegels eyeing her. The date of her wedding was consequently put forward from September to August, and in the intoxication of presents she recovered much of her good-humour.

Margaret found that she was expected to figure at this function, and to figure largely; it would be such an opportunity, said Henry, for her to get to know his set. Sir James Bidder would be there, and all the Cahills and the Fussells, and his sister-in-law, Mrs Warrington Wilcox, had fortunately got back from her tour round the world. Henry she loved, but his set promised to be another matter. He had not the knack of surrounding himself with nice people—indeed, for a man of ability and virtue his choice had been singularly unfortunate; he had no guiding principle beyond a certain preference for mediocrity; he was content to settle one of the greatest things in life haphazard, and so, while his investments went right, his friends generally went wrong. She would be told, 'Oh, So-and-so's a good sort—a thundering good sort,' and find, on meeting him, that he was a brute or a bore. If Henry had shown real affection, she would have understood, for affection explains everything. But he seemed without sentiment. The 'thundering good sort' might at any moment become 'a fellow for whom I never did have much use, and have less now,' and be shaken off cheerily into oblivion. Margaret had done the same as a schoolgirl. Now she never forgot anyone for whom she had once cared; she connected, though the connection might be bitter, and she hoped that some day Henry would do the same.

Evie was not to be married from Ducie Street. She had a fancy for something rural, and, besides, no one would be in London then, so she left her boxes for a few weeks at Oniton Grange, and her banns were duly published in the parish church, and for a couple of days the little town, dreaming between the ruddy hills, was roused by the clang of our civilization, and drew up by the roadside to let the motors pass. Oniton had been a discovery of Mr Wilcox's—a discovery of which he was not altogether proud. It was up towards the Welsh border, and so difficult of access that he had concluded it must be something special. A ruined castle stood in the grounds. But having got there, what was one to do? The shooting was bad, the fishing indifferent, and women-folk reported the scenery as nothing much. The place turned out to be in the wrong part of Shropshire, damn it, and though he never damned his own property aloud, he was only waiting to get it off his hands, and then to let fly. Evie's marriage was its last appearance in public. As soon as a tenant was found, it became a house for which he never had had much use, and had less now, and, like Howards End, faded into Limbo.

But on Margaret Oniton was destined to make a lasting impression. She regarded it as her future home, and was anxious to start straight with the clergy, etc., and, if possible, to see something of the local life. It was a market-town—as tiny a one as England possesses—and had for ages served that lonely valley, and guarded our marches against the Kelt. In spite of the occasion, in spite of the numbling hilarity that greeted her as soon as she got into the reserved saloon at Paddington, her senses were awake and watching, and though Oniton was to prove one of her innumerable false starts, she never forgot it, nor the things that happened there.

The London party only numbered eight—the Fussells, father and son, two Anglo-Indian ladies named Mrs Plynlimmon and Lady Edser, Mrs

Warrington Wilcox and her daughter, and, lastly, the little girl, very smart and quiet, who figures at so many weddings, and who kept a watchful eye on Margaret, the bride-elect. Dolly was absent—a domestic event detained her at Hilton; Paul had cabled a humorous message; Charles was to meet them with a trio of motors at Shrewsbury. Helen had refused her invitation; Tibby had never answered his. The management was excellent, as was to be expected with anything that Henry undertook; one was conscious of his sensible and generous brain in the background. They were his guests as soon as they reached the train; a special label for their luggage; a courier; a special lunch; they had only to look pleasant and, where possible, pretty. Margaret thought with dismay of her own nuptials—presumably under the management of Tibby. 'Mr Theobald Schlegel and Miss Helen Schlegel request the pleasure of Mrs Plynlimmon's company on the occasion of the marriage of their sister Margaret.' The formula was incredible, but it must soon be printed and sent, and though Wickham Place need not compete with Oniton, it must feed its guests properly, and provide them with sufficient chairs. Her wedding would either be ramshackly or bourgeois—she hoped the latter. Such an affair as the present, staged with a deftness that was almost beautiful, lay beyond her powers and those of her friends.

The low rich purr of a Great Western express is not the worst background for conversation, and the journey passed pleasantly enough. Nothing could have exceeded the kindness of the two men. They raised windows for some ladies, and lowered them for others, they rang the bell for the servant, they identified the colleges as the train slipped past Oxford, they caught books or bag-purses in the act of tumbling on to the floor. Yet there was nothing finicking about their politeness: it had the Public School touch, and, though sedulous, was virile. More battles than Waterloo have been won on our playing-fields, and Margaret bowed to a charm of which she did not wholly approve, and said nothing when the Oxford colleges were identified wrongly. 'Male and female created He them'; the journey to Shrewsbury confirmed this questionable statement, and the long glass saloon, that moved so easily and felt so comfortable, became a forcing-house for the idea of sex.

At Shrewsbury came fresh air. Margaret was all for sightseeing, and while the others were finishing their tea at the Raven, she annexed a motor and hurried over the astonishing city. Her chauffeur was not the faithful Crane, but an Italian, who dearly loved making her late. Charles, watch in hand, though with a level brow, was standing in front of the hotel when they returned. It was perfectly all right, he told her; she was by no means the last. And then he dived into the coffee-room, and she heard him say, 'For God's sake, hurry the women up; we shall never be off,' and Albert Fussell reply, 'Not I; I've done my share,' and Colonel Fussell opine that the ladies were getting themselves up to kill. Presently Myra (Mrs Warrington's daughter) appeared, and as she was his cousin, Charles blew her up a little: she had been changing her smart travelling hat for a smart motor hat. Then Mrs Warrington herself, leading the quiet child; the two Anglo-Indian ladies were always last. Maids, courier, heavy luggage, had already gone on by a branch-line to a station nearer Oniton, but there were five hat-boxes and four dressing-bags to be packed, and five dust-cloaks to be put on, and to be put off at the last moment, because Charles declared them not necessary. The men presided over everything with unfailing good-humour. By half-past five the party was ready, and went out of Shrewsbury by the Welsh Bridge.

Shropshire had not the reticence of Hertfordshire. Though robbed of half its magic by swift movement, it still conveyed the sense of hills. They were nearing the buttresses that force the Severn eastward and make it an English stream, and the sun, sinking over the Sentinels of Wales, was straight in their eyes. Having picked up another guest, they turned southward, avoiding the greater mountains, but conscious of an occasional summit, rounded and mild, whose colouring differed in quality from that of the lower earth, and whose contours altered more slowly. Quiet mysteries were in progress behind those tossing horizons: the West, as ever, was retreating with some secret which may not be worth the discovery, but which no practical man will ever discover.

They spoke of Tariff Reform.

Mrs Warrington was just back from the Colonies. Like many other critics of Empire, her mouth had been stopped with food, and she could only exclaim at the hospitality with which she had been received and warn the Mother Country against trifling with young Titans. 'They threaten to cut the painter,' she cried, 'and where shall we be then? Miss Schlegel, you'll undertake to keep Henry sound about Tariff Reform? It is our last hope.'

Margaret playfully confessed herself on the other side, and they began to quote from their respective hand-books while the motor carried them deep into the hills. Curious these were rather than impressive, for their outlines lacked beauty, and the pink fields on their summits suggested the handkerchiefs of a giant spread out to dry. An occasional outcrop of rock, an occasional wood, an occasional 'forest,' treeless and brown, all hinted at wildness to follow, but the main colour was an agricultural green. The air grew cooler; they had surmounted the last gradient, and Oniton lay below them with its church, its radiating houses, its castle, its river-girt peninsula. Close to the castle was a grey mansion, unintellectual but kindly, stretching with its grounds across the peninsula's neck—the sort of mansion that was built all over England in the beginning of the last century, while architecture was still an expression of the national character. That was the Grange, remarked Albert, over his shoulder, and then he jammed the break on, and the motor slowed down and stopped. 'I'm sorry,' said he, turning round. 'Do you mind getting out—by the door on the right. Steady on.'

'What's happened?' asked Mrs Warrington.

Then the car behind them drew up, and the voice of Charles was heard saying: 'Get out the women at once.' There was a concourse of males, and Margaret and her companions were hustled out and received into the second car. What had happened? As it started off again, the door of a cottage opened, and a girl screamed wildly at them.

'What is it?' the ladies cried.

Charles drove them a hundred yards without speaking. Then he said: 'It's all right. Your car just touched a dog.'

'But stop!' cried Margaret, horrified.

'It didn't hurt him.'

'Didn't really hurt him?' asked Myra.

'No.'

'Do *please* stop!' said Margaret, leaning forward. She was standing up in the car, the other occupants holding her knees to steady her. 'I want to go back, please.'

Charles took no notice.

'We've left Mr Fussell behind,' said another: 'and Angelo, and Crane.'

'Yes, but no woman.'

'I expect a little of'—Mrs Warrington scratched her palm—'will be more to the point than one of us!'

'The insurance company see to that,' remarked Charles, 'and Albert will do the talking.'

'I want to go back, though, I say!' repeated Margaret, getting angry.

Charles took no notice. The motor, loaded with refugees, continued to travel very slowly down the hill. 'The men are there,' chorused the others. 'Men will see to it.'

'The men *can't* see to it. Oh, this is ridiculous! Charles, I ask you to stop.'

'Stopping's no good,' drawled Charles.

'Isn't it?' said Margaret, and jumped straight out of the car.

She fell on her knees, cut her gloves, shook her hat over her ear. Cries of alarm followed her. 'You've hurt yourself,' exclaimed Charles, jumping after her.

'Of course I've hurt myself!' she retorted.

'May I ask what—'

'There's nothing to ask,' said Margaret.

'Your hand's bleeding.'

'I know.'

'I'm in for a frightful row from the pater.'

'You should have thought of that sooner, Charles.'

Charles had never been in such a position before. It was a woman in revolt who was hobbling away from him, and the sight was too strange to leave any room for anger. He recovered himself when the others caught them up: their sort he understood. He commanded them to go back.

Albert Fussell was seen walking towards them.

'It's all right!' he called. 'It wasn't a dog, it was a cat.'

'There!' exclaimed Charles triumphantly. 'It's only a rotten cat.'

'Got room in your car for a little un? I cut as soon as I saw it wasn't a dog; the chauffeurs are tackling the girl.' But Margaret walked forward steadily. Why should the chauffeurs tackle the girl? Ladies sheltering behind men, men sheltering behind servants—the whole system's wrong, and she must challenge it.

'Miss Schlegel! 'Pon my word, you've hurt your hand.'

'I'm just going to see,' said Margaret. 'Don't you wait Mr Fussell.'

The second motor came round the corner. 'It is all right madam,' said Crane in his turn. He had taken to call her madam.

'What's all right? The cat?'

'Yes, madam. The girl will receive compensation for it.'

'She was a very ruda girla,' said Angelo from the third motor thoughtfully.

'Wouldn't you have been rude?'

The Italian spread out his hands, implying that he had not thought of rudeness, but would produce it if it pleased her. The situation became absurd. The gentlemen were again buzzing round Miss Schlegel with offers of assistance, and Lady Edser began to bind up her hand. She yielded, apologizing slightly, and was led back to the car, and soon the landscape resumed its motion, the lonely cottage disappeared, the castle swelled on its cushion of turf, and they had arrived. No doubt she had disgraced herself. But she felt their whole journey from London had been unreal. They had no part with the earth and its emotions. They were dust, and a stink, and cosmopolitan chatter, and the girl whose cat had been killed had lived more deeply than they.

'Oh, Henry,' she exclaimed, 'I have been so naughty,' for she had decided to take up this line. 'We ran over a cat. Charles told me not to jump out, but I would, and look!' She held out her bandaged hand. 'Your poor Meg went such a flop.'

Mr Wilcox looked bewildered. In evening dress, he was standing to welcome his guests in the hall.

'Thinking it was a dog,' added Mrs Warrington.

'Ah, a dog's a companion!' said Colonel Fussell. 'A dog'll remember you.'

'Have you hurt yourself, Margaret?'

'Not to speak about; and it's my left hand.'

'Well, hurry up and change.'

She obeyed, as did the others. Mr Wilcox then turned to his son.

'Now, Charles, what's happened?'

Charles was absolutely honest. He described what he believed to have happened. Albert had flattened out a cat, and Miss Schlegel had lost her nerve, as any woman might. She had been got safely into the other car, but when it was in motion had leapt out again, in spite of all that they could say. After walking a little on the road, she had calmed down and had said that she was sorry. His father accepted this explanation, and neither knew that Margaret had artfully prepared the way for it. It fitted in too well with their view of feminine nature. In the smoking-room, after dinner, the Colonel put forward the view that Miss Schlegel had jumped it out of devilry. Well he remembered as a young man, in the harbour of Gibraltar once, how a girl—a handsome girl, too—had jumped overboard for a bet. He could see her now, and all the lads overboard after her. But Charles and Mr Wilcox agreed it was much more probably nerves in Miss Schlegel's case. Charles was depressed. That woman had a tongue. She would bring worse disgrace on his father before she had done with them. He strolled out on to the castle mound to think the matter over. The evening was exquisite. On three sides of him a little river whispered, full of messages from the west; above his head the ruins made patterns against the sky. He carefully reviewed their dealings with this family, until he fitted Helen, and Margaret, and Aunt Juley into an orderly conspiracy. Paternity had made him suspicious. He had two children to look after, and more coming, and day by day they seemed less likely to grow up rich men. 'It is all very well,' he reflected, 'the pater saying that he will be just to all, but one can't be just indefinitely. Money isn't elastic. What's to happen if Evie has a family? And, come to that, so may the pater. There'll not be enough to go round, for there's none coming in, either through Dolly or Percy. It's damnable!' He looked enviously at the Grange, whose windows poured light and laughter. First and last, this wedding would cost a pretty penny. Two ladies were strolling up and down the garden terrace, and as the syllables 'Imperialism' were wafted to his ears, he guessed that one of them was his aunt. She might have helped him, if she too had not had a family to provide for. 'Everyone for himself,' he repeated—a maxim which had cheered him in the past, but which rang grimly enough among the ruins of Oniton. He lacked his father's ability in business, and so had an ever higher regard for money; unless he could inherit plenty, he feared to leave his children poor.

As he sat thinking, one of the ladies left the terrace and walked into the meadow; he recognized her as Margaret by the white bandage that gleamed on her arm, and put out his cigar, lest the gleam should betray him. She climbed up the mound in zigzags, and at times stooped down, as if she was stroking the turf. It sounds absolutely incredible, but for a moment Charles thought that she was in love with him, and had come out to tempt him. Charles believed in temptresses, who are indeed the strong man's necessary complement, and having no sense of humour, he could not purge himself of the thought by a smile. Margaret, who was engaged to his father, and his sister's wedding-guest, kept on her way without noticing him, and he admitted that he had wronged her on this point. But what was she doing? Why was she stumbling about amongst the rubble and catching her dress in brambles and burrs? As she edged round the keep, she must have got to windward and smelt his cigar-smoke, for she exclaimed, 'Hullo! Who's that?'

Charles made no answer.

'Saxon or Kelt?' she continued, laughing in the darkness. 'But it doesn't matter. Whichever you are, you will have to listen to me. I love this place. I love Shropshire. I hate London. I am glad that this will be my home. Ah, dear'—she was now moving back towards the house—'what a comfort to have arrived!'

'That woman means mischief,' thought Charles, and compressed his lips. In a few minutes he followed her indoors, as the ground was getting damp. Mists were rising from the river, and presently it became invisible, though it whispered more loudly. There had been a heavy downpour in the Welsh hills.

Chapter Twenty-six

Next morning a fine mist covered the peninsula. The weather promised well, and the outline of the castle mound grew clearer each moment that Margaret watched it. Presently she saw the keep, and the sun painted the rubble gold, and charged the white sky with blue. The shadow of the house gathered itself together, and fell over the garden. A cat looked up at her window and mewed. Lastly the river appeared, still holding the mists between its banks and its overhanging alders, and only visible as far as a hill, which cut off its upper reaches.

Margaret was fascinated by Oniton. She had said that she loved it, but it was rather its romantic tension that held her. The rounded Druids of whom she had caught glimpses in her drive, the rivers hurrying down from them to England, the carelessly modelled masses of the lower hills, thrilled her with poetry. The house was insignificant, but the prospect from it would be an eternal joy, and she thought of all the friends she would have to stop in it, and of the conversion of Henry himself to a rural life. Society, too, promised favourably. The rector of the parish had dined with them last night, and she found that he was a friend of her father's, and so knew what to find in her. She liked him. He would introduce her to the town. While, on her other side, Sir James Bidder sat, repeating that she only had to give the word, and he would whip up the county families for twenty miles round. Whether Sir James, who was Garden Seeds, had promised what he could perform, she doubted, but so long as Henry mistook them for the county families when they did call, she was content.

Charles and Albert Fussell now crossed the lawn. They were going for a morning dip, and a servant followed them with their bathing-dresses. She had meant to take a stroll herself before breakfast, but saw that the day was still sacred to men, and amused herself by watching their contretemps. In the first place the key of the bathing-shed could not be found. Charles stood by the riverside with folded hands, tragical, while the servant shouted, and was misunderstood by another servant in the garden. Then came a difficulty about a spring-board, and soon three people were running backwards and forwards over the meadow, with orders and counter orders and recriminations and apologies. If Margaret wanted to jump from a motor-car, she jumped; if Tibby thought paddling would benefit his ankles, he paddled; if a clerk desired adventure, he took a walk in the dark. But these athletes seemed paralyzed. They could not bathe without their appliances, though the morning sun was calling and the last mists were rising from the dimpling stream. Had they found the life of the body after all? Could not the men whom they despised as milksops beat them, even on their own ground?

She thought of the bathing arrangements as they should be in her day—no worrying of servants, no appliances, beyond good sense. Her reflections were disturbed by the quiet child, who had come out to speak to the cat, but was now watching her watch the men. She called, 'Good-morning, dear,' a little sharply. Her voice spread consternation. Charles looked round, and though completely attired in indigo blue, vanished into the shed, and was seen no more.

'Miss Wilcox is up—' the child whispered, and then became unintelligible.

'What's that?'

It sounded like, '—cut-yoke–sack-back—'

'I can't hear.'

'–On the bed–tissue-paper—'

Gathering that the wedding-dress was on view, and that a visit would be seemly, she went to Evie's room. All was hilarity here. Evie, in a petticoat, was dancing with one of the Anglo-Indian ladies, while the other was adoring yards of white satin. They screamed, they laughed, they sang, and the dog barked.

Margaret screamed a little too, but without conviction. She could not feel that a wedding was so funny. Perhaps something was missing in her equipment.

Evie gasped: 'Dolly is a rotter not to be here! Oh, we would rag just then!' Then Margaret went down to breakfast.

Henry was already installed; he ate slowly and spoke little, and was, in Margaret's eyes, the only member of their party who dodged emotion successfully. She could not suppose him indifferent either to the loss of his daughter or to the presence of his future wife. Yet he dwelt intact, only issuing orders occasionally–orders that promoted the comfort of his guests. He inquired after her hand; he set her to pour out the coffee and Mrs Warrington to pour out the tea. When Evie came down there was a moment's awkwardness, and both ladies rose to vacate their places. 'Burton,' called Henry, 'serve tea and coffee from the sideboard!' It wasn't genuine tact, but it was tact, of a sort–the sort that is as useful as the genuine, and saves even more situations at Board meetings. Henry treated a marriage like a funeral, item by item, never raising his eyes to the whole, and 'Death, where is they sting? Love, where is thy victory?' one would exclaim at the close.

After breakfast she claimed a few words with him. It was always best to approach him formally. She asked for the interview, because he was going on to shoot grouse to-morrow, and she was returning to Helen in town.

'Certainly, dear,' said he. 'Of course, I have the time. What do you want?'

'Nothing.'

'I was afraid something had gone wrong.'

'No; I have nothing to say, but you may talk.'

Glancing at his watch, he talked of the nasty curve at the lych-gate. She heard him with interest. Her surface could always respond to his without contempt, though all her deeper being might be yearning to help him. She had abandoned any plan of action. Love is the best, and the more she let herself love him, the more chance was there that he would set his soul in order. Such a moment as this, when they sat under fair weather by the walks of their future home, was so sweet to her that its sweetness would surely pierce to him. Each lift of his eyes, each parting of the thatched lip from the clean-shaven, must prelude the tenderness that kills the Monk and the Beast at a single blow. Disappointed a hundred times, she still hoped. She loved him with too clear a vision to fear his cloudiness. Whether he droned trivialities, as to-day, or sprang kisses on her in the twilight, she could pardon him, she could respond.

'If there is this nasty curve,' she suggested, 'couldn't we walk to the church? Not, of course, you and Evie; but the rest of us might very well go on first, and that would mean fewer carriages.'

'One can't have ladies walking through the Market Square. The Fussells wouldn't like it; they were awfully particular at Charles's wedding. My—she—one of our party was anxious to walk, and certainly the church was just round the corner, and I shouldn't have minded; but the Colonel made a great point of it.'

'You men shouldn't be so chivalrous,' said Margaret thoughtfully.

'Why not?'

She knew why not, but said that she did not know. He then announced that, unless she had anything special to say, he must visit the wine-cellar, and they went off together in search of Burton. Though clumsy and a little inconvenient, Oniton was a genuine country-house. They clattered down flagged passages, looking into room after room, and scaring unknown maids from the performance of obscure duties. The wedding-breakfast must be in readiness when they come back from church, and tea would be served in the garden. The sight of so many agitated and serious people made Margaret smile, but she reflected that they were paid to be serious, and enjoyed being agitated. Here were the lower wheels of the machine that was tossing Evie up into nuptial glory. A little boy blocked their way with pig-pails. His mind could not grasp their greatness, and he said: 'By your leave; let me pass, please.' Henry asked him where Burton was. But the servants were so new that they did not know one another's names. In the still-room sat the band, who had stipulated for champagne as part of their fee, and who were already drinking beer. Scents of Araby came from the kitchen, mingled with cries. Margaret knew what had happened there, for it happened at Wickham Place. One of the wedding dishes had boiled over, and the cook was throwing cedar-shavings to hide the smell. At last they came upon the butler. Henry gave him the keys, and handed Margaret down the cellar-stairs. Two doors were unlocked. She, who kept all her wine at the bottom of the linen-cupboard, was astonished at the sight. 'We shall never get through it!' she cried, and the two men were suddenly drawn into brotherhood, and exchanged smiles. She felt as if she had again jumped out of the car while it was moving.

Certainly Oniton would take some digesting. It would be no small business to remain herself, and yet to assimilate such an establishment. She must remain herself, for his sake as well as her own, since a shadowy wife degrades the husband whom she accompanies; and she must assimilate for reasons of common honesty, since she had no right to marry a man and make him uncomfortable. Her only ally was the power of Home. The loss of Wickham Place had taught her more than its possession. Howards End had repeated the lesson. She was determined to create new sanctities among these hills.

After visiting the wine-cellar, she dressed, and then came the wedding, which seemed a small affair when compared with the preparations for it. Everything went like one o'clock. Mr Cahill materialized out of space, and was waiting for his bride at the church door. No one dropped the ring or mispronounced the responses, or trod on Evie's train, or cried. In a few minutes the clergymen performed their duty, the register was signed, and they were back in their carriages, negotiating the dangerous curve by the lych-gate. Margaret was convinced that they had not been married at all, and that the Norman church had been intent all the time on other business.

There were more documents to sign at the house, and the breakfast to eat, and then a few more people dropped in for the garden party. There had been a great many refusals, and after all it was not a very big affair—not as big as Margaret's would be. She noted the dishes and the strips of red carpet, that outwardly she might give Henry what was proper. But inwardly she hoped for something better than this blend of Sunday church and fox-hunting. If only someone had been upset! But this wedding had gone off so particularly well—'quite like a Durbar' in the opinion of Lady Edser, and she thoroughly agreed with her.

So the wasted day lumbered forward, the bride and bridegroom drove off, yelling with laughter, and for the second time the sun retreated towards the hills of Wales. Henry, who was more tired than he owned, came up to her in the castle meadow, and, in tones of unusual softness, said that he was pleased. Everything had gone off so well. She felt that he was praising her, too, and blushed; certainly she had done all she could with his intractable friends, and had made a special point of kow-towing to the men. They were breaking camp this evening: only the Warringtons and quiet child would stay the night, and the others were already moving towards the house to finish their packing. 'I think it did go off well,' she agreed. 'Since I had to jump out of the motor, I'm thankful I lighted on my left hand. I am so very glad about it, Henry dear; I only hope that the guests at ours may be half as comfortable. You must all remember that we have no practical person among us, except my aunt, and she is not used to entertainments on a large scale.'

'I know,' he said gravely. 'Under the circumstances, it would be better to put everything into the hands of Harrod's or Whiteley's, or even to go to some hotel.'

'You desire a hotel?'

'Yes, because—well, I mustn't interfere with you. No doubt you want to be married from your old home.'

'My old home's falling into pieces, Henry. I only want my new. Isn't it a perfect evening—'

'The Alexandrina isn't bad—'

'The Alexandrina,' she echoed, more occupied with the threads of smoke that were issuing from their chimneys, and ruling the sunlit slopes with parallels of grey.

'It's off Curzon Street.'

'Is it? Let's be married from off Curzon Street.'

Then she turned westward, to gaze at the swirling gold. Just where the river rounded the hill the sun caught it. Fairyland must lie above the bend, and its precious liquid was pouring towards them past Charles's bathing-shed. She gazed so long that her eyes were dazzled, and when they moved back to the house, she could not recognize the faces of people who were coming out of it. A parlour-maid was preceding them.

'Who are those people?' she asked.

'They're callers!' exclaimed Henry. 'It's too late for callers.'

'Perhaps they're town people who want to see the wedding presents.'

'I'm not at home yet to townees.'

'Well, hide among the ruins, and if I can stop them, I will.'

He thanked her.

Margaret went forward, smiling socially. She supposed that these were unpunctual guests, who would have to be content with vicarious civility, since Evie and Charles were gone, Henry tired, and the others in their rooms. She assumed the airs of a hostess; not for long. For one of the group was Helen–Helen in her oldest clothes, and dominated by that tense, wounding excitement that had made her a terror in their nursery days.

'What is it?' she called. 'Oh, what's wrong? Is Tibby ill?'

Helen spoke to her two companions, who fell back. Then she bore forward furiously.

'They're starving!' she shouted. 'I found them starving!'

'Who? Why have you come?'

'The Basts.'

'Oh, Helen!' moaned Margaret. 'Whatever have you done now?'

'He has lost his place. He has been turned out of his bank. Yes, he's done for. We upper classes have ruined him, and I suppose you'll tell me it's the battle of life. Starving. His wife is ill. Starving. She fainted in the train.'

'Helen, are you mad?'

'Perhaps. Yes. If you like, I'm mad. But I've brought them. I'll stand injustice no longer. I'll show up the wretchedness that lies under this luxury, this talk of impersonal forces, this cant about God doing what we're too slack to do ourselves.'

'Have you actually brought two starving people from London to Shropshire, Helen?'

Helen was checked. She had not thought of this, and her hysteria abated. 'There was a restaurant car on the train,' she said.

'Don't be absurd. They aren't starving, and you know it. Now, begin from the beginning. I won't have such theatrical nonsense. How dare you! Yes, how dare you!' she repeated, as anger filled her, 'bursting in to Evie's wedding in this heartless way. My goodness! but you've a perverted notion of philanthropy. Look'—she indicated the house—'servants, people out of the windows. They think it's some vulgar scandal, and I must explain, "Oh no, it's only my sister screaming, and only two hangers-on of ours, whom she has brought here for no conceivable reason."'

'Kindly take back that word "hangers-on,"' said Helen, ominously calm.

'Very well,' conceded Margaret, who for all her wrath was determined to avoid a real quarrel. 'I, too, am sorry about them, but it beats me why you've brought them here, or why you're here yourself.'

'It's our last chance of seeing Mr Wilcox.'

Margaret moved towards the house at this. She was determined not to worry Henry.

'He's going to Scotland. I know he is. I insist on seeing him.'

'Yes, to-morrow.'

'I knew it was our last chance.'

'How do you do, Mr Bast?' said Margaret, trying to control her voice. 'This is an odd business. What view do you take of it?'

'There is Mrs Bast, too,' prompted Helen.

Jacky also shook hands. She, like her husband, was shy, and, furthermore, ill, and, furthermore, so bestially stupid that she could not grasp what was happening. She only knew that the lady had swept down like a whirlwind last night, had paid the rent, redeemed the furniture, provided them with a dinner and a breakfast, and ordered them to meet her at Paddington next morning. Leonard had feebly protested, and when the morning came, had suggested that they shouldn't go. But she, half mesmerized, had obeyed. The lady had told them to, and they must, and their bed-sitting-room had accordingly changed into Paddington, and Paddington into a railway carriage, that shook, and grew hot, and grew cold, and vanished entirely, and reappeared amid torrents of expensive scent. 'You have fainted,' said the lady in an awe-struck voice. 'Perhaps the air will do you good.' And perhaps it had, for here she was, feeling rather better among a lot of flowers.

'I'm sure I don't want to intrude,' begun Leonard, in answer to Margaret's question. 'But you have been so kind to me in the past in warning me about the Porphyrion that I wondered—why, I wondered whether—'

'Whether we could get him back into the Porphyrion again,' supplied Helen. 'Meg, this has been a cheerful business. A bright evening's work that was on Chelsea Embankment.'

Margaret shook her head and returned to Mr Bast.

'I don't understand. You left the Porphyrion because we suggested it was a bad concern, didn't you?'

'That's right.'

'And went into a bank instead?'

'I told you all that,' said Helen; 'and they reduced their staff after he had been in a month, and now he's penniless, and I consider that we and our informant are directly to blame.'

'I hate all this,' Leonard muttered.

'I hope you do, Mr Bast. But it's no good mincing matters. You have done yourself no good by coming here. If you intend to confront Mr Wilcox, and to call him to account for a chance remark, you will make a very great mistake.'

'I brought them. I did it all,' cried Helen.

'I can only advise you to go at once. My sister has put you in a false position, and it is kindest to tell you so. It's too late to get to town, but you'll find a comfortable hotel in Oniton, where Mrs Bast can rest, and I hope you'll be my guests there.'

'That isn't what I want, Miss Schlegel,' said Leonard. 'You're very kind, and do doubt it's a false position, but you make me miserable. I seem no good at all.'

'It's work he wants,' interpreted Helen. 'Can't you see?'

Then he said: 'Jacky, let's go. We're more bother than we're worth. We're costing these ladies pounds and pounds already to get work for us, and they never will. There's nothing we're good enough to do.'

'We would like to find you work,' said Margaret rather conventionally. 'We want to–I, like my sister. You're only down in your luck. Go to the hotel, have a good night's rest, and some day you shall pay me back the bill, if you prefer it.'

But Leonard was near the abyss, and at such moments men see clearly. 'You don't know what you're talking about,' he said. 'I shall never get work now. If rich people fail at one profession, they can try another. Not I. I had my groove, and I've got out of it. I could do one particular branch of insurance in one particular office well enough to command a salary, but that's all. Poetry's nothing, Miss Schlegel. One's thoughts about this and that are nothing. Your money, too, is nothing, if you'll understand me. I mean if a man over twenty once loses his own particular job, it's all over with him. I have seen it happen to others. Their friends gave them money for a little, but in the end they fall over the edge. It's no good. It's the whole world pulling. There always will be rich and poor.'

He ceased. 'Won't you have something to eat?' said Margaret. 'I don't know what to do. It isn't my house, and though Mr Wilcox would have been glad to see you at any other time–as I say, I don't know what to do, but I undertake to do what I can for you. Helen, offer them something. Do try a sandwich, Mrs Bast.

They moved to a long table behind which a servant was still standing. Iced cakes, sandwiches innumerable, coffee, claret-cup, champagne, remained almost intact: their overfed guests could do no more. Leonard refused. Jacky thought she could manage a little. Margaret left them whispering together, and had a few more words with Helen.

She said: 'Helen, I like Mr Bast. I agree that he's worth helping. I agree that we are directly responsible.'

'No, indirectly. Via Mr Wilcox.'

'Let me tell you once and for all that if you take up that attitude, I'll do nothing. No doubt you're right logically, and are entitled to say a great many scathing things about Henry. Only, I won't have it. So choose.'

Helen looked at the sunset.

'If you promise to take them quietly to the George, I will speak to Henry about them—in my own way, mind; there is to be none of this absurd screaming about justice. I have no use for justice. If it was only a question of money, we could do it ourselves. But he wants work, and that we can't give him, but possibly Henry can.'

'It's his duty to,' grumbled Helen.

'Nor am I concerned with duty. I'm concerned with the characters of various people whom we know, and how, things being as they are, things may be made a little better. Mr Wilcox hates being asked favours: all business men do. But I am going to ask him, at the risk of a rebuff, because I want to make things a little better.'

'Very well. I promise. You take it very calmly.'

'Take them off to the George, then, and I'll try. Poor creatures! but they look tired.' As they parted, she added: 'I haven't nearly done with you, though, Helen. You have been most self-indulgent. I can't get over it. You have less restraint rather than more as you grow older. Think it over and alter yourself, or we shan't have happy lives.'

She rejoined Henry. Fortunately he had been sitting down: these physical matters were important. 'Was it townees?' he asked, greeting her with a pleasant smile.

'You'll never believe me,' said Margaret, sitting down beside him. 'It's all right now, but it was my sister.'

'Helen here?' he cried, preparing to rise. 'But she refused the invitation. I thought she despised weddings.'

'Don't get up. She has not come to the wedding. I've bundled her off to the George.'

Inherently hospitable, he protested.

'No; she has two of her protégés with her, and must keep with them.'

'Let 'em all come.'

'My dear Henry, did you see them?'

'I did catch sight of a brown bunch of a woman, certainly.'

'The brown bunch was Helen, but did you catch sight of a sea-green and salmon bunch?'

'What! are they out beanfeasting?'

'No; business. They wanted to see me, and later on I want to talk to you about them.'

She was ashamed of her own diplomacy. In dealing with a Wilcox, how tempting it was to lapse from comradeship, and to give him the kind of woman that he desired! Henry took the hint at once, and said: 'Why later on? Tell me now. No time like the present.'

'Shall I?'

'If it isn't a long story.'

'Oh, not five minutes; but there's a sting at the end of it, for I want you to find the man some work in your office.'

'What are his qualifications?'

'I don't know. He's a clerk.'

'How old?'

'Twenty-five, perhaps.'

'What's his name?'

'Bast,' said Margaret, and was about to remind him that they had met at Wickham Place, but stopped herself. It had not been a successful meeting.

'Where was he before?'

'Dempster's Bank.'

'Why did he leave?' he asked, still remembering nothing.

'They reduced their staff.'

'All right; I'll see him.'

It was the reward of her tact and devotion through the day. Now she understood why some women prefer influence to rights. Mrs Plynlimmon, when condemning suffragettes, had said: 'The woman who can't influence her husband to vote the way she wants ought to be ashamed of herself.' Margaret had winced, but she was influencing Henry now, and though pleased at her little victory, she knew that she had won it by the methods of the harem.

'I should be glad if you took him,' she said, 'but I don't know whether he's qualified.'

'I'll do what I can. But, Margaret, this mustn't be taken as a precedent.'

'No, of course—of course—'

'I can't fit in your protégés every day. Business would suffer.'

'I can promise you he's the last. He—he's rather a special case.'

'Protégés always are.'

She let it stand at that. He rose with a little extra touch of complacency, and held out his hand to help her up. How wide the gulf between Henry as he was and Henry as Helen thought he ought to be! And she herself—hovering as usual between the two, now accepting men as they are, now yearning with her sister for Truth. Love and Truth—their warfare seems eternal. Perhaps the whole visible world rests on it, and if they were one, life itself, like the spirits when Prospero was reconciled to his brother, might vanish into air, into thin air.

'Your protégé has made us late,' said he. 'The Fussells will just be starting.'

On the whole she sided with men as they are. Henry would save the Basts as he had saved Howards End, while Helen and her friends were discussing the ethics of salvation. His was a slap-dash method, but the world has been built slap-dash, and the beauty of mountain and river and sunset may be but the varnish with which the unskilled artificer hides his joins. Oniton, like herself, was imperfect. Its apple-trees were stunted, its castle ruinous. It, too, had suffered in the border warfare between the Anglo-Saxon and the Kelt, between things as they are and as they ought to be. Once more the west was retreating, once again the orderly stars were dotting the eastern sky. There is certainly no rest for us on the earth. But there is happiness, and as Margaret descended the mound on her lover's arm, she felt that she was having her share.

To her annoyance, Mrs Bast was still in the garden; the husband and

Helen had left her there to finish her meal while they went to engage rooms. Margaret found this woman repellent. She had felt, when shaking her hand, an overpowering shame. She remembered the motive of her call at Wickham Place, and smelt again odours from the abyss—odours the more disturbing because they were involuntary. For there was no malice in Jacky. There she sat, a piece of cake in one hand, an empty champagne glass in the other, doing no harm to anybody.

'She's overtired,' Margaret whispered.

'She's something else,' said Henry. 'This won't do. I can't have her in my garden in this state.'

'Is she—' Margaret hesitated to add 'drunk.' Now that she was going to marry him, he had grown particular. He discountenanced risqué conversations now.

Henry went up to the woman. She raised her face, which gleamed in the twilight like a puff-ball.

'Madam, you will be more comfortable at the hotel,' he said sharply.

Jacky replied: 'If it isn't Hen!'

'Ne crois pas que le mari lui ressemble,' apologized Margaret. 'Il est tout à fait différent.'

'Henry!' she repeated, quite distinctly.

Mr Wilcox was much annoyed. 'I can't congratulate you on your protégés,' he remarked.

'Hen, don't go. You do love me, dear, don't you?'

'Bless us, what a person!' sighed Margaret, gathering up her skirts.

Jacky pointed with her cake. 'You're a nice boy, you are.' She yawned. 'There now, I love you.'

'Henry, I am awfully sorry.'

'And pray why?' he asked, and looked at her so sternly that she feared he was ill. He seemed more scandalized than the facts demanded.

'To have brought this down on you.'

'Pray don't apologize.'

The voice continued.

'Why does she call you "Hen"?' said Margaret innocently. 'Has she ever seen you before?'

'Seen Hen before!' said Jacky. 'Who hasn't seen Hen? He's serving you like me, my dear. These boys! You wait—Still we love 'em.'

'Are you now satisfied?' Henry asked.

Margaret began to grow frightened. 'I don't know what it is all about,' she said. 'Let's come in.'

But he thought she was acting. He thought he was trapped. He saw his whole life crumbling. 'Don't you indeed?' he said bitingly. 'I do. Allow me to congratulate you on the success of your plan.'

'This is Helen's plan, not mine.'

'I now understand your interest in the Basts. Very well thought out. I am amused at your caution, Margaret. You are quite right—it was necessary. I am a man, and have lived a man's past. I have the honour to release you from your engagement.'

Still she could not understand. She knew of life's seamy side as a theory; she could not grasp it as a fact. More words from Jacky were necessary–words unequivocal, undenied.

'So that—' burst from her, and she went indoors. She stopped herself from saying more.

'So what?' asked Colonel Fussell, who was getting ready to start in the hall.

'We were saying–Henry and I were just having the fiercest argument, my point being—' Seizing his fur coat from a footman, she offered to help him on. He protested, and there was a playful little scene.

'No, let me do that,' said Henry, following.

'Thanks so much! You see–he has forgiven me!'

The Colonel said gallantly: 'I don't expect there's much to forgive.'

He got into the car. The ladies followed him after an interval. Maids, courier, and heavier luggage had been sent on earlier by the branch-line. Still chattering, still thanking their host and patronizing their future hostess, the guests were borne away.

Then Margaret continued: 'So that woman has been your mistress?'

'You put it with your usual delicacy,' he replied.

'When please?'

'Why?'

'When, please?'

'Ten years ago.'

She left him without a word. For it was not her tragedy: it was Mrs Wilcox's.

Chapter Twenty-seven

Helen began to wonder why she had spent a matter of eight pounds in making some people ill and others angry. Now that the wave of excitement was ebbing, and had left her, Mr Bast, and Mrs Bast stranded for the night in a Shropshire hotel, she asked herself what forces had made the wave flow. At all events, no harm was done. Margaret would play the game properly now, and though Helen disapproved of her sister's methods, she knew that the Basts would benefit by them in the long run.

'Mr Wilcox is so illogical,' she explained to Leonard, who had put his wife to bed, and was sitting with her in the empty coffee room. 'If we told him it was his duty to take you on, he might refuse to do it. The fact is, he isn't properly educated. I don't want to set you against him, but you'll find him a trial.'

'I can never thank you sufficiently, Miss Schlegel,' was all that Leonard felt equal to.

'I believe in personal responsibility. Don't you? And in personal everything. I hate—I suppose I oughtn't to say that—but the Wilcoxes are on the wrong tack surely. Or perhaps it isn't their fault. Perhaps the little thing that says "I" is missing out of the middle of their heads, and then it's a waste of time to blame them. There's a nightmare of a theory that says a special race is being born which will rule the rest of us in the future just because it lacks the little thing that says "I." Had you heard that?'

'I get no time for reading.'

'Had you thought it, then? That there are two kinds of people—our kind, who live straight from the middle of their heads, and the other kind who can't, because their heads have no middle? They can't say "I." They *aren't* in fact, and so they're supermen. Pierpont Morgan has never said "I" in his life.'

Leonard roused himself. If his benefactress wanted intellectual conversation, she must have it. She was more important than his ruined past. 'I never got on to Nietzsche,' he said. 'But I always understood that those supermen were rather what you may call egoists.'

'Oh no, that's wrong,' replied Helen. 'No superman ever said "I want," because "I want" must lead to the question, "Who am I?" and so to Pity and to Justice. He only says "want." "Want Europe," if he's Napoleon; "want wives," if he's Bluebeard; "want Botticelli," if he's Pierpont Morgan. Never the "I"; and if you could pierce through him, you'd find panic and emptiness in the middle.'

Leonard was silent for a moment. Then he said: 'May I take it, Miss Schlegel, that you and I are both the sort that say "I"?'

'Of course.'

'And your sister too?'

'Of course,' repeated Helen, a little sharply. She was annoyed with Margaret, but did not want her discussed. 'All presentable people say "I."'

'But Mr Wilcox—he is not perhaps—'

'I don't know that it's any good discussing Mr Wilcox either.'

'Quite so, quite so,' he agreed. Helen asked herself why she had snubbed him. Once or twice during the day she had encouraged him to criticize, and then had pulled him up short. Was she afraid of him presuming? If so, it was disgusting of her.

But he was thinking the snub quite natural. Everything she did was natural, and incapable of causing offence. While the Miss Schlegels were together he had felt them scarcely human—a sort of admonitory whirligig. But a Miss Schlegel alone was different. She was in Helen's case unmarried, in Margaret's about to be married, in neither case an echo of her sister. A light had fallen at last into this rich upper world, and he saw that it was full of men and women, some of whom were more friendly to him than others. Helen had become 'his' Miss Schlegel, who scolded him and corresponded with him, and had swept down yesterday with grateful vehemence. Margaret, though not unkind, was severe and remote. He would not presume to help her, for instance. He had never liked her, and began to think that his original impression was true, and that her sister did not like her either. Helen was certainly lonely. She, who gave away so much, was receiving too little. Leonard was pleased to think that he could spare her vexation by holding his tongue and concealing what he knew about Mr Wilcox. Jacky had announced her discovery when he fetched her from the lawn. After the first shock, he did not mind for himself. By now he had no illusions about his wife, and this was only one new stain on the face of a love that had never been pure. To keep perfection perfect, that should be his ideal, if the future gave him time to have ideals. Helen, and Margaret for Helen's sake, must not know.

Helen disconcerted him by turning the conversation to his wife. 'Mrs Bast—does she ever say "I"?' she asked, half mischievously, and then, 'Is she very tired?'

'It's better she stops in her room,' said Leonard.

'Shall I sit up with her?'

'No, thank you; she does not need company.'

'Mr Bast, what kind of woman is your wife?'

Leonard blushed up to his eyes.

'You ought to know my ways by now. Does that question offend you?'

'No, oh no, Miss Schlegel, no.'

'Because I love honesty. Don't pretend your marriage has been a happy one. You and she can have nothing in common.'

He did not deny it, but said shyly: 'I suppose that's pretty obvious; but Jacky never meant to do anybody any harm. When things went wrong, or I heard things, I used to think it was her fault, but, looking back, it's more mine. I needn't have married her, but as I have I must stick to her and keep her.'

'How long have you been married?'

'Nearly three years.'

'What did your people say?'

'They will not have anything to do with us. They had a sort of family council when they heard I was married, and cut us off altogether.'

Helen began to pace up and down the room. 'My good boy, what a mess!' she said gently. 'Who are your people?'

He could answer this. His parents, who were dead, had been in trade; his sisters had married commercial travellers; his brother was a lay-reader.

'And your grandparents?'

Leonard told her a secret that he had held shameful up to now. 'They were just nothing at all,' he said—'agricultural labourers and that sort.'

'So! From which part?'

'Lincolnshire mostly, but my mother's father—he, oddly enough, came from these parts round here.'

'From this very Shropshire. Yes, that is odd. My mother's people were Lancashire. But why do your brother and your sisters object to Mrs Bast?'

'Oh, I don't know.'

'Excuse me, you do know. I am not a baby. I can bear anything you tell me, and the more you tell the more I shall be able to help. Have they heard anything against her?'

He was silent.

'I think I have guessed now,' said Helen very gravely.

'I don't think so, Miss Schlegel; I hope not.'

'We must be honest, even over these things. I have guessed. I am frightfully, dreadfully sorry, but it does not make the least difference to me. I shall feel just the same to both of you. I blame, not your wife for these things, but men.'

Leonard left it at that—so long as she did not guess the man. She stood at the window and slowly pulled up the blinds. The hotel looked over a dark square. The mists had begun. When she turned back to him her eyes were shining.

'Don't you worry,' he pleaded. 'I can't bear that. We shall be all right if I get work. If I could only get work—something regular to do. Then it wouldn't be so bad again. I don't trouble after books as I used. I can imagine that with regular work we should settle down again. It stops one thinking.'

'Settle down to what?'

'Oh, just settle down.'

'And that's to be life!' said Helen, with a catch in her throat. 'How can you, with all the beautiful things to see and do—with music—with walking at night—'

'Walking is well enough when a man's in work,' he answered. 'Oh, I did talk a lot of nonsense once, but there's nothing like a bailiff in the house to drive it out of you. When I saw him fingering my Ruskins and Stevensons, I seemed to see life straight real, and it isn't a pretty sight. My books are back again, thanks to you, but they'll never be the same to me again, and I shan't ever again think night in the woods is wonderful.'

'Why not?' asked Helen, throwing up the window.

'Because I see one must have money.'

'Well, you're wrong.'

'I wish I was wrong, but—the clergyman—he has money of his own, or else he's paid; the poet or the musician—just the same; the tramp—he's no different. The tramp goes to the workhouse in the end, and is paid for with other people's money. Miss Schlegel, the real thing's money, and all the rest is a dream.'

'You're still wrong. You've forgotten Death.'

Leonard could not understand.

'If we lived for ever, what you say would be true. But we have to die, we have to leave life presently. Injustice and greed would be the real thing if we lived for ever. As it is, we must hold to other things, because Death is coming. I love Death—not morbidly, but because He explains. He shows me the emptiness of Money. Death and Money are the eternal foes. Not Death and Life. Never mind what lies behind Death, Mr Bast, but be sure that the poet and the musician and the tramp will be happier in it than the man who has never learnt to say, "I am I."'

'I wonder.'

'We are all in a mist—I know, but I can help you this far—men like the Wilcoxes are deeper in the mist than any. Sane, sound Englishmen! building up empires, levelling all the world into what they call common sense. But mention Death to them and they're offended, because Death's really Imperial, and He cries out against them for ever.'

'I am as afraid of Death as anyone.'

'But not of the idea of Death.'

'But what is the difference?'

'Infinite difference,' said Helen, more gravely than before.

Leonard looked at her wondering, and had the sense of great things sweeping out of the shrouded night. But he could not receive them, because his heart was still full of little things. As the lost umbrella had spoilt the concert at Queen's Hall, so the lost situation was obscuring the diviner harmonies now. Death, Life and Materialism were fine words, but would Mr Wilcox take him on as a clerk? Talk as one would, Mr Wilcox was king of this world, the superman, with his own morality, whose head remained in the clouds.

'I must be stupid,' he said apologetically.

While to Helen the paradox became clearer and clearer. 'Death destroys a man: the idea of Death saves him.' Behind the coffins and the skeletons that stay the vulgar mind lies something so immense that all that is great in us responds to it. Men of the world may recoil from the charnel-house that they will one day enter, but Love knows better. Death is his foe, but his peer, and in their age-long struggle the thews of Love have been strengthened, and his vision cleared, until there is no one who can stand against him.

'So never give in,' continued the girl, and restated again and again the vague yet convincing plea that the Invisible lodges against the Visible. Her excitement grew as she tried to cut the rope that fastened Leonard to the earth. Woven of bitter experience, it resisted her. Presently the waitress entered and gave her a letter from Margaret. Another note, addressed to Leonard, was inside. They read them, listening to the murmurings of the river.

Chapter Twenty-eight

For many hours Margaret did nothing; then she controlled herself, and wrote some letters. She was too bruised to speak to Henry; she could pity him, and even determine to marry him, but as yet all lay too deep in her heart for speech. On the surface the sense of his degradation was too strong. She could not command voice or look, and the gentle words that she forced out through her pen seemed to proceed from some other person.

'My dearest boy,' she began, 'this is not to part us. It is everything or nothing, and I mean it to be nothing. It happened long before we ever met, and even if it had happened since, I should be writing the same, I hope. I do understand.'

But she crossed out 'I do understand'; it struck a false note. Henry could not bear to be understood. She also crossed out, 'It is everything or nothing.' Henry would resent so strong a grasp of the situation. She must not comment; comment is unfeminine.

'I think that'll about do,' she thought.

Then the sense of his degradation choked her. Was he worth all this bother? To have yielded to a woman of that sort was everything, yes, it was, and she could not be his wife. She tried to translate his temptation into her own language, and her brain reeled. Men must be different, even to want to yield to such a temptation. Her belief in comradeship was stifled, and she saw life as from that glass saloon on the Great Western, which sheltered male and female alike from the fresh air. Are the sexes really races, each with its own code of morality, and their mutual love a mere device of Nature to keep things going? Strip human intercourse of the proprieties, and is it reduced to this? Her judgment told her no. She knew that out of Nature's device we have built a magic that will win us immortality. Far more mysterious than the call of sex to sex is the tenderness that we throw into that call; far wider is the gulf between us and the farmyard than between the farmyard and the garbage that nourishes it. We are evolving, in ways that Science cannot measure, to ends that Theology dares not contemplate. 'Men did produce one jewel,' the gods will say, and, saying, will give us immortality. Margaret knew all this, but for the moment she could not feel it, and transformed the marriage of Evie and Mr Cahill into a carnival of fools, and her own marriage—too miserable to think of that, she tore up the letter, and then wrote another:

Dear Mr Bast,
    I have spoken to Mr Wilcox about you, as I promised, and am sorry to say that he has no vacancy for you.
                                                        Yours truly,
                                                        M. J. Schlegel.

She enclosed this in a note to Helen, over which she took less trouble than she might have done; but her head was aching, and she could not stop to pick her words:

Dear Helen,
    Give him this. The Basts are no good. Henry found the woman drunk on the lawn. I am having a room got ready for you here, and will you please come round at once on getting this? The Basts are not at all the type we should trouble about. I may go round to them myself in the morning, and do anything that is fair.
                                                        M.

In writing this, Margaret felt that she was being practical. Something might be arranged for the Basts later on, but they must be silenced for the moment. She hoped to avoid a conversation between the woman and Helen. She rang the bell for a servant, but no one answered it; Mr Wilcox and the Warringtons were gone to bed, and the kitchen was abandoned to Saturnalia. Consequently she went over to the George herself. She did not enter the hotel, for discussion would have been perilous, and, saying that the letter was important, she gave it to the waitress. As she recrossed the square she saw Helen and Mr Bast looking out of the window of the coffee-room, and feared she was already too late. Her task was not yet over; she ought to tell Henry what she had done.

This came easily, for she saw him in the hall. The night wind had been rattling the pictures against the wall, and the noise had disturbed him.

'Who's there?' he called, quite the householder.

Margaret walked in and past him.

'I have asked Helen to sleep,' she said. 'She is best here; so don't lock the front-door.'

'I thought someone had got in,' said Henry.

'At the same time I told the man that we could do nothing for him. I don't know about later, but now the Basts must clearly go.'

'Did you say that your sister is sleeping here, after all?'

'Probably.'

'Is she to be shown up to your room?'

'I have naturally nothing to say to her; I am going to bed. Will you tell the servants about Helen? Could someone go to carry her bag?'

He tapped a little gong, which had been bought to summon the servants.

'You must make more noise than that if you want them to hear.'

Henry opened a door, and down the corridor came shouts of laughter. 'Far too much screaming there,' he said, and strode towards it. Margaret went upstairs, uncertain whether to be glad that they had met, or sorry. They had behaved as if nothing had happened, and her deepest instincts told her that this was wrong. For his own sake, some explanation was due.

And yet – what could an explanation tell her? A date, a place, a few details, which she could imagine all too clearly. Now that the first shock was over, she saw that there was every reason to premise a Mrs Bast. Henry's inner life had long laid open to her – his intellectual confusion, his obtuseness to personal influence, his strong but furtive passions. Should she refuse him because his outer life corresponded? Perhaps. Perhaps, if the dishonour had been done to her, but it was done long before her day. She struggled against the feeling. She told herself that Mrs Wilcox's wrong was her own. But she was not a barren theorist. As she undressed, her anger, her regard for the dead, her desire for a scene, all grew weak. Henry must have it as he liked, for she loved him and some day she would use her love to make him a better man.

Pity was at the bottom of her actions all through this crisis. Pity, if one may generalize, is at the bottom of woman. When men like us, it is for our better qualities, and however tender their liking, we dare not be unworthy of it, or they will quietly let us go. But unworthiness stimulates woman. It brings out her deeper nature, for good or for evil.

Here was the core of the question. Henry must be forgiven, and made better by love; nothing else mattered. Mrs Wilcox, that unquiet yet kindly ghost, must be left to her own wrong. To her everything was in proportion now, and she, too, would pity the man who was blundering up and down their lives. Had Mrs Wilcox known of his trespass? An interesting question, but Margaret fell asleep, tethered by affection, and lulled by the murmurs of the river that descended all the night from Wales. She felt herself at one with her future home, colouring it and coloured by it, and awoke to see, for the second time, Oniton Castle conquering the morning mists.

Chapter Twenty-nine

'Henry dear—' was her greeting.

He had finished his breakfast, and was beginning the 'Times.' His sister-in-law was packing. She knelt by him and took the paper from him, feeling that it was unusually heavy and thick. Then, putting her face where it had been, she looked up in his eyes.

'Henry dear, look at me. No, I won't have you shirking. Look at me. There. That's all.'

'You're referring to last evening,' he said huskily. 'I have released you from your engagement. I could find excuses, but I won't. No, I won't. A thousand times no. I'm a bad lot, and must be left at that.'

Expelled from his old fortress, Mr Wilcox was building a new one. He could no longer appear respectable to her, so he defended himself instead in a lurid past. It was not true repentance.

'Leave it where you will, boy. It's not going to trouble us: I know what I'm talking about, and it will make no difference.'

'No difference?' he inquired. 'No difference, when you find that I am not the fellow you thought?' He was annoyed with Miss Schlegel here. He would have preferred her to be prostrated by the blow, or even to rage. Against the tide of his sin flowed the feeling that she was not altogether womanly. Her eyes gazed too straight; they had read books that are suitable for men only. And though he had dreaded a scene, and though she had determined against one, there was a scene, all the same. It was somehow imperative.

'I am unworthy of you,' he began. 'Had I been worthy, I should not have released you from your engagement. I know what I am talking about. I can't bear to talk of such things. We had better leave it.'

She kissed his hand. He jerked it from her, and, rising to his feet, went on: 'You, with your sheltered life, and refined pursuits, and friends, and books, you and your sister, and women like you—I say, how can you guess the temptations that lie round a man?'

'It is difficult for us,' said Margaret; 'but if we are worth marrying, we do guess.'

'Cut off from decent society and family ties, what do you suppose happens to thousands of young fellows overseas? Isolated. No one near. I know by bitter experience, and yet you say it makes "no difference."'

'Not to me.'

He laughed bitterly. Margaret went to the sideboard and helped herself to one of the breakfast dishes. Being the last down, she turned out the spirit-lamp that kept them warm. She was tender, but grave. She knew that Henry was not so much confessing his soul as pointing out the gulf between the male soul and the female, and she did not desire to hear him on this point.

'Did Helen come?' she asked.

He shook his head.

'But that won't do at all, at all! We don't want her gossiping with Mrs Bast.'

'Good God! no!' he exclaimed, suddenly natural. Then he caught himself up. 'Let them gossip. My game's up, though I thank you for your unselfishness—little as my thanks are worth.'

'Didn't she send me a message or anything?'

'I heard of none.'

'Would you ring the bell, please?'

'What to do?'

'Why, to inquire.'

He swaggered up to it tragically, and sounded a peal. Margaret poured herself out some coffee. The butler came, and said that Miss Schlegel had slept at the George, so far as he had heard. Should he go round to the George?

'I'll go, thank you,' said Margaret, and dismissed him.

'It is no good,' said Henry. 'Those things leak out; you cannot stop a story once it has started. I have known cases of other men—I despised them once, I thought that *I'm* different, *I* shall never be tempted. Oh, Margaret—' He came and sat down near her, improvising emotion. She could not bear to listen to him. 'We fellows all come to grief once in our time. Will you believe that? There are moments when the strongest man— "Let him who standeth, take heed lest he fall." That's true, isn't it? If you knew all, you would excuse me. I was far from good influences—far even from England. I was very, very lonely, and longed for a woman's voice. That's enough. I have told you too much already for you to forgive me now.'

'Yes, that's enough, dear.'

'I have'—he lowered his voice—'I have been through hell.'

Gravely she considered this claim. Had he? Had he suffered tortures of remorse, or had it been, 'There! that's over. Now for respectable life again'? The latter, if she read him rightly. A man who has been through hell does not boast of his virility. He is humble and hides it, if, indeed, it still exists. Only in legend does the sinner come forth penitent, but terrible, to conquer pure woman by his resistless power. Henry was anxious to be terrible, but had not got it in him. He was a good average Englishman, who had slipped. The really culpable point—his faithlessness to Mrs Wilcox—never seemed to strike him. She longed to mention Mrs Wilcox.

And bit by bit the story was told her. It was a very simple story. Ten years ago was the time, a garrison town in Cyprus the place. Now and then he asked her whether she could possibly forgive him, and she answered, 'I have already forgiven you, Henry.' She chose her words carefully, and so saved him from panic. She played the girl, until he could rebuild his fortress and hide his soul from the world. When the butler came to clear away, Henry was in a very different mood—asked the fellow what he was in such a hurry for, complained of the noise last night in the servants' hall. Margaret looked intently at the butler. He, as a handsome young man, was faintly attractive to her as a woman—an attraction so faint as scarcely to be perceptible, yet the skies would have fallen if she had mentioned it to Henry.

On her return from the George the building operations were complete, and the old Henry fronted her, competent, cynical, and kind. He had made a clean breast, had been forgiven, and the great thing now was to forget his failure, and to send it the way of other unsuccessful investments. Jacky rejoined Howards End and Ducie Street, and the vermilion motor-car, and the Argentine Hard Dollars, and all the things and people for whom he had never had much use, and had less now. Their memory hampered him. He could scarcely attend to Margaret, who brought back disquieting news from the George. Helen and her clients had gone.

'Well, let them go—the man and his wife, I mean, for the more we see of your sister the better.'

'But they have gone separately—Helen very early, the Basts just before I arrived. They have left no message. They have answered neither of my notes. I don't like to think what it all means.'

'What did you say in the notes?'

'I told you last night.'

'Oh—ah—yes! Dear, would you like one turn in the garden?'

Margaret took his arm. The beautiful weather soothed her. But the wheels of Evie's wedding were still at work, tossing the guests outwards as deftly as they had drawn them in, and she could not be with him long. It had been arranged that they should motor to Shrewsbury, whence he would go north, and she back to London with the Warringtons. For a fraction of time she was happy. Then her brain recommenced.

'I am afraid there has been gossiping of some kind at the George. Helen would not have left unless she had heard something. I mismanaged that. It is wretched. I ought to have parted her from that woman at once.'

'Margaret!' he exclaimed, loosing her arm impressively.

'Yes—yes, Henry?'

'I am far from a saint—in fact, the reverse—but you have taken me, for better or worse. Bygones must be bygones. You have promised to forgive me. Margaret, a promise is a promise. Never mention that woman again.'

'Except for some practical reason—never.'

'Practical! You practical!'

'Yes, I'm practical,' she murmured, stooping over the mowing-machine and playing with the grass which trickled through her fingers like sand.

He had silenced her, but her fears made him uneasy. Not for the first time, he was threatened with blackmail. He was rich and supposed to be moral; the Basts knew that he was not, and might find it profitable to hint as much.

'At all events, you mustn't worry,' he said. 'This is a man's business.' He thought intently. 'On no account mention it to anybody.'

Margaret flushed at advice so elementary, but he was really paving the way for a lie. If necessary he would deny that he had ever known Mrs Bast, and prosecute her for libel. Perhaps he never had known her. Here was Margaret, who behaved as if he had not. There the house. Round them were half a dozen gardeners, clearing up after his daughter's wedding. All was so solid and spruce, that the past flew up out of sight like a spring-blind, leaving only the last five minutes unrolled.

Glancing at these, he saw that the car would be round during the next five, and plunged into action. Gongs were tapped, orders issued, Margaret was sent to dress, and the housemaid to sweep up the long trickle of grass that she had left across the hall. As is Man to the Universe, so was the mind of Mr Wilcox to the minds of some men—a concentrated light upon a tiny spot, a little Ten Minutes moving self-contained through its appointed years. No Pagan he, who lives for the Now, and may be wiser than all philosophers. He lived for the five minutes that have past, and the five to come; he had the business mind.

How did he stand now, as his motor slipped out of Oniton and breasted the great round hills? Margaret had heard a certain rumour, but was all right. She had forgiven him, God bless her, and he felt the manlier for it. Charles and Evie had not heard it, and never must hear. No more must Paul. Over his children he felt great tenderness, which he did not try to track to a cause: Mrs Wilcox was too far back in his life. He did not connect her with the sudden aching love that he felt for Evie. Poor little Evie! he trusted that Cahill would make her a decent husband.

And Margaret? How did she stand?

She had several minor worries. Clearly her sister had heard something. She dreaded meeting her in town. And she was anxious about Leonard, for whom they certainly were responsible. Nor ought Mrs Bast to starve. But the main situation had not altered. She still loved Henry. His actions, not his disposition, had disappointed her, and she could bear that. And she loved her future home. Standing up in the car, just where she had leapt from it two days before, she gazed back with deep emotion upon Oniton. Beside the Grange and the Castle keep, she could now pick out the church and the black-and-white gables of the George. There was the bridge, and the river nibbling its green peninsula. She could even see the bathing-shed, but while she was looking for Charles's new spring-board, the forehead of the hill rose up and hid the whole scene.

She never saw it again. Day and night the river flows down into England, day after day the sun retreats into the Welsh mountains, and the tower chimes, 'See the Conquering Hero.' But the Wilcoxes have no part in the place, nor in any place. It is not their names that recur in the parish register. It is not their ghosts that sigh among the alders at evening. They have swept into the valley and swept out of it, leaving a little dust and a little money behind.

Chapter Thirty

Tibby was now approaching his last year at Oxford. He had moved out of college, and was contemplating the Universe, or such portions of it as concerned him, for his comfortable lodgings in Long Wall. He was not concerned with much. When a young man is untroubled by passions and sincerely indifferent to public opinion, his outlook is necessarily limited. Tibby neither wished to strengthen the position of the rich nor to improve that of the poor, and so was well content to watch the elms nodding behind the mildly embattled parapets of Magdalen. There are worse lives. Though selfish, he was never cruel; though affected in manner, he never posed. Like Margaret, he disdained the heroic equipment, and it was only after many visits that men discovered Schlegel to possess a character and a brain. He had done well in Mods, much to the surprise of those who attended lectures and took proper exercise, and was now glancing disdainfully at Chinese in case he should some day consent to qualify as a Student Interpreter. To him thus employed Helen entered. A telegram had preceded her.

He noticed, in a distant way, that his sister had altered. As a rule he found her too pronounced, and had never come across this look of appeal, pathetic yet dignified—the look of a sailor who has lost everything at sea.

'I have come from Oniton,' she began. 'There has been a great deal of trouble there.'

'Who's for lunch?' said Tibby, picking up the claret, which was warming in the hearth. Helen sat down submissively at the table. 'Why such an early start?' he asked.

'Sunrise or something—when I could get away.'

'So I surmise. Why?'

'I don't know what's to be done, Tibby. I am very much upset at a piece of news that concerns Meg, and do not want to face her, and I am not going back to Wickham Place. I stopped here to tell you this.'

The landlady came in with the cutlets. Tibby put a marker in the leaves of his Chinese Grammar and helped them. Oxford – the Oxford of the vacation—dreamed and rustled outside, and indoors the little fire was coated with grey where the sunshine touched it. Helen continued her odd story.

'Give Meg my love and say that I want to be alone. I mean to go to Munich or else Bonn.'

'Such a message is easily given,' said her brother.

'As regards Wickham Place and my share of the furniture, you and she are to do exactly as you like. My own feeling is that everything may just as well be sold. What does one want with dusty economic books, which have made the world no better, or with mother's hideous cheffoniers? I have also another commission for you. I want you to deliver a letter.' She got up. 'I haven't written it yet. Why shouldn't I post it, though?' She sat down again. 'My head is rather wretched. I hope that none of your friends are likely to come in.'

Tibby locked the door. His friends often found it in this condition. Then he asked whether anything had gone wrong at Evie's wedding.

'Not there,' said Helen, and burst into tears.

He had known her hysterical—it was one of her aspects with which he had no concern—and yet these tears touched him as something unusual. They were nearer the things that did concern him, such as music. He laid down his knife and looked at her curiously. Then, as she continued to sob, he went on with his lunch.

The time came for the second course, and she was still crying. Apple Charlotte was to follow, which spoils by waiting. 'Do you mind Mrs Martlett coming in?' he asked, 'or shall I take it from her at the door?'

'Could I bathe my eyes, Tibby?'

He took her to his bedroom, and introduced the pudding in her absence. Having helped himself, he put it down to warm in the hearth. His hand stretched towards the Grammar, and soon he was turning over the pages, raising his eyebrows scornfully, perhaps at human nature, perhaps at Chinese. To him thus employed Helen returned. She had pulled herself together, but the grave appeal had not vanished from her eyes.

'Now for the explanation,' she said. 'Why didn't I begin with it? I have found out something about Mr Wilcox. He has behaved very wrongly indeed, and ruined two people's lives. It all came on me very suddenly last night; I am very much upset, and I do not know what to do. Mrs Bast—'

'Oh, those people!'

Helen seemed silenced.

'Shall I lock the door again?'

'No thanks, Tibbikins. You're being very good to me. I want to tell you the story before I go abroad. You must do exactly what you like—treat it as part of the furniture. Meg cannot have heard it yet, I think. But I cannot face her and tell her that the man she is going to marry has misconducted himself. I don't even know whether she ought to be told. Knowing as she does that I dislike him, she will suspect me, and think that I want to ruin her match. I simply don't know what to make of such a thing. I trust your judgment. What would you do?'

'I gather he has had a mistress,' said Tibby.

Helen flushed with shame and anger. 'And ruined two people's lives. And goes about saying that personal actions count for nothing, and there always will be rich and poor. He met her when he was trying to get rich out in Cyprus—I don't wish to make him worse than he is, and no doubt she was ready enough to meet him. But there it is. They met. He goes his way and she goes hers. What do you suppose is the end of such women?'

He conceded that it was a bad business.

'They end in two ways: Either they sink till the lunatic asylums and the workhouses are full of them, and cause Mr Wilcox to write letters to the papers complaining of our national degeneracy, or else they entrap a boy into marriage before it is too late. She—I can't blame her.'

'But this isn't all,' she continued after a long pause, during which the landlady served them with coffee. 'I come now to the business that took us to Oniton. We went all three. Acting on Mr Wilcox's advice, the man throws up a secure situation and takes an insecure one, from which he is dismissed. There are certain excuses, but in the main Mr Wilcox is to blame, as Meg herself admitted. It is only common justice that he should employ the man himself. But he meets the woman, and, like the cur that he is, he refuses, and tries to get rid of them. He makes Meg write. Two notes came from her late that evening—one for me, one for Leonard, dismissing him with barely a reason. I couldn't understand. Then it comes out that Mrs Bast had spoken to Mr Wilcox on the lawn while we left her to get rooms, and was still speaking about him when Leonard came back to her. This Leonard knew all along. He thought it natural he should be ruined twice. Natural! Could you have contained yourself?'

'It is certainly a very bad business,' said Tibby.

His reply seemed to calm his sister. 'I was afraid that I saw it out of proportion. But you are right outside it, and you must know. In a day or two—or perhaps a week—take whatever steps you think fit. I leave it in your hands.'

She concluded her charge.

'The facts as they touch Meg are all before you,' she added; and Tibby sighed and felt it rather hard that, because of his open mind, he should be empanelled to serve as a juror. He had never been interested in human beings, for which one must blame him, but he had had rather too much of them at Wickham Place. Just as some people cease to attend when books are mentioned, so Tibby's attention wandered when 'personal relations' came under discussion. Ought Margaret to know what Helen knew the Basts to know? Similar questions had vexed him from infancy, and at Oxford he had learned to say that the importance of human beings has been vastly overrated by specialists. The epigram, with its faint whiff of the eighties, meant nothing. But he might have let it off now if his sister had not been ceaselessly beautiful.

'You see, Helen—have a cigarette—I don't see what I'm to do.'

'Then there's nothing to be done. I dare say you are right. Let them marry. There remains the question of compensation.'

'Do you want me to adjudicate that too? Had you not better consult an expert?'

'This part is in confidence,' said Helen. 'It has nothing to do with Meg, and do not mention it to her. The compensation—I do not see who is to pay it if I don't, and I have already decided on the minimum sum. As soon as possible I am placing it to your account, and when I am in Germany you will pay it over for me. I shall never forget your kindness, Tibbikins, if you do this.'

'What is the sum?'

'Five thousand.'

'Good God alive!' said Tibby, and went crimson.

'Now, what is the good of driblets? To go through life having done one thing—to have raised one person from the abyss: not these puny gifts of shillings and blankets—making the grey more grey. No doubt people will think me extraordinary.'

'I don't care a damn what people think!' cried he, heated to unusual manliness of diction. 'But it's half what you have.'

'Not nearly half.' She spread out her hands over her soiled skirt. 'I have far too much, and we settled at Chelsea last spring that three hundred a year is necessary to set a man on his feet. What I give will bring in a hundred and fifty between two. It isn't enough.'

He could not recover. He was not angry or even shocked, and he saw that Helen would still have plenty to live on. But it amazed him to think what haycocks people can make of their lives. His delicate intonations would not work, and he could only blurt out that the five thousand pounds would mean a great deal of bother for him personally.

'I didn't expect you to understand me.'

'I? I understand nobody.'

'But you'll do it?'

'Apparently.'

'I leave you two commissions, then. The first concerns Mr Wilcox, and you are to use your discretion. The second concerns the money, and is to be mentioned to no one, and carried out literally. You will send a hundred pounds on account tomorrow.'

He walked with her to the station, passing through those streets whose serried beauty never bewildered him and never fatigued. The lovely creature raised domes and spires into the cloudless blue, and only the ganglion of vulgarity round Carfax showed how evanescent was the phantom, how faint its claim to represent England. Helen, rehearsing her commission, noticed nothing: the Basts were in her brain, and she retold the crisis in a meditative way, which might have made other men curious. She was seeing whether it would hold. He asked her once why she had taken the Basts right into the heart of Evie's wedding. She stopped like a frightened animal and said, 'Does that seem to you so odd?' Her eyes, the hand laid on the mouth, quite haunted him, until they were absorbed into the figure of St Mary the Virgin, before whom he paused for a moment on the walk home.

It is convenient to follow him in the discharge of his duties. Margaret summoned him the next day. She was terrified at Helen's flight, and he had to say that she had called in at Oxford. Then she said: 'Did she seem worried at any rumour about Henry?' He answered, 'Yes.' 'I knew it was that!' she exclaimed. 'I'll write to her.' Tibby was relieved.

He then sent the cheque to the address that Helen gave him, and stated that later on he was instructed to forward five thousand pounds. An answer came back, very civil and quiet in tone—such an answer as Tibby himself would have given. The cheque was returned, the legacy refused, the writer being in no need of money. Tibby forwarded this to Helen, adding in the fullness of his heart that Leonard Bast seemed somewhat a monumental person after all. Helen's reply was frantic. He was to take no notice. He was to go down at once and say that she commanded acceptance. He went. A scurf of books and china ornaments awaited him. The Basts had just been evicted for not paying their rent, and had wandered no one knew whither. Helen had begun bungling with her money by this time, and had even sold out her shares in the Nottingham and Derby Railway. For some weeks she did nothing. Then she reinvested, and, owing to the good advice of her stockbrokers, became rather richer than she had been before.

Chapter Thirty-one

Houses have their own ways of dying, falling as variously as the generations of men, some with a tragic roar, some quietly, but to an after-life in the city of ghosts, while from others–and thus was the death of Wickham Place–the spirit slips before the body perishes. It had decayed in the spring, disintegrating the girls more than they knew, and causing either to accost unfamiliar regions. By September it was a corpse, void of emotion, and scarcely hallowed by the memories of thirty years of happiness. Through its round-topped doorway passed furniture, and pictures, and books, until the last room was gutted and the last van had rumbled away. It stood for a week or two longer, open-eyed, as if astonished at its own emptiness. Then it fell. Navvies came, and spilt it back into the grey. With their muscles and their beery good temper, they were not the worst of undertakers for a house which had always been human, and had not mistaken culture for an end.

The furniture, with a few exceptions, went down into Hertfordshire, Mr Wilcox having most kindly offered Howards End as a warehouse. Mr Bryce had died abroad–an unsatisfactory affair–and as there seemed little guarantee that the rent would be paid regularly, he cancelled the agreement, and resumed possession himself. Until he relet the house, the Schlegels were welcome to stack their furniture in the garage and lower rooms. Margaret demurred, but Tibby accepted the offer gladly; it saved him from coming to any decision about the future. The plate and the more valuable pictures found a safer home in London, but the bulk of the things went country-ways, and were entrusted to the guardianship of Miss Avery.

Shortly before the move, our hero and heroine were married. They have weathered the storm, and may reasonably expect peace. To have no illusions and yet to love–what stronger surety can a woman find? She had seen her husband's past as well as his heart. She knew her own heart with a thoroughness that commonplace people believe impossible. The heart of Mrs Wilcox was alone hidden, and perhaps it is superstitious to speculate on the feelings of the dead. They were married quietly—really quietly, for as the day approached she refused to go through another Oniton. Her brother gave her away, her aunt, who was out of health, presided over a few colourless refreshments. The Wilcoxes were represented by Charles, who witnessed the marriage settlement, and by Mr Cahill. Paul did send a cablegram. In a few minutes, and without the aid of music, the clergyman made them man and wife, and soon the glass shade had fallen that cuts off married couples from the world. She, a monogamist, regretted the cessation of some of life's innocent odours; he, whose instincts were polygamous, felt morally braced by the change, and less liable to the temptations that had assailed him in the past.

They spent their honeymoon near Innsbruck. Henry knew of a reliable hotel there, and Margaret hoped for a meeting with her sister. In this she was disappointed. As they came south, Helen retreated over the Brenner, and wrote an unsatisfactory postcard from the shores of the Lake of Garda, saying that her plans were uncertain and had better be ignored. Evidently she disliked meeting Henry. Two months are surely enough to accustom an outsider to a situation which a wife has accepted in two days, and Margaret had again to regret her sister's lack of self-control. In a long letter she pointed out the need of charity in sexual matters: so little is known about them; it is hard enough for those who are personally touched to judge; then how futile must be the verdict of Society. 'I don't say there is no standard, for that would destroy morality; only that there can be no standard until our impulses are classified and better understood.' Helen thanked her for her kind letter—rather a curious reply. She moved south again, and spoke of wintering in Naples.

Mr Wilcox was not sorry that the meeting failed. Helen left him time to grow skin over his wound. There were still moments when it pained him. Had he only known that Margaret was awaiting him—Margaret, so lively and intelligent, and yet so submissive—he would have kept himself worthier of her. Incapable of grouping the past, he confused the episode of Jacky with another episode that had taken place in the days of his bachelorhood. The two made one crop of wild oats, for which he was heartily sorry, and he could not see that those oats are of a darker stock which are rooted in another's dishonour. Unchastity and infidelity were as confused to him as to the Middle Ages, his only moral teacher. Ruth (poor old Ruth!) did not enter into his calculations at all, for poor old Ruth had never found him out.

His affection for his present wife grew steadily. Her cleverness gave him no trouble, and, indeed, he liked to see her reading poetry or something about social questions; it distinguished her from the wives of other men. He had only to call, and she clapped the book up and was ready to do what he wished. Then they would argue so jollily, and once or twice she had him in quite a tight corner, but as soon as he grew really serious, she gave in. Man is for war, woman for the recreation of the warrior, but he does not dislike it if she makes a show of fight. She cannot win in a real battle, having no muscles, only nerves. Nerves make her jump out of a moving motor-car, or refuse to be married fashionably. The warrior may well allow her to triumph on such occasions; they move not the imperishable plinth of things that touch his peace.

Margaret had a bad attack of these nerves during the honeymoon. He told her—casually, as was his habit—that Oniton Grange was let. She showed her annoyance, and asked rather crossly why she had not been consulted.

'I didn't want to bother you,' he replied. 'Besides, I have only heard for certain this morning.'

'Where are we to live?' said Margaret, trying to laugh. 'I loved the place extraordinarily. Don't you believe in having a permanent home, Henry?'

He assured her that she misunderstood him. It is home life that distinguishes us from the foreigner. But he did not believe in a damp home.

'This is news. I never heard till this minute that Oniton was damp.'

'My dear girl!'—he flung out his hand—'have you eyes? have you a skin? How could it be anything but damp in such a situation? In the first place, the Grange is on clay, and built where the castle moat must have been; then there's that detestable little river, steaming all night like a kettle. Feel the cellar walls; look up under the eaves. Ask Sir James or anyone. Those Shropshire valleys are notorious. The only possible place for a house in Shropshire is on a hill; but, for my part, I think the country is too far from London, and the scenery nothing special.'

Margaret could not resist saying, 'Why did you go there, then?'

'I—because—' He drew his head back and grew rather angry. 'Why have we come to the Tyrol, if it comes to that? One might go on asking such questions indefinitely.'

One might; but he was only gaining time for a plausible answer. Out it came, and he believed it as soon as it was spoken.

'The truth is, I took Oniton on account of Evie. Don't let this go any further.'

'Certainly not.'

'I shouldn't like her to know that she nearly let me in for a very bad bargain. No sooner did I sign the agreement than she got engaged. Poor little girl! She was so keen on it all, and wouldn't even wait to make proper inquiries about the shooting. Afraid it would get snapped up—just like all of your sex. Well, no harm's done. She has had her country wedding, and I've got rid of my house to some fellows who are starting a preparatory school.'

'Where shall we live, then, Henry? I should enjoy living somewhere.'

'I have not yet decided. What about Norfolk?'

Margaret was silent. Marriage had not saved her from the sense of flux. London was but a foretaste of this nomadic civilization which is altering human nature so profoundly, and throws upon personal relations a stress greater than they have ever borne before. Under cosmopolitanism, if it comes, we shall receive no help from the earth. Trees and meadows and mountains will only be a spectacle, and the binding force that they once exercised on character must be entrusted to Love alone. May Love be equal to the task!

'It is now what?' continued Henry. 'Nearly October. Let us camp for the winter at Ducie Street, and look out for something in the spring.'

'If possible, something permanent. I can't be as young as I was, for these alterations don't suit me.'

'But, my dear, which would you rather have—alterations or rheumatism?'

'I see your point,' said Margaret, getting up. 'If Oniton is really damp, it is impossible, and must be inhabited by little boys. Only, in the spring, let us look before we leap. I will take warning by Evie, and not hurry you. Remember that you have a free hand this time. These endless moves must be bad for the furniture, and are certainly expensive.'

'What a practical little woman it is! What's it been reading? Theo—theo—how much?'

'Theosophy.'

So Ducie Street was her first fate—a pleasant enough fate. The house, being only a little larger than Wickham Place, trained her for the immense establishment that was promised in the spring. They were frequently away, but at home life ran fairly regularly. In the morning Henry went to the business, and his sandwich—a relic this of some prehistoric craving—was always cut by her own hand. He did not rely upon the sandwich for lunch, but liked to have it by him in case he grew hungry at eleven. When he had gone, there was the house to look after, and the servants to humanize, and several kettles of Helen's to keep on the boil. Her conscience pricked her a little about the Basts; she was not sorry to have lost sight of them. No doubt Leonard was worth helping, but being Henry's wife, she preferred to help someone else. As for theatres and discussion societies, they attracted her less and less. She began to 'miss' new movements, and to spend her spare time re-reading or thinking, rather to the concern of her Chelsea friends. They attributed the change to her marriage, and perhaps some deep instinct did warn her not to travel further from her husband than was inevitable. Yet the main cause lay deeper still; she had outgrown stimulants, and was passing from words to things. It was doubtless a pity not to keep up with Wedekind or John, but some closing of the gates is inevitable after thirty, if the mind itself is to become a creative power.

Chapter Thirty-two

She was looking at plans one day in the following spring—they had finally decided to go down into Sussex and build—when Mrs Charles Wilcox was announced.

'Have you heard the news?' Dolly cried, as soon as she entered the room. 'Charles is so ang—I mean he is sure you know about it, or, rather, that you don't know.'

'Why, Dolly!' said Margaret, placidly kissing her. 'Here's a surprise! How are the boys and the baby?'

Boys and the baby were well, and in describing a great row that there had been at the Hilton Tennis Club, Dolly forgot her news. The wrong people had tried to get in. The rector, as representing the older inhabitants, had said—Charles had said—the tax-collector had said—Charles had regretted not saying—and she closed the description with, 'But lucky you, with four courts of your own at Midhurst.'

'It will be very jolly,' replied Margaret.

'Are those the plans? Does it matter me seeing them?'

'Of course not.'

'Charles has never seen the plans.'

'They have only just arrived. Here is the ground floor—no, that's rather difficult. Try the elevation. We are to have a good many gables and a picturesque sky-line.'

'What makes it smell so funny?' said Dolly, after a moment's inspection. She was incapable of understanding plans or maps.

'I suppose the paper.'

'And *which* way up is it?'

'Just the ordinary way up. That's the sky-line, and the part that smells strongest is the sky.'

'Well, ask me another. Margaret—oh—what was I going to say? How's Helen?'

'Quite well.'

'Is she never coming back to England? Everyone thinks it's awfully odd she doesn't.'

'So it is,' said Margaret, trying to conceal her vexation. She was getting rather sore on this point. 'Helen is odd, awfully. She has now been away eight months.'

'But hasn't she any address?'

'A poste restante somewhere in Bavaria is her address. Do write her a line. I will look it up for you.'

'No, don't bother. That's eight months she has been away, surely?'

'Exactly. She left just after Evie's wedding. It would be eight months.'

'Just when baby was born, then?'

'Just so.'

Dolly sighed, and stared enviously round the drawing-room. She was beginning to lose her brightness and good looks. The Charles' were not well off, for Mr Wilcox, having brought up his children with expensive tastes, believed in letting them shift for themselves. After all, he had not treated them generously. Yet another baby was expected, she told Margaret, and they would have to give up the motor. Margaret sympathized, but in a formal fashion, and Dolly little imagined that the step-mother was urging Mr Wilcox to make them a more liberal allowance. She sighed again, and at last the particular grievance was remembered. 'Oh yes,' she cried, 'that is it: Miss Avery has been unpacking your packing-cases.'

'Why has she done that? How unnecessary!'

'Ask another. I suppose you ordered her to.'

'I gave no such orders. Perhaps she was airing the things. She did undertake to light an occasional fire.'

'It was far more than an air,' said Dolly solemnly. 'The floor sounds covered with books. Charles sent me to know what is to be done, for he feels certain you don't know.'

'Books!' cried Margaret, moved by the holy word. 'Dolly, are you serious? Has she been touching our books?'

'Hasn't she, though! What used to be the hall's full of them. Charles thought for certain you knew of it.'

'I am very much obliged to you, Dolly. What can have come over Miss Avery? I must go down about it at once. Some of the books are my brother's, and are quite valuable. She had no right to open any of the cases.'

'I say she's dotty. She was the one that never got married, you know. Oh, I say, perhaps she thinks your books are wedding-presents to herself. Old maids are taken that way sometimes. Miss Avery hates us all like poison ever since her frightful dust-up with Evie.'

'I hadn't heard of that,' said Margaret. A visit from Dolly had its compensations.

'Didn't you know she gave Evie a present last August, and Evie returned it, and then—oh, goloshes! You never read such a letter as Miss Avery wrote.'

'But it was wrong of Evie to return it. It wasn't like her to do such a heartless thing.'

'But the present was so expensive.'

'Why does that make any difference, Dolly?'

'Still, when it costs over five pounds—I didn't see it, but it was a lovely enamel pendant from a Bond Street shop. You can't very well accept that kind of thing from a farm woman. Now, can you?'

'You accepted a present from Miss Avery when you were married.'

'Oh, mine was old earthenware stuff—not worth a halfpenny. Evie's was quite different. You'd have to ask anyone to the wedding who gave you a pendant like that. Uncle Percy and Albert and father and Charles all said it was quite impossible, and when four men agree, what is a girl to do? Evie didn't want to upset the old thing, so thought a sort of joking letter best, and returned the pendant straight to the shop to save Miss Avery trouble.'

'But Miss Avery said—'

Dolly's eyes grew round. 'It was a perfectly awful letter. Charles said it was the letter of a madman. In the end she had the pendant back again from the shop and threw it into the duck-pond.'

'Did she give any reasons?'

'We think she meant to be invited to Oniton, and so climb into society.'

'She's rather old for that,' said Margaret pensively. 'May not she have given the present to Evie in remembrance of her mother?'

'That's a notion. Give everyone their due, eh? Well, I suppose I ought to be toddling. Come along Mr Muff—you want a new coat, but I don't know who'll give it you, I'm sure;' and addressing her apparel with mournful humour, Dolly moved from the room.

Margaret followed her to ask whether Henry knew about Miss Avery's rudeness.

'Oh yes.'

'I wonder, then, why he let me ask her to look after the house.'

'But she's only a farm woman,' said Dolly, and her explanation proved correct. Henry only censured the lower classes when it suited him. He bore with Miss Avery as with Crane—because he could get good value out of them. 'I have patience with a man who knows his job,' he would say, really having patience with the job, and not the man. Paradoxical as it may sound, he had something of the artist about him; he would pass over an insult to his daughter sooner than lose a good charwoman for his wife.

Margaret judged it better to settle the little trouble herself. Parties were evidently ruffled. With Henry's permission, she wrote a pleasant note to Miss Avery, asking her to leave the cases untouched. Then, at the first convenient opportunity, she went down herself, intending to repack her belongings and store them properly in the local warehouse: the plan had been amateurish and a failure. Tibby promised to accompany her, but at the last moment begged to be excused. So, for the second time in her life, she entered the house alone.

Chapter Thirty-three

The day of her visit was exquisite, and the last of unclouded happiness that she was to have for many months. Her anxiety about Helen's extraordinary absence was still dormant, and as for a possible brush with Miss Avery—that only gave zest to the expedition. She had also eluded Dolly's invitation to luncheon. Walking straight up from the station, she crossed the village green and entered the long chestnut avenue that connects it with the church. The church itself stood in the village once. But it there attracted so many worshippers that the devil, in a pet, snatched it from its foundations, and poised it on an inconvenient knoll, three-quarters of a mile away. If this story is true, the chestnut avenue must have been planted by the angels. No more tempting approach could be imagined for the lukewarm Christian, and if he still finds the walk too long, the devil is defeated all the same, Science having built Holy Trinity, a Chapel of Ease, near the Charles', and roofed it with tin.

Up the avenue Margaret strolled slowly, stopping to watch the sky that gleamed through the upper branches of the chestnuts, or to finger the little horseshoes on the lower branches. Why has not England a great mythology? Our folklore has never advanced beyond daintiness, and the greater melodies about our country-side have all issued through the pipes of Greece. Deep and true as the native imagination can be, it seems to have failed here. It has stopped with the witches and the fairies. It cannot vivify one fraction of a summer field, or give names to half a dozen stars. England still waits for the supreme moment of her literature—for the great poet who shall voice her, or, better still, for the thousand little poets whose voices shall pass into our common talk.

At the church the scenery changed. The chestnut avenue opened into a road, smooth but narrow, which led into the untouched country. She followed it for over a mile. Its little hesitations pleased her. Having no urgent destiny, it strolled downhill or up as it wished, taking no trouble about the gradients, nor about the view, which nevertheless expanded. The great estates that throttle the south of Hertfordshire were less obtrusive here, and the appearance of the land was neither aristocratic nor suburban. To define it was difficult, but Margaret knew what it was not: it was not snobbish. Though its contours were slight, there was a touch of freedom in their sweep to which Surrey will never attain, and the distant brow of the Chilterns towered like a mountain. 'Left to itself,' was Margaret's opinion, 'this county would vote Liberal.' The comradeship, not passionate, that is our highest gift as a nation, was promised by it, as by the low brick farm where she called for the key.

But the inside of the farm was disappointing. A most finished young person received her. 'Yes, Mrs Wilcox; no, Mrs Wilcox; oh yes, Mrs Wilcox, auntie received your letter quite duly. Auntie has gone up to your little place at the present moment. Shall I send the servant to direct you?' Followed by: 'Of course, auntie does not generally look after your place; she only does it to oblige a neighbour as something exceptional. It gives her something to do. She spends quite a lot of her time there. My husband says to me sometimes, "Where's auntie?" I say, "Need you ask? She's at Howards End." Yes, Mrs Wilcox. Mrs Wilcox, could I prevail upon you to accept a piece of cake? Not if I cut it for you?'

Margaret refused the cake, but unfortunately this acquired her gentility in the eyes of Miss Avery's niece.

'I cannot let you go on alone. Now don't. You really mustn't. I will direct you myself if it comes to that. I must get my hat. Now'—roguishly—'Mrs Wilcox, don't you move while I'm gone.'

Stunned, Margaret did not move from the best parlour, over which the touch of art nouveau had fallen. But the other rooms looked in keeping, though they conveyed the peculiar sadness of a rural interior. Here had lived an elder race, to which we look back with disquietude. The country which we visit at week-ends was really a home to it, and the graver sides of life, the deaths, the partings, the yearnings for love, have their deepest expression in the heart of the fields. All was not sadness. The sun was shining without. The thrush sang his two syllables on the budding guelder-rose. Some children were playing uproariously in heaps of golden straw. It was the presence of sadness at all that surprised Margaret, and ended by giving her a feeling of completeness. In these English farms, if anywhere, one might see life steadily and see it whole, group in one vision its transitoriness and its eternal youth, connect—connect without bitterness until all men are brothers. But her thoughts were interrupted by the return of Miss Avery's niece, and were so tranquillizing that she suffered the interruption gladly.

It was quicker to go out by the back door, and, after due explanations, they went out by it. The niece was now mortified by innumerable chickens, who rushed up to her feet for food, and by a shameless and maternal sow. She did not know what animals were coming to. But her gentility withered at the touch of the sweet air. The wind was rising, scattering the straw and ruffling the tails of the ducks as they floated in families over Evie's pendant. One of those delicious gales of spring, in which leaves still in bud seem to rustle, swept over the land and then fell silent. 'Georgie,' sang the thrush. 'Cuckoo,' came furtively from the cliff of pine-trees. 'Georgie, pretty Georgie,' and the other birds joined in with nonsense. The hedge was a half-painted picture which would be finished in a few days. Celandines grew on its banks, lords and ladies and primroses in the defended hollows; the wild rose-bushes, still bearing their withered hips, showed also the promise of blossom. Spring had come, clad in no classical garb, yet fairer than all springs; fairer even than she who walks through the myrtles of Tuscany with the graces before her and the zephyr behind.

The two women walked up the lane full of outward civility. But Margaret was thinking how difficult it was to be earnest about furniture on such a day, and the niece was thinking about hats. Thus engaged, they reached Howards End. Petulant cries of 'Auntie!' severed the air. There was no reply, and the front door was locked.

'Are you sure that Miss Avery is up here?' asked Margaret.

'Oh yes, Mrs Wilcox, quite sure. She is here daily.'

Margaret tried to look in through the dining-room window, but the curtain inside was drawn tightly. So were the drawing-room and the hall. The appearance of these curtains was familiar, yet she did not remember them being there on her other visit: her impression was that Mr Bryce had taken everything away. They tried the back. Here again they received no answer, and could see nothing; the kitchen-window was fitted with a blind, while the pantry and scullery had pieces of wood propped up against them, which looked ominously like the lids of packing-cases. Margaret thought of her books, and she lifted up her voice also. At the first cry she succeeded.

'Well, well!' replied someone inside the house. 'If it isn't Mrs Wilcox come at last!'

'Have you got the key, auntie?'

'Madge, go away,' said Miss Avery, still invisible.

'Auntie, it's Mrs Wilcox—'

Margaret supported her. 'Your niece and I have come together—'

'Madge, go away. This is no moment for your hat.'

The poor woman went red. 'Auntie gets more eccentric lately,' she said nervously.

'Miss Avery!' called Margaret. 'I have come about the furniture. Could you kindly let me in?'

'Yes, Mrs Wilcox,' said the voice, 'of course.' But after that came silence. They called again without response. They walked round the house disconsolately.

'I hope Miss Avery is not ill,' hazarded Margaret.

'Well, if you'll excuse me,' said Madge, 'perhaps I ought to be leaving you

now. The servants need seeing to at the farm. Auntie is so odd at times.'
Gathering up her elegancies, she retired defeated, and, as if her departure
had loosed a spring, the front door opened at once.

Miss Avery said, 'Well, come right in, Mrs Wilcox!' quite pleasantly and
calmly.

'Thank you so much,' began Margaret, but broke off at the sight of an
umbrella-stand. It was her own.

'Come right into the hall first,' said Miss Avery. She drew the curtain, and
Margaret uttered a cry of despair. For an appalling thing had happened. The
hall was fitted up with the contents of the library from Wickham Place. The
carpet had been laid, the big work-table drawn up near the window; the
bookcases filled the wall opposite the fireplace, and her father's sword–this
is what bewildered her particularly–had been drawn from its scabbard and
hung naked amongst the sober volumes. Miss Avery must have worked for
days.

'I'm afraid this isn't what we meant,' she began. 'Mr Wilcox and I never
intended the cases to be touched. For instance, these books are my brother's.
We are storing them for him and for my sister, who is abroad. When you
kindly undertook to look after things, we never expected you to do so much.'

'The house has been empty long enough,' said the old woman.

Margaret refused to argue. 'I dare say we didn't explain,' she said civilly.
'It has been a mistake, and very likely our mistake.'

'Mrs Wilcox, it has been mistake upon mistake for fifty years. The house
is Mrs Wilcox's, and she would not desire it to stand empty any longer.'

To help the poor decaying brain, Margaret said:

'Yes, Mrs Wilcox's house, the mother of Mr Charles.'

'Mistake upon mistake,' said Miss Avery. 'Mistake upon mistake.'

'Well, I don't know,' said Margaret, sitting down in one of her own chairs.
'I really don't know what's to be done.' She could not help laughing.

The other said: 'Yes, it should be a merry house enough.'

'I don't know–I dare say. Well, thank you very much, Miss Avery. Yes,
that's all right. Delightful.'

'There is still the parlour.' She went through the door opposite and drew a
curtain. Light flooded the drawing-room and the drawing-room furniture
from Wickham Place. 'And the dining-room.' More curtains were drawn,
more windows were flung open to the spring. 'Then through here—' Miss
Avery continued passing and repassing through the hall. Her voice was lost,
but Margaret heard her pulling up the kitchen blind. 'I've not finished here
yet,' she announced, returning. 'There's still a deal to do. The farm lads will
carry your great wardrobes upstairs, for there is no need to go into expense at
Hilton.'

'It is all a mistake,' repeated Margaret, feeling that she must put her foot
down. 'A misunderstanding. Mr Wilcox and I are not going to live at
Howards End.'

'Oh, indeed. On account of his hay fever?'

'We have settled to build a new home for ourselves in Sussex, and part of
this furniture–my part–will go down there presently.' She looked at Miss

Avery intently, trying to understand the kink in her brain. Here was no maundering old woman. Her wrinkles were shrewd and humorous. She looked capable of scathing wit and also of high but unostentatious nobility.

'You think that you won't come back to live here, Mrs Wilcox, but you will.'

'That remains to be seen,' said Margaret, smiling. 'We have no intention of doing so for the present. We happen to need a much larger house. Circumstances oblige us to give big parties. Of course, some day—one never knows, does one?'

Miss Avery retorted: 'Some day! Tcha! tcha! Don't talk about some day. You are living here now.'

'Am I?'

'You are living here, and have been for the last ten minutes, if you ask me.'

It was a senseless remark, but with a queer feeling of disloyalty Margaret rose from her chair. She felt that Henry had been obscurely censured. They went into the dining-room, where the sunlight poured in upon her mother's cheffonier, and upstairs, where many an old god peeped from a new niche. The furniture fitted extraordinarily well. In the central room—over the hall, the room that Helen had slept in four years ago—Miss Avery had placed Tibby's old bassinette.

'The nursery,' she said.

Margaret turned away without speaking.

At last everything was seen. The kitchen and lobby were still stacked with furniture and straw, but, as far as she could make out, nothing had been broken or scratched. A pathetic display of ingenuity! Then they took a friendly stroll in the garden. It had gone wild since her last visit. The gravel sweep was weedy, and grass had sprung up at the very jaws of the garage. And Evie's rockery was only bumps. Perhaps Evie was responsible for Miss Avery's oddness. But Margaret suspected the the cause lay deeper, and that the girl's silly letter had but loosed the irritation of years.

'It's a beautiful meadow,' she remarked. It was one of those open-air drawing-rooms that have been formed, hundreds of years ago, out of the smaller fields. So the boundary hedge zigzagged down the hill at right angles, and at the bottom there was a little green annex—a sort of powder-closet for the cows.

'Yes, the maidy's well enough,' said Miss Avery, 'for those, that is, who don't suffer from sneezing.' And she cackled maliciously. 'I've seen Charlie Wilcox go out to my lads in hay time—oh, they ought to do this—they mustn't do that—he'd learn them to be lads. And just then the tickling took him. He has it from his father, with other things. There's not one Wilcox that can stand up against a field in June—I laughed fit to burst while he was courting Ruth.'

'My brother gets hay fever too,' said Margaret.

'This house lies too much on the land for them. Naturally, they were glad enough to slip in at first. But Wilcoxes are better than nothing, as I see you've found.'

Margaret laughed.

'They keep a place going, don't they? Yes, it is just that.'

'They keep England going, it is my opinion.'

But Miss Avery upset her by replying: 'Ay, they breed like rabbits. Well, well, it's a funny world. But He who made it knows what He wants in it, I suppose. If Mrs Charlie is expecting her fourth, it isn't for us to repine.'

'They breed and they also work,' said Margaret, conscious of some invitation to disloyalty, which was echoed by the very breeze and by the songs of the birds. 'It certainly is a funny world, but so long as men like my husband and his sons govern it, I think it'll never be a bad one—never really bad.'

'No, better'n nothing,' said Miss Avery, and turned to the wych-elm.

On their way back to the farm she spoke of her old friend much more clearly than before. In the house Margaret had wondered whether she quite distinguished the first wife from the second. Now she said: 'I never saw much of Ruth after her grandmother died, but we stayed civil. It was a very civil family. Old Mrs Howard never spoke against anybody, nor let anyone be turned away without food. Then it was never "Trespassers will be prosecuted" in their land, but would people please not come in? Mrs Howard was never created to run a farm.'

'Had they no men to help them?' Margaret asked.

Miss Avery replied: 'Things went on until there were no men.'

'Until Mr Wilcox came along,' corrected Margaret, anxious that her husband should receive his dues.

'I suppose so; but Ruth should have married a—no disrespect to you to say this, for I take it you were intended to get Wilcox any way, whether she got him first or no.'

'Whom should she have married?'

'A soldier!' exclaimed the old woman. 'Some real soldier.'

Margaret was silent. It was a criticism of Henry's character far more trenchant than any of her own. She felt dissatisfied.

'But that's all over,' she went on. 'A better time is coming now, though you've kept me long enough waiting. In a couple of weeks I'll see your lights shining through the hedge of an evening. Have you ordered in coals?'

'We are not coming,' said Margaret firmly. She respected Miss Avery too much to humour her. 'No. Not coming. Never coming. It has all been a mistake. The furniture must be repacked at once, and I am very sorry, but I am making other arrangements, and must ask you to give me the keys.'

'Certainly, Mrs Wilcox,' said Miss Avery, and resigned her duties with a smile.

Relieved at this conclusion, and having sent her compliments to Madge, Margaret walked back to the station. She had intended to go to the furniture warehouse and give directions for removal, but the muddle had turned out more extensive than she expected, so she decided to consult Henry. It was as well that she did this. He was strongly against employing the local man whom he had previously recommended, and advised her to store in London after all.

But before this could be done an unexpected trouble fell upon her.

Chapter Thirty-four

It was not unexpected entirely. Aunt Juley's health had been bad all the winter. She had had a long series of colds and coughs, and had been too busy to get rid of them. She had scarcely promised her niece 'to really take my tiresome chest in hand,' when she caught a chill and developed acute pneumonia. Margaret and Tibby went down to Swanage. Helen was telegraphed for, and that spring party that after all gathered in that hospitable house had all the pathos of fair memories. On a perfect day, when the sky seemed blue porcelain, and the waves of the discreet little bay beat gentlest of tattoos upon the sand, Margaret hurried up through the rhododendrons, confronted again by the senselessness of Death. One death may explain itself, but it throws no light upon another: the groping inquiry must begin anew. Preachers or scientists may generalize, but we know that no generality is possible about those whom we love; not one heaven awaits them, not even one oblivion. Aunt Juley, incapable of tragedy, slipped out of life with odd little laughs and apologies for having stopped in it so long. She was very weak; she could not rise to the occasion, or realize the great mystery which all agree must await her; it only seemed to her that she was quite done up—more done up than ever before; that she saw and heard and felt less every moment; and that, unless something changed, she would soon feel nothing. Her spare strength she devoted to plans: could not Margaret take some steamer expeditions? were mackerel cooked as Tibby liked them? She worried herself about Helen's absence, and also that she should be the cause of Helen's return. The nurses seemed to think such interests quite natural, and perhaps hers was an average approach to the Great Gate. But Margaret saw Death stripped of any false romance; whatever the idea of Death may contain, the process can be trivial and hideous.

'Important—Margaret dear, take the Lulworth when Helen comes.'

'Helen won't be able to stop, Aunt Juley. She has telegraphed that she can only get away just to see you. She must go back to Germany as soon as you are well.'

'How very odd of Helen! Mr Wilcox—'

'Yes, dear?'

'Can he spare you?'

Henry wished her to come, and had been very kind. Yet again Margaret said so.

Mrs Munt did not die. Quite outside her will, a more dignified power took hold of her and checked her on the downward slope. She returned, without emotion, as fidgety as ever. On the fourth day she was out of danger.

'Margaret—important,' it went on: 'I should like you to have some companion to take walks with. Do try Miss Conder.'

'I have been a litte walk with Miss Conder.'

'But she is not really interesting. If only you had Helen.'

'I have Tibby, Aunt Juley.'

'No, but he has to do his Chinese. Some real companion is what you need. Really, Helen is odd.'

'Helen is odd, very,' agreed Margaret.

'Not content with going abroad, why does she want to go back there at once?'

'No doubt she will change her mind when she sees us. She has not the least balance.'

That was the stock criticism about Helen, but Margaret's voice trembled as she made it. By now she was deeply pained at her sister's behaviour. It may be unbalanced to fly out of England, but to stop away eight months argues that the heart is awry as well as the head. A sick-bed could recall Helen, but she was deaf to more human calls; after a glimpse at her aunt, she would retire into her nebulous life behind some poste restante. She scarcely existed; her letters had become dull and infrequent; she had no wants and no curiosity. And it was all put down to poor Henry's account! Henry, long pardoned by his wife, was still too infamous to be greeted by his sister-in-law. It was morbid, and, to her alarm, Margaret fancied that she could trace the growth of morbidity back in Helen's life for nearly four years. The flight from Oniton; the unbalanced patronage of the Basts; the explosion of grief up on the Downs—all connected with Paul, an insignificant boy whose lips had kissed hers for a fraction of time. Margaret and Mrs Wilcox had feared that they might kiss again. Foolishly: the real danger was reaction. Reaction against the Wilcoxes had eaten into her life until she was scarcely sane. At twenty-five she had an idée fixe. What hope was there for her as an old woman?

The more Margaret thought about it the more alarmed she became. For many months she had put the subject away, but it was too big to be slighted now. There was almost a taint of madness. Were all Helen's actions to be governed by a tiny mishap, such as may happen to any young man or woman? Can human nature be constructed on lines so insignificant? The blundering little encounter at Howards End was vital. It propagated itself where graver intercourse lay barren; it was stronger than sisterly intimacy, stronger than reason or books. In one of her moods Helen had confessed that she still 'enjoyed' it in a certain sense. Paul had faded, but the magic of his caress endured. And where there is enjoyment of the past there may also be reaction—propagation at both ends.

Well, it is odd and sad that our minds should be such seed-beds, and we without power to choose the seed. But man is an odd, sad creature as yet, intent on pilfering the earth, and heedless of the growths within himself. He cannot be bored about psychology. He leaves it to the specialist, which is as if he should leave his dinner to be eaten by a steam-engine. He cannot be bothered to digest his own soul. Margaret and Helen have been more patient, and it is suggested that Margaret has succeeded—so far as success is yet possible. She does understand herself, she has some rudimentary control over her own growth. Whether Helen has succeeded one cannot say.

The day that Mrs Munt rallied Helen's letter arrived. She had posted it at Munich, and would be in London herself on the morrow. It was a disquieting letter, though the opening was affectionate and sane.

> Dearest Meg,
>   Give Helen's love to Aunt Juley. Tell her that I love, and have loved, her ever since I can remember. I shall be in London Thursday.
>   My address will be care of the bankers. I have not yet settled on a hotel, so write or wire to me there and give me detailed news. If Aunt Juley is much better, or if, for a terrible reason, it would be no good my coming down to Swanage, you must not think it odd if I do not come. I have all sorts of plans in my head. I am living abroad at present, and want to get back as quickly as possible. Will you please tell me where our furniture is. I should like to take out one or two books; the rest are for you.
>   Forgive me, dearest Meg. This must read like rather a tiresome letter, but all letters are from your loving
>
>   Helen.

It was a tiresome letter, for it tempted Margaret to tell a lie. If she wrote that Aunt Juley was still in danger her sister would come. Unhealthiness is contagious. We cannot be in contact with those who are in a morbid state without ourselves deteriorating. To 'act for the best' might do Helen good, but would do herself harm, and, at the risk of disaster, she kept her colours flying a little longer. She replied that their aunt was much better, and awaited developments.

Tibby approved of her reply. Mellowing rapidly, he was a pleasanter companion than before. Oxford had done much for him. He had lost his peevishness, and could hide his indifference to people and his interest in food. But he had not grown more human. The years between eighteen and twenty-two, so magical for most, were leading him gently from boyhood to middle age. He had never known young-manliness, that quality which warms the heart till death, and gives Mr Wilcox an imperishable charm. He was frigid, through no fault of his own, and without cruelty. He thought Helen wrong and Margaret right, but the family trouble was for him what a scene behind footlights is for most people. He had only one suggestion to make, and that was characteristic.

'Why don't you tell Mr Wilcox?'

'About Helen?'

'Perhaps he has come across that sort of thing.'

'He would do all he could, but—'

'Oh, you know best. But he is practical.'

It was the student's belief in experts. Margaret demurred for one or two reasons. Presently Helen's answer came. She sent a telegram requesting the address of the furniture, as she would now return at once. Margaret replied, 'Certainly not; meet me at the bankers at four.' She and Tibby went up to London. Helen was not at the bankers, and they were refused her address.

Helen had passed into chaos.

Margaret put her arm round her brother. He was all that she had left, and never had he seemed more unsubstantial.

'Tibby love, what next?'

He replied: 'It is extraordinary.'

'Dear, your judgment's often clearer than mine. Have you any notion what's at the back?'

'None, unless it's something mental.'

'Oh–that!' said Margaret. 'Quite impossible.' But the suggestion had been uttered, and in a few minutes she took it up herself. Nothing else explained. And London agreed with Tibby. The mask fell off the city, and she saw it for what it really is–a caricature of infinity. The familiar barriers, the streets along which she moved, the houses between which she had made her little journeys for so many years, became negligible suddenly. Helen seemed one with grimy trees and the traffic and the slowly-flowing slabs of mud. She had accomplished a hideous act of renunciation and returned to the One. Margaret's own faith held firm. She knew the human soul will be merged, if it be merged at all, with the stars and the sea. Yet she felt that her sister had been going amiss for many years. It was symbolic the catastrophe should come now, on a London afternoon, while rain fell slowly.

Henry was the only hope. Henry was definite. He might know of some paths in the chaos that were hidden from them, and she determined to take Tibby's advice and lay the whole matter in his hands. They must call at his office. He could not well make it worse. She went for a few moments into St Paul's, whose dome stands out of the welter so bravely, as if preaching the gospel of form. But within, St Paul's is as its surroundings–echoes and whispers, inaudible songs, invisible mosaics, wet footmarks crossing and recrossing the floor. Si monumentum requiris, circumspice: it points us back to London. There was no hope of Helen here.

Henry was unsatisfactory at first. That she had expected. He was overjoyed to see her back from Swanage, and slow to admit the growth of a new trouble. When they told him of their search, he only chaffed Tibby and the Schlegels generally, and declared that it was 'just like Helen' to lead her relatives a dance.

'That is what we all say,' replied Margaret. 'But why should it be just like Helen? Why should she be allowed to be so queer, and to grow queerer?'

'Don't ask me. I'm a plain man of business. I live and let live. My advice to you both is, don't worry. Margaret, you've got black marks again under your eyes. You know that's strictly forbidden. First your aunt–then your sister. No, we aren't going to have it. Are we, Theobald?' He rang the bell. 'I'll give you some tea, and then you go straight to Ducie Street. I can't have my girl looking as old as her husband.'

'All the same, you have not quite seen our point,' said Tibby.

Mr Wilcox, who was in good spirits, retorted, 'I don't suppose I ever shall.' He leant back, laughing at the gifted but ridiculous family, while the fire flickered over the map of Africa. Margaret motioned to her brother to go on. Rather diffident, he obeyed her.

'Margaret's point is this,' he said. 'Our sister may be mad.'

Charles, who was working in the inner room, looked round.

'Come in, Charles,' said Margaret kindly. 'Could you help us at all? We are again in trouble.'

'I'm afraid I cannot. What are the facts? We are all mad more or less, you know, in these days.'

'The facts are as follows,' replied Tibby, who had at times a pedantic lucidity. 'The facts are that she has been in England for three days and will not see us. She has forbidden the bankers to give us her address. She refuses to answer questions. Margaret finds her letters colourless. There are other facts, but these are the most striking.'

'She has never behaved like this before, then?' asked Henry.

'Of course not!' said his wife, with a frown.

'Well, my dear, how am I to know?'

A senseless spasm of annoyance came over her. 'You know quite well that Helen never sins against affection,' she said. 'You must have noticed that much in her, surely.'

'Oh yes; she and I have always hit it off together.'

'No, Henry—can't you see?—I don't mean that.'

She recovered herself, but not before Charles had observed her. Stupid and attentive, he was watching the scene.

'I was meaning that when she was eccentric in the past, one could trace it back to the heart in the long-run. She behaved oddly because she cared for someone, or wanted to help them. There's no possible excuse for her now. She is grieving us deeply, and that is why I am sure that she is not well. "Mad" is too terrible a word, but she is not well. I shall never believe it. I shouldn't discuss my sister with you if I thought she was well—trouble you about her, I mean.'

Henry began to grow serious. Ill-health was to him something perfectly definite. Generally well himself, he could not realize that we sink to it by slow gradations. The sick had no rights; they were outside the pale; one could lie to them remorselessly. When his first wife was seized, he had promised to take her down into Hertfordshire, but meanwhile arranged with a nursing-home instead. Helen, too, was ill. And the plan that he sketched out for her capture, clever and well-meaning as it was, drew its ethics from the wolf-pack.

'You want to get hold of her?' he said. 'That's the problem, isn't it? She has got to see a doctor.'

'For all I know she has seen one already.'

'Yes, yes; don't interrupt.' He rose to his feet and thought intently. The genial, tentative host disappeared, and they saw instead the man who had carved money out of Greece and Africa, and bought forests from the natives for a few bottles of gin. 'I've got it,' he said at last. 'It's perfectly easy. Leave it to me. We'll send her down to Howards End.'

'How will you do that?'

'After her books. Tell her that she must unpack them herself. Then you can meet her there.'

'But, Henry, that's just what she won't let me do. It's part of her—whatever it is—never to see me.'

'Of course you won't tell her you're going. When she is there, looking at the cases, you'll just stroll in. If nothing is wrong with her, so much the better. But there'll be the motor round the corner, and we can run her up to a specialist in no time.'

Margaret shook her head. 'It's quite impossible.'

'Why?'

'It doesn't seem impossible to me,' said Tibby; 'it is surely a very tippy plan.'

'It is impossible, because—' She looked at her husband sadly. 'It's not the particular language that Helen and I talk, if you see my meaning. It would do splendidly for other people, whom I don't blame.'

'But Helen doesn't talk,' said Tibby. 'That's our whole difficulty. She won't talk your particular language, and on that account you think she's ill.'

'No, Henry; it's sweet of you, but I couldn't.'

'I see,' he said; 'you have scruples.'

'I suppose so.'

'And sooner than go against them you would have your sister suffer. You could have got her down to Swanage by a word, but you have scruples. And scruples are all very well. I am as scrupulous as any man alive, I hope; but when it is a case like this, when there is a question of madness—'

'I deny it's madness.'

'You said just now—'

'It's madness when I say it, but not when you say it.'

Henry shrugged his shoulders. 'Margaret! Margaret!' he groaned. 'No education can teach a woman logic. Now, my dear, my time is valuable. Do you want me to help you or not?'

'Not in that way.'

'Answer my question. Plain question, plain answer. Do—'

Charles surprised them by interrupting. 'Pater, we may as well keep Howards End out of it,' he said.

'Why, Charles?'

Charles could give no reason; but Margaret felt as if, over tremendous distance, a salutation had passed between them.

'The whole house is at sixes and sevens,' he said crossly. 'We don't want any more mess.'

'Who's "we"?' asked his father. 'My boy, pray, who's "we"?'

'I am sure I beg your pardon,' said Charles. 'I appear always to be intruding.'

By now Margaret wished she had never mentioned her trouble to her husband. Retreat was impossible. He was determined to push the matter to a satisfactory conclusion, and Helen faded as he talked. Her fair, flying hair and eager eyes counted for nothing, for she was ill, without rights, and any of her friends might hunt her. Sick at heart, Margaret joined in the chase. She wrote her sister a lying letter, at her husband's dictation; she said the furniture was all at Howards End, but could be seen on Monday next at

3 p.m., when a charwoman would be in attendance. It was a cold letter, and the more plausible for that. Helen would think she was offended. And on Monday next she and Henry were to lunch with Dolly, and then ambush themselves in the garden.

After they had gone, Mr Wilcox said to his son: 'I can't have this sort of behaviour, my boy. Margaret's too sweet-natured to mind, but I mind for her.'

Charles made no answer.

'Is anything wrong with you, Charles, this afternoon?'

'No, pater; but you may be taking on a bigger business than you reckon.'

'How?'

'Don't ask me.'

Chapter Thirty-five

One speaks of the moods of spring, but the days that are her true children have only one mood: they are all full of the rising and dropping of winds, and the whistling of birds. New flowers may come out, the green embroidery of the hedges increase, but the same heaven broods overhead, soft, thick, and blue, the same figures, seen and unseen, are wandering by coppice and meadow. The morning that Margaret had spent with Miss Avery, and the afternoon she set out to entrap Helen, were the scales of a single balance. Time might never have moved, rain never have fallen, and man alone, with his schemes and ailments, was troubling Nature until he saw her through a veil of tears.

She protested no more. Whether Henry was right or wrong, he was most kind, and she knew of no other standard by which to judge him. She must trust him absolutely. As soon as he had taken up a business, his obtuseness vanished. He profited by the slightest indications, and the capture of Helen promised to be staged as deftly as the marriage of Evie.

They went down in the morning as arranged, and he discovered that their victim was actually in Hilton. On his arrival he called at all the livery-stables in the village, and had a few minutes' serious conversation with the proprietors. What he said, Margaret did not know—perhaps not the truth; but news arrived after lunch that a lady had come by the London train, and had taken a fly to Howards End.

'She was bound to drive,' said Henry. 'There will be her books.'

'I cannot make it out,' said Margaret for the hundredth time.

'Finish your coffee, dear. We must be off.'

'Yes, Margaret, you know you must take plenty,' said Dolly.

Margaret tried, but suddenly lifted her hand to her eyes. Dolly stole glances at her father-in-law which he did not answer. In the silence the motor came round to the door.

'You're not fit for it,' he said anxiously. 'Let me go alone. I know exactly what to do.'

'Oh yes, I am fit,' said Margaret, uncovering her face. 'Only most frightfully worried. I cannot feel that Helen is really alive. Her letters and telegrams seem to have come from someone else. Her voice isn't in them. I don't believe your driver really saw her at the station. I wish I'd never mentioned it. I know that Charles is vexed. Yes, he is—' She seized Dolly's hand and kissed it. 'There, Dolly will forgive me. There. Now we'll be off.'

Henry had been looking at her closely. He did not like this breakdown.

'Don't you want to tidy yourself?'

'Have I time?'

'Yes, plenty.'

She went to the lavatory by the front door, and as soon as the bolt slipped, Mr Wilcox said quietly:

'Dolly, I'm going without her.'

Dolly's eyes lit up with vulgar excitement. She followed him on tip-toe out to the car.

'Tell her I thought it best.'

'Yes, Mr Wilcox, I see.'

'Say anything you like. All right.'

The car started well, and with ordinary luck would have got away. But Porgly-woggles, who was playing in the garden, chose this moment to sit down in the middle of the path. Crane, in trying to pass him, ran one wheel over a bed of wallflowers. Dolly screamed. Margaret, hearing the noise, rushed out hatless, and was in time to jump on the footboard. She said not a single word: he was only treating her as she had treated Helen, and her rage at his dishonesty only helped to indicate what Helen would feel against them. She thought, 'I deserve it: I am punished for lowering my colours.' And she accepted his apologies with a calmness that astonished him.

'I still consider you are not fit for it,' he kept saying.

'Perhaps I was not at lunch. But the whole thing is spread clearly before me now.'

'I was meaning to act for the best.'

'Just lend me your scarf, will you. This wind takes one's hair so.'

'Certainly, dear girl. Are you all right now?'

'Look! My hands have stopped trembling.'

'And have quite forgiven me? Then listen. Her cab should already have arrived at Howards End. (We're a little late, but no matter.) Our first move will be to send it down to wait at the farm, as, if possible, one doesn't want a scene before servants. A certain gentleman'–he pointed at Crane's back–'won't drive in, but will wait a little short of the front gate, behind the laurels. Have you still the keys of the house?'

'Yes.'

'Well, they aren't wanted. Do you remember how the house stands?'

'Yes.'

'If we don't find her in the porch, we can stroll round into the garden. Our object—'

Here they stopped to pick up the doctor.

'I was just saying to my wife, Mansbridge, that our main object is not to frighten Miss Schlegel. The house, as you know, is my property, so it should seem quite natural for us to be there. The trouble is evidently nervous—wouldn't you say so, Margaret?'

The doctor, a very young man, began to ask questions about Helen. Was she normal? Was there anything congenital or hereditary? Had anything occurred that was likely to alienate her from her family?

'Nothing,' answered Margaret, wondering what would have happened if she had added: 'Though she did resent my husband's immorality.'

'She always was highly strung,' pursued Henry, leaning back in the car as it shot past the church. 'A tendency to spiritualism and those things, though nothing serious. Musical, literary, artistic, but I should say normal—a very charming girl.'

Margaret's anger and terror increased every moment. How dare these men label her sister! What horrors lay ahead! What impertinences that shelter under the name of science! The pack was turning on Helen, to deny her human rights, and it seemed to Margaret that all Schlegels were threatened with her. 'Were they normal?' What a question to ask! And it is always those who know nothing about human nature, who are bored by psychology and shocked by physiology, who ask it. However piteous her sister's state, she knew that she must be on her side. They would be mad together if the world chose to consider them so.

It was now five minutes past three. The car slowed down by the farm, in the yard of which Miss Avery was standing. Henry asked her whether a cab had gone past. She nodded, and the next moment they caught sight of it, at the end of the lane. The car ran silently like a beast of prey. So unsuspicious was Helen that she was sitting in the porch, with her back to the road. She had come. Only her head and shoulders were visible. She sat framed in the vine, and one of her hands played with the buds. The wind ruffled her hair, the sun glorified it; she was as she had always been.

Margaret was seated next to the door. Before her husband could prevent her, she slipped out. She ran to the garden gate, which was shut, passed through it, and deliberately pushed it in his face. The noise alarmed Helen. Margaret saw her rise with an unfamiliar movement, and, rushing into the porch, learnt the simple explanation of all their fears—her sister was with child.

'Is the truant all right?' called Henry.

She had time to whisper: 'Oh, my darling—' The keys of the house were in her hand. She unlocked Howards End and thrust Helen into it. 'Yes, all right,' she said, and stood with her back to the door.

Chapter Thirty-six

'Margaret, you look upset!' said Henry.

Mansbridge had followed. Crane was at the gate, and the flyman had stood up on the box. Margaret shook her head at them; she could not speak any more. She remained clutching the keys, as if all their future depended on them. Henry was asking more questions. She shook her head again. His words had no sense. She heard him wonder why she had let Helen in. 'You might have given me a knock with the gate,' was another of his remarks. Presently she heard herself speaking. She, or someone for her, said 'Go away.' Henry came nearer. He repeated, 'Margaret, you look upset again. My dear, give me the keys. What are you doing with Helen?'

'Oh, dearest, do go away, and I will manage it all.'

'Manage what?'

He stretched out his hand for the keys. She might have obeyed if it had not been for the doctor.

'Stop that at least,' she said piteously; the doctor had turned back, and was questioning the driver of Helen's cab. A new feeling came over her; she was fighting for women against men. She did not care about rights, but if men came into Howards End, it should be over her body.

'Come, this is an odd beginning,' said her husband.

The doctor came forward now, and whispered two words to Mr Wilcox—the scandal was out. Sincerely horrified, Henry stood gazing at the earth.

'I cannot help it,' said Margaret. 'Do wait. It's not my fault. Please all four of you to go away now.'

Now the flyman was whispering to Crane.

'We are relying on you to help us, Mrs Wilcox,' said the young doctor. 'Could you go in and persuade your sister to come out?'

'On what grounds?' said Margaret, suddenly looking him straight in the eyes.

Thinking it professional to prevaricate, he murmured something about a nervous breakdown.

'I beg your pardon, but it is nothing of the sort. You are not qualified to attend my sister, Mr Mansbridge. If we require your services, we will let you know.'

'I can diagnose the case more bluntly if you wish,' he retorted.

'You could, but you have not. You are, therefore, not qualified to attend my sister.'

'Come, come, Margaret!' said Henry, never raising his eyes. 'This is a terrible business, an appalling business. It's doctor's orders. Open the door.'

'Forgive me, but I will not.'

'I don't agree.'

Margaret was silent.

'This business is as broad as it's long,' contributed the doctor. 'We had better all work together. You need us, Mrs Wilcox, and we need you.'

'Quite so,' said Henry.

'I do not need you in the least,' said Margaret.

The two men looked at each other anxiously.

'No more does my sister, who is still many weeks from her confinement.'

'Margaret, Margaret!'

'Well, Henry, send your doctor away. What possible use is he now?'

Mr Wilcox ran his eye over the house. He had a vague feeling that he must stand firm and support the doctor. He himself might need support, for there was trouble ahead.

'It all turns on affection now,' said Margaret. 'Affection. Don't you see?' Resuming her usual methods, she wrote the word on the house with her finger. 'Surely you see. I like Helen very much, you not so much. Mr Mansbridge doesn't know her. That's all. And affection, when reciprocated, gives rights. Put that down in your note-book, Mr Mansbridge. It's a useful formula.'

Henry told her to be calm.

'You don't know what you want yourselves,' said Margaret, folding her arms. 'For one sensible remark I will let you in. But you cannot make it. You would trouble my sister for no reason. I will not permit it. I'll stand here all the day sooner.'

'Mansbridge,' said Henry in a low voice, 'perhaps not now.'

The pack was breaking up. At a sign from his master, Crane also went back into the car.

'Now, Henry, you,' she said gently. None of her bitterness had been directed at him. 'Go away now, dear. I shall want your advice later, no doubt. Forgive me if I have been cross. But, seriously, you must go.'

He was too stupid to leave her. Now it was Mr Mansbridge who called in a low voice to him.

'I shall soon find you down at Dolly's,' she called, as the gate at last clanged between them. The fly moved out of the way, the motor backed, turned a little, backed again, and turned in the narrow road. A string of farm carts came up in the middle; but she waited through all, for there was no hurry. When all was over and the car had started, she opened the door. 'Oh, my darling!' she said. 'My darling, forgive me.' Helen was standing in the hall.

Chapter Thirty-seven

Margaret bolted the door on the inside. Then she would have kissed her sister, But Helen, in a dignified voice, that came strangely from her, said:

'Convenient! You did not tell me that the books were unpacked. I have found nearly everything that I want.'

'I told you nothing that was true.'

'It has been a great surprise, certainly. Has Aunt Juley been ill?'

'Helen, you wouldn't think I'd invent that?'

'I suppose not,' said Helen, turning away, and crying a very little. 'But one loses faith in everything after this.'

'We thought it was illness, but even then— I haven't behaved worthily.'

Helen selected another book.

'I ought not to have consulted anyone. What would our father have thought of me?'

She did not think of questioning her sister, nor of rebuking her. Both might be necessary in the future, but she had first to purge a greater crime than any that Helen could have committed–that want of confidence that is the work of the devil.

'Yes, I am annoyed,' replied Helen. 'My wishes should have been respected. I would have gone through this meeting if it was necessary, but after Aunt Juley recovered, it was not necessary. Planning my life, as I now have to do—'

'Come away from those books,' called Margaret. 'Helen, do talk to me.'

'I was just saying that I have stopped living haphazard. One can't go through a great deal of—' she missed out the noun–'without planning one's actions in advance. I am going to have a child in June, and in the first place conversation, discussions, excitement, are not good for me. I will go through them if necessary, but only then. In the second place I have no right to trouble people. I cannot fit in with England as I know it. I have done something that the English never pardon. It would not be right for them to pardon it. So I must live where I am not known.'

'But why didn't you tell me, dearest?'

'Yes,' replied Helen judicially. 'I might have, but decided to wait.'

'I believe you would never have told me.'

'Oh yes, I should. We have taken a flat in Munich.'

Margaret glanced out of the window.

'By "we" I mean myself and Monica. But for her, I am and have been and always wish to be alone.'

'I have not heard of Monica.'

'You wouldn't have. She's an Italian—by birth at least. She makes her living by journalism. I met her originally on Garda. Monica is much the best person to see me through.'

'You are very fond of her, then.'

'She has been extraordinarily sensible with me.'

Margaret guessed at Monica's type—'Italiano Inglesiato' they had named it: the crude feminist of the South, whom one respects but avoids. And Helen had turned to it in her need?

'You must not think that we shall ever meet,' said Helen, with a measured kindness. 'I shall always have a room for you when you can be spared, and the longer you can be with me the better. But you haven't understood yet, Meg, and of course it is very difficult for you. This is a shock to you. It isn't to me, who have been thinking over our futures for many months, and they won't be changed by a slight contretemps, such as this. I cannot live in England.'

'Helen, you've not forgiven me for my treachery. You *couldn't* talk like this to me if you had.'

'Oh, Meg dear, why do we talk at all?' She dropped a book and sighed wearily. Then, recovering herself, she said: 'Tell me, how is it that all the books are down here?'

'Series of mistakes.'

'And a great deal of the furniture has been unpacked.'

'All.'

'Who lives here, then?'

'No one.'

'I suppose you are letting it, though.'

'The house is dead,' said Margaret, with a frown. 'Why worry on about it?'

'But I am interested. You talk as if I had lost all my interest in life. I am still Helen, I hope. Now this hasn't the feel of a dead house. The hall seems more alive even than in the old days, when it held the Wilcoxes' own things.'

'Interested, are you? Very well, I must tell you, I suppose. My husband lent it on condition we—but by a mistake all our things were unpacked, and Miss Avery, instead of—' She stopped. 'Look here, I can't go on like this. I warn you I won't. Helen, why should you be so miserably unkind to me, simply because you hate Henry?'

'I don't hate him now,' said Helen. 'I have stopped being a schoolgirl, and Meg, once again, I'm not being unkind. But as for fitting in with your English life—no, put it out of your head at once. Imagine a visit from me at Ducie Street! It's unthinkable.'

Margaret could not contradict her. It was appalling to see her quietly moving forward with her plans, not bitter or excitable, neither asserting innocence nor confessing guilt, merely desiring freedom and the company of those who would not blame her. She had been through—how much? Margaret did not know. But it was enough to part her from old habits as well as old friends.

'Tell me about yourself,' said Helen, who had chosen her books, and was lingering over the furniture.

'There's nothing to tell.'

'But your marriage has been happy, Meg?'

'Yes, but I don't feel inclined to talk.'

'You feel as I do.'

'Not that, but I can't.'

'No more can I. It is a nuisance, but no good trying.'

Something had come between them. Perhaps it was Society, which henceforward would exclude Helen. Perhaps it was a third life, already potent as a spirit. They could find no meeting-place. Both suffered acutely, and were not comforted by the knowledge that affection survived.

'Look here, Meg, is the coast clear?'

'You mean that you want to go away from me?'

'I suppose so—dear old lady! it isn't any use. I knew we should have nothing to say. Give my love to Aunt Juley and Tibby, and take more yourself than I can say. Promise to come and see me in Munich later.'

'Certainly, dearest.'

'For that is all we can do.'

It seemed so. Most ghastly of all was Helen's common sense: Monica had been extraordinarily good for her.

'I am glad to have seen you and the things.' She looked at the bookcase lovingly, as if she was saying farewell to the past.

Margaret unbolted the door. She remarked: 'The car has gone, and here's your cab.'

She led the way to it, glancing at the leaves and the sky. The spring had never seemed more beautiful. The driver, who was leaning on the gate, called out, 'Please, lady, a message,' and handed her Henry's visiting-card through the bars.

'How did this come?' she asked.

Crane had returned with it almost at once.

She read the card with annoyance. It was covered with instructions in domestic French. When she and her sister had talked she was to come back for the night to Dolly's. 'Il faut dormir sur ce sujet.' While Helen was to be found 'une comfortable chambre à l'hotel.' The final sentence displeased her greatly until she remembered that the Charles' had only one spare room, and so could not invite a third guest.

'Henry would have done what he could,' she interpreted.

Helen had not followed her into the garden. The door once open, she lost her inclination to fly. She remained in the hall, going from bookcase to table. She grew more like the old Helen, irresponsible and charming.

'This *is* Mr Wilcox's house?' she inquired.

'Surely you remember Howards End?'

'Remember? I who remember everything! But it looks to be ours now.'

'Miss Avery was extraordinary,' said Margaret, her own spirits lightening a little. Again she was invaded by a slight feeling of disloyalty. But it brought her relief, and she yielded to it. 'She loved Mrs Wilcox, and would rather furnish her house with our things than think of it empty. In consequence here are all the library books.'

'Not all the books. She hasn't unpacked the Art Books, in which she may show her sense. And we never used to have the sword here.'

'The sword looks well, though.'

'Magnificent.'

'Yes, doesn't it?'

'Where's the piano, Meg?'

'I warehoused that in London. Why?'

'Nothing.'

'Curious, too, that the carpet fits.'

'The carpet's a mistake,' announced Helen. 'I know that we had it in London, but this floor ought to be bare. It is far too beautiful.'

'You still have a mania for under-furnishing. Would you care to come into the dining-room before you start? There's no carpet there.'

They went in, and each minute their talk became more natural.

'Oh, *what* a place for mother's cheffonier!' cried Helen.

'Look at the chairs, though.'

'Oh, look at them! Wickham Place faced north, didn't it?'

'North-west.'

'Anyhow, it is thirty years since any of those chairs have felt the sun. Feel. Their dear little backs are quite warm.'

'But why has Miss Avery made them set to partners? I shall just—'

'Over here, Meg. Put it so that anyone sitting will see the lawn.'

Margaret moved a chair. Helen sat down in it.

'Ye-es. The window's too high.'

'Try a drawing-room chair.'

'No, I don't like the drawing-room so much. The beam has been match-boarded. It would have been so beautiful otherwise.'

'Helen, what a memory you have for some things! You're perfectly right. It's a room that men have spoilt through trying to make it nice for women. Men don't know what we want—'

'And never will.'

'I don't agree. In two thousand years they'll know.'

'But the chairs show up wonderfully. Look where Tibby spilt the soup.'

'Coffee, It was coffee surely.'

Helen shook her head. 'Impossible. Tibby was far too young to be given coffee at that time.'

'Was father alive?'

'Yes.'

'Then you're right and it must have been soup. I was thinking of much later—that unsuccessful visit of Aunt Juley's, when she didn't realize that Tibby had grown up. It was coffee then, for he threw it down on purpose. There was some rhyme, "Tea, coffee—coffee, tea," that she said to him every morning at breakfast. Wait a minute—how did it go?'

'I know—no, I don't. What a detestable boy Tibby was!'

'But the rhyme was simply awful. No decent person could have put up with it.'

'Ah, that greengage tree,' cried Helen, as if the garden was also part of their childhood. 'Why do I connect it with dumb-bells? And there come the chickens. The grass wants cutting. I love yellowhammers—'

Margaret interrupted her. 'I have got it,' she announced.

'Tea, tea, coffee, tea,
Or chocolaritee.'

'That every morning for three weeks. No wonder Tibby was wild.'

'Tibby is moderately a dear now,' said Helen.

'There! I knew you'd say that in the end. Of course he's a dear.'

A bell rang.

'Listen! What's that?'

Helen said, 'Perhaps the Wilcoxes are beginning the siege.'

'What nonsense—listen!'

And the triviality faded from their faces, though it left something behind—the knowledge that they never could be parted because their love was rooted in common things. Explanations and appeals had failed; they had tried for a common meeting-ground, and had only made each other unhappy. And all the time their salvation was lying round them—the past sanctifying the present; the present, with wild heart-throb, declaring that there would after all be a future, with laughter and the voices of children. Helen, still smiling, came up to her sister. She said, 'It is always Meg.' They looked into each other's eyes. The inner life had paid.

Solemnly the clapper tolled. No one was in the front. Margaret went to the kitchen, and struggled between packing-cases to the window. Their visitor was only a little boy with a tin can. And triviality returned.

'Little boy, what do you want?'

'Please, I am the milk.'

'Did Miss Avery send you?' said Margaret, rather sharply.

'Yes, please.'

'Then take it back and say we require no milk.' While she called to Helen, 'No, it's not the siege, but possibly an attempt to provision us against one.'

'But I like milk, cried Helen. 'Why send it away?'

'Do you? Oh, very well. But we've nothing to put it in, and he wants the can.'

'Please, I'm to call in the morning for the can,' said the boy.

'The house will be locked up then.'

'In the morning would I bring eggs, too?'

'Are you the boy whom I saw playing in the stacks last week?'

The child hung his head.

'Well, run away and do it again.'

'Nice little boy,' whispered Helen. 'I say, what's your name? Mine's Helen.'

'Tom.'

That was Helen all over. The Wilcoxes, too, would ask a child its name, but they never told their names in return.

'Tom, this one here is Margaret. And at home we've another called Tibby.'

'Mine are lop-eared,' replied Tom, supposing Tibby to be a rabbit.

'You're a very good and rather a clever little boy. Mind you come again—Isn't he charming?'

'Undoubtedly,' said Margaret. 'He is probably the son of Madge, and Madge is dreadful. But this place has wonderful powers.'

'What do you mean?'

'I don't know.'

'Because I probably agree with you.'

'It kills what is dreadful and makes what is beautiful live.'

'I do agree,' said Helen, as she sipped the milk. 'But you said that the house was dead not half an hour ago.'

'Meaning that I was dead. I felt it.'

'Yes, the house has a surer life than we, even if it was empty, and, as it is, I can't get over that for thirty years the sun has never shone full on our furniture. After all, Wickham Place was a grave. Meg, I've a startling idea.'

'What is it?'

'Drink some milk to steady you.'

Margaret obeyed.

'No, I won't tell you yet,' said Helen, 'because you may laugh or be angry. Let's go upstairs first and give the rooms an airing.'

They opened window after window, till the inside, too, was rustling to the spring. Curtains blew, picture-frames tapped cheerfully. Helen uttered cries of excitement as she found this bed obviously in its right place, that in its wrong one. She was angry with Miss Avery for not having moved the wardrobes up. 'Then one would see really.' She admired the view. She was the Helen who had written the memorable letters four years ago. As they leant out, looking westward, she said: 'About my idea. Couldn't you and I camp out in this house for the night?'

'I don't think we could well do that,' said Margaret.

'Here are beds, tables, towels—'

'I know; but the house isn't supposed to be slept in, and Henry's suggestion was—'

'I require no suggestions. I shall not alter anything in my plans. But it would give me so much pleasure to have one night here with you. It will be something to look back on. Oh, Meg lovely, do let's!'

'But, Helen, my pet,' said Margaret, 'we can't without getting Henry's leave. Of course, he would give it, but you said yourself that you couldn't visit at Ducie Street now, and this is equally intimate.'

'Ducie Street is his house. This is ours. Our furniture, our sort of people coming to the door. Do let us camp out, just one night, and Tom shall feed us on eggs and milk. Why not? It's a moon.'

Margaret hesitated. 'I feel Charles wouldn't like it,' she said at last. 'Even our furniture annoyed him, and I was going to clear it out when Aunt Juley's illness prevented me. I sympathize with Charles. He feels it's his mother's house. He loves it in rather an untaking way. Henry I could answer for—not Charles.'

'I know he won't like it,' said Helen. 'But I am going to pass out of their lives. What difference will it make in the long run if they say, "And she even spent the night at Howards End"?'

'How do you know you'll pass out of their lives? We have thought that twice before.'

'Because my plans—'

'—which you change in a moment.'

'Then because my life is great and theirs are little,' said Helen, taking fire. 'I know of things they can't know of, and so do you. We *know* that there's poetry. We *know* that there's death. They can only take them on hearsay. We know this is our house, because it feels ours. Oh, they may take the title-deeds and the doorkeys, but for this one night we are at home.'

'It would be lovely to have you once more alone,' said Margaret. 'It may be a chance in a thousand.'

'Yes, and we could talk.' She dropped her voice. 'It won't be a very glorious story. But under that wych-elm—honestly, I see little happiness ahead. Cannot I have this one night with you?'

'I needn't say how much it would mean to me.'

'Then let us.'

'It is no good hesitating. Shall I drive down to Hilton now and get leave?'

'Oh, we don't want leave.'

But Margaret was a loyal wife. In spite of imagination and poetry—perhaps on account of them—she could sympathize with the technical attitude that Henry would adopt. If possible, she would be technical, too. A night's lodging—and they demanded no more—need not involve the discussion of general principles.

'Charles may say no,' grumbled Helen.

'We shan't consult him.'

'Go if you like; I should have stopped without leave.'

It was the touch of selfishness, which was not enough to mar Helen's character, and even added to its beauty. She would have stopped without leave, and escaped to Germany the next morning. Margaret kissed her.

'Expect me back before dark. I am looking forward to it so much. It is like you to have thought of such a beautiful thing.'

'Not a thing, only an ending;' said Helen rather sadly; and the sense of tragedy closed in on Margaret again as soon as she left the house.

She was afraid of Miss Avery. It is disquieting to fulfil a prophecy, however superficially. She was glad to see no watching figure as she drove past the farm, but only little Tom, turning somersaults in the straw.

Chapter Thirty-eight

The tragedy began quietly enough, and, like many another talk, by the man's deft assertion of his superiority. Henry heard her arguing with the driver, stepped out and settled the fellow, who was inclined to be rude, and then led the way to some chairs on the lawn. Dolly, who had not been 'told,' ran out with offers of tea. He refused them, and ordered them to wheel baby's perambulator away, as they desired to be alone.

'But the diddums can't listen; he isn't nine months old,' she pleaded.

'That's not what I was saying,' retorted her father-in-law.

Baby was wheeled out of earshot, and did not hear about the crisis till later years. It was now the turn of Margaret.

'Is it what we feared?' he asked.

'It is.'

'Dear girl,' he began, 'there is a troublesome business ahead of us, and nothing but the most absolute honesty and plain speech will see us through.' Margaret bent her head. 'I am obliged to question you on subjects we'd both prefer to leave untouched. As you know, I am not one of your Bernard Shaws who consider nothing sacred. To speak as I must will pain me, but there are occasions— We are husband and wife, not children. I am a man of the world, and you are a most exceptional woman.'

All Margaret's senses forsook her. She blushed, and looked past him at the Six Hills, covered with spring herbage. Noting her colour, he grew still more kind.

'I see that you feel as I felt when— My poor little wife! Oh, be brave! Just one or two questions, and I have done with you. Was your sister wearing a wedding-ring?'

Margaret stammered a 'No.'

There was an appalling silence.

'Henry, I really came to ask a favour about Howards End.'

'One point at a time. I am now obliged to ask for the name of her seducer.'

She rose to her feet and held the chair between them. Her colour had ebbed, and she was grey. It did not displease him that she should receive his question thus.

'Take your time,' he counselled her. 'Remember that this is far worse for me than for you.'

She swayed; he feared she was going to faint. Then speech came, and she said slowly: 'Seducer? No; I do not know her seducer's name.'

'Would she not tell you?'

'I never even asked her who seduced her,' said Margaret, dwelling on the hateful word thoughtfully.

'That is singular.' Then he changed his mind. 'Natural perhaps, dear girl, that you shouldn't ask. But until his name is known, nothing can be done. Sit down. How terrible it is to see you so upset! I knew you weren't fit for it. I wish I hadn't taken you.'

Margaret answered, 'I like to stand, if you don't mind, for it gives me a pleasant view of the Six Hills.'

'As you like.'

'Have you anything else to ask me, Henry?'

'Next you must tell me whether you have gathered anything. I have often noticed your insight, dear. I only wish my own was as good. You may have guessed something, even though your sister said nothing. The slightest hint would help us.'

'Who is "we"?'

'I thought it best to ring up Charles.'

'That was unnecessary,' said Margaret, growing warmer. 'This news will give Charles disproportionate pain.'

'He has at once gone to call on your brother.'

'That too was unnecessary.'

'Let me explain, dear, how the matter stands. You don't think that I and my son are other than gentlemen? It is in Helen's interests that we are acting. It is still not too late to save her name.'

Then Margaret hit out for the first time. 'Are we to make her seducer marry her?' she asked.

'If possible. Yes.'

'But, Henry, suppose he turned out to be married already? One had heard of such cases.'

'In that case he must pay heavily for his misconduct, and be thrashed within an inch of his life.'

So her first blow missed. She was thankful of it. What had tempted her to imperil both of their lives? Henry's obtuseness had saved her as well as himself. Exhausted with anger, she sat down again, blinking at him as he told her as much as he thought fit. At last she said: 'May I ask you my question now?'

'Certainly, my dear.'

'To-morrow Helen goes to Munich—'

'Well, possibly she is right.'

'Henry, let a lady finish. To-morrow she goes; to-night, with your permission, she would like to sleep at Howards End.'

It was the crisis of his life. Again she would have recalled the words as soon as they were uttered. She had not led up to them with sufficient care. She longed to warn him that they were far more important than he supposed. She saw him weighing them, as if they were a business proposition.

'Why Howards End?' he said at last. 'Would she not be more comfortable, as I suggested, at the hotel?'

Margaret hastened to give him reasons. 'It is an odd request, but you know what Helen is and what women in her state are.' He frowned, and moved irritably. 'She has the idea that one night in your house would give her pleasure and do her good. I think she's right. Being one of those imaginative girls, the presence of all our books and furniture soothes her. This is a fact. It is the end of her girlhood. Her last words to me were, "A beautiful ending."'

'She values the old furniture for sentimental reasons, in fact.'

'Exactly. You have quite understood. It is her last hope of being with it.'

'I don't agree there, my dear! Helen will have her share of the goods wherever she goes—possibly more than her share, for you are so fond of her that you'd give her anything of yours that she fancies, wouldn't you? and I'd raise no objection. I could understand it if it was her old home, because a home, or a house'—he changed the word, designedly; he had thought of a telling point—'because a house in which one has once lived becomes in a sort of way sacred, I don't know why. Associations and so on. Now Helen has no associations with Howards End, though I and Charles and Evie have. I do not see why she wants to stay the night there. She will only catch cold.'

'Leave it that you don't see,' cried Margaret. 'Call it fancy. But realize that fancy is a scientific fact. Helen is fanciful, and wants to.'

Then he surprised her—a rare occurrence. He shot an unexpected bolt. 'If she wants to sleep one night, she may want to sleep two. We shall never get her out of the house, perhaps.'

'Well?' said Margaret, with the precipice in sight. 'And suppose we don't get her out of the house? Would it matter? She would do no one any harm.'

Again the irritated gesture.

'No, Henry,' she panted, receding. 'I didn't mean that. We will only trouble Howards End for this one night. I take her to London to-morrow—'

'Do you intend to sleep in a damp house, too?'

'She cannot be left alone.'

'That's quite impossible! Madness. You must be here to meet Charles.'

'I have already told you that your message to Charles was unnecessary, and I have no desire to meet him.'

'Margaret—my Margaret—'

'What has this business to do with Charles? If it concerns me little, it concerns you less, and Charles not at all.'

'As the future owner of Howards End,' said Mr Wilcox, arching his fingers, 'I should say that it did concern Charles.'

'In what way? Will Helen's condition depreciate the property?'

'My dear, you are forgetting yourself.'

'I think you yourself recommended plain speaking.'

They looked at each other in amazement. The precipice was at their feet now.

'Helen commands my sympathy,' said Henry. 'As your husband, I shall do all for her that I can, and I have no doubt that she will prove more sinned against than sinning. But I cannot treat her as if nothing has happened. I should be false to my position in society if I did.'

She controlled herself for the last time. 'No, let us go back to Helen's request,' she said. 'It is unreasonable, but the request of an unhappy girl.

To-morrow she will go to Germany, and trouble society no longer. To-night she asks to sleep in your empty house—a house which you do not care about, and which you have not occupied for over a year. May she? Will you give my sister leave? Will you forgive her—as you hope to be forgiven, and as you have actually been forgiven? Forgive her for one night only. That will be enough.'

'As I have actually been forgiven—?'

'Never mind for the moment what I mean by that,' said Margaret. 'Answer my question.'

Perhaps some hint of her meaning did dawn on him. If so, he blotted it out. Straight from his fortress he answered: 'I seem rather unaccommodating, but I have some experience of life, and know how one thing leads to another. I am afraid that your sister had better sleep at the hotel. I have my children and the memory of my dear wife to consider. I am sorry, but see that she leaves my house at once.'

'You have mentioned Mrs Wilcox.'

'I beg your pardon?'

'A rare occurrence. In reply, may I mention Mrs Bast?'

'You have not been yourself all day,' said Henry, and rose from his seat with face unmoved. Margaret rushed at him and seized both his hands. She was transfigured.

'Not any more of this!' she cried. 'You shall see the connection if it kills you, Henry! You have had a mistress—I forgave you. My sister has a lover—you drive her from the house. Do you see the connection? Stupid, hypocritical, cruel—oh, contemptible—a man who insults his wife when she's alive and cants with her memory when she's dead. A man who ruins a woman for his pleasure, and casts her off to ruin other men. And gives bad financial advice, and then says he is not responsible. These men are you. You can't recognize them, because you cannot connect. I've had enough of your unweeded kindness. I've spoilt you long enough. All your life you have been spoiled. Mrs Wilcox spoiled you. No one has ever told what you are—muddled, criminally muddled. Men like you use repentance as a blind, so don't repent. Only say to yourself, "What Helen has done, I've done."'

'The two cases are different,' Henry stammered. His real retort was not quite ready. His brain was still in a whirl, and he wanted a little longer.

'In what way different? You have betrayed Mrs Wilcox, Helen only herself. You remain in society, Helen can't. You have had only pleasure, she may die. You have the insolence to talk to me of differences, Henry?'

Oh, the uselessness of it! Henry's retort came.

'I perceive you are attempting blackmail. It is scarcely a pretty weapon for a wife to use against her husband. My rule through life has been never to pay the least attention to threats, and I can only repeat what I said before: I do not give you and your sister leave to sleep at Howards End.'

Margaret loosed his hands. He went into the house, wiping first one and then the other on his handkerchief. For a little she stood looking at the Six Hills, tombs of warriors, breasts of the spring. Then she passed out into what was now the evening.

Chapter Thirty-nine

Charles and Tibby met at Ducie Street, where the latter was staying. Their interview was short and absurd. They had nothing in common but the English language, and tried by its help to express what neither of them understood. Charles saw in Helen the family foe. He had singled her out as the most dangerous of the Schlegels, and, angry as he was, looked forward to telling his wife how right he had been. His mind was made up at once: the girl must be got out of the way before she disgraced them further. If occasion offered she might be married to a villain or, possibly, to a fool. But this was a concession to morality, it formed no part of his main scheme. Honest and hearty was Charles's dislike, and the past spread itself out very clearly before him; hatred is a skilful compositor. As if they were heads in a note-book, he ran through all the incidents of the Schlegel's campaign: the attempt to compromise his brother, his mother's legacy, his father's marriage, the introduction of the furniture, the unpacking of the same. He had not yet heard of the request to sleep at Howards End; that was to be their master-stroke and the opportunity for his. But he already felt that Howards End was the objective, and, though he disliked the house, was determined to defend it.

Tibby, on the other hand, had no opinions. He stood above the conventions: his sister had a right to do what she thought right. It is not difficult to stand above the conventions when we leave no hostages among them; men can always be more unconventional than women, and a bachelor of independent means need encounter no difficulties at all. Unlike Charles, Tibby had money enough; his ancestors had earned it for him, and if he shocked the people in one set of lodgings he had only to move into another. His was the Leisure without sympathy—an attitude as fatal as the strenuous: a little cold culture may be raised on it, but no art. His sisters had seen the family danger, and had never forgotten to discount the gold islets that raised them from the sea. Tibby gave all the praise to himself, and so despised the struggling and the submerged.

Hence the absurdity of the interview; the gulf between them was economic as well as spiritual. But several facts passed: Charles pressed for them with an impertinence that the undergraduate could not withstand. On what date had Helen gone abroad? To whom? (Charles was anxious to fasten the scandal on Germany.) Then, changing his tactics, he said roughly: 'I suppose you realize that you are your sister's protector?'

'In what sense?'

'If a man played about with my sister, I'd send a bullet through him, but perhaps you don't mind.'

'I mind very much,' protested Tibby.

'Who d'ye suspect, then? Speak out, man. One always suspects someone.'

'No one. I don't think so.' Involuntarily he blushed. He had remembered the scene in his Oxford rooms.

'You are hiding something,' said Charles. As interviews go, he got the best of this one. 'When you saw her last, did she mention anyone's name? Yes or no!' he thundered, so that Tibby started.

'In my rooms she mentioned some friends, called the Basts—'

'Who are the Basts?'

'People–friends of hers at Evie's wedding.'

'I don't remember. But, by great Scott! I do. My aunt told me about some tag-rag. Was she full of them when you saw her? Is there a man? Did she speak of the man? Or–look here–have you had any dealings with him?'

Tibby was silent. Without intending it, he had betrayed his sister's confidence; he was not enough interested in human life to see where things will lead to. He had a strong regard for honesty, and his word, once given, had always been kept up to now. He was deeply vexed, not only for the harm he had done Helen, but for the flaw he had discovered in his own equipment.

'I see–you are in his confidence. They met at your rooms. Oh, what a family, what a family! God help the poor pater—'

And Tibby found himself alone.

Chapter Forty

Leonard–he could figure at length in a newspaper report, but that evening he did not count for much. The foot of the tree was in shadow, since the moon was still hidden behind the house. But above, to right, to left, down the long meadow the moonlight was streaming. Leonard seemed not a man, but a cause.

Perhaps it was Helen's way of falling in love–a curious way to Margaret, whose agony and whose contempt of Henry were yet imprinted with his image. Helen forgot people. They were husks that had enclosed her emotion. She could pity, or sacrifice herself, or have instincts, but had she ever loved in the noblest way, where man and woman, having lost themselves in sex, desire to lose sex itself in comradeship?

Margaret wondered, but said no word of blame. This was Helen's evening. Troubles enough lay ahead of her–the loss of friends and of social advantages, the agony, the supreme agony, of motherhood, which is even yet not a matter of common knowledge. For the present let the moon shine brightly and the breezes of the spring blow gently, dying away from the gale of the day, and let the earth, who brings increase, bring peace. Not even to herself dare she blame Helen. She could not assess her trespass by any moral code; it was everything or nothing. Morality can tell us that murder is worse then stealing, and group most sins in an order all must approve, but it cannot group Helen. The surer its pronouncements on this point, the surer may we be that morality is not speaking. Christ was evasive when they questioned Him. It is those that cannot connect who hasten to cast the first stone.

This was Helen's evening—won at what cost, and not to be marred by the sorrows of others. Of her own tragedy Margaret never uttered a word.

'One isolates,' said Helen slowly. 'I isolated Mr Wilcox from the other forces that were pulling Leonard downhill. Consequently, I was full of pity, and almost of revenge. For weeks I had blamed Mr Wilcox only, and so, when your letters came—'

'I need never have written them,' sighed Margaret. 'They never shielded Henry. How hopeless it is to tidy away the past, even for others!'

'I did not know that it was your own idea to dismiss the Basts.'

'Looking back, that was wrong of me.'

'Looking back, darling, I know that it was right. It is right to save the man whom one loves. I am less enthusiastic about justice now. But we both thought you wrote at his dictation. It seemed the last touch of his callousness. Being very much wrought up by this time—and Mrs Bast was upstairs. I had not seen her, and had talked for a long time to Leonard—I had snubbed him for no reason, and that should have warned me I was in danger. So when the notes came I wanted us to go to you for an explanation. He said that he guessed the explanation—he knew of it, and you mustn't know. I pressed him to tell me. He said no one must know; it was something to do with his wife. Right up to the end we were Mr Bast and Miss Schlegel. I was going to tell him that he must be frank with me when I saw his eyes, and guessed that Mr Wilcox had ruined him in two ways, not one. I drew him to me. I made him tell me. I felt very lonely myself. He is not to blame. He would have gone on worshipping me. I want never to see him again, though it sounds appalling. I wanted to give him money and feel finished. Oh, Meg, the little that is known about these things!'

She laid her face against the tree.

'The little, too, that is known about growth! Both times it was loneliness, and the night, and panic afterwards. Did Leonard grow out of Paul?'

Margaret did not speak for a moment. So tired was she that her attention had actually wandered to the teeth—the teeth that had been thrust into the tree's bark to medicate it. From where she sat she could see them gleam. She had been trying to count them. 'Leonard is a better growth than madness,' she said. 'I was afraid that you would react against Paul until you went over the verge.'

'I did react until I found poor Leonard. I am steady now. I shan't ever *like* your Henry, dearest Meg, or even speak kindly about him, but all that blinding hate is over. I shall never rave against Wilcoxes any more. I understand how you married him, and you will now be very happy.'

Margaret did not reply.

'Yes,' repeated Helen, her voice growing more tender, 'I do at last understand.'

'Except Mrs Wilcox, dearest; no one understands our little movements.'

'Because in death—I agree.'

'Not quite. I feel that you and I and Henry are only fragments of that woman's mind. She knows everything. She is everything. She is the house, and the tree that leans over it. People have their own deaths as well as their own lives, and even if there is nothing beyond death, we shall differ in our nothingness. I cannot believe that knowledge such as hers will perish with knowledge such as mine. She knew about realities. She knew when people were in love, though she was not in the room. I don't doubt that she knew when Henry deceived her.'

'Good-night, Mrs Wilcox,' called a voice.

'Oh, good-night, Miss Avery.'

'Why should Miss Avery work for us?' Helen murmured.

'Why, indeed?'

Miss Avery crossed the lawn and merged into the hedge that divided it from the farm. An old gap, which Mr Wilcox had filled up, had reappeared, and her track through the dew followed the path that he had turfed over, when he improved the garden and made it possible for games.

'This is not quite our house yet,' said Helen. 'When Miss Avery called, I felt we are only a couple of tourists.'

'We shall be that everywhere, and for ever.'

'But affectionate tourists—'

'But tourists who pretend each hotel is their home.'

'I can't pretend very long,' said Helen. 'Sitting under this tree one forgets, but I know that to-morrow I shall see the moon rise out of Germany. Not all your goodness can alter the facts of the case. Unless you will come with me.'

Margaret thought for a moment. In the past year she had grown so fond of England that to leave it was a real grief. Yet what detained her? No doubt Henry would pardon her outburst, and go on blustering and muddling into a ripe old age. But what was the good? She had just as soon vanish from his mind.

'Are you serious in asking me, Helen? Should I get on with your Monica?'

'You would not, but I am serious in asking you.'

'Still, no more plans now. And no more reminiscences.'

They were silent for a little. It was Helen's evening.

The present flowed by them like a stream. The tree rustled. It had made music before they were born, and would continue after their deaths, but its song was of the moment. The moment had passed. The tree rustled again. Their senses were sharpened, and they seemed to apprehend life. Life passed. The tree rustled again.

'Sleep now,' said Margaret.

The peace of the country was entering into her. It has no commerce with memory, and little with hope. Least of all is it concerned with the hopes of the next five minutes. It is the peace of the present, which passes understanding. Its murmur came 'now,' and 'now' once more as they trod the gravel, and 'now,' as the moonlight fell upon their father's sword. They passed upstairs, kissed, and amidst the endless iterations fell asleep. The house had enshadowed the tree at first, but as the moon rose higher the two disentangled, and were clear for a few moments at midnight. Margaret awoke and looked into the garden. How incomprehensible that Leonard Bast should have won her this night of peace! Was he also part of Mrs Wilcox's mind?

Chapter Forty-one

Far different was Leonard's development. The months after Oniton, whatever minor troubles they might bring him, were all overshadowed by Remorse. When Helen looked back she could philosophize, or she could look into the future and plan for her child. But the father saw nothing beyond his own sin. Weeks afterwards, in the midst of other occupations, he would suddenly cry out, 'Brute–you brute, I couldn't have—' and be rent into two people who held dialogues. Or brown rain would descend, blotting out faces and the sky. Even Jacky noticed the change in him. Most terrible were his sufferings when he awoke from sleep. Sometimes he was happy at first, but grew conscious of a burden hanging to him and weighing down his thoughts when they would move. Or little irons scorched his body. Or a sword stabbed him. He would sit at the edge of his bed, holding his heart and moaning, 'Oh what *shall* I do, whatever *shall* I do?' Nothing brought ease. He could put distance between him and the trespass, but it grew in his soul.

Remorse is not among the eternal verities. The Greeks were right to dethrone her. Her action is too capricious, as though the Erinyes selected for punishment only certain men and certain sins. And of all means to regeneration Remorse is surely the most wasteful. It cuts away healthy tissues with the poisoned. It is a knife that probes far deeper than the evil. Leonard was driven straight through its torments and emerged pure, but enfeebled–a better man, who would never lose control of himself again, but also a smaller man, who had less to control. Nor did purity mean peace. The use of the knife can become a habit as hard to shake off as passion itself, and Leonard continued to start with a cry out of dreams.

He built up a situation that was far enough from the truth. It never occurred to him that Helen was to blame. He forgot the intensity of their talk, the charm that had been lent him by sincerity, the magic of Oniton under darkness and of the whispering river. Helen loved the absolute. Leonard had been ruined absolutely, and had appeared to her as a man apart, isolated from the world. A real man, who cared for adventure and beauty, who desired to live decently and pay his way, who could have travelled more gloriously through life than the Juggernaut car that was crushing him. Memories of Evie's wedding had warped her, the starched servants, the yards of uneaten food, the rustle of overdressed women, motor-cars oozing grease on the gravel rubbish on a pretentious band. She had tasted the lees of this on her arrival: in the darkness, after failure, they intoxicated her. She and the victim seemed alone in a world of unreality, and she loved him absolutely, perhaps for half an hour.

In the morning she was gone. The note that she left, tender and hysterical in tone, and intended to be most kind, hurt her lover terribly. It was as if some work of art had been broken by him, some picture in the National Gallery slashed out of its frame. When he recalled her talents and her social position, he felt that the first passer-by had a right to shoot him down. He was afraid of the waitress and the porters at the railway-station. He was afraid at first of his wife, though later he was to regard her with a strange new tenderness, and to think, 'There is nothing to choose between us, after all.'

The expedition to Shropshire crippled the Basts permanently. Helen in her flight forgot to settle the hotel bill, and took their return tickets away with her; they had to pawn Jacky's bangles to get home, and the smash came a few days afterwards. It is true that Helen offered him five thousand pounds, but such a sum meant nothing to him. He could not see that the girl was desperately righting herself, and trying to save something out of the disaster, if it was only five thousand pounds. But he had to live somehow. He turned to his family, and degraded himself to a professional beggar. There was nothing else for him to do.

'A letter from Leonard,' thought Blanche, his sister; 'and after all this time.' She hid it, so that her husband should not see, and when he had gone to his work read it with some emotion, and sent the prodigal a little money out of her dress allowance.

'A letter from Leonard!' said the other sister, Laura, a few days later. She showed it to her husband. He wrote a cruel, insolent reply, but sent more money than Blanche, so Leonard soon wrote to him again.

And during the winter the system was developed. Leonard realized that they need never starve, because it would be too painful for his relatives. Society is based on the family, and the clever wastrel can exploit this indefinitely. Without a generous thought on either side, pounds and pounds passed. The donors disliked Leonard, and he grew to hate them intensely. When Laura censured his immoral marriage, he thought bitterly, 'She minds that! What would she say if she knew the truth?' When Blanche's husband offered him work he found some pretext for avoiding it. He had wanted work keenly at Oniton, but too much anxiety had shattered him, he was joining the unemployable. When his brother, the lay-reader, did not reply to a letter, he wrote again, saying that he and Jacky would come down to his village on foot. He did not intend this as blackmail. Still, the brother sent a postal order, and it became part of the system. And so passed his winter and his spring.

In the horror there are two bright spots. He never confused the past. He remained alive, and blessed are those who live, if it is only to a sense of sinfulness. The anodyne of muddledom, by which most men blur and blend their mistakes, never passed Leonard's lips—

And if I drink oblivion of a day,
So shorten I the stature of my soul.

It is a hard saying, and a hard man wrote it, but it lies at the foot of all character.

And the other bright spot was his tenderness for Jacky. He pitied her with nobility now—not the contemptuous pity of a man who sticks to a woman through thick and thin. He tried to be less irritable. He wondered what her hungry eyes desired—nothing that she could express, or that he or any man could give her. Would she ever receive the justice that is mercy—the justice for by-products that the world is too busy to bestow? She was fond of flowers, generous with money, and not revengeful. If she had borne him a child he might have cared for her. Unmarried, Leonard would never have begged; he would have flickered out and died. But the whole of life is mixed. He had to provide for Jacky, and went down dirty paths that she might have a few feathers and the dishes of food that suited her.

One day he caught sight of Margaret and her brother. He was in St Paul's. He had entered the cathedral partly to avoid the rain and partly to see a picture that had educated him in former years. But the light was bad, the picture ill placed, and Time and Judgment were inside him now. Death alone still charmed him, with her lap of poppies, on which all men shall sleep. He took one glance, and turned aimlessly away towards a chair. Then down the nave he saw Miss Schlegel and her brother. They stood in the fairway of passengers, and their faces were extremely grave. He was perfectly certain that they were in trouble about their sister.

Once outside—and he fled immediately—he wished that he had spoken to them. What was his life? What were a few angry words, or even imprisonment? He had done wrong—that was the true terror. Whatever they might know, he would tell them everything he knew. He re-entered St Paul's. But they had moved in his absence, and had gone to lay their difficulties before Mr Wilcox and Charles.

The sight of Margaret turned remorse into new channels. He desired to confess, and though the desire is proof of a weakened nature, which is about to lose the essence of human intercourse, it did not take an ignoble form. He did not suppose that confession would bring him happiness. It was rather that he yearned to get clear of the tangle. So does the suicide yearn. The impulses are akin, and the crime of suicide lies rather in its disregard for the feelings of those whom we leave behind. Confession need harm no one—it can satisfy that test—and though it was un-English, and ignored by our Anglican cathedral, Leonard had a right to decide upon it.

Moreover, he trusted Margaret. He wanted her hardness now. That cold, intellectual nature of hers would be just, if unkind. He would do whatever she told him, even if he had to see Helen. That was the supreme punishment she would exact. And perhaps she would tell him how Helen was. That was the supreme reward.

He knew nothing about Margaret, not even whether she was married to Mr Wilcox, and tracking her out took several days. That evening he toiled through the wet to Wickham Place, where the new flats were now appearing. Was he also the cause of their move? Were they expelled from society on his account? Thence to a public library, but could find no satisfactory Schlegel in the directory. On the morrow he searched again. He hung about outside Mr Wilcox's office at lunch time, and, as the clerks came out said: 'Excuse me, sir, but is your boss married?' Most of them stared, some said, 'What's that to you?' but one, who had not yet acquired reticence, told him what he wished. Leonard could not learn the private address. That necessitated more trouble with directories and tubes. Ducie Street was not discovered till the Monday, the day that Margaret and her husband went down on their hunting expedition to Howards End.

He called at about four o'clock. The weather had changed, and the sun shone gaily on the ornamental steps—black and white marble in triangles. Leonard lowered his eyes to them after ringing the bell. He felt in curious health: doors seemed to be opening and shutting inside his body, and he had been obliged to sleep sitting up in bed, with his back propped against the wall. When the parlourmaid came he could not see her face; the brown rain had descended suddenly.

'Does Mrs Wilcox live here?' he asked.

'She's out,' was the answer.

'When will she be back?'

'I'll ask,' said the parlourmaid.

Margaret had given instructions that no one who mentioned her name should ever be rebuffed. Putting the door on the chain—for Leonard's appearance demanded this—she went through to the smoking-room, which was occupied by Tibby. Tibby was asleep. He had had a good lunch. Charles Wilcox had not yet rung him up for the distracting interview. He said drowsily: 'I don't know. Hilton. Howards End. Who is it?'

'I'll ask, sir.'

'No, don't bother.'

'They have taken the car to Howards End,' said the parlourmaid to Leonard.

He thanked her, and asked whereabouts that place was.

'You appear to want to know a good deal,' she remarked. But Margaret had forbidden her to be mysterious. She told him against her better judgment that Howards End was in Hertfordshire.

'Is it a village, please?'

'Village! It's Mr Wilcox's private house—at least, it's one of them. Mrs Wilcox keeps her furniture there. Hilton is the village.'

'Yes. And when will they be back?'

'Mr Schlegel doesn't know. We can't know everything, can we?' She shut him out, and went to attend to the telephone, which was ringing furiously.

He loitered away another night of agony. Confession grew more difficult. As soon as possible he went to bed. He watched a patch of moonlight cross the floor of their lodging, and, as sometimes happens when the mind is overtaxed, he fell asleep for the rest of the room, but kept awake for the patch of moonlight. Horrible! Then began one of those disintegrating dialogues.

Part of him said: 'Why horrible? It's ordinary light from the moon.' 'But it moves.' 'So does the moon.' 'But it is a clenched fist.' 'Why not?' 'But it is going to touch me.' 'Let it.' And, seeming to gather motion, the patch ran up his blanket. Presently a blue snake appeared; then another, parallel to it. 'Is there life in the moon?' 'Of course.' 'But I thought it was uninhabited.' 'Not by Time, Death, Judgment, and the smaller snakes.' 'Smaller snakes!' said Leonard indignantly and aloud. 'What a notion!' By a rending effort of the will he woke the rest of the room up. Jacky, the bed, their food, their clothes on the chair, gradually entered his consciousness, and the horror vanished outwards, like a ring that is spreading through water.

'I say, Jacky, I'm going out for a bit.'

She was breathing regularly. The patch of light fell clear of the striped blanket, and began to cover the shawl that lay over her feet. Why had he been afraid? He went to the window, and saw that the moon was descending through a clear sky. He saw her volcanoes, and the bright expanses that a gracious error has named seas. They paled, for the sun, who had lit them up, was coming to light the earth. Sea of Serenity, Sea of Tranquillity, Ocean of the Lunar Storms, merged into one lucent drop, itself to slip into the sempiternal dawn. And he had been afraid of the moon!

He dressed among the contending lights, and went through his money. It was running low again, but enough for a return ticket to Hilton. As it clinked Jacky opened her eyes.

'Hullo, Len! What ho, Len!'

'What ho, Jacky! see you again later.'

She turned over and slept.

The house was unlocked, their landlord being a salesman at Covent Garden. Leonard passed out and made his way down to the station. The train, though it did not start for an hour, was already drawn up at the end of the platform, and he lay down in it and slept. With the first jolt he was in daylight; they had left the gateways of King's Cross, and were under blue sky. Tunnels followed, and after each the sky grew bluer, and from the embankment at Finsbury Park he had his first sight of the sun. It rolled along behind the eastern smokes—a wheel, whose fellow was the descending moon—and as yet it seemed the servant of the blue sky, not its lord. He dozed again. Over Tewin Water it was day. To the left fell the shadow of the embankment and its arches; to the right Leonard saw up into the Tewin Woods and towards the church, with its wild legend of immortality. Six forest trees—that is a fact—grow out of one of the graves in Tewin churchyard. The grave's occupant—that is the legend—is an artist, who declared that if God existed, six forest trees would grow out of her grave. These things in Hertfordshire; and farther afield lay the house of a hermit—Mrs Wilcox had known him—who barred himself up, and wrote prophecies, and gave all he had to the poor. While, powdered in between, were the villas of business men, who saw life more steadily, though with the steadiness of the half-closed eye. Over all the sun was streaming, to all the birds were singing, to all the primroses were yellow, and the speedwell blue, and the country, however they interpreted her, was uttering her cry of 'now'.

She did not free Leonard yet, and the knife plunged deeper into his heart as the train drew up at Hilton. But remorse had become beautiful.

Hilton was asleep, or at the earliest, breakfasting. Leonard noticed the contrast when he stepped out of it into the country. Here men had been up since dawn. Their hours were ruled, not by a London office, but by the movements of the crops and the sun. That they were men of the finest type only the sentimentalist can declare. But they kept to the life of daylight. They are England's hope. Clumsily they carry forward the torch of the sun, until such time as the nation sees fit to take it up. Half clodhopper, half board-school prig, they can still throw back to a nobler stock, and breed yeomen.

At the chalk pit a motor passed him. In it was another type, whom Nature favours—the Imperial. Healthy, ever in motion, it hopes to inherit the earth. It breeds as quickly as the yeoman, and as soundly; strong in the temptation to acclaim it as a super-yeoman, who carries his country's virtue overseas. But the Imperialist is not what he thinks or seems. He is a destroyer. He prepares the way for cosmopolitanism, and though his ambitions may be fulfilled, the earth that he inherits will be grey.

To Leonard, intent on his private sin, there came the conviction of innate goodness elsewhere. It was not the optimism which he had been taught at school. Again and again must the drums tap, and the goblins stalk over the universe before joy can be purged of the superficial. It was rather paradoxical, and arose from his sorrow. Death destroys a man, but the idea of death saves him—that is the best account of it that has yet been given. Squalor and tragedy can beckon to all that is great in us, and strengthen the wings of love. They can beckon; it is not certain that they will, for they are not love's servants. But they can beckon, and the knowledge of this incredible truth comforted him.

As he approached the house all thought stopped. Contradictory notions stood side by side in his mind. He was terrified but happy, ashamed, but had done no sin. He knew the confession: 'Mrs Wilcox, I have done wrong,' but sunrise had robbed its meaning, and he felt rather on a supreme adventure.

He entered a garden, steadied himself against a motor-car that he found in it, found a door open and entered a house. Yes, it would be very easy. From a room to the left he heard voices, Margaret's amongst them. His own name was called aloud, and a man whom he had never seen said, 'Oh, is he there? I am not surprised. I now thrash him within an inch of his life.'

'Mrs Wilcox,' said Leonard, 'I have done wrong.'

The man took him by the collar and cried, 'Bring me a stick.' Women were screaming. A stick, very bright, descended. It hurt him, not where it descended, but in the heart. Books fell over him in a shower. Nothing had sense.

'Get some water,' commanded Charles, who had all through kept very calm. 'He's shamming. Of course I only used the blade. Here, carry him out into the air.'

Thinking that he understood these things, Margaret obeyed him. They laid Leonard, who was dead, on the gravel; Helen poured water over him.

'That's enough,' said Charles.

'Yes, murder's enough,' said Miss Avery, coming out of the house with the sword.

Chapter Forty-two

When Charles left Ducie Street he had caught the first train home, but had no inkling of the newest development until late at night. Then his father, who had dined alone, sent for him, and in very grave tones inquired for Margaret.

'I don't know where she is, pater,' said Charles. 'Dolly kept back dinner nearly an hour for her.'

'Tell me when she comes in.'

Another hour passed. The servants went to bed, and Charles visited his father again, to receive further instructions. Mrs Wilcox had still not returned.

'I'll sit up for her as late as you like, but she can hardly be coming. Isn't she stopping with her sister at the hotel?'

'Perhaps,' said Mr Wilcox thoughtfully–'perhaps.'

'Can I do anything for you sir?'

'Not to-night, my boy.'

Mr Wilcox liked being called sir. He raised his eyes and gave his son more open a look of tenderness than he usually ventured. He saw Charles as little boy and strong man in one. Though his wife had proved unstable his children were left to him.

After midnight he tapped on Charles's door. 'I can't sleep,' he said. 'I had better have a talk with you and get it over.'

He complained of the heat. Charles took him out into the garden, and they paced up and down in their dressing-gowns. Charles became very quiet as the story unrolled; he had known all along that Margaret was as bad as her sister.

'She will feel differently in the morning,' said Mr Wilcox, who had of course said nothing about Mrs Bast. 'But I cannot let this kind of thing continue without comment. I am morally certain that she is with her sister at Howards End. The house is mine–and, Charles, it will be yours–and when I say that no one is to live there, I mean that no one is to live there.' I won't have it. He looked angrily at the moon. 'To my mind this question is connected with something far greater, the rights of property itself.'

'Undoubtedly,' said Charles.

Mr Wilcox lined his arm in his son's, but somehow liked him less as he told him more. 'I don't want you to conclude that my wife and I had anything of the nature of a quarrel. She was only overwrought, as who would not be? I shall do what I can for Helen, but on the understanding that they clear out of the house at once. Do you see? That is a sine qua non.'

'Then at eight to-morrow I may go up in the car?'

'Eight or earlier. Say that you are acting as my representative, and, of course, use no violence, Charles.'

On the morrow, as Charles returned, leaving Leonard dead upon the gravel, it did not seem to him that he had used violence. Death was due to heart disease. His stepmother herself had said so, and even Miss Avery had acknowledged that he only used the flat of the sword. On his way through the village he informed the police, who thanked him, and said there must be an inquest. He found his father in the garden shading his eyes from the sun.

'It has been pretty horrible,' said Charles gravely. 'They were there, and they had the man up there with them too.'

'What—what man?'

'I told you last night. His name was Bast.'

'My God! is it possible?' said Mr Wilcox. 'In your mother's house! Charles, in your mother's house?'

'I know, pater. That was what I felt. As a matter of fact, there is no need to trouble about the man. He was in the last stages of heart disease, and just before I could show him what I thought of him he went off. The police are seeing about it at this moment.'

Mr Wilcox listened attentively.

'I got up there—oh, it couldn't have been more than half-past seven. The Avery woman was lighting a fire for them. They were still upstairs. I waited in the drawing-room. We were all moderately civil and collected, though I had my suspicions. I gave them your message, and Mrs Wilcox said, "Oh yes, I see; yes," in that way of hers.'

'Nothing else?'

'I promised to tell you, "with her love," that she was going to Germany with her sister this evening. That was all we had time for.'

Mr Wilcox seemed relieved.

'Because by then I suppose the man got tired of hiding, for suddenly Mrs Wilcox screamed out his name. I recognized it, and I went for him in the hall. Was I right, pater? I thought things were going a little too far.'

'Right, my dear boy? I don't know. But you would have been no son of mine if you hadn't. Then did he just—just—crumple up as you said?' He shrunk from the simple word.

'He caught hold of the bookcase, which came down over him. So I merely put the sword down and carried him into the garden. We all thought he was shamming. However, he's dead right enough. Awful business!'

'Sword?' cried his father, with anxiety in his voice. 'What sword? Whose sword?'

'A sword of theirs.'

'What were you doing with it?'

'Well, didn't you see, pater, I had to snatch up the first thing handy. I hadn't a riding-whip or stick. I caught him once or twice over the shoulders with the flat of their old German sword.'

'Then what?'

'He pulled over the bookcase, as I said, and fell,' said Charles, with a sigh. It was no fun doing errands for his father, who was never quite satisfied.

'But the real cause was heart disease? Of that you're sure?'

'That or a fit. However, we shall hear more than enough at the inquest on such unsavoury topics.'

They went into breakfast. Charles had a racking headache, consequent on motoring before food. He was also anxious about the future, reflecting that the police must detain Helen and Margaret for the inquest and ferret the whole thing out. He saw himself obliged to leave Hilton. One could not afford to live near the scene of a scandal—it was not fair on one's wife. His comfort was that the pater's eyes were opened at last. There would be a horrible smash up, and probably a separation from Margaret; then they would all start again, more as they had been in his mother's time.

'I think I'll go round to the police-station,' said his father when breakfast was over.

'What for?' cried Dolly, who had still not been 'told.'

'Very well, sir. Which car will you have?'

'I think I'll walk.'

'It's a good half-mile,' said Charles, stepping into the garden. 'The sun's very hot for April. Shan't I take you up, and then, perhaps, a little spin round by Tewin?'

'You go on as if I didn't know my own mind,' said Mr Wilcox fretfully. Charles hardened his mouth. 'You young fellows' one idea is to get into a motor. I tell you, I want to walk: I'm very fond of walking.'

'Oh, all right; I'm about the house if you want me for anything. I thought of not going up to the office to-day, if that is your wish.'

'It is, indeed, my boy,' said Mr Wilcox, and laid a hand on his sleeve.

Charles did not like it; he was uneasy about his father, who did not seem himself this morning. There was a petulant touch about him—more like a woman. Could it be that he was growing old? The Wilcoxes were not lacking in affection; they had it royally, but did not know how to use it. It was the talent in the napkin, and, for a warm-hearted man, Charles had conveyed very little joy. As he watched his father shuffling up the road, he had a vague regret—a wish that something had been different somewhere—a wish (though he did not express it thus) that he had been taught to say 'I' in his youth. He meant to make up for Margaret's defection, but knew that his father had been very happy with her until yesterday. How had she done it? By some dishonest trick, no doubt—but how?

Mr Wilcox reappeared at eleven, looking very tired. There was to be an inquest on Leonard's body to-morrow, and the police required his son to attend.

'I expected that,' said Charles. 'I shall naturally be the most important witness there.'

Chapter Forty-three

Out of the turmoil and horror that had begun with Aunt Juley's illness and was not even to end with Leonard's death, it seemed impossible to Margaret that healthy life should re-emerge. Events succeeded in a logical, yet senseless, train. People lost their humanity, and took values as arbitrary as those in a pack of playing-cards. It was natural that Henry should do this and cause Helen to do that, and then think her wrong for doing it; natural that she herself should think him wrong; natural that Leonard should want to know how Helen was, and come, and Charles be angry with him for coming—natural, but unreal. In this jangle of causes and effects what had become of their true selves? Here Leonard lay dead in the garden, from natural causes; yet life was a deep, deep river, death a blue sky, life was a house, death a wisp of hay, a flower, a tower, life and death were anything and everything, except this ordered insanity, where the king takes the queen, and the ace the king. Ah, no; there was beauty and adventure behind, such as the man at her feet had yearned for; there was hope this side of the grave; there were truer relationships beyond the limits that fetter us now. As a prisoner looks up and sees stars beckoning, so she, from the turmoil and horror of those days, caught glimpses of the diviner wheels.

And Helen, dumb with fright, but trying to keep calm for the child's sake, and Miss Avery, calm, but murmuring tenderly, 'No one ever told the lad he'll have a child'—they also reminded her that horror is not the end. To what ultimate harmony we tend she did not know, but there seemed great chance that a child would be born into the world, to take the great chances of beauty and adventure that the world offers. She moved through the sunlit garden, gathering narcissi, crimson-eyed and white. There was nothing else to be done; the time for telegrams and anger was over, and it seemed wisest that the hands of Leonard should be folded on his breast and be filled with flowers. Here was the father; leave it at that. Let Squalor be turned into Tragedy, whose eyes are the stars, and whose hands hold the sunset and the dawn.

And even the influx of officials, even the return of the doctor, vulgar and acute, could not shake her belief in the eternity of beauty. After long centuries among the bones and muscles it might be advancing to knowledge of the nerves, but this would never give understanding. One could open the heart to Mr Mansbridge and his sort without discovering its secrets to them, for they wanted everything down in black and white, and black and white was exactly what they were left with.

They questioned her closely about Charles. She never suspected why. Death had come, and the doctor agreed that it was due to heart disease. They asked to see her father's sword. She explained that Charles's anger was natural, but mistaken. Miserable questions about Leonard followed, all of which she answered unfalteringly. Then back to Charles again. 'No doubt Mr Wilcox may have induced death,' she said, 'but if it wasn't one thing it would have been another, as you yourselves know.' At last they thanked her, and took the sword and the body down to Hilton. She began to pick up the books from the floor.

Helen had gone to the farm. It was the best place for her, since she had to wait for the inquest. Though, as if things were not hard enough, Madge and her husband had raised trouble; they did not see why they should receive the offscourings of Howards End. And, of course, they were right. The whole world was going to be right, and amply avenge any brave talk against the conventions. 'Nothing matters,' the Schlegels had said in the past, 'except one's self-respect and that of one's friends.' When the time came, other things mattered terribly. However, Madge had yielded, and Helen was assured of peace for one day and night, and to-morrow she would return to Germany.

As for herself, she determined to go too. No message came from Henry; perhaps he expected her to apologize. Now that she had time to think over her own tragedy, she was unrepentant. She neither forgave him for his behaviour nor wished to forgive him. Her speech to him seemed perfect. She would not have altered a word. It had to be uttered once in a life, to adjust the lopsidedness of the world. It was spoken not only to her husband, but to thousands of men like him—a protest against the inner darkness in high places that comes with a commercial age. Though he would build up his life without hers, she could not apologize. He had refused to connect, on the clearest issue that can be laid before a man, and their love must take the consequences.

No, there was nothing more to be done. They had tried not to go over the precipice, but perhaps the fall was inevitable. And it comforted her to think that the future was certainly inevitable: cause and effect would go jangling forward to some goal doubtless, but to none that she could imagine. At such moments the soul retires within, to float upon the bosom of a deeper stream, and has communion with the dead, and sees the world's glory not diminished, but different in kind to what she has supposed. She alters her focus until trivial things are blurred. Margaret had been tending this way all the winter. Leonard's death brought her to the goal. Alas! that Henry should fade away as reality emerged, and only her love for him should remain clear, stamped with his image like the cameos we rescue out of dreams.

With unfaltering eye she traced his future. He would soon present a healthy mind to the world again, and what did he or the world care if he was rotten at the core? He would grow into a rich, jolly old man, at times a little sentimental about women, but emptying his glass with anyone. Tenacious of power, he would keep Charles and the rest dependent, and retire from business reluctantly and at an advanced age. He would settle down—though she could not realize this. In her eyes Henry was always moving and causing others to move, until the ends of the earth met. But in time he must get too tired to move, and settle down. What next? The inevitable word. The release of the soul to its appropriate Heaven.

Would they meet in it? Margaret believed in immortality for herself. An eternal future had always seemed natural to her. And Henry believed in it for himself. Yet, would they meet again? Are there not rather endless levels beyond the grave, as the theory that he had censured teaches? And his level, whether higher or lower, could it possibly be the same as hers?

Thus gravely meditating, she was summoned by him. He sent up Crane in the motor. Other servants passed like water, but the chauffeur remained, though impertinent and disloyal. Margaret disliked Crane, and he knew it.

'Is it the keys that Mr Wilcox wants?' she asked.

'He didn't say, madam.'

'You haven't any note for me?'

'He didn't say, madam.'

After a moment's thought she locked up Howards End. It was pitiable to see in it the stirrings of warmth that would be quenched for ever. She raked out the fire that was blazing in the kitchen, and spread the coals in the gravelled yard. She closed the windows and drew the curtains. Henry would probably sell the place now.

She was determined not to spare him, for nothing new had happened as far as they were concerned. Her mood might never have altered from yesterday evening. He was standing a little outside Charles's gate, and motioned the car to stop. When his wife got out he said hoarsely: 'I prefer to discuss things with you outside.'

'It will be more appropriate in the road, I am afraid,' said Margaret. 'Did you get my message?'

'What about?'

'I am going to Germany with my sister. I must tell you now that I shall make it my permanent home. Our talk last night was more important than you have realized. I am unable to forgive you and am leaving you.'

'I am extremely tired,' said Henry, in injured tones. 'I have been walking about all the morning, and wish to sit down.'

'Certainly, if you will consent to sit on the grass.'

The Great North Road should have been bordered all its length with glebe. Henry's kind had filched most of it. She moved to the scrap opposite, wherein were the Six Hills. They sat down on the farther side, so that they could not be seen by Charles or Dolly.

'Here are your keys,' said Margaret. She tossed them towards him. They fell on the sunlit slope of grass, and he did not pick them up.

'I have something to tell you,' he said gently.

She knew this superficial gentleness, this confession of hastiness, that was only intended to enhance her admiration of the male.

'I don't want to hear it,' she replied. 'My sister is going to be ill. My life is going to be with her now. We must manage to build up something, she and I and her child.'

'Where are you going?'

'Munich. We start after the inquest, if she is not too ill.'

'After the inquest?'

'Yes.'

'Have you realized what the verdict at the inquest will be?'

'Yes, heart disease.'

'No, my dear; manslaughter.'

Margaret drove her fingers through the grass. The hill beneath her moved as if it was alive.

'Manslaughter,' repeated Mr Wilcox. 'Charles may go to prison. I dare not tell him. I don't know what to do—what to do. I'm broken—I'm ended.'

No sudden warmth arose in her. She did not see that to break him was her only hope. She did not enfold the sufferer in her arms. But all through that day and the next a new life began to move. The verdict was brought in. Charles was committed for trial. It was against all reason that he should be punished, but the law, being made in his image, sentenced him to three years' imprisonment. Then Henry's fortress gave way. He could bear no one but his wife, he shambled up to Margaret afterwards and asked her to do what she could with him. She did what seemed easiest—she took him down to recruit at Howards End.

Chapter Forty-four

Tom's father was cutting the big meadow. He passed again and again amid whirring blades and sweet odours of grass, encompassing with narrowing circles the sacred centre of the field. Tom was negotiating with Helen.

'I haven't any idea,' she replied. 'Do you suppose baby may, Meg?'

Margaret put down her work and regarded them absently. 'What was that?' she asked.

'Tom wants to know whether baby is old enough to play with hay?'

'I haven't the least notion,' answered Margaret, and took up her work again.

'Now, Tom, baby is not to stand; he is not to lie on his face; he is not to lie so that his head wags; he is not to be teased or tickled; and he is not to be cut into two or more pieces by the cutter. Will you be as careful as all that?'

Tom held out his arms.

'That child is a wonderful nursemaid,' remarked Margaret.

'He is fond of baby. That's why he does it!' was Helen's answer. 'They're going to be lifelong friends.'

'Starting at the ages of six and one?'

'Of course. It will be a great thing for Tom.'

'It may be a greater thing for baby.'

Fourteen months had passed, but Margaret still stopped at Howards End.

No better plan had occurred to her. The meadow was being recut, the great red poppies were reopening in the garden. July would follow with the little red poppies among the wheat, August with the cutting of the wheat. These little events would become part of her year after year. Every summer she would fear lest the well should give out, every winter lest the pipes should freeze; every westerly gale might blow the wych-elm down and bring the end of all things, and so she could not read or talk during a westerly gale. The air was tranquil now. She and her sister were sitting on the remains of Evie's rockery, where the lawn merged into the field.

'What a time they all are!' said Helen. 'What can they be doing inside?' Margaret, who was growing less talkative, made no answer. The noise of the cutter came intermittently, like the breaking of waves. Close by them a man was preparing to scythe out one of the dell-holes.

'I wish Henry was out to enjoy this,' said Helen. 'This lovely weather and to be shut up in the house! It's very hard.'

'It has to be,' said Margaret. 'The hay-fever is his chief objection against living here, but he thinks it worth while.'

'Meg, is or isn't he ill? I can't make out.'

'Not ill. Eternally tired. He has worked very hard all his life, and noticed nothing. Those are the people who collapse when they do notice a thing.'

'I suppose he worries dreadfully about his part of the tangle.'

'Dreadfully. That is why I wish Dolly had not come, too, to-day. Still, he wanted them all to come. It has to be.'

'Why does he want them?'

Margaret did not answer.

'Meg, may I tell you something? I like Henry.'

'You'd be odd if you didn't,' said Margaret.

'I usen't to.'

'Usen't!' She lowered her eyes a moment to the black abyss of the past. They had crossed it, always excepting Leonard and Charles. They were building up a new life, obscure, yet gilded with tranquillity. Leonard was dead; Charles had two years more in prison. One usen't always to see clearly before that time. It was different now.

'I like Henry because he does worry.'

'And he likes you because you don't.'

Helen sighed. She seemed humiliated, and buried her face in her hands. After a time she said: 'About love,' a transition less abrupt than it appeared.

Margaret never stopped working.

'I mean a woman's love for a man. I supposed I should hang my life on to that once, and was driven up and down and about as if something was worrying through me. But everything is peaceful now; I seem cured. That Herr Förstmeister, whom Frieda keeps writing about, must be a noble character, but he doesn't see that I shall never marry him or anyone. It isn't shame or mistrust of myself. I simply couldn't. I'm ended. I used to be so dreamy about a man's love as a girl, and think that for good or evil love must be the great thing. But it hasn't been; it has been itself a dream. Do you agree?'

'I do not agree. I do not.'

'I ought to remember Leonard as my lover,' said Helen, stepping down into the field. 'I tempted him, and killed him, and it is surely the least I can do. I would like to throw out all my heart to Leonard on such an afternoon as this. But I cannot. It is no good pretending. I am forgetting him.' Her eyes filled with tears. 'How nothing seems to match—how, my darling, my precious—' She broke off. 'Tommy!'

'Yes, please?'

'Baby's not to try and stand—There's something wanting in me. I see you loving Henry, and understanding him better daily, and I know that death wouldn't part you in the least. But I— Is it some awful appalling, criminal defect?'

Margaret silenced her. She said: 'It is only that people are far more different than is pretended. All over the world men and women are worrying because they cannot develop as they are supposed to develop. Here and there they have the matter out, and it comforts them. Don't fret yourself, Helen. Develop what you have; love your child. I do not love children. I am thankful to have none. I can play with their beauty and charm, but that is all—nothing real, not one scrap of what there ought to be. And others—others go farther still, and move outside humanity altogether. A place, as well as a person, may catch the glow. Don't you see that all this leads to comfort in the end? It is part of the battle against sameness. Differences—eternal differences, planted by God in a single family, so that there may always be colour; sorrow perhaps, but colour in the daily grey. Then I can't have you worrying about Leonard. Don't drag in the personal when it will not come. Forget him.'

'Yes, yes, but what has Leonard got out of life?'

'Perhaps an adventure.'

'Is that enough?'

'Not for us. But for him.'

Helen took up a bunch of grass. She looked at the sorrel, and the red and white and yellow clover, and the quaker grass, and the daisies, and the bents that composed it. She raised it to her face.

'Is it sweetening yet?' asked Margaret.

'No, only withered.'

'It will sweeten to-morrow.'

Helen smiled. 'Oh, Meg, you are a person,' she said. 'Think of the racket and torture this time last year. But now I couldn't stop unhappy if I tried. What a change—and all through you!'

'Oh, we merely settled down. You and Henry learnt to understand one another and to forgive, all through the autumn and the winter.'

'Yes, but who settled us down?'

Margaret did not reply. The scything had begun, and she took off her pince-nez to watch it.

'You!' cried Helen. 'You did it all, sweetest, though you're too stupid to see. Living here was your plan—I wanted you; he wanted you; and everyone said it was impossible, but you knew. Just think of our lives without you,

Meg—I and baby with Monica, revolting by theory, he handed about from Dolly to Evie. But you picked up the pieces, and made us a home. Can't it strike you—even for a moment—that your life has been heroic? Can't you remember the two months after Charles's arrest, when you began to act, and did all?'

'You were both ill at the time,' said Margaret. 'I did the obvious things. I had two invalids to nurse. Here was a house, ready furnished and empty. It was obvious. I didn't know myself it would turn into a permanent home. No doubt I have done a little towards straightening the tangle, but things that I can't phrase have helped me.'

'I hope it will be permanent,' said Helen, drifting away to other thoughts.

'I think so. There are moments when I feel Howards End peculiarly our own.'

'All the same, London's creeping.'

She pointed over the meadow—over eight or nine meadows, but at the end of them was a red dust.

'You see that in Surrey and even Hampshire now,' she continued. 'I can see it from the Purbeck Downs. And London is only part of something else, I'm afraid. Life's going to be melted down, all over the world.'

Margaret knew that her sister spoke truly. Howards End, Oniton, the Purbeck Downs, the Oderberge, were all survivals, and the melting-pot was being prepared for them. Logically, they had no right to be alive. One's hope was in the weakness of logic. Were they possibly the earth beating time?

'Because a thing is going strong now, it need not go strong for ever,' she said. 'This craze for motion has only set in during the last hundred years. It may be followed by a civilization that won't be a movement, because it will rest on the earth. All the signs are against it now, but I can't help hoping, and very early in the morning in the garden I feel that our house is the future as well as the past.'

They turned and looked at it. Their own memories coloured it now, for Helen's child had been born in the central room of the nine. Then Margaret said, 'Oh, take care—!' for something moved behind the window of the hall, and the door opened.

'The conclave's breaking at last. I'll go.'

It was Paul.

Helen retreated with the children far into the field. Friendly voices greeted her. Margaret rose, to encounter a man with a heavy black moustache.

'My father has asked for you,' he said with hostility.

She took her work and followed him.

'We have been talking business,' he continued, 'but I dare say you knew all about it beforehand.'

'Yes, I did.'

Clumsy of movement—for he had spent all his life in the saddle—Paul drove his foot against the paint of the front door. Mrs Wilcox gave a little cry of annoyance. She did not like anything scratched; she stopped in the hall to take Dolly's boa and gloves out of a vase.

Her husband was lying in a great leather chair in the dining-room, and by his side, holding his hand rather ostentatiously, was Evie. Dolly, dressed in purple, sat near the window. The room was a little dark and airless; they were obliged to keep it like this until the carting of the hay. Margaret joined the family without speaking; the five of them had met already at tea, and she knew quite well what was going to be said. Averse to wasting her time, she went on sewing. The clock struck six.

'Is this going to suit everyone?' said Henry in a weary voice. He used the old phrases, but their effect was unexpected and shadowy. 'Because I don't want you all coming here later on and complaining that I have been unfair.'

'It's apparently got to suit us,' said Paul.

'I beg your pardon, my boy. You have only to speak, and I will leave the house to you instead.'

Paul frowned ill-temperedly, and began scratching at his arm. 'As I've given up the outdoor life that suited me, and I have come home to look after the business, it's no good my settling down here,' he said at last. 'It's not really the country, and it's not the town.'

'Very well. Does my arrangement suit you, Evie?'

'Of course, father.'

'And you, Dolly?'

Dolly raised her faded little face, which sorrow could wither but not steady. 'Perfectly splendidly,' she said. 'I thought Charles wanted it for the boys, but last time I saw him he said no, because we cannot possibly live in this part of England again. Charles says we ought to change our name, but I cannot think what to, for Wilcox just suits Charles and me, and I can't think of any other name.'

There was a general silence. Dolly looked nervously round, fearing that she had been inappropriate. Paul continued to scratch his arm.

'Then I leave Howards End to my wife absolutely,' said Henry. 'And let everyone understand that; and after I am dead let there be no jealousy and no surprise.'

Margaret did not answer. There was something uncanny in her triumph. She, who had never expected to conquer anyone, had charged straight through these Wilcoxes and broken up their lives.

'In consequence, I leave my wife no money,' said Henry. 'That is her own wish. All that she would have had will be divided among you. I am also giving you a great deal in my lifetime, so that you may be independent of me. That is her wish, too. She also is giving away a great deal of money. She intends to diminish her income by half during the next ten years; she intends when she dies to leave the house to her–to her nephew, down in the field. Is all that clear? Does everyone understand?'

Paul rose to his feet. He was accustomed to natives, and a very little shook him out of the Englishman. Feeling manly and cynical, he said: 'Down in the field? Oh, come! I think we might have had the whole establishment, piccaninnies included.'

Mrs Cahill whispered: 'Don't, Paul. You promised you'd take care.' Feeling a woman of the world, she rose and prepared to take her leave.

Her father kissed her. 'Good-bye, old girl,' he said; 'don't you worry about me.'

'Good-bye, dad.'

Then it was Dolly's turn. Anxious to contribute, she laughed nervously, and said: 'Good-bye, Mr Wilcox. It does seem curious that Mrs Wilcox should have left Margaret Howards End, and yet she get it, after all.'

From Evie came a sharply-drawn breath. 'Good-bye,' she said to Margaret, and kissed her.

And again and again fell the word, like the ebb of a dying sea.

'Good-bye.'

'Good-bye, Dolly.'

'So long, father.'

'Good-bye, my boy; always take care of yourself.'

'Good-bye, Mrs Wilcox.'

'Good-bye.'

Margaret saw their visitors to the gate. Then she returned to her husband and laid her head in his hands. He was pitiably tired. But Dolly's remark had interested her. At last she said: 'Could you tell me, Henry, what was that about Mrs Wilcox having left me Howards End?'

Tranquilly he replied: 'Yes, she did. But that is a very old story. When she was ill and you were so kind to her she wanted to make you some return, and, not being herself at the time, scribbled "Howards End" on a piece of paper. I went into it thoroughly, and, as it was clearly fanciful, I set it aside, little knowing what my Margaret would be to me in the future.'

Margaret was silent. Something shook her life in its inmost recesses, and she shivered.

'I didn't do wrong, did I?' he asked, bending down.

'You didn't, darling. Nothing has been done wrong.'

From the garden came laughter. 'Here they are at last!' exclaimed Henry, disengaging himself with a smile. Helen rushed into the gloom, holding Tom by one hand and carrying her baby on the other. There were shouts of infectious joy.

'The field's cut!' Helen cried excitedly–'the big meadow! We've seen to the very end, and it'll be such a crop of hay as never!'

WEYBRIDGE, 1908–1910.

A Passage to India

A PASSAGE TO INDIA

To
SYED ROSS MASOOD
and to the seventeen years of our friendship

Mosque

Chapter One

Except for the Marabar Caves—and they are twenty miles off—the city of Chandrapore presents nothing extraordinary. Edged rather than washed by the river Ganges, it trails for a couple of miles along the bank, scarcely distinguishable from the rubbish it deposits so freely. There are no bathing-steps on the river front, as the Ganges happens not to be holy here; indeed there is no river front, and bazaars shut out the wide and shifting panorama of the stream. The streets are mean, the temples ineffective, and though a few fine houses exist they are hidden away in gardens or down alleys whose filth deters all but the invited guest. Chandrapore was never large or beautiful, but two hundred years ago it lay on the road between Upper India, then imperial, and the sea, and the fine houses date from that period. The zest for decoration stopped in the eighteenth century, nor was it ever democratic. There is no painting and scarcely any carving in the bazaars. The very wood seems made of mud, the inhabitants of mud moving. So abased, so monotonous is everything that meets the eye, that when the Ganges comes down it might be expected to wash the excrescence back into the soil. Houses do fall, people are drowned and left rotting, but the general outline of the town persists, swelling here, shrinking there, like some low but indestructible form of life.

Inland, the prospect alters. There is an oval Maidan, and a long sallow hospital. Houses belonging to Eurasians stand on the high ground by the railway station. Beyond the railway—which runs parallel to the river—the land sinks, then rises again rather steeply. On the second rise is laid out the little civil station, and viewed hence Chandrapore appears to be a totally different place. It is a city of gardens. It is no city, but a forest sparsely scattered with huts. It is a tropical pleasaunce washed by a noble river. The toddy palms and neem trees and mangoes and pepul that were hidden behind the bazaars now become visible and in their turn hide the bazaars. They rise from the gardens where ancient tanks nourish them, they burst out of stifling purlieus and unconsidered temples. Seeking light and air, and endowed with more strength than man or his works, they soar above the lower deposit to greet one another with branches and beckoning leaves, and to build a city for the birds. Especially after the rains do they screen what passes below, but at all times, even when scorched or leafless, they glorify the city to the English people who inhabit the rise, so that new-comers cannot believe it to be as meagre as it is described, and have to be driven down to acquire disillusionment. As for the civil station itself, it provokes no emotion. It charms not, neither does it repel. It is sensibly planned, with a red-brick club on its brow, and farther back a grocer's and a cemetery, and the bungalows are disposed along roads that intersect at right angles. It has nothing hideous in it, and only the view is beautiful; it shares nothing with the city except the overarching sky.

The sky too has its changes, but they are less marked than those of the vegetation and the river. Clouds map it up at times, but it is normally a dome of blending tints, and the main tint blue. By day the blue will pale down into white where it touches the white of the land, after sunset it has a new circumference—orange, melting upwards into tenderest purple. But the core of blue persists, and so it is by night. Then the stars hang like lamps from the immense vault. The distance between the vault and them is as nothing to the distance behind them, and that farther distance, though beyond colour, last freed itself from blue.

The sky settles everything—not only climates and seasons but when the earth shall be beautiful. By herself she can do little—only feeble outbursts of flowers. But when the sky chooses, glory can rain into the Chandrapore bazaars or a benediction pass from horizon to horizon. The sky can do this because it is so strong and so enormous. Strength comes from the sun, infused in it daily, size from the prostrate earth. No mountains infringe on the curve. League after league the earth lies flat, heaves a little, is flat again. Only in the south, where a group of fists and fingers are thrust up through the soil, is the endless expanse interrupted. These fists and fingers are the Marabar Hills, containing the extraordinary caves.

Chapter Two

Abandoning his bicycle, which fell before a servant could catch it, the young man sprang up on to the verandah. He was all animation. 'Hamidullah, Hamidullah! am I late?' he cried.

'Do not apologize,' said his host. 'You are always late.'

'Kindly answer my question. Am I late? Has Mahmoud Ali eaten all the food? If so I go elsewhere. Mr Mahmoud Ali, how are you?'

'Thank you, Dr Aziz, I am dying.'

'Dying before your dinner? Oh, poor Mahmoud Ali!'

'Hamidullah here is actually dead. He passed away just as you rode up on your bike.'

'Yes, that is so,' said the other. 'Imagine us both as addressing you from another and a happier world.'

'Does there happen to be such a thing as a hookah in that happier world of yours?'

'Aziz, don't chatter. We are having a very sad talk.'

The hookah had been packed too tight, as was usual in his friend's house, and bubbled sulkily. He coaxed it. Yielding at last, the tobacco jetted up into his lungs and nostrils, driving out the smoke of burning cow dung that had filled them as he rode through the bazaar. It was delicious. He lay in a trance, sensuous but healthy, through which the talk of the two others did not seem particularly sad—they were discussing as to whether or no it is possible to be friends with an Englishman. Mahmoud Ali argued that it was not, Hamidullah disagreed, but with so many reservations that there was no friction between them. Delicious indeed to lie on the broad verandah with the moon rising in front and the servants preparing dinner behind, and no trouble happening.

'Well, look at my own experience this morning.'

'I only contend that it is possible in England,' replied Hamidullah, who had been to that country long ago, before the big rush, and had received a cordial welcome at Cambridge.

'It is impossible here. Aziz! The red-nosed boy has again insulted me in Court. I do not blame him. He was told that he ought to insult me. Until lately he was quite a nice boy, but the others have got hold of him.'

'Yes, they have no chance here, that is my point. They come out intending to be gentlemen, and are told it will not do. Look at Lesley, look at Blakiston, now it is your red-nosed boy, and Fielding will go next. Why, I remember when Turton came out first. It was in another part of the Province. You fellows will not believe me, but I have driven with Turton in his carriage— Turton! Oh yes, we were once quite intimate. He has shown me his stamp collection.'

'He would expect you to steal it now. Turton! But red-nosed boy will be far worse than Turton!'

'I do not think so. They all become exactly the same, not worse, not better. I give any Englishman two years, be he Turton or Burton. It is only the difference of a letter. And I give any Englishwoman six months. All are exactly alike. Do you not agree with me?'

'I do not,' replied Mahmoud Ali, entering into the bitter fun, and feeling both pain and amusement at each word that was uttered. 'For my own part I find such profound differences among our rulers. Red-nose mumbles, Turton talks distinctly, Mrs Turton takes bribes, Mrs Red-nose does not and cannot, because so far there is no Mrs Red-nose.'

'Bribes?'

'Did you not know that when they were lent to Central India over a Canal

Scheme, some Rajah or other gave her a sewing machine in solid gold so that the water should run through his state.'

'And does it?'

'No, that is where Mrs Turton is so skilful. When we poor blacks take bribes, we perform what we are bribed to perform, and the law discovers us in consequence. The English take and do nothing. I admire them.'

'We all admire them. Aziz, please pass me the hookah.'

'Oh, not yet—hookah is so jolly now.'

'You are a very selfish boy.' He raised his voice suddenly, and shouted for dinner. Servants shouted back that it was ready. They meant that they wished it was ready, and were so understood, for nobody moved. Then Hamidullah continued, but with changed manner and evident emotion.

'But take my case—the case of young Hugh Bannister. Here is the son of my dear, my dead friends, the Reverend and Mrs Bannister, whose goodness to me in England I shall never forget or describe. They were father and mother to me, I talked to them as I do now. In the vacations their Rectory became my home. They entrusted all their children to me—I often carried little Hugh about—I took him up to the Funeral of Queen Victoria, and held him in my arms above the crowd.'

'Queen Victoria was different,' murmured Mahmoud Ali.

'I learn now that this boy is in business as a leather merchant at Cawnpore. Imagine how I long to see him and to pay his fare that this house may be his home. But it is useless. The other Anglo-Indians will have got hold of him long ago. He will probably think that I want something, and I cannot face that from the son of my old friends. Oh, what in this country has gone wrong with everything, Vakil Sahib? I ask you.'

Aziz joined in. 'Why talk about the English? Brrrr . . . ! Why be either friends with the fellows or not friends? Let us shut them out and be jolly. Queen Victoria and Mrs Bannister were the only exceptions, and they're dead.'

'No, no, I do not admit that, I have met others.'

'So have I,' said Mahmoud Ali, unexpectedly veering. 'All ladies are far from alike.' Their mood was changed, and they recalled little kindnesses and courtesies. 'She said "Thank you so much" in the most natural way.' 'She offered me a lozenge when the dust irritated my throat.' Hamidullah could remember more important examples of angelic ministration, but the other, who only knew Anglo-India, had to ransack his memory for scraps, and it was not surprising that he should return to 'But of course all this is exceptional. The exception does not prove the rule. The average woman is like Mrs Turton, and, Aziz, you know what she is.' Aziz did not know, but said he did. He too generalized from his disappointments—it is difficult for members of a subject race to do otherwise. Granted the exceptions, he agreed that all Englishwomen are haughty and venal. The gleam passed from the conversation, whose wintry surface unrolled and expanded interminably.

A servant announced dinner. They ignored him. The elder men had reached their eternal politics, Aziz drifted into the garden. The trees smelt sweet–green-blossomed champak–and scraps of Persian poetry came into his head. Dinner, dinner, dinner . . . but when he returned to the house for it, Mahmoud Ali had drifted away in his turn, to speak to his sais. 'Come and see my wife a little then,' said Hamidullah, and they spent twenty minutes behind the purdah. Hamidullah Begum was a distant aunt of Aziz, and the only female relative he had in Chandrapore, and she had much to say to him on this occasion about a family circumcision that had been celebrated with imperfect pomp. It was difficult to get away, because until they had had their dinner she would not begin hers, and consequently prolonged her remarks in case they should suppose she was impatient. Having censured the circumcision, she bethought her of kindred topics, and asked Aziz when he was going to be married.

Respectful but irritated, he answered, 'Once is enough.'

'Yes, he has done his duty,' said Hamidullah. 'Do not tease him so. He carries on his family, two boys and their sister.'

'Aunt, they live most comfortably with my wife's mother, where she was living when she died. I can see them whenever I like. They are such very, very small children.'

'And he sends them the whole of his salary and lives like a low-grade clerk, and tells no one the reason. What more do you require him to do?'

But this was not Hamidullah Begum's point, and having courteously changed the conversation for a few moments she returned and made it. She said, 'What is to become of all our daughters if men refuse to marry? They will marry beneath them, or—' And she began the oft-told tale of a lady of Imperial descent who could find no husband in the narrow circle where her pride permitted her to mate, and had lived on unwed, her age now thirty, and would die unwed, for no one would have her now. While the tale was in progress, it convinced the two men, the tragedy seemed a slur on the whole community; better polygamy almost, than that a woman should die without the joys God has intended her to receive. Wedlock, motherhood, power in the house–for what else is she born, and how can the man who has denied them to her stand up to face her creator and his own at the last day? Aziz took his leave saying 'Perhaps . . . but later . . .'–his invariable reply to such an appeal.

'You mustn't put off what you think right,' said Hamidullah. 'That is why India is in such a plight, because we put off things.' But seeing that his young relative looked worried, he added a few soothing words, and thus wiped out any impression that his wife might have made.

During their absence, Mahmoud Ali had gone off in his carriage leaving a message that he should be back in five minutes, but they were on no account to wait. They sat down to meat with a distant cousin of the house, Mohammed Latif, who lived on Hamidullah's bounty and who occupied the position neither of a servant nor of an equal. He did not speak unless spoken to, and since no one spoke kept unoffended silence. Now and then he belched, in compliment to the richness of the food. A gentle, happy and dishonest old man; all his life he had never done a stroke of work. So long as some one of his relatives had a house he was sure of a home, and it was unlikely that so large a family would all go bankrupt. His wife led a similar existence some hundreds of miles away—he did not visit her, owing to the expense of the railway ticket. Presently Aziz chaffed him, also the servants, and then began quoting poetry, Persian, Urdu, a little Arabic. His memory was good, and for so young a man he had read largely; the themes he preferred were the decay of Islam and the brevity of love. They listened delighted, for they took the public view of poetry, not the private which obtains in England. It never bored them to hear words, words; they breathed them with the cool night air, never stopping to analyse; the name of the poet, Hafiz, Hali, Iqbal, was sufficient guarantee. India—a hundred Indias—whispered outside beneath the indifferent moon, but for the time India seemed one and their own, and they regained their departed greatness by hearing its departure lamented, they felt young again because reminded that youth must fly. A servant in scarlet interrupted him; he was the chuprassi of the Civil Surgeon, and he handed Aziz a note.

'Old Callendar wants to see me at his bungalow,' he said, not rising. 'He might have the politeness to say why.'

'Some case, I daresay.'

'I daresay not, I daresay nothing. He has found out our dinner hour, that's all, and chooses to interrupt us every time, in order to show his power.'

'On the one hand he always does this, on the other it may be a serious case, and you cannot know,' said Hamidullah, considerately paving the way towards obedience. 'Had you not better clean your teeth after pan?'

'If my teeth are to be cleaned, I don't go at all. I am an Indian, it is an Indian habit to take pan. The Civil Surgeon must put up with it. Mohammed Latif, my bike, please.'

The poor relation got up. Slightly immersed in the realms of matter, he laid his hand on the bicycle's saddle, while a servant did the actual wheeling. Between them they took it over a tintack. Aziz held his hands under the ewer, dried them, fitted on his green felt hat, and then with unexpected energy whizzed out of Hamidullah's compound.

'Aziz, Aziz, imprudent boy. . . .' But he was far down the bazaar, riding furiously. He had neither light nor bell nor had he a brake, but what use are such adjuncts in a land where the cyclist's only hope is to coast from face to face, and just before he collides with each it vanishes? And the city was fairly empty at this hour. When his tyre went flat, he leapt off and shouted for a tonga.

He did not at first find one, and he had also to dispose of his bicycle at a friend's house. He dallied furthermore to clean his teeth. But at last he was rattling towards the civil lines, with a vivid sense of speed. As he entered their arid tidiness, depression suddenly seized him. The roads, named after victorious generals and intersecting at right angles, were symbolic of the net Great Britain had thrown over India. He felt caught in their meshes. When he turned into Major Callendar's compound he could with difficulty restrain himself from getting down from the tonga and approaching the bungalow on foot, and this not because his soul was servile but because his feelings—the sensitive edges of him—feared a gross snub. There had been a 'case' last year—an Indian gentleman had driven up to an official's house and been turned back by the servants and been told to approach more suitably—only one case among thousands of visits to hundreds of officials, but its fame spread wide. The young man shrank from a repetition of it. He compromised, and stopped the driver just outside the flood of light that fell across the verandah.

The Civil Surgeon was out.

'But the sahib has left me some message?'

The servant returned an indifferent 'No.' Aziz was in despair. It was a servant whom he had forgotten to tip, and he could do nothing now because there were people in the hall. He was convinced that there was a message, and that the man was withholding it out of revenge. While they argued, the people came out. Both were ladies. Aziz lifted his hat. The first, who was in evening dress, glanced at the Indian and turned instinctively away.

'Mrs Lesley, it *is* a tonga,' she cried.

'Ours?' enquired the second, also seeing Aziz, and doing likewise.

'Take the gifts the gods provide, anyhow,' she screeched, and both jumped in. 'O Tonga wallah, club, club. Why doesn't the fool go?'

'Go, I will pay you to-morrow,' said Aziz to the driver, and as they went off he called courteously, 'You are most welcome, ladies.' They did not reply, being full of their own affairs.

So it had come, the usual thing—just as Mahmoud Ali said. The inevitable snub—his bow ignored, his carriage taken. It might have been worse, for it comforted him somehow that Mesdames Callendar and Lesley should both be fat and weigh the tonga down behind. Beautiful women would have pained him. He turned to the servant, gave him a couple of rupees, and asked again whether there was a message. The man, now very civil, returned the same answer. Major Callendar had driven away half an hour before.

'Saying nothing?'

He had as a matter of fact said, 'Damn Aziz'—words that the servant understood, but was too polite to repeat. One can tip too much as well as too little, indeed the coin that buys the exact truth has not yet been minted.

'Then I will write him a letter.'

He was offered the use of the house, but was too dignified to enter it. Paper and ink were brought on to the verandah. He began: 'Dear Sir,—At your express command I have hastened as a subordinate should—' and then stopped. 'Tell him I have called, that is sufficient,' he said, tearing the protest up. 'Here is my card. Call me a tonga.'

'Huzoor, all are at the club.'

'Then telephone for one down to the railway station.' And since the man hastened to do this he said, 'Enough, enough, I prefer to walk.' He commandeered a match and lit a cigarette. These attentions, though purchased, soothed him. They would last as long as he had rupees, which is something. But to shake the dust of Anglo-India off his feet! To escape from the net and be back among manners and gestures that he knew! He began a walk, an unwonted exercise.

He was an athletic little man, daintily put together, but really very strong. Nevertheless walking fatigued him, as it fatigues everyone in India except the new-comer. There is something hostile in that soil. It either yields, and the foot sinks into a depression, or else it is unexpectedly rigid and sharp, pressing stones or crystals against the tread. A series of these little surprises exhausts; and he was wearing pumps, a poor preparation for any country. At the edge of the civil station he turned into a mosque to rest.

He had always liked this mosque. It was gracious, and the arrangement pleased him. The courtyard—entered through a ruined gate—contained an ablution tank of fresh clear water, which was always in motion, being indeed part of a conduit that supplied the city. The courtyard was paved with broken slabs. The covered part of the mosque was deeper than is usual; its effect was that of an English parish church whose side has been taken out. Where he sat, he looked into three arcades whose darkness was illuminated by a small hanging lamp and by the moon. The front—in full moonlight—had the appearance of marble, and the ninety-nine names of God on the frieze stood out black, as the frieze stood out white against the sky. The contest between this dualism and the contention of shadows within pleased Aziz, and he tried to symbolize the whole into some truth of religion or love. A mosque by winning his approval let loose his imagination. The temple of another creed, Hindu, Christian, or Greek, would have bored him and failed to awaken his sense of beauty. Here was Islam, his own country, more than a Faith, more than a battle-cry, more, much more . . . Islam, an attitude towards life both exquisite and durable, where his body and his thoughts found their home.

His seat was the low wall that bounded the courtyard on the left. The ground fell away beneath him towards the city, visible as a blur of trees, and in the stillness he heard many small sounds. On the right, over in the club, the English community contributed an amateur orchestra. Elsewhere some Hindus were drumming—he knew they were Hindus, because the rhythm was uncongenial to him,—and others were bewailing a corpse—he knew whose, having certified it in the afternoon. There were owls, the Punjab mail . . . and flowers smelt deliciously in the station-master's garden. But the mosque—that alone signified, and he returned to it from the complex appeal of the night, and decked it with meanings the builder had never intended. Some day he too would build a mosque, smaller than this but in perfect taste, so that all who passed by should experience the happiness he felt now. And near it, under a low dome, should be his tomb, with a Persian inscription:

> *Alas, without me for thousands of years*
> *The Rose will blossom and the Spring will bloom,*
> *But those who have secretly understood my heart—*
> *They will approach and visit the grave where I lie.*

He had seen the quatrain on the tomb of a Deccan king and regarded it as profound philosophy—he always held pathos to be profound. The secret understanding of the heart! He repeated the phrase with tears in his eyes, and as he did so one of the pillars of the mosque seemed to quiver. It swayed in the gloom and detached itself. Belief in ghosts ran in his blood, but he sat firm. Another pillar moved, a third, and then an Englishwoman stepped out into the moonlight. Suddenly he was furiously angry and shouted: 'Madam! Madam! Madam!'

'Oh! Oh!' the woman gasped.

'Madam, this is a mosque, you have no right here at all; you should have taken off your shoes; this is a holy place for Moslems.'

'I have taken them off.'

'You have?'

'I left them at the entrance.'

'Then I ask your pardon.'

Still startled, the woman moved out, keeping the ablution tank between them. He called after her, 'I am truly sorry for speaking.'

'Yes, I was right, was I not? If I remove my shoes, I am allowed?'

'Of course, but so few ladies take the trouble, especially if thinking no one is there to see.'

'That makes no difference. God is here.'

'Madam!'

'Please let me go.'

'Oh, can I do you some service now or at any time?'

'No, thank you, really none – good night.'

'May I know your name?'

She was now in the shadow of the gateway, so that he could not see her face, but she saw his, and she said with a change of voice, 'Mrs Moore.'

'Mrs—' Advancing, he found that she was old. A fabric bigger than the mosque fell to pieces, and he did not know whether he was glad or sorry. She was older than Hamidullah Begum, with a red face and white hair. Her voice had deceived him.

'Mrs Moore, I am afraid I startled you. I shall tell my community – our friends – about you. That God is here – very good, very fine indeed. I think you are newly arrived in India.'

'Yes – how did you know?'

'By the way you address me. No, but can I call you a carriage?'

'I have only come from the club. They are doing a play that I have seen in London, and it was so hot.'

'What was the name of the play?'

'*Cousin Kate.*'

'I think you ought not to walk at night alone, Mrs Moore. There are bad characters about and leopards may come across from the Marabar Hills. Snakes also.'

She exclaimed; she had forgotten the snakes.

'For example, a six-spot beetle,' he continued. 'You pick it up, it bites, you die.'

'But you walk about yourself.'

'Oh, I am used to it.'

'Used to snakes?'

They both laughed. 'I'm a doctor,' he said. 'Snakes don't dare bite me.' They sat down side by side in the entrance, and slipped on their evening shoes. 'Please may I ask you a question now? Why do you come to India at this time of year, just as the cold weather is ending?'

'I intended to start earlier, but there was an unavoidable delay.'

'It will soon be so unhealthy for you! And why ever do you come to Chandrapore?'

'To visit my son. He is the City Magistrate here.'

'Oh no, excuse me, that is quite impossible. Our City Magistrate's name is Mr Heaslop. I know him intimately.'

'He's my son all the same,' she said, smiling.

'But, Mrs Moore, how can he be?'

'I was married twice.'

'Yes, now I see, and your first husband died.'

'He did, and so did my second husband.'

'Then we are in the same box,' he said cryptically. 'Then is the City Magistrate the entire of your family now?'

'No, there are the younger ones—Ralph and Stella in England.'

'And the gentleman here, is he Ralph and Stella's half-brother?'

'Quite right.'

'Mrs Moore, this is all extremely strange, because like yourself I have also two sons and a daughter. Is not this the same box with a vengeance?'

'What are their names? Not also Ronny, Ralph, and Stella, surely?'

The suggestion delighted him. 'No, indeed. How funny it sounds! Their names are quite different and will surprise you. Listen, please. I am about to tell you my children's names. The first is called Ahmed, the second is called Karim, the third—she is the eldest—Jamila. Three children are enough. Do not you agree with me?'

'I do.'

They were both silent for a little, thinking of their respective families. She sighed and rose to go.

'Would you care to see over the Minto Hospital one morning?' he enquired. 'I have nothing else to offer at Chandrapore.'

'Thank you, I have seen it already, or I should have liked to come with you very much.'

'I suppose the Civil Surgeon took you.'

'Yes, and Mrs Callendar.'

His voice altered. 'Ah! A very charming lady.'

'Possibly, when one knows her better.'

'What? What? You didn't like her?'

'She was certainly intending to be kind, but I did not find her exactly charming.'

He burst out with: 'She has just taken my tonga without my permission—do you call that being charming?—and Major Callendar interrupts me night after night from where I am dining with my friends and I go at once, breaking up a most pleasant entertainment, and he is not there and not even a message. Is this charming, pray? But what does it matter? I can do nothing and he knows it. I am just a subordinate, my time is of no value, the verandah is good enough for an Indian, yes, yes, let him stand, and Mrs Callendar takes my carriage and cuts me dead . . .'

She listened.

He was excited partly by his wrongs, but much more by the knowledge that someone sympathized with them. It was this that led him to repeat, exaggerate, contradict. She had proved her sympathy by criticizing her fellow-countrywoman to him, but even earlier he had known. The flame that not even beauty can nourish was springing up, and though his words were querulous his heart began to glow secretly. Presently it burst into speech.

'You understand me, you know what others feel. Oh, if others resembled you!'

Rather surprised, she replied: 'I don't think I understand people very well. I only know whether I like or dislike them.'

'Then you are an Oriental.'

She accepted his escort back to the club, and said at the gate that she wished she was a member, so that she could have asked him in.

'Indians are not allowed into the Chandrapore Club even as guests,' he said simply. He did not expatiate on his wrongs now, being happy. As he strolled downhill beneath the lovely moon, and again saw the lovely mosque, he seemed to own the land as much as anyone owned it. What did it matter if a few flabby Hindus had preceded him there, and a few chilly English succeeded?

Chapter Three

The third act of *Cousin Kate* was well advanced by the time Mrs Moore re-entered the club. Windows were barred, lest the servants should see their mem-sahibs acting, and the heat was consequently immense. One electric fan revolved like a wounded bird, another was out of order. Disinclined to return to the audience, she went into the billiard room, where she was greeted by 'I want to see the *real* India,' and her appropriate life came back with a rush. This was Adela Quested, the queer, cautious girl whom Ronny had commissioned her to bring from England, and Ronny was her son, also cautious, whom Miss Quested would probably though not certainly marry, and she herself was an elderly lady.

'I want to see it too, and I only wish we could. Apparently the Turtons will arrange something for next Tuesday.'

'It'll end in an elephant ride, it always does. Look at this evening. *Cousin Kate*! Imagine, *Cousin Kate*! But where have you been off to? Did you succeed in catching the moon in the Ganges?'

The two ladies had happened, the night before, to see the moon's reflection in a distant channel of the stream. The water had drawn it out, so that it had seemed larger than the real moon, and brighter, which had pleased them.

'I went to the mosque, but I did not catch the moon.'

'The angle would have altered—she rises later.'

'Later and later,' yawned Mrs Moore, who was tired after her walk. 'Let me think—we don't see the other side of the moon out here, no.'

'Come, India's not as bad as all that,' said a pleasant voice. 'Other side of the earth, if you like, but we stick to the same old moon.' Neither of them knew the speaker nor did they ever see him again. He passed with his friendly word through red-brick pillars into the darkness.

'We aren't even seeing the other side of the world; that's our complaint,' said Adela. Mrs Moore agreed; she too was disappointed at the dullness of their new life. They had made such a romantic voyage across the Mediterranean and through the sands of Egypt to the harbour of Bombay, to find only a gridiron of bungalows at the end of it. But she did not take the disappointment as seriously as Miss Quested, for the reason that she was forty years older, and had learnt that Life never gives us what we want at the moment that we consider appropriate. Adventures do occur, but not punctually. She said again that she hoped that something interesting would be arranged for next Tuesday.

'Have a drink,' said another pleasant voice. 'Mrs Moore—Miss Quested—have a drink, have two drinks.' They knew who it was this time—the Collector, Mr Turton, with whom they had dined. Like themselves, he had found the atmosphere of *Cousin Kate* too hot. Ronny, he told them, was stage-managing in place of Major Callendar, whom some native subordinate or other had let down, and doing it very well; then he turned to Ronny's other merits, and in quiet, decisive tones said much that was flattering. It wasn't that the young man was particularly good at the games or the lingo, or that he had much notion of the Law, but—apparently a large but—Ronny was dignified.

Mrs Moore was surprised to learn this, dignity not being a quality with which any mother credits her son. Miss Quested learnt it with anxiety, for she had not decided whether she liked dignified men. She tried indeed to discuss this point with Mr Turton, but he silenced her with a good-humoured motion of his hand, and continued what he had come to say. 'The long and the short of it is Heaslop's a sahib; he's the type we want, he's one of us,' and another civilian who was leaning over the billiard table said, 'Hear, hear!' The matter was thus placed beyond doubt, and the Collector passed on, for other duties called him.

Meanwhile the performance ended, and the amateur orchestra played the National Anthem. Conversation and billiards stopped, faces stiffened. It was the Anthem of the Army of Occupation. It reminded every member of the club that he or she was British and in exile. It produced a little sentiment and a useful accession of willpower. The meagre tune, the curt series of demands on Jehovah, fused into a prayer unknown in England, and though they perceived neither Royalty nor Deity they did perceive something, they were strengthened to resist another day. Then they poured out, offering one another drinks.

'Adela, have a drink; mother, a drink.'

They refused—they were weary of drinks—and Miss Quested, who always said exactly what was in her mind, announced anew that she was desirous of seeing the real India.

Ronny was in high spirits. The request struck him as comic, and he called out to another passer-by: 'Fielding! how's one to see the real India?'

'Try seeing Indians,' the man answered, and vanished.

'Who was that?'

'Our schoolmaster—Government College.'

'As if one could avoid seeing them,' sighed Mrs Lesley.

'I've avoided,' said Miss Quested. 'Excepting my own servant, I've scarcely spoken to an Indian since landing.'

'Oh, lucky you.'

'But I want to see them.'

She became the centre of an amused group of ladies. One said, 'Wanting to see Indians! How new that sounds!' Another, 'Natives! why, fancy!' A third, more serious, said, 'Let me explain. Natives don't respect one any the more after meeting one, you see.'

'That occurs after so many meetings.'

But the lady, entirely stupid and friendly, continued: 'What I mean is, I was a nurse before my marriage, and came across them a great deal, so I know. I really do know the truth about Indians. A most unsuitable position for any Englishwoman—I was a nurse in a Native State. One's only hope was to hold sternly aloof.'

'Even from one's patients?'

'Why, the kindest thing one can do to a native is to let him die,' said Mrs Callendar.

'How if he went to heaven?' asked Mrs Moore, with a gentle but crooked smile.

'He can go where he likes as long as he doesn't come near me. They give me the creeps.'

'As a matter of fact I have thought what you were saying about heaven, and that is why I am against Missionaries,' said the lady who had been a nurse. 'I am all for Chaplains, but all against Missionaries. Let me explain.'

But before she could do so, the Collector intervened.

'Do you really want to meet the Aryan Brother, Miss Quested? That can be easily fixed up. I didn't realize he'd amuse you.' He thought a moment. 'You can practically see any type you like. Take your choice. I know the Government people and the landowners, Heaslop here can get hold of the barrister crew, while if you want to specialize on education, we can come down on Fielding.'

'I'm tired of seeing picturesque figures pass before me as a frieze,' the girl explained. 'It was wonderful when we landed, but that superficial glamour soon goes.'

Her impressions were of no interest to the Collector; he was only concerned to give her a good time. Would she like a Bridge Party? He explained to her what that was—not the game, but a party to bridge the gulf between East and West; the expression was his own invention, and amused all who heard it.

'I only want those Indians whom you come across socially—as your friends.'

'Well, we don't come across them socially,' he said, laughing. 'They're full of all the virtues, but we don't, and it's now eleven-thirty, and too late to go into the reasons.'

'Miss Quested, what a name!' remarked Mrs Turton to her husband as they drove away. She had not taken to the new young lady, thinking her ungracious and cranky. She trusted that she hadn't been brought out to marry nice little Heaslop, though it looked like it. Her husband agreed with her in his heart, but he never spoke against an Englishwoman if he could avoid doing so, and he only said that Miss Quested naturally made mistakes. He added: 'India does wonders for the judgment, especially during the hot weather; it has even done wonders for Fielding.' Mrs Turton closed her eyes at this name and remarked that Mr Fielding wasn't pukka, and had better marry Miss Quested, for she wasn't pukka. Then they reached their bungalow, low and enormous, the oldest and most uncomfortable bungalow in the civil station, with a sunk soup plate of a lawn, and they had one drink more, this time of barley water, and went to bed. Their withdrawal from the club had broken up the evening, which, like all gatherings, had an official tinge. A community that bows the knee to a Viceroy and believes that the divinity that hedges a king can be transplanted, must feel some reverence for any viceregal substitute. At Chandrapore the Turtons were little gods; soon they would retire to some suburban villa, and die exiled from glory.

'It's decent of the great man,' chattered Ronny, much gratified at the civility that had been shown to his guests. 'Do you know he's never given a Bridge Party before? Coming on top of the dinner too! I wish I could have arranged something myself, but when you know the natives better you'll realize it's easier for the Burra Sahib than for me. They know him—they know he can't be fooled—I'm still fresh comparatively. No one can even begin to think of knowing this country until he has been in it twenty years.—Hello, the mater! Here's your cloak.—Well: for an example of the mistakes one makes. Soon after I came out I asked one of the Pleaders to have a smoke with me—only a cigarette, mind. I found afterwards that he had sent touts all over the bazaar to announce the fact—told all the litigants, "Oh, you'd better come to my Vakil Mahmoud Ali—he's in with the City Magistrate." Ever since then I've dropped on him in Court as hard as I could. It's taught me a lesson, and I hope him.'

'Isn't the lesson that you should invite all the Pleaders to have a smoke with you?'

'Perhaps, but time's limited and the flesh weak. I prefer my smoke at the club amongst my own sort, I'm afraid.'

'Why not ask the Pleaders to the club?' Miss Quested persisted.

'Not allowed.' He was pleasant and patient, and evidently understood why she did not understand. He implied that he had once been as she, though not for long. Going to the verandah, he called firmly to the moon. His sais answered, and without lowering his head, he ordered his trap to be brought round.

Mrs Moore, whom the club had stupefied, woke up outside. She watched the moon, whose radiance stained with primrose the purple of the surrounding sky. In England the moon had seemed dead and alien; here she was caught in the shawl of night together with earth and all the other stars. A sudden sense of unity, of kinship with the heavenly bodies, passed into the old woman and out, like water through a tank, leaving a strange freshness behind. She did not dislike *Cousin Kate* or the National Anthem, but their note had died into a new one, just as cocktails and cigars had died into invisible flowers. When the mosque, long and domeless, gleamed at the turn of the road, she exclaimed, 'Oh, yes—that's where I got to—that's where I've been.'

'Been there when?' asked her son.

'Between the acts.'

'But, mother, you can't do that sort of thing.'

'Can't mother?' she replied.

'No, really not in this country. It's not done. There's the danger from snakes for one thing. They are apt to lie out in the evening.'

'Ah yes, so the young man there said.'

'That sounds very romantic,' said Miss Quested, who was exceedingly fond of Mrs Moore, and was glad she should have had this little escapade. 'You meet a young man in a mosque, and then never let me know!'

'I was going to tell you, Adela, but something changed the conversation and I forgot. My memory grows deplorable.'

'Was he nice?'

She paused, then said emphatically: 'Very nice.'

'Who was he?' Ronny enquired.

'A doctor. I don't know his name.'

'A doctor? I know of no young doctor in Chandrapore. How odd! What was he like?'

'Rather small, with a little moustache and quick eyes. He called out to me when I was in the dark part of the mosque—about my shoes. That was how we began talking. He was afraid I had them on, but I remembered luckily. He told me about his children, and then we walked back to the club. He knows you well.'

'I wish you had pointed him out to me. I can't make out who he is.'

'He didn't come into the club. He said he wasn't allowed to.'

Thereupon the truth struck him, and he cried 'Oh, good gracious! Not a Mohammedan? Why ever didn't you tell me you'd been talking to a native? I was going all wrong.'

'A Mohammedan! How perfectly magnificent!' exclaimed Miss Quested. 'Ronny, isn't that like your mother? While we talk about seeing the real India, she goes and sees it, and then forgets she's seen it.'

But Ronny was ruffled. From his mother's description he had thought the doctor might be young Muggins from over the Ganges, and had brought out all the comradely emotions. What a mix-up! Why hadn't she indicated by the tone of her voice that she was talking about an Indian? Scratchy and dictatorial, he began to question her. 'He called to you in the mosque, did he? How? Impudently? What was he doing there himself at that time of night?—No, it's not their prayer time.'—This in answer to a suggestion of Miss Quested's, who showed the keenest interest. 'So he called to you over your shoes. Then it was impudence. It's an old trick. I wish you had had them on.'

'I think it was impudence, but I don't know about a trick,' said Mrs Moore. 'His nerves were all on edge—I could tell from his voice. As soon as I answered he altered.'

'You oughtn't to have answered.'

'Now look here,' said the logical girl, 'wouldn't you expect a Mohammedan to answer if you asked him to take off his hat in church?'

'It's different, it's different; you don't understand.'

'I know I don't, and I want to. What is the difference, please?'

He wished she wouldn't interfere. His mother did not signify—she was just a globe-trotter, a temporary escort, who could retire to England with what impressions she chose. But Adela, who meditated spending her life in the country, was a more serious matter; it would be tiresome if she started crooked over the native question. Pulling up the mare, he said, 'There's your Ganges.'

Their attention was diverted. Below them a radiance had suddenly appeared. It belonged neither to water nor moonlight, but stood like a luminous sheaf upon the fields of darkness. He told them that it was where the new sand-bank was forming, and that the dark ravelled bit at the top was the sand, and that the dead bodies floated down that way from Benares, or would if the crocodiles let them. 'It's not much of a dead body that gets down to Chandrapore.'

'Crocodiles down in it too, how terrible!' his mother murmured. The young people glanced at each other and smiled; it amused them when the old lady got these gentle creeps, and harmony was restored between them consequently. She continued: 'What a terrible river! what a wonderful river!' she sighed. The radiance was already altering, whether through shifting of the moon or of the sand; soon the bright sheaf would be gone, and a circlet, itself to alter, be burnished upon the streaming void. The women discussed whether they would wait for the change or not, while the silence broke into patches of unquietness and the mare shivered. On her account they did not wait, but drove on to the City Magistrate's bungalow, where Miss Quested went to bed, and Mrs Moore had a short interview with her son.

He wanted to enquire about the Mohammedan doctor in the mosque. It was his duty to report suspicious characters and conceivably it was some disreputable hakim who had prowled up from the bazaar. When she told him that it was someone connected with the Minto Hospital, he was relieved, and said that the fellow's name must be Aziz, and that he was quite all right, nothing against him at all.

'Aziz! what a charming name!'

'So you and he had a talk. Did you gather he was well disposed?'

Ignorant of the force of this question, she replied, 'Yes, quite, after the first moment.'

'I meant, generally. Did he seem to tolerate us—the brutal conqueror, the sundried bureaucrat, that sort of thing?'

'Oh, yes, I think so, except the Callendars—he doesn't care for the Callendars at all.'

'Oh. So he told you that, did he? The Major will be interested. I wonder what was the aim of the remark.'

'Ronny, Ronny! you're never going to pass it on to Major Callendar?'

'Yes, rather, I must in fact!'

'But, my dear boy—'

'If the Major heard I was disliked by any native subordinate of mine, I should expect him to pass it on to me.'

'But, my dear boy—a private conversation!'

'Nothing's private in India. Aziz knew that when he spoke out, so don't you worry. He had some motive in what he said. My personal belief is that the remark wasn't true.'

'How not true?'

'He abused the Major in order to impress you.'

'I don't know what you mean, dear.'

'It's the educated native's latest dodge. They used to cringe, but the younger generation believe in a show of manly independence. They think it will pay better with the itinerant M.P. But whether the native swaggers or cringes, there's always something behind every remark be makes, always something, and if nothing else he's trying to increase his izzat—in plain Anglo-Saxon, to score. Of course there are exceptions.'

'You never used to judge people like this at home.'

'India isn't home,' he retorted, rather rudely, but in order to silence her he had been using phrases and arguments that he had picked up from older officials, and he did not feel quite sure of himself. When he said 'of course there are exceptions' he was quoting Mr Turton, while 'increasing the izzat' was Major Callendar's own. The phrases worked and were in current use at the club, but she was rather clever at detecting the first from the second hand, and might press him for definite examples.

She only said, 'I can't deny that what you say sounds very sensible, but you really must not hand on to Major Callendar anything I have told you about Doctor Aziz.'

He felt disloyal to his caste, but he promised, adding, 'In return please don't talk about Aziz to Adela.'

'Not talk about him? Why?'

'There you go again, mother—I really can't explain every thing. I don't want Adela to be worried, that's the fact; she'll begin wondering whether we treat the natives properly, and all that sort of nonsense.'

'But she came out to be worried—that's exactly why she's here. She discussed it all on the boat. We had a long talk when we went on shore at

Aden. She knows you in play, as she put it, but not in work, and she felt she must come and look round, before she decided—and before you decided. She is very, very fair-minded.'

'I know,' he said dejectedly.

The note of anxiety in his voice made her feel that he was still a little boy, who must have what he liked, so she promised to do as he wished, and they kissed good night. He had not forbidden her to think about Aziz, however, and she did this when she retired to her room. In the light of her son's comment she reconsidered the scene at the mosque, to see whose impression was correct. Yes, it could be worked into quite an unpleasant scene. The doctor had begun by bullying her, had said Mrs Callendar was nice, and then—finding the ground safe—had changed; he had alternately whined over his grievances and patronized her, had run a dozen ways in a single sentence, had been unreliable, inquisitive, vain. Yes, it was all true, but how false as a summary of the man; the essential life of him had been slain.

Going to hang up her cloak, she found that the tip of the peg was occupied by a small wasp. She had known this wasp or his relatives by day; they were not as English wasps, but had long yellow legs which hung down behind when they flew. Perhaps he mistook the peg for a branch—no Indian animal has any sense of an interior. Bats, rats, birds, insects will as soon nest inside a house as out; it is to them a normal growth of the eternal jungle, which alternately produces houses trees, houses trees. There he clung, asleep, while jackals in the plain bayed their desires and mingled with the percussion of drums.

'Pretty dear,' said Mrs Moore to the wasp. He did not wake, but her voice floated out, to swell the night's uneasiness.

Chapter Four

The Collector kept his word. Next day he issued invitation cards to numerous Indian gentlemen in the neighbourhood, stating that he would be at home in the garden of the club between the hours of five and seven on the following Tuesday, also that Mrs Turton would be glad to receive any ladies of their families who were out of purdah. His action caused much excitement and was discussed in several worlds.

'It is owing to orders from the L.G,' was Mahmoud Ali's explanation. 'Turton would never do this unless compelled. Those high officials are different—they sympathize, the Viceroy sympathizes, they would have us treated properly. But they come too seldom and live too far away. Meanwhile—'

'It is easy to sympathize at a distance,' said an old gentleman with a beard. 'I value more the kind word that is spoken close to my ear. Mr Turton has spoken it, from whatever cause. He speaks, we hear. I do not see why we need discuss it further.' Quotations followed from the Koran.

'We have not all your sweet nature, Nawab Bahadur, nor your learning.'

'The Lieutenant-Governor may be my very good friend, but I give him no trouble.—How do you do, Nawab Bahadur?—Quite well, thank you, Sir Gilbert; how are you?—And all is over. But I can be a thorn in Mr Turton's flesh, and if he asks me I accept the invitation. I shall come in from Dilkusha specially, though I have to postpone other business.'

'You will make yourself chip,' suddenly said a little black man.

There was a stir of disapproval. Who was this illbred upstart, that he should criticize the leading Mohammedan landowner of the district? Mahmoud Ali, though sharing his opinion, felt bound to oppose it. 'Mr Ram Chand!' he said, swaying forward stiffly with his hands on his hips.

'Mr Mahmoud Ali!'

'Mr Ram Chand, the Nawab Bahadur can decide what is cheap without our valuation, I think.'

'I do not expect I shall make myself cheap,' said the Nawab Bahadur to Mr Ram Chand, speaking very pleasantly, for he was aware that the man had been impolite and he desired to shield him from the consequences. It had passed through his mind to reply, 'I expect I shall make myself cheap,' but he rejected this as the less courteous alternative. 'I do not see why we should make ourselves cheap. I do not see why we should. The invitation is worded very graciously.' Feeling that he could not further decrease the social gulf between himself and his auditors, he sent his elegant grandson, who was in attendance on him, to fetch his car. When it came, he repeated all that he had said before, though at greater length, ending up with 'Till Tuesday, then, gentlemen all, when I hope we may meet in the flower gardens of the club.'

This opinion carried great weight. The Nawab Bahadur was a big proprietor and a philanthropist, a man of benevolence and decision. His character among all the communities in the province stood high. He was a straightforward enemy and a staunch friend, and his hospitality was proverbial. 'Give, do not lend; after death who will thank you?' was his favourite remark. He held it a disgrace to die rich. When such a man was prepared to motor twenty-five miles to shake the Collector's hand, the entertainment took another aspect. For he was not like some eminent men, who give out that they will come, and then fail at the last moment, leaving the small fry floundering. If he said he would come, he would come, he would never deceive his supporters. The gentlemen whom he had lectured now urged one another to attend the party, although convinced at heart that his advice was unsound.

He had spoken in the little room near the Courts where the pleaders waited for clients; clients, waiting for pleaders, sat in the dust outside. These had not received a card from Mr Turton. And there were circles even beyond these—people who wore nothing but a loincloth, people who wore not even that, and spent their lives in knocking two sticks together before a scarlet doll—humanity grading and drifting beyond the educated vision, until no earthly invitation can embrace it.

All invitations must proceed from heaven perhaps; perhaps it is futile for men to initiate their own unity, they do but widen the gulfs between them by the attempt. So at all events thought old Mr Graysford and young Mr Sorley, the devoted missionaries who lived out beyond the slaughterhouses, always travelled third on the railways, and never came up to the club. In our Father's house are many mansions, they taught, and there alone will the incompatible multitudes of mankind be welcomed and soothed. Not one shall be turned away by the servants on that verandah, be he black or white, not one shall be kept standing who approaches with a loving heart. And why should the divine hospitality cease here? Consider, with all reverence, the monkeys. May there not be a mansion for the monkeys also? Old Mr Graysford said No, but young Mr Sorley, who was advanced, said Yes; he saw no reason why monkeys should not have their collateral share of bliss, and he had sympathetic discussions about them with his Hindu friends. And the jackals? Jackals were indeed less to Mr Sorley's mind, but he admitted that the mercy of God, being infinite, may well embrace all mammals. And the wasps? He became uneasy during the descent to wasps, and was apt to change the conversation. And oranges, cactuses, crystals and mud? and the bacteria inside Mr Sorley? No, no, this is going too far. We must exclude someone from our gathering, or we shall be left with nothing.

Chapter Five

The Bridge Party was not a success—at least it was not what Mrs Moore and Miss Quested were accustomed to consider a successful party. They arrived early, since it was given in their honour, but most of the Indian guests had arrived even earlier, and stood massed at the farther side of the tennis lawns, doing nothing.

'It is only just five,' said Mrs Turton. 'My husband will be up from his office in a moment and start the thing. I have no idea what we have to do. It's the first time we've every given a party like this at the club. Mr Heaslop, when I'm dead and gone will you give parties like this? It's enough to make the old type of Burra Sahib turn in his grave.'

Ronny laughed deferentially. 'You wanted something not picturesque and we've provided it,' he remarked to Miss Quested. 'What do you think of the Aryan Brother in a topi and spats?'

Neither she nor his mother answered. They were gazing rather sadly over the tennis lawn. No, it was not picturesque; the East, abandoning its secular magnificence, was descending into a valley whose farther side no man can see.

'The great point to remember is that no one who's here matters; those who matter don't come. Isn't that so, Mrs Turton?'

'Absolutely true,' said the great lady, leaning back. She was 'saving herself up,' as she called it—not for anything that would happen that afternoon or even that week, but for some vague future occasion when a high official might come along and tax her social strength. Most of her public appearances were marked by this air of reserve.

Assured of her approbation, Ronny continued: 'The educated Indians will be no good to us if there's a row, it's simply not worth while conciliating them, that's why they don't matter. Most of the people you see are seditious at heart, and the rest 'ld run squealing. The cultivator—he's another story. The Pathan—he's a man if you like. But these people—don't imagine they're India.' He pointed to the dusky line beyond the court, and here and there it flashed a pince-nez or shuffled a shoe, as if aware that he was despising it. European costume had lighted like a leprosy. Few had yielded entirely, but none were untouched. There was a silence when he had finished speaking, on both sides of the court; at least, more ladies joined the English group, but their words seemed to die as soon as uttered. Some kites hovered overhead, impartial, over the kites passed the mass of a vulture, and with an impartiality exceeding all, the sky, not deeply coloured but translucent, poured light from its whole circumference. It seemed unlikely that the series stopped here. Beyond the sky must not there be something that overarches all the skies, more impartial even than they? Beyond which again . . .

They spoke of *Cousin Kate*.

They had tried to reproduce their own attitude to life upon the stage, and to dress up as the middle-class English people they actually were. Next year they would do *Quality Street* or *The Yeomen of the Guard*. Save for this annual incursion, they left literature alone. The men had no time for it, the women did nothing that they could not share with the men. Their ignorance of the Arts was notable, and they lost no opportunity of proclaiming it to one another; it was the Public School attitude, flourishing more vigorously than it can yet hope to do in England. If Indians were shop, the Arts were bad form, and Ronny had repressed his mother when she enquired after his viola; a viola was almost a demerit, and certainly not the sort of instrument one mentioned in public. She noticed now how tolerant and conventional his judgments had become; when they had seen *Cousin Kate* in London together in the past, he had scorned it; now he pretended that it was a good play, in order to hurt nobody's feelings. An 'unkind notice' had appeared in the local paper, 'the sort of thing no white man could have written,' as Mrs Lesley said. The play was praised, to be sure, and so were the stage management and the performance as a whole, but the notice contained the following sentence: 'Miss Derek, though she charmingly looked her part, lacked the necessary experience, and occasionally forgot her words.' This tiny breath of genuine criticism had given deep offence, not indeed to Miss Derek, who was as hard as nails, but to her friends. Miss Derek did not belong to Chandrapore. She was stopping for a fortnight with the McBrydes, the police people, and she had been so good as to fill up a gap in the cast at the last moment. A nice impression of local hospitality she would carry away with her.

'To work, Mary, to work,' cried the Collector, touching his wife on the shoulder with a switch.

Mrs Turton got up awkwardly. 'What do you want me to do? Oh, those purdah women! I never thought any would come. Oh dear!'

A little group of Indian ladies had been gathering in a third quarter of the grounds, near a rustic summer-house in which the more timid of them had already taken refuge. The rest stood with their backs to the company and their faces pressed into a bank of shrubs. At a little distance stood their male relatives, watching the venture. The sight was significant: an island bared by the turning tide, and bound to grow.

'I consider they ought to come over to me.'

'Come along, Mary, get it over.'

'I refuse to shake hands with any of the men, unless it has to be the Nawab Bahadur.'

'Whom have we so far?' He glanced along the line. 'H'm! h'm! much as one expected. We know why he's here, I think—over that contract, and he wants to get the right side of me for Mohurram, and he's the astrologer who wants to dodge the municipal building regulations, and he's that Parsi, and he's—Hullo! there he goes—smash into our hollyhocks. Pulled the left rein when he meant the right. All as usual.'

'They ought never to have been allowed to drive in; it's so bad for them,' said Mrs Turton, who had at last begun her progress to the summer-house, accompanied by Mrs Moore, Miss Quested, and a terrier. 'Why they come at all I don't know. They hate it as much as we do. Talk to Mrs McBryde. Her husband made her give purdah parties until she struck.'

'This isn't a purdah party,' corrected Miss Quested.

'Oh, really,' was the haughty rejoinder.

'Do kindly tell us who these ladies are,' asked Mrs Moore.

'You're superior to them, anyway. Don't forget that. You're superior to everyone in India except one or two of the Ranis, and they're on an equality.'

Advancing, she shook hands with the group and said a few words of welcome in Urdu. She had learnt the lingo, but only to speak to her servants, so she knew none of the politer forms and of the verbs only the imperative mood. As soon as her speech was over, she enquired of her companions, 'Is that what you wanted?'

'Please tell these ladies that I wish we could speak their language, but we have only just come to their country.'

'Perhaps we speak yours a little,' one of the ladies said.

'Why, fancy, she understands!' said Mrs Turton.

'Eastbourne, Piccadilly, High Park Corner,' said another of the ladies.

'Oh yes, they're English-speaking.'

'But now we can talk: how delightful!' cried Adela, her face lighting up.

'She knows Paris also,' called one of the onlookers.

'They pass Paris on the way, no doubt,' said Mrs Turton, as if she was describing the movements of migratory birds. Her manner had grown more distant since she had discovered that some of the group was Westernized, and might apply her own standards to her.

'The shorter lady, she is my wife, she is Mrs Bhattacharya,' the onlooker explained. 'The taller lady, she is my sister, she is Mrs Das.'

The shorter and the taller ladies both adjusted their saris, and smiled.

There was a curious uncertainty.about their gestures, as if they sought for a new formula which neither East nor West could provide. When Mrs Bhattacharya's husband spoke, she turned away from him, but she did not mind seeing the other men. Indeed all the ladies were uncertain, cowering, recovering, giggling, making tiny gestures of atonement or despair at all that was said, and alternately fondling the terrier or shrinking from him. Miss Quested now had her desired opportunity; friendly Indians were before her, and she tried to make them talk, but she failed, she strove in vain against the echoing walls of their civility. Whatever she said produced a murmur of deprecation, varying into a murmur of concern when she dropped her pocket-handkerchief. She tried doing nothing, to see what that produced, and they too did nothing. Mrs Moore was equally unsuccessful. Mrs Turton waited for them with a detached expression; she had known what nonsense it all was from the first.

When they took their leave, Mrs Moore had an impulse, and said to Mrs Bhattacharya, whose face she liked, 'I wonder whether you would allow us to call on you some day.'

'When?' she replied, inclining charmingly.

'Whenever is convenient.'

'All days are convenient.'

'Thursday . . .'

'Most certainly.'

'We shall enjoy it greatly, it would be a real pleasure. What about the time?'

'All hours.'

'Tell us which you would prefer. We're quite strangers to your country: we don't know when you have visitors,' said Miss Quested.

Mrs Bhattacharya seemed not to know either. Her gesture implied that she had known, since Thursdays began, that English ladies would come to see her on one of them, and so always stayed in. Everything pleased her, nothing surprised. She added, 'We leave for Calcutta to-day.'

'Oh, do you?' said Adela, not at first seeing the implication. Then she cried, 'Oh, but if you do we shall find you gone.'

Mrs Bhattacharya did not dispute it. But her husband called from the distance, 'Yes, yes, you come to us Thursday.'

'But you'll be in Calcutta.'

'No, no, we shall not.' He said something swiftly to his wife in Bengali. 'We expect you Thursday.'

'Thursday . . .' the woman echoed.

'You can't have done such a dreadful thing as to put off going for our sake?' exclaimed Mrs Moore.

'No, of course not, we are not such people.' He was laughing.

'I believe that you have. Oh, please—it distresses me beyond words.'

Everyone was laughing now, but with no suggestion that they had blundered. A shapeless discussion occurred, during which Mrs Turton retired, smiling to herself. The upshot was that they were to come Thursday, but early in the morning, so as to wreck the Bhattacharya plans as little as possible, and Mr Bhattacharya would send his carriage to fetch them, with servants to point out the way. Did he know where they lived? Yes, of course he knew, he knew everything; and he laughed again. They left among a flutter of compliments and smiles, and three ladies, who had hitherto taken no part in the reception, suddenly shot out of the summer-house like exquisitely coloured swallows, and salaamed them.

Meanwhile the Collector had been going his rounds. He made pleasant remarks and a few jokes, which were applauded lustily, but he knew something to the discredit of nearly every one of his guests, and was consequently perfunctory. When they had not cheated, it was bhang, women, or worse, and even the desirables wanted to get something out of him. He believed that a 'Bridge Party' did good rather than harm, or he would not have given one, but he was under no illusions, and at the proper moment he retired to the English side of the lawn. The impressions he left behind him were various. Many of the guests, especially the humbler and less anglicized, were genuinely grateful. To be addressed by so high an official was a permanent asset. They did not mind how long they stood, or how little happened, and when seven o'clock struck, they had to be turned out. Others were grateful with more intelligence. The Nawab Bahadur, indifferent for himself and for the distinction with which he was greeted, was moved by the mere kindness that must have prompted the invitation. He knew the difficulties. Hamidullah also thought that the Collector had played up well. But others, such as Mahmoud Ali, were cynical; they were firmly convinced that Turton had been made to give the party by his official superiors and was all the time consumed with impotent rage, and they infected some who were inclined to a healthier view. Yet even Mahmoud Ali was glad he had come. Shrines are fascinating, especially when rarely opened, and it amused him to note the ritual of the English club, and to caricature it afterwards to his friends.

After Mr Turton, the official who did his duty best was Mr Fielding, the Principal of the little Government College. He knew little of the district and less against the inhabitants, so he was in a less cynical state of mind. Athletic and cheerful, he romped about, making numerous mistakes which the parents of his pupils tried to cover up, for he was popular among them. When the moment for refreshments came, he did not move back to the English side, but burnt his mouth with gram. He talked to anyone and he ate anything. Amid much that was alien, he learnt that the two new ladies from England had been a great success, and that their politeness in wishing to be Mrs Bhattacharya's guests had pleased not only her but all Indians who heard of it. It pleased Mr Fielding also. He scarcely knew the two new ladies, still he decided to tell them what pleasure thay had given by their friendliness.

He found the younger of them alone. She was looking through a nick in the cactus hedge at the distant Marabar Hills, which had crept near, as was their custom at sunset; if the sunset had lasted long enough, they would have reached the town, but it was swift, being tropical. He gave her his information, and she was so much pleased and thanked him so heartily that he asked her and the other lady to tea.

'I'ld like to come very much indeed, and so would Mrs Moore, I know.'

'I'm rather a hermit, you know.'

'Much the best thing to be in this place.'

'Owing to my work and so on, I don't get up much to the club.'

'I know, I know, and we never get down from it. I envy you being with Indians.'

'Do you care to meet one or two?'

'Very, very, much indeed; it's what I long for. This party to-day makes me so angry and miserable. I think my countrymen out here must be mad. Fancy inviting guests and not treating them properly! You and Mr Turton and perhaps Mr McBryde are the only people who showed any common politeness. The rest make me perfectly ashamed, and it's got worse and worse.'

It had. The Englishmen had intended to play up better, but had been prevented from doing so by their women folk, whom they had to attend, provide with tea, advise about dogs, etc. When tennis began, the barrier grew impenetrable. It had been hoped to have some sets between East and West, but this was forgotten, and the courts were monopolized by the usual club couples. Fielding resented it too, but did not say so to the girl, for he found something theoretical in her outburst. Did she care about Indian music? he enquired; there was an old professor down at the College, who sang.

'Oh, just what we wanted to hear. And do you know Doctor Aziz?'

'I know all about him. I don't know him. Would you like him asked too?'

'Mrs Moore says he is so nice.'

'Very well, Miss Quested. Will Thursday suit you?'

'Indeed it will, and that morning we go to this Indian lady's. All the nice things are coming Thursday.'

'I won't ask the City Magistrate to bring you. I know he'll be busy at that time.'

'Yes, Ronny is always hard-worked,' she replied, contemplating the hills. How lovely they suddenly were! But she couldn't touch them. In front, like a shutter, fell a vision of her married life. She and Ronny would look into the club like this every evening, then drive home to dress; they would see the Lesleys and the Callendars and the Turtons and the Burtons, and invite them and be invited by them, while the true India slid by unnoticed. Colour would remain—the pageant of birds in the early morning, brown bodies, white turbans, idols whose flesh was scarlet or blue—and movement would remain as long as there were crowds in the bazaar and bathers in the tanks. Perched up on the seat of a dogcart, she would see them. But the force that lies behind colour and movement would escape her even more effectually than it did now. She would see India always as a frieze, never as a spirit, and she assumed that it was a spirit of which Mrs Moore had had a glimpse.

And sure enough they did drive away from the club in a few minutes, and they did dress, and to dinner came Miss Derek and the McBrydes, and the menu was: Julienne soup full of bullety bottled peas, pseudo-cottage bread, fish full of branching bones, pretending to be plaice, more bottled peas with the cutlets, trifle, sardines on toast: the menu of Anglo-India. A dish might be added or subtracted as one rose or fell in the official scale, the peas might rattle less or more, the sardines and the vermouth be imported by a different firm, but the tradition remained; the food of exiles, cooked by servants who did not understand it. Adela thought of the young men and women who had come out before her, P. & O. full after P. & O. full, and had been set down to the same food and the same ideas, and been snubbed in the same good-humoured way until they kept to the accredited themes and began to snub others. 'I should never get like that,' she thought, for she was young herself; all the same she knew that she had come up against something that was both insidious and tough, and against which she needed allies. She must gather around her at Chandrapore a few people who felt as she did, and she was glad to have met Mr Fielding and the Indian lady with the unpronounceable name. Here at all events was a nucleus; she should know much better where she stood in the course of the next two days.

Miss Derek—she companioned a Maharani in a remote Native State. She was genial and gay and made them all laugh about her leave, which she had taken because she felt she deserved it, not because the Maharani said she might go. Now she wanted to take the Maharaja's motor-car as well; it had gone to a Chiefs' Conference at Delhi, and she had a great scheme for burgling it at the junction as it came back in the train. She was also very funny about the Bridge Party—indeed she regarded the entire peninsula as a comic opera. 'If one couldn't see the laughable side of these people one 'ld be done for,' said Miss Derek. Mrs McBryde—it was she who had been the nurse—ceased not to exclaim, 'Oh, Nancy, how topping! Oh, Nancy, how killing! I wish I could look at things like that.' Mr McBryde did not speak much; he seemed nice.

When the guests had gone, and Adela gone to bed, there was another interview between mother and son. He wanted her advice and support—while resenting interference. 'Does Adela talk to you much?' he began. 'I'm so driven with work, I don't see her as much as I hoped, but I hope she finds things comfortable.'

'Adela and I talk mostly about India. Dear, since you mention it, you're quite right—you ought to be more alone with her than you are.'

'Yes, perhaps, but then people 'ld gossip.'

'Well, they must gossip sometime! Let them gossip.'

'People are so odd out here, and it's not like home—one's always facing the footlights, as the Burra Sahib said. Take a silly little example: when Adela went out to the boundary of the club compound, and Fielding followed her. I saw Mrs Callendar notice it. They notice everything, until they're perfectly sure you're their sort.'

'I don't think Adela 'll ever be quite their sort—she's much too individual.'

'I know, that's so remarkable about her,' he said thoughtfully. Mrs Moore thought him rather absurd. Accustomed to the privacy of London, she could not realize that India, seemingly so mysterious, contains none, and that consequently the conventions have greater force. 'I suppose nothing's on her mind,' he continued.

'Ask her, ask her yourself, my dear boy.'

'Probably she's heard tales of the heat, but of course I should pack her off to the Hills every April—I'm not one to keep a wife grilling in the Plains.'

'Oh, it wouldn't be the weather.'

'There's nothing in India but the weather, my dear mother; it's the Alpha and Omega of the whole affair.'

'Yes, as Mr McBryde was saying, but it's much more the Anglo-Indians themselves who are likely to get on Adela's nerves. She doesn't think they behave pleasantly to Indians, you see.'

'What did I tell you?' he exclaimed, losing his gentle manner. 'I knew it last week. Oh, how like a woman to worry over a side-issue!'

She forgot about Adela in her surprise. 'A side-issue, a side-issue?' she repeated. 'How can it be that?'

'We're not out here for the purpose of behaving pleasantly!'

'What do you mean?'

'What I say. We're out here to do justice and keep the peace. Them's my sentiments. India isn't a drawing-room.'

'Your sentiments are those of a god,' she said quietly, but it was his manner rather than his sentiments that annoyed her.

Trying to recover his temper, he said, 'India likes gods.'

'And Englishmen like posing as gods.'

'There's no point in all this. Here we are, and we're going to stop, and the country's got to put up with us, gods or no gods. Oh, look here,' he broke out, rather pathetically, 'what do you and Adela want me to do? Go against my class, against all the people I respect and admire out here? Lose such power as I have for doing good in this country because my behaviour isn't pleasant? You neither of you understand what work is, or you 'ld never talk such eyewash. I hate talking like this, but one must occasionally. It's morbidly sensitive to go on as Adela and you do. I noticed you both at the club to-day—after the Collector had been at all that trouble to amuse you. I am out here to work, mind, to hold this wretched country by force. I'm not a missionary or a Labour Member or a vague sentimental sympathetic literary man. I'm just a servant of the Government; it's the profession you wanted me to choose myself, and that's that. We're not pleasant in India, and we don't intend to be pleasant. We've something more important to do.'

He spoke sincerely. Every day he worked hard in the court trying to decide which of two untrue accounts was the less untrue, trying to dispense justice fearlessly, to protect the weak against the less weak, the incoherent against the plausible, surrounded by lies and flattery. That morning he had convicted a railway clerk of overcharging pilgrims for their tickets, and a Pathan of attempted rape. He expected no gratitude, no recognition for this, and both clerk and Pathan might appeal, bribe their witnesses more effectually in the interval, and get their sentences reversed. It was his duty. But he did expect sympathy from his own people, and except from new-comers he obtained it. He did think he ought not to be worried about 'Bridge Parties' when the day's work was over and he wanted to play tennis with his equals or rest his legs upon a long chair.

He spoke sincerely, but she could have wished with less gusto. How Ronny revelled in the drawbacks of his situation! How he did rub it in that he was not in India to behave pleasantly, and derived positive satisfaction therefrom! He reminded her of his public-schooldays. The traces of young-man humanitarianism had sloughed off, and he talked like an intelligent and embittered boy. His words without his voice might have impressed her, but when she heard the self-satisfied lilt of them, when she saw the mouth moving so complacently and competently beneath the little red nose, she felt, quite illogically, that this was not the last word on India. One touch of regret—not the canny substitute but the true regret from the heart—would have made him a different man, and the British Empire a different institution.

'I'm going to argue, and indeed dictate,' she said, clinking her rings. 'The English *are* out here to be pleasant.'

'How do you make that out, mother?' he asked, speaking gently again, for he was ashamed of his irritability.

'Because India is part of the earth. And God has put us on the earth in order to be pleasant to each other. God . . . is . . . love.' She hesitated, seeing how much he disliked the argument, but something made her go on. 'God has put us on earth to love our neighbours and to show it, and He is omnipresent, even in India, to see how we are succeeding.'

He looked gloomy, and a little anxious. He knew this religious strain in her, and that it was a symptom of bad health; there had been much of it when his step-father died. He thought, 'She is certainly ageing, and I ought not to be vexed with anything she says.'

'The desire to behave pleasantly satisfies God. . . . The sincere if impotent desire wins His blessing. I think every one fails, but there are so many kinds of failure. Good will and more good will and more good will. Though I speak with the tongues of . . .'

He waited until she had done, and then said gently, 'I quite see that. I suppose I ought to get off to my files now, and you'll be going to bed.'

'I suppose so, I suppose so.' They did not part for a few minutes, but the conversation had become unreal since Christianity had entered it. Ronny approved of religion as long as it endorsed the National Anthem, but he objected when it attempted to influence his life. Then he would say in respectful yet decided tones, 'I don't think it does to talk about these things, every fellow has to work out his own religion,' and any fellow who heard him muttered, 'Hear!'

Mrs Moore felt that she had made a mistake in mentioning God, but she found him increasingly difficult to avoid as she grew older, and he had been constantly in her thoughts since she entered India, though oddly enough he satisfied her less. She must needs pronounce his name frequently, as the greatest she knew, yet she had never found it less efficacious. Outside the arch there seemed always an arch, beyond the remotest echo a silence. And she regretted afterwards that she had not kept to the real serious subject that had caused her to visit India—namely the relationship between Ronny and Adela. Would they, or would they not, succeed in becoming engaged to be married?

Chapter Six

Aziz had not gone to the Bridge Party. Immediately after his meeting with Mrs Moore he was diverted to other matters. Several surgical cases came in, and kept him busy. He ceased to be either outcaste or poet, and became the medical student, very gay, and full of details of operations which he poured into the shrinking ears of his friends. His profession fascinated him at times, but he required it to be exciting, and it was his hand, not his mind, that was scientific. The knife he loved and used skilfully, and he also liked pumping in the latest serums. But the boredom of régime and hygiene repelled him, and after inoculating a man for enteric, he would go away and drink unfiltered water himself. 'What can you expect from the fellow?' said dour Major Callendar. 'No grits, no guts.' But in his heart he knew that if Aziz and not he had operated last year on Mrs Graysford's appendix, the old lady would probably have lived. And this did not dispose him any better towards his subordinate.

There was a row the morning after the mosque–they were always having rows. The Major, who had been up half the night, wanted damn well to know why Aziz had not come promptly when summoned.

'Sir, excuse me, I did. I mounted my bike, and it bust in front of the Cow Hospital. So I had to find a tonga.'

'Bust in front of the Cow Hospital, did it? And how did you come to be there?'

'I beg your pardon?'

'Oh Lord, oh Lord! When I live here'–he kicked the gravel–'and you live there–not ten minutes from me–and the Cow Hospital is right ever so far away the other side of you–*there*–then how did you come to be passing the Cow Hospital on the way to me? Now do some work for a change.'

He strode away in a temper, without waiting for the excuse, which as far as it went was a sound one: the Cow Hospital was in a straight line between Hamidullah's house and his own, so Aziz had naturally passed it. He never realized that the educated Indians visited one another constantly, and were weaving, however painfully, a new social fabric. Caste 'or something of the sort' would prevent them. He only knew that no one ever told him the truth, although he had been in the country for twenty years.

Aziz watched him go with amusement. When his spirits were up he felt that the English are a comic institution, and he enjoyed being misunderstood by them. But it was an amusement of the emotions and nerves, which an accident or the passage of time might destroy; it was apart from the fundamental gaiety that he reached when he was with those whom he trusted. A disobliging simile involving Mrs Callendar occurred to his fancy. 'I must tell that to Mahmoud Ali, it'll make him laugh,' he thought. Then he got to work. He was competent and indispensable, and he knew it. The simile passed from his mind while he exercised his professional skill.

During these pleasant and busy days, he heard vaguely that the Collector was giving a party, and that the Nawab Bahadur said every one ought to go to it. His fellow-assistant, Doctor Panna Lal, was in ecstasies at the prospect, and was urgent that they should attend it together in his new tum-tum. The arrangement suited them both. Aziz was spared the indignity of a bicycle or the expense of hiring, while Dr Panna Lal, who was timid and elderly, secured someone who could manage his horse. He could manage it himself, but only just, and he was afraid of the motors and of the unknown turn into the club grounds. 'Disaster may come,' he said politely, 'but we shall at all events get there safe, even if we do not get back.' And with more logic: 'It will, I think, create a good impression should two doctors arrive at the same time.'

But when the time came, Aziz was seized with a revulsion, and determined not to go. For one thing his spell of work, lately concluded, left him independent and healthy. For another, the day chanced to fall on the anniversary of his wife's death. She had died soon after he had fallen in love with her; he had not loved her at first. Touched by Western feeling, he disliked union with a woman whom he had never seen; moreover, when he did see her, she disappointed him, and he begat his first child in mere animality. The change began after its birth. He was won by her love for him, by a loyalty that implied something more than submission, and by her efforts to educate herself against that lifting of the purdah that would come in the next generation if not in theirs. She was intelligent, yet had old-fashioned grace. Gradually he lost the feeling that his relatives had chosen wrongly for him. Sensuous enjoyment—well, even if he had had it, it would have dulled in a year, and he had gained something instead, which seemed to increase the longer they lived together. She became the mother of a son . . . and in giving him a second son she died. Then he realized what he had lost, and that no woman could ever take her place; a friend would come nearer to her than another woman. She had gone, there was no one like her, and what is that uniqueness but love? He amused himself, he forgot her at times: but at other times he felt that she had sent all the beauty and joy of the world into Paradise, and he meditated suicide. Would he meet her beyond the tomb? Is there such a meeting-place? Though orthodox, he did not know. God's unity was indubitable and indubitably announced, but on all other points he wavered like the average Christian; his belief in the life to come would pale to a hope, vanish, reappear, all in a single sentence or a dozen heart-beats, so that the corpuscles of his blood rather than he seemed to decide which opinion he should hold, and for how long. It was so with all his opinions. Nothing stayed, nothing passed that did not return; the circulation was ceaseless and kept him young, and he mourned his wife the more sincerely because he mourned her seldom.

It would have been simpler to tell Dr Lal that he had changed his mind about the party, but until the last minute he did not know that he had changed it; indeed, he didn't change it, it changed itself. Unconquerable aversion welled. Mrs Callendar, Mrs Lesley—no, he couldn't stand them in his sorrow: they would guess it—for he dowered the British matron with strange insight—and would delight in torturing him, they would mock him to their husbands. When he should have been ready, he stood at the Post Office, writing a telegram to his children, and found on his return that Dr Lal had called for him, and gone on. Well, let him go on, as befitted the coarseness of his nature. For his own part, he would commune with the dead.

And unlocking a drawer, he took out his wife's photograph. He gazed at it, and tears spouted from his eyes. He thought, 'How unhappy I am!' But because he really was unhappy, another emotion soon mingled with his self-pity: he desired to remember his wife and could not. Why could he remember people whom he did not love? They were always so vivid to him, whereas the more he looked at this photograph, the less he saw. She had eluded him thus, ever since they had carried her to her tomb. He had known that she would pass from his hands and eyes, but had thought she could live in his mind, not realizing that the very fact that we have loved the dead increases their unreality, and that the more passionately we invoke them the further they recede. A piece of brown cardboard and three children—that was all that was left of his wife. It was unbearable, and he thought again, 'How unhappy I am!' and became happier. He had breathed for an instant the mortal air that surrounds Orientals and all men, and he drew back from it with a gasp, for he was young. 'Never, never shall I get over this,' he told himself. 'Most certainly my career is a failure, and my sons will be badly brought up.' Since it was certain, he strove to avert it, and looked at some notes he had made on a case at the hospital. Perhaps some day a rich person might require this particular operation, and he gain a large sum. The notes interesting him on their own account, he locked the photograph up again. Its moment was over, and he did not think about his wife any more.

After tea his spirits improved, and he went round to see Hamidullah. Hamidullah had gone to the party, but his pony had not, so Aziz borrowed it, also his friend's riding breeches and polo mallet. He repaired to the Maidan. It was deserted except at its rim, where some bazaar youths were training. Training for what? They would have found it hard to say, but the word had got into the air. Round they ran, weedy and knock-kneed—the local physique was wretched—with an expression on their faces not so much of determination as of a determination to be determined. 'Maharajah, salaam,' he called for a joke. The youths stopped and laughed. He advised them not to exert themselves. They promised they would not, and ran on.

Riding into the middle, he began to knock the ball about. He could not play, but his pony could, and he set himself to learn, free from all human tension. He forgot the whole damned business of living as he scurried over the brown platter of the Maidan, with the evening wind on his forehead, and the encircling trees soothing his eyes. The ball shot away towards a stray subaltern who was also practising; he hit it back to Aziz and called, 'Send it along again.'

'All right.'

The new-comer had some notion of what to do, but his horse had none, and forces were equal. Concentrated on the ball, they somehow became fond of one another, and smiled when they drew rein to rest. Aziz liked soldiers—they either accepted you or swore at you, which was preferable to the civilian's hauteur—and the subaltern liked anyone who could ride.

'Often play?' he asked.

'Never.'

'Let's have another chukker.'

As he hit, his horse bucked and off he went, cried, 'Oh God!' and jumped on again. 'Don't you ever fall off?'

'Plenty.'

'Not you.'

They reined up again, the fire of good fellowship in their eyes. But it cooled with their bodies, for athletics can only raise a temporary glow. Nationality was returning, but before it could exert its poison they parted, saluting each other. 'If only they were all like that,' each thought.

Now it was sunset. A few of his co-religionists had come to the Maidan, and were praying with their faces towards Mecca. A Brahminy Bull walked towards them, and Aziz, though disinclined to pray himself, did not see why they should be bothered with the clumsy and idolatrous animal. He gave it a tap with his polo mallet. As he did so, a voice from the road hailed him: it was Dr Panna Lal, returning in high distress from the Collector's party.

'Dr Aziz, Dr Aziz, where you been? I waited ten full minutes' time at your house, then I went.'

'I am so awfully sorry—I was compelled to go to the Post Office.'

One of his own circle would have accepted this as meaning that he had changed his mind, an event too common to merit censure. But Dr Lal, being of low extraction, was not sure whether an insult had not been intended, and he was further annoyed because Aziz had buffeted the Brahminy Bull. 'Post Office? Do you not send your servants?' he said.

'I have so few—my scale is very small.'

'Your servant spoke to me. I saw your servant.'

'But, Dr Lal, consider. How could I send my servant when you were coming: you come, we go, my house is left alone, my servant comes back perhaps, and all my portable property has been carried away by bad characters in the meantime. Would you have that? The cook is deaf—I can never count on my cook—and the boy is only a little boy. Never, never do I and Hassan leave the house at the same time together. It is my fixed rule.' He said all this and much more out of civility, to save Dr Lal's face. It was not offered as truth and should not have been criticized as such. But the other demolished it—an easy and ignoble task. 'Even if this so, what prevents leaving a chit saying where you go?' and so on. Aziz detested ill breeding, and made his pony caper. 'Farther away, or mine will start out of sympathy,' he wailed, revealing the true source of his irritation. 'It has been so rough and wild this afternoon. It spoiled some most valuable blossoms in the club garden, and had to be dragged back by four men. English ladies and gentlemen looking on, and the Collector Sahib himself taking a note. But, Dr Aziz, I'll not take up your valuable time. This will not interest you, who have so many engagements and telegrams. I am just a poor old doctor who thought right to pay my respects when I was asked and where I was asked. Your absence, I may remark, drew commentaries.'

'They can damn well comment.'

'It is fine to be young. Damn well! Oh, very fine. Damn whom?'

'I go or not as I please.'

'Yet you promise me, and then fabricate this tale of a telegram. Go forward, Dapple.'

They went, and Aziz had a wild desire to make an enemy for life. He could do it so easily by galloping near them. He did it. Dapple bolted. He thundered back on to the Maidan. The glory of his play with the subaltern remained for a little, he galloped and swooped till he poured with sweat, and until he returned the pony to Hamidullah's stable he felt the equal of any man. Once on his feet, he had creeping fears. Was he in bad odour with the powers that be? Had he offended the Collector by absenting himself? Dr Panna Lal was a person of no importance, yet was it wise to have quarrelled even with him? The complexion of his mind turned from human to political. He thought no longer, 'Can I get on with people?' but 'Are they stronger than I?' breathing the prevalent miasma.

At his home a chit was awaiting him, bearing the Government stamp. It lay on his table like a high explosive, which at a touch might blow his flimsy bungalow to bits. He was going to be cashiered because he had not turned up at the party. When he opened the note, it proved to be quite different; an invitation from Mr Fielding, the Principal of Government College, asking him to come to tea the day after to-morrow. His spirits revived with violence. They would have revived in any case, for he possessed a soul that could suffer but not stifle, and led a steady life beneath his mutability. But this invitation gave him particular joy, because Fielding had asked him to tea a month ago, and he had forgotten about it—never answered, never gone, just forgotten And here came a second invitation, without a rebuke or even an allusion to his slip. Here was true courtesy—the civil deed that shows the good heart—and snatching up his pen he wrote an affectionate reply, and hurried back for news to Hamidullah's. For he had never met the Principal, and believed that the one serious gap in his life was going to be filled. He longed to know everything about the splendid fellow—his salary, preferences, antecedents, how best one might please him. But Hamidullah was still out, and Mahmoud Ali, who was in, would only make silly rude jokes about the party.

Chapter Seven

This Mr Fielding had been caught by India late. He was over forty when he entered that oddest portal, the Victoria Terminus at Bombay, and–having bribed a European ticket inspector–took his luggage into the compartment of his first tropical train. The journey remained in his mind as significant. Of his two carriage companions one was a youth, fresh to the East like himself, the other a seasoned Anglo-Indian of his own age. A gulf divided him from either; he had seen too many cities and men to be the first or to become the second. New impressions crowded on him, but they were not the orthodox new impressions; the past conditioned them, and so it was with his mistakes. To regard an Indian as if he were an Italian is not, for instance, a common error, nor perhaps a fatal one, and Fielding often attempted analogies between this peninsula and that other, smaller and more exquisitely shaped, that stretches into the classic waters of the Mediterranean.

His career, though scholastic, was varied, and had included going to the bad and repenting thereafter. By now he was a hard-bitten, good-tempered, intelligent fellow on the verge of middle age, with a belief in education. He did not mind whom he taught; public schoolboys, mental defectives and policemen, had all come his way, and he had no objection to adding Indians. Through the influence of friends, he was nominated Principal of the little college at Chandrapore, liked it, and assumed he was a success. He did succeed with his pupils, but the gulf between himself and his countrymen, which he had noticed in the train, widened distressingly. He could not at first see what was wrong. He was not unpatriotic, he always got on with Englishmen in England, all his best friends were English, so why was it not the same out here? Outwardly of the large shaggy type, with sprawling limbs and blue eyes, he appeared to inspire confidence until he spoke. Then something in his manner puzzled people and failed to allay the distrust which his profession naturally inspired. There needs must be this evil of brains in India, but woe to him through whom they are increased! The feeling grew that Mr Fielding was a disruptive force, and rightly, for ideas are fatal to caste, and he used ideas by that most potent method–interchange. Neither a missionary nor a student, he was happiest in the give-and-take of a private conversation. The world, he believed, is a globe of men who are trying to reach one another and can best do so by the help of good will plus culture and intelligence–a creed ill suited to Chandrapore, but he had come out too late to lose it. He had no racial feeling–not because he was superior to his brother civilians, but because he had matured in a different atmosphere, where the herd-instinct does not flourish. The remark that did him most harm at the club was a silly aside to the effect that the so-called white races are really pinko-grey. He only said this to be cheery, he did not realize that 'white' has no more to do with a colour than 'God save the King' with a god, and that it is the height of impropriety to consider what it does connote. The pinko-grey male whom he addressed was subtly scandalized; his sense of insecurity was awoken, and he communicated it to the rest of the herd.

Still, the men tolerated him for the sake of his good heart and strong body; it was their wives who decided that he was not a sahib really. They disliked him. He took no notice of them, and this, which would have passed without comment in feminist England, did him harm in a community where the male is expected to be lively and helpful. Mr Fielding never advised one about dogs or horses, or dined, or paid his midday calls, or decorated trees for one's children at Christmas, and though he came to the club, it was only to get his tennis or billiards, and to go. This was true. He had discovered that it is possible to keep in with Indians and Englishmen, but that he who would also keep in with Englishwomen must drop the Indians. The two wouldn't combine. Useless to blame either party, useless to blame them for blaming one another. It just was so, and one had to choose. Most Englishmen preferred their own kinswomen, who, coming out in increasing numbers, made life on the home pattern yearly more possible. He had found it convenient and pleasant to associate with Indians and he must pay the price. As a rule no Englishwoman entered the College except for official functions, and if he invited Mrs Moore and Miss Quested to tea, it was because they were new-comers who would view everything with an equal if superficial eye, and would not turn on a special voice when speaking to his other guests.

The College itself had been slapped down by the Public Works Department, but its grounds included an ancient garden and a garden-house, and here he lived for much of the year. He was dressing after a bath when Dr Aziz was announced. Lifting up his voice, he shouted from the bedroom, 'Please make yourself at home.' The remark was unpremeditated, like most of his actions; it was what he felt inclined to say.

To Aziz it had a very definite meaning. 'May I really, Mr Fielding? It's very good of you,' he called back; 'I like unconventional behaviour so extremely.' His spirits flared up, he glanced round the living-room. Some luxury in it, but no order—nothing to intimidate poor Indians. It was also a very beautiful room, opening into the garden through three high arches of wood. 'The fact is I have long wanted to meet you,' he continued. 'I have heard so much about your warm heart from the Nawab Bahadur. But where is one to meet in a wretched hole like Chandrapore?' He came close up to the door. 'When I was greener here, I'll tell you what. I used to wish you to fall ill so that we could meet that way.' They laughed, and encouraged by his success he began to improvise. 'I said to myself, How does Mr Fielding look this morning? Perhaps pale. And the Civil Surgeon is pale too, he will not be able to attend upon him when the shivering commences. I should have been sent for instead. Then we would have had jolly talks, for you are a celebrated student of Persian poetry.'

'You know me by sight, then.'

'Of course, of course. You know me?'

'I know you very well by name.'

'I have been here such a short time, and always in the bazaar. No wonder you have never seen me, and I wonder you know my name. I say, Mr Fielding?'

'Yes?'

'Guess what I look like before you come out. That will be a kind of game.'

'You're five feet nine inches high,' said Fielding, surmising this much through the ground glass of the bedroom door.

'Jolly good. What next? Have I not a venerable white beard?'

'Blast!'

'Anything wrong?'

'I've stamped on my last collar stud.'

'Take mine, take mine.'

'Have you a spare one?'

'Yes, yes, one minute.'

'Not if you're wearing it yourself.'

'No, no, one in my pocket.' Stepping aside, so that his outline might vanish, he wrenched off his collar, and pulled out of his shirt the back stud, a gold stud, which was part of a set that his brother-in-law had brought him from Europe. 'Here it is,' he cried.

'Come in with it if you don't mind the unconventionality.'

'One minute again.' Replacing his collar, he prayed that it would not spring up at the back during tea. Fielding's bearer, who was helping him to dress, opened the door for him.

'Many thanks.' They shook hands smiling. He began to look round, as he would have with any old friend. Fielding was not surprised at the rapidity of their intimacy. With so emotional a people it was apt to come at once or never, and he and Aziz, having heard only good of each other, could afford to dispense with preliminaries.

'But I always thought that Englishmen kept their rooms so tidy. It seems that this is not so. I need not be so ashamed.' He sat down gaily on the bed; then, forgetting himself entirely, drew up his legs and folded them under him. 'Everything ranged coldly on shelves was what *I* thought.—I say, Mr Fielding, is the stud going to go in?'

'I hae ma doots.'

'What's that last sentence, please? Will you teach me some new words and so improve my English?'

Fielding doubted whether 'everything ranged coldly on shelves' could be improved. He was often struck with the liveliness with which the younger generation handled a foreign tongue. They altered the idiom, but they could say whatever they wanted to say quickly; there were none of the babuisms ascribed to them up at the club. But then the club moved slowly; it still declared that few Mohammedans and no Hindus would eat at an Englishman's table, and that all Indian ladies were in impenetrable purdah. Individually it knew better; as a club it declined to change.

'Let me put in your stud. I see . . . the shirt back's hole is rather small and to rip it wider a pity.'

'Why in hell does one wear collars at all?' grumbled Fielding as he bent his neck.

'We wear them to pass the Police.'

'What's that?'

'If I'm biking in English dress—starch collar, hat with ditch—they take no notice. When I wear a fez, they cry, "Your lamp's out!" Lord Curzon did not consider this when he urged natives of India to retain their picturesque costumes.—Hooray! Stud's gone in.—Sometimes I shut my eyes and dream I have splendid clothes again and am riding into battle behind Alamgir. Mr Fielding, must not India have been beautiful then, with the Mogul Empire at its height and Alamgir reigning at Delhi upon the Peacock Throne?'

'Two ladies are coming to tea to meet you—I think you know them.'

'Meet me? I know no ladies.'

'Not Mrs Moore and Miss Quested?'

'Oh yes—I remember.' The romance at the mosque had sunk out of his consciousness as soon as it was over. 'An excessively aged lady; but will you please repeat the name of her companion?'

'Miss Quested.'

'Just as you wish.' He was disappointed that other guests were coming, for he preferred to be alone with his new friend.

'You can talk to Miss Quested about the Peacock Throne if you like—she's artistic, they say.'

'Is she a Post Impressionist?'

'Post Impressionism, indeed! Come along to tea. This world is getting too much for me altogether.'

Aziz was offended. The remark suggested that he, an obscure Indian, had no right to have heard of Post Impressionism—a privilege reserved for the Ruling Race, that. He said stiffly, 'I do not consider Mrs Moore my friend, I only met her accidentally in my mosque,' and was adding 'a single meeting is too short to make a friend,' but before he could finish the sentence the stiffness vanished from it, because he felt Fielding's fundamental good will. His own went out to it, and grappled beneath the shifting tides of emotion which can alone bear the voyager to an anchorage but may also carry him across it on to the rocks. He was safe really—as safe as the shore-dweller who can only understand stability and supposes that every ship must be wrecked, and he had sensations the shore-dweller cannot know. Indeed, he was sensitive rather than responsive. In every remark he found a meaning, but not always the true meaning, and his life though vivid was largely a dream. Fielding, for instance, had not meant that Indians are obscure, but that Post Impressionism is; a gulf divided his remark from Mrs Turton's 'Why, they speak English,' but to Aziz the two sounded alike. Fielding saw that something had gone wrong, and equally that it had come right, but he didn't fidget, being an optimist where personal relations were concerned, and their talk rattled on as before.

'Besides the ladies I am expecting one of my assistants—Narayan Godbole.'

'Oho, the Deccani Brahman!'

'He wants the past back too, but not precisely Alamgir.'

'I should think not. Do you know what Deccani Brahmans say: That England conquered India from them—from them, mind, and not from the Moguls. Is not that like their cheek? They have even bribed it to appear in text-books, for they are so subtle and immensely rich. Professor Godbole must be quite unlike all other Deccani Brahmans from all I can hear say. A most sincere chap.'

'Why don't you fellows run a club in Chandrapore, Aziz?'

'Perhaps—some day . . . just now I see Mrs Moore and—what's her name—coming.'

How fortunate that it was an 'unconventional' party, where formalities are ruled out! On this basis Aziz found the English ladies easy to talk to, he treated them like men. Beauty would have troubled him, for it entails rules of its own, but Mrs Moore was so old and Miss Quested so plain that he was spared this anxiety. Adela's angular body and the freckles on her face were terrible defects in his eyes, and he wondered how God could have been so unkind to any female form. His attitude towards her remained entirely straightforward in consequence.

'I want to ask you something, Dr Aziz,' she began. 'I heard from Mrs Moore how helpful you were to her in the mosque, and how interesting. She learnt more about India in those few minutes' talk with you than in the three weeks since we landed.'

'Oh, please do not mention a little thing like that. Is there anything else I may tell you about my country?'

'I want you to explain a disappointment we had this morning; it must be some point of Indian etiquette.'

'There honestly is none,' he replied. 'We are by nature a most informal people.'

'I am afraid we must have made some blunder and given offence,' said Mrs Moore.

'That is even more impossible. But may I know the facts?'

'An Indian lady and gentleman were to send their carriage for us this morning at nine. It has never come. We waited and waited and waited; we can't think what happened.'

'Some misunderstanding,' said Fielding, seeing at once that it was the type of incident that had better not be cleared up.

'Oh no, it wasn't that,' Miss Quested persisted. 'They even gave up going to Calcutta to entertain us. We must have made some stupid blunder, we both feel sure.'

'I wouldn't worry about that.'

'Exactly what Mr Heaslop tells me,' she retorted, reddening a little. 'If one doesn't worry, how's one to understand?'

The host was inclined to change the subject, but Aziz took it up warmly, and on learning fragments of the delinquents' name pronounced that they were Hindus.

'Slack Hindus—they have no idea of society; I know them very well because of a doctor at the hospital. Such a slack, unpunctual fellow! It is as well you did not go to their house, for it would give you a wrong idea of India. Nothing sanitary. I think for my own part they grew ashamed of their house and that is why they did not send.'

'That's a notion,' said the other man.

'I do so hate mysteries,' Adela announced.

'We English do.'

'I dislike them not because I'm English, but from my own personal point of view,' she corrected.

'I like mysteries but I rather dislike muddles,' said Mrs Moore.

'A mystery is a muddle.'

'Oh, do you think so, Mr Fielding?'

'A mystery is only a high-sounding term for a muddle. No advantage in stirring it up, in either case. Aziz and I know well that India's a muddle.'

'India's— Oh, what an alarming idea!'

'There'll be no muddle when you come to see me,' said Aziz, rather out of his depth. 'Mrs Moore and everyone—I invite you all—oh, please.'

The old lady accepted: she still thought the young doctor excessively nice; moreover, a new feeling, half languor, half excitement, bade her turn down any fresh path. Miss Quested accepted out of adventure. She also liked Aziz, and believed that when she knew him better he would unlock his country for her. His invitation gratified her, and she asked him for his address.

Aziz thought of his bungalow with horror. It was a detestable shanty near a low bazaar. There was practically only one room in it, and that infested with small black flies. 'Oh, but we will talk of something else now,' he exclaimed. 'I wish I lived here. See this beautiful room! Let us admire it together for a little. See those curves at the bottom of the arches. What delicacy! It is the architecture of Question and Answer. Mrs Moore, you are in India; I am not joking.' The room inspired him. It was an audience hall built in the eighteenth century for some high official, and though of wood had reminded Fielding of the Loggia de' Lanzi at Florence. Little rooms, now Europeanized, clung to it on either side, but the central hall was unpapered and unglassed, and the air of the garden poured in freely. One sat in public—on exhibition, as it were—in full view of the gardeners who were screaming at the birds and of the man who rented the tank for the cultivation of water chestnut. Fielding let the mango trees too—there was no knowing who might not come in—and his servants sat on his steps night and day to discourage thieves. Beautiful certainly, and the Englishman had not spoilt it, whereas Aziz in an occidental moment would have hung Maude Goodmans on the walls. Yet there was no doubt to whom the room really belonged. . . .

'I am doing justice here. A poor widow who has been robbed comes along and I give her fifty rupees, to another a hundred, and so on and so on. I should like that.'

Mrs Moore smiled, thinking of the modern method as exemplified in her son. 'Rupees don't last for ever, I'm afraid,' she said.

'Mine would. God would give me more when he saw I gave. Always be giving, like the Nawab Bahadur. My father was the same, that is why he died poor.' And pointing about the room he peopled it with clerks and officials, all benevolent because they lived long ago. 'So we would sit giving for ever—on a carpet instead of chairs, that is the chief change between now and then, but I think we would never punish anyone.'

The ladies agreed.

'Poor criminal, give him another chance. It only makes a man worse to go to prison and be corrupted.' His face grew very tender—the tenderness of one incapable of administration, and unable to grasp that if the poor criminal is let off he will again rob the poor widow. He was tender to everyone except a few family enemies whom he did not consider human: on these he desired revenge. He was even tender to the English; he knew at the bottom of his heart that they could not help being so cold and odd and circulating like an ice stream through his land. 'We punish no one, no one,' he repeated, 'and in the evening we will give a great banquet with a nautch and lovely girls shall shine on every side of the tank with fireworks in their hands, and all shall be feasting and happiness until the next day, when there shall be justice as before—fifty rupees, a hundred, a thousand—till peace comes. Ah, why didn't we live in that time?—But are you admiring Mr Fielding's house? Do look how the pillars are painted blue, and the verandah's pavilions—what do you call them?—that are above us inside are blue also. Look at the carving on the pavilions. Think of the hours it took. Their little roofs are curved to imitate bamboo. So pretty—and the bamboos waving by the tank outside. Mrs Moore! Mrs Moore!'

'Well?' she said, laughing.

'You remember the water by our mosque? It comes down and fills this tank—a skilful arrangement of the Emperors. They stopped here going down into Bengal. They loved water. Wherever they went they created fountains, gardens, hammams. I was telling Mr Fielding I would give anything to serve them.'

He was wrong about the water, which no Emperor, however skilful, can cause to gravitate uphill; a depression of some depth together with the whole of Chandrapore lay between the mosque and Fielding's house. Ronny would have pulled him up, Turton would have wanted to pull him up, but restrained himself. Fielding did not even want to pull him up; he had dulled his craving for verbal truth and cared chiefly for truth of mood. As for Miss Quested, she accepted everything Aziz said as true verbally. In her ignorance, she regarded him as 'India,' and never surmised that his outlook was limited and his method inaccurate, and that no one is India.

He was now much excited, chattering away hard, and even saying damn when he got mixed up in his sentences. He told them of his profession, and of the operations he had witnessed and performed, and he went into details that scared Mrs Moore, though Miss Quested mistook them for proofs of his broad-mindedness; she had heard such talk at home in advanced academic circles, deliberately free. She supposed him to be emancipated as well as reliable, and placed him on a pinnacle which he could not retain. He was high enough for the moment, to be sure, but not on any pinnacle. Wings bore him up, and flagging would deposit him.

The arrival of Professor Godbole quieted him somewhat, but it remained his afternoon. The Brahman, polite and enigmatic, did not impede his eloquence, and even applauded it. He took his tea at a little distance from the outcasts, from a low table placed slightly behind him, to which he stretched back, and as it were encountered food by accident; all feigned indifference to Professor Godbole's tea. He was elderly and wizen with a grey moustache and grey-blue eyes, and his complexion was as fair as a European's. He wore a turban that looked like pale purple macaroni, coat, waistcoat, dhoti, socks with clocks. The clocks matched the turban, and his whole appearance suggested harmony—as if he had reconciled the products of East and West, mental as well as physical, and could never be discomposed. The ladies were interested in him, and hoped that he would supplement Dr Aziz by saying something about religion. But he only ate—ate and ate, smiling, never letting his eyes catch sight of his hand.

Leaving the Mogul Emperors, Aziz turned to topics that could distress no one. He described the ripening of the mangoes, and how in his boyhood he used to run out in the Rains to a big mango grove belonging to an uncle and gorge there. 'Then back with water streaming over you and perhaps rather a pain inside. But I did not mind. All my friends were paining with me. We have a proverb in Urdu: "What does unhappiness matter when we are all unhappy together?" which comes in conveniently after mangoes. Miss Quested, do wait for mangoes. Why not settle altogether in India?'

'I'm afraid I can't do that,' said Adela. She made the remark without thinking what it meant. To her, as to the three men, it seemed in key with the rest of the conversation, and not for several minutes—indeed, not for half an hour—did she realize that it was an important remark, and ought to have been made in the first place to Ronny.

'Visitors like you are too rare.'

'They are indeed,' said Professor Godbole. 'Such affability is seldom seen. But what can we offer to detain them?'

'Mangoes, mangoes.'

They laughed. 'Even mangoes can be got in England now,' put in Fielding. 'They ship them in ice-cold rooms. You can make India in England apparently, just as you can make England in India.'

'Frightfully expensive in both cases,' said the girl.

'I suppose so.'

'And nasty.'

But the host wouldn't allow the conversation to take this heavy turn. He turned to the old lady, who looked flustered and put out—he could not imagine why—and asked about her own plans. She replied that she should like to see over the College. Everyone immediately rose, with the exception of Professor Godbole, who was finishing a banana.

'Don't you come too, Adela; you dislike institutions.'

'Yes, that is so,' said Miss Quested, and sat down again.

Aziz hesitated. His audience was splitting up. The more familiar half was going, but the more attentive remained. Reflecting that it was an 'unconventional' afternoon, he stopped.

Talk went on as before. Could one offer the visitors unripe mangoes in a fool? 'I speak now as a doctor: no.' Then the old man said, 'But I will send you up a few healthy sweets. I will give myself that pleasure.'

'Miss Quested, Professor Godbole's sweets are delicious,' said Aziz sadly, for he wanted to send sweets too and had no wife to cook them. 'They will give you a real Indian treat. Ah, in my poor position I can give you nothing.'

'I don't know why you say that, when you have so kindly asked us to your house.'

He thought again of his bungalow with horror. Good heavens, the stupid girl had taken him at his word! What was he to do? 'Yes, all that is settled,' he cried. 'I invite you all to see me in the Marabar Caves.'

'I shall be delighted.'

'Oh, that is a most magnificent entertainment compared to my poor sweets. But has not Miss Quested visited our caves already?'

'No. I've not even heard of them.'

'Not heard of them?' both cried. 'The Marabar Caves in the Marabar Hills?'

'We hear nothing interesting up at the club. Only tennis and ridiculous gossip.'

The old man was silent, perhaps feeling that it was unseemly of her to criticize her race, perhaps fearing that if he agreed she would report him for disloyalty. But the young man uttered a rapid 'I know.'

'Then tell me everything you will, or I shall never understand India. Are they the hills I sometimes see in the evening? What are these caves?'

Aziz undertook to explain, but it presently appeared that he had never visited the caves himself—had always been 'meaning' to go, but work or private business had prevented him, and they were so far. Professor Godbole chaffed him pleasantly. 'My dear young sir, the pot and the kettle! Have you ever heard of that useful proverb?'

'Are they large caves?' she asked.

'No, not large.'

'Do describe them, Professor Godbole.'

'It will be a great honour.' He drew up his chair and an expression of tension came over his face. Taking the cigarette box, she offered to him and to Aziz, and lit up herself. After an impressive pause he said: 'There is an entrance in the rock which you enter, and through the entrance is the cave.'

'Something like the caves at Elephanta?'

'Oh no, not at all; at Elephanta there are sculptures of Siva and Parvati. There are no sculptures at Marabar.'

'They are immensely holy, no doubt,' said Aziz, to help on the narrative.

'Oh no, oh no.'

'Still, they are ornamented in some way.'

'Oh no.'

'Well, why are they so famous? We all talk of the famous Marabar Caves. Perhaps that is our empty brag.'

'No, I should not quite say that.'

'Describe them to this lady, then.'

'It will be a great pleasure.' He forewent the pleasure, and Aziz realized that he was keeping back something about the caves. He realized because he often suffered from similar inhibitions himself. Sometimes, to the exasperation of Major Callendar, he would pass over the one relevant fact in a position, to dwell on the hundred irrelevant. The Major accused him of disingenuousness, and was roughly right, but only roughly. It was rather that a power he couldn't control capriciously silenced his mind. Godbole had been silenced now; no doubt not willingly, he was concealing something. Handled subtly, he might regain control and announce that the Marabar Caves were—full of stalactites, perhaps; Aziz led up to this, but they weren't.

The dialogue remained light and friendly, and Adela had no conception of its underdrift. She did not know that the comparatively simple mind of the Mohammedan was encountering Ancient Night. Aziz played a thrilling game. He was handling a human toy that refused to work—he knew that much. If it worked, neither he nor Professor Godbole would be the least advantaged, but the attempt enthralled him and was akin to abstract thought. On he chattered, defeated at every move by an opponent who would not even admit that a move had been made, and further than ever from discovering what, if anything, was extraordinary about the Marabar Caves.

Into this Ronny dropped.

With an annoyance he took no trouble to conceal, he called from the garden: 'What's happened to Fielding? Where's my mother?'

'Good evening!' she replied coolly.

'I want you and mother at once. There's to be polo.'

'I thought there was to be no polo.'

'Everything's altered. Some soldier men have come in. Come along and I'll tell you about it.'

'Your mother will return shortly, sir,' said Professor Godbole, who had risen with deference. 'There is but little to see at our poor college.'

Ronny took no notice, but continued to address his remarks to Adela; he had hurried away from his work to take her to see the polo, because he thought it would give her pleasure. He did not mean to be rude to the two men, but the only link he could be conscious of with an Indian was the official, and neither happened to be his subordinate. As private individuals he forgot them.

Unfortunately Aziz was in no mood to be forgotten. He would not give up the secure and intimate note of the last hour. He had not risen with Godbole, and now, offensively friendly, called from his seat, 'Come along up and join us, Mr Heaslop; sit down till your mother turns up.'

Ronny replied by ordering one of Fielding's servants to fetch his master at once.

'He may not understand that. Allow me—' Aziz repeated the order idiomatically.

Ronny was tempted to retort; he knew the type; he knew all the types, and this was the spoilt Westernized. But he was a servant of the Government, it was his job to avoid 'incidents,' so he said nothing, and ignored the provocation that Aziz continued to offer. Aziz was provocative. Everything he said had an impertinent flavour or jarred. His wings were failing, but he refused to fall without a struggle. He did not mean to be impertinent to Mr Heaslop, who had never done him harm, but here was an Anglo-Indian who must become a man before comfort could be regained. He did not mean to be greasily confidential to Miss Quested, only to enlist her support; nor to be loud and jolly towards Professor Godbole. A strange quartette—he fluttering to the ground, she puzzled by the sudden ugliness, Ronny fuming, the Brahman observing all three, but with downcast eyes and hands folded, as if nothing was noticeable. A scene from a play, thought Fielding, who now saw them from the distance across the garden grouped among the blue pillars of his beautiful hall.

'Don't trouble to come, mother,' Ronny called; 'we're just starting.' Then he hurried to Fielding, drew him aside and said with pseudo-heartiness, 'I say, old man, do excuse me, but I think perhaps you oughtn't to have left Miss Quested alone.'

'I'm sorry, what's up?' replied Fielding, also trying to be genial.

'Well . . . I'm the sun-dried bureaucrat, no doubt; still, I don't like to see an English girl left smoking with two Indians.'

'She stopped, as she smokes, by her own wish, old man.'

'Yes, that's all right in England.'

'I really can't see the harm.'

'If you can't see, you can't see. . . . Can't you see that fellow's a bounder?' Aziz flamboyant, was patronizing Mrs Moore.

'He isn't a bounder,' protested Fielding. 'His nerves are on edge, that's all.'

'What should have upset his precious nerves?'

'I don't know. He was all right when I left.'

'Well, it's nothing I've said,' said Ronny reassuringly. 'I never even spoke to him.'

'Oh well, come along now, and take your ladies away; the catastrophe over.'

'Fielding . . . don't think I'm taking it badly, or anything of that sort. . . . I suppose you won't come on to the polo with us? We should all be delighted.'

'I'm afraid I can't, thanks all the same. I'm awfully sorry you feel I've been remiss. I didn't mean to be.'

So the leave-taking began. Every one was cross or wretched. It was as if irritation exuded from the very soil. Could one have been so petty on a Scotch moor or an Italian alp? Fielding wondered afterwards. There seemed no reserve of tranquillity to draw upon in India. Either none, or else tranquillity swallowed up everything, as it appeared to do for Professor Godbole. Here was Aziz all shoddy and odious, Mrs Moore and Miss

Quested both silly, and he himself and Heaslop both decorous on the surface, but detestable really, and detesting each other.

'Good-bye, Mr Fielding, and thank you so much. . . . What lovely College buildings!'

'Good-bye, Mrs Moore.'

'Good-bye Mr Fielding. Such an interesting afternoon. . . .'

'Good-bye, Miss Quested.'

'Good-bye, Dr Aziz.'

'Good-bye, Mrs Moore.'

'Good-bye, Dr Aziz.'

'Good-bye, Miss Quested.' He pumped her hand up and down to show that he felt at ease. 'You'll jolly jolly well not forget those caves, won't you? I'll fix the whole show up in a jiffy.'

'Thank you. . . .'

Inspired by the devil to a final effort, he added, 'What a shame you leave India so soon! Oh, do reconsider your decision, do stay.'

'Good-bye, Professor Godbole,' she continued, suddenly agitated. 'It's a shame we never heard you sing.'

'I may sing now,' he replied, and did.

His thin voice rose, and gave out one sound after another. At times there seemed rhythm, at times there was the illusion of a Western melody. But the ear, baffled repeatedly, soon lost any clue, and wandered in a maze of noises, none harsh or unpleasant, none intelligible. It was the song of an unknown bird. Only the servants understood it. They began to whisper to one another. The man who was gathering water chestnut came naked out of the tank, his lips parted with delight, disclosing his scarlet tongue. The sounds continued and ceased after a few moments as casually as they had begun—apparently half through a bar, and upon the subdominant.

'Thanks so much: what was that?' asked Fielding.

'I will explain in detail. It was a religious song. I placed myself in the position of a milkmaiden. I say to Shri Krishna, "Come! come to me only." The god refuses to come. I grow humble and say: "Do not come to me only. Multiply yourself into a hundred Krishnas, and let one go to each of my hundred companions, but one, O Lord of the Universe, come to me." He refuses to come. This is repeated several times. The song is composed in a raga appropriate to the present hour, which is the evening.'

'But He comes in some other song, I hope?' said Mrs Moore gently.

'Oh no, he refuses to come,' repeated Godbole, perhaps not understanding her question. 'I say to Him, Come, come, come, come, come, come. He neglects to come.'

Ronny's steps had died away, and there was a moment of absolute silence. No ripple disturbed the water, no leaf stirred.

Chapter Eight

Although Miss Quested had known Ronny well in England, she felt well advised to visit him before deciding to be his wife. India had developed sides of his character that she had never admired. His self-complacency, his censoriousness, his lack of subtlety, all grew vivid beneath a tropic sky; he seemed more indifferent than of old to what was passing in the minds of his fellows, more certain that he was right about them or that if he was wrong it didn't matter. When proved wrong, he was particularly exasperating; he always managed to suggest that she needn't have bothered to prove it. The point she made was never the relevant point, her arguments conclusive but barren, she was reminded that he had expert knowledge and she none, and that experience would not help her because she could not interpret it. A Public School, London University, a year at a crammer's, a particular sequence of posts in a particular province, a fall from a horse and a touch of fever were presented to her as the only training by which Indians and all who reside in their country can be understood; the only training she could comprehend, that is to say, for of course above Ronny there stretched the higher realms of knowledge, inhabited by Callendars and Turtons, who had been not one year in the country but twenty and whose instincts were superhuman. For himself he made no extravagant claims; she wished he would. It was the qualified bray of the callow official, the 'I am not perfect, but—' that got on her nerves.

How gross he had been at Mr Fielding's—spoiling the talk and walking off in the middle of the haunting song! As he drove them away in the tum-tum, her irritation became unbearable, and she did not realize that much of it was directed against herself. She longed for an opportunity to fly out at him, and since he felt cross too, and they were both in India, an opportunity soon occurred. They had scarcely left the College grounds before she heard him say to his mother, who was with him on the front seat, 'What was that about caves?' and she promptly opened fire.

'Mrs Moore, your delightful doctor has decided on a picnic, instead of a party in his house; we are to meet him out there—you, myself, Mr Fielding, Professor Godbole—exactly the same party.'

'Out where?' asked Ronny.

'The Marabar Caves.'

'Well, I'm blessed,' he murmured after a pause. 'Did he descend to any details?'

'He did not. If you had spoken to him, we could have arranged them.'

He shook his head laughing.

'Have I said anything funny?'

'I was only thinking how the worthy doctor's collar climbed up his neck.'

'I thought you were discussing the caves.'

'So I am. Aziz was exquisitely dressed, from tie-pin to spats, but he had forgotten his back collar-stud, and there you have the Indian all over: inattention to detail; the fundamental slackness that reveals the race. Similarly, to "meet" in the caves as if they were the clock at Charing Cross, when they're miles from a station and each other.'

'Have you been to them?'

'No, but I know all about them, naturally.'

'Oh naturally!'

'Are you too pledged to this expedition, mother?'

'Mother is pledged to nothing,' said Mrs Moore, rather unexpectedly. 'Certainly not to this polo. Will you drive up to the bungalow first, and drop me there, please? I prefer to rest.'

'Drop me too,' said Adela. 'I don't want to watch polo either, I'm sure.'

'Simpler to drop the polo,' said Ronny. Tired and disappointed, he quite lost self-control, and added in a loud lecturing voice, 'I won't have you messing about with Indians any more! If you want to go to the Marabar Caves, you'll go under British auspices.'

'I've never heard of these caves, I don't know what or where they are,' said Mrs Moore, 'but I really can't have'–she tapped the cushion beside her–'so much quarrelling and tiresomeness!'

The young people were ashamed. They dropped her at the bungalow and drove on together to the polo, feeling it was the least they could do. Their crackling bad humour left them, but the heaviness of their spirit remained; thunderstorms seldom clear the air. Miss Quested was thinking over her own behaviour, and didn't like it at all. Instead of weighing Ronny and herself, and coming to a reasoned conclusion about marriage, she had incidentally, in the course of a talk about mangoes, remarked to mixed company that she didn't mean to stop in India. Which meant that she wouldn't marry Ronny: but what a way to announce it, what a way for a civilized girl to behave! She owed him an explanation, but unfortunately there was nothing to explain. The 'thorough talk' so dear to her principles and temperament had been postponed until too late. There seemed no point in being disagreeable to him and formulating her complaints against his character at this hour of the day, which was the evening. . . . The polo took place on the Maidan near the entrance of Chandrapore city. The sun was already declining and each of the trees held a premonition of night. They walked away from the governing group to a distant seat, and there, feeling that it was his due and her own, she forced out of herself the undigested remark: 'We must have a thorough talk, Ronny, I'm afraid.'

'My temper's rotten, I must apologize,' was his reply. 'I didn't mean to order you and mother about, but of course the way those Bengalis let you down this morning annoyed me, and I don't want that sort of thing to keep happening.'

'It's nothing to do with them that I . . .'

'No, but Aziz would make some similar muddle over the caves. He meant nothing by the invitation, I could tell by his voice: it's just their way of being pleasant.'

'It's something very different, nothing to do with caves, that I wanted to talk over with you.' She gazed at the colourless grass. 'I've finally decided we are not going to be married, my dear boy.'

The news hurt Ronny very much. He had heard Aziz announce that she would not return to the country, but had paid no attention to the remark, for he never dreamt that an Indian could be a channel of communication between two English people. He controlled himself and said gently, 'You never said we should marry, my dear girl; you never bound either yourself or me—don't let this upset you.'

She felt ashamed. How decent he was! He might force his opinions down her throat, but did not press her to an 'engagement,' because he believed, like herself, in the sanctity of personal relationships: it was this that had drawn them together at their first meeting, which had occurred among the grand scenery of the English Lakes. Her ordeal was over, but she felt it should have been more painful and longer. Adela will not marry Ronny. It seemed slipping away like a dream. She said, 'But let us discuss things; it's all so frightfully important, we mustn't make false steps. I want next to hear your point of view about me—it might help us both.'

His manner was unhappy and reserved. 'I don't much believe in this discussing—besides, I'm so dead with all this extra work Mohurram's bringing, if you'll excuse me.'

'I only want everything to be absolutely clear between us, and to answer any questions you care to put to me on my conduct.'

'But I haven't got any questions. You've acted within your rights, you were quite right to come out and have a look at me doing my work, it was an excellent plan, and anyhow it's no use talking further—we should only get up steam.' He felt angry and bruised; he was too proud to tempt her back, but he did not consider that she had behaved badly, because where his compatriots were concerned he had a generous mind.

'I suppose that there is nothing else; it's unpardonable of me to have given you and your mother all this bother,' said Miss Quested heavily, and frowned up at the tree beneath which they were sitting. A little green bird was observing her, so brilliant and neat that it might have hopped straight out of a shop. On catching her eye it closed its own, gave a small skip and prepared to go to bed. Some Indian wild bird. 'Yes, nothing else,' she repeated, feeling that a profound and passionate speech ought to have been delivered by one or both of them. 'We've been awfully British over it, but I suppose that's all right.'

'As we are British, I suppose it is.'

'Anyhow we've not quarrelled, Ronny.'

'Oh, that would have been too absurd. Why should we quarrel?'

'I think we shall keep friends.'

'I know we shall.'

'Quite so.'

As soon as they had exchanged this admission, a wave of relief passed through them both, and then transformed itself into a wave of tenderness, and passed back. They were softened by their own honesty, and began to feel lonely and unwise. Experiences, not character, divided them; they were not dissimilar, as humans go; indeed, when compared with the people who stood nearest to them in point of space they became practically identical. The Bhil who was holding an officer's polo pony, the Eurasian who drove the Nawab Bahadur's car, the Nawab Bahadur himself, the Nawab Bahadur's debauched grandson—none would have examined a difficulty so frankly and coolly. The mere fact of examination caused it to diminish. Of course they were friends, and for ever. 'Do you know what the name of that green bird up above us is?' she asked, putting her shoulder rather nearer to his.

'Bee-eater.'

'Oh no, Ronny, it has red bars on its wings.'

'Parrot,' he hazarded.

'Good gracious no.'

The bird in question dived into the dome of the tree. It was of no importance, yet they would have liked to identify it, it would somehow have solaced their hearts. But nothing in India is identifiable, the mere asking of a question causes it to disappear or to merge in something else.

'McBryde has an illustrated bird book,' he said dejectedly. 'I'm no good at all at birds, in fact I'm useless at any information outside my own job. It's a great pity.'

'So am I. I'm useless at everything.'

'What do I hear?' shouted the Nawab Bahadur at the top of his voice, causing both of them to start. 'What most improbable statement have I heard? An English lady useless? No, no, no, no, no.' He laughed genially, sure, within limits, of his welcome.

'Hallo, Nawab Bahadur! Been watching the polo again?' said Ronny tepidly.

'I have, sahib, I have.'

'How do you do?' said Adela, likewise pulling herself together. She held out her hand. The old gentleman judged from so wanton a gesture that she was new to his country, but he paid little heed. Women who exposed their face became by that one act so mysterious to him that he took them at the valuation of their men folk rather than at his own. Perhaps they were not immoral, and anyhow they were not his affair. On seeing the City Magistrate alone with a maiden at twilight, he had borne down on them with hospitable intent. He had a new little car, and wished to place it at their disposal; the City Magistrate would decide whether the offer was acceptable.

Ronny was by this time rather ashamed of his curtness to Aziz and Godbole, and here was an opportunity of showing that he could treat Indians with consideration when they deserved it. So he said to Adela, with the same sad friendliness that he had employed when discussing the bird, 'Would half an hour's spin entertain you at all?'

'Oughtn't we to get back to the bungalow.'

'Why?' He gazed at her.

'I think perhaps I ought to see your mother and discuss future plans.'

'That's as you like, but there's no hurry, is there?'

'Let me take you to the bungalow, and first the little spin,' cried the old man, and hastened to the car.

'He may show you some aspect of the country I can't, and he's a real loyalist. I thought you might care for a bit of a change.'

Determined to give him no more trouble, she agreed, but her desire to see India had suddenly decreased. There had been a factitious element in it.

How should they seat themselves in the car? The elegant grandson had to be left behind. The Nawab Bahadur got up in front, for he had no intention of neighbouring an English girl. 'Despite my advanced years, I am learning to drive,' he said. 'Man can learn everything if he will but try.' And foreseeing a further difficulty, he added, 'I do not do the actual steering. I sit and ask my chauffeur questions, and thus learn the reason for everything that is done before I do it myself. By this method serious and I may say ludicrous accidents, such as befell one of my compatriots during that delightful reception at the English Club, are avoided. Our good Panna Lal! I hope, sahib, that great damage was not done to your flowers. Let us have our little spin down the Gangavati road. Half one league onwards!' He fell asleep.

Ronny instructed the chauffeur to take the Marabar road rather than the Gangavati, since the latter was under repair, and settled himself down beside the lady he had lost. The car made a burring noise and rushed along a chaussée that ran upon an embankment above melancholy fields. Trees of a poor quality bordered the road, indeed the whole scene was inferior, and suggested that the country-side was too vast to admit of excellence. In vain did each item in it call out, 'Come, come.' There was not enough god to go round. The two young people conversed feebly and felt unimportant. When the darkness began, it seemed to well out of the meagre vegetation, entirely covering the fields each side of them before it brimmed over the road. Ronny's face grew dim—an event that always increased her esteem for his character. Her hand touched his, owing to a jolt, and one of the thrills so frequent in the animal kingdom passed between them, and announced that all their difficulties were only a lovers' quarrel. Each was too proud to increase the pressure, but neither withdrew it, and a spurious unity descended on them, as local and temporary as the gleam that inhabits a firefly. It would vanish in a moment, perhaps to reappear, but the darkness is alone durable. And the night that encircled them, absolute as it seemed, was itself only a spurious unity, being modified by the gleams of day that leaked up round the edges of the earth, and by the stars.

They gripped . . . bump, jump, a swerve, two wheels lifted in the air, brakes on, bump with tree at edge of embankment, standstill. An accident. A slight one. Nobody hurt. The Nawab Bahadur awoke. He cried out in Arabic, and violently tugged his beard.

'What's the damage?' enquired Ronny, after the moment's pause that he permitted himself before taking charge of a situation. The Eurasian, inclined to be flustered, rallied to the sound of his voice, and, every inch an

Englishman, replied, 'You give me five minutes' time, I'll take you any damn anywhere.'

'Frightened, Adela?' He released her hand.

'Not a bit.'

'I consider not to be frightened the height of folly,' cried the Nawab Bahadur quite rudely.

'Well, it's all over now, tears are useless,' said Ronny, dismounting. 'We had some luck butting that tree.'

'All over . . . oh yes, the danger is past, let us smoke cigarettes, let us do anything we please. Oh yes . . . enjoy ourselves—oh my merciful God . . .' His words died into Arabic again.

'Wasn't the bridge. We skidded.'

'We didn't skid,' said Adela, who had seen the cause of the accident, and thought everyone must have seen it too. 'We ran into an animal.'

A loud cry broke from the old man: his terror was disproportionate and ridiculous.

'An animal?'

'A large animal rushed up out of the dark on the right and hit us.'

'By Jove, she's right,' Ronny exclaimed. 'The paint's gone.'

'By Jove, sir, your lady is right,' echoed the Eurasian. Just by the hinges of the door was a dent, and the door opened with difficulty.

'Of course I'm right. I saw its hairy back quite plainly.'

'I say, Adela, what was it?'

'I don't know the animals any better than the birds here—too big for a goat.'

'Exactly, too big for a goat . . .' said the old man.

Ronny said, 'Let's go into this; let's look for its tracks.'

'Exactly; you wish to borrow this electric torch.'

The English people walked a few steps back into the darkness, united and happy. Thanks to their youth and upbringing, they were not upset by the accident. They traced back the writhing of the tyres to the source of their disturbance. It was just after the exit from a bridge; the animal had probably come up out of the nullah. Steady and smooth ran the marks of the car, ribbons neatly nicked with lozenges, then all went mad. Certainly some external force had impinged, but the road had been used by too many objects for any one track to be legible, and the torch created such high lights and black shadows that they could not interpret what it revealed. Moreover, Adela in her excitement knelt and swept her skirts about, until it was she if anyone who appeared to have attacked the car. The incident was a great relief to them both. They forgot their abortive personal relationship, and felt adventurous as they muddled about in the dust.

'I believe it was a buffalo,' she called to their host, who had not accompanied them.

'Exactly.'

'Unless it was a hyena.'

Ronny approved this last conjecture. Hyenas prowl in nullahs and headlights dazzle them.

'Excellent, a hyena,' said the Indian with an angry irony and a gesture at the night. 'Mr Harris!'

'Half a mo-ment. Give me ten minutes' time.'

'Sahib says hyena.'

'Don't worry Mr Harris. He saved us from a nasty smash. Harris, well done!'

'A smash, sahib, that would not have taken place had he obeyed and taken us Gangavati side, instead of Marabar.'

'My fault that. I told him to come this way because the road's better. Mr Lesley has made it pukka right up to the hills.'

'Ah, now I begin to understand.' Seeming to pull himself together, he apologized slowly and elaborately for the accident. Ronny murmured, 'Not at all,' but apologies were his due, and should have started sooner: because English people are so calm at a crisis, it is not to be assumed that they are unimportant. The Nawab Bahadur had not come out very well.

At that moment a large car approached from the opposite direction. Ronny advanced a few steps down the road, and with authority in his voice and gesture stopped it. It bore the inscription 'Mudkul State' across its bonnet. All friskiness and friendliness, Miss Derek sat inside.

'Mr Heaslop, Miss Quested, what are you holding up an innocent female for?'

'We've had a breakdown.'

'But how putrid!'

'We ran into a hyena!'

'How absolutely rotten!'

'Can you give us a lift?'

'Yes, indeed.'

'Take me too,' said the Nawab Bahadur.

'Heh, what about me?' cried Mr Harris.

'Now what's all this? I'm not an omnibus,' said Miss Derek with decision. 'I've a harmonium and two dogs in here with me as it is. I'll take three of you if one'll sit in front and nurse a pug. No more.'

'I will sit in front,' said the Nawab Bahadur.

'Then hop in: I've no notion who you are.'

'Heh no, what about my dinner? I can't be left alone all the night.' Trying to look and feel like a European, the chauffeur interposed aggressively. He still wore a topi, despite the darkness, and his face, to which the Ruling Race had contributed little beyond bad teeth, peered out of it pathetically, and seemed to say, 'What's it all about? Don't worry me so, you blacks and whites. Here I am, stuck in damn India same as you, and you got to fit me in better than this.'

'Nussu will bring you out some suitable dinner upon a bicycle,' said the Nawab Bahadur, who had regained his usual dignity. 'I shall despatch him with all possible speed. Meanwhile, repair my car.'

They sped off, and Mr Harris, after a reproachful glance, squatted down upon his hams. When English and Indians were both present, he grew self-conscious, because he did not know to whom he belonged. For a little he was vexed by opposite currents in his blood, then they blended, and he belonged to no one but himself.

But Miss Derek was in tearing spirits. She had succeeded in stealing the Mudkul car. Her Maharajah would be awfully sick, but she didn't mind, he could sack her if he liked. 'I don't believe in these people letting you down,' she said. 'If I didn't snatch like the devil, I should be nowhere. He doesn't want the car, silly fool! Surely it's to the credit of his State I should be seen about in it at Chandrapore during my leave. He ought to look at it that way. Anyhow he's got to look at it that way. My Maharani's different—my Maharani's a dear. That's her fox terrier, poor little devil. I fished them out both with the driver. Imagine taking dogs to a Chiefs' Conference! As sensible as taking Chiefs, perhaps.' She shrieked with laughter. 'The harmonium—the harmonium's my little mistake, I own. They rather had me over the harmonium. I meant it to stop on the train. Oh lor'!'

Ronny laughed with restraint. He did not approve of English people taking service under the Native States, where they obtain a certain amount of influence, but at the expense of the general prestige. The humorous triumphs of a free lance are of no assistance to an administrator, and he told the young lady that she would outdo Indians at their own game if she went on much longer.

'They always sack me before that happens, and then I get another job. The whole of India seethes with Maharanis and Ranis and Begums who clamour for such as me.'

'Really. I had no idea.'

'How could you have any idea, Mr Heaslop? What should he know about Maharanis, Miss Quested? Nothing. At least I should hope not.'

'I understand those big people are not particularly interesting,' said Adela, quietly, disliking the young woman's tone. Her hand touched Ronny's again in the darkness, and to the animal thrill there was now added a coincidence of opinion.

'Ah, there you're wrong. They're priceless.'

'I would scarcely call her wrong,' broke out the Nawab Bahadur, from his isolation on the front seat, whither they had relegated him. 'A Native State, a Hindu State, the wife of a ruler of a Hindu State, may beyond doubt be a most excellent lady, and let it not be for a moment supposed that I suggest anything against the character of Her Highness and Maharani of Mudkul. But I fear she will be uneducated, I fear she will be superstitious. Indeed, how could she be otherwise? What opportunity of education has such a lady had? Oh, superstition is terrible, terrible! oh, it is the great defect in our Indian character!'—and as if to point his criticism, the lights of the civil station appeared on a rise to the right. He grew more and more voluble. 'Oh, it is the duty of each and every citizen to shake superstition off, and though I have little experience of Hindu States, and none of this particular one, namely Mudkul (the Ruler, I fancy, has a salute of but eleven guns)—yet I cannot imagine that they have been as successful as British India, where we see reason and orderliness spreading in every direction, like a most health-giving flood!'

Miss Derek said 'Golly!'

Undeterred by the expletive, the old man swept on. His tongue had been loosed and his mind had several points to make. He wanted to endorse Miss Quested's remark that big people are not interesting, because he was bigger himself than many an independent chief; at the same time, he must neither remind nor inform her that he was big, lest she felt she had committed a discourtesy. This was the groundwork of his oration; worked in with it was his gratitude to Miss Derek for the lift, his willingness to hold a repulsive dog in his arms, and his general regret for the trouble he had caused the human race during the evening. Also he wanted to be dropped near the city to get hold of his cleaner, and to see what mischief his grandson was up to. As he wove all these anxieties into a single rope, he suspected that his audience felt no interest, and that the City Magistrate fondled either maiden behind the cover of the harmonium, but good breeding compelled him to continue; it was nothing to him if they were bored, because he did not know what boredom is, and it was nothing to him if they were licentious, because God has created all races to be different. The accident was over, and his life, equally useful, distinguished, happy, ran on as before and expressed itself in streams of well-chosen words.

When this old geyser left them, Ronny made no comment, but talked lightly about polo; Turton had taught him that it is sounder not to discuss a man at once, and he reserved what he had to say on the Nawab's character until later in the evening. His hand, which he had removed to say good-bye, touched Adela's again; she caressed it definitely, he responded, and their firm and mutual pressure surely meant something. They looked at each other when they reached the bungalow, for Mrs Moore was inside it. It was for Miss Quested to speak, and she said nervously, 'Ronny, I should like to take back what I said on the Maidan.' He assented, and they became engaged to be married in consequence.

Neither had foreseen such a consequence. She had meant to revert to her former condition of important and cultivated uncertainty, but it had passed out of her reach at its appropriate hour. Unlike the green bird or the hairy animal, she was labelled now. She felt humiliated again, for she deprecated labels, and she felt too that there should have been another scene between her lover and herself at this point, something dramatic and lengthy. He was pleased instead of distressed, he was surprised, but he had really nothing to say. What indeed is there to say? To be or not to be married, that was the question, and they had decided it in the affirmative.

'Come along and let's tell the mater all this'—opening the perforated zinc door that protected the bungalow from the swarms of winged creatures. The noise woke the mater up. She had been dreaming of the absent children who were so seldom mentioned, Ralph and Stella, and did not at first grasp what was required of her. She too had become used to thoughtful procrastination, and felt alarmed when it came to an end.

When the announcement was over, he made a gracious and honest remark. 'Look here, both of you, see India if you like and as you like—I know I made myself rather ridiculous at Fielding's, but . . . it's different now. I wasn't quite sure of myself.'

'My duties here are evidently finished, I don't want to see India now; now for my passage back,' was Mrs Moore's thought. She reminded herself of all that a happy marriage means, and of her own happy marriages, one of which had produced Ronny. Adela's parents had also been happily married, and excellent it was to see the incident repeated by the younger generation. On and on! the number of such unions would certainly increase as education spread and ideals grew loftier, and characters firmer. But she was tired by her visit to Government College, her feet ached, Mr Fielding had walked too fast and far, the young people had annoyed her in the tum-tum, and given her to suppose they were breaking with each other, and though it was all right now she could not speak as enthusiastically of wedlock or of anything as she should have done. Ronny was suited, now she must go home and help the others, if they wished. She was past marrying herself, even unhappily; her function was to help others, her reward to be informed that she was sympathetic. Elderly ladies must not expect more than this.

They dined alone. There was much pleasant and affectionate talk about the future. Later on they spoke of passing events, and Ronny reviewed and recounted the day from his own point of view. It was a different day from the women's, because while they had enjoyed themselves or thought, he had worked. Mohurram was approaching, and as usual the Chandrapore Mohammedans were building paper towers of a size too large to pass under the branches of a certain pepul tree. One knew what happened next; the tower stuck, a Mohammedan climbed up the pepul and cut the branch off, the Hindus protested, there was a religious riot, and Heaven knew what, with perhaps the troops sent for. There had been deputations and conciliation committees under the auspices of Turton, and all the normal work of Chandrapore had been hung up. Should the procession take another route, or should the towers be shorter? The Mohammedans offered the former, the Hindus insisted on the latter. The Collector had favoured the Hindus, until he suspected that they had artificially bent the tree nearer the ground. They said it sagged naturally. Measurements, plans, an official visit to the spot. But Ronny had not disliked his day, for it proved that the British were necessary to India; there would certainly have been bloodshed without them. His voice grew complacent again; he was here not to be pleasant but to keep the peace, and now that Adela had promised to be his wife, she was sure to understand.

'What does our old gentleman of the car think?' she asked, and her negligent tone was exactly what he desired.

'Our old gentleman is helpful and sound, as he always is over public affairs. You've seen in him our show Indian.'

'Have I really?'

'I'm afraid so. Incredible, aren't they, even the best of them? They're all—they all forget their back collar studs sooner or later. You've had to do with three sets of Indians to-day, the Bhattacharyas, Aziz, and this chap, and it really isn't a coincidence that they've all let you down.'

'I like Aziz, Aziz is my real friend,' Mrs Moore interposed.

'When the animal runs into us the Nawab loses his head, deserts his unfortunate chauffeur, intrudes upon Miss Derek . . . no great crimes, no great crimes, but no white man would have done it.'

'What animal?'

'Oh, we had a small accident on the Marabar road. Adela thinks it was a hyena.'

'An accident?' she cried.

'Nothing; no one hurt. Our excellent host awoke much rattled from his dreams, appeared to think it was our fault, and chanted exactly, exactly.'

Mrs Moore shivered, 'A ghost!' But the idea of a ghost scarcely passed her lips. The young people did not take it up, being occupied with their own outlooks, and deprived of support it perished, or was reabsorbed into the part of the mind that seldom speaks.

'Yes, nothing criminal,' Ronny summed up, 'but there's the native, and there's one of the reasons why we don't admit him to our clubs, and how a decent girl like Miss Derek can take service under natives puzzles me. . . . But I must get on with my work. Krishna!' Krishna was the peon who should have brought the files from his office. He had not turned up, and a terrific row ensued. Ronny stormed, shouted, howled, and only the experienced observer could tell that he was not angry, did not much want the files, and only made a row because it was the custom. Servants, quite understanding, ran slowly in circles, carrying hurricane lamps. Krishna the earth, Krishna the stars replied, until the Englishman was appeased by their echoes, fined the absent peon eight annas, and sat down to his arrears in the next room.

'Will you play Patience with your future mother-in-law, dear Adela, or does it seem too tame?'

'I should like to—I don't feel a bit excited—I'm just glad it's settled up at last, but I'm not conscious of vast changes. We are all three the same people still.'

'That's much the best feeling to have.' She dealt out the first row of 'demon.'

'I suppose so,' said the girl thoughtfully.

'I feared at Mr Fielding's that it might be settled the other way . . . black knave on a red queen. . . .' They chatted gently about the game.

Presently Adela said: 'You heard me tell Aziz and Godbole I wasn't stopping in their country. I didn't mean it, so why did I say it? I feel I haven't been—frank enough, attentive enough, or something. It's as if I got everything out of proportion. You have been so very good to me, and I meant to be good when I sailed, but somehow I haven't been. . . . Mrs Moore, if one isn't absolutely honest, what is the use of existing?'

She continued to lay out her cards. The words were obscure, but she understood the uneasiness that produced them. She had experienced it twice herself, during her own engagements—this vague contrition and doubt. All had come right enough afterwards and doubtless would this time—marriage makes most things right enough. 'I wouldn't worry,' she said. 'It's partly the odd surroundings; you and I keep on attending to trifles instead of what's important; we are what the people here call "new."'

'You mean that my bothers are mixed up with India?'

'India's—' She stopped.

'What made you call it a ghost?'

'Call what a ghost?'

'The animal thing that hit us. Didn't you say "Oh, a ghost," in passing?'

'I couldn't have been thinking of what I was saying.'

'It was probably a hyena, as a matter of fact.'

'Ah, very likely.'

And they went on with their Patience. Down in Chandrapore the Nawab Bahadur waited for his car. He sat behind his town house (a small unfurnished building which he rarely entered) in the midst of the little court that always improvises itself round Indians of position. As if turbans were the natural product of darkness a fresh one would occasionally froth to the front, incline itself towards him, and retire. He was preoccupied, his diction was appropriate to a religious subject. Nine years previously, when first he had had a car, he had driven it over a drunken man and killed him, and the man had been waiting for him ever since. The Nawab Bahadur was innocent before God and the Law, he had paid double the compensation necessary; but it was no use, the man continued to wait in an unspeakable form, close to the scene of his death. None of the English people knew of this, nor did the chauffeur; it was a racial secret communicable more by blood than speech. He spoke now in horror of the particular circumstances; he had led others into danger, he had risked the lives of two innocent and honoured guests. He repeated, 'If I had been killed, what matter? It must happen sometime; but they who trusted me—' The company shuddered and invoked the mercy of God. Only Aziz held aloof, because a personal experience restrained him: was it not by despising ghosts that he had come to know Mrs Moore? 'You know, Nureddin,' he whispered to the grandson–an effeminate youth whom he seldom met, always liked, and invariably forgot–'you know, my dear fellow, we Moslems simply must get rid of these superstitions, or India will never advance. How long must I hear of the savage pig upon the Marabar Road?' Nureddin looked down. Aziz continued: 'Your grandfather belongs to another generation, and I respect and love the old gentleman, as you know. I say nothing against him, only that it is wrong for us, because we are young. I want you to promise me–Nureddin, are you listening?–not to believe in Evil Spirits, and if I die (for my health grows very weak) to bring up my three children to disbelieve in them too.' Nureddin smiled, and a suitable answer rose to his pretty lips, but before he could make it the car arrived, and his grandfather took him away.

The game of Patience up in the civil lines went on longer than this. Mrs Moore continued to murmur 'Red ten on a black knave,' Miss Quested to assist her, and to intersperse among the intricacies of the play details about the hyena, the engagement, the Maharani of Mudkul, the Bhattacharyas, and the day generally, whose rough desiccated surface acquired as it receded a definite outline, as India itself might, could it be viewed from the moon. Presently the players went to bed, but not before other people had woken up elsewhere, people whose emotions they could not share, and whose existence they ignored. Never tranquil, never perfectly dark, the night wore itself away, distinguished from other nights by two or three blasts of wind, which seemed to fall perpendicularly out of the sky and to bounce back into it, hard and compact, leaving no freshness behind them: the hot weather was approaching.

Chapter Nine

Aziz fell ill as he foretold–slightly ill. Three days later he lay abed in his bungalow, pretending to be very ill. It was a touch of fever, which he would have neglected if there was anything important at the hospital. Now and then he groaned and thought he should die, but did not think so for long, and a very little diverted him. It was Sunday, always an equivocal day in the East, and an excuse for slacking. He could hear church bells as he drowsed, both from the civil station and from the missionaries out beyond the slaughter house–different bells and rung with different intent, for one set was calling firmly to Anglo-India, and the other feebly to mankind. He did not object to the first set; the other he ignored, knowing their inefficiency. Old Mr Graysford and young Mr Sorley made converts during a famine, because they distributed food; but when times improved they were naturally left alone again, and though surprised and aggrieved each time this happened, they never learnt wisdom. 'No Englishman understands us except Mr Fielding,' he thought; 'but how shall I see him again? If he entered this room the disgrace of it would kill me.' He called to Hassan to clear up, but Hassan, who was testing his wages by ringing them on the step of the verandah, found it possible not to hear him; heard and didn't hear, just as Aziz had called and hadn't called. 'That's India all over . . . how like us . . . there we are . . .' He dozed again, and his thoughts wandered over the varied surface of life.

Gradually they steadied upon a certain spot–the Bottomless Pit according to missionaries, but he had never regarded it as more than a dimple, Yes, he did want to spend an evening with some girls, singing and all that, the vague jollity that would culminate in voluptuousness. Yes, that was what he did want. How could it be managed? If Major Callendar had been an Indian, he would have remembered what young men are, and granted two or three days' leave to Calcutta without asking questions. But the Major assumed either that his subordinates were made of ice, or that they repaired to the Chandrapore bazaars–disgusting ideas both. It was only Mr Fielding who—

'Hassan!'

The servant came running.

'Look at those flies, brother;' and he pointed to the horrible mass that hung from the ceiling. The nucleus was a wire which had been inserted as a homage to electricity. Electricity had paid no attention, and a colony of eye-flies had come instead and blackened the coils with their bodies.

'Huzoor, those are flies.'

'Good, good, they are, excellent, but why have I called you?'

'To drive them elsewhere,' said Hassan, after painful thought.

'Driven elsewhere, they always return.'

'Huzoor.'

'You must make some arrangement against flies; that is why you are my servant,' said Aziz gently.

Hassan would call the little boy to borrow the stepladder from Mahmoud Ali's house; he would order the cook to light the Primus stove and heat water; he would personally ascend the steps with a bucket in his arms, and dip the end of the coil into it.

'Good, very good. Now what have you to do?'

'Kill flies.'

'Good. Do it.'

Hassan withdrew, the plan almost lodged in his head, and began to look for the little boy. Not finding him, his steps grew slower, and he stole back to his post on the verandah, but did not go on testing his rupees, in case his master heard them clink. On twittered the Sunday bells; the East had returned to the East via the suburbs of England, and had become ridiculous during the detour.

Aziz continued to think about beautiful women.

His mind here was hard and direct, though not brutal. He had learnt all he needed concerning his own constitution many years ago, thanks to the social order into which he had been born, and when he came to study medicine he was repelled by the pedantry and fuss with which Europe tabulates the facts of sex. Science seemed to discuss everything from the wrong end. It didn't interpret his experiences when he found them in a German manual, because by being there they ceased to be his experiences. What he had been told by his father or mother or had picked up from servants—it was information of that sort that he found useful, and handed on as occasion offered to others.

But he must not bring any disgrace on his children by some silly escapade. Imagine if it got about that he was not respectable! His professional position too must be considered, whatever Major Callendar thought. Aziz upheld the proprieties, though he did not invest them with any moral halo, and it was here that he chiefly differed from an Englishman. His conventions were social. There is no harm in deceiving society as long as she does not find you out, because it is only when she finds you out that you have harmed her; she is not like a friend or God, who are injured by the mere existence of unfaithfulness. Quite clear about this, he meditated what type of lie he should tell to get away to Calcutta, and had thought of a man there who could be trusted to send him a wire and a letter that he could show to Major Callendar, when the noise of wheels was heard in his compound. Someone had called to enquire. The thought of sympathy increased his fever, and with a sincere groan he wrapped himself in his quilt.

'Aziz, my dear fellow, we are greatly concerned,' said Hamidullah's voice. One, two, three, four bumps, as people sat down upon his bed.

'When a doctor falls ill it is a serious matter,' said the voice of Mr Syed Mohammed, the assistant engineer.

'When an engineer falls ill, it is equally important,' said the voice of Mr Haq, a police inspector.

'Oh yes, we are all jolly important, our salaries prove it.'

'Dr Aziz took tea with our Principal last Thursday afternoon,' piped Rafi, the engineer's nephew. 'Professor Godbole, who also attended, has sickened too, which seems rather a curious thing, sir, does it not?'

Flames of suspicion leapt up in the breast of each man. 'Humbug!' exclaimed Hamidullah, in authoritative tones, quenching them.

'Humbug, most certainly,' echoed the others, ashamed of themselves. The wicked schoolboy, having failed to start a scandal, lost confidence and stood up with his back to the wall.

'Is Professor Godbole ill?' enquired Aziz, penetrated by the news. 'I am sincerely sorry.' Intelligent and compassionate, his face peeped out of the bright crimson folds of the quilt. 'How do you do, Mr Syed Mohammed, Mr Haq? How very kind of you to enquire after my health! How do you do, Hamidullah? But you bring me bad news. What is wrong with him, the excellent fellow?'

'Why don't you answer, Rafi? You're the great authority,' said his uncle.

'Yes, Rafi's the great man,' said Hamidullah, rubbing it in. 'Rafi is the Sherlock Holmes of Chandrapore. Speak up, Rafi.'

Less than the dust, the schoolboy murmured the word 'Diarrhoea,' but took courage as soon as it had been uttered, for it improved his position. Flames of suspicion shot up again in the breasts of his elders, though in a different direction. Could what was called diarrhoea really be an early case of cholera?

'If this is so, this is a very serious thing: this is scarcely the end of March. Why have I not been informed?' cried Aziz.

'Dr Panna Lal attends him, sir.'

'Oh yes, both Hindus; there we have it; they hang together like flies and keep everything dark. Rafi, come here. Sit down. Tell me all the details. Is there vomiting also?'

'Oh yes indeed, sir, and the serious pains.'

'That settles it. In twenty-four hours he will be dead.'

Everybody looked and felt shocked, but Professor Godbole had diminished his appeal by linking himself with a co-religionist. He moved them less than when he had appeared as a suffering individual. Before long they began to condemn him as a source of infection. 'All illness proceeds from Hindus,' Mr Haq said. Mr Syed Mohammed had visited religious fairs, at Allahabad and at Ujjain, and described them with biting scorn. At Allahabad there was flowing water, which carried impurities away, but at Ujjain the little river Sipra was banked up, and thousands of bathers deposited their germs in the pool. He spoke with disgust of the hot sun, the cowdung and marigold flowers, and the encampment of saddhus, some of whom strode stark naked through the streets. Asked what was the name of the chief idol at Ujjain, he replied that he did not know, he had disdained to enquire, he really could not waste his time over such trivialities. His outburst took some time, and in his excitement he fell into Punjabi (he came from that side) and was unintelligible.

Aziz liked to hear his religion praised. It soothed the surface of his mind, and allowed beautiful images to form beneath. When the engineer's noisy tirade was finished, he said, 'That is exactly my own view.' He held up his hand, palm outward, his eyes began to glow, his heart to fill with tenderness. Issuing still farther from his quilt, he recited a poem by Ghalib. It had no connection with anything that had gone before, but it came from his heart and spoke to theirs. They were overwhelmed by its pathos; pathos, they agreed, is the highest quality in art; a poem should touch the hearer with a sense of his own weakness, and should institute some comparison between mankind and flowers. The squalid bedroom grew quiet; the silly intrigues, the gossip, the shallow discontent were stilled, while words accepted as immortal filled the indifferent air. Not as a call to battle, but as a calm assurance came the feeling that India was one; Moslem; always had been; an assurance that lasted until they looked out of the door. Whatever Ghalib had felt, he had anyhow lived in India, and this consolidated it for them: he had gone with his own tulips and roses, but tulips and roses do not go. And the sister kingdoms of the north—Arabia, Persia, Ferghana, Turkestan—stretched out their hands as he sang, sadly, because all beauty is sad, and greeted ridiculous Chandrapore, where every street and house was divided against itself, and told her that she was a continent and a unity.

Of the company, only Hamidullah had any comprehension of poetry. The minds of the others were inferior and rough. Yet they listened with pleasure, because literature had not been divorced from their civilization. The police inspector, for instance, did not feel that Aziz had degraded himself by reciting, nor break into the cheery guffaw with which an Englishman averts the infection of beauty. He just sat with his mind empty, and when his thoughts, which were mainly ignoble, flowed back into it they had a pleasant freshness. The poem had done no 'good' to anyone, but it was a passing reminder, a breath from the divine lips of beauty, a nightingale between two worlds of dust. Less explicit than the call to Krishna, it voiced our loneliness nevertheless, our isolation, our need for the Friend who never comes yet is not entirely disproved. Aziz it left thinking about women again, but in a different way: less definite, more intense. Sometimes poetry had this effect on him, sometimes it only increased his local desires, and he never knew beforehand which effect would ensue: he could discover no rule for this or for anything else in life.

Hamidullah had called in on his way to a worrying committee of notables, nationalist in tendency, where Hindus, Moslems, two Sikhs, two Parsis, a Jain, and a Native Christian tried to like one another more than came natural to them. As long as someone abused the English, all went well, but nothing constructive had been achieved, and if the English were to leave India, the committee would vanish also. He was glad that Aziz, whom he loved and whose family was connected with his own, took no interest in politics, which ruin the character and career, yet nothing can be achieved without them. He thought of Cambridge–sadly, as of another poem that had ended. How happy he had been there, twenty years ago! Politics had not mattered in Mr and Mrs Bannister's rectory. There, games, work, and pleasant society had interwoven, and appeared to be sufficient substructure for a national life. Here all was wirepulling and fear. Messrs Syed Mohammed and Haq–he couldn't even trust them, although they had come in his carriage, and the schoolboy was a scorpion. Bending down, he said, 'Aziz, Aziz, my dear boy, we must be going, we are already late. Get well quickly, for I do not know what our little circle would do without you.'

'I shall not forget those affectionate words,' replied Aziz.

'Add mine to them,' said the engineer.

'Thank you, Mr Syed Mohammed, I will.'

'And mine,' 'And, sir accept mine,' cried the others, stirred each according to his capacity towards goodwill. Little ineffectual unquenchable flames! The company continued to sit on the bed and to chew sugar-cane, which Hassan had run for into the bazaar, and Aziz drank a cup of spiced milk. Presently there was the sound of another carriage. Dr Panna Lal had arrived, driven by horrid Mr Ram Chand. The atmosphere of a sick-room was at once re-established, and the invalid retired under his quilt.

'Gentlemen, you will excuse, I have come to enquire by Major Callendar's orders,' said the Hindu, nervous of the den of fanatics into which his curiosity had called him.

'Here he lies,' said Hamidullah, indicating the prostrate form.

'Dr Aziz, Dr Aziz, I come to enquire.'

Aziz presented an expressionless face to the thermometer.

'Your hand also, please.' He took it, gazed at the flies on the ceiling, and finally announced 'Some temperature.'

'I think not much,' said Ram Chand, desirous of fomenting trouble.

'Some; he should remain in bed,' repeated Dr Panna Lal, and shook the thermometer down, so that its altitude remained for ever unknown. He loathed his young colleague since the disasters with Dapple, and he would have liked to do him a bad turn and report to Major Callendar that he was shamming. But he might want a day in bed himself soon,–besides, though Major Callendar always believed the worst of natives, he never believed them when they carried tales about one another. Sympathy seemed the safer course. 'How is stomach?' he enquired, 'how head?' And catching sight of the empty cup, he recommended a milk diet.

'This is a great relief to us, it is very good of you to call, Doctor Sahib,' said Hamidullah, buttering him up a bit.

'It is only my duty.'

'We know how busy you are.'

'Yes, that is true.'

'And how much illness there is in the city.'

The doctor suspected a trap in this remark; if he admitted that there was or was not illness, either statement might be used against him. 'There is always illness,' he replied, 'and I am always busy–it is a doctor's nature.'

'He has not a minute, he is due double sharp at Government College now,' said Ram Chand.

'You attend Professor Godbole there perhaps?'

The doctor looked professional and was silent.

'We hope his diarrhoea is ceasing.'

'He progresses, but not from diarrhoea.'

'We are in some anxiety over him–he and Dr Aziz are great friends. If you could tell us the name of his complaint we should be grateful to you.'

After a cautious pause he said, 'Haemorrhoids.'

'And so much, my dear Rafi, for your cholera,' hooted Aziz, unable to restrain himself.

'Cholera, cholera, what next, what now?' cried the doctor, greatly fussed. 'Who spreads such untrue reports about my patients?'

Hamidullah pointed to the culprit.

'I hear cholera, I hear bubonic plague, I hear every species of lie. Where will it end, I ask myself sometimes. This city is full of misstatements, and the originators of them ought to be discovered and punished authoritatively.'

'Rafi, do you hear that? Now why do you stuff us up with all this humbug?'

The schoolboy murmured that another boy had told him, also that the bad English grammar the Government obliged them to use often gave the wrong meaning for words, and so led scholars into mistakes.

'That is no reason you should bring a charge against a doctor,' said Ram Chand.

'Exactly, exactly,' agreed Hamidullah, anxious to avoid an unpleasantness. Quarrels spread so quickly and so far, and Messrs Syed Mohammed and Haq looked cross, and ready to fly out. 'You must apologize properly, Rafi, I can see your uncle wishes it,' he said. 'You have not yet said that you are sorry for the trouble you have caused this gentleman by your carelessness.'

'It is only a boy,' said Dr Panna Lal, appeased.

'Even boys must learn,' said Ram Chand.

'Your own son failing to pass the lowest standard, I think,' said Syed Mohammed suddenly.

'Oh, indeed? Oh yes, perhaps. He has not the advantage of a relative in the Prosperity Printing Press,'

'Nor you the advantage of conducting their cases in the Courts any longer.'

Their voices rose. They attacked one another with obscure allusions and had a silly quarrel. Hamidullah and the doctor tried to make peace between them. In the midst of the din someone said, 'I say! Is he ill or isn't he ill?' Mr Fielding had entered unobserved. All rose to their feet, and Hassan, to do an Englishman honour, struck with a sugar-cane at the coil of flies.

Aziz said, 'Sit down,' coldly. What a room! What a meeting! Squalor and ugly talk, the floor strewn with fragments of cane and nuts, and spotted with ink, the pictures crooked upon the dirty walls, no punkah! He hadn't meant to live like this or among these third-rate people. And in his confusion he thought only of the insignificant Rafi, whom he had laughed at, and allowed to be teased. The boy must be sent away happy, or hospitality would have failed, along the whole line.

'It is good of Mr Fielding to condescend to visit our friend,' said the police inspector. 'We are touched by this great kindness.'

'Don't talk to him like that, he doesn't want it, and he doesn't want three chairs; he's not three Englishmen,' he flashed. 'Rafi, come here. Sit down again. I'm delighted you could come with Mr Hamidullah, my dear boy; it will help me to recover, seeing you.'

'Forgive my mistakes,' said Rafi, to consolidate himself.

'Well, are you ill, Aziz, or aren't you?' Fielding repeated.

'No doubt Major Callendar has told you that I am shamming.'

'Well, are you?' The company laughed, friendly and pleased. 'An Englishman at his best,' they thought; 'so genial.'

'Enquire from Dr Panna Lal.'

'You're sure I don't tire you by stopping?'

'Why, no! There are six people present in my small room already. Please remain seated, if you will excuse the informality.' He turned away and continued to address Rafi, who was terrified at the arrival of his Principal, remembered that he had tried to spread slander about him, and yearned to get away.

'He is ill and he is not ill,' said Hamidullah, offering a cigarette. 'And I suppose that most of us are in that same case.'

Fielding agreed; he and the pleasant sensitive barrister got on well. They were fairly intimate and beginning to trust each other.

'The whole world looks to be dying, still it doesn't die, so we must assume the existence of a beneficent Providence.'

'Oh, that is true, how true!' said the policeman, thinking religion had been praised.

'Does Mr Fielding think it's true?'

'Think which true? The world isn't dying. I'm certain of that!'

'No, no–the existence of Providence.'

'Well, I don't believe in Providence.'

'But how then can you believe in God?' asked Syed Mohammed.

'I don't believe in God.'

A tiny movement as of 'I told you so!' passed round the company, and Aziz looked up for an instant, scandalized. 'Is it correct that most are atheists in England now?' Hamidullah enquired.

'The educated thoughtful people? I should say so, though they don't like the name. The truth is that the West doesn't bother much over belief and disbelief in these days. Fifty years ago, or even when you and I were young, much more fuss was made.'

'And does not morality also decline?'

'It depends what you call–yes, yes, I suppose morality does decline.'

'Excuse the question, but if this is the case, how is England justified in holding India?'

There they were! Politics again. 'It's a question I can't get my mind on to,' he replied. 'I'm out here personally because I needed a job. I cannot tell you why England is here or whether she ought to be here. It's beyond me.'

'Well-qualified Indians also need jobs in the educational.'

'I guess they do; I got in first,' said Fielding, smiling.

'Then excuse me again—is it fair an Englishman should occupy one when Indians are available? Of course I mean nothing personally. Personally we are delighted you should be here, and we benefit greatly by this frank talk.'

There is only one answer to a conversation of this type: 'England holds India for her good.' Yet Fielding was disinclined to give it. The zeal for honesty had eaten him up. He said, 'I'm delighted to be here too—that's my answer, there's my only excuse. I can't tell you anything about fairness. It mayn't have been fair I should have been born. I take up some other fellow's air, don't I, whenever I breathe? Still, I'm glad it's happened, and I'm glad I'm out here. However big a badmash one is—if one's happy in consequence, that is some justification.'

The Indians were bewildered. The line of thought was not alien to them, but the words were too definite and bleak. Unless a sentence paid a few compliments to Justice and Morality in passing, its grammar wounded their ears and paralysed their minds. What they said and what they felt were (except in the case of affection) seldom the same. They had numerous mental conventions and when these were flouted they found it very difficult to function. Hamidullah bore up best. 'And those Englishmen who are not delighted to be in India—have they no excuse?' he asked.

'None. Chuck 'em out.'

'It may be difficult to separate them from the rest,' he laughed.

'Worse than difficult, wrong,' said Mr Ram Chand. 'No Indian gentleman approves chucking out as a proper thing. Here we differ from those other nations. We are so spiritual.'

'Oh that is true, how true!' said the police inspector.

'Is it true, Mr Haq? I don't consider us spiritual. We can't co-ordinate, we can't co-ordinate, it only comes to that. We can't keep engagements, we can't catch trains. What more than this is the so-called spirituality of India? You and I ought to be at the Committee of Notables, we're not; our friend Dr Lal ought to be with his patients, he isn't. So we go on, and so we shall continue to go, I think, until the end of time.'

'It is not the end of time, it is scarcely ten-thirty, ha, ha!' cried Dr Panna Lal, who was again in confident mood. 'Gentlemen, if I may be allowed to say a few words, what an interesting talk, also thankfulness and gratitude to Mr Fielding in the first place teaches our sons and gives them all the great benefits of his experience and judgment—'

'Dr Lal!'

'Dr Aziz?'

'You sit on my leg.'

'I beg pardon, but some might say your leg kicks.'

'Come along, we tire the invalid in either case,' said Fielding, and they filed out—four Mohammedans, two Hindus and the Englishman. They stood on the verandah while their conveyances were summoned out of various patches of shade.

'Aziz has a high opinion of you, he only did not speak because of his illness.'

'I quite understand,' said Fielding, who was rather disappointed with his call. The Club comment, 'making himself cheap as usual,' passed through his mind. He couldn't even get his horse brought up. He had liked Aziz so much at their first meeting, and had hoped for developments.

Chapter Ten

The heat had leapt forward in the last hour, the street was deserted as if a catastrophe had cleaned off humanity during the inconclusive talk. Opposite Aziz' bungalow stood a large unfinished house belonging to two brothers, astrologers, and a squirrel hung head-downwards on it, pressing its belly against burning scaffolding and twitching a mangy tail. It seemed the only occupant of the house, and the squeals it gave were in tune with the infinite, no doubt, but not attractive except to other squirrels. More noises came from a dusty tree, where brown birds creaked and floundered about looking for insects; another bird, the invisible coppersmith, had started his 'ponk ponk.' It matters so little to the majority of living beings what the minority, that calls itself human, desires or decides. Most of the inhabitants of India do not mind how India is governed. Nor are the lower animals of England concerned about England, but in the tropics the indifference is more prominent, the inarticulate world is closer at hand and readier to resume control as soon as men are tired. When the seven gentlemen who had held such various opinions inside the bungalow came out of it, they were aware of a common burden, a vague threat which they called 'the bad weather coming.' They felt that they could not do their work, or would not be paid enough for doing it. The space between them and their carriages, instead of being empty, was clogged with a medium that pressed against their flesh, the carriage cushions scalded their trousers, their eyes pricked, domes of hot water accumulated under their head-gear and poured down their cheeks. Salaaming feebly, they dispersed for the interior of other bungalows, to recover their self-esteem and the qualities that distinguished them from each other.

All over the city and over much of India the same retreat on the part of humanity was beginning, into cellars, up hills, under trees. April, herald of horrors, is at hand. The sun was returning to his kingdom with power but without beauty—that was the sinister feature. If only there had been beauty! His cruelty would have been tolerable then. Through excess of light, he failed to triumph, he also; in his yellowy-white overflow not only matter, but brightness itself lay drowned. He was not the unattainable friend, either of men or birds or other suns, he was not the eternal promise, the never-withdrawn suggestion that haunts our consciousness; he was merely a creature, like the rest, and so debarred from glory.

Chapter Eleven

Although the Indians had driven off, and Fielding could see his horse standing in a small shed in the corner of the compound, no one troubled to bring it to him. He started to get it himself, but was stopped by a call from the house. Aziz was sitting up in bed, looking dishevelled and sad. 'Here's your home,' he said sardonically. 'Here's the celebrated hospitality of the East. Look at the flies. Look at the chunam coming off the walls. Isn't it jolly? Now I suppose you want to be off, having seen an Oriental interior.'

'Anyhow, you want to rest.'

'I can rest the whole day, thanks to worthy Dr Lal. Major Callendar's spy, I suppose you know, but this time it didn't work. I am allowed to have a slight temperature.'

'Callendar doesn't trust anyone, English or Indian: that's his character, and I wish you weren't under him; but you are, and that's that.'

'Before you go, for you are evidently in a great hurry, will you please unlock that drawer? Do you see a piece of brown paper at the top?'

'Yes.'

'Open it.'

'Who is this?'

'She was my wife. You are the first Englishman she has ever come before. Now put her photograph away.'

He was astonished, as a traveller who suddenly sees, between the stones of the desert, flowers. The flowers have been there all the time, but suddenly he sees them. He tried to look at the photograph, but in itself it was just a woman in a sari, facing the world. He muttered, 'Really, I don't know why you pay me this great compliment, Aziz, but I do appreciate it.'

'Oh, it's nothing, she was not a highly educated woman or even beautiful, but put it away. You would have seen her, so why should you not see her photograph?'

'You would have allowed me to see her?'

'Why not? I believe in the purdah, but I should have told her you were my brother, and she would have seen you. Hamidullah saw her, and several others.'

'Did she think they were your brothers?'

'Of course not, but the word exists and is convenient. All men are my brothers, and as soon as one behaves as such he may see my wife.'

'And when the whole world behaves as such, there will be no more purdah?'

'It is because you can say and feel such a remark as that, that I show you the photograph,' said Aziz gravely. 'It is beyond the power of most men. It is because you behave well while I behave badly that I show it you. I never expected you to come back just now when I called you. I thought, "He has certainly done with me; I have insulted him." Mr Fielding, no one can ever realize how much kindness we Indians need, we do not even realize it ourselves. But we know when it has been given. We do not forget, though we may seem to. Kindness, more kindness, and even after that more kindness. I assure you it is the only hope.' His voice seemed to arise from a dream. Altering it, yet still deep below his normal surface, he said, 'We can't build up India except on what we feel. What is the use of all these reforms, and Conciliation Committees for Mohurram, and shall we cut the tazia short or shall we carry it another route, and Councils of Notables and official parties where the English sneer at our skins?'

'It's beginning at the wrong end, isn't it? I know, but institutions and the governments don't.' He looked again at the photograph. The lady faced the world at her husband's wish and her own, but how bewildering she found it, the echoing contradictory world!

'Put her away, she is of no importance, she is dead,' said Aziz gently. 'I showed her to you because I have nothing else to show. You may look round the whole of my bungalow now, and empty everything. I have no other secrets, my three children live away with their grandmamma, and that is all.'

Fielding sat down by the bed, flattered at the trust reposed in him, yet rather sad. He felt old. He wished that he too could be carried away on waves of emotion. The next time they met, Aziz might be cautious and standoffish. He realized this, and it made him sad that he should realize it. Kindness, kindness, and more kindness—yes, that he might supply, but was that really all that the queer nation needed? Did it not also demand an occasional intoxication of the blood? What had he done to deserve this outburst of confidence, and what hostage could he give in exchange? He looked back at his own life. What a poor crop of secrets it had produced! There were things in it that he had shown to no one, but they were so uninteresting, it wasn't worth while lifting a purdah on their account. He'd been in love, engaged to be married, lady broke it off, memories of her and thoughts about her had kept him from other women for a time; then indulgence, followed by repentance and equilibrium. Meagre really except the equilibrium, and Aziz didn't want to have that confided to him—he would have called it 'everything ranged coldly on shelves.'

'I shall not really be intimate with this fellow,' Fielding thought, and then 'nor with anyone.' That was the corollary. And he had to confess that he really didn't mind, that he was content to help people, and like them as long as they didn't object, and if they objected pass on serenely. Experience can do much, and all that he had learnt in England and Europe was an assistance to him, and helped him towards clarity, but clarity prevented him from experiencing something else.

'How did you like the two ladies you met last Thursday?' he asked.

Aziz shook his head distastefully. The question reminded him of his rash remark about the Marabar Caves.

'How do you like Englishwomen generally?'

'Hamidullah liked them in England. Here we never look at them. Oh no, much too careful. Let's talk of something else.'

'Hamidullah's right: they are much nicer in England. There's something that doesn't suit them out here.'

Aziz after another silence said, 'Why are you not married?'

Fielding was pleased that he had asked. 'Because I have more or less come through without it,' he replied. 'I was thinking of telling you a little about myself some day if I can make it interesting enough. The lady I liked wouldn't marry me—that is the main point, but that's fifteen years ago and now means nothing.'

'But you haven't children.'

'None.'

'Excuse the following question: have you any illegitimate children?'

'No. I'ld willingly tell you if I had.'

'Then your name will entirely die out.'

'It must.'

'Well.' He shook his head. 'This indifference is what the Oriental will never understand.'

'I don't care for children.'

'Caring has nothing to do with it,' he said impatiently.

'I don't feel their absence, I don't want them weeping around my death-bed and being polite about me afterwards, which I believe is the general notion. I'd far rather leave a thought behind me than a child. Other people can have children. No obligation, with England getting so chock-a-block and overrunning India for jobs.'

'Why don't you marry Miss Quested?'

'Good God! why, the girl's a prig.'

'Prig, prig? Kindly explain. Isn't that a bad word?'

'Oh, I don't know her, but she struck me as one of the more pathetic products of Western education. She depresses me.'

'But prig, Mr Fielding? How's that?'

'She goes on and on as if she's at a lecture—trying ever so hard to understand India and life, and occasionally taking a note.'

'I thought her so nice and sincere.'

'So she probably is,' said Fielding, ashamed of his roughness: any suggestion that he should marry always does produce overstatements on the part of the bachelor, and a mental breeze. 'But I can't marry her if I wanted to, for she has just become engaged to the City Magistrate.'

'Has she indeed? I am so glad!' he exclaimed with relief, for this exempted him from the Marabar expedition: he would scarcely be expected to entertain regular Anglo-Indians.

'It's the old mother's doing. She was afraid her dear boy would choose for himself, so she brought out the girl on purpose, and flung them together until it happened.'

'Mrs Moore did not mention that to me among her plans.'

'I may have got it wrong—I'm out of club gossip. But anyhow they're engaged to be married.'

'Yes, you're out of it, my poor chap,' he smiled. 'No Miss Quested for Mr Fielding. However, she was not beautiful. She has practically no breasts, if you come to think of it.'

He smiled too, but found a touch of bad taste in the reference to a lady's breasts.

'For the City Magistrate they shall be sufficient perhaps, and he for her. For you I shall arrange a lady with breasts like mangoes. . . .'

'No, you won't.'

'I will not really, and besides your position makes it dangerous for you.' His mind had slipped from matrimony to Calcutta. His face grew grave. Fancy if he had persuaded the Principal to accompany him there, and then got him into trouble! And abruptly he took up a new attitude towards his friend, the attitude of the protector who knows the dangers of India and is admonitory. 'You can't be too careful in every way, Mr Fielding; whatever you say or do in this damned country there is always some envious fellow on the look-out. You may be surprised to know that there were at least three spies sitting here when you came to enquire. I was really a good deal upset that you talked in that fashion about God. They will certainly report it.'

'To whom?'

'That's all very well, but you spoke against morality also, and you said you had come to take other people's jobs. All that was very unwise. This is an awful place for scandal Why, actually one of your own pupils was listening.'

'Thanks for telling me that; yes, I must try and be more careful. If I'm interested, I'm apt to forget myself. Still, it doesn't do real harm.'

'But speaking out may get you into trouble.'

'It's often done so in the past.'

'There, listen to that! But the end of it might be that you lost your job.'

'If I do, I do. I shall survive it. I travel light.'

'Travel light! You are a most extraordinary race,' said Aziz, turning away as if he were going to sleep, and immediately turning back again. 'Is it your climate, or what?'

'Plenty of Indians travel light too—saddhus and such. It's one of the things I admire about your country. Any man can travel light until he has a wife or children. That's part of my case against marriage. I'm a holy man minus the holiness. Hand that on to your three spies, and tell them to put it in their pipes.'

Aziz was charmed and interested, and turned the new idea over in his mind. So this was why Mr Fielding and a few others were so fearless! They had nothing to lose. But he himself was rooted in society and Islam. He belonged to a tradition which bound him, and he had brought children into the world, the society of the future. Though he lived so vaguely in this flimsy bungalow, nevertheless he was placed, placed.

'I can't be sacked from my job, because my job's Education. I believe in teaching people to be individuals, and to understand other individuals. It's the only thing I do believe in. At Government College, I mix it up with trigonometry, and so on. When I'm a saddhu, I shall mix it up with something else.'

He concluded his manifesto, and both were silent. The eye-flies became worse than ever and danced close up to their pupils, or crawled into their ears. Fielding hit about wildly. The exercise made him hot, and he got up to go.

'You might tell your servant to bring my horse. He doesn't seem to appreciate my Urdu.'

'I know. I gave him orders not to. Such are the tricks we play on unfortunate Englishmen. Poor Mr Fielding! But I will release you now. Oh dear! With the exception of yourself and Hamidullah, I have no one to talk to in this place. You like Hamidullah, don't you?'

'Very much.'

'Do you promise to come at once to us when you are in trouble?'

'I never can be in trouble.'

'There goes a queer chap, I trust he won't come to grief,' thought Aziz, left alone. His period of admiration was over, and he reacted towards patronage. It was difficult for him to remain in awe of anyone who played with all his cards on the table. Fielding, he discovered on closer acquaintance, was truly warm-hearted and unconventional, but not what can be called wise. That frankness of speech in the presence of Ram Chand, Rafi and Co. was dangerous and inelegant. It served no useful end.

But they were friends, brothers. That part was settled, their compact had been subscribed by the photograph, they trusted one another, affection had triumphed for once in a way. He dropped off to sleep amid the happier memories of the last two hours—poetry of Ghalib, female grace, good old Hamidullah, good Fielding, his honoured wife and dear boys. He passed into a region where these joys had no enemies but bloomed harmoniously in an eternal garden, or ran down watershoots of ribbed marble, or rose into domes whereunder were inscribed, black against white, the ninety-nine attributes of God.

Caves

Chapter Twelve

The Ganges, though flowing from the foot of Vishnu and through Siva's hair, is not an ancient stream. Geology, looking further than religion, knows of a time when neither the river nor the Himalayas that nourished it existed, and an ocean flowed over the holy places of Hindustan. The mountains rose, their debris silted up the ocean, the gods took their seats on them and contrived the river, and the India we call immemorial came into being. But India is really far older. In the days of the prehistoric ocean the southern part of the peninsula already existed, and the high places of Dravidia have been land since land began, and have seen on the one side the sinking of a continent that joined them to Africa, and on the other the upheaval of the Himalayas from a sea. They are older than anything in the world. No water has ever covered them, and the sun who has watched them for countless aeons may still discern in their outlines forms that were his before our globe was torn from his bosom. If flesh of the sun's flesh is to be touched anywhere, it is here, among the incredible antiquity of these hills.

Yet even they are altering. As Himalayan India rose, this India, the primal, has been depressed, and is slowly re-entering the curve of the earth. It may be that in aeons to come an ocean will flow here too, and cover the sun-born rocks with slime. Meanwhile the plain of the Ganges encroaches on them with something of the sea's action. They are sinking beneath the newer lands. Their main mass is untouched, but at the edge their outposts have been cut off and stand knee-deep, throat-deep, in the advancing soil. There is something unspeakable in these outposts. They are like nothing else in the world, and a glimpse of them makes the breath catch. They rise abruptly, insanely, without the proportion that is kept by the wildest hills elsewhere, they bear no relation to anything dreamt or seen. To call them 'uncanny' suggests ghosts, and they are older than all spirit. Hinduism has scratched and plastered a few rocks, but the shrines are unfrequented, as if pilgrims, who generally seek the extraordinary, had here found too much of it. Some saddhus did once settle in a cave, but they were smoked out, and even Buddha, who must have passed this way down to the Bo Tree of Gya, shunned a renunciation more complete than his own, and has left no legend of struggle or victory in the Marabar.

The caves are readily described. A tunnel eight feet long, five feet high, three feet wide, leads to a circular chamber about twenty feet in diameter. This arrangement occurs again and again throughout the group of hills, and this is all, this is a Marabar Cave. Having seen one such cave, having seen two, having seen three, four, fourteen, twenty-four, the visitor returns to Chandrapore uncertain whether he has had an interesting experience or a dull one or any experience at all. He finds it difficult to discuss the caves, or to keep them apart in his mind, for the pattern never varies, and no carving, not even a bees'-nest or a bat distinguishes one from another. Nothing, nothing attaches to them, and their reputation—for they have one—does not depend upon human speech. It is as if the surrounding plain or the passing birds have taken upon themselves to exclaim 'extraordinary,' and the word has taken root in the air, and been inhaled by mankind.

They are dark caves. Even when they open towards the sun, very little light penetrates down the entrance tunnel into the circular chamber. There is little to see, and no eye to see it, until the visitor arrives for his five minutes, and strikes a match. Immediately another flame rises in the depths of the rock and moves towards the surface like an imprisoned spirit: the walls of the circular chamber have been most marvellously polished. The two flames approach and strive to unite, but cannot, because one of them breathes air, the other stone. A mirror inlaid with lovely colours divides the lovers, delicate stars of pink and grey interpose, exquisite nebulae, shadings fainter than the tail of a comet or the midday moon, all the evanescent life of the granite, only here visible. Fists and fingers thrust above the advancing soil—here at last is their skin, finer than any covering acquired by the animals, smoother than windless water, more voluptuous than love. The radiance increases, the flames touch one another, kiss, expire. The cave is dark again, like all the caves.

Only the wall of the circular chamber has been polished thus. The sides of the tunnel are left rough, they impinge as an afterthought upon the internal perfection. An entrance was necessary, so mankind made one. But elsewhere, deeper in the granite, are there certain chambers that have no entrances? Chambers never unsealed since the arrival of the gods. Local report declares that these exceed in number those that can be visited, as the dead exceed the living—four hundred of them, four thousand or million. Nothing is inside them, they were sealed up before the creation of pestilence or treasure; if mankind grew curious and excavated, nothing, nothing would be added to the sum of good or evil. One of them is rumoured within the boulder that swings on the summit of the highest of the hills; a bubble-shaped cave that has neither ceiling nor floor, and mirrors its own darkness in every direction infinitely. If the boulder falls and smashes, the cave will smash too–empty as an Easter egg. The boulder because of its hollowness sways in the wind, and even moves when a crow perches upon it: hence its name and the name of its stupendous pedestal: the Kawa Dol.

Chapter Thirteen

These hills look romantic in certain lights and at suitable distances, and seen of an evening from the upper verandah of the club they caused Miss Quested to say conversationally to Miss Derek that she should like to have gone, that Dr Aziz at Mr Fielding's had said he would arrange something, and that Indians seem rather forgetful. She was overheard by the servant who offered them vermouths. This servant understood English. And he was not exactly a spy, but he kept his ears open, and Mahmoud Ali did not exactly bribe him, but did encourage him to come and squat with his own servants, and would happen to stroll their way when he was there. As the story travelled, it accreted emotion and Aziz learnt with horror that the ladies were deeply offended with him, and had expected an invitation daily. He thought his facile remark had been forgotten. Endowed with two memories, a temporary and a permanent, he had hitherto relegated the caves to the former. Now he transferred them once for all, and pushed the matter through. They were to be a stupendous replica of the tea party. He began by securing Fielding and old Godbole, and then commissioned Fielding to approach Mrs Moore and Miss Quested when they were alone–by this device Ronny, their official protector, could be circumvented. Fielding didn't like the job much; he was busy, caves bored him, he foresaw friction and expense, but he would not refuse the first favour his friend had asked from him, and did as required. The ladies accepted. It was a little inconvenient in the present press of their engagements, still, they hoped to manage it after consulting Mr Heaslop. Consulted, Ronny raised no objection, provided Fielding undertook full responsibility for their comfort. He was not enthusiastic about the picnic, but, then, no more were the ladies–no one was enthusiastic, yet it took place.

Aziz was terribly worried. It was not a long expedition–a train left Chandrapore just before dawn, another would bring them back for tiffin–but he was only a little official still, and feared to acquit himself dishonourably. He had to ask Major Callendar for half a day's leave, and be refused because of his recent malingering; despair; renewed approach of Major Callendar through Fielding, and contemptuous snarling permission. He had to borrow cutlery from Mahmoud Ali without inviting him. Then there was the question of alcohol; Mr Fielding, and perhaps the ladies, were drinkers, so must he provide whisky-sodas and ports? There was the problem of transport from the wayside station of Marabar to the caves. There was the problem of Professor Godbole and his food, and of Professor Godbole and other people's food–two problems, not one problem. The

Professor was not a very strict Hindu—he would take tea, fruit, soda-water and sweets, whoever cooked them, and vegetables and rice if cooked by a Brahman; but not meat, not cakes lest they contained eggs, and he would not allow anyone else to eat beef: a slice of beef upon a distant plate would wreck his happiness. Other people might eat mutton, they might eat ham. But over ham Aziz' own religion raised its voice: he did not fancy other people eating ham. Trouble after trouble encountered him, because he had challenged the spirit of the Indian earth, which tries to keep men in compartments.

At last the moment arrived.

His friends thought him most unwise to mix himself up with English ladies, and warned him to take every precaution against unpunctuality. Consequently he spent the previous night at the station. The servants were huddled on the platform, enjoined not to stray. He himself walked up and down with old Mohammed Latif, who was to act as major-domo. He felt insecure and also unreal. A car drove up, and he hoped Fielding would get out of it, to lend him solidity. But it contained Mrs Moore, Miss Quested, and their Goanese servant. He rushed to meet them, suddenly happy. 'But you've come, after all. Oh how very very kind of you!' he cried. 'This is the happiest moment in all my life.'

The ladies were civil. It was not the happiest moment in their lives, still, they looked forward to enjoying themselves as soon as the bother of the early start was over. They had not seen him since the expedition was arranged, and they thanked him adequately.

'You don't require tickets—please stop your servant. There are no tickets on the Marabar branch line; it is its peculiarity. You come to the carriage and rest till Mr Fielding joins us. Did you know you are to travel purdah? Will you like that?'

They replied that they should like it. The train had come in, and a crowd of dependents were swarming over the seats of the carriage like monkeys. Aziz had borrowed servants from his friends, as well as bringing his own three, and quarrels over precedence were resulting. The ladies' servant stood apart, with a sneering expression on his face. They had hired him while they were still globe-trotters, at Bombay. In a hotel or among smart people he was excellent, but as soon as they consorted with anyone whom he thought second-rate he left them to their disgrace.

The night was still dark, but had acquired the temporary look that indicates its end. Perched on the roof of a shed, the station-master's hens began to dream of kites instead of owls. Lamps were put out, in order to save the trouble of putting them out later; the smell of tobacco and the sound of spitting arose from third-class passengers in dark corners; heads were unshrouded, teeth cleaned on the twigs of a tree. So convinced was a junior official that another sun would rise, that he rang a bell with enthusiasm. This upset the servants. They shrieked that the train was starting, and ran to both ends of it to intercede. Much had still to enter the purdah carriage—a box bound with brass, a melon wearing a fez, a towel containing guavas, a step-ladder and a gun. The guests played up all right. They had no race-consciousness—Mrs Moore was too old, Miss Quested too new—and they behaved to Aziz as to any young man who had been kind to them in the country. This moved him deeply. He had expected them to arrive with Mr Fielding, instead of which they trusted themselves to be with him a few moments alone.

'Send back your servant,' he suggested. 'He is unnecessary. Then we shall all be Moslems together.'

'And he is such a horrible servant. Antony, you can go; we don't want you,' said the girl impatiently.

'Master told me to come.'

'Mistress tells you to go.'

'Master says, keep near the ladies all the morning.'

'Well, your ladies won't have you.' She turned to the host. 'Do get rid of him, Dr Aziz!'

'Mohammed Latif!' he called.

The poor relative exchanged fezzes with the melon, and peeped out of the window of the railway carriage, whose confusion he was superintending.

'Here is my cousin, Mr Mohammed Latif. Oh no, don't shake hands. He is an Indian of the old-fashioned sort, he prefers to salaam. There, I told you so. Mohammed Latif, how beautifully you salaam. See, he hasn't understood; he knows no English.'

'You spick lie,' said the old man gently.

'I spick a lie! Oh, jolly good. Isn't he a funny old man? We will have great jokes with him later. He does all sorts of little things. He is not nearly as stupid as you think, and awfully poor. It's lucky ours is a large family.' He flung an arm round the grubby neck. 'But you get inside, make yourselves at home; yes, you lie down.' The celebrated Oriental confusion appeared at last to be at an end. 'Excuse me, now I must meet our other two guests!'

He was getting nervous again, for it was ten minutes to the time. Still, Fielding was an Englishman, and they never do miss trains, and Godbole was a Hindu and did not count, and, soothed by this logic, he grew calmer as the hour of departure approached. Mohammed Latif had bribed Antony not to come. They walked up and down the platform, talking usefully. They agreed that they had overdone the servants, and must leave two or three behind at Marabar station. And Aziz explained that he might be playing one or two practical jokes at the caves—not out of unkindness, but to make the guests laugh. The old man assented with slight sideway motions of the head: he was always willing to be ridiculed, and he bade Aziz not spare him. Elated by his importance, he began an indecent anecdote.

'Tell me another time, brother, when I have more leisure, for now, as I have already explained, we have to give pleasure to non-Moslems. Three will be Europeans, one a Hindu, which must not be forgotten. Every attention must be paid to Professor Godbole, lest he feel that he is inferior to my other guests.'

'I will discuss philosophy with him.'

'That will be kind of you; but the servants are even more important. We must not convey an impression of disorganization. It can be done, and I expect you to to it . . .'

A shriek from the purdah carriage. The train had started.

'Merciful God!' cried Mohammed Latif. He flung himself at the train, and leapt on to the footboard of a carriage. Aziz did likewise. It was an easy feat, for a branch-line train is slow to assume special airs. 'We're monkeys, don't worry,' he called, hanging on to a bar and laughing. Then he howled, 'Mr Fielding! Mr Fielding!'

There were Fielding and old Godbole, held up at the level-crossing. Appalling catastrophe! The gates had been closed earlier than usual. They leapt from their tonga; they gesticulated, but what was the good. So near and yet so far! As the train joggled past over the points, there was time for agonized words.

'Bad, bad, you have destroyed me.'

'Godbole's pujah did it,' cried the Englishman.

The Brahman lowered his eyes, ashamed of religion. For it was so: he had miscalculated the length of a prayer.

'Jump on, I must have you,' screamed Aziz, beside himself.

'Right, give a hand.'

'He's not to, he'll kill himself,' Mrs Moore protested. He jumped, he failed, missed his friend's hand, and fell back on to the line. The train rumbled past. He scrambled on to his feet, and bawled after them, 'I'm all right, you're all right, don't worry,' and then they passed beyond range of his voice.

'Mrs Moore, Miss Quested, our expedition is a ruin.' He swung himself along the footboard, almost in tears.

'Get in, get in; you'll kill yourself as well as Mr Fielding. I see no ruin.'

'How is that? Oh, explain to me!' he said piteously, like a child.

'We shall be all Moslems together now, as you promised.'

She was perfect as always, his dear Mrs Moore. All the love for her he had felt at the mosque welled up again, the fresher for forgetfulness. There was nothing he would not do for her. He would die to make her happy.

'Get in, Dr Aziz, you make us giddy,' the other lady called. 'If they're so foolish as to miss the train, that's their loss, not ours.'

'I am to blame. I am the host.'

'Nonsense, go to your carriage. We're going to have a delightful time without them.'

Not perfect like Mrs Moore, but very sincere and kind. Wonderful ladies, both of them, and for one precious morning his guests. He felt important and competent. Fielding was a loss personally, being a friend, increasingly dear, yet if Fielding had come, he himself would have remained in leading-strings. 'Indians are incapable of responsibility,' said the officials, and Hamidullah sometimes said so too. He would show those pessimists that they were wrong. Smiling proudly, he glanced outward at the country, which was still invisible except as a dark movement in the darkness; then upwards at the sky, where the stars of the sprawling Scorpion had begun to pale. Then he dived through a window into a second-class carriage.

'Mohammed Latif, by the way, what is in these caves, brother? Why are we all going to see them?'

Such a question was beyond the poor relative's scope. He could only reply that God and the local villagers knew, and that the latter would gladly act as guides.

Chapter Fourteen

Most of life is so dull that there is nothing to be said about it, and the books and talk that would describe it as interesting are obliged to exaggerate, in the hope of justifying their own existence. Inside its cocoon of work or social obligation, the human spirit slumbers for the most part, registering the distinction between pleasure and pain, but not nearly as alert as we pretend. There are periods in the most thrilling day during which nothing happens, and though we continue to exclaim, 'I do enjoy myself,' or, 'I am horrified,' we are insincere. 'As far as I feel anything, it is enjoyment, horror'—it's no more than that really, and a perfectly adjusted organism would be silent.

It so happened that Mrs Moore and Miss Quested had felt nothing acutely for a fortnight. Ever since Professor Godbole had sung his queer little song, they had lived more or less inside cocoons, and the difference between them was that the elder lady accepted her own apathy, while the younger resented hers. It was Adela's faith that the whole stream of events is important and interesting, and if she grew bored she blamed herself severely and compelled her lips to utter enthusiasms. This was the only insincerity in a character otherwise sincere, and it was indeed the intellectual protest of her youth. She was particularly vexed now because she was both in India and engaged to be married, which double event should have made every instant sublime.

India was certainly dim this morning, though seen under the auspices of Indians. Her wish had been granted, but too late. She could not get excited over Aziz and his arrangements. She was not the least unhappy or depressed, and the various odd objects that surrounded her—the comic 'purdah' carriage, the piles of rugs and bolsters, the rolling melons, the scent of sweet oils, the ladder, the brass-bound box, the sudden irruption of Mahmoud Ali's butler from the lavatory with tea and poached eggs upon a tray—they were all new and amusing, and led her to comment appropriately, but they wouldn't bite into her mind. So she tried to find comfort by reflecting that her main interest would henceforward be Ronny.

'What a nice cheerful servant! What a relief after Antony!'

'They startle one rather. A strange place to make tea in,' said Mrs Moore, who had hoped for a nap.

'I want to sack Antony. His behaviour on the platform has decided me.'

Mrs Moore thought that Antony's better self would come to the front at Simla. Miss Quested was to be married at Simla; some cousins, with a house looking straight on to Thibet, had invited her.

'Anyhow, we must get a second servant, because at Simla you will be at the hotel, and I don't think Ronny's Baldeo . . .' She loved plans.

'Very well, you get another servant, and I'll keep Antony with me. I am used to his unappetizing ways. He will see me through the Hot Weather.'

'I don't believe in the Hot Weather. People like Major Callendar who always talk about it—it's in the hope of making one feel inexperienced and small, like their everlasting, "I've been twenty years in this country."'

'I believe in the Hot Weather, but never did I suppose it would bottle me up as it will.' For owing to the sage leisureliness of Ronny and Adela, they could not be married till May, and consequently Mrs Moore could not return to England immediately after the wedding, which was what she had hoped to do. By May a barrier of fire would have fallen across India and the adjoining sea, and she would have to remain perched up in the Himalayas waiting for the world to get cooler.

'I won't be bottled up,' announced the girl. 'I've no patience with these women here who leave their husbands grilling in the plains. Mrs McBryde hasn't stopped down once since she married; she leaves her quite intelligent husband alone half the year, and then's surprised she's out of touch with him.'

'She has children, you see.'

'Oh yes, that's true,' said Miss Quested, disconcerted.

'It is the children who are the first consideration. Until they are grown up, and married off. When that happens one has again the right to live for oneself—in the plains or the hills, as suits.'

'Oh yes, you're perfectly right. I never thought it out.'

'If one has not become too stupid and old.' She handed her empty cup to the servant.

'My idea now is that my cousins shall find me a servant in Simla, at all events to see me through the wedding, after which Ronny means to reorganize his staff entirely. He does it very well for a bachelor; still, when he is married no doubt various changes will have to be made—his old servants won't want to take their orders from me, and I don't blame them.'

Mrs Moore pushed up the shutters and looked out. She had brought Ronny and Adela together by their mutual wish, but really she could not advise them further. She felt increasingly (vision or nightmare?) that, though people are important, the relations between them are not, and that in particular too much fuss has been made over marriage; centuries of carnal embracement, yet man is no nearer to understanding man. And to-day she felt this with such force that it seemed itself a relationship, itself a person who was trying to take hold of her hand.

'Anything to be seen of the hills?'

'Only various shades of the dark.'

'We can't be far from the place where my hyena was.' She peered into the timeless twilight. The train crossed a nullah. 'Pomper, pomper, pomper,' was the sound that the wheels made as they trundled over the bridge, moving very slowly. A hundred yards on came a second nullah, then a third, suggesting the neighbourhood of higher ground. 'Perhaps this is mine; anyhow, the road runs parallel with the railway.' Her accident was a pleasant memory; she felt in her dry, honest way that it had given her a good shake up, and taught her Ronny's true worth. Then she went back to her plans; plans had been a passion with her from girlhood. Now and then she paid tribute to the present, said how friendly and intelligent Aziz was, ate a guava, couldn't eat a fried sweet, practised her Urdu on the servant; but her thoughts ever veered to the manageable future, and to the Anglo-Indian life she had decided to endure. And as she appraised it with its adjuncts of Turtons and Burtons, the train accompanied her sentences, 'pomper, pomper,' the train half asleep, going nowhere in particular and with no passenger of importance in any of its carriages, the branch-line train, lost on a low embankment between dull fields. Its message—for it had one—avoided her well-equipped mind. Far away behind her, with a shriek that meant business, rushed the Mail, connecting up important towns such as Calcutta and Lahore, where interesting events occur and personalities are developed. She understood that. Unfortunately, India has few important towns. India is the country, fields, fields, then hills, jungle, hills, and more fields. The branch line stops, the road is only practicable for cars to a point, the bullock-carts lumber down the side tracks, paths fray out into the cultivation, and disappear near a splash of red paint. How can the mind take hold of such a country? Generations of invaders have tried, but they remain in exile. The important towns they build are only retreats, their quarrels the malaise of men who cannot find their way home. India knows of their trouble. She knows of the whole world's trouble, to its uttermost depth. She calls 'Come' through her hundred mouths, through objects ridiculous and august. But come to what? She has never defined. She is not a promise, only an appeal.

'I will fetch you from Simla when it's cool enough. I will unbottle you in fact,' continued the reliable girl. 'We then see some of the Mogul stuff—how appalling if we let you miss the Taj!—and then I will see you off at Bombay. Your last glimpse of this country really shall be interesting.' But Mrs Moore had fallen asleep, exhausted by the early start. She was in rather low health, and ought not to have attempted the expedition, but had pulled herself together in case the pleasure of the others should suffer. Her dreams were of the same texture, but there it was her other children who were wanting something, Stella and Ralph, and she was explaining to them that she could not be in two families at once. When she awoke, Adela had ceased to plan, and leant out of a window, saying, 'They're rather wonderful.'

Astonishing even from the rise of the civil station, here the Marabar were gods to whom earth is a ghost. Kawa Dol was nearest. It shot up in a single slab, on whose summit one rock was poised—if a mass so great can be called one rock. Behind it, recumbent, were the hills that contained the other caves, isolated each from his neighbour by broad channels of the plain. The assemblage, ten in all, shifted a little as the train crept past them, as if observing its arrival.

'I'ld not have missed this for anything,' said the girl, exaggerating her enthusiasm. 'Look, the sun's rising—this'll be absolutely magnificent—come quickly—look. I wouldn't have missed this for anything. We should never have seen it if we'd stuck to the Turtons and their eternal elephants.'

As she spoke, the sky to the left turned angry orange. Colour throbbed and mounted behind a pattern of trees, grew in intensity, was yet brighter, incredibly brighter, strained from without against the globe of the air. They awaited the miracle. But at the supreme moment, when night should have died and day lived, nothing occurred. It was as if virtue had failed in the celestial fount. The hues in the east decayed, the hills seemed dimmer though in fact better lit, and a profound disappointment entered with the morning breeze. Why, when the chamber was prepared, did the bridegroom not enter with trumpets and shawms, as humanity expects? The sun rose without splendour. He was presently observed trailing yellowish behind the trees, or against insipid sky, and touching the bodies already at work in the fields.

'Ah, that must be the false dawn—isn't it caused by dust in the upper layers of the atmosphere that couldn't fall down during the night? I think Mr McBryde said so. Well, I must admit that England has it as regards sunrises. Do you remember Grasmere?'

'Ah, dearest Grasmere!' Its little lakes and mountains were beloved by them all. Romantic yet manageable, it sprang from a kindlier planet. Here an untidy plain stretched to the knees of the Marabar.

'Good morning, good morning, put on your topis,' shouted Aziz from farther down the train. 'Put on your topis at once, the early sun is highly dangerous for heads. I speak as a doctor.'

'Good morning, good morning, put on your own.'

'Not for my thick head,' he laughed, banging it and holding up pads of his hair.

'Nice creature he is,' murmured Adela.

'Listen—Mohammed Latif says "Good morning" next.' Various pointless jests.

'Dr Aziz, what's happened to your hills? The train has forgotten to stop.'

'Perhaps it is a circular train and goes back to Chandrapore without a break. Who knows!'

Having wandered off into the plain for a mile, the train slowed up against an elephant. There was a platform too, but it shrivelled into insignificance. An elephant, waving her painted forehead at the morn! 'Oh, what a surprise!' called the ladies politely. Aziz said nothing, but he nearly burst with pride and relief. The elephant was the one grand feature of the picnic, and God alone knew what he had gone through to obtain her. Semi-official, she was best approached through the Nawab Bahadur, who was best approached through Nureddin, but he never answered letters, but his mother had great influence with him and was a friend of Hamidullah Begum's, who had been excessively kind and had promised to call on her provided the broken shutter of the purdah carriage came back soon enough from Calcutta. That an elephant should depend from so long and so slender a string filled Aziz with content, and with humorous appreciation of the East, where the friends of friends are a reality, where everything gets done sometime, and sooner or later every one gets his share of happiness. And Mohammed Latif was likewise content, because two of the guests had missed the train, and consequently he could ride on the howdah instead of following in a cart, and the servants were content because an elephant increased their self-esteem, and they tumbled out the luggage into the dust with shouts and bangs, issuing orders to one another, and convulsed with goodwill.

'It takes an hour to get there, an hour to get back, and two hours for the caves, which we will call three,' said Aziz, smiling charmingly. There was suddenly something regal about him. 'The train back is at eleven-thirty, and you will be sitting down to your tiffin in Chandrapore with Mr Heaslop at exactly your usual hour, namely, one-fifteen. I know everything about you. Four hours—quite a small expedition—and an hour extra for misfortunes, which occur somewhat frequently among my people. My idea is to plan everything without consulting you; but you, Mrs Moore, or Miss Quested, you are at any moment to make alterations if you wish, even if it means giving up the caves. Do you agree? Then mount this wild animal.'

The elephant had knelt, grey and isolated, like another hill. They climbed up the ladder, and he mounted shikar fashion, treading first on the sharp edge of the heel and then into the looped-up tail. When Mohammed Latif followed him, the servant who held the end of the tail let go of it according to previous instructions, so that the poor relative slipped and had to cling to the netting over the buttocks. It was a little piece of court buffoonery, and distressed only the ladies, whom it was intended to divert. Both of them disliked practical jokes. Then the beast rose in two shattering movements, and poised them ten feet above the plain. Immediately below was the scurf of life that an elephant always collects round its feet—villagers, naked babies. The servants flung crockery into tongas. Hassan annexed the stallion intended for Aziz, and defied Mahmoud Ali's man from its altitude. The Brahman who had been hired to cook for Professor Godbole was planted under an acacia tree, to await their return. The train, also hoping to return, wobbled away through the fields, turning its head this way and that like a centipede. And the only other movement to be seen was a movement as of antennae, really the counterpoises of the wells which rose and fell on their pivots of mud all over the plain and dispersed a feeble flow of water. The scene was agreeable rather than not in the mild morning air, but there was little colour in it, and no vitality.

As the elephant moved towards the hills (the pale sun had by this time saluted them to the base, and pencilled shadows down their creases) a new quality occurred, a spiritual silence which invaded more senses than the ear. Life went on as usual, but had no consequences, that is to say, sounds did not echo or thoughts develop. Everything seemed cut off at its root, and therefore infected with illusion. For instance, there were some mounds by the edge of the track, low, serrated, and touched with whitewash. What were these mounds—graves, breasts of the goddess Parvati? The villagers beneath gave both replies. Again, there was a confusion about a snake which was never cleared up. Miss Quested saw a thin, dark object reared on end at the farther side of a watercourse, and said, 'A snake!' The villagers agreed, and Aziz explained: yes, a black cobra, very venomous, who had reared himself up to watch the passing of the elephant. But when she looked through Ronny's field-glasses, she found it wasn't a snake, but the withered and twisted stump of a toddy-palm. So she said, 'It isn't a snake.' The villagers contradicted her. She had put the word into their minds, and they refused to abandon it. Aziz admitted that it looked like a tree through the glasses, but insisted that it was a black cobra really, and improvised some rubbish about protective mimicry. Nothing was explained, and yet there was no romance. Films of heat, radiated from the Kawa Dol precipices, increased the confusion. They came at irregular intervals and moved capriciously. A patch of field would jump as if it was being fried, and then lie quiet. As they drew closer the radiation stopped.

The elephant walked straight at the Kawa Dol as if she would knock for admission with her forehead, then swerved, and followed a path round its base. The stones plunged straight into the earth, like cliffs into the sea, and while Miss Quested was remarking on this, and saying that it was striking, the plain quietly disappeared, peeled off, so to speak, and nothing was to be seen on either side but the granite, very dead and quiet. The sky dominated as usual, but seemed unhealthily near, adhering like a ceiling to the summits of the precipices. It was as if the contents of the corridor had never been changed. Occupied by his own munificence, Aziz noticed nothing. His guests noticed a little. They did not feel that it was an attractive place or quite worth visiting, and wished it could have turned into some Mohammedan object, such as a mosque, which their host would have appreciated and explained. His ignorance became evident, and was really rather a drawback. In spite of his gay, confident talk, he had no notion how to treat this particular aspect of India; he was lost in it without Professor Godbole, like themselves.

The corridor narrowed, then widened into a sort of tray. Here, more or less, was their goal. A ruined tank held a little water which would do for the animals, and close above the mud was punched a black hole—the first of the caves. Three hills encircled the tray. Two of them pumped out heat busily, but the third was in shadow, and here they camped.

'A horrid, stuffy place really,' murmured Mrs Moore to herself.

'How quick your servants are!' Miss Quested exclaimed. For a cloth had already been laid, with a vase of artificial flowers in its centre, and Mahmoud Ali's butler offered them poached eggs and tea for the second time.

'I thought we would eat this before our caves, and breakfast after.'

'Isn't this breakfast?'

'This breakfast? Did you think I should treat you so strangely?' He had been warned that English people never stop eating, and that he had better nourish them every two hours until a solid meal was ready.

'How very well it is all arranged.'

'That you shall tell me when I return to Chandrapore. Whatever disgraces I bring upon myself, you remain my guests.' He spoke gravely now. They were dependent on him for a few hours, and he felt grateful to them for placing themselves in such a position. All was well so far; the elephant held a fresh cut bough to her lips, the tonga shafts stuck up into the air, the kitchen-boy peeled potatoes, Hassan shouted, and Mohammed Latif stood as he ought, with a peeled switch in his hand. The expedition was a success, and it was Indian; an obscure young man had been allowed to show courtesy to visitors from another country, which is what all Indians long to do—even cynics like Mahmoud Ali—but they never have the chance. Hospitality had been achieved, they were 'his' guests; his honour was involved in their happiness, and any discomfort they endured would tear his own soul.

Like most Orientals, Aziz overrated hospitality, mistaking it for intimacy, and not seeing that it is tainted with the sense of possession. It was only when Mrs Moore or Fielding was near him that he saw further, and knew that it is more blessed to receive than to give. These two had strange and beautiful effects on him—they were his friends, his for ever, and he theirs for ever; he loved them so much that giving and receiving became one. He loved them even better than the Hamidullahs, because he had surmounted obstacles to meet them, and this stimulates a generous mind. Their images remained somewhere in his soul up to his dying day, permanent additions. He looked at her now as she sat on a deck-chair, sipping his tea, and had for a moment a joy that held the seeds of its own decay, for it would lead him to think, 'Oh, what more can I do for her?' and so back to the dull round of hospitality. The black bullets of his eyes filled with soft expressive light, and he said, 'Do you ever remember our mosque, Mrs, Moore?'

'I do, I do,' she said, suddenly vital and young.

'And how rough and rude I was, and how good you were.'

'And how happy we both were.'

'Friendships last longest that begin like that, I think. Shall I ever entertain your other children?'

'Do you know about the others? She will never talk about them to me,' said Miss Quested, unintentionally breaking a spell.

'Ralph and Stella, yes, I know everything about them. But we must not forget to visit our caves. One of the dreams of my life is accomplished in having you both here as my guests. You cannot imagine how you have honoured me. I feel like the Emperor Babur.'

'Why like him?' she enquired, rising.

'Because my ancestors came down with him from Afghanistan. They joined him at Herat. He also had often no more elephants than one, none sometimes, but he never ceased showing hospitality. When he fought or hunted or ran away, he would always stop for a time among hills, just like us; he would never let go of hospitality and pleasure, and if there was only a little food, he would have it arranged nicely, and if only one musical instrument, he would compel it to play a beautiful tune. I take him as my ideal. He is the poor gentleman, and he became a great king.'

'I thought another Emperor is your favourite—I forget the name—you mentioned him at Mr Fielding's: what my book calls Aurangzebe.'

'Alamgir? Oh yes, he was of course the more pious. But Babur—never in his whole life did he betray a friend, so I can only think of him this morning. And you know how he died? He laid down his life for his son. A death far more difficult than battle. They were caught in the heat. They should have gone back to Kabul for the bad weather, but could not for reasons of state, and at Agra Humayun fell sick. Babur walked round the bed three times, and said, 'I have borne it away,' and he did bear it away; the fever left his son and came to him instead, and he died. That is why I prefer Babur to Alamgir. I ought not to do so, but I do. However, I mustn't delay you. I see you are ready to start.'

'Not at all,' she said, sitting down by Mrs Moore again. 'We enjoy talk like this very much.' For at last he was talking about what he knew and felt, talking as he had in Fielding's garden-house; he was again the Oriental guide whom they appreciated.

'I always enjoy conversing about the Moguls. It is the chief pleasure I know. You see, those first six emperors were all most wonderful men, and as soon as one of them is mentioned, no matter which, I forget everything else in the world except the other five. You could not find six such kings in all the countries of the earth, not, I mean, coming one after the other—father, son.'

'Tell us something about Akbar.'

'Ah, you have heard the name of Akbar. Good. Hamidullah—whom you shall meet—will tell you that Akbar is the greatest of all. I say, "Yes, Akbar is very wonderful, but half a Hindu; he was not a true Moslem," which makes Hamidullah cry, "No more was Babur, he drank wine." But Babur always repented afterwards, which makes the entire difference, and Akbar never repented of the new religion he invented instead of the Holy Koran.'

'But wasn't Akbar's new religion very fine? It was to embrace the whole of India.'

'Miss Quested, fine but foolish. You keep your religion, I mine. That is the best. Nothing embraces the whole of India, nothing, nothing, and that was Akbar's mistake.'

'Oh, do you feel that, Dr Aziz?' she said thoughtfully. 'I hope you're not right. There will have to be something universal in this country—I don't say religion, for I'm not religious, but something, or how else are barriers to be broken down?'

She was only recommending the universal brotherhood he sometimes dreamed of, but as soon as it was put into prose it became untrue.

'Take my own case,' she continued—it was indeed her own case that had animated her. 'I don't know whether you happen to have heard, but I'm going to marry Mr Heaslop.'

'On which my heartiest congratulations.'

'Mrs Moore, may I put our difficulty to Dr Aziz—I mean our Anglo-Indian one?'

'It is your difficulty, not mine, my dear.'

'Ah, that's true. Well, by marrying Mr Heaslop, I shall become what is known as an Anglo-Indian.'

He held up his hand in protest. 'Impossible. Take back such a terrible remark.'

'But I shall; it's inevitable. I can't avoid the label. What I do hope to avoid is the mentality. Women like—' She stopped, not quite liking to mention names; she would boldly have said 'Mrs Turton and Mrs Callendar' a fortnight ago. 'Some women are so—well, ungenerous and snobby about Indians, and I should feel too ashamed for words if I turned like them, but—and here's my difficulty—there's nothing special about me, nothing specially good or strong, which will help me to resist my environment and avoid becoming like them. I've most lamentable defects. That's why I want Akbar's "universal religion" or the equivalent to keep me decent and sensible. Do you see what I mean?'

Her remarks pleased him, but his mind shut up tight because she had alluded to her marriage. He was not going to be mixed up in that side of things. 'You are certain to be happy with any relative of Mrs Moore's,' he said with a formal bow.

'Oh, my happiness—that's quite another problem. I want to consult you about this Anglo-Indian difficulty. Can you give me any advice?'

'You are absolutely unlike the others, I assure you. You will never be rude to my people.'

'I am told we all get rude after a year.'

'Then you are told a lie,' he flashed, for she had spoken the truth and it touched him on the raw; it was itself an insult in these particular circumstances. He recovered himself at once and laughed, but her error broke up their conversation—their civilization it had almost been—which scattered like the petals of a desert flower, and left them in the middle of the hills. 'Come along,' he said, holding out a hand to each. They got up a little reluctantly, and addressed themselves to sightseeing.

The first cave was tolerably convenient. They skirted the puddle of water, and then climbed up over some unattractive stones, the sun crashing on their backs. Bending their heads, they disappeared one by one into the interior of the hills. The small black hole gaped where their varied forms and colours had momentarily functioned. They were sucked in like water down a drain. Bland and bald rose the precipices; bland and glutinous the sky that connected the precipices; solid and white, a Brahminy kite flapped between the rocks with a clumsiness that seemed intentional. Before man, with his itch for the seemly, had been born, the planet must have looked thus. The kite flapped away. . . . Before birds, perhaps. . . . And then the hole belched and humanity returned.

A Marabar cave had been horrid as far as Mrs Moore was concerned, for she had nearly fainted in it, and had some difficulty in preventing herself from saying so as soon as she got into the air again. It was natural enough: she had always suffered from faintness, and the cave had become too full, because all their retinue followed them. Crammed with villagers and servants, the circular chamber began to smell. She lost Aziz and Adela in the dark, didn't know who touched her, couldn't breathe, and some vile naked thing struck her face and settled on her mouth like a pad. She tried to regain the entrance tunnel, but an influx of villagers swept her back. She hit her head. For an instant she went mad, hitting and gasping like a fanatic. For not only did the crush and stench alarm her; there was also a terrifying echo.

Professor Godbole had never mentioned an echo; it never impressed him, perhaps. There are some exquisite echoes in India; there is the whisper round the dome at Bijapur; there are the long, solid sentences that voyage through the air at Mandu, and return unbroken to their creator. The echo in a Marabar cave is not like these, it is entirely devoid of distinction. Whatever is said, the same monotonous noise replies, and quivers up and down the walls until it is absorbed into the roof. 'Boum' is the sound as far as the human alphabet can express it, or 'bou-oum,' or 'ou-boum,'—utterly dull. Hope, politeness, the blowing of a nose, the squeak of a boot, all produce 'boum.' Even the striking of a match starts a little worm coiling, which is too small to complete a circle but is eternally watchful. And if several people talk at once, an overlapping howling noise begins, echoes generate echoes, and the cave is stuffed with a snake composed of small snakes, which writhe independently.

After Mrs Moore all the others poured out. She had given the signal for the reflux. Aziz and Adela both emerged smiling and she did not want him to think his treat was a failure, so smiled too. As each person emerged she looked for a villain, but none was there, and she realized that she had been among the mildest individuals, whose only desire was to honour her, and that the naked pad was a poor little baby, astride its mother's hip. Nothing evil had been in the cave, but she had not enjoyed herself; no, she had not enjoyed herself, and she decided not to visit a second one.

'Did you see the reflection of his match—rather pretty?' asked Adela.

'I forget . . .'

'But he says this isn't a good cave, the best are on the Kawa Dol.'

'I don't think I shall go on to there. I dislike climbing.'

'Very well, let's sit down again in the shade until breakfast's ready.'

'Ah, but that'll disappoint him so; he has taken such trouble. You should go on; you don't mind.'

'Perhaps I ought to,' said the girl, indifferent to what she did, but desirous of being amiable.

The servants, etc., were scrambling back to the camp, pursued by grave censures from Mohammed Latif. Aziz came to help the guests over the rocks. He was at the summit of his powers, vigorous and humble, too sure of himself to resent criticism, and he was sincerely pleased when he heard they were altering his plans. 'Certainly, Miss Quested, so you and I will go together, and leave Mrs Moore here, and we will not be long, yet we will not hurry, because we know that will be her wish.'

'Quite right. I'm sorry not to come too, but I'm a poor walker.'

'Dear Mrs Moore, what does anything matter so long as you are my guests? I am very glad you are *not* coming, which sounds strange, but you are treating me with true frankness, as a friend.'

'Yes, I am your friend,' she said, laying her hand on his sleeve, and thinking, despite her fatigue, how very charming, how very good, he was, and how deeply she desired his happiness. 'So may I make another suggestion? Don't let so many people come with you this time. I think you may find it more convenient.'

'Exactly, exactly,' he cried, and, rushing to the other extreme, forbade all except one guide to accompany Miss Quested and him to the Kawa Dol. 'Is that all right?' he enquired.

'Quite right, now enjoy yourselves, and when you come back tell me all about it.' And she sank into the deck-chair.

If they reached the big pocket of caves, they would be away nearly an hour. She took out her writing-pad, and began, 'Dear Stella, Dear Ralph,' then stopped, and looked at the queer valley and their feeble invasion of it. Even the elephant had become a nobody. Her eye rose from it to the entrance tunnel. No, she did not wish to repeat that experience. The more she thought over it, the more disagreeable and frightening it became. She minded it much more now than at the time. The crush and the smells she could forget, but the echo began in some indescribable way to undermine her hold on life. Coming at a moment when she chanced to be fatigued, it had managed to murmur, 'Pathos, piety, courage—they exist, but are identical, and so is filth. Everything exists, nothing has value.' If one had spoken vileness in that place, or quoted lofty poetry, the comment would have been the same—'ou-boum.' If one had spoken with the tongues of angels and pleaded for all the unhappiness and misunderstanding in the world, past, present, and to come, for all the misery men must undergo whatever their opinion and position, and however much they dodge or bluff—it would amount to the same, the serpent would descend and return to the ceiling. Devils are of the North, and poems can be written about them, but no one could romanticize the Marabar because it robbed infinity and eternity of their vastness, the only quality that accommodates them to mankind.

She tried to go on with her letter, reminding herself that she was only an elderly woman who had got up too early in the morning and journeyed too far, that the despair creeping over her was merely her despair, her personal weakness, and that even if she got a sunstroke and went mad the rest of the world would go on. But suddenly, at the edge of her mind, Religion appeared, poor little talkative Christianity, and she knew that all its divine words from 'Let there be Light' to 'It is finished' only amounted to 'boum.' Then she was terrified over an area larger than usual; the universe, never comprehensible to her intellect, offered no repose to her soul, the mood of the last two months took definite form at last, and she realized that she didn't want to write to her children, didn't want to communicate with anyone, not even with God. She sat motionless with horror, and, when old Mohammed Latif came up to her, thought he would notice a difference. For a time she thought, 'I am going to be ill,' to comfort herself, then she surrendered to the vision. She lost all interest, even in Aziz, and the affectionate and sincere words that she had spoken to him seemed no longer hers but the air's.

Chapter Fifteen

Miss Quested and Aziz and a guide continued the slightly tedious expedition. They did not talk much, for the sun was getting high. The air felt like a warm bath into which hotter water is trickling constantly, the temperature rose and rose, the boulders said, 'I am alive,' the small stones answered, 'I am almost alive.' Between the chinks lay the ashes of little plants. They meant to climb to the rocking-stone on the summit, but it was too far, and they contented themselves with the big group of caves. *En route* for these, they encountered several isolated caves, which the guide persuaded them to visit, but really there was nothing to see; they lit a match, admired its reflection in the polish, tested the echo and came out again. Aziz was 'pretty sure they should come on some interesting old carvings soon,' but only meant he wished there were some carvings. His deeper thoughts were about the breakfast. Symptoms of disorganization had appeared as he left the camp. He ran over the menu: an English breakfast, porridge and mutton chops, but some Indian dishes to cause conversation, and pan afterwards. He had never liked Miss Quested as much as Mrs Moore, and had little to say to her, less than ever now that she would marry a British official.

Nor had Adela much to say to him. If his mind was with the breakfast, hers was mainly with her marriage. Simla next week, get rid of Antony, a view of Thibet, tiresome wedding bells, Agra in October, see Mrs Moore comfortably off from Bombay—the procession passed before her again, blurred by the heat, and then she turned to the more serious business of her life at Chandrapore. There were real difficulties here—Ronny's limitations and her own—but she enjoyed facing difficulties, and decided that if she could control her peevishness (always her weak point), and neither rail against Anglo-India nor succumb to it, their married life ought to be happy and profitable. She mustn't be too theoretical; she would deal with each problem as it came up, and trust to Ronny's common sense and her own. Luckily, each had abundance of common sense and good will.

But as she toiled over a rock that resembled an inverted saucer, she thought, 'What about love?' The rock was nicked by a double row of footholds, and somehow the question was suggested by them. Where had she seen footholds before? Oh yes, they were the pattern traced in the dust by the wheels of the Nawab Bahadur's car. She and Ronny—no, they did not love each other.

'Do I take you too fast?' enquired Aziz, for she had paused, a doubtful expression on her face. The discovery had come so suddenly that she felt like a mountaineer whose rope had broken. Not to love the man one's going to marry! Not to find it out till this moment! Not even to have asked oneself the question until now! Something else to think out. Vexed rather than appalled, she stood still, her eyes on the sparkling rock. There was esteem and animal contact at dusk, but the emotion that links them was absent. Ought she to break her engagement off? She was inclined to think not—it would cause so much trouble to others; besides, she wasn't convinced that love is necessary to a successful union. If love is everything, few marriages would survive the honeymoon. 'No, I'm all right, thanks,' she said, and, her emotions well under control, resumed the climb, though she felt a bit dashed. Aziz held her hand, the guide adhered to the surface like a lizard and scampered about as if governed by a personal centre of gravity.

'Are you married, Dr Aziz?' she asked, stopping again, and frowning.

'Yes, indeed, do come and see my wife'—for he felt it more artistic to have his wife alive for a moment.

'Thank you,' she said absently.

'She is not in Chandrapore just now.'

'And have you children?'

'Yes, indeed, three,' he replied in firmer tones.

'Are they a great pleasure to you?'

'Why, naturally, I adore them,' he laughed.

'I suppose so.' What a handsome little Oriental he was, and no doubt his wife and children were beautiful too, for people usually get what they already possess. She did not admire him with any personal warmth, for there was nothing of the vagrant in her blood, but she guessed he might attract women of his own race and rank, and she regretted that neither she nor Ronny had physical charm. It does make a difference in a relationship—beauty, thick hair, a fine skin. Probably this man had several wives—Mohammedans always insist on their full four, according to Mrs Turton. And having no one else to speak to on that eternal rock, she gave rein to the subject of marriage and said in her honest, decent, inquisitive way: 'Have you one wife or more than one?'

The question shocked the young man very much. It challenged a new conviction of his community, and new convictions are more sensitive than old. If she had said, 'Do you worship one god or several?' he would not have objected. But to ask an educated Indian Moslem how many wives he has—appalling, hideous! He was in trouble how to conceal his confusion. 'One, one in my own particular case,' he sputtered, and let go of her hand. Quite a number of caves were at the top of the track, and thinking, 'Damn the English even at their best,' he plunged into one of them to recover his balance. She followed at her leisure, quite unconscious that she had said the wrong thing, and not seeing him, she also went into a cave, thinking with half her mind 'sight-seeing bores me,' and wondering with the other half about marriage.

Chapter Sixteen

He waited in his cave a minute, and lit a cigarette so that he could remark on rejoining her, 'I bolted in to get out of the draught,' or something of the sort. When he returned, he found the guide, alone, with his head on one side. He had heard a noise, he said, and then Aziz heard it too: the noise of a motor-car. They were now on the outer shoulder of the Kawa Dol, and by scrambling twenty yards they got a glimpse of the plain. A car was coming towards the hills down the Chandrapore road. But they could not get a good view of it, because the precipitous bastion curved at the top, so that the base was not easily seen and the car disappeared as it came nearer. No doubt it would stop almost exactly beneath them, at the place where the pukka road degenerated into a path, and the elephant had turned to sidle into the hills.

He ran back, to tell the strange news to his guest.

The guide explained that she had gone into a cave.

'Which cave?'

He indicated the group vaguely.

'You should have kept her in sight, it was your duty,' said Aziz severely. 'Here are twelve caves at least. How am I to know which contains my guest? Which is the cave I was in myself?'

The same vague gesture. And Aziz, looking again, could not even be sure he had returned to the same group. Caves appeared in every direction–it seemed their original spawning place–and the orifices were always the same size. He thought, 'Merciful Heavens, Miss Quested is lost,' then pulled himself together, and began to look for her calmly.

'Shout!' he commanded.

When they had done this for awhile, the guide explained that to shout is useless, because a Marabar cave can hear no sound but its own. Aziz wiped his head, and sweat began to stream inside his clothes. The place was so confusing; it was partly a terrace, partly a zigzag, and full of grooves that led this way and that like snaketracks. He tried to go into every one, but he never knew where he had started. Caves got behind caves or confabulated in pairs, and some were at the entrance of a gully.

'Come here!' he called gently, and when the guide was in reach, he struck him in the face for a punishment. The man fled, and he was left alone. He thought, 'This is the end of my career, my guest is lost.' And then he discovered the simple and sufficient explanation of the mystery.

Miss Quested wasn't lost. She had joined the people in the car–friends of hers, no doubt, Mr Heaslop perhaps. He had a sudden glimpse of her, far down the gully—only a glimpse, but there she was quite plain, framed between rocks, and speaking to another lady. He was so relieved that he did not think her conduct odd. Accustomed to sudden changes of plan, he supposed that she had run down the Kawa Dol impulsively, in the hope of a little drive. He started back alone towards his camp, and almost at once caught sight of something which would have disquieted him very much a moment before: Miss Quested's field glasses. They were lying at the verge of a cave, half-way down an entrance tunnel. He tried to hang them over his shoulder, but the leather strap had broken, so he put them into his pocket instead. When he had gone a few steps, he thought she might have dropped something else, so he went back to look. But the previous difficulty recurred: he couldn't identify the cave. Down in the plain he heard the car starting; however, he couldn't catch a second glimpse of that. So he scrambled down the valley-face of the hill towards Mrs Moore, and here he was more successful: the colour and confusion of his little camp soon appeared, and in the midst of it he saw an Englishman's topi, and beneath it—oh joy!—smiled not Mr Heaslop, but Fielding.

'Fielding! Oh, I have so wanted you!' he cried, dropping the 'Mr' for the first time.

And his friend ran to meet him, all so pleasant and jolly, no dignity, shouting explanations and apologies about the train. Fielding had come in the newly arrived car—Miss Derek's car—that other lady was Miss Derek. Chatter, chatter, all the servants leaving their cooking to listen. Excellent Miss Derek! She had met Fielding by chance at the post office, said, 'Why haven't you gone to the Marabar?' heard how he missed the train, offered to run him there and then. Another nice English lady. Where was she? Left with car and chauffeur while Fielding found camp. Car couldn't get up—no, of course not—hundreds of people must go down to escort Miss Derek and show her the way. The elephant in person. . . .

'Aziz, can I have a drink?'

'Certainly not.' He flew to get one.

'Mr Fielding!' called Mrs Moore, from her patch of shade; they had not spoken yet, because his arrival had coincided with the torrent from the hill.

'Good morning again!' he cried, relieved to find all well.

'Mr Fielding, have you seen Miss Quested?'

'But I've only just arrived. Where is she?'

'I do not know.'

'Aziz! Where have you put Miss Quested to?'

Aziz, who was returning with a drink in his hand, had to think for a moment. His heart was full of new happiness. The picnic, after a nasty shock or two, had developed into something beyond his dreams, for Fielding had not only come, but brought an uninvited guest. 'Oh, she's all right,' he said; 'she went down to see Miss Derek. Well, here's luck! Chin-chin!'

'Here's luck, but chin-chin I do refuse,' laughed Fielding, who detested the phrase. 'Here's to India!'

'Here's luck, and here's to England!'

Miss Derek's chauffeur stopped the cavalcade which was starting to escort his mistress up, and informed it that she had gone back with the other young lady to Chandrapore; she had sent him to say so. She was driving herself. 'Oh yes, that's quite likely,' said Aziz. 'I knew they'd gone for a spin.' 'Chandrapore? The man's made a mistake,' Fielding exclaimed. 'Oh no, why?' He was disappointed, but made light of it; no doubt the two young ladies were great friends. He would prefer to give breakfast to all four; still, guests must do as they wish, or they become prisoners. He went away cheerfully to inspect the porridge and the ice.

'What's happened?' asked Fielding, who felt at once that something had gone queer. All the way out Miss Derek had chattered about the picnic, called it an unexpected treat, and said that she preferred Indians who didn't invite her to their entertainments to those who did it. Mrs Moore sat swinging her foot, and appeared sulky and stupid. She said: 'Miss Derek is most unsatisfactory and restless, always in a hurry, always wanting something new; she will do anything in the world except go back to the Indian lady who pays her.'

Fielding, who didn't dislike Miss Derek, replied: 'She wasn't in a hurry when I left her. There was no question of returning to Chandrapore. It looks to me as if Miss Quested's in the hurry.'

'Adela?—she's never been in a hurry in her life,' said the old lady sharply.

'I say it'll prove to be Miss Quested's wish, in fact I know it is,' persisted the schoolmaster. He was annoyed—chiefly with himself. He had begun by missing a train—a sin he was never guilty of—and now that he did arrive it was to upset Aziz' arrangements for the second time. He wanted someone to share the blame, and frowned at Mrs Moore rather magisterially. 'Aziz is a charming fellow,' he announced.

'I know,' she answered, with a yawn.

'He has taken endless trouble to make a success of our picnic.'

They knew one another very little, and felt rather awkward at being drawn together by an Indian. The racial problem can take subtle forms. In their case it had induced a sort of jealousy, a mutual suspicion. He tried to goad her enthusiasm; she scarcely spoke. Aziz fetched them to breakfast.

'It is quite natural about Miss Quested,' he remarked, for he had been working the incident a little in his mind, to get rid of its roughnesses. 'We were having an interesting talk with our guide, then the car was seen, so she decided to go down to her friend.' Incurably inaccurate, he already thought that this was what had occurred. He was inaccurate because he was sensitive. He did not like to remember Miss Quested's, remark about polygamy, because it was unworthy of a guest, so he put it from his mind, and with it the knowledge that he had bolted into a cave to get away from her. He was inaccurate because he desired to honour her, and—facts being entangled—he had to arrange them in her vicinity, as one tidies the ground after extracting a weed. Before breakfast was over, he had told a good many lies. 'She ran to her friend, I to mine,' he went on, smiling. 'And now I am with my friends and they are with me and each other, which is happiness.'

Loving them both, he expected them to love each other. They didn't want to. Fielding thought with hostility, 'I knew these women would make trouble,' and Mrs Moore thought, 'This man, having missed the train, tries to blame us'; but her thoughts were feeble; since her faintness in the cave she was sunk in apathy and cynicism. The wonderful India of her opening weeks, with its cool nights and acceptable hints of infinity, had vanished.

Fielding ran up to see one cave. He wasn't impressed. Then they got on the elephant and the picnic began to unwind out of the corridor and escaped under the precipice towards the railway station, pursued by stabs of hot air. They came to the place where he had quitted the car. A disagreeable thought now struck him, and he said: 'Aziz, exactly where and how did you leave Miss Quested?'

'Up there.' He indicated the Kawa Dol cheerfully.

'But how——' A gully, or rather a crease, showed among the rocks at this place; it was scurfy with cactuses. 'I suppose the guide helped her.'

'Oh, rather, most helpful.'

'Is there a path off the top?'

'Millions of paths, my dear fellow.'

Fielding could see nothing but the crease. Everywhere else the glaring granite plunged into the earth.

'But you saw them get down safe?'

'Yes, yes, she and Miss Derek, and go off in the car.'

'Then the guide came back to you?'

'Exactly. Got a cigarette?'

'I hope she wasn't ill,' pursued the Englishman. The crease continued as a nullah across the plain, the water draining off this way towards the Ganges.

'She would have wanted me, if she was ill, to attend her.'

'Yes, that sounds sense.'

'I see you're worrying, let's talk of other things,' he said kindly. 'Miss Quested was always to do what she wished, it was our arrangement. I see you are worrying on my account, but really I don't mind, I never notice trifles.'

'I do worry on your account. I consider they have been impolite!' said Fielding, lowering his voice. 'She had no right to dash away from your party, and Miss Derek had no right to abet her.'

So touchy as a rule, Aziz was unassailable. The wings that uplifted him did not falter, because he was a Mogul emperor who had done his duty. Perched on his elephant, he watched the Marabar Hills recede, and saw again, as provinces of his kingdom, the grim untidy plain, the frantic and feeble movements of the buckets, the white shrines, the shallow graves, the suave sky, the snake that looked like a tree. He had given his guests as good a time as he could, and if they came late or left early that was not his affair. Mrs Moore slept, swaying against the rods of the howdah, Mohammed Latif embraced her with efficiency and respect, and by his own side sat Fielding, whom he began to think of as 'Cyril.'

'Aziz, have you figured out what this picnic will cost you?'

'Sh! my dear chap, don't mention that part. Hundreds and hundreds of rupees. The completed account will be too awful; my friends' servants have robbed me right and left, and as for an elephant, she apparently eats gold. I can trust you not to repeat this. And M.L.–please employ initials, he listens—is far the worst of all.'

'I told you he's no good.'

'He is plenty of good for himself; his dishonesty will ruin me.'

'Aziz, how monstrous!'

'I am delighted with him really, he has made my guests comfortable; besides, it is my duty to employ him, he is my cousin. If money goes, money comes. If money stays, death comes. Did you ever hear that useful Urdu proverb? Probably not, for I have just invented it.'

'My proverbs are: A penny saved is a penny earned; A stitch in time saves nine; Look before you leap; and the British Empire rests on them. You will never kick us out, you know, until you cease employing M.L.'s and such.'

'Oh, kick you out? Why should I trouble over that dirty job? Leave it to the politicians. . . . No, when I was a student I got excited over your damned countrymen, certainly; but if they'll let me get on with my profession and not be too rude to me officially, I really don't ask for more.'

'But you do; you take them to a picnic.'

'This picnic is nothing to do with English or Indian; it is an expedition of friends.'

So the cavalcade ended, partly pleasant, partly not; the Brahman cook was picked up, the train arrived, pushing its burning throat over the plain, and the twentieth century took over from the sixteenth. Mrs Moore entered her carriage, the three men went to theirs, adjusted the shutters, turned on the electric fan and tried to get some sleep. In the twilight, all resembled corpses, and the train itself seemed dead though it moved—a coffin from the scientific north which troubled the scenery four times a day. As it left the Marabars, their nasty little cosmos disappeared, and gave place to the Marabars seen from a distance, finite and rather romantic. The train halted once under a pump, to drench the stock of coal in its tender. Then it caught sight of the main line in the distance, took courage, and bumped forward, rounded the civil station, surmounted the level-crossing (the rails were scorching now), and clanked to a standstill. Chandrapore, Chandrapore! The expedition was over.

And as it ended, as they sat up in the gloom and prepared to enter ordinary life, suddenly the long drawn strangeness of the morning snapped. Mr Haq, the Inspector of Police, flung open the door of their carriage and said in shrill tones: 'Dr Aziz, it is my highly painful duty to arrest you.'

'Hullo, some mistake,' said Fielding, at once taking charge of the situation.

'Sir, they are my instructions. I know nothing.'

'On what charge do you arrest him?'

'I am under instructions not to say.'

'Don't answer me like that. Produce your warrant.'

'Sir, excuse me, no warrant is required under these particular circumstances. Refer to Mr McBryde.'

'Very well, so we will. Come along, Aziz, old man; nothing to fuss about, some blunder.'

'Dr Aziz, will you kindly come?—a closed conveyance stands in readiness.'

The young man sobbed—his first sound—and tried to escape out of the opposite door on to the line.

'That will compel me to use force,' Mr Haq wailed.

'Oh, for God's sake—' cried Fielding, his own nerves breaking under the contagion, and pulled him back before a scandal started, and shook him like a baby. A second later, and he would have been out, whistles blowing, a man-hunt. . . . 'Dear fellow, we're coming to McBryde together, and enquire what's gone wrong—he's a decent fellow, it's all unintentional . . . he'll apologize. Never, never act the criminal.'

'My children and my name!' he gasped, his wings broken.

'Nothing of the sort. Put your hat straight and take my arm. I'll see you through.'

'Ah, thank God, he comes,' the Inspector exclaimed.

They emerged into the midday heat, arm in arm. The station was seething. Passengers and porters rushed out of every recess, many Government servants, more police. Ronny escorted Mrs Moore. Mohammed Latif began wailing. And before they could make their way through the chaos, Fielding was called off by the authoritative tones of Mr Turton, and Aziz went on to prison alone.

Chapter Seventeen

The Collector had watched the arrest from the interior of the waiting-room, and throwing open its perforated doors of zinc, he was now revealed like a god in a shrine. When Fielding entered the doors clapped to, and were guarded by a servant, while a punkah, to mark the importance of the moment, flapped dirty petticoats over their heads. The Collector could not speak at first. His face was white, fanatical, and rather beautiful—the expression that all English faces were to wear at Chandrapore for many days. Always brave and unselfish, he was now fused by some white and generous heat; he would have killed himself, obviously, if he had thought it right to do so. He spoke at last. 'The worst thing in my whole career has happened,' he said. 'Miss Quested has been insulted in one of the Marabar caves.'

'Oh no, oh no, no,' gasped the other, feeling sickish.

'She escaped—by God's grace.'

'Oh no, no, but not Aziz . . . not Aziz . . .'

He nodded.

'Absolutely impossible, grotesque.'

'I called you to preserve you from the odium that would attach to you if you were seen accompanying him to the Police Station,' said Turton, paying no attention to his protest, indeed scarcely hearing it.

He repeated 'Oh no,' like a fool. He couldn't frame other words. He felt that a mass of madness had arisen and tried to overwhelm them all; it had to be shoved back into its pit somehow, and he didn't know how to do it, because he did not understand madness: he had always gone about sensibly and quietly until a difficulty came right. 'Who lodges this infamous charge?' he asked, pulling himself together.

'Miss Derek and–the victim herself. . . .' He nearly broke down, unable to repeat the girl's name.

'Miss Quested herself definitely accuses him of—'

He nodded and turned his face away.

'Then she's mad.'

'I cannot pass that last remark,' said the Collector, waking up to the knowledge that they differed, and trembling with fury. 'You will withdraw it instantly. It is the type of remark you have permitted yourself to make ever since you came to Chandrapore.'

'I'm excessively sorry, sir; I certainly withdraw it unconditionally.' For the man was half mad himself.

'Pray, Mr Fielding, what induced you to speak to me in such a tone?'

'The news gave me a very great shock, so I must ask you to forgive me. I cannot believe that Dr Aziz is guilty.'

He slammed his hand on the table. 'That–that is a repetition of your insult in an aggravated form.'

'If I may venture to say so, no,' said Fielding, also going white, but sticking to his point. 'I make no reflection on the good faith of the two ladies, but the charge they are bringing against Aziz rests upon some mistake, and five minutes will clear it up. The man's manner is perfectly natural; besides, I know him to be incapable of infamy.'

'It does indeed rest upon a mistake,' came the thin, biting voice of the other. 'It does indeed. I have had twenty-five years' experience of this country'–he paused, and 'twenty-five years' seemed to fill the waiting-room with their staleness and ungenerosity–'and during those twenty-five years I have never known anything but disaster result when English people and Indians attempt to be intimate socially. Intercourse, yes. Courtesy, by all means. Intimacy–never, never. The whole weight of my authority is against it. I have been in charge at Chandrapore for six years, and if everything has gone smoothly, if there has been mutual respect and esteem, it is because both peoples kept to this simple rule. New-comers set our traditions aside, and in an instant what you see happens, the work of years is undone and the good name of my District ruined for a generation. I–I–can't see the end of this day's work, Mr Fielding. You, who are imbued with modern ideas–no doubt you can. I wish I had never lived to see its beginning, I know that. It is the end of me. That a lady, that a young lady engaged to my most valued subordinate–that she–an English girl fresh from England–that I should have lived—'

Involved in his own emotions, he broke down. What he had said was both dignified and pathetic, but had it anything to do with Aziz? Nothing at all, if Fielding was right. It is impossible to regard a tragedy from two points of view, and whereas Turton had decided to avenge the girl, he hoped to save the man. He wanted to get away and talk to McBryde, who had always been friendly to him, was on the whole sensible, and could, anyhow, be trusted to keep cool.

'I came down particularly on your account–while poor Heaslop got his mother away. I regarded it as the most friendly thing I could do. I meant to tell you that there will be an informal meeting at the club this evening to discuss the situation, but I am doubtful whether you will care to come. Your visits there are always infrequent.'

'I shall certainly come, sir, and I am most grateful to you for all the trouble you have taken over me. May I venture to ask–where Miss Quested is.'

He replied with a gesture; she was ill.

'Worse and worse, appalling,' he said feelingly.

But the Collector looked at him sternly, because he was keeping his head. He had not gone mad at the phrase 'an English girl fresh from England,' he had not rallied to the banner of race. He was still after facts, though the herd had decided on emotion. Nothing enrages Anglo-India more than the lantern of reason if it is exhibited for one moment after its extinction is decreed. All over Chandrapore that day the Europeans were putting aside their normal personalities and sinking themselves in their community. Pity, wrath, heroism, filled them, but the power of putting two and two together was annihilated.

Terminating the interview, the Collector walked on to the platform. The confusion there was revolting. A chuprassi of Ronny's had been told to bring up some trifles belonging to the ladies, and was appropriating for himself various articles to which he had no right; he was a camp follower of the angry English. Mohammed Latif made no attempt to resist him. Hassan flung off his turban, and wept. All the comforts that had been provided so liberally were rolled about and wasted in the sun. The Collector took in the situation at a glance, and his sense of justice functioned though he was insane with rage. He spoke the necessary word, and the looting stopped. Then he drove off to his bungalow and gave rein to his passions again. When he saw the coolies asleep in the ditches or the shopkeepers rising to salute him on their little platforms, he said to himself: 'I know what you're like at last; you shall pay for this, you shall squeal.'

Chapter Eighteen

Mr McBryde, the District Superintendent of Police, was the most reflective and best educated of the Chandrapore officials. He had read and thought a good deal, and, owing to a somewhat unhappy marriage, had evolved a complete philosophy of life. There was much of the cynic about him, but nothing of the bully; he never lost his temper or grew rough, and he received Aziz with courtesy, was almost reassuring. 'I have to detain you until you get bail,' he said, 'but no doubt your friends will be applying for it, and of course they will be allowed to visit you, under regulations. I am given certain information, and have to act on it—I'm not your judge.' Aziz was led off weeping. Mr McBryde was shocked at his downfall, but no Indian ever surprised him, because he had a theory about climatic zones. The theory ran: 'All unfortunate natives are criminals at heart, for the simple reason that they live south of latitude 30. They are not to blame, they have not a dog's chance—we should be like them if we settled here.' Born at Karachi, he seemed to contradict his theory, and would sometimes admit as much with a sad, quiet smile.

'Another of them found out,' he thought, as he set to work to draft his statement to the Magistrate.

He was interrupted by the arrival of Fielding.

He imparted all he knew without reservations. Miss Derek had herself driven in the Mudkul car about an hour ago, she and Miss Quested both in a terrible state. They had gone straight to his bungalow where he happened to be, and there and then he had taken down the charge and arranged for the arrest at the railway station.

'What is the charge, precisely?'

'That he followed her into the cave and made insulting advances. She hit at him with her field-glasses: he pulled at them and the strap broke, and that is how she got away. When we searched him just now, they were in his pocket.'

'Oh no, oh no, no; it'll be cleared up in five minutes,' he cried again.

'Have a look at them.'

The strap had been newly broken, the eye-piece was jammed. The logic of evidence said 'Guilty.'

'Did she say any more?'

'There was an echo that appears to have frightened her. Did you go into those caves?'

'I saw one of them. There was an echo. Did it get on her nerves?'

'I couldn't worry her overmuch with questions. She'll have plenty to go through in the witness-box. They don't bear thinking about, these next weeks. I wish the Marabar Hills and all they contain were at the bottom of the sea. Evening after evening one saw them from the club, and they were just a harmless name. . . . Yes, we start already.' For a visiting card was brought; Vakil Mahmoud Ali, legal adviser to the prisoner, asked to be allowed to see him. McBryde sighed, gave permission, and continued: 'I heard some more from Miss Derek—she is an old friend of us both and talks freely; well—her account is that you went off to locate the camp, and almost at once she heard stones falling on the Kawa Dol and saw Miss Quested running straight down the face of a precipice. Well. She climbed up a sort of gully to her, and found her practically done for—her helmet off—'

'Was a guide not with her?' interrupted Fielding.

'No. She had got among some cactuses. Miss Derek saved her life coming just then—she was beginning to fling herself about. She helped her down to the car. Miss Quested couldn't stand the Indian driver, cried, "Keep him away"—and it was that that put our friend on the track of what had happened. They made straight for our bungalow, and are there now. That's the story as far as I know it yet. She sent the driver to join you. I think she behaved with great sense.'

'I suppose there's no possibility of my seeing Miss Quested?' he asked suddenly.

'I hardly think that would do. Surely.'

'I was afraid you'ld say that. I should very much like to.'

'She is in no state to see anyone. Besides, you don't know her well.'

'Hardly at all. . . . But you see I believe she's under some hideous delusion, and that that wretched boy is innocent.'

The policeman started in surprise, and a shadow passed over his face, for he could not bear his dispositions to be upset. 'I had no idea that was in your mind,' he said, and looked for support at the signed deposition, which lay before him.

'Those field-glasses upset me for a minute, but I've thought since: it's impossible that, having attempted to assault her, he would put her glasses into his pocket.'

'Quite possible, I'm afraid; when an Indian goes bad, he goes not only very bad, but very queer.'

'I don't follow.'

'How should you? When you think of crime you think of English crime. The psychology here is different. I dare say you'll tell me next that he was quite normal when he came down from the hill to greet you. No reason he should not be. Read any of the Mutiny records; which, rather than the Bhagavad Gita, should be your Bible in this country. Though I'm not sure that the one and the other are not closely connected. Am I not being beastly? But, you see, Fielding, as I've said to you once before, you're a schoolmaster, and consequently you come across these people at their best. That's what puts you wrong. They can be charming as boys. But I know them as they really are, after they have developed into men. Look at this, for instance.' He held up Aziz' pocket-case. 'I am going through the contents. They are not edifying. Here is a letter from a friend who apparently keeps a brothel.'

'I don't want to hear his private letters.'

'It'll have to be quoted in Court, as bearing on his morals. He was fixing up to see women at Calcutta.'

'Oh, that'll do, that'll do.'

McBryde stopped, naïvely puzzled. It was obvious to him that any two sahibs ought to pool all they knew about any Indian, and he could not think where the objection came in.

'I dare say you have the right to throw stones at a young man for doing that, but I haven't. I did the same at his age.'

So had the Superintendent of Police, but he considered that the conversation had taken a turn that was undesirable. He did not like Fielding's next remark either.

'Miss Quested really cannot be seen? You do know that for a certainty?'

'You have never explained to me what's in your mind here. Why on earth do you want to see her?'

'On the off chance of her recanting before you send in that report and he's committed for trial, and the whole thing goes to blazes. Old man, don't argue about this, but do of your goodness just ring up your wife or Miss Derek and enquire. It'll cost you nothing.'

'It's no use ringing up them,' he replied, stretching out for the telephone. 'Callendar settles a question like that, of course. You haven't grasped that she's seriously ill.'

'He's sure to refuse, it's all he exists for,' said the other desperately.

The expected answer came back: the Major would not hear of the patient being troubled.

'I only wanted to ask her whether she is certain, dead certain, that it was Aziz who followed her into the cave.'

'Possibly my wife might ask her that much.'

'But *I* wanted to ask her. I want someone who believes in him to ask her.'

'What difference does that make?'

'She is among people who disbelieve in Indians.'

'Well, she tells her own story, doesn't she?'

'I know, but she tells it to you.'

McBryde raised his eyebrows, murmuring: 'A bit too finespun. Anyhow, Callendar won't hear of you seeing her. I'm sorry to say he gave a bad account just now. He says that she is by no means out of danger.'

They were silent. Another card was brought into the office–Hamidullah's. The opposite army was gathering.

'I must put this report through now, Fielding.'

'I wish you wouldn't.'

'How can I not?'

'I feel that things are rather unsatisfactory as well as most disastrous. We are heading for a most awful smash. I can see your prisoner, I suppose.'

He hesitated. 'His own people seem in touch with him all right.'

'Well, when he's done with them.'

'I wouldn't keep you waiting; good heavens, you take precedence of any Indian visitor, of course. I meant what's the good. Why mix yourself up with pitch?'

'I say he's innocent—'

'Innocence or guilt, why mix yourself up? What's the good?'

'Oh, good, good,' he cried, feeling that every earth was being stopped. 'One's got to breathe occasionally, at least I have. I mayn't see her, and now I mayn't see him. I promised him to come up here with him to you, but Turton called me off before I could get two steps.'

'Sort of all-white thing our Collector would do,' he muttered sentimentally. And trying not to sound patronizing, he stretched his hand over the table, and said: 'We shall all have to hang together, old man, I'm afraid. I'm your junior in years, I know, but very much your senior in service; you don't happen to know this poisonous country as well as I do, and you must take it from me that the general situation is going to be nasty at Chandrapore during the next few weeks, very nasty indeed.'

'So I have just told you.'

'But at a time like this there's no room for–well–personal views. The man who doesn't toe the line is lost.'

'I see what you mean.'

'No, you don't see entirely. He not only loses himself, he weakens his friends. If you leave the line, you leave a gap in the line. These jackals'–he pointed at the lawyers' cards–'are looking with all their eyes for a gap.'

'Can I visit Aziz?' was his answer.

'No.' Now that he knew of Turton's attitude, the policeman had no doubts. 'You may see him on a magistrate's order, but on my own responsibility I don't feel justified. It might lead to more complications.'

He paused, reflecting that if he had been either ten years younger or ten years longer in India, he would have responded to McBryde's appeal. The bit between his teeth, he then said, 'To whom do I apply for an order?'

'City Magistrate.'

'That sounds comfortable!'

'Yes, one can't very well worry poor Heaslop.'

More 'evidence' appeared at this moment–the tabledrawer from Aziz' bungalow, borne with triumph in a corporal's arms.

'Photographs of women. Ah!'

'That's his wife,' said Fielding, wincing.

'How do you know that?'

'He told me.'

McBryde gave a faint, incredulous smile, and started rummaging in the drawer. His face became inquisitive and slightly bestial. 'Wife indeed, I know those wives!' he was thinking. Aloud he said: 'Well, you must trot off now, old man, and the Lord help us, the Lord help us all. . . .'

As if his prayer had been heard, there was a sudden rackety-dacket on a temple bell.

Chapter Nineteen

Hamidullah was the next stage. He was waiting outside the Superintendent's office, and sprang up respectfully when he saw Fielding. To the English-man's passionate 'It's all a mistake,' he answered, 'Ah, ah, has some evidence come?'

'It will come,' said Fielding, holding his hand.

'Ah, yes, Mr Fielding; but when once an Indian has been arrested, we do not know where it will stop.' His manner was deferential. 'You are very good to greet me in this public fashion, I appreciate it; but, Mr Fielding, nothing convinces a magistrate except evidence. Did Mr McBryde make any remark when my card came in? Do you think my application annoyed him, will prejudice him against my friend at all? If so, I will gladly retire.'

'He's not annoyed, and if he was, what does it matter?'

'Ah, it's all very well for you to speak like that, but we have to live in this country.'

The leading barrister of Chandrapore, with the dignified manner and Cambridge degree, had been rattled. He too loved Aziz, and knew he was calumniated; but faith did not rule his heart, and he prated of 'policy' and 'evidence' in a way that saddened the Englishman. Fielding, too, had his anxieties—he didn't like the field-glasses or the discrepancy over the guide—but he relegated them to the edge of his mind, and forbade them to infect its core. Aziz *was* innocent, and all action must be based on that, and the people who said he was guilty were wrong, and it was hopeless to try to propitiate them. At the moment when he was throwing in his lot with Indians, he realized the profundity of the gulf that divided him from them. They always do something disappointing. Aziz had tried to run away from the police, Mohammed Latif had not checked the pilfering. And now Hamidullah!—instead of raging and denouncing, he temporized. Are Indians cowards? No, but they are bad starters and occasionally jib. Fear is everywhere; the British Raj rests on it; the respect and courtesy Fielding himself enjoyed were unconscious acts of propitiation. He told Hamidullah to cheer up, all would end well; and Hamidullah did cheer up, and became pugnacious and sensible. McBryde's remark, 'If you leave the line, you leave a gap in the line,' was being illustrated.

'First and foremost, the question of bail . . .'

Application must be made this afternoon. Fielding wanted to stand surety. Hamidullah thought the Nawab Bahadur should be approached.

'Why drag in him, though?'

To drag in everyone was precisely the barrister's aim. He then suggested that the lawyer in charge of the case would be a Hindu; the defence would then make a wider appeal. He mentioned one or two names—men from a distance who would not be intimidated by local conditions—and said he should prefer Amritrao, a Calcutta barrister, who had a high reputation professionally and personally, but who was notoriously anti-British.

Fielding demurred; this seemed to him going to the other extreme. Aziz must be cleared, but with a minimum of racial hatred. Amritrao was loathed at the club. His retention would be regarded as a political challenge.

'Oh no, we must hit with all our strength. When I saw my friend's private papers carried in just now in the arms of a dirty policeman, I said to myself, "Amritrao is the man to clear up this." '

There was a lugubrious pause. The temple bell continued to jangle harshly. The interminable and disastrous day had scarcely reached its afternoon. Continuing their work, the wheels of Dominion now propelled a messenger on a horse from the Superintendent to the Magistrate with an official report of arrest. 'Don't complicate, let the cards play themselves' entreated Fielding, as he watched the man disappear into dust. 'We're bound to win, there's nothing else we can do. She will never be able to substantiate the charge.'

This comforted Hamidullah, who remarked with complete sincerity, 'At a crisis, the English are really unequalled.'

'Good-bye, then, my dear Hamidullah (we must drop the 'Mr' now). Give Aziz my love when you see him, and tell him to keep calm, calm, calm. I shall go back to the College now. If you want me, ring me up; if you don't, don't, for I shall be very busy.'

'Good-bye, my dear Fielding, and you actually are on our side against your own people?'

'Yes. Definitely.'

He regretted taking sides. To slink through India unlabelled was his aim. Henceforward he would be called 'anti-British,' 'seditious'–terms that bored him, and diminished his utility. He foresaw that besides being a tragedy, there would be a muddle; already he saw several tiresome little knots, and each time his eye returned to them, they were larger. Born in freedom, he was not afraid of muddle, but he recognized its existence.

This section of the day concluded in a queer vague talk with Professor Godbole. The interminable affair of the Russell's Viper was again in question. Some weeks before, one of the masters at the College, an unpopular Parsi, had found a Russell's Viper nosing round his class-room. Perhaps it had crawled in of itself, but perhaps it had not, and the staff still continued to interview their Principal about it, and to take up his time with their theories. The reptile is so poisonous that he did not like to cut them short, and this they knew. Thus when his mind was bursting with other troubles and he was debating whether he should compose a letter of appeal to Miss Quested, he was obliged to listen to a speech which lacked both basis and conclusion, and floated through air. At the end of it Godbole said, 'May I now take my leave?'–always an indication that he had not come to his point yet. 'Now I take my leave, I must tell you how glad I am to hear that after all you succeeded in reaching the Marabar. I feared my unpunctuality had prevented you, but you went (a far pleasanter method) in Miss Derek's car. I hope the expedition was a successful one.'

'The news has not reached you yet, I can see.'

'Oh yes.'

'No; there has been a terrible catastrophe about Aziz.'

'Oh yes. That is all round the College.'

'Well, the expedition where that occurs can scarcely be called a successful one,' said Fielding, with an amazed stare.

'I cannot say. I was not present.'

He stared again–a most useless operation, for no eye could see what lay at the bottom of the Brahman's mind, and yet he had a mind and a heart too, and all his friends trusted him, without knowing why. 'I am most frightfully cut up,' he said.

'So I saw at once on entering your office. I must not detain you, but I have a small private difficulty on which I want your help; I am leaving your service shortly, as you know.'

'Yes, alas!'

'And am returning to my birthplace in Central India to take charge of education there. I want to start a High School there on sound English lines, that shall be as like Government College as possible.'

'Well?' he sighed, trying to take an interest.

'At present there is only vernacular education at Mau. I shall feel it my duty to change all that. I shall advise His Highness to sanction at least a High School in the Capital, and if possible another in each pargana.'

Fielding sunk his head on his arms; really, Indians were sometimes unbearable.

'The point—the point on which I desire your help is this: what name should be given to the school?'

'A name? A name for a school?' he said, feeling sickish suddenly, as he had done in the waiting-room.

'Yes, a name, a suitable title, by which it can be called, by which it may be generally known.'

'Really—I have no names for schools in my head. I can think of nothing but our poor Aziz. Have you grasped that at the present moment he is in prison?'

'Oh yes. Oh no, I do not expect an answer to my question now. I only meant that when you are at leisure, you might think the matter over, and suggest two or three alternative titles for schools. I had thought of the 'Mr Fielding High School,' but failing that, the 'King-Emperor George the Fifth.''

'Godbole!'

The old fellow put his hands together, and looked sly and charming.

'Is Aziz innocent or guilty?'

'That is for the Court to decide. The verdict will be in strict accordance with the evidence, I make no doubt.'

'Yes, yes, but your personal opinion. Here's a man we both like, generally esteemed; he lives here quietly doing his work. Well, what's one to make of it? Would he or would he not do such a thing?'

'Ah, that is rather a different question from your previous one, and also more difficult: I mean difficult in our philosophy. Dr Aziz is a most worthy young man, I have a great regard for him; but I think you are asking me whether the individual can commit good actions or evil actions, and that is rather difficult for us.' He spoke without emotion and in short tripping syllables.

'I ask you: did he do it or not? Is that plain? I know he didn't, and from that I start. I mean to get at the true explanation in a couple of days. My last notion is that it's the guide who went round with them. Malice on Miss Quested's part—it couldn't be that, though Hamidullah thinks so. She has certainly had some appalling experience. But you tell me, oh no—because good and evil are the same.'

'No, not exactly, please, according to our philosophy. Because nothing can be performed in isolation. All perform a good action, when one is performed, and when an evil action is performed, all perform it. To illustrate my meaning, let me take the case in point as an example.

'I am informed that an evil action was performed in the Marabar Hills, and that a highly esteemed English lady is now seriously ill in consequence. My answer to that is this: that action was performed by Dr Aziz.' He stopped and sucked in his thin cheeks. 'It was performed by the guide.' He stopped again. 'It was performed by you.' Now he had an air of daring and of coyness. 'It was performed by me.' He looked shyly down the sleeve of his own coat. 'And by my students. It was even performed by the lady herself. When evil occurs, it expresses the whole of the universe. Similarly when good occurs.'

'And similarly when suffering occurs, and so on and so forth, and everything is anything and nothing something,' he muttered in his irritation, for he needed the solid ground.

'Excuse me, you are now again changing the basis of our discussion. We were discussing good and evil. Suffering is merely a matter for the individual. If a young lady has sunstroke, that is a matter of no significance to the universe. Oh no, not at all. Oh no, not the least. It is an isolated matter, it only concerns herself. If she thought her head did not ache, she would not be ill, and that would end it. But it is far otherwise in the case of good and evil. They are not what we think them, they are what they are, and each of us has contributed to both.'

'You're preaching that evil and good are the same.'

'Oh no, excuse me once again. Good and evil are different, as their names imply. But, in my own humble opinion, they are both of them aspects of my Lord. He is present in the one, absent in the other, and the difference between presence and absence is great, as great as my feeble mind can grasp. Yet absence implies presence, absence is not non-existence, and we are therefore entitled to repeat, "Come, come, come, come."' And in the same breath, as if to cancel any beauty his words might have contained, he added, 'But did you have time to visit any of the interesting Marabar antiquities?'

Fielding was silent, trying to meditate and rest his brain.

'Did you not even see the tank by the usual camping ground?' he nagged.

'Yes, yes,' he answered distractedly, wandering over half a dozen things at once.

'That is good, then you saw the Tank of the Dagger.' And he related a legend which might have been acceptable if he had told it at the tea-party a fortnight ago. It concerned a Hindu Rajah who had slain his own sister's son, and the dagger with which he performed the deed remained clamped to his hand until in the course of years he came to the Marabar Hills, where he was thirsty and wanted to drink but saw a thirsty cow and ordered the water to be offered to her first, which, when done, 'dagger fell from his hand, and to commemorate miracle he built Tank.' Professor Godbole's conversations frequently culminated in a cow. Fielding received this one in gloomy silence.

In the afternnoon he obtained a permit and saw Aziz, but found him unapproachable through misery. 'You deserted me,' was the only coherent remark. He went away to write his letter to Miss Quested. Even if it reached her, it would do no good, and probably the McBrydes would withhold it. Miss Quested did pull him up short. She was such a dry, sensible girl, and quite without malice: the last person in Chandrapore wrongfully to accuse an Indian.

Chapter Twenty

Although Miss Quested had not made herself popular with the English, she brought out all that was fine in their character. For a few hours an exalted emotion gushed forth, which the women felt even more keenly than the men, if not for so long. 'What can we do for our sister?' was the only thought of Mesdames Callendar and Lesley, as they drove through the pelting heat to enquire. Mrs Turton was the only visitor admitted to the sick-room. She came out ennobled by an unselfish sorrow. 'She is my own darling girl,' were the words she spoke, and then, remembering that she had called her 'not pukka' and resented her engagement to young Heaslop, she began to cry. No one had ever seen the Collector's wife cry. Capable of tears—yes, but always reserving them for some adequate occasion, and now it had come. Ah, why had they not all been kinder to the stranger, more patient, given her not only hospitality but their hearts? The tender core of the heart that is so seldom used—they employed it for a little, under the stimulus of remorse. If all is over (as Major Callendar implied), well, all is over, and nothing can be done, but they retained some responsibility in her grievous wrong that they couldn't define. If she wasn't one of them, they ought to have made her one, and they could never do that now, she had passed beyond their invitation. 'Why don't one think more of other people?' sighed pleasure-loving Miss Derek. These regrets only lasted in their pure form for a few hours. Before sunset, other considerations adulterated them, and the sense of guilt (so strangely connected with our first sight of any suffering) had begun to wear away.

People drove into the club with studious calm—the jog-trot of country gentlefolk between green hedgerows, for the natives must not suspect that they were agitated. They exchanged the usual drinks, but everything tasted different, and then they looked out at the palisade of cactuses stabbing the purple throat of the sky; they realized that they were thousands of miles from any scenery that they understood. The club was fuller than usual, and several parents had brought their children into the rooms reserved for adults, which gave the air of the Residency at Lucknow. One young mother—a brainless but most beautiful girl—sat on a low ottoman in the smoking-room with her baby in her arms; her husband was away in the district, and she dared not return to her bungalow in case the 'niggers attacked.' The wife of a small railway official, she was generally snubbed; but this evening, with her abundant figure and masses of corn-gold hair, she symbolized all that is worth fighting and dying for; more permanent a symbol, perhaps, than poor Adela. 'Don't worry, Mrs Blakiston, those drums are only Mohurram,' the men would tell her. 'Then they've started,' she moaned, clasping the infant and rather wishing he would not blow bubbles down his chin at such a moment as this. 'No, of course not, and anyhow, they're not coming to the club.' 'And they're not coming to the Burra Sahib's bungalow either, my dear, and that's where you and your baby'll sleep tonight,' answered Mrs Turton, towering by her side like Pallas Athene, and determining in the future not to be such a snob.

The Collector clapped his hands for silence. He was much calmer than when he had flown out at Fielding. He was indeed always calmer when he addressed several people than in a *tête-à-tête*. 'I want to talk specially to the ladies,' he said. 'Not the least cause for alarm. Keep cool, keep cool. Don't go out more than you can help, don't go into the city, don't talk before your servants. That's all.'

'Harry, is there any news from the city?' asked his wife, standing at some distance from him, and also assuming her public-safety voice. The rest were silent during the august colloquy.

'Everything absolutely normal.'

'I gathered as much. Those drums are merely Mohurram, of course.'

'Merely the preparations for it–the Procession is not till next week.'

'Quite so, not till Monday.'

'Mr McBryde's down there disguised as a Holy Man,' said Mrs Callendar.

'That's exactly the sort of thing that must not be said,' he remarked, pointing at her. 'Mrs Callendar, be more careful than that, please, in these times.'

'I . . . well, I . . .' She was not offended, his severity made her feel safe.

'Any more questions? Necessary questions.'

'Is the–where is he—' Mrs Lesley quavered.

'Jail. Bail has been refused.'

Fielding spoke next. He wanted to know whether there was an official bulletin about Miss Quested's health, or whether the grave reports were due to gossip. His question produced a bad effect, partly because he had pronounced her name; she, like Aziz, was always referred to by a periphrasis.

'I hope Callendar may be able to let us know how things are going before long.'

'I fail to see how that last question can be termed a necessary question,' said Mrs Turton.

'Will all ladies leave the smoking-room now, please?' he cried, clapping his hands again. 'And remember what I have said. We look to you to help us through a difficult time, and you can help us by behaving as if everything is normal. It is all I ask. Can I rely on you?'

'Yes, indeed, oh indeed,' they chorused out of peaked, anxious faces. They moved out, subdued yet elated, Mrs Blakiston in their midst like a sacred flame. His simple words had reminded them that they were an outpost of Empire. By the side of their compassionate love for Adela another sentiment sprang up which was to strangle it in the long run. Its first signs were prosaic and small. Mrs Turton made her loud, hard jokes at bridge, Mrs Lesley began to knit a comforter.

When the smoking-room was clear, the Collector sat on the edge of a table, so that he could dominate without formality. His mind whirled with contradictory impulses. He wanted to avenge Miss Quested and punish Fielding, while remaining scrupulously fair. He wanted to flog every native that he saw, but to do nothing that would lead to a riot or to the necessity for military intervention. The dread of having to call in the troops was vivid to him; soldiers put one thing straight, but leave a dozen others crooked, and they love to humiliate the civilian administration. One soldier was in the room this evening–a stray subaltern from a Gurkha regiment; he was a little drunk, and regarded his presence as providential. The Collector sighed. There seemed nothing for it but the old weary business of compromise and moderation. He longed for the good old days when an Englishman could satisfy his own honour and no questions asked afterwards. Poor young Heaslop had taken a step in this direction, by refusing bail, but the Collector couldn't feel this was wise of poor young Heaslop. Not only would the Nawab Bahadur and others be angry, but the Government of India itself also watches–and behind it is that caucus of cranks and cravens, the British Parliament. He had constantly to remind himself that, in the eyes of the law, Aziz was not yet guilty, and the effort fatigued him.

The others, less responsible, could behave naturally. They had started speaking of 'women and children'–that phrase that exempts the male from sanity when it has been repeated a few times. Each felt that all he loved best in the world was at stake, demanded revenge, and was filled with a not unpleasing glow, in which the chilly and half-known features of Miss Quested vanished, and were replaced by all that is sweetest and warmest in the private life. 'But it's the women and children,' they repeated, and the Collector knew he ought to stop them intoxicating themselves, but he hadn't the heart. 'They ought to be compelled to give hostages,' etc. Many of the said women and children were leaving for the Hill Station in a few days, and the suggestion was made that they should be packed off at once in a special train.

'*And* a jolly suggestion,' the subaltern cried. 'The army's got to come in sooner or later. (A special train was in his mind inseparable from troops.) This would never have happened if Barabas Hill was under military control. Station a bunch of Gurkhas at the entrance of the cave was all that was wanted.'

'Mrs Blakiston was saying if only there were a few Tommies,' remarked someone.

'English no good,' he cried, getting his loyalties mixed. 'Native troops for this country. Give me the sporting type of native, give me Gurkhas, give me Rajputs, give me Jats, give me the Punjabi, give me Sikhs, give me Marathas, Bhils, Afridis and Pathans, and really if it comes to that, I don't mind if you give me the scums of the bazaars. Properly led, mind. I'd lead them anywhere—'

The Collector nodded at him pleasantly, and said to his own people: 'Don't start carrying arms about. I want everything to go on precisely as usual, until there's cause for the contrary. Get the womenfolk off to the hills, but do it quietly, and for Heaven's sake no more talk of special trains. Never mind what you think or feel. Possibly I have feelings too. One isolated Indian has attempted–is charged with an attempted crime.' He flipped his forehead hard with his finger-nail, and they all realized that he felt as deeply as they did, and they loved him, and determined not to increase his difficulties. 'Act upon that fact until there are more facts,' he concluded. 'Assume every Indian is an angel.'

They murmured, 'Right you are, so we will. . . . Angels. . . . Exactly. . . .' From the subaltern: 'Exactly what I said. The native's all right if you get him alone. Lesley! Lesley! You remember the one I had a knock with on your Maidan last month. Well, he was all right. Any native who plays polo is all right. What you've got to stamp on is these educated classes, and, mind, I do know what I'm talking about this time.'

The smoking-room door opened, and let in a feminine buzz. Mrs Turton called out, 'She's better,' and from both sections of the community a sigh of joy and relief rose. The Civil Surgeon, who had brought the good news, came in. His cumbrous, pasty face looked ill-tempered. He surveyed the company, saw Fielding crouched below him on an ottoman, and said, 'H'm!' Everyone began pressing him for details. 'No one's out of danger in this country as long as they have a temperature,' was his answer. He appeared to resent his patient's recovery, and no one who knew the old Major and his ways was surprised at this.

'Squat down, Callendar; tell us all about it.'

'Take me some time to do that.'

'How's the old lady?'

'Temperature.'

'My wife heard she was sinking.'

'So she may be. I guarantee nothing. I really can't be plagued with questions, Lesley.'

'Sorry, old man.'

'Heaslop's just behind me.'

At the name of Heaslop a fine and beautiful expression was renewed on every face. Miss Quested was only a victim, but young Heaslop was a martyr; he was the recipient of all the evil intended against them by the country they had tried to serve; he was bearing the sahib's cross. And they fretted because they could do nothing for him in return; they felt so craven sitting on softness and attending the course of the law.

'I wish to God I hadn't given my jewel of an assistant leave. I'ld cut my tongue out first. To feel I'm responsible, that's what hits me. To refuse, and then give in under pressure. That is what I did, my sons, that is what I did.'

Fielding took his pipe from his mouth and looked at it thoughtfully. Thinking him afraid, the other went on: 'I understood an Englishman was to accompany the expedition. That is why I gave in.'

'No one blames you, my dear Callendar,' said the Collector, looking down. 'We are all to blame in the sense that we ought to have seen the expedition was insufficiently guaranteed, and stopped it. I knew about it myself; we lent our car this morning to take the ladies to the station. We are all implicated in that sense, but not an atom of blame attaches to you personally.'

'I don't feel that. I wish I could. Responsibility is a very awful thing, and I've no use for the man who shirks it.' His eyes were directed on Fielding. Those who knew that Fielding had undertaken to accompany and missed the early train were sorry for him; it was what is to be expected when a man mixes himself up with natives; always ends in some indignity. The Collector, who knew more, kept silent, for the official in him still hoped that Fielding would toe the line. The conversation turned to women and children again, and under its cover Major Callendar got hold of the subaltern, and set him on to bait the schoolmaster. Pretending to be more drunk than he really was, he began to make semi-offensive remarks.

'Heard about Miss Quested's servant?' reinforced the Major.

'No, what about him?'

'Heaslop warned Miss Quested's servant last night never to lose sight of her. Prisoner got hold of this and managed to leave him behind. Bribed him. Heaslop has just found out the whole story, with names and sums—a well-known pimp to those people gave the money, Mohammed Latif by name. So much for the servant. What about the Englishman—our friend here? How did they get rid of him? Money again.'

Fielding rose to his feet, supported by murmurs and exclamations, for no one yet suspected his integrity.

'Oh, I'm being misunderstood, apologies,' said the Major offensively. 'I didn't mean they bribed Mr Fielding.'

'Then what do you mean?'

'They paid the other Indian to make you late—Godbole. He was saying his prayers. I know those prayers!'

'That's ridiculous . . .' He sat down again, trembling with rage; person after person was being dragged into the mud.

Having shot this bolt, the Major prepared the next. 'Heaslop also found out something from his mother. Aziz paid a herd of natives to suffocate her in a cave. That was the end of her, or would have been only she got out. Nicely planned, wasn't it? Neat. Then he could go on with the girl. He and she and a guide, provided by the same Mohammed Latif. Guide now can't be found. Pretty.' His voice broke into a roar. 'It's not the time for sitting down. It's the time for action. Call in the troops and clear the bazaars.'

The Major's outbursts were always discounted, but he made everyone uneasy on this occasion. The crime was even worse than they had supposed—the unspeakable limit of cynicism, untouched since 1857. Fielding forgot his anger on poor old Godbole's behalf, and became thoughtful; the evil was propagating in every direction, it seemed to have an existence of its own, apart from anything that was done or said by individuals, and he understood better why both Aziz and Hamidullah had been inclined to lie down and die. His adversary saw that he was in trouble, and now ventured to say, 'I suppose nothing that's said inside the club will go outside the club?' winking the while at Lesley.

'Why should it?' responded Lesley.

'Oh, nothing. I only heard a rumour that a certain member here present has been seeing the prisoner this afternoon. You can't run with the hare and hunt with the hounds, at least not in this country.'

'Does anyone here present want to?'

Fielding was determined not to be drawn again. He had something to say, but it should be at his own moment. The attack failed to mature, because the Collector did not support it. Attention shifted from him for a time. Then the buzz of women broke out again. The door had been opened by Ronny.

The young man looked exhausted and tragic, also gentler than usual. He always showed deference to his superiors, but now it came straight from his heart. He seemed to appeal for their protection in the insult that had befallen him, and they, in instinctive homage, rose to their feet. But every human act in the East is tainted with officialism, and while honouring him they condemned Aziz and India. Fielding realized this, and he remained seated. It was an ungracious, a caddish thing to do, perhaps an unsound thing to do, but he felt he had been passive long ennugh, and that he might be drawn into the wrong current if he did not make a stand. Ronny, who had not seen him, said in husky tones, 'Oh please—please all sit down, I only want to listen what has been decided.'

'Heaslop, I'm telling them I'm against any show of force,' said the Collector apologetically. 'I don't know whether you will feel as I do, but that is how I am situated. When the verdict is obtained, it will be another matter.'

'You are sure to know best; I have no experience, I can't tell.'

'How is your mother, old boy?'

'Better, thank you. I wish everyone would sit down.'

'Some have never got up,' the young soldier said.

'And the Major brings us an excellent report of Miss Quested,' Turton went on.

'I do, I do, I'm satisfied.'

'You thought badly of her earlier, did you not, Major? That's why I refused bail.'

Callendar laughed with friendly inwardness, and said, 'Heaslop, Heaslop, next time bail's wanted, ring up the old doctor before giving it; his shoulders are broad, and, speaking in the strictest confidence, don't take the old doctor's opinion too seriously. He's a blithering idiot, we can always leave it at that, but he'll do the little he can towards keeping in quod the—' He broke off with affected politeness. 'Oh, but he has one of his friends here.'

The subaltern called, 'Stand up, you swine.'

'Mr Fielding, what has prevented you from standing up?' said the Collector, entering the fray at last. It was the attack for which Fielding had waited, and to which he must reply.

'May I make a statement, sir?'

'Certainly.'

Seasoned and self-contained, devoid of the fervours of nationality or youth, the schoolmaster did what was for him a comparatively easy thing. He stood up and said, 'I believe Dr Aziz to be innocent.'

'You have a right to hold that opinion if you choose, but pray is that any reason why you should insult Mr Heaslop?'

'May I conclude my statement?'

'Certainly.'

'I am waiting for the verdict of the courts. If he is guilty I resign from my service, and leave India. I resign from the club now.'

'Hear, hear!' said voices, not entirely hostile, for they liked the fellow for speaking out.

'You have not answered my question. Why did you not stand when Mr Heaslop entered?'

'With all deference, sir, I am not here to answer questions, but to make a personal statement, and I have concluded it.'

'May I ask whether you have taken over charge of this District?'

Fielding moved towards the door.

'One moment, Mr Fielding. You are not to go yet, please. Before you leave the club, from which you do very well to resign, you will express some detestation of the crime, and you will apologize to Mr Heaslop.'

'Are you speaking to me officially, sir?'

The Collector, who never spoke otherwise, was so infuriated that he lost his head. He cried, 'Leave this room at once, and I deeply regret that I demeaned myself to meet you at the station. You have sunk to the level of your associates; you are weak, weak, that is what is wrong with you—'

'I want to leave the room, but cannot while this gentleman prevents me,' said Fielding lightly; the subaltern had got across his path.

'Let him go,' said Ronny, almost in tears.

It was the only appeal that could have saved the situation. Whatever Heaslop wished must be done. There was a slight scuffle at the door, from which Fielding was propelled, a little more quickly than is natural, into the room where the ladies were playing cards. 'Fancy if I'd fallen or got angry,' he thought. Of course he was a little angry. His peers had never offered him violence or called him weak before, besides Heaslop had heaped coals of fire on his head. He wished he had not picked the quarrel over poor suffering Heaslop, when there were cleaner issues at hand.

However, there it was, done, muddled through, and to cool himself and regain mental balance he went on to the upper verandah for a moment, where the first object he saw was the Marabar Hills. At this distance and hour they leapt into beauty; they were Monsalvat, Walhalla, the towers of a cathedral, peopled with saints and heroes, and covered with flowers. What miscreant lurked in them, presently to be detected by the activities of the law? Who was the guide, and had he been found yet? What was the 'echo' of which the girl complained? He did not know, but presently he would know. Great is information, and she shall prevail. It was the last moment of the light, and as he gazed at the Marabar Hills they seemed to move graciously towards him like a queen, and their charm became the sky's. At the moment they vanished they were everywhere, the cool benediction of the night descended, the stars sparkled, and the whole universe was a hill. Lovely, exquisite moment—but passing the Englishman with averted face and on swift wings. He experienced nothing himself; it was as if someone had told him there was such a moment, and he was obliged to believe. And he felt dubious and discontented suddenly, and wondered whether he was really and truly successful as a human being. After forty years' experience, he had learnt to manage his life and make the best of it on advanced European lines, had developed his personality, explored his limitations, controlled his passions—and he had done it all without becoming either pedantic or worldly. A creditable achievement, but as the moment passed, he felt he ought to have been working at something else the whole time,—he didn't know at what, never would know, never could know, and that was why he felt sad.

Chapter Twenty-one

Dismissing his regrets, as inappropriate to the matter in hand, he accomplished the last section of the day by riding off to his new allies. He was glad that he had broken with the club, for he would have picked up scraps of gossip there, and reported them down in the city, and he was glad to be denied this opportunity. He would miss his billiards, and occasional tennis, and cracks with McBryde, but really that was all, so light did he travel. At the entrance of the bazaars, a tiger made his horse shy—a youth dressed up as a tiger, the body striped brown and yellow, a mask over the face. Mohurram was working up. The city beat a good many drums, but seemed good-tempered. He was invited to inspect a small tazia—a flimsy and frivolous erection, more like a crinoline than the tomb of the grandson of the Prophet, done to death at Kerbela. Excited children were pasting coloured paper over its ribs. The rest of the evening he spent with the Nawab Bahadur, Hamidullah, Mahmoud Ali, and others of the confederacy. The campaign was also working up. A telegram had been sent to the famous Amritrao, and his acceptance received. Application for bail was to be renewed—it could not well be withheld now that Miss Quested was out of danger. The conference was serious and sensible, but marred by a group of itinerant musicians, who were allowed to play in the compound. Each held a large earthenware jar, containing pebbles, and jerked it up and down in time to a doleful chant. Distracted by the noise, he suggested their dismissal, but the Nawab Bahadur vetoed it; he said that musicians, who had walked many miles, might bring good luck.

Late at night, he had an inclination to tell Professor Godbole of the tactical and moral error he had made in being rude to Heaslop, and to hear what he would say. But the old fellow had gone to bed, and slipped off unmolested to his new job in a day or two: he always did possess the knack of slipping off.

Chapter Twenty-two

Adela lay for several days in the McBrydes' bungalow. She had been touched by the sun, also hundreds of cactus spines had to be picked out of her flesh. Hour after hour Miss Derek and Mrs McBryde examined her through magnifying glasses, always coming on fresh colonies, tiny hairs that might snap off and be drawn into the blood if they were neglected. She lay passive beneath their fingers, which developed the shock that had begun in the cave. Hitherto she had not much minded whether she was touched or not: her senses were abnormally inert and the only contact she anticipated was that of mind. Everything now was transferred to the surface of her body, which began to avenge itself, and feed unhealthily. People seemed very much alike, except that some would come close while others kept away. 'In space things touch, in time things part,' she repeated to herself while the thorns were being extracted–her brain so weak that she could not decide whether the phrase was a philosophy or a pun.

They were kind to her, indeed over-kind, the men too respectful, the women too sympathetic; whereas Mrs Moore, the only visitor she wanted, kept away. No one understood her trouble, or knew why she vibrated between hard commonsense and hysteria. She would begin a speech as if nothing particular had happened. 'I went into this detestable cave,' she would say dryly, 'and I remember scratching the wall with my finger-nail, to start the usual echo, and then as I was saying there was this shadow, or sort of shadow, down the entrance tunnel, bottling me up. It seemed like an age, but I suppose the whole thing can't have lasted thirty seconds really. I hit at him with the glasses, he pulled me round the cave by the strap, it broke, I escaped, that's all. He never actually touched me once. It all seems such nonsense.' Then her eyes would fill with tears. 'Naturally I'm upset, but I shall get over it.' And then she would break down entirely, and the women would feel she was one of themselves and cry too, and men in the next room murmur: 'Good God, good God!' No one realized that she thought tears vile, a degradation more subtle than anything endured in the Marabar, a negation of her advanced outlook and the natural honesty of her mind. Adela was always trying to 'think the incident out,' always reminding herself that no harm had been done. There was 'the shock,' but what is that? For a time her own logic would convince her, then she would hear the echo again, weep, declare she was unworthy of Ronny, and hope her assailant would get the maximum penalty. After one of these bouts, she longed to go out into the bazaars and ask pardon from everyone she met, for she felt in some vague way that she was leaving the world worse than she found it. She felt that it was her crime, until the intellect, reawakening, pointed out to her that she was inaccurate here, and set her again upon her sterile round.

If only she could have seen Mrs Moore! The old lady had not been well either, and was disinclined to come out, Ronny reported. And consequently the echo flourished, raging up and down like a nerve in the faculty of her hearing, and the noise in the cave, so unimportant intellectually, was prolonged over the surface of her life. She had struck the polished wall—for no reason—and before the comment had died away, he followed her, and the climax was the falling of her field-glasses. The sound had spouted after her when she escaped, and was going on still like a river that gradually floods the plain. Only Mrs Moore could drive it back to its source and seal the broken reservoir. Evil was loose . . . she could even hear it entering the lives of others. . . . And Adela spent days in this atmosphere of grief and depression. Her friends kept up their spirits by demanding holocausts of natives, but she was too worried and weak to do that.

When the cactus thorns had all been extracted, and her temperature fallen to normal, Ronny came to fetch her away. He was worn with indignation and suffering, and she wished she could comfort him; but intimacy seemed to caricature itself, and the more they spoke the more wretched and self-conscious they became. Practical talk was the least painful, and he and McBryde now told her one or two things which they had concealed from her during the crisis, by the doctor's orders. She learnt for the first time of the Mohurram troubles. There had nearly been a riot. The last day of the festival, the great procession left its official route, and tried to enter the civil station, and a telephone had been cut because it interrupted the advance of one of the larger paper towers. McBryde and his police had pulled the thing straight—a fine piece of work. They passed on to another and very painful subject: the trial. She would have to appear in court, identify the prisoner, and submit to cross-examination by an Indian lawyer.

'Can Mrs Moore be with me?' was all she said.

'Certainly, and I shall be there myself,' Ronny replied. 'The case won't come before me; they've objected to me on personal grounds. It will be at Chandrapore—we thought at one time it would be transferred elsewhere.'

'Miss Quested realizes what all that means, though,' said McBryde sadly. 'The case will come before Das.'

Das was Ronny's assistant—own brother to the Mrs Bhattacharya whose carriage had played them false last month. He was courteous and intelligent, and with the evidence before him could only come to one conclusion; but that he should be judge over an English girl had convulsed the station with wrath, and some of the women had sent a telegram about it to Lady Mellanby, the wife of the Lieutenant-Governor.

'I must come before someone.'

'That's—that's the way to face it. You have the pluck, Miss Quested.' He grew very bitter over the arrangements, and called them 'the fruits of democracy.' In the old days an Englishwoman would not have had to appear, nor would any Indian have dared to discuss her private affairs. She would have made her deposition, and judgment would have followed. He apologized to her for the condition of the country, with the result that she gave one of her sudden little shoots of tears. Ronny wandered miserably about the room while she cried, treading upon the flowers of the Kashmir carpet that so inevitably covered it or drumming on the brass Benares bowls. 'I do this less every day, I shall soon be quite well,' she said, blowing her nose and feeling hideous. 'What I need is something to do. That is why I keep on with this ridiculous crying.'

'It's not ridiculous, we think you wonderful,' said the policeman very sincerely. 'It only bothers us that we can't help you more. Your stopping here—at such a time—is the greatest honour this house—' He too was overcome with emotion. 'By the way, a letter came here for you while you were ill,' he continued. 'I opened it, which is a strange confession to make, Will you forgive me? The circumstances are peculiar. It is from Fielding.'

'Why should he write to me?'

'A most lamentable thing has happened. The defence got hold of him.'

'He's a crank, a crank,' said Ronny lightly.

'That's your way of putting it, but a man can be a crank without being a cad. Miss Quested had better know how be behaved to you. If you don't tell her, somebody else will.' He told her. 'He is now the mainstay of the defence, I needn't add. He is the one righteous Englishman in a horde of tyrants. He receives deputations from the bazaar, and they all chew betel nut and smear one another's hands with scent. It is not easy to enter into the mind of such a man. His students are on strike—out of enthusiasm for him they won't learn their lessons. If it weren't for Fielding one would never have had the Mohurram trouble. He has done a very grave disservice to the whole community. The letter lay here a day or two, waiting till you were well enough, then the situation got so grave that I decided to open it in case it was useful to us.'

'Is it?' she said feebly.

'Not at all. He only has the impertinence to suggest you have made a mistake.'

'Would that I had!' She glanced through the letter, which was careful and formal in its wording. 'Dr Aziz is innocent,' she read. Then her voice began to tremble again. 'But think of his behaviour to you, Ronny. When you had already to bear so much for my sake! It was shocking of him. My dear, how can I repay you? How can one repay when one has nothing to give? What is the use of personal relationships when everyone brings less and less to them? I feel we ought all to go back into the desert for centuries and try and get good. I want to begin at the beginning. All the things I thought I'd learnt are just a hindrance, they're not knowledge at all. I'm not fit for personal relationships. Well, let's go, let's go. Of course Mr Fielding's letter doesn't count; he can think and write what he likes, only he shouldn't have been rude to you when you had so much to bear. That's what matters. . . . I don't want your arm, I'm a magnificent walker, so don't touch me, please.'

Mrs McBryde wished her an affectionate good-bye—a woman with whom she had nothing in common and whose intimacy oppressed her. They would have to meet now, year after year, until one of their husbands was super-annuated. Truly Anglo-India had caught her with a vengeance, and perhaps it served her right for having tried to take up a line of her own. Humbled yet repelled, she gave thanks. 'Oh, we must help one another, we must take the rough with the smooth,' said Mrs McBryde. Miss Derek was there too, still making jokes about her comic Maharajah and Rani. Required as a witness at the trial, she had refused to send back the Mudkul car; they would be frightfully sick. Both Mrs McBryde and Miss Derek kissed her, and called her by her Christian name. Then Ronny drove her back. It was early in the morning, for the day, as the hot weather advanced, swelled like a monster at both ends, and left less and less room for the movements of mortals.

As they neared his bungalow, he said: 'Mother's looking forward to seeing you, but of course she's old, one mustn't forget that. Old people never take things as one expects, in my opinion.' He seemed warning her against approaching disappointment, but she took no notice. Her friendship with Mrs Moore was so deep and real that she felt sure it would last, whatever else happened. 'What can I do to make things easier for you? it's you who matter,' she sighed.

'Dear old girl to say so.'

'Dear old boy.' Then she cried: 'Ronny, she isn't ill too?'

He reassured her; Major Callendar was not dissatisfied.

'But you'll find her—irritable. We are an irritable family. Well, you'll see for yourself. No doubt my own nerves are out of order, and I expected more from mother when I came in from the office than she felt able to give. She is sure to make a special effort for you; still, I don't want your home-coming to be a disappointing one. Don't expect too much.'

The house came in sight. It was a replica of the bungalow she had left. Puffy, red, and curiously severe, Mrs Moore was revealed upon a sofa. She didn't get up when they entered, and the surprise of this roused Adela from her own troubles.

'Here you are both back,' was the only greeting.

Adela sat down and took her hand. It withdrew, and she felt that just as others repelled her, so did she repel Mrs Moore.

'Are you all right? You appeared all right when I left,' said Ronny, trying not to speak crossly, but he had instructed her to give the girl a pleasant welcome, and he could not but feel annoyed.

'I am all right,' she said heavily. 'As a matter of fact I have been looking at my return ticket. It is interchangeable, so I have a much larger choice of boats home than I thought.'

'We can go into that later, can't we?'

'Ralph and Stella may be wanting to know when I arrive.'

'There is plenty of time for all such plans. How do you think our Adela looks?'

'I am counting on you to help me through; it is such a blessing to be with you again, everyone else is a stranger,' said the girl rapidly.

But Mrs Moore showed no inclination to be helpful. A sort of resentment emanated from her. She seemed to say: 'Am I to be bothered for ever?' Her

Christian tenderness had gone, or had developed into a hardness, a just irritation against the human race; she had taken no interest at the arrest, asked scarcely any questions, and had refused to leave her bed on the awful last night of Mohurram, when an attack was expected on the bungalow.

'I know it's all nothing; I must be sensible, I do try—' Adela continued, working again towards tears. 'I shouldn't mind if it had happened anywhere else; at least I really don't know where it did happen.'

Ronny supposed that he understood what she meant: she could not identify or describe the particular cave, indeed almost refused to have her mind cleared up about it, and it was recognized that the defence would try to make capital out of this during the trial. He reassured her: the Marabar caves were notoriously like one another; indeed, in the future they were to be numbered in sequence with white paint.

'Yes, I mean that, at least not exactly; but there is this echo that I keep on hearing.'

'Oh, what of the echo?' asked Mrs Moore, paying attention to her for the first time.

'I can't get rid of it.'

'I don't suppose you ever will.'

Ronny had emphasized to his mother that Adela would arrive in a morbid state, yet she was being positively malicious.

'Mrs Moore, what is this echo?'

'Don't you know?'

'No—what is it? oh, do say! I felt you would be able to explain it . . . this will comfort me so. . . .'

'If you don't know, you don't know, I can't tell you.'

'I think you're rather unkind not to say.'

'Say, say, say,' said the old lady bitterly. 'As if anything can be said! I have spent my life in saying or in listening to sayings; I have listened too much. It is time I was left in peace. Not to die,' she added sourly. 'No doubt you expect me to die, but when I have seen you and Ronny married, and seen the other two and whether they want to be married—I'll retire then into a cave of my own.' She smiled, to bring down her remark into ordinary life and thus add to its bitterness. 'Somewhere where no young people will come asking questions and expecting answers. Some shelf.'

'Quite so, but meantime a trial is coming on,' said her son hotly, 'and the notion of most of us is that we'd better pull together and help one another through, instead of being disagreeable. Are you going to talk like that in the witness-box?'

'Why should I be in the witness-box?'

'To confirm certain points in our evidence.'

'I have nothing to do with your ludicrous law courts,' she said, angry. 'I will not be dragged in at all.'

'I won't have her dragged in, either; I won't have any more trouble on my account,' cried Adela, and again took the hand, which was again withdrawn. 'Her evidence is not the least essential.'

'I thought she would want to give it. No one blames you, mother, but the fact remains that you dropped off at the first cave, and encouraged Adela to go on with him alone, whereas if you'd been well enough to keep on too nothing would have happened. He planned it, I know. Still, you fell into his trap just like Fielding and Antony before you. . . . Forgive me for speaking so plainly, but you've no right to take up this high and mighty attitude about law courts. If you're ill, that's different; but you say you're all right and you seem so, in which case I thought you'ld want to take your part, I did really.'

'I'll not have you worry her whether she's well or ill,' said Adela, leaving the sofa and taking his arm; then dropped it with a sigh and sat down again. But he was pleased she had rallied to him and surveyed his mother patronizingly. He had never felt easy with her. She was by no means the dear old lady outsiders supposed, and India had brought her into the open.

'I shall attend your marriage, but not your trial,' she informed them, tapping her knee; she had become very restless, and rather ungraceful. 'Then I shall go to England.'

'You can't go to England in May, as you agreed.'

'I have changed my mind.'

'Well, we'd better end this unexpected wrangle,' said the young man, striding about. 'You appear to want to be left out of everything, and that's enough.'

'My body, my miserable body,' she sighed. 'Why isn't it strong? Oh, why can't I walk away and be gone? Why can't I finish my duties and be gone? Why do I get headaches and puff when I walk? And all the time this to do and that to do and this to do in your way and that to do in her way, and everything sympathy and confusion and bearing one another's burdens. Why can't this be done and that be done in my way and they be done and I at peace? Why has anything to be done, I cannot see. Why all this marriage, marriage? . . . The human race would have become a single person centuries ago if marriage was any use. And all this rubbish about love, love in a church, love in a cave, as if there is the least difference, and I held up from my business over such trifles!'

'What do you want?' he said, exasperated. 'Can you state it in simple language? If so, do.'

'I want my pack of patience cards.'

'Very well, get them.'

He found, as he expected, that the poor girl was crying. And, as always, an Indian close outside the window, a mali in this case, picking up sounds. Much upset, he sat silent for a moment, thinking over his mother and her senile intrusions. He wished he had never asked her to visit India, or become under any obligation to her.

'Well, my dear girl, this isn't much of a home-coming,' he said at last. 'I had no idea she had this up her sleeve.'

Adela had stopped crying. An extraordinary expression was on her face, half relief, half horror. She repeated, 'Aziz, Aziz.'

They all avoided mentioning that name. It had become synonymous with the power of evil. He was 'the prisoner,' 'the person in question,' 'the defence,' and the sound of it now rang out like the first note of new symphony.

'Aziz . . . have I made a mistake?'

'You're over-tired,' he cried, not much surprised.

'Ronny, he's innocent; I made an awful mistake.'

'Well, sit down anyhow.' He looked round the room, but only two sparrows were chasing one another. She obeyed and took hold of his hand. He stroked it and she smiled, and gasped as if she had risen to the surface of the water, then touched her ear.

'My echo's better.'

'That's good. You'll be perfectly well in a few days, but you must save yourself up for the trial. Das is a very good fellow, we shall all be with you.'

'But Ronny, dear Ronny, perhaps there oughtn't to be any trial.'

'I don't quite know what you're saying, and I don't think you do.'

'If Dr Aziz never did it he ought to be let out.'

A shiver like impending death passed over Ronny. He said hurriedly, 'He was let out—until the Mohurram riot, when he had to be put in again.' To divert her, he told her the story, which was held to be amusing. Nureddin had stolen the Nawab Bahadur's car and driven Aziz into a ditch in the dark. Both of them had fallen out, and Nureddin had cut his face open. Their wailing had been drowned by the cries of the faithful, and it was quite a time before they were rescued by the police. Nureddin was taken to the Minto Hospital, Aziz restored to prison, with an additional charge against him of disturbing the public peace. 'Half a minute,' he remarked when the anecdote was over, and went to the telephone to ask Callendar to look in as soon as he found it convenient, because she hadn't borne the journey well.

When he returned, she was in a nervous crisis, but it took a different form—she clung to him, and sobbed, 'Help me to do what I ought. Aziz is good, You heard your mother say so.'

'Heard what?'

'He's good; I've been so wrong to accuse him.'

'Mother never said so.'

'Didn't she?' she asked, quite reasonable, open to every suggestion anyway.

'She never mentioned that name once.'

'But, Ronny, I heard her.'

'Pure illusion. You can't be quite well, can you, to make up a thing like that.'

'I suppose I can't. How amazing of me!'

'I was listening to all she said, as far as it could be listened to; she gets very incoherent.'

'When her voice dropped she said it—towards the end, when she talked about love—love—I couldn't follow, but just then she said: "Doctor Aziz never did it."'

'Those words?'

'The idea more than the words.'

'Never, never, my dear girl. Complete illusion. His name was not mentioned by anyone. Look here—you are confusing this with Fielding's letter.'

'That's it, that's it,' she cried, greatly relieved. I knew I'd heard his name somewhere. I am so grateful to you for clearing this up–it's the sort of mistake that worries me, and proves I'm neurotic.'

'So you won't go saying he's innocent again, will you? for every servant I've got is a spy.' He went to the window. The mali had gone, or rather had turned into two small children–impossible they should know English, but he sent them packing. 'They all hate us,' he explained. 'It'll be all right after the verdict, for I will say this for them, they do accept the accomplished fact; but at present they're pouring out money like water to catch us tripping, and a remark like yours is the very thing they look out for. It would enable them to say it was a put-up job on the part of us officials. You see what I mean.'

Mrs Moore came back, with the same air of ill-temper, and sat down with a flump by the card-table. To clear the confusion up, Ronny asked her point-blank whether she had mentioned the prisoner. She could not understand the question and the reason of it had to be explained. She replied: 'I never said his name,' and began to play patience.

'I thought you said, "Aziz is an innocent man," but it was in Mr Fielding's letter.'

'Of course he is innocent,' she answered indifferently: it was the first time she had expressed an opinion on the point.

'You see, Ronny, I was right,' said the girl.

'You were not right, she never said it.'

'But she thinks it.'

'Who cares what she thinks?'

'Red nine on black ten—' from the card-table.

'She can think, and Fielding too, but there's such a thing as evidence, I suppose.'

'I know, but—'

'Is it again my duty to talk?' asked Mrs Moore, looking up. 'Apparently, as you keep interrupting me.'

'Only if you have anything sensible to say.'

'Oh, how tedious . . . trivial . . .' and as when she had scoffed at love, love, love, her mind seemed to move towards them from a great distance and out of darkness. 'Oh, why is everything still my duty? when shall I be free from your fuss? Was he in the cave and were you in the cave and on and on . . . and Unto us a Son is born, unto us a Child is given . . . and am I good and is he bad and are we saved? . . . and ending everything the echo.'

'I don't hear it so much,' said Adela, moving towards her. 'You send it away, you do nothing but good, you are so good.'

'I am not good, no, bad.' She spoke more calmly and resumed her cards, saying as she turned them up, 'A bad old woman, bad, bad, detestable. I used to be good with the children growing up, also I meet this young man in his mosque, I wanted him to be happy. Good, happy, small people. They do not exist, they were a dream. . . . But I will not help you to torture him for what he never did. There are different ways of evil and I prefer mine to yours.'

'Have you any evidence in the prisoner's favour?' said Ronny in the tones of the just official. 'If so, it is your bounden duty to go into the witness-box for him instead of for us. No one will stop you.'

'One knows people's characters, as you call them,' she retorted disdainfully, as if she really knew more than character but could not impart it. 'I have heard both English and Indians speak well of him, and I felt it isn't the sort of thing he would do.'

'Feeble, mother, feeble.'

'Most feeble.'

'And most inconsiderate to Adela.'

Adela said: 'It would be so appalling if I was wrong. I should take my own life.'

He turned on her with: 'What was I warning you just now? You know you're right, and the whole station knows it.'

'Yes, he . . . This is very, very awful. I'm as certain as ever he followed me . . . only, wouldn't it be possible to withdraw the case? I dread the idea of giving evidence more and more, and you are all so good to women here and you have so much more power than in England—look at Miss Derek's motor-car. Oh, of course it's out of the question, I'm ashamed to have mentioned it; please forgive me.'

'That's all right,' he said inadequately. 'Of course I forgive you, as you call it. But the case has to come before a magistrate now; it really must, the machinery has started.'

'She has started the machinery; it will work to its end.'

Adela inclined towards tears in consequence of this unkind remark, and Ronny picked up the list of steamship sailings with an excellent notion in his head. His mother ought to leave India at once: she was doing no good to herself or to anyone else there.

Chapter Twenty-three

Lady Mellanby, wife to the Lieutenant-Governor of the Province, had been gratified by the appeal addressed to her by the ladies of Chandrapore. She could not do anything—besides, she was sailing for England; but she desired to be informed if she could show sympathy in any other way. Mrs Turton replied that Mr Heaslop's mother was trying to get a passage, but had delayed too long, and all the boats were full; could Lady Mellanby use her influence? Not even Lady Mellanby could expand the dimensions of a P. and O., but she was a very, very nice woman, and she actually wired offering the unknown and obscure old lady accommodation in her own reserved cabin. It was like a gift from heaven; humble and grateful, Ronny could not but reflect that there are compensations for every woe. His name was familiar at Government House owing to poor Adela, and now Mrs Moore would stamp it on Lady Mellanby's imagination, as they journeyed across the Indian Ocean and up the Red Sea. He had a return of tenderness for his mother—as we do for our relatives when they receive conspicuous and unexpected honour. She was not negligible, she could still arrest the attention of a high official's wife.

So Mrs Moore had all she wished; she escaped the trial, the marriage, and the hot weather; she would return to England in comfort and distinction, and see her other children. At her son's suggestion, and by her own desire, she departed. But she accepted her good luck without enthusiasm. She had come to that state where the horror of the universe and its smallness are both visible at the same time—the twilight of the double vision in which so many elderly people are involved. If this world is not to our taste, well, at all events there is Heaven, Hell, Annihilation—one or other of those large things, that huge scenic background of stars, fires, blue or black air. All heroic endeavour, and all that is known as art, assumes that there is such a background, just as all practical endeavour, when the world is to our taste, assumes that the world is all. But in the twilight of the double vision, a spiritual muddledom is set up for which no high-sounding words can be found; we can neither act nor refrain from action, we can neither ignore nor respect Infinity. Mrs Moore had always inclined to resignation. As soon as she landed in India it seemed to her good, and when she saw the water flowing through the mosque-tank, or the Ganges, or the moon, caught in the shawl of night with all the other stars, it seemed a beautiful goal and an easy one. To be one with the universe! So dignified and simple. But there was always some little duty to be performed first, some new card to be turned up from the diminishing pack and placed, and while she was pottering about, the Marabar struck its gong.

What had spoken to her in that scoured-out cavity of the granite? What dwelt in the first of the caves? Something very old and very small. Before time, it was before space also. Something snub-nosed, incapable of generosity—the undying worm itself. Since hearing its voice, she had not entertained one large thought, she was actually envious of Adela. All this fuss over a frightened girl! Nothing had happened, 'and if it had,' she found herself thinking with the cynicism of a withered priestess, 'if it had, there are worse evils than love.' The unspeakable attempt presented itself to her as love: in a cave, in a church—Boum, it amounts to the same. Visions are supposed to entail profundity, but— Wait till you get one, dear reader! The abyss also may be petty, the serpent of eternity made of maggots; her constant thought was: 'Less attention should be paid to my future daughter-in-law and more to me, there is no sorrow like my sorrow,' although when the attention was paid she rejected it irritably.

Her son couldn't escort her to Bombay, for the local situation continued acute, and all officials had to remain at their posts. Antony couldn't come either, in case he never returned to give his evidence. So she travelled with no one who could remind her of the past. This was a relief. The heat had drawn back a little before its next advance, and the journey was not unpleasant. As she left Chandrapore the moon, full again, shone over the Ganges and touched the shrinking channels into threads of silver, then veered and looked into her window. The swift and comfortable mail-train slid with her through the night, and all the next day she was rushing through Central India, through landscapes that were baked and bleached but had not the hopeless melancholy of the plain. She watched the indestructible life of man and his changing faces, and the houses he has built for himself and God, and they appeared to her not in terms of her own trouble but as things to see. There was, for instance, a place called Asirgarh which she passed at sunset and identified on a map—an enormous fortress among wooded hills. No one had ever mentioned Asirgarh to her, but it had huge and noble bastions and to the right of them was a mosque. She forgot it. Ten minutes later, Asirgarh reappeared. The mosque was to the left of the bastions now. The train in its descent through the Vindyas had described a semicircle round Asirgarh. What could she connect it with except its own name? Nothing; she knew no one who lived there. But it had looked at her twice and seemed to say: 'I do not vanish.' She woke in the middle of the night with a start, for the train was falling over the western cliff. Moonlit pinnacles rushed up at her like the fringes of a sea; then a brief episode of plain, the real sea, and the soupy dawn of Bombay. 'I have not seen the right places,' she thought, as she saw embayed in the platforms of the Victoria Terminus the end of the rails that had carried her over a continent and could never carry her back. She would never visit Asirgarh or the other untouched places; neither Delhi nor Agra nor the Rajputana cities nor Kashmir, nor the obscurer marvels that had sometimes shone through men's speech: the bilingual rock of Girnar, the statue of Shri Belgola, the ruins of Mandu and Hampi, temples of Khajraha, gardens of Shalimar. As she drove through the huge city which the West has built and abandoned with a gesture of despair, she longed to stop, though it was only Bombay, and disentangle the hundred Indias that passed each other in its streets. The feet of the horses moved her on, and presently the boat sailed and thousands of coco-nut palms appeared all round the anchorage and climbed the hills to wave her farewell. 'So you thought an echo was India; you took the Marabar caves as final?' they laughed. 'What have we in common with them, or they with Asirgarh? Good-bye!' Then the steamer rounded Colaba, the continent swung about, the cliff of the Ghats melted into the haze of a tropic sea. Lady Mellanby turned up and advised her not to stand in the heat: 'We are safely out of the frying-pan,' said Lady Mellanby, 'it will never do to fall into the fire.'

Chapter Twenty-four

Making sudden changes of gear, the heat accelerated its advance after Mrs Moore's departure until existence had to be endured and crime punished with the thermometer at a hundred and twelve. Electric fans hummed and spat, water splashed on to screens, ice clinked, and outside these defences, between a greyish sky and a yellowish earth, clouds of dust moved hesitatingly. In Europe life retreats out of the cold, and exquisite fireside myths have resulted—Balder, Persephone—but here the retreat is from the source of life, the treacherous sun, and no poetry adorns it because disillusionment cannot be beautiful. Men yearn for poetry though they may not confess it; they desire that joy shall be graceful and sorrow august and infinity have a form, and India fails to accommodate them. The annual helter-skelter of April, when irritability and lust spread like a canker, is one of her comments on the orderly hopes of humanity. Fish manage better; fish, as the tanks dry, wriggle into the mud and wait for the rains to uncake them. But men try to be harmonious all the year round, and the results are occasionally disastrous. The triumphant machine of civilization may suddenly hitch and be immobilized into a car of stone, and at such moments the destiny of the English seems to resemble their predecessors', who also entered the country with intent to refashion it, but were in the end worked into its pattern and covered with its dust.

Adela, after years of intellectualism, had resumed her morning kneel to Christianity. There seemed no harm in it, it was the shortest and easiest cut to the unseen, and she could tack her troubles on to it. Just as the Hindu clerks asked Lakshmi for an increase in pay, so did she implore Jehovah for a favourable verdict. God who saves the King will surely support the police. Her deity returned a consoling reply, but the touch of her hands on her face started prickly heat, and she seemed to swallow and expectorate the same insipid clot of air that had weighed on her lungs all the night. Also the voice of Mrs Turton disturbed her. 'Are you ready, young lady?' it pealed from the next room.

'Half a minute,' she murmured. The Turtons had received her after Mrs Moore left. Their kindness was incredible, but it was her position not her character that moved them; she was the English girl who had had the terrible experience, and for whom too much could not be done. No one, except Ronny, had any idea of what passed in her mind, and he only dimly, for where there is officialism every human relationship suffers. In her sadness she said to him, 'I bring you nothing but trouble; I was right on the Maidan, we had better just be friends,' but he protested, for the more she suffered the more highly he valued her. Did she love him? This question was somehow draggled up with the Marabar, it had been in her mind as she entered the fatal cave. Was she capable of loving anyone?

'Miss Quested, Adela, what d'ye call yourself, it's half-past seven; we ought to think of starting for that Court when you feel inclined.'

'She's saying her prayers,' came the Collector's voice.

'Sorry, my dear; take your time. . . . Was your chhota hazri all right?'

'I can't eat; might I have a little brandy?' she asked, deserting Jehovah. When it was brought, she shuddered, and said she was ready to go.

'Drink it up; not a bad notion, a peg.'

'I don't think it'll really help me, Burra Sahib.'

'You sent brandy down to the Court, didn't you, Mary?'

'I should think I did, champagne too.'

'I'll thank you this evening, I'm all to pieces now,' said the girl, forming each syllable carefully as if her trouble would diminish if it were accurately defined. She was afraid of reticence, in case something that she herself did not perceive took shape beneath it, and she had rehearsed with Mr McBryde in an odd, mincing way her terrible adventure in the cave, how the man had never actually touched her but dragged her about, and so on. Her aim this morning was to announce, meticulously, that the strain was appalling, and she would probably break down under Mr Amritrao's cross-examination and disgrace her friends. 'My echo has come back again badly,' she told them.

'How about aspirin?'

'It is not a headache, it is an echo.'

Unable to dispel the buzzing in her ears, Major Callendar had diagnosed it as a fancy, which must not be encouraged. So the Turtons changed the subject. The cool little lick of the breeze was passing over the earth, dividing night from day; it would fail in ten minutes, but they might profit by it for their drive down into the city.

'I am sure to break down,' she repeated.

'You won't,' said the Collector, his voice full of tenderness.

'Of course she won't, she's a real sport.'

'But Mrs Turton . . .'

'Yes, my dear child?'

'If I do break down, it is of no consequence. It would matter in some trials, not in this. I put it to myself in the following way: I can really behave as I like, cry, be absurd, I am sure to get my verdict, unless Mr Das is most frightfully unjust.'

'You're bound to win,' he said calmly, and did not remind her that there was bound to be an appeal. The Nawab Bahadur had financed the defence, and would ruin himself sooner than let an 'innocent Moslem perish,' and other interests, less reputable, were in the background too. The case might go up from court to court, with consequences that no official could foresee. Under his very eyes, the temper of Chandrapore was altering. As his car turned out of the compound, there was a tap of silly anger on its paint—a pebble thrown by a child. Some larger stones were dropped near the mosque. In the Maidan, a squad of native police on motor cycles waited to escort them through the bazaars. The Collector was irritated and muttered, 'McBryde's an old woman'; but Mrs Turton said, 'Really, after Mohurram a show of force will do no harm; it's ridiculous to pretend they don't hate us, do give up that farce.' He replied in an odd, sad voice, 'I don't hate them, I don't know why,' and he didn't hate them; for if he did, he would have had to condemn his own career as a bad investment. He retained a contemptuous affection for the pawns he had moved about for so many years, they must be worth his pains. 'After all, it's our women who make everything more difficult out here,' was his inmost thought, as he caught sight of some obscenities upon a long blank wall, and beneath his chivalry to Miss Quested resentment lurked, waiting its day—perhaps there is a grain of resentment in all chivalry. Some students had gathered in front of the City Magistrate's Court—hysterical boys whom he would have faced if alone, but he told the driver to work round to the rear of the building. The students jeered, and Rafi (hiding behind a comrade that he might not be identified) called out the English were cowards.

They gained Ronny's private room, where a group of their own sort had collected. None were cowardly, all nervy, for queer reports kept coming in. The Sweepers had just struck, and half the commodes of Chandrapore remained desolate in consequence—only half, and Sweepers from the District, who felt less strongly about the innocence of Dr Aziz, would arrive in the afternoon, and break the strike, but why should the grotesque incident occur? And a number of Mohammedan ladies had sworn to take no food until the prisoner was acquitted; their death would make little difference, indeed, being invisible, they seemed dead already, nevertheless it was disquieting. A new spirit seemed abroad, a rearrangement, which no one in the stern little band of whites could explain. There was a tendency to see Fielding at the back of it: the idea that he was weak and cranky had been dropped. They abused Fielding vigorously: he had been seen driving up with the two counsels, Amritrao and Mahmoud Ali; he encouraged the Boy Scout movement for seditious reasons; he received letters with foreign stamps on them, and was probably a Japanese spy. This morning's verdict would break the renegade, but he had done his country and the Empire incalculable disservice. While they denounced him, Miss Quested lay back with her hands on the arms of her chair and her eyes closed, reserving her strength. They noticed her after a time, and felt ashamed of making so much noise.

'Can we do nothing for you?' Miss Derek said.

'I don't think so, Nancy, and I seem able to do nothing for myself.'

'But you're strictly forbidden to talk like that; you're wonderful.'

'Yes indeed,' came the reverent chorus.

'My old Das is all right,' said Ronny, starting a new subject in low tones.

'Not one of them's all right,' contradicted Major Callendar.

'Das is, really.'

'You mean he's more frightened of acquitting than convicting, because if he acquits he'll lose his job,' said Lesley with a clever little laugh.

Ronny did mean that, but he cherished 'illusions' about his own subordinates (following the finer traditions of his service here), and he liked to maintain that his old Das really did possess moral courage of the Public School brand. He pointed out that—from one point of view—it was good that an Indian was taking the case. Conviction was inevitable; so better let an Indian pronounce it, there would be less fuss in the long run. Interested in the argument, he let Adela become dim in his mind.

'In fact, you disapprove of the appeal I forwarded to Lady Mellanby,' said Mrs Turton with considerable heat. 'Pray don't apologize, Mr Heaslop; I am accustomed to being in the wrong.'

'I didn't mean that . . .'

'All right. I said don't apologize.'

'Those swine are always on the look-out for a grievance,' said Lesley, to propitiate her.

'Swine, I should think so,' the Major echoed. 'And what's more, I'll tell you what. What's happened is a damn good thing really, barring of course its application to present company. It'll make them squeal and it's time they did squeal. I've put the fear of God into them at the hospital anyhow. You should see the grandson of our so-called leading loyalist.' He tittered brutally as he described poor Nureddin's present appearance. 'His beauty's gone, five upper teeth, two lower and a nostril. . . . Old Panna Lal brought him the looking-glass yesterday and he blubbered. . . . I laughed; I laughed, I tell you, and so would you; that used to be one of these buck niggers, I thought, now he's all septic; damn him, blast his soul—er—I believe he was unspeakably immoral—er—' He subsided, nudged in the ribs, but added, 'I wish I'd had the cutting up of my late assistant too; nothing's too bad for these people.'

'At last some sense is being talked,' Mrs Turton cried, much to her husband's discomfort.

'That's what I say; I say there's not such a thing as cruelty after a thing like this.'

'Exactly, and remember it afterwards, you men. You're weak, weak, weak. Why, they ought to crawl from here to the caves on their hands and knees whenever an Englishwoman's in sight, they oughtn't to be spoken to, they ought to be spat at, they ought to be ground into the dust, we've been far too kind with our Bridge Parties and the rest.'

She paused. Profiting by her wrath, the heat had invaded her. She subsided into a lemon squash, and continued between the sips to murmur, 'Weak, weak.' And the process was repeated. The issues Miss Quested had raised were so much more important than she was herself that people inevitably forgot her.

Presently the case was called.

Their chairs preceded them into the Court, for it was important that they should look dignified. And when the chuprassies had made all ready, they filed into the ramshackly room with a condescending air, as if it was a booth at a fair. The Collector made a small official joke as he sat down, at which his entourage smiled, and the Indians, who could not hear what he said, felt that some new cruelty was afoot, otherwise the sahibs would not chuckle.

The Court was crowded and of course very hot, and the first person Adela noticed in it was the humblest of all who were present, a person who had no bearing officially upon the trial: the man who pulled the punkah. Almost naked, and splendidly formed, he sat on a raised platform near the back, in the middle of the central gangway, and he caught her attention as she came in, and he seemed to control the proceedings. He had the strength and beauty that sometimes come to flower in Indians of low birth. When that strange race nears the dust and is condemned as untouchable, then nature remembers the physical perfection that she accomplished elsewhere, and throws out a god—not many, but one here and there, to prove to society how little its categories impress her. This man would have been notable anywhere: among the thin-hammed, flat-chested mediocrities of Chandrapore he stood out as divine, yet he was of the city, its garbage had nourished him, he would end on its rubbish heaps. Pulling the rope towards him, relaxing it rhythmically, sending swirls of air over others, receiving none himself, he seemed apart from human destinies, a male fate, a winnower of souls. Opposite him, also on a platform, sat the little assistant magistrate, cultivated, self-conscious, and conscientious. The punkah wallah was none of these things: he scarcely knew that he existed and did not understand why the Court was fuller than usual, indeed he did not know that it was fuller than usual, didn't even know he worked a fan, though he thought he pulled a rope. Something in his aloofness impressed the girl from middle-class England, and rebuked the narrowness of her sufferings. In virtue of what had she collected this roomful of people together? Her particular brand of opinions, and the suburban Jehovah who sanctified them—by what right did they claim so much importance in the world, and assume the title of civilization? Mrs Moore—she looked round, but Mrs Moore was far away on the sea; it was the kind of question they might have discussed on the voyage out before the old lady had turned disagreeable and queer.

While thinking of Mrs Moore she heard sounds, which gradually grew more distinct. The epoch-making trial had started, and the Superintendent of Police was opening the case for the prosecution.

Mr McBryde was not at pains to be an interesting speaker; he left eloquence to the defence, who would require it. His attitude was, 'Everyone knows the man's guilty, and I am obliged to say so in public before he goes to the Andamans.' He made no moral or emotional appeal, and it was only by degrees that the studied negligence of his manner made itself felt, and lashed part of the audience to fury. Laboriously did he describe the genesis of the picnic. The prisoner had met Miss Quested at an entertainment given by the Principal of Government College, and had there conceived his intentions concerning her: prisoner was a man of loose life, as documents found upon him at his arrest would testify, also his fellow-assistant, Dr Panna Lal, was in a position to throw light on his character, and Major Callendar himself would speak. Here Mr McBryde paused. He wanted to keep the proceedings as clean as possible, but Oriental Pathology, his favourite theme, lay around him, and he could not resist it. Taking off his spectacles, as was his habit before enunciating a general truth, he looked into them sadly, and remarked that the darker races are physically attracted by the fairer, but not *vice versa*—not a matter for bitterness this, not a matter for abuse, but just a fact which any scientific observer will confirm.

'Even when the lady is so uglier than the gentleman?'

The comment fell from nowhere, from the ceiling perhaps. It was the first interruption, and the Magistrate felt bound to censure it. 'Turn that man out,' he said. One of the native policemen took hold of a man who had said nothing, and turned him out roughly. Mr McBryde resumed his spectacles and proceeded. But the comment had upset Miss Quested. Her body resented being called ugly, and trembled.

'Do you feel faint, Adela?' asked Miss Derek, who tended her with loving indignation.

'I never feel anything else, Nancy. I shall get through, but it's awful, awful.'

This led to the first of a series of scenes. Her friends began to fuss around her, and the Major called out, 'I must have better arrangements than this made for my patient; why isn't she given a seat on the platform? She gets no air.'

Mr Das looked annoyed and said: 'I shall be happy to accommodate Miss Quested with a chair up here in view of the particular circumstances of her health.' The chuprassies passed up not one chair but several, and the entire party followed Adela on to the platform, Mr Fielding being the only European who remained in the body of the hall.

'That's better,' remarked Mrs Turton, as she settled herself.

'Thoroughly desirable change for several reasons,' replied the Major.

The Magistrate knew that he ought to censure this remark, but did not dare to. Callendar saw that he was afraid, and called out authoritatively, 'Right, McBryde, go ahead now; sorry to have interrupted you.'

'Are you all right yourselves?' asked the Superintendent.

'We shall do, we shall do.'

'Go on, Mr Das, we are not here to disturb you,' said the Collector patronizingly. Indeed, they had not so much disturbed the trial as taken charge of it.

While the prosecution continued, Miss Quested examined the hall— timidly at first, as though it would scorch her eyes. She observed to left and right of the punkah man many a half-known face. Beneath her were gathered all the wreckage of her silly attempt to see India—the people she had met at the Bridge Party, the man and his wife who hadn't sent their carriage, the old man who would lend his car, various servants, villagers, officials, and the prisoner himself. There he sat—strong, neat little Indian with very black hair, and pliant hands. She viewed him without special emotion. Since they last met, she had elevated him into a principle of evil, but now he seemed to be what he had always been—a slight acquaintance. He was negligible, devoid of significance, dry like a bone, and though he was 'guilty' no atmosphere of sin surrounded him. 'I suppose he *is* guilty. Can I possibly have made a mistake?' she thought. For this question still occurred to her intellect, though since Mrs Moore's departure it had ceased to trouble her conscience.

Pleader Mahmoud Ali now arose, and asked with ponderous and ill-judged irony whether his client could be accommodated on the platform too: even Indians felt unwell sometimes, though naturally Major Callendar did not think so, being in charge of a Government Hospital. 'Another example of their exquisite sense of humour,' sang Miss Derek. Ronny looked at Mr Das to see how he would handle the difficulty, and Mr Das became agitated, and snubbed Pleader Mahmoud Ali severely.

'Excuse me—' It was the turn of the eminent barrister from Calcutta. He was a fine-looking man, large and bony, with grey closely cropped hair. 'We object to the presence of so many European ladies and gentlemen upon the platform,' he said in an Oxford voice. 'They will have the effect of intimidating our witnesses. Their place is with the rest of the public in the body of the hall. We have no objection to Miss Quested remaining on the platform, since she has been unwell; we shall extend every courtesy to her throughout, despite the scientific truths revealed to us by the District Superintendent of Police; but we do object to the others.'

'Oh, cut the cackle and let's have the verdict,' the Major growled.

The distinguished visitor gazed at the Magistrate respectfully.

'I agree to that,' said Mr Das, hiding his face desperately in some papers. 'It was only to Miss Quested that I gave permission to sit up here. Her friends should be so excessively kind as to climb down.'

'Well done, Das, quite sound,' said Ronny with devastating honesty.

'Climb down, indeed, what incredible impertinence!' Mrs Turton cried.

'Do come quietly, Mary,' murmured her husband.

'Hi! my patient can't be left unattended.'

'Do you object to the Civil Surgeon remaining, Mr Amritrao?'

'I should object. A platform confers authority.'

'Even when it's one foot high; so come along all,' said the Collector, trying to laugh.

'Thank you very much, sir,' said Mr Das, greatly relieved. 'Thank you, Mr Heaslop; thank you ladies all.'

And the party, including Miss Quested, descended from its rash eminence. The news of their humiliation spread quickly, and people jeered outside. Their special chairs followed them. Mahmoud Ali (who was quite silly and useless with hatred) objected even to these; by whose authority had special chairs been introduced, why had the Nawab Bahadur not been given one? etc. People began to talk all over the room, about chairs ordinary and special, strips of carpet, platforms one foot high.

But the little excursion had a good effect on Miss Quested's nerves. She felt easier now that she had seen all the people who were in the room. It was like knowing the worst. She was sure now that she should come through 'all right'–that is to say, without spiritual disgrace, and she passed the good news on·to Ronny and Mrs Turton. They were too much agitated with the defeat to British prestige to be interested. From where she sat, she could see the renegade Mr Fielding. She had had a better view of him from the platform, and knew that an Indian child perched on his knee. He was watching the proceedings, watching her. When their eyes met, he turned his away, as if direct intercourse was of no interest to him.

The Magistrate was also happier. He had won the battle of the platform, and gained confidence. Intelligent and impartial, he continued to listen to the evidence, and tried to forget that later on he should have to pronounce a verdict in accordance with it. The Superintendent trundled steadily forward: he had expected these outbursts of insolence–they are the natural gestures of an inferior race, and he betrayed no hatred of Aziz, merely an abysmal contempt.

The speech dealt at length with the 'prisoner's dupes,' as they were called–Fielding, the servant Antony, the Nawab Bahadur. This aspect of the case had always seemed dubious to Miss Quested, and she had asked the police not to develop it. But they were playing for a heavy sentence, and wanted to prove that the assault was premeditated. And in order to illustrate the strategy, they produced a plan of the Marabar Hills, showing the route that the party had taken, and the 'Tank of the Dagger' where they had camped.

The Magistrate displayed interest in archaeology.

An elevation of a specimen cave was produced; it was lettered 'Buddhist Cave.'

'Not Buddhist, I think, Jain. . . .'

'In which cave is the offence alleged, the Buddhist or the Jain?' asked Mahmoud Ali, with the air of unmasking a conspiracy.

'All the Marabar caves are Jain.'

'Yes, sir; then in which Jain cave?'

'You will have an opportunity of putting such questions later.'

Mr McBryde smiled faintly at their fatuity. Indians invariably collapse over some such point as this. He knew that the defence had some wild hope of establishing an alibi, that they had tried (unsuccessfully) to identify the guide, and that Fielding and Hamidullah had gone out to the Kawa Dol and paced and measured all one moonlit night. 'Mr Lesley says they're Buddhist, and he ought to know if anyone does. But may I call attention to the shape?' And he described what had occurred there. Then he spoke of Miss Derek's arrival, of the scramble down the gully, of the return of the two ladies to Chandrapore, and of the document Miss Quested signed on her arrival, in which mention was made of the field-glasses. And then came the culminating evidence: the discovery of the field-glasses on the prisoner. 'I have nothing to add at present,' he concluded, removing his spectacles. 'I will now call my witnesses. The facts will speak for themselves. The prisoner is one of those individuals who have led a double life. I dare say his degeneracy gained upon him gradually. He has been very cunning at concealing, as is usual with the type, and pretending to be a respectable member of society, getting a Government position even. He is now entirely vicious and beyond redemption, I am afraid. He behaved most cruelly, most brutally, to another of his guests, another English lady. In order to get rid of her, and leave him free for his crime, he crushed her into a cave among his servants. However, that is by the way.'

But his last words brought on another storm, and suddenly a new name, Mrs Moore, burst on the court like a whirlwind. Mahmoud Ali had been enraged, his nerves snapped; he shrieked like a maniac, and asked whether his client was charged with murder as well as rape, and who was this second English lady.

'I don't propose to call her.'

'You don't because you can't, you have smuggled her out of the country; she is Mrs Moore, she would have proved his innocence, she was on our side, she was poor Indians' friend.'

'You could have called her yourself,' cried the Magistrate. 'Neither side called her, neither must quote her as evidence.'

'She was kept from us until too late—I learn too late—this is English justice, here is your British Raj. Give us back Mrs Moore for five minutes only, and she will save my friend, she will save the name of his sons; don't rule her out, Mr Das; take back those words as you yourself are a father; tell me where they have put her, oh, Mrs Moore. . . .'

'If the point is of any interest, my mother should have reached Aden,' said Ronny dryly; he ought not to have intervened, but the onslaught had startled him.

'Imprisoned by you there because she knew the truth.' He was almost out of his mind, and could be heard saying above the tumult: 'I ruin my career, no matter; we are all to be ruined one by one.'

'This is no way to defend your case,' counselled the Magistrate.

'I am not defending a case, nor are you trying one. We are both of us slaves.'

'Mr Mahmoud Ali, I have already warned you, and unless you sit down I shall exercise my authority.'

'Do so; this trial is a farce, I am going.' And he handed his papers to Amritrao and left, calling from the door histrionically yet with intense passion, 'Aziz, Aziz—farewell for ever.' The tumult increased, the invocation of Mrs Moore continued, and people who did not know what the syllables meant repeated them like a charm. They became Indianized into Esmiss Esmoor, they were taken up in the street outside. In vain the Magistrate threatened and expelled. Until the magic exhausted itself, he was powerless.

'Unexpected,' remarked Mr Turton.

Ronny furnished the explanation. Before she sailed, his mother had taken to talk about the Marabar in her sleep, especially in the afternoon when servants were on the verandah, and her disjointed remarks on Aziz had doubtless been sold to Mahmoud Ali for a few annas: that kind of thing never ceases in the East.

'I thought they'd try something of the sort. Ingenious.' He looked into their wide-open mouths. 'They get just like over their religion,' he added calmly. 'Start and can't stop. I'm sorry for your old Das, he's not getting much of a show.'

'Mr Heaslop, how disgraceful dragging in your dear mother,' said Miss Derek, bending forward.

'It's just a trick, and they happened to pull it off. Now one sees why they had Mahmoud Ali—just to make a scene on the chance. It is his speciality.' But he disliked it more than he showed. It was revolting to hear his mother travestied into Esmiss Esmoor, a Hindu goddess.

Esmiss Esmoor
Esmiss Esmoor
Esmiss Esmoor
Esmiss Esmoor. . . .

'Ronny—'
'Yes, old girl?'

'Isn't it all queer.'

'I'm afraid it's very upsetting for you.'

'Not the least. I don't mind it.'

'Well, that's good.'

She had spoken more naturally and healthily than usual. Bending into the middle of her friends, she said: 'Don't worry about me, I'm much better than I was; I don't feel the least faint; I shall be all right, and thank you all, thank you, thank you for your kindness.' She had to shout her gratitude, for the chant, Esmiss Esmoor, went on.

Suddenly it stopped. It was as if the prayer had been heard, and the relics exhibited. 'I apologize for my colleague,' said Mr Amritrao, rather to everyone's surprise. 'He is an intimate friend of our client, and his feelings have carried him away.'

'Mr Mahmoud Ali will have to apologize in person,' the Magistrate said.

'Exactly, sir, he must. But we had just learnt that Mrs Moore had important evidence which she desired to give. She was hurried out of the country by her son before she could give it; and this unhinged Mr Mahmoud Ali–coming as it does upon an attempt to intimidate our only other European witness, Mr Fielding. Mr Mahmoud Ali would have said nothing had not Mrs Moore been claimed as a witness by the police.' He sat down.

'An extraneous element is being introduced into the case,' said the Magistrate. 'I must repeat that as a witness Mrs Moore does not exist. Neither you, Mr Amritrao, nor, Mr McBryde, you, have any right to surmise what that lady would have said. She is not here, and consequently she can say nothing.'

'Well, I withdraw my reference,' said the Superintendent wearily. 'I would have done so fifteen minutes ago if I had been given the chance. She is not of the least importance to me.'

'I have already withdrawn it for the defence.' He added with forensic humour: 'Perhaps you can persuade the gentlemen outside to withdraw it too,' for the refrain in the street continued.

'I am afraid my powers do not extend so far,' said Das, smiling.

So peace was restored, and when Adela came to give her evidence the atmosphere was quieter than it had been since the beginning of the trial. Experts were not surprised. There is no stay in your native. He blazes up over a minor point, and has nothing left for the crisis. What he seeks is a grievance, and this he had found in the supposed abduction of an old lady. He would now be less aggrieved when Aziz was deported.

But the crisis was still to come.

Adela had always meant to tell the truth and nothing but the truth, and she had rehearsed this as a difficult task–difficult, because her disaster in the cave was connected, though by a thread, with another part of her life, her engagement to Ronny. She had thought of love just before she went in, and had innocently asked Aziz what marriage was like, and she supposed that her question had roused evil in him. To recount this would have been incredibly painful, it was the one point she wanted to keep obscure; she was willing to give details that would have distressed other girls, but this story of her private failure she dared not allude to, and she dreaded being examined in public in case something came out. But as soon as she rose to reply, and heard the sound of her own voice, she feared not even that. A new and unknown sensation protected her, like magnificent armour. She didn't think what had happened, or even remember in the ordinary way of memory, but she returned to the Marabar Hills, and spoke from them across a sort of darkness to Mr McBryde. The fatal day recurred, in every detail, but now she was of it and not of it at the same time, and this double relation gave it indescribable splendour. Why had she thought the expedition 'dull'? Now the sun rose again, the elephant waited, the pale masses of the rock flowed round her and presented the first cave; she entered, and a match was reflected in the polished walls—all beautiful and significant, though she had been blind to it at the time. Questions were asked, and to each she found the exact reply; yes, she had noticed the 'Tank of the Dagger,' but not known its name; yes, Mrs Moore had been tired after the first cave and sat in the shadow of a great rock, near the dried-up mud. Smoothly the voice in the distance proceeded, leading along the paths of truth, and the airs from the punkah behind her wafted her on. . . .

'. . . the prisoner and the guide took you on to the Kawa Dol, no one else being present?'

'The most wonderfully shaped of those hills. Yes.' As she spoke, she created the Kawa Dol, saw the niches up the curve of the stone, and felt the heat strike her face. And something caused her to add: 'No one else was present to my knowledge. We appeared to be alone.'

'Very well, there is a ledge half-way up the hill, or broken ground rather, with caves scattered near the beginning of a nullah.'

'I know where you mean.'

'You went alone into one of those caves?'

'That is quite correct.'

'And the prisoner followed you.'

'Now we've got 'im,' from the Major.

She was silent. The court, the place of question, awaited her reply. But she could not give it until Aziz entered the place of answer.

'The prisoner followed you, didn't he?' he repeated in the monotonous tones that they both used; they were employing agreed words throughout, so that this part of the proceedings held no surprises.

'May I have half a minute before I reply to that, Mr McBryde?'

'Certainly.'

Her vision was of several caves. She saw herself in one, and she was also outside it, watching its entrance, for Aziz to pass in. She failed to locate him. It was the doubt that had often visited her, but solid and attractive, like the hills, 'I am not—' Speech was more difficult than vision. 'I am not quite sure.'

'I beg your pardon?' said the Superintendent of Police.

'I cannot be sure . . .'

'I didn't catch that answer.' He looked scared, his mouth shut with a snap. 'You are on that landing, or whatever we term it, and you have entered a cave. I suggest to you that the prisoner followed you.'

She shook her head.

'What do you mean, please?'

'No,' she said in a flat, unattractive voice. Slight noises began in various parts of the room, but no one yet understood what was occurring except Fielding. He saw that she was going to have a nervous breakdown and that his friend was saved.

'What is that, what are you saying? Speak up, please.' The Magistrate bent forward.

'I'm afraid I have made a mistake.'

'What nature of mistake?'

'Dr Aziz never followed me into the cave.'

The Superintendent slammed down his papers, then picked them up and said calmly: 'Now, Miss Quested, let us go on. I will read you the words of the deposition which you signed two hours later in my bungalow.'

'Excuse me, Mr McBryde, you cannot go on. I am speaking to the witness myself. And the public will be silent. If it continues to talk, I have the court cleared. Miss Quested, address your remarks to me, who am the Magistrate in charge of the case, and realize their extreme gravity. Remember you speak on oath, Miss Quested.'

'Dr Aziz never—'

'I stop these proceedings on medical grounds,' cried the Major on a word from Turton, and all the English rose from their chairs at once, large white figures behind which the little magistrate was hidden. The Indians rose too, hundreds of things went on at once, so that afterwards each person gave a different account of the catastrophe.

'You withdraw the charge? Answer me,' shrieked the representative of Justice.

Something that she did not understand took hold of the girl and pulled her through. Though the vision was over, and she had returned to the insipidity of the world, she remembered what she had learnt. Atonement and confession—they could wait. It was in hard prosaic tones that she said, 'I withdraw everything.'

'Enough—sit down. Mr McBryde, do you wish to continue in the face of this?'

The Superintendent gazed at his witness as if she was a broken machine, and said, 'Are you mad?'

'Don't question her, sir; you have no longer the right.'

'Give me time to consider—'

'Sahib, you will have to withdraw; this becomes a scandal,' boomed the Nawab Bahadur suddenly from the back of the court.

'He shall not,' shouted Mrs Turton against the gathering tumult. 'Call the other witnesses; we're none of us safe—' Ronny tried to check her, and she gave him an irritable blow, then screamed insults at Adela.

The Superintendent moved to the support of his friends, saying nonchalantly to the Magistrate as he did so, 'Right, I withdraw.'

Mr Das rose, nearly dead with the strain. He had controlled the case, just controlled it. He had shown that an Indian can preside. To those who could hear him he said, 'The prisoner is released without one stain on his character; the question of costs will be decided elsewhere.'

And then the flimsy framework of the court broke up, the shouts of derision and rage culminated, people screamed and cursed, kissed one another, wept passionately. Here were the English, whom their servants protected, there Aziz fainted in Hamidullah's arms. Victory on this side, defeat on that—complete for one moment was the antithesis. Then life returned to its complexities, person after person struggled out of the room to their various purposes, and before long no one remained on the scene of the fantasy but the beautiful naked god. Unaware that anything unusual had occurred, he continued to pull the cord of his punkah, to gaze at the empty dais and the overturned special chairs, and rhythmically to agitate the clouds of descending dust.

Chapter Twenty-five

Miss Quested had renounced her own people. Turning from them, she was drawn into a mass of Indians of the shopkeeping class, and carried by them towards the public exit of the court. The faint, indescribable smell of the bazaars invaded her, sweeter than a London slum, yet more disquieting: a tuft of scented cotton wool, wedged in an old man's ear, fragments of pan between his black teeth, odorous powders, oils—the Scented East of tradition, but blended with human sweat as if a great king had been entangled in ignominy and could not free himself, or as if the heat of the sun had boiled and fried all the glories of the earth into a single mess. They paid no attention to her. They shook hands over her shoulder, shouted through her body—for when the Indian does ignore his rulers, he becomes genuinely unaware of their existence. Without part in the universe she had created, she was flung against Mr Fielding.

'What do you want here?'

Knowing him for her enemy, she passed on into the sunlight without speaking.

He called after her, 'Where are you going, Miss Quested?'

'I don't know.'

'You can't wander about like that. Where's the car you came in?'

'I shall walk.'

'What madness . . . there's supposed to be a riot on . . . the police have struck, no one knows what'll happen next. Why don't you keep to your own people?'

'Ought I to join them?' she said, without emotion. She felt emptied, valueless; there was no more virtue in her.

'You can't, it's too late. How are you to get round to the private entrance now? Come this way with me—quick—I'll put you into my carriage.'

'Cyril, Cyril, don't leave me,' called the shattered voice of Aziz.

'I'm coming back. . . . This way, and don't argue.' He gripped her arm. 'Excuse manners, but I don't know anyone's position. Send my carriage back any time to-morrow, if you please.'

'But where am I to go in it?'

'Where you like. How should I know your arrangements?'

The victoria was safe in a quiet side lane, but there were no horses, for the sais, not expecting the trial would end so abruptly, had led them away to visit a friend. She got into it obediently. The man could not leave her, for the confusion increased, and spots of it sounded fanatical. The main road through the bazaars was blocked, and the English were gaining the civil station by by-ways; they were caught like caterpillars, and could have been killed off easily.

'What—what have you been doing?' he cried suddenly. 'Playing a game, studying life, or what?'

'Sir, I intend these for you, sir,' interrupted a student, running down the lane with a garland of jasmine on his arm.

'I don't want the rubbish; get out.'

'Sir, I am a horse, we shall be your horses,' another cried as he lifted the shafts of the victoria into the air.

'Fetch my sais, Rafi; there's a good chap.'

'No, sir, this is an honour for us.'

Fielding wearied of his students. The more they honoured him the less they obeyed. They lassoed him with jasmine and roses, scratched the splash-board against a wall, and recited a poem, the noise of which filled the lane with a crowd.

'Hurry up, sir; we pull you in a procession.' And, half affectionate, half impudent, they bundled him in.

'I don't know whether this suits you, but anyhow you're safe,' he remarked. The carriage jerked into the main bazaar, where it created some sensation. Miss Quested was so loathed in Chandrapore that her recantation was discredited, and the rumour ran that she had been stricken by the Deity in the middle of her lies. But they cheered when they saw her sitting by the heroic Principal (some addressed her as Mrs Moore!), and they garlanded her to match him. Half gods, half guys, with sausages of flowers round their necks, the pair were dragged in the wake of Aziz' victorious landau. In the applause that greeted them some derision mingled. The English always stick together! That was the criticism. Nor was it unjust. Fielding shared it himself, and knew that if some misunderstanding occurred, and an attack was made on the girl by his allies, he would be obliged to die in her defence. He didn't want to die for her, he wanted to be rejoicing with Aziz.

Where was the procession going? To friends, to enemies, to Aziz' bungalow, to the Collector's bungalow, to the Minto Hospital where the Civil Surgeon would eat dust and the patients (confused with prisoners) be released, to Delhi, Simla. The students thought it was going to Government College. When they reached a turning, they twisted the victoria to the right, ran it by side lanes down a hill and through a garden gate into the mango plantation, and, as far as Fielding and Miss Quested were concerned, all was peace and quiet. The trees were full of glossy foliage and slim green fruit, the tank slumbered; and beyond it rose the exquisite blue arches of the garden-house. 'Sir, we fetch the others; sir, it is a somewhat heavy load for our arms,' were heard. Fielding took the refugee to his office, and tried to telephone to McBryde. But this he could not do; the wires had been cut. All his servants had decamped. Once more he was unable to desert her. He assigned her a couple of rooms, provided her with ice and drinks and biscuits, advised her to lie down, and lay down himself—there was nothing else to do. He felt restless and thwarted as he listened to the retreating sounds of the procession, and his joy was rather spoilt by bewilderment. It was a victory, but such a queer one.

At that moment Aziz was crying, 'Cyril, Cyril . . .' Crammed into a carriage with the Nawab Bahadur, Hamidullah, Mahmoud Ali, his own little boys, and a heap of flowers, he was not content; he wanted to be surrounded by all who loved him. Victory gave no pleasure, he had suffered too much. From the moment of his arrest he was done for, he had dropped like a wounded animal; he had despaired, not through cowardice, but because he knew that an Englishwoman's word would always outweigh his own. 'It is fate,' he said; and, 'It is fate,' when he was imprisoned anew after Mohurram. All that existed, in that terrible time, was affection, and affection was all that he felt in the first painful moments of his freedom. 'Why isn't Cyril following? Let us turn back.' But the procession could not turn back. Like a snake in a drain, it advanced down the narrow bazaar towards the basin of the Maidan, where it would turn about itself, and decide on its prey.

'Forward, forward,' shrieked Mahmoud Ali, whose every utterance had become a yell. 'Down with the Collector, down with the Superintendent of Police.'

'Mr Mahmoud Ali, this is not wise,' implored the Nawab Bahadur: he knew that nothing was gained by attacking the English, who had fallen into their own pit and had better be left there; moreover, he had great possessions and deprecated anarchy.

'Cyril, again you desert,' cried Aziz.

'Yet some orderly demonstration is necessary,' said Hamidullah, 'otherwise they will still think we are afraid.'

'Down with the Civil Surgeon . . . rescue Nureddin.'

'Nurredin?'

'They are torturing him.'

'Oh, my God . . .'—for this, too, was a friend.

'They are not. I will not have my grandson made an excuse for an attack on the hospital,' the old man protested.

'They are. Callendar boasted so before the trial. I heard through the tatties; he said, "I have tortured that nigger."'

'Oh, my God, my God. . . . He called him a nigger, did he?'

'They put pepper instead of antiseptic on the wounds.'

'Mr Mahmoud Ali, impossible; a little roughness will not hurt the boy, he needs discipline.'

'Pepper. Civil Surgeon said so. They hope to destroy us one by one; they shall fail.'

The new injury lashed the crowd to fury. It had been aimless hitherto, and had lacked a grievance. When they reached the Maidan and saw the sallow arcades of the Minto they shambled towards it howling. It was near midday. The earth and sky were insanely ugly, the spirit of evil again strode abroad. The Nawab Bahadur alone struggled against it, and told himself that the rumour must be untrue. He had seen his grandson in the ward only last week. But he too was carried forward over the new precipice. To rescue, to maltreat Major Callendar in revenge, and then was to come the turn of the civil station generally.

But disaster was averted, and averted by Dr Panna Lal.

Dr Panna Lal had offered to give evidence for the prosecution in the hope of pleasing the English, also because he hated Aziz. When the case broke down, he was in a very painful position. He saw the crash coming sooner than most people, slipped from the court before Mr Das had finished, and drove Dapple off through the bazaars, in flight from the wrath to come. In the hospital he should be safe, for Major Callendar would protect him. But the Major had not come, and now things were worse than ever, for here was a mob, entirely desirous of his blood, and the orderlies were mutinous and would not help him over the back wall, or rather hoisted him and let him drop back, to the satisfaction of the patients. In agony he cried, 'Man can but die the once,' and waddled across the compound to meet the invasion, salaaming with one hand and holding up a pale yellow umbrella in the other. 'Oh, forgive me,' he whined as he approached the victorious landau. 'Oh, Dr Aziz, forgive the wicked lies I told.' Aziz was silent, the others thickened their throats and threw up their chins in token of scorn. 'I was afraid, I was mislaid,' the suppliant continued. 'I was mislaid here, there, and everywhere as regards your character. Oh, forgive the poor old hakim who gave you milk when ill! Oh, Nawab Bahadur, whoever merciful, is it my poor little dispensary you require? Take every cursed bottle.' Agitated, but alert, he saw them smile at his indifferent English, and suddenly he started playing the buffoon, flung down his umbrella, trod through it, and struck himself upon the nose. He knew what he was doing, and so did they. There was nothing pathetic or eternal in the degradation of such a man. Of ignoble origin, Dr Panna Lal possessed nothing that could be disgraced, and he wisely decided to make the other Indians feel like kings, because it would put them into better tempers. When he found they wanted Nureddin, he skipped like a goat, he scuttled like a hen to do their bidding, the hospital was saved, and to the end of his life he could not understand why he had not obtained promotion on the morning's work. 'Promptness, sir, promptness similar to you,' was the argument he employed to Major Callendar when claiming it.

When Nureddin emerged, his face all bandaged, there was a roar of relief as though the Bastille had fallen. It was the crisis of the march, and the Nawab Bahadur managed to get the situation into hand. Embracing the young man publicly, he began a speech about Justice, Courage, Liberty, and

Prudence, ranged under heads, which cooled the passion of the crowd. He further announced that he should give up his British-conferred title, and live as a private gentleman, plain Mr Zulfiqar, for which reason he was instantly proceeding to his country seat. The landau turned, the crowd accompanied it, the crisis was over. The Marabar caves had been a terrible strain on the local administration; they altered a good many lives and wrecked several careers, but they did not break up a continent or even dislocate a district.

'We will have rejoicings to-night,' the old man said. 'Mr Hamidullah, I depute you to bring out our friends Fielding and Amritrao, and to discover whether the latter will require special food. The others will keep with me. We shall not go out to Dilkusha until the cool of the evening, of course. I do not know the feelings of other gentlemen; for my own part, I have a slight headache, and I wish I had thought to ask our good Panna Lal for aspirin.'

For the heat was claiming its own. Unable to madden, it stupefied, and before long most of the Chandrapore combatants were asleep. Those in the civil station kept watch a little, fearing an attack, but presently they too entered the world of dreams—that world in which a third of each man's life is spent, and which is thought by some pessimists to be a premonition of eternity.

Chapter Twenty-six

Evening approached by the time Fielding and Miss Quested met and had the first of their numerous curious conversations. He had hoped, when he woke up, to find someone had fetched her away, but the College remained isolated from the rest of the universe. She asked whether she could have 'a sort of interview,' and, when he made no reply, said, 'Have you any explanation of my extraordinary behaviour?'

'None,' he said curtly. 'Why make such a charge if you were going to withdraw it?'

'Why, indeed.'

'I ought to feel grateful to you, I suppose, but—'

'I don't expect gratitude. I only thought you might care to hear what I have to say.'

'Oh, well,' he grumbled, feeling rather schoolboyish. 'I don't think a discussion between us is desirable. To put it frankly, I belong to the other side in this ghastly affair.'

'Would it not interest you to hear my side?'

'Not much.'

'I shouldn't tell you in confidence, of course. So you can hand on all my remarks to your side, for there is one great mercy that has come out of all to-day's misery: I have no longer any secrets. My echo has gone—I call the buzzing sound in my ears an echo. You see, I have been unwell ever since that expedition to the caves, and possibly before it.'

The remark interested him rather; it was what he had sometimes suspected himself. 'What kind of illness?' he enquired.

She touched her head at the side, then shook it.

'That was my first thought, the day of the arrest: hallucination.'

'Do you think that would be so?' she asked with great humility. 'What should have given me an hallucination?'

'One of three things certainly happened in the Marabar,' he said, getting drawn into a discussion against his will. 'One of four things. Either Aziz is guilty, which is what your friends think; or you invented the charge out of malice, which is what my friends think; or you have had an hallucination. I'm very much inclined'–getting up and striding about–'now that you tell me that you felt unwell before the expedition–it's an important piece of evidence–I believe that you yourself broke the strap of the field-glasses; you were alone in that cave the whole time.'

'Perhaps. . . .'

'Can you remember when you first felt out of sorts?'

'When I came to tea with you there, in that garden-house.'

'A somewhat unlucky party. Aziz and old Godbole were both ill after it too.'

'I was not ill–it is far too vague to mention: it is all mixed up with my private affairs. I enjoyed the singing . . . but just about then a sort of sadness began that I couldn't detect at the time . . . no, nothing as solid as sadness: living at half pressure expresses it best. Half pressure. I remember going on to polo with Mr Heaslop at the Maidan. Various other things happened–it doesn't matter what, but I was under par for all of them. I was certainly in that state when I saw the caves, and you suggest (nothing shocks or hurts me)–you suggest that I had an hallucination there, the sort of thing–though in an awful form–that makes some women think they've had an offer of marriage when none was made.'

'You put it honestly, anyhow.'

'I was brought up to be honest; the trouble is it gets me nowhere.'

Liking her better, he smiled and said, 'It'll get us to heaven.'

'Will it?'

'If heaven existed.'

'Do you not believe in heaven, Mr Fielding, may I ask?' she said, looking at him shyly.

'I do not. Yet I believe that honesty gets us there.'

'How can that be?'

'Let us go back to hallucinations. I was watching you carefully through your evidence this morning, and if I'm right, the hallucination (what you call half pressure–quite as good a word) disappeared suddenly.'

She tried to remember what she had felt in court, but could not; the vision disappeared whenever she wished to interpret it. 'Events presented themselves to me in their logical sequence,' was what she said, but it hadn't been that at all.

'My belief–and of course I was listening carefully, in hope you would make some slip–my belief is that poor McBryde exorcised you. As soon as he asked you a straightforward question, you gave a straightforward answer, and broke down.'

'Exorcise in that sense. I thought you meant I'd seen a ghost.'

'I don't go to that length!'

'People whom I respect very much believe in ghosts,' she said rather sharply. 'My friend Mrs Moore does.'

'She's an old lady.'

'I think you need not be impolite to her, as well as to her son.'

'I did not intend to be rude. I only meant it is difficult, as we get on in life, to resist the supernatural. I've felt it coming on me myself. I still jog on without it, but what a temptation, at forty-five, to pretend that the dead live again; one's own dead; no one else's matter.'

'Because the dead don't live again.'

'I fear not.'

'So do I.'

There was a moment's silence, such as often follows the triumph of rationalism. Then he apologized handsomely enough for his behaviour to Heaslop at the club.

'What does Dr Aziz say of me?' she asked, after another pause.

'He–he has not been capable of thought in his misery, naturally he's very bitter,' said Fielding, a little awkward, because such remarks as Aziz had made were not merely bitter, they were foul. The underlying notion was, 'It disgraces me to have been mentioned in connection with such a hag.' It enraged him that he had been accused by a woman who had no personal beauty; sexually, he was a snob. This had puzzled and worried Fielding. Sensuality, as long as it is straightforward, did not repel him, but this derived sensuality–the sort that classes a mistress among motor-cars if she is beautiful, and among eye-flies if she isn't–was alien to his own emotions, and he felt a barrier between himself and Aziz whenever it arose. It was, in a new form, the old, old trouble that eats the heart out of every civilization: snobbery, the desire for possessions, creditable appendages; and it is to escape this rather than the lusts of the flesh that saints retreat into the Himalayas. To change the subject, he said, 'But let me conclude my analysis. We are agreed that he is not a villain and that you are not one, and we aren't really sure that it was an hallucination. There's a fourth possibility which we must touch on: was it somebody else?'

'The guide.'

'Exactly, the guide. I often think so. Unluckily Aziz hit him on the face, and he got a fright and disappeared. It is most unsatisfactory, and we hadn't the police to help us, the guide was of no interest to them.'

'Perhaps it was the guide,' she said quietly; the question had lost interest for her suddenly.

'Or could it have been one of that gang of Pathans who have been drifting through the district?'

'Someone who was in another cave, and followed me when the guide was looking away? Possibly.'

At that moment Hamidullah joined them, and seemed not too pleased to find them closeted together. Like everyone else in Chandrapore, he could make nothing of Miss Quested's conduct. He had overheard their last remark. 'Hullo, my dear Fielding,' he said. 'So I run you down at last. Can you come out at once to Dilkusha?'

'At once?'

'I hope to leave in a moment, don't let me interrupt,' said Adela.

'The telephone has been broken; Miss Quested can't ring up her friends,' he explained.

'A great deal has been broken, more than will ever be mended,' said the other. 'Still, there should be some way of transporting this lady back to the civil lines. The resources of civilization are numerous.' He spoke without looking at Miss Quested, and he ignored the slight movement she made towards him with her hand.

Fielding, who thought the meeting might as well be friendly, said, 'Miss Quested has been explaining a little about her conduct of this morning.'

'Perhaps the age of miracles has returned. One must be prepared for everything, our philosophers say.'

'It must have seemed a miracle to the onlookers,' said Adela, addressing him nervously. 'The fact is that I realized before it was too late that I had made a mistake, and had just enough presence of mind to say so. That is all my extraordinary conduct amounts to.'

'All it amounts to, indeed,' he retorted, quivering with rage but keeping himself in hand, for he felt she might be setting another trap. 'Speaking as a private individual, in a purely informal conversation, I admired your conduct, and I was delighted when our warm-hearted students garlanded you. But, like Mr Fielding, I am surprised; indeed, surprise is too weak a word. I see you drag my best friend into the dirt, damage his health and ruin his prospects in a way you cannot conceive owing to your ignorance of our society and religion, and then suddenly you get up in the witness-box: "Oh no, Mr McBryde, after all I am not quite sure, you may as well let him go." Am I mad? I keep asking myself. Is it a dream, and if so, when did it start? And without doubt it is a dream that has not yet finished. For I gather you have not done with us yet, and it is now the turn of the poor old guide who conducted you round the caves.'

'Not at all, we were only discussing possibilities,' interposed Fielding.

'An interesting pastime, but a lengthy one. There are one hundred and seventy million Indians in this notable peninsula, and of course one or other of them entered the cave. Of course some Indian is the culprit, we must never doubt that. And since, my dear Fielding, these possibilities will take you some time'—here he put his arm over the Englishman's shoulder and swayed him to and fro gently—'don't you think you had better come out to the Nawab Bahadur's—or I should say to Mr Zulfiqar's, for that is the name he now requires us to call him by.'

'Gladly, in a minute . . .'

'I have just settled my movements,' said Miss Quested. 'I shall go to the Dak Bungalow.'

'Not the Turtons?' said Hamidullah, goggle-eyed. 'I thought you were their guest.'

The Dak Bungalow of Chandrapore was below the average, and certainly servantless. Fielding, though he continued to sway with Hamidullah, was thinking on independent lines, and said in a moment: 'I have a better idea than that, Miss Quested. You must stop here at the College. I shall be away at least two days, and you can have the place entirely to yourself, and make your plans at your convenience.'

'I don't agree at all,' said Hamidullah, with every symptom of dismay. 'The idea is a thoroughly bad one. There may quite well be another demonstration to-night, and suppose an attack is made on the College. You would be held responsible for this lady's safety, my dear fellow.'

'They might equally attack the Dak Bungalow.'

'Exactly, but the responsibility there ceases to be yours.'

'Quite so. I have given trouble enough.'

'Do you hear? The lady admits it herself. It's not an attack from our people I fear—you should see their orderly conduct at the hospital; what we must guard against is an attack secretly arranged by the police for the purpose of discrediting you. McBryde keeps plenty of roughs for this purpose, and this would be the very opportunity for him.'

'Never mind. She is not going to the Dak Bungalow,' said Fielding. He had a natural sympathy for the down-trodden—that was partly why he rallied from Aziz—and had become determined not to leave the poor girl in the lurch. Also, he had a new-born respect for her, consequent on their talk. Although her hard schoolmistressy manner remained, she was no longer examining life, but being examined by it; she had become a real person.

'Then where is she to go? We shall never have done with her!' For Miss Quested had not appealed to Hamidullah. If she had shown emotion in court, broke down, beat her breast, and invoked the name of God, she would have summoned forth his imagination and generosity—he had plenty of both. But while relieving the Oriental mind, she had chilled it, with the result that he could scarcely believe she was sincere, and indeed from his standpoint she was not. For her behaviour rested on cold justice and honesty; she had felt, while she recanted, no passion of love for those whom she had wronged. Truth is not truth in that exacting land unless there go with it kindness and more kindness and kindness again, unless the Word that was with God also is God. And the girl's sacrifice—so creditable according to Western notions—was rightly rejected, because, though it came from her heart, it did not include her heart. A few garlands from students was all that India ever gave her in return.

'But where is she to have her dinner, where is she to sleep? I say here, here, and if she is hit on the head by roughs, she is hit on the head. That is my contribution. Well, Miss Quested?'

'You are very kind. I should have said yes, I think, but I agree with Mr Hamidullah. I must give no more trouble to you. I believe my best plan is to return to the Turtons, and see if they will allow me to sleep, and if they turn me away I must go to the Dak. The Collector would take me in, I know, but

Mrs Turton said this morning that she would never see me again.' She spoke without bitterness, or, as Hamidullah thought, without proper pride. Her aim was to cause the minimum of annoyance.

'Far better stop here than expose yourself to insults from that preposterous woman.'

'Do you find her preposterous? I used to. I don't now.'

'Well, here's our solution,' said the barrister, who had terminated his slightly minatory caress and strolled to the window. 'Here comes the City Magistrate. He comes in a third-class band-ghari for purposes of disguise, he comes unattended, but here comes the City Magistrate.'

'At last,' said Adela sharply, which caused Fielding to glance at her.

'He comes, he comes, he comes. I cringe. I tremble.'

'Will you ask him what he wants, Mr Fielding?'

'He wants you, of course.'

'He may not even know I'm here.'

'I'll see him first, if you prefer.'

When he had gone, Hamidullah said to her bitingly: 'Really, really. Need you have exposed Mr Fielding to this further discomfort? He is far too considerate.' She made no reply, and there was complete silence between them until their host returned.

'He has some news for you,' he said. 'You'll find him on the verandah. He prefers not to come in.'

'Does he tell me to come out to him?'

'Whether he tells you or not, you will go, I think,' said Hamidullah.

She paused, then said, 'Perfectly right,' and then said a few words of thanks to the Principal for his kindness to her during the day.

'Thank goodness, that's over,' he remarked, not escorting her to the verandah, for he held it unnecessary to see Ronny again.

'It was insulting of him not to come in.'

'He couldn't very well after my behaviour to him at the Club. Heaslop doesn't come out badly. Besides, Fate has treated him pretty roughly to-day. He has had a cable to the effect that his mother's dead, poor old soul.'

'Oh, really. Mrs Moore. I'm sorry,' said Hamidullah rather indifferently.

'She died at sea.'

'The heat, I suppose.'

'Presumably.'

'May is no month to allow an old lady to travel in.'

'Quite so. Heaslop ought never to have let her go, and he knows it. Shall we be off?'

'Let us wait until the happy couple leave the compound clear . . . they really are intolerable dawdling there. Ah well, Fielding, you don't believe in Providence, I remember. I do. This is Heaslop's punishment for abducting our witness in order to stop us establishing our alibi.'

'You go rather too far there. The poor old lady's evidence could have had no value, shout and shriek Mahmoud Ali as he will. She couldn't see through the Kawa Dol even if she had wanted to. Only Miss Quested could have saved him.'

'She loved Aziz, he says, also India, and he loved her.'

'Love is of no value in a witness, as a barrister ought to know. But I see there is about to be an Esmiss Esmoor legend at Chandrapore, my dear Hamidullah, and I will not impede its growth.'

The other smiled, and looked at his watch. They both regretted the death, but they were middle-aged men, who had invested their emotions elsewhere, and outbursts of grief could not be expected from them over a slight acquaintance. It's only one's own dead who matter. If for a moment the sense of communion in sorrow came to them, it passed. How indeed is it possible for one human being to be sorry for all the sadness that meets him on the face of the earth, for the pain that is endured not only by men, but by animals and plants, and perhaps by the stones? The soul is tired in a moment, and in fear of losing the little she does understand, she retreats to the permanent lines which habit or chance have dictated, and suffers there. Fielding had met the dead woman only two or three times, Hamidullah had seen her in the distance once, and they were far more occupied with the coming gathering at Dilkusha, the 'victory' dinner, for which they would be most victoriously late. They agreed not to tell Aziz about Mrs Moore till the morrow, because he was fond of her, and the bad news might spoil his fun.

'Oh, this is unbearable!' muttered Hamidullah. For Miss Quested was back again.

'Mr Fielding, has Ronny told you of this new misfortune?'

He bowed.

'Ah me!' She sat down, and seemed to stiffen into a monument.

'Heaslop is waiting for you, I think.'

'I do so long to be alone. She was my best friend, far more to me than to him. I can't bear to be with Ronny . . . I can't explain . . . Could you do me the very great kindness of letting me stop after all?'

Hamidullah swore violently in the vernacular.

'I should be pleased, but does Mr Heaslop wish it?'

'I didn't ask him, we are too much upset—it's so complex, not like what unhappiness is supposed to be. Each of us ought to be alone, and think. Do come and see Ronny again.'

'I think he should come in this time,' said Fielding, feeling that this much was due to his own dignity. 'Do ask him to come.'

She returned with him. He was half miserable, half arrogant—indeed, a strange mix-up—and broke at once into uneven speech. 'I came to bring Miss Quested away, but her visit to the Turtons has ended, and there is no other arrangement so far, mine are bachelor quarters now—'

Fielding stopped him courteously. 'Say no more, Miss Quested stops here. I only wanted to be assured of your approval. Miss Quested, you had better send for your own servant if he can be found, but I will leave orders with mine to do all they can for you, also I'll let the Scouts know. They have guarded the College ever since it was closed, and may as well go on. I really think you'll be as safe here as anywhere. I shall be back Thursday.'

Meanwhile Hamidullah, determined to spare the enemy no incidental pain, had said to Ronny: 'We hear, sir, that your mother has died. May we ask where the cable came from?'

'Aden.'

'Ah, you were boasting she had reached Aden, in court.'

'But she died on leaving Bombay,' broke in Adela. 'She was dead when they called her name this morning. She must have been buried at sea.'

Somehow this stopped Hamidullah, and he desisted from his brutality, which had shocked Fielding more than anyone else. He remained silent while the details of Miss Quested's occupation of the College were arranged, merely remarking to Ronny, 'It is clearly to be understood, sir, that neither Mr Fielding nor any of us are responsible for this lady's safety at Government College,' to which Ronny agreed. After that, he watched the semi-chivalrous behavings of the three English with quiet amusement; he thought Fielding had been incredibly silly and weak, and he was amazed by the younger people's want of proper pride. When they were driving out to Dilkusha, hours late, he said to Amritrao, who accompanied them: 'Mr Amritrao, have you considered what sum Miss Quested ought to pay as compensation?'

'Twenty thousand rupees.'

No more was then said, but the remark horrified Fielding. He couldn't bear to think of the queer honest girl losing her money and possibly her young man too. She advanced into his consciousness suddenly. And, fatigued by the merciless and enormous day, he lost his usual sane view of human intercourse, and felt that we exist not in ourselves, but in terms of each others' minds—a notion for which logic offers no support and which had attacked him only once before, the evening after the catastrophe, when from the verandah of the club he saw the fists and fingers of the Marabar swell until they included the whole night sky.

Chapter Twenty-seven

'Aziz, are you awake?'

'No, so let us have a talk; let us dream plans for the future.'

'I am useless at dreaming.'

'Good night then, dear fellow.'

The Victory Banquet was over, and the revellers lay on the roof of plain Mr Zulfiqar's mansion, asleep, or gazing through mosquito nets at the stars. Exactly above their heads hung the constellation of the Lion, the disc of Regulus so large and bright that it resembled a tunnel, and when this fancy was accepted all the other stars seemed tunnels too.

'Are you content with our day's work, Cyril?' the voice on his left continued.

'Are you?'

'Except that I ate too much. "How is stomach, how head?"—I say, Panna

Lal and Callendar'll get the sack.'

'There'll be a general move at Chandrapore.'

'And you'll get promotion.'

'They can't well move me down, whatever their feelings.'

'In any case we spend our holidays together, and visit Kashmir, possibly Persia, for I shall have plenty of money. Paid to me on account of the injury sustained by my character,' he explained with cynical calm. 'While with me you shall never spend a single pie. This is what I have always wished, and as the result of my misfortunes it has come.'

'You have won a great victory . . .' began Fielding.

'I know, my dear chap, I know; your voice need not become so solemn and anxious. I know what you are going to say next: Let, oh let Miss Quested off paying, so that the English may say, "Here is a native who has actually behaved like a gentleman; if it was not for his black face we would almost allow him to join our club." The approval of your compatriots no longer interests me, I have become anti-British, and ought to have done so sooner, it would have saved me numerous misfortunes.'

'Including knowing me.'

'I say, shall we go and pour water on to Mohammed Latif's face? He is so funny when this is done to him asleep.'

The remark was not a question but a full-stop. Fielding accepted it as such and there was a pause, pleasantly filled by a little wind which managed to brush the top of the house. The banquet, though riotous, had been agreeable, and now the blessings of leisure–unknown to the West, which either works or idles–descended on the motley company. Civilization strays about like a ghost here, revisiting the ruins of empire, and is to be found not in great works of art or mighty deeds, but in the gestures well-bred Indians make when they sit or lie down. Fielding, who had dressed up in native costume, learnt from his excessive awkwardness in it that all his motions were makeshifts, whereas when the Nawab Bahadur stretched out his hand for food or Nureddin applauded a song, something beautiful had been accomplished which needed no development. This restfulness of gesture–it is the Peace that passeth Understanding, after all, it is the social equivalent of Yoga. When the whirring of action ceases, it becomes visible, and reveals a civilization which the West can disturb but will never acquire. The hand stretches out for ever, the lifted knee has the eternity though not the sadness of the grave. Aziz was full of civilization this evening, complete, dignified, rather hard, and it was with diffidence that the other said: 'Yes, certainly you must let off Miss Quested easily. She must pay all your costs, that is only fair, but do not treat her like a conquered enemy.'

'Is she wealthy? I depute you to find out.'

'The sums mentioned at dinner when you all got so excited–they would ruin her, they are perfectly preposterous. Look here . . .'

'I am looking, though it gets a bit dark. I see Cyril Fielding to be a very nice chap indeed and my best friend, but in some ways a fool. You think that by letting Miss Quested off easily I shall make a better reputation for myself and Indians generally. No, no. It will be put down to weakness and the attempt to gain promotion officially. I have decided to have nothing more to do with British India, as a matter of fact. I shall seek service in some Moslem State, such as Hyderabad, Bhopal, where Englishmen cannot insult me any more. Don't counsel me otherwise.'

'In the course of a long talk with Miss Quested . . .'

'I don't want to hear your long talks.'

'Be quiet. In the course of a long talk with Miss Quested I have begun to understand her character. It's not an easy one, she being a prig. But she is perfectly genuine and very brave. When she saw she was wrong, she pulled herself up with a jerk and said so. I want you to realize what that means. All her friends around her, the entire British Raj pushing her forward. She stops, sends the whole thing to smithereens. In her place I should have funked it. But she stopped, and almost did she become a national heroine, but my students ran us down a side street before the crowd caught flame. Do treat her considerately. She really mustn't get the worst of both worlds. I know what all these'—he indicated the shroud'will want, but you mustn't listen to them. Be merciful. Act like one of your six Mogul Emperors, or all the six rolled into one.'

'Not even Mogul Emperors showed mercy until they received an apology.'

'She'll apologize if that's the trouble,' he cried, sitting up. 'Look, I'll make you an offer. Dictate to me whatever form of words you like, and this time to-morrow I'll bring it back signed. This is not instead of any public apology she may make you in law. It's an addition.'

' "Dear Dr Aziz, I wish you had come into the cave; I am an awful old hag, and it is my last chance." Will she sign that?'

'Well good night, good night, it's time to go to sleep, after that.'

'Good night, I suppose it is.'

'Oh, I wish you wouldn't make that kind of remark,' he continued after a pause. 'It is the one thing in you I can't put up with.'

'I put up with all things in you, so what is to be done?'

'Well, you hurt me by saying it; good night.'

There was silence, then dreamily but with deep feeling the voice said: 'Cyril, I have had an idea which will satisfy your tender mind: I shall consult Mrs Moore.'

Opening his eyes, and beholding thousands of stars, he could not reply, they silenced him.

'Her opinion will solve everything; I can trust her so absolutely. If she advises me to pardon this girl, I shall do so. She will counsel me nothing against my real and true honour, as you might.'

'Let us discuss that to-morrow morning.'

'Is it not strange? I keep on forgetting she has left India. During the shouting of her name in court I fancied she was present. I had shut my eyes, I confused myself on purpose to deaden the pain. Now this very instant I forgot again. I shall be obliged to write. She is now far away, well on her way towards Ralph and Stella.'

'To whom?'

'To those other children.'

'I have not heard of other children.'

'Just as I have two boys and a girl, so has Mrs Moore. She told me in the mosque.'

'I knew her so slightly.'

'I have seen her but three times, but I know she is an Oriental.'

'You are so fantastic. . . . Miss Quested, you won't treat her generously; while over Mrs Moore there is this elaborate chivalry. Miss Quested anyhow behaved decently this morning, whereas the old lady never did anything for you at all, and it's pure conjecture that she would have come forward in your favour, it only rests on servants' gossip. Your emotions never seem in proportion to their objects, Aziz.'

'Is emotion a sack of potatoes, so much the pound, to be measured out? Am I a machine? I shall be told I can use up my emotions by using them, next.'

'I should have thought you could. It sounds common sense. You can't eat your cake and have it, even in the world of the spirit.'

'If you are right, there is no point in any friendship; it all comes down to give and take, or give and return, which is disgusting, and we had better all leap over this parapet and kill ourselves. Is anything wrong with you this evening that you grow so materialistic?'

'Your unfairness is worse than my materialism.'

'I see. Anything further to complain of?' He was good-tempered and affectionate but a little formidable. Imprisonment had made channels for his character, which would never fluctuate as widely now as in the past. 'Because it is far better you put all your difficulties before me, if we are to be friends for ever. You do not like Mrs Moore, and are annoyed because I do; however, you will like her in time.'

When a person, really dead, is supposed to be alive, an unhealthiness infects the conversation. Fielding could not stand the tension any longer and blurted out: 'I'm sorry to say Mrs Moore's dead.'

But Hamidullah, who had been listening to all their talk, and did not want the festive evening spoilt, cried from the adjoining bed: 'Aziz, he is trying to pull your leg; don't believe him, the villain.'

'I do not believe him,' said Aziz; he was inured to practical jokes, even of this type.

Fielding said no more. Facts are facts, and everyone would learn of Mrs Moore's death in the morning. But it struck him that people are not really dead until they are felt to be dead. As long as there is some misunderstanding about them, they possess a sort of immortality. An experience of his own confirmed this. Many years ago he had lost a great friend, a woman, who believed in the Christian heaven, and assured him that after the changes and chances of this mortal life they would meet in it again. Fielding was a blank, frank atheist, but he respected every opinion his friend held: to do this is essential in friendship. And it seemed to him for a time that the dead awaited him, and when the illusion faded it left behind it an emptiness that was almost guilt: 'This really is the end,' he thought, 'and I gave her the final blow.' He had tried to kill Mrs Moore this evening, on the roof of the Nawab

Bahadur's house; but she still eluded him, and the atmosphere remained tranquil. Presently the moon rose—the exhausted crescent that precedes the sun—and shortly after men and oxen began their interminable labour, and the gracious interlude, which he had tried to curtail, came to its natural conclusion.

Chapter Twenty-eight

Dead she was—committed to the deep while still on the southward track, for the boats from Bombay cannot point towards Europe until Arabia has been rounded; she was further in the tropics than ever achieved while on shore, when the sun touched her for the last time and her body was lowered into yet another India—the Indian Ocean. She left behind her sore discomfort, for a death gives a ship a bad name. Who was this Mrs Moore? When Aden was reached, Lady Mellanby cabled, wrote, did all that was kind, but the wife of a Lieutenant-Governor does not bargain for such an experience; and she repeated: 'I had only seen the poor creature for a few hours when she was taken ill; really this has been needlessly distressing, it spoils one's home-coming.' A ghost followed the ship up the Red Sea, but failed to enter the Mediterranean. Somewhere about Suez there is always a social change: the arrangements of Asia weaken and those of Europe begin to be felt, and during the transition Mrs Moore was shaken off. At Port Said the grey blustery north began. The weather was so cold and bracing that the passengers felt it must have broken in the land they had left, but it became hotter steadily there in accordance with its usual law.

The death took subtler and more lasting shapes in Chandrapore. A legend sprang up that an Englishman had killed his mother for trying to save an Indian's life—and there was just enough truth in this to cause annoyance to the authorities. Sometimes it was a cow that had been killed—or a crocodile with the tusks of a boar had crawled out of the Ganges. Nonsense of this type is more difficult to combat than a solid lie. It hides in rubbish heaps and moves when no one is looking. At one period two distinct tombs containing Esmiss Esmoor's remains were reported: one by the tannery, the other up near the goods station. Mr McBryde visited them both and saw signs of the beginning of a cult—earthenware saucers and so on. Being an experienced official, he did nothing to irritate it, and after a week or so, the rash died down. 'There's propaganda behind all this,' he said, forgetting that a hundred years ago, when Europeans still made their home in the country-side and appealed to its imagination, they occasionally became local demons after death—not a whole god, perhaps, but part of one, adding an epithet or gesture to what already existed, just as the gods contribute to the great gods, and they to the philosophic Brahm.

Ronny reminded himself that his mother had left India at her own wish, but his conscience was not clear. He had behaved badly to her, and he had either to repent (which involved a mental overturn), or to persist in unkindness towards her. He chose the latter course. How tiresome she had been with her patronage of Aziz! What a bad influence upon Adela! And now she still gave trouble with ridiculous 'tombs,' mixing herself up with natives. She could not help it, of course, but she had attempted similar exasperating expeditions in her lifetime, and he reckoned it against her. The young man had much to worry him—the heat, the local tension, the approaching visit of the Lieutenant-Governor, the problems of Adela—and threading them all together into a grotesque garland were these Indianizations of Mrs Moore. What does happen to one's mother when she dies? Presumably she goes to heaven, anyhow she clears out. Ronny's religion was of the sterilized Public School brand, which never goes bad, even in the tropics. Wherever he entered, mosque, cave, or temple, he retained the spiritual outlook of the Fifth Form, and condemned as 'weakening' any attempt to understand them. Pulling himself together, he dismissed the mater from his mind. In due time he and his half-brother and -sister would put up a tablet to her in the Northamptonshire church where she had worshipped, recording the dates of her birth and death and the fact that she had been buried at sea. This would be sufficient.

And Adela—she would have to depart too; he hoped she would have made the suggestion herself ere now. He really could not marry her—it would mean the end of his career. Poor lamentable Adela. . . . She remained at Government College, by Fielding's courtesy—unsuitable and humiliating, but no one would receive her at the civil station. He postponed all private talk until the award against her was decided. Aziz was suing her for damages in the sub-judge's court. Then he would ask her to release him. She had killed his love, and it had never been very robust; they would never have achieved betrothal but for the accident to the Nawab Bahadur's car. She belonged to the callow academic period of his life which he had out-grown—Grasmere, serious talks and walks, that sort of thing.

Chapter Twenty-nine

The visit of the Lieutenant-Governor of the Province formed the next stage in the decomposition of the Marabar. Sir Gilbert, though not an enlightened man, held enlightened opinions. Exempted by a long career in the Secretariat from personal contact with the peoples of India, he was able to speak of them urbanely, and to deplore racial prejudice. He applauded the outcome of the trial, and congratulated Fielding on having taken 'the broad, the sensible, the only possible charitable view from the first. Speaking confidentially . . .' he proceeded. Fielding deprecated confidences, but Sir Gilbert insisted on imparting them; the affair had been 'mishandled by certain of our friends up the hill' who did not realize that 'the hands of the clock move forward, not back,' etc., etc. One thing he could guarantee: the Principal would receive a most cordial invitation to rejoin the club, and he begged, nay commanded him, to accept. He returned to his Himalayan altitudes well satisfied; the amount of money Miss Quested would have to pay, the precise nature of what had happened in the caves—these were local details, and did not concern him.

Fielding found himself drawn more and more into Miss Quested's affairs. The College remained closed and he ate and slept at Hamidullah's, so there was no reason she should not stop on if she wished. In her place he would have cleared out, sooner than submit to Ronny's half-hearted and distracted civilities, but she was waiting for the hour-glass of her sojourn to run through. A house to live in, a garden to walk in during the brief moment of the cool—that was all she asked, and he was able to provide them. Disaster had shown her her limitations, and he realized now what a fine loyal character she was. Her humility was touching. She never repined at getting the worst of both worlds; she regarded it as the due punishment of her stupidity. When he hinted to her that a personal apology to Aziz might be seemly, she said sadly: 'Of course. I ought to have thought of it myself, my instincts never help me. Why didn't I rush up to him after the trial? Yes, of course I will write him an apology, but please will you dictate it?' Between them they concocted a letter, sincere, and full of moving phrases, but it was not moving as a letter. 'Shall I write another?' she enquired. 'Nothing matters if I can undo the harm I have caused. I can do this right, and that right; but when the two are put together they come wrong. That's the defect of my character. I have never realized it until now. I thought that if I was just and asked questions I would come through every difficulty.' He replied: 'Our letter is a failure for a simple reason which we had better face: you have no real affection for Aziz, or Indians generally.' She assented. 'The first time I saw you, you were wanting to see India, not Indians, and it occurred to me: Ah, that won't take us far. Indians know whether they are liked or not—they cannot be fooled here. Justice never satisfies them, and that is why the British Empire rests on sand.' Then he said: 'Do I like anyone, though?' Presumably she liked Heaslop, and he changed the subject, for this side of her life did not concern him.

His Indian friends were, on the other hand, a bit above themselves. Victory, which would have made the English sanctimonious, made them aggressive. They wanted to develop an offensive, and tried to do so by discovering new grievances and wrongs, many of which had no existence. They suffered from the usual disillusion that attends warfare. The aims of battle and the fruits of conquest are never the same; the latter have their value and only the saint rejects them, but their hint of immortality vanishes as soon as they are held in the hand. Although Sir Gilbert had been courteous, almost obsequious, the fabric he represented had in no wise bowed its head. British officialism remained, as all-pervading and as unpleasant as the sun; and what was next to be done against it was not very obvious, even to Mahmoud Ali. Loud talk and trivial lawlessness were attempted, and behind them continued a genuine but vague desire for education. 'Mr Fielding, we must all be educated promptly.'

Aziz was friendly and domineering. He wanted Fielding to 'give in to the East,' as he called it, and live in a condition of affectionate dependence upon it. 'You can trust me, Cyril.' No question of that, and Fielding had no roots among his own people. Yet he really couldn't become a sort of Mohammed Latif. When they argued about it something racial intruded—not bitterly, but inevitably, like the colour of their skins: coffee-colour versus pinko-grey. And Aziz would conclude: 'Can't you see that I'm grateful to you for your help and want to reward you?' And the other would retort: 'If you want to reward me, let Miss Quested off paying.'

The insensitiveness about Adela displeased him. It would, from every point of view, be right to treat her generously, and one day he had the notion of appealing to the memory of Mrs Moore. Aziz had this high and fantastic estimate of Mrs Moore. Her death had been a real grief to his warm heart; he wept like a child and ordered his three children to weep also. There was no doubt that he respected and loved her. Fielding's first attempt was a failure. The reply was: 'I see your trick. I want revenge on them. Why should I be insulted and suffer and the contents of my pockets read and my wife's photograph taken to the police station? Also I want the money—to educate my little boys, as I explained to her.' But he began to weaken, and Fielding was not ashamed to practise a little necromancy. Whenever the question of compensation came up, he introduced the dead woman's name. Just as other propagandists invented her a tomb, so did he raise a questionable image of her in the heart of Aziz, saying nothing that he believed to be untrue, but producing something that was probably far from the truth. Aziz yielded suddenly. He felt it was Mrs Moore's wish that he should spare the woman who was about to marry her son, that it was the only honour he could pay her, and he renounced with a passionate and beautiful outburst the whole of the compensation money, claiming only costs. It was fine of him, and, as he foresaw, it won him no credit with the English. They still believed he was guilty, they believed it to the end of their careers, and retired Anglo-Indians in Tunbridge Wells or Cheltenham still murmur to each other: 'That Marabar case which broke down because the poor girl couldn't face giving her evidence—that was another bad case.'

When the affair was thus officially ended, Ronny, who was about to be transferred to another part of the Province, approached Fielding with his usual constraint and said: 'I wish to thank you for the help you have given Miss Quested. She will not of course trespass on your hospitality further; she has as a matter of fact decided to return to England. I have just arranged about her passage for her. I understand she would like to see you.'

'I shall go round at once.'

On reaching the College, he found her in some upset. He learnt that the engagement had been broken by Ronny. 'Far wiser of him,' she said pathetically. 'I ought to have spoken myself, but I drifted on wondering what would happen. I would willingly have gone on spoiling his life through inertia—one has nothing to do, one belongs nowhere and becomes a public nuisance without realizing it.' In order to reassure him, she added: 'I speak only of India. I am not astray in England. I fit in there–no, don't think I shall do harm in England. When I am forced back there, I shall settle down to some career. I have sufficient money left to start myself, and heaps of friends of my own type. I shall be quite all right.' Then sighing: 'But oh, the trouble I've brought on everyone here. . . . I can never get over it. My carefulness as to whether we should marry or not . . . and in the end Ronny and I part and aren't even sorry. We ought never to have thought of marriage. Weren't you amazed when our engagement was originally announced?'

'Not much. At my age one's seldom amazed,' he said, smiling. 'Marriage is too absurd in any case. It begins and continues for such very slight reasons. The social business props it up on one side, and the theological business on the other, but neither of them are marriage, are they? I've friends who can't remember why they married, no more can their wives. I suspect that it mostly happens haphazard, though afterwards various noble reasons are invented. About marriage I am cynical.'

'I am not. This false start has been all my own fault. I was bringing to Ronny nothing that ought to be brought, that was why he rejected me really. I entered that cave thinking: Am I fond of him? I have not yet told you that, Mr Fielding. I didn't feel justified. Tenderness, respect, personal intercourse–I tried to make them take the place–of—'

'I no longer want love,' he said, supplying the word.

'No more do I. My experiences here have cured me. But I want others to want it.'

'But to go back to our first talk (for I suppose this is our last one)–when you entered that cave, who did follow you, or did no one follow you? Can you now say? I don't like it left in air.'

'Let us call it the guide,' she said indifferently. 'It will never be known. It's as if I ran my finger along that polished wall in the dark, and cannot get further. I am up against something, and so are you. Mrs Moore–she did know.'

'How could she have known what we don't?'

'Telepathy, possibly.'

The pert, meagre word fell to the ground. Telepathy? What an explanation! Better withdraw it, and Adela did so. She was at the end of her spiritual tether, and so was he. Were there worlds beyond which they could never touch, or did all that is possible enter their consciousness? They could not tell. They only realized that their outlook was more or less similar, and found in this a satisfaction. Perhaps life is a mystery, not a muddle; they could not tell. Perhaps the hundred Indias which fuss and squabble so tiresomely are one, and the universe they mirror is one. They had not the apparatus for judging.

'Write to me when you get to England.'

'I shall, often. You have been excessively kind. Now that I'm going, I realize it. I wish I could do something for you in return, but I see you've all you want.'

'I think so,' he replied after a pause. 'I have never felt more happy and secure out here. I really do get on with Indians, and they do trust me. It's pleasant that I haven't had to resign my job. It's pleasant to be praised by an L.-G. Until the next earthquake I remain as I am.'

'Of course this death has been troubling me.'

'Aziz was so fond of her too.'

'But it has made me remember that we must all die: all these personal relations we try to live by are temporary. I used to feel death selected people, it is a notion one gets from novels, because some of the characters are usually left talking at the end. Now "death spares no one" begins to be real.'

'Don't let it become too real, or you'll die yourself. That is the objection to meditating upon death. We are subdued to what we work in. I have felt the same temptation, and had to sheer off. I want to go on living a bit.'

'So do I.'

A friendliness, as of dwarfs shaking hands, was in the air. Both man and woman were at the height of their powers–sensible, honest, even subtle. They spoke the same language, and held the same opinions, and the variety of age and sex did not divide them. Yet they were dissatisfied. When they agreed, 'I want to go on living a bit,' or, 'I don't believe in God,' the words were followed by a curious backwash as though the universe had displaced itself to fill up a tiny void, or as though they had seen their own gestures from an immense height–dwarfs talking, shaking hands and assuring each other that they stood on the same footing of insight. They did not think they were wrong, because as soon as honest people think they are wrong instability sets up. Not for them was an infinite goal behind the stars, and they never sought it. But wistfulness descended on them now, as on other occasions; the shadow of the shadow of a dream fell over their clear-cut interests, and objects never seen again seemed messages from another world.

'And I do like you so very much, if I may say so,' he affirmed.

'I'm glad, for I like you. Let's meet again.'

'We will, in England, if I ever take home leave.'

'But I suppose you're not likely to do that yet.'

'Quite a chance. I have a scheme on now as a matter of fact.'

'Oh, that would be very nice.'

So it petered out. Ten days later Adela went off, by the same route as her dead friend. The final beat up before the monsoon had come. The country was stricken and blurred. Its houses, trees and fields were all modelled out of the same brown paste, and the sea at Bombay slid about like broth against the quays. Her last Indian adventure was with Antony, who followed her on to the boat and tried to blackmail her. She had been Mr Fielding's mistress, Antony said. Perhaps Antony was discontended with his tip. She rang the cabin bell and had him turned out, but his statement created rather a scandal, and people did not speak to her much during the first part of the voyage. Through the Indian Ocean and the Red Sea she was left to herself, and to the dregs of Chandrapore.

With Egypt the atmosphere altered. The clean sands, heaped on each side of the canal, seemed to wipe off everything that was difficult and equivocal, and even Port Said looked pure and charming in the light of a rose-grey morning. She went on shore there with an American missionary, they walked out to the Lesseps statue, they drank the tonic air of the Levant. 'To what duties, Miss Quested, are you returning in your own country after your taste of the tropics?' the missionary asked. 'Observe, I don't say to what do you turn, but to what do you *re*-turn. Every life ought to contain both a turn and a *re*-turn. This celebrated pioneer (he pointed to the statue) will make my question clear. He turns to the East, he *re*-turns to the West. You can see it from the cute position of his hands, one of which holds a string of sausages.' The missionary looked at her humorously, in order to cover the emptiness of his mind. He had no idea what he meant by 'turn' and 'return,' but he often used words in pairs, for the sake of moral brightness. 'I see,' she replied. Suddenly, in the Mediterranean clarity, she had seen. Her first duty on returning to England was to look up those other children of Mrs Moore's, Ralph and Stella, then she would turn to her profession. Mrs Moore had tended to keep the products of her two marriages apart, and Adela had not come across the younger branch so far.

Chapter Thirty

Another local consequence of the trial was a Hindu-Moslem entente. Loud protestations of amity were exchanged by prominent citizens, and there went with them a genuine desire for a good understanding. Aziz, when he was at the hospital one day, received a visit from rather a sympathetic figure: Mr Das. The magistrate sought two favours from him: a remedy for shingles and a poem for his brother-in-law's new monthly magazine. He accorded both.

'My dear Das, why, when you tried to send me to prison, should I try to send Mr Bhattacharya a poem? Eh? That is naturally entirely a joke. I will write him the best I can, but I thought your magazine was for Hindus.'

'It is not for Hindus, but Indians generally,' he said timidly.

'There is no such person in existence as the general Indian.'

'There was not, but there may be when you have written a poem. You are our hero; the whole city is behind you, irrespective of creed.'

'I know, but will it last?'

'I fear not,' said Das, who had much mental clearness. 'And for that reason, if I may say so, do not introduce too many Persian expressions into the poem, and not too much about the bulbul.'

'Half a sec,' said Aziz, biting his pencil. He was writing out a prescription. 'Here you are. . . . Is not this better than a poem?'

'Happy the man who can compose both.'

'You are full of compliments to-day.'

'I know you bear me a grudge for trying that case,' said the other, stretching out his hand impulsively. 'You are so kind and friendly, but always I detect irony beneath your manner.'

'No, no, what nonsense!' protested Aziz. They shook hands, in a half-embrace that typified the entente. Between people of distant climes there is always the possibility of romance, but the various branches of Indians know too much about each other to surmount the unknowable easily. The approach is prosaic. 'Excellent,' said Aziz, patting a stout shoulder and thinking, 'I wish they did not remind me of cow-dung'; Das thought, 'Some Moslems are very violent.' They smiled wistfully, each spying the thought in the other's heart, and Das, the more articulate, said: 'Excuse my mistakes, realize my limitations. Life is not easy as we know it on the earth.'

'Oh, well, about this poem—how did you hear I sometimes scribbled?' he asked, much pleased, and a good deal moved—for literature had always been a solace to him, something that the ugliness of facts could not spoil.

'Professor Godbole often mentioned it, before his departure for Mau.'

'How did he hear?'

'He too was a poet; do you not divine each other?'

Flattered by the invitation, he got to work that evening. The feel of the pen between his fingers generated bulbuls at once. His poem was again about the decay of Islam and the brevity of love; as sad and sweet as he could contrive, but not nourished by personal experience, and of no interest to these excellent Hindus. Feeling dissatisfied, he rushed to the other extreme, and wrote a satire, which was too libellous to print. He could only express pathos or venom, though most of his life had no concern with either. He loved poetry—science was merely an acquisition, which he laid aside when unobserved like his European dress—and this evening he longed to compose a new song which should be acclaimed by multitudes and even sung in the fields. In what language shall it be written? And what shall it announce? He vowed to see more of Indians who were not Mohammedans, and never to look backward. It is the only healthy course. Of what help, in this latitude and hour, are the glories of Cordova and Samarcand? They have gone, and while we lament them the English occupy Delhi and exclude us from East Africa. Islam itself, though true, throws cross-lights over the path to freedom. The song of the future must transcend creed.

The poem for Mr Bhattacharya never got written, but it had an effect. It led him towards the vague and bulky figure of a mother-land. He was without natural affection for the land of his birth, but the Marabar Hills drove him to it. Half closing his eyes, he attempted to love India. She must imitate Japan. Not until she is a nation will her sons be treated with respect. He grew harder and less approachable. The English, whom he had laughed at or ignored, persecuted him everywhere; they had even thrown nets over his dreams. 'My great mistake has been taking our rulers as a joke,' he said to Hamidullah next day; who replied with a sigh: 'It is far the wisest way to take them, but not possible in the long run. Sooner or later a disaster such as yours occurs, and reveals their secret thoughts about our character. If God himself descended from heaven into their club and said you were innocent, they would disbelieve him. Now you see why Mahmoud Ali and self waste so much time over intrigues and associate with creatures like Ram Chand.'

'I cannot endure committees. I shall go right away.'

'Where to? Turtons and Burtons, all are the same.'

'But not in an Indian state.'

'I believe the Politicals are obliged to have better manners. It amounts to no more.'

'I do want to get away from British India, even to a poor job. I think I could write poetry there. I wish I had lived in Babur's time and fought and written for him. Gone, gone, and not even any use to say "Gone, gone," for it weakens us while we say it. We need a king, Hamidullah; it would make our lives easier. As it is, we must try to appreciate these quaint Hindus. My notion now is to try for some post as doctor in one of their states.'

'Oh, that is going much too far.'

'It is not going as far as Mr Ram Chand.'

'But the money, the money—they will never pay an adequate salary, those savage Rajahs.'

'I shall never be rich anywhere, it is outside my character.'

'If you had been sensible and made Miss Quested pay—'

'I chose not to. Discussion of the past is useless,' he said, with sudden sharpness of tone. 'I have allowed her to keep her fortune and buy herself a husband in England, for which it will be very necessary. Don't mention the matter again.'

'Very well, but your life must continue a poor man's; no holidays in Kashmir for you yet, you must stick to your profession and rise to a highly paid post, not retire to a jungle-state and write poems. Educate your children, read the latest scientific periodicals, compel European doctors to respect you. Accept the consequences of your own actions like a man.'

Aziz winked at him slowly and said: 'We are not in the law courts. There are many ways of being a man; mine is to express what is deepest in my heart.'

'To such a remark there is certainly no reply,' said Hamidullah, moved. Recovering himself and smiling, he said: 'Have you heard this naughty rumour that Mohammed Latif has got hold of?'

'Which?'

'When Miss Quested stopped in the College, Fielding used to visit her . . . rather too late in the evening, the servants say.'

'A pleasant change for her if he did,' said Aziz, making a curious face.

'But you understand my meaning?'

The young man winked again and said: 'Just! Still, your meaning doesn't help me out of my difficulties. I am determined to leave Chandrapore. The problem is, for where? I am determined to write poetry. The problem is, about what? You give me no assistance.' Then, surprising both Hamidullah and himself, he had an explosion of nerves. 'But who does give me assistance? No one is my friend. All are traitors, even my own children. I have had enough of friends.'

'I was going to suggest we go behind the purdah, but your three treacherous children are there, so you will not want too.'

'I am sorry, it is ever since I was in prison my temper is strange; take me, forgive me.'

'Nureddin's mother is visiting my wife now. That is all right, I think.'

'They come before me separately, but not so far together. You had better prepare them for the united shock of my face.'

'No, let us surprise them without warning, far too much nonsense still goes on among our ladies. They pretended at the time of your trial they would give up purdah; indeed, those of them who can write composed a document to that effect, and now it ends in humbug. You know how deeply they all respect Fielding, but not one of them has seen him. My wife says she will, but always when he calls there is some excuse–she is not feeling well, she is ashamed of the room, she has no nice sweets to offer him, only Elephants' Ears, and if I say Elephants' Ears are Mr Fielding's favourite sweet, she replies that he will know how badly hers are made, so she cannot see him on their account. For fifteen years, my dear boy, have I argued with my begum, for fifteen years, and never gained a point, yet the missionaries inform us our women are down-trodden. If you want a subject for a poem, take this: The Indian lady as she is and not as she is supposed to be.'

Chapter Thirty-one

Aziz had no sense of evidence. The sequence of his emotions decided his beliefs, and led to the tragic coolness between himself and his English friend. They had conquered but were not to be crowned. Fielding was away at a conference, and after the rumour about Miss Quested had been with him undisturbed for a few days, he assumed it was true. He had no objection on moral grounds to his friends amusing themselves, and Cyril, being middle-aged, could no longer expect the pick of the female market, and must take his amusement where he could find it. But he resented him making up to this particular woman, whom he still regarded as his enemy; also, why had he not been told? What is friendship without confidences? He himself had told things sometimes regarded as shocking, and the Englishman had listened, tolerant, but surrendering nothing in return.

He met Fielding at the railway station on his return, agreed to dine with him, and then started taxing him by the oblique method, outwardly merry. An avowed European scandal there was–Mr McBryde and Miss Derek. Miss Derek's faithful attachment to Chandrapore was now explained: Mr McBryde had been caught in her room, and his wife was divorcing him. 'That pure-minded fellow. However, he will blame the Indian climate. Everything is our fault really. Now, have I not discovered an important piece of news for you, Cyril?'

'Not very,' said Fielding, who took little interest in distant sins. 'Listen to mine.' Aziz' face lit up. 'At the conference, it was settled. . . .'

'This evening will do for schoolmastery. I should go straight to the Minto now, the cholera looks bad. We begin to have local cases as well as imported.

In fact, the whole of life is somewhat sad. The new Civil Surgeon is the same as the last, but does not dare to be. That is all any administrative change amounts to. All my suffering has won nothing for us. But look here, Cyril, while I remember it. There's gossip about you as well as McBryde. They say that you and Miss Quested became also rather too intimate friends. To speak perfectly frankly, they say you and she have been guilty of impropriety.'

'They would say that.'

'It's all over the town, and may injure your reputation. You know, everyone is by no means your supporter. I have tried all I could to silence such a story.'

'Don't bother. Miss Quested has cleared out at last.'

'It is those who stop in the country, not those who leave it, whom such a story injures. Imagine my dismay and anxiety. I could scarcely get a wink of sleep. First my name was coupled with her and now it is yours.'

'Don't use such exaggerated phrases.'

'As what?'

'As dismay and anxiety.'

'Have I not lived all my life in India? Do I not know what produces a bad impression here?' His voice shot up rather crossly.

'Yes, but the scale, the scale. You always get the scale wrong, my dear fellow. A pity there is this rumour, but such a very small pity—so small that we may as well talk of something else.'

'You mind for Miss Quested's sake, though. I can see from your face.'

'As far as I do mind. I travel light.'

'Cyril, that boastfulness about travelling light will be your ruin. It is raising up enemies against you on all sides, and makes me feel excessively uneasy.'

'What enemies?'

Since Aziz had only himself in mind, he could not reply. Feeling a fool, he became angrier. 'I have given you list after list of the people who cannot be trusted in this city. In your position I should have the sense to know I was surrounded by enemies. You observe I speak in a low voice. It is because I see your sais is new. How do I know he isn't a spy?' He lowered his voice: 'Every third servant is a spy.'

'Now, what is the matter?' he asked, smiling.

'Do you contradict my last remark?'

'It simply doesn't affect me. Spies are as thick as mosquitoes, but it's years before I shall meet the one that kills me. You've something else in your mind.'

'I've not; don't be ridiculous.'

'You have. You're cross with me about something or other.'

Any direct attack threw him out of action. Presently he said: 'So you and Madamsell Adela used to amuse one another in the evening, naughty boy.'

Those drab and high-minded talks had scarcely made for dalliance. Fielding was so startled at the story being taken seriously, and so disliked being called a naughty boy, that he lost his head and cried: 'You little rotter!

Well, I'm damned. Amusement indeed. Is it likely at such a time?'

'Oh, I beg your pardon, I'm sure. The licentious Oriental imagination was at work,' he replied, speaking gaily, but cut to the heart; for hours after his mistake he bled inwardly.

'You see, Aziz, the circumstances . . . also the girl was still engaged to Heaslop, also I never felt . . .'

'Yes, yes; but you didn't contradict what I said, so I thought it was true. Oh dear, East and West. Most misleading. Will you please put your little rotter down at his hospital?'

'You're not offended?'

'Most certainly I am not.'

'If you are, this must be cleared up later on.'

'It has been,' he answered, dignified. 'I believe absolutely what you say, and of that there need be no further question.'

'But the way I said it must be cleared up. I was unintentionally rude. Unreserved regrets.'

'The fault is entirely mine.'

Tangles like this still interrupted their intercourse. A pause in the wrong place, an intonation misunderstood, and a whole conversation went awry. Fielding had been startled, not shocked, but how convey the difference? There is always trouble when two people do not think of sex at the same moment, always mutual resentment and surprise, even when the two people are of the same race. He began to recapitulate his feelings about Miss Quested. Aziz cut him short with: 'But I believe you, I believe. Mohammed Latif shall be severely punished for inventing this.'

'Oh, leave it alone, like all gossip—it's merely one of those half-alive things that try to crowd out real life. Take no notice, it'll vanish, like poor old Mrs Moore's tombs.'

'Mohammed Latif has taken to intriguing. We are already much displeased with him. Will it satisfy you if we send him back to his family without a present?'

'We'll discuss M.L. at dinner.'

His eyes went clotted and hard. 'Dinner. This is most unlucky— I forgot. I have promised to dine with Das.'

'Bring Das to me.'

'He will have invited other friends.'

'You are coming to dinner with me as arranged,' said Fielding, looking away. 'I don't stand this. You are coming to dinner with me. You come.'

They had reached the hospital now. Fielding continued round the Maidan alone. He was annoyed with himself, but counted on dinner to pull things straight. At the post office he saw the Collector. Their vehicles were parked side by side while their servants competed in the interior of the building. 'Good morning; so you are back,' said Turton icily. 'I should be glad if you will put in your appearance at the club this evening.'

'I have accepted re-election, sir. Do you regard it as necessary I should come? I should be glad to be excused; indeed, I have a dinner engagement this evening.'

'It is not a question of your feelings, but of the wish of the Lieutenant-Governor. Perhaps you will ask me whether I speak officially. I do. I shall expect you this evening at six. We shall not interfere with your subsequent plans.'

He attended the grim little function in due course. The skeletons of hospitality rattled–'Have a peg, have a drink.' He talked for five minutes to Mrs Blakiston, who was the only surviving female. He talked to McBryde, who was defiant about his divorce, conscious that he had sinned as a sahib. He talked to Major Roberts, the new Civil Surgeon; and to young Milner, the new City Magistrate; but the more the club changed, the more it promised to be the same thing. 'It is no good,' he thought, as he returned past the mosque, 'we all build upon sand; and the more modern the country gets, the worse'll be the crash. In the old eighteenth century, when cruelty and injustice raged, an invisible power repaired their ravages. Everything echoes now; there's no stopping the echo. The original sound may be harmless, but the echo is always evil.' This reflection about an echo lay at the verge of Fielding's mind. He could never develop it. It belonged to the universe that he had missed or rejected. And the mosque missed it too. Like himself, those shallow arcades provided but a limited asylum. 'There is no God but God' doesn't carry us far through the complexities of matter and spirit; it is only a game with words, really, a religious pun, not a religious truth.

He found Aziz overtired and dispirited, and he determined not to allude to their misunderstanding until the end of the evening; it would be more acceptable then. He made a clean breast about the club–said he had only gone under compulsion, and should never attend again unless the order was renewed. 'In other words, probably never; for I am going quite soon to England.'

'I thought you might end in England,' he said very quietly, then changed the conversation. Rather awkwardly they ate their dinner, then went out to sit in the Mogul garden-house.

'I am only going for a little time. On official business. My service is anxious to get me away from Chandrapore for a bit. It is obliged to value me highly, but does not care for me. The situation is somewhat humorous.'

'What is the nature of the business? Will it leave you much spare time?'

'Enough to see my friends.'

'I expected you to make such a reply. You are a faithful friend. Shall we now talk about something else?'

'Willingly. What subject?'

'Poetry,' he said, with tears in his eyes. 'Let us discuss why poetry has lost the power of making men brave. My mother's father was also a poet, and fought against you in the Mutiny. I might equal him if there was another mutiny. As it is, I am a doctor, who has won a case and has three children to support, and whose chief subject of conversation is official plans.'

'Let us talk about poetry.' He turned his mind to the innocuous subject. 'You people are sadly circumstanced. Whatever are you to write about? You cannot say, "The rose is faded," for evermore. We know it's faded. Yet you can't have patriotic poetry of the "India, my India" type, when it's nobody's India.'

'I like this conversation. It may lead to something interesting.'

'You are quite right in thinking that poetry must touch life. When I knew you first, you used it as an incantation.'

'I was a child when you knew me first. Everyone was my friend then. The Friend: a Persian expression for God. But I do not want to be a religious poet either.'

'I hoped you would be.'

'Why, when you yourself are an atheist?'

'There is something in religion that may not be true, but has not yet been sung.'

'Explain in detail.'

'Something that the Hindus have perhaps found.'

'Let them sing it.'

'Hindus are unable to sing.'

'Cyril, you sometimes make a sensible remark. That will do for poetry for the present. Let us now return to your English visit.'

'We haven't discussed poetry for two seconds,' said the other, smiling.

But Aziz was addicted to cameos. He held the tiny conversation in his hand, and felt it epitomized his problem. For an instant he recalled his wife, and, as happens when a memory is intense, the past became the future, and he saw her with him in a quiet Hindu jungle native state, far away from foreigners. He said: 'I suppose you will visit Miss Quested.'

'If I have time. It will be strange seeing her in Hampstead.'

'What is Hampstead?'

'An artistic and thoughtful little suburb of London—'

'And there she lives in comfort: you will enjoy seeing her. . . . Dear me, I've got a headache this evening. Perhaps I am going to have cholera. With your permission, I'll leave early.'

'When would you like the carriage?'

'Don't trouble–I'll bike.'

'But you haven't got your bicycle. My carriage fetched you–let it take you away.'

'Sound reasoning,' he said, trying to be gay. 'I have not got my bicycle. But I am seen too often in your carriage. I am thought to take advantage of your generosity by Mr Ram Chand.' He was out of sorts and uneasy. The conversation jumped from topic to topic in a broken-backed fashion. They were affectionate and intimate, but nothing clicked tight.

'Aziz, you have forgiven me the stupid remark I made this morning?'

'When you called me a little rotter?'

'Yes, to my eternal confusion. You know how fond I am of you.'

'That is nothing, of course, we all of us make mistakes. In a friendship such as ours a few slips are of no consequence.'

But as he drove off, something depressed him–a dull pain of body or mind, waiting to rise to the surface. When he reached the bungalow he wanted to return and say something very affectionate; instead, he gave the sais a heavy tip, and sat down gloomily on the bed, and Hassan massaged him incompetently. The eye-flies had colonized the top of an almeira; the red stains on the durry were thicker, for Mohammed Latif had slept here during his imprisonment and spat a good deal; the table drawer was scarred where the police had forced it open; everything in Chandrapore was used up, including the air. The trouble rose to the surface now: he was suspicious; he suspected his friend of intending to marry Miss Quested for the sake of her money, and of going to England for that purpose.

'Huzoor?'–for he had muttered.

'Look at those flies on the ceiling. Why have you not drowned them?'

'Huzoor, they return.'

'Like all evil things.'

To divert the conversation, Hassan related how the kitchen-boy had killed a snake, good, but killed it by cutting it in two, bad, because it becomes two snakes.

'When he breaks a plate, does it become two plates?'

'Glasses and a new teapot will similarly be required, also for myself a coat.'

Aziz sighed. Each for himself. One man needs a coat, another a rich wife; each approaches his goal by a clever detour. Fielding had saved the girl a fine of twenty thousand rupees, and now followed her to England. If he desired to marry her, all was explained; she would bring him a larger dowry. Aziz did not believe his own suspicions–better if he had, for then he would have denounced and cleared the situation up. Suspicion and belief could in his mind exist side by side. They sprang from different sources, and need never intermingle. Suspicion in the Oriental is a sort of malignant tumour, a mental malady, that makes him self-conscious and unfriendly suddenly; he trusts and mistrusts at the same time in a way the Westerner cannot comprehend. It is his demon, as the Westerner's is hypocrisy. Aziz was seized by it, and his fancy built a satanic castle, of which the foundation had been laid when he talked at Dilkusha under the stars. The girl had surely been Cyril's mistress when she stopped in the College–Mohammed Latif was right. But was that all? Perhaps it was Cyril who followed her into the cave. . . . No; impossible. Cyril hadn't been on the Kawa Dol at all. Impossible. Ridiculous. Yet the fancy left him trembling with misery. Such treachery–if true–would have been the worst in Indian history; nothing so vile, not even the murder of Afzul Khan by Sivaji. He was shaken, as though by a truth, and told Hassan to leave him.

Next day he decided to take his children back to Mussoorie. They had come down for the trial, that he might bid them farewell, and had stayed on at Hamidullah's for the rejoicings. Major Roberts would give him leave, and during his absence Fielding would go off to England. The idea suited both his beliefs and his suspicions. Events would prove which was right, and preserve, in either case, his dignity.

Fielding was conscious of something hostile, and because he was really fond of Aziz his optimism failed him. Travelling light is less easy as soon as affection is involved. Unable to jog forward in the serene hope that all would come right, he wrote an elaborate letter in the rather modern style: 'It is on my mind that you think me a prude about women. I had rather you thought anything else of me. If I live impeccably now, it is only because I am well on the forties—a period of revision. In the eighties I shall revise again. And before the nineties come—I shall be revised! But, alive or dead, I am absolutely devoid of morals. Do kindly grasp this about me.' Aziz did not care for the letter at all. It hurt his delicacy. He liked confidences, however gross, but generalizations and comparisons always repelled him. Life is not a scientific manual. He replied coldly, regretting his inability to return from Mussoorie before his friend sailed: 'But I must take my poor little holiday while I can. All must be economy henceforward, all hopes of Kashmir have vanished for ever and ever. When you return I shall be slaving far away in some new post.'

And Fielding went, and in the last gutterings of Chandrapore—heaven and earth both looking like toffee—the Indian's bad fancies were confirmed. His friends encouraged them, for though they had liked the Principal, they felt uneasy at his getting to know so much about their private affairs. Mahmoud Ali soon declared that treachery was afoot. Hamidullah murmured, 'Certainly of late he no longer addressed us with his former frankness,' and warned Aziz 'not to expect too much—he and she are, after all, both members of another race.' 'Where are my twenty thousand rupees?' he thought. He was absolutely indifferent to money—not merely generous with it, but promptly paying his debts when he could remember to do so—yet these rupees haunted his mind, because he had been tricked about them, and allowed them to escape overseas, like so much of the wealth of India. Cyril would marry Miss Quested—he grew certain of it, all the unexplained residue of the Marabar contributing. It was the natural conclusion of the horrible senseless picnic, and before long he persuaded himself that the wedding had actually taken place.

Chapter Thirty-two

Egypt was charming—a green strip of carpet and walking up and down it four sorts of animals and one sort of man. Fielding's business took him there for a few days. He re-embarked at Alexandria—bright blue sky, constant wind, clean low coast-line, as against the intricacies of Bombay. Crete welcomed him next with the long snowy ridge of its mountains, and then came Venice. As he landed on the piazzetta a cup of beauty was lifted to his lips, and he drank with a sense of disloyalty. The buildings of Venice, like the mountains of Crete and the fields of Egypt, stood in the right place, whereas in poor India everything was placed wrong. He had forgotten the beauty of form among idol temples and lumpy hills; indeed, without form, how can there be beauty? Form stammered here and there in a mosque, became rigid through nervousness even, but oh these Italian churches! San Giorgio standing on the island which could scarcely have risen from the waves without it, the Salute holding the entrance of a canal which, but for it, would not be the Grand Canal! In the old undergraduate days he had wrapped himself up in the many-coloured blanket of St Mark's, but something more precious than mosaics and marbles was offered to him now: the harmony between the works of man and the earth that upholds them, the civilization that has escaped muddle, the spirit in a reasonable form, with flesh and blood subsisting. Writing picture post-cards to his Indian friends, he felt that all of them would miss the joys he experienced now, the joys of form, and that this constituted a serious barrier. They would see the sumptuousness of Venice, not its shape, and though Venice was not Europe, it was part of the Mediterranean harmony. The Mediterranean is the human norm. When men leave that exquisite lake, whether through the Bosphorus or the Pillars of Hercules, they approach the monstrous and extraordinary; and the southern exit leads to the strangest experience of all. Turning his back on it yet again, he took the train northward, and tender romantic fancies that he thought were dead for ever, flowered when he saw the buttercups and daisies of June.

Temples

Chapter Thirty-three

Some hundreds of miles westward of the Marabar Hills, and two years later in time, Professor Narayan Godbole stands in the presence of God. God is not born yet—that will occur at midnight—but He has also been born centuries ago, nor can He ever be born, because He is the Lord of the Universe, who transcends human processes. He is, was not, is not, was. He and Professor Godbole stood at opposite ends of the same strip of carpet.

> *Tukaram, Tukaram,*
> *Thou art my father and mother and everybody.*
> *Tukaram, Tukaram,*
> *Thou art my father and mother and everybody.*
> *Tukaram, Tukaram,*
> *Thou art my father and mother and everybody.*
> *Tukaram, Tukaram,*
> *Thou art my father and mother and everybody.*
> *Tukaram. . . .*

This corridor in the palace at Mau opened through other corridors into a courtyard. It was of beautiful hard white stucco, but its pillars and vaulting could scarcely be seen behind coloured rags, iridescent balls, chandeliers of opaque pink glass, and murky photographs framed crookedly. At the end was the small but famous shrine of the dynastic cult, and the God to be born was largely a silver image the size of a teaspoon. Hindus sat on either side of the carpet where they could find room, or overflowed into the adjoining corridors and the courtyard—Hindus, Hindus only, mild-featured men, mostly villagers, for whom anything outside their villages passed in a dream.

They were the toiling ryot, whom some call the real India. Mixed with them sat a few tradesmen out of the little town, officials, courtiers, scions of the ruling house. Schoolboys kept inefficient order. The assembly was in a tender, happy state unknown to an English crowd, it seethed like a beneficent potion. When the villagers broke cordon for a glimpse of the silver image, a most beautiful and radiant expression came into their faces, a beauty in which there was nothing personal, for it caused them all to resemble one another during the moment of its indwelling, and only when it was withdrawn did they revert to individual clods. And so with the music. Music there was, but from so many sources that the sum-total was untrammelled. The braying banging crooning melted into a single mass which trailed round the palace before joining the thunder. Rain fell at intervals throughout the night.

It was the turn of Professor Godbole's choir. As Minister of Education, he gained this special honour. When the previous group of singers dispersed into the crowd, he pressed forward from the back, already in full voice, that the chain of sacred sounds might be uninterrupted. He was barefoot and in white, he wore a pale blue turban; his gold pince-nez had caught in a jasmine garland, and lay sideways down his nose. He and the six colleagues who supported him clashed their cymbals, hit small drums, droned upon a portable harmonium, and sang:

> *Tukaram, Tukaram,*
> *Thou art my father and mother and everybody.*
> *Tukaram, Tukaram,*
> *Thou art my father and mother and everybody.*
> *Tukaram, Tukaram. . . .*

They sang not even to the God who confronted them, but to a saint; they did not one thing which the non-Hindu would feel dramatically correct; this approaching triumph of India was a muddle (as we call it), a frustration of reason and form. Where was the God Himself, in whose honour the congregation had gathered? Indistinguishable in the jumble of His own altar, huddled out of sight amid images of inferior descent, smothered under rose-leaves, overhung by oleographs, outblazed by golden tablets representing the Rajah's ancestors, and entirely obscured, when the wind blew, by the tattered foliage of a banana. Hundreds of electric lights had been lit in His honour (worked by an engine whose thumps destroyed the rhythm of the hymn). Yet His face could not be seen. Hundreds of His silver dishes were piled around Him with the minimum of effect. The inscriptions which the poets of the State had composed were hung where they could not be read, or had twitched their drawing-pins out of the stucco, and one of them (composed in English to indicate His universality) consisted, by an unfortunate slip of the draughtsman, of the words, 'God si Love.'

God si Love. Is this the final message of India?

> *Tukaram, Tukaram . . .,*

continued the choir, reinforced by a squabble behind the purdah curtain, where two mothers tried to push their children at the same moment to the front. A little girl's leg shot out like an eel. In the courtyard, drenched by the rain, the small Europeanized band stumbled off into a waltz. 'Nights of Gladness' they were playing. The singers were not perturbed by this rival, they lived beyond competition. It was long before the tiny fragment of Professor Godbole that attended to outside things decided that his pince-nez was in trouble, and that until it was adjusted he could not choose a new hymn. He laid down one cymbal, with the other he clashed the air, with his free hand he fumbled at the flowers round his neck. A colleague assisted him. Singing into one another's grey moustaches, they disentangled the chain from the tinsel into which it had sunk. Godbole consulted the music-book, said a word to the drummer, who broke rhythm, made a thick little blur of sound, and produced a new rhythm. This was more exciting, the inner images it evoked more definite, and the singers' expressions became fatuous and languid. They loved all men, the whole universe, and scraps of their past, tiny splinters of detail, emerged for a moment to melt into the universal warmth. Thus Godbole, though she was not important to him, remembered an old woman he had met in Chandrapore days. Chance brought her into his mind while it was in this heated state, he did not select her, she happened to occur among the throng of soliciting images, a tiny splinter, and he impelled her by his spiritual force to that place where completeness can be found. Completeness, not reconstruction. His senses grew thinner, he remembered a wasp seen he forgot where, perhaps on a stone. He loved the wasp equally, he impelled it likewise, he was imitating God. And the stone where the wasp clung—could he . . . no, he could not, he had been wrong to attempt the stone, logic and conscious effort had seduced, he came back to the strip of red carpet and discovered that he was dancing upon it. Up and down, a third of the way to the altar and back again, clashing his cymbals, his little legs twinkling, his companions dancing with him and each other. Noise, noise, the Europeanized band louder, incense on the altar, sweat, the blaze of lights, wind in the bananas, noise, thunder, eleven-fifty by his wrist-watch, seen as he threw up his hands and detached the tiny reverberation that was his soul. Louder shouts in the crowd. He danced on. The boys and men who were squatting in the aisles were lifted forcibly and dropped without changing their shapes into the laps of their neighbours. Down the path thus cleared advanced a litter.

It was the aged ruler of the state, brought against the advice of his physicians to witness the Birth ceremony.

No one greeted the Rajah, nor did he wish it; this was no moment for human glory. Nor could the litter be set down, lest it defiled the temple by becoming a throne. He was lifted out of it while its feet remained in air, and deposited on the carpet close to the altar, his immense beard was straightened, his legs tucked under him, a paper containing red powder was placed in his hand. There he sat, leaning against a pillar, exhausted with illness, his eyes magnified by many unshed tears.

He had not to wait long. In a land where all else was unpunctual, the hour of the Birth was chronometrically observed. Three minutes before it was due, a Brahman brought forth a model of the village of Gokul (the Bethlehem in that nebulous story) and placed it in front of the altar. The model was on a wooden tray about a yard square; it was of clay, and was gaily blue and white with streamers and paint. Here, upon a chair too small for him and with a head too large, sat King Kansa, who is Herod, directing the murder of some Innocents, and in a corner, similarly proportioned, stood the father and mother of the Lord, warned to depart in a dream. The model was not holy, but more than a decoration, for it diverted men from the actual image of the God, and increased their sacred bewilderment. Some of the villagers thought the Birth had occurred, saying with truth that the Lord must have been born, or they could not see Him. But the clock struck midnight, and simultaneously the rending note of the conch broke forth, followed by the trumpeting of elephants; all who had packets of powder threw them at the altar, and in the rosy dust and incense, and clanging and shouts, Infinite Love took upon itself the form of SHRI KRISHNA, and saved the world. All sorrow was annihilated, not only for Indians, but for foreigners, birds, caves, railways, and the stars; all became joy, all laughter; there had never been disease nor doubt, misunderstanding, cruelty, fear. Some jumped in the air, others flung themselves prone and embraced the bare feet of the universal lover; the women behind the purdah slapped and shrieked; the little girl slipped out and danced by herself, her black pigtails flying. Not an orgy of the body; the tradition of that shrine forbade it. But the human spirit had tried by a desperate contortion to ravish the unknown, flinging down science and history in the struggle, yes, beauty herself. Did it succeed? Books written afterwards say 'Yes.' But how, if there is such an event, can it be remembered afterwards? How can it be expressed in anything but itself? Not only from the unbeliever are mysteries hid, but the adept himself cannot retain them. He may think, if he chooses, that he has been with God, but as soon as he thinks it, it becomes history, and falls under the rules of time.

A cobra of papier-mâché now appeared on the carpet, also a wooden cradle swinging from a frame. Professor Godbole approached the latter with a red silk napkin in his arms. The napkin was God, not that it was, and the image remained in the blur of the altar. It was just a napkin, folded into a shape which indicated a baby's. The Professor dandled it and gave it to the Rajah, who, making a great effort, said, 'I name this child Shri Krishna,' and tumbled it into the cradle. Tears poured from his eyes, because he had seen the Lord's salvation. He was too weak to exhibit the silk baby to his people, his privilege in former years. His attendants lifted him up, a new path was cleared through the crowd, and he was carried away to a less sacred part of the palace. There, in a room accessible to Western science by an outer staircase, his physician, Dr Aziz, awaited him. His Hindu physician, who had accompanied him to the shrine, briefly reported his symptoms. As the ecstasy receded, the invalid grew fretful. The bumping of the steam engine that worked the dynamo disturbed him, and he asked for what reason it had been introduced into his home. They replied that they would enquire, and administered a sedative.

Down in the sacred corridors, joy had seethed to jollity. It was their duty to play various games to amuse the newly born God, and to simulate his sports with the wanton dairymaids of Brindaban. Butter played a prominent part in these. When the cradle had been removed, the principal nobles of the state gathered together for an innocent frolic. They removed their turbans, and one put a lump of butter on his forehead, and waited for it to slide down his nose into his mouth. Before it could arrive, another stole up behind him, snatched the melting morsel, and swallowed it himself. All laughed exultantly at discovering that the divine sense of humour coincided with their own. 'God si love!' There is fun in heaven. God can play practical jokes upon Himself, draw chairs away from beneath His own posteriors, set His own turbans on fire, and steal His own petticoats when He bathes. By sacrificing good taste, this worship achieved what Christianity has shirked: the inclusion of merriment. All spirit as well as all matter must participate in salvation, and if practical jokes are banned, the circle is incomplete. Having swallowed the butter, they played another game which chanced to be graceful: the fondling of Shri Krishna under the similitude of a child. A pretty red and gold ball is thrown, and he who catches it chooses a child from the crowd, raises it in his arms, and carries it round to be caressed. All stroke the darling creature for the Creator's sake, and murmur happy words. The child is restored to his parents, the ball thrown on, and another child becomes for a moment the World's Desire. And the Lord bounds hither and thither through the aisles, chance, and the sport of chance, irradiating little mortals with His immortality. . . . When they had played this long enough—and being exempt from boredom, they played it again and again, they played it again and again—they took many sticks and hit them together, whack smack, as though they fought the Pandava wars, and threshed and churned with them, and later on they hung from the roof of the temple, in a net, a great black earthenware jar, which was painted here and there with red, and wreathed with dried figs. Now came a rousing sport. Springing up, they struck at the jar with their sticks. It cracked, broke, and a mass of greasy rice and milk poured on to their faces. They ate and smeared one another's mouths, and dived between each other's legs for what had been pashed upon the carpet. This way and that spread the divine mess, until the line of schoolboys, who had somewhat fended off the crowd, broke for their share. The corridors, the courtyard, were filled with benign confusion. Also the flies awoke and claimed their share of God's bounty. There was no quarrelling, owing to the nature of the gift, for blessed is the man who confers it on another, he imitates God. And those 'imitations,' those 'substitutions,' continued to flicker through the assembly for many hours, awaking in each man, according to his capacity, an emotion that he would not have had otherwise. No definite image survived; at the Birth it was questionable whether a silver doll or a mud village, or a silk napkin, or an intangible spirit, or a pious resolution, had been born. Perhaps all these things! Perhaps none! Perhaps all birth is an allegory! Still, it was the main event of the religious year. It caused strange thoughts. Covered with grease and dust, Professor Godbole had once more developed the life of his spirit. He had, with increasing vividness, again seen Mrs Moore, and round her faintly clinging forms of trouble. He was a Brahman, she Christian, but it made no difference, it made no difference whether she was a trick of his memory or a telepathic appeal. It was his duty, as it was his desire, to place himself in the position of the God and to love her, and to place himself in her position and to say to the God, 'Come, come, come, come.' This was all he could do. How inadequate! But each according to his own capacities, and he knew that his own were small. 'One old Englishwoman and one little, little wasp,' he thought, as he stepped out of the temple into the grey of a pouring wet morning. 'It does not seem much, still it is more than I am myself.'

Chapter Thirty-four

Dr Aziz left the palace at the same time. As he returned to his house–which stood in a pleasant garden further up the main street of the town–he could see his old patron paddling and capering in the slush ahead. 'Hullo!' he called, and it was the wrong remark, for the devotee indicated by circular gestures of his arms that he did not desire to be disturbed. He added, 'Sorry,' which was right, for Godbole twisted his head till it didn't belong to his body, and said in a strained voice that had no connection with his mind: 'He arrived at the European Guest House perhaps–at least possibly.'

'Did he? Since when?'

But time was too definite. He waved his arm more dimly and disappeared. Aziz knew who 'he' was–Fielding–but he refused to think about him, because it disturbed his life, and he still trusted the floods to prevent him from arriving. A fine little river issued from his garden gate and gave him much hope. It was impossible that anyone could get across from Deora in such weather as this. Fielding's visit was official. He had been transferred from Chandrapore, and sent on a tour through Central India to see what the remoter states were doing with regard to English education. He had married, he had done the expected with Miss Quested, and Aziz had no wish to see him again.

'Dear old Godbole,' he thought, and smiled. He had no religious curiosity, and had never discovered the meaning of this annual antic, but he was well assured that Godbole was a dear old man. He had come to Mau through him and remained on his account. Without him he could never have grasped problems so totally different from those of Chandrapore. For here the cleavage was between Brahman and non-Brahman; Moslems and English were quite out of the running, and sometimes not mentioned for days. Since Godbole was a Brahman, Aziz was one also for purposes of intrigue: they would often joke about it together. The fissures in the Indian soil are infinite: Hinduism, so solid from a distance, is riven into sects and clans, which radiate and join, and change their names according to the aspect from which they are approached. Study it for years with the best teachers, and when you raise your head, nothing they have told you quite fits. Aziz, the day of his inauguration, had remarked: 'I study nothing, I respect'–making an excellent impression. There was now a minimum of prejudice against him. Nominally under a Hindu doctor, he was really chief medicine man to the court. He had to drop inoculation and such Western whims, but even at Chandrapore his profession had been a game, centring round the operating table, and here in the backwoods he let his instruments rust, ran his little hospital at half steam, and caused no undue alarm.

His impulse to escape from the English was sound. They had frightened him permanently, and there are only two reactions against fright: to kick and scream on committees, or to retreat to a remote jungle, where the sahib seldom comes. His old lawyer friends wanted him to stop in British India and help agitate, and might have prevailed, but for the treachery of Fielding. The news had not surprised him in the least. A rift had opened between them after the trial when Cyril had not joined in his procession; those advocacies of the girl had increased it; then came the post-cards from Venice, so cold, so unfriendly that all agreed that something was wrong; and finally, after a silence, the expected letter from Hampstead. Mahmoud Ali was with him at the time. 'Some news that will surprise you. I am to marry someone whom you know. . . .' He did not read further. 'Here it comes, answer for me—' and he threw it to Mahmoud Ali. Subsequent letters he destroyed unopened. It was the end of a foolish experiment. And though sometimes at the back of his mind he felt that Fielding had made sacrifices for him, it was now all confused with his genuine hatred of the English. 'I am an Indian at last,' he thought, standing motionless in the rain.

Life passed pleasantly, the climate was healthy so that the children could be with him all the year round, and he had married again–not exactly a marriage, but he liked to regard it as one–and he read his Persian, wrote his poetry, had his horse, and sometimes got some shikar while the good Hindus looked the other way. His poems were all on one topic–Oriental womanhood. 'The purdah must go,' was their burden, 'otherwise we shall never be free.' And he declared (fantastically) that India would not have been conquered if women as well as men had fought at Plassy. 'But we do not show our women to the foreigner'–not explaining how this was to be managed, for he was writing a poem. Bulbuls and roses would still persist, the pathos of defeated Islam remained in his blood and could not be expelled by modernities. Illogical poems–like their writer. Yet they struck a true note: there cannot be a mother-land without new homes. In one poem–the only one funny old Godbole liked–he had skipped over the mother-land (whom he did not truly love) and gone straight to internationality. 'Ah, that is bhakti; ah, my young friend, that is different and very good. Ah, India, who seems not to move, will go straight there while the other nations waste their time. May I translate this particular one into Hindi? In fact, it might be rendered into Sanskrit almost, it is so enlightened. Yes, of course, all your other poems are very good too. His Highness was saying to Colonel Maggs last time he came that we are proud of you'—simpering slightly.

Colonel Maggs was the Political Agent for the neighbourhood and Aziz' dejected opponent. The Criminal Investigation Department kept an eye on Aziz ever since the trial—they had nothing actionable against him, but Indians who have been unfortunate must be watched, and to the end of his life he remained under observation, thanks to Miss Quested's mistake. Colonel Maggs learnt with concern that a suspect was coming to Mau, and, adopting a playful manner, rallied the old Rajah for permitting a Moslem doctor to approach his sacred person. A few years ago, the Rajah would have taken the hint, for the Political Agent then had been a formidable figure, descending with all the thunders of Empire when it was most inconvenient, turning the polity inside out, requiring motor-cars and tiger-hunts, trees cut down that impeded the view from the Guest House, cows milked in his presence, and generally arrogating the control of internal affairs. But there had been a change of policy in high quarters. Local thunders were no longer endorsed, and the group of little states that composed the agency discovered this and began comparing notes with fruitful result. To see how much, or how little, Colonel Maggs would stand, became an agreeable game at Mau, which was played by all the departments of State. He had to stand the appointment of Dr Aziz. The Rajah did not take the hint, but replied that Hindus were less exclusive than formerly, thanks to the enlightened commands of the Viceroy, and he felt it his duty to move with the times.

Yes, all had gone well hitherto, but now, when the rest of the state was plunged in its festival, he had a crisis of a very different sort. A note awaited him at his house. There was no doubt that Fielding had arrived overnight, nor much doubt that Godbole knew of his arrival, for the note was addressed to him, and he had read it before sending it on to Aziz, and had written in the margin, 'Is not this delightful news, but unfortunately my religious duties prevent me from taking any action.' Fielding announced that he had inspected Mudkul (Miss Derek's former preserve), that he had nearly been drowned at Deora, that he had reached Mau according to time-table, and hoped to remain there two days, studying the various educational innovations of his old friend. Nor had he come alone. His wife and her brother accompanied him. And then the note turned into the sort of note that always did arrive from the State Guest House. Wanting something. No eggs. Mosquito nets torn. When would they pay their respects to His Highness? Was it correct that a torchlight procession would take place? If so, might they view it? They didn't want to give trouble, but if they might stand in a balcony, or if they might go out in a boat. . . . Aziz tore the note up. He had had enough of showing Miss Quested native life. Treacherous hideous harridan! Bad people altogether. He hoped to avoid them, though this might be difficult, for they would certainly be held up for several days at Mau. Down country, the floods were even worse, and the pale grey faces of lakes had appeared in the direction of the Asirgarh railway station.

Chapter Thirty-five

Long before he discovered Mau, another young Mohammedan had retired there—a saint. His mother said to him, 'Free prisoners.' So he took a sword and went up to the fort. He unlocked a door, and the prisoners streamed out and resumed their previous occupations, but the police were too much annoyed and cut off the young man's head. Ignoring its absence, he made his way over the rocks that separate the fort and the town, killing policemen as he went, and he fell outside his mother's house, having accomplished her orders. Consequently there are two shrines to him to-day—that of the Head above, and that of the Body below—and they are worshipped by the few Mohammedans who live near, and by Hindus also. 'There is no God but God'; that symmetrical injunction melts in the mild airs of Mau; it belongs to pilgrimages and universities, not to feudalism and agriculture. When Aziz arrived, and found that even Islam was idolatrous, he grew scornful, and longed to purify the place, like Alamgir. But soon he didn't mind, like Akbar. After all, this saint had freed prisoners, and he himself had lain in prison. The Shrine of the Body lay in his own garden and produced a weekly crop of lamps and flowers, and when he saw them he recalled his sufferings. The Shrine of the Head made a nice short walk for the children. He was off duty the morning after the great pujah, and he told them to come. Jemila held his hand. Ahmed and Karim ran in front, arguing what the body looked like as it came staggering down, and whether they would have been frightened if they met it. He didn't want them to grow up superstitious, so he rebuked them, and they answered yes father, for they were well brought up, but, like himself, they were impervious to argument, and after a polite pause they continued saying what their natures compelled them to say.

A slim, tall eight-sided building stood at the top of the slope, among some bushes. This was the Shrine of the Head. It had not been roofed, and was indeed merely a screen. Inside it crouched a humble dome, and inside that, visible through a grille, was a truncated gravestone, swathed in calico. The inner angles of the screen were cumbered with bees' nests, and a gentle shower of broken wings and other aerial oddments kept falling, and had strewn the damp pavement with their flue. Ahmed, apprized by Mohammed Latif of the character of the bee, said, 'They will not hurt us, whose lives are chaste,' and pushed boldly in; his sister was more cautious. From the shrine they went to a mosque, which, in size and design, resembled a fire-screen; the arcades of Chandrapore had shrunk to a flat piece of ornamental stucco, with protuberances at either end to suggest minarets. The funny little thing didn't even stand straight, for the rock on which it had been put was slipping down the hill. It, and the shrine, were a strange outcome of the protests of Arabia.

They wandered over the old fort, now deserted, and admired the various views. The scenery, according to their standards, was delightful–the sky grey and black, bellyfuls of rain all over it, the earth pocked with pools of water and slimy with mud. A magnificent monsoon–the best for three years, the tanks already full, bumper crops possible. Out towards the river (the route by which the Fieldings had escaped from Deora) the downpour had been enormous, the mails had to be pulled across by ropes. They could just see the break in the forest trees where the gorge came through, and the rocks above that marked the site of the diamond mine, glistening with wet. Close beneath was the suburban residence of the Junior Rani, isolated by floods, and Her Highness, lax about purdah, to be seen paddling with her handmaidens in the garden and waving her sari at the monkeys on the roof. But better not look close beneath, perhaps–nor towards the European Guest House either. Beyond the Guest House rose another grey-green gloom of hills, covered with temples like little white flames. There were over two hundred gods in that direction alone, who visited each other constantly, and owned numerous cows, and all the betel-leaf industry, besides having shares in the Asirgarh motor omnibus. Many of them were in the palace at this moment, having the time of their lives; others, too large or proud to travel, had sent symbols to represent them. The air was thick with religion and rain.

Their white shirts fluttering, Ahmed and Karim ran about over the fort, shrieking with joy. Presently they intersected a line of prisoners, who were looking aimlessly at an old bronze gun. 'Which of you is to be pardoned?' they asked. For to-night was the procession of the Chief God, when He would leave the palace, escorted by the whole power of the State, and pass by the Jail, which stood down in the town now. As He did so, troubling the waters of our civilization, one prisoner would be released, and then He would proceed to the great Mau tank that stretched as far as the Guest House garden, where something else would happen, some final or subsidiary apotheosis, after which He would submit to the experience of sleep. The Aziz family did not grasp as much as this, being Moslem, but the visit to the Jail was common knowledge. Smiling, with downcast eyes, the prisoners discussed with the gentry their chances of salvation. Except for the irons on their legs they resembled other men, nor did they feel different. Five of them, who had not yet been brought to trial, could expect no pardon, but all who had been convicted were full of hope. They did not distinguish between the God and the Rajah in their minds, both were too far above them; but the guard was better educated, and ventured to enquire after His Highness's health.

'It always improves,' replied the medicine man. As a matter of fact, the Rajah was dead, the ceremony overnight had overtaxed his strength. His death was being concealed lest the glory of the festival were dimmed. The Hindu physician, the Private Secretary, and a confidential servant remained with the corpse, while Aziz had assumed the duty of being seen in public, and misleading people. He had liked the ruler very much, and might not prosper under his successor, yet he could not worry over such problems yet, for he was involved in the illusion he helped to create. The children continued to run about, hunting for a frog to put in Mohammed Latif's bed, the little fools. Hundreds of frogs lived in their own garden, but they must needs catch one up on the fort. They reported two topis below. Fielding and his brother-in-law, instead of resting after their journey, were climbing the slope to the saint's tomb!

'Throw stones?' asked Karim.

'Put powdered glass in their pan?'

'Ahmed, come here for such wickedness.' He raised his hand to smite his firstborn, but allowed it to be kissed instead. It was sweet to have his sons with him at this moment, and to know they were affectionate and brave. He pointed out that the Englishmen were State guests, so must not be poisoned, and received, as always, gentle yet enthusiastic assent to his words.

The two visitors entered the octagon, but rushed out at once pursued by some bees. Hither and thither they ran, beating their heads; the children shrieked with derision, and out of heaven, as if a plug had been pulled, fell a jolly dollop of rain. Aziz had not meant to greet his former friend, but the incident put him into an excellent temper. He felt compact and strong. He shouted out, 'Hullo, gentlemen, are you in trouble?'

The brother-in-law exclaimed; a bee had got him.

'Lie down in a pool of water, my dear sir—here are plenty. Don't come near me. . . . I cannot control them, they are State bees; complain to His Highness of their behaviour.' There was no real danger, for the rain was increasing. The swarm retired to the shrine. He went up to the stranger and pulled a couple of stings out of his wrist, remarking, 'Come, pull yourself together and be a man.'

'How do you do, Aziz, after all this time? I heard you were settled in here,' Fielding called to him, but not in friendly tones. 'I suppose a couple of stings don't signify.'

'Not the least. I'll send an embrocation over to the Guest House. I heard you were settled in there.'

'Why have you not answered my letters?' he asked, going straight for the point, but not reaching it, owing to buckets of rain. His companion, new to the country, cried, as the drops drummed on his topi, that the bees were renewing their attack. Fielding checked his antics rather sharply, then said: 'Is there a short cut down to our carriage? We must give up our walk. The weather's pestilential.'

'Yes. That way.'

'Are you not coming down yourself?'

Aziz sketched a comic salaam; like all Indians, he was skilful in the slighter impertinences. 'I tremble, I obey,' the gesture said, and it was not lost upon Fielding. They walked down a rough path to the road—the two men first; the brother-in-law (boy rather than man) next, in a state over his arm, which hurt; the three Indian children last, noisy and impudent—all six wet through.

'How goes it, Aziz?'

'In my usual health.'

'Are you making anything out of your life here?'

'How much do you make out of yours?'

'Who is in charge of the Guest House?' he asked, giving up his slight effort to recapture their intimacy, and growing more official; he was older and sterner.

'His Highness's Private Secretary, probably.'

'Where is he, then?'

'I don't know.'

'Because not a soul's been near us since we arrived.'

'Really.'

'I wrote beforehand to the Durbar, and asked if a visit was convenient. I was told it was, and arranged my tour accordingly; but the Guest House servants appear to have no definite instructions, we can't get any eggs, also my wife wants to go out in the boat.'

'There are two boats.'

'Exactly, and no oars.'

'Colonel Maggs broke the oars when here last.'

'All four?'

'He is a most powerful man.'

'If the weather lifts, we want to see your torchlight procession from the water this evening,' he pursued. 'I wrote to Godbole about it, but he has taken no notice; it's a place of the dead.'

'Perhaps your letter never reached the Minister in question.'

'Will there be any objection to English people watching the procession?'

'I know nothing at all about the religion here. I should never think of watching it myself.'

'We had a very different reception both at Mudkul and Deora, they were kindness itself at Deora, the Maharajah and Maharani wanted us to see everything.'

'You should never have left them.'

'Jump in, Ralph'—they had reached the carriage.

'Jump in, Mr Quested, and Mr Fielding.'

'Who on earth is Mr Quested?'

'Do I mispronounce that well known name? Is he not your wife's brother?'

'Who on earth do you suppose I've married?'

'I'm only Ralph Moore,' said the boy, blushing, and at that moment there fell another pailful of the rain, and made a mist round their feet. Aziz tried to withdraw, but it was too late.

'Quested? Quested? Don't you know that my wife was Mrs Moore's daughter?'

He trembled, and went purplish grey; he hated the news, hated hearing the name Moore.

'Perhaps this explains your odd attitude?'

'And pray what is wrong with my attitude?'

'The preposterous letter you allowed Mahmoud Ali to write for you.'

'This is a very useless conversation, I consider.'

'However did you make such a mistake?' said Fielding, more friendly than before, but scathing and scornful. 'It's almost unbelievable. I should think I wrote you half a dozen times, mentioning my wife by name. Miss Quested! What an extraordinary notion!' From his smile, Aziz guessed that Stella was beautiful. 'Miss Quested is our best friend, she introduced us, but . . . what an amazing notion. Aziz, we must thrash this misunderstanding out later on. It is clearly some devilry of Mahmoud Ali's. He knows perfectly well I married Miss Moore. He called her 'Heaslop's sister' in his insolent letter to me.'

The name woke furies in him. 'So she is, and here is Heaslop's brother, and you his brother-in-law, and good-bye.' Shame turned into a rage that brought back his self-respect. 'What does it matter to me who you marry? Don't trouble me here at Mau is all I ask. I do not want you, I do not want one of you in my private life, with my dying breath I say it. Yes, yes, I made a foolish blunder; despise me and feel cold. I thought you married my enemy. I never read your letter. Mahmoud Ali deceived me. I thought you'd stolen my money, but'—he clapped his hands together, and his children gathered round him—'it's as if you stole it. I forgive Mahmoud Ali all things, because he loved me.' Then pausing, while the rain exploded like pistols, he said, 'My heart is for my own people henceforward,' and turned away. Cyril followed him through the mud, apologizing, laughing a little, wanting to argue and reconstruct, pointing out with irrefragable logic that he had married, not Heaslop's betrothed, but Heaslop's sister. What difference did it make at this hour of the day? He had built his life on a mistake, but he had built it. Speaking in Urdu, that the children might understand, he said: 'Please do not follow us, whomever you marry. I wish no Englishman or Englishwoman to be my friend.'

He returned to the house excited and happy. It had been an uneasy, uncanny moment when Mrs Moore's name was mentioned, stirring memories. 'Esmiss Esmoor . . .'—as though she was coming to help him. She had always been so good, and that youth whom he had scarcely looked at was her son, Ralph Moore, Stella and Ralph, whom he had promised to be kind to, and Stella had married Cyril.

Chapter Thirty-six

All the time the palace ceased not to thrum and tumtum. The revelation was over, but its effect lasted, and its effect was to make men feel that the revelation had not yet come. Hope existed despite fulfilment, as it will be in heaven. Although the God had been born, His procession—loosely supposed by many to be the birth—had not taken place. In normal years, the middle hours of this day were signalized by performances of great beauty in the private apartments of the Rajah. He owned a consecrated troupe of men and boys, whose duty it was to dance various actions and meditations of his faith before him. Seated at his ease, he could witness the Three Steps by which the Saviour ascended the universe to the discomfiture of Indra, also the death of the dragon, the mountain that turned into an umbrella, and the saddhu who (with comic results) invoked the God before dining. All culminated in the dance of the milkmaidens before Krishna, and in the still greater dance of Krishna before the milkmaidens, when the music and the musicians swirled through the dark blue robes of the actors into their tinsel crowns, and all became one. The Rajah and his guests would then forget that this was a dramatic performance, and would worship the actors. Nothing of the sort could occur to-day, because death interrupts. It interrupted less here than in Europe, its pathos was less poignant, its irony less cruel. There were two claimants to the throne, unfortunately, who were in the palace now and suspected what had happened, yet they made no trouble, because religion is a living force to the Hindus, and can at certain moments fling down everything that is petty and temporary in their natures. The festival flowed on, wild and sincere, and all men loved each other, and avoided by instinct whatever could cause inconvenience or pain.

Aziz could not understand this, any more than an average Christian could. He was puzzled that Mau should suddenly be purged from suspicion and self-seeking. Although he was an outsider, and excluded from their rites, they were always particularly charming to him at this time; he and his household received small courtesies and presents, just because he was outside. He had nothing to do all day, except to send the embrocation over to the Guest House, and towards sunset he remembered it, and looked round his house for a local palliative, for the dispensary was shut. He found a tin of ointment belonging to Mohammed Latif, who was unwilling it should be removed, for magic words had been spoken over it while it was being boiled down, but Aziz promised that he would bring it back after application to the stings: he wanted an excuse for a ride.

The procession was beginning to form as he passed the palace. A large crowed watched the loading of the State palanquin, the prow of which protruded in the form of a silver dragon's head through the lofty half-opened door. Gods, big and little, were getting aboard. He averted his eyes, for he never knew how much he was supposed to see, and nearly collided with the Minister of Education. 'Ah, you might make me late'—meaning that the touch of a non-Hindu would necessitate another bath; the words were spoken without moral heat. 'Sorry,' said Aziz. The other smiled, and again mentioned the Guest House party, and when he heard that Fielding's wife was not Miss Quested after all, remarked 'Ah, no, he married the sister of Mr Heaslop. Ah, exactly, I have known that for over a year'—also without heat. 'Why did you not tell me? Your silence plunged me into a pretty pickle.' Godbole, who had never been known to tell anyone anything, smiled again, and said in deprecating tones: 'Never be angry with me. I am, as far as my limitations permit, your true friend; besides, it is my holy festival.' Aziz

always felt like a baby in that strange presence, a baby who unexpectedly
receives a toy. He smiled also, and turned his horse into a lane, for the crush
increased. The Sweepers' Band was arriving. Playing on sieves and other
emblems of their profession, they marched straight at the gate of the palace
with the air of a victorious army. All other music was silent, for this was
ritually the moment of the Despised and Rejected; the God could not issue
from his temple until the unclean Sweepers played their tune, they were the
spot of filth without which the spirit cannot cohere. For an instant the scene
was magnificent. The doors were thrown open, and the whole court was seen
inside, barefoot and dressed in white robes; in the fairway stood the Ark of
the Lord, covered with cloth of gold and flanked by peacock fans and by stiff
circular banners of crimson. It was full to the brim with statuettes and
flowers. As it rose from the earth on the shoulders of its bearers, the friendly
sun of the monsoons shone forth and flooded the world with colour, so that
the yellow tigers painted on the palace walls seemed to spring, and pink and
green skeins of cloud to link up the upper sky. The palanquin moved. . . .
The lane was full of State elephants, who would follow it, their howdahs
empty out of humility. Aziz did not pay attention to these sanctities, for they
had no connection with his own; he felt bored, slightly cynical, like his own
dear Emperor Babur, who came down from the north and found in
Hindustan no good fruit, no fresh water or witty conversation, not even a
friend.

The lane led quickly out of the town on to high rocks and jungle. Here he
drew rein and examined the great Mau tank, which lay exposed beneath him
to its remotest curve. Reflecting the evening clouds, it filled the nether-
world with an equal splendour, so that earth and sky leant toward one
another, about to clash in ecstasy. He spat, cynical again, more cynical than
before. For in the centre of the burnished circle a small black blot was
advancing–the Guest House boat. Those English had improvised
something to take the place of oars, and were proceeding in their work of
patrolling India. The sight endeared the Hindus by comparison, and
looking back at the milk-white hump of the palace, he hoped that they would
enjoy carrying their idol about, for at all events it did not pry into other
people's lives. This pose of 'seeing India' which had seduced him to Miss
Quested at Chandrapore was only a form of ruling India; no sympathy lay
behind it; he knew exactly what was going on in the boat as the party gazed at
the steps down which the image would presently descend, and debated how
near they might row without getting into trouble officially.

He did not give up his ride, for there would be servants at the Guest House
whom he could question; a little information never comes amiss. He took the
path by the sombre promontory that contained the royal tombs. Like the
palace, they were of snowy stucco, and gleamed by their internal light, but
their radiance grew ghostly under approaching night. The promontory was
covered with lofty trees, and the fruit-bats were unhooking from the boughs
and making kissing sounds as they grazed the surface of the tank; hanging
upside down all the day, they had grown thirsty. The signs of the contented
Indian evening multiplied; frogs on all sides, cow-dung burning eternally; a

flock of belated hornbills overhead, looking like winged skeletons as they flapped across the gloaming. There was death in the air, but not sadness; a compromise had been made between destiny and desire, and even the heart of man acquiesced.

The European Guest House stood two hundred feet above the water, on the crest of a rocky and wooded spur that jutted from the jungle. By the time Aziz arrived, the water had paled to a film of mauve-grey, and the boat vanished entirely. A sentry slept in the Guest House porch, lamps burned in the cruciform of the deserted rooms. He went from one room to another, inquisitive, and malicious. Two letters lying on the piano rewarded him, and he pounced and read them promptly. He was not ashamed to do this. The sanctity of private correspondence has never been ratified by the East. Moreover, Mr McBryde had read all his letters in the past, and spread their contents. One letter—the more interesting of the two—was from Heaslop to Fielding. It threw light on the mentality of his former friend, and it hardened him further against him. Much of it was about Ralph Moore, who appeared to be almost an imbecile. 'Hand on my brother whenever suits you. I write to you because he is sure to make a bad bunderbust.' Then: 'I quite agree—life is too short to cherish grievances, also I'm relieved you feel able to come into line with the Oppressors of India to some extent. We need all the support we can get. I hope that next time Stella comes my way she will bring you with her, when I will make you as comfortable as a bachelor can—it's certainly time we met. My sister's marriage to you coming after my mother's death and my own difficulties did upset me, and I was unreasonable. It is about time we made it up properly, as you say—let us leave it at faults on both sides. Glad about your son and heir. When next any of you write to Adela, do give her some sort of message from me, for I should like to make my peace with her too. You are lucky to be out of British India at the present moment. Incident after incident, all due to propaganda, but we can't lay our hands on the connecting thread. The longer one lives here, the more certain one gets that everything hangs together. My personal opinion is, it's the Jews.'

Thus far the red-nosed boy. Aziz was distracted for a moment by blurred sounds coming from over the water; the procession was under way. The second letter was from Miss Quested to Mrs Fielding. It contained one or two interesting touches. The writer hoped that 'Ralph will enjoy his India more than I did mine,' and appeared to have given him money for this purpose—'my debt which I shall never repay in person.' What debt did Miss Quested imagine she owed the country? He did not relish the phrase. Talk of Ralph's health. It was all 'Stella and Ralph,' even 'Cyril' and 'Ronny'—all so friendly and sensible, and written in a spirit he could not command. He envied the easy intercourse that is only possible in a nation whose women are free. These five people were making up their little difficulties, and closing their broken ranks against the alien. Even Heaslop was coming in. Hence the strength of England, and in a spurt of temper he hit the piano, and since the notes had swollen and stuck together in groups of threes, he produced a remarkable noise.

'Oh, oh, who is that?' said a nervous and respectful voice; he could not remember where he had heard its tones before. Something moved in the twilight of an adjoining room. He replied, 'State doctor, ridden over to enquire, very little English,' slipped the letters into his pocket, and to show that he had free entry to the Guest House, struck the piano again.

Ralph Moore came into the light.

What a strange-looking youth, tall, prematurely aged, the big blue eyes faded with anxiety, the hair impoverished and tousled! Not a type that is often exported imperially. The doctor in Aziz thought, 'Born of too old a mother,' the poet found him rather beautiful.

'I was unable to call earlier owing to pressure of work. How are the celebrated bee-stings?' he asked patronizingly.

'I—I was resting, they thought I had better; they throb rather.'

His timidity and evident 'newness' had complicated effects on the malcontent. Speaking threateningly, he said, 'Come here, please, allow me to look.' They were practically alone, and he could treat the patient as Callendar had treated Nureddin.

'You said this morning—'

'The best of doctors make mistakes. Come here, please, for the diagnosis under the lamp. I am pressed for time.'

'Aough—'

'What is the matter, pray?'

'Your hands are unkind.'

He started and glanced down at them. The extraordinary youth was right, and he put them behind his back before replying with outward anger: 'What the devil have my hands to do with you? This is a most strange remark. I am a qualified doctor, who will not hurt you.'

'I don't mind pain, there is no pain.'

'No pain?'

'Not really.'

'Excellent news,' sneered Aziz.

'But there is cruelty.'

'I have brought you some salve, but how to put it on in your present nervous state becomes a problem,' he continued, after a pause.

'Please leave it with me.'

'Certainly not. It returns to my dispensary at once.' He stretched forward, and the other retreated to the farther side of a table. 'Now, do you want me to treat your stings, or do you prefer an English doctor? There is one at Asirgarh. Asirgarh is forty miles away, and the Ringnod dam broken. Now you see how you are placed. I think I had better see Mr Fielding about you; this is really great nonsense, your present behaviour.'

'They are out in a boat,' he replied, glancing about him for support.

Aziz feigned intense surprise. 'They have not gone in the direction of Mau, I hope. On a night like this the people become most fanatical.' And, as if to confirm him, there was a sob, as though the lips of a giant had parted; the procession was approaching the Jail.

'You should not treat us like this,' he challenged, and this time Aziz was checked, for the voice, though frightened, was not weak.

'Like what?'

'Dr Aziz, we have done you no harm.'

'Aha, you know my name, I see. Yes, I am Aziz. No, of course your great friend Miss Quested did me no harm at the Marabar.'

Drowning his last words, all the guns of the State went off. A rocket from the Jail garden gave the signal. The prisoner had been released, and was kissing the feet of the singers. Rose-leaves fall from the houses, sacred spices and coco-nut are brought forth. . . . It was the half-way moment; the God had extended His temple, and paused exultantly. Mixed and confused in their passage, the rumours of salvation entered the Guest House. They were startled and moved on to the porch, drawn by the sudden illumination. The bronze gun up on the fort kept flashing, the town was a blur of light, in which the houses seemed dancing, and the palace waving little wings. The water below, the hills and sky above, were not involved as yet; there was still only a little light and song struggling among the shapeless lumps of the universe. The song became audible through much repetition; the choir was repeating and inverting the names of deities.

Radhakrishna Radhakrishna,
Radhakrishna Radhakrishna,
Krishnaradha Radhakrishna,
Radhakrishna Radhakrishna,

they sang, and woke the sleeping sentry in the Guest House; he leant upon his iron-tipped spear.

'I must go back now, good night,' said Aziz, and held out his hand, completely forgetting that they were not friends, and focusing his heart on something more distant than the caves, something beautiful. His hand was taken, and then he remembered how detestable he had been, and said gently, 'Don't you think me unkind any more?'

'No.'

'How can you tell, you strange fellow?'

'Not difficult, the one thing I always know.'

'Can you always tell whether a stranger is your friend?'

'Yes.'

'Then you are an Oriental.' He unclasped as he spoke, with a little shudder. Those words–he had said them to Mrs Moore in the mosque in the beginning of the cycle, from which, after so much suffering, he had got free. Never be friends with the English! Mosque, caves, mosque, caves. And here he was starting again. He handed the magic ointment to him. 'Take this, think of me when you use it. I shall never want it back. I must give you one little present, and it is all I have got; you are Mrs Moore's son.'

'I am that,' he murmured to himself; and a part of Aziz' mind that had been hidden seemed to move and force its way to the top.

'But you are Heaslop's brother also, and alas, the two nations cannot be friends.'

'I know. Not yet.'

'Did your mother speak to you about me?'

'Yes.' And with a swerve of voice and body that Aziz did not follow he added, 'In her letters, in her letters. She loved you.'

'Yes, your mother was my best friend in all the world.' He was silent, puzzled by his own great gratitude. What did this eternal goodness of Mrs Moore amount to? To nothing, if brought to the test of thought. She had not borne witness in his favour, nor visited him in the prison, yet she had stolen to the depths of his heart, and he always adored her. 'This is our monsoon, the best weather,' he said, while the lights of the procession waved as though embroidered on an agitated curtain. 'How I wish she could have seen them, our rains. Now is the time when all things are happy, young and old. They are happy out there with their savage noise, though we cannot follow them; the tanks are all full so they dance, and this is India. I wish you were not with officials, then I would show you my country, but I cannot. Perhaps I will just take you out on the water now, for one short half-hour.'

Was the cycle beginning again? His heart was too full to draw back. He must slip out in the darkness, and do this one act of homage to Mrs Moore's son. He knew where the oars were—hidden to deter the visitors from going out—and he brought the second pair, in case they met the other boat; the Fieldings had pushed themselves out with long poles, and might get into difficulties, for the wind was rising.

Once on the water, he became easy. One kind action was with him always a channel for another, and soon the torrent of his hospitality gushed forth and he began doing the honours of Mau and persuading himself that he understood the wild procession, which increased in lights and sounds as the complications of its ritual developed. There was little need to row, for the freshening gale blew them in the direction they desired. Thorns scratched the keel, they ran into an islet and startled some cranes. The strange temporary life of the August flood-water bore them up and seemed as though it would last for ever.

The boat was a rudderless dinghy. Huddled up in the stern, with the spare pair of oars in his arms, the guest asked no questions about details. There was presently a flash of lightning, followed by a second flash—little red scratches on the ponderous sky. 'Was that the Rajah?' he asked.

'What—what do you mean?'

'Row back.'

'But there's no Rajah—nothing—'

'Row back, you will see what I mean.'

Aziz found it hard work against the advancing wind. But he fixed his eyes on the pin of light that marked the Guest House and backed a few strokes.

'There . . .'

Floating in the darkness was a king, who sat under a canopy, in shining royal robes. . . .

'I can't tell you what that is, I'm sure,' he whispered. 'His Highness is dead. I think we should go back at once.'

They were close to the promontory of the tombs, and had looked straight into the chhatri of the Rajah's father through an opening in the trees. That was the explanation. He had heard of the image—made to imitate life at enormous expense—but he had never chanced to see it before, though he frequently rowed on the lake. There was only one spot from which it could be seen, and Ralph had directed him to it. Hastily he pulled away, feeling that his companion was not so much a visitor as a guide. He remarked, 'Shall we go back now?'

'There is still the procession.'

'I'd rather not go nearer—they have such strange customs, and might hurt you.'

'A little nearer.'

Aziz obeyed. He knew with his heart that this was Mrs Moore's son, and indeed until his heart was involved he knew nothing. 'Radhakrishna Radhakrishna Radhakrishna Radhakrishna Krishnaradha,' went the chant, then suddenly changed, and in the interstice he heard, almost certainly, the syllables of salvation that had sounded during his trial at Chandrapore.

'Mr Moore, don't tell anyone that the Rajah is dead. It is a secret still, I am supposed not to say. We pretend he is alive until after the festival, to prevent unhappiness. Do you want to go still nearer?'

'Yes.'

He tried to keep the boat out of the glare of the torches that began to star the other shore. Rockets kept going off, also the guns. Suddenly, closer than he had calculated, the palanquin of Krishna appeared from behind a ruined wall, and descended the carven glistening watersteps. On either side of it the singers tumbled, a woman prominent, a wild and beautiful young saint with flowers in her hair. She was praising God without attributes—thus did she apprehend Him. Others praised Him without attributes, seeing Him in this or that organ of the body or manifestation of the sky. Down they rushed to the foreshore and stood in the small waves, and a sacred meal was prepared, of which those who felt worthy partook. Old Godbole detected the boat, which was drifting in on the gale, and he waved his arms—whether in wrath or joy Aziz never discovered. Above stood the secular power of Mau—elephants, artillery, crowds—and high above them a wild tempest started, confined at first to the upper regions of the air. Gusts of wind mixed darkness and light, sheets of rain cut from the north, stopped, cut from the south, began rising from below, and across them struggled the singers, sounding every note but terror, and preparing to throw God away, God Himself, (not that God can be thrown) into the storm. Thus was He thrown year after year, and were others thrown—little images of Ganpati, baskets of ten-day corn, tiny tazias after Mohurram—scapegoats, husks, emblems of passage; a passage not easy, not now, not here, not to be apprehended except when it is unattainable: the God to be thrown was an emblem of that.

The village of Gokul reappeared upon its tray. It was the substitute for the silver image, which never left its haze of flowers; on behalf of another symbol, it was to perish. A servitor took it in his hands, and tore off the blue and white streamers. He was naked, broad-shouldered, thin-waisted—the Indian body again triumphant—and it was his hereditary office to close the gates of salvation. He entered the dark waters, pushing the village before

him, until the clay dolls slipped off their chairs and began to gutter in the
rain, and King Kansa was confounded with the father and mother of the
Lord. Dark and solid, the little waves sipped, then a great wave washed and
then English voices cried 'Take care!'

The boats had collided with each other.

The four outsiders flung out their arms and grappled, and, with oars
and poles sticking out, revolved like a mythical monster in the whirlwind.
The worshippers howled with wrath or joy, as they drifted forward helplessly against the servitor. Who awaited them, his beautiful dark face
expressionless, and as the last morsels melted on his tray, it struck them.

The shock was minute, but Stella, nearest to it, shrank into her husband's
arms, then reached forward, then flung herself against Aziz, and her motions
capsized them. They plunged into the warm, shallow water, and rose
struggling into a tornado of noise. The oars, the sacred tray, the letters of
Ronny and Adela, broke loose and floated confusedly. Artillery was fired,
drums beaten, the elephants trumpeted, and drowning all an immense peal
of thunder, unaccompanied by lightning, cracked like a mallet on the dome.

That was the climax, as far as India admits of one. The rain settled in
steadily to its job of wetting everybody and everything through, and soon
spoiled the cloth of gold on the palanquin and the costly disc-shaped
banners. Some of the torches went out, fireworks didn't catch, there began
to be less singing, and the tray returned to Professor Godbole, who picked
up a fragment of the mud adhering and smeared it on his forehead without
much ceremony. Whatever had happened had happened, and while the
intruders picked themselves up, the crowds of Hindus began a desultory
move back into the town. The image went back too, and on the following day
underwent a private death of its own, when some curtains of magenta and
green were lowered in front of the dynastic shrine. The singing went on even
longer . . . ragged edges of religion . . . unsatisfactory and undramatic
tangles. . . . 'God si love.' Looking back at the great blur of the last twenty-
four hours, no man could say where was the emotional centre of it, any more
than he could locate the heart of a cloud.

Chapter Thirty-seven

Friends again, yet aware that they could meet no more, Aziz and Fielding
went for their last ride in the Mau jungles. The floods had abated and the
Rajah was officially dead, so the Guest House party were departing next
morning, as decorum required. What with the mourning and the festival,
the visit was a failure. Fielding had scarcely seen Godbole, who promised
every day to show him over the King-Emperor George Fifth High School,
his main objective, but always made some excuse. This afternoon Aziz let
out what had happened: the King-Emperor had been converted into a

granary, and the Minister of Education did not like to admit this to his former Principal. The school had been opened only last year by the Agent to the Governor-General, and it still flourished on paper; he hoped to start it again before its absence was remarked and to collect its scholars before they produced children of their own. Fielding laughed at the tangle and waste of energy, but he did not travel as lightly as in the past; education was a continuous concern to him, because his income and the comfort of his family depended on it. He knew that few Indians think education good in itself, and he deplored this now on the widest grounds. He began to say something heavy on the subject of Native States, but the friendliness of Aziz distracted him. This reconciliation was a success, anyhow. After the funny shipwreck there had been no more nonsense or bitterness, and they went back laughingly to their old relationship as if nothing had happened. Now they rode between jolly bushes and rocks. Presently the ground opened into full sunlight and they saw a grassy slope bright with butterflies, also a cobra, which crawled across doing nothing in particular, and disappeared among some custard-apple trees. There were round white clouds in the sky, and white pools on the earth; the hills in the distance were purple. The scene was as park-like as England, but did not cease being queer. They drew rein, to give the cobra elbow-room, and Aziz produced a letter that he wanted to send to Miss Quested. A charming letter. He wanted to thank his old enemy for her fine behaviour two years back: perfectly plain was it now that she had behaved well. 'As I fell into our largest Mau tank under circumstances our other friends will relate, I thought how brave Miss Quested was, and decided to tell her so, despite my imperfect English. Through you I am happy here with my children instead of in a prison, of that I make no doubt. My children shall be taught to speak of you with the greatest affection and respect.'

'Miss Quested will be greatly pleased. I am glad you have seen her courage at last.'

'I want to do kind actions all round and wipe out the wretched business of the Marabar for ever. I have been so disgracefully hasty, thinking you meant to get hold of my money: as bad a mistake as the cave itself.'

'Aziz, I wish you would talk to my wife. She too believes that the Marabar is wiped out.'

'How so?'

'I don't know, perhaps she might tell you, she won't tell me. She has ideas I don't share—indeed, when I'm away from her I think them ridiculous. When I'm with her, I suppose because I'm fond of her, I feel different, I feel half dead and half blind. My wife's after something. You and I and Miss Quested are, roughly speaking, not after anything. We jog on as decently as we can, you a little in front—a laudable little party. But my wife is not with us.'

'What are you meaning? Is Stella not faithful to you, Cyril? This fills me with great concern.'

Fielding hesitated. He was not quite happy about his marriage. He was passionate physically again—the final flare-up before the clinkers of middle age—and he knew that his wife did not love him as much as he loved her, and he was ashamed of pestering her. But during the visit to Mau the situation had improved. There seemed a link between them at last—that link outside either participant that is necessary to every relationship. In the language of theology, their union had been blessed. He could assure Aziz that Stella was not only faithful to him, but likely to become more so; and trying to express what was not clear to himself, he added dully that different people had different points of view. 'If you won't talk about the Marabar to Stella, why won't you talk to Ralph? He is a wise boy really. And (same metaphor) he rides a little behind her, though with her.'

'Tell him also, I have nothing to say to him, but he is indeed a wise boy and has always one Indian friend. I partly love him because he brought me back to you to say good-bye. For this is good-bye, Cyril, though to think about it will spoil or ride and make us sad.'

'No, we won't think about it.' He too felt that this was their last free intercourse. All the stupid misunderstandings had been cleared up, but socially they had no meeting-place. He had thrown in his lot with Anglo-India by marrying a countrywoman, and he was acquiring some of its limitations, and already felt surprise at his own past heroism. Would he to-day defy all his own people for the sake of a stray Indian? Aziz was a memento, a trophy, they were proud of each other, yet they must inevitably part. And, anxious to make what he could of this last afternoon, he forced himself to speak intimately about his wife, the person most dear to him. He said: 'From her point of view, Mau has been a success. It calmed her—both of them suffer from restlessness. She found something soothing, some solution of her queer troubles here.' After a silence—myriads of kisses around them as the earth drew the water in—he continued: 'Do you know anything about this Krishna business?'

'My dear chap, officially they call it Gokul Ashtami. All the State offices are closed, but how else should it concern you and me?'

'Gokul is the village where Krishna was born—well, more or less born, for there's the same hovering between it and another village as between Bethlehem and Nazareth. What I want to discover is its spiritual side, if it has one.'

'It is useless discussing Hindus with me. Living with them teaches me no more. When I think I annoy them, I do not. When I think I don't annoy them, I do. Perhaps they will sack me for tumbling on to their dolls'-house; on the other hand, perhaps they will double my salary. Time will prove. Why so curious about them?'

'It's difficult to explain. I never really understood or liked them, except an occasional scrap of Godbole. Does the old fellow still say "Come, come?"'

'Oh, presumably.'

Fielding sighed, opened his lips, shut them, then said with a little laugh, 'I can't explain, because it isn't in words at all, but why do my wife and her brother like Hinduism, though they take no interest in its forms? They won't talk to me about this. They know I think a certain side of their lives is a mistake, and are shy. That's why I wish you would talk to them, for at all events you're Oriental.'

Aziz refused to reply. He didn't want to meet Stella and Ralph again, knew they didn't want to meet him, was incurious about their secrets, and felt good old Cyril to be a bit clumsy. Something—not a sight, but a sound—flitted past him, and caused him to re-read his letter to Miss Quested. Hadn't he wanted to say something else to her? Taking out his pen, he added: 'For my own part, I shall henceforth connect you with the name that is very sacred in my mind, namely, Mrs Moore.' When he had finished, the mirror of the scenery was shattered, the meadow disintegrated into butterflies. A poem about Mecca—the Caaba of Union—the thorn-bushes where pilgrims die before they have seen the Friend—they flitted next; he thought of his wife; and then the whole semi-mystic, semi-sensuous overturn, so characteristic of his spiritual life, came to end like a landslip and rested in its due place, and he found himself riding in the jungle with his dear Cyril.

'Oh, shut up,' he said. 'Don't spoil our last hour with foolish questions. Leave Krishna alone, and talk about something sensible.'

They did. All the way back to Mau they wrangled about politics. Each had hardened since Chandrapore, and a good knock about proved enjoyable. ·They trusted each other, although they were going to part, perhaps because they were going to part. Fielding had 'no further use for politeness,' he said, meaning that the British Empire really can't be abolished because it's rude. Aziz retorted, 'Very well, and we have no use for you,' and glared at him with abstract hate. Fielding said: 'Away from us, Indians go to seed at once. Look at the King-Emperor High School! Look at you, forgetting your medicine and going back to charms. Look at your poems.'—'Jolly good poems, I'm getting published Bombay side.'—'Yes, and what do they say? Free our women and India will be free. Try it, my lad. Free your own lady in the first place, and see who'll wash Ahmed Karim and Jamila's faces. A nice situation!'

Aziz grew more excited. He rose in his stirrups and pulled at his horse's head in the hope it would rear. Then he should feel in a battle. He cried: 'Clear out, all you Turtons and Burtons. We wanted to know you ten years back—now it's too late. If we see you and sit on your committees, it's for political reasons, don't you make any mistake.' His horse did rear. 'Clear out, clear out, I say. Why are we put to so much suffering? We used to blame you, now we blame ourselves, we grow wiser. Until England is in difficulties we keep silent, but in the next European war—aha, aha! Then is our time.' He paused, and the scenery, though it smiled, fell like a gravestone on any human hope. They cantered past a temple to Hanuman—God so loved the world that he took monkey's flesh upon him—and past a Saivite temple, which invited to lust, but under the semblance of eternity, its obscenities bearing no relation to those of our flesh and blood. They splashed through butterflies and frogs; great trees with leaves like plates rose among the brushwood. The divisions of daily life were returning, the shrine had almost shut.

'Who do you want instead of the English? The Japanese?' jeered Fielding, drawing rein.

'No, the Afghans. My own ancestors.'

'Oh, your Hindu friends will like that, won't they?'

'It will be arranged—a conference of Oriental statesmen.'

'It will indeed be arranged.'

'Old story of "We will rob every man and rape every woman from Peshawar to Calcutta," I suppose, which you get some nobody to repeat and then quote every week in the *Pioneer* in order to frighten us into retaining you! We know!' Still he couldn't quite fit in Afghans at Mau, and, finding he was in a corner, made his horse rear again until he remembered that he had, or ought to have, a mother-land. Then he shouted: 'India shall be a nation! No foreigners of any sort! Hindu and Moslem and Sikh and all shall be one! Hurrah! Hurrah for India! Hurrah! Hurrah!'

India a nation! What an apotheosis! Last comer to the drab nineteenth-century sisterhood! Waddling in at this hour of the world to take her seat! She, whose only peer was the Holy Roman Empire, she shall rank with Guatemala and Belgium perhaps! Fielding mocked again. And Aziz in an awful rage danced this way and that, not knowing what to do, and cried: 'Down with the English anyhow. That's certain. Clear out, you fellows, double quick, I say. We may hate one another, but we hate you most. If I don't make you go, Ahmed will, Karim will, if it's fifty five-hundred years we shall get rid of you, yes, we shall drive every blasted Englishman into the sea, and then'—he rode against him furiously—'and then,' he concluded, half kissing him, 'you and I shall be friends.'

'Why can't we be friends now?' said the other, holding him affectionately. 'It's what I want. It's what you want.'

But the horses didn't want it—they swerved apart; the earth didn't want it, sending up rocks through which riders must pass single file; the temples, the tank, the jail, the palace, the birds, the carrion, the Guest House, that came into view as they issued from the gap and saw Mau beneath: they didn't want it, they said in their hundred voices, 'No, not yet,' and the sky said, 'No, not there.'

Weybridge, 1924.

Distinguished broadcaster and writer **Jonathan Dimbleby** is the presenter of LWT's flagship political programme *Jonathan Dimbleby* and BBC Radio 4's *Any Questions* and *Any Answers*. He was the ITV anchorman for the 1997 general election. His books include two highly acclaimed biographies, *Richard Dimbleby* (1975), and *The Prince of Wales* (1994).

An award-winning reporter, he has made current affairs and documentary films in more than sixty countries around the world. They include *Charles: The Private Man, The Public Role* (1994), which provoked international headlines and a significant reappraisal of the Prince of Wales in the British media, and *The Last Governor* (1997), a five-part television series on Chris Patten and the handover of Hong Kong, an independent production for the BBC.

Jonathan Dimbleby is married to the novelist and broadcaster Bel Mooney. They live in Somerset.

THE LAST GOVERNOR

*Chris Patten
and the Handover
of Hong Kong*

JONATHAN DIMBLEBY

PEN & SWORD HISTORY

First published in Great Britain in 1997,
Reprinted in this format in 2018 by
PEN & SWORD HISTORY
an imprint of
Pen & Sword Books Ltd
47 Church Street
Barnsley, South Yorkshire
S70 2AS

A CIP record for this book is available from the British Library

HB ISBN 978 1 52670 063 6
PB ISBN 978 1 52670 183 1

Printed and bound in England by
CPI Group (UK) Ltd, Croydon, CR0 4YY

Pen & Sword Books Ltd incorporates the Imprints of Aviation, Atlas,
Family History, Fiction, Maritime, Military, Discovery, Politics, History,
Archaeology, Select, Wharncliffe Local History, Wharncliffe True Crime,
Military Classics, Wharncliffe Transport, Leo Cooper, The Praetorian Press,
Remember When, Seaforth Publishing and Frontline Publishing.

For a complete list of Pen & Sword titles please contact
PEN & SWORD BOOKS LIMITED
47 Church Street, Barnsley, South Yorkshire, S70 2AS, England
E-mail: enquiries@pen-and-sword.co.uk
Website: www.pen-and-sword.co.uk

For Bel

CONTENTS

CONTENTS

ACKNOWLEDGEMENTS

Over the five years of this project, I have received kindness and hospitality in abundance from many people in Hong Kong and London. For that and more I owe them a huge debt of gratitude. All of those listed below have not only been generous with their time but have helped me to a better understanding of the issues that form the subject matter of this book. Many of them have spent long hours exploring with me their differing and frequently rivalrous viewpoints on Hong Kong. Some of them will disagree bitterly with my interpretation and judgement. None of them should be blamed for my opinions. One or two of those who have offered particularly helpful insights have asked not to be identified. I am in their debt no less than I am to the following.

David Akers-Jones, Martin Barrow, Sir Jack Cater, Anson Chan, Professor Edward Chen, George and Rowena Chen, Cheung Man Yee, David Chu, Francis Cornish, William Courtauld, Sir Percy Cradock, Hugh Davies, Dr Michael Degoylyer, Martin Dinham, Jamie Dundas, Baroness Lydia Dunn, Major-General Bryan Dutton, William Ehrman, Sir David Ford, Sir Alastair Goodlad, Leo Goodstadt, Han Dongfang, Mike Hanson, Hari Harilela and his family, Richard Hoare, Michael Howard, Lord Howe of Aberavon, Christopher Hum, Douglas Hurd, Jimmy Lai, Albert Lam, Norris Lam, Emily Lau, Allen Lee, Commander Dick Lee, Martin Lee, Dr C. H. Leong, Bowen Leung, Edward Llewellyn, Vincent Lo, Christine Loh, Ma Yuzhen, Kerry McGlynn, Sir Robin McLaren, the Lord MacLehose of Beoch, Richard Margolis, Simon Murray, Ng Koon Leung, Margaret Ng, Bob Peirce, Sir Charles Powell, Peter

Ricketts, Malcolm Rifkind, William Shawcross, Michael Sze, David Tang, Baroness Thatcher, Nancy Thompson, Peter Thompson, Hank Townsend, Tsang Yok Sing, Simon Vickers, Wong Oi Ying, Lord Wilson of Tillyorn, Peter Woo, Minky Worden, Grace Wu, Gordon Wu and Lord Young of Graffham.

Chris and Lavender Patten have had many burdens to bear in Hong Kong. I added to these by consuming many hours of their precious time. Like many others over the last five years, I have been a beneficiary of their goodwill, their kindness, the warmth of their hospitality, and – wondrously – their sense of perspective.

Caroline Courtauld has been a consummate guide and mentor. Her diaries, which have been a delight to read, were also an invaluable source of illumination. Sister Helen Kenny's religious duties command many hours of commitment and yet for the love of the subject, she managed to find time, throughout the last five years, to create and maintain a beautifully ordered cuttings library without which I would frequently have been lost. Both Sister Helen and Caroline Courtauld were assisted by Fanny Wong, who also helped to organise my life on most of my whistle-stop visits. Gary Pollard provided me with his extensive research notes into the Hong Kong media and related issues. Jonathan Mirsky, a distinguished foreign correspondent, was generous with his knowledge, his opinions and his Italian home cooking. He took the trouble to make available to me the original drafts of many of his articles for *The Times*, and for this, and more, I am in his debt. Stella Ma was a skilful and sensitive interpreter. I am grateful, too, to Robin Allison Smith for the care and speed with which he took many of the photographs in this book.

As a longstanding colleague and friend, Francis Gerard was in at the start of this project. His judgement, his enthusiasm and his company have made a sometimes daunting task far easier to accomplish than it would otherwise have been. These qualities are shared by my PA, Georgie Grindlay, who not only transcribed hundreds of hours of taped interviews (forming her own fierce views about Hong Kong in the process), but made sense of incoherent notes and half-formed ideas written on the backs of envelopes. I have benefited greatly from her opinions and her commitment.

Philippa Harrison, the chief executive of Little, Brown, had the original faith to commission the book and has been astute and wise throughout. Caroline North, my editor, has not only been meticulous but contrived to restructure key parts of my original manuscript with skill and tact and at great speed. Cheung Man Yee, Francis Gerard, Mike Hanson and Caroline Courtauld read all or parts of my text and made many helpful criticisms and suggestions. All of them should share the credit for any virtues that may be detected in *The Last Governor*, they bear no responsibility for any of its vices.

Bel, my wife, has been stoical, wise and my unfailing support in times of stress. But then, she always is.

FOREWORD

The first edition of *The Last Governor* was published a few days after the handover of Hong Kong to China at midnight on 30 June 1997. Britain's departure had been accomplished with dignity. After a turbulent five years, Chris Patten, the last governor, was garlanded in accolades. In the subsequent months his stature has been, if anything, enhanced. In the 1998 New Year Honours he was duly appointed a Companion of Honour, and in April he was asked by the prime minister, Tony Blair, to chair the independent commission examining the future of the Royal Ulster Constabulary. *The Last Governor* itself has provoked bitter controversy as those who are disposed to believe that Chris Patten did well by Hong Kong have taken issue with others – a minority – who think otherwise. The matters which have given rise to the strongest debate cluster around the conduct of British foreign policy on Hong Kong in the years leading up to Patten's appointment in 1992; around the battles between Whitehall and Patten during his tenure; and around Patten's own outspoken observations about his adversaries, not only in Beijing and Hong Kong, but in London as well.

Writing in *The Times* on the eve of publication of *The Last Governor*, the influential columnist Simon Jenkins argued that what he described as 'this remarkable book' contained 'allegations against British ministers and officials as astonishing as anything in recent imperial history', which, if true, amounted, in his judgement, to 'treason'. In furious response, Sir Percy Cradock, the architect of British policy until 1992 and Patten's most venomous critic, insisted that the 'grotesque' charges of 'dishonourable conduct' against him and others 'would not bear serious examination'.

In *The Sunday Times*, the former foreign secretary Lord Howe wrote of the 'surreal and unjust accusations of treachery and foul play' made in *The Last Governor*. Nor did he neglect to express his 'sadness' at Patten's readiness to question the motives of 'almost all but himself' while describing me as the governor's 'Iago-like' accomplice.

The 'accusations' which stung Lord Howe to such an uncharacteristic excess of language were given even greater prominence – and an unexpected spin – by the sudden intervention of the new Labour government's minister without portfolio, Peter Mandelson. On 3 August, the front page of *The Sunday Times* was splashed with an 'exclusive' report claiming that the Foreign Office had launched a full-scale inquiry to discover whether I had been in receipt of 'secret intelligence material' from Chris Patten. It had been a difficult weekend for the government. Much press attention had been devoted to the private life of the foreign secretary, Robin Cook. In the absence of any identified source for the *Sunday Times* story, the rest of the media was swift to put two and two together: the 'smear' against Patten, they concluded, rightly or wrongly, was clearly a diversionary tactic, likely to have been devised by Mandelson. The minister without portfolio, in uneasy partnership with the deputy prime minister, John Prescott, was standing in for prime minister Tony Blair, who was on holiday.

The suspicion of 'dirty tricks' gained credence when, the following day, a respected BBC political correspondent, John Sopel, revealed that, in the face of BBC scepticism, Labour officials had sought to 'talk up' the 'Patten story'. In the absence of confirmation of any 'investigation' from the Foreign Office, they had reassured the BBC that Mandelson would be happy to confirm the substance of the *Sunday Times* report in a Radio 4 interview already scheduled. The fact that the Foreign Office – despite the animosity towards Patten of some of its senior officials – seemed anxious to distance itself from Mandelson's announcement appeared to substantiate the flimsiness of the *Sunday Times* article. When Patten swiftly and vehemently repudiated the 'allegations' against him, the story disappeared, to be all but forgotten except by his close associates, who felt that he had been exceptionally badly treated for cheap political ends.

Nonetheless, the security services were, it seems, instructed to investigate – though the forensic intensity of their inquiries may be gauged from the fact that they apparently did not deem it necessary to seek an interview with either Patten or the author. In November, the solicitor-general informed the House of Commons in writing that 'after consultation with his colleagues', he had decided that the director of public prosecutions would not be instituting criminal proceedings against the former governor of Hong Kong. Coinciding with the public celebration of the Queen and Prince Philip's fiftieth wedding anniversary, this news excited little notice.

Yet the underlying issues which created this furore have not gone away. One of the principal themes that runs through *The Last Governor* is the view, pervasive in Hong Kong, that successive British governments frustrated the colony's demand for democracy because they were overly fearful of China's reaction. It is this interpretation of the events in which, for a time, they were key participants that so rankles with Sir Percy Cradock, Lord Howe and their acolytes. Contemptuous of anyone who fails to view Hong Kong from their own perspective, they display hurt feelings but fail to offer a convincing rebuttal of the case against them.

The substance of this case is not that British officials acted treasonably or treacherously (though many people in Hong Kong do believe themselves to have been betrayed), but that their priorities were woefully misplaced, and that, as a result, they not only underplayed Britain's hand in their dealings with China, but, as I argue, at a key period in this tortured history – between 1986 and 1987 – they knowingly subverted the will of the people of Hong Kong in collusion with China. They rage at that analysis (I suspect) because, in the absence of clear evidence to the contrary, they emerge from this episode less as statesmen than as diplomatic wheeler-dealers preferring almost any agreement to none. The reputations of British officials at that time are indeed likely to be tarnished unless they are able to demonstrate that the diplomatic manoeuvres I ascribe to them either did not occur or have been significantly distorted in the telling.

Reacting publicly to my account of the secret negotiations with the Chinese, Patten has refrained from making accusations of betrayal against any of those who were party to what he has caustically described as a 'gents' understanding' with China. However, choosing his words with care, he deprecated the performance of the British officials involved, noting devastatingly that 'their judgement did not seem to be in line with the Joint Declaration or with our historic and substantial responsibilities to six million people'.

On 5 August, after reading the relevant passages from *The Last Governor*, the leader of the Liberal Democrats, Paddy Ashdown, wrote to the prime minister, Tony Blair, to urge a formal inquiry into whether or not there had been 'collusion or worse with the Chinese authorities'. If such allegations were true, he argued, they would 'cast a very serious shadow on the actions of the then government, and on the exercise of our duties on behalf of, and in the interests of, the people of Hong Kong'. As Ashdown noted, the appropriate forum for such an inquiry would be the Foreign Affairs Select Committee of the House of Commons. Although he has not chosen to echo Ashdown's demand, Patten has indicated that, 'if people want to know what happened', he cannot see 'any reason' why the appropriate documents from that period should not be forthcoming. Nonetheless, given the likely resistance of the Foreign Office and some of the key players involved at the time, it seems unlikely that Ashdown's proposal will be heeded, at least in the near future.

Since *The Last Governor* was first published, I have been in illuminating correspondence with several readers. Although I have not made any significant alterations to the text for this edition as a result, I am grateful to those who have pointed out errors of factual detail, which I have duly sought to correct. In his review of the first edition, Lord Howe quite properly took me to task for incorrectly placing him on the board of GEC, which invests heavily in China. I regret my error. I should have written (though he did not take the opportunity to point this out himself) that he was a consultant to the board of Cable and Wireless, which similarly invests heavily in China. Both he and Sir Percy Cradock, who also has business interests in China, have complained that I allege (in the words of the latter) that the 'prospect of commercial gain' in China influenced their judgement about

Hong Kong. I have imputed no such motive. However, it would be surprising if the high-level contacts with officials in Beijing afforded to them by their commercial responsibilities had made no impression on them at all – which is a quite different matter.

There is a handful of omissions from the original text that I regret. One of them is glaring. As prime minister, Margaret Thatcher played a crucial role, which I describe extensively, in the negotiations which led up to the 1984 Joint Declaration. However, since her elevation to the House of Lords, she has continued to take a close interest in Hong Kong. Her support for Patten was consistent throughout and indeed was a source of immense comfort to him, and to his supporters in Hong Kong, when the going got rough. Although Baroness Thatcher has made no complaint about my oversight, my failure to reflect the significance of her role during this period is a lapse which I am glad to remedy here.

The Last Governor was written as events in Hong Kong unfolded. In retrospect, therefore, the emphasis I placed on some matters is in need of reappraisal. A number of constructive critics have suggested that I exaggerated the extent to which Patten was beleaguered in Hong Kong. They point out that, despite the intense pressures on them, the governor's local (Hong Kong Chinese) civil servants remained staunchly supportive. Although I have accurately reported what I was told by senior civil servants – when some officials complained bitterly about the governor's decision to 'confront' China and when, more generally, morale among them was undeniably at a low ebb – Patten himself appeared to be largely unaffected. As he was always unstinting in his praise for the civil service, it may be presumed that any disaffection in their ranks had a negligible influence on the conduct of policy. It is also true that broadly, whatever doubts there may have been in moments of crisis, the Hong Kong civil service remained loyal, efficient and cohesive. This was due in no small part to the presence of Anson Chan, Patten's choice as chief secretary (a post which she has retained since the handover). As I make clear, her administrative gifts and her political courage are not in doubt. Nor is her unswerving dedication to Hong Kong. Yet her friends and admirers (among whom Patten is to the fore) feel that I have been ungenerous in highlighting occasional moments in her career which appeared to me, and to others, to place a small question-mark over her enthusiasm for democracy and open government. They insist that her commitment cannot fairly be called into question on either count. I am more than happy to acknowledge that in general, and especially latterly, she has revealed herself as a principled exponent both of open government, and – insofar as it is within her power – of democracy as well. My minor caveats should also be viewed in the context of the great weight of responsibility that rests on her shoulders. Hong Kong is fortunate to have so formidable a figure in such a pivotal role.

In the foreword to the first edition of *The Last Governor*, I made it clear that Chris Patten was one among many of my sources. Yet some have nevertheless assumed that every judgement, every interpretation and even every anecdote in the book sprang from his lips. This is frustrating for the author and doubtless for Patten himself, not to mention my other sources. For example, some readers have leaped to the conclusion that it was Patten who supplied me with a couple of critical stories about Anson Chan. He did not. Not only was he entirely loyal to his senior lieutenant, in private as well as in public, but, as should be apparent from the text, he never spoke to me about her except in laudatory and affectionate terms. I cannot in this case, as in many others, acknowledge my sources without infringing their confidentiality.

Although several months have passed since the first edition of *The Last Governor* was published, I would not in general wish to alter the thrust of my account in any significant way. I have told the story as I witnessed it, and as it was told to me by those directly involved. I believe it to be fair and accurate. Of course, it lacks the benefit of hindsight and future historians will doubtless have a better perspective. After all, it was Chou Enlai, when asked about the importance of the French Revolution, who is said to have replied, 'It is too early to tell.'

Jonathan Dimbleby, July 1998

Somewhere a strange and shrewd To-morrow goes to bed,
Planning a test for men from Europe; no one guesses
Who will be most ashamed, who richer, and who dead.

from *The Ship*
by W.H. Auden

INTRODUCTION

Hong Kong brags shamelessly. In all Asia it lays claim to the boldest tycoons, the best-educated and most industrious workers, the most important financial centre, the most innovative trading houses, the highest living standards, the most billionaires, the most spendthrift gamblers, the largest gold market, the largest diamond market, the busiest port, the most crowded skies, the most exciting skyscrapers, the widest range of luxury shops, the most expensive apartments, the lowest taxes, the most efficient civil service and the least corrupt police force. Hong Kong spews out statistics about itself which show that – on one level – it is indeed a jewel in Asia; at another, deeper, level it reveals the fragility of the identity about which its apologists boast with such abandon. If this city state has any culture, it is that of the marketplace – a free-for-all world where the pursuit of profit is unashamed and the possession of wealth is admired, not envied. If Hong Kong has a commitment, it is to today and tomorrow. The day after tomorrow will take care of itself – or so many of its denizens have wished to believe.

On 1 July 1997, Hong Kong was to be released from British colonial status to be incorporated as a special administrative region (SAR) of the last major communist power in the world, the People's Republic of China. With a population of 1.3 billion people, which accounts for about a quarter of the world's population, China is still in the throes of a social and economic upheaval caused by an attempt to graft the practice of capitalism on to the precepts of totalitarianism. It is an awesome venture fraught with uncertainty.

This book is about the last five years of British rule in Hong

Kong and its principal focus is the remarkable political drama which began to unfold once it became clear, within a few months of his arrival, that the new governor, Chris Patten, and the rulers of China were on a collision course. From July 1992 to the end of June 1997, Patten had to make judgements of a nature and on a scale unimaginable to most men and women. Uniquely in the history of British colonialism, he had the responsibility of accomplishing the peaceful transfer of sovereign power from one state to another, rather than into independence.

The book's main vantage point is the perch I was allowed to occupy inside Government House, where I had easy access to the governor and his team. With the proviso that what he said would be embargoed until after the handover, Patten agreed in advance to discuss – for the future record – his strategy and his tactics at every stage of what was to become a serious and sustained diplomatic crisis, the consequences of which are still uncertain. He not only did so with extraordinary candour but, self-evidently, without benefit of hindsight. As a result, his own testimony will surely be of unusual historical interest.

Patten's task was to meet three overlapping but not necessarily compatible challenges. First, he was to negotiate the final stages of the transfer of sovereignty over Hong Kong from Britain to China. Secondly, he had to prepare the people of the colony to face the uncertainties enshrined in that prospect. Thirdly, he had to convince public opinion in the United Kingdom and internationally that Britain's withdrawal from Hong Kong had been accomplished with at least a modicum of dignity and honour. Patten did not himself enumerate his objectives in precisely these terms, but, from the standpoint of history, they serve as useful yardsticks by which to evaluate his governorship in the sunset years of British colonialism.

Inheriting a basket of unfinished business which affected the basic rights and freedoms of more than 6 million people, Patten was charged with assessing how best to prepare Hong Kong to face the unpredictable imperatives of the gerontocracy which formed the ruling politburo in Beijing. Sino–British relations had long been marked by suspicion, which, in the case of China, verged on paranoia. Disposed to regard the outgoing colonial power as an agent of 'Western imperialism', the old men in Beijing were swift to conclude that any failure by Britain to yield to the 'principles' of sovereignty to which they adhered was evidence of a Western plot to subvert the People's Republic.

The prospects for a smooth transfer had been dramatically and immeasurably undermined by the gathering storm of protest in China during the early months of 1989 which culminated in the killings in Tiananmen Square – and in other major cities beyond Beijing – on 4 June 1989. This atrocity shattered the illusions harboured about the nature of the regime by those who had chosen to interpret the economic reforms introduced by Deng Xiaoping, China's 'paramount leader', a decade earlier as an irreversible process leading inevitably to fundamental social and political reform. Hong Kong's horror at the shedding of so much innocent blood was matched by China's fear that Hong Kong would become a base for internal subversion against their regime. The fact that the constitution of the People's Republic pledges to uphold democracy and to protect human rights throughout China, including the SAR of Tibet, did little to reassure the people of Hong Kong that the principle of 'one country, two systems' – the term used by Deng Xiaoping to express the ideal relationship between the mainland and the new SAR of Hong Kong – would survive for long.

Even under conditions of mutual amity, negotiations between Britain and China were bound to be fraught with difficulty and misunderstandings. As it was, the distrust which had bedevilled their relationship before Patten's arrival was compounded by the intense suspicions harboured by the people of Hong Kong about both present and future sovereign powers.

Although I have sought to preserve an observer's detachment throughout, my proximity to Government House is bound to have shaped, if not distorted, my authorial perspective. In an attempt to remedy this, my narrative is also driven by the experiences and opinions of many other individuals in Hong Kong and, to a lesser extent, in Britain, whose competing aspirations formed part of the backdrop against which Patten defined his own priorities. On the understanding that nothing they said would be published until 1 July 1997, several of these people freely confided their thoughts and feelings about the drama in which they were all central characters. I have variously attributed motives, opinions, and beliefs to all these individuals, and especially to Chris Patten. Although my judgements are based on close observation, they remain mine alone unless they are duly attributed. This book may have the authority of first-hand experience, but it is my own account of events and not 'authorised' by anyone.

As an outsider, I cannot claim to 'understand' Hong Kong, and this book makes little attempt therefore to penetrate what remain to me the cultural and social opacities of its 6 million inhabitants. However, in charting the crucial milestones along the 150-year history of Britain's last significant colony, I have drawn extensively on the scholarship of others to chronicle the most pertinent episodes in the long march from the Opium Wars to Patten's appointment as Hong Kong's last governor. Since it is impossible to understand the predicament inherited by Patten without some appreciation of the colony's recent political history, I have explored in some detail, with the help of those most closely involved (including the former prime minister, Baroness Thatcher, her former political adviser Sir Percy Cradock and two former foreign secretaries, Lord Howe and Douglas Hurd), Britain's diplomatic objectives in the years between 1979 and 1992.

It was originally my hope to balance this portrait of Hong Kong's last years by including the 'Beijing perspective'. At first, in the person of the Chinese ambassador to London, the authorities of the People's Republic showed keen interest in this idea. However, they soon retreated into vague promises about what they might be able to deliver once the 'misunderstandings between our two countries' had been resolved. I gave up. As the text shows, I have been obliged as a result to rely on the authority of press conferences, official statements and other much-quoted 'sources'. However, I suspect that these have yielded as much of the truth as I would have discovered for myself if I had been able to penetrate the carapace of secrecy in China to forge a more productive relationship with one or more of its luminaries.

Inevitably, *The Last Governor* has been written on the run. For that reason alone, it is essentially a work of extended journalism of the sort that its proponents like to describe as 'contemporary history'. That it contains material which has historical significance I have no doubt, but even though I have been privileged to witness at close quarters 'history in the making', my perspective lacks the enchantment of distance. At the time of writing, the future of Hong Kong is uncertain and precarious. I have to declare a twofold bias: first in favour of the last governor of Hong Kong, and secondly in favour of democracy. As a friend, I am disposed to judge Chris Patten sympathetically; more pertinently, as a democrat, I am inclined to look askance at those who use their own freedom to argue that others can do very well, thank you, without democracy.

Of great matters in contention, it is sometimes said that 'history will judge'. History, of course, does no such thing. People judge and, as of now, we can only guess at what, in the case of Chris Patten, that judgement will be. I like to believe that he will be shown to have been on the 'right' side of history; that his faith in individual freedom is well founded, and that, for this reason, future generations in Hong Kong, and even in China, will look back on his struggle on their behalf with gratitude.

I

'A TERRIBLE FEELING OF FALLING'

The New Governor Arrives in Hong Kong

Western writers have been by turns entranced and appalled by their experience of Hong Kong. Ian Fleming, writing in the early sixties, described the city as 'the last stronghold of feudal luxury in the world . . . a gay and splendid colony humming with vitality and progress, and pure joy to the senses and spirits'. A decade later, John le Carré set a memorable episode of *The Honourable Schoolboy* in Hong Kong. Describing a taxi ride in bad weather up the winding road from the city centre to the top of the Peak, he wrote that the car 'sobbed slowly up the concrete cliffs', which were engulfed by 'a fog thick enough to choke on'. Outside the taxi, 'it was even worse. A hot, unbudgeable curtain had spread itself across the summit, reeking of petrol and crammed with the din of the valley. The moisture floated in hot, fine swarms.' On a clear day it would have been possible to see far out over the harbour across Kowloon towards the New Territories, and beyond a vagueness of mountains that marked the border with the People's Republic of China.

The Peak has long been de rigueur for tourists, who usually prefer to travel to the top in the Peak Tram which clanks up the sheer side of the mountain. Jan Morris, Hong Kong's finest apologist, took this route in the seventies, accompanied by a 'foreign devil' who showed her the 'kingdoms of the world' which lay below them: 'The skyscrapers of Victoria, jam-packed at the foot of the hill, seemed to vibrate with pride, greed, energy and success, and all among them the traffic swirled, and the crowds milled, and the shops glittered, and the money rang.' By no means starry-eyed, however, she also saw this throbbing megalopolis as a 'permanent parasite' upon the skin of China, wherein the British and the Chinese, springing from 'two utterly alien cultures, from opposite ends of the world' are 'fused in the furnace of Hong Kong, and made colleagues by the hope of profit'.

The last governor of Britain's last colony landed at Kai Tak Airport on 9 July 1992, on schedule at two o'clock in the afternoon. Accompanied by his wife, Lavender, and two of his three daughters, Laura and Alice, Chris Patten stepped off the aircraft to face a battery of television cameras and journalists corralled on the tarmac by officials of the Government Information Services. The weather was routinely sweltering and the humidity nudged towards 100 per cent. Hong Kong's new first family, the source of much excited chatter in the local media since the announcement of Patten's appointment, smiled self-consciously and disappeared into the merciful cool of the VIP lounge.

After a pause for refreshments, the Patten motorcade left the airport to drive through the heart of Kowloon to the public pier, where the family boarded the *Lady Maurine*, the elderly and elegant motor yacht provided by the Hong Kong government for the personal use of the governor and which, along with an equally ancient Rolls–Royce, was one of the gubernatorial perks to provoke in some a titter of envy. Led by a Royal Navy warship and surrounded by a flotilla of naval and police launches and a convoy of pleasure craft, the Patten family made stately progress across the harbour to disembark at Queen's Pier. A couple of fireboats sprayed a welcoming spume of water as she passed. RAF jets and army helicopters flew low overhead. Foghorns blasted and the sound of a seventeen-gun salute from the naval landbase *HMS Tamar* ricocheted around the waiting crowd. There was a guard of honour and a Gurkha band played the national anthem. Patten took the salute with his wife and children beside him, their dresses swishing slowly in a sultry breeze. For aficionados it was colonialism encapsulated in a single image – even if their new overlord, surrounded by so much gold braid, did cut an underwhelming figure in a plain grey suit and without the gubernatorial plumed hat favoured by his predecessors.

In the dog days of colonialism it had become customary for the media in London to caricature the motley selection of superannuated politicians dispatched to govern Britain's dwindling possessions as faintly ridiculous refugees from a Gilbert and Sullivan opera strutting their way into the imperial sunset. Patten had no intention of either joining that twilight galaxy or dressing the part, which was one of the reasons why he had decided to forgo both the plumed hat and the ceremonial uniform. There was also an aesthetic consideration: 'If you are built like one of those sketches for a Daks suit from Simpson's, you can get away with wearing a hat – as someone said to me rather indelicately – with a chicken on top and that wonderful white tropical kit. If you are built like me, medium-sized and lumpy, you do look extremely foolish.' His friends had been disappointed. 'The prime minister said that I had been a frightful spoilsport. Lots of people who were looking forward to a rather more cheerful breakfast when they looked at photographs of me in the paper were to be denied that pleasure.' A more pertinent, if no less self-conscious reason for his abstinence lay in his determination to impress upon popular opinion in Hong Kong that in style and character he was cast in a quite different mould from his predecessors; that his governorship would be 'more open and accessible and without some of the flummery' which had been traditionally associated with the post.

The power vested in the governor of Hong Kong under the Letters Patent, which gave him absolute executive authority over the colony as the head of government and commander-in-chief of the armed forces, was a sharp reminder to Patten that he lacked the popular legitimacy of an elected leader, and it made him vaguely queasy. With this in mind, he not only resisted the 'flummery' of his new office but also turned down the knighthood that traditionally went with it. 'There were negotiations and the Palace was receptive and helpful,' he confided. 'I've got my house colours as a privy councillor, which, for a politician, is the most important honour you can have . . . I think the time for an additional honour, if there does come a time, should be when I've actually done something for Hong Kong, not just because I've taken a job.'

The welcome he was given was friendly but not effusive. Foreign tourists and expatriates, as intrigued by the Patten daughters as by the new governor himself, all but outnumbered the local population. The people of Hong Kong had seen too many British officials alight on their soil to be anything other than sceptical about the latest arrival. However, even the sceptics acknowledged that Patten was a little different. For weeks the local media had regaled their public with every recycled titbit about the new governor and his family: how Lavender had been a barrister in London; that their eldest daughter Kate was in South America before starting a degree course at Newcastle University; that Laura, a photogenic seventeen and given to stylishly short dresses, would stay for a while but might return to work in London; and that twelve-year-old Alice would be living at Government House and would become a pupil at the Island School in the Midlevels. Patten himself was a good deal younger than any of his recent predecessors, who had been rewarded with the governorship towards the close of their careers. And unlike his predecessors, he was already a public figure, even – in Britain at least – something of a star. As written up by the assiduous Hong Kong press, the Pattens had all the makings of a genuine first family: politically glamorous and pleasingly enthusiastic about the adventure ahead of them.

It was not merely that Patten exuded bonhomie; nor that he waved from the Rolls and searched for hands to shake with the manic energy of a campaigning politician; nor that his face easily creased in what seemed to be a genuinely eager smile, even if, on the first humid day, his complexion assumed an ever-deepening shade of puce. All that helped, but there was something else: from the start, he exuded a self-confidence and certainty which implied, even via the unyieldingly attentive television cameras recording his arrival, that he had a purpose and he knew what it was. Even the cynical – which included most of those of whatever viewpoint who had taken more than a spasmodic interest in the unfolding drama of the previous decade, and who knew Albion to be perfidious – could not help feeling a frisson of anticipatory excitement. For better, for worse, life with the new governor – Peng Dingkang in the official Cantonese translation, or Fat Pang, as he soon came to be called – at least promised to be far from boring.

Chris Patten had been preceded to Hong Kong by a formidable reputation as one of the Conservative government's heavyweights. The prime minister's close friend and most trusted confidant, he was deemed to have snatched electoral victory for his party from what the polls had predicted to be certain defeat. In the process, he became, in his own characteristic phrase, 'the only Cabinet minister careless enough to lose his seat' in his own west-country constituency of Bath.

In Britain, Patten had been a skilled political communicator. His way with the English language had earned him a reputation as a thoughtful and fastidious politician who avoided the coarse public dialogue in which so many of his colleagues indulged. His was by no means a high Tory background: his father worked in what was then called Tin Pan Alley (Patten would recall proudly that he published the hit song 'She Wears Red Feathers and a Hooly-Hooly Skirt'). A scholarship boy, he was educated at Catholic schools and read history at Balliol College, Oxford, where he co-authored the annual college review in which he updated fragments by the Greek writer Aristophanes. Patten evinced no interest in politics until, having won a Coolidge Travelling Scholarship to the United States, he was given a job as a researcher with the team running John Lindsay's 1965 campaign to become mayor of New York. Enthused by this experience of politics in the raw, he returned to London and eschewed a BBC traineeship to join the Conservative Research Department. After four years he went to the Cabinet Office, and two years later, in 1972, he became private secretary to the party chairman, Peter Carrington. On his return to the research department as director in 1974, he soon fell foul of the new party leader, Margaret Thatcher, who regarded him as deplorably hostile to her radical vision. Although he remained at the research department he was effectively ostracised by Thatcher. As one of his friends told the writer John Newhouse, 'Chris protested and then went into outer darkness.'

In the 1979 election Patten won the marginal seat of Bath, going on to serve his ministerial apprenticeship as a PPS at Social Services and a parliamentary under-secretary at the Northern Ireland Office before rising to become minister of state, first at the Department of Education and Science and then, between 1986 and 1989, in the Foreign Office, where he was in charge of overseas development. Despite his relatively slow progress, he had already been cast by his peers in all parties in the role of 'future leader'. Although he was averse to the style of Thatcherism, and semi-detached from much of its content, he had managed to overcome his distaste to the point of toiling annually in the arid vineyard of the prime minister's speeches to the Conservative Party Conference, attempting to bring eloquence to her thought and life to her prose. His reward, in 1989, was a place in the Cabinet as secretary of state for the environment, charged with 'bedding down' Thatcher's community charge, steered on to the statute book by Nicholas Ridley. Though Patten regarded the poll tax as a catastrophe, the last gasp of a leader who had lost touch with political reality, he did not hesitate to bludgeon the bill's opponents in the House of Commons – to their amazement and to the dismay of his admirers beyond Westminster, who could not understand how such an apparently decent politician could be party to so manifest an injustice. In failing to appreciate the iron laws of collective responsibility, they also underestimated the careful ambition of a politician which was obscured by a beguiling persona in which high seriousness and dry humour were, in that grey age, refreshingly entwined.

Patten had comforted himself by letting it be known at Westminster that he found the 'old girl' faintly ridiculous. In private he was also scathing about the vainglory of lesser colleagues. Contemptuous of romantic argument, whether it emanated from the right or the left, his response to it had been to acquire the disconcerting habit of slowly rolling his eyes in exaggerated bewilderment, as if to indicate that its proponent had to be off his – or, in the case of Thatcher, her – trolley.

Patten's 'success' in imposing the community charge on a resentful populace helped precipitate Thatcher's downfall. Forced to defend her leadership in a party election, she failed to win outright in the first ballot. Believing her to be mortally wounded, Patten joined the health secretary, Kenneth Clarke, in telling her that it was time to retire gracefully. He warned that if she did not follow their advice, they, like many of their colleagues, would be unable to support her in the second round. She departed for the House of Lords, blessing John Major as her successor in the Commons. Major duly defeated the foreign secretary, Douglas Hurd, and the former defence secretary, Michael Heseltine, to emerge as leader and prime minister.

Patten was appointed chairman of the party to mastermind John Major's victory over a resurgent Labour party. The 1992 campaign was not an elevated affair. Bending himself to the task of achieving victory, Patten started to deploy terms like 'double whammy', 'gobsmacked' and 'porkies', as if to demonstrate to genuine street-brawlers like Lord Tebbit (a predecessor in the post) that he, too, was an upper-echelon bruiser. Many commentators were genuinely taken aback by his vulgarity, while his opponents affected dismay that such an eminently reasonable politician should stoop to such abuse. Yet those who knew him well were already accustomed to his private, if quaintly anachronistic earthiness, and were surprised only that this trait had not emerged earlier in his career. The Patten they knew was a complex individual, a man of pragmatic conviction, blessed with religious faith, who lived for politics but also had what Denis Healey had memorably called 'a hinterland'. He had one of the best political brains of his generation among the Tory high-flyers. An ideologue who wore his commitment lightly, he was a Conservative in the mould of 'Rab' Butler and Sir Edward Boyle, formal photographs of whom had become part of his office furniture. Yet unlike those icons of 'one-nation' Toryism, he was also, in the political sense, more of a thug than his genial demeanour suggested.

Armed with a swift wit and a gift for the apposite phrase, he had long been the leading figure in a group of sympathetic contemporaries which included such luminaries as William Waldegrave, Tristan Garel-Jones, his namesake, John Patten, and John Major, before the latter's meteoric rise at the behest of Margaret Thatcher. Perhaps not as clever as Waldegrave, nor so artful as Garel-Jones, and less volatile than John Patten, he nonetheless dominated the group with effortless aplomb. To the chagrin of political journalists, even the most ambitious of his colleagues, who were usually swift to deprecate each other in private, stayed their hands. He was the one to whom others turned for advice and reassurance, and whose judgement was trusted, even by his fiercest rivals. Some likened him to Lord Whitelaw, whose benign countenance disguised a shrewd political wisdom on which Margaret Thatcher had learned to rely. But the comparison was inapt: Whitelaw lacked ambition and the 'killer' instinct to go with it. Patten wanted to be prime minister, and he was not nearly so squeamish about it as his self-deprecatory manner might have implied. His asperity in argument left none of his friends in any doubt that the master of the emollient soundbite was very much tougher than his image might suggest.

In his final weeks as the Conservative MP for Bath, that political armour was tested to the limit. Patten had been resigned to the prospect of defeat from the start of the election campaign. Damaged by his association with the poll tax, he was also held responsible for the injustices of the uniform business rate – not least in his own constituency, where some traders faced consequential ruin. As party chairman he was obliged to be in London under the daily scrutiny of the media, and although he was ferried to Bath by helicopter, his campaign in what had long been a marginal seat was inevitably spasmodic. In his constituency he became a scapegoat for the government's unpopularity and, as the canvass returns seemed to confirm, enough of his sophisticated electorate had resolved to vote 'tactically' against him to ensure that at least one member of the Cabinet would be driven from office.

The rejection was more painful than he had anticipated. Afterwards he tried to draw comfort from Adlai Stevenson's reaction after his defeat in the 1952 US presidential elections. Like a small boy who had stubbed his toe, 'It hurt too much to laugh but I was too grown up to cry.' Patten resisted the temptation to blame the burghers of Bath, but he was to harbour lasting resentment about the raucous delight with which some of his opponents at the count greeted his defeat. His farewell speech was dignified, decent and generous, but his successor, the Liberal Democrat Don Foster, failed to offer the customary condolences, an omission or oversight which rankled. Reports that some right-wingers at an election gathering in London hosted by the party's treasurer, Lord McAlpine, had toasted his demise even as they celebrated the victory of which he had been the principal architect did little to soothe his wounded spirits. Exhausted by an election campaign which, as usual, had been demeaned by personal abuse and vilification, Patten left Central Office in the early hours of Friday morning, sustained by the gratitude of a jubilant prime minister but conscious that, for the moment, his own career in British politics was at an end.

Knowing that Patten was unlikely to hold his seat in Bath, the prime minister had held out the promise of the Hong Kong governorship to his friend some weeks earlier. On the day after the election, Major renewed the offer, but at the same time intimated that he would dearly like Patten to reject the Hong Kong option in favour of remaining in his Cabinet. It was common knowledge that the prime minister had come to rely heavily on Patten's acute political intelligence as well as on his skills as a communicator. Patten exuded that air of relaxed assurance that Major could never master; it would be invaluable to have such a 'safe pair of hands' close by to help navigate the government through the turbulent waters of domestic politics that lay ahead. As Patten recalled their conversation a few days later, Major made it clear that 'he'd have liked me to stay around, but he recognised that Hong Kong was a big job . . . [and that] without being too vain, I sort of fitted the bill . . . I guess quite a lot of my friends, while recognising the importance of the job and flattering me into thinking I could do it, also flatteringly, hoped that I'd stay in London.'

Indeed, within hours of the election some of his closest friends were counselling him to find a 'safe' seat (in Chelsea, for instance, former minister and fellow 'wet' Nicholas Scott had indicated that he would be ready to stand down in favour of such a formidable successor), or to accept John Major's offer of a peerage and a place in the Cabinet with the prospect of succeeding Douglas Hurd as foreign secretary. Patten demurred. 'I did have a very strong feeling,' he said privately a few weeks later, 'that I didn't want to hang around on the margins of contemporary domestic politics, collecting directorships, doing a bit of writing, with the terrible danger of starting to be afflicted with a sense of what might have been. I think it's important, since we're only here once, to look forward, not backward.'

Patten had long stated his private aversion to political carpet-bagging, or joining the 'chicken run', as the demeaning search for a safe seat was later disparagingly described. Moreover, he was too astute to presume that any Conservative seat would be safe in a high-profile by-election following the return of an unloved government. If he accepted a peerage, his future in public life would depend exclusively on the prime minister's patronage: for an ambitious individual who was not yet fifty years old, the Lords seemed a remarkably precarious pinnacle from which to establish a position of sustained influence. He had no wish to become a supplicant at the court of Westminster.

Yet party politics had been his life, and he felt bereaved. On the Saturday following the election he helped the prime minister to select the new Cabinet and, he said, felt 'a certain wry detachment' when three of the new appointees rang him for advice about what to do and how to do it. Yet he had no sense that he should have been in their shoes: the 'stabs and twists of anguish' that did assail him sprang from the inevitable loss of companionship, the feeling that he was no longer a member of an intimate club and the recognition that half a dozen of his closest friends now inhabited a world from which he was excluded. He resolved to resist the temptation to resort to envy or bitterness. 'Some people might find this barking mad, but the first time I had dinner with them, and practically all of them had to go off to vote at ten to ten, I did feel slightly gutted,' he confessed later. 'What really came nearest to emotional disembowelling, though, was not just missing them, but realising they were going to miss you.'

By this time, Patten had virtually decided to accept John Major's offer to become the last governor of Britain's last significant colony, Hong Kong. Despite the passionate entreaties of Tristan Garel-Jones, one of the wiliest insiders at Westminster, who organised an informal lobby of sympathetic Tories to ring

Patten urging him to stay, he was not to be persuaded. On the Sunday he told Douglas Hurd on the phone that he was 'very attracted' to the job. Lavender, his wife, was also enthusiastic. From the outset, she had said, 'If you don't take it, you'll spend the rest of your life regretting it.' Only his loyalty to the prime minister still made him hesitate. That evening the Pattens and the Hurds dined together. Although other names had been canvassed for the governorship (including that of the former foreign secretary David Owen), Hurd made it clear that Patten was, in his judgement, the best available choice. The two men and their wives rehearsed the pros and cons, but the foreign secretary was gently adamant: 'Without pushing me into doing it, Douglas made the point that it would be much more interesting than most of the jobs I might have been doing in domestic politics,' Patten recalled. 'It is unique in public service. Dangerous – not in a physical sense – but difficult enough to be fascinating . . . Almost the second the prime minister knocked the ball over the net, I wanted to knock it back again.' As Hurd put it, 'I was very sad for Chris when he lost his seat, but when the thought was sown that he might go to Hong Kong, I jumped at it, because I could see there were going to be problems.'

It was later reported that Patten was so agonised by the decision facing him that he and Lavender had to remove themselves to France for a heart-searching weekend. 'Pretty average bilge,' Patten commented. The die had already been cast.

The decision to replace a diplomat, Sir David Wilson, with a politician for the final years of British rule had been mooted by Douglas Hurd some months before the election. Hurd explained later that this 'had nothing to do with Chris Patten', although, as he saw it, the argument in favour of a 'political' governor was compelling: 'The last five years were going to be very difficult, and we needed someone in Hong Kong who was in tune with the world of Westminster and the British media; someone who could operate in Hong Kong in a more political way than had been traditional, finding allies and supporters in a way which a traditional governor had no need to do.' It was, he insisted, no criticism of David Wilson, just 'a clear view on my part that we needed a different kind of governor for the last five years of British rule'.

When the decision to replace Wilson became known, it was rumoured that the prime minister and the foreign secretary (both of whom had been recently bruised by a joint mission to Beijing) regarded the outgoing governor as one of the principal advocates of the 'appeasement' of China, an approach which they believed could no longer be sustained after the atrocity of Tiananmen Square in June 1989. Hurd has conceded that his visit with the prime minister to Beijing in 1991 – to follow up a 'memorandum of understanding' about the construction of a new airport for Hong Kong initialled by Major's foreign affairs adviser, Sir Percy Cradock, earlier that year, on which Beijing was soon to renege – had been 'extremely frustrating'. The groundwork for this doomed effort had been prepared by Wilson in co-operation with Sir Percy. As a result, both sinologists fell foul of the media, which – led notably by *The Times* and the *Spectator* – were scathing about the 'kowtowing' diplomats in the Foreign Office who had masterminded Britain's relations with the 'butchers of Beijing'. Hurd has dismissed as 'a journalistic cliché' the suggestion that his and the prime minister's experiences in Beijing turned them against the Foreign Office 'kowtowers', but he has acknowledged that the decision to replace a diplomat with a politician did involve a shift of emphasis by the government: while 'co-operation and consultation', he explained, remained 'highly desirable and necessary', they 'don't mean waiting to establish what the government of the People's Republic wants and then doing it'. The implied rebuke was self-evident.

For his part, Lord Wilson has been reticent about his departure, confirming only that he was 'very sorry to leave', and that had he been asked to remain, 'I'd certainly have regarded it as my duty to do so.' It was 'very crude indeed' to suggest that he had been sacked for failing to stand up to the Chinese and to make way for someone who would. However, Wilson shared the view held by many of his peers in the Foreign Office that the restoration of good relations with China following the shootings in Tiananmen Square was of paramount importance. 'I was trying to build a house that had decent foundations,' he has since explained. 'Now that meant . . . Chinese support is perhaps putting it too strongly; Chinese acquiescence, yes, for sure.'

To this end, he confided to at least one senior colleague in Government House that he was quite ready to be pilloried by the media in Britain and Hong Kong as one of the 'arch-appeasers' of China. Appointed in 1987, Wilson had been expected to retire before the handover, but he was bitterly disappointed by the prime minister's decision to remove him at a moment when, he claimed, 'We had recovered in a quite remarkable way from all the problems of 1989.' According to his friends, he felt especially betrayed by the failure of government ministers to quash publicly the rumours that he had been sacked to make way for a figure of greater resolution and substance.

The prospective governor had been to Hong Kong as overseas development minister and before that, in 1979, as one of a group of backbenchers, led by the Labour MP Ted Rowlands, who took it upon themselves, in the words of one official who was present, to 'harangue' the governor of the time, Sir Murray MacLehose, about democracy. Why, Patten and his colleagues wanted to know, had the colonial authorities been so dilatory about the introduction of democracy? Were not the Hong Kong people mature enough to accept a parliamentary system? And would not democratic reform reinforce Hong Kong's precious 'way of life'? By the prevailing standards in Government House, such questions must have seemed irredeemably jejune. Nevertheless, this encounter between the young Turks and the colonial old guard did, in fact, help to nudge the colonial admin-istration towards the establishment, in embryonic form, of the hydra-headed quasi-democracy which the new governor was to inherit over a decade later.

Aside from these brief encounters, Patten's knowledge of Hong Kong was rudimentary, while his acquaintance with the delicate latticework of diplomacy between Britain and China in the intervening years was negligible. He was tangentially famil-iar with the Joint Declaration (the 1984 treaty, lodged at the United Nations, defining the terms under which the sovereignty of Hong Kong would revert from Britain to China in 1997), and the Basic Law (China's codification of the Joint Declaration into a constitutional and legal framework for the governance of Hong Kong as a special administrative region of the People's Republic of China). However, he had had no cause to pay close attention to the recent history of Hong Kong and he was thus not au fait with the carefully contrived ambiguities of either document, or with the tortuous diplomacy through which, under relentless pressure from China, Britain had negotiated its retreat from sovereignty.

Throughout May and June of 1992, therefore, Patten immersed himself in the detail of Hong Kong's recent history. Briefed by Foreign Office officials and former diplomats, he was also lobbied by industrialists, financiers and several of Hong Kong's most prominent public figures, who flew to London to deliver their competing recipes for triumph and disaster. He worked his way through a daunting collection of files – memoranda, briefing notes, telegrams and correspondence – reading between the lines to piece together not only the order of events but the aspirations and assumptions which underlay the process of diplomacy. As he noted at the end of those two months, 'It's dragged me up the learning curve and in the process I've acquired some prejudices. But I'm absolutely convinced that when I actually get to Hong Kong and see things for myself, and allow my nostrils to twitch in the breeze – if there is any in July – it'll feel different.'

Sir Percy Cradock – who had been the principal architect of Sino–British relations in the 1980s and who, as foreign affairs adviser to Margaret Thatcher and, latterly, to John Major, was still the most influential sinologist in Whitehall – had opposed the appointment of a 'political' governor. His aversion, which pre-dated Patten's availability for the post, sprang from his fierce belief that the accommodations he had engineered with Beijing would be jeopardised by the more aggressive approach that a politician, driven by other imperatives, would almost certainly adopt. In particular he was convinced that a politician as governor would be overly swayed by the media in Hong Kong and London, a large sector of which, to Cradock's chagrin, had already decided that his own approach had been pusillanimous. Cradock thought that 'there were great springs of emotion bubbling away below the surface about this' in the hothouse of Westminster, and that these threatened to undermine the prospect of a smooth transition which, he believed, his 'realism' had managed to secure. He feared that a politician would too easily yield to unrealistic but vociferous demands to extend the bounds of democracy in Hong Kong before 1997, and that any project of this kind would be doomed to fail amid acrimony and conflict with China. By his own account, Cradock told Major, as he had previously told Thatcher, 'It's no good shuffling the cards; you are not going to change the situation.'

He made no headway with the prime minister; Douglas Hurd, meanwhile, privately believed that Cradock and his fellow sinologists had 'missed the change in Hong Kong' following the killings in Tiananmen Square and the new strength of the demand in Hong Kong for political advance. This internal conflict was concealed until some months after Patten's appointment, but it went to the heart of the bitter divisions, within Whitehall and between the Foreign Office and Government House, which were soon to provoke an undeclared war of attrition between them. This was only resolved in Patten's favour precisely because he was the kind of heavyweight politician to which Cradock had taken such exception.

Patten had foreseen that there would be tensions. 'I'm sure that, from time to time, there will be differences of view. I'm sure there will be people who say, "It just shows what happens when you appoint a politician,"' he commented on the eve of his departure for Hong Kong. 'I guess there'll be people who'd say, "It just shows that with a job like that at the crossroads of Asia, you really needed to have an old Asia hand stroking their nose. Needed a sinologist. Good lad – but didn't speak Mandarin."' However, he had no premonition of how prolonged, how vituperative and – in the case of Cradock and a motley array of superannuated diplomats and politicians – how public this fundamental dispute would become.

The new governor's insouciance was underpinned by his confidence that Major and Hurd would, in his own phrase, give him 'a great deal of authority and a great deal of elbow room to manufacture policy with them'. Indeed, according to Patten, the three of them never even discussed the issue because: 'They both

know I'm not a turf warrior . . . it didn't need to be said that I
would have the authority I needed.' The mutual trust that existed
between Major, Hurd and Patten would, they all three recognised, be critical in sustaining that authority as Patten sought to
navigate Hong Kong through the political and diplomatic rapids
ahead. At the Rio Summit soon after the announcement of
Patten's appointment, John Major duly described the elevated
status of the new governor to the Chinese premier, Li Peng. As
reported to Patten, the prime minister in effect said, 'This is one
of my closest personal and political friends in Britain. He's one of
the leading politicians in my party and the country, and there is
no point in thinking you can slip bits of tissue paper between him
and Number Ten. If you are talking to him, you are talking to
me.' This blunt statement served only to intensify Beijing's growing suspicion – paranoia is perhaps a better term – about Britain's
purpose in Hong Kong in the run-up to the handover. It also
confirmed Cradock and his allies in the Foreign Office in their
belief that Britain was about to embark on a hazardous course of
confrontation rather than conciliation.

Patten was clear about the competing pressures that would be
placed on him by China, Britain and a volatile community in
Hong Kong. He also knew that if he was to impose himself on
the drift of events – not to turn the tide but to direct the flow –
he would have to act swiftly, and to be seen to do so. As he
focused more precisely on his objectives, he was sharply conscious
that the eyes of the world would be on Hong Kong, and on
him. 'This is the last big job in our colonial history. I don't mean
to give the impression that I want a place in history – I think
politicians who talk like that are pretty dangerous – but it is a literal description . . . Britain's colonial history is going to be
judged, to a considerable extent, through the prism of the next
five years in Hong Kong.' He was also aware that the decolonisation of Hong Kong was quite different from any other. Hong
Kong was not to acquire independence, but to be transferred
from one sovereign power to another; from a liberal democracy
to a communist dictatorship. In 1980 the Chinese leader, Deng
Xiaoping, had used the phrase 'one country, two systems' to
characterise the prospective relationship between the 1.3 billion

people on the mainland and the 6 million of Hong Kong. This slogan had acquired an almost mystical significance, becoming a mantra for optimists and pessimists alike, to be chanted with ritual fervour in the knowledge that, like all phrases devoid of intrinsic meaning, it was reassuring precisely because it was opaque.

To define his own objective as governor, Patten had taken to using – or, by his account, abusing – an intergalactic metaphor. The traditional process of decolonisation, he noted, involved 'designing' a constitution, complete with an independent judiciary, an honest civil service and the Westminster model of democracy. The next step was to 'put this on the launchpad, light the blue touchpaper and hope the satellite will go into orbit. Sometimes it is successful and sometimes it isn't – which is when you fetch up with judges being murdered, the public service corrupt and Sandhurst having rather more influence on government than Westminster.' In the case of Hong Kong, however, there had to be 'a docking of shuttles in outer space'. If this intricate manoeuvre were to succeed, the applause would be muted and, in the case of 'a lot of Americans and others who take sometimes a rather dangerously moralistic view of global issues', absent altogether. However, failure to dock would be calamitous. One of his mentors commented: 'Of course, if it goes smoothly it'll be frightfully boring. If it doesn't, you'll have people rioting on the streets and you'll have civil disorder. You'll have a collapsing Hang Seng Index. You'll have half the people wanting to run you out of town for causing instability and the other half for not standing up to China with sufficient vigour.'

The prospect of severing his ties with the intimacies of the political club to which he had belonged for most of his adult life for the uncertainties of Hong Kong was bittersweet. By the time of Patten's departure, the shock of his election defeat had given way to a lingering sense that this new appointment had brought his career in domestic politics to an end. 'It is difficult,' he noted wistfully, 'to think of anybody who has taken off for a flight round the airfield and has managed to touch down again. Christopher Soames [the last governor of Rhodesia] didn't manage. I don't know whether Sir Leon Brittan [a European commissioner] will manage . . . Our system slightly distrusts those who show from time to time that Westminster isn't the only place in the world.

'I have woken up once or twice early in the morning with a terrible feeling of falling. It's an adventure.'

'RECKLESS AND UNSCRUPULOUS ADVENTURES'

Britain Acquires a Colony

The new governor lacked the reverential approach to China's past with which so many British sinologists were afflicted. A few days after his arrival at Government House, he stood in his study examining a map of China as he reflected breezily on Beijing's attitude to the handover of sovereignty in 1997. 'I think for most Chinese, but certainly for the immortals, the Long March generation — pretty fatal, literally, once you start calling yourself an immortal — for that generation, it is about the national humiliation of the Opium Wars. It is about reasserting Chinese sovereignty and, in the process, closing a humiliating episode in Chinese history.' His own knowledge of that history was, as he readily acknowledged, decidedly sparse.

The British flag was planted on Hong Kong for the first time in January 1841. The foreign secretary, Lord Palmerston, was dismayed when he heard the news, and reprimanded Captain Elliot, who had taken this 'barren island', pronouncing that Hong Kong would never be 'a mart of trade'. The Chinese emperor, Daoguang, was no less baffled, but concluded of the invaders: 'These barbarians always look on trade as their chief occupation . . . It is plain they are not worth attending to.'

The seizure of Hong Kong was a classic if accidental triumph of gunboat diplomacy. The island was one of a hundred or more scattered around the estuary of the Pearl River, seventy miles downstream from the capital of southern China, Canton. By the early eighteenth century, Canton was already an elegant city whose grandest quarters, graced by fine squares and magnificent triumphal arches, reminded one contemporary correspondent of St Germain in Paris. By the end of the century it had become an established entrepôt where the great trading nations of the world had taken up residence to exploit the huge but virtually untapped market of an ancient but ramshackle empire which already had a population of 300 million subjects. In Britain, liberal ideology was in the ascendant, most aggressively in the form of a commitment to free trade, which had acquired the status of a quasi-moral imperative. It was underpinned by a genuine belief that international peace and prosperity could not otherwise be secured: the alternative to free trade, it was argued, was war. British merchant venturers, with the Royal Navy in support, criss-crossed the trading routes of the globe in pursuit of the rapidly growing opportunities for trade and investment. In Canton, these buccaneers operated under the protective authority of the East India Company, which was formally entrusted with quasi-governmental responsibilities on behalf of the British empire. Like their European rivals, the scions of the great trading houses, such as Messrs Jardine and Matheson, regarded themselves, in the words of the latter, as the 'princes of the earth', the advance guard of a new world order.

Unhappily for these self-appointed 'princes', this obeisance before the altar of commerce clashed fundamentally with some of the basic tenets of Confucianism. In the celestial empire, the deference owed to traditional hierarchies was rigidly enforced. The merchant class was to be found almost at the bottom of the social scale, above beggars and prostitutes but beneath peasants and craftsmen. In Canton, the self-esteem of the 'princes of the earth' was thus put severely to the test. As *fan-kwais,* or 'barbarians', foreign merchants were required to segregate themselves from contact with the indigenous population, which regarded them with suspicion and even hostility. Forbidden to live inside the city walls, they were restricted to their own compounds while their womenfolk were banned altogether from landing on Cantonese soil. Even more frustratingly, their terms of trade were severely restricted and they were only permitted to do business with

China during the summer months, after which they decamped, reluctantly, to the island of Macau at the mouth of the Pearl River delta.

These constraints were not only irksome but, far more importantly, they violated the new Western orthodoxy according to which all nations not only had the right but the obligation to open their borders in the cause of free trade. This imperative, it was widely agreed, was a cause which could legitimately be pressed to the point of war. In 1793, following pressure from the East India Company, the British government sent Lord Macartney on the first 'embassy' to Peking to urge His Celestial Majesty to liberalise Chinese trading regulations and, more broadly, to put Britain's diplomatic relations with China on a more substantial footing by allowing His Britannic Majesty's government to establish a presence at the Imperial Court. He failed. In a courteous but firm rebuff, the old emperor, Qianlong, sent Macartney back with a missive for George III informing the British monarch that the changes he sought were 'not in harmony with the state system of our dynasty and will definitely not be tolerated'.

By the end of the eighteenth century, opium, cultivated in India and shipped to Canton, had become the most valuable commodity traded with China. An imperial edict banning the import of this addictive substance had been widely ignored by local merchants, who smuggled the contraband ashore under the eyes of well-bribed officials. Everyone – with the possible exception of opium addicts – benefited. As Frank Welsh has observed in his masterly *History of Hong Kong*, 'It was in everyone's interest that the Canton trade continued uninterrupted: the prosperity of Canton, the comforts of Peking, the livelihood of thousands of officials, and, through the duties levied on tea [the celestial empire's principal export], a substantial part of the revenue of the British government, all depended on it.' As a result, efforts by the Chinese authorities to stamp out the illegal trade were at best desultory. On one occasion, after a ritual engagement with a departing convoy of opium traders, the Chinese naval authorities issued a proclamation stating: 'His Celestial Majesty's Imperial fleet, after a desperate conflict, has made the Fan-kwais run before it.' This sound and fury concealed the fact that, as always, the Chinese gunboats had followed the British merchant ships, as Welsh puts it, 'at a respectful distance and at a deliberate pace, but with the minimum discharge of ordnance'. Great care was taken to ensure that no one was hurt and no ships suffered more than superficial damage.

In Britain opium was still highly regarded as both a painkiller and a soporific. Its addictive properties were well known, but caused concern only to a minority. In China, the use of the narcotic was as commonplace as that of tobacco in Britain. So opium itself was not a casus belli between the two countries. As Welsh has argued persuasively, the underlying cause of the Opium Wars between Britain and China was principally the dispute over free trade which sprang from mutually incompatible attitudes. It is conceivable that if the emperor had been willing to open negotiations with the first British envoy to visit Peking, the 'embassy' led by Lord Macartney in 1793, armed conflict between Britain and China, and more than two centuries of resentment and distrust, might have been avoided. It is clear from the available evidence that the British authorities would have been quite willing to suppress the opium trade in return for the liberalisation of legitimate trade, which had far greater potential. That happy outcome, however, would have required the statesmen of both sides to bridge the cultural chasm that separated their two empires – an improbable vision to contemplate, even with the benefit of hindsight.

Throughout this period, the British government came under growing domestic pressure from the merchant classes, who demanded the right to trade as directly and freely with China as with the other parts of the world over which Britannia held sway. Towards the end of the eighteenth century British exporters were facing intense competition from rival European nations and from the United States of America. They were anxious for new outlets in which to market the products of the industrial revolution. For them, China was an untapped source of unimaginable wealth: if only they could trade freely through Canton and move unhindered about China, then, as Welsh has noted, 'the Chinese masses would rejoice at being able to buy Staffordshire mugs,

Birmingham trays and Lancashire frocks, all brought to them cheaply by British-built railways'. A petition to Parliament in 1820 demanded action; the government of Lord Liverpool, its collective mind elsewhere, for the moment demurred.

In Canton, the British merchants became ever more fretful. In 1831, they petitioned London again, complaining that the Cantonese authorities were 'a venal and corrupt class of persons, who, having purchased their appointments, study only the means of amassing wealth by extortion and injustice'. Worse, they subjected the foreign community to 'privations and treatment to which it would be difficult to find parallel in any part of the world'. The petitioners proposed that if the Cantonese authorities could not be persuaded to mend their ways, the British government should 'by the acquisition of an insular possession near the coast of China place British Commerce in this remote quarter of the globe beyond the reach of further despotism and oppression'.

The imperial arrogance of this demand did not find immediate favour in London, where the government faced conflict rather closer to home: an agrarian uprising, riots in major cities, a financial crisis, and, in the form of the Great Reform Bill, a constitutional drama of the first magnitude. Indeed, in 1833, even with the bellicose Lord Palmerston as foreign secretary, a British government mission to Canton was enjoined to 'cautiously abstain from all unnecessary use of menacing language . . . to ensure that all British subjects understood their duty to obey the laws and usages of the Chinese empire . . . to avoid any conduct, language, or demeanour, which should excite jealousy or distrust among the Chinese people or government . . .' Evidently the British empire's policy towards China had yet to live up to the bloodcurdling reputation that later mythology was to bestow on that period. However, this injunction failed to impress the man chosen by Palmerston to lead the mission, Lord Napier, a former naval officer without experience of diplomacy or trade, who, in the words of the Tory *Morning Post*, knew as much about Canton as an orang-utan.

The reaction of the Chinese to the British envoy at the start of what was intended to be a confidence-building exercise was instructive. Reporting the 'arrival of a ship's boat at Canton, about midnight, bringing four English devils', one of the local viceroy's officials warned: 'We think that such coming as this is manifestly stealing into Canton.' And as a representative of the British government, Napier had indeed violated Chinese proto- col. Instead of announcing his arrival to the local viceroy by letter, he should first have presented himself at the court in Peking. As it was, he lacked the requisite permits even to land at Canton. The viceroy, however, stayed his hand, choosing to give an impudent but ignorant 'barbarian' the benefit of the doubt.

At a meeting with the viceroy's representatives, Napier dis- played all those attributes of British imperialism that the Chinese most deplored. Upbraiding his hosts for keeping him waiting, his Lordship declared that the delay was an 'insult to His Britannic Majesty'. Moreover, he made it clear that he was quite ready to deploy armed force to secure Britain's diplomatic and mercantile objectives in China.

The relationship between two mutually uncomprehending cul- tures rapidly deteriorated. In a wholly unprovoked gesture, the British envoy engineered a skirmish between two British war- ships, which happened to be in the vicinity, and a couple of lightly armed Chinese patrol boats, near the Chinese fortress at Whampoa, downriver from Canton. The Chinese response was immediate and, for once, unequivocal. They announced a boy- cott of all British goods and the death sentence for any local merchant caught trading with the barbarians. The British envoy's foray into diplomacy had been a disaster. He departed soon after- wards for Macau in disgrace. His enduring, if only, legacy was a dispatch to London in which he urged the occupation of 'the island of Hong Kong, in the entrance of the Canton River, which is admirably adapted for every purpose'.

The tensions did not abate. There were misunderstandings, disputes and skirmishes. If the Chinese were stubborn and dis- dainful, the British merchants in Canton were arrogant and uncouth. The quality of their collective character was embodied in the person of James Matheson, who wrote in 1836, 'It has pleased Providence to assign to the Chinese – a people charac- terised by a marvellous degree of imbecility, avarice, conceit and obstinacy – the possession of a vast portion of the most desirable parts of the earth, and a population estimated as amounting to nearly one third of the human race.' There was, Matheson avowed, only one course of action open to the thwarted British empire: 'We must resolve upon vindicating our insulted honour as a nation, and protecting the injured innocence of our commerce.' The alternative was to humble ourselves in 'ignominious submission, at the feet of the most insolent, the most ungrateful, the most pusillanimous people on earth'. Matheson's grandiloquence was patently absurd, but in his vulgar way he voiced the opinion of many leading figures of the British merchant class.

As free trade faltered, the smugglers continued to flourish, and by 1838, the drug-runners were landing no fewer than 40,000 chests of opium a year at various points along the south China coast. Increasingly frustrated by this impertinence, the authorities in Peking faced two options. Either they could concede defeat and legalise the opium trade, or they could opt to stamp it out altogether. There seemed to be no middle path. After intense debate with his advisers at court, the emperor decided on the latter course of action.

It was not the barbarians but the local Chinese who were the first to experience the full sting of the imperial lash. James Matheson's business partner, William Jardine, recounted: 'The Governor-General has been seizing, trying, and strangling poor devils without mercy . . . We have never seen so serious a persecution.' Napier's successor in Canton, Lord Admiral Sir Charles Elliot – a man of greater sensitivity and judgement who genuinely supported the imperial edict against opium – warned his recalcitrant compatriots that owners of craft 'engaged in the said illicit opium trade' would receive no support from Her Majesty's Government 'if the Chinese Government shall think fit to seize [them]'. He also warned them that any smuggler causing the death of a Chinese in the course of his illicit trade should expect the death sentence.

On 18 March 1839, the imperial commissioner, Lin Zexu, who had been dispatched from the celestial court in Peking to oversee the clampdown, had sixty of the most notorious Chinese smugglers detained. Four of them were later executed. However, he was swift to reassure the expatriate community that it would come to no harm unless the imperial diktat was defied. To this end he ordered that all stocks of opium were to be surrendered and that all foreigners should pledge themselves never again to deal in the contraband. Otherwise, he warned, they would face the full rigour of the Chinese law: imprisonment, expropriation, and perhaps decapitation. Lin, who was both famously incorruptible and notably sophisticated, laced these warnings with an eloquent reminder that the opium smugglers were undermining the growth of the legal trade in properly bartered goods, which alone was the proper basis on which to conduct economic relations between nations. In a note to the emperor he advised that 'the said barbarians are from a far-off country . . . our policy is to be rigorous without resorting to any offensive action'. Nevertheless he ordered a military cordon to be thrown round the compound of foreign-owned factories outside the walls of the city, incarcerating its European inhabitants until every last ounce of opium had been surrendered. After six weeks, Lin and Elliot (who had himself been immured in the compound) contrived to secure the surrender of more than 1,000 tons of opium, valued at more than £2 million, which was ceremoniously burned on the banks of the Pearl River by the Chinese authorities.

In Britain, the London East India and China Association, which represented the merchants trading in the Far East, tendered their advice to Palmerston. 'We have no desire that it should for one instance be supposed that we are advocating the continuance of a trade against which the Chinese government formally protest,' they insisted. 'British merchants trading in China must obey the laws of that country.' The association urged the government to press the case with China for free trade and for the opening of specified ports to make that possible. These recommendations were adopted, yet soon afterwards a delegation from the association, led by William Jardine, managed to convince Palmerston that the Chinese should nonetheless be persuaded to compensate the British traders for the destruction of the opium which they had quite legally purchased from India. The foreign secretary was further assured that the dispatch of a naval task force to the South China Seas would help expedite this outcome.

One member of the British Cabinet recalled in a dry aside, 'We had resolved . . . on a war with the master of one third of the human race.'

In Canton, the imperial commissioner pressed his advantage. Explaining to the emperor that 'the barbarians never break an agreement', he demanded that every British trader put his signature to a formal document promising that if 'one little bit of opium was found out in any part of my ship by examination, I am willingly deliver up the transgressor and he shall be punish to death according to the correctness law of the Government of the Heavenly Dynasty'. Lin's translators may not have served him well, but the import of the document was self-evident and, to Admiral Sir Charles Elliot, unacceptable. Recognising the scope for abuse it offered the Chinese authorities, and mindful of the vagaries of celestial justice, he instead ordered the British community in Canton to cease trading with China and to withdraw to the Portuguese colony of Macau.

A drunken brawl between some British sailors and local Chinese in Tsim Sha Tsui on the southernmost point of China was enough to cause a deteriorating relationship to plummet. One of the Chinese involved in the fracas died of his injuries. Elliot at once ordered an official inquiry into the 'grave offences' which had been committed. Although it proved impossible to identify a single culprit, five sailors were arraigned to stand trial before a special court convened by the British envoy and conducted according to British domestic law. Although the jury threw out the charge of murder, all five of the accused were convicted of riotous assault, fined and sentenced to short terms of imprisonment. This did not satisfy the imperial commissioner, who demanded that a culprit – any culprit – be handed over to the Chinese authorities. When Elliot refused, Lin Zexu's response was to pressurise the governor of Macau to expel the British community. On 15 August 1839, the several hundred men, women and children were, as described by Elliot's wife, Clara, 'turned out of our houses' to be transferred into British ships moored in the natural harbour formed between the protective land mass of Kowloon on the southern coastal tip of mainland China and the island of Hong Kong.

In an attempt to maintain the pressure, Lin decreed that the British ships should be denied fresh food and water by the Chinese traders on Kowloon. Elliot went ashore to persuade the local traders to ignore the edict. He had some success: on 4 September, a convoy of small craft set off to supply the British fleet, only to be intercepted by Chinese naval junks. Exasperated by this obduracy, Elliot ordered three of his vessels to fire on the Chinese. In what was the first of the several skirmishes which were to enter Chinese mythology as the 'Opium Wars', no casualties were reported by either side.

On 3 November, despite frantic efforts by Elliot to broker a truce, an assemblage of Chinese naval junks challenged the local might of the British navy: four junks were destroyed and one British sailor was wounded. Thereafter hostilities were suspended until, early in 1840, with some reluctance, Palmerston dispatched a small task force to the South China Seas. Its mission was to demonstrate the potential of the British navy rather than to pursue a still undeclared war, but this 'diplomacy' could hardly have been more provocative, even if in military terms it was largely free of risk. The task force first blockaded the Pearl River, then the Yangtze, and later the Yellow River. After this show of force, it proceeded to the approaches to Peking and awaited orders.

In the late autumn the British fleet sailed south again to regroup in the Pearl River. On 7 January 1841, the *Nemesis*, a prototype for the British gunboat, led an attack against the Chinese fortifications which guarded the approaches to Canton. Lin's successor as imperial commissioner was swift to negotiate with Elliot. On 28 January, knowing that his own demands had fallen far short of Palmerston's orders to secure a commercial treaty opening up every major Chinese port to the benefits of free trade, Elliot secured 'the cession of the island and harbour of Hong Kong to the British Crown'. Under the Convention of Ch'uen-pi, he also secured payment of a $6 million indemnity and the right both to trade again in Canton and in future to conduct official negotiations 'upon equal footing'. At 8.15am on 26 January, Captain Edward Belcher RN of the *Sulphur* raised the Union Jack on Hong Kong and Admiral Sir Charles Elliot, aboard *HMS Wellesley*, declared himself governor of Britain's first colonial acquisition in the Far East.

The shame and grievance at the seizure of Hong Kong was deeply felt in Peking. In London, Lord Palmerston was no less aggrieved by Elliot's decision to settle for the 'barren island'. In consequence the governments of both empires declined to accept the terms of the convention which their respective emissaries had agreed on their behalf. The imperial commissioner was escorted back to Peking in chains; Charles Elliot, rebuked by the foreign secretary for treating his instructions 'as if they were waste paper', was summoned back to London to be replaced by Sir Henry Pottinger, an altogether cruder exponent of gunboat diplomacy.

The Opium Wars were in military terms more a splutter of skirmishes than a struggle of Titans. The Treaty of Nanking (1842) ended the First Anglo–Chinese War by securing in perpetuity British sovereignty over the thirty square miles of the island of Hong Kong and the opening of five Chinese ports (including Canton) to foreign trade. Officially, and only with the reluctant consent of a sceptical British government, Hong Kong became a crown colony on 26 June 1843. But this did not settle matters: in the struggle for free trade, one skirmish led to another. After the Second Anglo–Chinese War (1856–8), the emperor gave his approval to the Treaty of Tientsin, which granted Britain the right to permanent diplomatic representation in Peking. However, the military sparring resumed the following year, and as a result, in 1860 the Convention of Peking formally ceded the southern tip of Kowloon (fifteen square miles) to Britain as a base for a garrison. The physical framework for the early development of Hong Kong as a British trading station, a minor entrepôt in the Far East, was now in place. The cost in military terms had been negligible; in diplomatic terms, however, though it was not yet apparent, the price would prove far higher.

The 'unequal treaties' (as, more than a century later, the People's Republic of China would refer to the cession 'in perpetuity' of both the island of Hong Kong and the southern tip of Kowloon) did not complete the process of British acquisition. Following the Japanese invasion of China in 1895, the European powers scrambled for advantage against each other. Britain, anxious to ward off the marauding interest of France and the United States, extracted a further concession from the Celestial Empire. Under the second Convention of Peking in 1898, the British secured a ninety-nine-year lease on the so-called New Territories, which comprised 287 square miles of the Chinese mainland to the north of Kowloon and 235 small and largely uninhabited islands around Hong Kong. It was agreed that the lease would expire on 1 July 1997.

In the years following the establishment of the People's Republic, the Chinese politburo constructed a version of the nineteenth-century conflict with Britain from which no deviation was permitted. According to this mantra-like revision, the 'motherland' had been ruled by a succession of weak and corrupt Manchu emperors. Among their subjects, however, were a number of patriotic soldiers who fought heroically against the opium trade and its British sponsors. The obstinacy shown by the British imperialists forced China to take up arms, but despite great resistance, the imperialists were able to impose their will on a dynasty that was physically and psychologically on the point of collapse. Thereafter, the struggle in China took place on two fronts: emancipation from feudalism and liberation from Western imperialism. In the words of the usually urbane Chinese ambassador to St James's, Ma Yuzhen, speaking in 1992, the loss of Hong Kong was 'a national humiliation' that was followed by a number of 'unequal treaties' which were unacceptable to the Chinese people. This outrage was compounded by the attempted 'carve-up' of China by the European powers at the end of the nineteenth century which left Britain in occupation of the New Territories. Thus, as judged from Beijing, 1997 offered a restoration of 'national dignity, national independence and national sovereignty' by erasing for ever an historic mortification at the hands of Britain.

The sincerity of this communist revisionism was not doubted by the sinologists at the Foreign Office, and it had a powerful impact on British diplomacy in the years leading up to Patten's arrival in Hong Kong. According to Percy Cradock, for instance, 'When it comes to the crunch, memories of 1840 are at the top of the bill. China's determination to expunge those humiliations and to recover their national territory on their own terms comes absolutely top . . . I can't emphasise the importance of this too much.'

Under Britain's colonial administration, the fruits of China's defeat slowly began to blossom in Hong Kong. The population of the island at the time of the seizure was no more than 2,000; within a year it had grown to 15,000. In large measure this was due to the foresight of Charles Elliot. Before his recall in August 1841, the disgraced plenipotentiary had not only authorised the sale of commercial land along the harbour's edge but had witnessed the auction of the first tranche of potentially valuable real estate on 14 June 1841, before the British government had even acknowledged the acquisition of Hong Kong to be anything more than a tactical manoeuvre. By the spring of the following year, the Royal Engineers had built a four-mile road along the foreshore. Storage sheds had started to sprout from building plots; merchants oversaw the construction of grand mansions. Soon there were police stations, post offices and a jail, as well as the inevitable sprinkling of gambling dens and whorehouses. By the following year the first of many theatrical touring companies performed in the Opera House and the first newspaper (the *Friend of China*, later named the *China Mail*) went on sale in the streets. Within four years, the waterfront had taken shape: naval and military installations of a permanent nature rose elegantly alongside the two- and three-storey warehouses and offices.

Elliot's swift move to authorise the sale or lease of development land which had not been sanctioned by London was reinforced by the decision of his successor, Sir Henry Pottinger, to allow the publication of official statements implying a British commitment to Hong Kong which had not yet been made. As a result the establishment of Hong Kong as a British colony had become a fait accompli before the Cabinet had resolved the matter one way or the other.

In the official summary of the colony's history, compiled by the Hong Kong Information Services, it is recorded, in an otherwise somewhat Panglossian account, that 'the new settlement did not go well at first. It attracted unruly elements, while fever and typhoons threatened life and property. Crime was rife.' In fact Hong Kong rapidly acquired the nastiest characteristics of the worst kind of frontier town. Piracy on and around the coastline was matched in the centre by a violence and lawlessness which made the streets quite unsafe for all but those accompanied by bodyguards. In the absence of an effective police force, the Europeans armed themselves with handguns against marauding bands of murderous thieves.

This anarchy was attributed to a rapid influx of Chinese from the mainland in search of easy pickings. Within the first ten years of the seizure, the Chinese community multiplied sixteenfold to over 32,000. According to the Rev. Charles Gutzlaff, one of the colony's most influential figures of that time, 'Many of them are of the worst characters, and ready to commit any atrocity . . . It is very natural that depraved, idle and bad characters . . . should flock to the colony where money can be made . . . The moral standard of the people . . . is of the lowest description.' Fugitives from mainland justice mingled easily with the local population. As one observer noted, 'The shelter and protection afforded by the presence of our fleet soon made our shores the resort of outlaws, opium-smugglers, and, indeed, of all persons who had made themselves obnoxious to the Chinese laws . . . Hong Kong has been invested by numbers of the Triad Society, the members of which . . . perpetrate the grossest enormities.' The triads had emerged in the eighteenth century as a quasi-liberation movement with a mission to rid China of its Manchu – 'foreign' – rulers. However they had soon degenerated into a Mafia-like alliance of criminals and their activities had already begun to pollute both China and Hong Kong.

By 1845, the situation had become so bad that the governor of the time, Sir John Bowring, introduced a range of emergency measures to combat the lawlessness. These included pass laws providing that 'any Chinaman found at large . . . elsewhere than in his own Habitation not having a pass . . . shall be summarily punished by any Justice of the Peace . . .' The available chastisements ranged from fines and imprisonment to 'Public Whipping and Personal Exposure in the Stocks'. Vigilante groups, defined as 'every person lawfully acting as Sentry or Patrol', were authorised 'to fire upon with intent or effect to kill'. They were doubtless stiffened in their resolve by the knowledge that 'no Act done or attempted in pursuance of this Ordinance shall be questioned in any court'. In the early years exemplary punishment in the form of public hangings and floggings had little impact. Public hangings were later abandoned, but that Victorian favourite, corporal punishment (administered with the cat-o'-nine-tails), persisted.

In their own way, the expatriate community behaved no less deplorably than those over whom they held sway. As if to compensate for their own treatment in Canton, the British lost no time in reminding the Chinese who were now the masters. Some of them behaved with such arrogance, braggadocio and brutality that one Anglican cleric was driven to comment that the merchant venturers of Hong Kong treated the Chinese as though they were 'a degraded race of people'. A later traveller, Miss Isabella Bird, noted: 'You cannot be two minutes in Hong Kong without seeing Europeans striking coolies with their canes or umbrellas.'

The social niceties of colonial life, while less formally applied than in other outposts of the empire, were nonetheless carefully observed. The Chinese were effectively barred from the Midlevels and the Peak, the high ground with a view on which the Europeans set about creating an outpost of Western civilisation. The segregation on the Peak was later extended to a 20,000-acre site on Kowloon, ostensibly in the name of (European) public health. The Chinese were also forbidden to enter the 'whites-only' clubs and sports grounds, those semblances of British culture without which colonial settlers of that era would have been bereft. Miss Bird was not altogether impressed by expatriate Hong Kong, with 'its cliques, its boundless hospitalities, its extravagances in living, its quarrels, its gaieties, its picnics, balls, regattas, races, dinner parties, lawn tennis parties, amateur theatricals, afternoon teas, and all its other modes of creating a whirl which passes for pleasure', from all of which, of course, the Chinese were wholly excluded, except in the role of servant.

The Victorian settlers not only found the Chinese culture hard to fathom but were evidently reluctant to make the effort. Prejudice was much simpler – and there was ample opportunity

for its indulgence. Although the authorities in Hong Kong outlawed infanticide, they were unable to make much impression on
the traditions of foot-binding, child marriage and concubinage,
despite much hand-wringing outrage on the subject from social
reformers in London. The living conditions in the Chinese community served to reinforce European prejudices. As the
population of the indigenous Chinese expanded (by the turn of
the century, with a population of 240,000, they outnumbered the
Europeans by twenty-five to one), their quarters became synonymous in the minds of the uptown settlers with disease and
squalor. Governor Sir John Pope-Hennessy, who took up office
in 1877, noted: 'The dwellings of the Chinese working classes are
inconvenient, filthy and unwholesome. Accumulations of filth
occur in and around them . . . Above all, the water supply is miserable.' But he added, as if to reproach his fellow countrymen, 'It
is unjust to condemn them as a hopelessly filthy race 'til they have
been provided with reasonable means for cleanliness. I conceive
that it is the duty of the Government to see that these means are
provided and applied . . .' Unfortunately, the resources to achieve
this were not readily forthcoming in a colony of free-traders
which was already prone to regard all taxation as a form of
administrative theft, and where subsequent overlords were not
always so enlightened. Sir William Robinson, for example, writing in the last decade of the nineteenth century, detected that the
Chinese were 'educated to insanitary habits, and accustomed
from infancy to herd together, they were quite unable to grasp
the necessity of segregation; they were quite content to die like
sheep, spreading disease around them so long as they were left
undisturbed'.

Although the Chinese were gradually to emerge from the
degrading status imposed on them by the settlers, the process
took a very long time. In 1896, a leading businessman by the
name of Granville Sharp deplored the beginnings of change:
'When first I came to Hong Kong every Chinese coolie doffed his
cap and stood to one side to allow you to pass. When do you see
a coolie do that now? We do not exercise our undoubted superiority. We must rule by power.' His attitude was widely shared, and
remained institutionalised until well into the twentieth century. It

was defined in 1935 by an incoming governor as a form of 'mental arrogance', the basis for which, he wrote, was 'the assumption that the European is inherently superior to the Asian'. At least until 1940, one of Hong Kong's leading hospitals, the Matilda, which Granville Sharp had endowed, still reserved admission for Europeans only. Chinese subjects of the crown were not allowed to serve in the police force until the Second World War, and it was not until 1942 that the Colonial Office dropped its requirement that all candidates should be 'of pure European descent'. It was only in 1946 that the ordinance imposing residential segregation was finally repealed.

The two communities did have some occasion for closer intercourse. As befitted the 'new frontier' atmosphere of Hong Kong's market economy, the red-light zone, with its illegal gambling dens and brothels, grew to accommodate an apparently insatiable need. The Chinese, in particular, were addicted to gambling, and for them games of chance carried no whiff of moral opprobrium. In Victorian England a range of complex (and, from a late twentieth-century perspective, arcane) set of laws sought to control the popular taste for what was regarded as a degrading appetite. However, it soon became evident to the administration in Hong Kong that gambling was impossible to suppress. Ignoring the cries of anguish from social reformers and Christian missionaries, Sir Richard MacDonnell (who became governor in 1867) therefore sanctioned the opening of eleven gaming houses. However, Victorian humbug was not to be thwarted. The MacDonnell reform was soon reversed and a veil of discretion was once again draped over a 'vice' which prospered to the great benefit of the triads, whose 'protection' soon became an ineradicable feature of the colony's subculture.

Like gambling, prostitution proved impossible to abolish by administrative fiat. The official statistics for venereal disease revealed that by 1880, a quarter of the soldiers and sailors stationed in Hong Kong were so adversely affected by syphilis – known locally as Havana flu – that they were unfit for duty. In an attempt to control the disease, which not only incapacitated its victims but caused them terrible suffering, the colonial authorities had instituted a system of licences for 'approved' brothels and inspections for those which were not registered (except for those used exclusively by the Chinese, which were exempt from scrutiny). Unhappily, this pragmatic approach appeared to condone in Hong Kong a 'vice' which was outlawed in Britain. Upon the repeal of the Contagious Diseases Act (which permitted the forcible medical examination of those at risk) by the Westminster Parliament, Hong Kong was driven to abandon licences and inspections. By the turn of the century, no less than half the Hong Kong garrison was infected by venereal disease, a problem which was only solved with the discovery of penicillin some years later.

The expatriate community protected themselves from these disagreeable aspects of Hong Kong by a veneer of gentility which over the years ossified into a set of small-town snobberies that were cruelly observed by the novelist Stella Benson, writing in the 1930s. 'There is nobody here who reads, nobody who is interested in European politics,' she noted. 'Really nobody likes even the mildest honesty here . . . Faces shut like doors unless we talk about games or the weather.'

The stifling mores that ruled social intercourse in the European ghetto contrasted sharply with the economic rapacity of its occupants, whose character found little favour with the British civil servants dispatched to impose administrative order on their buccaneering fellow countrymen. In the words of a senior official from the Board of Trade, writing in 1863, 'The class of Britons who press into this new and untrodden field of enterprise is mainly composed of reckless and unscrupulous adventurers who seek nothing but enormous profits on particular transactions and care little for the permanent interests of commerce – still less for the principles of truth and justice. These men always cloak their injustices under the guise of patriotism and civilisation.'

Even so, Hong Kong did not at first prosper; indeed, it remained a colonial backwater until the second half of the twentieth century. Widely regarded, in the words of one contemporary, as a 'remote and completely unimportant settlement', the colony bore no comparison to Canton and Shanghai as a trading port. In 1845, a deputation of merchants complained to the colonial secretary that 'Hong Kong has no trade at all and is a mere place of residence of the government and its officers with a few British merchants and a very scanty, poor population'. Yet, as Frank Welsh has noted, the overblown expectations of the merchants themselves were almost certainly the root cause of their disappointment. Even as Hong Kong built its basic infra-structure, utilities and services, the throughput of goods in the port grew sluggishly and the economy remained virtually stag-nant. The merchants' investment in Hong Kong, in the form of seventy-five-year leases for their waterfront warehouses, seemed, for a time, distinctly insecure.

The most fundamental change in Hong Kong's prospects did not occur until after the Second World War, during which the colony was occupied by the Japanese and its inhabitants subjected to the harsh treatment characteristic of the Japanese Imperial Army. The governor, Sir Mark Young, who had been held in captivity by the Japanese and suffered terrible privations at their hands, was reinstated at Government House in 1946. In 1949 hundreds of thousands of refugees began to pour across the border from southern China and to arrive by boat from Shanghai. The former were peasants fleeing from hunger; the latter were princi-pally merchants fleeing from expropriation and repression after the fall of Beijing, Shanghai and Canton to the Communists. Mao Zedong's Long March had reached its revolutionary desti-nation, and those who feared that the People's Republic would not be to their taste saw in Hong Kong an alternative route to individual and communal salvation.

As a result the population of Hong Kong virtually doubled within a single year, and by the end of 1950, altogether upwards of 2 million people had crossed the border. The authorities in the British colony, mindful of the need to preserve diplomatic rela-tions with the new regime in Beijing, referred to these hapless people as squatters to avoid the implication that they had fled from persecution. This linguistic obfuscation sprang in part from the fear that Mao might use the excuse of nationalist subversion in Hong Kong to launch a pre-emptive strike against the colony to restore Chinese sovereignty by force. Tens of thousands of the opponents of the Nationalists, led by Chiang Kai Shek, had fled to Hong Kong before the Nationalist army collapsed, and it would have been a simple matter for Beijing to stimulate an internal uprising of communist sympathisers against the latest wave of refugees which would almost certainly have been beyond the powers of the war-weary colonial authorities to contain. Similarly, Chiang could easily have roused the no less fervent nationalist supporters of his 'exiled' regime in Taiwan. Hong Kong faced a social, economic and political problem on an alarming scale.

In the literal sense, the refugees were indeed squatters. Camped on the hills around Hong Kong and Kowloon, filling every available piece of land, they lacked any basic amenities. Gradually the authorities imposed a semblance of administrative order: they screened the squatters for resettlement, marked out plots of land on which they could build, provided standpipes and paved the paths through each settlement as it was established. Nothing was done to indicate that these migrants had any right to settle in the colony, or that the authorities had any responsibility for them. Then, on Christmas Day 1953, a fire in the squatter camp at Shek Kip Mei made 50,000 people homeless. Overnight, the governor, Sir Alexander Grantham, was forced into taking a fateful decision: the government would have to build houses for the squatters. By 1956, 200,000 former refugees had been accommodated in tenement rooms, each individual allocated a living area somewhat smaller than the square footage of a double bed. It was a modest but, given the resources of the Hong Kong government, gallant effort to rehouse the dispossessed. More significantly, Grantham's initiative established a principle from which the British government could not possibly retreat. As a result, within a generation the phrase 'refugee community' had come to denote not a physical environment, but the psyche of most of the territory's inhabitants.

To the relief of the authorities, the new settlers were, in general, peaceable, law-abiding and hard-working. Sir Jack Cater, then a junior official, later to become chief secretary, was astonished by the degree to which the immigrants accommodated the privations of this period: 'It was extraordinary for me to visit one of these areas where many thousands of people were living, with one standpipe for two hundred people, and then to see the girls going off to work in the factories in the morning looking pretty, smooth and clean. It was absolutely fantastic.'

The fears of internal upheaval gradually faded until, in 1956, on the anniversary of the 1911 October Revolution (which had led to the downfall of the Ch'ing dynasty), a British resettlement officer took it upon himself to order the removal of some nationalist flags. This crass decision provoked a riot: shops were looted and factories owned by communists came under attack; known communists were rounded up, taken to Nationalist headquarters and brutally assaulted. They were forced to chant nationalist slogans and some of them were killed in cold blood. It took two days for the police and army to restore order, by which time fifty-nine people were dead, forty-four shot by the police, who had been ordered to fire 'without hesitation', and fifteen murdered by the rioters. The adjournment debate in the Commons on this grave breakdown of order in a British colony did not take place for almost a month after the riots, and then it lasted a mere thirty minutes – an accurate measure, as Frank Welsh has pointed out, of the 'very low priority accorded Hong Kong'. After guttering for a moment, the candle of curiosity about Hong Kong was soon snuffed out by more pressing matters closer to home.

In the sixties Hong Kong's economy took off. Under the direction of financial secretary Sir John Cowperthwaite, a laissez-faire economist, the British colony acquired all the characteristics of a free-trade port. Long before Milton Friedman or Margaret Thatcher summoned up the gods of the free market, Cowperthwaite imposed a regime of minimum public spending and minimal restraint on the maximisation of profits. Between 1960 and 1970, wages rose on average by 50 per cent and the number of people living in acute poverty fell from over 50 per cent of the population to under 16 per cent. The annual report for 1971 was able to boast that Hong Kong had become a 'stable and increasingly affluent society comparable with the developed world in nearly every respect'. This was an exaggeration: an ideological hostility towards the concept of the welfare state, combined with the financial secretary's refusal to countenance public borrowing, left Hong Kong's basic services woefully underfunded. Health and education in particular languished far behind what the developed world would regard as appropriate for a thriving modern society. Yet, in the latter half of the sixties, the

departments of education, health and social welfare managed to
record large budget surpluses apparently without provoking
criticism.

Across the border, the People's Republic of China lurched
from one slogan to another. The 'Let a Hundred Flowers Bloom'
years of the early fifties gave way to the 'Great Leap Forward' in
1958 – and between 20 and 40 million people starved to death in
the process. Mao's authority soared. In 1966, he initiated the
Cultural Revolution, a regime of persecution and terror under
which the intelligentsia were purged and the Red Guards held
terrifying sway. It was not difficult to visualise how the same
generation in Hong Kong, appropriately subverted from the
mainland, might erupt with similar revolutionary fervour. In
April of that year, a protest against a rise in fares on the Star
Ferry which plied its trade between Hong Kong and Kowloon
was the pretext for an outbreak of unrest in Kowloon, in which
one demonstrator was killed. In comparison with neighbouring
Macau, where rioting Red Guards were fired on by Portuguese
troops, the Hong Kong disturbances were easily contained.
However, any complacency was misplaced. The frustration of
the young and the poor, the badly housed and ill educated, was
tinder waiting to be ignited. And in May 1967, a rash of demonstrations did escalate quickly into full-scale rioting. Day after day
thousands of people, old as well as young, took to the streets in
the name of the Cultural Revolution. There was arson and looting. Urged on from the mainland by Red Guards, who had
seized control of Canton, saboteurs in Hong Kong planted bombs
which killed fifteen people.

Meanwhile, the lives of ordinary citizens were frighteningly
disrupted. Loudspeakers from the Bank of China directed an
incessant bombardment of anti-British propaganda into the centre
of the city. Even schoolchildren were urged to rise up against the
British colonialists. The police, stretched to capacity, reacted
severely, using batons and tear gas. On one occasion they chased
a group of rioters to a power station, where five young revolutionaries leaped into an empty bucket on a conveyor-belt which
scooped coal to the furnaces. They were drawn down into the
coalstack, and buried alive. This incident, along with one or two

others, was later used to support claims that the police had acted with great brutality.

Bearing in mind, however, that ten police officers had been killed and scores more seriously wounded, it might be fairer to say that in general the police acted with remarkable restraint. Nonetheless hundreds of people were arrested, charged and imprisoned, some of whom would never forgive the British for what they complained was the summary justice handed down by the courts. Although the Hong Kong authorities affected an air of insouciance, they were close to despair. According to Sir David Ford, a civil servant with military and media expertise who was drafted in to liaise between the government and the army, the insurrection put the administration under extreme pressure.

> People were very apprehensive. A lot of people were saying that Hong Kong was finished . . . the fear was that China would simply take over . . . There were bodies floating down the Pearl River in their hundreds every day. In Hong Kong, there were major marches up to Government House, with everybody chanting Maoist slogans. And underneath that, there was the ferment of labour strikes, transport strikes, food strikes. There is no doubt that if it had continued, and if the Chinese government had sanctioned the cutting off of water or food supplies, that would have been the end of Hong Kong.

In August, a crowd laid siege to the British embassy in Beijing and, on the night of 22 August, a mob invaded the compound and broke into the embassy building. Soon the embassy was on fire, and the British officials who had barricaded themselves inside were forced to surrender. They were paraded through the crowd by the police, who did little to prevent frenzied onlookers from beating and kicking these emissaries of 'stern imperialism'. Eventually they were taken into what passed for protective custody before the authorities finally sanctioned their release. This episode had a lasting effect on the victims, who included Percy Cradock, then chargé d'affaires, who has vividly described the incident in his memoirs, *Experiences of China*.

In Hong Kong this episode fuelled the authorities' fears of a similar fate. As it turned out, Beijing was not so incautious as to attempt such a démarche. According to Ford: 'The Chinese government clearly made the decision to tell the compatriots in Hong Kong who were causing the trouble to stop.' Even in this period of acute turmoil, the leaders in Beijing had evidently not entirely lost their reason.

Despite the setbacks of 1967, Hong Kong's economy continued to grow. By the early seventies, the Chinese entrepreneurs who had fled to Hong Kong twenty years earlier had not only restored their fortunes but added to them. Men like Sir Y.K. Pao, who began with one small cargo boat, and K.S. Li, a manufacturer of plastic flowers, who had started businesses in the early fifties with almost no assets, had become international tycoons, rivalling (in influence and acumen, if not yet in scale) the long-established British companies like Swires and Jardine Matheson. The stock exchange flourished; banks multiplied. Takeovers and reverse takeovers accelerated as 'old' money merged with 'new' to generate fabulous wealth for speculators and investors alike in a market that was artificially sustained by the soaring value of land and property.

Under the governorship of Sir Murray MacLehose, the authorities reinforced Hong Kong's burgeoning international reputation by instigating an all-out drive against the corruption endemic in Hong Kong from the early years. The problem was personified by Joseph Godber, an expatriate chief superintendent in the Royal Hong Kong Police who had distinguished himself in the 1967 riots. Godber was also at the heart of a web of corruption which had made him a Hong Kong-dollar millionaire several times over. His exposure as a criminal led to the creation of the Independent Commission Against Corruption (ICAC). Under the unrelenting leadership of Sir Jack Cater, the ICAC set about its task with a vengeance. Hundreds of police officers were arrested in a drive against bribery and back-handers that penetrated deep into the world of organised crime and came perilously close to exposing some of the colony's most prominent entrepreneurs. The realisation that the ICAC was in earnest appeared to have a transforming effect on behaviour, if not on attitudes, in both the public and private sectors. The consequent dawning awareness that Hong Kong, unlike almost every other entrepôt in Asia except for Singapore, was now relatively free of corruption enhanced the colony's standing as the most attractive financial-services centre in the region. Following Deng Xiaoping's economic 'reforms', which began in 1978, mainland China began to invest in Hong Kong with growing self-assurance, helping to propel the colony to the very centre of the Far Eastern stage. By the end of the seventies, Hong Kong thus found itself at both the trading and the financial hub of a region that was developing with spectacular speed.

So in the twenty years before Chris Patten's arrival, the face of what had once been a colonial backwater had been transformed as Hong Kong grew upwards and outwards at an astonishing rate. A network of new bridges, roads, tunnels, railways and a metro system gave the colony the appearance of a great American metropolis, a cross between New York and Los Angeles. This hugely ambitious transport programme, financed by the vast government surpluses that flowed from the city's runaway economic expansion, included the development of a clutch of satellite cities linked umbilically to Hong Kong and Kowloon by every means of modern communication. Taipo, Shatin, Sheungshui and Fanling were designed to accommodate upwards of 2 million people between them. They would have schools, hospitals, universities, sports stadia and, in one case, even a racecourse. The New Territories, which had been a quiet, rural area dotted with traditional villages, now sprouted great clusters of high-rise apartment blocks, sports grounds, shopping malls, stations and car parks. It was a bold vision, planned unequivocally to embrace a refugee community as permanent residents of what had become one of the most dynamic societies in the world. Of course, you could still find poverty, squalor and homelessness, but in this, as in other respects, Hong Kong was much like any Western society.

There was one glaring omission: the failure of the colonial authorities to make any significant concession to a cardinal principle of twentieth-century governance – that no society could claim to be civilised until the will of the people, as expressed freely through the ballot box, was held to be inviolable. This shameful, if explicable, failure of foresight, imagination and courage by the British government would soon return to haunt Hong Kong.

3

'WE HAD NO OPTION'

Deciding Hong Kong's Fate

In 1949, flushed with victory though they were, the Communists had stopped short of crossing the border and overrunning Hong Kong. Of course, they made it clear that they rejected the 'unequal treaties' by which Hong Kong had been prised away from the motherland and asserted that Hong Kong had always been part of China, but stated that the issue could be resolved by negotiation at an appropriate date in the future. During the extreme privations wrought by the Great Leap Forward in the late fifties, China was preoccupied with the internal crisis generated by Mao's programme of economic 'reform', but even during the heady days of the Cultural Revolution, Beijing (Peking) took no action. However, the Chinese premier, Zhou Enlai, warned that the future of Hong Kong would be settled by 'patriots' and not 'imperialists'. In 1971, during the hangover induced by the excesses of the Cultural Revolution, he was more specific, indicating that the Chinese would indeed seek to recover Hong Kong, but not until the expiry of the leases on the New Territories – the area north of Kowloon and the 235 small islands surrounding Hong Kong – which was then still more than a quarter of a century away.

The issue lay dormant until 1979. According to Sir Percy Cradock, 'Up to this point Hong Kong had been only one refrain of the sometimes dissonant music of Sino–British relations. Never absent, and, on occasion, as in the Cultural Revolution, harsh and threatening. But still a secondary theme. From 1979 onwards, however, it gathered strength and from 1982 became the main motif, drowning virtually all others.' As Britain's chargé d'affaires in Beijing at the height of the Cultural Revolution, Cradock's experience of that 'collective madness' as a de facto hostage in the embassy scarred him permanently. 'It was like having the French Revolution at the bottom of the garden and being asked every now and then to join in. It is participatory theatre of a very violent and brutal kind. It was a great hardship,' he acknowledged after his retirement in 1992. Although he was later to be labelled by critics in Britain and Hong Kong one of China's arch-appeasers, a charge he bitterly repudiates, his analysis of the Chinese leadership was caustic if not lacking in awe. Even before the Cultural Revolution, he had found Maoism, 'that unholy marriage of Chinese culture and Western communism', an almost overpowering force. The leaders who orchestrated the cruelties of the revolution seemed isolated, arrogant, inflexible and secretive. Appearing to believe themselves predestined to be at the centre of the world, they were acutely suspicious of the West, and in particular of Britain, and – although they no longer used the term in public – it seemed to Cradock that they considered the description 'barbarian' to be as apt in the twentieth century as they had in the nineteenth. They were 'a very emotional, violent people who feel they have to assert themselves'.

Cradock was never in any doubt, therefore, that for the old guard in Beijing, the issue of Hong Kong was both real and symbolic, a struggle against Britain, an adversary which would use every wile capitalism could devise to frustrate the recovery of their territory. Cradock also believed that the Chinese held virtually all the cards and that 'the ground was slipping away under the British feet every day'. To him, therefore, the question had always been not whether, but when, they would assert their claim on Hong Kong. For Cradock, the 'bottom line' was that China was the preponderant political and military power: the People's Liberation Army could overrun Hong Kong at any time and Britain could do nothing about it. This bleak assessment thoroughly infected the handful of Foreign Office officials who, under Cradock's intellectual leadership, were responsible for defining Britain's stance throughout the tortuous negotiations which led to the 1984 Joint Declaration and beyond. If this entailed what his critics were to describe as a policy of appeasement, Cradock was irritated but not ashamed to be so castigated: in his mind, it was 'a policy of co-operation. The only sensible policy. The policy of realism.'

Nevertheless, until 1979, in London:

There was no clear view of the likely terms of any such settlement. It was acknowledged that the long-term trend was probably unfavourable to Hong Kong's existence as a colony. But there was always the chance that the status quo might quietly be maintained, particularly if there was a bow in the direction of Chinese sovereignty.

In Hong Kong, the matter was regarded with rather less insouciance. China's assertion of sovereign rights over the colony hovered perpetually in the background, menacingly to some, beguilingly to others. The economic reform programme initiated by Deng Xiaoping, however, gave confidence that the post-Mao generation of Chinese elders would at least not deliberately undermine Hong Kong's crucial role as a rapidly expanding entrepôt. In a community which lived for the short term and where entrepreneurs took high risks and expected quick returns, 1997 was a faraway precipice which almost no one greatly cared to contemplate and which was, therefore, only discussed sotto voce.

It was against this background that in 1979 Hong Kong's governor, Lord MacLehose, flew to Beijing as the guest of the Chinese government. Unlike Sir Percy Cradock, MacLehose was an unabashed enthusiast for China. Recalling his postwar experiences there, he remembered: 'The thrill of that different world . . . It has a strong effect on people. Either they love it or they hate it. I love it . . . You know what they say about the Foreign Office "always loving our enemies"? I think they are a fascinating people, and provided you take them on their own terms, very rewarding.'

As the governor of Hong Kong, MacLehose had been preoccupied with social and economic matters: driving through a vast housing programme; reforming a police service which, in the aftermath of the Cultural Revolution, had become exhausted and excessively prone, for a consideration, to turn a blind eye to the protection rackets operated by the triads; and enhancing Hong Kong's identity as the region's economic miracle. Although the 'bamboo curtain' between Hong Kong and China was still firmly in place, MacLehose did what he could to filter his own goodwill across the border, becoming the first governor to celebrate China Day and signing the book of condolence at the New China News Agency on the death of Mao.

In a sense, the invitation to Beijing was a reward for his assiduous efforts to cultivate better relations with the mainland. His would be the first official visit to China by a Hong Kong governor since 1949, and he made it clear to his Chinese counterparts that he would only go if he could meet 'leading personalities' and if the visit were to 'have some substance'. With this confirmed, it was MacLehose who advised the Foreign Office, that, inter alia, the future of Hong Kong should form part of Britain's agenda for the talks.

The Foreign Office assented at once. Although Hong Kong was flourishing, the Foreign Office took the view, in Cradock's recollection, that there would shortly come a point when fears about the future would begin to overshadow that prosperity. He and his officials concurred with MacLehose's opinion that, with land mortgages in Hong Kong lasting usually for fifteen years, prospective purchasers were likely to shy away, and that business confidence might rapidly evaporate. It was imperative to give investors at least some security about their holdings after 1997. This, combined with the apparently reformist character of the Deng leadership, made the moment seem propitious. The question, therefore, was not whether but how to raise what was recognised to be a matter of the very greatest delicacy.

Instead of tackling the issue head on, MacLehose suggested that they should take what Cradock described as a 'sidelong' approach, treating the matter as if the issue at stake were merely a technical one. The British side would seek Chinese authority for the sale of individual leases in the New Territories that would straddle 1997, in the hope that the constitutional deadline might

thereby be blurred. Were the Chinese to assent to this in principle, it might then be possible to amend the Order in Council
under which Britain administered the New Territories until 1997
by simply removing the terminal date. In retrospect, given the
well-known suspicions of the Chinese, this ruse seems almost
comically transparent and diplomatically inept, but Cradock, at
this time British ambassador in Beijing, has explained that he
thought it worth a try. The game plan was endorsed by the
Labour foreign secretary, Dr David Owen – although, according
to his own account, he gave instructions that MacLehose should
not go so far as to mention the Order in Council.

The decision to raise the issue at all was taken in the teeth of
opposition from one or two of MacLehose's most senior colleagues, including his chief secretary, Sir Jack Cater, who argued,
'Don't go and see the Chinese; they are reactive, not proactive.
Don't raise the question at all.' Cater relates:

> I was being told by Murray that there was grave concern
> about the leases in the New Territories; that the subleases
> were getting shorter and shorter; that people and the
> bankers were getting worried about the mortgages. This
> was nonsense. We did not even have mortgages at that
> time – or at least in no great number. And I'd certainly not
> heard about it and obviously I would have done.
>
> There was concern [in the Foreign Office] about the
> leases. No doubt. But basically it seemed to me that they
> wanted to get shot of Hong Kong but in the nicest possible
> way . . . It was simply the East of Suez policy of 1964. Hong
> Kong was indefensible. It was the government's policy for
> Hong Kong to be handed back.

It is true that MacLehose presumed that China would reclaim
Hong Kong. It is also true that David Owen had put the future of
Hong Kong high on his own agenda for discussion during a
forthcoming visit scheduled for April, and that he was intending
to propose a 'pre-emptive' transfer of sovereignty in return for a
guarantee of continued British administration after 1997. As it
was, to Cradock's great relief, the Owen visit was torpedoed by

the fall of the Callaghan government in the wake of the 'winter of discontent'. Yet even if Cater's analysis of the Labour government's intention to 'surrender' Hong Kong contained an element of truth, it is, with the benefit of hindsight, naive to suppose that his alternative strategy – studiously to ignore the problem – might have prevailed. In MacLehose's view it was 'bunkum' to think that 'the Chinese might have drifted past 1997 . . . [or] that we could drift by without any arrangements being made for four million people who had no legal title to Hong Kong under international law and no domestic title as landowners . . . The mind boggles.'

The British team was ushered into the Great Hall of the People in a state of some trepidation. In Hong Kong the visit was the subject of much press excitement and speculation, but only a handful of people were aware of MacLehose's real purpose: any rumour to the effect that Hong Kong's future was 'up for grabs' would have been certain to trigger precisely those fears which they hoped this meeting could be used to allay. But what if Deng Xiaoping were to rebuff them? Or if he simply refused to discuss the matter? They felt themselves to be on a high wire without a safety net.

As it was – and as if to confirm the British contention that the issue could not have been allowed to drift – Deng at once wrong-footed MacLehose by seizing the initiative himself. Like other British envoys, the Hong Kong governor was magnetised by Deng's presence. He was relieved when the Chinese leader spoke in mollifying terms, conveying in a somewhat rambling way (as summarised by Cradock): 'Of course Hong Kong will return to China. Sovereignty belongs to China. But 1997 is quite a long way off. Don't worry down there, you'll be all right.'

According to Beijing's official version of the chairman's statement, Deng reasserted China's sovereignty over Hong Kong and insisted that a negotiated settlement should be based on that premise. At the same time he conceded that Hong Kong would be a 'special region' where capitalism would be allowed to flourish 'for a considerable length of time'.

MacLehose took the cue from Deng to raise the issue of the leases in the New Territories. Deng either failed to grasp the point or affected to misunderstand what the governor had said. When MacLehose tried again, Deng cautioned him that, in any mention of land leases, there should be no reference to British administration. He also advised that China had not yet decided on a political structure for Hong Kong after 1997. However, he repeated, in what Cradock has described as 'an all-weather quote' upon which the British seized to use later for public consumption, that investors should 'set their hearts at ease'. And that, for the next three years, was that.

The British had not been entirely rebuffed, but they had failed to make any headway. The future for Hong Kong after 1997 was essentially no clearer after the visit than it had been before. Cradock was frustrated: 'We were not satisfied because we had dropped a rock into the Chinese pool and seen some ripples but we weren't quite sure even yet that the full meaning of what we said had been taken aboard.' In a further attempt to broach the issue, Cradock had a meeting with the vice-foreign minister. The response was unequivocal: 'We advise you not to go ahead with any proposal to extend British sovereignty beyond 1997.'

Cradock was anxious to maintain the dialogue but MacLehose was nervous. London sided with the governor, and Cradock was refused the go-ahead. In the following months the subject of Hong Kong was raised in 'bilateral' meetings between British and Chinese officials, but in a desultory fashion. It was clear that Beijing had temporarily redirected its diplomatic attention to the even more formidable problem of Taiwan, which for a moment seemed to offer China a promise of peaceful reincorporation. This hope proved forlorn following the election of President Reagan, who was all but ready to offer Taiwan a place in the United Nations as an independent state. However, it was not until 1982 that Chinese officials began to indicate that Hong Kong was again on their minds. Just before the outbreak of the Falklands War, the former British prime minister Sir Edward Heath, known as a 'friend of China', returned from Beijing to report that Deng Xiaoping had told him bluntly that China intended to reassert its sovereignty over the entire territory of Hong Kong. The 'unequal treaties' would be abrogated accordingly, and while Hong Kong would continue to enjoy economic and social autonomy, there would be no role for Britain after 1997. Deng coined his 'one country, two systems' slogan to embrace the concept to which China was now wedded. His message to the British elder statesman was clearly intended for 10 Downing Street, but the new prime minister was preoccupied by the conflict with Argentina and, as Heath no longer had government status, Whitehall decided that his message did not require an official response. It did, however, provoke serious discussion among the sinologists at the Foreign Office, whose own prejudices were confirmed by Deng's words.

The trigger for the next stage was the official visit the British prime minister, Margaret Thatcher, was due to make to Beijing in September 1982. Rather late in the day, the Foreign Office briefed her for the first time on the unappetising options facing her government. Three years into her premiership, Thatcher was not only viscerally opposed to communism but, fresh from leading Britain to victory against the Argentinian junta, she had also become the most charismatic leader of the 'free world'. In the view of one of her closest advisers on China, 'This had left her with a great disposition to military solutions, tough solutions and a certain degree of suspicion of the Foreign Office.' According to Sir Percy Cradock, Thatcher's attitude towards the policy of the Foreign Office on Hong Kong was essentially: 'Here is another colonial outpost they want to sell off.'

By this time, the Foreign Office – where the views of Sir Percy Cradock held sway, although he himself was still in Beijing – had decided to ditch the 'sidelong' approach essayed by Lord MacLehose. In its place Cradock now favoured what was in effect a pre-emptive retreat on sovereignty, arguing that the best Britain could now expect was to persuade Beijing to agree to leave the administration of Hong Kong after 1997 in British hands in return for 'making a bow' in the direction of the Chinese claim to the island. Since it was clear to him that the Chinese intended to take over the territory in 1997, when the lease on the New Territories expired, there was little practical point in counter-asserting the legality of the 'unequal treaties' by which Hong Kong and the southern tip of Kowloon had been ceded to Britain in perpetuity.

Margaret Thatcher was not at all impressed. 'Look, I would have loved to have kept it,' she recalled fourteen years later.

> Sovereignty means something to us. We recognised sover-
> eignty. I believe it would have been recognised in
> international law . . . Being brought up on the rule of law,
> it hadn't occurred to me that the sovereignty of Hong Kong
> would not be respected. I thought they would respect it
> because it's a treaty . . . I would have liked to have kept the
> sovereignty of Hong Kong island for Britain . . . [Or, alter-
> natively] I would have loved for them to have their
> independence and to be a small member of the United
> Nations . . . It would have been marvellous.

The hapless officials at the Foreign Office were the victims of the whirlwind whipped up by that assumption. Evidently contemp-tuous of what she regarded as their timid approach, Thatcher was at her most relentless and abrasive – or as Cradock has put it, 'combative and unco-operative'. Her approach, he recalled, was 'one of free, not to say hostile, inquiry, with a predisposition to solutions based on legal, or even military strength'. In the words of one official, 'She looked quite hard at the idea that we should simply stand pat, hold our own, and tell the Chinese to take a running jump.'

Margaret Thatcher only succumbed when she was persuaded, as she later described it, that Britain had no option.

> Hong Kong island is less than 8 per cent of the territory. All
> the rest is China mainland. There is no way we could say,
> 'We're going to keep the sovereignty of Hong Kong.' There
> was no way in which we could defend it. More than that:
> they didn't need to march in. The Chinese could have just
> turned off the supply of water and food which came from
> the mainland. So I had very few cards in my hand.

Nonetheless, the prime minister remained a reluctant convert. On more than one occasion in the months ahead, she sought to recant. Cradock described her stubbornness. 'There was resolution in plenty at those meetings, but it tended to resolution of a one-dimensional kind, with little or no sense of the other side of the struggle, their prejudices, strengths and likely reactions; and in such an embattled setting it was not always easy to supply the missing elements in the equation – in other words, to give a realistic assessment of the prospects – without sounding negative or even faint-hearted.' On more than one occasion, according to Cradock, the defence secretary, Michael Heseltine, was summoned to the prime minister's presence to confirm the Foreign Office line that Hong Kong could indeed not be held by force of arms against a regime which, Cradock says, she regarded as 'bad, tough and cruel'.

Eventually even the prime minister was driven to concede Cradock's case for beating the retreat: since Hong Kong was indefensible by military means, there had to be a negotiated settlement. Whether Britain liked it or not, there would be a reversion of the whole territory in 1997, and what would matter would be the terms of that reversion. Strategically, Cradock's view was straightforward, if somewhat lacking in heroism: 'If there was to be a retreat, it had to be an orderly retreat from one carefully defended point to another . . . and this was the first position: sovereignty to China, administration staying with Britain.'

It was in this spirit that in September 1982 the prime minister followed the well-trodden path into the Great Hall of the People. Cradock's strategy, accepted by Thatcher, was to negotiate for continued British administration of Hong Kong after 1997 in return for which Britain would be willing to 'consider' the question of sovereignty. The proposition was, as Cradock intended, highly qualified, but it also dangled the carrot of concession.

The prime minister's first meeting was with her opposite number, the Chinese premier Zhao Ziyang. Although in Thatcher's view he was 'the kindest, the most understanding of the lot', he was also unyielding. He insisted that in 1997 China would recover sovereignty over both the New Territories and Hong Kong itself, and it was, he indicated, nonsense to suppose that any other state would be permitted to administer any of the territory on China's behalf.

The following day, 24 September, Thatcher was ushered into the presence of Deng Xiaoping. Like Lord MacLehose, she was impressed:

> The volume of personality compared with the physical volume – he is small, not very tall – makes the personality even more obvious. Very much in charge. Oh, very much . . . Now, this man had known what it was like to be put in prison by the communist system. His son had been grievously injured during the Cultural Revolution – thrown from the top of a building and left to lie there for twenty-four hours. Now we think, 'That must have been a terrible experience for Deng; it must have made him more human and sympathetic.' Do you know, I don't believe it did . . . He is a really tough guy.

The meeting did not go well. Thatcher rehearsed the British position with what Cradock called 'great charm and clarity'. Deng, chain-smoking and gesticulating dismissively, was unmoved. He would allow up to two years for consultations, and then China would announce its decision. The British prime minister retorted that, while of course Britain accepted the termination of the lease on the New Territories, the treaties ceding Hong Kong to Britain were valid in international law and therefore could not be abrogated unilaterally. Deng became tetchy. Thatcher responded forcefully, on the grounds that: 'If you are going to argue with someone, you might as well be frank; there is no point to me in putting it all in diplomatic language. They don't understand that.' As she recalled the meeting in 1996, the two leaders then had the following exchange:

> Deng: 'Look, I could walk in and take the whole lot this afternoon.'
> Thatcher: 'Yes. There is nothing I could do to stop you. But the eyes of the world would now know what China is like. Everything would leave Hong Kong. You'd have its prosperity and you would suddenly have lost the lot.'

This was the heart of the matter: would China really risk the destruction of Hong Kong and international obloquy to reclaim sovereignty? Or would it have been possible to call Deng's bluff and to have counter-proposed a diplomatic and economic modus vivendi between the British island and the Chinese mainland? Although the British side had already half ceded the case, Deng's response to Thatcher's riposte was instructive: 'The whole atmosphere changed. I think he and the people watching him were absolutely amazed . . . He had never been brought face to face with what he could do to China in the eyes of the world.' Allowing for any histrionic quality in the former prime minister's recollection of the moment, Deng's reaction does raise the question of whether Cradock's readiness to concede the reversion of Hong Kong essentially on the terms demanded by Beijing was not infected by a touch of defeatism.

As it was, the die was cast. The two sides tussled over a communiqué – which was sufficiently ambiguous to cause months of mutual recrimination afterwards – to the effect that negotiations over the future of Hong Kong would begin in earnest. Whether or not these were to be conducted on the premise that Hong Kong would revert to China, as Beijing demanded, or whether the issue of reversion was one of several yet to be decided, as the British claimed, remained unresolved. Sovereignty would revert to China in 1997, but for a while, the Foreign Office would negotiate as if the maintenance of British administration were crucial to the colony's future. It is not clear whether Whitehall really expected Beijing to accept this compromise or whether officials saw it as a negotiating ploy to decelerate further and inevitable retreat.

The prime minister left Beijing for Hong Kong with a sense of some foreboding. She has recalled:

I realised that the people of Hong Kong somehow thought that we could pull something out of the hat. And I realised we weren't going to be able to. Just as they didn't understand our system, I didn't realise that the Chinese would overturn a treaty which gave us sovereignty over Hong Kong; that they would take this view of law. Because if you do that, you've no international law and no treaty is ever worth anything.

If the British prime minister was touched by a degree of self-delusion, the pro-Chinese media responded with characteristic bombast: Thatcher's 'fallacy imbued with colonialism', Hong Kong's leading pro-Beijing paper, *Wen Wei Po*, thundered, 'has aroused the indignation of Hong Kong patriots and has once again recalled to the 1 billion Chinese people the history of aggression against China by the British Empire . . . Is it not that she wishes to enjoy once again the aggressions of the past?' There was much more in the same vein. In the view of Sir Percy Cradock, who would have preferred reticence on Thatcher's part, the impact of her words in Beijing 'provoked an angry reaction which had the effect of complicating the already arduous task of getting negotiations started'. In what now became a gruesome war of diplomatic attrition, Britain began to retreat inch by inch towards China's bottom line. On the question of sovereignty Cradock has insisted, 'They were prepared to go to the brink of breakdown and virtually ruin Hong Kong financially.'

The evidence for this claim is persuasive, though whether this prospective démarche would have been a deliberate act of economic sabotage or simply a byproduct of incompetence is debatable. During Margaret Thatcher's visit, Hong Kong investors had one of their periodic bouts of anxiety and the Hang Seng Index began to plummet. According to the former prime minister, at one point Deng turned to her and rasped, 'Money is going out. You must stop it.' Thatcher replied, 'I can't. I have no powers to stop it.'

'Of course you can!'

Thatcher repeated, 'I can't. I have no power suddenly to step in and stop the market operating. I have no powers under the law.' She was bewildered: 'He didn't understand. He just had no comprehension at all.'

The negotiations stalled. In the spring of 1983, to Cradock's horror, the prime minister fell to canvassing a host of ideas, including a UN-sponsored referendum on the future of Hong Kong, or even independence. Instead she was persuaded to write to the Chinese premier shifting Britain's stance. If the two sides could reach agreement over the administration of what China had designated the 'special administrative region' of Hong Kong, then she would not only 'consider' the sovereignty issue, but she would be prepared to recommend to Parliament the reversion of sovereignty to China. Cradock called this the 'first finesse'. It was not enough; by the autumn of 1983 the negotiations had reached the point of collapse.

Although key officials at the Foreign Office, where Sir Geoffrey Howe had become foreign secretary a few months earlier, had acknowledged among themselves that the Chinese would never accept the prospect of a British administration of Hong Kong after 1997, even one operating under Chinese sovereignty, they had continued to press the case. This tactic was designed in part to extract better terms from the Chinese in the process of retreat. It was also thought to be important, in the words of Sir Robin McLaren, political adviser in Hong Kong from 1981 to 1985, to 'convince British ministers, and above all the prime minister, that we had done everything possible'. Thatcher remained sceptical. 'Margaret's heart kept on cherishing the alternative,' Lord Howe recalled in 1995, 'dreaming of a way in which we could have something more permanent and more durable. And heart and mind were constantly in conflict. And we had to keep on restoring the sovereignty of mind over heart.'

The Foreign Office also had to cope with fierce resistance from within the colony itself, led by Lord MacLehose's replacement as governor, Sir Teddy Youde, and his principal officials, and leading members of the community.

Much against the will of the British diplomats involved, the prime minister had insisted that the leading members of the Executive Council, the governor's appointed advisers, should be kept abreast of the negotiations and allowed to comment on their progress. 'Diplomats are a coterie who rather prefer the idea of negotiating with their fellows in secret,' noted McLaren. 'I think it was their instinct that it is better, and easier and tidier, to deal with these things in private rather than negotiating in public.' In this hall of mirrors, the British negotiators were under no less pressure from London and Hong Kong than they were from

Beijing. It is at least arguable that Britain would have been free to retreat more rapidly to China's bottom line, as defined by Cradock, if there had not been a countervailing imperative to persuade the most influential figures in Hong Kong that the territory had only been surrendered after fierce and prolonged resistance. As it was, the Chinese proved as obdurate as the British team had always presumed they would be, insisting that their Twelve-Point Plan, which appeared to confirm Hong Kong's future status as an independent economic entity, should allay any residual doubts, and that to suggest otherwise was mere colonial arrogance on Britain's part.

On paper at least, the Twelve-Point Plan appeared to offer the reassurances that the people of Hong Kong would need. Stipulating the basic principles which would govern Hong Kong's future under Chinese sovereignty, the twelve points confirmed, inter alia, that Hong Kong would become a special administrative region with 'a high degree of autonomy, except in foreign and defence affairs', which would become the 'responsibilities of the Central People's Government'. The SAR would be vested with 'executive, legislative and independent judicial power, including that of final adjudication', while the laws currently in force in Hong Kong would remain 'basically' unchanged. The current social and economic systems and 'lifestyle' would also remain unchanged: 'Rights and freedoms, including those of the person, of speech, of the press, of assembly, of association, of travel, of movement, of correspondence, of strike, of choice of occupation, of academic research and of religious belief' would be protected by law. Hong Kong would retain its status as an international financial centre.

Although they were encouraged by the tenor of the twelve points, the British negotiators were unwilling to accept these commitments at their face value. They sought clarification, precision and exegesis. The diplomatic impasse between the two sides had already provoked an atmosphere of crisis. Earlier in September, the Hang Seng Index had fallen precipitously and, more alarmingly, the value of the Hong Kong dollar dropped by 8 per cent in one day. Huge queues formed at Hong Kong supermarkets as the population panicked itself into stocking up on

essential goods. In London, treasury officials worried that the
sterling reserves would have to be called upon to support the local
dollar, a prospect which was averted when, in October, officials
rushed through a decision to peg the Hong Kong currency to the
US dollar. In a mood of suspicion and recrimination, there were
strong rumours that the Bank of China had been used by Beijing
to precipitate the collapse of the currency, while Beijing accused
the British of manipulating the Hong Kong dollar for the same
duplicitous purpose. The financial crisis served only to confirm
Cradock's pessimism about Beijing's determination to regain sovereignty over Hong Kong regardless of the economic
consequences. The foreign secretary was easily persuaded to
Cradock's view, explaining that he soon realised: 'There was no
stopping that, whatever we tried to do. We couldn't stop them by
force or by appeal to world opinion or anything of the sort.'

In the summer Cradock had drafted what he liked to describe
as a 'second finesse', the next staging post on the long retreat 'in
good order' to which he sought to commit the government. He
urged that Britain should now be willing to 'explore' whether the
foundations of lasting prosperity in Hong Kong could be established in the absence of continued administration by Britain. If
they could, Her Majesty's government would no longer resist
the transfer of sovereignty required by the Chinese. But even
after the autumn financial crisis, a majority of Hong Kong officials and advisers still opposed further concessions, declaring that
the Chinese were still bluffing and that there was no need for further retreat. Although Thatcher and Howe both accepted the
Foreign Office view that the Chinese were deadly serious, it was
only when the Hong Kong establishment had been assured that
the proposal was 'conditional' that they assented to Cradock's
'second finesse'.

In truth, the 'conditionality' of the talks which now began in
earnest was of an entirely theoretical kind. The British had
already concluded that Beijing's claim on Hong Kong could not
be resisted and that this should not be permitted to precipitate a
breakdown in negotiations. Although the prime minister still
yearned – romantically, in the view of her advisers – either to
retain British sovereignty or to achieve independence for Hong

Kong and Kowloon, the Foreign Office had implicitly accepted both the premises and the preconditions set by China. As a result, the deadlock was at last broken, and the negotiations, even if they were intense and sometimes combative, now took place in an altered and more cordial atmosphere. Howe and Cradock still had trouble with both what Cradock described later as the 'unyielding' British officials of the Hong Kong government and Hong Kong's appointed politicians, who, he later recalled acidly, were 'poised uneasily on the windowledge, threatening to jump, with myself desperately clutching their coat-tails'.

In April 1984 the foreign secretary finally acknowledged in public that British administration over Hong Kong would terminate in July 1997. Sir Geoffrey Howe had flown to Hong Kong from Beijing, where he had endured a two-hour audience with Deng Xiaoping. It had been, he said, a 'daunting' experience. In an earlier meeting with the Chinese foreign secretary, Wu Xueqian, Howe had devised a metaphor to express the common interest of each side. Hong Kong, he told his interlocutors, was like 'a Ming vase, an object of priceless value', which was to be handed over like the baton in a relay race. It would be disastrous to drop it. His emollience paved the way for agreement on a timetable for negotiations leading to the restoration of Chinese sovereignty which did not yet formally exclude a continued but unspecified 'British role' in Hong Kong after 1997.

The Sino–British negotiations had been conducted in secret. Although there had been much speculation about them, it still came as a shock to hear the British foreign secretary inform Hong Kong's Legislative Council in his 'unveiling statement' that 'it would not be realistic to think in terms of an agreement that provides for British administration in Hong Kong after 1997'. There were gasps in the assembly and many people broke down in tears at the recognition of a finality which, in the interests of diplomacy, had been kept from them for so long.

By the autumn of 1984, the final deal was almost in place. It was agreed that the twelve points should, as the Chinese had insisted from the beginning, form the basis of a Joint Declaration which would define the terms under which sovereignty over Hong Kong would revert to China. However, the Chinese conceded that these principles would be elaborated in an annex of substantially more detail than they had originally been willing to accept. The two sides also agreed that the twelve points and the elaboration of them in the annex would be stipulated 'in a Basic Law of the Hong Kong Administrative Region of the People's Republic of China, by the National People's Congress', and that these policies would remain unchanged for fifty years.

The only outstanding Chinese demand – that they should be free to establish a commission in Hong Kong to oversee the final phase of transition – was also agreed, although, at Britain's request, this body was to be renamed the Joint Liaison Group (JLG). After prolonged haggling, it was determined that the JLG would begin work in July 1988, a small concession by the Chinese, who had wanted it to be set up in January of that year. This modest triumph of diplomacy seems to have given the British team an inordinate amount of satisfaction.

After another marathon set of negotiations in Beijing, the two sides finally reached agreement on the key clauses of the Joint Declaration. Deng Xiaoping emerged from the last round of talks in ebullient mood, smiling and joshing with an equally relaxed Sir Geoffrey Howe, who was delighted when Deng declared: 'We have decided that we can trust the British people and the British government. Please convey to your prime minister our hope that she will come to sign the agreement. And to Her Majesty, your Queen, our hope that she too will be able to visit our country.'

The Joint Declaration was initialled in September 1984, thus meeting the deadline set by Deng two years earlier. In December the prime minister flew to Beijing to join Deng for the official signing ceremony, at which point the Joint Declaration became the basis for all future discussions about Hong Kong's future with China. Before long, the agreement was acknowledged across the political spectrum in Hong Kong and in Britain to have been a consummate achievement, and one for which Sir Percy Cradock's sinuous intellect and strategic perspective were very largely responsible. The media in Hong Kong, reflecting widespread relief, commented with jubilation on China's apparent commitment to preserving Hong Kong's social and economic freedoms in the name of lasting prosperity and stability. In London, *The*

Times was more cautious, asserting: 'Just as it would be wrong to celebrate the agreement as a victory, so too it would be wrong to criticise it too severely. It has managed to secure some unusually specific assurances from Peking, and as such holds out the prospect of order, stability and business confidence in Hong Kong at least for the next few years.'

In 1990, six years after Margaret Thatcher and Deng Xiaoping put their signatures to the Joint Declaration, the National Congress of the People's Republic rubber-stamped the Basic Law, which codified the principles outlined in the Joint Declaration in the form of a detailed mini-constitution for Hong Kong.

And what of democracy? Not a mention of that issue seems to have passed the lips of any negotiator until, as if it were an after-thought, a mere seven days before the Joint Declaration was submitted to both governments for approval, Sir Geoffrey Howe raised the question of Hong Kong's internal governance. 'My important proposal', as he would later describe it, was that the post-1997 Legislative Council should be constituted by elections and that the executive should be accountable to the legislature. This cryptic commitment, inserted into the agreement at the very last moment, is the only reference to the concept of democracy in the entire 8,000-word document. Given Sir Percy Cradock's assertion twelve years later that the phrase 'constituted by elections' was approved by the British in the full knowledge that the Chinese had therein made no commitment to democracy whatsoever, it is hard to understand Howe's later self-satisfaction. Nonetheless, this fragile clause was Chris Patten's most vital inheritance – a conceptual chalice filled in equal measure with the elixir of ambiguity and the poison of self-deception.

4

'No One is Safe'

Alarm Bells Across the Border

A few months before Chris Patten's arrival in Hong Kong, Professor Gong Xiang Rui of Beijing University concluded the draft of a lecture which he intended to deliver at the Hong Kong Human Rights Conference in 1992. The words he wrote eloquently expressed Patten's own conviction.

> There are some rights which are inherent in a system of democracy, whether it is capitalist or socialist. So long as there are free elections based on public opinion, it is always possible to compel the government not to overstep the boundaries of its powers, for there is a minority who would give attention to any abuses, and persuade the electorate to oppose those abuses. And if the government is not responsive, it may be turned out. There will be no democracy if minority opinions cannot be expressed, or if people cannot meet together to discuss their opinions and their actions, or if those who think alike on any subject cannot associate for mutual support and for the propagation of their common ideas. Yet these rights are vulnerable and they are most likely to be subject to attack. Therefore the fundamental liberty is not only of free election but also of the limitation of government powers.

The lecture was never delivered. Just before the Human Rights

Conference, Professor Gong Xiang Rui was informed by the authorities in Beijing that he was forbidden to leave China for Hong Kong.

In China the gerontocracy was still in control. Deng Xiaoping, lingering for an apparent eternity on his deathbed, held a dead hand over the regime he had created. The old guard and the new guard were both imprisoned by his immobile authority. China's conversion to capitalism was irrepressible but wayward. Impoverished peasants drifting from the countryside to the towns and cities in search of work formed a migratory army of perhaps 20 million people competing for jobs with a similar number of unemployed urban workers. Higher up the economic scale the pickings were rich. Businessmen, lawyers, soldiers, party cadres – any individuals with a place to protect in the anarchic web of negotiation and transaction by which an arthritic socialist economy stumbled into the new age of global capitalism – survived and prospered by demonstrating their commitment to the new order which involved, inter alia, endemic corruption on a massive, if unquantifiable, scale.

The price of rampant growth was not only inflation but social insecurity and, in so vast a country, a perpetual sense of incipient disorder. The political freedoms and civil liberties elaborately enshrined in the constitution of the People's Republic were conspicuous only by the severity of the punishment imposed on those seeking to exercise these rights. The cynicism with which the regime espoused the cause of freedom while crushing any perceived threat to the arbitrary exercise of its 'revolutionary' authority made even the most insouciant observer recoil. In Hong Kong, the idea of 1997 was inseparable from an anticipatory shiver of anxiety.

On 19 May 1989, the Chinese premier, Li Peng, introduced martial law in China to combat the students and workers who, exercising their rights under Article 35 of the constitution, had taken to the boulevards of Beijing to campaign for democracy. Two days later in Hong Kong, 50,000 people braved a typhoon to stage the first of several huge demonstrations in the colony supporting the democracy movement on the mainland. They

marched through torrential rain and high winds to the headquarters of China's de facto embassy, the headquarters of the
New China News Agency (NCNA) in Happy Valley, where they
staged a protest. At a request from the platform they all sat on the
sodden ground and, to enable everyone to see the proceedings,
they obediently folded their umbrellas as the leaders of the
demonstration spoke in support of the Chinese students who, in
defiance of Li Peng, had occupied Tiananmen Square in Beijing.

The organiser of the Hong Kong protest was Martin Lee, a
leading barrister and a member of the colony's Legislative
Council, who had recently emerged to prominence after conducting a well-orchestrated media campaign for fully democratic
elections and a Bill of Rights. In a second demonstration a week
later, a million people – one sixth of the entire population of
Hong Kong – took to the streets.

On Saturday 4 June 1989, in Beijing, the People's Liberation
Army was ordered to cleanse Tiananmen Square of the 'subversive elements' occupying it. At 8pm the tanks rolled in and the
first of several hundred unarmed civilians were mown to the
ground. The massacre horrified the world. The following day, a
million people of all races and creeds again took to the streets of
Hong Kong. Once more they walked in silence through the city
to Happy Valley, in mourning and dread. In a gesture of despair
and defiance, Martin Lee, who was a member of the Drafting
Committee responsible for formulating the Basic Law, symbolically burned his copy of the draft. In Beijing the Queen's counsel
was accused of violating Article 1 of the Chinese constitution,
branded a subversive and formally expelled from the committee.

In Britain, the public feeling of disgust and impotent rage
found powerful expression in the British media, notably in newspapers like *The Times*, the *Telegraph* and the *Spectator*, which, with
varying degrees of vehemence, warned that the diplomatic triumphalism over the Joint Declaration five years before now
seemed horribly misplaced. The *Spectator*, indeed, urged that the
document be torn up altogether. Margaret Thatcher later admitted to feeling such revulsion that she, too, wondered whether she
had been right to put her signature to what was by now a binding international treaty. She was one of the first world leaders to

denounce the perpetrators of Tiananmen Square and the very first to endorse a range of (albeit modest) sanctions against the regime.

Martin Lee was born in southern China in 1938, the son of a Chinese army officer. His father had been a student activist in France, where he was a contemporary of Zhou Enlai, but despite the entreaties of the latter, he supported the Kuomintang nationalists rather than Mao Zedong's revolutionaries. When the Long March reached the Yangtze, the Lee family fled to Hong Kong, where Martin's father spent much time resisting Zhou Enlai's efforts to enlist him in the revolutionary cause.

Martin himself did not become involved in politics until he was in his forties. He was chairman of the Hong Kong Bar Association from 1980 to 1983, and it was in that capacity that in 1982, shortly before Margaret Thatcher's visit, he had been invited to Beijing. It was there that, for the first time, he had become aware of China's determination to resume sovereignty over Hong Kong in 1997. The prospect made his heart sink. Though he soon discovered that many local tycoons, who had likewise become aware of China's intentions, had chosen to sell their assets in Hong Kong to buy US dollars and thus to secure American passports for themselves, he decided that he would stay in the colony to oppose a takeover by the communists.

Lee had been selected by China to join the Basic Law Drafting Committee in 1985. As a supporter of the Joint Declaration, he had soon become disillusioned by the way in which that hard-won treaty was gradually being eroded. 'I felt China was really trying to control Hong Kong,' he said later. He and his colleague Szeto Wah had found themselves at odds with other members of the committee, who seemed far too ready to yield on points of substance that, once surrendered, would drain Deng's original concept of 'one country, two systems' of its unique potential. The two of them were keenly aware that the Basic Law was itself subordinate to the Chinese constitution, Article 1 of which stated: 'The People's Republic of China is a socialist state . . . Disruption of the socialist system by any organisation or individual is prohibited.' Martin Lee argued not only that more 'democracy' should be written into the Basic Law itself, but that interpretation of it should be exclusively a matter for the Hong Kong courts to settle rather than for the Standing Committee of the National People's Congress in Beijing, which he knew to be a 'paper tiger' mouthpiece of the politburo. It was to no avail. It was pointed out to him that he should not be alarmed: after all, Article 35 of the Chinese constitution also stated that 'citizens of the People's Republic of China enjoy freedom of speech, of the press, of assembly, of association, of procession and of demonstration'.

In 1987, Deng Xiaoping had addressed the members of the Basic Law Drafting Committee in Beijing, warning them that the Chinese leadership would not permit any activities which, in the guise of 'democracy', would turn Hong Kong into a base for sub-version against China. The next day, in response, Martin Lee departed from his prepared speech to declare that those who 'genuinely loved Hong Kong' had an inalienable right to criticise the Chinese government when mistakes were made. From then on, so far as Beijing was concerned, he had been a marked man.

During the pro-democracy demonstrations in Hong Kong which immediately preceded Tiananmen Square, members of both the Legislative Council and the Executive Council, swept along by the wave of public feeling, had agreed unanimously that the pace of democratic change in Hong Kong had to be acceler-ated. They called then for 50 per cent of the sixty-seat Legislative Council to be elected directly, on the basis of universal adult suf-frage, in 1991, rising to 100 per cent in 1995.

On his first secret mission to Beijing at the end of 1989, Sir Percy Cradock raised the question of increasing the number of directly elected seats to the Legislative Council. He was given a dusty answer. Tiananmen Square, he said later, had exacerbated the 'profound suspicion on the Chinese side of Western-style democracy as a force for political change and instability, even chaos'. Nevertheless, after two further months of negotiation involving a formal exchange of letters between the British and Chinese, the two governments agreed, in principle, to the cre-ation of eighteen directly elected seats in 1991, rising to twenty by the handover, and to thirty by 2003. For good measure, however, the Chinese made it clear that any unilateral departure from those figures would lead to what was described to Cradock as 'big trouble'.

To the dismay of Martin Lee and others, and despite strenuous argument from the British, Article 23 of the Basic Law contained a general prohibition of 'subversion against the Central People's Government', while Articles 158 and 159 respectively vested the power of interpretation of, and amendment to, the Basic Law in the National People's Congress. In the same month Martin Lee and like-minded liberals formed the United Democrats to campaign for greater freedom and democracy than the Basic Law appeared to envisage.

In the 1991 elections the United Democrats took seventeen of the eighteen seats elected on the basis of universal adult suffrage. Martin Lee's landslide was a fierce rebuke not only to China, but to the colonial administration as well. Lee had become an outspoken critic of the British government and contemptuous of the outgoing governor, Sir David Wilson, whom he regarded as one of the archetypal Foreign Office diplomats 'who only believe in kowtowing to Beijing' and whose philosophy was 'to push a little for Hong Kong', but only to the point that 'they consider to be China's bottom line'. In China the United Democrats were regarded as a threat to the state, and Martin Lee himself was routinely excoriated in the Beijing press as a 'subversive'.

The killings in Tiananmen Square had alerted the world to the fact that, in one vital respect, Deng Xiaoping's regime was no different from its predecessors. According to a detailed report by Amnesty International, 'Death in Beijing', published a few months later, 'at least 1,000 civilians – most of them unarmed – were killed and several thousands injured by troops firing indiscriminately into crowds in Beijing between 3 and 9 June 1989 . . . Since early June, at least 4,000 people are officially reported to have been arrested throughout China in connection with pro-democracy protests, but the total number of those detained is believed to be much higher . . .' Reports reaching Amnesty suggested that many of those who had been detained were subjected to severe beatings and torture; others, it was said, had been sent for show trials followed by summary execution.

The introduction to Amnesty's report was written by Jonathan Mirsky, who was in Tiananmen Square as the correspondent for the *Observer*. He had witnessed PLA troops firing indiscriminately into the huddled mass of demonstrators, and seen the dead and wounded lying in pools of blood. He put the atrocity in illuminating context. 'Any Tibetan could have foretold the violence to come, after years of experience of the PLA, most recently in March, when Chinese soldiers mowed down monks and nuns.' He recalled China's long record of brutality. In April 1956, Chairman Mao had informed the politburo that 2 to 3 million counter-revolutionaries had been executed, imprisoned, or placed under control in the past. The term 'counter-revolutionaries' has long been used by the Chinese Communist party as a justification for abusing its adversaries – a 'catch-all for rapists, thieves, murderers and "troublemakers"'. Although Beijing had occasionally expressed regret for some excess or other, the use of 'extra-judicial execution' was regarded as routine punishment for what the party referred to as 'evil members of the herd'. During what Chinese commentators have since described as the 'terrible decade' of the Cultural Revolution, from 1966 to 1976, nearly 1 million people were killed by mobs urged on by Chairman Mao. A further 100 million were officially acknowledged to have been treated illegally. Between 1986 and 1989, it was estimated that as many as 10,000 'counter-revolutionaries' were shot, usually on the day of sentence and without right of appeal. Mirsky wrote: 'During this horrendous period, which equalled anything in Stalin's Russia, few voices arose from the international community and none from any government, except in the case of the UK, when its own nationals were badly treated. On the whole China is treated as a grand exception. Its assertion that human rights is an internal matter is barely challenged.' He was scathing about those in the West who chose to claim that 'the Chinese have different concepts of human rights and democracy from our own, and therefore the routine use by the Chinese of the familiar tools of repression – execution, torture, labour camps, and internal exile – that Amnesty has detailed, is somehow acceptable'.

Three years on, little had changed, except that there was no longer any reason for the world to be ignorant of the repression of their own citizens and in their name by the rulers of the People's Republic of China. Thanks to individuals like Jonathan Mirsky and human-rights organisations like Asia Watch and Amnesty International, it was virtually impossible in the early nineties to be unaware of China's continuing brutality. From 1989 onwards, Amnesty accumulated a body of convincing evidence which demonstrated that, despite the economic reforms in China, the authorities still used the law, the administrative system and the prison service to persecute those who dared to oppose their will. Citing well-documented individual cases, Amnesty identified the victims as political dissidents, human-rights activists, workers' representatives, peasants, Tibetan nationalists, ethnic minorities and religious groups. 'No one,' Amnesty judged, 'is safe in China . . . political repression and abuse of power mean that everyone is at risk.'

The authorities have invariably denied that the People's Republic holds any political prisoners. China has acknowledged, however, that thousands of 'counter-revolutionaries' have been jailed or executed. The provisions of the criminal law most widely used to jail 'prisoners of conscience' have been Articles 98 and 102, which outlaw respectively 'organising, leading or taking part in a counter-revolutionary group' and promoting 'counter-revolutionary propaganda'. Dissidents have also been detained as common criminals for 'disturbing public order' or 'hooliganism'.

Two years after the events in Tiananmen Square, Chen Yanbin and Zhang Yafei were arrested and charged with carrying out 'counter-revolutionary propaganda and incitement' by writing articles in a political journal called *Iron Currents*, wherein they allegedly 'slandered' the rule of the Chinese Communist party. They were further charged with forming an organisation, the Chinese Revolutionary Democratic Front, 'with the purpose of overthrowing the leadership of the CCP and the political power of the people's democratic dictatorship'. The two men were found guilty and sentenced to terms of imprisonment of fifteen and eleven years respectively.

In July 1992, in one of the most infamous of many examples of political persecution, a senior Communist party apparatchik, Bao

Tong, was given a seven-year sentence for 'leaking' state secrets. A former assistant to Zhao Ziyang, who was forced to resign in disgrace as the CCP general secretary just before the imposition of martial law in Beijing on 20 May 1989, Bao Tong was arrested the following week. He was held for a year in solitary confinement and then put under house arrest until his detention and trial in January 1992. His conviction was based solely on a conversation he was alleged to have had with another senior official of the party, the content of which, of course, had to remain a state secret.

A formal trial, however arbitrary in character, was not the only means available to the state for persecuting dissidents. The use of 'administrative detention' was also widespread. According to official Chinese statistics, hundreds of thousands of citizens are detained each year either for 'shelter and investigation' or for 're-education through labour'. Under the former provision, the police are given the authority to hold anyone suspected of committing a crime for up to three months without charge, even for 'minor acts of law infringement'. In 1990, the Ministry of Public Security reported that 902,000 individuals were held for 'shelter and investigation', up to 40 per cent of whom, according to Chinese legal scholars who examined the official figures, were detained for longer than the prescribed three-month period. Despite Article 48 of the 1979 Criminal Procedure Law, which imposed a ten-day limit on detention without charge, some held for 'shelter and investigation' were subsequently 'sentenced' by local government committees to a term of 're-education through labour' lasting up to three years.

A handful of cases have reached international attention, but they constitute only a minute proportion of the several thousand unearthed by Amnesty International over the years. The leaders of the democracy movement have been targeted with particular venom. Since 1989, according to Amnesty, 'large-scale arbitrary arrests have been carried out around the anniversary of the 4 June massacre'. Fifteen such 'dissidents' held in Beijing in 1991 were indicted the following year on a range of 'counter-revolutionary' charges. Having spent two and a half years in detention they were eventually to be convicted in December

1994, after a trial lasting five months, of forming dissident groups and writing and printing political pamphlets for publication. Five of these 'counter-revolutionaries' were 'exempted' from further punishment, one was given two 'supervision orders' and nine were jailed for terms ranging from three to twenty years.

Throughout this period, the use of torture, explicitly banned by Chinese law, remained endemic. The most common forms of torture identified by Amnesty include 'severe beatings with fists or a variety of instruments, whipping, kicking, the use of electric batons which give powerful electric shocks, the use of handcuffs or leg-irons in ways that cause intense pain, and suspension by the arms, often combined with beatings'. Amnesty documented further forms of torture or 'cruel, inhuman or degrading treatment' such as incarceration in unlit cells without heat, ventilation or sanitation; exposure to intense cold or heat; and deprivation of food and sleep.

A group of political prisoners held at the Lingyan Number 2 Labour Reform Detachment in Liaoning province claimed that they were repeatedly tortured between 1991 and 1992. The abuse apparently started when a group of eleven newly arrived dissidents refused to acknowledge that they were 'criminals'. All were severely beaten and four were sent to the 'correction unit'. Here, they said, they were stripped naked, held down on the floor and repeatedly given shocks with high-voltage electric batons to their heads, necks, shoulders, armpits, stomachs and the insides of the legs. One of their number, Leng Wanhao, who remained silent during this ordeal, had an electric baton forced into his mouth.

In a number of the reported cases, the victims did not survive such ordeals. According to the *Henan Legal Daily* of 7 October 1993, forty-one prisoners and 'innocent suspects' died from torture under interrogation between 1990 and 1992 in Henan province alone. Among the forms of torture listed by the newspaper were instances of victims being hung up, having boiling water poured over them, being hit with bottles, burned with cigarettes, whipped with leather or plastic belts or having electric prods placed on their genitals. Citing this and other reports in the Chinese press, Amnesty International has noted starkly that 'deaths as a result of torture are not rare'.

According to a former police officer in Shanghai, for every case investigated by the authorities and reported in the press, there were hundreds of unacknowledged cases. A few of the allegations have apparently been investigated by the judiciary but, Amnesty says, the Chinese authorities have 'erected a wall of silence around torture and ill-treatment' from which the only conclusion to be drawn is that the Communist party acquiesces in this massive violation of human rights.

Throughout this period the authorities in Beijing forbade any reputable international organisation or group to investigate the grave allegations against China. Refusing to accept the terms on which the International Committee of the Red Cross conducts its inquiries, the foreign minister, Qian Qichen, was to offer the view that these standard requirements were 'hardly feasible for China'. Amnesty's own efforts to gain access to China have yielded no response. This refusal to permit outside scrutiny led Amnesty to the view that China has much to hide; that the scale of human-rights violations may be far worse than can be documented, and that the Chinese authorities still believe that they can do what they like to people and are not accountable for their actions, either internally or externally.

Across the border in Britain's last significant colony, the persecution and punishment of dissidents and the repression of political freedom was observed with growing alarm. In 1976, Britain had ratified the two UN covenants (the International Covenant on Civil and Political Rights and the International Covenant on Economic, Social and Cultural Rights) which codified in treaty form the Universal Declaration of Human Rights adopted by the UN General Assembly in 1948. The ratification of both covenants applied simultaneously to all British dependent territories, including Hong Kong. In 1984, the two signatories of the Joint Declaration agreed that the provisions of both treaties should remain in force in Hong Kong after 1997, an agreement confirmed in Article 39 of the Basic Law of 1990. In the meantime, pressure grew in the community for a single piece of legislation, a Bill of Rights, to bring together under domestic law all relevant rights included in the covenants. During 1989, in the diplomatic phrase of an official British booklet on the issue, 'public support for such a bill increased'. Backed by an overwhelming majority of the Legislative Council, the bill came into force on 8 June 1991. With characteristic bluntness, Chris Patten was later to volunteer that the Bill of Rights was a 'measure introduced in the wake of the killings in Tiananmen Square in 1989 to meet understandable anxieties at the time'.

Except in the case of six ordinances, any previous legislation that was held to be 'plainly' in conflict with the Bill of Rights was automatically repealed, and any future legislation that failed to conform to the twenty-three articles in the new bill would be invalid. The over-arching authority of the Bill of Rights meant that a number of key laws relating to the rights and freedoms of the individual would have to be withdrawn or amended. Patten's inheritance, therefore, was the obligation to oversee draft legislation to amend the Societies Ordinance, the Public Order Ordinance, the Emergency Regulations Ordinance and the Crimes Ordinance – all of which gave draconian powers to the Hong Kong authorities in clear violation of the new Bill of Rights. The Emergency Regulations, for example, enabled the police to ban demonstrations and assemblies, to detain suspects without trial and to suspend habeus corpus.

Although the Joint Declaration and the Basic Law did contain a commitment to protect the individual rights and freedoms enshrined in the UN Declaration of Human Rights, the relevant articles did not identify how, after the handover, China proposed to implement this laudable objective within a framework that placed 'affairs of state' outside Hong Kong's jurisdiction and in the hands of the National People's Congress. Indeed, neither the Joint Declaration nor the Basic Law provided a final blueprint for the principles they both appeared to embody. The ambiguities and opacities in both documents reflected a set of conceptual imprecisions that left open a range of possibilities which still had to be negotiated. The new governor was thus trapped between his obligation – and his desire – to reform these anachronistic laws and the likelihood that to do so would provoke the wrath of China.

Indeed, Chris Patten had taken on a whole basket of

unresolved and contentious issues dating back to the colonial mists of time. One matter which went to the heart of Hong Kong's survival as a free and prosperous society was the judicial system, and, in particular, the status and composition of the Court of Final Appeal, which was due to replace the Privy Council after 1 July 1997 as Hong Kong's court of last resort. Under Clause 3 of the Joint Declaration it had been agreed that the Hong Kong SAR would be vested with 'independent judicial power, including that of final adjudication'. In the Basic Law, China elaborated this point, indicating that the judicial system in Hong Kong after 1997 would remain as it had been under British rule, 'except for those changes consequent upon the establishment of the Court of Final Appeal'. Following the publication of the Basic Law in April 1990, a number of legal matters remained in negotiation between China and Britain, at the conclusion of which it was hoped that the powers of the Privy Council could be transferred smoothly to those of the Court of Final Appeal.

The prevailing ethos before Patten's arrival dictated that these negotiations were conducted in absolute secrecy. However, in a society like Hong Kong, where the rule of law was universally regarded as a vital element in preserving the community's unique way of life, the core issues were not hard to identify.

As a member of the Basic Law Drafting Committee in the late eighties, Martin Lee had challenged Beijing to insert a clause guaranteeing the autonomy of the Court of Final Appeal against interference by China, pointing out that, in the absence of such a guarantee, the court's independence would be undermined by the powers given elsewhere in the Basic Law to the National People's Congress. He lost the argument. As promulgated, Article 17 of the Basic Law gave the Standing Committee of the National People's Congress the power to invalidate any law enacted by the legislature of the SAR of Hong Kong which the committee considered to be not in conformity with the provisions of the Basic Law 'regarding affairs within the responsibility of the Central Authorities, or regarding the relationship between the Central Authorities and the region'. These 'responsibilities' were not precisely defined, but were held to include, inter alia, foreign affairs and security. In addition, under Article 18, the National People's

Congress reserved the power to issue an order applying the relevant national laws to Hong Kong if, 'by reason of turmoil . . .
which endangers national unity or security', it were to decide that
the region was in a state of emergency. Article 19 explicitly
underlined this, stating that Hong Kong courts would have no
jurisdiction over 'acts of state, such as defence and foreign affairs'.
The question of what activities, if any, apart from foreign affairs
and defence, would constitute 'acts of state' hung in the air, unanswered. However, it was already clear that 'internal security' – a
term dreaded by human-rights activists in China – was unlikely to
be excluded by Beijing from the list of 'acts of state' over which,
at best, Hong Kong would have limited jurisdiction.

The ambiguities of the Joint Declaration and Basic Law were
not confined to the fundamental questions of human rights and
democracy. The fact that Britain and China were unable to
resolve the complex issues of nationality in the Joint Declaration
was a further cause of concern in Hong Kong. In 1962, following large-scale immigration from the 'new' (i.e., non-white)
commonwealth countries, the Commonwealth Immigration Act
had for the first time imposed tight controls over the number of
immigrants allowed into Britain from these newly independent
states. Under the 1981 Nationality Act, the concept of British citizenship was redefined to exclude the 'right of abode' from these
British passport-holders. Among them, more than 3 million
Hong Kong subjects of the crown suddenly found themselves
reincarnated as 'second-class' British citizens free to travel on
their new 'dependent territory' BDTC passports, free to enter the
United Kingdom without a visa, but, for the first time in 150
years, denied the right to settle in Britain.

But the predicament of Hong Kong's British subjects was
unique: unlike every other major community affected by the
1981 act, they were not citizens of a new independent state but
colonial subjects due to be transferred from the sovereignty of
Britain to that of the People's Republic of China. For this reason,
Britain's 'betrayal' of its citizens in Hong Kong caused not only
deep offence but a great fear. In Hong Kong, 'right of abode in
Britain' had become virtually synonymous with 'means of escape
from China'. Britain itself had long ceased to be the chosen

destination for more than a handful of the 20,000 to 30,000 people who emigrated from Hong Kong each year; the United States, Australia and Canada were far more enticing destinations to those anxious to establish a base outside the British colony. Moreover, the overwhelming majority of Hong Kong's citizens had no desire whatsoever to leave their homes or their jobs in one of the most prosperous communities on earth for the uncertain prospects of a Britain in relative decline. For those people, the right of abode in Britain had represented not a licence to swamp Britain with their presence but a safety net against persecution, a reassurance that in case of catastrophe they would not be left entirely at the mercy of the People's Liberation Army. From the perspective of almost everyone in Hong Kong, the removal of that precious shield by the 1981 act was an abdication by the British government of a moral duty to protect its own citizens, and it was greatly resented.

In the Joint Declaration, Britain and China exchanged memoranda on the status of BDTC passport-holders. As Hong Kong would cease to be a dependent territory on the handover, Britain undertook to replace the BDTC passport (which would be invalid after 1 July 1997) with a document of similar status, except that it could not be passed on to the next generation and would only provide consular protection outside China. It was later decided to call this document the BNO (British National Overseas) passport. The Chinese memorandum confirmed that former holders of BDTC passports could use travel documents issued by the British government 'for purposes of travelling to other states and regions', and that, as Chinese nationals, they would not be entitled to British consular protection on Chinese soil.

Year after year, throughout the remainder of the 1980s, campaigners from Hong Kong took their case to Westminster, lobbying politicians of all parties in the forlorn hope of amending the 1981 act to take account of the colony's unique situation. When the People's Liberation Army's tanks rolled into Tiananmen Square in 1989, and a million people in Hong Kong responded by taking to the streets, the governor, Sir David Wilson, hurried to London for a meeting with the prime minister, Margaret Thatcher. At 10 Downing Street, in the presence of

Sir Geoffrey Howe, the foreign secretary, he proposed that full British passports should be granted to all BDTC passport-holders to help restore confidence to a community in despair about the future. His case was, as he recalled five years later, that such a move 'would give a sense of security to those people; they would feel that if things went really badly wrong, there was a door out – and it would have rooted in Hong Kong those people most necessary for its success'. Margaret Thatcher, whose own fear of a Britain swamped by immigrants had paved the way for the 1981 Nationalities Act, gave Wilson short shrift. Howe was no more sympathetic, arguing then, as he related later:

> The risk of three and a half million Hong Kong people actually claiming their right to come here would have created the most impossible social problems in this country, however brilliant and marvellous they are . . . Even the most generous society in the world could not have accommodated what could have happened . . . A government cannot give an undertaking that it will receive those people as British citizens unless it is prepared to mean what it says. We couldn't deliver, and it would have been quite wrong to suggest that we could.

In the House of Commons, the underlying consensus was so firm that even when the foreign secretary saw fit to point out that the arrival of over 3 million people from Hong Kong would sharply increase Britain's 'ethnic-minority population', no senior politician, with the exception of the leader of the Liberal Democrats, Paddy Ashdown, murmured in protest, or even squirmed with embarrassment. None felt it relevant to mention that 30 million or more white commonwealth citizens living in Australia, Canada and New Zealand – not to mention the 260 million citizens of the European Community – all had the right to 'swamp' Britain at will; or indeed that many of the 100,000 ethnic Chinese inhabitants of Hong Kong's neighbouring colony, Macau, also enjoyed right of abode in Britain as holders of full Portuguese passports with the same freedom of movement as any other citizen of the European Community.

Nonetheless, the Cabinet realised that Britain could not ignore the risk that the brightest and best in the civil service and the professions might lead an exodus from Hong Kong, draining the colony of precisely the talent it most needed to weather the transition into 1997. So, ten months after Tiananmen Square, the government introduced the British Nationalities (Hong Kong) Bill, under which 50,000 heads of household would be offered full British citizenship, giving them, their spouses and their offspring under the age of eighteen the right of abode in the United Kingdom. This elite would acquire a BNS (British Nationality Scheme) passport, carrying identical rights to those enjoyed by any other UK citizen. The selection of the 50,000 heads of household was to be made on a points system designed to favour those whose skills and services were thought most vital to Hong Kong, or who had the education, training and resources to make a 'positive contribution' to life in Britain.

The debate on the bill was a shabby and ill-tempered affair in which the House of Commons showed itself in its worst light. The home secretary, David Waddington, plodded through his set-piece speech without conviction; Norman Tebbit reinforced his reputation as the leader of the 'little England' tendency of the Commons by warning in sub-Powellite rhetoric of 'social upheaval'. The shadow home secretary, Roy Hattersley, was splenetic but inconsequential, scoring cheap points off the government without offering a serious alternative of his own (the Labour party being as fearful of appearing 'soft' on immigration as the Conservatives). Once again, only the Liberal Democrats found the measure of the moment, but as they would not have to take the responsibility for their principles, their opinions were widely discounted. Aside from Paddy Ashdown, no significant politician ventured the opinion that the government's bill was mean-spirited, nor hinted that it was riddled with racism. It was duly passed.

Sir Percy Cradock, who had become Margaret Thatcher's foreign policy adviser, regarded her horrified reaction to the events in Tiananmen Square as an understandable but regrettable emotional spasm which threatened to cloud the underlying realities of the relationship with China and thereby to make it even more difficult to resolve the vital issues which had not been settled in the Joint Declaration. By December 1989, Cradock had again prevailed. Encouraged by the intervention of Dame Lydia Dunn, Hong Kong's most senior politician, the prime minister agreed that Cradock, accompanied by Robin McLaren, the assistant under-secretary at the Foreign Office, should fly to Beijing in an attempt to break the diplomatic impasse.

The visit was undertaken in great secrecy to avoid further accusations about Britain's readiness to 'kowtow' to Beijing, which was, even now, putting its 'subversives' on 'trial' before their summary execution. Cradock took with him a mollifying message from the prime minister, which he had drafted himself, and which said, in effect, 'We are two great powers, fellow members of the Security Council. We have worked together very well. It is very sad to have these rifts. We have important issues to discuss.'

The two diplomats were welcomed by every senior member of the regime, including the prime minister, Li Peng (widely credited as the principal agent of the killings), the secretary general, Jiang Zemin, and the foreign minister, Qian Qichen. Ostracised by the world community for its complicity in mass murder, the Chinese leadership was delighted by the timing of Cradock's arrival and by the prime minister's readiness, as Cradock put it, to 'pick up the threads again' so soon. They warmly consented to his proposal that they should look forward rather than dwell on the past, and agreed that it was in both countries' interests to abide by the Joint Declaration.

According to Cradock, the Chinese were 'touchy' about Tiananmen Square, and reminded the British envoy that they had been dealing with 'rebellion, a counter-revolutionary act; that they were entitled to act as they had done; that they had done no harm to Britain, and yet [the British] had been one of the first in the cabal to produce sanctions against us'. They went on to inform the British duo that Hong Kong was a base for subversion against China, producing evidence which Cradock claims he was unable to refute: money had indeed been sent from Hong Kong to provide tents used by the demonstrators in Tiananmen

Square, while political activists in the territory had indeed taken it upon themselves to denounce the leadership of the People's Republic. Cradock did not respond to this complaint with the contempt which others might have thought it deserved. Instead he reiterated on Britain's behalf that

> we had no intention of allowing Hong Kong to be used as a base for subversion against the mainland; that while of course each country applied its own laws – and those of the British were different from those operating in China – it remained the policy of the British government that if any individuals arrived in Hong Kong seeking deliberately to make trouble with China, they would be expelled.

From the standpoint of a Western liberal, this was an unedifying exchange, but it served its immediate purpose: to restore some of the trust without which it would be impossible to explore further three vital and interrelated issues – the Chinese commitment to 'elections' in Hong Kong, the status of British passports held by residents of Hong Kong after 1997, and the airport at Chek Lap Kok, which, since the project spanned 1997, could not be realised without Chinese consent. The airport was the last item on that agenda to be raised, but from the perspective of the business community and even some of the diplomats involved, it was the most critical of the three.

The development of the new airport was a precondition for sustaining the phenomenal growth rates to which it had become accustomed. The old airport at Kai Tak was reaching saturation point; it was antiquated and dangerous. Although the runway was constructed on reclaimed land jutting into the harbour, the final approach involved a sharp bank to the right only a few hundred feet over the surrounding densely populated high-rise apartments, a flight path regarded by pilots as one of the most hazardous in the world. The prospect of a catastrophe in the heart of Kowloon was too terrible to contemplate.

By 1990, Beijing's traditional paranoia about Britain had resurfaced to be focused, inter alia, on the new airport. Prone in any case to believe that the outgoing colonialists intended to empty

the public coffers before their departure, they were by now suspicious that the British would use the Chek Lap Kok project to
enrich British companies in the process. As Cradock was swift to
detect, they were also mindful that such a major undertaking
gave them a very powerful lever with which to extend their
efforts to control Hong Kong in advance of the handover. 'One
of the bad effects of Tiananmen was their view that the relationship with the British was much more struggle than co-operation:
the hostile elements took control.'

Throughout 1990 the airport project remained in limbo as the
Chinese made more and more extreme and strident demands for
a central role in Hong Kong affairs generally. Clearly dismayed by
the increasingly vocal calls for greater democracy emanating from
Hong Kong, they were also, it seemed to Cradock, extremely
worried by the speed with which communism in Europe had
collapsed. With the fall of the Romanian dictator Nicolae
Ceausescu, they were friendless and ideologically exposed.
Although they claimed that they wanted to reach a 'consensus', it
was plain that they really sought a veto over Hong Kong's development. From the British standpoint, this implicit insistence flew
in the face of the Joint Declaration.

In the spring of 1991, in an attempt to break the deadlock, the
new foreign secretary, Douglas Hurd, flew out to Beijing. After
what he would later describe, with characteristic understatement,
as a 'frustrating' encounter with the leadership, he returned
empty-handed. Two months later, in June, the Chinese threatened to leak details of Cradock's secret negotiations which, the
diplomat foresaw, would lead to 'a slanging match in which
everything would get out of hand'. To avoid that, Hong Kong's
governor, David Wilson, proposed that the new prime minister,
John Major, should write to Li Peng warning, in the mildest
terms, that if 'clarity and certainty' were not forthcoming, then
the airport project should simply be cancelled.

A few days later, David Tang, a ubiquitous and colourful Hong
Kong businessman, accompanied by another prominent, if precariously successful entrepreneur, T.T. Tsui (who had intimate
links with the Beijing leadership), asked to see the prime minister. These unlikely envoys, ushered into 10 Downing Street on

the advice of Sir Percy Cradock, suggested that the time had
arrived for some 'personal diplomacy'. Towards the end of the
meeting, Major slipped his foreign-policy adviser a note asking
for his opinion. Cradock scribbled, 'Worth a try.' Within a fortnight, Cradock was once more on his way to Beijing, where his
old ally, Robin McLaren, had recently been appointed British
ambassador. Cradock, who relished such cloak-and-dagger diplomacy, called this 'secret visit number two'. He thought the
position was 'fairly desperate' and that the chances of a breakthrough were at best 50 per cent.

As it turned out, the talks went far better than either British
diplomat had dared to hope. The two sides agreed on the size of
the reserves to be left in the Hong Kong treasury on Britain's
departure, and instead of a bruising battle of 'principle' over
Beijing's right to have a veto over the airport project, they devised
a form of words that merely conceded China's right to be consulted – and then only within the terms of the Joint Declaration.
At first the two British diplomats were bemused that the Chinese
were suddenly so amenable. Then, in their meeting with the
Chinese premier, 'the scales fell from our eyes', as one of them
put it. Li Peng was clearly interested in only one thing: that John
Major should be prevailed upon to fly out to Beijing to sign a
'memorandum of understanding' on the airport which had
eluded them for eighteen months. The trade-off was obvious: a
visit from the British prime minister would do much to rehabilitate the discredited regime in the eyes of the outside world.
From Cradock's perspective it had the makings of a very good
deal indeed.

The agreement was announced on 4 July 1991 and Major duly
arranged to fly to Beijing for the official signing, where he would
be obliged to become the first Western leader to shake hands with
the 'butcher of Beijing' under the glare of the media's sceptical
spotlight. Cradock was delighted with the breakthrough he had
helped to negotiate. It was 'big stuff', he claimed later, convincing evidence that relations between the two nations were about to
enter what he then saw as a 'new golden age'. Some officials in
the Foreign Office were reluctant for the prime minister to be
seen saluting the Chinese flag or inspecting a guard of honour in

Tiananmen Square itself, but Cradock, who had no sympathy
with such squeamishness, knew that the Chinese would demand
no less. Yet again he prevailed over not only his colleagues in the
Foreign Office but ministers as well. For the one or two ministers
who were 'mooning around, viewing the visit as a shameful
episode', his contempt was boundless: 'You cannot help Hong
Kong unless you talk to China. It is self-defeating, indeed, it is
self-indulgent, to say we are not going to talk to these people.'

The prime minister arrived in Beijing in September 1991. As
a sop to the liberal sentiment which Cradock so despised, he was
careful to raise the issue of 'human rights' and to make sure that
it was known that he had done so. However, the television coverage showing a British prime minister exchanging pleasantries
with Li Peng left some commentators aghast. It was widely
judged that Major had allowed himself to be manipulated by
the Chinese into endorsing their campaign for international
rehabilitation.

It was rumoured that the prime minister, who had looked
decidedly ill at ease as he inspected the guard of honour provided
by the People's Liberation Army, soon came to regret the visit
Cradock had orchestrated. Although Cradock had been the decisive figure throughout, Sir David Wilson had to shoulder much of
the subsequent opprobrium. Wilson's friends blamed Cradock
for offloading on to Wilson his responsibility for the prime minister's damaging international foray. However, Cradock
maintained that Major 'was very pleased with the outcome – as
well he might have been . . . As regards Sino–British relations,
they were back to a peak.'

Not for long, however. Within weeks the Chinese were once
again jibbing over the airport, arguing over issues which the
British assumed had been settled with the prime minister's visit
and insisting on guarantees over the financial arrangements. In
short, despite the negotiations, despite the memorandum of
understanding, and despite the prime minister's trip, the airport
project was once more in limbo, a hostage to China's paranoia
about the British.

5

'NO MORE GAMES'

The Governor Assesses his Options

The Hong Kong people are often spoken of as if they formed an undifferentiated mass with uniform aspirations and values and a shared belief in the means required to attain their common goals. In reality, Hong Kong was a disparate and divided community with competing objectives, though the political conflicts thereby generated had been skilfully muzzled by the informal alliance of senior civil servants and business leaders who between them had charted the colony's meteoric rise to prosperity.

Even before setting foot in Hong Kong, Chris Patten had convinced himself that he could not navigate honourably towards 1997 without widespread public support within the colony itself. Since as governor he had no formal mandate from the electorate, he had already resolved to take to the streets to secure the popular endorsement for his leadership without which, he feared, he would soon become a 'lame duck'.

> I've got to earn people's trust and understanding by trying to appeal directly to them. To try through my presence on the streets to establish that I'm working in the interests of the six million people who live out there . . . And the more they think I'm a decent bloke and think that at least I'm trying to understand them, the more likely it is that I'll

be able to penetrate the carapace of the newspapers and the media.

To this end, on his second day in Hong Kong, more in the manner of an American president than of a British politician, Patten strode through the heart of Kowloon with Lavender at his side, flanked by police and bodyguards, to 'press the flesh'. Given that this personal approach was beyond the experience of the security services, the media and the public among whom he had so miraculously descended, the resulting 'Australian rugby league scrum' was inevitable. 'I want to meet the people of Hong Kong as well as the photographers,' he complained to an aide, but he was hemmed in by both. In the narrow streets of Mong Kok, he surrendered to the enthusiasm of a bewildered populace which clearly welcomed the governor's démarche as a novel form of street theatre. The camera teams duly recorded the scene for the next day's news. For their benefit as well as his own, he grasped outstretched hands, kissed at least two toddlers (only one of which cried), lifted another into his arms, and accepted petitions from two groups of protesters who immediately joined in the applause for what was, everyone agreed, a bravura performance. He seemed genuinely touched by the reception he was given. Here, said the reporters to one another, was a real political star: 'Who could imagine any of his predecessors behaving like this?'

It was indeed a break with tradition, and those of more conservative opinion in Hong Kong were not overly impressed. Muttering to each other about the dignity of the governor's office, they also worried that the Chinese would not approve. It began to dawn on them that Patten's 'charm offensive' could only too easily be deployed against Beijing. The prospect that Patten might use public opinion as a diplomatic weapon, an informal court of appeal, was almost as distasteful to Hong Kong's elite as it was alien to the gerontocracy in Beijing. This, the first of many walkabouts, was indeed a pre-emptive strike – part of a strategy which Patten had already planned before his departure from London, from which the Hong Kong establishment had been deliberately excluded. As he confided two days after his arrival, his ploy was to 'get the benefit of the doubt' on the home front before advancing on Beijing with a set of proposals that was bound to produce tremors in the Chinese capital, if not an earthquake.

The new governor found the resources of his private office quite inadequate for his needs. Accustomed to running a government department with a well-oiled bureaucratic machine at his disposal, he had inherited a ramshackle arrangement in which the responsibilities of the officials closest to him were at best ill defined. At his very first meeting with them he asked, 'Who keeps my diary?' To his amusement, three people put up their hands.

His inclination was to create within Government House a replica in miniature of the structure at 10 Downing Street.

> Without, I hope, folie de grandeur, I want to establish an office a bit like the one the prime minister has, which can provide a transmission mechanism between me and the government machine – one hundred and eighty thousand civil servants responsible for the eleventh- largest trading territory in the world. It has a vast housing programme, educational programme. There is law and order and security. All that as well as politics. One of the bits of jargon which Beijing is keen on is 'executive-led government', and I don't think we've got the machinery to have that . . . Maybe all that is the most appalling vainglory, but that's the way I feel about it.

A priority was the establishment of a secure telephone link between Government House and Whitehall. The absence of such a line was a telling illustration of the status in the diplomatic hierarchy enjoyed by his predecessors. 'I've been used to phoning the prime minister once or twice over the weekend and maybe a couple of times in the week,' he explained. 'I've nattered at Douglas [Hurd] on the phone, and other colleagues – I'm not suddenly going to stop doing that . . . I don't want to spend all my time writing telegrams. I want to go on dealing directly with people.' The scrambler was installed at once.

The governor's principal advisers were drawn partly from the

Hong Kong civil service and partly from Foreign Office diplomats seconded to the colony. They were highly trained, well informed and capable, but they were not his own appointees. Feeling the need to have about him one or two people whom he could trust absolutely, he had circumvented the official structure by bringing with him two personal advisers, neither of whom had significant experience of either China or Hong Kong: Martin Dinham as his senior adviser, and Edward Llewellyn as his political adviser. Dinham, 'the best private secretary I ever had', had worked for Patten when he was the minister for overseas aid. The governor respected his strategic judgement, his insider's knowledge of Whitehall, his skill as a draughtsman (if not as a speech-writer) and his toughness as an infighter. Llewellyn had been fresh from university when he became a private secretary to Margaret Thatcher in the last years of her premiership. He joined John Major's team at Number 10 for the 1992 election campaign, where he worked closely with Patten, then party chairman, who learned to respect his political acumen and to admire his 'networking' skills within the Conservative party and the British media. Both men were blessed with personal charm; Patten enjoyed their company and knew that they would be unswervingly loyal. With Dinham and Llewellyn, more than the others, he could freely share doubts and anxieties in the knowledge that neither adviser would leak them into the wider community of the civil service or the media.

Unlike other senior aides, Dinham and Llewellyn worked in Patten's private office, a few yards away from his study and only a short walk down the stairs from his private apartment. Initially, their privileged position caused some resentment among less favoured colleagues, who feared – correctly, as it turned out – that the two outsiders would enjoy an influence greater than their own. Foreign Office diplomats, especially those in Beijing, who were in any case dubious about Patten's appointment, discerned in his choice of lieutenants a deplorable tendency to buck the Whitehall system which had hitherto largely left China and Hong Kong in the hands of the sinologists.

The inadequacies of Patten's press team proved another cause for concern. The cultivation of local and international media was a crucial plank in his efforts to secure popular goodwill, and Patten devoted much thought to the subject.

> I hope I'll get my message through and my argument through by being as open and accessible as is reasonable to the media. I think if I take the initiative with the press in a fairly deliberate and calm way, it might help me to reduce some of the frenzy with which political events are covered. I don't want to find myself constantly driven by the rather frantic preoccupation of the media with each nuance of somebody's remark or speech . . . It doesn't make delivering a sensible policy terribly easy if one allows oneself to be buffeted by all that.

Patten's goal, commonplace in Western democracies, but hitherto untested in Hong Kong, was to charm the media into unwitting complicity with his efforts to woo public opinion, and thereby to protect his flank from potential critics within the foreign-policy establishment in Britain and the business community in Hong Kong.

On that second day in office, the governor broke with precedent to call a press conference in the grounds of Government House. The media were corralled on the lawn by the director of information services, Mrs Irene Yau, with a brusqueness to which local correspondents had long been inured. Patten came down the steps from his office to deliver what he intended to be a genial but authoritative statement at the start of what, in his mind, was to be an extremely important relationship. One reporter described the moment to his readers: 'Facing the media behind a yellow and black nylon cord ten paces away, the great man spoke. "Good morning," he probably said. A bank of incredulous faces opposite said something was seriously wrong. "Is the microphone working?" It wasn't. He tapped it. Nothing doing. And again. Eventually he decided to shout. "Speak up!" yelled the assembled press.' It went from bad to worse, and, finally conceding defeat, a clearly exasperated governor concluded his first press conference by saying, 'I dare say we'll meet in these circumstances again in the future.'

'I hope not,' one intrepid reporter yelled back. 'Not without a microphone.'

Patten did not need to be told that the press conference had been, in his words, 'a pretty spectacular shambles'. From his point of view, it merely served to highlight some of the problems which were waiting to be sorted out. The GIS, on which his predecessors had relied to impart their occasional public utterances to the populace, was, in Patten's view, 'very good at producing glossy brochures on Hong Kong economic policy', but hopeless at conveying any political message. 'The whole thing needs pulling together and to be given a sense of direction – not least in relation to getting across what the government is trying to do and handling the media. I think the operation tends to be firefighting and damage-limitation rather than getting out and selling what we are up to.'

To remedy this shortcoming, Patten decided to import another idea from the prime minister's office. 'I'm going to have a spokesman for me, here in Government House, just as Bernard Ingham was at Number Ten. Someone who can speak for me but can also make sure that the operation of the information service right across the departments is pulled together.' The man he chose was an energetic and approachable government official on the GIS staff, Mike Hanson. Hanson had served as refugee co-ordinator during the critical period of 1989–91, when tension over the Vietnamese refugees in Hong Kong was at its peak, and his experience had honed his natural flair for public relations. At first the chief secretary, Sir David Ford, looked askance at Patten's decision to appoint someone else to the task which had hitherto been his responsibility, but he soon came to appreciate Hanson's ability to promote the governor's cause. Patten himself was to judge that Hanson hardly put a foot wrong. As information co-ordinator, Hanson joined Dinham and Llewellyn in the inner circle surrounding Patten. They became a devoted triumvirate which helped to refine his ideas, protect his flank and articulate his case both privately and publicly. Other key players included Ford, whose bland and jovial manner concealed a shrewd and edgy intelligence; Leo Goodstadt, who combined an air of semi-detached all-knowingness with a sceptical intellect and a deep understanding of Hong Kong; Michael Sze, one of the first 'local' civil servants to be entrusted, as constitutional secretary, with a role worthy of his ability; Hamish McLeod, the reliable and diligent financial secretary, and William Ehrman, his political adviser, a shy and languid official on secondment from the Foreign Office, who was far more loyal to Patten than some of his peers.

With the help of others in the Foreign Office, the embassy in Beijing and the local community, Patten and his advisers had a little over two months in which to draft his first policy address to the Legislative Council, in which he had committed himself to define the parameters of the historic task ahead.

Government House was built in a neoclassical style reminiscent of the American deep south. Completed in 1855, it had once enjoyed a fine view over the nineteenth-century harbour. Surrounded by a well-manicured garden which ran down steeply towards the waterfront, and which, in March, displayed the best show of azaleas in the colony, Government House was a very splendid little mansion. Viewed from any one of the towerblocks by which it was now entirely surrounded, it had the air of a colonial amphitheatre, an appropriate setting for Scarlett O'Hara and Rhett Butler to stroll down the front steps and pause awhile in the soft evening breeze. From the opposite perspective, it was disconcerting for the mansion's inhabitants to be so obviously exposed, hemmed in and dwarfed by the brilliant, brassy and assertive monuments to modern capitalism which reared up from the stalls to the gods with intimidating disinterest. The Hong Kong and Shanghai Bank, designed by the British architect Sir Norman Foster, presented its backside – likened by traditionalists to the rear of a giant fridge – to the main verandah of the house, entirely obliterating the view towards Kowloon. A little way away to the east, the Bank of China rose effortlessly above its myriad rivals, by common consent the most elegant high-rise in the colony – all silvery steel and reflecting glass, austerely delicate, but, according to local superstition, directing its shards of bad *feng shui* towards the Pattens' drawing room. During the day, the sounds of the city ricocheted around this colonial oasis; by night, when all else was still, the throb of air-conditioning units gave no peace.

The Pattens' new home provided a private flat in the east wing, a range of reception rooms for official entertaining, and a substantial private office. Several commentators in Britain had adopted a reproachful if not envious tone about the tax-free £150,000 salary and expense allowance which went with his new job, which greatly exceeded his earnings as a government minister. Slightly needled by this media focus, he commented before leaving Britain: 'They write as though it were a matter of hitting the jackpot. I think it fair to say that I could have been pretty comfortably looked after doing all sorts of other things I was asked to do. This job is well paid. The facilities, the houses [Government House itself, and the 'country' residence in the New Territories on the edge of a golf course at Fanling] are all very comfortable. But there is an awful lot of responsibility that goes with them.'

Once in Hong Kong, he and Lavender did not allow themselves to dwell on the tabloid murmurings back home. Patten reflected with some contentment:

> For the first time in our lives as a family we're not going to be slightly concerned about the bank statement at the end of every month . . . I have never believed in much mortification of the flesh, Catholic though I am, and I certainly don't bear a metal-studded thong around my upper thigh. I therefore confess freely to looking forward with some enthusiasm to living in a bit of style. And I think that a lot of Lavender's friends would look forward to not having to do the ironing.

To take possession of Government House, was, he volunteered, 'terrific fun'. The Pattens thought that their new residence needed to be spruced up; that it had become somewhat faded and dated, and that the public areas, at least, needed a facelift. 'There are some nice pictures here,' the new proprietor remarked, wandering through the hall and into the drawing room. He cast a baleful glance at the anodyne designs for the armchairs and the sofas chosen by the previous incumbents. 'One has to do something about the covers, which are a bit tacky . . .'

Until a couple of months before, Hong Kong's new first family

had commuted between a modest flat in Victoria and a small cottage in Patten's Bath constituency. As a government minister, he
was used to 'doing' his red boxes on a dining room table spread
with his daughters' homework. The last governor was determined, at the very least, to relish the experience of such
unaccustomed space. 'I don't think it is impossible to be both
quite grand and quite welcoming.' Certainly he was not to
acquire the reputation locally for miserliness with which, perhaps
unfairly, his predecessors had been burdened. The empty wine
cellar left by the Wilsons was to be filled with the best that a substantial budget could afford – or at least, wine good enough to
match the quality of the multicultured cuisine on offer from the
Chinese chefs, which, in the opinion of the many connoisseurs
who would pass through in the months ahead, rivalled all but the
best restaurants in either China or the West. Every room would
be employed to the full. 'At present there is an awful lot of kit
which is simply unused,' Patten mused. 'There are rooms we've
discovered that haven't been used for years.'

Unaware of the sensitivities involved, he later observed, in the
presence of a journalist, that he and Lavender wanted to get rid of
'all that Laura Ashley' with which several of the official rooms had
been decorated. Those who had helped the Wilsons to implement their taste in decor were greatly offended when this remark
was duly published, and Patten was accused of denigrating a great
fashion house. He responded that he and Lavender intended to
redecorate the house to reflect the best of Chinese design and to
capture the feel of Hong Kong. This aspiration was later for-
malised in a glossy booklet in which the theme of the restoration
work was defined as 'East meets West'. The plan, according to the
design team responsible, was 'to treat this renovation project as an
opportunity to display to world leaders who come calling on the
territory – as well as to local leaders and the general public – the
impressive workmanship of Hong Kong's craftsmen and engineers in architectural, interior and industrial design and
manufacturing.'

The idea of combining occidental taste with oriental colours,
patterns and fabrics, led to a blueprint (produced by the Taoho
Design Architects Ltd) which stressed 'a soft, warm, muted' look.

There were lavish new rugs in pinks and greens, each woven around the motif of Hong Kong's 'official' flower, the pink bauhinia. Out went almost all the existing furniture, utilitarian but characterless, which was described tactfully by the design department of the Hong Kong Trade Development Council, under whose auspices the renovation was commissioned, as symbolising 'the legacy of the building's previous residents'; in came a collection of rosewood chairs, tables and sideboards reproduced in the light but elegant style of the seventeenth-century Ming dynasty. There was a nineteenth-century camphor-wood chest with an elm stand, two elm money chests, and two solid elm armchairs, all chosen by the Pattens and carefully restored to their original patina. They also selected a set of twenty-eight light green clay pots, each one individually knife-carved with Chinese designs created by local artists. Four of them were filled with plants and flowers to decorate the portico at the main entrance, the galleried lobby and the main corridor leading to the grand ballroom. The floors were to be relaid in polished limestone of the mildest pink hue; balustrades, latticework and bookshelves were stripped of tarnished paint to reveal the teak, cherry and oak wood beneath. The formal drawing room was decorated in soft shades of peach, rust and cream, colours echoed in the striped curtains into which a delicate oriental pattern of flowers was woven. The sofas, large, squashy and European, were upholstered in cream and rust damask. The dining room, over which the Annigoni portrait of the Queen reigned supreme, featured a mahogany dining table which could seat up to thirty guests. Its formality was softened by walls sponged in two shades of yellow and an oval carpet in a pattern of green leaves edged in gold.

The royal portraits were to remain in place over the lofty entrance hall, but they would be joined by a selection of the best of contemporary Chinese art and artifacts – a celebration of local culture in an otherwise quintessentially British environment. It was a choice which the governor was resolved to make himself, indulging a passion which, perforce, as a mere minister of the crown, he had been obliged to restrain. Sculpture and paintings by Chinese artists from Taiwan, Hong Kong and the mainland adorned the main hall and all the principal rooms; some works

were donated, others borrowed from museums and galleries and
one or two were bought for what became a rotating collection of
the best of Asian modern art.

Then there was the ballroom – bare on the Pattens' arrival
apart from a stack of chairs and the faded aura of grand entertainments long since forgotten. It had been used by his
predecessors on formal occasions, but Patten planned to exploit
its grandeur far more frequently. 'I think we should have a concert once every month on a Sunday evening. We should have
people in for drinks, have a buffet – you can fit a hundred people
in with no difficulty. I think we should get a bit of sponsorship
and have the Pavilion Opera here – it's a stunning room.'

The overall effect of the restoration was to create an atmosphere that contrived to be elegant rather than sumptuous;
imposing and yet informal. The dowdiness of earlier decades
yielded to a last colonial hurrah which looked to the future, not
to the past – even if, as some wags remarked, Government House
was to be re-established as the Museum of Colonial Atrocities
after 1997.

Hong Kong does not encourage self-doubt. True, the city may
be cramped, noisy, overcrowded, polluted and often foul-
smelling; its air laden with fumes from belching trucks and
commuter-crowded highways. It may vibrate with the sound of
a million air-conditioners throbbing against the swirling humidity which engulfs the island for nine months of the year. Its
surrounding waters may be a cesspit of toxic waste and its landscape may be pock-marked by sprawling junkyards. It may offer
little other source of refreshment than the betting windows at the
racecourse in Happy Valley, a clutch of manicured golf courses
and a number of breathtaking views from the well-trodden foot-
paths that criss-cross the tropical hillsides, too steep for even the
most rapacious developer to destroy. Hong Kong may lack a
developed taste for literature and the arts, importing virtually all
its music and theatre from elsewhere in Europe and Asia. In
short, it may lack many of those ingredients which the affluent
Westerner has come to regard as prerequisites for a civilised existence. But, as its elite are quick to point out, such disdain misses

the point. Hong Kong, they explain, using a weary cliché, is 'a borrowed place living on borrowed time' – and its purpose is to make money.

John Krich, an American travel writer visiting the city in the early eighties, described it as 'a long shot . . . one bookie joint operating under the nose of the Maoist vice . . . a high volume, low overhead trading post', where the British offered 'one prize rock's worth of real estate on which cling the addicts of property'. If his tone was jaundiced, Krich nonetheless went to the heart of the matter. Hong Kong's raison d'être as an entrepôt was, and is, defined physically and psychologically in terms of property. Yes, the harbour is the most exciting in the world, the water churned permanently by aggressive flotillas competing for right of way: glossy liners, dilapidated coasters, container ships, tugs, lighters, barges, fishing smacks, hydrofoil ferries and a vulgar glitter of private motor yachts. Yes, Kai Tak Airport, which reaches out into the harbour on a spit of reclaimed land, does growl with Jumbo jets coming in from and going out to every continent, a layman's measure of Hong Kong's financial and commercial pre-eminence. Yes, the traffic between Hong Kong and China is ceaseless, the defining purpose of a parasitical community. But for the great majority of the people of Britain's last colony – whether they sit before computers, thirty, forty or fifty floors up a towerblock, insulated in artificially cool isolation from the throbbing streets below, or whether they toil on the new bridges, roads and subways, or in the factories, warehouses, shopping malls and street markets – property, or the promise of property, is all.

Simon Murray, one of the handful of expatriates with a genuine feel for Hong Kong's recent history, understood this cast of mind and approved of it.

> This is a refugee community. It is tough to say it, but they are on the run. People in Hong Kong are mesmerised by money. Not so much because of greed – it is to get security . . . Today China is getting closer, and they think, 'We've got to make some money, because with that money we can buy our security. We can buy our ticket out of here.

We can buy some property overseas. We'll be OK.' Without money you are dead.

Murray had arrived in Hong Kong twenty years earlier, almost penniless, himself a refugee, from six years in the French Foreign Legion, where he had survived to acquit himself with distinction. He applied himself with verve, charm and talent to making money in Hong Kong. 'I was turned on by this place,' he explained. 'I like selling things, I like people, I like the Chinese. Genuinely. People say they do, but they don't. I think they are fabulous. And, yes, I saw a chance to make some money.' By the late eighties he had risen to become the chief executive of one of Hong Kong's largest conglomerates, Hutchison Whampoa, and the trusted lieutenant of its tycoon owner, K. S. Li, one of the richest men in the colony. Murray had no illusions about the world in which he now moved with such aplomb. 'It is absolutely as bloody as you could possibly imagine. Lots of grins and shaking hands and banquets, but underneath that, it is lethal. There are huge jealousies. It is very clannish: they really gang together and they have their loves and hates. They are very tough.'

Murray, by now a millionaire, was a member of an influential elite, many of whose most powerful figures – men like K. S. Li, Stanley Ho, Peter Woo, Robert Kuok, Cheng Yu Tung, Sir Run Run Shaw, H. C. Lee, Walter Kuok and Ronnie Chan – had prudently diverted a hefty proportion of their assets into financial havens well away from the uncertainties of 1997. The biggest players were not only traders, but gamblers in real estate who had made most of their money out of land. Given that over 6 million inhabitants had to be squashed into an area only half the size of greater London, the better part of which was composed of steep hills, the demand would have been intense even if Hong Kong had not been the eighth-largest trading community in the world. As it was, the supply was controlled by the government, which released development land in annual tranches at a rate which did not begin to meet the ever-growing need. As a result, property prices inflated in value far faster even than the Hang Seng Index, the fastest-growing stock market in the world. Simon Murray tells how he bought a flat for HK$1.5 million. The following day he left for his summer retreat in southern France. Two weeks later the telephone rang. 'There was a man on the phone who said he wanted to buy my flat for ten million dollars. I thought it was a joke. Hysterical. But it was for real. Imagine the guys who were doing this on a scale not of one flat, but of ten thousand flats.'

The thought that such riches might not be entirely beyond the realms of their reasonable aspirations was never far from the collective consciousness of the restless millions who comprised the great majority of the population. The great disparities in wealth in the colony appeared to provoke no significant discontent among those at the bottom of the pile: on the contrary, their vision seemed unclouded by envy and untrammelled by the odds against them. They laboured furiously to work their way up towards the edge of that financial future which for them was measured in square feet and bounded in bricks and mortar, a cornucopia that remained elusively just out of reach but always in sight.

In the street markets of Kowloon, you enter a world which is far removed from the ersatz elegance of Hong Kong's commercial centre. Trucks and vans and taxis, belching diesel fumes, thread their way through line upon line of hawkers and vendors. Everyone is in a hurry, buying and selling. A van stops outside a butcher's and the carcasses of five fat, freshly slaughtered pigs are thrown on to the road, slithering across the tarmac to be picked up and carried fireman-style to a long wooden slab of a table, where they are slapped down on the knife-scarred surface. Within minutes, each carcass has been hacked into neat pieces of instantly cookable flesh for the gathering crowd to purchase. At a nearby stall, there are large green frogs, eyes popping, sliding over one another in a wire colander. A few feet away, snakes in a basket wait to be killed and skinned. Sitting beside a small tank in which fish thrash helplessly in three inches of water, there is an old woman, her face leathery and lined, dressed like the Western image of a coolie. She is selling vegetables discarded by other vendors, piled higgledy-piggledy on a battered handcart. The awnings over the booths selling cheap and garish T-shirts, blouses, shorts, slacks and trainers have been faded by the sun and rotted by the humidity; tattered and frayed, they sway listlessly in a fetid breeze. The streets here are overshadowed by decrepit apartment blocks, paint blistered, plaster falling. Wires trail from one window to another; television aerials sprout haphazardly. Air-conditioners whirr and rattle, incompetent against the weight of humidity and heat. There are balconies crowded against each other, filled with fresh flowers and washing lines.

It is tempting for the liberal commentator to detect in such grime-laden localities a great social injustice, an unforgivable Dickensian squalor. This would be to miss the point. In Hong Kong, as the official statisticians are quick to remind the sceptic, malnutrition is almost unknown, education is universal and free, and unemployment is lower than in any country in Western Europe. Even the tenements which now cover virtually all the habitable terrain of the New Territories, transforming this rural oasis into a cityscape of identikit towerblocks, can mislead. Most of these apartments, so drearily monochrome in design and structure, were owned privately, family assets of rapidly growing value in a market where the scramble for real estate seemed never to be tempered by the fear that the property bubble might one day burst.

By 1992, Hong Kong's economic prosperity was already entwined with that of China, itself careering anarchically towards capitalism with a growth rate in excess of 9 per cent a year. For this reason, from the viewpoint of Peter Woo – chairman of the Wheelock Group, which had assets worth US$10 billion in property, telecommunications, hotels, retailing and distribution, financial services, public transport and a container terminal – it made no commercial sense to view Hong Kong in isolation. 'We are not just talking about the six million people of this city. We are talking about an economic region that is composed of Hong Kong and southern China. That's almost sixty million people – the size of the UK.'

Woo was one of Hong Kong's grandees, a member of one of the most powerful families in the colony. He had easy access to Government House and top civil servants would juggle their diaries to suit his. Appointed by China to the Basic Law Consultative Committee, he was also a vice-president of the Prince of Wales' Business Leaders Forum. His office was ritually adorned with photographs of himself with world leaders and members of the royal family, the Chinese gerontocracy competing for space with President Bush, Margaret Thatcher and the heir to the British throne. In such a competitive environment, rival members of the good and the great did not shy away from self-promotion, but Peter Woo was inclined to reticence and lacked that Hong Kong taste for vulgar ostentation which makes the colonial classes cringe. Tall and sleek, he was suave in style and calculating in conversation. He gave no indication that he was troubled by self-doubt or an overdeveloped social conscience. Although he liked it to be known that he was a public benefactor who gave away several million US dollars each year in charitable donations, he was coldly hostile to Western ideals of social welfare. He regarded the United States, from his own elevated perspective, as an exemplar of the 'socialist' model of development which had drained the West of its competitive potential.

Happily gliding through the harbour on his motor yacht, he pointed out his possessions on either side of the busiest waterway in the world. 'See this?' he said, indicating a long expanse of newly reclaimed land on the Kowloon waterfront, which was already sprouting embryo office blocks and apartments. 'As far as you can see in either direction, it belongs to the company.'

Peter Woo's manner was deceptively bland, his analysis of Hong Kong's success embalmed in the smooth jargon of the Columbia Business School, of which he was among many of Hong Kong's alumnae. The raw certainties of Hong Kong's business ethic pepper his discourse. Hong Kong, he has explained, is 'the world's only merchant city', a conveyor-belt for goods between China and the rest of the world. 'Cargo is the essence of Hong Kong. The creation of cargo and the movement of cargo. That is our prosperity. You know that Felixstowe is the largest port in the UK? Our growth is one Felixstowe every year.'

The liberalisation of the Chinese economy authorised by Deng Xiaoping had further inflamed the entrepreneurial senses of the community. Peter Woo explained the enthusiasm this had generated:

Someone will say, 'Look, I haven't got much money but I have a flat. I'll mortgage the flat to buy two hundred sewing machines . . . and suddenly I am in business.' And before long they say, 'I've got to move across the border into mainland China. Then I can start up an eight hundred-sewing-machine factory.' And before long he's got two hundred workers. Soon this guy's a multimillionaire through hard work and the opportunity to move very, very fast. Those guys are our champions.

For Peter Woo the vitality of the 'borrowed place, borrowed time' cliché sprang from the need to secure the economic growth of Hong Kong beyond the last five years of British rule. 'We knew the British lease was running out. So we shrink our timetables. We work faster. The returns are faster.' The sense of an ending is untouched by false sentiment. The merchant city could collapse almost overnight. 'You've got to have freedom of movement – freedom of goods, services and capital . . . If the entrepreneurs see the environment has changed, they'll vote very quietly with their feet and you won't even know they have left until you see that, rather than cargo throughput increasing by one Felixstowe a year, it is decreasing by one Felixstowe a year.'

In his analysis of Hong Kong's achievements, Peter Woo volunteered not a single mention of freedom of speech or assembly, of civil rights or democracy. Like the overwhelming majority of his peers, he had enjoyed the benefits of a liberal education under the British or (usually at graduate level) in the United States. Yet concepts of freedom and democracy, at least in the context of Hong Kong, had remained, for them, alien and problematic. Pressed about his apparent disregard for these Western values, Peter Woo's opinions, in comparison with those of some of his opposite numbers, sounded remarkably sophisticated. 'I don't think anybody in Hong Kong has anything against democracy, but people know that democracy has its own limitations. The issue is not whether we have democracy or not, the issue is how to maintain Hong Kong as a merchant city.' Though he held these views tenaciously, he refrained from expressing them in public, or even, although he had ample opportunity to do so, in

private with the governor. Peter Woo disdained Patten's principles, but, for a while, liked to bask in the reflected glory of his
company.

Apologists for this view in the Hong Kong civil service and the
Foreign Office chose to focus world-wearily on the need to protect the future prosperity of the 'merchant city' by
accommodating China's distaste for democracy. Their guru, Sir
Percy Cradock, would freely acknowledge that, under Deng
Xiaoping, the gerontocracy in Beijing was composed of an unre-
constructed communist tyranny or, as he once noted, 'a bunch of
thugs'. More than a decade earlier, Jiang Zemin, already a leading figure in the Chinese Communist party, had warned him, in
effect: 'We want Hong Kong back. We want it back, of course,
prosperous. Like everyone else we want to have our cake and eat
it. But if it comes to the crunch, we'll have it back a wasteland.'
Cradock did not for a moment doubt that the Chinese leader
meant what he said – and his response, as a British negotiator, had
been to make accommodations accordingly.

The international business community had fastened on
Cradock's rationale with alacrity and relief. With one bound, he
seemed to have liberated them from the charge of collaborating
with the 'tyrants' in Beijing in a purblind scramble for a slice of
the lucrative Chinese market. Yet they also knew that the widespread aversion to democracy among their Chinese counterparts
in Hong Kong was not merely driven by 'realism' about the
recidivists in Beijing. Though they rarely put it so baldly in
public, the Hong Kong elite had persuaded themselves that
democracy was intrinsically a threat to their 'merchant city'. In
private, Peter Woo was delicately explicit: 'I think democracy
arouses debate, and debates are healthy. But what is the ultimate
objective? To ensure Hong Kong's prosperity and stability. Hong
Kong is the only merchant city in the world, and that happens
because of sovereign policy . . . Now, if you look at the Basic Law,
it spells out very, very clearly that the Chinese want Hong Kong
to be a merchant city.' Throughout the eighties he thought that
Hong Kong had heard a great deal, indeed too much, from what
he referred to as 'the so-called democratic lobby'. Now, he
advised, the business people were venting their concerns about

democracy, which they believed threatened to erode Hong Kong's pre-eminence: 'For me it would be a shame to destroy Hong Kong's role as a merchant city because it can never be created again.' The trouble with Western democracy, he averred, was that it too often produced 'one-party control'; in Asia, and especially in Hong Kong, people wanted a political system where different segments of the community had an opportunity to express their views. 'So the whole debate is basically on the basis of "Let's have a system whereby the consensus of the community becomes the rule of the day rather than anyone who has more votes than anyone else."'

Did this mean, in essence, that Hong Kong's elite should make the decisions in collaboration with the elite in Beijing? 'We know what happens in Washington or Whitehall . . . things don't happen. I mean, it's a joke,' declared Peter Woo. 'In business, when you don't want something to happen, you put it through a committee . . . If you want Hong Kong to be a merchant city then there have to be certain parameters. If you don't want that, then I think "one man, one vote" seems very plausible – to a Western eye.' Why, though, should 'one person, one vote' be inherently incompatible with the prosperity of a 'merchant city'?

> Very simply, it is this. If you look at the electorate in any society, they are a small minority. And therefore if you go to a one-man, one-vote situation, then the so-called bottom of the pyramid – where people are concerned for their own welfare – will dominate the way the government is run . . . Hong Kong has been successful and the entire population has benefited. We really should not tamper with it.

The self-satisfaction with which so many of the Chinese elite in Hong Kong displayed their 'robber-baron' status was a source of entertainment, laced with admiration, to the expatriates whom they had gradually usurped. By the 1990s, only a tiny proportion of the colony's population were offspring of the colonial power and the British had ceased to dominate the expatriate community. Although they still held the key posts at the top of the civil service, they were of dwindling significance in trade and commerce. The senior positions in Hong Kong's most important international conglomerates were still occupied by white expatriates, but the Indians, Eurasians and, latterly, the indigenous Chinese had begun to take an increasing share of senior management jobs.

The leading banks and legal firms proved the most reluctant to accommodate non-white talent in the boardroom. The latent rivalries between the expatriate minority and the Chinese majority sprang from a variety of cultural and social divisions, of which racial antagonism – covert in public, overt in private – played no small part. In this respect, Hong Kong was stiflingly parochial, and from an outsider's perspective, embarrassingly trapped in its colonial past. The Hong Kong Club and the Captain's Bar at the Mandarin Hotel were both haunts which most Chinese preferred to avoid. The former preserved the traditions of a Pall Mall club in the environment of an upmarket American hotel. Secure in these cloisters, the prejudices of those who were nostalgic for the colony's *ancien régime* could still be heard above the tinkle of ice in a whisky glass.

The Captain's Bar was altogether less subtle. A bolt-hole for youngish men on the make – some of whom lacked the talent to make it elsewhere – it was occupied every evening by noisy advocates of Thatcherite brutalism. Stuffed into city uniforms, their faces flushed by expensive claret, they brayed about financial deals, sexual conquests and, when the spirit took them, about the deficiencies of the Chinese – 'chinks' or 'little yellow buggers' – among whom they were obliged to live and work. In the last outpost of British rule, they disported themselves with the arrogance of the worst of their forebears. Incurious and insensitive, they lived in self-delusion cushioned by self-regard, and protected by the ersatz authority which, even in its dying days, colonialism still bestowed upon the second rate. They lived for the moment: for quick money, flash apartments, glossy cars, motor yachts, weekend parties, the cheap supply of domestic servants and the pleasure of reinforcing each other's certainties.

Mercifully, these arrivistes were not in the majority among the expatriate community. Hong Kong was also peopled by academics, writers, journalists, civil servants, doctors, nurses, clerics and community workers who were ashamed of their raucous and racist compatriates. Many of the colony's established emigrés understood Hong Kong's past and cared greatly about its future – not for their own sake, but for that of an indigenous community which they did not necessarily understand but which they held in high regard and even affection. Although many of them looked towards the uncertainties of 1997 with trepidation, others were determined to remain in Hong Kong after the handover, apparently indifferent to the change of sovereign. For them, Hong Kong was not merely about money: it had become their home, and they felt themselves to be part of its peculiar culture and civilisation. Hong Kong was more comprehensible and more secure to them than the 'old world' to which they now felt themselves to be formally but elusively attached by the possession of what, after 1997, would become a foreign passport.

British expatriates were easily lost among other Europeans and Americans who had come to Hong Kong for one purpose only: to maximise their own profits or those of the international conglomerates for which they worked. None of them cared much for democracy: safe in the knowledge that they were temporary exiles from a free society, they were, in general, dismissive about the virtues of democracy in the context of Asia and Hong Kong. The more established among them had developed a genuine regard for the Chinese entrepreneurs who had displaced them or their forebears. In private conversation they seemed anxious to demonstrate the baldness of their commitment to capitalism without the constraints of democracy. In their entrepreneurial dynamism, they could not fail to impress; within these limits, it was easy to appreciate why they were more at ease with the short-term certainties of autocracy than with the vagaries of twentieth-century liberal democracy.

Vincent Lo, a property developer, was like Peter Woo, an influential voice in both Hong Kong and Beijing. 'We are obviously not an idealistic people,' he volunteered. 'Hong Kong is not an idealistic place. To put it bluntly, we are very materialistic, very capitalistic – and that's how we survive. That's how we prosper. We make no apologies for that.' And democracy? 'I don't think we necessarily associate freedom with democracy, because we believe that economic prosperity is our protector, our guarantee for the future, the assurance of individual rights.'

In the judgement of the majority of people like Peter Woo and Vincent Lo, Hong Kong was fortunate to have been spared the draconian levels of taxation needed to finance state pensions, unemployment benefits and a national-health service, all of which they regarded as crippling burdens imposed by the West's commitment to the welfare state. 'Western observers say, "Boom, democracy! You like it, you're a good guy. You don't, you're a bad guy,"' said Peter Woo. 'I don't think it is as simple as that.'

If in 1992 it was thought to be impolitic to avow such sentiments in public, they were nonetheless the common currency of off-the-record and private conversations. It was clear to any close observer that long before the arrival of Chris Patten, the business community in Hong Kong found themselves in collusion with Beijing against democracy, a situation tacitly but powerfully endorsed by their international counterparts. This was not so much because they feared a Chinese démarche against the subversive threat allegedly posed by the democratic aspirations of their fellow citizens, but because they detected from the same source an equally insidious political threat to their established position as Hong Kong's ruling elite. Their overriding concern was that a new governor, driven by other imperatives, would upset the delicate balance of power in Hong Kong which, for several decades, had given them an effective veto on political and social progress and had preserved their financial and trading citadels intact. In this respect, Hong Kong's capitalists and Beijing's communists formed a potent coalition against the kind of freedom and democracy for which the majority of Hong Kong's citizens had already declared their enthusiasm.

This enthusiasm was embodied in the person of Martin Lee, who, in 1989, had spearheaded the mass demonstrations in Hong Kong in support of China's fledgling democracy movement and to protest against the atrocities of Tiananmen Square. Having led his party, the United Democrats, to a handsome – but, for the business community, spine-chilling – victory in Hong Kong's first quasi-national elections in 1991, he had become something of a popular hero in the colony, albeit an

unlikely one. Mild-mannered, ascetic and studious in appearance, he possessed neither obvious charisma nor the politician's
gift for soundbite rhetoric. Yet his evident gentleness and
integrity, combined with the courage of a prospective martyr,
made him a potent symbol of Hong Kong's fate.

Although the 1991 elections were regarded as the first to be
freely and openly contested, they were far from democratic in any
conventional sense of the word. Forty-two of the sixty members
of the Legislative Council were either appointed directly by the
governor or selected by 'election committees' and from 'functional constituencies' representing the dominant professional and
business groups in the colony. The intrinsic absurdities of this
deformed and flagrantly gerrymandered franchise would have
been ridiculed out of existence long ago in any genuinely open
society. It was no surprise, therefore, that Lee's United Democrats
won seventeen of the eighteen directly elected seats.

Insofar as the citizens of Hong Kong had been given a voice in
the 1991 elections, they had spoken with remarkable unanimity in
favour of precisely those principles and aspirations that so alarmed
both the business community in Hong Kong and the gerontocracy in Beijing. Although only a minority of the electorate had
been confident or assertive enough to enter the polling booths,
there had been little doubt that those who did spoke for most of
those who did not. Even before Patten's arrival, the potential for
a political confrontation within Hong Kong, let alone between
Hong Kong and China, could hardly have been more apparent.

This was certainly clear to the Hong Kong government and
the Foreign Office. To those diplomats who were charged with
the delicate task of negotiating the transfer of sovereignty from
Britain to China, Martin Lee was neither villain nor hero. From
their perspective, his principal offence was not that he argued for
universal adult suffrage, nor that he was bitterly critical of the collective tyranny which ruled China, but that he seemed to attract
overwhelming popular support for his heresies – support which
was bound to make their project even more difficult to accomplish. Traditionally accustomed to exercising their benign and
usually efficient authority over a generally compliant legislature,
Hong Kong's civil servants – especially the 'local', that is Chinese,

members of the service – tended to be ambivalent about the virtues of democracy. Their attitude towards Martin Lee was touched by disdain: yes, he was a brave man, but he was also foolhardy and naive. In challenging China so directly, he had been provocative to the point of irresponsibility. It irked them that this local hero was also fêted in Britain by the handful of politicians and journalists who made it their business to take an interest in Hong Kong, and who were likewise unhealthily addicted to democratic reform. They faced enough problems effecting a smooth transfer as it was without the agitation of well-meaning but ill-informed commentators 'back home'.

Patten had pledged himself to work in the interests of all 6 million people of Hong Kong, but what did this mean? Was it to deliver what they wanted, assuming this could be established, or was it to deliver an outcome which they could be persuaded was in their interests?

> I suppose, if I'm honest, both. I hope I'll be able to comprehend what they want, though what they want sounds more than a shade paradoxical. They say, 'You've got to stand up for Hong Kong, show you're firm.' At the same time they say, 'Don't have a fuss with China. We've got to have a nice smooth life with China.' Somehow one has to square that circle.

The governor used his swearing-in ceremony, which took place in the City Hall in the presence of local dignitaries, the representatives of foreign governments and a massive contingent of local and international journalists, to make his first speech on Hong Kong soil. Though it contained the usual genuflections towards the colony's 'formidable assets' and its status as 'one of the most spectacular examples of a free economy known to man . . . a capitalist heart beating at the centre of Asia, pumping prosperity even more widely', Patten identified some guiding principles, expressing them more bluntly than was usual in Hong Kong. His focus confirmed the impression that he was 'different'.

Stressing the importance of the rule of law, freedom of speech and democratic participation, he undertook to listen carefully but to lead from the front. 'To govern is to choose, and choice is invariably difficult. Good political leadership involves facing up to hard decisions, taking them, setting out clearly what has to be done when all the talking is over, and winning consent for the course that has to be pursued . . . the ultimate responsibility of government rests with me.' Promising to devote all his energies to representing the interests of the people of Hong Kong as strongly and wisely as he could, he undertook to stand up for the colony 'courteously and firmly'. Of all his tasks, the most vital and challenging was to remove misunderstanding and to build up trust between Britain and China which was, he avowed, his sincere aim and his profound wish. But trust, he added, was a 'two-way street'. Departing from his written text, he added, as if to reassure – or, perhaps, to rebuke – Beijing, 'I have no secret agenda.' It was a confident performance in front of a sceptical audience – and it was his own speech. 'I dictated what I wanted to say . . . It was circulated round the world for comments by embassies, and we managed to avoid taking too much notice of what people said . . .' Nonetheless he contrived to avoid causing offence to anyone.

Hong Kong's most prominent figures, protecting themselves against an uncertain future, publicly offered him a wary welcome. Tycoons praised his 'balanced approach', and Peter Woo, in particular, commended his 'refreshing' style. A deputy to the National People's Congress in Beijing was reported to have said, 'I'm moved by the governor's pledge to remove misunderstandings', while Martin Lee promised to co-operate with the new governor. Yet of those quoted, only Simon Murray, the managing director of Hutchison Whampoa, appeared to register the full import of Patten's speech. 'He is terrific,' Murray declared. 'His message [to China] is very clear. No more games.'

In private, Patten's critics had been swift to deride his walk-abouts as attempts to earn cheap applause from the Hong Kong gallery. The new governor's instinctive populism confirmed their intuitive prejudice against Major's decision to appoint a politician – especially one so skilled in the black arts of public relations – to such a sensitive diplomatic post. Had they known that the cultivation of public opinion was at the very heart of Patten's strategy for seizing the diplomatic initiative, they would have been even more disconcerted. In the endgame to which he was now committed, the apparently trivial decisions about the plumed hat and the knighthood were in fact the first shots in a 'hearts-and-minds' campaign which he would pursue with vigour.

Martin Lee confided:

> Here you have the consummate politician kissing babies and always appealing to the people. I almost feel he's trying to run against me in the next elections . . . But I've got to be cautious because I don't know ultimately what the British government's intentions are: whether they just want to do a better PR job so that the free world will look at them trying to discharge obligations towards Hong Kong, and yet finally failing – or whether they really want to do something for Hong Kong even at the risk of offending China.

It was the latter prospect which most worried Martin Lee's name-sake and political rival, Allen Lee. An appointed member of both the Legislative Council (LegCo), and the Executive Council (ExCo, the governor's official advisory body), Allen Lee had been in public life for longer than any other of Hong Kong's emerging political leaders. Always responsive to the wind blowing from Beijing, he was a toughened but compliant advocate of the business community and their allies in China. 'I fear that Mr Patten will do things by himself without consulting the Chinese,' he admitted. 'I don't believe he will, but he is a very powerful politician.' Immediately before Patten's arrival Lee had been in Beijing to see Lu Ping, the director of the Hong Kong and Macau Affairs Office, who had told him, 'We want to talk to Chris Patten as soon as possible.' Lee was swift to pass this message on to Government House and optimistic that Patten would act accordingly before settling on his priorities in the run-up to 1997.

Emily Lau, an elected member of LegCo and a searing critic of both Britain and China, was the only public figure to be openly sceptical of Patten's credentials:

We are like people swimming and drowning, and we will grasp at anything which is thrown at us. Now we are being thrown Chris Patten . . . He sounds tough, a skilful politician and so on. Doesn't cut any ice with me. I only believe in actions, and I wait to see what he's going to do. The next six months or even less is going to be decisive. If he's not going to do anything in the next six months I think we can kiss ourselves goodbye.

6

'A DEMOCRATIC TIME BOMB'

Patten Draws Up a Blueprint

The Pattens adjusted easily to the regular routine imposed on them by their responsibilities. At least twice a week, soon after daybreak, the governor began the day with a game of tennis on the Government House court a few yards from the front door. He usually played with a coach, but some-times with Lavender or one of his guests. By 8.30am he was back in the flat at the top of Government House, showered and ready for the day. After breakfasting with his wife, he invariably went down to his study to face the first of the day's official papers and meetings. Every morning, at 'prayers', he met his personal aides to talk through the day ahead, to monitor the local media and to discuss the most pressing dilemmas facing the team. Then there would be routine meetings with departmental officials, business leaders, local politicians and other representatives of the commu-nity, as well as the steady stream of visiting dignitaries from Britain and elsewhere who invariably stopped off in Hong Kong en route to other destinations in the Far East. In the afternoon, there were more meetings, public and private consultations, and, frequently, visits to housing estates, schools, shopping centres or factories throughout the community.

Patten soon realised that local officials were prone to treat these visits as quasi-royal tours, and therefore took pains to escort him round the most modern and cleanest block of flats, the refur-bished home for the elderly, or the school which had just acquired a new science laboratory. To avoid becoming the star character in a self-serving, if well-meaning, pantomime, he decided to make unannounced visits to outlying districts, giving local officials and the police only as much notice as they needed to arrange the itinerary he had chosen. As a result he began to discover more about the genuine worries and grievances of the public: the leaking roofs, broken lifts, toilets which flooded in rainstorms, officials who failed to respond to repeated requests for assistance. His 'subjects' treated him with a combination of deference and frankness that was reminiscent of petitioners in a feudal monarchy. He listened, took note, and, sometimes directly, but more frequently through his staff, agitated on their behalf with the appropriate branch of the civil service. In so small a community, his reputation as someone who genuinely cared about 'ordinary' people spread rapidly; to his great political advantage, this perception was played back in the opinion polls, which confirmed and entrenched his reputation as a sincere and honourable governor.

In the last week of August 1992, Patten put the finishing touches to his plan for the reform of Hong Kong's electoral system. At the core of his proposals was the creation of a constitutional framework for the 1995 elections, which, it was hoped, would be adopted by the Chinese for the first elections after the transfer of sovereignty, which were due to be held in 1998. In the jargon of their earlier negotiations, the British and Chinese had alighted on the metaphor of the 'through train' to describe the guiding principle that any electoral system put in place by the British before 1997 should remain after the handover. Although he knew that his reforms would raise eyebrows in Beijing, Patten had convinced himself that they would not derail the 'through train', not least because he was confident that they fell within the ground rules established by the Basic Law, which was itself designed to be consistent with the Joint Declaration.

Patten's proposals were the product of his determination to open up new ground. While they were still in preparation he said privately:

What I feel very strongly is that we have to break out of the cul-de-sacs in which all the political arguments have been taking place; that I have to make it into open country . . . I think there is quite a lot I can do to broaden and deepen democracy in Hong Kong without necessarily taking on the Chinese on things which they have said they won't accept. They still might not much like the agenda I put forward, but I think we'll be in rather better country when it comes to manoeuvring.

It was a bold vision, even more fraught with hazard than Patten appreciated. In retrospect his insouciance would seem precariously optimistic. Hitherto, public debate about the framework for the 1995 elections had focused on the demand made by Martin Lee, and endorsed by Dame Lydia Dunn, the doyenne of Hong Kong's politicians, that the number of directly elected seats in the sixty-seat Legislative Council should be increased from twenty to thirty by the handover date, 1 July 1997. Patten knew, because it had been made unequivocally clear to him by the Foreign Office, that any such increase would be unacceptable to the Chinese, and that for Beijing this was a fundamental issue. Consequently he had no intention of allowing himself to be sidetracked into a dead-end route by reopening the question. Instead he resolved to 'raise some of the issues which I think are actually more important and interesting'. The only room for manoeuvre available to him, therefore, lay in the arcane electoral system for the thirty seats representing the 'functional' constituencies, and the ten chosen by an Election Committee – both of which had been originally devised for the precise purpose of restricting democratic participation to those inside the charmed circle of Hong Kong's commercial barons and political powerbrokers.

In London Patten had pored over the Basic Law and discovered that nowhere did it proscribe either an extension of the voting base in the functional constituencies or a change in the composition of the Election Committee. In both cases, he realised, with a frisson of cautious delight, there was 'quite a lot of space, quite a lot of elbow room between the Joint Declaration and the Basic

Law. What I propose to do is to find all those bits of elbow room for bedding down democracy or extending it.'

Notwithstanding his optimism, he was not indifferent to the pitfalls ahead. 'I could find myself with a very sensible, rational, carefully worked out policy that is politically adroit, guileful and wily, but which no one agrees with . . . I'm only too well aware of the fact that I could find myself in no-man's-land without a compass.' The Chinese in particular would be exceptionally dubious: 'I think some of them suspect that, having come to democracy rather late in Hong Kong, we're trying to construct some democratic time bomb to blow their system to smithereens.' This prospective reaction could only have been sharpened by his refusal to attend in person upon the leadership in Beijing before his arrival in Hong Kong. On the announcement of his appointment, Beijing had used the 'usual channels' to invite him to visit China to discuss the development of Hong Kong's new airport on Chek Lap Kok Island, the construction of which had been delayed by the disputes between the two sovereign powers. According to Patten, Beijing intimated that 'I could have the airport if I'd give them certain undertakings on political issues.' He had refused to accept this linkage, confiding, 'Even if we had – which I wouldn't have done – it would have leaked straight away, and I'd have been a completely lame duck for five years: somebody who'd kowtowed even before he'd arrived in Hong Kong.' Patten's first stand-off was not widely known about. Likewise, he shared his ideas on extending democracy only with his most trusted colleagues. By mid-September, however, he and his team had honed his ideas into a fully fledged – and wholly transparent – constitutional proposal ready to present to LegCo in early October.

Contrary to the myth long peddled by some of the Foreign Office's most influential sinologists, the debate about the future of democracy in Hong Kong long predated the 1989 massacre in Tiananmen Square. Indeed, it first surfaced almost 150 years ago. The charter establishing Hong Kong as a colony in 1843 included provision for both an Executive Council and a Legislative Council. The former was to consist exclusively of crown servants, who were to meet only when summoned by the governor, and then to discuss matters which he alone had tabled. The latter was to have no powers, except those of scrutiny, and its members could be dismissed by the governor at will.

Hong Kong's fourth governor, Sir John Bowring, who arrived to take up his duties in 1854, tried to put his reformist instincts to good effect by proposing that Hong Kong should be given at least an element of genuinely 'representative government', from which the Chinese should not be excluded. His suggestion was that LegCo should be expanded to accommodate three 'unofficial' members, elected directly by all residents of the colony in possession of land worth £10 per annum, and that they should hold office for three years. The response from the colonial secretary, Henry Labouchere, sharply illuminates subsequent policy:

> I believe that the present is the first proposal that has been made for introducing those institutions amongst an Asiatic population, containing but a very small proportion of British or even European residents: I have, therefore, thought it the more necessary to weigh carefully the reasons for and against it . . . The testimony of those best acquainted with them represent the Chinese race as endowed with much intelligence, but as very deficient in the most essential elements of morality. The Chinese population of Hong Kong is, with perhaps a few honourable exceptions, admitted to stand very low in this respect.

The British community, too, was disqualified by the colonial secretary, but for different, and arguably sounder, reasons:

> Few if any of the British residents in Hong Kong are persons who go to establish themselves and their descendants permanently in that place; they merely sojourn there during a limited time, engaged in commercial or professional pursuits, but intending to quit the colony as soon as circumstances will permit.
>
> To whatever extent the control of local affairs might be conferred on this class by the partial introduction of representative government, the effect would be, to give power

over the permanent population to temporary settlers, differing from them in race, language, and religion, and not influenced by their opinions. However respectable the character of the residents may be, I cannot believe that such an arrangement could work satisfactorily.

Thus thwarted, Bowring abandoned his cause. The assumptions underlying the colonial secretary's rebuff, being unchallenged, remained intact. Notwithstanding his decision, Labouchere's colonial instincts were liberal – far more so than those of the settlers for whom he had ultimate responsibility. He advised Bowring that if the governor could find suitable candidates from within the Chinese community 'whom you may think fit' to hold administrative office, 'I should be willing to assent to such appointments'. Encouraged at least to this extent, Bowring began the process of incorporating the leaders of the Chinese community into the public life of the colony by allowing them access to the legal profession with a view to appointing the first tranche of Chinese magistrates. For this, as for all progressive decisions, he was bitterly vilified by the expatriate community, which was delighted to see the back of him in 1859.

The slow process of Chinese emancipation was accelerated by the arrival of refugees fleeing from the long and bloody Taiping rebellion on the mainland. Unlike the rapacious 'coolies' of the early days, the new immigrants were prosperous families. By the year of Bowring's departure, sixty-five Chinese firms were registered as 'Hongs', a title accorded to the larger, well-established merchants. Within the next twenty years, several famous Hong Kong families entrenched themselves as major entrepreneurs, or in the middle ranks of the civil service, and in 1880, one of their scions, Ng-Choy, became the first Chinese member of the Legislative Council. The influence of the Chinese community soon grew to the point where their needs and aspirations could no longer be ignored by the expatriate minority or by the colonial administration, whose response was to cede them greater institutional authority.

The emerging concepts of Western democracy played no part in the complex structure of relationships within which the

Chinese community organised its own affairs and began to play a more assertive, albeit still segregated, part in the life of Hong Kong. Guided by Confucian principles of family and hierarchy, and driven by the imperatives of Western commerce, its leadership was profoundly conservative in attitude. To this extent, and no further, it found common cause with the expatriate elite, which had no patience at all with the highfalutin notions of emancipation and universal suffrage which emanated from English radicals far away in London.

In the 1880s, under the governorship of Sir George Bowen, the composition of the Legislative Council was modestly adapted to take account of Hong Kong's growing sophistication. Five seats of the sixty-member council were to be taken by 'unofficial' appointees selected to represent specific interests. One of these went automatically to a representative from Jardine Matheson, which had graduated from the murky waters of the illicit opium trade to become the most powerful 'Hong' in the colony. Another seat was reserved for one or other of the lesser business houses. The third went to the justices of the peace, the fourth to the Chamber of Commerce, and the last was reserved for a Chinese subject of the crown, also selected by the governor. Except for one or two minor changes, the structure created by Bowen survived intact for very nearly a hundred years.

This constitutional inertia has been explained away by recent apologists with the breezy assertion that until very recently the issue had not arisen because there was no popular demand for democracy. This self-serving revision of history, which was to be blandly repeated by a succession of government ministers and Foreign Office officials, does not do justice to the available evidence, or to those who sought fundamental constitutional reform but were repeatedly outmanoeuvred by a powerful coalition of timid diplomats in Whitehall and over-mighty merchants in the colony itself.

The modern argument for democracy in Hong Kong had its birthplace in London towards the end of the Second World War and was enthusiastically backed by the wartime governor, Sir Mark Young – who had been held in captivity by the Japanese and subjected to appalling privations – when he was reinstated at

Government House. Based on the widely accepted premise that the outcome of the war had been a triumph of democracy over dictatorship, the Young Plan, as it became known, advocated a fundamental restructuring of Hong Kong's antiquated political system to bring it more into line with the democratic precepts of the postwar world. The British civil servants who had been instrumental in preparing the ground for this plan assumed that the people of Hong Kong would expect and demand more than the restoration of the prewar status quo.

Young's original plan was to create a forty-eight-member Municipal Council representing the urban areas of the territory (the term 'colony' gradually faded from use in official communiqués), with thirty-two directly elected members, sixteen representing the Chinese and sixteen the non-Chinese communities. A further sixteen members would be 'nominated' by Chinese and non-Chinese bodies, again in equal numbers, to represent the two communities. Young envisaged that the Municipal Council would be given a high degree of financial autonomy and that it would have responsibility for public sanitation, education, social welfare, building, town planning, the supervision of public utilities, general licensing, the fire brigade and the management of parks and playgrounds. Although the franchise was to be restricted by age limits, literacy and property standards and residency qualifications, his proposals nonetheless represented a huge step along the road towards democracy. The council would have enjoyed complete control over its own affairs within the framework of an overall budget allocated by the administration and approved by the Legislative Council. Young also wanted to extend the principle of direct representation for a number of seats in the legislative assembly. It was his hope that Hong Kong would steadily develop the idea of representative government at central and local level, on the basis of a combination of directly and indirectly elected seats.

Young made it clear that his plan was open to debate. Indeed, he believed that the education in democracy which such public participation would entail was crucial to the success of self-government in Hong Kong, especially given the uncertainties which were bound to arise if and when China reasserted its claim on a territory it considered to have been snatched from the motherland. In such an uncertain climate, democracy could only take root with the understanding and commitment of public opinion. Young envisaged that the consultation period would last nine months. In fact, for a number of reasons which he had failed to foresee, the debate turned into a war of diplomatic and political attrition which took place largely over the heads of the people of Hong Kong and endured for almost six years.

The spectrum of opinion in 1946 ranged from the standpoint of the colonial secretary, Arthur Creech-Jones, who thought the Young Plan did not go far enough, and who favoured the immediate reform of the legislative assembly on the basis of direct elections, to the fears of the colony's merchant venturers that any democratic reforms would pose a threat to the economic hegemony they enjoyed, and which they identified as Hong Kong's raison d'être. That the latter view was to prevail is testimony not only to the enduring power of the business community in Hong Kong. For those who believed, even in the late forties, that Hong Kong's 'unique way of life' could be protected in the long term only by entrenching individual rights and freedoms within a democratic framework of law and administration, it also testified to the moral astigmatism which afflicts those whose vision is transfixed by the Hang Seng Index.

The Young Plan foundered in uncharted waters. Some civil servants feared that whatever the outcome of the civil war then ravaging China, any attempt at extending democracy in Hong Kong would fall foul of subversion either by the Kuomintang or by Mao Zedong's communist revolutionaries. Many British expatriates were viscerally prejudiced against Chinese emancipation. The Hong Kong General Chamber of Commerce argued against any extension of democracy which did not guarantee to leave a majority of the votes in the hands of the 'responsible' minority of the population (namely themselves), a view echoed by the China Association, which represented British Far East trading interests in London. This demand for a British veto was endorsed by a majority of the expatriate members of the Legislative Council, several of whom were also leading members of the Chamber of Commerce. The Chinese members of the Legislative Council chose, conspicuously, to refrain from making any public comment, on the astonishing grounds that they did not wish to exercise undue influence on the debate. Not unnaturally, this was widely interpreted as a statement of tacit opposition to reform.

Ranged against this weight of opinion, the response of the Chinese community at large was initially muted. Most of its members were too shell-shocked by their experiences, too uncertain as refugees and too desperate to claw a living for themselves and their families to pay any attention to the debate, let alone to follow its intricacies. Their leaders had no expertise in constitutional affairs, and it is likely, in any case, that they assumed the Young Plan was a blueprint for reform which would be imposed from above, regardless of their views. However, in the autumn of 1946, the grass roots began to stir. According to a survey of several thousand Chinese citizens, there was overwhelming support for the Young Plan, even though the electoral system would conceivably yield only a token majority for their community.

As the Chinese scholar Steve Tsang has pointed out in his monograph *Democracy Shelved*, any assessment of this response must take into account the 'traditional' Chinese character: 'Important policy ought to originate at the top . . . the local leaders would support it if it was acceptable . . . The vast majority of the illiterate and semi-literate considered public affairs to be the domain of the government and of the educated; their main concern was to make ends meet.'

Despite these inhibitions, Chinese opinion slowly coalesced around the need for constitutional reform. By 1949, three years after the prospect of extending democracy to their community had first been mooted, no fewer than 142 representative bodies were, according to Steve Tsang, 'clamouring' for reform. By this time, however, Young had retired to be replaced as governor by Sir Alexander Grantham, who came from a very different school of thought.

Grantham arrived in Hong Kong in July 1947. Having announced his support for the Young Plan, he at once set about dismantling it. With the active support of the business community, the majority of the appointed members of LegCo and a growing number of Foreign Office officials who, like him, feared communist subversion in Hong Kong, Grantham contrived to delay, prevaricate and obstruct until, two years later, he was ready to introduce what were in effect a set of elaborately contrived counter-proposals. Stripped of its cosmetic modifications, Grantham's blueprint tore the democratic heart out of his predecessor's plan. Effectively abandoning the idea of a Municipal Council, he argued instead that a proportion of seats on the Legislative Council should be directly elected. It was claimed on his behalf that this constituted a more radical reform than that advanced by Young. However, by insisting that only British subjects should be given the vote, he effectively excluded the overwhelming majority of the Hong Kong community who would have been enfranchised by the Young Plan: in 1949 Hong Kong's population had risen to 1.8 million, of whom a mere 14,000 were non-Chinese. Of the 16,000 British subjects entitled to vote, only 4,000 would be Chinese.

Later Grantham explained confidentially to a newly receptive Colonial Office that the great merit of his plan was that it safeguarded Hong Kong from communist infiltration while the allocation of seats in LegCo was so devised as to guarantee that potentially 'unreliable' members could never defeat the administration on any issue of political substance. By this time, the Colonial Office, once so enthusiastic about the Young Plan, had come to the view that the electoral system for LegCo should be so gerrymandered to ensure that votes would always stack up in favour of the government. When pressed by the Committee of Inquiry into the Constitutional Development of the Smaller Territories, which judged that his approach 'left the election of the legislature in the hands of the representatives of the richer classes' and was 'undemocratic', Grantham merely countered that any Chinese government, communist or nationalist, would press for the return of Hong Kong, and that the advent of direct elections in the colony would 'result in the dominance in Hong Kong of Chinese politics'.

It had now become impossible to assert with any credibility that Hong Kong was 'apathetic' about democracy. A cursory glance at the press or at petitions from more than a hundred

communal institutions showed conclusively that support for genuine constitutional reform had become widespread among both
the Chinese majority and expatriate professionals in the media
and the law. However, Grantham remained adamant that articulate opinion in the colony was not to be trusted, particularly
when it was non-British.

By this time other forces were at work. While the debate about
constitutional reform in Hong Kong stumbled irresolutely
onward, the Long March in China had reached its destination. In
October 1949, with the formal establishment of the People's
Republic of China, the flow of refugees from the mainland into
Hong Kong became a flood. The Colonial Office now joined the
Foreign Office in fearing internal subversion or a guerrilla attack
from across the border.

To make any announcement about constitutional reform in
Hong Kong, they believed, would be to tempt fate. It could
easily be criticised by the communists in Beijing as an 'instance of
the hypocritical insincerity of the imperialist oppressors' aimed at
'brutally crushing the rightful interests of the Chinese in the
colony'. To press ahead with the reforms was bound to provoke
the Chinese communists into a propaganda attack on Britain at a
time when the Far Eastern position was 'particularly serious'.

The outbreak of the Korean War further fuelled the case
against any constitutional change in Hong Kong. Members of the
British garrison there had been dispatched to face Chinese communists on that battlefield, and the Colonial Office had to prepare
itself for the 'international police action' in Korea to spill over
into Hong Kong. Sir Alexander Grantham, who had always
regretted the 1946 commitment to democratic reform, willingly
conceded that the issue should be temporarily put aside.
Although it was briefly resurrected again late in 1951, by which
time the Conservatives, led by Winston Churchill, had replaced
Clement Attlee's Labour party in government, the new colonial
secretary, Oliver Lyttelton, was swift to judge that 'responsible and
professional' people had not demanded reform; only a 'vocal
minority' at 'a lower level' who 'could not be regarded as responsible' were still agitating for the introduction of democracy.

On 20 October 1952, Lyttelton announced in the House of

Commons that the time for significant constitutional change in Hong Kong was 'inopportune'. In the colony, Grantham announced that he at least was 'at all times ready to consider further proposals for constitutional changes, provided they are not of a major character'. Thus the foremost agent of British 'betrayal' managed to leave the impression that, far from sabotaging the reform process, he was willing to resuscitate it. In any event, democratisation was dead. The repercussions on the future rights and freedoms of the people of Hong Kong, and on the international reputation of Britain, were to be incalculable.

Twenty-five years later, in a momentary spasm of resolve, an attempt was made to resurrect the corpse. In 1979, the colony's chief secretary, Sir Jack Cater (who had worked closely with the Chinese community as the first registrar of co-operative societies in Hong Kong), was one of the small handful of expatriate civil servants to decide that 'the time was right for us to have a good dose of democracy'. As chief secretary, Cater was aware that Britain, in the person of the governor, Sir Murray MacLehose, was about to approach China directly at the start of the process which led to the Joint Declaration five years later. For this reason he was anxious to move swiftly so that, in terms of democracy, 'we would have something on which to base our future'. MacLehose was unlikely to be sympathetic: in private, he had never disguised his opinion that the principal threat to Hong Kong's survival was any suspicion in Beijing that the British colony might become a base for subversion against the mainland. In MacLehose's view (which, by the late seventies, had congealed into the diplomatic consensus), a democratic election in Hong Kong would constitute just such a threat by turning the hustings into the battlefield for a civil war between nationalists and communists. As he explained much later, 'If the communists won, that would be the end of Hong Kong. If the nationalists won, that would bring in the communists. So it seemed a thoroughly unhelpful line to develop.'

Early in 1979, while MacLehose was away in London, Cater summoned a small group to his official residence, Victoria House, to work out 'possible plans for democracy – or more democracy – in Hong Kong'. Those present included two future chief secretaries: David Akers-Jones (who subsequently became a 'China adviser' and one of Patten's bitterest critics), and David Ford, who was in the post for the first two years of Patten's governorship. The 'Victoria House Group' conducted their discussions in secret because Cater knew how unpopular he would become with his colleagues for even convening such a gathering. After several meetings, according to Cater, 'we worked out a skeleton of what might have been . . . When Murray returned, I put our proposal to him. He was not very happy.'

Cater persisted, and as a result he was allowed to present a much watered-down proposal to the governor's advisory body, the Executive Council. At that meeting, MacLehose made it clear to Cater that he still disapproved of any constitutional change and that Cater was on his own. In the face of such resistance, Cater made very little ground. 'It was quite clear that the majority of ExCo, including the Chinese members, were certainly dead set against democracy in principle . . . To me it was a great disappointment. If we had had those ten, twelve years to experience democracy . . .'

Cater's efforts were not entirely in vain, however. In 1981, the Executive Council agreed to the introduction of direct elections for eighteen newly created District Boards. Although the powers of these quasi-parish councils were very limited and their elected members were again in a minority, at least a principle had been established. Campaigning occurred, votes were counted and the roof did not fall in. Perhaps more importantly, as the contemporary historian of these events, Robert Cottrell, has astutely observed, 'It enabled British politicians to talk a few years later . . . about the "continued development" of "representative government" in Hong Kong as though it were a longstanding process rather than merely an adjunct of 1997.'

Even this claim was far less valid than it might have been. More to the point, Hong Kong still lacked any significant degree of democratic accountability by the time negotiations with China on Hong Kong's future began, at which stage it was almost too late to make any significant progress.

In retrospect, MacLehose was to concede that the fear of provoking Beijing which led him to sidestep the pressure for democracy 'sounds remarkably feeble'. But he has explained: 'I felt my job was to make Hong Kong as contented and prosperous and cohesive as possible . . . Insofar as I don't sleep at nights, that is the sort of thing one looks back at and wonders whether one should have done it. I still think I was right.' According to John Walden, director of home affairs between 1975 and 1980, democracy was a 'dirty word' throughout his thirty years as an official in Hong Kong. Walden has written that the handful of expatriate civil servants who favoured democratic reform were regarded as disloyal, or even dangerous.

> Pressure groups advocating political reform or grass-roots democracy were carefully monitored by the government and the Special Branch of the Hong Kong Police and, where possible, their activities were discreetly obstructed or frustrated, sometimes by the use of highly questionable tactics. This deliberate and active discouragement of the growth of the democratic process by the government continued right up to 1980, to my certain knowledge.

These allegations are dismissed by MacLehose as 'absolute moonshine', and it is fair to say that they have not been given great currency except by the most ardent conspiracy theorists in Hong Kong.

Whatever the truth, as Robert Cottrell has pointed out, the civil servants at the heart of this history lacked both foresight and imagination. Their defence has been that Hong Kong enjoyed the benefit of an admittedly authoritarian executive which was, nonetheless, itself bound to the precepts of Britain's democratic tradition. However, this rationalisation of their inertia founders on their failure to think coherently beyond 1997; their failure to accommodate the argument of those who believed, as Lord MacLehose dismissively phrased it, that 'somehow the democratic process would insulate Hong Kong against China', or to appreciate that, in Cottrell's words, 'should any rendition of Hong Kong eventually occur, the seeding of democracy there would encourage British public opinion to feel slightly nobler about the process, and probably also make rendition more acceptable to Hong Kong itself'.

It was perhaps with these considerations in mind, but almost as an afterthought, that the concept of a representative government for Hong Kong 'constituted by elections' was slipped into the final draft of the Joint Declaration at Britain's request. As we have seen, neither party interpreted this to mean that a future legislature would be elected by universal suffrage (except 'ultimately', whatever that term was supposed to mean in this context). The British were reconciled to the view that such elections might be 'indirect' and that the franchise might be severely limited. As Cottrell says, 'In the Chinese political lexicon "elections" could have meant almost anything.' It is difficult to resist his scathing conclusion that 'the British government was more concerned at this juncture with the political benefits which would derive from the *idea* of democracy for Hong Kong, than it was with the implementation of democracy as such.'

In November 1984, following agreement on the final draft of the Joint Declaration, the government published a White Paper advocating that the Legislative Council should be restructured to the extent that two fifths of its membership would be indirectly elected through the creation of the twelve 'functional' constituencies representing various professional and business interests, while twelve more seats would be allocated by an 'electoral college' formed by local government organisations. 'A very small number of directly elected members' was proposed for 1988, building up to what was carefully described as 'a significant number' by 1997.

In both Houses of Parliament, ministers expressed in the most sententious language that they all fully accepted that a firmly based democratic administration should be built up in Hong Kong before 1997. Backbenchers, among them the former prime minister Sir Edward Heath, who was later to become one of Patten's most strident critics, urged the government to move rapidly towards that goal. More than 140 years after the seizure of Hong Kong, this belated commitment carried little conviction among those on whose behalf the Mother of Parliaments had been so dilatory.

The sceptics were right. In perhaps the most blatant act of perfidy in this shabby little history, the British soon reneged on even the modest commitment made in the 1984 White Paper. Within a year the Chinese had made it clear that Britain's unilateral decision to promise a 'very small number' of directly elected seats in the 1988 elections constituted a violation of the commitment made in the Joint Declaration to securing 'a smooth transition'. According to the Chinese, this objective could only be achieved if Britain refrained from any change to the political structure of Hong Kong that might be construed as a contravention of the Basic Law – by which Hong Kong would be bound after 1997, but which, in a Kafkaesque tweak of diplomacy, had yet to be finalised, let alone promulgated. 'Convergence' was the buzzword used by the Beijing officials to characterise Britain's 'obligation' to honour this self-serving interpretation of the 1984 agreement. Nonetheless, Britain consented to what one government minister described as this 'important' principle with no apparent qualms. As a result, as Cottrell has noted, 'China could claim the right to co-determine pre-1997 policy decisions, and also, prior to the Basic Law's publication, to delay any major decisions which Britain might wish to take until China, too, was ready to pronounce on the matter.' To this extent, Britain had meekly submitted to a Chinese armlock over all major political developments relating to Hong Kong for the next decade and, in a shameless volte face, conceded that direct elections, after all, should not be essayed in 1988.

Given the strength of feeling on the issue, a Green Paper in 1987 did not entirely rule out the option of direct elections for the following year, but buried the prospect in the small print. This subterfuge backfired, however. Altogether 368,431 individuals exercised their right to register a formal response to the Green Paper. Of these, 361,398 expressed an opinion about direct elections: 265,078 were in favour, 94,565 against, and 1,755 had no definite view. The verdict in favour of direct elections could hardly have been more clear cut.

Yet, in a breathtaking sleight of hand, the Hong Kong Survey Office, which had the task of collating these responses, under instructions from Government House, and at the behest of the Foreign Office, contrived to suggest that the reverse was true. The campaign against direct elections was orchestrated by the

'united front' pro-China groups, led by the trades unions, working with the business elite. They distributed preprinted forms
around offices and factories which respondents merely had to
sign and return to the Survey Office. By contrast, most of the signatures in favour of direct elections were attached to petitions
collected by liberal groups led by the United Democrats. Offering
no explanation for its decision, the Survey Office decided to
treat every signature on the preprinted form as an individual submission, but not to accord the same value to the signatures on the
petitions. Thus, with an effrontery usually associated only with
totalitarian states and banana republics, the Hong Kong government blithely announced that, on the basis of the submissions to
the Survey Office, 'more were against than in favour of the introduction of direct elections in 1988'. Progress towards the ultimate
goal was postponed yet again.

In fact it was not until 1991, by which time the principle of
'convergence' had been called into question by the atrocities in
Tiananmen Square, that a system of direct elections was at last
introduced for a minority (eighteen) of seats in a legislative assembly which (despite its honorific title) was still essentially a debating
chamber without significant legislative authority. Following that
year's elections, the constitutional structure of Hong Kong
remained much as it had been for the previous 150 years.
Absolute power still resided at Government House in the hands of
the present sovereign power, very much as the future sovereign
power might have wished. Yet although Martin Lee's victorious
United Democrats were still outnumbered two to one in the
sixty-seat assembly by those either indirectly elected or appointed
by the governor, they had a legitimacy, conferred on them by the
endorsement of a genuine electorate, which threatened to con-
found the Tammany Hall assumptions on which the legislative
assembly had been constructed almost a century and a half earlier.

Against such a background Chris Patten's self-imposed goal of
escaping from the 'cul-de-sacs' of the past would have been
fraught even in normal circumstances. As it was, he was not yet
fully acquainted with this convoluted history, and his predicament
was massively aggravated by the fact that the handover was a

mere five years away. China was bound to be even more dubious about any further tinkering with the electoral system, while the people of Hong Kong, who had learned to view any proposals for reform emanating from Britain with suspicion, were themselves divided about how far to appease or to challenge China. At the very least, the new governor had set himself a daunting task.

Patten's informal drafting committee included Sir David Ford, William Ehrman, Michael Sze, Martin Dinham and Edward Llewellyn. Other groups and individuals also played a part. In other circumstances, the product of their work during the summer of 1992, though novel, would hardly be described as controversial. The voting age, for example, was to be lowered from twenty-one to eighteen, which did no more than bring it into line with China's own constitution. The number of seats in the Legislative Council which were to be contested by direct elections was in any case due to rise from eighteen to twenty, again with Beijing's tacit consent: despite pressure from Martin Lee and others to increase the number to thirty, Patten did not deviate from his original intention to refrain from incurring the wrath of China by 'revisiting' that issue. Neither of these proposals was therefore expected to provoke an adverse reaction in Beijing.

Patten focused his search for the 'elbow room' exactly where he expected to find it: in the future structure of the functional constituencies and the Election Committee. So far as he understood it, neither of these anachronistic arrangements had been the subject of negotiation with China, and to that extent, he believed himself to have a free hand to democratise them. The structure of both, as Patten was well aware, was a coruscating indictment of a deeply flawed and often corrupt process for which the term gerrymandering was barely adequate.

As Patten well knew, the immediate 'victims' of his reforms would be Hong Kong's mercantile and financial elite, the corporate voters heavily overrepresented in LegCo. Patten's blueprint, as it became known, proposed that in the functional constituencies 'all forms of corporate voting should be replaced by individuals who own or control the management of the corporations concerned'. Thus, for example, 'all directors of companies that are members of the General Chamber of Commerce would be able to vote, instead of just the companies themselves, as was the case hitherto'.

The importance of this seemingly modest reform was far greater than it might at first appear. In 1992, Simon Murray, who, as group managing director of Hutchison Whampoa, was directly responsible for assets in excess of £11 billion and for 20,000 employees, was almost alone among his peers in acknowledging the failings of the existing structure. 'Take my group, which has thirty companies which are members of the Chamber of Commerce,' he explained. 'Theoretically, each of those companies has a vote. But of course, if I tell them to vote for Smith, they are likely to do that.' Under Patten's proposals, which Murray was to endorse with enthusiasm, the individual directors of the thirty companies in the Hutchison Whampoa group – some 150 people – would each cast a personal vote by secret ballot, making the outcome very much more difficult to gerrymander. The repercussions would not only echo through every boardroom in Hong Kong but ricochet all the way to Beijing.

Patten had quite deliberately not only challenged the entrenched power of Hong Kong's mercantile autarchies but also threatened their discreet but cosy relationship with Beijing. Once again, the General Chamber of Commerce was to supply a pertinent example. In 1992, a few months before five directors of its Executive Committee were due to retire, but expecting to stand again and to be voted in automatically, Beijing intervened. Simon Murray explained at the time: 'China let it be known that they had their own list, people who they wanted to stand against the five guys who were retiring. They passed that list round to many of the 3,000 companies in the Chamber of Commerce. They also got many Chinese companies, which weren't members, to join the chamber.' In eighteen months membership of the Chamber of Commerce increased by 900, the fastest-ever growth in its long history. As Murray was to observe later, 'When the votes came in, the five guys on China's list all got 900 votes. Of course, it was the Chinese companies voting them in. Over time, if that were to continue, the committee of the Chamber of Commerce – theoretically – will be run by people put in by

China.' As a result, under the existing system, the selection of the chamber's representative in LegCo would, in effect, be determined by Beijing. And, Murray went on, 'they operate in the same way with the lawyers and with the banks'. So, in the absence of reform, he had no doubt that China would acquire 'a very menacing control over LegCo, which cannot be good for anybody, because they will just be puppets doing what they are told'.

Patten's proposed reforms of the existing twenty-one functional constituencies were designed to cut the ground from under this form of corruption. Extending the franchise in all of them would increase the potential number of eligible voters by a factor of five; moreover, by loosening the grip of a few powerful individuals over the votes of their subordinates, he would ensure that the democratic gain was likely to be greater than the bare arithmetic would suggest. It would not be surprising, therefore, if the thin skein of trust between Britain and China unravelled in this constitutional knot to the point where the architect of these reforms would be reviled in language not heard since the Cultural Revolution.

This was not all. As agreed with China, Patten was also obliged to create nine new functional constituencies to replace the seats hitherto taken by government appointees. It was here that he found the further 'elbow room' to advance the cause of democracy quite dramatically. Under the chief secretary's direction, a small team of civil servants constructed these new constituencies to meet Patten's requirement that, as far as possible, they should embrace 'the entire working population'. This was to be achieved by giving a vote to all those working in Hong Kong's existing industrial and commercial sectors: in agriculture and the fishing industry, power and construction, manufacturing, import and export, textiles and garments, wholesale and retail, hotels and catering, transport and communication, financing, insurance, real estate and business services, as well as in community, social and personal services. At a stroke, Patten had contrived to extend the franchise through the functional constituencies to 2.7 million people without, he believed, violating the terms of the Joint Declaration or the Basic Law.

In addition to the twenty directly elected seats and the thirty elected by the functional constituencies, the sixty-seat chamber was to be completed by ten seats selected by an Election Committee, itself elected by the District Boards. Hitherto, these seats had been directly appointed by the governor. Here Patten had alighted on another aspect of Hong Kong's gerrymandered political system: that the District Boards were themselves composed of appointees. Without condemning the prevailing structure, he advocated that this system should be abolished in favour of direct elections. A group led by one of the colony's foremost legislators, Jimmy McGregor, came up with a proposal that the Election Committee for the 1995 elections should 'draw all or most of its members' from the District Boards which, for the first time, would themselves be overwhelmingly composed of individuals who had been directly elected into local government. This would not only have the effect of enhancing local democracy but would yet again serve to strengthen the democratic credentials of the Legislative Council. As McGregor would later explain to the legislative assembly: 'The ideal would be to ensure that the Election Committee became genuinely representative of the community.' If all members of LegCo were to be elected in 1995, it made sense that the electors on the committee should themselves have been elected. 'Anything less,' he observed dryly, 'might be taken as appointment by proxy.'

Taken together, Patten's proposals would seriously impair Beijing's ability to influence, directly or indirectly, the outcome of an election in Hong Kong. Although the leadership of the People's Republic had subscribed in principle to the concept of elections for Hong Kong, this commitment, it was tacitly acknowledged – even by Beijing's most ardent advocates in the expatriate community – had been made on the assumption that the electoral system could be guaranteed to deliver a compliant majority in the Legislative Council. From Beijing's crabbed and fearful perspective, the governor was indeed proposing to place a 'democratic time bomb' in Hong Kong. Patten was in little doubt that Beijing would react badly, regardless of whether his proposals did or did not violate either the Joint Declaration or the Basic Law. His schemes to promote the democratisation of Hong Kong violated a cardinal principle of colonial governance, to which, from their differing viewpoints, both the outgoing and incoming masters of the colony had long tacitly subscribed: that the electoral process should be so structured and manipulated as to ensure that its people could not mount a significant challenge to either sovereign power in the name of democracy. This complicity, which was a source of growing resentment among Hong Kong's thwarted intelligentsia, was about to be blown asunder in the name of freedom and, albeit in a stunted form, democratic accountability.

Once completed, the Patten blueprint was sent to the Foreign Office and to a number of key embassies around the world, including those in Beijing and Washington. Not one official raised any objection of substance to what was proposed, although Sir Robin McLaren, the recently appointed British ambassador in Beijing, warned that the Chinese would react badly to it. On 25 September 1992, with the full support of the prime minister and the rest of the Cabinet, the foreign secretary, Douglas Hurd, handed a copy of Patten's proposals to his Chinese counterpart, Qian Qichen, in New York, where they were both attending the autumn session of the United Nations. Patten himself sent a written message to Lu Ping, who, as the director of the Hong Kong and Macau Affairs Office, was, strictly speaking, his opposite number.

To Hurd's surprise they heard nothing for a week. Then, on the first Saturday in October, the British ambassador in Beijing was summoned to receive what Patten described privately as 'a stern note from Lu Ping'. Two calls 'along private channels' confirmed that the Chinese were 'furious'. The message was clear and simple: Patten should shelve his proposals until he had discussed them with China. For once, the British government refused to allow itself to become trapped in this familiar diplomatic cul-de-sac. According to Hurd, the Chinese 'expected a long period of confidential discussions in which they would express their views and we would accede to them. Well, that was unrealistic.'

'We've been getting storm warnings, rather than signals, for the best part of a week,' Patten elucidated a few days later. 'Of course, it is the way Peking customarily does business, so it's a bit difficult to know whether it's any different from other times. But I expect Peking to be pretty savage and to try to frighten the community here . . . I imagine that the rhetorical thunderbolts will start raining down.' He was aware of the precariousness of his own position. 'Of course, it's true that if, after a couple of months of banging the dustbins and making a lot of noise, the community here has flooded away from supporting any notion of more democracy, then it will be difficult to get any package through the Legislative Council or to make it stand up. But I hope that doesn't happen. I hope the community has some self-confidence. We shall see.'

7

'YOU DESERVE BETTER'

An Agenda for Hong Kong

On 7 October 1992, the day of Patten's first policy address to the Legislative Council, Hong Kong was abuzz with rumour and speculation. Overworked phrases like 'moment of truth' and 'turning point' filled the newspapers; politicians, some of whom had been briefed by Patten on the broad thrust of his proposals, were quoted extensively on what they thought he might say. There were warnings of a 'backlash' from disgruntled legislators, while 'sources in Beijing' warned that if the governor's speech breached the Joint Declaration then the Foreign Ministry would register a formal protest. The columnist Margaret Ng, writing in the *South China Morning Post*, discerned that his speech would clarify two fundamental questions about the new governor: whether his style of government was to be 'co-operative' or 'confrontational', and whether he was in the colony 'to do the greater good for Hong Kong or for Chris Patten'. The mood of excited anticipation in the Legislative Council, and in the wider community, was almost palpable as Patten launched into what he described self-mockingly as a speech of Castro-length proportions, entitled 'Our Next Five Years: The Agenda for Hong Kong'.

His address was not, nor was it intended to be, entertainment: it was devoid of the jokes and rhetorical flourishes for which he was renowned, and delivered with a deliberation reminiscent of the sovereign's speech at the state opening of the British Parliament. 'My goal is simply this: to safeguard Hong Kong's way of life,' he declared emphatically at the start. He dealt with local issues first, unveiling a massive five-year programme of public spending on health, education, housing and law and order. There would be enough teachers to reduce average class sizes to twenty; the public housing authorities would build an average of a hundred new flats a day; an extra 800 police officers would be recruited in the forthcoming financial year; spending on health would rise by almost 5 per cent per annum. He also announced a public-works programme on infrastructural projects and community buildings worth $HK78 billion. As a result of these and other plans, annual public spending – the former Conservative Cabinet minister was proud to boast – would rise by 21 per cent in real terms over the five years to 1997, a figure that could comfortably be maintained by economic performance and without depleting Hong Kong's traditionally prudent level of reserves.

Then there was the proposal to construct the new airport at Chek Lap Kok which, he reminded his delighted audience, would confirm Hong Kong's position at the crossroads of Asia. Designed to be the largest and most modern airport in Asia, it promised to be one of the world's greatest engineering feats. It would require a small but mountainous island off the coast to be levelled; a supporting network of new motorways; a suspension bridge to rival the Golden Gate, and a new metro system. Although the project had fallen prey to the mutual antipathy and mistrust which had bedevilled Sino–British relations following Tiananmen Square, work was already underway, underwritten for the moment by the Hong Kong government. But it had become an issue of such financial, commercial and political magnitude that the word 'crisis' hovered around every mention of the subject. By 1992, the Chinese had once again decided to use the airport in a blatant attempt to exert leverage on the political process in Hong Kong. This time, however, they found themselves hoist by their own petard.

Instead of displaying the constructive ambiguity favoured by diplomats, Patten was unequivocal. 'I will not be judged on whether in 1997 I fly out for the last time from Chek Lap Kok,' he reminded his audience in the legislative chamber and beyond.

I remain convinced that if we discuss the airport on its merits, then our very able negotiators could sort things out in a morning, perhaps even with a break for coffee. . . . If, in the event, we cannot achieve the breakthrough we need, and if, because the timetable slips, the costs rise and I have to fly out of Kai Tak or leave on the *Lady Maurine*, it will not be for want of effort or ingenuity in seeking out a timely solution. But the delay would be a great pity for Hong Kong; and it would be just as great a pity for China.

The message was clear: Patten was not going to allow anxiety over the new airport to derail his proposals for constitutional reform.

I owe it to the community to make my own position plain. I have spent my entire career engaged in a political system based on representative democracy. It would be surprising if that had not marked me. It has. I have always been moved by Isaiah Berlin's description of democracy as 'the view that the promotion of social justice and individual liberty does not necessarily mean the end of all efficient government; that power and order are not identical with a straitjacket of doctrine, whether economic or political; that it is possible to reconcile individual liberty – a loose texture of society – with the indispensable minimum of organising and authority'. I bring those opinions to the task of governing Hong Kong, where the ink of international agreements and the implacable realities of history, geography and economics shape and determine the way in which such views can be applied.

It was a powerful credo, plainly stated in terms which the citizens of Hong Kong had not heard before from any British official. The words were spoken slowly and with great emphasis, and with a touch of defiance. Yes, Patten acknowledged, the pace of democratisation was necessarily constrained, but, he stressed, 'It is *constrained*, not stopped dead in its tracks.' That established, he defined a crucial role for democracy in a way which was to cause great controversy within Hong Kong and, when he elaborated on his theme elsewhere, throughout the region. 'Democracy,' he declared, 'is more than just a philosophical ideal. It is, for instance, an essential element in pursuit of economic progress.'

This sentiment flew in the face of the received wisdom to which the business elite in Hong Kong had always clung. It challenged the premise on which the authoritarian leaders of several Asian 'tigers' had constructed their economic miracles; and, implicitly, at least, it was a rebuke to the Chinese leadership, which was struggling to establish capitalism within the political and bureaucratic constraints of its own deformed 'dictatorship of the proletariat'. Patten was unrepentant. In the absence of the rule of law buttressed by democratic institutions, and without an independent judiciary enforcing laws democratically enacted, he insisted, investors were vulnerable to 'arbitrary political decisions taken on a whim'. The new governor could hardly have described his outlook more bluntly or more precisely. Many of his listeners were visibly affected by what he said: some mesmerised by his vision, others aghast at his temerity. These contrasting responses reflected precisely the profound schism by which the community had long been divided.

Patten then revealed his blueprint for electoral reform, prefacing it with two crucial commitments. First, that most of the community, he was sure, wished any constitutional reform to be compatible 'as far as possible' with the Basic Law, and, accordingly, to transcend 1997, which meant that his proposals would require 'serious discussions with Peking'. Secondly, that while 'it would be very easy diplomatically and, perhaps, politically, to draw a line here and to declare that, in due course, this council will be informed of the outcome of the negotiations', he had not been so tempted. 'You deserve better,' he promised, 'and I believe my first duty is one of frankness to this council and to the community.'

In that brief statement of intent, Patten repudiated the stance which had been adopted by all his predecessors, and which had been enshrined in the Cradock doctrine of secret diplomacy endorsed by all previous British ministers. Two related factors were at the root of his approach: the fundamentally altered environment created by Tiananmen Square, and the growing demand for democracy in Hong Kong which that atrocity had accelerated. He had taken it upon himself to invest the Joint Declaration with a passion for democratisation that neither signatory had intended their complicit ambiguities to imply. More than that, he had pledged himself to a style of diplomacy which reflected that commitment. Any lingering doubts that the appointment of Patten might have been a cosmetic diversion had now been swept away. For better or for worse, the people of Hong Kong were to be put to the test in ways which had not been demanded of them before. Some shrank from the prospect; others rejoiced. Most resolved to wait and see.

The headlines in Hong Kong the following day reflected the excitement and concern Patten's speech had provoked. 'PATTEN "VOTES FOR ALL" PLAN', trumpeted the front page of the *South China Morning Post*. In an enthusiastic editorial which carefully refrained from judging the package itself, the leading English-language newspaper commented:

> Chris Patten has never been one to duck a fight . . . Yesterday he demonstrated to a new audience in Hong Kong that he is not short of political courage . . . Those who thought he would back away from confrontation ahead of his first visit to Beijing later this month were proved wrong. Fears of jeopardising an agreement on airport financing did not sway him from his purpose yesterday . . . He pressed on with his ambitious plan to extend the franchise to include every eligible member of Hong Kong's working population through an extension of the functional constituency system. China will denounce the move as bringing in more democracy through the back door, in contravention of the Basic Law . . . After three months of shadow boxing, the first appearance in the ring of Hong Kong's new champion was no let-down . . . Let nobody say that the territory is short of leadership, however controversial it proves.

On the first page of an eight-page supplement, under the headline 'CHINA HITS OUT AT PLANS FOR POLITICAL SHAKE-OUT', the

Post confirmed that the private 'storm warnings' from China a few weeks earlier were in earnest. A 'Hong Kong-based senior Chinese official, who declined to be named' was quoted as saying that the proposed reforms were 'incompatible with the Joint Declaration and the Basic Law' and 'a far cry from the provisions of the two documents'. Moreover, the source indicated:

> What Mr Patten said was contrary to repeated assurances by the British side that Britain would consult China on major issues concerning Hong Kong . . . We are gravely disappointed that he did not have the intention of consulting us in the first place. Sincerity is absent from his speech. Against this background, it would be difficult to expect Mr Patten's policy outline, in its present form, would be accepted by the Chinese side.

The same criticism was echoed in almost identical terms by Beijing apologists like Edmond Lau Ting Chung, a Hong Kong affairs 'adviser' to Beijing, who warned, 'If China does not agree, all these changes will be dropped by 1997 when China will organise another round of elections according to the present arrangements . . .' For good measure, he added, 'He's just putting on a show for the British people and for his future career in Britain.'

Other members of the Legislative Council were more reticent. Even the most ardent advocate of 'standing up' to China, Martin Lee, who was prone to denounce almost any statement emanating from Government House as some form of 'sell-out', had been wrong-footed by the governor's speech and merely expressed the hope that the governor would 'do what was right' even if Beijing were to oppose him.

After the United Democrats' landslide victory in the 1991 elections, Martin Lee had been in no doubt about the message that result had conveyed to Beijing. As he said later, 'The battle lines were drawn thus: on the Chinese side they said, "Be careful in casting this sacred vote. Vote for those who can work with China. Don't vote for those who can't" – namely us. The verdict from the ballot box was crystal clear.' Buoyed up by their result, the United Democrats had persisted in their campaign for half the Legislative Council – thirty seats – to be directly elected in 1995, rather than 2003, as Beijing had insisted. Lee was to recall a conversation of that time with Sir David Wilson, in which the governor chided him for adopting a confrontational approach towards the mainland. 'You know that China is not going to let you have that sort of democracy,' Wilson told him. 'And is it really in the interests of Hong Kong to go on fighting for it in these circumstances?' Martin Lee was convinced that by this stage, the British government simply 'wanted us to go quietly and to accept our fate. They didn't want trouble from us, because if we were to shout it would make Britain look bad in the eyes of the world. After all, which other government in the world was handing over six million people to a repressive communist regime?'

On the basis of his first meeting with Patten, which took place before the new governor's arrival in Hong Kong, Martin Lee had immediately concluded that Patten was different. Nonetheless, when the governor invited him for a briefing a few hours before the announcement of his proposals, Lee remained sceptical. The outline of what Patten intended to say was, however, enough to send the leader of the Democratic party (as the United Democrats had by this time renamed themselves) hurrying back to his colleagues to prepare them for a remarkable turnabout in British policy. They were not convinced.

A few hours later, when they heard Patten lay out his proposals in full, they were incredulous. 'They were so thrilled,' said Martin Lee. 'They just couldn't believe it. Disbelief. The good ideas . . . I mean, it is almost like a fully democratic election . . . Last night, after a long session, some of our people actually went and had drinks to celebrate. We've never celebrated anything before.'

Yet Patten's 'modest proposals' posed a dilemma for the Democrats. Hitherto the essence of their stance as a political party had been fierce opposition to both China and Britain: to the former as a despotic regime bent on the destruction of freedom and human rights; to the latter for 'kowtowing' to the malign purposes of the former. Now Patten had rudely unbalanced the neat symmetry of this political platform. Martin Lee described his problem and his solution to it with candour.

> I think our official line will be that we still want ten more directly elected seats; that we expect the British government to talk to the Chinese to give us those ten; and that even if they don't get Chinese approval, there is nothing to stop them going ahead. But we won't be able to go too hard on that or we'll lose the support of the people of Hong Kong. They will think, 'These people are idealists. They are just banging their heads against the wall. They are not realistic because the alternative [the Patten proposals] is perfectly acceptable already . . .' When they have an alternative which is almost as democratic as the American system of electing their president, and which is not inconsistent with the Basic Law, and we can go ahead without Chinese agreement, they will say, 'Of course, ten directly elected seats is more democratic, but China will go through the roof. Let's take the lesser option. It is not as good, but it has the advantage of not really offending China.' So if we continue our present policy, we will have real difficulty bringing the people behind us.

After prolonged internal discussion, the Democrats agreed to maintain their commitment to direct elections but to soften their rhetoric. Their objective now was to manoeuvre into a position where they could retain both their democratic credentials and their public support by endorsing the Patten proposals without appearing to compromise the principles on which they had been elected. For a group of individuals who were fresh to the realities of party politics, and who belonged to a community which was still widely regarded by the British and Hong Kong civil service as politically immature, they showed a remarkable understanding of the realities of the democratic process.

And how would Martin Lee carry off this triumph of compromise? Would he be able to conceal his delight? To celebrate in private while in public continuing to insist that Patten should have gone further? 'Oh, that's not difficult. I mean, I just pull a long face in public,' he explained disarmingly. The following day he duly wrote an article for the *Guardian* in Britain in which he accused Patten, who 'does not seem willing to stand up to pressure from Beijing', of appeasing China by failing to increase the number of democratically elected seats in the Legislative Council and thereby failing to fulfil Britain's responsibilities towards its major colony.

Martin Lee was astute, but it did not occur to him that this criticism from the Democrats could be used by Patten as a tactical weapon, a counter to those strident voices who decried his proposals as 'irresponsible' – or, in the words of Sir Percy Cradock, 'fatal, fatal, fatal'. To have Martin Lee, China's bête noir, pay tribute to him in the eye of that gathering storm would, as Patten was only too well aware, only have intensified its violence. As it was, the governor was able to assert that he had contrived to steer a careful course between the competing aspirations of the community he served. And if Martin Lee was to have a serious go at him, would that be a problem? 'No. And I don't think he will. It would be more of a problem if he was hagiographical about me.' Patten had been convinced from the start that:

> The alternative to an argument with China wasn't a quiet life, but four or five years of argument with pro-democracy politicians in Hong Kong, and with pretty well everyone one respects here and outside . . . I could have had hunger strikes and people chained to railings and people resigning from the Legislative Council and forcing by-elections and political turmoil of that sort without any great difficulty at all if I'd simply gone along with whatever China had wanted.

Later Martin Lee was to embroil himself in a bitter row with Patten over another unresolved 1997 issue – the powers and structure of the Court of Final Appeal – in which each would be wounded by the other. At this stage, however, his admiration for the governor was unclouded, while Patten, for his part, already viewed the Democrats' leader as 'the most formidable politician in Hong Kong', and felt a strong political affinity with him. The thought was never far from the governor's mind that individuals like Lee, of high, even self-destructive, principles, might one day find themselves behind the iron bars of a Chinese jail for asserting those principles and campaigning for objectives from which no one educated even minimally in the concepts of freedom and democracy could conceivably resile. 'I think one of my tasks,' Patten explained in these early days, 'is to ensure that people like Martin Lee, along with the whole notion of a more plural approach to government, are accepted by China by 1997. And I've got to ensure that people like Martin Lee don't push it too far with China. To help in some accommodation between Martin Lee and China would be a great success . . . It may well be beyond me.'

Other politicians in Hong Kong, who were inclined to believe that the mantle Chris Patten had privately thrown around Martin Lee should more properly be theirs, were distinctly less enthusiastic about the governor's proposals. Martin Lee's rival, Allen Lee, was now the leader of the recently formed and quaintly named Co-operative Resources Centre (CRC), a quasi-political party representing the interests of the business community, but anxious to be seen as independent of Chinese influence. When pressed, he tended to speak in favour of democracy, but he preferred to regard himself as a political realist: in the fragile hothouse of Hong Kong politics, he was regarded more as a weathervane than as a leader, and he had long been treasured by civil servants because he could be relied upon to take a 'sensible' if sometimes opaque position on matters of controversy.

Allen Lee had been, for many years, an uncomplaining colonial subject. Born in Shanghai in 1940, he was smuggled into Hong Kong fourteen years later aboard a cargo ship. His father, a merchant, had already fled to the United States, so as a teenager, Lee lived alone in Hong Kong until the family was reunited in 1957. When Allen Lee had finished his schooling, his father sent him to the United States, where he studied engineering and mathematics at the University of Michigan. He returned to Hong Kong in 1966 as an employee of Lockheed Electronics, but was soon headhunted to become managing director of what was then the colony's largest engineering company, employing 3,800 people. In 1977, he was introduced to the governor of the time, Sir Murray MacLehose, who was evidently impressed by the eager young executive. The following year, at the age of thirty-eight, he became the youngest person ever to be appointed to the Legislative Council. In 1986 he was also appointed to the Executive Council. In the 1980s Lee had been an assiduous champion of open government and democracy; by the time of Patten's arrival he had fallen under the influence of the tycoon Sir S. Y. Chung and, along with his mentor, had switched allegiance to the future sovereign.

On the day of Chris Patten's address, Allen Lee was one of several public figures summoned to Government House to be relieved of their duties as advisers to the government on the Executive Council. It is true that Patten had not been greatly impressed by Lee, but the ExCo member's dismissal was not a reflection on him personally: he was a casualty of the governor's decision to separate the function of the Executive from that of the Legislative Council, a distinction which had previously been blurred.

Patten's reform of these functions, which he had announced in his address, was straightforward: henceforth no member of LegCo could simultaneously serve on ExCo. As the former would be an exclusively elected body, the members of the latter would be appointed from the existing pool of senior civil servants and co-opted leaders of the wider community. ExCo's role, on a miniature scale, would be similar to that of the US Cabinet. 'My intention,' Patten said, 'is to ensure that we have vigorous and effective executive-led government that is properly accountable to this Legislative Council.' The 'confusion and muddle' which was endemic in the existing structure was a threat to the effective development of the legislature as an independent check on government. 'It is the legislature which is the main constitutional element, and which must be developed.'

By separating ExCo from LegCo, Patten hoped to streamline the process of government and to reinforce open political debate. As his chosen advisers, members of the Executive Council were bound by confidentiality and collective responsibility. 'What kind of democracy,' he asked rhetorically, 'seeks to take open political debate away from the legislature and shut it up in confidential discussion hidden from the eyes of the voters who elect the legislature?' This reform fell well within the terms of the Joint Declaration. Patten had carefully preserved the concept of 'executive-led government', a phrase which had become a mantra recited by both governments in the full knowledge that, if driven to assert their constitutional authority, the British governor or his Chinese successor could legitimately override the wishes of a troublesome majority in the Legislative Council by exercising their 'executive-led' veto. Patten did not add that his reform of the Executive Council extricated him from a grave dilemma: as the leader of the largest democratically elected party, Martin Lee would previously have had a powerful claim to a place on ExCo, which Patten would have found it hard to deny him. To have appointed China's 'subversive-in-chief' as one of his senior advisers would have angered Beijing and alarmed the Foreign Office. So Patten's reform not only had intrinsic merit but also the rare virtue of defusing a potential battle with both Chinese officials and British mandarins.

In public, Martin Lee again excoriated the governor for deciding to 'bar elected representatives from sitting on the Executive Council', a decision which, he asserted, 'constitutes a significant backward step in Hong Kong's democratic development. Put simply, he is thumbing his nose at the voters.' In private, he acknowledged, 'I can't push too hard . . . It would be very bad for the Chinese community in Hong Kong to get the message: "Martin is doing all this just to get himself a place on ExCo."' He was honest enough to add: 'Of course, I wouldn't, in any case, enjoy the prospect of going to ExCo, because that would mean giving up the best part of my legal practice.' As in the case of direct elections, the Democrats made their point but soft-pedalled the issue and soon dropped it altogether.

Patten also used his reform of the relationship between LegCo and ExCo to rid himself of another lurking problem. In their first meeting with him, several members of ExCo had informed him that they would not be willing to support a significant extension of democracy. Though he did not admit it in these terms, the 'constitutional' argument for the reform of ExCo provided a convenient cover for the expulsion from his inner council of potential adversaries whose loyalty was extremely uncertain.

Some of the Executive Council members who lost their positions through the reform were disgruntled. Patten confirmed, 'I'll be hearing more from one or two of them . . . There will be a certain lack of "house spirit". And in a sixty-member Legislative Council, one or two people can cause a lot of difficulty. They will feel that they did their best to support the administration. If the administration doesn't want their help, maybe they should kick over the traces.' But Allen Lee, the leading casualty, insisted that he felt no resentment: 'I don't feel bruised . . . His options are very limited. Either he has to separate LegCo from ExCo, or he has to appoint people like Martin Lee to the Executive Council and the Chinese will give him hell.' In his own time and his own style, however, Allen Lee was indeed to 'kick over the traces' in ways which irritated the governor and confirmed his instinct that Allen Lee was a distinctly less substantial figure than Martin Lee.

In public, Allen Lee confined himself to bromide statements about the desirability of a 'smooth transition' and 'convergence', but confidentially he was more forthcoming.

> Mr Patten is going to use his charm and his political wisdom to try to convince the Chinese, but I don't think they will be convinced. They're going to give him a very difficult time. So what's he going to do? That's the key question. When he comes back from his visit to China, he will have a choice: either negotiate with the Chinese again and come up with a package which leads to his being accused in Hong Kong of 'kowtowing', or take unilateral action. Now, if he takes unilateral action, we can throw convergence out of the door . . . Don't forget, after 1997, the consequences will be lived by the Hong Kong people, not Chris Patten. He will be leaving Hong Kong. How is China going to treat Hong Kong then? That is the important question.

While he stressed that he supported Patten's drive towards greater democracy, Allen Lee privately signalled his shift towards 'realism' by confessing that he had some sympathy with the complaint from Chinese sources that Patten's proposals had violated the spirit of the Basic Law. 'I mean, the Chinese expected to have dialogue with Chris Patten on this particular issue and the dialogue isn't really there,' he explained. 'Mr Patten wants to give Hong Kong as much democracy as he can, so he's looking at the loopholes in the Basic Law . . . and that, too, causes a problem with the spirit of the Basic Law.'

In October 1992, the message from Beijing was still not clear. The Foreign Ministry spokesman had been relatively restrained, but Patten's 'other channels' of intelligence, about which the governor was coy, were less encouraging. 'We've had some private messages from those who claim to be in the know, whose role in life I should perhaps not describe,' he confided, 'that the Chinese are furious and that Li Peng is furious.' The gist of the information was that the 'important people' in Beijing would refuse to meet him and that the airport project would be held hostage to his intransigence. In short, according to Patten, they were saying, 'We'll get you for this.'

As an accomplished public figure, Chris Patten was familiar with the round of official meetings, luncheons and dinners which consume so much of a politician's working life. He was blessed with an easy authority and a relaxed approach towards the public duties of high office. As the sovereign's representative in Hong Kong, he delighted in referring to himself mockingly in private as Hong Kong's 'Queen'. At the newly refurbished Government House, the Pattens were generous hosts. Dispensing with much of the formality favoured by some professional diplomats, they presided over luncheons and dinner parties with bonhomie, though they took care not to destroy that sense of occasion many of their guests craved. While her husband held court at one end of the table, affable, anecdotal, but dryly ferocious in argument, Lavender contrived to be solicitous, but never ingratiating, at the other. It was to become a testing role. Given to the expression of strong, independent opinions behind closed doors, she contrived to conceal her distaste for her husband's critics and adversaries, who were, according to protocol, only too often seated on her left and right. If it was disagreeable to entertain guests from Britain and Hong Kong whom Lavender knew were bent on frustrating his purpose, she never allowed her guard to slip. Invariably charming and discreet, she waited until they had departed before venting her loyal wrath against the 'rats' and 'traitors' whose company she had been obliged to endure on Patten's behalf.

Lavender had never been at ease with her husband's political ideology – 'I'm not one of your Tory wives,' she retorted defiantly when Patten teased her about failing to wear a hat for one official engagement – but she had been an assiduous campaigner in his Bath constituency. When Patten was in the Cabinet, she had pursued an independent career as a barrister specialising in family law. Now she had to play the part of first lady. Not all of her friends thought she would succeed. Her reserve, which disguised a gentle and affectionate nature, could be faintly intimidating. Lacking any streak of flamboyance, she did not display that superficial panache which leads social commentators to describe a hostess as 'legendary'. Nor, at first, did it seem that she would enjoy the round of duties that would inevitably envelop her: how, her friends wondered, would she adapt to the tedious obligations of a public spouse under constant, critical scrutiny? Would she dress the part? Would she *play* the part? Or would she succumb to frustration and irritation at what they imagined to be the suffocating proprieties imposed upon her? They need not have worried. With no inherited wealth, and with three daughters to educate, the Pattens had lived modestly, if not with frugality, in Britain. Now, blessed for the first time with a substantial income, Lavender blossomed. Elegant in dress, modest in demeanour and sympathetic in manner, she swiftly reinvented herself as the very model of a modern first lady. Before long, it was established in the community that Mrs Patten, unlike her husband, could do no wrong. She started to learn Cantonese (though she never mastered more than a few phrases and soon gave up); she patronised important charities with sustained conviction; she discovered how to make effective speeches – short, simply expressed and genuinely felt – and she became a familiar sight around town or walking on the Peak, accompanied by her two terriers, Whisky and Soda, who became local stars and the subject of affectionate cartoons. When Soda disappeared one afternoon, Mrs Patten was correctly reported to be distraught. A clumsy joke by an Australian diplomat, who speculated that the dog had been spirited across the border to be consumed as a delicacy by the Chinese leadership, offended the local community no less than its first lady. When the dog was recovered, the rejoicing was not confined to the Patten household.

In the days following his address, Chris Patten and his team sifted through the mound of press cuttings culled from Hong Kong's seventy-eight newspapers and the British press. In general they were encouraged. The English-language dailies were supportive, one of them describing Patten admiringly as a 'marathon man' for taking his case to the people via phone-ins and a quartet of public meetings. The latter innovation caused great excitement, and he was able to demonstrate his popular touch – though not without testing the mettle of his translator with his characteristic irony and colloquialisms like 'sick as a parrot'. One or two pro-Beijing papers referred to Patten 'playing the public-opinion card' at these rallies. The gulf of incomprehension between China's apologists and the former chairman of the British Conservative party on the question of the status of 'public opinion' in a free society was ominous. Patten detected in his critics an 'awful contempt' for their fellow human beings and only just resisted saying so.

The public meetings bore little relation to their nearest equivalents in Britain. Patten was greeted more like a royal visitor than a politician. Many of those in the audience seemed to have come simply to be able to tell their grandchildren about it. The only questions which contained an element of confrontation were from pro-China activists, who had evidently been closely briefed. The form of words used was virtually identical, focusing either on Britain's colonial record or on Patten's apparent failure to understand the importance of 'convergence'. The governor was, in either case, brusquely dismissive. 'I could tell straight away who they were. They were close to the microphones and it was the standard line you get in polite conversation with Chinese negotiators – that we wrecked every country we ever left, and that we'll wreck Hong Kong. It's standard Chinese Marxist kit. Crap, of course.'

If the Hong Kong citizenry appreciated their governor's eagerness to press the flesh, the encounters also boosted his own resolve. Although his demeanour was unflappable, his style concealed an intellectual restlessness which led him to constantly re-examine every option facing him. By nature he was pragmatic: the grand gesture or the high risk was not greatly to his taste. Yet he had found himself, by political conviction and through his sense of history, driven to occupy the high ground. It frequently disconcerted him to be thus exposed, so perilously close to the territory favoured in 'gesture' politics, and, although he sought to hide his moods from even the closest of his advisers, the pressure of the great political gamble on which he had embarked sometimes told heavily. Direct contact with a supportive public, therefore, was not merely a matter of shoring up the polls but an experience from which to draw encouraging conclusions, however extravagant they might seem in the cold light of the morrow. After one of his public meetings, which was attended by 3,000 people, Patten said:

> You saw tonight – even though there were some loonies in the audience, and even though there was every opportunity for people to react in an excitable way – they actually behaved perfectly well. So I think we can make things work and, if they work, the Chinese are not going to change them. Because, boy, are they going to be worried about how to make this work as well as we've made it work.

Exactly who were these Hong Kong citizens whose support the governor was going to such lengths to retain? It is impossible, of course, to generalise, except by stating the obvious: that most were either refugees from mainland China or the offspring of refugees; that they worked, by European standards, very long hours; that for them capitalism was not a political question but the only economic answer; that the individual and the family mattered more than the community or the state; that the future mattered more than the past; and that, in their individual lives, they were more usually given to optimism than to pessimism. Though their differing attitudes were doubtless reflected in the opinion polls which so assiduously charted the shifting hopes and fears of an insecure and shallow-rooted society, their horizons were not bound by the vicissitudes of the 'through train'. To the outsider, they represented Hong Kong only in the most imprecise fashion, as representatives of some of the most significant sectors of the community and, unusually, in being willing to talk about their lives openly to a stranger.

Ng Koon Leung, for example, ran a market stall when Chris Patten first arrived in Hong Kong. He was not interested in politics and for him, Patten was merely another British overlord. He was intrigued to see the new governor in the streets among the people, but his life was bounded by a set of basic imperatives which gave him no time to follow in any detail the tortuous details of the diplomatic drama which was to be played out not only over his head but without his participation. He worked hard, but he was unable to earn enough from selling cigarettes and trinkets to support his two children, aged fourteen and eight. His wife, Wong Oi Ying, a lively and practical woman, supplemented his income by working part-time as a seamstress. They lived in a high-rise flat in a vast concrete block on one of the public housing estates that had mushroomed all over the New Territories in the 1970s. They had a small living room, which was dominated by a television set; a bedroom just large enough to take a double bed, a bunk room, six feet by six; a galley kitchen, six feet by four; a shower and toilet. It was cramped but spotless, and it did not cross their minds that they were in any way deprived.

Ng Koon Leung's father had arrived in Hong Kong in 1948, aged eighteen, driven out of China by poverty and the depredations of the Japanese. He found work as a labourer, and after a few months he returned to his village across the border to meet the bride who had been chosen for him and brought her back to Hong Kong. Like hundreds of thousands of similar immigrants, the couple worked with the tenacity of desperation until they had secured for themselves the basic means of subsistence. They had virtually no contact with the British, except in the form of officialdom, and then only remotely. Their abiding memory of their colonial masters was of their vast physical size: the white man was tall and intimidating.

Soon after Patten's arrival Ng Koon Leung gave up his market stall to become a lorry-driver, collecting scrap. He was efficient and trustworthy, and soon became a foreman. The work was dirty and tiring but he relished the responsibility: 'We collect anything and everything, and you have to try to assess how much the stock is worth. For machinery you have to decide if it can be reconditioned or whether it should be scrapped. You have to decide that for yourself . . . Yes, it is satisfying.' He worked eight hours a day, six days a week for HK$10,000 (£850) a month. His wages were soon put up to HK$13,000, and he considered himself fairly rewarded in what he knew to be a fiercely competitive sector of the economy. Each month he handed over HK$10,000 to his wife to keep the family. Their basic living expenses – food, rent, water and electricity – consumed half that amount, while extra tuition for the children and clothing cost another HK$2,000. The remainder, according to Wong Oi Ying, 'we put aside for a rainy day'. In the absence of a state insurance scheme to cover healthcare, unemployment benefit or a pension, HK$3,000 was scarcely enough to provide for their future security, let alone for the luxury of an occasional outing or holiday.

For this reason, Wong Oi Ying decided to boost their income by babysitting two small children, a boy aged three and a girl of eight months. Both children were brought to her on Monday mornings by their parents and collected again five days later, after work on Fridays. The elder child slept on a mattress in the living room, the baby in a cot in the Ngs' bedroom. Wong Oi Ying enjoyed looking after them, but it was 'quite hard work – twenty-four hours a day'. The extra HK$5,500 a month, however, made all the difference. She explained that the practice of 'boarding out' children in this way was becoming increasingly common: 'In Hong Kong both partners have to go out to work to keep their family. The working day is long: they must be at the office for a nine o'clock start, and with overtime, they are frequently not home until after eight in the evening.'

Despite their own economic insecurity, the Ngs did not resent the absence of a welfare state. Though they could appreciate the advantages of unemployment benefit, they thought that, on balance, it would mainly benefit the idle and incompetent. 'Of course it would be nice to have it, but in other countries people live on benefits rather than going out to work. Here, if you are disabled or off sick, the Welfare Council will help, but it is only a thousand dollars a month, which is not enough even for the basics. If they gave more it would be a burden on the economy.' As for pensions and healthcare, they shared the view that, since there was no state scheme, it was incumbent on individuals to look after themselves, and not to take a 'shortsighted view of the future'.

The Ngs had recently started to follow the debate about the destiny of Hong Kong and had formed the impression that Patten was 'smart'. But they could not understand why Britain and China could not resolve their differences amicably. 'There is no need to shout at each other,' Wong Oi Ying said. 'They should just sit down together and discuss these things.' They felt there was little they could do to influence matters: 'We are just ordinary citizens. We just listen and let others speak.' Although the concept of democracy was still alien, they were not indifferent to its attractions. 'It is better to have the right to speak out. If you have the right to put forward your views, it doesn't matter if what you say is accepted. At least you have the chance to say it.' Wong Oi Ying was optimistic about the future, her husband less so. 'At the moment you can say anything and you can sign any petition, but after 1997, the Chinese can do what they like. There is nothing you can do. They might be more open than one expects but, in my opinion, it will be very much like China here in Hong Kong after 1997 . . . If there is restriction on freedom of speech it will not make much difference to us ordinary citizens.'

Hong Kong's freedoms, however, mattered greatly to Grace Wu, an antiques-dealer specialising in Ming furniture, on which she had become an authority with a rapidly growing international reputation. An elegant woman in her forties, she was as much at home in London and New York as in Hong Kong, where she now lived with her teenage daughter. Grace was born in China but her parents fled Shanghai soon after the Communist takeover for Singapore, where she spent her early childhood until her family decided to settle permanently in Hong Kong. She was sent to school in Canada and the United States, and later lived in England for a time. Despite her Western demeanour, she had always considered herself to be an exile from her homeland, a refugee, loyal to Hong Kong but, culturally at least, a 'Chinese patriot'.

Like others in the thriving antiques trade in Hong Kong, Grace Wu's business was expanding quickly. The delicate fifteenth- and seventeenth-century chairs, tables, bedsteads and wardrobes she imported from China were particularly in demand in the United States, where the best-quality items in her glossy catalogue could sell for upwards of $100,000. The handover loomed large in her mind, not least because of the Chinese government's ambivalent attitude towards the export of antiques. On one hand, some officials tacitly endorsed – and, in the case of the Cultural Relics Bureau, openly supported – international auctions in Beijing, Shanghai and Guangzhou (Canton); on the other, as Grace Wu put it, 'One does hear the constant noise of condemnation of "those who trade in our heritage" et cetera.' The future, therefore, was very uncertain. 'It is guesswork. We don't know.'

In China the trade was governed by the Antiquities Law, which made it illegal for any object over a hundred years old to be exported. However, its enforcement was the responsibility of the Chinese customs, who were well known for turning a blind eye for a small consideration. Grace Wu bought much of her stock from outside China itself, but when importing from the mainland, she was careful to work within the law – at least, insofar as she understood it. Inexplicably, antique furniture itself was exempt from the hundred-year rule, but it was forbidden to export the ancient and precious woods often used to make Ming furniture. The legality of her trade was not in doubt so long as customs officials could be convinced that the wood in her antiques did not fall into the prohibited category. Although she had been scrupulous in demanding an official stamp of approval from the Chinese authorities for every piece which passed through her hands, she was only too aware that she operated in a 'grey area' of the law. Many of her colleagues sidestepped it entirely, thereby — theoretically at least — leaving themselves open to charges which in China carried the death penalty.

The dealers feared that in the 'patriotic' fervour of postcolonial Hong Kong, they would be treated like scavengers. They expected their trade to be sharply curtailed and their possessions to be impounded. Consequently no antiques-dealer or collector of substance had failed to make contingency plans against a crack-down by the post-1997 authorities. Many works of art had already been shipped abroad to second homes or loaned to for-eign museums. Of those that were left, every glazed vase had its packing case, each carved goddess its precisely contoured crate, complete with well-oiled casters, ready for a smooth, if unsched-uled, departure by air. It was said that the contents of the T.T. Tsui Museum, a breathtaking collection of immeasurable value, had been similarly protected against the prospective vagaries of the Antiquities Law.

Grace Wu wanted to stay in Hong Kong. However, her deci-sion would not be based merely on the prospects for the antiques business but on whether the 'one country, two systems' concept could survive the handover. She lived in a precise but elegant apartment, sparsely furnished in a mixture of modernist and Ming. Sitting there with three friends, all in the antiques trade, she said: 'I think we all feel the same way. We have overwhelm-ing feelings for Hong Kong. I joke that I'm going to be out on the last helicopter, but this is my home. I would leave only if I thought that my personal freedoms were under threat.'

Her friends, for a variety of reasons, were less committed. One, a woman who had been born in Malaysia, educated in the United States, trained at Sotheby's, and now lived in Hong Kong because it was still a 'charmed world' for the collector, was plan-ning to move to England before the handover. Another, a refugee from Shanghai who was a dealer in ceramics, was deter-mined to stay on. 'My concern is to make money,' he explained. He was optimistic that the Chinese would not stand in his way after 1997. Politics did not interest him; as for freedom, he thought that it would still be possible 'to sit at dinner and criti-cise the government as long as we are not voicing our opinions publicly', and that was fine by him. The third friend, a painter, concurred.

> What is there to complain about if you can have a comfort-able living, if you can have your friends around you? You can still enjoy good food in the restaurants and good clothes in the stores. Nothing has changed. There is just a different government . . . You know, artistic freedom is not some-thing that has been important in the past. It's not something we ever had. So I don't think many people understand democracy, or care whether or not we have it. Most people want stability.

Grace Wu disagreed, but seemed uncomfortable doing so openly, as if unwilling to cast aspersions on the narrowly mercantile values flaunted by her friends, and which she, in part, shared. 'In our long history it has always been true that if you did not agree with the ruling dynasty, then you could not voice your opinion. You'd be caught and thrown in jail.' But was it important to her, for example, that newspapers should be free to tell the truth and free to express divergent opinions? 'It is important.' How important? 'Important enough to make me leave, but, having said that, because of our long tradition, I understand why people can feel that it is possible to say, "If I keep out of politics I can be happy." I can understand that.'

Patten's early performance as governor seemed to achieve its pri-mary purpose. A poll conducted by one television station showed over 70 per cent support for his LegCo speech; another sug-gested that almost 50 per cent of the colony thought he should press ahead even if China were to object. Sixty per cent of the respondents to a poll by Radio and Television Hong Kong (RTHK), the government-owned public-service station, said they believed that the proposed reforms were of the right kind and were being advanced at the right pace.

The pro-Chinese press in Hong Kong was predictably hostile, but in the absence of an unequivocal line from Beijing to guide them, they confined their criticism to vague generalities. Two days after the speech, a Chinese Foreign Ministry spokesman was quoted as saying that Beijing would not be held responsible for maintaining the Patten proposals after 1997, while the Hong Kong and Macau Affairs Office said that the SAR government would reverse any changes that were not in line with the Joint Declaration. Five days later, the deputy director of the NCNA accused the governor, without identifying him by name, of 'masquerading as the saviour of Hong Kong' by offering democratic reform and by appearing to commit the Hong Kong government to proceeding with the new airport regardless of Chinese approval. A columnist in the pro-China *Wen Wei Po* argued that Patten's reforms did indeed violate both the Joint Declaration and the Basic Law, which gave China 'the right to discuss matters relating to the smooth transfer of government in 1997 and the right to be involved in the procedures to be adopted for that transition, both of which Patten has ostentatiously overlooked'. The author was a reliable indicator of Beijing's latent paranoia about what he described as the determination of the British government 'to violate the Joint Declaration and to ignore the need for convergence . . . [and] to impose its representative government system on Hong Kong so that after 1997 it could exert the maximum influence and preserve its interests here'.

The attitude of the British press could hardly have been more different, or more reassuring to a governor who always had one eye on reactions at home. *The Times*, in a leading article entitled 'TYPHOON PATTEN', acclaimed the governor for taking 'a calculated political gamble, on the success of which rests Hong Kong's hopes for giving lasting meaning to the "one country, two systems" formula . . . Mr Patten has set out to recapture the policy initiative from Peking, after a decade of defensive British manoeuvring – and to do so, significantly, from Hong Kong. In this pace setting, he has succeeded.' Peppered with words like 'audacious' and 'challenging', it conceded that Patten would have made himself enemies, and that he had yet to demonstrate 'how effective his bulwarks can be made against post-1997 misrule', but its eulogistic conclusion was that the new governor had made 'a brilliant, eloquent debut'. In similar vein, the *Daily Telegraph* prefaced its accolade with a side thrust at the 'succession of Foreign Office mandarins' who had 'bent before every slightest breeze out of Peking, on the grounds that to attempt to answer back would amount to confronting Peking over the Basic Law on the introduction of democracy and might expose the people of Hong Kong to Chinese retribution'. In taking a calculated gamble, Patten had 'dealt brusquely with this attitude. Someone like Mr Patten should have been made governor decades ago.' In the British media no dissenting voice was to be heard.

The foreign secretary rang to offer his congratulations and the prime minister wrote a warm note of appreciation. Moreover, Patten was advised by Number 10 that Major was due to say what the governor judged to be 'some excessively flattering things' about him in his annual speech to the Conservative party conference. Although Patten was duly grateful, he feared that one phrase in the leader's eulogy would be 'misunderstood' in the febrile atmosphere of Hong Kong:

> He's going to say that he looks forward to me returning to British politics in due course, which I would have deleted from the speech if I'd had any choice in the matter. One of the Peking attacks on me is that I'm not doing this for the people of Hong Kong and that I'm just interested in becoming prime minister or foreign secretary or something. But I couldn't conceivably go back to the prime minister and say that . . . even though the likelihood of my returning to British politics is remote.

Fortified by these public and private endorsements from Britain, Patten kept up a whirlwind round of public appearances, media interviews and private meetings with Hong Kong politicians, diplomats and civil servants, maintaining the momentum in the run-up to his official visit to Beijing, which he had announced in his speech. He was due to leave on 19 October, twelve days after his LegCo address. The Chinese, he judged, were 'confused and angry. They don't quite know what I'm up to . . . It is changing the rules of the game to decline to spend the next five years with one hand tied behind your back.' Although he had the impression that at the most sophisticated level they were anxious about the governability of Hong Kong after 1997, and 'paranoid' about Martin Lee, and despite the fact that the pro-Chinese media in Hong Kong had started to be 'pretty vitriolic', he felt confident enough to dismiss this as an orchestrated onslaught by Chinese officials of only passing significance. He was likewise resigned to facing 'one or two little humiliations along the road . . . Remember, the old emperors, if they had a provincial governor who hadn't entirely behaved, used to send a simple peremptory command: "Tremble and obey." And they will want to try to get me to tremble.'

Patten was anxious to try to establish a personal relationship with his opposite number, the director of the Hong Kong and Macau Office, Lu Ping. 'I've got to have one or two people there who at least start to listen to what I say and take me seriously.' He was concerned, too, about Hong Kong's financial and commercial elite. So far their public reaction had been muted, but he was well aware that, 'on the whole, the business community has never been at the forefront of those who believe in democracy'. At this stage, however, he hoped to win over the sceptics.

> The best way of maintaining political stability is by accommodating, in a modest way, people's demands for greater democracy rather than standing up to them for the next five years. The biggest threat to our wellbeing is an outbreak of trade war between China and the US. I will be incomparably more convincing in Washington in arguing the case for a continuation of most-favoured-nation [MFN] status for China if I'm thought by American public opinion and American politicians to be somebody who battles for Hong Kong.

Although Patten had already tried to persuade some leading businessmen of this argument, he was under no illusion that it had carried much weight. Emissaries from the business community had reported their anxieties to him with some precision. The MFN status conferred by the USA on other countries to set quotas and tariffs at favourable levels defined their standard trading relationship with those nations. Around half the world enjoyed MFN status – only pariahs such as North Korea and Cuba were exempt. If the USA were to withdraw MFN status and place higher tariff barriers in the way of Chinese exports, trade between the two states (and others locked into the same system of preferences) would be certain to decline. As the main conduit for the transfer of goods and services between China and the rest of the world, Hong Kong would suffer at once. The prospect that senators and congressmen in the United States, either from a deep-rooted hostility towards communism or from a concern for human rights, might persuade the US administration to remove China's MFN status was the stuff of nightmares for Hong Kong's business leaders. However, their greater fear was that, in the name of democracy, Patten would – from their perspective – goad China into an overreaction that would frighten the markets and lead to a downward economic spiral which might easily run out of control.

Up to a point Patten shared their concern that Chinese officials 'might be able to roar and shout sufficiently loudly to unsettle the market', and he was uncomfortably aware that there were 'certainly a lot of businessmen around with cold feet. But they haven't broken cover yet.'

Vincent Lo was one of those to keep his counsel, despite his misgivings. As chairman of the Hong Kong General Chamber of Commerce and president of the Business and Professionals Federation of Hong Kong (BPF), he confided that most of his members were 'expressing grave concern about [Patten's] proposals and what they would do to Hong Kong'. Although they did not wish to voice their concerns in public, their antagonism towards Patten was deeper than he supposed. 'We hoped that democratisation in Hong Kong would go step by step, not trying to create everything in one go. So I think in that sense we do see eye to eye with China.' At this stage Lo was already certain that Beijing would reject the reforms.

We know that China will react very strongly because we've been dealing with them for years . . . we know that head-on confrontation will not serve our purpose, and we know exactly how China is going to react . . . It's really a myth to think that they will not kill the goose that lays the golden egg. Today, I would say, we need China more than they need us . . . I think we are very close to a breakdown.

Baroness Lydia Dunn, the most senior of Patten's advisers on LegCo, maintained a loyally aloof silence. Although she had none of Lo's ambitious devotion to the Chinese leadership, she shared some of his pessimism. She thought that Beijing must have felt outmanoeuvred by Patten, that they had 'lost face', that they were genuinely angry, and that their sense of paranoia about a 'British conspiracy' would intensify. Although she endorsed Patten's planned reforms, her fear was that China would say 'categorically and publicly, "If you do this we will dismantle whatever you have put in place in 1997." Now, that would be a very serious statement, and it would present us with a major dilemma. It would derail the programme; it would, in fact, destroy everything we're trying to achieve.'

Unlike Vincent Lo, who hoped to see the Patten project derailed, Baroness Dunn was cautiously optimistic that the governor could retain public support. Though sustained by the polls, Patten was permanently anxious about the fragility of the backing he appeared to enjoy. Acutely aware that without popular support his plans would collapse, he knew that he was just as likely to become a 'lame duck' governor for 'confronting' as for 'kowtowing' to China.

> The Chinese have a tactic, which has worked again and again, which is to scare people, scare public opinion – and it's pretty volatile . . . I've got to know Hong Kong as well as you could get to know any place in four months, but I still have no real comprehension of what makes people tick when they are under pressure or what they really want, or how they'll trade off a bit of short-term security for longer-term security.

Moreover, Patten had not given himself much negotiating leeway in Beijing. 'I'm pretty close to my bottom line,' he admitted.

I finessed on two cards they put on the table: no Martin Lee on ExCo – I wouldn't have put him on anyway, but they were terrified about that for some preposterous reason – and no increase in directly elected seats . . . We are still keeping the question of directly elected seats in play, but by and large they've got those cards . . . You could come up with a different form of Election Committee, but for me it would have to be a democratically elected Election Committee. You could talk a bit about functional constituencies . . . but I haven't got much room for manoeuvre.

He had also set himself a very tight timescale: any agreement with Beijing, he thought, would have to be reached quite early in the New Year – less than three months away. And would he delay beyond that? 'No, because otherwise I'll get into endless discussions.' His reluctance to find himself embroiled in such 'endless discussions' sprang from his fear that the longer the talks continued, the more Beijing would gain the upper hand by frightening the men and women on the 'Wanchai omnibus'.

Patten believed that the prospects for reaching an accommodation with China would be greatly enhanced by a change at the top of the communist hierarchy. 'What I find astonishing is to see people behaving in what is so self-evidently not their best interest. There are things one can't say, but does anybody expect that it will be quite the same establishment in 1997 actually running things in Peking?' To hope that key members of the Beijing gerontocracy might meet their maker or fall from grace in the intervening years was perhaps to place undue faith in the fates. Nevertheless, it was widely assumed that the 'paramount leader', Deng Xiaoping, was close to death, and that, after his demise, China would be sufficiently liberated from its political sclerosis to see the light about Hong Kong. In the meantime, Patten had to consider Britain's interests as well as those of Hong Kong. 'What is the sense in me making accommodations – dishonourable accommodations – now on the assumption that the establishment in Peking is going to remain exactly the same until 1997? What would I look like then? I'd be an ornament – and not a very attractive ornament – for most of my time here. And it would all look like a very dishonourable way for Britain to end an important story.'

As he set off for what he was confident would be the first of many visits to the Chinese capital, Patten expected to be on the receiving end of 'a half beating-up', but he was not in a mood to be cowed. 'I think there is a certain awe about dealing with China, which surprises me,' he commented, 'I think they are bullies in that they've got used, over the years, to other countries applying different criteria in their relations with China [from those] they use in their relations with others. I mean, why should one play the game by their rules?' His hope was that, at the end of the encounter, he would be able to invite Lu Ping and others to his country house at Fanling, near the border, for a follow-up meeting. What he was unable to judge, despite the intelligence available to him from Beijing, was whether the Chinese would want to talk seriously, or 'whether they will want to have a break-down and say, "That's it. No point in talking about this any more. Good afternoon."'

Despite his reserves of optimism, it was hardly the most auspicious beginning to what he presumed would be the first of many discussions he would have with China over the next five years.

8

'RESTRAINT IN DIFFICULT CIRCUMSTANCES'

Britain and China at Odds

The governor's visit to Beijing for two days of official talks
began with a snub. Lu Ping was not at the airport to greet
him and sent a junior official instead. Every Chinese with
a smattering of Confucian values knew that the message was
unambiguous, and accordingly the incident was widely reported
in these terms. The governor was resilient and affected indifference the following day.

> The press are frightfully silly about this business of snubs . . .
> Lu Ping had his first meeting of the Central Committee at
> the time. He apologised profusely when we met – actually
> while we were walking past the press – but nobody took a
> blind bit of notice. But even if there were calculated and
> deliberate snubs, the idea that anyone who has been through
> the British political system and lost his seat could actually
> feel frightfully snubbed by not meeting someone or other is
> preposterous.

This was not quite the point. Beijing's carefully calibrated attitude
towards the Patten visit was calculated not so much to affect him
personally as to define the significance the leadership placed on a
visit by a wayward emissary of the outgoing colonial power.
Patten was cushioned from the impact partly by his failure to
appreciate the peculiar obsession that the Chinese have with

'face', and partly by his determination to negotiate on his terms and in his style, regardless of the niceties on which, in his view, the sinologists in the Foreign Office had focused for far too long.

The meeting with Lu Ping took place in a guest house at the government's Diao Yu Tai complex for foreign VIPs. Patten arrived to face a battery of jostling cameras and journalists. He was greeted by a smiling Lu Ping, and the two men proceeded into an elegant chamber, preserving as much dignity as they could amid the almost uncontrollable media excitement. Patten sat opposite Lu Ping at the centre of an oval table, and their respective teams assembled beside them. They delivered themselves of a few pleasantries for the benefit of the cameras and then began a long session of talks punctuated by a brief luncheon. It was, Patten acknowledged the following day, 'six hours of pretty tough grind'.

Although to begin with the meeting with this 'highly intelligent man' was, according to Patten, 'infinitely courteous', their exchanges were rigorous. The governor reiterated his firm belief that his proposals converged with the Basic Law and were within the framework of the Joint Declaration ('I mean, their arguments that we're in breach of the Basic Law are pretty pathetic'), and that they were designed to secure the stability of Hong Kong. It was soon brought home to him that the Chinese disagreed, and that Lu Ping and his colleagues were even more obsessed with Martin Lee, with Hong Kong becoming a focus for unrest in China, and with the consequent threat to their control over Hong Kong, than he had been aware. He reacted by pointing out that 'if they really wanted to ensure that Martin Lee wins every election there is, they'll go on treating him as a demon'. It was also clear to Patten that the Chinese 'thought we'd pulled a fast one on them by finding ways of extending democracy indirectly'.

Lu Ping adopted what Patten called 'fairly familiar language' to charge the British with breaches of the Joint Declaration, the memorandum of understanding on the airport, the Basic Law and 'past understandings', about the last of which he was, at first, imprecise. Patten noticed that his counterpart had a written text before him which he was waiting to introduce into the argument. Lu Ping delayed reading from this until the late afternoon, and when he did so, Patten gained the impression that he 'toned it

down as he went along'. At the end, however, the Chinese negotiator became rather emotional, and as the governor described it
immediately afterwards, 'We had a bit of heat in the argument
and the allegation that we'd broken understandings that we'd
reached in 1989 and 1990.' This was the first and only charge
which Patten felt unable to deny with confidence.

The 'past understandings' to which Lu Ping referred were the
outcome of the secret visits made by Sir Percy Cradock to Beijing
after Tiananmen Square, the subsequent negotiations and an
'exchange of letters' between the foreign secretary and the
Chinese foreign minister in January and February 1990. The specific thrust of Lu Ping's case was that Patten's proposals for the
Election Committee, which he'd announced in his speech to
LegCo, breached these 'understandings', which Douglas Hurd, as
foreign secretary, had reached with the Chinese government. It
was clear to Patten that what he thought to be a 'rather false
point' was one about which Lu Ping felt strongly. The governor's
initial instinct was to ascribe this 'flare-up' to pressure from Lu
Ping's colleagues demanding, 'How's this guy managing to exploit
the Basic Law and the Joint Declaration? You were responsible for
the Basic Law. Why has it got these holes in it?'

The meeting broke up in bad humour. Lu Ping stalked out of
the chamber, pausing only to inform his guest that if the British
could not stick to agreements they had reached in apparent good
faith, then there was precious little point in any dialogue between
the two sides. He declined to set a date for any future meeting.
The British ambassador, Sir Robin McLaren, telegraphed
London afterwards to impart the bad news: the session had been
grim, the atmosphere appalling. Patten, who underestimated the
significance of these 'past understandings' to the Chinese, was less
pessimistic. Looking back on the talks at the end of the day, he
allowed himself a modicum of satisfaction.

When you know you are going to get a rough ride, it's
quite encouraging to discover that even if you have no
saddle and you are going over rather rocky ground, you
know what you are doing. And the most encouraging thing
of all is to find your arguments are pretty good . . . I've been

to European Council meetings, having to put dreadful arguments on things like greenhouse-gas emissions – one against
eleven. Now that's a rough ride, because you are arguing
from a bloody awful brief. You know you are wrong and
you feel cornered. If you feel quite intellectually well
defended, even a rough ride isn't too bad. And I think – I
hope this isn't vainglory – that I've deployed the arguments
pretty well.

Whether or not Lu Ping's 'flare-up' was sincere, the issue which
lay behind it was far more explosive than Patten had either imagined or was in an adequate position to appreciate. In all his
briefings before he left London, no one had referred to these 'past
understandings' or to a correspondence which the Chinese evidently felt to be of genuine significance: not one Foreign Office
official; not the prime minister's adviser, Sir Percy Cradock; not
Sir Robin McLaren, who had drafted the British documents;
nor, indeed, the foreign secretary himself, whose political adviser
in Hong Kong, Alan Galsworthy – on secondment from the
Foreign Office and the author of the FO 'bible' on Hong Kong –
was similarly silent. As a result, Patten had devised his reforms in
ignorance of the exchange of letters between Hurd and Qian
Qichen that had in fact formed the most recent round of a protracted negotiation about an important component of the most
controversial issue facing Hong Kong.

It was only by chance that, a mere two days before the
Government House team set off for Beijing, one of Patten's advisers, Edward Llewellyn, making a final trawl through the papers
relating to earlier negotiations with China, came across a brief reference to a set of telegrams of which he and his colleagues had
not previously been aware. Thus alerted, Llewellyn contacted the
Foreign Office, where an official in the Hong Kong Department
drew his attention to the existence of this buried and apparently
forgotten correspondence. It was at this point that Patten learned
of the predicament in which he had been placed. It was, to put it
mildly, a most remarkable gap in his knowledge, and one that he
could not possibly acknowledge, at least in public. If the truth
were to emerge, his colleagues in the Foreign Office, including

those sinologists seconded to Hong Kong, would be open to the charge of negligence and the Chinese would be handed a devastating propaganda coup. In the process, his own credibility, through no fault of his own, would be severely dented, while the validity of his reforms would assuredly be called even more sharply into question, even by those inclined to endorse them.

For this reason Patten's only public reference to this embarrassing discovery was made fifteen months later, in testimony before the Foreign Affairs Select Committee. On 20 January 1994, he volunteered that his reforms had been the product of 'extensive' discussions with a wide range of people and 'some months of advice' from his advisers in Hong Kong and officials in London. He was asked by the committee's chairman, David Howell: 'You had seen at that stage all the exchanges between Mr Hurd and the Chinese foreign minister, and these were known to you and your advisers fully?' Patten replied:

They were completely known to my advisers, because some of my advisers had taken part, not least in drafting the exchanges. I read in detail all the exchanges before I went to Peking for the discussions that I had with Director Lu Ping shortly after my LegCo speech. My officials, I repeat, were well aware of the exchanges and therefore they were taken into account in framing my proposals in the October speech.

This was not strictly true: neither Leo Goodstadt nor Mike Hanson, who between them had drafted most of the speech, had any knowledge of these contentious documents.

Patten's response was carefully crafted to protect his officials. To his relief, the committee did not take the matter further. Nobody thought to draw attention to Patten's tacit admission that he had not himself been aware of these exchanges in drafting his proposals, or to ask how, in that case, he could be so certain that they had been taken into account when he was preparing his blueprint. Nor was he questioned about when he had seen the documents, or how detailed his study of the material might have been in the few hours available to him before his meeting with Lu Ping.

In fact Patten had had almost no time to assess the importance of the secret negotiations which had led to the 1990 exchange of letters – and certainly not enough to prepare an informed or detailed rebuttal. As a result he went into the meeting prepared to counter any thrust from his Chinese counterpart, but knowing that he had little choice other than to treat the documents as if they were of peripheral importance. He could not possibly concede that his proposals might have been framed in different terms had he been in a position, three months earlier, to form a clear judgement about the status and role which each side had attached to them. Afterwards, Patten reflected, 'It would, I suppose – particularly when I was under a lot of pressure on all of this – have been easier to dump on officials and say, "If I'd known about this it could all have been different."' Although he was furious about this oversight, and it led him to doubt the competence of the relevant officials at the Foreign Office, he also castigated himself for failing to ask whether there were any agreements with the Chinese beyond those limiting the number of directly elected seats to LegCo, on which he had been fully briefed. Although his distrust of the Foreign Office was to grow, Patten was somewhat mollified when the head of the Hong Kong Department, Peter Ricketts – one of the few officials whom he both liked and respected – apologised profusely for his department's failure.

The importance of the correspondence was soon to become a matter of very public and acrimonious debate. Later in the year, the Foreign Office took the unprecedented step of releasing the full text of the disputed, and hitherto secret, papers. This decision was not taken, as the Foreign Office claimed, in the cause of open government, but to pre-empt a leak from the Chinese side. As it was, the British beat them by a mere four hours. It was enough time, however, for Mike Hanson to 'spin' the significance of the documents – momentarily, at least – to Patten's advantage. The British hoped, somewhat desperately, that by giving the appearance of openness they would avoid being put on the defensive by Beijing. In the short term the tactic was partially successful. Few people bothered to read the papers in detail, so, while the conflicting gloss put on their contents by the rival camps carried weight with their own respective supporters, most chose to interpret the row as yet another illustration of the propensity of diplomats to squabble over fine print.

The correspondence consisted of eight letters in all, comprising, for the most part, an attempt by both sides to find a compromise over the rate at which directly elected seats to the Legislative Council should be introduced. In the second of these letters, Douglas Hurd wrote, 'We are not far apart on directly elected seats,' which, it had been agreed by both sides, would reach thirty, or 50 per cent of the total, by 2003. Two letters later, in the same context, the foreign secretary stated: 'I am now able to confirm an understanding with the Chinese government.' Subject only to the proviso that the Chinese included their commitment to this understanding in the Basic Law, which they were already disposed to do, the two sides evidently had a deal. To this extent, the 'exchange of letters' clearly had the status of at least a heads of agreement.

The correspondence dealt similarly with the role and composition of the Election Committee. In his third, and most technically detailed, letter, the foreign secretary suggested five principles which he thought 'could best form the framework for creating an Election Committee system for the legislature'. These included the principles that the Election Committee should be as representative as possible, and that the procedure for the nomination by the Election Committee should be simple, open and prescribed in the electoral law. Nowhere, however, did the five principles prescribe that the 'representative' character of the Election Committee should be secured by a process of democratic elections. This was presumably why the Chinese foreign minister felt free to respond that, 'with regard to the Electoral Committee, the Chinese side agrees with the five principles proposed by the British side'. It must be assumed that for the Chinese, the 'representative' nature of the Election Committee could be achieved as effectively – and certainly more desirably – by a process of selection rather than election.

The British also argued that no member of the Chinese National People's Congress should be allowed to sit on the Election Committee. On this point, the Chinese foreign minister was adamant: the composition of the Election Committee 'should not be subject to change', because it had already been endorsed by the Basic Law Drafting Committee. In response, the foreign secretary noted: 'I agree in principle with the arrangements you propose for an Electoral Committee which could be established in 1995. The precise details of how this should be done can be discussed between our two sides in due course. Meanwhile, I hope that the five principles to which you have agreed can be reflected in the Basic Law.' It was this 'agreement in principle' which formed the basis of – or the excuse for – China's charge that the Patten proposals had violated a clear understanding between the two sovereign powers.

While the foreign secretary could not be held to have made any secret deal, his 'agreement in principle' and his commitment to discuss the 'precise details' of how the Election Committee might be established for the 1995 elections, is clearly far from the non-committal exchange of views that the British side now tried to claim their correspondence to have been. Certainly, while there were important questions which had yet to be resolved, it was disingenuous of the Foreign Office to claim that 'at the end of these exchanges, the question of electoral arrangements in Hong Kong up to 1997 remained open'. Not closed perhaps, but hardly open. As Mike Hanson noted cryptically soon afterwards, the words 'agreement in principle' had caused the governor 'particular difficulty'. Hanson and his embarrassed colleagues now recognised that parts of the Basic Law had been drafted as if there had been an agreement between the two sides: a 'specific performance' to which contract lawyers, in other circumstances, would attach great importance.

The schism between Britain and China over this exchange of letters was echoed, discreetly but at the highest level, within the British foreign policy establishment as well. Six years later, Douglas Hurd was to maintain:

[I was] amazed later to hear it suggested that that exchange of letters was thought to govern the framework for the second round [1995] of legislative elections. They never did in my mind. Obviously, we were going to need to consult the Chinese about the second round, but that was common sense . . . But I never supposed that my hands or my successor's hands were tied by what had happened in 1990 as to what would happen in the second round.

However, Sir Percy Cradock has insisted that at the time his interpretation of the letters was that:

> Both sides regarded them as of great significance. The Chinese finalised their Basic Law on the strength of them. And in conjunction with the Joint Declaration of 1984, the 1990 exchange of letters constituted, you might say, a constitutional and political settlement for Hong Kong . . . and I venture to think this was the view of other figures on the British side at that time . . . There is no doubt at all that the thing was regarded by China as being a settlement on which they could build. And they were taken aback and felt they had been sandbagged when we said this wasn't a settlement, and we were going to do something else.

Significantly, Cradock's interpretation was to be endorsed by Hurd's predecessor, Sir Geoffrey (now Lord) Howe, who helped finalise the terms of the Joint Declaration. Choosing his words with the caution for which he has long been renowned, he said in 1996 of Patten's proposals:

> I must say I was startled when I heard of the proposal to reshape and redefine the flightpath towards democracy which had been agreed in correspondence, which had been embodied, as I understand it, in the Basic Law as a fulfilment of the Joint Declaration . . . I think the attempt to change that by redefining some of the components – turning oranges into apples – could certainly be regarded as a departure from the spirit of the Joint Declaration.

Douglas Hurd is dismissive of that view, arguing instead that what really angered the Chinese about Patten's proposals was not so much their content but that their author had failed to conduct negotiations with them on the same terms as before. It is this issue, according to Hurd, which goes to the heart of the whole disagreement he and Patten had with Cradock. In Hurd's opinion it would not have been either right or possible to discuss these matters 'week after week, month after month, in secret', and to inform the people of Hong Kong of the outcome only at the end of a negotiating process from whose terms they had been entirely excluded. 'Certainly the Chinese had rights. They had the right to express a view. But they didn't have a right to insist that that view must be expressed in secret.' To which argument Cradock, supported by Howe in very similar language, has retorted, 'I'm afraid it doesn't lie with us to shuffle off responsibility for Hong Kong on to Hong Kong public opinion which we have helped to create. In the end, we are responsible for Hong Kong up to the last minute of the handover, and it's for us to negotiate with the Chinese. They will only talk to us. They will take no account of Hong Kong, LegCo or the like.'

Underlying this conflict was another, which was sharper and of greater significance. While Cradock genuinely believed that the virtue of secret negotiation was that it allowed the British diplomats to clothe their retreat to China's 'bottom line' with some dignity, Patten, supported by Major and Hurd, was equally convinced that open diplomacy was a precondition for securing public support in Hong Kong for whatever might be agreed in Beijing.

Whatever the case, there can be no doubt that the belated discovery of the 1990 correspondence caused severe embarrassment to the governor. Already committed to proposals for the Election Committee which had been explicitly rejected by the Chinese, he was now exposed to the charge that he had consciously ridden roughshod over the delicate understandings reached between the foreign secretary and the Chinese foreign minister. Moreover, he had been obliged to defend his corner against a sustained and angry barrage from the Chinese, who had at their disposal chapter and verse from the foreign secretary's own pen, which appeared to commit the British to continuing the dialogue between the two sides in a similarly confidential form. It was clearly open to the Chinese to argue that the same 'principle' applied, implicitly, to all the outstanding questions relating to the 1995 elections, not least the most controversial of them: the functional constituencies.

Quite why Patten was not informed of the existence of a formal exchange of correspondence dealing with matters of substance and sensitivity remains unclear. Douglas Hurd believes that there must have been an oversight by Foreign Office officials. 'Chris was not told of them, and I was not reminded of them,' he later recalled. 'It never occurred to officials that there was a read-across from one negotiation to the other. But they should have told him. I mean, he was a newcomer to it. They should have told him of that background, and they should have reminded me of that background.' Sir Percy Cradock, who had two meetings with Patten before the governor took up his appointment, has also acknowledged that he failed to raise the exchange of letters, but he claimed that 'everybody' knew about them, and that 'it was inconceivable that a governor going out to Hong Kong would not have had all of these documents in front of him, and have read them several times. And indeed, many of my comments related to them.'

Patten was not persuaded by Cradock's apologia. 'I think if they were significant to the democratic development of Hong Kong, it's amazing that Sir Percy didn't mention them to me, because he has an all-embracing knowledge of these matters,' he commented later, adding icily: 'Except, of course, that since he doesn't believe there's any commitment to the democratic development of Hong Kong, perhaps he put it to one side.'

It is common ground between Patten and Cradock – almost the only common ground – that Cradock warned the new governor against any attempt to increase the number of directly elected seats, but that he failed to explore with him the implications of tampering unilaterally with the Election Committee. Patten's only public reference to this failure was made, again, in front of the Select Committee. He said then, with strained jocularity: 'When we discussed the difficulties we might have in putting in place electoral arrangements . . . Sir Percy never said to me: "You can forget about any other ideas on political development, old boy. We have agreed all that with the Chinese side. That is all cut and dried. We have had these exchanges with the Chinese side. Everybody has agreed the way forward."'

In a letter to the Foreign Affairs Committee written soon after that testimony, Cradock stated that the main subject of his comments in their conversation had been the 'very limited room we had for manoeuvre, given the existing agreements, which we both understood as meaning in particular the Joint Declaration and the agreement on elected seats of 1990'. He went on: 'My remarks concentrated on directly elected seats because at that time [May 1992] they seemed the problem area. There was no inkling at that time of the plan to circumvent existing agreements.' Patten has since insisted to friends that he made it clear in the meeting with Cradock that he intended to 'look at' ways of reforming the Election Committee, but that Cradock – otherwise so free with his advice – dispensed none at all on this matter.

Although the issue refused to go away, Patten was never to take the view that his ignorance of the exchange of letters had any lasting effect on the crisis in Sino–British relations which followed his visit to Beijing. And in Hong Kong, opinion polls showed that the governor had not been damaged in this skirmish. Convinced from early on that any attempt on his part to establish a fair and open electoral system within the framework of the Joint Declaration and the Basic Law was bound to lead to a row with China in any case, he was unrepentant. Even if he had been in a position to take account of the correspondence in drafting his reforms, it is inconceivable that he would have been willing to modify them either in character or on a scale that would have had any serious impact on the conflict. But there can be no doubt that he would have accommodated the weight given to the exchange of letters by both sides: at the very least, as he has acknowledged to the author, he would have couched his reforms in language which made it clear that he was aware that there had been a set of significant, if indeterminate, negotiations, and that he was not insensitive to them.

On the second day of his official visit to Beijing, the governor met the vice-foreign minister, Jiang Enzhu, who was later to become Chinese ambassador in London. This meeting went no better than the one with Lu Ping, though it was much shorter. According to Patten, the Chinese made it clear that their opposition to his proposals was pretty much root and branch. At one point during a tough exchange, the governor could not resist reminding his interlocutor that, 'Hong Kong, unlike other places, is a place where there hasn't been any social turmoil or political instability for twenty-five years . . . And you worry about instability in Hong Kong in the future? My proposals are likely to produce even more stability.' The message was plain: the Cultural Revolution and Tiananmen Square had not occurred in Hong Kong.

That evening, at the end of an even frostier meeting with the foreign minister, Qian Qichen, Patten was told, 'After our prime minister, Li Peng, saw your prime minister in Rio, we had great hopes of you. But it is clear we have to discuss these matters at foreign secretary or prime-ministerial level in order to resolve these problems.' Undeterred by this put-down, which he chose to ignore, Patten commented afterwards:

> I just thought it was a sign of weakness. There isn't going to be any difference between what John Major says and what I say. And that's one of the things that bothers them, I guess . . . I've made it plain that co-operate means co-operate and consult means consult. Co-operate doesn't mean we'll do anything they want, and consult doesn't mean they've got a veto on anything. It's come as a shock.

Patten suspected that some members of the Chinese team may have wanted a 'complete breach' and to have walked away, which, he acknowledged, would have been unsettling. He was relieved, therefore, by the foreign minister's suggestion that the dialogue should continue, albeit in a forum which would exclude his own participation. Conceding that 'they won't give up, and, in that sense, I don't know where it will end', he had at least averted a total breakdown in communications. Or so he thought.

That evening Patten returned to the embassy to discover that the foreign minister's personal rebuff had already been reported to 10 Downing Street, where the prime minister had become so incensed on his friend's behalf that he had instructed the Foreign Office to withdraw the invitation to the Chinese vice-premier, Zhu Rongji, who was due to arrive in London for an official

ministerial visit within the next fortnight. Appalled by the collapse of diplomatic relations which this would herald, a senior
official in the Foreign Office at once rang the British embassy in
Beijing in the hope of persuading Patten to try to talk the prime
minister out of a decision which, he stressed, would 'send a deteriorating relationship into nosedive'.

Patten did not need to be persuaded. He was soon at the
switchboard, surrounded by his own team and the British ambassador, who, summoned from his shower, was swathed in a
dressing gown, his hair standing on end. Patten was unable to
speak to John Major personally as he was chairing Thursday's regular Cabinet meeting. Instead he talked to Jonathan Hill, one of
the prime minister's political secretaries. Expressing his gratitude
for the prime minister's concern but his horror at what was proposed, Patten urged Hill to ask Major on his behalf to rescind his
decision. 'What has happened today,' he told Hill, 'is that they
have agreed to further discussions. They've been very tough, but
they haven't broken everything off. We've actually come out of it
pretty well . . . and not looking too battered and bruised.' He
spoke slowly and deliberately but with urgency. If the Chinese
were to be rebuffed in the way proposed by the prime minister,
he said, 'I think it would bring matters to a head in such a way
that it would be more difficult for me to hold public opinion in
Hong Kong. It would be regarded with incredulity by the people
of Hong Kong, as gratuitously offensive. It would actually lose me
support rather than gain it. That is my very strong advice.'

The problem was, as Patten knew only too well, that once a
prime-ministerial instruction has been issued it acquires the
authority of an edict. The governor told Hill that if necessary he
would take the first plane to London to explain his case more
fully. 'I'd be very grateful if you would say to him that you hope
nothing final would be done until I've managed to make my
position clear. I think that would be fatal. All right?'

Within thirty minutes, Patten was in the embassy drawing
room exchanging pleasantries with the ambassador's guest of
honour for that evening's banquet, Lu Ping. Meanwhile his political adviser, Edward Llewellyn, was on the phone to Stephen
Wall, the prime minister's foreign-affairs adviser, who had left the

Cabinet room to take the call. Wall reminded Llewellyn that the prime minister's instruction could not easily be countermanded, explaining: 'The PM said that he knew the governor would object or protest that the PM had no need to go to such extremes on his behalf, but that we should go ahead regardless.' However, Wall, appreciating Patten's predicament, agreed to raise the issue again. Slipping back into the Cabinet meeting, he gave Major a note summarising the governor's views. When the prime minister was told that Patten was ready to bring his case to London, he relented, scribbling 'OK' on Wall's message. The immediate crisis was over.

Yet the signs were far from promising. From his vantage point in Beijing, Robin McLaren had been pessimistic from the moment Patten had decided to ignore the Chinese demand that he discuss his proposals with them in secret before announcing them to the world. Nor did he refrain from advising the new governor accordingly.

> I certainly made clear that they wouldn't like it. The Chinese were warned beforehand of exactly what he was going to say. Their reaction was, 'Don't do it.' It was inevitable that they would react badly once we ignored that advice . . . Now the governor was faced with a very difficult dilemma . . . but he was pretty well aware that the Chinese reaction would be extremely hostile. I think he probably thought he could wear that, but that in due course, after time and with difficulty, the Chinese might be persuaded to enter into discussions.

McLaren did not share Patten's optimism, but he did not attempt to dissuade him from the course of action he had proposed. 'You can give advice, but I think that the ambassador's role should not be, "You should not do this." That is, if at all, for ministers in London to do. The ambassador's role is to say, "If you do this, these are likely to be the consequences."' And that, repeatedly, is exactly what McLaren had done. It did not endear him to Patten's team at Government House, one or two of whom had taken to calling him, rather unfairly, the 'White Rabbit'.

Nevertheless, Patten's advisers were impressed by the performance of McLaren and his aides throughout the talks. 'We
suspect that they don't like the governor's package very much,
and that most of them are very uncomfortable with what's going
on,' Mike Hanson confided after the first day of talks. 'They
would never have recommended it, but they have been incredibly professional about it. Patten has had superb support from
the embassy this week . . . One could have expected a lot of I-
told-you-so noises from them, particularly after the meeting with
Lu Ping. And we didn't have any of that.' And Patten himself
was swift to acknowledge that McLaren had been extremely
supportive.

The events of the previous forty-eight hours had confirmed all
McLaren's instincts. As he waited to receive his guest, Lu Ping,
the ambassador stood unhappily in the foyer of the embassy and
forecast for the future record the next move from the Chinese
side:

> They will say, I think, 'If the governor won't listen to reason,
> then we will do our own thing in 1997. We will form the
> legislature in accordance with the provisions of the Basic
> Law . . .' In other words, you can do what you like in 1995,
> but there will be no through train. It won't continue . . .
> And then they will try, through their propaganda, to
> frighten LegCo off so that it doesn't pass the necessary leg-
> islation, and to frighten public opinion. In the meantime,
> they won't reach agreement over the airport, either. So there
> will be a feeling that there is no progress on any front. So it
> will be pretty hard for the governor to maintain leader-
> ship . . . The question is, will the Hong Kong people follow
> when the Chinese turn the heat on?

The ambassador's customary telegram to London reporting on
the visit included these points, and was, according to its author, 'a
description from me of the extent of Chinese anger that was
exhibited during the governor's visit . . . saying that this is something we have to take account of in planning where we go from
here'. This was not how his missive was interpreted by the

governor, who, according to members of his entourage, regarded it privately as 'McLaren's surrender document', adding with heavy sarcasm that the part which he had most enjoyed was the advice that the British should pay reparations to the Chinese to make amends for their governor's egregious behaviour. According to his officials, Patten's irritation with the telegram lay less with McLaren's account of what had occurred than with his implicit prescription that, 'in the light of these grim circumstances, the only course of action I can see is to find out whether the proposals can be changed without surrendering their central character'.

The governor was dismayed by the British diplomat's eagerness to make concessions so quickly. He was also perplexed by McLaren's assumption that such concessions might secure an agreement with the Chinese, even if the proposals could be amended 'without destroying their central character', which he thought extremely unlikely. McLaren's view, which was widely shared by his senior colleagues in the Foreign Office, was that the governor's stance had been ill judged and that now, before it was too late, he should step back from the democratic brink to arrest the inevitable sharp deterioration in Sino–British relations. To Patten's team, the McLaren telegram embodied all that they most despised about the traditional Foreign Office approach to China.

Patten was furious when the broad thrust of this 'surrender document' somehow found its way from the Foreign Office into the British press. 'I don't honestly think it was Robin McLaren, but I think there are those in the embassy in Peking who've been muttering in that way,' he said. He was more irritated by the fact that more than one foreign diplomat in Hong Kong had told him, 'Some of our officials in Peking are critical of the approach we've been taking on Hong Kong.' He did not approve of such loose talk, especially as no British diplomat had offered such a view to his face. Was there no suggestion from any of them that he had got it wrong? 'No,' Patten replied.

He thought it imperative to conceal any friction in the British camp. Patten had left the Chinese capital secure in the belief that the embassy and his own Government House team had managed to put a constructive gloss on what everyone who had been

closely involved recognised to be a damaging stand-off between
Britain and China. Before going off to brief the media, Patten
told Mike Hanson, 'You want them to say that we've done rather
well to avoid a breakdown.'

Hanson suggested dryly, 'Restraint in difficult circumstances?'
The governor laughed, and repeated the phrase approvingly in
mock-Churchillian tones. 'We want to get the message out
that . . . we've had a very severe exchange of views but the relationship is intact,' Hanson explained. 'We can talk to each other.
We haven't taken the phone off the hook . . . that's what we want
to get out, because all the instincts of the press in Hong Kong are
to declare a breakdown.'

The only light relief in a dismal forty-eight hours came at the
dinner for Lu Ping, when the governor accidentally tipped his
pudding into his guest's lap. As the staff rushed to make amends,
the governor rescued the moment by recalling a similar incident
at Chequers in which Sir Geoffrey Howe was the victim.
Margaret Thatcher had been swift to offer her commiserations –
to the waitress.

As the governor's party departed for Hong Kong, Lu Ping
held a press conference in which, for the first time, he publicly
made clear the extent of the Chinese government's anger. In his
'post-visit blast', as the US secretary of state George Schultz had
once described this Chinese ritual to Patten, the director of the
Hong Kong and Macau Affairs office said:

> We do not want to make public the differences between our
> sides. Before Mr Patten made public his policy address, the
> Chinese government said he should not make public his
> proposals. He should not engage in microphone diplomacy
> and he should not stir up a public debate between the two
> sides . . . Regrettably, however, Mr Patten simply did not
> take into account the views of the Chinese side. He believed
> he should make public our difference. Since he did that we
> have to do the same. In my letters to him I told him that if
> he starts to stir up an open debate then we have to partici-
> pate in this debate . . . The essence of our differences is not
> whether the pace of democracy should be accelerated but

whether there will still be co-operation or confrontation. If the other side insists on confrontation we have no other choice.

It was the declaration of diplomatic war which McLaren had foreseen, and to which Patten now had to find a response.

9

'THE CRIMINAL
OF ALL TIME'

Beijing Campaigns Against
the Governor

On 28 October 1992, a week after the governor's return
from Beijing, a senior executive from one of Hong
Kong's most important companies was invited to breakfast at the NCNA, Beijing's headquarters in Hong Kong
Afterwards he wrote a confidential note to his colleagues about
what he billed dryly as a 'discussion among old friends', which
was in truth used by his hosts to launch a sustained diatribe against
the governor:

> They said that Sino–British relations were at the lowest
> point since the signing of the Joint Declaration. The main
> focus was on CP himself: 'He totally lacks sincerity. Had no
> understanding of China. No understanding of the back-
> ground of a 150-year relationship and did not understand
> the character of the Chinese people.' They had warned sev-
> eral times through various channels against letting this
> situation arise and were very sorry about it as the losers
> would be the people of Hong Kong . . . It was a great pity
> that with relations recovering from the events of 1989, there
> now had to be this setback. The top leaders in Beijing were
> very upset. It was surprising to them that British business
> groups in Hong Kong had been appearing to support CP as
> his proposals would be to their long-term detriment.'

The threat this predictable view contained was characteristically blatant. It also signalled the beginning of a sustained assault against the governor with the clear purpose of undermining his credibility and forcing his departure from Hong Kong. In the closing weeks of 1992, the Chinese escalated their campaign, using ever more strident and vituperative language. Patten fought to maintain his public support while worrying his way through the narrow range of options available to him.

This public excoriation of Patten, which he chose to describe without great conviction as 'background noise', was peculiarly crude and, to a Western mind honed on the invective of Swift or Voltaire, faintly ridiculous as well. How was it possible to take seriously a regime whose mouthpieces chose to denounce the governor of Hong Kong variously as a 'sly lawyer', a 'dirty trickster' a 'clown', a 'tango dancer', a 'strutting prostitute', a 'serpent', an 'assassin', and – Patten's own favourite – the 'Triple Violator'. Lu Ping himself was quoted as saying that 'in the history of Hong Kong the governor should be regarded as the criminal of all time'. These insults seemed more suited to the bar or the playground, yet to patronise Beijing's rhetoric was to miss the point.

As a measurement of China's mood and its determination to unnerve the Hong Kong public, the shrillness of this diatribe, echoed day after day by mainland spokesmen or by unnamed sources in Hong Kong's Beijing-controlled Chinese press, at least demonstrated that the communist leadership was in earnest. Although Patten's personal ratings withstood the onslaught, support for his proposals slipped sharply. By the late autumn, as Sir Robin McLaren had warned, it was not at all clear that the community would stand by him. In a poll taken in mid-November for the *South China Morning Post*, 48 per cent of respondents, compared with 19 per cent a month earlier, said that Patten should abandon his package rather than proceed and thereby derail the through train. Likewise, offered the choice between the governor's blueprint and an agreement on the new airport, a choice which Patten had explicitly rejected, 46 per cent opted for the airport. At the same time the Hang Seng Index, which was monitored with all the care physicians bestow on a severe case of cardiac infarction, began to falter as investors either took fright or realised that it was time to play the market. Hamish McLeod, the financial secretary, was obliged to call a press conference on 19 November. 'I will just say that we must keep things in perspective,' he said. 'Investors should be calm.' But analysts took a different view, prompting the *South China Morning Post* to warn, 'MARKET BRACED FOR NERVOUS SWINGS'. For the first time, China had the upper hand in the propaganda war against Patten.

The chairman of Wheelock, Peter Woo, one of the most influential members of the business elite, had been consulted by the governor on several occasions, and his wife Bessie had become Lavender Patten's golfing companion. They were frequent visitors to Government House and the Pattens liked to think of them as friends. But Woo was also an ambitious man with a highly developed sense of his own worth, who, even by the rapacious standards of Hong Kong, enjoyed a reputation for ruthlessness which had endeared him to very few of his peers. Whatever his personal regard for Patten might have been, he did not allow it to cloud his judgement or perspective. Discreet to the point of opacity in public, he was more forthcoming for the historical record. The essential character of the relationship between Hong Kong and China, he insisted, was economic and financial. All the rest – democracy and human rights, though of course they were not without value – was of secondary importance. Any threat to Hong Kong's role as a 'conveyor-belt' for international trade was, by definition, bad for Hong Kong. The governor's proposals would, he feared, place Hong Kong 'in a very difficult position'.

Justifying the mounting, but still discreet, criticism of Patten by the business community, the Wheelock chairman explained that the effect of the stand-off with China was 'negative'.

> Hong Kong has its own economic agenda and this agenda is being disrupted. We hope that it is not severe. We hope that it is short. But that's hoping. And businessmen don't plan their businesses on hope . . . And that is why the stock market went down . . . It also affects banks. When banks feel uncomfortable they may go back to a borrower and say,

'Look, the margin has shrunk. We may need some more margin.' And this is a sort of momentum; a downward spiral.

At the same time, through the good offices of the NCNA, Beijing started to seed the thought in briefings for business leaders, newspaper editors and sympathetic commentators that Patten's departure was a prerequisite for the restoration of normal relations. As a result, the refrain 'Patten must go' was soon being whispered around the corridors of financial and commercial power. Vincent Lo, the president of the Business and Professionals Federation of Hong Kong, was swift to pass the whisper along. Although the BPF, which listed 130 of Hong Kong's most important companies among its membership, claimed to be non-aligned, it never strayed far from the Beijing stance. While very few of them would speak their minds openly, the luminaries on the BPF's Executive Committee were among Patten's most formidable critics. On 4 November, they had agreed a draft 'position paper' repudiating the proposed reforms and urging the governor to return to the status quo ante. When the paper was released a few days later, it was front-page news. Its publication confirmed the general impression that Patten had 'lost' Hong Kong's business elite. At a press conference on 9 November, Vincent Lo became the first business leader to voice the majority view: 'Democracy is important, but it is not the only goal. A smooth transition is more important.' In private, Lo claimed: 'Even people in the street are asking, "Is he really doing this for us? What is he after? . . . Why should we gamble our future when he says it is just a slight and modest increase in democracy? Why do we have to face all this?"'

As if that were not enough, the rumblings of opposition in the Foreign Office began to find a public outlet in Britain. Among others, the former governor Lord MacLehose emerged from obscurity in the same month to inform his colleagues in the Upper House at Westminster: 'I greatly admire the way in which Mr Patten has endeared himself to people in Hong Kong in such a very short time.' But, he added, they should know that the reforms he had proposed would be 'quite valueless' to them unless they could be carried through 1997. 'Having so much in common with the Chinese government over Hong Kong, is it not a great pity that this dispute has developed into what amounts to a major confrontation?' he asked witheringly. Patten's critics in the Lords were joined by a motley group of backbenchers in the Commons, members of his own party who had identified themselves as 'friends of China' and whose egos were heavily massaged by the hospitality bestowed on them whenever they visited Beijing. The most prominent of these was the former prime minister Sir Edward Heath, who was regarded by the intelligentsia in Hong Kong with some contempt. He was known to fall asleep at dinners given in his honour and had a reputation for delivering himself of the most portentous inanities, of which the most notable was his judgement of the Tiananmen Square massacre: 'Probably the students ought to have been told to go home before Mr Gorbachev arrived.' Heath was churlish and rude to those who ventured to prick his certainties with an alternative view of the gerontocracy in Beijing of which he was so ineffably enamoured.

In this febrile atmosphere, Patten flew to London towards the end of November for a highly publicised set of meetings with the foreign secretary and the prime minister – both of whom, like the governor, had underestimated the Chinese reaction to the proposed reforms. Patten reflected ruefully, 'It's certainly at the noisier end of what we were anticipating. And that is, I think, because Deng Xiaoping is himself said to have taken an interest. There is some evidence that he's muttered a few words into his daughter's tape-recorder and that he has said there must be no compromise with the British.' On the other hand, Patten found it hard to believe that Beijing would manage to 'keep up the decibel count indefinitely . . . It's a problem to keep up the same level of hysteria for two, three, four years.'

The ferocity of Beijing's assault was disconcerting, but he was determined not to be swayed by it. 'I don't think one ever cares much for a storm raging around one's head,' he confessed, 'but on this occasion, since I think we're doing the right thing, I don't find it unendurable.' He was far more concerned about the brittle frailty of public opinion in Hong Kong. On the basis of anecdote and intelligence available to him, Patten maintained that he knew 'for an eighteen-carat fact' that China was overtly blackmailing the business community with 'old-fashioned threats and intimidation'. The Chinese, he said, were warning them: 'Unless you denounce Patten and all his works, you'll have great difficulty in getting this or that franchise after 1997. You'll have great difficulty doing business in Guangdong.'

The governor was in no doubt that the business elite could be 'very dangerous'. It had the potential to undermine public confidence to the point where the wider community might conclude that 'the game's just not worth the candle. I am worried by the danger of them driving a wedge not between me and the UK government, but between me and the people of Hong Kong . . . I've also got to stop the sniping getting completely out of hand. I mean, there is a lot of "get the governor" in it all; the illusion that somehow it's my policy, and that if ever they get rid of me everything will return to normality.' The trip to London was, in large measure, designed to counteract that threat. 'It is essential to set in concrete the government's support for what we are doing and to prevent any backsliding,' he confided. 'I think the prime minister and the foreign secretary intend to manifest their support for me in a pretty straightforward way. I think the foreign secretary will want to make it clear to one or two people who are starting to suggest, if not that we offer reparations, at least that we should start throwing away bits of policy . . . that this is not on.' Patten himself was in no mood to back off.

> I don't think that there is a great mystique about foreign policy, and about representing what you believe to be in your own interests. I think that diplomacy is sometimes identified as having a comfortable ride and avoiding rows and avoiding fuss, which isn't very sensible if you are dealing with people who don't care about having a fuss or a bumpy ride. If that's diplomacy, you always lose out . . . I think the Chinese are bullies. I think there's a certain amount of awe in dealing with China, which surprises me. Why should one play the game entirely by their rules? Why should one accept their definition of what a 'principled position' is or what 'consultation' is? We wouldn't do it with others, so

why should we do it with China? If being a sinologist is taking that view, then I'm quite glad I'm not a sinologist.

Although Patten's immediate predecessor, Sir David (now Lord) Wilson, had been more circumspect than Lord MacLehose, he was known to share similar reservations. Likewise, Sir Alan Donald, who had preceded Sir Robin McLaren as ambassador to China – although an altogether less substantial player than the others involved – made no secret of his aversion to Patten. Sir Percy Cradock's bitter hostility was also well known in Whitehall. One or two officials in the Foreign Office had been so indiscreet that even the foreign minister of Canada had got wind of the conflict within the British camp, a fact which, Patten pointed out grimly, was 'pretty remarkable'. He had little patience with any of these critics.

> Presumably they think they left a policy which was in perfect shape, which helped to produce this jewel in Hong Kong, and that what I'm doing may wreck that inheritance. It's also possible, I suppose, that some of them think that if the policy we're pursuing succeeds, it may raise question-marks about the approach that's been taken in the past . . . In the past the assumption has been that really China has all the cards and that the bottom line has to be getting on with China and accepting finally whatever China's world view is . . . I think it is not self-evidently the case that whatever China wants, China must get.

Indeed, oddly, if not perversely, Patten began to derive added strength from his Foreign Office detractors. It was almost as if to be attacked by sinologists was a mark of honour. As for dealing with 'old warhorses' like MacLehose, Patten liked to borrow Stanley Baldwin's adage: 'When you've left the bridge, you shouldn't spit on the deck.' He added: 'I think one or two of the most distinguished governors would have been outraged if their predecessors had criticised what they were up to. It just doesn't seem to me that that's an acceptable way of behaving in public life.'

Nonetheless, the effect of this muffled cacophony of offstage mutterings against him threatened to exacerbate Patten's difficulties. 'I shall have a word with senior officials in the Foreign Office and the secretary of state. To be fair, I don't think there are many people within the diplomatic service who are doing this. I think it's done by senior officials in London.' *The Times* noted with dismay the number of 'old friends' of Beijing who had clustered around the Chinese vice-premier, Zhu Rongji, whose trip to London, saved from cancellation by Patten's intervention, had been timed to overlap with that of the governor. On 20 November, the paper's leading article commented with acerbity:

> Many of them echo Peking's complaints that Mr Patten should have asked China's permission before lifting a finger . . . the real fear of these former architects of China policy is that the pusillanimous character of the advice they have been giving ministers for years will be exposed if he succeeds . . . Where Hong Kong is concerned, the old China hands have not exactly covered Britain in glory. They could usefully refrain from carping in the wings.

Patten was delighted by this thunderous support; the sinologists were furious. For Sir Percy Cradock, in particular, it was an intolerable slur on his reputation. He resolved to hit back openly, but in his own way and in his own time.

Behind the scepticism about his stance, Patten detected a cynicism towards the political future in Hong Kong. This mood was especially prevalent in the 'square mile' of the city, a significant proportion of which, in his words, appeared to believe the Joint Declaration to be 'just a frill, a curtain behind which Britain can withdraw, feeling modestly virtuous', and which did not for a moment imagine that the values it exemplified had any chance of surviving beyond 1997. Patten's tenacious belief that those values could endure was buttressed by two assumptions, neither of which could be said to be grounded in more than an imprecise optimism about China's potential to recast its political values in tune with a rapidly changing economic environment. The first was his confidence that the new leadership cadre emerging in

Beijing could be less obsessively concerned about a vestigial form of democracy in Hong Kong. Secondly, while 'I don't think that we're about to see an outbreak of liberal democracy in China,' he found it impossible to imagine that economic reform would not have some effect on politics. 'I don't think you can open up the Chinese economy and keep an absolutely tight grip on political structures . . . It hasn't been possible anywhere else, so why should it be possible in China?'

Patten's adherence to the Western view that authoritarian and repressive regimes invariably succumb to the political imperatives of a market economy, and thus yield to one or another form of representative democracy, was to become one of his recurrent themes. However, he was to win few converts in a region where the 'Asian values' of the kind asserted by Lee Kuan Yew in Singapore seemed no less appropriate. Whether or not one day he would be proved right, it was, in 1992, a fragile base for optimism about China's intentions for Hong Kong. In public, he appeared to have committed himself to the expression of two contrary views about the Chinese. On one hand, he argued that they were to be trusted when they asserted that they would abide by the terms of the Joint Declaration; on the other, that they should not be believed when they threatened, quite unequivocally, to dismantle his reforms in 1997. Patten readily conceded that it was very difficult to have it both ways in the broad light of day.

> It's an argument which is best put on a dark night with a following wind. It is easier to develop in private, because you can say things like, 'Power structures will change in Peking.' If you say that in public, you are challenging them to deny it. You're also making it more difficult for those who will be, one hopes, a more liberal generation of leaders. At the moment they are under intense pressure to demonstrate that they are just as hard-line as the old men in the compound.

As it was, Patten was surprised that only one journalist thought to tax him publicly on such a blatant self-contradiction. Brian Walden, a renowned British television interrogator, identified the inconsistency in late 1992, yet, in the words of Patten's press secretary, 'He set the trap but failed to spring it.' The governor was greatly relieved.

As a pragmatic Westminster politician, Patten had an inbuilt horror of finding himself exposed by his own policies in unfavourable terrain from which there was no discernible means of escape. As a result he spent much time, with his colleagues, with friends and alone, exploring alternative routes, peering ahead into the unknown to reassure himself that whatever he did or said, there was always a way out, even from the worst alley. Despite his contempt for the siren voices urging him to withdraw his proposals, he had already started to prepare his ground for a partial retreat by the time of his London visit, hoping to discover ways in which a compromise could be created in the Legislative Council. The most likely area to do it would be in that of the new proposed functional constituencies, he thought, conceding, 'It would only be a way of shoring up a position. It won't satisfy China, because China's got herself into the position in which nothing except going straight back to the drawing board is satisfactory.' Yet he was hopeful that some such compromise might spike the guns of the business community in Hong Kong and London, and reassure the public that their governor was not bent on confrontation for its own sake. He kept these thoughts to himself, mentioning them to neither Douglas Hurd nor even his most trusted advisers in Government House. 'As soon as anybody thinks I've blinked, I'll be in big trouble,' he explained to the author at the time.

Despite the misgivings in Whitehall, Patten was encouraged to find that the foreign secretary remained robustly supportive. Douglas Hurd, dryly contemptuous of the mindset of the governor's detractors, admonished them as Patten had predicted. He was similarly dismissive of those British businessmen who now started to call in growing numbers for a rapprochement with China. 'There are people who stay in the Mandarin Hotel and listen to a few people and think they know Hong Kong,' he commented. 'They don't see that what is actually happening inside that amazing society is change. And when it is put under their noses they don't like it, because, of course, life would be much easier, more comfortable, if everything went on as before and there were no politics in Hong Kong. There *are* politics in

Hong Kong, and ministers have to take account of that the way that *taipans* don't have to.'

The prime minister backed Patten unequivocally, but he had too many other troubles to concentrate for long on those of Hong Kong. John Major's government had just lost the battle to keep sterling in the exchange-rate mechanism of the European Union. Under pressure from currency speculators and despite the frantic efforts of the Bank of England, the pound had plunged through the floor, provoking a financial and political crisis of such a scale that the future of the government and the survival of Major himself had become a matter of intense public debate. On 16 September, the very day that sterling 'fell out' of the system, Patten had a private breakfast with the prime minister at the Admiralty. Not surprisingly, Major was somewhat distracted; inevitably, from his perspective, the governor's difficulties were something of a sideshow. Although Patten correctly defined his proposals as being those of the British government, it was only his relentless advocacy that prevented the sinologists in the Foreign Office from devising a retreat from them. The bonds of mutual respect and loyalty which bound Major, Hurd and Patten together were virtually inviolable, but Patten was walking on his own high wire. Had he wished to descend, neither of his colleagues would have instructed him to stay put; by the same token, for as long as he was able to maintain his balance, they would be there as his safety net against those seeking to topple him. Patten returned to Hong Kong confident of this, and hopeful that a measure of calm would be restored to the debate. Those hopes did not even survive the month.

On 30 November 1992, China suddenly announced that 'contracts, leases and agreements, signed and ratified by the Hong Kong government, which are not approved by the Chinese side, will be invalid after 30 June 1997'. The £14.8 billion airport project was now joined in financial limbo by an £800 million scheme to extend the cargo-handling facilities in the rapidly expanding container terminal known as CT9. A host of other projects in the pipeline were also under threat. As all infrastructure projects and public utilities in Hong Kong are operated by private companies

under government licence, Beijing's edict sent a chill through all
the businesses involved in communications, transport, gas and
electricity supply, as well as the colony's radio and television net-
works, which, with the exception of the government-owned
RTHK, were under franchise. The investment programmes of
some of the colony's most powerful companies, including Hong
Kong Telecom (Cable and Wireless's most profitable subsidiary),
China Light and Power, Hutchison Whampoa and Wharf, were
in doubt. Theoretically, at least, even the future of some hospitals
and public housing projects was uncertain.

The pessimism provoked by this announcement was exacerbated by a false report that the Chinese premier had written to
the governor upbraiding him for provoking an 'open confrontation', and warning that if Hong Kong followed his blueprint,
there was bound to be chaos in 1997. Earlier, the politburo's
mouthpiece, the *People's Daily*, had cautioned foreign investors:
'[Those] who support Patten's proposals are helping to wreak
chaos and disaster on the people of Hong Kong . . . Creating
chaos will not only bring calamity to the people of Hong Kong
but will harm the interests of investors of every nationality.'

The icy wind blowing from Beijing dismayed investors. In the
space of five days, the Hang Seng Index fell suddenly by 1,000
points (almost 20 per cent), a crash which seemed to confirm Sir
Percy Cradock's view that the Chinese 'patriots' in Beijing would
be quite prepared to inherit a wasteland rather than permit experiments with democracy of which they disapproved. Since China
was a major investor in Hong Kong, and especially in some of the
companies likely to be worst affected, the immediate consequence – as Beijing doubtless intended – was to tighten the screw
on the hostility of the business community towards the Patten
plans.

Early in December, Vincent Lo and some of his BPF colleagues
went to Government House to plead their cause. The BPF leader
was reticent about what was said, but later he confided: 'There was
no meeting of minds at all.'

Immediately afterwards, apparently more in sorrow than in
anger, he volunteered privately:

Maybe it would be better for him to go . . . I think that
unless he's prepared to withdraw his whole proposal and
start from scratch, they will not be prepared to come back to
the negotiating table . . . There is no way I can see the
Chinese government trusting him or working with him in
the next four and a half years . . . I think they really believe
strongly that there is a grand conspiracy going on in the
Western democracies to gang up on China. And I think
that is a very frightening thought to them.

However, Lo felt that it was impossible for Patten to go back to
the drawing board. 'His own credibility and his own reputation
will be ruined. That is why I say that his interests and the interests of Hong Kong may not be the same.'

This was another emerging theme that found a ready echo,
and not only in the Beijing lobby: that Patten had accepted the
governorship only to prove that he was not a 'broken reed', to
'rehabilitate' himself before a Westminster comeback, to make
a mark on the world stage or to 'salvage' Britain's honour. The
common thread of these naively disparaging attitudes was that
the governor had no intention of serving his full term, and
that once his immediate task had been accomplished, he would
beat a retreat to some well-paid bolthole in the West. Very
little of this conjecture was uttered in public, but conversations
about Patten's purpose and his future were the small change of
the political gossip which flew from lip to lip in the conspira-
torial atmosphere created by the impasse with China. Senior
members of the pro-Chinese establishment began to speculate
with incontinent enthusiasm about who might replace him. It
was suggested by one or two members of the Hong Kong old
guard that Sir Robin McLaren coveted the job, and there was
even a rumour to the effect that Sir Edward Heath, whose adu-
lation of his fellow gerontocrats in Beijing was much
appreciated by the business community, would be summoned
from Westminster to act as an 'honest broker' between the two
sides.

Of the major companies in Hong Kong, Jardine Matheson,
the colony's longest-established firm and still one of its most

powerful, was virtually alone in distancing itself from this speculation. The Keswick family, which still dominated the Jardine boardroom, had themselves fallen foul of Beijing but had survived. In 1984 the chairman, Henry Keswick, had authorised a decision to move the company's base from Hong Kong to the apparently more secure haven of Bermuda, which was widely and correctly interpreted as a vote of no confidence in Beijing. In 1989, after Tiananmen Square, Henry Keswick had used an invitation to address the Foreign Affairs Select Committee to denounce the Chinese government as a 'Marxist–Leninist, thuggish, oppressive regime'. It was no surprise, therefore, that the self-same 'oppressive regime' chose this moment to single out Jardine, the erstwhile opium-dealers, for denunciation. Although no one took the attacks seriously, Jardine's shares fell sharply amid a sudden fear that, after 1997, the company might find it impossible to operate effectively in the new SAR of Hong Kong.

The continuing Chinese assaults on Patten did cause genuine alarm, however. 'They really gave us hell last week,' confided Mike Hanson in December. 'They put immense pressure on the business community, from brutal threats to gentle persuasion . . . They panicked the business community, they panicked the Stock Exchange, they panicked a good proportion of the public and a fair proportion of the civil service.'

On 1 December Sir Percy Cradock broke cover to take revenge on his critics. In a letter to *The Times* defending the policies he and his colleagues had adopted before Patten's arrival, he argued that his policy towards China had been one of 'quiet but tenacious' negotiation,

> pressing hard, but avoiding open breaches and trials of strength for which Hong Kong will have to pay . . . Hong Kong's welfare depends on Sino–British co-operation. If that is a pusillanimous policy, I must plead guilty; and so must the ministers of two governments who endorsed it . . . The logic or fairness of the Chinese response is neither here nor there. What matters is whether they will carry out their threats. If we are sure they are bluffing, all well and good. If

we believe, as I do, that they are serious, that is a different matter.

In an interview on BBC's *Newsnight* he went further. Without naming Patten directly, he warned that while 'it might allow us to strike a heroic pose', failure to co-operate with China would do grave damage to Hong Kong. To dismiss warnings that China would overturn the Patten reforms in 1997 would, he said, 'be a serious, indeed a fatal, misjudgement . . . I'm sure they would be ready to dismantle them and impose what they think is a safer system, which by definition means a more repressive system.' He added: 'To find anything like the same state of tension, I think I'd have to go back to the Cultural Revolution in the sixties.' In Hong Kong, it was universally assumed that Cradock was not speaking only for himself but for the Foreign Office community of sinologists of which, until very recently, he had been the most influential member. Echoing Beijing's complaint, the former adviser to Thatcher and Major insisted that British policy had been through a 'one hundred and eighty-degree change' from co-operation to confrontation and, he averred privately: 'If I'd still been at Number Ten when the change happened, I would, of course, have resigned.' The governor had, he asserted later, 'to use a neutral word', been 'incompetent'.

The foreign secretary, who was well aware of Cradock's views, was not impressed by either his timing or his judgement. Hurd held that the former official quite failed to appreciate how, in the wake of Tiananmen Square, Hong Kong had, without British prompting, become 'a political city as well as a money-making city'. He confided that the question in the back of everybody's minds was always:

Are we really going to try to make the Joint Declaration work? Are we really going to try to hold the Chinese to something which we know is very uncomfortable for them; which is gradually turning Hong Kong into a democratic society? Or is that rather a façade, something to get round an awkward corner? Sir Percy would have preferred us simply to find out privately, in secret, without any reference to people in Hong Kong, what the Chinese will accept on a particular issue . . . and then go along with that, present it as best we could.

This dispute between Hurd and Cradock, which predated Patten's appointment, went to the very core of the conflict within the government which had been simmering well before the new governor set foot in Hong Kong. Although Patten had been given a free hand by the prime minister, the foreign secretary's unequivocal endorsement of his approach sprang from a deepening conviction that Cradock was profoundly wrong.

I think if we'd followed Sir Percy Cradock's view, we'd have had a very minimal degree of democracy in Hong Kong – no guarantees, no likelihood of an independent judiciary or a free press, because his argument would have applied at all those points . . . If we had simply accepted that on every occasion we had, at the end of the day, to agree to whatever the Chinese were willing to do, it wouldn't be very long before Hong Kong would be indistinguishable from Shanghai, or perhaps even from Tibet.

In Hong Kong, lesser figures than Cradock took their cue from his public outburst against the government. Among them, Sir David Akers-Jones, a former chief secretary and still on the government's payroll as chairman of the Housing Authority, chose this moment to side openly with China against the governor. As one of those expatriates who had decided to live out his days in Hong Kong, Akers-Jones was not ashamed either to accept an invitation from Beijing to become a formal Chinese adviser, or to join Vincent Lo in publicly endorsing the BPF's criticism of Patten. Though past retiring age, Akers-Jones was by no means a spent force in Hong Kong where, in sharp contrast to Cradock, it was perceived that he genuinely cared about the colony. Fearing that the breakdown was serious enough to prompt the Chinese to move swiftly to set up an 'alternative government' for Hong Kong well before 1997, he let it be known that he thought Beijing's claim that Patten had gone back on an understanding with China was valid. While he conceded that the 1990 correspondence did not constitute a legally binding document, he claimed privately, 'Everyone I've spoken to in Hong Kong believes there was an agreement.' This judgement, delivered as it was by a leading figure in the British community nominally still in Her Majesty's service, had a corrosive effect; moreover, Akers-Jones was known to speak for many more who preferred to stay silent but not loyal. One of his fellow expatriates, a senior civil servant, commented, 'He evidently hasn't taken sufficient notice of the impact of what he is doing on the morale of the civil service. And how he squares what he is doing with the old-fashioned concept of patriotism, I do not know.'

Amid the mood of darkening gloom which in some quarters seemed close to panic, Government House appeared eerily calm. The impression was superficial: for the first time since Patten's arrival there was an atmosphere of real crisis. A mere six months into his five-year tenure, the governor looked exhausted, the ever-present bags under his eyes etched deeper and greyer than before. Though he stayed outwardly calm, in private he seemed sometimes on the verge of succumbing to the view that his venture was in deep peril. In early December Mike Hanson described how the 'boss' would sink into a sombre silence which cast a pall over the office. Patten, who was not given to self-pity, acknowledged that he had a tendency to 'talk myself down' as he surrendered to what he called the 'black dog' of despair. Hanson sensed that his reaction to intense pressure was not coldly to analyse the predicament, but to 'live out' its potential ramifications by saying to himself, 'This could go wrong next. How would we respond? How could we cope? What would it feel like to have to cope?' The self-mortification invariably worked: 'He comes out of the other end. He knows what might go wrong; he knows where the downside is, and he knows how he will cope.'

It was clear now that, in addition to the business community, the traditional elites from both the expatriate and the Chinese population were for the most part antagonistic. To make matters worse, the chief secretary, Sir David Ford, felt bound to report that the civil service, unnerved by the Chinese onslaught, were also 'no longer behind the governor'. As Mike Hanson, himself a senior civil servant, put it, 'There isn't a great deal of stomach for a fight with the PRC in the civil service. There is no doubt about that . . . They ask us, "Why on earth are you leading us into a battle we can't possibly win? You're prepared to make yourself heroes and save your own consciences. But it is we that are going to be here after 1997."'

Privately, Sir David Ford had been sceptical about the rationale behind Patten's appointment. As chief secretary under his predecessor, Sir David Wilson, Ford had been intimately involved in the events leading up to and following the diplomatic watershed of Tiananmen Square. 'Until that moment there was a developing relationship, a relationship even on personal terms,' he recalled. 'If one had a banquet with Chinese officials, one could expect to make good progress on the margins of that banquet . . . they'd talk about the Cultural Revolution and what had happened to their families.' After 4 June 1989 that atmosphere 'absolutely and totally changed', and these genial encounters ceased altogether, despite the most elaborate attempts to restore them. In Ford's view, the Chinese officials were both terrified of making 'mistakes' with the outside world and, by 1992, intensely suspicious of the political process in Hong Kong. In this context Ford did not believe that either Major or Hurd had given sufficient thought to the impact of a 'political' governor on the relationship with China.

Ford and Patten had met in London soon after the announcement of Patten's appointment, and the chief secretary had at once formed the impression that the new governor was 'a man with a real political reputation . . . a man who would find it extremely difficult to abandon his principles in a negotiation with China and simply give up his bottom line to find an agreement'. For this reason, he judged Patten to be the wrong choice for the job, and believed that Sir David Wilson should have been retained to ride the hostility of the democrats and continue the policy of accommodation with China.

Yet Ford conceded that the political environment in Hong Kong was rapidly changing. Nor was he immune to the argument that 'to engage in another secret negotiation would have made it very difficult to maintain confidence in the government'. Patten's appointment had represented a dramatic shift in the authority vested in the governor. 'You don't put a political heavyweight in, such as Chris Patten, and then start to second-guess whether he's right or not . . . It was a sea change in the whole channel of communication and the way in which policy was made.' Hitherto, however strong the individual, and however forceful his advocacy, a 'diplomatic' governor was in the end no more than 'another voice in Whitehall'.

Despite his misgivings, Ford was swift to appreciate Patten's virtues and soon became a loyal lieutenant on whose calm and measured judgement Patten, subjected as he was to a torrent of conflicting advice, came to place great reliance. Ford explained:

> This wasn't a headstrong governor who was overruling his officials . . . He was extremely open to argument; he liked to have things discussed fully. He had no amour propre at all. He was a real person who accepted criticism and voices of dissent. And he was refreshing and easy to work with. One never felt inhibited from speaking one's mind . . . I think what shone through was his principle and integrity . . . and he translated that into the Hong Kong situation in a way which was immensely commendable. I never thought for one moment that his interest was anything other than doing his best for Hong Kong.

For Patten, the situation was made worse by the fact that, with the exception of his wife Lavender, he felt unable to confide fully in anyone, or to share with them the weight of his responsibility. Far away from the Westminster club, he relied heavily on the occasional phone call or brief visit from friends in Britain. Only then could he to some extent unburden himself without risk of undermining the morale of his team. 'You can't help having the odd self-doubt, waking up in the middle of the night and not getting back to sleep again, night after night,' he confided. 'I wouldn't discount the unnerving nature of what's been happening, and I wouldn't underestimate the extent to which one does sometimes wonder, was it worth it? Should I have settled for improving my tennis and having a quiet life and giving in gracefully? But the way the Chinese are behaving actually makes me feel even more strongly that what we're trying to do is right.'

Convinced that he had to win, or at least, not lose a 'very important argument', he drew strength from the fact that, even if the elites might crumble under the threats and inducements from Beijing about their future prosperity, the people on the 'Wanchai omnibus' were still with him. Moreover, his support in the polls had recovered. 'It's amazing and cheering,' he said, as if to comfort himself, 'how much public support has held up. I wouldn't have been at all surprised to see the community simply upping sticks and heading for the hills as soon as the serious noise started.' He cited a degree ceremony at the Chinese University, where he had been guest of honour. 'There were twelve hundred kids and their dads and mums at the back,' and as he walked through their ranks, he reported gleefully, there was a 'sort of rippling of applause down this huge esplanade'.

The Pattens managed to maintain enough of a genuinely private life to keep self-importance at bay and Hong Kong in perspective. On the rare evenings when they were alone or with the intimate circle of trusted friends which they built around them, they dispensed with ceremony, if not with the service of their cooks and orderlies. As a family, they wore their hearts on their sleeves: opinionated, argumentative, affectionate and emotional, they were never constrained by any sense of internal hierarchy. Each voiced what he or she thought and felt, and did so with unabashed vehemence and persistence. If either parent was tempted to presume that gubernatorial status invested an opinion with particular authority or merit, one or more of their daughters would soon puncture that assumption, with affection but emphatically.

At weekends, whenever possible, they usually retreated to their 'country house' at Fanling. It was spacious without being stately: the drawing room was ideal for the family to sprawl in; a verandah overlooked the sloping lawn and there they sipped wine before lunch and sat in the evening. The Pattens used this semi-rural retreat as many other middle-class English families might: they played music, they swam in the pool, they lay in the sun, and in the evening they played tennis. After dinner, they would watch a film on video, usually chosen by Alice. Patten, who worked at his official boxes late into the night during the week, often spent his weekend evenings writing speeches or broadcasts and updating his diary, in which he recorded the confidential details of his governorship.

The whine and whirr of a helicopter fluttering down between violently swaying trees towards their front door signalled the end of their Fanling reprieve. Within minutes they were airborne, leapfrogging the traffic which snaked slowly towards the city. They flew back across the mountains, deeply shadowed in the evening light, over the tenements of Kowloon, skirted around the jets landing at Kai Tak and scudded across the harbour towards the helicopter pad on Hong Kong island itself, where a limousine waited to return them in stately fashion back to Government House in time for dinner.

The governor's advisers were still not sure quite how serious his predicament had become. 'It's difficult to know whether they will go on firing blanks – noisy blanks – or whether they'll try firing live rounds,' Patten noted. He was inclined to discount the plunge in the Hang Seng Index as the product of 'rhetoric, veiled threats and action by mainland firms and banks: you buy forward or sell forward on the futures market, and you drive the price down . . . We know that is what they have been doing.' Meanwhile the 'real' economy, which in Hong Kong meant the property market, had not been affected. Indeed, in the first week of December, one of the most respected credit-rating agencies had put Hong Kong at the top of the international league table. However, he feared that this might tempt the Chinese to 'rattle their sabres louder . . . by taking steps which would really hurt people's wellbeing – even, perhaps, undertaking "big military manoeuvres" on Hong Kong's borders'.

By this time the governor had been driven reluctantly to conclude that Deng Xiaoping did indeed regard his reform proposals as 'part of a global conspiracy to destroy the last communist power'. This disposition on the part of the ailing 'paramount leader' could only have been reinforced by the US decision to sell advanced F16 warplanes to Taiwan, reports that the Germans,

French and Dutch were preparing to sell other armaments to the same customer, a visit by the US trade representative to Taipei and doubts about whether the new Clinton administration would renew China's MFN status.

His advisers now presented him with three options, none of them free of danger. The boldest, urged by both his constitutional affairs secretary, Michael Sze, and his senior adviser, Martin Dinham, was to present his reforms to LegCo in their entirety. Another alternative, advocated by Sir David Ford, was to divide his proposals into sections and submit them to LegCo one by one. The third choice, favoured by some of the 'old guard' and by the British embassy in Beijing, was to go back to the drawing board in the hope of tempting the Chinese into reopening some form of constructive dialogue. Patten discarded the drawing-board option at once.

> Look what I am being asked to do. Would they have con-nived at keeping Martin Lee out of the 1995 Legislative Council? Because that was China's endgame. I think some of them would have done. Lord MacLehose, who was here the other day, was criticising Martin Lee – by any definition the most popular democratic politician in Hong Kong. Well, we've got experience of that in our imperial history . . . we went round the world locking up the Martin Lees. Would that have been a good way of finishing our great imperial story? . . . At what point do you draw the line and say, we can't possibly go beyond that?

It was far less easy to choose between the remaining options. Two schools of thought emerged among his senior advisers. One, according to Mike Hanson, argued: 'You must give something to China to head off this awful barrage.' The other urged the governor not to lose his nerve. If he were to start 'backing off', they said, the PRC would draw the conclusion that they could rattle him. The Hong Kong liberals would see this as the sign of betrayal they were anticipating and he might find himself with nothing but enemies on the Legislative Council. 'Get the reforms into the Legislative Council as they stand,' they insisted. The argument went back and forth, with 'all these things racing round in one's head', as Patten put it, until the issue came to a head at the end of that first week in December. Fearful that their boss was about to come down in favour of accommodation, Michael Sze, supported by Hanson and Llewellyn, submitted a paper arguing that Patten would be 'finished' if he were to adopt the option pre-ferred by the chief secretary. If he put the proposals into LegCo piecemeal, 'China would pick off each element of his reforms, one by one'. Sze, a forceful advocate, was, in Patten's view, one of the most brilliant and courageous civil servants he had encoun-tered. Nevertheless the governor was racked with doubt.

Far more cautious than his image suggested, he was tempted by the thought that the Ford alternative might reduce the intensity of the row with China. He was also tempted to propose a con-ciliatory modification to his blueprint for the functional constituencies. 'It's very difficult,' he confided.

> If the parameters were different – if there wasn't this back-ground of liberals feeling betrayed – I'd be, by nature, inclined to suggest a bit of flexibility in areas where I think our proposals will be changed in any case by the Legislative Council. But I feel very constrained about doing that. I don't want to fall down a hole in the middle. I don't want liberals to feel they've been led up the garden path and not to have any support on the other side, either.

It was only after a further protracted round of discussions at Government House that Patten finally decided in favour of the 'high-ground' option: his reforms would be put before LegCo as one package. And it would be done as quickly as possible, on the pragmatic grounds that 'by definition, you are cutting down the time for trouble'. With the decision made, the tension at Government House visibly eased. Of course, the inevitable con-frontation with China would be debilitating, but at least the issues would be fought openly and the choice would be made by the Legislative Council, whose members had recently shown them-selves to be reassuringly unflappable in the face of Chinese disapproval. A fortnight earlier, they had debated a motion, sponsored by one of Patten's own appointees to LegCo, Christine Loh, which offered 'general support' for the governor's blueprint; after extended discussion, the motion had been carried by 32 to 19. The angry reaction from the Chinese leadership, which asserted through the NCNA that as an 'advisory body', LegCo had no right to approve a resolution which overthrew Sino–British agreements, left most legislators unmoved. Even if a majority of their number were likely to favour amendments to the Patten proposals, the resultant compromise would at least be seen to have been the product of a quasi-democratic process. And, as Government House totted up the figures, it looked as though the governor could expect to secure a small majority in favour of his reforms.

Patten was given another small boost when, only a few days after its collapse, the Hang Seng Index confounded the specialists by contriving to rise by 6 per cent in one trading session. However, he did not for a moment share the optimism of those financial analysts who attributed this unexpected recovery to the view taken by European investors that the Sino–British conflict would soon blow over.

The excitable Allen Lee expressed his own pessimism in apocalyptic terms – although, for the time being, he shared it only with his fellow members of the CRC. In no doubt that Hong Kong now faced a 'disaster' that could only be resolved by a Sino–British summit, he warned confidentially that the Chinese would set up a shadow government in Hong Kong, which would undermine the current government.

> Chris Patten's power will be gradually diminishing. In other words, the people of Hong Kong will not listen to him any more . . . I am told that they are drafting such a proposal already in Beijing . . . And they will implement it – I'm a hundred per cent certain of that – because they can't work with the British any more . . . It's a disastrous situation for Hong Kong, for Britain and for China. And for what? For a few seats in the legislative assembly.

Lee was so agitated by this prospective calamity that he wrote to

John Major seeking an urgent meeting. A few days later he said heatedly:

> The prime minister has got to answer me. And don't tell me he hasn't got time for us over this great impasse between the two countries. If he doesn't want to see us, that leads me to the conclusion that they don't give a damn about Hong Kong and the Hong Kong people; that they don't want to handle it, and they will let Chris Patten do his thing . . . The British rule over Hong Kong will be completely finished and the Chinese hand will be over Hong Kong. If Chris Patten goes on in this way – I put it very grossly – he is digging his own grave.

In his barely suppressed panic, Allen Lee not only spoke for a significant constituency in Hong Kong but also had access to senior members of the Chinese government. Chris Patten, who was well aware of this, recommended to Downing Street that the leader of the CRC should be granted his prime-ministerial audience. Lee could not easily be dismissed as a mere hysteric. The dry-eyed chairman of the Hongkong and Shanghai Bank, Sir William Purves, was no less critical of British policy, although, as one of the advisers appointed by Patten to his Executive Council, he refrained from saying so for the time being. In private he was scathing about Patten. According to Allen Lee, Purves had recently approached him saying, 'Come on, you've got to provide him with a ladder to climb down.' Lee replied, 'Look, the governor doesn't want a ladder. You must know that.'

Patten had resigned himself to the prospect that Allen Lee would 'go public' after his meeting with Major, which had been arranged for the New Year, but he was taken by surprise when a figure of far greater stature and influence in Asia chose to abuse the conventions of international diplomacy by joining the onslaught against him. On 12 December 1992, the governor was at the Hong Kong University to welcome the senior minister of Singapore, Lee Kuan Yew, who had been invited there to address a gathering of the colony's leading figures. Patten had met Singapore's 'strong man', as he was usually described in the international press, on his way to Hong Kong nine months before. Somewhat in awe of Asia's eminence gris, the new governor had allowed himself to overlook Singapore's abysmal human-rights record, which had earned Lee Kuan Yew a long-established place in Amnesty International's pantheon of states which routinely violated the guiding precepts upon which Hong Kong's unique 'way of life' had been so painstakingly constructed.

Patten's illusions about Lee Kuan Yew were rapidly demolished. The cold venom with which Asia's elder statesman consigned the governor's proposals to the ashcan of history left his host visibly taken aback. 'I have never believed that democracy brings progress,' Lee Kuan Yew informed his admiring audience. 'I know it to have brought regression. I watch it year by year, and it need not have been thus.' In a reference to the recent attacks on Patten by Cradock and others, he commented with arch sarcasm:

> I have been intrigued in the last few days by some very unusual developments, to me unthinkable. Three British professional diplomats, all retired, have come out to state their position on Hong Kong against their political masters. I am truly amazed . . . I think they are signalling something desperately to their political masters – that they have misjudged the situation . . . I therefore expect a real scrap in Hong Kong.

Patten endured this and more in the same vein in silent fury. When the Singaporean leader had finished, he commented, with an irony which most of the audience seemed to miss, 'I hope that some time, perhaps after 1997, I shall have the right of reply . . .' He paused. 'Maybe in Singapore.'

By the end of 1992, it could not be said that the governor relished the prospect of his remaining four and a half years in Hong Kong. 'Deo volente,' he noted wearily, 'I strongly suspect that I'll be here until the thirtieth of June 1997. I try to brace myself up in the morning. It's something I'm not greatly looking forward to, but it's got to be done.'

10

'PEBBLES IN A BLACK HOLE'

Talks About Talks

On 2 February 1993, Chris Patten entered Queen Mary's Hospital in Hong Kong for heart surgery. For several weeks he had complained of extreme tiredness, which he attributed to stress and overwork. However, his family had a history of heart disease (both his parents had died of heart attacks) and the prospect that he too might be affected by it often hovered in the back of his mind. Although he took regular exercise – strenuously on the tennis court – he was significantly overweight. By his own admission, he ate too much of the kind of food of which health enthusiasts disapprove and enjoyed liberal quantities of good wine.

One Sunday in January, he and Lavender were invited for lunch and tennis at a friend's house. Halfway through the match, he was forced to stop playing and lie down beside the court, suffering from what he at first presumed to be acute indigestion brought on by an indulgent lunch of boeuf bourguignon and claret. When the pain became more severe, he decided to return to Government House, where a team of doctors was summoned. They immediately gave him an ECG, which revealed nothing, and a blood test, which showed that he had had an 'episode', though whether it was a full heart attack remained unclear. They told him that he should go into hospital at once for further tests. Anxious to fulfil a dinner engagement the following night with Sir Charles Powell, the former foreign-affairs adviser to Margaret

Thatcher, and now a director of Jardine Matheson, he refused. The specialists debated whether to insist, or whether to allow him to remain at his post, a deliberation that was interrupted by a Patten family holiday in Bali over the Chinese New Year.

On his return to Hong Kong, still feeling listless and weary, Patten told the doctors that he had suffered from sunburn but had enjoyed several vigorous walks. Evidently aghast at his folly, they prevailed on him to go into hospital at once, a prospect which filled him with foreboding. They asked him to take a treadmill test, which confirmed within seconds that, in his words, 'something was seriously wrong'. With reluctance, he agreed to undergo a full examination, which revealed that his arteries had 'furred up' and the blood supply to his heart was severely constricted. He had feared that the doctors would recommend a coronary bypass, but the medical team at Queen Mary's decided that they could restore his arteries to full function using the far less taxing procedure of angioplasty. The operation was routine, if disconcerting, but Patten was aggrieved at having to be out of action for even a few days.

The announcement that the governor was to have angioplasty, the medical details of which were explored in colourful detail by the media, provoked a rash of speculation about both the physical causes of his condition and the strain he had been under during the previous few months. The director of the Hong Kong branch of the NCNA, Zhou Nan, whose diplomatic skills had been honed as an interrogator of British prisoners in the Korean War, and whom Patten regarded as a 'nasty piece of work', momentarily suspended his vendetta against the governor to send him best wishes for a quick recovery. Not all of his adversaries were so cordial. In a characteristically vinegarish commentary, T.S. Lo, one of Beijing's official 'advisers', and the owner and editor of *Windows*, a virulently anti-British weekly magazine, suggested to his readers that the angioplasty was Patten's way out of the diplomatic dead end into which he had led himself. Others, who were unnamed, speculated that Patten's condition had provided the British government with a heaven-sent excuse to replace its troublesome plenipotentiary with a figure more amenable to China.

On his admission to Queen Mary's, Patten pledged publicly to stay on as governor until 1997, and his spokesman was repeatedly quoted accordingly. Yet the possibility of his demise had enough resonance in the financial world to produce a rush of buyers for Hong Kong stock in London, with the result that the local closing prices were driven upwards. The going rate for a photograph of Patten on a stretcher was also rising. In pursuit of a fee said to be in the region of HK$400,000, Hong Kong's paparazzi embarked on a form of guerrilla warfare with the hospital security guards. They hid in corners, they climbed scaffolding, they tried bribery, but they failed to hunt down their quarry. After only two days he was out of hospital, and within a fortnight he was back at his desk.

After a lull in hostilities over the Chinese New Year, the conflict was soon resumed in earnest. Deng Xiaoping himself issued a warning (contained in a report from the Central Military Commission, published on 17 February 1993) that China might break its pledges on Hong Kong if Patten refused to withdraw his reforms. The Chinese leader was further quoted as saying that the proposals were part of a Western 'plot' to wage a 'new cold war' against China. He had ordered a harsh policy towards Britain because he believed London's aim was to 'internationalise' Hong Kong and to turn it into a political entity that could not be controlled by China. The conventional wisdom in Hong Kong was that Patten would find it excessively difficult to extricate himself from this impasse.

Just before Christmas, Patten had committed himself to introducing his proposals into the Legislative Council early in February in the belief that, suitably amended to reduce the ferocity of Beijing's objections, they would be on the statute book before the end of the 1993 session in June. Accordingly, the proposals were drafted into legislative form by the end of January. Early in February, the governor's appointed advisers on ExCo endorsed the bill, despite the private opposition of at least three members and the doubts of others. At this point, the British ambassador, Robin McLaren, was instructed to take a copy of the bill into the Foreign Ministry and the Hong Kong and Macau

Affairs Office in Beijing with separate accompanying letters from the foreign secretary and the governor which explained the proposed legislative procedure and reaffirmed the readiness of the British side to hold talks. They informed the Chinese that the bill would be 'gazetted' (published, but not tabled for debate in LegCo) a few days later, on 12 February.

A few hours before this deadline, the Chinese Foreign Ministry delivered their response to Douglas Hurd's letter. Beijing was willing to talk 'on the basis of the Joint Declaration, the Basic Law and the understandings between us'. Suspicious of the ministry's motives but cautiously encouraged, Patten decided that he had no alternative but to postpone publication of the bill. On 16 February, the British contacted the Chinese Foreign Ministry to express their pleasure at this development and to inform Beijing that the British team would be led by Robin McLaren and would include a number of named officials of the Hong Kong government. The British proposed that the first round of talks should begin on 24 February, in order to ensure that the Hong Kong authorities could meet the legislative timetable required to establish a new constitutional framework in time for the 1995 elections.

At this point the diplomatic lines to Beijing suddenly went dead. According to Patten, 'It was like throwing a pebble into a black hole. There was obviously a debate going on in Peking, and I think there were some efforts by Zhou Nan to kibosh the whole process.' The governor now postponed publication of the bill for the second time. Against a background of public anxiety about this delay, he decided, on 26 February, on yet another postponement because, as he explained, 'I felt we had to be falling over backwards to appear to be giving every opportunity for the Chinese to talk.' Patten's suspicion that the hold-up in Beijing was caused by divisions in the Chinese hierarchy was confirmed unofficially (though not to him) by Tsang Yok Sing, the influential leader of the pro-Beijing Democratic Alliance for the Betterment of Hong Kong (DAB). In his role as an official adviser, the DAB leader had attended a 'summit meeting' in Guangzhou, where it became clear that the 'doves', led by Lu Ping, were keen to develop the dialogue with the British, while the 'hawks', led by Zhou Nan, the most ardently anti-British of any Chinese official, wanted to end it. The businessman Vincent Lo, who was also at the meeting, confirmed Tsang Yok Sing's analysis.

It was another two weeks before the Chinese broke what the governor dryly referred to as their 'radio silence' to reiterate their willingness to negotiate. They insisted, however, on a number of preconditions – 'trivial debating points', they seemed to Patten – which included the demand that the proposed talks should not merely be confidential, but that their very existence should remain a carefully guarded secret. The British responded to this with some impatience, telling the Chinese Foreign Ministry, as Patten put it: 'You must be joking. You can't make the existence of these talks secret, because everyone will know they are going on. If senior officials are seen at Kai Tak Airport clutching tickets for Peking, nobody's going to think they are going up there to see their mothers-in-law. It's inconceivable that you can have talks in secret.' Beijing also disputed the right of the British side to include Hong Kong officials in its negotiating team, insisting that, since formal talks could only take place between the two sovereign powers, no servant of the Hong Kong government was entitled to a place at the table. 'It was a rather elaborate, theological point,' Patten commented at the time, 'and you certainly couldn't explain it to a Martian. You couldn't actually explain it to any rational human being.'

So far these manoeuvres had been conducted without any public explanation of what was afoot. Always aware of the need to maintain public support, and acutely sensitive to the suspicions of the liberals that he was going to back away from his commitment to democracy, Patten now felt he could no longer hold the line against a growing public feeling that a deal was indeed being concocted in secret. Unable to stall members of LegCo any longer, he decided that he would have to give them a 'bowdlerised version' of what was going on. On 3 March, in a local television interview, he reiterated, albeit guardedly, his own readiness to talk to Beijing on a basis which would not exclude the alleged 'understandings' contained in the 1990 exchange of letters. This prompted an immediate response from the United

Democrats. Though he was very much more discreet in public, Martin Lee was alarmed.

> It's really a repeat performance of the Percy Cradock era . . . The only conclusion I can draw is that he is backing down . . . They have deferred gazetting the bill for three weeks now – and we don't even know when the bill will reach us, because the moment they sit down and talk, and if they should arrive at some sort of agreement, then the actual bill will be presented to us according to the agreement, and no longer according to the Patten proposals. I think they are giving in to the Chinese side too much, even before they sit down.

Even so, Martin Lee was somewhat more disposed than his colleagues to give Patten the benefit of the doubt: 'Hopefully he will have the courage in the crucial moment to tell the Chinese, "If you insist on such a bad deal I will not continue with these negotiations but simply present the bill to LegCo and let LegCo decide." But that takes a lot of courage. Once you sit down, you get sucked into the process. Experience tells us that it is very difficult to break off.'

Patten was concerned that Martin Lee would soon broadcast his party's fears, a prospect which put additional pressure on him to maintain a momentum that the Chinese seemed determined to frustrate. 'We've got to deal first of all with the incessant suspicion of the liberals that the British always lose when they negotiate with China, that Hong Kong will be cut out of the debate, and that you can't trust perfidious Albion,' he complained as he and his team prepared three alternative statements for his LegCo appearance the following day. He had to choose between saying, 'There will be no talks, and the bill will be gazetted forthwith,' or, 'Yes, we are going to talk and the date is this,' or, 'I think we will talk – there are just minor points of detail to be worked out, and the sooner we can get a response on these minor points from China, the better.'

In the absence of any word from Beijing, he decided to plump for discretion rather than valour by choosing the third option, on the grounds, yet again, that he had to be able to demonstrate to the community that he could not have tried more; that he had gone the extra mile. As well as informing LegCo that the publication of the bill would be postponed again (an announcement which inevitably provoked headlines the following day of the 'PATTEN'S CREDIBILITY AT STAKE' variety), he used his statement to signal to the Chinese that he would accept Beijing's precise formulation of the terms on which any talks should take place, which included the pertinence of the 1990 exchange of letters.

At this stage Patten was optimistic that his concession would allow the two sides to 'wind up everything in another couple of meetings', and confident that the opening of negotiations would be announced the following week. Once again, though, he was foiled when Sir Robin McLaren (described by Martin Lee as 'a good civil servant, but every cell in his body is Percy Cradock') and Jiang Enzhu (described by Patten as China's 'extremely plodding, bureaucratic vice-foreign minister') became bogged down in an arcane and lengthy debate. It concerned the two unresolved – and what an exasperated governor now called 'ridiculous' – issues: the 'secrecy' of the prospective talks, and the composition of the British team at them.

In themselves the details of these exchanges are of such inconsequence that they are worth exploring only because they reveal something of what was involved in attempting to open serious negotiations on the future of Hong Kong. On 11 March, after five further days of 'talks about talks', the British minister of state, Alastair Goodlad, was finally driven to summon the Chinese ambassador to the Foreign Office to inform him that unless Beijing could agree these outstanding questions by the following day, the governor would go ahead and publish his bill. According to Patten, Goodlad also told Ma Yuzhen that 'the question of membership of the British team wasn't negotiable. We weren't going to change the basis on which previous talks had taken place.' The following morning in Beijing, McLaren and Jiang Enzhu had another marathon session at which, McLaren reported, the Chinese agreed that they would not insist on differentiating between the London and Hong Kong members of the British team. On that basis, Patten decided to extend his deadline by one more day. That same afternoon, however, the 'hard men' in Beijing, as Patten called them, evidently regained the upper hand: Jiang Enzhu contacted the British embassy to inform McLaren that the Chinese side had, on reflection, decided to withdraw their 'concession'. His government was not now willing to permit the Hong Kong members of the British team to be treated on an equal footing in the negotiations.

To break this deadlock, the governor suggested a compromise: the British would not make any public statement about the role allotted to individual members of the negotiating team, and only if pressed would he or his colleagues feel obliged to say, in effect, that there was no apartheid on their side. If the Chinese wished to describe McLaren's team as advisers and experts, the British would refrain from contradicting them. This attempt to fudge the issue failed absolutely. 'We got nowhere,' revealed Patten with a mixture of incredulity and relief.

These fruitless exchanges over status and nomenclature had now lasted a full fortnight, forcing Patten into yet another post-ponement and prompting the *Hong Kong Standard*, among others, to assert that if the governor dared to announce another such deferral, 'his credibility and the leadership of the government would fall through the floor'. Patten had in any case already decided that he could delay no longer: the more or less secret 'talks about talks' had now lasted for more than six weeks. 'If the talks about talks were going to be like that, I hate to think what the talks themselves would have been like,' he commented.

The Patten bill was duly published on 15 March to a pre-dictable display of outrage from the Chinese. The first blast was delivered by a spokesman from the NCNA in Hong Kong, who declared that there was now no basis for talks between the two sides. The following day, far more seriously, the Chinese premier, Li Peng, in the strongest language yet publicly deployed by the Beijing leadership, denounced Patten for 'perfidiously and uni-laterally' crafting proposals designed to alter Hong Kong's political system. Deng Rong, a daughter of Deng Xiaoping, added weight to this peculiarly personal onslaught by saying that the Sino–British row had been entirely the governor's fault. According to Zhou Nan, Britain now had no way out of the controversy. By common consent the intensity of the Chinese response reflected a genuine rage, at least among the Beijing 'hawks', at Patten's temerity. The Hang Seng Index, which had partially recovered from its December fall, reacted by plummeting 201 points (a drop of almost 4 per cent) in thirty minutes.

Patten's public response to the attack by Li Peng was to remonstrate mildly that the interests of Hong Kong were not served by 'excessive language'. Inside Government House, he and his team assessed the situation. Of one thing they were certain: further delay would have been impossible. 'Each week we had to send my press spokesman or even me to the gate to say, "Er . . . um . . . sorry, it's not this week."' The decision to publish the bill had been made only after close consultation with Douglas Hurd: 'If the foreign secretary had thought we were up the pole, he or the prime minister would have said so,' the governor commented. 'In the last twenty-four hours, when London was asleep, we had absolute carte blanche to play the hand.' Although it had been a finely balanced decision, he insisted, 'I don't think there was anybody among my advisers – anybody at all – who thought that another deferral was an option . . . I'm absolutely sure that we'd have been finished, or at least badly wounded.'

Although he was reluctant to admit it, the governor had already compromised his December position. At that time he had been determined to have the bill debated in February. Six weeks later, he reflected ruefully:

> If we had put the bill into the Legislative Council back in February, we'd now be in the middle of a huge ding-dong, but at least things would be happening, and people would have to accommodate themselves to reality rather than rhetoric. But we really, I think, never had a choice, because we're endlessly having to manoeuvre to keep in touch with the middle ground of the community, and that keeps changing . . .

Indeed, the volatility of the community was a major preoccupation at Government House; of greater importance than the condition of the Hang Seng Index, and of no less concern than the diatribes from Beijing. At the end of March, Patten was dismayed by polling evidence which seemed to show that the people of Hong Kong were in 'a pretty odd mood'. While they still supported his reforms, they were divided about whether he had been right to call off the 'talks about talks' merely on the question of the status of Hong Kong's representatives at the negotiating table. For the first time since his arrival in Hong Kong, the governor felt that he had misjudged the community's resolve, and that he was now 'on the back foot'. However, he was certain that he would have been 'shredded' if he had accepted the Chinese terms. He was resigned to the conclusion that, in their confusion and ambivalence, people were bound to 'criticise us for not having a bottom line until we stand on one, at which point they will say, "Perhaps we didn't mean that."'

As evidence of this frustrating mood, Patten cited a member of his Executive Council who had insisted that the question of who should represent Hong Kong at the talks should be non-negotiable. Following the breakdown of the 'talks about talks', the same stalwart suddenly changed his ground, suggesting, 'Maybe we've made too much fuss about representation. Maybe we can look at it again.' Patten remonstrated with him, reminding him of what he had said with such conviction seven days before. 'Ah,' his adviser said, quite unembarrassed. 'That was last week.'

Even more blatant was the volte face made by Allen Lee, who, before the breakdown, had urged Patten to gazette his bill on the basis that 'he could not wait for ever'. Now Lee condemned him for following that very advice: the governor, he complained, had not given himself enough time 'to find out if the Chinese were sincere – which, in my view, they are'. Lee's gyrations provoked some derision in the media, and led one cartoonist to portray the senior legislator as a toad (adding insult by offering apologies to the toad, which, the cartoonist explained helpfully, at least had a backbone). Allen Lee was indignant, not, he claimed, at the imagery, but at the implication: 'I'd rather be accused of being pro-China than pro-British, because I am Chinese. I was furious because I think I am working in Hong Kong's interests.'

The legislator's oscillating judgements were by no means unique in Hong Kong: others, in large numbers, shared his rudderless anxieties but lacked his willingness to unburden themselves so openly. Their volatility, though, was the litmus test by which Patten had to assess the potential of every move he now made. The problem was that the long march to the high ground was bound to take the governor and his team through dangerously exposed terrain. Moreover, their room for manoeuvre was circumscribed by the imbalance of power between the two adversaries and a timetable which was against them. The immediate question facing them was not whether to table the bill, but when. Patten's instinct was to move quickly, but a number of legislators, including some of Martin Lee's supporters, were privately urging him to delay, suggesting that a cooling-off period was needed, and that the proposals should be considered after the Easter recess. A number of sympathetic editorials adopted the same line. Patten was aware that he was now approaching the decisive point of his governorship: 'It's going to be a difficult, cathartic, political moment,' he confided. 'We'll be told it's the end not just of the Hang Seng Index, but of humanity as we know it – or at least, as China knows it.'

At this point, to complicate matters, a number of contradictory signals began to emerge from Beijing. Despite the wrath he had heaped on Patten only a few days earlier, Lu Ping was, according to Patten's sources of intelligence in the Chinese capital, along with Li Peng, 'still trying to flag up their interest in talks'. Making a distinction between publishing and tabling the bill, the Chinese leaders had indicated informally that they had not yet entirely abjured talk of 'co-operation'. Patten was, somewhat reluctantly, drawn to the conclusion that it was just possible that something would start moving. 'I rather doubt it. It's equally possible that something sufficiently provocative will happen to push us into introducing the bill earlier.'

Far from believing that the Chinese were honourably at odds with the British over matters of principle and procedure, Patten was by now more than ever convinced that they were acting in bad faith. In this respect, his indicator was China's attitude to Martin Lee and his colleague, Szeto Wah. Would these Democratic party leaders be allowed to remain as members of the legislature after the handover, or would they be expelled as subversives? For Patten, this was a simple matter of principle. 'I think it goes right to the heart of the argument, and it's what we are fighting about before 1997 . . . If I look at it now, I don't think that they have any conception of a credible Legislative Council after 1997, any more than they have a real conception of the rule of law.'

As he considered how best to nudge his way ahead, Patten parried all public attempts to pin him down to any particular course of action. Meanwhile, he and his advisers identified two alternative ways forward. The first option was, as they put it, to 'buy' peace by contriving arrangements for the 1995 Legislative Council that would guarantee China an acquiescent majority, and from which recalcitrant members could be swiftly removed. As one or two of his advisers were quick to remind him, this would probably secure an agreement on contracts for the new airport, for the container terminal, CT9, and would be very likely to produce a more secure economic environment in the process. The other option was to risk an economic rough ride, but 'at least to fight for some sort of decency surviving 1997' with a chance, Patten thought, that China would find it difficult to overthrow a 'reasonable set of arrangements' after the handover. By adopting the latter course, Patten argued, 'we'll have established at least some sense of political propriety in that period, and, at the very least, we won't have been behaving in a thoroughly shaming way'.

The question was, what would be judged to be a 'reasonable set of arrangements', and by whom? Many of his admirers in Hong Kong were reluctant to see him rush prematurely into legislation. They believed that the governor's repeated invocation of a deadline which was constantly allowed to slip both exposed the weakness of his hand and was unnecessarily provocative. Patten conceded that: 'Our weakest ground has always been the determination to get things through quickly,' but he was still driven by the conviction that, sooner or later, the community would have to decide whether or not it had a bottom line. 'Let's get it over and done with: if the community decides that we haven't really given it any alternative but to cave in, there is not much I'd be able to do about it, but let's know that soon.' Nonetheless he remained fearful that the public might lack the stomach for such a robust approach.

Judging by the opinion polls, the public was still bewildered. In a telephone poll conducted at the beginning of April for the *Hong Kong Standard*, 78 per cent of respondents said they favoured efforts to achieve more democracy before 1997, even if the territory's economic prosperity were affected as a result. However, 57 per cent also declared that they wanted the governor either to amend or to withdraw his plans in the face of Chinese hostility. A similar poll in the *South China Morning Post* showed that while only 25 per cent of the sample supported the British position, a mere 19 per cent supported the Chinese. No less than 56 per cent of the population was undecided.

With this ambiguity in the forefront of his mind, Patten flew to London at Easter for another round of meetings at the Foreign Office and with the prime minister. The informal evidence from private sources – and in the form of a surprisingly conciliatory statement from the director of the NCNA – appeared to suggest that, despite the governor's obduracy to date, the door was still open for further negotiations if he could be persuaded to desist from further 'criminal' action: in other words, from tabling his bill. To this extent, if to this extent only, the Chinese appeared to have ceded ground. At the same time, Patten began to realise that Beijing had tumbled the fact that the legislative constraints on him – as opposed to the political attractions of an early decision by LegCo – were in fact somewhat less pressing than he had repeatedly insisted. They could therefore pursue their delaying tactics by hinting at the prospect of further Sino–British negotiations without in reality risking the constitutional crisis in Hong Kong that his own statements seemed to suggest would occur. Patten was angry but not surprised to discover, through intelligence sources, that at least one former diplomat, apparently thoroughly briefed by ex-colleagues in the Foreign Office, had taken it upon himself to inform his contacts in the Chinese government that the timing constraints on which Government House had laid such stress were fictitious, and that the pressure from that source could safely be discounted. Even so, he was astonished by such brazen treachery.

On 13 April, Patten was scheduled to have a lunchtime working session with the prime minister. To his irritation, this meeting was prefigured by yet another Whitehall 'source', who commented for the benefit of several attentive journalists: 'I'm afraid that unless Patten is reined in, China will withdraw all co-operation as Hong Kong heads for the 1997 handover of power, and that would be disastrous for the people living in the territory. Talks between Britain and China could restart tomorrow but for Patten's insistence on having members of Hong Kong's government on his negotiating team.' Even in the new age of 'leaking' civil servants, specific briefing of this kind was rare. Patten knew that the source could only inhabit the Foreign Office or the Department of Trade and Industry, which was now led by Michael Heseltine, who had recently reinvented himself as the 'president of the Board of Trade'. Heseltine was known to have a rapacious eye on the potential of China's booming economy, and it was no secret that he shared the view prevailing in both departments that Sino–British relations should not be allowed to founder over the intricacies of the electoral arrangements for a territory that would soon be consigned to the margins of Britain's colonial history. Though he did not suspect Heseltine of being in any way implicated personally, Patten was uncomfortably aware that his former Cabinet colleague was likely to share the broad thrust of this anonymous and potentially devastating remark.

In Hong Kong, this 'revelation' served to confirm the impression that Patten was now isolated from mainstream opinion in the government and that he was a 'problem', an obstacle to progress and harmony. It was a perception that was reinforced in Britain by commentators like the former Irish government minister Conor Cruise O'Brien, who called for his resignation, and the ineffable Lord Jenkins of Hillhead, the leader of the Liberal Democrats in the House of Lords, who used a discussion with the governor on BBC Radio's *Any Questions* to express a fastidious disdain for Britain's efforts to introduce greater democracy into Hong Kong at so late a date. The conventional wisdom in the colony, voiced by the ubiquitous Allen Lee, was that the tête-à-tête between Major and Patten would be 'a waste of time'. The legislator was further quoted as saying, 'I do not think Britain has ever given anything to Hong Kong, nor do I either think China will be bad for Hong Kong. If they are going to talk, that is fine. If not, China will have to do what it thinks it needs to do. That is also fine.'

Before the governor and the prime minister had the opportunity to 'waste their time' over lunch the conventional wisdom had been confounded. On the morning of 13 April, Robin McLaren's patience finally bore fruit in the form of a simultaneous announcement from London and Beijing that Sino–British negotiations would after all take place, and that they would begin in the middle of the following week. They would be conducted on precisely the terms which Patten had been demonstrably willing to accept some six weeks earlier, and which involved no discernible retreat by the British on the question of either the 'secrecy' of the talks or of the composition of the British negotiating team. The British side was to be led by Robin McLaren, the British ambassador, supported by Peter Ricketts, the head of the Hong Kong Department at the Foreign Office; Michael Sze, the secretary for constitutional affairs in the Hong Kong government; his deputy, Peter Lai; and William Ehrman, seconded from the Foreign Office to the Hong Kong government as one of Patten's political advisers. The governor contented himself with saying that the breakthrough had been 'a victory for common sense'. Allen Lee was greatly cheered by 'this excellent news' and the Hang Seng Index responded with Pavlovian predictability by leaping 371 points to 6,789.7 – a record one-day rise to a record high.

Patten was not carried away by this euphoria, estimating that chances of a successful outcome to the negotiations were no better than 'three to one against'. Though he confided that he was ready to dilute his original proposals, he was not prepared to give ground unless the Chinese offered something in exchange, which, he noted, 'may come as a rude shock' to them. Moreover, he was unwilling to let the talks drag on indefinitely, predicting that they would not last more than a couple of months at most. He was right about the odds, but wrong about the timetable.

As agreed by both sides, the talks began within a few days. Three weeks later, and after two rounds of negotiation, neither side had advanced one millimetre. Using the traditional tactic that had proved so effective in the past, the Chinese began by attempting to bind the British side into agreeing a set of broad 'principles' about constitutional structure before moving on to the precise details of the electoral scaffolding. Patten's team was wary, suspecting that to give any such commitment on the functional constituencies or the Election Committee, which were the two most contentious issues, would leave the British with no room for genuine negotiation on either. To make matters worse, Patten also had to accept that it would now be impossible to meet his self-imposed deadline of late July for the passage of his reform bill through the Legislative Council. Instead he began to consider the idea of 'decoupling' those parts of his reform package which applied to the 1994 'local' District Board elections from those which affected the 1995 Legislative Council elections, in which case he would have to table two bills rather than one.

In an effort to make some progress with the Chinese, Patten prevailed upon the foreign secretary to send a message to his counterpart, Qian Qichen, saying, in effect, 'Come on, we can't go on like this: we've got to get down to serious negotiation.' In the absence of a positive response from Beijing, he and his team proposed to bring into play what he liked to describe, with a touch of vainglory, as 'Patten's Maggie Factor': the unstated threat that the governor might suddenly do something wild and unpredictable, such as introducing the legislation without any warning. Whether he could in reality risk putting any such threat into practice at this stage was questionable. Were the British to walk away from the negotiations on the grounds that they were heading nowhere, he feared that a majority of LegCo members would say, 'We're not having any of this. Go back to the Chinese and negotiate something.' And he detected a similar mood among his advisers in ExCo.

Patten now felt himself to be not merely on the defensive but on the retreat. 'I'm in a weaker position because we started negotiating as late as this,' he confided in early May. 'The truth of the matter is that negotiation is inevitable, and a bit of a slippery slope, because people want a successful outcome . . . the further along a road you go like this, there are always a declining number of options.' In the hope of making genuine progress, he had identified two areas for compromise as soon as the Chinese betrayed a willingness to talk in earnest. He was prepared to give ground to Beijing on both the composition of the Election Committee and the size of the electorate for the functional constituencies. The latter, he calculated, could be reduced from some 2.5 million to as little as half a million without undermining their pluralistic flavour. He was insistent that in return he would need guarantees that every member of the legislature elected in 1995 would retain a place on the 'through train'. 'There's not much point in agreeing institutional arrangements that will go through 1997 if people can't as well,' he noted.

During these weeks, Patten's own resolve was put to the test persistently, not only by his own team, which he encouraged to debate every discernible option, but, far less agreeably, by the continuing sniping from the unnamed 'sources' in the Foreign Office, who he had hoped would have been silenced by the foreign secretary's admonition some months earlier.

While Patten professed himself to have been 'overwhelmingly well served' by most of the Foreign Office officials who had worked for him, this handful of dissidents irked him more than he liked to admit. Some, such as John Coles, the permanent secretary, and David Wright, his deputy (whom Patten thought had been overpromoted), frequently adopted an air of courteous but faintly disapproving scepticism. Although Patten dismissed others as 'some old sinologists on the fringes', he detected a disinclination generally in the Foreign Office to stand up to the bitter prejudice of Sir Percy Cradock, even after the latter's retirement. Although he did not put it in precisely such terms, Patten thought of Cradock as the Foreign Office's deus ex machina. It was also plain to him that the former diplomat had 'moved from being a critic on the sidelines to actively working to screw up what we are doing'. Patten harboured the thought that any success on his part would be too painful for Cradock to bear: he remarked acerbically, 'It's curious to take a view of public service that everything you do has to be vindicated, accepted by the outside world as the virtuous activities of a wise senator. Barmy.'

Patten raged against Cradock and his acolytes less for their opinions than for the influence that Beijing might assume they exercised in Whitehall. This concern came vividly into focus just before he made a visit to the States in May 1993, at the invitation (inspired by the prime minister at a meeting with the new president, Bill Clinton) of the White House. As he prepared for his own trip, Patten discovered that Cradock was about to embark on a visit to China. Given that Cradock could oil the hinges of almost any door in Beijing, it came as no shock that, on his retirement from the civil service, he had been able to sell his services to the merchant bankers Kleinwort Benson, who were anxious for a foothold in the People's Republic. However, Patten was surprised to discover that a diplomat so recently retired had considered it appropriate to travel to Beijing, 'purportedly' on his new employer's behalf. He was even more surprised to learn that Cradock's former colleagues in the Foreign Office not only knew about the proposed trip but, so Patten was informed, had been briefing him accordingly.

The governor only discovered what was afoot as a result of a casual conversation between Jiang Enzhu and William Ehrman at the customary banquet following the second round of Sino–British talks. The Chinese official told Ehrman that he and his colleagues were greatly looking forward to Sir Percy's visit to Beijing. Ehrman, a loyal if sceptical lieutenant, at once told the governor, who was not amused. He was even less amused when he discovered that the Foreign Office had known for two months that a group of British officials in Hong Kong were proposing to entertain Sir Percy to dinner, but that 'it slipped everybody's mind to tell me. They hadn't thought it was important. I was, as they say in Noël Coward plays, "crawss".'

Patten contacted the Foreign Office at once. 'I insisted they asked Sir Percy Cradock not to go, and I also insisted that they stopped briefing him.' Aware that there was little he could do to snuff out the spirit of freemasonry in London, Patten was sufficiently frustrated to summon his 'local' Foreign Office advisers to Government House where, according to one of those present, he gave them a full-scale dressing down, stating, among other things, that Cradock was now officially 'beyond the pale', and reminding them that 'when we are retreating under fire, it does help us if we keep good order'. Some of those summoned, who were not implicated except by association, were upset to have been treated as if they were dissidents; however, one official – Tony Galsworthy, the Foreign Office's unofficial historian of the Sino–British negotiations – was overhead to say with relish: 'So he does realise that it's a retreat. It's the first time he has acknowledged that.' Cradock's visit to China went ahead, and so did the dinner party.

Patten departed for America encouraged by the rough ride given to Lu Ping by the outgoing Bush administration the previous year. Although he was well aware that the Chinese were super-sensitive about the United States, and that to invoke American support would open him to the charge of 'internationalising' the Sino–British dispute, Patten was hopeful that President Clinton and sympathetic members of the US Senate could be persuaded to use the bait of most-favoured-nation status to tempt Beijing to be more accommodating about democracy in Hong Kong. It would be a delicate manoeuvre on his part. In public, no governor of Hong Kong could be seen to argue against the renewal of MFN for the People's Republic because the British colony's own prosperity was so intimately bound to China's MFN status. However, he thought that it might be possible to exert pressure on Beijing discreetly by persuading the Americans to hint obliquely that there was a link, however slight, between the renewal of MFN and the enhancement of democracy in Hong Kong. To this end Patten proposed to encourage Washington to confirm, implicitly but publicly, that by 'standing up' for Hong Kong's way of life, Britain was in a much stronger position to argue in favour of MFN renewal.

Patten was in his element in the politics of Washington, which had entranced him as a student when he briefly worked as part of Mayor Lindsay's campaign team. He was not too blasé to experience a frisson of pleasure as his limousine swept him through the White House gates on Pennsylvania Avenue for his audience with the president. The two men found an easy rapport and the meeting overran by fifteen minutes. To Patten's delight, Clinton went further than he could have wished in supporting his stance.

Sitting in the Oval Office with the governor beside him, the president informed the world's media:

> I think that the democracy initiative in Hong Kong is a good thing, and I'm encouraged the parties have agreed to talk about it. You know, it is one of the world's most vibrant, thriving, important cities. It is an incredible centre of commerce, and a haven of opportunity for millions of people. Many of them had not a thing but the clothes on their backs when they came there. And I think the idea of trying to keep it an open and free society after 1997 is in the best interests of the Chinese. So I think this is an issue which is well founded, and I support it. And I hope it doesn't offend anybody, but how can the United States be against democracy? It's our job to go out there and promote it.

Afterwards, Patten could hardly contain his enthusiasm: 'If you are a politician, being in Washington is like a cricket fan being at Lord's, or a Jesuit being in Rome. It's the centre of all that is most interesting and exciting between politics and the way the world works.' The governor had been far more impressed with Clinton than he had expected; by his physique ('He's so big!'), and by the speed and flexibility of his political intelligence. In addition to his audience at the White House, Patten had been given what seemed to him 'astonishing' access – to the Treasury, the State Department, leading senators and the vice-president, Al Gore. He was confident that this 'red–carpet treatment' would send a clear message to Beijing. 'I hope they will take the point that the US and the rest of the world will be looking at the way Peking treats Hong Kong as a touchstone for how much China can be encouraged to join polite international society,' he said. 'I think it's quite important that China recognises that behaving badly in Hong Kong isn't a cost-free option for them.' In public, however, he took care to ensure that the 'internationalisation card' did not appear to be being played.

The USA visit was judged a success. However, given China's propensity to ignore world opinion, it was perhaps optimistic of Patten to suppose that even the subtlest efforts to 'internationalise'

Hong Kong would have a beneficial impact in Beijing. He anticipated the 'usual crude and silly attacks' from China on him for
having the temerity to visit the United States at all, but he was
not at all prepared to find, on opening *The Times* on the day after
his meeting with Clinton, that one of the Foreign Office's freelance communicators had been at work again. The newspaper
quoted an unnamed Foreign Office official as saying – in Patten's
gloss – 'what a pity it was that President Clinton had expressed
support for my proposals on Hong Kong's democratic institutions because that might cock things up. He should have just had
his picture taken with me. It was a great pity that he was so effusive.' Patten chose to attribute this war of attrition being waged
against him to 'mutterings in the bar at the Travellers Club', but
he was angry that a minority of Douglas Hurd's officials should
feel free to ignore the foreign secretary's recent strictures, given
in his presence, 'about how everyone must be loyal and
supportive'.

The pressure sometimes seemed unremitting. With the exception of Lady Thatcher, the procession of grandees from Britain
who filed through Government House as his guests frequently
exacerbated his sense of isolation. When the former Labour
prime minister Lord Callaghan arrived in Hong Kong en route to
a gathering of elder statesmen in Beijing, he did not spare his
host's feelings. Callaghan argued his case with impressive clarity
and courtesy. Patten observed afterwards that this was preferable
to the blandishments of those who came to stay at Government
House and 'tell me what a wonderful job I'm doing and then go
round town sounding gloomy'. Callaghan's view, as reported by
Patten, was essentially that Britain should not be overly concerned about 'doing the right thing by Hong Kong'. British
interests in China and relations with Beijing were of far greater
moment. It was important to protect Britain's commercial interests, to promote British trade with China, and to secure a greater
share of China's expanding market. Callaghan's conclusion – 'We
can't make very much difference to what Hong Kong is like after
1997, and therefore basically we shouldn't have any arguments
with China' – was thoroughly disheartening.

Pessimistically predicting that the conclave of former statesmen gathered in Beijing was likely to share Callaghan's opinion, Patten confessed:

> I do get depressed by the amount of time I inevitably have to spend explaining to people why I'm not a grand poseur. Why what we are doing matters. Why we've taken the decisions we have taken . . . I've got to keep showing them that I'm not just grandstanding; that what we are doing has rational grounds for it and is important for the prosperity of Hong Kong.

As he approached the end of his first twelve months in office, the governor seemed to have lost much of his early bounce. Though he worked tirelessly and sounded no less confident in public, he seemed burdened and careworn in private, his usually bullish stance often yielding to doubt and anxiety. In confidential conversation about his tactics with China, he contrived to be both defiant and defensive. Insisting that his adversaries in Beijing had to believe that the British were serious, he added, in the same breath, 'I mean, we do want to do business. Having got on to this inevitable and slippery slope, we have to complete the journey.'

'THE MAD GOVERNOR FACTOR'

Negotiating in Earnest but in Vain

In the summer of 1993, after two months of negotiation (which had taken them well past the governor's self-imposed deadline), the British team saw a glimmer of hope. Even Chris Patten found himself grasping at the straws which seemed to blow in with the wind from Beijing. Despite China's insistence that the two sides should agree on a list of principles before dealing with matters of substance, the British had not given way. 'If we compromised first, we would have found that the bargain was between our "compromise" position and whatever their position was,' explained Patten. 'So it was imperative that they set out their stall first . . . if there is going to be a compromise, it'll be somewhere between where we started and where they've dug their trenches.' On his instructions, the British side had continued to press the Chinese on the need to establish objective criteria for allowing Hong Kong's elected representatives to travel on the 'through train' across the 1997 barrier. By the end of round three, there had been stalemate.

At this point, however, the Chinese began to shift ground. Although there was no tangible movement in rounds four and five, the British side noticed that the Chinese negotiators had quietly dropped their insistence on establishing 'principles' as a precondition for progress and agreed to proceed to the matters of substance. In the sixth round, the Chinese even laid out their position on the composition of the functional constituencies.

Reiterating that the British should drop Patten's proposals for extending the franchise to embrace some 2.7 million people, they demanded that the nine new constituencies should be based on corporate, not popular, votes. It was hardly a leap forward, but it was a step in the right direction, however crabbed. Patten noted dryly, 'Hey presto. They moved. So we did make progress.' Indeed, he even allowed himself to be reassured by the fact that some 'experienced old sinologists' thought the progress made 'spectacular'. For the first time, it seemed to him that the Chinese were serious about negotiating a compromise.

His advisers in Government House were less optimistic. 'The PRC would not ever do a deal, except on their terms,' said one of them. Patten presumed that Beijing's apparent amenability was attributable at least in part to economic factors: 'When the insults were first raining down on the Triple Violator last autumn, if there was economic pressure, it was thought to be on us: British businessmen and Hong Kong businessmen concerned about losing markets in China; concerned that, by standing up to China, we'd ruin the Hong Kong economy.' At that time there had been euphoria about the Chinese economy; nine months later, the Hang Seng Index had risen by almost 30 per cent, while the Chinese economy seemed to be dangerously overheating. 'The Chinese, I think, are feeling they don't want to wreck the Hong Kong economy if they are going to have economic troubles themselves.' To support this theory, Patten cited the fact that the Chinese were about to float ten of their largest companies on the Hong Kong stock market.

> Do they want to carry out these privatisations on a falling, plummeting Hong Kong stock market or one that is stable and rising? The question answers itself . . . The more they worry about their own currency, the more they are stuffing money into Hong Kong . . . So all the signs are that, with Hong Kong representing a fifth – and the healthiest fifth – of China's economy, they aren't going to wreck it.

He was sufficiently confident that China wished to avoid a break-down to revise his pessimistic assessment of the chances of a deal from three to one against to fifty-fifty. From his vantage point, it now seemed that British resolution was reaping its just reward.

> They wouldn't talk unless the Triple Violator dropped his proposals. They wouldn't talk unless members of the Hong Kong administration were travelling third class. They would-n't talk if anybody knew talks were taking place. They wouldn't make any progress in the talks unless we compro-mised first. They wouldn't tell us what they wanted to do until we compromised. At every stage you sit there quietly for a time and they shout and rave and then it happens.

Patten thought that the Chinese, accustomed to a very different style of Sino–British negotiations before his arrival as governor, were now 'recognising that there is slightly less disposition on our side to try to get round substantial issues by clever words . . . We haven't backed off anything. It doesn't mean that we are not going to try to find a compromise, but that it will be a compro-mise we come to rationally.'

If he was right, then, for the first time, the Chinese were preparing to yield on matters which they had claimed publicly to be issues of overriding 'principle'. For them to cede ground, perhaps to the extent of compromising in favour of Britain's commitment to the 'through train', would be a diplomatic tri-umph for which Patten would properly be given much, if not all, the credit. Such an outcome would also turn on its head the conventional sinological wisdom about the gerontocracy in Beijing, and call into question the past conduct of relations with China over Hong Kong. Patten was not so incontinent as to speculate in this fashion, but he was, by now, more than ever con-vinced that Britain had underestimated its position and its strength in the past.

In his new positive mood, the governor was careful to avoid any further public commitment to a timetable for the completion of the talks, a tacit acknowledgement that his previous attempts to do so had been ineffectual, if not counterproductive. Nonetheless he and his team had decided that it would be quite impossible to delay tabling his bill (probably revised as a result of the negotiations with China) beyond the end of the year, which was already five months later than the date he had originally announced.

Patten now flew to London for a well-publicised meeting of the Cabinet subcommittee on 1 July, which was chaired by the prime minister and attended by the foreign secretary and the home secretary, Michael Howard. Its purpose, Patten confided, was to demonstrate 'the harmony between London and Hong Kong and the complete commitment to the approach we've taken, our mild but growing impatience and our shared objectives in the talks – and to give a little burnishing to the threat of the mad governor breaking loose again'. It was duly conveyed to the media afterwards that while the governor had set no deadline for the talks, time was running out, and that, in the absence of a deal, he would press ahead unilaterally by tabling his package in LegCo. The Hong Kong newspapers responded predictably. Pro-democracy commentators noted that the Cabinet endorsement of his approach was a 'victory' for Patten, although they fretted that the British were about to cede too much ground to the Chinese. Conversely, the pro-Beijing press declared that the line adopted by Britain was bound to make the negotiations 'more difficult'. If the British side persisted with Patten's 'three-violation' package, the talks would fail. While China had always been 'sincere', the 'petty tricks' and unspecified 'unreasonable demands' of the British undermined the prospect of a settlement.

It was soon obvious that this response reflected a renewed obduracy in Beijing, and that Patten and his advisers had misread the signals emerging from the Chinese capital. Within days, the governor's optimism began to evaporate. A meeting between the foreign secretary and the Chinese foreign minister on 9 July – at which, according to Patten, Douglas Hurd intended to 'make it pretty clear that we need to get a move on, that we are serious about trying to negotiate a settlement but we are also serious about walking away from the table if they are just mucking about' – yielded nothing of substance. Hurd was reduced to flan-nelling in public, effectively saying that the proof of whether or not the visit was worthwhile would be seen in what actually hap-pened later.

During rounds eight and nine of the talks Britain offered

further concessions on the composition of the functional constituencies and the Election Committee, but, reverting to their
earlier stance, the Chinese refused to shift ground. As for the
'through train', which was for Patten a core issue, they simply
refused to discuss it. By the end of round nine the governor was
reluctantly forced to reverse his judgement that the Chinese were
serious about securing a compromise. Two insurmountable obstacles blocked the way: Beijing's obsession with China's sovereign
rights over Hong Kong, which Patten was persuaded would
endure until the 'immortals' had finally departed, and the bureaucratic shambles and infighting by which the Chinese
administration was so obviously afflicted. As if that were not
enough, he was, in blacker moods, also frustrated by what he saw
as the innate cowardice of too many members of the Hong Kong
community and the greed of the business elite, both of which
played into Beijing's hands.

In August the Pattens flew to Italy for a month in the sun. They
stayed with friends in an Umbrian villa, where they relaxed in the
traditional English way. Patten sat in the full glare of the sun, covered himself with lotion and read Jonathan Spence's *The Search for
Modern China*. He played tennis, went for extended walks, swam
and almost every day explored the surrounding towns and villages
in search of paintings and churches. His friends noted that despite
his genial demeanour, he often seemed distracted, his bonhomie
uncharacteristically forced. He consumed spaghetti and red wine
with his usual enthusiasm, but he often drifted away from the
conversation as if wrapped in private worries. On more than one
occasion his reveries were punctured by telephone calls from a
troubled John Major in London – for the prime minister (though
Patten would never have said so) continued to treat his absent
mentor as a fount of rare wisdom and understanding – complaining about his treatment at the hands of a hostile Eurosceptical
media. Patten did his best to reassure Major and to offer advice,
but these interruptions at this time did little to restore his spirits.
    It was during these weeks that he began to think his way into
the collapse of negotiations which he now considered to be all
but inevitable. Although he felt that he had only a little more

ground to give, he was still willing to make further modifications
to his reforms which would bring them more closely into line
with what he would have proposed originally had he been told
about the 1990 'understandings', the principal source of his troubles in Beijing nine months earlier. He envisaged a further
revision of the composition and size of the functional constituencies, which, he was ready to concede, might be scaled
down to 840,000 electors. In the case of the Election Committee,
he allowed that it should be formed 'precisely' on the model
prescribed in the Basic Law, except that the places on it reserved
for those Hong Kong residents who were also members of the
Chinese legislature should be filled by election rather than, as the
Chinese wanted, by appointment. This prospective retreat, which
would have horrified the Democrats had they known of it, was as
far as Patten felt he could go without reneging on his own commitment to an electoral process that was palpably 'fair, open, and
acceptable to the people of Hong Kong'. It was precisely because
he believed that his modified proposals still met these criteria
that he was now so dubious about the prospect of agreement with
Beijing. As one of Beijing's favoured 'advisers', Sir David Akers-
Jones, was to explain, with no sense of irony, to the Foreign
Affairs Committee at Westminster a few weeks later: 'The
Chinese style is not to rig elections, but they do like to know the
results before they are held.'

In the space of a month, Patten's analysis of the Chinese stance
had been through a 180-degree about-turn, a fact which he readily acknowledged. As the summer waned he resigned himself to
the prospect that any further talks were destined for the quick-
sands. The one hope was that the Chinese were preparing to
make a last-minute concession which might be wrung out of
them in New York in a further meeting between Douglas Hurd
and Qian Qichen scheduled for early October. It was a remote
possibility, but one to which the sinologists in the Foreign Office
clung. Meanwhile, Patten began to plan for the anticipated breakdown. He thought it would strengthen his hand as far as public
opinion was concerned if the British were to publish a White
Paper explaining how and why the two sides had failed to reach
a compromise. He nurtured the hope that this might demonstrate

to both Hong Kong and the international community that he had gone as far as it was reasonable to go in a genuine attempt to accommodate Beijing's doubts and suspicions. His immediate inclination was to table his original, unmodified bill in the hope of thus avoiding a confrontation with Martin Lee and the Democrats, but at the same time leaving room for LegCo to amend his reforms if that was the will of the majority. Although he would be denounced by China, he soon convinced himself that this was the only credible way ahead.

With some weariness he predicted a renewed outbreak of panic in Hong Kong at the prospect of a head-on confrontation with China, which might, he feared, provoke one or two of his less stalwart advisers on the Executive Council to resign in protest. However, he thought that his approach would at least be seen as morally defensible and – in political terms – more 'saleable' at Westminster and on Capitol Hill. A collapse of the talks on the grounds he foresaw would at least allow him to argue that the issue between Britain and China was not essentially the previous 'understandings', or whether his proposals constituted a helter-skelter dash for democracy, but whether Hong Kong's electoral system should be conspicuously fair or self-evidently rigged. He was still inclined to believe that if the 1995 Hong Kong elections were conducted on the terms proposed in his original bill, the Chinese would preserve the structure after the handover – regardless of the rhetorical thunderbolts which would be hurled from Beijing in the meantime. If the outcome of the 1995 elections should prove 'so terrifying' that the old men in Beijing felt obliged to dismantle an electoral system approved by LegCo, he thought they would find it exceptionally difficult to justify such vandalism in the eyes of the world. In these circumstances, Britain would emerge somewhat bowed but not entirely dishonoured – a concern which was never far from the mind of a Westminster politician who cared for the national interest, and who wished to retain at least the option of a role in public life after 1997.

Some of his former colleagues in the Conservative party did not want him to wait that long. In the summer of 1993, Douglas Hurd rang Patten to suggest that he might like to return within the next twelve months and re-enter the cabinet as leader of the

House of Lords. From that vantage point, Hurd reasoned, he could help shepherd the government, and a beleaguered prime minister, towards the next election. Major's standing had plummeted following the débâcle of Black Wednesday the previous autumn. A catastrophic performance in the 1993 local elections had led to a mood of panic and rebellion in the parliamentary party. Some senior colleagues who were ideologically at odds with Major's imprecise and vacillating commitment to be 'at the heart of Europe', were in more or less open revolt. Such was the disarray that he was being privately vilified, and none too discreetly, even by members of his own Cabinet – a disloyalty which drove him soon afterwards to refer to the 'bastards' therein. The view that the prime minister was indecisive, weak and incompetent had begun to stalk his leadership to the extent that only a very determined politician was likely to survive the onslaught from his own party and the government's erstwhile supporters in the media, notably the *Daily Mail*, the *Daily Telegraph* and the *Sunday Telegraph*. In vain Major's friends advised him to ignore a media campaign which he believed, with some justification, was being orchestrated to bring him down in favour of a successor committed to leading Britain from the 'heart' to the periphery of the European Union – a prospect from which the prime minister himself recoiled.

As the implications of the Maastricht Treaty began to take effect, the debate over the single currency degenerated into a verbal brawl between senior colleagues, while what had once been an anti-European rump in the Conservative party began to affect the public mood with a potent combination of anti-Brussels rhetoric and jingoism. 'Some pretty nasty people', as Patten described these backbench rebels, had done their best to undermine the prime minister by voting against the treaty, which, Patten said, 'viewed from Hong Kong, is a bit of a fight up a cul-de-sac'. They very nearly succeeded in forcing a vote of no confidence in the administration. The Hong Kong governor shared the view which soon became fashionable in and around Westminster that, with a majority in single figures, the prime minister was in such a perilous position that he might well be driven out of the leadership. Although Major had not yet hinted at this himself, Patten was in little doubt that Hurd's informal overture reflected the prime minister's own sense of impending crisis and his faith that the return of his most trusted colleague could somehow turn the tide.

But it was not a prospect that tempted the governor even for a moment. He was honest enough to confess in private that he was reluctant to mortgage his political future to a permanent seat but a transitory role in the House of Lords. And, while he knew that the prime minister would appreciate his strategic perspective, he was not at all sure that he would be able to help Major steer a more persuasive course through the shoals which beset the government. Nonetheless, if the prime minister had asked him unequivocally, his ties of personal loyalty and political conviction would have obliged him to return. One of Patten's team recalled later that he had come out of a breakfast meeting with Major, sunk into the back of the car and 'heaved a sigh of relief' that the prime minister had not broached the issue directly on that occasion. Patten informed the foreign secretary that unless the prime minister were expressly to summon him back, he intended to remain at his post until the handover.

The negotiations with China dragged on through the summer and into the autumn. Twelve rounds of talks brought half-promises of a modest harvest while, week by week, delivering only fruit that withered on the branch. Throughout Patten remained in direct command of the negotiations. At the end of each session, he and his team in Government House gathered in his study to read through the telegrams from the Beijing embassy. The governor listened to the advice of his specialists and responded by sending McLaren his 'riding instructions' for the next day. It became an increasingly exhausting process.

On 1 October, three days before his meeting with Qian Qichen in New York, Douglas Hurd reminded an audience in Singapore that Hong Kong had become a 'political city', contradicting a statement by the Chinese foreign minister three months earlier. A day before their meeting, Qian Qichen retaliated by quoting the words of Deng Xiaoping in his meeting with Margaret Thatcher eleven years before: an 'early takeover' of

Hong Kong might be necessary, he said, if there were 'major disturbances' in the colony before 1997. This theme was echoed on the same day, the forty-fourth anniversary of the establishment of the People's Republic, by Li Peng in an address to the party faithful in the Great Hall of the People. Patten shrugged off the warning, declaring that if there was any political instability in the region, it was not to be found in Hong Kong. However, the inflammatory tone of the Chinese statement reinforced his doubts.

To no one's surprise, the discussions between the two foreign ministers on 4 October failed to break the deadlock. To the dismay of the British, Qian Qichen made it clear that China intended to reserve the 'right' to exclude from LegCo after 1997 any elected politician of whom he and his colleagues did not approve. After two hours of discussion, Douglas Hurd emerged to comment bleakly, 'There is a considerable gap, and I can't say we have narrowed it today.' It was particularly dispiriting because the British were prone to regard Qian Qichen as a reasonable figure, whom Patten contrasted favourably with 'the hard men who, at the drop of a hat, start to sound like cultural revolutionary nutters'.

In his second annual policy address to LegCo, in October 1993, Patten confirmed: 'We now have only weeks rather than months to conclude these talks . . . We are not prepared to give away our principles in order to sign a piece of paper. What would that be worth?' Preparing what his team felt to be a 'very shaky LegCo' for the prospect of a vengeful response from China, he urged its members to meet the challenge of Hong Kong's predicament, declaring emotionally: 'We cannot be bolder than you, because liberty stands in the heart. When it shrivels there, nothing can save it.' At a press conference afterwards, he was challenged by pro-Beijing reporters who accused him of delivering an ultimatum to China. Concealing his true feelings in the hope of retaining the diplomatic high ground, he responded breezily. He still had boundless optimism, he said, that a few more rounds of talks could deliver a solution, although he added: 'As the weeks and months tick by, hope becomes a little shadowed by reality.' In his speech, he had been circumspect about the

lack of progress in the talks and made no reference to China's failure to make concessions. Afterwards he was asked if the Chinese
had moved at all. 'You had better ask them. I don't know how
long the answer might take.' Away from the reporters, his answer
to the question was that it would take 'about four and a half seconds . . . The Chinese haven't, in practice, budged an inch.
Indeed, the more you get ideas out of them, the more alarming
they become.' In LegCo he refrained from sharing with his audience his conviction that the Chinese were obsessed with the
need to control the legislature after 1997.

Although it was inconceivable that he would even hint at such
a bleak appraisal in public while ostensibly the talks had not yet
run their course, he was by now quite clear that 'unless something
astonishing' were to occur within the next few weeks, he would
fly to London for a Cabinet committee meeting in late October
at which he would recommend that 'we pull the plug' in
November. With this in their minds, Patten's advisers began to
shift the emphasis away from the diminishing prospect of a deal
towards the 'endgame': making sure that the British side emerged
from the breakdown 'looking as good as possible'.

Three more rounds of negotiations had been planned for
October, and the revisions that Patten's team had conceived in the
summer were duly presented to the Chinese side in the middle of
the month. To the governor's astonishment, Beijing once again
appeared to shift ground by suddenly proposing, in round fifteen,
that the two sides record an 'interim understanding' on five points
which had not hitherto been agreed. Once more driven to revise
his expectations, Patten concluded that this move was 'substantial
enough to be real', and could not be dismissed merely as an
attempt to wrong-foot the forthcoming Cabinet committee
meeting. The proposed 'interim understanding' related to the
reduction of the voting age in Hong Kong to eighteen (the age
qualification already in force for 'elections' in China); the right of
Hong Kong citizens who were also members of the National
People's Congress to stand in local and LegCo elections; a single-
vote, single-member system for local elections (but not for LegCo
elections); the nature and function of District Board and
Municipal Councils (the local authorities); and the composition

of these two local assemblies. In the last case, the Chinese appeared to concede the right of the British to replace the appointed members of District Boards and Municipal Councils by elected representatives, but reserved the right of the future SAR government to revert to a system of appointees. These were far from the most contentious issues that divided the two sides, but Patten was encouraged to believe that further concessions would be forthcoming and that, even as it stood, the Chinese proposal held the prospect of a genuine deal.

In the governor's view this eleventh-hour response conceded 'three quarters, maybe half, of the Triple Violator's original package', even though it still left the really awkward issues to be resolved. It was a measure of his eagerness to emerge from these negotiations with an agreement that he allowed himself to be so enthused by what, especially in retrospect, would seem such a nugatory shift by the Chinese. But it was enough to persuade him to change tack. In London at the end of October, he persuaded the Cabinet committee, not to 'pull the plug', but to endorse the notion of splitting his bill in two, 'decoupling' the non-controversial matters referred to in the 'interim understanding' from the less tractable issues in the hope that they could be finessed into an agreed form of words during the sixteenth round of talks and then introduced into LegCo before Christmas. This, he hoped, would at least introduce some momentum into the process. The really divisive issues – the Election Committee, the functional constituencies and the 'through train' – could then be negotiated separately and without quite the same pressure to reach an early agreement.

This way ahead would only be possible if the Chinese were willing to concede that the single-seat, single-vote principle should apply not only to the local elections but to the LegCo elections as well. Otherwise, Patten judged, the deal would not be politically acceptable to opinion in Hong Kong. The Cabinet was sympathetic. After the president of the Board of Trade, Michael Heseltine, had asked 'some perfectly reasonable, legitimate questions' about the impact on Britain's economic interests if China were to start 'trying to take it out on us', Patten was given unquestioning support, both for his handling of the crisis so far and for the strategy he now proposed to adopt. At the conclusion of what was to prove a decisive meeting, the prime minister sent a message to the Chinese premier welcoming the progress made, but indicating that, for practical reasons, it would be necessary to reach agreement very soon. In broad terms, he suggested that he thought agreement should be made forthwith on the 'immediate issues', while the less easily solved questions could be handled in an intensive final phase of negotiations.

Patten's cautious optimism was tempered by his belief that on the more divisive matters, 'the gap between their bottom line and our bottom line is so huge that it's going to be difficult to bridge'. In the case of the 'through train', for example, the Chinese had set out in round fifteen a range of criteria which prospective travellers would have to satisfy, which included a reference to 'sedition'. It was not clear either what they had in mind, or whether their anxiety was about past or future conduct. There was, as Patten observed, 'a world of difference between people promising they won't commit seditious acts in the future and people being pinned for what the Chinese may regard as seditious in the past, like protesting against Tiananmen Square'.

The governor's ambivalence about the negotiating process in which he was ensnared was almost palpable. On one hand, he was inclined to believe that the group in Peking which wanted a settlement was in the ascendant; on the other, he conceded: 'Our assessments of what is going on in Peking are always subject to the caveat that I'm not sure any of us knows what happens in that secret society . . . Who is running China? Is China being run by the president of the All-China Bridge Federation [Deng Xiaoping]? Is China being run by the daughter of the president of the All-China Bridge Federation?'

Patten's private sentiments about the 'Alice in Wonderland' world of Sino–British diplomacy were barely printable.

It's mad. Utterly crazy. Take one issue – the 'through train'. It's inconceivable that with any other country or government you'd actually be arguing about these matters with part of the world standing by and nodding away as though it were a rational thing to be arguing about. And with large numbers of the business community, many of them educated in liberal, plural societies, actually thinking, 'China's got a point. Perhaps we should throw people out of the Legislative Council if they protested against Tiananmen Square.' I mean, it's cloud-cuckoo land.

We are devising the most complicated elections, I should think, in the history of civilisation, with the Chinese trying to devise them in a way that rigs them . . . At the moment there are five functional constituencies where there has never been an election. It's always been a shoe in. In the Chinese commercial functional constituency, which is, by and large, the Chinese Chamber of Commerce – a completely open-and-shut job for Peking – there was a legislator called Mr Ho . . . who, in the run-up to the last LegCo elections, expressed some views about the airport which China didn't like. It was made clear to him that his business interests would suffer. So he stands down and is replaced by a man who's just been chucked out of the stock exchange for his practices . . .

Then there was the regional council functional constituency. The chap representing that is now in Stanley Prison, having been found to have bribed several of the electors. And so you go on. We can't conceivably allow that sort of rot to continue, and we must ensure that the nine new functional constituencies are set up on rather cleaner lines. If not, it will make absolutely certain that it is a rotten legislature in the palm of Peking.

The governor's angry indictment of the prevailing structure contained an implicit criticism, not only of those who had devised it, but also of his own predecessors in Government House, the Foreign Office and the British Cabinet. It was, after all, British officials, endorsed by British ministers, who had invented these rotten boroughs and who had concocted an electoral system – essentially at the behest of Hong Kong's merchant elite – which appeared to accommodate the concepts of freedom and justice, but in reality flouted them. It was not a glorious record, and Hong Kong's last governor was very far from proud of it.

In early November the British returned to the negotiating table for round sixteen with a revised 'memorandum of understanding' based on the Chinese document submitted in the previous round. In an effort to move towards an agreement on objective criteria for the 'through train', the British side submitted a draft oath of allegiance to the special administrative region. But now the British suddenly found themselves in what Patten called 'serious Lewis Carroll country' as the Chinese retreated from what the British believed to be their stated position on the appointment of members to the District Boards and Municipal Councils. Although the leader of the British negotiating team, Robin McLaren, thought he had elucidated the Chinese view (and 'replayed' it back to them twice to make sure), they insisted during rounds sixteen and seventeen that there had been a misunderstanding. According to Patten, the Chinese were only prepared to explain what they had really meant if the British were willing to give up a point of substance in return. In effect they were arguing that their explanation would itself be a concession. They also rejected the British proposal that a first-stage agreement should incorporate a commitment to the single-seat, single-vote formula for LegCo elections as well as the local elections, without which Patten was sure any agreement would be rejected by a majority of Hong Kong's legislators. Acknowledging that Beijing appeared to have 'caught us for another couple of months' of negotiations – which would take them past the December deadline which he had argued only recently would be impossible to postpone – the governor steeled himself for the inevitable complaints from Martin Lee and his democratic cohorts that he was allowing himself to be 'strung along' by China.

At the end of round sixteen – during which, according to Patten, the Chinese made their case with 'pretty ill grace' – Christopher Hum, a Foreign Office official deputising for Robin McLaren, who was ill, was instructed to inform his Chinese counterparts that if they reneged on the agreement the British thought they had made in round fifteen, then it would not be possible to go on discussing these so-called first-stage issues in round seventeen. At the traditional banquet that night, the

Chinese were in angry mood. 'There was,' said Patten, 'a huge fuss, and the leader of the Chinese negotiating team behaved in a very ill-mannered and uncouth way.' The atmosphere was the ugliest British negotiators could recall. For the governor's colleagues in Government House, there was a delicious irony in this moment. Christopher Hum, who bore the brunt of the hostility, was one of the governor's most persistent critics in the Foreign Office. Rightly or wrongly, Patten's team believed that Hum was the principal agent of the anonymous leaks from those 'sources in Whitehall' which had so irritated the governor. On this occasion, however, Hum obeyed his instructions to the letter.

At the end of another fruitless round, Hum said simply: 'I have no more authority to go on talking about "first-stage" issues.' After 200 hours of negotiation, the two sides had managed to agree that, whatever form elections might take, the voting age should be reduced from twenty-one to eighteen. And that was it.

Patten now wanted to publish his 'first-stage' bill as soon as the lawyers completed the final draft, and to introduce it into LegCo for debate before Christmas. However, Anson Chan, his choice to succeed Sir David Ford as chief secretary, felt that it should not appear to have been rushed. She advised that what the governor described as a 'more deliberate, orderly' introduction would look better to the community, and so he decided to delay the bill just a little longer. Anson Chan was a formidable character whom Patten had identified within six months of his arrival in Hong Kong as the most suitable 'local' civil servant to inherit a role which had hitherto been the preserve of British officials. She had taken up the post in September, and already her influence was pervasive. Patten readily admitted that he would only take a decision against her advice in extremis. 'I think,' he commented, 'that the most difficult aspect of decision-making and political leadership isn't making up your own mind, but trying to square others.'

Indeed, the question of timing was discussed by ExCo with great passion. Four members, led by Denis Chang, a respected liberal lawyer, felt strongly that Patten should move rapidly. 'If you think something is right,' declared Chang, 'put it in place and – hopefully – it will survive . . .' However, the prevailing view among his colleagues was that the governor should 'be realistic', and Patten was determined to ensure that the majority in ExCo was willing, however reluctantly, to endorse his decision. Denis Chang watched his style with detached admiration: 'He has a very brilliant mind in summing things up, but you can almost hear between the lines what he wants!' he observed. In this case, as Patten explained, 'I summed up against the minority despite the fact that the more I heard of the argument [advanced by Denis Chang], the more convinced I was by it. But . . . I didn't want to make those who were anyway pretty lukewarm or iffy about the course of action we were pursuing to feel they'd had two bloody noses in one day.' It was his constitutional obligation to consult his advisers on ExCo, but it was also good politics to carry them with him: to face resignations from those members of the community whom he had been seen to select as those most able to give him sound and detached advice would have been very much more than an embarrassment.

Patten was more sensitive to the awkward task of dealing with ExCo than some of its members presumed. 'It would be much easier if one just listened to one's own voices and followed one's own instinct,' he ruminated. 'It is quite difficult and a curious exercise, because the Executive Council doesn't have much clout in the community. They are all distinguished people and they very often give good advice very bravely, but . . . I have to think about managing them, and that probably slows me down a bit sometimes.' As it was, several members of ExCo, of fainter heart than he realised, lobbied Patten's team furiously, urging them to intervene with the governor in a last-ditch attempt to persuade him to back away from a showdown with China. They refused.

China's obstinacy was hard for Patten to bear. He found a release for his pent-up frustrations in meetings with his senior staff, who had by now grown accustomed to his expletive-undeleted remarks on the subject. Before his regular question-and-answer sessions in LegCo, a ritual he had instituted soon after his arrival, he prepared himself in dry runs with his advisers so that together they could establish the line to take and he could tailor his responses accordingly. In one such session, on the day before Patten was due to announce that the talks had broken down, Martin Dinham asked him mildly, 'So why was it that in the end you could not reach agreement?'

The governor twirled his glasses, looked at the ceiling as if in search of inspiration, and replied thoughtfully: 'Because they are wankers.'

The decision to delay the first-stage bill would, Patten feared, create more time for 'Chinese intimidation and pressure to work on individual members of the Legislative Council'. Indeed, that pressure had already begun: several LegCo members who had been 'very solid and supportive' the previous week were, Patten detected, already 'peeling off' and, he reported, saying, 'Maybe we could agree all this in a couple of days, and postpone putting in the legislation for another month or six weeks . . .' The reason for this prevarication was, in Patten's mind, self-evident: 'They've had a telephone call from the NCNA.'

There were other reasons for delay. First, even at this late stage, the foreign secretary still harboured a residual hope that the Chinese would return to the negotiating table. Secondly, since Douglas Hurd was to be away from London at a NATO meeting, it would be some days before he could deliver an appropriate par- liamentary statement. He therefore advised Patten that it would be wise to proceed with caution. 'London has been extremely supportive,' explained the governor, '[but] I think Douglas's judgement was that London wasn't quite prepared for a break- down in the way that the community here was.'

Patten continued to insist publicly that the door was wide open for further discussion, and to reiterate his confidence in the willingness of the Chinese to abide by the terms of the Joint Declaration and the Basic Law. Away from the spotlight he noted: 'I hope I'm wrong – and things may change between now and 1997; things may change in Peking – but they give every indica- tion of simply not believing in Hong Kong people running Hong Kong under "one country, two systems". It's all there in the text, but everything they do tells a different story.' It was a dismal thought when he was committed to spending the next three and a half years pretending to the outside world that the reality might be otherwise.

On 6 December 1993 Hurd formally announced that the talks

had collapsed. The leader of the Liberal Democrats, Paddy Ashdown, gave the government his support. The Labour party, in the person of the shadow foreign secretary, Jack Cunningham, failed to rise to the moment. In a carping speech in which party points-scoring took precedence over shadow statesmanship, he smirked, 'The central question in response to the right honourable gentleman's speech is what on earth has gone wrong? . . . It seems, Madam Speaker, as though the "through train" of democratic reform has just come off the rails.' In the Lords, the former Labour prime minister James Callaghan was similarly unhelpful. 'The government,' he observed, 'have got themselves into a cul-de-sac. And the cul-de-sac is that they cannot now satisfy the people of Hong Kong and we are endangering our long-term relations with China. This is a terrible example of ineptitude.'

Patten voiced his feelings of isolation.

I suspect one reason why it feels more uncomfortable than most political dramas in which I've been embroiled is precisely that feeling that nobody back home quite knows what it's like. London is in every sense a long way off. Look at the coverage of Hong Kong at the moment in the British media. It's negligible apart from some pretty third-rate sort of Angela Brazil reporting on the BBC . . . There is a bit in *The Times* and in one or two other newspapers . . . but not really the sort of coverage which people here would expect the subject to deserve.

Eighteen months into his governorship, Patten knew that he had reached the point of no return; that the future was all the more daunting for being quite unpredictable.

'WITHOUT FEAR
OR FAVOUR'

Defending Free Speech

The ambivalence and uncertainty about the future under China which preoccupied many Hong Kong citizens was typified by the conflicting feelings of one member of the younger generation. In 1992, when Chris Patten arrived in Hong Kong, Norris Lam was a fourteen-year-old schoolgirl living with her parents and her brother in a cramped flat on one of the ubiquitous estates in the New Territories. She had been born in Fujian province in China, where her father was a doctor. In 1980 the family, ostensibly on their way to the Philippines, stopped off in Hong Kong and stayed put. After three months her father, Lam Koon Ying, found a job as an editor at a local news agency.

Norris Lam was already driven by the imperative to succeed that distinguishes Hong Kong teenagers from their Western counterparts. She attended the neighbourhood school, where she was marked out as a star pupil and a natural leader. In addition to her knapsack of books, she invariably carried a mobile phone, which she used to organise a variety of school and community activities with her fellow students. She was studying mathematics, physics, economics and English for A-Level and expected to go on to the Chinese University.

Norris had won a school award for her academic and social record. A member of the school debating team (in both English and Cantonese), she was also chair of the school Community Youth Club, editor of the school magazine, house captain, leader of the Civic Education Group, and, proudly, a member of the

Hong Kong Outstanding Students' Association. Cheerful and direct in manner, she talked without priggishness about her urge to make money but also to serve the community. 'We have to show that we can contribute to our society. I am a volunteer at a home for the aged. And we also organised a "workathon" to raise money for World Vision. We like organising camping vacations, and we are hoping to have three days in China.'

Her intention was to use her return to the 'motherland' to discuss the future of Hong Kong with her Chinese counterparts. Although she had not been to the mainland since arriving in Hong Kong as an infant, she thought that it was important to share experiences and to tell her peers about Hong Kong.

> I will tell them about the pace of life here, which is so fast, and about our way of life, which is the trend all over the world. We care about the environment, and about technology, which makes us very efficient. I will tell them that in a democratic country we have the right to speak freely and to have religious freedom. Also voting is important. These are our rights, our human rights. And I think they should know of them, too.

Although Norris had not followed the course of Chris Patten's conflict with Beijing, she was worried that he was moving Hong Kong too far, too fast. 'We are very conservative. I am not even sure that the voting age should be brought down to eighteen. We are not mature enough, I think, for that. But Mr Patten is a real star. Very strong-willed and very hard-working. I think he wants Hong Kong to be a democratic society.'

In July 1993, Norris was able to make her longed-for trip to China. As her bus approached the Lo Wu Bridge, she could see the border. 'I became more and more excited. I kept saying to myself, "I'm nearly there." We all had the same feeling in our group, that we had finally reached Chinese soil and we were back in the motherland at last. Maybe it is because we are Chinese that we have this patriotic feeling.'

This guileless enthusiasm was soon tempered by experience. In the city of Guangzhou, which was growing even faster than

Hong Kong, she was struck by the dirt and the drabness. The endless march of new skyscrapers from the impersonal heart of the business centre to the far horizon could not disguise the drudgery, and despite an abundance of Mercedes swirling between new banks and new hotels or from grand apartments to garish nightclubs, the people on the streets seemed down at heel. When the Hong Kong visitors sat down to talk to their Chinese hosts, also students, she voiced her feelings to one of them. 'The things I saw made me a bit depressed. I saw these people in the train station, and they gave me the impression that they were lost and confused.' She was told that they were probably the 'blind flow', migrants from the north travelling south in search of work. The Chinese student explained:

> Economically, Guangdong is quite advanced, but the rest of China is poorer. You can imagine the situation in the north, where fields have been taken out of agricultural production to meet the needs of urban expansion. There are fewer jobs on the land as a result. There are better prospects in the south. If one person from the north finds work in Guangdong this year, he'll go back and bring ten friends down for work next year. Then that ten might bring down a further hundred the following year. Of course, this makes employment more difficult. And when they can't find work, they often commit suicide.

Others in the party from Hong Kong mentioned their own observations. One had seen groups of peasants in a shanty town which looked as if it had been burned down. The government had tried to help these people by resettling them in a better place, but they moved around in search of work, the students were told. The city of Guangzhou had become more unstable and chaotic, and the crime rate had risen. 'These people have no money and no jobs. They are too ashamed to go back home, so they steal and rob from others. As the "blind flow" is always increasing, the government has been unable to cope. Even though some of them will be locked up as vagrants, they will return to the same situation as soon as they are released.'

The candour of the Chinese teenager's response encouraged Norris Lam to ask: 'You witness this depressing fact about this society, and yet you still love your country? What motivates this?' His reply was equally frank: 'I believe,' he said, 'it is the education. The government's emphasis on moral and civil education is very pronounced, especially at primary level. The young are taught about the ideology of the government to make them become more patriotic.'

'And what is the most important aspect of political education?' Norris wanted to know.

'First, you have to be patriotic and passionate towards your motherland, able to understand the basics of the law. Also we have to understand the basic changes of development of the country by the time we reach Form Three. From Forms Four to Six we learn about the basics of business and management. In the beginning, the core thinking is mainly political.' The Chinese student asked Norris about Hong Kong. Was there the same emphasis on political education?

'In Hong Kong they teach you about the basic structure of the government, and they illustrate the rights and responsibilities of the citizen,' she explained. 'We don't usually learn any specific "thinking", as you do. You have lots of activities organised by the government. Students receive their thinking from the government, and pursue these activities. Why are you so obedient to the government?'

Her host's response was simple. 'It's largely because of the political education. The government wishes the young to understand the importance of obedience, loyalty towards your superiors and to the country.'

'We don't have to be obedient towards our parents. We always feel that parents and children will get on better if they are more like friends,' Norris said.

Another Chinese student suggested: 'Maybe we are still inclined to the old traditions. Obeying your superiors is still very important.'

'Tradition may not be as bad as it seems,' offered a third. 'At least it has preserved our society from collapse.'

Norris Lam was a serious teenager, divided from her peers in mainland China by history, not by ethnicity. She wanted to understand, and not to judge, yet she could not begin to comprehend the culture from which she herself sprang, but on which had been superimposed an ideology – communism – which she found alien, and, in her innocence, quite bizarre. Yet she sensed that, if she were to make a place for herself in Hong Kong, which was her home, she would have to adjust to the values her hosts appeared to accept so willingly. Lacking any clear ideological perspective herself, she was troubled by the encounter. Initially she thought it would be a simple, patriotic exploration. Instead it left her feeling that the gulf between her and her counterparts in China was far wider than she had supposed.

In February 1993, nearly four years after Tiananmen Square, the National People's Congress in China had adopted the State Security Law, which criminalised acts 'harmful to state security', either committed by or financed by groups outside the state or carried out 'in collusion with them'. Proscribed activities included 'plotting to subvert the government', 'secretly gathering . . . and illegally providing state secrets for an enemy' and 'other activities against state security'. These 'other activities' related directly to freedom of speech, publication, association and religion. The catch-all nature of these 'offences' was not accidental. Although the law has not been widely deployed, except in respect of 'state secrets', it created, as it must have been intended to do, a climate in which any 'dissident' activity was fraught with even greater uncertainty and danger than before. Potentially, almost any act of defiance against the authorities became subject to severe criminal penalties, not excluding execution.

The same year a well-known journalist, Gao Yu, was arrested and charged with leaking important state secrets. Amnesty International has highlighted her case as an illustration of a judicial system in which the verdict is invariably decided in advance of a trial. This inversion of justice reflected the explicit subservience of the judiciary to the diktat of the Communist party. As the procurator general, Zhang Siqing, later stated in his report to the National People's Congress: 'We should closely rely on the leadership of the party committees and voluntarily accept supervision by the people's congresses. Procuratorial bodies should regularly report to party committees and the people's congresses, seek their advice and consciously carry out their instructions and opinions.'

The implications for Hong Kong of China's attitude towards human rights was brought into sharp focus by the arrest, on 7 October 1993, of Xi Yang, a reporter working in Beijing for one of Hong Kong's leading Chinese-language newspapers, *Ming Pao*. He was held in detention for eleven days before allegedly 'confessing' that he had been 'spying on national financial secrets', the character of which was not disclosed. It appeared, however, that the offence related to a report in *Ming Pao* on 28 July 1993 revealing that the Chinese People's Bank had decided to sell part of its gold reserves to build up its foreign-exchange holdings and that, as interest rates had already been increased twice that year, a third increase was unlikely. The alleged source for Xi Yang's article, an employee of the People's Bank, also 'confessed' to the same 'crime'. The Hong Kong Journalists' Association, a doughty, if isolated, defender of press freedom, pointed out that it was not readily apparent how China's national security might have been endangered by this report.

Margaret Ng, a high-profile columnist and barrister, writing in the *South China Morning Post* a few days after Xi Yang's arrest, offered a disconcerting analysis of the danger facing Hong Kong. Noting that the Chinese law on national security was drawn so widely that what was viewed as perfectly normal journalistic investigation in Hong Kong could be regarded as an unlawful activity in China, she argued that the very existence of a free press in Hong Kong posed a threat to the authorities in Beijing. As China's political, financial, economic and social policies and struggles had an increasingly powerful influence on Hong Kong affairs, so more and more of the colony's journalists would be sent north to cover these developments. Their discoveries would be published in Hong Kong's newspapers, and these in turn would become ever more easily available on the mainland – unless the authorities in Beijing could rupture the cycle of information. 'Not only is China likely to deal harshly with Hong Kong reporters once they are in China,' wrote Ng, 'but [it] is more likely to do everything it can to curtail the freedom of the press in Hong Kong after 1997, probably by getting a similar national security law enacted in Hong Kong if it can.'

One of the troubling features of this case was the way the owners of *Ming Pao* responded to their employee's arrest. They were told by Beijing that they should use the good offices of the British embassy in Beijing to secure Xi Yang's release, and informed that introducing 'self-censorship' in *Ming Pao* would be more likely to bring this about. In these circumstances, the paper understandably refrained from reporting the news of its journalist's detention. However, when the Chinese authorities then pressed charges against Xi Yang, *Ming Pao* abandoned that approach and gave full coverage to this alarming incident. Yet two days later, the chairman of the Ming Pao Group, Yu Pun Hoi, not only took it upon himself to apologise to the Chinese authorities, but declared he had reason to believe that his reporter was indeed guilty as charged – a statement he made without even attempting to consult Xi Yang himself. As Margaret Ng reminded her readers, 'The implication for future freedom of the press is grim.'

The case of Xi Yang not only highlighted the fragility of Hong Kong's freedom; it also threw into sharp relief the shifting attitudes towards that freedom adopted by those of its elite who wished to keep a place in the sun for themselves after July 1997.

By the early 1990s, seventy-six daily newspapers and 663 periodicals were published in Hong Kong, a higher proportion per capita than anywhere else in the world. In this highly competitive marketplace the pressure to cut costs was intense. The culture of investigative journalism was not nearly as developed as it was in the West, and the finance for it was even more limited. While the level of technology was as high as anywhere in the world, the use to which it was put did little to promote adventurous or challenging journalism – to the relief of both the business community and the upper echelons of the civil service, where press freedom was generally regarded as an irritant rather than a virtue. By 1993, the deferential attitude with which Hong Kong's media had long been infected was perceptibly beginning to shift towards self-censorship as more and more journalists, either voluntarily or at the behest of their proprietors, began to heed the pressure from

Beijing. Depressingly, it was also clear that the majority in Hong Kong believed this process to be inevitable and irreversible.

In a poll conducted in September 1993, 70 per cent of respondents indicated that they believed the freedom of the press would be eroded after 1997. In the same month, it was reported that the chairman of the Newspaper Society of Hong Kong, Shum Choi Sang, had told the Information Policy Panel of the Legislative Council that many journalists exercised self-censorship because they feared retaliation after 1997. He also estimated that almost three quarters of the profession were worried that they would no longer be able to work in a free environment after the handover.

On 28 March 1994, this pessimism deepened when Xi Yang, who had been held incommunicado for eight months (except for one brief visit from his father), was convicted of 'probing into and stealing state financial secrets'. He was sentenced to twelve years' imprisonment, and his 'accomplice' in the People's Bank received fifteen years. The punishment horrified Hong Kong, and hundreds of local journalists took to the streets to march on the local headquarters of the NCNA in protest. A further 1,300 signed a petition deploring the conviction and the absence of a fair and open trial. The Legislative Council took an unprecedented decision to debate the issue. Nonetheless the message from Beijing was clearly understood: in a poll commissioned by the *South China Morning Post*, 56 per cent of the sample concluded that the sentence was a warning to Hong Kong journalists to be careful and not to do anything with which the Chinese government might disagree.

Almost by definition, it was hard to gauge the full extent of such a closet and insidious practice as self-censorship. However, enough individuals were ready to acknowledge off the record that they exercised it to illustrate the degree to which the independence of the media – one of the defining characteristics of Hong Kong's 'way of life' which was supposed to have been consecrated in both the Joint Declaration and the Basic Law – was under assault. Although all journalists who discover, digest and select facts for publication frequently censor themselves to honour a confidence or to protect a source, it was not this normal filtering process which worried those in Hong Kong who cared about press freedom. In its 1994 annual report, the Hong Kong Journalists' Association explored a phenomenon which it held would 'increasingly play a key role in undermining freedom of expression in the territory', and which, it believed, was infecting the entire industry.

Among other instances, the 1994 report cited the case of Chan Ya, a columnist on the *Express Daily News*, a Chinese-language newspaper which had generally adopted a neutral position on the most controversial issues facing Hong Kong's future. In 1993, shortly after Xi Yang's arrest, Chan Ya's employers told her that they had decided to veto any comment on the case to 'avoid sensitivity'. She agreed to abide by the ruling until Xi Yang's boss made his notorious apology to the Chinese authorities. Incensed, she wrote two articles on the subject, both of which were 'spiked'. In January 1994 she submitted a piece which was critical of David Chu Yiu Lin, a member of the Preliminary Working Committee, a group of pro-Beijing activists appointed by China to help 'prepare' the ground for the transfer of sovereignty. The article was dropped because, according to her editor, it contained an 'indecent metaphor' which he did not choose to identify. Then the paper's chief editor told her that the report was not merely obscene but 'misleading'. Chan Ya's contract was terminated two months later.

A later poll conducted by the Social Sciences Research Centre revealed that over 60 per cent of Hong Kong's journalists felt that their colleagues were apprehensive about criticising the Chinese government, while almost one in three (28.5 per cent) acknowledged that they themselves felt such apprehension.

The term 'self-discipline' was often substituted by editors and reporters, without any obvious sense of irony, for 'self-censorship'. From its own research, the Hong Kong Journalists' Association identified the principal motives for 'self-discipline' from the responses to two related questions: 'Will work which is perceived to be unfavourable to or critical of the Chinese authorities draw repercussions after 1997?' and 'What might the degree of these repercussions be – greater pressures to conform, the loss of one's job, harassment by the authorities, or threats of prosecution for subversion or theft of state secrets?' According to the association, many publishers found it impossible to distinguish their editorial responsibilities from their entrepreneurial priorities. Their attitudes were increasingly dominated by commercial and financial imperatives, which made them unwilling to offend China. Several newspaper proprietors already had extensive investments in China and, whereas Hong Kong's media market was reaching saturation point, the commercial opportunities in China appeared limitless.

The direct but insidious pressure exerted by Beijing on the Hong Kong media played a crucial role in this process. In October 1993, Kam Yiu Yu, the former chief editor of the daily newspaper *Wen Wei Po*, China's unofficial voice in Hong Kong, gave an interview in which he explained, with the authority of an insider, the methods used by Beijing to secure greater compliance from Hong Kong's sometimes wayward media. Some of them were uniquely despotic. Selecting correspondents from supportive papers for favoured attention by giving them 'inside' stories or even headline news is a technique frequently deployed by democratic governments. The Chinese went further. Targeting what Kam Yiu Yu called the 'economic bases' of Hong Kong's media, they set about acquiring a controlling stake in individual newspapers or media groups by encouraging pro-Beijing investors to purchase the requisite number of shares on their behalf. The purpose of this infiltration, according to this former chief editor, was to gain control of editorial policy and the newspaper's direction of public opinion.

An even more direct pressure was exerted through advertising. Guided by Beijing, Chinese-owned companies had started to offer lucrative but conditional advertising contracts to targeted newspapers, magazines and broadcasting companies. Beijing's trade-off was crude but effective: a boost to company revenue in return for a supportive editorial line. Evidence of this tactic surfaced on 4 June 1993, when *Ming Pao*, one of the few independent Chinese-language papers, published the contents of two internal notices issued by the Bank of China's Hong Kong and Macau office. These instructed all organisations under the bank's extensive control not to place advertisements in eight newspapers and eleven magazines, including *Ming Pao* itself.

CHINESE DIPLOMACY.

The relationship between Britain and China has been characterised for more than two centuries by misunderstandings, disputes and skirmishes, encompassing the Opium Wars and an enduring sense of shame and grievance in China at Britain's seizure of Hong Kong.
Illustrated London News

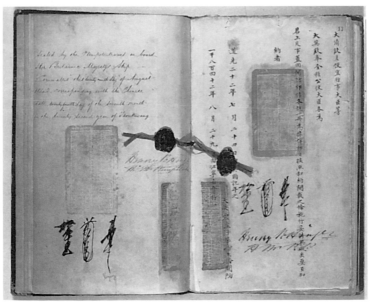

The Treaty of Nanking, signed in 1842, the first of the 'unequal treaties' under which the island of Hong Kong was ceded in perpetuity to Britain.
Public Record Office Image Library

Hong Kong justice, circa 1900.
*Lawlessness was rife, but in
their own way the expatriate
community behaved no less
deplorably than those over
whom they held sway.*
Foreign Office

*By the end of the eighteenth century, opium had become the most valuable commodity
traded by Britain with China, where its use was commonplace. This contemporary cartoon
offers a succinct comment on the relationship between the two nations.*
Bibliothèque Nationale de France

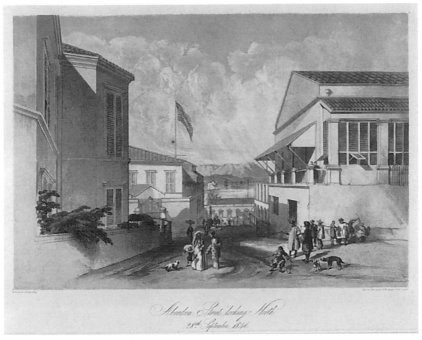

Aberdeen Street, 1846. Hong Kong remained a colonial backwater until the second half of the twentieth century. Expatriates protected themselves from its disagreeable aspects with a veneer of gentility.
HSBC Holdings plc

Demonstrators plaster the gateway of Government House with posters during the riots of 1967. Day after day, thousands took to the streets in the name of the Cultural Revolution, and the authorities were close to despair.
Hong Kong Government

The 'policy of co-operation' in action. Governor Sir Edward Youde (second right) and British ambassador Sir Percy Cradock at talks with the Chinese in 1983 about Hong Kong's future. Associated Press

Lord MacLehose, governor of Hong Kong from 1971 to 1982.
Hong Kong Government

Chris Patten's predecessor, Sir David Wilson, governor from 1987 to 1992.
Hong Kong Government

Prime minister Margaret Thatcher meets Deng Xiaoping in the Great Hall of the People in Beijing in 1984. Associated Press

On 4 June 1989 hundreds of people were killed or injured when the People's Liberation Army forced an end to a student demonstration in Tiananmen Square in Beijing. The atrocity was to have a lasting impact on Sino–British relations and on the negotiations over Hong Kong. Associated Press

Prime minister John Major was obliged to become the first Western leader to publicly shake hands with Chinese premier Li Peng after the Tiananmen Square massacre when the two leaders signed a 'memorandum of understanding' on the new Hong Kong airport in 1991. It was rumoured that Major later came to regret the visit. Associated Press

John Major with his choice as Hong Kong's last governor in April 1992. Patten was the first politician to be given the governorship – 'If you are talking to him, you are talking to me,' Major is said to have told Li Peng. Hong Kong Government

The new governor arrives in Hong Kong with his wife, Lavender, and daughters Laura (far left) and Alice.
Hong Kong Government

Chris Patten sets about his momentous task, flanked by the trusted personal advisers he brought with him to Hong Kong, political adviser Edward Llewellyn (left) and senior adviser Martin Dinham. Robin Allison Smith

Patten's walkabouts, a novelty in Hong Kong, reflected the importance to him of public opinion. His 'charm offensive' did not please his critics, but it certainly enhanced his reputation among the people of the colony. Hong Kong Government

Open day at Government House. The cultivation of local and international media was another crucial plank in Patten's efforts to secure popular goodwill. Robin Allison Smith

The throbbing megalopolis of Hong Kong, until 1997 the last significant jewel in Britain's colonial crown, has been variously described by Western writers as 'pure joy to the senses' and a 'permanent parasite' upon the skin of China. Robin Allison Smith

The leader of the Liberal party, Allen Lee, a toughened but compliant advocate of the business community and their allies in China.
Robin Allison Smith

Margaret Ng (below), the fearless political columnist elected to the Legislative Council in 1995.
Robin Allison Smith

Martin Lee, the leader of the Democrats, who recorded a landslide victory in 1991, when, for the first time, a proportion of the seats on the Legislative Council were directly elected.
Robin Allison Smith

The Legislative Council chamber (below), the setting of many scenes in the remarkable political drama which unfolded during Patten's governorship.
Robin Allison Smith

The redoubtable Emily Lau. 'Emily is a sort of yardstick against which the rest of us have to measure ourselves,' remarked Patten. Robin Allison Smith

Christine Loh, originally the governor's own appointee to the Legislative Council, emerged as a politician in her own right in the countdown to the handover. Robin Allison Smith

The author in conversation with Tsang Yok Sing, the leader of the Democratic Alliance for the Betterment of Hong Kong. Robin Allison Smith

*Property developer Vincent Lo,
an influential voice in both
Hong Kong and Beijing.*
Robin Allison Smith

*The trials and the triumphs of
Patten's term of office were
monitored assiduously by the
local press.* FormAsia Books Ltd

British ambassador to China Sir Robin McLaren faces the press after the fourth round of talks in 1993. Associated Press

Sir David Ford, chief secretary in Hong Kong from 1986 to 1993.
Hong Kong Government

Sir Len Appleyard, McLaren's successor as British ambassador in Beijing during the final years of British rule in Hong Kong.
London Pictures Service

The prime minister's former adviser Sir Percy Cradock arrives at Kai Tak Airport in 1993 en route for Beijing, a visit undertaken against the governor's wishes.
David Wong, South China Morning Post

Foreign secretary Malcolm Rifkind, watched by the governor, performs the topping-out ceremony at the British consulate building in Hong Kong on his first official visit to the territory in January 1996.
Hong Kong Government

The country retreat at Fanling provided some respite from the pressures of Government House, but there were always official boxes to attend to. Robin Allison Smith

'Being gubernatorial'. Patten with the Prince of Wales, on an official visit to Hong Kong (top), and inspecting a guard of honour (below). His decision to dispense with the ceremonial uniform traditionally associated with the post was a disappointment to some.
FormAsia Books Ltd

The people of Hong Kong look forward to the future with mixed feelings. The Ngs and their children (top left); Hari Harilela and his extended family (below left); George and Rowena Chen (top right); and Norris Lam.
Robin Allison Smith

Will the freedoms enshrined in the Joint Declaration survive the handover? Dick Lee of the Hong Kong Police (top) is optimistic about China's intentions, but street demonstrations by Hong Kong citizens, such as this one photographed in 1997 (below), are under threat.
Robin Allison Smith

Two of Hong Kong's most prominent characters: David Chu (top), posing with his beloved motorbike, and the irrepressible Jimmy Lai (left), proprietor of the hugely popular newspaper Apple Daily.

Robin Allison Smith

Chris Patten with Baroness Thatcher in 1997 *(top) and in conversation with a supportive President Clinton during his successful visit to the USA in* 1993. FormAsia Books

The governor with chief secretary Anson Chan. Patten considered her a vital link in ensuring a smooth transition between the outgoing and incoming administrations. 'If she goes, it will be a very bad blow,' he noted. FormAsia Books Ltd

Chris Patten pictured with the author shortly before the handover. Robin Allison Smith

The last governor with his family in front of Government House – from left to right: Laura, Lavender, Alice and Kate – not forgetting local stars Whisky and Soda.
Government House

These diverse periodicals shared one feature: none of them had been willing to toe the Beijing line.

The task of securing the undivided loyalty of Hong Kong's media was reinforced by what Kam Yiu Yu referred to as 'under-cover agents': loyal party members sent to work as reporters and editors for Hong Kong papers, usually on the 'China beat'. Many of these mainland correspondents were veterans of the official China News Agency or the semi-official New China News Agency. They were readily hired by Hong Kong editors because their links with the communist hierarchy in Beijing were held to be valuable in themselves; moreover, they held the promise of a major 'scoop'. After the failure of Hong Kong's media, including otherwise loyal newspapers, to endorse the 1989 massacre in Tiananmen Square, Beijing had apparently redoubled its use of these 'agents', first to recover the loyalty of the errant communist press, and secondly to work on the rest.

According to what the 1995 report of the Hong Kong Journalists' Association referred to as 'informed sources', the second of these two objectives was tackled with some sophistica-tion. In addition to direct infiltration, some agents were instructed to offer freelance articles to a variety of newspapers and maga-zines – an important way, apparently, of 'occupying more bases of public opinion'. Others were to befriend journalists with the purpose of influencing their judgement. As with the other forms of pressure, it was impossible to quantify how widespread or effective these efforts were, but in the tense atmosphere of Hong Kong, they were enough to perturb those who wished to remain journalists after 1997.

In addition the Chinese used the NCNA to bully and threaten recalcitrant journalists, to castigate 'hostile' publications and to instruct editors to undertake their 'patriotic' task with greater dedication. In July 1993, Next magazine, a Chinese-language weekly similar to Time or Newsweek, drew attention to allegations of self-censorship within the Sing Tao Group of newspapers, owned by Sally Aw, who had a reputation in Hong Kong as a tough proprietor with strongly pro–Beijing sympathies. After the sudden resignation of Sing Tao's editor in chief, Next reported that Aw had berated her editorial team, complaining that the Chinese had expressed unhappiness about a *Sing Tao* editorial on human rights, which they adjudged to be 'biased', a view with which she concurred. She issued instructions that future editorials should be 'fair, neutral, and objective', but did not specify how these standards were to be measured. Sources at *Sing Tao* interpreted the ruling to mean that any news about the pro-democracy movement in China, or about hostility towards Deng Xiaoping, should be regarded as 'unhelpful'. Soon afterwards, reports that a group of students on a Beijing university campus had dared to demonstrate against the authorities, which received extensive coverage elsewhere, were ignored by every paper in the Sing Tao chain. Was it a coincidence that the Sing Tao Group had decided to co-operate with a subsidiary of the *People's Daily* in Beijing to produce a monthly magazine called *Starlight*? Or that, at the same time, *Sing Tao*'s office in Guangzhou had set up a TV magazine called *Screen Friends* in collaboration with an official Cantonese television station? Independent observers drew the obvious conclusion.

Yet the trade-offs were not quite as simple as such a bald analysis might imply. At least in comparison with the mainland, the consumer in Hong Kong was highly sophisticated and would certainly be alienated by any overt sign of subservience to Beijing. Few editors were willing to curry favour with the politburo at the risk of decimating their circulation, and therefore only a handful of Hong Kong's newspapers openly campaigned against the principles of democracy. Although it was still easy to distinguish between pro-British and pro-Chinese coverage of the Sino–British conflict, every newspaper of note liked to claim that its editorial stance was merely 'pro-Hong Kong'. Of the mainstream Chinese-language papers, only the *Hong Kong Economic Journal* was stalwart in support of democratic reform; most of the rest sheltered behind the demand for 'consensus' and 'compromise' without specifying how these admirable objectives might be achieved in the circumstances.

In 1994, the chairman of the Hong Kong Journalists' Association, Daisy Lee, contributed an article for a programme compiled by the Hong Kong News Association for the Three Coast Forums, an annual seminar on journalism attended by delegates from Hong Kong, Taiwan and China. 'The Hong Kong media is in a state of growth and crisis; an era of hope and challenge,' she wrote. 'As long as we don't rush to censor ourselves and compromise our principles, the present freedom of the press can be maintained after 1997.' The piece was removed from the programme. Denying that this decision was a precise illustration of Daisy Lee's warning, the Hong Kong News Association told Radio and Television Hong Kong that the issue of press freedom was both 'too minor' and 'too sensitive' for discussion at the forum.

Broadcasters, too, came under pressure. RTHK was financed directly by the Hong Kong government but prided itself on exercising a similar independence to that enshrined in the charter of the BBC. RTHK's director was Cheung Man Yee, a former civil servant who had emerged as a tenacious advocate of broadcasting freedom. Under her leadership, RTHK maintained its reputation for fair and impartial journalism and as a station that did not shrink from contentious public debate. To protect RTHK from interference after 1997, Cheung Man Yee had pressed for the state broadcasting system to be incorporated as an independent public institution. However, China at once made it clear that this would be regarded as a hostile move by the colonial authorities, and the Hong Kong government decided that it would be a bridge too far, a decision reluctantly endorsed by Chris Patten. Morale at RTHK was severely affected, and it took all Cheung Man Yee's formidable powers of leadership to prevent her colleagues from succumbing to fatalism about 1997 – especially when it became ever more obvious that Beijing was unable to distinguish public-service broadcasting from state propaganda.

The colony's other two terrestrial broadcasters, the commercial stations TVB and ATV, were less stalwart. They competed for audiences with the mix of game shows, comedy and serials which form the staple diet of 'tabloid' television all over the world. Their most popular current-affairs programmes were frothy in content and sensationalist in tone, and shared a penchant for voyeuristic reporting of 'human-interest' dramas and crime. 'Is A.A. Ying's sex drive really strong?' inquired one TVB programme, reporting the alleged rape by a taxi-driver of a sexually promiscuous woman. The manager of TVB's 'Enrichment' Department justified their prurient coverage: 'There were reports in the press about this amazing woman. We had to support our story with in-depth reporting . . . If you stop reporting things you consider bad taste, then I think you are adopting an undesirable attitude as far as disseminating information and communicating are concerned.'

This intrepid approach did not extend to what might more usually be regarded as 'current affairs'. In 1993, TVB bought the rights to a BBC documentary called *Mao Zedong: The Last Emperor*, which took a distinctly less reverent view of the 'great helmsman' than the two portraits already transmitted by local commercial channels. Although it was the programme's revelations about Mao's sexual proclivities which attracted headlines in the West, its contention that he was indeed an emperor of the old school, remote from his people and ruthless in his means, was far more likely to inflame opinion in Beijing. Indeed, the Chinese had already unsuccessfully attempted to pressurise the Foreign Office into asking the BBC to drop the programme, and the Foreign Correspondents' Club in Hong Kong to cancel a private screening. When TVB failed to transmit *The Last Emperor*, it was widely presumed that either the station had yielded to pressure from Beijing, or, at China's behest, had bought the rights precisely to prevent its transmission in Hong Kong. TVB also acquired the rights to another BBC documentary, about China's labour camps, which contained secretly shot footage of prisoners toiling in the fields and on their way to work in prison factories. The film included interviews which revealed the appalling conditions under which 're-education through labour' took place. As in the case of *The Last Emperor*, the documentary was not shown, a decision which angered some legislators. TVB explained: 'It is just one of the documentaries we've bought in and we do not have a schedule for it yet.'

Whether or not TVB was exercising 'self-discipline' in these two cases, it was notable that both TVB and ATV refrained from featuring news likely to provoke Beijing's wrath. When Jung Chang, the author of *Wild Swans*, arrived in Hong Kong, both stations declined to interview her, even though her book was a world bestseller and she herself was generally fêted wherever she went. *Wild Swans* was not only a history of modern China, but a searing indictment of the Cultural Revolution, written from the author's first-hand perspective with an eye for coruscating detail. Similarly, in November 1993, both TVB and ATV decided to ban further interviews with the veteran dissident Wei Jingsheng, who was at the time nominally, though temporarily, a free man. He had served fourteen years in jail in China for trying to protect rights granted by the law but systematically violated in practice before being released that September – nine days before China's thwarted bid to host the Olympics in 2000. The two broadcasters vehemently denied the ban, but when an enterprising journalist rang Wei Jingsheng in Beijing, he confirmed that TVB, at least, had recently cancelled an appointment to interview him.

Other examples abounded, among them the decision by ATV to drop *News Tease*, which, with an audience of over half a million, was one of the most highly rated and discussed programmes on Hong Kong television, compared locally with CNN's *Larry King Live*. ATV's management explained the cancellation as an editorial decision, claiming that the programme had lost its flair. Yet it was widely recognised that – certainly by Chinese standards – the programme was remarkably sharp-edged and tenacious. It was also noted that one of its interviewers, Wong Yuk Man, had made no secret of his antipathy to communism. Without naming him, a number of pro-Beijing papers, led by *Sing Tao*, had mounted a campaign against the programme, accusing Wong Yuk Man of abusing the freedom of the media, of being 'anti-China', and of 'talking too loudly and being too hostile'.

ATV was embarrassed when, in the spring of 1994, six senior members of the News Department resigned in protest against the decision by its chief executive to cancel the planned broadcast of a documentary made by a Spanish television company to commemorate the fifth anniversary of Tiananmen Square. As edited by ATV, the documentary included a brief segment filmed in the square in the early hours of 4 June 1989. In later evidence before the Legislative Council, the senior managers who had taken the decision to withdraw the programme explained that the film failed to show the 'overall' situation in Tiananmen Square, and that, in any case, they thought it would be 'unhelpful' to pore over the details of that unfortunate episode yet again.

After a protracted debate in the media about this decision, ATV shifted their ground, insisting that there had not been a ban but a misunderstanding: it had always been their intention to transmit the documentary, but in a different slot from that proposed by the News Department. In the event, the programme was transmitted on the anniversary as originally scheduled, but none of the six journalists accepted ATV's offer of reinstatement, preferring instead to use the incident to campaign against the growing threat of self-censorship. 'I don't think there is any room for compromise,' one of them commented. 'One alternative is to give up. But if you carry on, you have to take a journalistic stance. The most important thing is that we journalists are able to maintain our journalistic ethics. Of course, journalists are only one part of the media. The companies themselves, and the public, should also act as watchdogs if they want to maintain press freedom.'

An even more craven example of 'self-discipline' was provided by the world's most powerful media proprietor, Rupert Murdoch. In 1994, as part of his restless search for global supremacy, the owner of News International bought Star TV, a rapidly growing satellite station owned by one of Hong Kong's most powerful entrepreneurs, K.S. Li. K.S., as he was known locally, had sold space on Star's northern beam to the BBC, which used this access to transmit its new World Television Service into Hong Kong and China. In the past Murdoch had made much of the virtues of satellite broadcasting, declaring that global communications of the kind he owned would be the 'biggest catalyst for peaceful coexistence'. The freedom of the airwaves, he intimated, transcended national borders and would liberate countless millions of people trapped in ignorance by the propaganda of oppressive regimes. Soon after his takeover of Star TV, he made a speech in which he reiterated that 'the march of telecommunications technology has been the key factor in the enormous spread of freedom that is the distinguishing characteristic of recent years'. Within weeks of that speech, however, Murdoch informed the

BBC that Star TV satellite system would no longer be available for its World Television Service.

Had this decision merely been the product of the tycoon's insatiable urge to crush his rivals, it might have been understandable; indeed, Star TV insisted at first that it had been taken for entirely commercial reasons. It was left to Murdoch himself to reveal the precise character of those 'commercial reasons' for denying viewers in China access to the freedom of the airwaves about which he had recently waxed so eloquent. In an interview with his biographer, William Shawcross, for *Esquire*, he acknowledged that his decision would appear cowardly and that he was 'well aware the freedom fighters of the world would abuse me for it', but, he explained, the Chinese authorities 'hate the BBC'. As a result, 'We said that in order to get in there . . . we'd cut the BBC out.' Shamelessly, Murdoch also volunteered that the reason why he had sold most of his shares in the *South China Morning Post* before his acquisition of Star TV was another move to minimise the risk of conflict with China. 'We certainly don't want Star to be shut down because of the opinions of some of our newspaper editors,' he said. Perhaps the only virtue of Murdoch's confession was that he gave expression in public to attitudes shared in private by the overwhelming majority of his peers in the international business community.

It was in this context that Chris Patten decided to give vent to his own fears about the freedom of the press in Hong Kong. Worried about the growing extent to which the Chinese, through the NCNA locally, were 'leaning' on the broadcasting companies and individual newspapers, he used an invitation to address the World Press Freedom Conference in Hong Kong in the autumn of 1994 to urge journalists and proprietors to stand firm. 'This governor will defend the freedom of the press up hill and down dale . . . All of us in Hong Kong need our free press now, more than ever.' Entreating the media to give the news 'true and straight, without fear or favour', to 'investigate, analyse and explain', and to 'ask the difficult questions and insist on the answers', he spoke with a conviction that clearly touched his audience. 'For our system in Hong Kong to survive and prosper,' he declared, 'proprietors, editors and journalists will have to demonstrate that they too believe passionately in the values of an open society. I am sure they will not betray that trust.' In truth he had no such confidence. He knew that in the scramble for trade with China, proprietors were suggestible and biddable, and, with a handful of exceptions, indifferent to the principles on behalf of which he was so agitated. He knew, too, that many of their employees lacked the stomach for a prolonged struggle on behalf of cultural values which were still novel, if not alien. Even if some of them had the courage of his convictions, they would not easily withstand such political and mercantile pressures.

As the tide in favour of an accommodation with China became more and more difficult to resist, it became evident that fewer and fewer media outlets in Hong Kong could be trusted persistently to champion the values of an open society in the way that the colony's last governor had hoped. The peculiarly personal character of China's onslaught against Patten, combined with the deep-seated if anonymous resentment against him in the business community, found a ready welcome in an increasingly ambivalent media.

By the end of 1993, it was almost impossible to find a British investor in China with a good word to say about Patten's policies for Hong Kong. The governor was the principal subject of dinner-party gossip as bankers and investors gave free rein to their resentment and disdain. Those of his friends who monitored the shifting attitudes of this elite detected from the dismissive hubbub that Patten's standing in this sector of the community was at its lowest since his arrival. Late in 1993, a private dinner party given by Peter Woo and his wife, Bessie, for the chairman of the Hongkong and Shanghai Bank, Sir William Purves, who was relocating to London, exemplified the mood. Peter Woo made a speech heaping praise on Purves. Purves spoke about his sadness at leaving Hong Kong. He uttered not a word about freedom or democracy or human rights, but made a promise that, back in London, he would 'raise the flag' for Hong Kong as much as he possibly could. Reminding his approving audience that Hong Kong had to 'get on' with China, he expressed the hope that relations would soon be restored and that the 'cack-handed' manner in which these had been handled in recent months would soon be rectified.

When he heard about this, the governor was not so much surprised as disappointed at the disloyalty of a senior adviser who, as a member of ExCo, had not only been privy to his strategy but had failed to speak against it at the time. Word of what Purves had said at his valedictory dinner soon swept through Hong Kong's establishment, as he must have known it would. Indeed, when he returned to his table he had commented in a gleeful aside, 'Well, I expect I have lost some of my more liberal friends now.' A few nights later, at a dinner for Purves at Government House, Patten made a glancing reference to the banker's assessment of his conduct of Hong Kong affairs. According to one guest, 'It was gently done, but Purves was flattened. He had very great trouble making a coherent response.'

Patten's contempt for Purves originated in an incident which had taken place some months earlier. The chairman of the Hongkong Bank had come to Government House to threaten Patten that if he did not change course, he would face dire consequences. In so many words he told the governor, 'The prime minister is in very considerable political difficulty, a very weak position. I'm thinking of taking along a lot of businessmen to see him to tell him he has to change his policy on Hong Kong and China. You'd better understand that.' On another occasion, the chairman of Shell came to see him and made similar threats. He behaved, as Patten put it, 'with the sort of crudeness which I don't think the Mafia would show'. Patten was not used to such raw conduct and it genuinely shocked him.

One of the more painful episodes for Patten in this period was a visit from a former Cabinet minister, Lord Prior, who had re-emerged into prominence as the chairman of GEC. In government, where he had served as minister of agriculture and secretary of state for Northern Ireland, Prior had earned a reputation for affability and decency, if not for strength of purpose or intellect. Patten, who had served under him in Northern Ireland, had grown to like and respect him. As a prominent 'wet', Prior had had an uncomfortable relationship with Margaret Thatcher, who made no secret of her disdain for his 'one-nation' Toryism.

As chairman of GEC, however, he was a surrogate for Lord Weinstock, and in this role he appeared to shed these values – at least in relation to Hong Kong. Those close to the governor revealed that Prior used his visit to Government House to berate his former colleague, showing a disconcerting lack of perspective and an embarrassing ignorance of the colony. The governor was by now familiar with Prior's message, which had already been delivered to him by other panjandrums of British industry for whom the rights and aspirations of the people of Hong Kong were apparently of little moment. Nonetheless it distressed him that Prior could so easily discard the principles which he had once seemed to hold dear.

He was less surprised by the animosity of another former colleague, Lord Young, the chairman of Cable and Wireless. Unlike Prior, Young had been one of Thatcher's favourites, an abrasive businessman who had never claimed a serious interest in political ideas. He was an entrepreneur by instinct and talent, a man of energy and enthusiasm whose 'can-do' attitude to apparently intractable problems prompted the prime minister to bring him into the Cabinet for a brief but inconsequential spell in the eighties. His contempt for the niceties of diplomacy was well known. In the case of China he believed simply, as he explained in 1996, 'It is trade that strengthens relationships, not treaties.' In 1984, following the signing of the Joint Declaration, he had led a British trade mission to Beijing during which he laid the foundations of a productive relationship with the Chinese leadership. As a former secretary of state for trade and industry, he liked to regard himself as an 'old friend' of China. Moreover, as the chairman of a company hungry for business in China, he conveniently found himself in sympathy with many of the attitudes of the country's leaders. By the early nineties he had come to the view that 'if you allowed too much openness in China . . . it would go back to warlordism'. The danger, he thought, lay in disparities in living standards between the north and, for instance, Shanghai, where, in 1995, 'Ferrari opened a car showroom and sold four cars in the first weekend to local Chinese. Well, they don't do that in London.'

It was from this standpoint that Lord Young assessed Patten's programme for Hong Kong. 'I think a number of us saw that there were opportunities in China on a heroic scale. That we could go back and reclaim markets that were ours in the last century. And that, I thought, would be a great prize: to retreat with honour and actually have a relationship.' Tiananmen Square, he conceded, was 'of course, appalling; it was a terrible miscalculation', but he was encouraged when one or two of his friends in Beijing acknowledged that this 'miscalculation' was the product of inexperience. Indeed, he had some sympathy when they told him, 'This was the first demonstration we'd had since 1949 which we had not organised ourselves. We were clumsy.' The problem, as it was explained to him, was that they had 'put in people who had no idea about crowd control'. Young was also persuaded by his Chinese hosts that the demonstrators were not entirely blameless, either. Although he did not know how many had died, he suspected that 'a lot of these people' had been 'stoked up'.

> They had been talked into democracy and they got talked into doing a number of things which an ageing leadership felt, I suspect, struck at the very heart of what they were trying to do . . . They were humiliated. The worst thing you can ever do is to make people lose face in that part of the world . . . And then I suppose they reacted – and that's not to apologise for them; what they did was wrong in every way – but you could begin to understand.

This 'understanding' had allowed Lord Young, among others, to nurture his relationship with China – even when, as a member of the Cabinet, he was subject to the bar on ministerial meetings with the Chinese imposed by the European Community after the Tiananmen Square 'miscalculation'. Young thought that it was 'extraordinarily important to keep the relationship going', regardless of the sanctions. To this end he even managed to arrange a meeting to discuss the expansion of the Anglo–French nuclear plant at Daya Bay by inviting the relevant Chinese general to meet him in a box at Ascot Races. 'I passed a very pleasant five minutes with him and off I went,' Young said. The general was able to report back that he had 'met' the trade secretary, while

Young could claim that their 'chance encounter' did not breach the sanctions. As Young put it, 'Everything was plain sailing from then on.'

Soon after his appointment as governor, Patten had been invited to lunch at Cable and Wireless, where Young and his colleagues had put their case for accommodating China in the interests of British industry. According to Young, they went out of their way to tell Patten how things should be done in private rather than in public, and how 'face' was very important. Patten did not seem overly impressed, and made it clear, Young says, that he was going to 'look at this with different eyes'. Afterwards Young recalls turning to a colleague and saying of Patten's appointment: 'I'm very worried. I am not sure this is going to be such a good idea.'

Young's doubts turned to dismay when he heard that Patten had decided to forgo the governor's plumed hat and official dress.

> You see, the governor is not an elected individual. The governor should be an aloof person who represents authority . . . Chris behaved as if he was canvassing for votes . . . you know, going round and kissing babies . . . I thought it demeaned the position of governor. I was concerned at his whole style . . . it is not the way to deal with the Beijing leadership where, in my book, you should say everything to them privately and agree what you're going to say publicly. It's not kowtowing to Beijing; it's simply the best way of getting agreement out of them.

At that time Cable and Wireless was the only foreign telecommunications company – through its subsidiary, Hong Kong Telecom – permitted to operate inside China. Young had worked hard to secure a closer relationship with the Chinese leadership. 'I had invested an enormous amount of time and effort seeing everybody – the president, Jiang Zemin, the premier, Li Peng – in order to find a way in which we could play a role . . . in what would be by far the largest market in the world,' he explained. 'It was incredibly important.' As he saw it, Patten's desire for democracy in Hong Kong not only threatened his own company's interests, but, more generally, promised to cause unnecessary damage to Britain's trading prospects with China. 'I do not believe that it was his job to sell out the people of Hong Kong for the benefit of the United Kingdom,' he said later. 'But I do believe there was a balance . . . and I think that balance went too far.'

Patten's refusal to be swayed rankled with Young. During a trip to Hong Kong, Young visited Government House on three occasions to press his case, all to no avail. If Patten managed to conceal his contempt for what he felt to be Young's crude approach and narrow focus, he gave the chairman of Cable and Wireless no comfort. 'We'd started on a confrontational approach, and I was trying my very best to plead the course of agreement with him,' Young recalled. 'We didn't have a row – my personal relationship [with Patten] was very good, and I think he's a very honourable, decent human being – but it was obvious I was not being listened to. And if you think you are not being listened to, you think to yourself, why bother?' After the third visit he did not seek any further meetings. Nor, he reflected, was he invited.

After his departure from Cable and Wireless following a long and highly publicised boardroom struggle, Young was unrepentant. Insisting that his overriding concern was the 'people of Hong Kong', the 'vast majority' of whom were 'entirely unpolitical', he declared Patten's term to have been a 'disaster'. 'The business community in Britain is totally against the governor,' he volunteered, 'and the business community in Hong Kong is totally against the governor.' He added: 'When you find this unanimity of opinion, you have to ask yourself why.' For Young the answer to the question was as honourable as it was self-evident.

Patten found it very difficult to take Young seriously. 'He never put those arguments to my face, though I used to hear what he said behind my back. That happened regularly over the years,' the governor commented dismissively. 'I think that is perhaps characteristic of Lord Young's style. But I can never remember him coming and having a serious discussion with me about our obligations to the people of Hong Kong.'

Young's response to the charge of cowardice was to say, somewhat limply, 'I did not risk having an argument with him because

I didn't want to bring any animus into the relationship we had, because that would react on my company.'

Patten's contempt for individuals like Purves and Young extended to many of their Chinese counterparts in Hong Kong. 'Some of the business leaders in the community appear to have been prepared to accept a sort of Faustian deal,' he noted with disdain. 'In effect they say to the Chinese leadership, "Well, nobody gives a button about a free press or all this other stuff the Brits went on about and stuck into the Joint Declaration. So long as we can go on making money, everything is all right."'

Patten's critics in the business community were now becoming more outspoken. Even the silkily oblique Peter Woo allowed something of his resistance to the Patten reforms to emerge, if only for the future record. While he and his wife, Bessie, continued to cultivate the Pattens socially, he spoke insinuatingly of the damage caused by the proposals 'the governor is supposed to have put on the table'. In so doing Patten had provoked the raising of a voice which had hitherto been silent: 'The business voice, saying, "We don't like it." Look, we don't try to control Hong Kong – it is not the business people's desire to control Hong Kong. But they don't want to see that they have no say in the future.'.

Vincent Lo expressed his hostility with less guile. 'To be blunt,' he said towards the end of 1993, 'I think he has done what he has done. So if there is a good assignment for him in London or elsewhere, maybe he can go and we can have a new governor who can really understand the reality of Hong Kong and work with Beijing so that we can get a better deal.'

Among the few unequivocal champions Patten had in Hong Kong was the flamboyant and outspoken Simon Murray, former managing director of Hutchison Whampoa. Murray's endorsement of Patten had irritated the company's chairman, K.S. Li, who was avowedly pro-Beijing. Though neither of them would concede the point publicly, their conflict over this issue was instrumental in Murray's decision, late in 1993, to resign. As he moved easily between the expatriate and the local elite, Murray was in a unique position to assess the motives of his fellow businessmen. Visitors always asked him similar questions: 'Why doesn't Patten keep quiet?' 'Why doesn't he shut up?' 'Why doesn't Britain co-operate?' Some of them, assuming that Murray shared their views, would complain about 'this bloody Patten'. Murray gave them no quarter.

> You simply do not understand. Who the hell are you, coming from France, or London, or wherever, to start telling me that Patten is wrong? You haven't even understood one fraction of the issue, and yet you are coming out here telling us what the score is . . . You say, 'Patten seems to be the problem.' Well, he may be the problem for your particular business. But there are five or six million people here for whom Patten is not the problem. Patten is their life-saver. OK? Have you thought about their position? The ordinary Hong Kong citizen has run away from China. He's a refugee. We are handing over Hong Kong to a third party which happens to be the last bastion of hard-nosed communism in the world. Examine the human-rights record. Every so often they release a guy who's been in jail for twenty-seven years and never actually been on trial, and they'll say 'It's all getting better.' Yes, it is getting better, but China's record is still pretty bad, and this leaves a lot of people in this place who are absolutely terrified of what comes next.

Murray was resigned to the fact that his would remain a lone voice, even though his listeners sometimes appeared to be impressed that one of their own should speak with such convic-tion. He was by no means self-righteous. It was simply as a matter of fact that he noted: 'Businessmen are interested in their money, and that is all they are interested in.'

Murray pressed Patten's cause with his counterparts in terms which Patten could not himself deploy, even in informal gather-ings. Insisting that only a more broadly based, and thus more democratic, Legislative Council could protect Hong Kong from the corruption that was endemic on the mainland, he argued that if LegCo were to be elected on Beijing's terms, it would be a very small body and dangerously open to bribery and coercion. 'Anybody in his right mind would say that we've got to have a wider electoral body to ensure that we do not have a corrupt Legislative Council, and that we can throw them out if they turn bad on us.' Murray believed that many of his peers privately shared this opinion but were afraid to speak out. He persevered.

The only way we can have any hope of continued success is by being different. Who needs Hong Kong? The weather's OK, and it is quite a nice place to live, but it would be irrelevant for our business. We'll all go and open our offices in Shanghai. Outsiders will not invest in Hong Kong if the business is exactly the same as in China. Hong Kong's GDP will begin to fall, and Hong Kong will begin to fade. It will cease to be important. It is important today because of the freedoms and because of the law.

Murray often found that he could 'swing a dinner table round', but his success was invariably short-lived. 'The following day they are back under their tables. They are fearful and they want to keep their mouths shut and hope it will all go away. In many ways it's pathetic.'

Patten only occasionally gave vent to his own frustration. Rarely raising his voice, even in private, he invariably encased his feelings with a carapace of heavy irony. At a particularly exasperating moment in December 1993, when his responsibilities seemed 'fairly nerve-racking', he noted that he had 'learned to worry less about the ammunition which is going to be fired at you from the other side than the ammunition which comes zinging at you from behind your back'. A few months later he was less oblique. The most depressing thing about the first two years of his governorship was the extent to which the business community had been prepared to 'sell out completely without really bothering whether or not China lives up to the bargain it undertook in the Joint Declaration, and without bothering whether China actually lives up to all its commitments on preserving the values of Hong Kong. I think that is pretty treacherous.'

13

'A Bracing and Bruising Experience'

Charges and Counter-Charges

The collapse of negotiations with China at the end of 1993 provoked a protracted bout of political soul-searching in Government House. Although he could hardly admit it publicly, Chris Patten felt a sharp sense of liberation and relief that the Chinese negotiators had at the last moment reneged on their apparent readiness to do a deal. In particular he had not enjoyed having to concede ground on the electoral franchise; nor could he rid himself of the sense that to negotiate with Beijing involved a through-the-looking-glass journey in which the awareness of delusion was always mockingly at hand. The future was daunting, but at least he was once again in control of events – insofar as it was possible to dictate a process so fraught with uncertainty.

The governor knew that he had to regain the initiative and to reinvigorate Hong Kong with the confidence and enthusiasm for his reforms which had noticeably dissipated in the long months of haggling. On 3 December 1993, he announced that ExCo had sanctioned his plan to introduce the first (and least controversial) part of his reform package into the Legislative Council on 15 December. The Chinese responded with a predictable outcry and, taking its cue from Beijing and the business community, Allen Lee's Liberal party (the Co-operative Resources Centre had reinvented itself in March) voiced severe misgivings about Patten's decision to press ahead in the absence of China's blessing.

Patten was far more concerned about the Democrats. Martin

Lee had expressed his dismay that the governor had ever allowed himself to be drawn into the charade of negotiations with China. By now the two men knew each other well, and Martin Lee had privately left Patten in no doubt about his party's 'bottom line'. Patten's decision to table his original bill, albeit in two parts, was not only a matter of political instinct. It was also governed by the knowledge that he would lose the support of the Democrats if he were to table the 1993 version of his proposals watered down in an attempt to reach agreement with China. Martin Lee's Democrats might well join Allen Lee's Liberals in an unholy alliance to wreck any bill thus amended. In these circumstances, public confidence, already fragile, would be shattered, as would his own credibility. The demands for his departure would reach a crescendo and, as he privately acknowledged, it would be very difficult for him to remain in office.

As it was the path on which he now had little choice but to embark was hazardous. Even if he could muster the votes for the relatively innocuous first stage of the bill, he knew that LegCo would be split down the middle over the second stage. He was not at all confident that he would emerge triumphant from such a fracas. Whatever the final outcome, he was all too conscious that the months ahead would put his political acumen severely to the test. He had a foretaste of this when Martin Lee, ostensibly one of his few allies in Hong Kong, attacked his approach while on a trip to Washington to drum up congressional support. Warning that the governor's decision to table the bill in two parts would give the Chinese even more time to derail the reforms, Martin Lee declared that he no longer trusted Patten to fight for democracy in Hong Kong. In characteristically exaggerated language, he claimed that the governor had 'talked a great deal but delivered nothing'.

The days leading up to Christmas were consumed by a dreary routine of charge and countercharge which aggravated the deteriorating relationship between Britain and China. Beijing accused the British of being responsible for the breakdown; London retorted that it was the other way round. Each side claimed that it was willing to recommence negotiations and blamed the other for failing to respond. On 17 December a Chinese Foreign

Ministry spokesman reiterated that any legislation passed by LegCo in the absence of a Sino–British accord would not straddle 1997. He added that trade relations between the two sovereign powers would be adversely affected, although he did not specify in what way or to what extent. Patten reacted swiftly by pointing out that China enjoyed a trade surplus with Britain, and that he could not imagine that Beijing would wish to damage that advantageous imbalance. On 27 December, in their most unequivocal statement so far, the Chinese issued a formal warning that there would be no 'through train' for the legislative assembly, or for the two tiers of local government, the District Boards and the Municipal Councils. On 1 July 1997, they announced, all individuals elected to these three bodies would cease to hold office, and a new three-tier structure of government would be 're-established in accordance with the relevant Basic Law stipulations'. This was the most unnerving declaration of intent yet to issue from Beijing.

To add to the mood of pessimism in Hong Kong, a leading NCNA official served notice that senior government officials would not automatically be allowed to remain in office following the handover. This threat to derail the administrative 'through train' along with its political counterpart was calculated to alarm not only civil servants but also the business community, for whom the survival of an experienced and independent civil service was critical to ensure stability. The Basic Law stipulated that all civil servants would have the right to remain in service after 1997. However, the NCNA spokesman said, the mechanism by which this process was to have been achieved had been severely damaged by Patten's insistence on pressing ahead with his constitutional reforms in defiance of China's will. As a result, the first chief executive of the SAR would (as stipulated elsewhere in the Basic Law) nominate senior officials who would be appointed by the central government of the People's Republic. The implied threat was self-evident: senior civil servants who had the temerity to honour their obligations as loyal servants of the British crown might have to look elsewhere for employment after 1997.

Anson Chan, the chief secretary, responded mildly but firmly that it was 'important to maintain the continuity of the civil service'. Her words disguised the anxiety felt by all her colleagues in the upper echelons of the government, many of whom had already privately made it clear that they had no faith in Patten's 'confrontational' approach. The governor's press secretary, Mike Hanson, one of his most loyal officials and himself a civil servant, was frustrated by the erosion of morale among his colleagues, some of whom complained to him that the governor had been too distracted by the conflict with China to address other important issues. They felt isolated from the policy-making process, and, they told Hanson, they no longer trusted Patten to act wisely in Hong Kong's interests. Hanson noticed that on a number of domestic issues they were becoming increasingly recalcitrant – one or two of them even failed to co-operate in the preparation of the governor's 1993 address to LegCo. Instead of identifying and exploring a range of alternative policy options, a few chose, in Hanson's words, to 'cut off the options in advance'.

Simon Vickers, another expatriate who had joined the Hong Kong civil service in 1979, was equally disturbed. He had served in various departments, including the chief secretary's office, before joining the Security Department in 1992, with responsibility for immigration and nationality policy. The impact of Tiananmen Square had forced him, like so many others, radically to adjust his views about the future of Hong Kong. The optimism of the mid-eighties, when he had been sure that he and his family would be able to stay on after 1997, swiftly gave way to uncertainty and then to pessimism. After Patten's arrival and the outbreak of diplomatic hostilities between Britain and China, he had noticed a shift of attitude among 'local' civil servants. Though ostensibly loyal to their present sovereign, he sensed that a lot of them had 'fallen away' from Patten because 'he was causing too many problems for them in their daily lives'. According to Vickers, they were frustrated that many of their otherwise non-contentious policy proposals for the development of Hong Kong were being blocked by Beijing in the Joint Liaison Group (JLG), the forum through which the Chinese exercised their right to be consulted on all matters relating to the handover. Rather than blame their future masters for this impasse, they tended instead to blame Patten, lamenting, 'It wasn't like this in the old days.' The warnings from China that their jobs would not be secure after 1997 served only to sharpen this alienation which, Vickers detected, was accompanied by a surge in 'patriotic' sentiment. He saw this as a threat to the colony's post-1997 prospects. 'It doesn't leave room for Hong Kong to say, "Well, we are part of China, but we do things in a different way."'

One incident was to lodge in Vickers' mind to illustrate this anxiety. A year or so on, in 1995, as a reliable expatriate, he was transferred to the Judiciary Department, where he was charged with the sensitive task of separating those personnel files that would be made available to the Chinese in 1997 from those to be retained or shredded. On one occasion, when he was deputising for the department's senior administrator, he came across a note from one of the colony's most senior Chinese judges, which was clearly not intended for his eyes. Attached to a clipping from a newspaper article about the alleged superiority of the Chinese IQ over that of other ethnic groups, the judge had written: 'How much longer must we carry on this charade of subordination?' The latent hostility towards the British from such an important member of Hong Kong's judicial establishment intensified Vickers' own growing sense of isolation and reinforced his intention to take his family back to Britain before the handover of sovereignty. Vickers shared Hanson's view that the governor would have great difficulty retaining the loyalty of the most senior civil servants in the final stages of the handover. Hanson was reluctant to add to Patten's troubles by voicing such fears. 'I don't think the governor realises how isolated he is,' he said.

As Christmas approached, in his rare moments of respite from the increasing pressures of his governorship, Patten tried to make the most of the personal comforts his surroundings offered. If Hong Kong is light on culture, it is a cornucopia for those in need of retail therapy, and the governor was an avid shopper. In Bath, he had been a familiar sight in supermarkets, delicatessens and wine stores, not propositioning constituents but buying the weekend groceries. On holiday in France (where the Pattens were to buy a house in 1994), his daily routine was constructed around his mission to attend every local market of significance. As these occurred at least three times a week, he was kept very busy. Despite Lavender's attempts to curtail his enthusiasm, he invariably returned from such expeditions heavily laden with cheeses, wines, meats, fruit and pastries, concerned only about whether he had purchased enough to meet their needs before his next foray.

In Hong Kong, where he did not need to buy his own food, he browsed in the antique shops which line Hollywood Road, a mere ten minutes from Government House. He also enjoyed buying clothes for himself and for his family, choosing dresses for his wife and daughters – even for Laura, who now worked in London for *Harpers & Queen*. On one occasion he selected for her a scarlet slip of a dress designed by Jean-Paul Gaultier: it fitted perfectly. He was also taken with Shanghai Tang, owned by one of Hong Kong's most imaginative entrepreneurs, David Tang. Here he bought a long green *cheong sam* as a surprise for Lavender and a velvet Chinese jacket lined with vivid cartoon prints for himself. When friends came to stay he took them to Shanghai Tang and urged them to follow his example.

In Hollywood Road, calling in on the way to buy his favourite sweetmeats from a corner store which proudly displayed a photograph of him with the owner, he would happily spend a couple of hours wandering from shop to shop, admiring the ceramics, bronzes, ivory and jade on display. Patten soon acquired enough antiques to adorn both the private quarters at Government House and the main rooms at Fanling. A cleaner at Fanling, evidently unaware of the importance attached by collectors to the original pigment on 2,000-year-old ceramics, noticed one day that the rough pieces of ancient pottery seemed grubby. She decided to attack them with hot water and cloth. Soon they were free of all dirt – and almost all colour. The Pattens sighed, but did not complain.

In January 1994, Patten flew to London to give evidence before the Foreign Affairs Committee of the House of Commons. In his opening statement to the assembled MPs, he intimated something of the pressure to which he had been subjected. Offering an otherwise robust account of his stewardship, he volunteered that the attempt to negotiate the transfer of sovereignty was 'occasionally a more bracing and bruising experience than any of us would like'. Answering the charge that he had been responsible for violating the Joint Declaration, the Basic Law and other agreements between Britain and China, he asserted that no Chinese official had yet 'been able to identify precisely where these perfidious crimes have taken place'. As for Sir Percy Cradock's accusation, made before the same committee a month earlier, that Patten had 'refused consultations with the Chinese', it was, he insisted, 'completely untrue – whether the result of misunderstanding or whether the result of other motivations is for Sir Percy to explain in due course'.

In an indirect riposte to Cradock, who had gone on to accuse him of a 'reckless' disregard for the interests of the people of Hong Kong, Patten poured scorn on those unnamed officials who liked to approach negotiations in the belief that 'if you find a suitably opaque form of words, full of strong nouns and weak verbs, it can provide a curtain behind which you can retreat on matters of substance'. A little later in his evidence, he challenged Cradock directly to 'say openly that basically his point of view is that we should settle for whatever China will provide'. Remarkably, this swingeing assault – his only public reprimand until that point for the prime minister's former adviser – was barely noticed by the media, whose attention was otherwise engaged. Privately, Patten expressed his contempt for the 'appeasement' policy advanced by Cradock, his loyalists in and around Whitehall and a significant proportion of the international business community. 'You know, I dare say there are some who, if China was saying, "Well, our price is slaughter of the first-born," who would say, "Well, maybe it is not unreasonable in the circumstances. You know, you have to allow for different cultural traditions." I mean, do we ever have a bottom line?'

The animosity between the governor and the former diplomat not only reflected their mutual contempt but their mutual incomprehension. The non-debate between them exposed contradictory certainties about Britain's responsibilities towards Hong Kong and, consequently, about what strategy to adopt with China. These divisions, long suppressed by the diplomatic evasions and self-delusions of the Foreign Office, had allowed both Britain and China to pretend to themselves that fundamental questions about freedom and justice could be avoided or postponed. By insisting that these issues could not honourably be ignored, and that, diplomatically, Britain should not be intimidated by China, Patten had not only brought them to the surface but had obliged Hong Kong, China and Britain to confront the perilous realities which faced them.

But Patten had now advanced too far down his chosen path to be diverted for long by a thwarted ex-official who refused to keep his own counsel. Bombarding the committee with carefully marshalled arguments, he reiterated his belief that his proposals were not only modest but well within the terms of the Joint Declaration and the Basic Law. He concluded – carried away more by his own rhetoric than by a genuine conviction – with the assertion: 'I am optimistic about Hong Kong's future. I am optimistic about the likelihood of our values and our way of life surviving, because I think that what Hong Kong represents is the future, not the past.'

Meanwhile, there was the present. Asked about the deadline by which the two parts of his bill would have to complete their passage through the Legislative Council, he answered, 'We need to have the main legislation in place by July . . . these are fantastically complicated elections. They involve, as honourable members can, I am sure, imagine, about forty different pieces of subordinate legislation or administrative guidelines . . . All these things are hugely complicated and July is cutting things very fine indeed.' This was the first deadline he had set which genuinely could not be extended without severely disrupting Hong Kong's electoral timetable.

On 24 January, the Cabinet once again endorsed the governor's approach and strategy. In what by now had become a routine procedure, the foreign secretary stood beside Patten at a press conference after the Cabinet meeting to make it clear that the governor had the 'unanimous support' of his colleagues in government. This statement of the predictable was ignored by the British media, for which, in any case, it was not principally intended. It played well in Hong Kong, however, where a distinctly more credulous school of journalism prevailed, and where every inconsequential phrase from a figure of authority was likely to be treated as a tablet from the mount. It also served to remind Beijing that the 'Triple Violator' and the British prime minister were not easily to be unyoked, however rough the terrain might become. Both men genuflected towards a resumption of talks, but the press conference did elicit two points of substance: that the governor had not yet decided when to table the second part of his reform package, and that the decision was to be his alone, subject only to consultation with the foreign secretary.

Meanwhile, the possibility of Patten returning to London to help restore the fortunes of an ailing government was given an airing in the British press. The *Daily Telegraph* reported that a number of senior officials had privately urged that the governor should be summoned back from Hong Kong in the hope of restoring Sino–British relations. His skills, they noted dryly, could perhaps be put to better use in a less sensitive role. More flatteringly, an editorial in the same paper observed: 'Minister after minister has lamented privately that Mr Patten, among the ablest of Tory strategists, is absent from the bridge in the government's hour of need.' This was certainly true: the Conservatives were still stricken by divisions over Europe and the failure of the 'feel-good' factor to emerge at the end of Britain's longest postwar recession. The party had also exposed itself to contempt and ridicule with a succession of financial and sexual scandals, and the term 'sleaze' had attached itself, limpet-like, to the reputation of an unpopular government. Whether or not Patten could have made a significant difference was, however, open to question. Although he sometimes allowed himself the thought that he might have been able to steer Major around some of the pitfalls into which he had fallen, the government's problems were as much matters of substance as of presentation, and Patten had been far too preoccupied with his own drama in Hong Kong to do more than commiserate with his friends and colleagues at Westminster. In any case, he was as robustly determined to stay as he had been six months earlier when Douglas Hurd had first mooted the possibility of a premature return to the government. In an attempt to deter further wishful thinking by his former colleagues, Patten used an interview with Max Hastings to scotch rumours that he had his sights on an early departure from Hong Kong. He was only too aware that if they were to gather force, his credibility would be further endangered. Hastings clearly got the message: although he ruminated on the prospect of the governor's return, the burden of the *Telegraph's* editorial on the subject was summed up in the headline, 'PATTEN SHOULD STAY'.

In Hong Kong, it was widely presumed that the first part of Patten's bill would emerge unscathed from LegCo. Regardless of the mutterings from Beijing, it seemed unlikely that the anti-Patten coalition within LegCo could mount a significant threat to a set of proposals whose most controversial point was lowering the voting age to eighteen. All attention was therefore now focused on the fate of the second part of the package. The question lobbed back and forth in the media and between the competing political parties was whether Patten should table his original 1992 proposals or the 1993 version watered down in the vain attempt to secure a deal with China. Patten, of course, had already made up his mind in favour of the 1992 proposals the previous summer, but had not disclosed this to his colleagues until his return from holiday. Although the Cabinet meeting on 24 January 1994 had formally endorsed his decision, he refrained from committing himself in public. Indeed, as a precautionary measure, the lawyers in the Constitutional Affairs Department had been instructed to draft a parallel bill based on the 1993 concessions. The governor and his team resolutely denied the existence of such a draft, knowing that it would be used by his adversaries to undermine the case for the original bill.

In early February, Patten made an official visit to Australia, where the foreign minister, Gareth Evans, paid fulsome tribute to his 'modest' reforms. In contrast, the premier, Paul Keating, whose anti-British chippiness was well known, was notably reticent about the need for greater democracy in the British colony, an omission which was gloatingly picked up by the NCNA. At the same time, Beijing reacted to news that, on Patten's advice, the Foreign Office was about to release a White Paper detailing the background to the breakdown of the Sino–British talks with a tit-for-tat promise to produce their own version. Irreverent observers noted wryly that only a serious breakdown in relations could prompt either Britain or China into such an uncharacteristic display of open government.

In fact Government House had been involved in a fierce argument with both the Foreign Office (where Christopher Hum, one of Cradock's acolytes, was particularly influential) and the embassy in Beijing about whether it was necessary or advisable to give the Chinese formal notice of the decision to publish the White Paper and of the proposed timetable for the LegCo debate. In the end, as one of Patten's disgruntled aides put it, 'the diplomats won'. It was agreed that the British ambassador, Sir Robin McLaren, would deliver a letter to Lu Ping on 17 February. But the day before a member of ExCo leaked the proposed LegCo timetable to the *Economic Journal*, which duly published the details. When the British embassy pressed for a meeting with Lu Ping, there was no response. As a result McLaren had to leave the letter at the Hong Kong and Macau Affairs Office without even seeing its director. A measure of the relationship between Government House and the embassy may be gauged from the report of one of Patten's aides that the governor had chortled mirthlessly: 'The cowardly sods gave it to the receptionist and ran.' A few hours later, Lu Ping's office rang wanting to know why the British ambassador had not had the courtesy to await a response. When this was finally delivered, down the phone line, it was, said Mike Hanson, 'terrible'.

The Foreign Office released their White Paper on 24 February, timing it to coincide with the passage of the first stage of Patten's reform bill through LegCo in the early hours of the same day. The Electoral Provisions (Miscellaneous Amendments) (No. 2) Bill, as it was officially known, confirmed that in the 'geographical' constituencies at all three levels of government elections would be on the basis of a single-seat, single-vote system; that appointments to Municipal Councils and District Boards would be abolished; that the voting age would be reduced to eighteen; and that restrictions on the rights of Hong Kong residents who were simultaneously members of the Chinese People's Congress to stand for election in the territory would be lifted. The bill was passed on second reading by a majority of 48 to 2 after a motion proposing its postponement had been rejected by 36 votes to 23.

Anson Chan welcomed the outcome, and despite Beijing's fury at Britain's unilateral decision to forge ahead with the unamended second-stage bill, made emollient noises about future co-operation with China. Moving forward with the second stage was complicated by the fact that several senior civil servants, increasingly fearful of Beijing's wrath, had hoped to appease China by running with the 1993 version. The secretary for constitutional affairs, Nicholas Ng, who had replaced Michael Sze, was ill at ease with the decision to press on with Patten's original proposals. His attempt to defend it in public reflected his doubts and was at times incompetent.

Patten formally announced his decision to proceed with his 1992 proposals a few hours after the publication of the White Paper, at one of his regular question-and-answer sessions in LegCo. The bill, he informed the legislators, would be tabled on 9 March. The response from China and the pro-Beijing lobby in Hong Kong was immediate and predictable. Patten was denounced for 'sabotaging' the Sino–British negotiations and, yet again, for violating the Joint Declaration and the Basic Law. Beijing fulminated that the decision to publish the White Paper was both a breach of confidentiality and a 'bid to deceive the public and mislead public opinion'. Anson Chan countered that the White Paper was 'the truth', and a Foreign Office spokesman reiterated that the decision to table the second stage of Patten's reform bill had been made after close consultation between the governor and the British Cabinet. Beijing responded by restating that as the bill had no status in Chinese law, the three tiers of councils 'unilaterally established by the British side' would be abolished at the handover.

Bracing themselves for further Chinese reprisals, the independent *Ming Pao* and an official Beijing newspaper, *Overseas China Daily*, warned that Beijing might also exact an economic price for Britain's political démarche by retaliating against British firms trading with the mainland. The *Overseas China Daily* warned that the Chinese might form their own 'shadow' tiers of government before 1997, or even make moves to take Hong Kong back earlier. It was unavoidable, the paper declared, that China would strike back. The *South China Morning Post* summed up the general view of relations between Britain and China with the headline 'NOW IT'S ROCK BOTTOM'.

Patten now found the ranks of his detractors swelled by the Democrats, apparently fearful that the governor was only half-hearted in his commitment to electoral reform. Martin Lee, in particular, was agitated by Patten's persistent public reminders that the Legislative Council had the authority to amend or annul any legislation proposed by the government. As the governor had tried to intimate to Martin Lee, this did not mean that he would refrain from advocating the virtues of his proposals or, indeed, from lobbying for them. Lee was not impressed. His anxiety that the reforms would be shredded by hostile amendments was exacerbated by the suspicion that Patten had done a secret deal with China. He confided his concerns soon after the bill had been tabled.

> I am afraid Patten may be doing a very clever thing and a very dangerous thing. He knows that he could not possibly have introduced the '93 version of his reforms, so he introduced the '92 version, which is more democratic. But as for telling members, 'Well, if you want to amend it, I will accept it,' I have never heard of a government which says to its Parliament, 'Look, we are presenting this bill to you because we think it is good, but please, if you don't like it amend it in any way you like and we will accept it.' He calls this 'an executive-led government'. I think this is very dishonest.

Martin Lee's suspicions had been fuelled some weeks earlier, before the publication of the White Paper, at a lunch with Tsang Yok Sing, the leader of Hong Kong's most significant pro-Beijing party, the DAB. Asked by others at the table if, despite the breakdown of negotiations, agreement between Britain and China was still possible, Martin Lee responded with an unequivocal no. 'I don't agree,' countered Tsang Yok Sing, explaining, according to Martin Lee, that there would be an agreement because Patten had already made enough concessions (in the 1993 negotiations) to satisfy the Chinese. As Tsang Yok Sing was known to have the ear of Beijing, Martin Lee leaped to the conclusion that, in the course of those negotiations, the British had retreated far enough to ensure that Beijing could control the legislature. Knowing that amendments tabled by pro-Beijing legislators to the 9 March proposals would be designed to dilute them to satisfy China, Martin Lee was moved to complain privately that Patten's stance was a 'devious and dishonourable and dishonest way' of appeasing Beijing. Despite Patten's original insistence that he had no hidden agenda for Hong Kong, the colony was rife with rumours of plots and conspiracies and, not for the first time, Martin Lee allowed himself to fall foul of the prevailing atmosphere.

Although Patten had, in fact, engaged in no such legerdemain, Martin Lee's interpretation of his motives was closer to the mark than he would have liked to acknowledge.

> I suspect he is trying to make life easier for himself in two ways. He wants to make sure that when he leaves Hong Kong no one can say, 'How could you, the British government, sell Hong Kong down the river to a very repressive communist regime without leaving some democratic institution to protect human rights and the rule of law? . . . And he can do that by presenting a bill which, if passed in its present form, would give us those safeguards. But he then leaves it to the Legislative Council – which is highly undemocratic – to water it down so that the legislature which China inherits in 1997 is one that it controls . . . He can then say, 'Look, it's not my fault. I tried to give Hong Kong democracy but they were too nervous to accept.' In other words, he's trying to put the blame on the people of Hong Kong.

Martin Lee's assumption was unjust, but it reflected a genuine fear that by standing aloof from the legislative fray the governor would, by default, aid and abet Beijing's purpose. For the first time, but not for the last, Patten was irritated by Lee's lack of faith. 'The refusal to rule out any amendment at all produces, yet again, charges of conspiracy,' he protested wearily. 'But I went through the eight, nine, ten previous occasions on which Martin and his friends had said we were about to rat on them, and pointed out to them that after eighteen months there was still no rat. So maybe they should just be a bit more patient.'

Patten's analysis of China's attitude to the events now unfolding in Hong Kong was based as much on intuition as evidence. He was puzzled, confiding that he was unable to predict China's next move. 'I now have sufficient confidence in my knowledge of China to say we haven't got the faintest idea what they'll do next,' he said dryly. Yet he remained optimistic. 'I think there is a very good chance – though I don't intend saying it very much in public because it just pushes them into saying, "Ya boo, you're wrong" – of the electoral arrangements we put in place this year surviving through 1997.' Allen Lee reacted scathingly to this tentative prognosis, commenting with an air of finality, 'No way. That's a myth. That's Chris Patten's line. It will never have a future.' Patten had a delicate path to tread: to intervene strenuously in the debate about his reforms would lay him open to the charge of misusing his executive authority; to stand aside would allow Martin Lee and others to allege that, for all his rhetoric, he was indifferent to Hong Kong's fate. In an attempt to weave a path through this political minefield, he decided to increase his public appearances, carefully orchestrating them to ensure that he could react swiftly to criticism and, where possible, get his retaliation in first: 'I have to be, as they say, out and about pretty well every day, being seen in public.' Taking care to avoid proselytising for his reforms, he took every opportunity to reassure people that his proposals were good for Hong Kong; that they fell within the Basic Law; but that, of course, in the end, it was for the people of Hong Kong, through their representatives on LegCo, to decide.

As the July deadline drew close, the battle for votes in LegCo intensified. A visit to Hong Kong by Lu Ping at the beginning of May exemplified the contrasting behaviour of Patten and his Chinese counterpart. As soon as the visit was announced, Patten issued Lu Ping with an invitation to Government House, which he duly refused: Lu Ping, the governor was told, would be too busy to meet him. Government House expressed its regrets but assured the director of the Hong Kong and Macau Affairs Office that Patten would interrupt his own hectic schedule at any time to facilitate a meeting. Patten was in fact concerned that he would be marginalised by the visit but, in a generally successful attempt to turn it to his advantage, he repeated his invitation at every opportunity, even suggesting that Lu Ping might like to return to the territory to join the guests at his forthcoming fiftieth birthday party. For the next few days the two men circled each other in Hong Kong, vying for public attention as they respectively hurried from one pressing engagement to another. Farcical though this stand-off appeared, the media was swift to side with Patten. The week before, Government House had nudged the *Oriental Daily* into conducting an opinion poll which demonstrated overwhelming support for a meeting between the two leaders (though the sample of 206, as Patten's press aide gleefully admitted, was 'sentiment, not science'). The findings were widely reported and seemed genuinely to confirm the mood of the public.

Under pressure from the media Lu Ping issued a statement explaining that he would not be in a position to meet the governor until the differences between the two governments had been resolved. The contrast between the governor's openness at press conferences and during walkabouts and Lu Ping's stiff and formal style was widely noted, again to the former's advantage. Tsang Yok Sing confided, 'I believe Lu Ping should and could have done a lot better . . . we can't see what China or Lu Ping himself can lose by meeting the governor.' Except, he might have added, 'face'. Even Vincent Lo, China's most loyal advocate, admitted: 'I would like to see the two of them sit down and really thrash things out.' But he judged that China was making an explicit and fundamental point.

On the third day of his visit, Lu Ping and his entourage were stricken by food poisoning. Government House (which monitored the NCNA offices just as carefully as the Chinese were presumed to bug the British embassy in Beijing) discovered that Lu Ping himself had had to be given glucose intravenously. Muttering, 'It wouldn't have happened here,' Patten took malicious delight in sending Lu Ping his best wishes for a speedy recovery. By the time of the director's departure, it was quite clear that he had signally failed to dent Patten's image.

The concern within Government House about public opinion sometimes bordered on the neurotic, and the relief when Patten's ratings survived the visit intact was palpable. Yet his need to demonstrate that he remained at the centre of events, still confidently guiding Hong Kong's destiny, was not narrowly egotistical; his desire to secure the passage of his reforms through LegCo, notwithstanding Martin Lee's scepticism, governed his every move. Perhaps for this reason, Patten still allowed himself to believe that Lu Ping would have to meet him before long: nothing would do more to enhance his local standing and to undermine his critics. Patten's problem, which he sometimes seemed to forget, was that the Chinese were as aware of this as he was.

An illustration of the governor's sensitivity at this time was his response to the news that Sir Percy Cradock had once again chosen to intervene in Hong Kong's affairs. On a visit to the colony immediately before Lu Ping's arrival, Cradock had accepted an invitation to meet the director of the NCNA, Zhou Nan. According to Tsang Yok Sing, who leaked the story to journalists, Cradock advised Zhou Nan that Lu Ping should decline to meet the governor. He was reported to have warned that such a meeting would send the wrong message from China to the British government and would demonstrate that Beijing could be bullied into submission; that it would have overtones of the Opium Wars. As soon as this alleged act of treachery was reported to Government House, one of Patten's aides was on the line to the Foreign Office, demanding that Cradock issue a statement to clarify his comments. Disconcerted by the story, the former diplomat vehemently denied that such a conversation had occurred. Some days later, one of Patten's friends confided that the governor was still 'spitting' at this latest 'betrayal'.

Patten's resolve was also being tested from another quarter. Despite his brisk rejection of Douglas Hurd's suggestion the previous summer that he was needed back home, the issue had not gone away, and Westminster gossip continued to float his candidature for a senior position in the government. At the end of May 1994, these rumours reached Hong Kong, where newspapers reported that John Major had asked him to return as Conservative party chairman, an offer which he had refused. With the fate of Patten's reforms teetering in the balance, the suggestion that the prime minister wanted to withdraw him from Hong Kong was very far from helpful. Government House at once issued a statement dismissing the reports as nonsense and reiterating that the governor would stay until 1 July 1997. As it stood the statement was true – the prime minister had not asked Patten to return as party chairman – but it was also misleading. For while Patten was not seeking to leave Hong Kong prematurely, he knew that the prime minister was anxious to secure his services. Indeed, early in the summer, Major approached Patten directly 'as a friend', to ask whether, once he had steered his electoral reforms on to the statute book, he would consider returning to the Cabinet as his most senior colleague.

The prime minister offered his trusted political ally an astonishing brief: he could become leader of the Lords and foreign secretary, as well as taking over the vacant role of deputy prime minister. Apart from Major himself, Patten would become the most powerful man in the Cabinet. Patten was flattered, but once again he declined, observing gently that the prime minister really needed someone like Lord Whitelaw, who had served as Margaret Thatcher's shrewd and unflappable deputy prime minister in the eighties. Major replied that this was precisely why he wanted him back in London. But Patten insisted that, unless instructed otherwise, he could not honourably renege on his duty to Hong Kong.

Although he sympathised with Major's plight, Patten thought that the prime minister's approach reflected a failure to recognise the significance of the responsibility he was attempting to discharge on Britain's behalf as the colony's last governor. It was a feeling he had had when Douglas Hurd had approached him the year before. On that occasion it had seemed to him somewhat perverse that a British foreign secretary, of all people, should appear to place the difficulties of the Tory party above the reputation of a nation. Although he had by no means 'gone native', Patten retained an acute sense that his was a momentous assignment, and he was disappointed that Major, like Hurd, appeared unable to share that sense of history. Instead, yet again, and in an exceptionally demanding period, the prime minister had unwittingly left Patten with the impression that Britain's mission in

Hong Kong somehow mattered less in 10 Downing Street than the future of his troubled administration at Westminster. For a while Patten brooded on this: it did nothing to cheer him.

There were other irritations as well. Henry Keswick, the chairman of Jardine Matheson, one of the most powerful 'Hongs', had been one of the very few international business leaders not to have deserted the governor early on in his battle with Beijing. Now he, too, abandoned him – and in circumstances which infuriated Patten. After transferring the company's place of incorporation from Hong Kong to the apparently safer financial haven of Bermuda in 1984, the Jardine board had refrained from criticising the British stance as the company continued to weather China's outbursts of hostility. Although Patten was not so naive as to suppose that Keswick's tacit support sprang from altruism, he was dismayed when the magnate began to behave in a way which clearly suggested that he expected a return on his investment. It was Keswick's habit to fly into Hong Kong three times a year, usually accompanied by senior members of his 'absentee' board, for an intensive round of meetings with key executives in Hong Kong. Invariably on these occasions, they would expect, and duly received, an invitation to Government House. In March 1994, in his capacity as a member of Jardine's main board, Sir Charles Powell, Margaret Thatcher's former adviser at Number 10, made use of this access to press Patten to exercise his authority on Keswick's behalf.

In 1991, Henry Keswick had decided to move Jardine Matheson's primary stock-exchange listing to London, leaving only a secondary listing in Hong Kong. By 1993, Jardine was operational in thirty countries and employed a workforce of more than 200,000. Keswick was impatient to liberate the company from the constraints of the Hong Kong takeover code, and his lawyers embarked on discussions with the Securities and Futures Commission (SFC). Arguing that the company was soon to become subject to Bermuda's takeover code, they tried to convince the SFC that its shareholders would lose none of the protection afforded them by the Hong Kong code. The SFC was not impressed. Keswick was enraged by what he regarded as pettifogging and vindictive decisions by second-rate bureaucrats.

Powell was dispatched to Government House to demand that Patten exercise his gubernatorial powers to overturn the SFC's decision. Patten refused. The governor's aides, reflecting his own strong feelings, emerged from this meeting filled with indignation at what they saw as a blatant attempt to 'call in the favours' that the Keswicks had hitherto bestowed on the governor. At a subsequent meeting a few days later, at which Powell was joined by Henry Keswick's brother Simon, the two men made the case again. Once more they were rebuffed by Patten, who insisted that it would be quite improper for him to intervene. 'We won't be bullied,' he said afterwards.

Keswick ran Jardine as if it were his own fiefdom, although by now his family owned only some 15 per cent of the shares. In March 1994, thwarted by the SFC, the company took the drastic step of withdrawing its listing from the Hong Kong Stock Exchange. Keswick declared that his decision did not signal any lack of confidence in the future of Hong Kong itself. 'We are as confident as ever in Hong Kong's future . . . we wish to continue to expand our investment in and business links with Hong Kong, China and the whole Asia Pacific region,' he said. This did not find favour among his employees in Hong Kong, who regarded the decision to delist as an act of pique and a betrayal of their loyalty by an arrogant and distant board as indifferent to their individual fates as it was to that of Hong Kong. The governor had similar feelings. He was not surprised when the Keswicks ceased to press for invitations to Government House, although Sir Charles Powell remained one of his confidants. The discovery that Keswick now referred to him as 'that bloody little socialist' merely confirmed Patten's impression that the tycoon was faintly ridiculous.

At the end of May Patten found himself under assault from his democratic allies on another front. It emerged that he had authorised a decision to bar two Chinese dissidents now resident in the United States from coming to Hong Kong to take part in the annual 4 June rally in Victoria Park to commemorate Tiananmen Square. Under pressure from the local media, Government House insisted, without much conviction, that Hong Kong could not be used as a base for dissidents. The governor's apparent failure to live up to his own rhetoric about human rights provoked the censure of democratic activists, which embarrassed and irritated him. As one of his aides commented privately, 'I'm afraid we have handled this very badly. It has been looked on by some as another example of the government kowtowing to China.'

Patten earned even more opprobrium from the same quarter when he made it clear that he opposed the establishment of a Human Rights Commission for Hong Kong. Arguing that the Bill of Rights, which was already on the statute book, was protection enough, he claimed that his forthcoming Equal Opportunities Bill would take care of all outstanding issues, and faced down the human-rights activists in LegCo – even to the extent of barring Anna Wu, a respected independent member, from tabling a motion in favour of a commission. For good measure he made it clear that he would also reject an Access to Information Bill proposed by Christine Loh. Both these decisions were presented as if they had emanated from ExCo, but no one was in any doubt that they originated with the governor. His reason for refusing to countenance the 'all-singing, all-dancing legislative effort', as he described Anna Wu's motion, was that, as he confided later, he had come to the conclusion that the community would not stomach another huge fight with China. He argued that the same ends could be achieved by other means which might involve 'running skirmishes with the Chinese rather than another nuclear confrontation'.

Christine Loh was one of the governor's own appointees to LegCo. Brought up to enjoy the middle-class comforts of a prosperous merchant's family, as a teenager in the late 1960s she had been more interested in sport than politics. Her father was a refugee from Shanghai but unusually, her mother, who had been born in Hong Kong, could trace her family back through four generations as colonial subjects. Like that of most of her peers, Loh's knowledge of China was culled from newspapers and television; the vicissitudes of life in the People's Republic did not impinge significantly on her early life. At the end of that decade she was sent to :chool in England and did not return to Hong Kong until 1979. At the age of twenty-three, armed with a law degree and a belated zest for public affairs, she took lessons in Chinese and soon became involved in 'fringe' politics as a member of a group called the Hong Kong Observers, which lobbied for the extension of human rights and democracy in the colony. Although Loh had reservations about the Joint Declaration, it was not until the Tiananmen Square outrage that she became convinced that the 1997 transition would be fraught with danger. Encouraged by the appointment of Chris Patten as governor, she was astonished, in October 1992, to be invited up to Government House, where the chief secretary, Sir David Ford, asked if she would accept the governor's appointment to a seat on the Legislative Council. She thought, 'My God, I can't believe this!' Over the next few hours, she discussed the offer with other activists, all of whom advised her to accept. 'This is a vital opportunity to promote the liberal cause,' they told her. She took their advice. Six months later, she said, as if still off balance, 'Chris Patten has completely changed my life.'

But now some of the governor's liberal critics began to wonder whether his genial demeanour concealed an authoritarian streak. Six months earlier, in November 1993, Patten had made a speech at the Foreign Correspondents' Club in which he had attacked those moral relativists who liked to believe that the issue of human rights was essentially a Western obsession amounting to a 'neo-colonial incursion into Asian affairs'. Put the other way round, if it were argued that human rights weren't really appropriate for Asia, Latin America or Africa, the proposition would, he avowed, rightly be regarded as sanctimonious, if not racist.

> If you are a journalist locked up for months for telling the truth; if you are a trades-unionist incarcerated for championing workers' rights; if you're thrown out of your country and deprived of your rights; if you're beaten over the head, or worse, by a policeman, the brutal result is the same, whether it happens in Europe, or Asia, or America, or Africa. Human rights are indivisible and interdependent.

It was a stirring dissertation no previous governor would have essayed. That China was the principal object of his scorn was in no doubt, yet – or so it seemed to the activists in Hong Kong – the self-appointed champion of human rights seemed overly willing to retreat from these heady values when it came to the crunch. They were disappointed and angry.

To make matters even more tiresome, two of his senior officials disagreed in public about the scope of the government's Equal Opportunities Bill. Patten wanted Anson Chan to handle the presentation of the policy, but she insisted that it was the responsibility of the home affairs secretary, Michael Suen. Evidently ill briefed, he mishandled the press conference. On the most sensitive issue of all, he stated that the government's bill would not include proposals to outlaw sexual discrimination in the workplace. Mark Fisher, a British Labour politician who was in Hong Kong to support Christine Loh's unsuccessful attempt to introduce her Freedom of Information Bill, watched bemused as the hapless official stumbled through his brief. It was, Fisher judged, a 'pitiful performance'.

The following day, members of LegCo, led by Anna Wu and Christine Loh, expressed their fury at the government's apparent indifference to the issues at stake. To limit the damage, Patten's press secretary, Michael Hanson, rushed out a statement insisting that, despite what Michael Suen had appeared to say, the government's Equal Opportunities Bill would after all include measures relating to sexual harassment. The home affairs secretary doggedly stuck to his guns. He was not aware that the scope of the bill was to be extended in this way, he said, adding: 'Mr Hanson does not represent the government.' Patten was furious. Although he eventually prevailed, the incident could not have occurred at a worse moment. As one of his aides admitted, 'It was a huge cock-up.' It certainly confirmed the impression, seized on by his adversaries, that, as an administrator, Patten was not infallible.

The governor was under too much pressure to dwell on adversity. In early June he was censured by the Legislative Council in the unprecedented form of a vote of no confidence. The issue, which involved property rates, was of little significance constitutionally and the effect of the censure was merely symbolic. But in such a feverish atmosphere, symbolic gestures mattered. The episode served to remind the governor that the independence of

Hong Kong's legislators, for which he had so ardently proselytised, could backfire on him personally. With the vote on his reform package only three weeks away, anything that could undermine his authority was a potential threat to its passage. In this case he was quick to turn the setback to his advantage, using his question time at LegCo to declare, 'I will always defend the right of this council to criticise the government and the governor. I hope we can take this for granted after 1997.'

In the days leading up to the anniversary of Tiananmen Square, Beijing's 'friends', led shamelessly by the former prime minister Sir Edward Heath, urged Hong Kong to forget the massacre or at least to reinterpret it less harshly. In his weekly column in the *South China Morning Post*, Tsang Yok Sing, the most politically sensitive of Beijing's allies in the colony, advised his readers not to 'reopen the wound'. It was all the more telling, therefore, when, in an interview for CNN on the eve of the vigil, he broke down in tears as he remembered how the entire school where he was headmaster had wept that day in 1989. The trauma of Tiananmen Square still echoed through all discourse about democracy in Hong Kong, and it was not only the democrats who were offended by the crass intervention of Heath and others.

Tsang Yok Sing, the leader of the DAB, was born in Hong Kong in 1947 and educated at the colony's leading Roman Catholic school, St Paul's College. He went on to study at the University of Hong Kong, where he became caught up in the high drama of the Cultural Revolution. With his brother, Tsang Tak Sing, he helped to organise the student demonstrations against the British which erupted in the riots of 1967 and nearly brought colonial rule to a premature end. The authorities had been obliged to fall back on the draconian powers embodied in the Emergency Regulations, yet even these measures would not have prevailed had it not been for a simultaneous instruction from the Beijing Maoists to their Hong Kong cadres calling a halt to the uprising. The repressive methods adopted by the British, which led to Tsang Tak Sing being jailed for two years, confirmed his brother's antipathy towards colonial rule and his intellectual commitment to Marxism. Although Tsang Yok Sing was always to insist that he never joined the Communist party (which was, and remained, outlawed in Hong Kong), he soon established himself as one of the most loyal supporters of Beijing in the colony. In 1969 he became a mathematics teacher at the Pui Kiu Middle School, one of more than a dozen 'patriotic' schools. He took over as principal in 1986, by which time he had already been appointed by the politburo in Beijing as a delegate to the People's Congress in Guangdong.

The Tiananmen Square vigil, on 4 June in Victoria Park, took place only three weeks before the LegCo vote on Patten's reforms, which gave it a particular poignancy. It was a wet night, and a crowd of over 30,000 sat on plastic sheets or newspapers holding lighted candles protected by rice-paper shades. At a crescendo in the music the candles were held aloft and glittered through the rain across the park. The quiet resolution of the people affected even the most hardened observers, and it was impossible to conclude that the hunger for freedom and democracy in Hong Kong was a popular spasm exploited by irresponsible elements among the colony's chattering classes. Edward Llewellyn, the governor's political adviser, was spotted watching from the sidelines by a reporter from *Ming Pao*. The pro-Beijing *Wen Wei Po* picked this up and inevitably saw in the aide's presence a British plot. The following day the NCNA made two official complaints to the governor.

In the run-up to the decisive vote on Patten's reform package, Government House began to lobby intensively to secure its passage. To win, Patten needed at least half the votes in the sixty-seat council; to win convincingly he needed a big enough majority to offset the effect of the votes of three 'ex-officio' LegCo members (the chief secretary, the financial secretary and the attorney general) who, as government employees, were obliged to support the bill. With LegCo almost evenly split, the outcome hinged on a handful of wavering votes. These included those of the so-called 'Breakfast Group', an alliance of disparate interests featuring, among others, a senior executive of Jardine Matheson, Martin Barrow, who had a reputation for listening with very great care to his paymasters' voice; Hui Yin Fat, of the social workers' functional constituency; and Simon Ip, an amiable but lacklustre solicitor who represented the legal profession on LegCo. Patten homed in on this group, joining them for breakfast on several occasions to make his case. The task of corralling other floating votes was entrusted to Nicholas Ng, the constitutional affairs secretary, and his deputy, C.M. Leung, who spent long hours in the council antechambers openly lobbying against his adversaries in the Chinese camp.

Their job was made more difficult by the positions taken by Martin Lee and Emily Lau, the governor's two most impressive but unpredictable allies on LegCo. Lau, the most forceful and eloquent politician in Hong Kong, had argued vigorously that the three government officials appointed to LegCo should be released from their obligation to support Patten to join her in voting against his package in favour of her own bill, which called for direct elections to all sixty LegCo seats. Her proposal was regarded by Patten, in the words of one of his staff, as 'not only crazy, but certain to send China berserk'. Nonetheless it had the potential, as a grand but futile gesture, to scupper his reforms by luring away one or more of the Democrats' crucial votes. Even more seriously, opponents of the Patten reforms, notably the pro-Beijing Liberals, might decide to vote for Emily Lau's 'impossibilist' bill to embarrass him. From the perspective of Government House, Emily Lau's perversity was matched by Martin Lee's failure to rally support for the governor. Although he had been surprised and delighted by the Patten proposals, he had yet to endorse them in public; formally, the Democrats were still committed to an increase in the number of directly elected seats for the 1995 elections from twenty to thirty. To Government House this seemed pointless, as Lee had made it quite clear privately that his party would in the end endorse Patten's reforms. 'Martin seems to be doing nothing,' one of the governor's aides complained in exasperation a few days before the crucial debate.

To complicate the process, there were fourteen amendments to Patten's bill, the most dangerous of which had been tabled by the Liberals. At first the governor's team took comfort from the fact that this attempt to redraft his package was so clumsy that even some in the pro-China camp were embarrassed by it. In seeking to scale down the functional constituencies, for example, Allen Lee had found himself proposing restriction of the franchise in one functional constituency to a maximum of 153 senior executives. Patten's allies were optimistic that none of the 'floaters' would be attracted by such blatant efforts to subvert the democratic process. Nonetheless, they knew that the pro-Beijing bloc in LegCo would throw its weight behind the Liberal amendment. If so, Patten would need to secure every last possible vote for his bill to survive more or less intact.

14

'INSIDE I'M CROWING LIKE MAD'

LegCo Votes on Patten's Reforms

On the eve of the vote on the Legislative Council (Electoral Provisions) (Amendment) Bill 1994, the outcome still hung in the balance. In Government House the mood was gloomy. Though even his closest colleagues did not know it, Patten believed that it would be impossible for his governorship to survive a defeat at the hands of the Liberals. Lavender, whose public performance as the governor's wife had earned her plaudits throughout Hong Kong and across the political spectrum, knew this, but kept her nerve. Although she did not volunteer strong opinions in public, she understood his predicament with clarity, and did not hesitate to express her thoughts within Government House. In this case, she shared her husband's view: he had invested too much of his reputation in his reforms for his credibility to withstand their defeat.

Behind the scenes Martin Lee was almost in despair at what he regarded as the governor's failure to secure enough support for his bill, and complained that he had only himself to blame. 'I told him he had to lobby hard, but I think he thought all would be fine. Now they appear to have only twenty-eight votes, and that is not enough. I am very unhappy, and very annoyed. He is supposed to have a good reputation for twisting arms. I just cannot believe he could not have done better.' If Patten were to lose the vote, he fretted, 'It would be the cruellest thing that could happen to Hong Kong. It would have been better if Wilson had remained, toeing his line of appeasement. We will have been betrayed.'

Within twenty-four hours of the decisive vote, it began to look as though the bill would fall. Not only had LegCo's pro-Beijing bloc confirmed publicly that it would almost certainly support the Liberal amendment, but, despite Patten's breakfast appearances, the independents seemed likely to follow suit. The remaining waverers were wobbling so violently that it was impossible to tell which way they would eventually vote. One by one they were summoned to Government House to hear the governor make his case yet again. One or two of them indicated that he would have their vote; others listened intently but refused to declare themselves one way or the other. 'I've been Clintonising since the end of last week,' remarked Patten. 'I don't much like it. I'm not one of nature's whips. But there it is, it had to be done. I don't want to go through this again.'

At the eleventh hour, Martin Lee finally came to the governor's aid by agreeing to make a speech, at the request of Government House, in which he not only called on all instinctive democrats of whatever party to support the Patten proposals, but also named the remaining undecided voters who could tip the scales either way. In an intriguing development, he also undertook to lobby Lau Wong Fat, the deeply conservative leader of Heung Yee Kuk, a residents' association bloc from the New Territories, with whom he was deeply at odds on almost every issue. Indeed, his own amendment to the Patten bill proposed the abolition of Heung Yee Kuk's three seats in LegCo. Now, after much prompting from Patten, Lee promised that he would try to cut a deal with Lau Wong Fat by undertaking to withdraw this part of his amendment in return for a commitment from the Heung Yee Kuk leader that he and at least one of his colleagues would either vote against, or abstain on, the Liberal amendment.

On the night before the most crucial day in his political career, Chris Patten went to bed, well supplied with sleeping tablets, not knowing whether the next day would bring glorious victory or ignominious defeat.

The morning of 29 June 1994 began as usual for the governor with a workout on the tennis court. In his private office, his team vainly scoured the newspapers for developments. The only new story was in the *Eastern Express*, which reported that John Major had intervened to secure a crucial vote 'as the fate of Chris Patten's reform proposals hung in the balance'.

According to the *Post*, the prime minister had, in some unspecified way, persuaded Henry Keswick to secure the support of Martin Barrow, the Jardine Matheson executive on LegCo. The previous day, Barrow, whose own hostility to the Patten reforms was no secret, had suddenly upset all calculations by announcing that he would not after all be supporting the Liberal amendment of which he himself was a principal architect. When Patten arrived in the office, he dismissed the report. He had, he said, himself momentarily considered ringing the Jardine chairman, but had managed to resist the temptation. 'Hand on heart, I did not call Henry. I just thought it would put me in the position of a supplicant.' Barrow, too, insisted that it was his 'personal' decision. 'It was going to be such a dead-heat situation. I didn't think that I should be the one with the casting vote.' Yet it was widely presumed that Barrow would not have switched his loyalties so suddenly without instructions from his chairman. Despite Keswick's falling-out with Patten, Jardine Matheson was a significant contributor to Conservative party funds, and the family was believed to maintain close links with the government, not least through Keswick's wife, Tessa, who was the political adviser to the chancellor of the exchequer, Kenneth Clarke.

Whatever the truth, Allen Lee, who had been relying on Barrow's support for his Liberal amendment, was furious, though less with Barrow than with the governor. Before announcing his decision, the Jardine executive had rung the Liberal party leader to break the news of his defection. According to Lee, Barrow was reticent about his change of heart.

> He told me he had changed his mind for personal reasons, and that it had nothing to do with the governor, but I couldn't get any explanation. We've been working on this for two weeks. He was instrumental in designing our package. He had devised a lobbying plan; he told us how to lobby Chinese support and how to lobby local support; he

told us who we had to discuss our plan with in Beijing, and that this was the way to secure the support of pro-China legislators here . . . He was working with us day and night. Now, at the last moment, he drops out. There must be a reason . . . Somebody must have got to him. I told him, 'Martin, your heart must be bleeding.'

Allen Lee, never known to understate a case, claimed that Patten's lobbying tactics had been excessively brutal. 'Their limbs have been taken off by the governor. He is twisting their arms and legs . . . Is this fair? Is this British politics? Is this letting the Hong Kong people decide? We had thirty votes; now the fate of Hong Kong is being changed by one man. I've never seen anybody operating like that.'

Edward Llewellyn acknowledged that Government House had been like a whip's office on the previous day, and that Patten and his advisers had managed to 'square' Martin Barrow. While the governor admitted that he had lobbied 'vigorously', if with some distaste for the process, he was adamant that the proprieties had been scrupulously observed.

I can say hand on heart that we didn't promise anybody anything and we didn't threaten anybody. What we said was that we thought that a defeat would be extremely bad for the authority of the government; that it wouldn't end the political argument; that . . . it would make sure the argument rumbled on for the next two or three years with the pro-democracy politicians becoming increasingly difficult to handle. Why? Because they would feel, understandably, that they'd been robbed.

After breakfast, Patten's team huddled in the private office to project the impact of Barrow's about-turn. At first, on the basis of the latest reports from LegCo, it looked as though they were likely to scrape home with a 28–25 majority. Mike Hanson announced, to no one in particular, 'We've got it in the bag.' It was soon clear that his optimism was premature.

The debate began at 9am but it was expected to be at least ten hours before the crucial vote on the Liberal amendment was taken. With television and radio coverage of the proceedings droning in the background, Martin Dinham and Edward Llewellyn orchestrated the last-minute effort to keep the wavering legislators on side. But despite the assiduous lobbying of Nicholas Ng and C.M. Leung, at least three of them were still under intense pressure to abstain or vote against the Patten proposals, not only from their colleagues but, as it soon transpired, directly from Beijing. Patten's support was starting to crumble.

China's original tactic had been to remain aloof from the proceedings. But in the days leading up to 29 June, in the wake of the Barrow-inspired efforts of the Liberals, the Chinese had shifted their ground. Not only had Lu Ping issued his allies on LegCo with instructions to support Allen Lee's amendment, but now, on the day itself, he was secretly lobbying himself. In perhaps the most breathtaking attempt to destroy Patten's reforms, the now London-based chairman of the Hongkong and Shanghai Bank, Sir William Purves, also chose this moment to turn against the governor. The previous day, a respected member of LegCo, Vincent Cheng, who was on the board of the bank, told Government House that he had decided to abstain on the Liberal amendment. Now, twelve hours later, with the debate underway, he rang both Dinham and Nicholas Ng in some distress to tell them that he had come under great pressure from Purves to switch his vote in favour of the amendment and felt obliged to do so. Purves had, Cheng reported, made it clear to him that 'his job was on the line'. Purves's call had been followed up by another from Lu Ping. Patten knew that Purves had seen Lu Ping the previous day and half suspected that the two men were even now in the same office. He was aghast. 'That's Willie Purves, true to the last,' he said contemptuously. Later, still angry, he was more explicit:

The Hongkong Bank owes something to Hong Kong . . . the chairman of the Hongkong Bank was a member of my Executive Council when we were first pushing these proposals and knew about them before they were announced . . . but the most disgraceful aspect of this is that someone can phone up an employee on an open line from Peking and tell that employee how to vote. What's the employee supposed to say, knowing perfectly well that the phone call is probably being listened to by the Chinese? It is mind-boggling.

When Lavender Patten walked into the private office and heard the news, she spat, 'Bloody traitor,' before recovering her poise. An aide spluttered: 'If we win, we'll get him for this.'

Vincent Cheng's defection was likely to influence other unde-cided legislators to follow, and by mid-morning, Hanson was obliged to adjust his optimistic forecast. 'Down in the hothouse of LegCo, four or five votes are dodging around quite a bit. They keep changing their minds. At the moment we don't know which way it's going to go. It's very, very close.' In Government House, the atmosphere became more and more oppressive: faces were drawn and anxious; fingers drummed on desks against the background babble of the televised debate.

A little later, news came through of another intervention from Beijing. Lu Ping had been on the phone again, this time to Hui Yin Fat, the elected representative of the functional constituency representing the social workers. This time, however, Dinham was able to confirm: 'Hui has told Lu Ping to get lost, I'm glad to say.' According to Dinham, Lu Ping had urged Hui Yin Fat to abstain. 'All I ask of you,' the Beijing official had said, 'is that you leave the chamber when they vote.' Hui Yin Fat apparently had the courage to retort, 'I am not prepared to do that.' Another of Patten's aides reported that the legislator felt under such pressure that he had hidden himself away in his office, refusing to take calls from anyone.

Lu Ping tried the same tactic with one of Hui Yin Fat's col-leagues, Pan Chung Hoi, urging him: 'I don't care what you do. Just go to the toilet if necessary when the vote is cast.' Pan Chung Hoi, too, stood firm.

Patten mused: 'What's it going to be like after 1997? They won't have to make phone calls from Peking to get them to vote the right way then. Just a local call.' 'And they are free,' quipped Dinham.

Lavender Patten sat in the private sitting room upstairs. The last
week or two, she reflected, had been testing.

I try to give Chris a little bit of reassurance if I can, but it is
very hard. I can't reassure him that the votes are there if they
aren't. So I suppose all I can really do is say to him, 'There
is still time to capture the votes, and we'll deal with what
happens if we don't win afterwards.' There's no need to
anticipate disaster, because that can paralyse you. But it's
easy to say that, and impossible for him not to think about
the effects if it goes the wrong way . . . I've got to support
him and not panic. I wouldn't be much good to him if I was
screaming . . . Who knows, perhaps by this time next week
we will have retired.

By lunchtime, the figures were looking bad. All hope of a three-
vote majority had now evaporated, and defeat seemed to beckon.
Edward Llewellyn, who was keeping a running tally, estimated
that the race was neck and neck at 27–27. Patten's survival now
appeared to depend on Martin Lee's ability to deliver his deal
with Lau Wong Fat of Heung Yee Kuk. If this were to collapse,
one horrified aide whispered, 'It's awful, we fall.' Llewellyn hurried to warn Patten, who had temporarily retired to his study.

Unhappily, Martin Lee's flair as an advocate was not matched
by his skill as a broker. It rapidly became clear that his efforts were
foundering. In the early hours of the morning, the leader of the
Democrats had finally persuaded his own colleagues to accept the
proposed trade-off with Lau Wong Fat. As the morning wore on,
however, Allen Lee had discovered what was afoot and had
threatened that unless the Heung Yee Kuk leader and his colleagues voted for the Liberal amendment, the Liberals would
themselves vote to abolish his functional constituency, and
thereby his seat on LegCo.

Incomprehensibly, Martin Lee, apparently believing that he
could afford to increase the pressure on Lau Wong Fat, chose this
moment to jettison the deal which he had persuaded his colleagues to endorse only a few hours earlier. Not content with an
abstention, he now demanded that Lau Wong Fat and his

colleagues vote against Allen Lee's amendment. This was a miscalculation. In high indignation, Lau Wong Fat broke off
negotiations. When news of this reached Government House,
Patten was almost speechless with frustration. 'Martin is mad,' he
expostulated. 'It really is like trying to deal with the entire Society
of Jesus.' He could not understand how the leader of the
Democrats could be so incompetent and self-regarding as to jeop-
ardise the prospect of extending the franchise to 2.5 million new
voters. 'Martin has really fucked this up,' he finally exploded, and
retreated upstairs to the family sitting room.

Meanwhile, in a meeting room in the precincts of the
Legislative Council, Nicholas Ng tried desperately to persuade
Martin Lee to see sense. Llewellyn went upstairs to warn Patten
that defeat was not only possible but probable. The governor
said: 'I'll do anything Nicholas wants me to do. It'll be so annoying if Martin cocks up this deal. You know, actually arguing
about whether somebody should vote against the amendment or
abstain, I mean . . .' His voice trailed away as he returned to the
strained hubbub of the private office. An unidentified voice in the
LegCo chamber rose and could be heard to say, 'There are people
who appear to be gripped by horror and frightened to death.'
The governor paced abstractedly back and forth, then slumped
into an armchair, head in hands. He roused himself once to
remark, in self-mockery, 'I think what is called for is a prayer.
What time do we meet at the cathedral for early mass tomorrow
if it goes right?'

In the afternoon, there were public duties to briefly take
Patten's mind off the battle for votes. He departed by helicopter
for an official visit to Tsing Yi – 'being gubernatorial', as he
described it – where he inspected an environmental scheme and
planted a tree, cautioning the local officials, 'Don't let it die.'
Llewellyn, who accompanied him, monitored the LegCo debate
on a transistor radio. Patten reflected on the fragility of Hong
Kong's political courage. 'What I can't imagine is telling someone
I would do something and then not doing it,' he said, bemused by
the way votes were even now shifting from one side to the other.
He prepared himself for the recriminations which would follow
a defeat, especially from the Democrats. 'What will irritate me

most,' he sighed, 'will be the allegation that we didn't try; that we meant to lose all along.'

At a press conference he was asked about the LegCo proceedings. He replied smoothly, 'I think the issue is being resolved in the right way by the representatives of the people of Hong Kong: in the open, not in secret behind closed doors, and that is a very important step forward.'

Back in the helicopter, a call came through from 10 Downing Street: the prime minister wanted a progress report. Llewellyn replied that while he remained optimistic, the outcome was still uncertain.

Patten returned to his private office to resume his original position, slouched in an armchair alternately sucking his spectacles and whirling them round distractedly. At one point he exclaimed restlessly, to no one in particular, 'I'm no good to you in here like a jaded lemon,' and walked out, only to return to his post a few minutes later. As he waited, he crossed his fingers in unconscious supplication. On another occasion, he interrupted his silent ruminations to bewail the absence of Baroness Lydia Dunn, his most senior adviser on ExCo, who had left for Britain in the crucial run-up to the vote. 'She's not really in London arguing for passports, you know. She's been on holiday for the last three weeks.' He raised his eyes towards the ceiling as if to say, 'Why wasn't she here helping to get the bill through?'

There were only two hours to go before the first vote was due to be taken. The government's officials on LegCo redoubled their efforts to shore up their support. C.M. Leung lobbied two legislators who had confided separately to him that they were frightened about being out on a limb if they abstained on the Liberal amendment. Edward Llewellyn suggested, only half jokingly, that each should be told that if they were to abstain together, neither of them would be alone. Patten fretted about Simon Ip, the representative of the legal functional constituency, who was easily driven by the shifting winds. The night before, Ip had been frog-marched into a hastily arranged meeting of the Bar Council by Margaret Ng, the diminutive but forceful barrister-cum-columnist, where he had been lobbied furiously to vote for Patten and against the Liberal amendment. But the larger part of his constituency was made up of solicitors who were less enthusiastic about the Patten proposals, and twelve hours later, he was still adrift.

Margaret Ng, born in Hong Kong in 1946, had graduated from the University of Hong Kong with a degree in philosophy and comparative literature. She then studied in the United States at Boston University and in England at Cambridge, where she acquired respectively a PhD in philosophy and a BA in law. In the eighties she had worked variously as a university researcher and administrator, and, for a time, at the local headquarters of the Chase Manhattan Bank. In this period she wrote and broadcast prolifically for the Hong Kong media, earning herself a reputation for clinical analysis and fearless commentary. By the time of Patten's arrival, she combined a twice-weekly column in the *South China Morning Post* with a growing practice at the bar. She had at once warmed to Patten's style but, as she said at the time, she gave herself 'no room for pessimism or optimism' about the prospects of the 'one country, two systems' concept surviving the handover. Britain's impending departure made her 'very, very depressed' – not because she wished British rule to continue, but because 'we are to be returned to a communist regime over which we have almost no influence and over which I have no influence whatsoever. We are now going to be taken over by a government which will have no qualms about riding roughshod over our opinion, whatever we want.'

Like many other people, Ng had only realised the significance of the Liberal amendment to the governor's bill in the hours leading up to the debate. Until then she had merely been pleased that the decision was to be taken by Hong Kong's legislators and not 'rammed down our throats' as the result of a secret deal between Britain and China. However, on the eve of the debate, Denis Chang, a fellow lawyer and a Patten loyalist, whom the governor had appointed to ExCo soon after his arrival, had told her that China was working very hard to secure the Liberal amendment.

Mortified that Simon Ip, the representative of her own constituency, might have the decisive vote, she had deployed her formidable powers of argument to win him over. At first she had been optimistic, but later she discovered that he was backsliding under pressure from the solicitors. Now, only three hours before the vote, she rang Chang and told him, 'Frankly, my feeling is that it is very dodgy. It depends on who gets to him last.' With the moment of decision rapidly approaching, Denis Chang at once rang Government House to pass on this news. Martin Dinham tried to engineer a meeting between Simon Ip and C.M. Leung, in the hope that the latter might be able to stiffen the lawyer's resolve. 'I've got C.M. to lay a trap,' Dinham said. He had arranged for Denis Chang to waylay Ip and lead him casually into the LegCo meeting room, where C.M. Leung had taken up temporary residence on Patten's behalf.

In the meantime Margaret Ng called Government House to tell Llewellyn that she and Denis Chang were determined to see Simon Ip once more, 'just to make sure that he is on track'. She had some sympathy for Ip. 'It was a moment of crisis,' she recalled afterwards. 'I felt I was much involved in a moment of history . . . I was very tense, looking down at Simon to see which way he would vote. He looked pale and totally unhappy. I felt very sad for him, because he had obviously been subjected to a great deal of pressure.'

By six o' clock in the evening, Patten's team was assembled in the private office, watching the debate on television. The vote was still too close to call, but it was too late to do anything about it now.

'If anyone presses the wrong button, we're done,' the governor commented gloomily.

'You *are* a morale-booster,' retorted Llewellyn.

Dinham joined them to discuss the wording of two alternative telegrams, one of which would have to be sent to London. Martin Barrow, belatedly loyal, rang to say that he thought he had managed to secure Simon Ip's vote. Patten was nonplussed and unimpressed. 'The trouble is Simon is so weak. Anyway,' he went on disbelievingly, 'why is Martin now lobbying for us?' A few moments later, they heard that Ip had undertaken to abstain. Patten could barely control his relief. 'Fucking hell, fucking hell!' he muttered loudly, smashing his right fist into the palm of his left hand. 'Let's hope the vote comes before Simon changes his mind again.'

A few minutes later, Patten was given another break. Nicholas Ng phoned in to report that one, if not two, of the wavering Breakfast Group, infuriated by the tone of a speech in support of the Liberal amendment, were likely to vote for Patten after all. Sustained by this crumb of comfort, the governor retreated to his study to wait with Lavender.

By 7.30pm, thirty minutes before the vote, the phones in Government House had ceased to ring. At 7.45, the vote on the Liberal amendment was finally called. The legislators pushed their buttons, and the result flashed up on the television screens instantaneously: 28 in favour, 29 against. The governor's package had survived by one vote. His team erupted in triumph. All decorum vanished as they waved their arms in the air, clapped and embraced one another. 'Fucking hell!' yelled Llewellyn; Dinham, discarding his usual reserve to punch the air, repeated over and over again, 'Yes! Yes! Yes!' There were other amendments to follow, but this was the one that mattered. An elated Patten hurried to the office, flushed with relief, and called for champagne all round. Llewellyn rang the Foreign Office to report the good news.

It was not the margin of victory for which they had hoped. Without the three ex-officio votes, Patten's bill would have fallen to the Liberal amendment. Patten saw a way of pre-empting the mischief an embittered Allen Lee might try to cause by alleging that Government House had fixed the result. If a majority of those legislators who had been directly elected in 1991 had voted against the Liberal amendment, he could at least blunt any such attack by pointing out that a one-vote victory it may have been, but it had been sustained by a substantial majority of those who had been democratically elected. Sitting at Dinham's desk, he pored exultantly over a list of legislators, shouting out their names one by one: were they elected or appointed? As his team yelled back the answers, he was overjoyed to discover that only one of the eighteen directly elected members had voted against him, while Allen Lee's support came overwhelmingly from legislators appointed by his predecessor. The governor's relief was palpable: 'That's the answer we've got to keep on using if people talk about the "official" votes.'

In public Allen Lee contained his rancour, and refrained from identifying Martin Barrow as the defector who had helped to destroy his amendment. In private, however, he fulminated against Patten.

> He didn't win. He bulldozed it through. He won by one vote. He didn't let the Hong Kong people decide. He's been lying to the Hong Kong people. And finally he uses the three official votes to get it through. He now has a system for 1995 which has no future after 1997. His package has no chance, absolutely no chance . . . For Christ's sake, we're not morons. We're not kindergarten kids. I think he is bad for Hong Kong, really bad for Hong Kong. A failed politician coming here and playing politics. This feeling will never wash off me. I'm going to be here in 1997. He is not.

Meanwhile, Martin Lee, who had failed to deliver his deal, was blithely unaware of the frustration he had provoked at Government House. Instead he rejoiced in Allen Lee's defeat as though he had masterminded it himself. The Liberal leader's credibility, he chortled, had been severely damaged.

> You have to remember that the majority of the Liberals were appointed by Patten's predecessor, Sir David Wilson. The only way for them to preserve their position was to make sure that the future electoral arrangements would not be fair or open or democratic. With undemocratic elections, as proposed by their amendment, they would have stood a good chance of getting themselves, in effect, appointed to the Legislative Council – to serve China, no doubt. So they've had their own interests to serve.

Patten's bill was still not quite safe. The Democratic party now tabled an amendment designed to extend the number of directly elected seats for 1995 from twenty to thirty in accordance with their publicly stated objective. This was a clear violation of the Basic Law. The government team feared that Allen Lee might now urge his party members to vote for Martin Lee's amendment in the hope of wrecking the Patten reforms, which would, Llewellyn warned, leave them 'in deep shit'. This time, however, the leader of the Democrats saw the light. After a brief but genial conversation, Patten put down the phone to announce with relief, tinged by self-satisfaction, 'Martin is withdrawing his amendment.'

Now, at last, the governor knew that his bill was through, and that he and the British government had been spared a humiliation which would have had lasting personal and political consequences. In the end, his margin of victory on the substantive motion was larger than he had expected. Once every hostile amendment had been defeated, a number of jittery legislators finally screwed up enough courage to bow to the sentiment of LegCo's elected majority. As a result, after more than seventeen hours of debate, the Patten bill was endorsed by a comfortable majority of eight votes (32–24). Of the eighteen directly elected members of LegCo, only Emily Lau voted against it, and that was because it failed to satisfy her own rigid aspirations. Her decision combined principle and pragmatism, but it had caused a jolt of last-minute anxiety at Government House. Patten admired Lau, but not unequivocally. 'Emily is a sort of yardstick by which the rest of us have to measure ourselves. Every community needs a sea-green incorruptible,' he observed. Then he added: 'It does make her from time to time absolutely infuriating.' Immediately before the third reading of his bill, Patten had telephoned Lau to ask for her backing.

'Look, you may actually endanger the vote if you don't vote for it,' he said.

'You've got enough votes,' Emily Lau replied.

'We can't be sure of that. And at the end of the day, you're going to be voting with the Liberal party and all those pro-Peking legislators. Is that really the sort of company you want to be in?'

But Emily Lau did not yield. Her own bill, which demanded universal adult suffrage on the Westminster model, was due to be debated immediately after the vote on the Patten reforms, and it would clearly have weakened her cause to have supported the governor so soon before seeking LegCo's support for her far more radical proposal. Patten remarked, less than graciously, 'She voted against us just so that she could stay greener than green.'

If that was Emily Lau's inspiration, she was not alone. In the early hours of the following morning, the minority of legislators who had stayed up through the night to debate her bill did reject her passionately argued case, but only by the wafer-thin margin of one vote. Patten had not expected the result to be quite so close, and he was more relieved than he liked to admit to have escaped what would have been a severe embarrassment. Although he conceded that there was a moral case for complete democracy in Hong Kong, he would not have hesitated to veto her bill for the same reason that he would have felt obliged to reject Martin Lee's amendment: neither was compatible with the Basic Law. Acknowledging that if Emily Lau's amendment had been carried, 'it would have given her another stick to beat us with', he added, with greater generosity, that in the months ahead she would have 'plenty to shout about, and she will shout with great eloquence. The fact that she'll still be there shouting in 1997 is good for an awful lot of people in Hong Kong, who may think she is a pain in the backside. But you actually need people like that to be able to go on living in a free society.'

The next day, the liberal media expressed a widespread cautious relief. However, commentators were scathing about both Martin Barrow and Simon Ip. Regardless of the fact that their abstentions had helped to save the Patten bill, their reputations were destroyed. The *Eastern Express* declared that they had both 'shirked their duty' in failing to come out in favour of democracy. 'When for whatever pathetic reason, they are unable to take a stand on the most important political issue facing Hong Kong,' the paper thundered, 'they should vacate their seats to allow in someone who has more stomach for the job.' The two men stayed put.

Buoyed by his victory, Patten declared that the result was 'historic', but he was careful not to elaborate. He confided: 'I've got to avoid triumphalism, and I've got to build as many bridges as possible, not just with China, but with those people who feel bruised by what has happened.' He was reminded of something the former Conservative Cabinet minister William Whitelaw had once said: 'Everybody tells me I mustn't crow. I'm certainly not going to crow. But inside I'm crowing like mad.'

Patten's internal triumphalism was reinforced by the response of the community to LegCo's decision. 'The conventional wisdom was that we couldn't have a political argument about Hong Kong without the roof falling in here,' he said. 'Well, the Hang Seng Index went up by over a hundred points this morning . . . I think some of the conventional wisdom got heavily bombed over the last twenty-four hours.' Another piece of conventional wisdom to be called into question was, as Patten noted dryly, that 'you couldn't have an argument with China and at least in the short term – we don't know about the long term – do any other business with them'. The LegCo vote did not deter China from concluding – after seven years of frustrated negotiation – an agreement the following day in the Joint Liaison Group on the future of the colony's defence lands, which were due to be handed over to the People's Liberation Army in 1997. This deal, the first of several which would have to be struck for a smooth transition through 1997 to be secured, gave Patten reason to hope that the Chinese were indeed prepared, as some of their spokesmen had hinted, to separate economics from politics.

He even allowed himself to believe that he might restore his personal relationship with the Chinese leadership. Although Lu Ping had snubbed Patten a few weeks earlier on his official visit to Hong Kong, the governor was now sure that a meeting would, after all, take place. To this end, he resolved to be 'as positive as possible, and to avoid being unnecessarily provocative'. An embrace of this kind from China would not constitute the seal of approval from Beijing, but it would go a long way to restoring Patten's credibility with his critics. Did he really think that he would be given another chance to visit Beijing? 'Oh yes,' he replied airily. 'Sooner or later.' In this respect, as in others, he woefully overestimated his own hand, and greatly underestimated the unforgiving nature of Hong Kong's future overlord.

Immediately after the vote, Edward Llewellyn dictated a statement on behalf of the governor over the phone to the *Times* correspondent in Hong Kong, Jonathan Mirsky: '"This has been an important day and night for Hong Kong. I welcome the council's decision. This has been a vigorous debate which ends a significant chapter in Hong Kong's history. We must now turn the page." That's it.' As Mirsky, among others, prophesied, it wasn't.

The intoxication of victory was short-lived. Although the local elections in September, conducted on the basis of Patten's reforms, attracted a record turn-out of over 30 per cent, Beijing's attitude towards the governor did not soften. By the late autumn, various official spokesmen had made it clear that no Chinese official would conduct negotiations directly with the governor of Hong Kong. He was openly castigated by local critics, while further afield, politicians and businessmen kept asking him for assurances about the future which he felt unable to give against what he called a 'backdrop of growing anxiety, suspicion and concern about China'. Clear evidence that the mainland's economy was overheating combined with some glaring examples of endemic corruption to·dent what Patten referred to as the 'global euphoria' about China's economic miracle. Any disruption to the country's economy was bound to blow back into Hong Kong and, given the breakdown of political relations with Beijing, Patten was well aware that he would certainly take some of the blame, however unjust this might be. He was particularly worried about the property market in Hong Kong. If anxiety about the future were to translate into fears about property values, then prices could tumble sharply as people hurried to cash in their assets.

His worries were reinforced by evidence that morale in the civil service had plummeted. In an internal survey of opinion among the staff of the MRTC (Mass Transit Railway Corporation), 20 per cent of senior managers declared that they would leave Hong Kong before 1997. How many others in similar roles in the private and public sectors had made the same decision, or would do so if fears about their prospects after 1997 became widespread?

At the end of 1994 the columnist Margaret Ng spoke privately of her conviction that Hong Kong would face a 'very tough takeover'. It was, by now, quite clear to her that 'Peking is going to take control of this place before it will allow local people to

have any say . . . there may be a period when there will be a lot
of persecution with people like me being a target.' She was
depressed by the superficial appraisal of Hong Kong's prospects so
often parroted by outsiders.

> Every visitor will tell you, 'Hong Kong is a vibrant place.
> The economy is growing,' but you can feel that a lot of
> your fellow workers are on the edge of breakdown. You
> know, sometimes you feel that on a bad day all you have to
> do is to light a match and the whole house would blow up
> because everyone is under tremendous pressure. No one
> likes to acknowledge it, because that is not our style . . . but
> there are lots of inexplicable cases of people suddenly break-
> ing down and weeping. If you look at the broader picture,
> there is this tension. We are going berserk. There is no
> doubt about it.

Margaret Ng was not an excitable woman and she spoke reflec-
tively, more in the manner of a psychiatrist than a polemical writer.
    The governor was far from sanguine. 'My worry six months to
a year ago was that we might find ourselves in the last couple of
years facing a downturn in the Chinese economic cycle and a
shift of mood from euphoria to pessimism, which is more abrupt
in relation to China than anywhere else in the world,' he confided
in late 1994. 'Well, it seems to me that it is happening, all too
much on cue.' In such circumstances Patten's isolation would
place him in a most precarious position, and he knew it.

> We'll be pressed with increasing stridency by some sections
> of the community to do more to safeguard human rights . . .
> whereas ever more limited efforts to do that will draw down
> on our heads huge denunciations from the Chinese leader-
> ship . . . This will provoke even more rows each time . . . I
> think this job is going to be trickier in the coming year than
> it was last year.

Patten managed to mask his anxieties to enter into the spirit of his
social duties as governor. The Pattens' desire to make extensive

use of the ballroom at Government House was enthusiastically welcomed by the organisers of local charities, who knew that the cachet of a Government House event attended by the governor and his wife was a sure-fire fund-raiser in this competitively generous community. One evening in March 1995, organised by two local children's charities of which Lavender was patron, was typical. A visiting company from Britain, the European Chamber Opera, gave a performance of Mozart's *Cosí Fan Tutte*. The occasion, sponsored by two of Hong Kong's most formidable institutions in the Hang Seng Bank and Jardine Pacific, attracted a swathe of the colony's grandees.

Quite what the Chinese guests made of Mozart's most absurdly complicated plot was unclear, especially as the opera was sung uncompromisingly, if with verve, in Italian, and without the benefit of scenery. It was perhaps not surprising that at least some of the guests soon allowed their imagination and attention to wander. The Europeans present, if only to confirm their familiarity with the work or the Italian language, laughed noisily at appropriate moments. For the detached observer, no cultural occasion could more vividly have pinpointed the cultural divide between the races: the intense concentration of the Europeans set against the bemused indifference of the Chinese. Afterwards, Patten joined the performers for a late-night drink. His day of meetings and visits had begun at 8am and had been interrupted only by a luncheon for the Mayor of Westminster. Yet one of his guests remarked that he seemed more animated than he had been in the morning. He chatted to the young singers and musicians, praising their performance, listening to what they had to say about England and telling them about Hong Kong, until well after midnight. As his friend observed, 'Somehow, it seemed to make him feel at home again. These were his people, and his country.'

This was also the weekend of the Hong Kong Sevens rugby tournament, the highlight of the colony's sporting year, for which the world's leading teams arrive to compete in the fiercest seven-a-side competition on earth. As guests of honour, the Pattens were escorted to their blue-canopied box along with their house guests, who included the governor of Macau and his wife. Patten was in his element. Sweeping his binoculars around the crowd of 40,000, mainly Europeans, who danced and yelled their way through the afternoon, he grinned delightedly. 'Look at that! Isn't it a marvellous sight?' At school he had been fanatical about rugby; now he showed the restraint befitting the guest of honour as each match was battled out in front of him. Nevertheless he obeyed the entreaties of the abandoned crowd and rose self-consciously when a Mexican wave swept round the stadium engulfing the stand in which he and other VIPs were sitting. Afterwards he walked behind the stands, where young British expatriates were draining jugs of beer in convivial satisfaction. 'All right, then, Chris?' they asked, raising their glasses to him. He smiled easily, the politician at home among his own.

'A MATTER OF DECENCY'

A Row Over the
Court of Final Appeal

In the prevailing atmosphere of renewed anxiety, the governor now had to confront a raft of unfinished but highly contentious business which had been delayed by the protracted conflict with China over his political reforms. Detailed negotiations covering a wide range of crucial issues – including the airport project, the CT9 container terminal, the sale of defence lands, immigration and passports – had come to a virtual standstill. And then there was the matter of human rights. Patten's refusal to countenance a Human Rights Commission earlier in the year did not mean that the question had fallen off Hong Kong's agenda. To bring the legislation into line with the 1991 Bill of Rights, he had been advised by the government's lawyers that he should abolish a range of longstanding repressive laws which had been a source of embarrassment to the Hong Kong government for years. Britain had done little or nothing about the issue before Patten's appointment, and the desultory approach of his predecessors had left the governor doubly exposed: he now had to act not only under the critical scrutiny of human-rights activists in Hong Kong and the hard-line regime in Beijing, but against a very tight deadline. Patten thought that the readiness of officials in London and in the colony to see the protection of human rights in Hong Kong in terms of diplomatic settlements with China was another example of how Britain continually viewed Hong Kong 'through the prism of our relationship with

Peking'. It had made his task far more difficult than it would otherwise have been.

A case in point were the laws grouped together under the
colony's Emergency Regulations, last used in the riots of 1967,
when the authorities feared that the survival of Hong Kong hung
in the balance. To deploy the Emergency Powers Ordinance
would be tantamount to a declaration of martial law, and Patten
had no choice but to abolish it, not least because Hong Kong's
law officers were in no doubt that these residual powers contravened the Bill of Rights. Although China had undertaken in
Article 13 of the Basic Law to protect 'freedom of the person, of
speech, of assembly, of association . . . of strike, of demonstration'
in Hong Kong after the handover, Patten predicted that he would
face a hostile reaction from Beijing once he announced his decision to follow his own official advice.

> When we first go along to them, clearing our throat and
> saying, 'Well, you know, we've got to do something about
> these emergency powers, because they are not in line with
> the Bill of Rights,' they will say, 'But they've been all right
> for governors to have in their back pockets in case they
> needed them. Why are you now changing them? . . . You
> just want to create chaos. What you want is to go round
> unloosening all the screws.'

Although the Legislative Council had passed the appropriate
measure to abolish some of the harsher elements of the Public
Order Act, the governor was inclined to get rid of the
Emergency Regulations using a swifter and more surgical
method: exercising his executive powers, authorised, or rubber-
stamped, by his advisers on the Executive Council. Even though
Beijing was likely to 'blow a gasket', he had persuaded the
Cabinet in London to recognise that this was his best available
option. However, he confided, 'I still have to carry London on
the timing.'

He was well aware that the Chinese would be bound to interpret his decision as a deliberate indication to the outside world
that his successors could not be trusted to exercise the same

degree of restraint as his predecessors. As it turned out, when Patten did eventually abolish the Emergency Powers by executive fiat, to his relief and astonishment, Beijing seemed not to notice.

There was no chance of finessing past Beijing an even more controversial issue which had the potential to explode into a terminal conflict with China, and which was therefore almost certain to become yet another cause of friction between Government House and the Foreign Office. Once again the crisis he now foresaw had been inherited from a chain of events which predated his appointment, and once again, the focus was on human rights. In this case, the context was the judicial system, and notably the status and composition of the Court of Final Appeal, which was to replace the Privy Council as Hong Kong's court of last resort.

In 1991, the terms of the secret agreement between Britain and China on the Court of Final Appeal had been unveiled before a sceptical Hong Kong public, whose suspicions were duly confirmed. As Patten later commented, the deal reflected a 'particular style of diplomacy of which I am not wholly enamoured'. Britain, he complained, had been willing to reach 'pretty fundamental agreements with the Chinese without taking much notice of what people in Hong Kong thought'. The main area of contention concerned the Basic Law's imprecise definition of 'acts of state', over which, under Article 18, Hong Kong courts would have no jurisdiction. The issue of exactly what activities – if any – in addition to foreign affairs and defence, might fall into this category had been skirted by Britain and China and was still unresolved. Several legislators and a number of prominent lawyers, led by Martin Lee and Margaret Ng, also expressed their dismay that the British had apparently colluded in an interpretation of an ambiguity in Article 82 of the Basic Law which would, they argued, severely damage the credibility of the Court of Final Appeal.

This article stated that judges 'from other common-law jurisdictions' could be invited by the chief justice 'as required' to sit on the court. But the British negotiators had yielded to China's insistence that Article 82 should be taken to mean that only one 'foreign' judge could sit on the court at any one time. From the critics' perspective, the presence of expatriate judges sitting with their local counterparts at the highest level of the Hong Kong judiciary would both enhance the standing of the court internationally and act as a counterweight to any interference, however discreet, from Beijing. But limiting the court to one 'foreign' judge would invariably leave the verdict – by a potential majority of four to one – in 'domestic' hands, a prospect which threatened to undermine these twin objectives.

Patten had been warned before his arrival in Hong Kong that the Court of Final Appeal would cause him trouble. He was aware that the 1991 agreement had, as he put it, 'left one or two bits of shirt-tail flapping', but he thought, somewhat casually, that it still left Hong Kong with 'quite a reasonable' deal. The colony's legislators, kept in the dark during the course of the 1991 negotiations, had responded with predictable hostility once the terms of the agreement became public. 'As soon as it saw the light of day,' Patten reflected, 'the agreement was howled down by the legal profession in Hong Kong and voted down by the Legislative Council'. Nonetheless, the British felt that they had no option but to draw up a bill based on the agreement. It was this bill which was Patten's inheritance.

According to the terms of the Joint Declaration, the forum for discussing all these issues was the Joint Liaison Group between the British and the Chinese. In the wake of the collapse of relations between their respective sovereign masters, communication between the two sides in the JLG had reached a nadir. Before Patten's arrival, for example, it had been the tradition for the leaders of each delegation to entertain one another – at the theatre, the ballet, and even at home for dinner – during their regular sessions in Beijing or London, regardless of how fraught matters at the negotiating table had been. This display of social amity had been suspended during the seventeen rounds of inter-governmental negotiations about Patten's electoral reforms, and although the custom was re-established in the summer of 1994, it had done nothing to accelerate progress.

In May 1994, the head of the British delegation at the JLG, Hugh Davies, had presented the Chinese with Hong Kong's proposed bill establishing the Court of Final Appeal, but amid this dialogue of the deaf the Chinese refrained from making any response until almost four months later. Eventually, they deigned to raise what the British side considered some 'rather puerile questions' about the bill. According to one long-serving and long-suffering participant, the discussions now became impatient to the point of acrimony. 'Their tempers rise and so do ours. But we don't shout at each other . . . The only way out is to break and try to reassemble in smaller groups.' It was not until the early spring of 1995 that the Chinese returned to the table again, armed this time with a set of more serious questions which nevertheless served only to convince the British that they had 'decided they would prefer not to reach an agreement'.

In the face of such obduracy, the governor had to consider his options in earnest. Exasperated by the unwillingness or inability of the Chinese to reach any decision on any significant issue, he characterised their attitude as one of 'mendacity, fabrication, incompetence and wishful thinking'. They had raised three issues relating to the Court of Final Appeal Bill, all of which suggested that they had it in mind to curtail sharply, if not terminally, the independence of the Hong Kong judiciary. First, they argued that the court should not be permitted to pronounce on the 'constitutionality of laws' – for example, on cases arising out of the Bill of Rights. Secondly, they sought to include a mechanism for what they described as a 'post-remedial verdict', which would allow the National People's Congress to overturn any judgement reached by the Court of Appeal. Thirdly, they intimated that the definition of 'acts of state' would have to embrace 'other things' in addition to foreign affairs and defence. They also demanded that the bill should contain a clause specifically drawing attention to the fact that any 'acts of state' thus defined would not fall within the jurisdiction of the Court of Final Appeal, a requirement which the British had hitherto resisted. For Patten, the implication of these demands was as crude as its purpose was self-evident: 'If we – the Chinese – don't like the result, we've got to find some way to overturn it.'

Given the character of the objections of the Chinese and their refusal to negotiate, Patten came to the conclusion that it was going to be impossible to reach an agreement with their officials 'in their present mood'. Yet the Joint Declaration had specified that the court was to be established in advance of the 1997 handover. The governor was running out of time. Although this did not emerge publicly, he now faced his most daunting quandary since his appointment. For the first time, he found himself facing the prospect of conflict not only with officials in the Foreign Office, but potentially with senior members of the Cabinet as well – even those who trusted him most – and certainly with the president of the Board of Trade, Michael Heseltine. In March 1995 he explained his predicament:

> London accepts the argument for trying to set up a Court of Final Appeal before 1997. After all, we negotiated the agreement. But London also wants to minimise the number of rows that we have with China. There is still the view – more among diplomats than politicians – that if only we could somehow get on better with China, everything would be easier and Sino–British relations would produce an aura of sunlight in which problems could be solved and trade would be better.
>
> Here in Hong Kong, we feel very strongly that we've at least got to have a go at setting up the court, but we are still dealing with a Legislative Council which we don't think will vote in very large numbers for the court. So do we press ahead on our own without Chinese agreement? If we do, and there is a row, can we get the bill through the Legislative Council? What sort of situation is this in which to persuade London that we should go ahead? We have a row with China, and we fall flat on our face in the Legislative Council.
>
> The position I am in is one in which my political judgement is going to be taken rather less seriously by my former colleagues from now on. Over the electoral provisions we won. We had a row, but we won. But to go into the Legislative Council [on this issue] wondering whether we can win or not poses a real dilemma.

Indeed, the pro-China legislators would have been bound to

oppose any measure not approved by Beijing, while the
Democrats had made it plain that they would also vote against the
bill unless it was modified in ways which Patten believed would
violate the 1991 agreement with China. It was quite possible that
the Democrats might amend the bill in an effort to alter the
composition of the court to ensure that more than one foreign
judge could sit on it at the same time – the point on which the
British had given way in 1991. Were this to happen, Patten would
be constrained by what he regarded disdainfully as a 'sacred text
between Britain and China'. For the governor to give his assent
to a bill thus amended by the Legislative Council would, he
believed, be tantamount to advocating a breach of the agreement
between the two sovereign powers. 'I don't think I could have
done that. I don't think the foreign secretary or the prime minister could have accepted it,' he concluded.

Meanwhile, the British ambassador in Beijing, Sir Len
Appleyard, was sending anxious messages to London warning
that it would be 'ill advised' to press ahead with the CFA bill. He
argued in what Patten's team regarded as an 'unhelpful memo'
that to confront China over this issue would damage British interests in China and provoke Beijing to be even less conciliatory on
all matters in the run-up to 1997. Appleyard was known by
bolder spirits in the Foreign Office as 'Applecart'; at Government
House, he was roundly distrusted for what Patten's advisers
regarded as his readiness to appease his Beijing hosts. As on other
occasions, they believed he had succumbed to the temptation to
load the evidence and exaggerate the prospective damage to win
his case. 'Sir Len will do almost anything for an easy life,'
remarked one of them bitterly.

Although both the foreign secretary and the prime minister
had made it clear to Patten that if he thought it was right to go
ahead and try to legislate, they would back him, the Foreign
Office sinologists had other ideas. On this occasion they had a
powerful ally in Michael Heseltine. Officials in the Department of
Trade and Industry had spent several months putting together a
team of prominent British industrialists for a trade mission to
China, scheduled for mid-May 1995, to be led by the president of
the Board of Trade. The visit was being promoted as the first

major trip of its kind since the eighties, when Lord Young had been tour leader on the DTI's behalf, and Heseltine was expected to meet the most senior members of the politburo. It was soon clear that Heseltine's team was determined that his thunder should not be stolen by what they saw as an avoidable quarrel with China. Patten, they argued, should be restrained from pursuing his arcane obsession with the Court of Final Appeal with such undue haste.

The governor was intuitively sceptical about the value of the travelling circus of industrialists Heseltine was intending to parade around China. Although he refrained from expressing direct criticism of his former Cabinet colleague, his team in Government House was well aware that he had long been suspicious of the 'grandstanding' instincts of the Cabinet's most colourful character. Although there were those, Patten mused, who 'think that having receptions for ministers and businessmen, signing letters of intent and memoranda of understanding, is the same as getting contracts and winning exports', he also recalled, with a touch of savage satisfaction, that Lord Young's endeavours in this respect during the eighties had failed to stem a decline in either British exports to or Britain's share of trade with China. And he pointed out that, despite the political breakdown with Beijing in 1992, British trade with the People's Republic had grown rapidly ever since: there was no evidence that 'kowtowing' made any difference to the prospects for trade or investment.

Patten's overriding worry about the Heseltine mission was the potential it had to undermine the British government's stance over Hong Kong. He feared that it would be bound to signal to China that, from London's point of view, trade with the People's Republic mattered more than human rights or the rule of law in the future SAR. His concern was increased by the fact that China had already intimated to the British embassy in Beijing that a 'warming in the economic relationship' might be in the offing if only the political environment could be improved. Officials in the Department of Trade and Industry and the Foreign Office, supported by Sir Len Appleyard, pressed this argument vigorously. The disagreement continued back and forth between London and Government House without resolution throughout the spring of 1995. In the end, Patten decided against adopting what he described as the 'Rorke's Drift approach to politics'. He reluctantly agreed to postpone tabling the CFA bill, at least until Heseltine had returned from China.

During this period, the foreign secretary, Douglas Hurd, came under intense pressure from both Heseltine and Patten. 'I really did have very considerable difficulty with these two colleagues,' he commented later.

> Michael's preoccupation was entirely justified. He is different from Percy Cradock because Cradock's concern is mainly political. But Michael sees this immense market growing at a huge rate. He sees the Germans and the French powering in there with huge delegations, and he wants to do the same. And Hong Kong is an impediment to that process . . . Michael and I are friends. We've not had a real row in our lives, and we certainly didn't then. We circled round each other to a certain extent, and you assess the size of each other's arguments and who is likely to support them . . . I was always asking Chris, 'Can you not postpone it for a little [longer] while I handle Michael?' But for Chris, the Court of Final Appeal was an absolutely crucial point.

With the prime minister watching from the sidelines, Hurd advised Patten that he should stand by to return to London after Heseltine's visit to argue his case against the president of the Board of Trade face to face in the Cabinet. Patten was not at all certain that he would win, not least because he knew that he would have to share his fear that LegCo was likely to reject his proposals for the Court of Final Appeal, an admission of weakness which would make it even harder for him to prevail in Cabinet. Yet, although he was reluctant to make the CFA a resigning issue, he was by no means sure that he could return to Hong Kong as governor if he failed to get his way in London.

Patten was tempted to think that Heseltine had allowed himself to be flattered into seeing his visit to Beijing as a possible turning point in Sino–British relations. Certainly this was the line taken by the Foreign Office, and by Heseltine's prospective

Chinese hosts – egged on (it was presumed at Government House) by the ubiquitous Sir Percy Cradock, who had himself recently returned from Beijing. To the governor's team it was clear that the forceful head of the Hong Kong Department in the Foreign Office, Sherard Cowper-Coles, was using Appleyard's reports from Beijing to promote the view that Britain's relations with China should take priority over its concerns about Hong Kong – urging, in effect, as one of them put it, that 'we should wash our hands of Hong Kong and rebuild our relationship with China'.

Patten was contemptuous of the view that there was a 'cornucopia in China waiting to flow over our slippered feet if only we would recognise the importance of "restoring good relations" . . . I think the Chinese have managed to turn otherwise rational and sensible people inside out by dangling these great, fat carrots.' By the time of Heseltine's visit in May 1995, a year after the draft CFA bill had originally been submitted to the Chinese in the JLG, the governor's impatience with the Foreign Office sinologists and their allies in the DTI had reached a new intensity. The interminable conflict over how to deal with China over this issue, he confided, had become

more debilitating than the rows about anything else, and certainly more debilitating than having an argument with the Chinese about democracy . . . Looking over your shoulder while you are trying to take on an important issue is always rather tiresome. I've always thought that we were in a somewhat difficult position . . . trying to implement it in the teeth of opposition from China, and from parts of the local community. What I guess I hadn't entirely expected was that there would be opposition on one's own side, too.

Claiming that the ins and outs of bureaucratic politics did not usually engage him, he volunteered that in the case of the Court of Final Appeal he had been 'surprised and mildly shocked by some of the tricks and devices' which had been used against him by the sinologists. Though he was unwilling to go into detail, the precise cause of his deepening anger was easily apparent. His closest advisers, who shared his opinion, were furious at the way in which, as it seemed to them, both Appleyard and Cowper-Coles had usurped their proper roles as subordinate officials to undermine the governor's position. In particular Patten's aides resented the eagerness of one or two people in the Foreign Office to put it about that their 'boss' was not only intellectually arrogant, but refused to listen to counter-arguments or superior wisdom.

The Chinese treated the arrival of the British president of the Board of Trade as an event of great moment. According to most observers in Beijing, Heseltine was magnificently presidential in bearing and made an excellent impression on his hosts. He saw all the top leaders, with the exception of Deng Xiaoping, and, amid all the flummery and fanfare that such formalities invariably engender, the two sides duly signed letters of intent worth hundreds of millions of pounds. In Hong Kong, the governor's enthusiasm for Heseltine's coup de théâtre was muted.

> I think trade missions are important to any country, and I think it is absolutely fair to say that the president of the Board of Trade has been terrifically supportive of British business all around the world . . . I very much hope that Michael's visit will lead to big business coups for Britain. He carries these things off with more chutzpah than anybody else could manage. But at the end of the day the Chinese do business on business terms.

Reiterating that while Britain, the European Union's biggest investor in China, had enjoyed 'huge increases' in its exports to the People's Republic over the previous two years, he was also at pains to point out that British trade with Hong Kong was of even greater significance. 'I want to see the best possible trading relationship between Britain and China,' he maintained. 'But what I don't agree with is that in order to do business with China you should ignore your obligations to Hong Kong, not only because it is a matter of decency, honour, Britain's word and Britain's place in the world, but because I think that a huge commercial interest of Britain's is that Hong Kong should continue to succeed.'

Appleyard's valedictory telegram to London after Heseltine's trip confirmed all Patten's fears. Both oleaginous and, from the standpoint of Government House, defeatist in tone, it lavished praise on the president of the Board of Trade for what Appleyard described as an 'outstandingly successful visit'. As a direct result, he reported, British companies were now chasing business worth more than £5 billion, while deals to the tune of £1 billion had already been concluded. The showpiece of the event, a meeting between Heseltine and Li Peng, had, according to Appleyard, sent a message throughout China to the effect that Britain was greatly valued as a trading partner. Even more importantly, the visit had apparently been viewed by both sides as an important landmark in the process of the 'gradual restoration of good relations' between the two nations. In his tête-à-tête with Heseltine, Appleyard reported, Li Peng had made it clear that the two countries could have even closer ties if only the stumbling block of Hong Kong could be removed. While Beijing was anxious to co-operate and to reach agreement on the outstanding issues between them, the ambassador concluded, failure to achieve this desirable outcome would be bound to have an adverse effect on trade relations between the two nations. He and other British officials were careful to avoid using phrases such as 'turning point', but Appleyard nonetheless declared that the time was ripe to capitalise on the achievements of the mission.

This was precisely what Patten had expected from the outset. Although he took pains to avoid blaming Heseltine – who he knew had not once strayed from the Cabinet's agreed stance over Hong Kong while he was in Beijing – he was disconcerted to be told that, on one occasion, the president of the Board of Trade and the British ambassador, closeted in a Guangdong hotel owned by the People's Liberation Army, had discussed the best way of handling the 'Patten problem'. He was far more dismayed by the zeal with which, on his return to London, Heseltine set about attempting to shift the government's priorities towards Hong Kong. Arguing that British trade with China should take precedence, he claimed that, if it was not to be severely damaged in the months ahead, Patten had to be prevented from causing yet another showdown with the People's Republic over the Court of Final Appeal.

In Beijing Heseltine had formed the view that the Chinese were willing to compromise over the CFA. Indeed, according to a member of Patten's team, one of Li Peng's aides had even told the British Cabinet minister that the Chinese were willing to look again at the quota of foreign judges allowed to sit on the supreme court. Encouraged by this apparent flexibility, Heseltine urged that Patten should be instructed by the Cabinet to delay tabling his bill for a further six weeks to allow more time for the exploration of the potential for a negotiated settlement. On the face of it, as Patten ruefully acknowledged, the president of the Board of Trade had a powerful case.

In Hong Kong, where the Court of Final Appeal had now emerged publicly to become a subject of acrimonious debate, Patten's imperatives were of a quite different order. To delay tabling the CFA bill would, he was convinced, be interpreted as a sign of weakness on his part at the worst possible moment. Reiterating the governor's stance, his chief secretary, Anson Chan, had only recently voiced the opinion that failure to set up the court before 1997 would leave Hong Kong's legal system with a 'vacuum at the apex'. Any delay, she declared, would lead the Hong Kong government to be 'rightly criticised for not meeting our obligations under the 1991 agreement'. Rumours that Beijing was seeking to impose restrictions on the powers of the court had started to leak into the local press, and though Patten had managed to sidestep anxious questions from legislators, he knew he would have to act swiftly to avert a crisis of confidence. It was essential, he believed, to head off Heseltine. To this end he sent an impassioned telegram to London insisting that it was vital that the bill was tabled without further delay. If he were to acquiesce to Heseltine's plan, he wrote, his own authority in Hong Kong would be fatally undermined; it would be seen as a 'betrayal of the principles that we have constantly said we stand for'. Moreover, to postpone the decision would send precisely the wrong signals to both Beijing and the community in Hong Kong, and would almost certainly result in the establishment of a court 'even less to our liking'. He informed London that his approach had the support of the legal profession, the civil service and – for once – the business community as well; the media, apart from the irredeemably pro-Beijing press, were also urging him to forge ahead. It was extremely important, he maintained, that the Cabinet should not be 'seduced' by 'reassurances' from Li Peng about Hong Kong; in the past these had amounted to very little.

Patten knew that Michael Heseltine had been urging the prime minister to send a conciliatory message to Li Peng stating, in effect, that he was sure they could reach agreement on all sorts of matters that concerned Britain, including the outstanding issues in relation to Hong Kong, and that if it would help, Britain would certainly be willing to come to terms on the question of the appointment of judges to the Court of Final Appeal. The governor repeated that Heseltine's approach was, if well-meaning, misguided. Adamant that the government should put as much space as possible between Heseltine's visit and any action over the CFA, he advised that, if the Cabinet insisted on endorsing the approach suggested by the president of the Board of Trade, he would feel bound to fly back immediately to fight his corner. He warned that the mood in Hong Kong was now so volatile that this in itself would be enough to shatter the territory's confidence as it was bound to be interpreted as evidence of a serious rift with China.

The implicit, if unstated, message of Patten's telegram was 'back me or sack me'. The warning was not lightly given. Although he was sure that he still enjoyed the confidence of the prime minister, he also knew that, following a disastrous showing by the Conservatives in the 1995 local elections, John Major would find it hard to confront Heseltine directly on the issue. Heseltine had become the lynchpin of the administration, and the merest hint that he was unhappy with the prime minister's handling of affairs would give credence to the growing murmur that Major would face a leadership challenge in the autumn of the kind which had dealt Margaret Thatcher's premiership its fatal blow five years before. The Conservative backbenchers were dangerously demoralised and restless, and calls for Major's resignation had started to reverberate around Westminster. The continued support of Heseltine, his most powerful Cabinet colleague, was indispensable to Major's survival as leader of the party. In these circumstances Patten was less sanguine about his own position in Hong Kong than at any time since his arrival.

For several days, Major stood aloof as the battle over the CFA was fought out between the president of the Board of Trade and the foreign secretary, who remained entirely loyal to Patten despite pressure from his own civil servants. According to the reports which reached Government House, there was a 'real stand-off' between the two Cabinet heavyweights. Finally, prompted by Patten's telegram, the prime minister consulted the chancellor of the exchequer, who endorsed the governor's stance. Soon afterwards he summoned Douglas Hurd, Kenneth Clarke and Michael Heseltine to a meeting at Number 10. They had three papers before them – one from the embassy in Beijing, one from the Cabinet Office and one from the governor of Hong Kong – all offering conflicting opinions. As the story was relayed to Government House, Heseltine argued, in effect, 'For God's sake, I've made this trip. Don't screw up the prospects. I've had good conversations with the Chinese. They are saying we can make progress if we don't throw the CFA at them.' The same points were made by some of his officials in what Patten described as a distinctly less sophisticated way.

After a vigorous debate, Patten was informed by the Foreign Office that he had won the day and that Heseltine had yielded with characteristic grace. In the absence of agreement with China within the next few days, he was, free, as he interpreted it, to 'go ahead and legislate'. Government House had planned to gazette the CFA bill on the third Friday in June, which, it was calculated, would leave just enough time for the Legislative Council to vote on it before the summer recess. Heseltine was apparently molli-fied by the prime minister's decision to take his advice and send a message to the Chinese premier indicating, in Patten's gloss, that he 'very much hoped we would be able to reach an agreement, and that he welcomed the success of Michael Heseltine's visit to Peking'. This communication may or may not have had an impact on what happened next.

Events now moved with unexpected speed and in an unpre-dictable manner. The Cabinet had given Patten full authority to oversee a last-ditch attempt to secure a deal with China, and this decisive meeting of the Joint Liaison Group was held on 30 May 1995. Towards the end of the session, the leader of the Chinese side, Chen Zuo'er, made a number of suggestions and indicated for the first time that Beijing's principal anxiety was the timing of the establishment of the Court of Final Appeal. Even though the 1991 agreement committed both sides to establishing the court before the handover, he made it clear that, for reasons the British could not fathom, Beijing would prefer the court not to 'open for business' until 1 July 1997.

That evening, after a rapid round of consultations, Chris Patten authorised Richard Hoare, the acting head of the British negotiating team in the JLG, to inform his Chinese counterpart that, while the British would like the court to be set up before 1997, it was not as fundamental to them as the nature of the court that was actually to be established. Patten was to argue that this compromise (or climbdown, as his critics described it) was a sensible trade-off, a relatively modest price to pay for the possibility of an agreement with China on the structure and function of the court. On the plausible assumption that the Legislative Council would approve a bill endorsed by China, he asserted privately that his concession on timing would ensure that there would not be a rupture in the rule of law after the handover.

A week earlier, the Hong Kong government had redrafted parts of the bill to bring it in line with six of eight demands made by the Preliminary Working Committee, the body set up in Hong Kong in 1993 by Beijing as an alternative centre of influence to Government House, allegedly to assist the smooth transfer of power following the collapse of negotiations between the two sovereign states. Hitherto Patten had loftily ignored the ruminations of the PWC. Now, although the body's recommendations for the Court of Final Appeal dealt essentially with technical issues, the governor's willingness to redraft his bill basically on their terms was a significant shift towards the Chinese position which could not have gone unnoticed in Beijing.

Beijing responded by dropping its original demands that the bill should contain a 'post-remedial verdict mechanism' and that the court should be debarred from adjudicating on the 'constitutionality of laws'. China also backed away from its earlier intimation that the bill should define 'acts of state' more precisely than they were defined in the Basic Law. In return, the British side was authorised by Patten to concede that the bill would, as Beijing had insisted, contain a clause confirming that all 'acts of state', howsoever defined in the Basic Law, would be excluded from the jurisdiction of the Court of Final Appeal.

The British negotiators presented Patten's revised bill to their counterparts in the JLG at the beginning of June. The Chinese moved with surprising dispatch, and on 7 June, the two sides signed an agreement to set up the Court of Final Appeal on 1 July 1997. At first Patten was jubilant. Although he acknowledged that it would have been 'incomparably better if we'd been able to establish the court now', he explained that he had been boxed into a corner, not so much by pressure from London as by the prospect of certain defeat in the legislative assembly had he pressed ahead with the CFA bill without China's consent. 'The position we were in was very different from the argument over electoral reform,' he explained. 'On this occasion it looked more and more as if legislating on our own was going to be charging the guns. It would have been magnificent, but ultimately not wildly successful.' In this case it was, as he saw it, a straightforward choice between having a say in the nature of the court and not having the court set up until 1997, or not having a say in the court and still not having the court set up until 1997.

Quite why the Chinese had suddenly decided to compromise was the subject of much speculation at Government House. Patten had not yielded to Heseltine's argument for delay, nor had Britain ceded the right to table the bill in the absence of China's approval. Patten himself thought that Beijing must have reached the conclusion that they were 'running out of time to screw us up, just as we are running out of time as the sovereign power in Hong Kong'. He also felt that they had started to worry about the low morale among civil servants, for whom British standards of justice and law were a sine qua non of civil order, and about the possible exodus of capital from Hong Kong that could so easily be precipitated by a failure to resolve such a crucial issue. Indeed, if they agreed with Patten on few other matters, the colony's business leaders were united with him in the conviction that the survival of the 'rule of law' was vital to their prosperity after the handover. However, not one significant voice in the business community expressed anxiety about whether Beijing would interpret the controversial clause about 'acts of state' in a repressive fashion. Their worry was that Hong Kong's post-1997 judicial system might lack international credibility: it was essential that foreign banks and corporations should regard the Court of Final Appeal as a truly independent body with the power of ultimate adjudication, especially in relation to the law of contract. Otherwise, as they warned Beijing with growing urgency, the world's major investors would inevitably shy away from negotiating deals under Hong Kong law.

Patten was convinced that the Chinese had also been impressed by the 'mad governor' factor; by the evidence that, following the Cabinet decision in his favour, the British would not, in the end, be deterred from establishing a Court of Final Appeal even in the absence of an agreement with China. According to Patten, Douglas Hurd shared this assessment. 'I think the foreign secretary was as surprised at the outcome as we were. But I think, like us, he believed that the real reason we got a deal was because the Chinese believed we had a bottom line, and that we were going to go ahead if we reached the deadline.' Whatever the explanation, Patten was relieved that the deal 'enabled us to dig ourselves out of a hole', and freely conceded that, when the prospect of an agreement appeared, he 'grabbed at it with both hands'.

Throughout the process Patten had been scrupulous in closely consulting Martin Lee. He not only shared with the leader of the Democrats some of his frustrations and dilemmas, but even indicated in broad terms some of the pressures he had been under from London. The governor was indignant, therefore, when the CFA bill was published, that Martin Lee not only failed to applaud the breakthrough but chose to denounce the terms of the deal with China in the most strident and contemptuous fashion. The two erstwhile allies at once found themselves locked in an unusually vituperative public battle. For the first time, Government House experienced the full strength of the Democrats on the offensive. Patten's team reflected ruefully on how dangerously abrasive their relationship would have become if the governor had failed to introduce his political reforms.

Their bitter row went to the heart of an issue which deeply troubled both men: Britain's inability to impose limits on the action the Chinese government would be able to take in Hong Kong after 1997. The first round was fought in the pages of the *South China Morning Post* on 15 June, when Martin Lee accused Britain of allowing the sun 'to set in shame' over its colonial history and Patten of doing 'Beijing's dirty work'. The fundamental cause for the legislator's outburst was what he described as Britain's 'explicit acceptance of China's faulty definition of "acts of state"'. The following day, Patten responded in the same newspaper with a ferocity Hong Kong had not previously witnessed, and which betrayed the governor's acute sensitivity on the issue. Charging Martin Lee with resorting to 'pejorative clichés' and 'inventing quotes and ascribing them to me', he argued that, far from accepting China's definition of the 'acts of state', Britain had merely agreed to 'incorporate the precise wording of the Basic Law into the CFA bill'. He continued, in a tone of exasperation, 'The plain fact is that the Basic Law will be the law of Hong Kong after 1997, and whatever we do now, the CFA would have to be compatible with the Basic Law after 1997 anyway.' Urging Martin Lee to abandon his 'knee-jerk stuff', he criticised the leader of Hong Kong's only directly elected party for doing a 'disservice to Hong Kong people and to the rule of law which both he and I cherish so much'.

To illustrate the nub of his argument, Martin Lee cited a hypothetical but by no means far-fetched scenario.

> Supposing the People's Liberation Army, who will be stationed in Hong Kong, were to arrest somebody and just keep that person in prison without a trial. And suppose his family were to go to court and ask for habeas corpus, according to the common law which will apply in Hong Kong after 1997. And the court says, 'Quite right. You cannot imprison someone in this way without charge. What do you think you are doing?' But the PLA says, 'This is an act of state; we are acting to protect the security of the government in Beijing. This man is a dissident, a counter-revolutionary.' That could

be the end of that man's freedom . . . In other words, Beijing will decide, effectively, the cases which our courts can try and those they cannot try.

Patten could not contradict the point directly, and he knew it. Instead he claimed, wrongly and limply, that hitherto the issue of 'acts of state' had not been raised by Martin Lee and his civil-libertarian allies. As they were quick to counter, the issue had been central to their concern during the drafting of the Basic Law and one of the reasons why the Legislative Council had been so suspicious of the 1991 agreement between Britain and China. In any case, Patten's critics wondered, was the governor suggesting that the British would have been more stalwart if the Democrats had been more vociferous? Or was he merely seeking to blame them for delivering such an unpalatable message through the letterbox of Government House?

The slanging match lasted for almost a month as each side cast around in vain for the linguistic stiletto that might inflict the fatal wound to the other's case. The rawness of their exchanges, laced with sharp debating points and a genuine sense of grievance, owed a great deal to the fact that they shared very similar anxieties and a genuine dismay that they should find themselves at each other's throats. Lee agonised privately, 'I feel betrayed. I think he's betrayed the Hong Kong people's trust in him. When he came it was like a breath of fresh air. He effectively took over from us our banner for democracy . . . I feel terrible . . . I mean, what difference is it from the good old Percy Cradock days?'

Almost symmetrically, Patten confided, 'I think Martin Lee is the most important elected politician in Hong Kong, and that is why I think his attitude to this is so profoundly worrying.' Acknowledging that he was indeed in a 'terrific state' about Lee, Patten complained bitterly about the self-righteousness of the legislator's onslaught. 'It's as if Martin's got a monopoly on concern about – he'd almost go as far as to say knowledge of – the rule of law in Hong Kong.' However, the governor's dismay went deeper than this. It was, though he did not explicitly admit it, as much a manifestation of his own fears as it was a reflection on Martin Lee. 'The frustration is to have the argument turned to issues on which one can't give reassurance,' he said. 'Instead of being about the composition of the court, the argument has become about something which he knows we can't give a one hundred per cent answer on . . . The argument is now about China's understanding and comprehension of the law after 1997.' He appreciated the skill with which Lee had marshalled his case, but he protested that it was nonetheless neither particularly decent nor honourable. 'If Martin spends the next two years saying, "It is all going to be hopeless. Hong Kong is finished. It's a disaster," I can give my opinion, which is maybe matched against his, but I can't stop people in this community and elsewhere becoming either excessively fatalistic or excessively pessimistic about Hong Kong.'

As the two men traded blows they each attracted impressive support. Some of Britain's most important allies – the Americans, the Australians, the Japanese, the Hong Kong Chamber of Commerce and the chief justice – lined up behind the governor. Martin Lee was able to call on the Bar Council, every international human-rights organisation of any note and some of the most eloquent columnists in the colony. Privately, he also had the support of one or two of Patten's most trusted lieutenants who had not broken ranks before. One of them complained:

> The governor is just wrong. I've seen the Executive Council papers on this, and it was agreed that we must not yield on 'acts of state'. It was very clear that this should not be included in the bill as this would be to surrender on an important principle. Now this has been turned upside down overnight. Even if Chris can justify this on the grounds of force majeure – that he had no option on broader diplomatic or political grounds – he should not now turn round and blame Martin for defending a position which he himself once defended as being very important . . . He should have come clean and said, 'It is the best we could get.'

The aide was reminded uncomfortably of Sir David Wilson's governorship, and in this he was not alone. 'In those days they would identify a set of points on which they agreed they should not compromise. Then, after years of futile negotiation with the Chinese, they would meet again and redefine their definitions and then go and present abject defeat as astonishing triumph,' the official explained. 'That is exactly what the governor is trying to do now. It may be inevitable, but it leaves a bad taste.' Later Patten came to regret his decision to allow the Chinese to incorporate the 'acts of state' clause into the CFA bill – a lapse of judgement which perhaps should be attributed more to the intense and sustained pressure imposed on him by London and Beijing than to any indifference to the potential consequences of his retreat from what had once been an important point of principle.

On the eve of the debate on the bill in the Legislative Council, the principal combatants once more drew their swords in public. Patten accused Martin Lee and his supporters of talking in 'irresponsible and exaggerated terms about the destruction of the rule of law in Hong Kong', an approach, he warned, that created the real danger of doing before 1997 the damage they claimed the Chinese would do afterwards. Far from fighting for the rule of law, he said, Lee and his colleagues were virtually 'raising the white flag'. Lee countered that Patten and his officials had 'graduated from distortions to comical hyperbole'. He noted that his fellow barristers on the Bar Council had condemned the CFA bill in ten specific areas for undermining the rule of law and the independence of the judiciary. To rub salt into the wound, he also quoted Sir Percy Cradock, who, as one of the architects of the 1991 agreement, had made the most egregious intervention of all, taking it upon himself to warn that Patten's bill incorporated a 'dangerously broad definition of "acts of state"'. As Martin Lee observed caustically, 'When Sir Percy describes something as dangerous, it must be very dangerous indeed.' He concluded, with all the hyperbole of which he had accused the governor, 'By being craven and giving in to Beijing's demands, Mr Patten is not doing Hong Kong a favour. He is doing all Chinese people the gravest disservice in the long term, and dashing our hopes of Hong Kong helping to set an example for China in the future . . . He has abandoned ship.'

★

The outcome of the vote in LegCo was never in doubt, and on 26 July, after formal negotiations with China lasting seven years, the Legislative Council voted overwhelmingly, by a majority of 38–17, in favour of the CFA bill. The governor expressed his satisfaction. 'I am sure it will be welcomed by the whole community and by international investors as a vote of confidence in Hong Kong's future,' he said. The media were distinctly less euphoric. The *Eastern Express* commented that 'despondency carried the day', and elsewhere that it was a 'dark day' for the human rights of the Hong Kong people. While the *South China Morning Post* condemned Martin Lee for 'whipping up fears', it noted that many legislators were unhappy with the lack of a clear definition of acts of state. 'Every possible effort must now be made to find out how much broader the scope will be, so that real concerns – as well as scaremongering – can be laid to rest.' The paper's cartoonist depicted the governor at the wheel of a giant steamroller flattening Martin Lee into the ground.

The leader of the Democrats was defiant, informing his colleagues after the vote was cast, 'I'm down, but I'm not out.' The truth, on this issue at least, was that the juggernaut had already moved on.

16

'A GOOD MOMENT'

The First Fully Elected LegCo

Surrounded as he was by adversaries on so many fronts, Chris Patten rejoiced in the discovery of a new ally. Jimmy Lai was an immigrant from the mainland for whom the Hong Kong version of the American dream had come true. An enthusiast for Western notions of freedom and democracy, he was alone among his peers in the business sector in using his fortune to advocate these twin causes and to make money in the process. As a small boy in the 1950s, he had hustled in the streets of Shanghai, 'trying to sell this and that to make some money'. He noticed that visitors from Hong Kong were sleek and well dressed, and he was envious. One day one of them gave him a bar of chocolate. 'I tasted it and said, "What's this? Where's it from? Hong Kong?" I thought Hong Kong must be heaven.' Later he stowed away in the bottom of a boat, arriving in Hong Kong as an illegal immigrant. By 1981, he had accumulated enough capital to set up in business on his own. He opened a clothes shop which he called Giordano, selling cheap but fashionable designs for the young 'me' generation of the early eighties. The company grew at the rate of 30 per cent a year, and within little more than a decade, the Giordano empire owned 300 shops throughout Asia and was valued at around $US400 million.

Jimmy Lai did not belong to Hong Kong's elite and he did not share their reticence. A bulky man, restless and energetic, he dressed flamboyantly in casual suits and coloured shirts and sported loud braces. Nor was he ashamed to express his opinions or feelings. 'I'm always a troublemaker. I love trouble. I love the intensity of trouble,' he proclaims with the air of a naughty child who knows that no one, nowadays, is likely to gainsay him. It was in the spirit of entrepreneurial flair and personal iconoclasm that he decided to divert some of his fortune into publishing. His first venture was a weekly magazine called *Next*, which, under his idiosyncratic tutelage, swiftly emerged to challenge and then conquer the existing market in Hong Kong. Often scurrilous, sometimes investigative and frequently prurient, *Next* managed to combine the virtues of *Newsweek*, *Hello!* and *Private Eye*. It irritated, offended, entertained – and it made money. Never afraid to use *Next* to expose and lampoon the powerful, Lai soon acquired more enemies than friends, especially among the cadres in Beijing whose financial dealings in Hong Kong came under damaging scrutiny in the pages of his magazine.

Lai grew increasingly politicised as a result of his foray into journalism, and his criticism of the People's Republic was often vehement. After the 4 June massacre in 1989 he cast off restraint entirely, using what had now become a bestselling periodical to publish a coruscating 'open letter' of condemnation to the Chinese premier, Li Peng. 'I was so mad,' he explained later. 'It was a very nasty, rude letter. I called him . . .' – he paused at the reminder of the enormity of what he had written, and lowered his voice – 'I called him the son of the turtle egg, which is very rude. I don't want to translate it.' He had indeed caused grievous offence to the Chinese leadership, and Beijing's retribution was not long delayed. Within days of the appearance of the offending article, the authorities closed his Giordano shop in the Chinese capital and warned the company that it would not be permitted to trade there again as long as Jimmy Lai remained in control. And that was not all: 'I got bombs thrown into my house here in Hong Kong. I got people coming to my office, ransacking my computer.' Undaunted, Lai removed himself from the board of Giordano, divested himself of his shares and used some of the proceeds to expand into newspapers. In the spring of 1995, his *Apple Daily* hit the news-stands amid an avalanche of publicity. Cleverly targeted at the mass market, *Apple Daily* established itself within days as one of the colony's most popular daily newspapers. Scantily dressed girls vied for the reader's attention with reports on the criminal underworld and a political message which was unequivocally in favour of human rights and democracy.

Not everyone appreciated the new addition to Hong Kong's crowded and cut-throat media market. Jimmy Lai's journalists were threatened, news-vendors were warned not to stock the offending journal and, the proprietor reported, 'We got papers thrown in the harbour and our Giordano shop in Macau was set on fire. Maybe it was because some of the things we wrote offended the triads and they wanted us to know that they didn't like it.' Whatever the motive, these tactics had no effect other than to make Jimmy Lai rue his decision to spend so much on the launch of *Apple Daily*. 'Had I known they would do that, I would have spent much less on promotion. We had all the publicity we needed from these people trying to stop us.'

As the 1995 election approached, Lai's editorial message to his fast-growing readership was simple: 'Don't have fear.' Explaining his enthusiasm for Patten's reforms, he spoke with defiance and intensity. 'Hong Kong is our home. Hong Kong is where we want to protect our freedom. I don't give a shit what happens in China – this is my home.' And if, after 1997, the authorities were to suppress *Next* or *Apple Daily*? 'I will just lie low and wait for the right time to come back again. I am young. Unless my life is threatened I will stay here. This is my home.' As he reiterated the last four words, his face creased and his eyes filled with tears.

A few days before the voters of Hong Kong went to the polls to choose the first fully elected Legislative Council in the history of Hong Kong, David Chu Yiu Lin boarded his motor yacht for the outlying island of Ping Chau. His mission was to solicit one vote from the leader of the local council, which he was confident would be enough to secure his place in the legislature. The twenty seats on the Legislative Council which were to be directly elected would be decided on the first-past-the-post system in geographical constituencies covering the entire territory; another thirty were to be elected in the functional constituencies. The remaining ten would fall to candidates elected by the Election

Committee, which consisted of 266 people representing the
District Boards, who had themselves been elected in the 1994
local elections. It was one of these latter seats that David Chu
coveted.

Hong Kong's most ebullient apologist for Beijing had not run
for an election of any kind before, and, by his own account, it was
an exciting if daunting experience. Born in Shanghai in 1944,
David Chu had fled with his family to Hong Kong to escape the
rigours of early Maoism. When he was fourteen, they emigrated
to the United States, where he acquired an American accent,
some influential friends and an MBA from the Harvard Business
School. In 1977, now a senior financial executive, he returned to
Hong Kong, soon to be headhunted by Jardine Matheson. In
1984 he launched his own company specialising in property
development. Before long he was a multimillionaire.

His business acumen notwithstanding, he was better known in
Hong Kong for a penchant for fast motorbikes ('I go fast to scare
myself') and dangerous sports. In August 1995, at the age of fifty-
one, he was able to boast that his most recent escapade –
paragliding from Hong Kong to Beijing – had not only broken
three world records but raised US$130,000 for charity. His image
as a middle-aged playboy was complicated by his passion for
political debate and an irrepressible and apparently guileless optimism about Hong Kong's future under Chinese rule. In 1992 his
loyalty had been rewarded by Beijing with a role as an 'adviser' on
Hong Kong affairs, and the following year he was appointed to
the Preliminary Working Committee. In this capacity he wrote
articles for a variety of newspapers and magazines denouncing the
alleged perfidies of Chris Patten and his democratic allies in the
Legislative Council. His breezy disdain for the political freedoms
he had enjoyed as a naturalised citizen of the United States was
offset by a personal charm. As a result he was readily forgiven –
if not taken very seriously – by those he chastised in print.

Chu's sincerity was not in doubt. Unlike many of his colleagues in the business community who protested their allegiance
to China but, in the governor's phrase, had 'British passports
tucked in their back pockets', he had recently taken the rare step
of surrendering his Western (in this case, American) passport to

demonstrate his commitment to the mainland. In this campaign
his message was to be simple, if not simplistic: 'You may say I am
extremely optimistic. I fully expect things to be better after 1997.
I expect Chinese people will be able to rule Hong Kong even
better when the British have left . . . When Hong Kong is ruled
by Hong Kong people, we'll be so proud.' As for the danger that
China might intervene to repress personal liberties, he placed his
trust in the Basic Law. 'You know, China is not allowed to close
down democracy. It is not permitted by the Basic Law. I have
faith in the Basic Law, and in my ability to make China behave
according to the Basic Law. The Basic Law is not only a constitution for Hong Kong, it is also a contract between Hong Kong
and China, and neither side can break that contract for fifty years.'
He conceded that some Chinese officials were bemused that such
a colourful individual as himself could be so dedicated to Beijing's
cause. 'My personal lifestyle is vastly different from that of a
Chinese official, so they look upon me as a really strange animal,
but I am quietly friendly to them, and genuinely patriotic.'

For many liberals in Hong Kong, David Chu was the almost
acceptable face of a regime which they not only loathed but
feared. In the summer of 1995, however, only the most courageous individuals were still prepared to speak their minds
regardless of the consequences. With the business community
and its acolytes in the media ranged against them, they faced isolation and ridicule from those who damned them with the
faintest of praise as idealists or romantics or self-righteous publi-
cists. Along with Emily Lau, Martin Lee and his colleague Szeto
Wah, Christine Loh had emerged as one of the few public figures
to speak out publicly in favour of human rights and in defiance of
Beijing's animosity, and she shared none of David Chu's optimism
about their future sovereign. Although she had not yet decided
whether to give up a successful career in business for the vagaries
of full-time politics, her scepticism about China's readiness to
allow Hong Kong a 'high degree of autonomy' after 1997 had by
now turned to pessimism. By the end of 1993, she had made up
her mind to run as an independent candidate in the 1995 elections, commenting wryly, 'I never thought I would be in this
predicament, but I have to be positive, to say that there is a way

forward, because if we can't believe that, then the future is pretty bleak.'

As the 1995 election campaign approached, Christine Loh maintained this façade, but in private she was warding off despair. The repeated warnings from Beijing that after the handover the entire political structure of Hong Kong would, as she saw it, be 'liquidated' was 'really, really bad news'. Yet instead of taking to the streets to demonstrate their disapproval, as she had hoped and half expected, the people seemed to have 'numbed themselves' to the prospect. 'I am pessimistic,' she told her friends, 'but I can't do the job I do if I can't get up in the morning and believe that there are still some things we can do. I'm not going to rule out the Hong Kong people . . . Why should they take this lying down?'

Christine Loh was to stand against a veteran legislator called Peggy Lam, a vigorous ally of Beijing. Lam had nurtured her constituency in Central, and enjoyed a reputation as a doughty political infighter. It would not be an easy contest. Loh's overriding reason for running against such a stalwart opponent was, she declared, 'to fight for our own identity'. She believed that there were many who shared her inability to express any patriotic fervour for the motherland. 'I do not know whether I can ever stand up and say, "I'm a citizen of the People's Republic of China,"' she confessed privately. 'Maybe people like me will have to be phased out.' She had been angered by a conversation she had recently had with a senior Chinese official. He had told her, 'If you really feel this way about us, why don't you just leave?' She had replied, 'Hong Kong is my home. You can't say that to me.' She went into the campaign in this mood of defiance, reflecting, 'Of course, if we are talking about tanks rolling over the border, then I concede right away. But we have to continue to argue that that's not going to happen . . . It's a last stand, in a way.'

Margaret Ng shared Christine Loh's pessimism, but felt it even more keenly. After playing a decisive part in preventing the lawyers' representative, Simon Ip, from voting against Patten's reforms in 1994, she had found herself more directly involved in the political process, but with dwindling expectations. By the summer of 1995, she was not only despondent about China but

also bitter about what she regarded as the governor's acquiescence in a fatally flawed compromise with Beijing over the Court
of Final Appeal. 'Relying on logic,' she commented, 'there is
every reason to be pessimistic, to believe that the rule of law will
be non-existent after 1997. But, of course, hope defies logic.' It
was in this spirit that, at the last moment, she decided to run for
a place in the legislative assembly, aspiring to represent the legal
profession in a functional constituency whose size had been significantly increased by the Patten reforms to embrace almost
2,000 registered voters. Superficially, at least, her decision to enter
the political fray was paradoxical. 'There is nothing to stay here
for. People don't want people like me. I won't be able to find a
job. No one will hire me as a lawyer, no one will print my articles,' she had said to herself. Like many others who would never
admit it publicly, her growing despair had led her to start flat-
hunting in London, for a bolt-hole to which she could retreat in
a hurry, if necessary. She was well aware that it would be difficult
to earn a living in Britain, but she was ready to work, 'as a char-
lady' if she had to. 'I think it is a perfectly respectable way to live.
You offer a service which is needed, and you get paid for it. I
would still be able to amuse myself by reading books, even by
writing books. I think what is important is the inner life.'

But by September 1995 these plans had been put in abeyance
as Margaret Ng prepared to enter a political campaign which, if
she were successful, would almost certainly oblige her to stay in
Hong Kong until after the handover. A few weeks earlier, a group
of like-minded lawyers had approached her to ask her to stand in
the elections. She was neither flattered nor excited. She had never
contemplated a political life, and she knew enough about LegCo
to conclude that it was 'very boring' for most of the time and that
it would interfere with her personal freedom. She also sensed that
the focus of attention between 1995 and 1997 would shift from
the legislative assembly to the Preparatory Committee which,
under the terms of the Joint Declaration, was due to be set up in
1996 to replace the Preliminary Working Committee, ostensibly
to ensure a smooth handover. She was well aware that she would
therefore have limited influence, and, if successful, she expected
to have to fight hard for very little. She was not even looking

forward to the campaign itself. 'It involves thinking about problems you have found very boring to think about before. It
involves listening to the views of a lot of people. It involves
cheering the troops. It involves canvassing for votes. It involves
election meetings and giving people tea . . . It's all terribly
tedious.'

Nonetheless she felt obliged to submit herself to an ordeal to
which, with no false modesty, she thought herself to be particularly ill suited. Before acceding to her colleagues' request, she
asked herself whether there was something, despite all that, which
made it worth doing. Her answer was positive, and her certainties
lacked any hint of bravado or vainglory, but seemed to be driven
by a fierce moral imperative.

> There might come a moment when something needs to be
> said. You might be able to change the political culture. You
> may be able to bring into question a taboo that no one has
> realised before. You may be able to offer your time, your
> knowledge and your skill to ensure that certain bills are con-
> structed to protect the rule of law . . . It is very much a
> matter of 'maybe', but I do not see that it is impossible.
>
> What do I stand for? An uncompromising attitude
> towards all things which are fundamental to the liberty of
> the individual. For the quality of professional service. For
> integrity. Not being afraid to speak the truth. Not putting
> your own interests first. Being able to face whatever it takes
> to say the honest thing. I don't know if they are of use to
> anyone, but such as they are, I offer them.

These attitudes were not calculated to endear her to the post-
1997 sovereign, as Margaret Ng knew only too well.

Of the established politicians, Martin Lee was the most prominent figure in the campaign. The two most notable candidates
standing against his Democratic party were his old rival Allen Lee,
an appointed member of the Legislative Council and the leader of
the pro-Beijing Liberals, and Tsang Yok Sing of the Democratic
Alliance for the Betterment of Hong Kong, the pro-Beijing
coalition he had helped to found in 1992. Neither man had stood

for election before, and they formed an unlikely alliance: Allen Lee, the muddled voice of vacillating compromise, and Tsang Yok Sing, the Marxist intellectual, publicly loyal but privately troubled by the predatory instincts of the repressive regime in China.

In the 1980s Lee had been an assiduous champion of open government and democracy; by the time of Patten's arrival he had fallen under the influence of Sir S.Y. Chung and, along with his mentor, had switched allegiance from the colonial authorities to the future sovereign. 'I have thought many times,' he confided in the run-up to the 1995 elections, 'do we really need democracy in Hong Kong while we enjoy all the freedoms under British rule, where our businesses flourish and Hong Kong has become a great international centre?' His born-again reluctance to make any link between freedom under the law and democratic accountability was an attitude endemic in Hong Kong among civil servants, the business community and those like himself who had been plucked from obscurity and given some power and much prestige under Britain's relatively benign patronage.

After 1989, the language people chose to use about the killings in Tiananmen Square was a revealing indicator of feelings towards China. For some it was an 'atrocity'; for others, 'unfortunate'. Allen Lee saw it as a 'tragic' episode, a 'very sad' period that could have been resolved peacefully, not least if the student leaders had been less 'distasteful and impolite' to the Chinese premier, Li Peng. The sharpening divisions between Martin Lee's Democrats and Allen Lee's Liberals dated from this period, the Liberals taking the view that Beijing should not be shunned but 'engaged in discussion', a standpoint which coincided precisely with that of Allen Lee's political partner of convenience, Tsang Yok Sing.

Notwithstanding their assiduous attempts the previous year to torpedo the Patten reforms, both Tsang Yok Sing and Allen Lee decided that in order to retain any vestige of political credibility in Hong Kong, they would have to undergo the novel experience of running for direct election. Tsang Yok Sing's advisers selected what they thought to be the safest seat, Taipo in the New Territories. Embarrassingly, and for the same reason, Allen Lee made the same choice. Protracted negotiations ensued in an attempt to avoid certain defeat for one of them and conceivably, through splitting the pro-Beijing vote, for both. At first Tsang Yok Sing tried to persuade Allen Lee to bypass the test of a direct election and instead, as Hong Kong's 'most experienced legislator', to ensure himself a place in the chamber by running for a safe seat via the reformed Election Committee system. His suggestion fell on deaf ears. Beijing, in the person of Lu Ping, intervened directly to break the deadlock by instructing Tsang Yok Sing to withdraw his candidature for the Taipo seat. The DAB leader reluctantly obeyed this edict, only to come under intense pressure from his party colleagues, who urged him to take himself the indirect route on to LegCo which he had vainly pressed on Allen Lee. 'If there is any chance of winning in one of the geographical constituencies I should go for it,' Tsang Yok Sing argued. 'If I am to lead the election campaign, I want to do it as a participant, as someone standing for election, seeking a popular mandate.'

It was intriguing to witness how far both Tsang Yok Sing and Allen Lee had already been swayed by the process put in train by the Patten reforms. Although each deplored the governor's measures, neither could ignore the political lesson generated by the subsequent public debate about democracy. The prospect of two of Patten's principal adversaries seeking a popular mandate for their platform of public opposition to the very electoral system in which they were about to be such prominent participants did not go unnoticed at Government House, where it caused a degree of complacent mirth.

Tsang Yok Sing had to fight a fierce internal battle with his DAB colleagues to win their consent to stand in what some of them thought to be 'futile' elections. He maintained that it was vital 'to show people both in the pro-China camp and in society at large that we can win support from the voters'. However, this was not an end in itself. On the eve of the elections, in a confession which would have astonished the Hong Kong public and horrified those in China for whom he was an important apologist, he volunteered his hope that, if his party performed well in the elections, Beijing might be persuaded to withdraw its threat to dismantle the legislature in 1997. 'If most people were to agree that the results of the elections reflected the intentions of the voters it would be easier for us – for people who believe in the present system – to convince the Chinese officials that it won't be disastrous for the establishment of the SAR to keep the electoral system more or less the same.' Patten could hardly have wished for a more full-hearted endorsement of his reform package; unhappily, he did not even know of it, because Tsang Yok Sing, not through cowardice but in order to retain his moderating influence in Beijing, had at no stage felt able to rally support for the governor in public. The DAB leader eventually persuaded his colleagues that he should contest a seat in Kowloon, where he would be competing with a popular local democrat. His opponent would be sustained by a far more sophisticated electoral machine than the DAB possessed. The DAB had ample funds, but lacked any experience of electioneering.

By British standards, the election campaign was a muted affair. Although hoardings were littered with the portraits of the candidates, some of whom took to the streets with aplomb, complete with megaphones and video displays, the contest was remarkably free of vulgarity or venom. Contenders for the twenty seats to be directly elected set up their stalls outside underground stations or bus terminals or near busy markets. Supporters, carrying bright banners and wearing identical T-shirts, lined the pavements to exhort the public to back their candidate. Often two or three candidates arrived to occupy the same pitch at the same time. Once or twice there were scuffles but for the most part they contented themselves with out-shouting the opposition. Very few voters seemed to take much notice.

The media reflected this apparent lethargy. The newspapers carried summaries of the competing platforms and interviewed the most prominent candidates in the most closely contested seats, but election news rarely made the front pages. The tabloids preferred to focus on an unpublished government report suggesting that pornographic videos were a principal cause of rape in the colony's jails. And Typhoon Kent, which hit Hong Kong at the beginning of September, was a far bigger story: traffic was brought to a standstill for eight hours, railways and bus routes were closed and the Tuen Mun road, part of a main artery

between Hong Kong and the New Territories, had to be shut for
emergency repairs to prevent a landslide. By 6 September, the
papers were calling on the governor to apologise for the disruption caused by the road closure. Patten refused to oblige, and *Sing
Tao* editorialised: 'Patten's mentality is typical of a "sunset governor" who cannot be bothered even to go through the motions of
expressing his concern for the inconvenience caused to the
public.' Typhoon Kent eventually gave way to the arrest of three
police officers on corruption charges and the trial of Albert
Yeung, the chairman of a large corporation, who had close links
with Beijing, also on a corruption charge. On 12 September, five
days before the election, the media devoted front-page coverage
to a confrontation between Han Dongfang, a Chinese dissident
expelled from China and now living in Hong Kong, and officials
of the local branch of the NCNA. On 13 September, the lead
story in most newspapers was a road accident in which eleven
pregnant women, all illegal immigrants from the mainland, were
injured. They had been smuggled across the border to give birth
in the territory, thereby giving their children the right of abode
in Hong Kong. This drama all but smothered Patten's comments
expressing his hope for a large turnout and urging that this 'milestone' election should not be seen as the last which would be
conducted freely in Hong Kong. It was with only three days to
go that the 'milestone' election finally came to dominate the
news.

On Sunday 17 September, the voters went to the polls, filing
into schools and other public buildings in a quiet and orderly
fashion, confirming the view that the citizens of Hong Kong
were quite mature enough to participate in the democratic
process so belatedly bequeathed to them. It was, however, far
more complicated than the British elections which in other
respects it so closely resembled. Many voters had also registered
for their respective functional constituencies and therefore not
only had to select their chosen candidate for the geographical
constituency in which they lived but had to vote a second time
for a candidate on that slate as well. An overall turnout of 35 per
cent was lower than the governor might have hoped for, but,
given the complexity of the new system, it bore favourable

comparison with the presidential elections in the United States and with local elections in Britain. In the case of the twenty directly elected seats, the turnout was 3.5 per cent down on the 1991 elections, but the total number of voters had risen by 170,000 to a record 920,000. Although fewer than half a million of the 2.7 million people eligible had cast a vote in the functional constituencies, it was widely recognised that this was due less to apathy than to a failure by many voters to identify which of the nine new functional constituencies was 'theirs'.

When the polls closed, the ballot boxes were conveyed in sealed boxes under police escort to the International Trade Mart to be counted. Here, at last, it was possible to experience the 'election fever' hitherto so markedly absent from the campaign. The trade mart had been turned into a vast electronic theatre with a giant video wall relaying the images of frantic activity on the floor caught by endlessly roving cameras. Anxious candidates and their supporters watched as the votes piled up for and against them on long tables. Tellers and runners, dressed according to their role and status in uniform reds, yellows and greens, dashed back and forth across the hall with well-drilled urgency. Newspaper journalists from all over the world, there to record Hong Kong's first – and possibly last – genuinely free election, sat in a tier of reserved seats waiting for the results in an atmosphere of real excitement. Television and radio reporters from more than a dozen countries stood ready to deliver a well-turned phrase to their audiences. In an outer arena, four local television channels provided live coverage of the count, their star presenters, proficient and cool under the arc lights, talking endlessly despite the absence of news. Rumours abounded: the Democrats had won by a landslide; Allen Lee had lost; the DAB had been trounced. By midnight only a handful of votes had been counted. By two o'clock, the result was still uncertain. Famous local figures, a beaming governor to the fore, strode purposefully across the set. Anxious candidates wandered from table to table, going nowhere. The fast-food counters around the main hall were soon littered with empty bottles and screwed-up napkins and the residue of innumerable Cokes, Pepsis and pizzas. In the end it took fifteen hours to count all 1.4 million votes cast.

To those with feelings of foreboding about 1997, the good-natured enthusiasm of a new political class – men and women at last liberated to exercise rights which should, and could, have been theirs for a generation – was both impressive and touching. Before each result was announced, the candidates were summoned to a long dais to await the verdict of the voters. The winners stood for photographs and sometimes uttered a few words for the cameras before being swept away into the enfolding arms of friends and supporters. Christine Loh, who won Hong Kong Central with almost twice as many votes as Peggy Lam, was visibly moved at her startling share of the vote. Margaret Ng was even more astonished to emerge comfortably ahead of her two rivals for the legal functional constituency, but she declined to make a victory speech and could barely face the cameras. David Chu, who in the end failed to secure the support of the local councillor on Ping Chau Island, still garnered enough votes to win one of the ten seats chosen by the 283-member Election Committee. He could hardly contain his delight, but no one asked him to make a speech. Martin Lee won easily in Hong Kong Island East; and, despite his own pessimism, Allen Lee was victorious in a three-way contest in the New Territories North-East after what was widely regarded as one of the most effective campaigns in the entire contest. Emily Lau, the territory's most charismatic politician, who had poured scorn on China and Britain in equal measure while still demanding direct elections for every seat in the legislature, secured the largest personal vote (39,265) of the twenty geographical constituencies – almost 2,000 more than Martin Lee. However, they were both outdone by Elizabeth Wong, a much-admired civil servant who had taken early retirement to contest the community and social services functional constituency as an independent. She secured more than 40,000 votes from workers in that field, a turnout of over 40 per cent.

Aside from the defeats of Peggy Lam and her fellow pro-China veteran Elsie Tu, the most significant casualty was Tsang Yok Sing, who was comfortably beaten by a relatively unknown candidate from the Association for Democracy and People's Livelihood (ADPL), which had close links with Martin Lee's

Democratic party. Tsang Yok Sing's personal credibility had been damaged by a revelation about his family which had first surfaced six months earlier. Soon after Tiananmen Square, his wife and daughter had secured Canadian passports and retreated to Vancouver. Though Tsang Yok Sing himself had remained in Hong Kong, his opponent in the campaign had insinuated that the DAB leader could easily 'jump a plane' out of Hong Kong if he wished to escape Chinese sovereignty. Tsang Yok Sing indignantly denied that he possessed a foreign passport of any kind, but the mud stuck. The only smear of note in the campaign, it was, as Tsang Yok Sing himself conceded, remarkably effective.

Yet it was not in itself the reason for his downfall. It was clear that the voters had not been convinced by Tsang Yok Sing's assiduous efforts to distance himself from Beijing. His failure to persuade the electorate that he was not merely China's mouthpiece had not been helped by repeated warnings from Beijing – one on the very eve of the vote – that the entire electoral edifice would in any case be dismantled on 1 July 1997. Frustrated by China's clumsy belligerence, Tsang Yok Sing had gone out of his way to insist during the campaign that the 1995 election should be regarded as a valid test of opinion, and, immediately after his defeat, he reiterated publicly that there was 'no evidence to show that the elections were unfair'. Privately he went further: 'I will advise the Chinese government and the officials in charge of Hong Kong affairs to say nothing more against these elections. It will not help in any way . . . I do not think it is wise, although there are obviously some people in the Chinese government who think it necessary to remind people in Hong Kong that there will be no "through train".'

The DAB leader drew comfort from the fact that seven other members of his party had won seats in the Legislative Council. These, combined with the ten seats won by Allen Lee's Liberal party and a small bloc of pro-China independents, meant that the Democratic party, the largest single bloc with nineteen seats, would have to depend on the support of independents (among whom only Emily Lau, Christine Loh and Margaret Ng could be relied on) to form even a small majority in the legislature. Tsang Yok Sing saw this as precisely the 'balanced' outcome which should hold no fears for Beijing. 'If anybody in Beijing or Hong Kong believes that by scrapping the present system we could replace it with another that was acceptable to the people of Hong Kong yet composed of very different people from what we now have, then he is certainly wrong,' he confided. It was a judgement which revealed the depth of foreboding felt even by this honourable communist about Hong Kong's future.

If the DAB leader was dismayed by the behaviour of Beijing, he was appalled that so many of his 'friends' in the community, assuming his to be a sympathetic ear, went out of their way to stress to him that they shared China's concerns. The Legislative Council would have to be reconstituted in 1997, they said, both to maintain social stability and to create a 'conciliatory' relationship between the legislature and the government. Though he was not altogether surprised that such sentiments should emerge from the business community, it shocked him to discover that 'there are people within the Hong Kong government who believe it will be really difficult to work with a legislature dominated by members of populist political parties', and that there was still a 'proportion of our population who don't believe that democracy as we see it in some Western countries is really good for Hong Kong'.

Tsang Yok Sing was tempted to voice these concerns, but he concluded that to speak his mind openly would be counterproductive. 'If I am not mistaken, the Chinese government does not accept this form of lobbying. Doesn't like it.' Such honesty in the aftermath of his own defeat was remarkable, not least because he was determined to press this case behind the scenes with Beijing while being quite willing for his real views to be made public after the handover. If the old guard in Beijing were to live up to their well-earned reputation for vengefulness, Tsang Yok Sing's prospects after 1997 were likely to be dramatically diminished.

As if to confirm his anxieties, China reacted to the election result in precisely the way he had predicted. The NCNA in Hong Kong declared that the outcome had been 'unfair and unreasonable'. In Beijing, Li Peng announced that China would not recognise any political structure that violated the Joint Declaration and the Basic Law. A Foreign Ministry spokesman said that the election result 'did not reflect public opinion', and the Hong Kong and Macau Affairs Office confirmed that 'China's decision to terminate LegCo on 30 June 1997 is strong and firm: it will not be changed by the election results'. Unnamed 'sources close to China' advised that Beijing's attitude would become 'harsher' as the leadership was bound to conclude that 'Hong Kong people now support those who confront China'.

Martin Lee, whose party's nineteen seats included twelve of the twenty directly elected seats, was undeterred by China's response. 'The principal reason for our victory is that the voters trust us to stand up for Hong Kong . . . Hong Kong people cannot be intimidated into submission. They love democracy and they want their human rights to be preserved.' Chris Patten was almost as exuberant. Congratulating the Democrats on maintaining the momentum in the four years since their previous triumph, he declared that their 1991 victory had clearly not been a flash in the pan. 'Four years nearer to the transition, we have people standing up and saying the same things, and saying them with a great deal of conviction.' He countered China's threat to 'terminate' LegCo by warning of serious international repercussions if they were to contravene the Joint Declaration and the Basic Law. However, he was careful not to specify what would constitute contravention, or what action would be taken and by whom.

On the day after the vote, in the relative tranquillity of Government House, Patten struggled to express his mixed feelings. The election which he had devised, and for which he had fought for three years, was over. It had self-evidently been free and fair: it was not only a personal triumph, however transitory, but a huge relief. He said that he was 'sort of cheerful', but that he had a sense of 'slightly alarmed astonishment' because 'the people of Hong Kong couldn't have more decisively demonstrated that we haven't been entirely out of tune with them for the last three years'. This made him feel 'slightly emotional'. An American friend of his who had first introduced him to US politics, and who had been staying at Government House, had gone out touring the polling stations. Captivated by the experience, he returned to tell Patten, 'You know, what was wonderful was seeing all these people who are proud of their freedom practising it.' As he related his friend's thought, the governor found himself unable to continue. Tears came to his eyes, and there was a long pause before he said, with unintended bathos, 'So it was a good moment.'

His sang-froid restored, he went on: 'I don't see any way in which the Chinese can simply ignore this result. I imagine the New China News Agency will have a bit of trouble explaining it away, and that there will be those who'll say, "We've just got to look more positive if we are going to win a few hearts and minds before 1997." Because, as sure as hell, they haven't done that yet.' He was by no means confident that the gap could be bridged.

His situation was complicated by his anxieties about the civil service. In the face of Chinese attrition, he feared for their morale. The intention of Michael Sze – who was widely admired for the tenacity he had displayed, as secretary for constitutional affairs, in the face-to-face negotiations with China – to depart from government for a job in the private sector (though in the end he decided against this) deepened the gloom in Hong Kong's corridors of power. Patten was frustrated by the fact that 'a lot of my administration, a lot of my civil servants, will not want to be doing things which undermine "executive-led government"'. His words echoed Tsang Yok Sing's concerns. It would not be easy, he said, to bolster the standing of the legislature, but it was part of the democratisation of the community. He feared formidable opposition: indeed, earlier in the month, his own appointee as chief secretary, Anson Chan, had led a powerful delegation of civil servants to Government House to urge Patten to redraft the constitution to reinforce the concept of an 'executive-led government' by forbidding the introduction of any private member's bill without the prior approval of the governor.

Patten had been horrified by this proposal. It demonstrated an alarming failure on behalf of the colony's future administrators to appreciate an important channel for the expression of democratic opinion, and furthermore he knew that such a regressive change would fundamentally undermine his own position in the community. Patten respected Anson Chan for her judgement, intellect and integrity, and if he was aware of this authoritarian streak in her character, it was counterbalanced for him by her evident ability to 'stand up for Hong Kong'. He shared the wide-spread view that she would be the lynchpin of the post-1997 administration, and that if she was removed from office by the Chinese, the civil service would rapidly crumble. He was there-fore dismayed by her advocacy of what he regarded as a 'rotten case' for constitutional 'reform'.

Like many of her colleagues in the government, Anson Chan was ambivalent about the growth of the democratic spirit in Hong Kong. Ill at ease with the freedoms enjoyed by the media, whose practitioners she was prone to regard with disdain, she had rarely displayed great sympathy for the efforts of Hong Kong's elected politicians to flex their fledgling muscles. Whether this merely betrayed an efficient administrator's frustration at the messiness of democracy, or whether, as some of her critics feared, it revealed the narrow vision of a thwarted autocrat, her distrust of Hong Kong's democratic momentum troubled her admirers no less than her detractors.

Patten had listened to the case made by his most senior bureau-crats, but ended the meeting by making it clear that he would not contemplate acceding to his chief secretary's proposal. He pointed out to her and her colleagues that, as governor, he already had far-reaching constitutional powers, and that if he were to 'pick a constitutional row' with Hong Kong's legislators on the issue of private members' bills, they might refuse to co-operate with the executive by, for instance, refusing to approve the budget. If the civil servants were not convinced by his stance, they soon realised that the governor was not to be swayed.

Patten derived little consolation from this victory. He was well aware that he could not afford to alienate his senior colleagues. After the election he noted, 'I have a civil service which I want to keep loyal, which I don't want to see starting to look towards a less democratic future as the answer to their prayers.' At the same time, in the form of the Legislative Council, he had another constituency which he had to handle with care. Together, the members of a newly credible legislature and the traditionalist civil service represented, as it seemed to Patten, the 'political schizo-phrenia of Hong Kong . . . I want to persuade the administration to look for ways of co-operating more with the Legislative

Council. At the same time, I want to try to persuade the Legislative Council to do things which are sensible on the economic and social front rather than to go in for knee-jerk populism.'

Patten knew that much would depend on whether Martin Lee and his colleagues used their new power with discretion. If they did, he argued, it would be far harder for senior civil servants and the business community to point an accusing finger at Government House, complaining, 'You see? As soon as you have a more democratic legislature, they cock up the economy.' Moreover, it would be very much more difficult for China to remove Martin Lee and other 'subversives' from the 'through train', or to deny them a role in Hong Kong's political future. Patten believed that in this respect the future stability of the territory was at stake.

> What will be the consequence of the Chinese continuing to try to anathemise Martin Lee and the other Democrats? The consequence, if they do that beyond 1997, is, inevitably, political turbulence. You can't, in a community like Hong Kong, simply shut out the opinions, the views, the aspirations, the ambitions, the fears, without there being socio-political consequences.

Patten's faith in the colony's democratic potential was undimmed; indeed, in the wake of the elections, it burned even more powerfully. In his certainty, he had been a combative but measured campaigner, tenacious, eloquent and inspiring: now, his judgement about the people of Hong Kong vividly confirmed, he longed for a legislature that would display the kind of political maturity which would make it even harder for Beijing to snuff out the light of freedom after the handover.

For this reason he worried about the Democrats. 'The easy thing for Martin Lee to do now,' he confided, 'would be to spend the last two years of British sovereignty demonstrating that the last British governor wasn't elected, didn't have a democratic mandate and was the representative of an external colonial power a long way away.' Although Patten suspected that this would 'doubtless satisfy some of his American entourage' – the latest in a line of Martin Lee's political advisers, Minky Worden, had a born-again attitude towards democracy which so irritated Patten's team that, in schoolboy fashion, they had nicknamed their cheerful adversary Stinky – he hoped that the leader of the Democratic party might be both 'more open and more generous' and 'more responsible in the sense of less populist' than he feared would be the case.

As it was, Martin Lee had started to reflect on the fruits of victory in terms that would have delighted the governor and indeed even surprised himself. It was not until several hours after the final declaration of the results that the leader of the Democrats began to realise that he and his allies would be able to form a clear majority in the legislature on almost all issues of any substance. On the basis of his party's analysis of the Patten reforms, Martin Lee had long ago concluded that the Democrats would remain in opposition as a minority party after the election. 'We never thought that we could form a majority. It was a very very pleasant surprise.' He also felt somewhat chastened.

> People kept on saying, 'Look, the Tiananmen effect has gone. The people of Hong Kong have learned to be more pragmatic. They want to work with China . . . That means, if necessary, working on China's terms.' The British bought that line. And I almost bought it. I and my party assumed that the Hong Kong people didn't want trouble with China. So the results of the poll shook me. They were a very strong vindication of what we had been doing, although in our hearts we thought we had lost their support.

The following morning, his exhilaration rapidly ebbed away to be replaced by a political hangover. His electoral mandate, combined with the enhanced status devolved to the Legislative Council by the Patten reforms, was bound to alter the contours of political debate. With characteristic candour, he confessed that his party was uneasy with the unexpected authority bestowed on it by the voters.

I was extremely worried, thinking to myself that with this majority there comes responsibility. We have to be more careful in everything we say from now on . . . Every time we take a stance on anything, we really have to be very careful. If we get it wrong, maybe the government will actually do what we want them to do . . . We will have to be much more reasonable and sensible in all our statements, because it could make a difference. If we get it wrong, the community will suffer and we will have to take the blame.

In opposition, the only role he and his colleagues had effectively previously experienced, his task had been simple. As the colonial government had been able to ignore LegCo, individual legislators had been free to indulge in 'gesture' politics – a memory which already seemed to be provoking a glow of nostalgia in Martin Lee. 'Even if the government did something that was quite generous to our people – and which some of our members may have privately applauded – in public we could complain that it was not enough . . . No party had any obligation or responsibility, really. Whatever the government did, you could simply say that it was not enough.' To Martin Lee's frustration, his senior lieutenant, Szeto Wah, led a faction that was reluctant to adapt to the new situation. 'He wants to be in the minority all the time, and he thought we would be,' he said dismissively. However, the party leader reminded Szeto Wah and his colleagues:

It has happened: we are the majority, and if we don't take what I consider the sensible approach, and we merely criticise the government strongly for another two years, then at the end of that time we might not have done anything for our people. We will have criticised a lot, but what will we have done? With compromise the chances are that, with the co-operation of the government, we could actually do something.

Chris Patten was keen to restore the goodwill between himself and Martin Lee which had been ruptured by their public slanging match over the Court of Final Appeal. Although Lee was still fiercely critical of the governor's actions in that matter, he was by now ready to concede that Patten might have been under pressure from the Foreign Office and the British government. Personally, he still considered Patten a 'genuine and interesting person, a nice guy', and, as a fellow Catholic, he was enthusiastic about the prospect of future 'co-operation'. But he warned: 'Of course, we will never concede on principle on issues like the rule of law and individual liberty.'

The governor, not yet aware of Martin Lee's intentions, did not in any event have time to dwell on the happy outcome of the elections. Within a week the triumph of democracy was driven out of the headlines by an issue which had long been lurking in the political undergrowth, tinder waiting for a match: in this case, however, the governor's principal adversaries were not to be found in Hong Kong or China, but in Whitehall.

'NOT REMOTELY ACRIMONIOUS'

Tackling the Home Secretary

On Friday 22 September 1995, Chris Patten appeared in an edition of the BBC Radio 4 programme *Any Questions*, which was broadcast live from Government House. In response to a question from the former BBC correspondent Anthony Lawrence, the governor declared that more than 3 million subjects of the British crown in Hong Kong should be given right of abode in Britain. In elaboration he said:

> I don't think that a British passport should just be a more convenient way of getting on and off an aeroplane. I think that a British passport should be about more than helping you to travel comfortably around the world, and I think that those who qualify for a BDTC [British Dependent Territories Citizen] passport – a British passport – should qualify for something that, if necessary, gives them right of abode. I don't think that more than three million Hong Kong citizens are suddenly going to arrive at Heathrow. Nobody seriously supposes that. And, to be blunt, if they did that, they certainly wouldn't be living on the welfare state.

Patten had chosen his words with care. Knowing that the issue was likely to be raised in the programme, he had debated with his advisers how best to respond. He concluded that he would have to give a direct answer. Anything less, he explained afterwards, would have caused a 'huge fuss in Hong Kong'. As it was, his words caused a huge fuss in London. Traditionally xenophobic newspapers like the *Sunday Express* led the way. Patten had 'lost touch with reality', its leader-writer spluttered, 'for the reality is that the "full up" sign should have been hung up on these islands years ago. And Governor Patten doesn't seem to know it. Maybe he has spent too much time in his colonial mansion, decorated in exotic taste, surrounded by flunkies. Maybe the £150,000-a-year salary and the chauffeur-driven car have gone to his head.' With the notable, and surprising, exception of the *Daily Mail*, the other tabloids were scarcely more restrained. The broadsheets, led by *The Times* and the *Daily Telegraph*, reflecting longstanding editorial policies, were, however, supportive. Nonetheless, under the headline 'TORY FURY AT PATTEN CALL FOR 3M PASSPORTS', the *Observer* reported that many right-wingers on the government's backbenches were incensed that the former party chairman should seek to reopen an issue which they thought had been closed more than five years earlier when the House of Commons passed the 1990 British Nationalities (Hong Kong) Act in response to the killings in Tiananmen Square, and thereby marginally 'liberalised' Britain's strict immigration regulations for the first time in almost thirty years by offering the right of abode in the UK to 50,000 selected British subjects.

Since then, the formal policy of the Hong Kong government had remained that all existing BDTC passport-holders should be offered right of abode in the United Kingdom, and Patten's comments on *Any Questions* were, as he was ingeniously swift to remind the Home Office, merely a repetition of this. He was, however, under no illusion that the government (of which, incidentally, he had been a loyal member when the 1990 act came into force) would fail to respond to his challenge, and he was not at all surprised when, two days after the broadcast, the home secretary, Michael Howard, hurried to the microphone to reassure the public in Britain that there was no question of a change in policy and that the matter had been settled once and for all by Parliament in 1990. On immigration, at least, New Labour, like Old Labour, was not to be outflanked from the right: the shadow home secretary, Jack Straw, was similarly quick to criticise Patten. He could not resist a cheap political shot at the governor's expense, asserting that his plea for more passports 'must raise questions about his own confidence in the stability of the arrangements he has put in place for after 1997'. Despite this rebuff from Westminster, the Government House spokesman, Kerry McGlynn, who had succeeded Mike Hanson earlier in the year, confirmed that the governor would continue to raise the issue 'when appropriate'.

In reality, Patten had no such intention, because he knew per-fectly well that it would be a waste of his time. In any case, he had to face what was, to his mind, a far more important battle with the Home Office, and one he was determined to win against an obdurate home secretary. For some months his team had been sounding out their counterparts in Whitehall on two crucial issues which, Patten confided in September 1995, 'could cause us very, very considerable difficulty and embarrassment the closer we get to 1997'.

The first of these was the question of Hong Kong's non-Chinese 'ethnic minorities', which, as Patten said that autumn, 'still sits there waiting, I think, to hit us in the solar plexus as we're leaving'. To date Home Office officials had been adamant that none of Britain's 5,000 or so non-Chinese colonial subjects born in Hong Kong, who were mainly of Indian origin, would be eli-gible for full British passports unless they had been selected under the 1990 act for one of the 50,000 BNS passports. Similarly, although the imprecision of Beijing's concept of nationality as defined in Article 24 of the Basic Law made it difficult to be sure, it appeared to exclude Hong Kong's 'ethnic minorities' from the right to acquire Chinese citizenship either. If so, in the absence of a British passport, Hong Kong's Indian community would in effect become 'stateless', even if they were permitted to remain in Hong Kong as residents.

Privately, the governor sympathised strongly with their predicament, and he believed that the British government had a moral obligation to provide them, as British citizens, with full UK passports. A failure to do so had the potential, he felt, to inflict severe damage on Britain's international reputation. However, the public position of the government, as outlined in a carefully crafted 'information note' published before Patten's arrival, was that 'effectively no one will really be *stateless* in Hong Kong in 1997'. To those who might have been perturbed by the weasel words 'effectively' and 'really', the note made much of the fact that 'the small minority of Hong Kong people . . . who have no right of abode elsewhere than Hong Kong will automatically become British Overseas Citizens (BOC) with right of abode here [in Hong Kong] too'. However, the chief secretary's civil servants were careful to avoid mentioning the fact that the BOC passport was a travel document of extremely limited use, providing visa-free access to very few countries outside the United Kingdom and no right of abode in Britain itself. Indeed, in Hong Kong, as elsewhere, a BOC passport was held to do little more than identify with cruel precision the 'effective' and 'real' statelessness of its holder. The Hong Kong government was prone to reiterating the 'assurance' of the British government given to 'those with solely British nationality' that if they had to leave and had nowhere else to go, they would be 'considered sympathetically for entrance into Britain'. If anything, this attempt at reassurance served only to increase the level of anxiety among the Indian community.

The second of Patten's preoccupations had even greater potential to wreak havoc – indeed, he was afraid that it might make governing Hong Kong very difficult in the following eighteen months. This issue was whether the 3 million people who would automatically acquire HKSAR (Hong Kong Special Administrative Region) passports in 1997 should be offered visa-free access to the United Kingdom. The SAR passport was to replace the identity cards held by the ethnic Chinese and would also be available to all Hong Kong citizens who failed to qualify for BNO passports but were likely to satisfy Beijing's as yet ill-defined criteria concerning nationality.

Patten believed that it would be an act of great folly for Britain to withhold visa-free access from SAR passport-holders. Failure to grant SAR and BNO passports similar status would, he thought, have calamitous consequences, not only for Hong Kong but for British interests throughout the region. Yet, as in the case of the ethnic minorities, he suspected that the weight of opinion in the Cabinet would be against him. And he knew for certain that the secretary of state responsible for immigration, Michael Howard, was, as he put it, 'implacably opposed to making any change'.

In the autumn of 1995, the governor, Edward Llewellyn and Martin Dinham began what they knew would be a war of attrition with the Home Office. Their aim was to create a consensus in and around the Cabinet strong enough to force the home secretary to abandon his rigid stance. 'We have to persuade the Home Office in general, and the home secretary in particular, that, though his argument may be intellectually logical, it's politically, and, I think, morally, wrong,' Patten explained. 'What I have to do is mobilise support in London.' Failure would be intolerable, but the chances of success were not good. Not only had Howard staked out his opposition unambiguously, but any retreat would dent his carefully honed image as a populist hard-liner on immigration.

There were glimmers of hope. 'There isn't an MP who's come here in the last months who hasn't gone away convinced of the strength of our case,' said Patten, and he was confident that the media – 'at least the quality end' – would be supportive. But the issue of visa-free access for SAR passport-holders had yet to become a matter of public debate in Hong Kong, and, given the political minefield ahead of him, Patten was at this stage anxious that it shouldn't 'surface prematurely'. He wanted to start lobbying in London before any hint of the emerging conflict between the governor of Hong Kong and the British home secretary leaked out. If necessary, however, he was quite ready to turn a private negotiation into a public battle.

It was not simply a matter of two men's credibility. On the surface, at least, the home secretary had a formidable case. In political terms, he could argue that it would be hugely damaging for a Conservative administration, pledged to maintain strict limits on immigration, to approach the next election committed to giving millions of ethnic Chinese from Hong Kong the right to enter Britain at will, albeit without any right of abode. He could argue, as many of his most reactionary colleagues on the

Conservative backbenches were sure to do, that the electorate, egged on by a xenophobic tabloid media, would not easily distinguish between the right to enter Britain and the right to stay there. Not only would the Conservative party's already enfeebled electoral prospects be further weakened, but, as Patten recognised, a Cabinet decision to 'open the floodgates' would also be subject to merciless exploitation by a Labour party which, on such issues, was equally opportunistic. Perhaps more persuasively, Howard would be sure to point out that to grant visa-free access to SAR passport-holders would set an unwarranted precedent. As Patten summed it up: 'The home secretary could reasonably ask why we should be obliged to give people with Chinese passports in Hong Kong after 1997 – when we will not be sovereign – rights which they didn't have before 1997, when we were.' It was, he conceded, a good question.

The governor's counter-case centred on the likely repercussions of the denial of such access. First, there would be alarming consequences for BNO passport-holders. China would be infuriated by Britain's stance, and might well retaliate by lobbying every other member of the United Nations to treat BNO and SAR passports on the same footing. As most countries were already dubious about offering visa-free access to holders of BNO passports, there was a real risk that they would respond to Chinese pressure by barring that right to both categories. If this occurred, Patten had little doubt that prospective holders of BNO passports would become extremely nervous about whether their new travel documents would be worth anything after 1997. One of his team summed it up more bluntly: 'If we don't give free access to SAR passport-holders, we'll kill the BNO passport.'

Secondly, another, more direct, form of Chinese retaliation was likely. After the handover they could require all UK citizens to obtain visas before entering Hong Kong. In 1995, some 14,000 Hong Kong Chinese carrying Certificates of Identity (all of whom would become SAR passport-holders) travelled to Britain annually, whereas more than 400,000 British citizens travelled from London to Hong Kong. 'Given the extent to which Hong Kong is our jumping-off point for China and Asia,' Patten reasoned, 'it really would be a case of shooting oneself in the foot.'

More generally, and perhaps even more damagingly, another of the 'extremely disagreeable consequences' would be that the Chinese would portray Britain as having no real interest in the future wellbeing of Hong Kong. To refuse visa-free access to SAR passport-holders would, Patten believed, 'trigger a good deal of criticism of Britain, tinged with a certain view that we are behaving in a racist way'. The prospect exasperated him. 'I mean,' he said, clenching his fists in frustration, 'everybody now talks about us having a more assertive role in relation to Asia, and making the most of our opportunities in China through Hong Kong. If one's serious about that, how could one seriously lash oneself to a policy as misguided as the one we've been talking about?'

The Government House tactic against the Home Office was to lobby key members of the British government and their civil servants, reiterating and elaborating Patten's case, hoping to pick them off one by one. By mid-September 1995, the governor's 'campaign', as he called it, was already underway. By the end of the month he had rallied some key figures to his cause, including the Conservative chairman of the Hong Kong Parliamentary Group. He was also confident that the Labour party and the Liberal Democrats would not be 'difficult about it'. The affable minister of state at the Foreign Office, Jeremy Hanley (one of Patten's devotees), and the permanent secretary, John Coles, both of whom had just been in Hong Kong, were also supportive. However, he was less certain about three more important players: the foreign secretary, Malcolm Rifkind, who had replaced Douglas Hurd in a government reshuffle in July; the deputy prime minister, Michael Heseltine, promoted to that role following his part in securing John Major's self-imposed re-election as party leader in June; and the chancellor, Kenneth Clarke. Patten's team decided to direct their fire at Hanley and Coles in the hope that, according to one of those directly involved, they would 'go back and push the argument with Rifkind'.

In June, just before his departure from the government, Hurd, who strongly supported Patten on the issue, had called together a small group of senior Cabinet ministers for an initial discussion, prompted by an alarming proposal from immigration officials in

Brussels that Hong Kong should be placed on a list of countries whose citizens would require mandatory visas to enter the European Union. At that meeting, Howard had shown his colours, not only making his case against visa-free access for SAR passport-holders, but also seeking to pre-empt further debate by announcing the decision publicly. Moreover, he had made it clear that he was in favour of extending the visa requirement to BNO passports as well – a stance, according to Government House, that was supported by Clarke. Rifkind, as defence secretary, had been at best equivocal. Hurd was appalled by Howard's lack of perspective and, by his own account, told the home secretary: 'Hold your horses – don't let's stir up an unnecessary row in Hong Kong until we've all looked at it seriously.'

The governor knew he had no hope of victory without winning over the new foreign secretary; nor did he underestimate the magnitude of his task. 'I'm not saying he's hostile, it's just that he needs to be persuaded that this is an issue which demands a fight.' He suspected that Rifkind, for whose forensic cast of mind he had great respect, would not be won over until he had seen Hong Kong for himself. His first visit to the colony as foreign secretary was scheduled for November 1995, when, as one of Patten's team put it, 'we will really expose him to the arguments'. As the governor left for London in early October, he knew that, sooner or later, there would be a fight. The Home Office was still intransigent, or, as he put it, 'being a bit silly' about the possibility of Hong Kong citizens overstaying their official welcome: if there were to be a problem of 'visa abuse' after 1997, he complained, 'then they can deal with it as they've dealt with other examples . . . by slapping in a regime, a restrictive set of controls'.

Patten's arrival in London almost coincided with the departure of the Chinese vice-premier and foreign minister, Qian Qichen, making his first visit to Britain since the row over Patten's reforms. Qian Qichen had prefaced his trip with a sideswipe clearly directed at the governor for advocating that Britain should grant right of abode to the 3.3 million holders of BDTC passports. This intervention was, he said, one example of 'troublemaking' by the Hong Kong authorities which stood in the way of further improvements in the relationship between

Britain and China. Although he did not mention it himself, several pro-China newspapers in Hong Kong, citing sources in Beijing, reported that the Chinese foreign minister intended to use his London visit to demand visa-free access to Britain for SAR passport-holders. There was now a danger that Patten's own rift with the Home Office would leak into the British media, making his task even more difficult. The governor was in a most curious situation: singled out for condemnation by Beijing for promoting democracy in Hong Kong, he was about to become the most insistent – if not the only – significant advocate of China's case for SAR passports. If Beijing's renewed campaign to have him removed as governor were to succeed, the prospect of securing such access for those passport-holders would almost certainly vanish with him.

As it turned out, the passports issue was to be temporarily overshadowed by an unexpected, if superficial, thaw in Sino–British relations. On his first day in London, 2 October, Qian Qichen met the deputy prime minister, Michael Heseltine, after which it was reported that both men had agreed that closer co-operation between the two sovereign powers was required to secure a smooth transition and that, with this in mind, Qian Qichen had invited Heseltine to pay a return visit to Beijing in 1996. The following day, the Chinese vice-premier attended a three-hour session with Malcolm Rifkind at the Foreign Office, where they were joined briefly by the prime minister. Their discussions produced a number of 'understandings', or what was described as a 'consensus', designed to improve official contacts between Britain and China at all levels in the run-up to 1997 and beyond. They also agreed that the handover ceremony itself should be 'solemn and dignified'. Afterwards, the foreign secretary emerged with Qian Qichen at his side to inform the assembled media that they had had an 'extremely important and satisfactory session'. The Chinese foreign minister described it as 'positive, useful and productive'. Although the 'consensus' lacked any single measure of substance, the Hong Kong media promptly deduced that Sino–British relations were back to normal. One correspondent, writing in the South China Morning Post, was so carried away by the warm words emanating from each side that

he informed his readers that the two governments had managed
to 'draw up a new road map for a smooth transfer of the
territory'.

The Foreign Office did nothing to dispel this illusion. Indeed,
officials were on hand to point out for the benefit of attentive
journalists that no representative of the Hong Kong government
had been present at the talks. Just in case the significance of that
should fail to seep into the collective consciousness of the media,
at least one of them went on to confide, anonymously: 'We don't
always have to see Hong Kong through the prism of Chris
Patten's eyes.' It was a lethal remark, which, since it came from an
apparently unimpeachable source, drew both the British and
Hong Kong press to the obvious conclusion: Patten had been
sidelined and isolated in an effort to put Sino–British relations
back on course.

With the lines between London and Hong Kong humming,
Patten was at once caught in a new crossfire. Detecting a Foreign
Office 'sell-out', Martin Lee noted that Malcolm Rifkind had
failed to confront Qian Qichen over the latter's public reminder
that LegCo would be abolished on 1 July 1997. In their joint press
conference, the Chinese foreign minister had responded to a
question about the 'through train' with the words, 'We did not
discuss this question. The issue has already been resolved.'
However, the new British foreign secretary had failed to reiterate
the official British position, that there was no justification for preventing the members of LegCo from serving a full term, i.e., until
1998. 'It is obvious,' Martin Lee reasoned, 'that economic interests have become the primary concern of the British side in
dealing with China.'

The governor now had the delicate task of endorsing Rifkind's
bullish remarks about his meeting with Qian Qichen while denying that he himself had been sidelined or that the talks had been
a 'sell-out'. Officially he confined himself to saying that the proposals for improving co-operation between Britain and China
had emanated from Government House; that the position of the
British government remained that there was no reason why the
Legislative Council should be demolished; and that, as for his
own role, 'I continue to be in regular touch with the prime

minister and the foreign secretary.' Martin Lee was not mollified. 'As Britain and China tango cheek to cheek,' he said on RTHK's *Letter to Hong Kong* a few days later, 'they are trampling Hong Kong.' Any sense that the rapprochement between China and Britain would benefit Hong Kong was swept aside in a renewed bout of doubt and suspicion about the real purpose of the British government and the future role of the governor.

Patten seethed with frustration at the impact in Hong Kong of the words attributed by the media to 'senior officials' from the Foreign Office. 'It was irritating,' he confided, 'not really because it bruised my ego – though it would be dishonest in the extreme to pretend that occasionally that sort of thing doesn't piss one off in a fairly substantial way – but because there really was a good story for Hong Kong to tell, and quite an important story, which got completely screwed up.' The important story was that he and his colleagues had 'stood firm on a number of matters of principle – particularly on decent elections – and we've still managed to do serious business with China within a couple of weeks of those elections'. From his point of view, the significance of this was – or should have been – 'what we've argued all along: that they are obliged to do business on some issues as we get closer to 1997, and one shouldn't think one has to throw in all one's cards to do business with them at all'. All this had been put in jeopardy by the Foreign Office.

'So what happens? Instead of that being the story, the story which spins out – as though the New China News Agency were running the Foreign Affairs News Department – is, "Ah! We've managed to do all these deals with China because we've bypassed Hong Kong . . . and the clever old Foreign Office in London has done it all."' Patten was far from pacified by what he referred to as the 'Foreign Office line' relayed to Government House 'rather nervously', to the effect that the unnamed officials had been misquoted. Patten had no doubt that the newspaper reports were accurate: two of the three journalists involved were people, he said, who 'I know are straight, and on whom I would completely rely'.

Yet the governor was inclined to believe that the Foreign Office had been inept rather than treacherous. 'There was,' he complained, a 'complete lack of comprehension of the sensitivities in Hong Kong, of the extent to which people simply don't trust Britain and have, actually, in some respects, quite a good pedigree for that particular opinion or prejudice.' He was also sure that real damage had been done to Britain's negotiating stance with Beijing. 'I have no doubt that Qian Qichen would have left London thinking that there was a difference between the governor of Hong Kong and the British government. No doubt at all.'

This impression of disharmony could only have been exacerbated, to Patten's dismay, by the fact that, at the grand dinner given for Qian Qichen, one of the guests had been Sir Percy Cradock. Soon afterwards, Cradock was heard describing Patten as the 'incredible shrinking governor' in a radio interview, designed, in the latter's view, 'to do maximum damage and to create the impression that the only role I had in the future was to stamp on the Democrats when they got out of line'.

Patten was swift to exonerate the foreign secretary from any blame for the débâcle. It was clear to him that Rifkind had been mortified by his failure to rebut Qian Qichen at once over the 'through train'. As soon as the story broke, he had been on the phone to Hong Kong to say how unfortunate it was, and how he would immediately put his position on the record. Patten offered an explanation for Rifkind's uncharacteristic lapse. 'When you are a new foreign secretary coming to a brief which is as complicated as Hong Kong, it's a miracle if you get the main tune right. If you manage one or two grace notes as well, it is astonishing.' Moreover, the oversight was partly attributable to Patten himself. Before Rifkind's meeting with his Chinese counterpart, Government House had prepared a brief for the foreign secretary listing the main points Patten wanted him to raise with China. Assuming that he was bound to reiterate the British position on the 'through train', Patten's team failed to draw attention to the need to remind him of it. The governor conceded:

Maybe we should have banged our fists on the table more vigorously before the meeting, and said, 'It's imperative that before you start talking about anything else, you just remind the Chinese what our position is on the Legislative

Council'. . . But we are always sensitive to the charge that we are party-poopers, that we are not sufficiently concerned about – what's the phrase? – 'warming up the relationship with China'.

Patten's scorn for the in-house language of the Foreign Office and the 'exceptionally unhelpful' behaviour of some of its officials was fuelled by personal resentment, but it was driven by a genuine and deepening anxiety. The perception of disunity in the British camp was likely to encourage the Chinese to be even more intractable. In particular, he feared that they were likely to be much more assertive in their threats to dismantle Hong Kong's protection of human rights contained in the Bill of Rights.

To forestall this, Patten now resolved to challenge Beijing openly on both the Bill of Rights and the legislative assembly. If he was prone to overestimating the strength of his hand – in late 1995 he still allowed himself to believe that it would be 'extremely difficult' for the Chinese to dismantle his reforms – it was because he found it hard to credit that the gerontocracy in Beijing would, in the end, act so blatantly against China's own interests. To this extent he suffered from a form of intellectual schizophrenia, apparently convincing himself that a regime which he judged to be generally vindictive, irrational and incompetent would nonetheless act in this respect with goodwill, common sense and at least a modicum of competence. If officials at the Foreign Office continued in their efforts to baulk him, he intended to make an unequivocal response. 'I'll do what I've always done, which is to take the first opportunity in front of a television camera to set out my views.' He recognised that pressure of this kind was likely to increase up to the handover, and that it would be far more problematic to resist afterwards. In theory Britain had the right and duty to monitor, through the Joint Liaison Group, the execution of the Joint Declaration for a further decade. Given the attitude of the Foreign Office, he feared that, in practice, it would be 'even more difficult to win the argument that Britain has to demonstrate a commitment to Hong Kong. You can imagine the sighs of relief in some parts of the bureaucracy on 1 July. You know, "Now we can get back to trying to get the sort of relationship with China that Germany has . . ."'

The foreign secretary had not only intimated that he wished to make political amends for his failure to tackle Qian Qichen on the 'through train' issue: according to Patten, he wanted to be 'rather more supportive than we thought entirely sensible'. Rifkind was evidently appalled by the way in which Beijing saw fit to treat a British governor. His instinct was to respond by suggesting that Patten should, in future, accompany him whenever he met the Chinese leadership, either in London or in Beijing, to make it clear not only that Patten remained the driving force behind British policy towards China over Hong Kong, but that the territory remained the government's first priority. Patten was encouraged by Rifkind's robust attitude, but he resisted the proposition, explaining, 'In practice, it doesn't make very much difference, and I wouldn't like to become part of the problem.'

He was encouraged, too, by the response of a growing number of his former colleagues to the passport issue. Still intent on keeping the latent tensions within the Cabinet from surfacing too soon, he focused on his main concern now: restraining some members of Parliament, including those on the Conservative benches, from 'leaping in and starting to lobby too early'. None of his ministerial colleagues were yet prepared to commit themselves in favour of visa-free access, but the prime minister, the foreign secretary, the deputy prime minister and the new president of the Board of Trade, Ian Lang, had at least listened carefully to his case without argument – although Lang had seemed less than impressed.

With the home secretary, however, it was different. While their conversation, according to Patten, was 'not remotely acrimonious', the governor was frustrated by Michael Howard's 'slightly annoying barrister's habit of merely repeating his best point, while arguments you advance yourself are allowed to whizz overhead'. In any event, Howard remained firm. As Patten had predicted, the home secretary warned, as the governor phrased it, 'I'm not proposing to change anything. At the moment, if you are a Certificate of Identity holder – a future SAR passport-holder – and you want to go to London, you require a visa. And

you will require a visa after 1997 as an SAR passport-holder. So
what is the difference?' When Patten reminded Howard that visa
policy had changed dramatically since 1990, when visa-free access
to Britain was granted to Czechs, Hungarians, Poles, Latvians,
Lithuanians and Estonians, bringing the total number of foreigners who now enjoyed such access to over 2 billion, the home
secretary was dismissive. According to sources close to Howard,
he thought Patten's argument 'simply didn't wash' and that the
fact that 'hundreds of millions of people already have visa-free
access does not seem to be remotely a reason for deciding
whether a particular group of people should have visa-free access
in the future'. Patten disclosed that, as far as Howard was concerned, the only question at stake was not whether to introduce
visa-free access but when the government should announce publicly that SAR passport-holders would require a visa to enter
Britain after 1 July 1997. As Government House had forecast,
Howard seemed to take the view – mistakenly, in Patten's opinion – that the British public would not be able to distinguish
between immigration policy and ease of travel.

Patten returned to Hong Kong with the issue still unresolved.
The schedule for the foreign secretary's first visit to Hong Kong
happened to dovetail with the timetable for a set of related negotiations in the Joint Liaison Group, where, according to one of
Patten's aides: 'Our line with the Chinese is, "Of course we're
happy to give visa-free access for SAR passports, but we can't do
that until we know the form of the passport – who is eligible for
it, and how it will be issued; will it be properly secure?"' When
the foreign secretary's visit was put back from November to
January, Patten's team found itself in danger of reaching an agreement on the technicalities of the SAR passports without being at
all sure that London would be willing to deliver on the governor's
implicit, if provisional, undertaking to secure visa-free access for
them.

In December the British continued to press the Chinese
through the JLG on the 'integrity' of the SAR passport. In
London Qian Qichen had shown off what Patten described as a
'technologically gee-whizz' document which would be hard to
forge. However, there was still some doubt as to whether Hong

Kong would be the only authority permitted to issue SAR passports. In the absence of such a guarantee, few states would be willing to grant visa-free access, and some would be reluctant even to accept the new passport as a valid travel document. In Patten's blunt assessment: 'There are going to be immigration authorities all round the world who will see that it is a more useful document than the Chinese passport and will therefore – I am sure incorrectly – leap to the conclusion that there won't be a cadre's son or daughter in Peking who won't have a copy of it.'

It was important therefore for the Chinese to confirm unequivocally that the SAR passport would only be issued in Hong Kong by the appropriate authority, and would be available only to those citizens entitled to hold it. Although the Chinese had been characteristically oblique until now, Patten's hope was that they would satisfy these requirements before the foreign secretary's rescheduled visit to Hong Kong. If so, Patten was confident that Rifkind would endorse his case and go back to London ready to confront Howard directly. Patten suspected that the foreign secretary would fare no better than he had done himself. In this event Rifkind would almost certainly lay out his views in letters to his Cabinet colleagues. This would be followed by what Patten hoped would be a decisive meeting of the Cabinet Committee in the spring, at which, with luck, the home secretary would find himself outnumbered. In the meantime, the governor was determined to keep up the momentum with discreet but sustained lobbying in Whitehall and Westminster.

Back in Hong Kong, banquets and grand balls followed one another relentlessly. The Pattens were invariably invited as guests of honour and were duty-bound to attend the most important events of the social calendar. The highlight of the 1995 Christmas season was the party given by the barrister and former attorney general, Michael Thomas, at the end of December in honour of his wife, Baroness Dunn. Invitations to this function were prized above all others. Lydia Dunn, the political doyenne of Hong Kong, was the most elevated public figure in the Chinese community. Invariably dressed in white, perfectly coiffed, exquisitely poised, she looked deceptively like an alabaster doll, unlined and ageless, but she was a canny, tough and perceptive insider who knew most, if not all, Hong Kong's secrets. Patten had been impressed by her knowledge and judgement, and, in the early months of his governorship, he had had regular tête-à-têtes with her which had proved invaluable.

The banquet, held in the Grand Hyatt, was to be Baroness Dunn's formal farewell to Hong Kong as she and her husband had decided to move permanently to Britain. To mark the significance of the occasion, the banqueting room of the hotel had been remodelled for the evening, fitted with false walls and hung with paintings to provide a more intimate atmosphere for the 220 guests. That night Hong Kong's elite was on display. In one of several delicious ironies, Lavender Patten was seated next to William Purves, the man she had metaphorically denounced as a traitor for his covert efforts to destroy her husband's reforms during the marathon LegCo session the previous year. Purves's wife sat beside the governor. Paul Cheng, the LegCo representative of the Chamber of Commerce, one of Patten's smoothest but bitterest foes, was also there, as were critics such as the tycoons Sir S.Y. Chung, Robert Kuok and K.S. Li, who had long ago made their peace with China on Beijing's terms. They smiled politely and engaged in small talk with the governor whose efforts for Hong Kong they abhorred. Peter Woo and Bessie, his wife, were present. Bessie and Lavender Patten had forged a genuine regard for one another; Peter, who had not yet judged it impolitic to be regarded as a confidant of the governor, was, as ever, charming. Another guest was Peter Sutch, the *taipan* of Swires. The most powerful of the colony's expatriate entrepreneurs, Sutch had lived in Hong Kong for twenty years. He was a 'company' man who had risen through the ranks to become its unassuming chief executive. Respected for his business acumen and his far-sighted approach to management, he had made no secret of his reservations about Patten's reforms, but, unusually, he had at least expressed his views with courtesy and to the governor's face. As a result, the two men had remained on cordial and mutually respectful terms.

In this gathering of Hong Kong power-brokers it was not easy for the governor to count many allies. At a neighbouring table were Tung Chee Hwa and his wife, Betty. C.H., as Tung was known by everyone locally, was a shipping tycoon who had close links with the Beijing leadership. C.H. had a reputation for being incorruptible, his own man. Patten, seeking the authentic voice of traditional Chinese conservatism, had persuaded him to join the Executive Council in October 1992, where he had proved to be cautious, sincere and worldly-wise. One or two insiders had started to champion him as a possible successor to Patten as Hong Kong's first chief executive.

The chief executive would be the most important figure in post-handover Hong Kong. Appointed by Beijing, he would have full authority over the SAR as specified in the Joint Declaration – in theory, only foreign affairs and defence would remain with the government in Beijing. It was widely thought that C.H. possessed the attributes such a demanding role would require. However, in his deceptively avuncular manner, he had been quick to disown any such ambition. At dinner, insofar as conversation was possible above the cacophony from the dance floor, he intimated that, if the truth were known, he was really a man of very little importance. He spoke with affection of Liverpool, where he had attended university, and with adoration of his grandchildren whom, he said, he made a point of visiting every day. His wife, meanwhile, engaged in a discussion about democracy. Like C.H., Betty Tung was held in high regard. She worked for charity, she was generous, shrewd and kindly. But democracy – which she identified principally as a source of communal friction and potential disharmony – clearly remained an alien notion to her. She very much liked the governor, she said, but added, as if speaking for her husband as well, 'We do not really understand this idea of democracy. We believe in freedom, but democracy is complicated.' Another guest suggested that democracy and freedom were intertwined, arguing, 'Freedom cannot survive without accountability. In the West we believe that accountability is best secured by democracy in the form of universal adult suffrage.' Betty Tung shrugged, and the conversation moved on. 'What we would really like to do when C.H. retires is to live in San Francisco,' she confided. 'The weather is beautiful, the atmosphere is friendly. The only problem is that it is more expensive to hire staff in America, and it takes much longer to get a washing-machine mended. Sometimes it takes days. Here you make the call and someone is round immediately.'

By the late autumn, public attention in Hong Kong had begun to focus once again on human rights. Three weeks after Qian Qichen's 'successful' visit to London, Beijing had confirmed Patten's fear that the politburo would be ready to exploit any perceived divisions in the British camp. It was announced, in the guise of a 'recommendation' of the Preliminary Working Committee, that the Bill of Rights was in need of fundamental revision. Following the enactment of the Bill of Rights in 1992, scores of anachronistic ordinances had been amended or were in the process of revision. The most important of these concerned individual rights to free assembly, free speech and the free expression of opinion. The PWC's proposal, which was immediately endorsed by Chinese officials in Hong Kong and on the mainland, was that a number of vital safeguards should be removed from the Bill of Rights. In particular, the PWC recommended that three crucial articles – 2 (3), 3 and 4, which stated that no Hong Kong law enacted either before or after the Bill of Rights should contravene any of its provisions – should be deleted. They also argued that six ordinances which had already been amended should be restored to their original form. The Chinese claimed that the amended versions of these ordinances 'seriously weakened the government's authority and are not conducive to a smooth transition'. Citing three broadcasting ordinances, and three relating to public order and the use of emergency powers – all of which, before being amended, had not only contravened the relevant international covenants but had also been allowed to gather dust for almost two decades – the NCNA declared that the decision to introduce a Bill of Rights had been motivated by Britain's determination to 'undermine the authority of the post-1997 administration'. The British were, the Chinese asserted, gambling with the stability and prosperity of Hong Kong. For good measure, Beijing, in the person of a Foreign Ministry spokesman, offered a ritual denunciation of the Bill of Rights as a 'serious violation' of the Joint Declaration and the Basic Law.

So preposterous was this latest Chinese onslaught that even some of Beijing's most dutiful supporters were embarrassed. The business community, as usual, refrained from expressing any opinion that might have been taken as evidence of a collective conscience or moral backbone, but a number of 'anti-British' legislators like the Liberal party's Selina Chow condemned the PWC's proposal. Similarly, Tsang Yok Sing, speaking for the DAB, and effectively for a much wider constituency in the colony, was careful to distance himself from the recommendations, noting publicly that they were 'worrying' and set a 'bad precedent'. Answering questions from journalists, Patten said that the PWC's proposals called into question their commitment to the rule of law, and indeed, their understanding of it. 'It does immeasurable damage to confidence, and therefore immeasurable damage to Hong Kong's prospects . . . I very much hope that wiser counsel will prevail.'

His hopes were vain. Even before the 'Triple Violator' had arrived in Hong Kong, the Chinese had made clear that in devising the Bill of Rights, Britain had 'disregarded' what they chose to describe as a matter of principle, and that, accordingly, Beijing reserved the right to 'review' that document and all other legislation. Throughout the late autumn of 1995, competing lawyers examined the fine print of the Basic Law to establish to their own satisfaction that the Bill of Rights most certainly did, or did not, depending on which side they were representing, constitute a violation of the Basic Law. In reality, however, the controversy was far less a dispute about constitutional niceties than a bitter political conflict clothed in legal jargon which reflected the deep-seated insecurities of the totalitarian regime in Beijing. As with the Legislative Council, China's attitude, expressed through the PWC, provided unsettling evidence that, as 1997 approached, the politburo was finding it increasingly difficult to tolerate the vision of a genuinely autonomous Hong Kong.

Even the leader of the Liberal party, Allen Lee, was uneasy. The Chinese would have to find ways to back off, he said unofficially, or the public would become extremely demoralised. 'If you ask a common person in the streets about the content of the Bill of Rights, they don't know. But they feel . . . that it will protect them from abuses by the government . . . I think Hong Kong people don't want them to screw around with the Bill of Rights . . . The Chinese are walking on a very thin line.'

Then a single indiscretion by Hong Kong's chief justice, Sir Ti Liang Yang, detonated a furious public row. Towards the end of October, the colony's senior law officer had been invited to dinner by the deputy director of the NCNA, Zhang Junsheng. In the course of what he apparently considered a private conversation, the chief justice confided to his host that he shared Beijing's view that the Bill of Rights threatened to undermine Hong Kong's legal system. His comments were inevitably leaked to the media by the mischief-making official. At first, the hapless chief justice responded to the consequent uproar by claiming that he could not remember what he had said at dinner. Then, to make matters even worse, he shifted his ground, intimating that whatever he had said, it should not be regarded as the product of careful thought on his part as he had not yet studied the matter in any detail; for this reason, whatever he had said could not be taken to represent his final opinion. Zhang Junsheng immediately countered by observing that the chief justice's comments had been 'well thought out and delivered prudently'.

In other circumstances, this Ruritanian dialogue might have been entertaining; as it was, the prospective dismemberment of the Bill of Rights was the most sensitive legal question facing Hong Kong. The breathtaking incompetence displayed by the individual charged with interpreting and defending the law from political interference hardly inspired confidence in the attitude of the judiciary after 1997. Although the chief justice was ridiculed by liberal politicians and commentators, the incident left the impression that, if he remained in his post after the handover, Sir Ti Liang Yang was likely to prove as biddable as Beijing hoped and Hong Kong feared.

In the middle of November, the Legislative Council debated the PWC's recommendations for the Bill of Rights, and, by 40 votes to 15, passed a motion deploring them. The motion also urged the governor to review all existing laws to ensure that they were in line with the bill. A fortnight later, maintaining the pressure, Martin Lee led a delegation of Democrats to Government House to urge

Patten to press ahead with the repeal of all the 'colonial' legislation still on the statute book, including the Official Secrets Act and the Crimes Ordinance (which in any case required amendment to reflect the Basic Law prohibitions against subversion, secession, sedition and treason). Although Patten was not yet ready to show his hand, he gave the Democrats a sympathetic hearing.

As only his private office knew, his desire to face down the Chinese over the Bill of Rights and its associated legislation had not merely remained undiminished but had been actively fuelled by Beijing's animosity. 'It is exceptionally important . . . and it goes right to the heart of the central issue: whether the Chinese really are committed to upholding Hong Kong's way of life, and whether they are prepared to show that restraint in dealing with Hong Kong which is implied by the concept of "one country, two systems",' he remarked in December. The fact that the PWC had been 'ventriloquised' by Beijing into advocating the dilution of the bill so soon after Qian Qichen's visit to London was, for Patten, a 'nice reminder to those who subscribe to the notion that you have a nice meeting with the Chinese, and everything proceeds as it would with anybody else' of how little there was to be gained from that course of action. Phrases like 'warm afterglow', 'gradual restoration of relations' and 'preserving the channel to Qian' had become the small change of Foreign Office memoranda. They were held in such contempt at Government House that as soon as a new one entered the mandarinate's lexicon, Patten's advisers would pin it up on a pillar in his private office which he christened Democracy Wall. It was astonishing, Patten fumed, that within days of the Chinese foreign minister's return from London, Chinese officials had no qualms about threatening to dismantle the main protection for Hong Kong's civil liberties or making proposals which would involve absolute direct contraventions of the Basic Law.

It was inevitable that the clash between Government House and the Foreign Office which had long been simmering beneath the surface should now be exposed. In Government House, the obligation to protect Hong Kong's 'way of life' within the framework of the Joint Declaration was not merely a slogan but a commitment which coursed through the veins of those who now surrounded Chris Patten. His senior adviser, Martin Dinham, his personal political adviser, Edward Llewellyn, the government's political adviser, Bob Peirce, and several others, including his press secretary Kerry McGlynn, were unswerving in their belief that Britain had a moral duty to protect and enhance freedom and democracy in Hong Kong, even at the risk of alienating China. Nor did their attitude spring only from the feeling that the British should depart from their last significant colony with pride and honour. Many of them found it bizarre that Whitehall should set so much greater store by the bilateral relationship with China than by the indirect but organic growth in trade and influence which Britain enjoyed throughout the region as a result of its presence in the enterprise capital of Asia. Britain's trade with Hong Kong was three times more valuable than the direct flow of exports to the People's Republic. In any case, trade between Britain and China had grown sharply despite the presence of the 'Triple Violator' in Hong Kong. Between 1990 and 1995, Britain's exports to China had risen by 75 per cent. The share of this trade which flowed into the People's Republic through Hong Kong had risen from 24 to 36 per cent, and it was to rise dramatically again, to 46 per cent, in 1996.

Although he remained grateful for what he continued to regard as the generally excellent service provided to Government House by the Foreign Office, Patten viewed with mounting incredulity the gap between style and substance which often seemed to permeate the departments with which, through his advisers, he had most contact. 'There is a difference between real diplomacy and shaking hands and smiling,' he said. In some parts of the Foreign Office, the failure to make that distinction had become 'part of the wallpaper', a weakness which, he suspected, 'sometimes affects our dealings with, and attitudes to, other parts of the world as well'.

In respect of Hong Kong at least, this criticism was damning, but the implications of Whitehall's shortcomings were far less damaging than they might have been had anyone other than Patten been governor. None of his predecessors, diplomats rather than politicians, would have had either the authority or the willpower to withstand the persistent pressure from the Foreign

Office to compromise again and again to placate Beijing. Even if they had been blessed with an appetite for bureaucratic infighting, they lacked the institutional and political clout to prevail against a Whitehall consensus which implicitly, if not always consciously, favoured 'co-operation'. To the frustration of some mandarins, Patten's unique advantage, from the point of view of Government House, was that he could, and, whenever necessary, did, bypass the Whitehall machine to press his case directly with his former colleagues in the Cabinet. They did not easily forget that his predecessors had, in matters of policy, been answerable to them.

As he looked towards his final full year in office, Patten was in no mood to be diverted from his course. The public indignation in Hong Kong over China's brutish attitude towards the Bill of Rights could, he thought, increasingly give way to apprehension, and he was worried that people would begin to 'vote with their feet'. The demand for foreign passports was growing steadily; any surge in that demand would not only undermine confidence in the colony's future but had the potential to trigger the mass exodus which was the great unspoken fear of every senior official. Patten still retained a residual hope that the Chinese position was perhaps given a harder edge than they intended by the individuals they had chosen as spokesmen or advisers in Hong Kong. In his opinion, most of these representatives 'couldn't persuade their way out of a paper bag . . . They display all the finesse of a bacon-slicer when dealing with some of these issues.' In any case, his self-appointed and overriding task now was to promote Hong Kong's liberties in every possible forum in the colony itself, in London and in every other significant capital city.

It touches on something I'm beginning to feel more and more. That is that what happens here is at the heart of the debate about what happens in China, both economically and politically. And for Chinese spokesmen to be so nervous about what sort of slogans people should be allowed, under the law, to shout in the streets in Hong Kong, suggests a lack of self-confidence which doesn't bode particularly well.

Yet for many citizens, it was the economy rather than politics
which remained the most significant factor in their personal
lives. George Chen was born in Hong Kong in the 1950s. His
father was one of the thousands of Chinese who had fled
Shanghai when the Communists took over in 1949. George had
a conventional upbringing until he was a teenager, when he
met Rowena, the girl who was to become his wife, at their
piano-teacher's house. They fell in love almost at once, and
although they were both only seventeen, they were determined
to marry as soon as possible. Their parents thought that they
were too young, and said so. They decided to elope, and emigrated to Canada. When they arrived in Vancouver they had two
suitcases and 500 Canadian dollars between them. Financing
their way through college by working part-time as shop assistants, they graduated, and six years later went back to Hong
Kong as Canadian citizens to register their marriage. Two years
after their return they set up a trading company, buying and
selling cheap clothes. Rowena, who had always wanted to be a
fashion designer, taught herself how to sketch and to cut fabrics
and began to experiment with her own designs. Within a few
years the company had expanded enough to finance the purchase
of a garment factory in China, and Rowena was marketing her
designs under her own label.

    In the boom of the late 1980s, their principal market was in
Japan. 'We positioned ourselves to serve the better end of the
market . . . the only thing we worried about was how much
could we produce. Did we have enough capacity to meet the
demand?' George explained. Then the Far Eastern bubble burst
and suddenly their company was on the point of collapse. The
Chens decided to take advantage of the new opportunities opening up in China's rush towards capitalism. In corporate terms,
they were minnows, but they knew that to survive they had to
move faster than everyone else. In the fiercely competitive world
they had chosen to inhabit this meant ensuring that the Chinese
factories in which they had invested produced clothes of a range,
quality and price which would attract their customers – whole-
salers and retailers in other parts of Asia and Europe. By 1993
their high-turnover, high-risk business had seemed secure and the

Chens had laid plans to expand further in China, producing clothes to meet the burgeoning consumer demand in the north, which was starting to benefit from an economy growing at upwards of 15 per cent a year.

George Chen's world was bounded by horizons which seemed limitless. He dreamed of creating an 'information highway' for the clothes trade.

> The customer comes to see me. We sit down. I ask him, 'What do you want? Tell me your total concept.' After I've listened to him, I say: 'These are the fabrics you want. This is the factory you should go to. This is the design . . .' My customer is not buying a product, but a collection, so that he can create a market. My vision is to mastermind the whole process, from the production of the material right through to what the customer buys. We have a project in China for a million-square-foot shopping mall. We are going to put different retailers into the mall and we will manage them collectively, doing all their merchandise. Different labels for a specific market. That is two hundred shops with two hundred different needs all coming back to me along my information highway. So I am very excited.

George Chen was not only infatuated by his 'concepts', but with the jargon of hi-tech commerce. He explained that he and his wife could not realise their vision without their base in Hong Kong, because Hong Kong was at the 'interface' of China and his potential markets in the rest of the world. Likewise, in terms of fashion, it was the 'interface' between Western designs and the Chinese consumer. 'Without Hong Kong, I very much doubt that I could be in business. Singapore? I doubt it. Shanghai? Maybe in ten years' time.'

Except ethnically, both George and Rowena Chen seemed to be children of the West, embracing 'global-village' assumptions in style and manners. And yet their notion of freedom did not readily embrace the concept of democracy. For the Chens, freedom was defined vaguely in terms of 'lifestyle', not of political representation or the accountability of the executive, nor even of the right to free speech and assembly. When he spoke of such matters, George Chen's techno-fluency faltered.

> What is politics? This is a new language for us. I'm patriotic, but patriotic to what? Let's forget about it. Let's hold on to our normal life. Hong Kong is so busy, we have never had spare time to think about politics . . . You talk about freedom . . . The question is, does it affect me? I'm a very selfish guy . . . the monetary thing is very important to me. I have a young family. If the political situation changes so that I cannot make my living here, or I cannot maintain my lifestyle, then I would move on . . . If Hong Kong cannot give that to me, then in order to maintain our dreams and continue our life, maybe somewhere else could satisfy our needs.

The recurrence of the word 'lifestyle' spoke partly of glossy magazines and holiday brochures but, for the Chens, it clearly defined somewhat more than this, however imprecisely. Their work was all-consuming. They wanted the 'good things', but they seemed to have them already: they ate in good restaurants, they had a bright, fast car, and their apartment was expensively furnished. They did not seek leisure; on the contrary, leisure was for them a form of idleness, an indulgence they could not afford and did not crave. Their 'lifestyle' encompassed the right and the ability to travel freely and to set up their stall in the global marketplace. For them, freedom of speech and freedom of assembly lacked intrinsic merit but were accidental and agreeable, if inexplicable, byproducts of the capitalist system. They were clearly bewildered by the notion of representative democracy. From their perspective, Chris Patten's row with the Chinese was 'unnecessary', a conflict about 'face' between the two sovereign powers which threatened to damage their interests. Nevertheless it left them 'uneasy' and on the alert. If the outcome was good for business they would stay; if not, using their Canadian passports, they would quietly slip away. They had a choice, but they did not yet have to decide.

★

As if to confirm the governor's somewhat broader anxieties, on 13 December 1995 China sentenced its most prominent dissident, Wei Jingsheng, to another fourteen years' imprisonment for allegedly attempting to overthrow the government. Wei Jingsheng was familiar with Chinese prisons: he had served almost fifteen years in jail before being paroled in 1993 during China's unsuccessful bid to host the 2000 Olympic Games. He was re-arrested the following year after meeting a senior human-rights official from the United States and held incommunicado until the subversion charges which led to his sentence were finally laid against him. Although the Chinese authorities had said that he would have an 'open' trial, all journalists and foreign diplomats were barred from the proceedings, which were conducted in secret and lasted five hours. According to the evidence presented against him, Wei Jingsheng's capital offence included alleged plans to purchase newspapers and to establish a Hong Kong-registered company to organise non-governmental cultural and artistic activities, and thereby to set up a 'propaganda and liaison base [in an attempt] to raise a storm powerful enough to shake up the present government'. The three judges took thirty-five minutes to reach their verdict.

The United States and major European Union governments at once condemned the sentence, and in Hong Kong, even pro-Beijing legislators expressed their abhorrence of the harshness shown by the regime. As several commentators observed, Article 45 of the Chinese constitution, on which Wei Jingsheng had based his unsuccessful defence, was replicated almost word for word in Article 27 of the Basic Law, which reads: 'Hong Kong residents shall have freedom of speech, of the press and of publication; freedom of association, of assembly, of processions and of demonstration; and the right and freedom to form trades unions, and to strike.' Wei Jingsheng was convicted of subversion against the state, an offence which would be a crime under Article 23 of the Basic Law after the handover. It was hardly surprising that those in Hong Kong who treasured their legitimate freedom were consumed by trepidation.

For Chris Patten personally, it was discouraging to receive at precisely this moment an emissary from Lambeth Palace, who

told him that the archbishop of Canterbury, George Carey, would
not be accepting an open invitation to stay at Government House
on his forthcoming visit to the colony. Carey had evidently been
advised by the Anglican bishop of Hong Kong that it would be
'unhelpful' and an 'unnecessary provocation to China' to be seen
to consort with the governor. Recalling ruefully the enthusiasm
for democracy and human rights displayed by both Lambeth
Palace and the Synod before his departure from England in 1992,
Patten did not remonstrate with Lambeth Palace, but away from
the spotlight he was scornful of what he regarded as a feeble-
minded and cowardly decision.

Not to be outdone, Carey's predecessor as archbishop of
Canterbury, Robert Runcie, also chose to ally himself with what
Patten's closest friends regarded as Lambeth Palace's 'trahison des
clercs' by writing to say that he, too, would be declining the hospitality offered by Government House when he came to Hong
Kong. In explanation, he informed the governor that he had
consulted two specialists, Sir Percy Cradock and Sir Edward
Heath, both of whom had counselled him against accepting the
hospitality of Her Majesty's representative in Hong Kong. Patten
assumed that the clerics had been advised that the prospect of
ending religious persecution in China would be enhanced if they
took care to avoid causing the regime in Beijing unnecessary
offence. For him it was further dispiriting evidence that the
'warm-afterglow' school of diplomacy was not confined to the
Foreign Office or to the business community.

Patten shrugged off these discourtesies, although he was not
able to disguise the hurt they momentarily caused. More to the
point, the accumulation of petty slights reinforced his prediction
that the last year of his governorship would be no less testing than
the first four. He presumed that the Chinese would continue to
be difficult and obstructive in 1996 and he was resigned to the
likelihood of even more debilitating arguments with the Foreign
Office. He knew that the mandarins' case was, superficially, persuasive – even to the point where some members of the Cabinet
might begin to recycle it. 'Look, we've gone a long way with
Chris, it is now time to face up to reality,' he could hear them
saying to each other. 'What happens after 1997 will happen. We

have to deal with China, so let's not put unnecessary obstacles in the path of that relationship.'

There were rare moments to be relished. In the middle of December, the leadership of the People's Republic used a meeting of the Joint Liaison Group to express its dismay at Patten's proposal to increase Hong Kong's nugatory welfare budget to take better care of the elderly. The leader of the Chinese side, Chen Zuo'er, evidently encouraged by Lu Ping, denounced Patten in a sustained burst of petulance, culminating in the charge that the governor was a 'big dictator'. Entertained by the idea that China could regard him simultaneously as a big dictator and a lame duck, Patten nonetheless asked the Foreign Office to make an official complaint about this unwarranted interference in Hong Kong's internal affairs. In the absence of an ambassador (Ma Yuzhen had returned to Beijing, and his successor had not yet been appointed), the hapless Chinese chargé d'affaires, Wang Qilang, was summoned to the Foreign Office to receive a dressing-down from the deputy under-secretary, Andrew Burns, during which he was told that the Chinese outburst could be interpreted as jeopardising the level of autonomy for Hong Kong promised by China after 1997. The Chinese official appeared chastened and, evidently caught off guard, even acknowledged that welfare spending was important.

Such priceless incidents aside, Patten's pessimism was aggravated by a flurry of anecdotal evidence that a growing number of people in Hong Kong were losing their residual confidence in China's good faith. He had his own example, the case of a prominent doctor who told him that he was about to take early retirement. Patten asked him why. 'Well,' the doctor explained, 'if I retire now I can be sure of receiving my pension. But if I wait another five years, who knows?' The governor reminded him that he had rights under the law of contract; that there was an agreement with the Chinese government and that his pension entitlement would have to be honoured. The doctor replied, 'Yes, my wife said you'd say that.'

'What more could you say?' Patten reflected. It was a small but bleak reminder of Hong Kong's fragility.

'THANK YOU FOR THE VISAS, PRIME MINISTER'

John Major Brings Good News

Late in the evening of Saturday 6 January 1996, the British foreign secretary, Malcolm Rifkind, arrived in Hong Kong. The following day he joined the governor and his predecessor Douglas Hurd, who was in Hong Kong on private business as a director of the NatWest Bank, for a day-long walk on Lantau Island. It was, according to one of those involved, a 'very good bonding session'. At a three-hour working dinner that night at Government House, Chris Patten's ad hoc team of advisers (Martin Dinham, Bob Peirce and Edward Llewellyn were joined, significantly, on this occasion by the chief secretary, Anson Chan, and the financial secretary, Donald Tsang) briefed Rifkind in detail on the most pressing questions facing them. 'He'd read about all the issues in his briefing papers, but the case is much more persuasive when you're hearing about them from the individuals directly affected,' one of Patten's team noted. They lobbied him 'pretty hard' on visa-free access for SAR passport-holders. Rifkind also came under pressure from legislators, from the Executive Council and from businessmen, which 'helped finally to convince him that visa-free access was extremely important'.

At an open session in the Legislative Council, he parried questions about visa-free access, but he was given a rough ride when he informed his audience that the government's decision not to grant UK passports to Britain's soon-to-be former subjects was irreversible. Afterwards, in private, he said that Patten, as governor, was bound to act as Hong Kong's champion; as foreign secretary, he thought it would not be 'reasonable or appropriate' to give British citizenship to 'millions of people who have an identity that is essentially Chinese'. This was virtually the only point of disagreement between himself and Patten. However, on the eve of his departure, Rifkind reassured Patten that, in relation to visa-free access, he had finally been persuaded by the evidence to remove himself from the political fence on which he had perched for so long. For the future record, he confirmed this, albeit inexplicitly: 'I shall be making it very clear where I stand to my colleagues in the near future. I will be making a recommendation, because it needs collective discussion. I shall be making a clear and unequivocal recommendation.' His caution was understandable: like Patten, he knew very well that Michael Howard was not only a dogged opponent but that he might easily be joined by his predecessor as home secretary, Ken Clarke, who was an even more formidable member of the government.

Rifkind left Hong Kong on Tuesday 9 January for Beijing, where he was given a warm welcome by the Chinese leadership. Despite the fact that the visit coincided with the transmission in Britain of *The Dying Rooms*, a horrifying television documentary about the ill-treatment and neglect of Chinese orphans, Qian Qichen was evidently in 'warm-up' mood. He even invited the foreign secretary to look round the orphanage at the centre of the scandal to see it for himself, an invitation which Rifkind neatly sidestepped. After a three-hour formal meeting, the foreign secretary emerged to announce that the two sides had reached an understanding on a range of matters. As it happened, the Joint Liaison Group negotiations on the details of the SAR passport had progressed more slowly than had been anticipated, and so, fortuitously, Rifkind's delayed visit now coincided with an interim agreement on the main technical points. This meant that the two sides were able to sign a formal minute covering these issues, which had, in fact, been finalised only the previous day in the JLG. According to one of the individuals closely involved, the agreement, which was not published, stipulated that the SAR passport would be available only in Hong Kong, to people who had permanent Hong Kong identity cards, and that it could be issued only by the Hong Kong immigration authorities. Nor, he added dryly, could the passport easily be faked: 'We are to have a computer system which will digitise details of the passport . . . this is a facility which can't be replicated in Guangdong or the Chinese embassy in Bratislava.' As a result, Britain would now be willing to endorse the SAR passport as a bona-fide travel document, a commitment which would be crucial in persuading other states of its validity.

Rifkind also briefed the media that the Cabinet would decide within two to three months whether or not to grant visa-free access to people holding SAR passports. The one issue which was not yet resolved, and which the British side had originally asserted would be a sine qua non of granting visa-free access, was the 'eligibility' criterion: who would or would not be granted these passports? This question begged another: who would be granted right of abode in Hong Kong after 1997? Beijing's utterances on this matter had been so impenetrable as to confuse every constitutional specialist, each of whom was driven to the conclusion that China did not yet itself know the answer. Six weeks later, Beijing had still not responded to this question. Scores of thousands of Hong Kong Chinese living in Canada, the United States, Australia and elsewhere still had no idea whether, or on what terms, they would be granted right of abode in the future SAR, and therefore, whether they would be eligible for an SAR passport. In December, China had sent a diplomatic note to most UN states asking them to enter negotiations with Beijing about 'reciprocal' visa agreements, implying obliquely that in the absence of such an agreement, the SAR might require visas for visiting foreigners. As one of Patten's team put it, 'Some of these countries, I think, are likely to reply to the Chinese note that they'd love to be able to take a decision about visa arrangements, but that they will need a clarification on the right-of-abode issue before they do that.'

In London, despite the efforts of the foreign secretary, Michael Howard remained intransigent. Britain, he thought, had been unwise to grant UK citizenship to three million BNO passport-holders, and he was not going to compound that error by extending visa-free access to a further 3 million Hong Kong citizens. However, a decision could not be postponed indefinitely. The prime minister was due to make his last visit to Hong Kong at the beginning of March, by now only a matter of weeks away. If he failed to confirm the visa-free status of the SAR passport, the reputation of the British government would plummet. Patten's advisers made it clear to London that if Major were to arrive empty-handed, his visit would be a diplomatic disaster. According to Patten himself, Major's visit was to prove the decisive factor. 'It was the fact that he became personally interested in, and committed to the issues. At every stage of nuancing on all the issues we resolved, the prime minister's instincts and decency took him into a position nearer to Hong Kong rather than further away from Hong Kong,' he explained. With the prime minister on side, Rifkind had a one-to-one meeting with Howard ten days before Major's departure, at which, related a Patten aide, the foreign secretary 'set out all the arguments we've been using – in particular, of course, that this decision was one that could be reviewed, like all other visa arrangements: if there was abuse or trouble, a visa regime could be imposed'.

Howard, who was still obsessed by the prospect of a flood of Hong Kong Chinese pouring into Britain, now knew that he was not only outnumbered, but likely to be a lone voice in the Cabinet. He surrendered. His friends would later maintain that he was eventually persuaded by Rifkind's presentation of the case, and especially by the point that if a catastrophe in Hong Kong should lead to a stampede of refugees, Britain and all other countries would be obliged to impose a visa 'regime' on both BNO and SAR passport-holders to control the potential deluge of immigrants. Patten's colleagues, however, insist that Howard was well aware of these arguments from the start, and that his climb-down was calculated to avoid a debate in the Cabinet which he knew he would lose. As one of them put it, 'He wasn't overruled by the PM or by the Cabinet, because he was ultimately prepared to sign a recommendation to the Cabinet that visa-free access should be allowed.'

★

At the beginning of March 1996, John Major arrived in Hong Kong from London via Bangkok after a trying domestic week for his government. After the Commons debate on the Scott Report into the 'Arms to Iraq' scandal, a testy Anglo–Irish summit and many late-night phone conversations with the taoiseach, John Bruton, Major had flown to Thailand for the first heads-of-government meeting between European and Asian leaders, where he met the Chinese premier (to discuss Hong Kong) and the Vietnamese premier (to discuss the Boat People still languishing in camps in the British colony). After two days in Bangkok, he flew into Hong Kong and went immediately to the governor's country residence in the New Territories. There, in the relative balm of Fanling, he worked with Patten to put the finishing touches to a speech he was to make to the Chamber of Commerce, which was to be widely regarded as the most important statement of British attitudes towards Hong Kong and China since the Joint Declaration in 1984. It was certain to be the last such speech made by a British prime minister.

After their return from Fanling to Government House for a formal dinner in the banqueting hall on the eve of his speech, Major and Patten retreated upstairs to the governor's private sitting room for a final meeting with their closest aides. Very late on that Sunday night, Major made clear his view that it would not be enough merely to say that Britain would watch closely what happened in Hong Kong after 1997; it was vital to demonstrate that no future prime ministers, within the limits of their power and influence, would merely look on. The speech was once more adapted to reflect that very personal commitment.

On Monday 4 March, Major delivered the speech, which had been drafted by the government's political adviser, Bob Peirce, whose influence had grown rapidly since his recent appointment, and approved by Patten. It began with a lucid exposition of Hong Kong's remarkable economic development, highlighting the 'energy, dynamism, the sheer guts in business enterprise' and the vital contribution made to the territory's pre-eminent role in Asia that flowed from the commitment to the rule of law, individual freedom and the free movement of information. Reminding his audience at the British Chamber of

Commerce that these values had been underpinned by the Joint Declaration, Major reported bluntly that at his meeting with Li Peng the two leaders had reached no agreement on the future of the Legislative Council, or on the issues relating to the Bill of Rights. 'We did not agree to disagree, we just disagreed,' he added. 'We are not going to leave it there . . . We will say only what we do believe. We do not, and will not, simply lie down and accept what we are told.' He went on to warn China and to reassure Hong Kong. 'If there were any suggestion of a breach of the Joint Declaration, we would have a duty to pursue every legal and other avenue available to us . . . Britain's commitment to Hong Kong will not end next summer. Far from it.' Then, to Chris Patten's delight, in the passage he had rewritten the night before to toughen up the Government House draft, the prime minister announced:

We in Britain will have continuing responsibilities to the people of Hong Kong, not just a moral responsibility as the former colonial power, and as staunch friends of Hong Kong, but a specific responsibility as a signatory to the Joint Declaration. We shall watch, vigilant, over the implementation of the treaty to which Britain and China have solemnly committed themselves . . . Every member of the international community, all Hong Kong's friends and partners around the world, in both hemispheres and five continents, will be watching to see that the letter and spirit of the Joint Declaration are honoured, now, next year and for fifty years beyond. And we will be making sure that they do.

These were not the words of a sinologist anxious to retreat to China's 'bottom line', nor the product of the collective wisdom of those officials in the Foreign Office and the DTI whose priority was to 'warm up' the relationship with Beijing. As the democratic majority in Hong Kong recognised at once, the prime minister's declaration of intent was an act of statesmanship, an express commitment from which no future British government would find it easy to resile. Major's decision to throw down the gauntlet in these terms had not been taken lightly. The foreign

secretary, who was consulted, shared the view that the time was
right to be unequivocal about Britain's readiness to mobilise
international public opinion.

The prime minister had another piece of news, which he had
revealed an hour earlier at a closed session of the Legislative
Council, and repeated publicly in his speech. 'I have reflected
carefully on this with my Cabinet colleagues in London, in the
light of the powerful arguments made by the governor, the
Legislative Council, by business people and by the wider community in Hong Kong in recent months,' he told his audience.
'The answer is, yes, we shall extend visa-free access [to SAR
passport-holders].' Under the terms of Major's announcement,
SAR passport-holders would be free to enter Britain for up to six
months but, as in all other such cases, they would be forbidden to
work, study or draw social security.

News of Major's announcement, though it had not been
unexpected, spread fast. Within two hours of his address, the
prime minister went on a walkabout in the New Territories town
of Shatin, where, in places, the crowd was twenty feet deep.
Many shouted out, 'Thank you for the visas, Prime Minister.' At
a primary school he shook hands with six-year-old Yip Kwan
Ho. 'He is the King of England,' she beamed proudly. It was not
the kind of welcome to which the beleaguered leader of an
unpopular government was accustomed.

The media in Hong Kong were surprised and thrilled by this
prime ministerial pledge. 'YOU'LL NEVER WALK ALONE' was
the banner headline the following morning in the *Eastern
Express*, and, in its leading article, the *South China Morning Post*
commented,

> Just for once, a visiting minister did not fail to live up to
> expectations. Indeed he exceeded them . . . Mr Major
> struck an impressive note. After the trade-obsessed approach
> of deputy prime minister Michael Heseltine, whose eva-
> siveness so angered legislators during their recent visit to
> London, it was refreshing to hear yesterday's pledge . . .
> such a pledge provides that, in the unlikely event things did

go wrong after the handover, Britain would not wash its hands of the problem.

There was an unexpected bouquet from a newspaper which was not renowned for its enthusiasm for the colonial administration. 'MAJOR MOVE SAVES BRITAIN'S HONOUR', the *Hong Kong Standard* declared, praising his decision, after 'all the years of weasel words and humming and hawing that Hong Kong people have had to endure', to grant every holder of an SAR passport visa-free access to Britain after all.

Major's speech was somewhat less well received by some of his own backbenchers and their acolytes in the tabloid media who shared Michael Howard's prejudice. 'OPEN INVITE TO 2 MILLION' was the banner headline in the *Daily Express*. Charles Wardle, a former immigration minister, warned that the change would lead to further abuses of the system, and that anyone, like the foreign secretary, who thought otherwise was 'talking through his head'. Teresa Gorman, a 'rent-a-quote' right-winger, demanded 'urgent reassurance' from the government and warned shrilly, 'We had better be prepared for the worst.' Norman Tebbit, who had been bitterly opposed to the 1990 Nationality Scheme, commented caustically, 'I wonder how much money John Major has collected for the party in Hong Kong.' Yet this backlash lacked teeth: Major's enemies in his own party were far too preoccupied with plotting against him over Europe to waste more than a spasm of energy on the distant 'threat' from Hong Kong.

In the colony there was a further cause for rejoicing. At 8am, on the morning of Major's speech, Jack Edwards, a seventy-seven-year-old British expatriate who had for ten years led a one-person crusade on behalf of a dwindling band of Hong Kong war widows denied full UK citizenship, had arrived outside Government House with his Union Jack and a petition for the prime minister. Edwards, himself a former prisoner of war, was far from optimistic that the British government could be persuaded at this late stage to legislate in favour of the remaining twenty-nine wives and widows of ethnic Chinese subjects who had fought for king and country in the Second World War. Edwards did not know that the governor shared his view that the

British stance was both shameful and unsustainable, and that in fact Patten had been lobbying London accordingly for at least nine months, albeit to no apparent effect. He was surprised, therefore, when one of the governor's aides came down to the front gates and asked him to return at midday.

Once again, it was the home secretary who had been the stumbling block. His particular fear in this matter was that a host of other 'special cases' would be tacked on to any primary legislation designed to appease the war widows, thus, as he saw it, reopening the floodgates for a Chinese invasion from Hong Kong which he hoped had been dammed permanently in 1990. However, neither Howard nor indeed the British government had bargained for the wave of disgust the callousness of this attitude would create. In 1994, under pressure from Government House and the House of Lords, the home secretary had grudgingly agreed to send a letter to the twenty-nine widows reassuring each of them that, in return for their 'late husband's services to Hong Kong', they would, after all, be free to enter Britain at any time and to settle there if they so wished. However, he explained, they would not have a right to a British passport. This concession served only to inflame the moral outrage of Jack Edwards and the international body of opinion which he had helped to mobilise. The force of their case – that Britain owed these elderly women British citizenship in view of the sacrifice made by their husbands' service to the crown – continued to reverberate. Their cries left a powerful and potentially indelible impression that, on this issue, the British government had demonstrated at best an impoverished sense of honour. It was a failure of political imagination which left Patten quite incredulous.

The issue remained unresolved until the weekend before Major's departure for Hong Kong, when he was given his brief for the visit together with the draft of his speech to the British Chamber of Commerce. At this point he decided to act with the decency ascribed to him by the governor. According to a member of Patten's team, there began at once a 'great flurry of activity' which continued until after the prime minister's arrival in Bangkok. The Private Office at Number 10 was instructed to ask the Home Office for some new options for progress. Initially,

Michael Howard was reluctant to respond and, according to his friends, capitulated only when it became quite clear to him that the prime minister was determined to 'bear good tidings' with him to Hong Kong. In the volte-face necessary to accommodate this political imperative, Howard 'discovered' that, after all, it would be possible to introduce into Parliament a 'carefully circumscribed' private member's bill which would not have the damaging implications for immigration that he had until that moment foreseen.

When Jack Edwards returned to Government House at midday as instructed, he was unaware that at the time of his earlier visit the prime minister had been about to inform LegCo that the British government had relented. Now he was ushered in to see John Major, who walked up to him, placed a hand on his arm and said, 'I've got some good news for you.' Edwards left, visibly affected, for a round of radio and television interviews. In one of these, he said of Major, pointing to his now redundant petition, 'I have called him a hypocrite before and I have called him all sorts of names. But today he is a gentleman.'

The last-minute decision to provide passports for war widows and visa-free access for SAR passport-holders still left one group of British subjects without the protection of a full British passport or the right to carry an SAR passport – the 'ethnic minorities', most of whose families had emigrated to Hong Kong from the Indian subcontinent, where they had become subjects of the British crown. Although Beijing did propose to grant this group right of abode in Hong Kong, albeit as officially stateless persons, they would be unable to travel as Chinese citizens. Only those fortunate enough to have acquired one of the 50,000 British passports available under the 1990 British Nationality Act had the security, protection and identity of citizenship. The endemic anomalies and apparent arbitrary nature of this selection process had served only to exacerbate the anxiety and dismay of the leaders of the Indian community. The situation was particularly painful for a group which was not only closely knit and self-contained but also bound together by ties of blood in a network of extended families. Only a minority of the 5,000 or so citizens of Indian origin had been granted British passports, and the relief of these 'winners' was tempered by the knowledge that their friends, brothers, sisters, sons and daughters had emerged as losers.

One of the most prominent Indian families in Hong Kong was led by Hari Harilela, who emigrated to the colony as a young man in the mid-1930s. Working first as a newspaper-vendor and then as a salesman, he went on to create a chain of hotels which, by the time of Patten's arrival in Hong Kong, had given him a substantial entrepreneurial toe-hold throughout the region as well as in Britain, Canada and the United States. In the manner of a minor maharaja, he had built a palatial Indian compound in Kowloon containing separate apartments which were allocated to upwards of forty relations spanning three generations. His contribution as a pillar of the Indian community – he was a longstanding justice of the peace – had been recognised, in 1979, with the award of an OBE. Harilela was more perplexed than angry to discover that he and his wife would be granted British citizenship while his son, who was nineteen and had a shareholding in the family empire worth HK$100 million, had been rejected. Too proud, and perhaps too embarrassed, to suggest openly that the British government's attitude was tinged with racism, he could not fathom why his hard-working, law-abiding and prosperous family should be thought unfit to enjoy right of abode in Britain – which, as it happened, none of them wished to exercise, except in extremis. On their behalf, he felt humiliated.

> We are a British-orientated people. I was shocked when we realised that we would be refused British passports – in my immediate family, out of six members, four get it and two don't. After all, we have been here for sixty years. My son's accent is just like yours, just like a British accent. In the case of my elder brother, his elder son has a passport, his second son is denied. It is so piecemeal, so arbitrary. Can you tell me why we have been rejected? We took the oath of allegiance to Her Majesty the Queen. Now we will be a broken family.

Another relative, Leila, said: 'My husband and I got rejected last week. My husband's younger brother will be sworn in next month. I was very upset, hurt. I was in tears. It is like a betrayal. All of a sudden we are nowhere.'

Despite the entreaties of the Indian community the British government's position on the issue had not changed. Following a report of the Foreign Affairs Select Committee in March 1994, the Home Office had stated explicitly that discrimination against them would be a factor in determining whether members of the ethnic minorities in Hong Kong had come 'under pressure' and therefore whether 'sympathetic consideration' should be given to an application to settle in Britain. Michael Howard had regarded even this 'concession' as one too many, and he was not now willing to go further. Yet again – as in the case of the SAR passport-holders and the war widows – the governor believed Howard's stance to be untenable. He was sharply aware that it lacked moral credibility, and he knew that in the run-up to 1997 Britain would come under increasing pressure to relent.

At Patten's instigation, Government House had started to lobby discreetly on behalf of the ethnic minorities in mid-1995, urging the Home Office to provide them with at least the same degree of protection that Howard had originally been prepared to offer the war widows – namely the right to settle in Britain if they chose to do so, albeit without the right to a British passport. Howard refused on familiar grounds; indeed, in the case of the ethnic minorities he had been even more stubborn. However, he had reckoned without the prime minister's 'decency' and his tacit alliance with Patten. At the instigation of Number 10, Malcolm Rifkind had lobbied Howard with what Patten described as 'considerable verve and tenacity' both before and after the prime minister's departure for Bangkok. Memoranda and draft statements flew between London, Hong Kong and Bangkok, but still Howard did not relent. Finally, a few hours before Major's flight from Bangkok to Hong Kong, Michael Heseltine, as his deputy, was drafted in on the prime minister's behalf. In the course of a long three-way telephone conference between Heseltine, Howard and Rifkind, the home secretary was finally persuaded to accept a new formula, which was put to Patten a few hours before the prime minister's arrival. Although the governor thought the proposed offer was still inadequate, he decided not to press for more at that stage, hoping that Howard had been driven to shift just far enough to deal with what he described as the 'real anxiety' among the ethnic minorities. Two days later, in Hong Kong, the prime minister duly announced the revised British position in his speech to the Chamber of Commerce: 'Let me make it clear to this group that we are prepared to guarantee – repeat, guarantee – admission and settlement if, at any time after 1 July, they were to come under pressure to leave Hong Kong.' As if to reassure the home secretary and his right-wing backers in the media, Major added: 'It is the position, of course, that this group do not wish to leave Hong Kong; they are settled here; their businesses are here; their family ties are here. But they want to be sure that if they come under pressure to leave they will have a country to go to. From today, they have that assurance.'

Major's visit was a rare success for the British government. Martin Lee was moved to comment that the prime minister's speech was the 'strongest statement of support for Hong Kong yet from any British minister. At a time when we believe that the British interest in Hong Kong is only in terms of dollars, I think this is a very pleasant surprise.' Even Emily Lau, who had awarded Major 'ten out of a hundred' for passport commitments, was teased by him into conceding, 'Oh, all right, eleven, then.' The prime minister set off for London garlanded with accolades from the local media and reinvigorated by Patten's company. On the flight he was relaxed enough to share his feelings about the governor's virtues with the Westminster lobby correspondents travelling with him. His praise for Patten, particularly in an interview with the BBC's political editor, Robin Oakley, prompted that questing posse to draw the unanimous conclusion that the prime minister had deliberately chosen this moment to anoint the Hong Kong governor as his chosen successor as leader of the Conservative party.

Only thirty-six hours earlier the governor had himself said enough to persuade the Westminster media that he was intent on making a political comeback in Britain. Pressed by the assembled political editors, who betrayed distinctly more curiosity about his own future than they did about that of Hong Kong, he said, 'I am a political animal. I could not fail to be interested in the issues, and I follow what goes on at Westminster pretty closely.' Volunteering that he missed the atmosphere of the Commons, 'though not the clubbiness', he added, 'I am not ruling anything in, and I am not ruling anything out.' His remarks produced headlines in the British press the next day of the 'Patten signals his return to Commons' variety. Recalling that the governor had recently made a speech extolling the virtues of the so-called tiger economies of Asia, all of which maintained low levels of public spending, the journalists also reported that he had recently 'told friends' that he was becoming increasingly sceptical about the merits of a single currency. On this basis, they speculated that he was eager to shed his image as a Tory 'wet' in order to place himself in a stronger position from which to claim the Conservative crown.

In Britain, the apparent endorsement of the prime minister for Patten's supposed hunger for high office after the handover not only produced headlines, but led to a number of leading articles which fully exposed the raw wounds of a Conservative party racked by ideological conflict and personal animosity. When Patten saw these, he was shocked by the vituperation heaped on him by some commentators for daring to presume that the Conservative party would ever accept him as leader. Despite his tough political hide, he was hurt and bewildered. Attempting to make light of this hostility, he joked that at least he had managed to 'bring into an unholy union the *People's Daily* and some of the populist tabloids'. But a few days later he admitted, 'It didn't make me any more enthusiastic about the prospect of going back into British politics.' He knew that Major's remarks had been injudicious, if well meant, but, somewhat disingenuously, he observed, 'The prime minister did no more than say that he thought I was a decent bloke. I guess it would have been more of a story if he'd said what a terrible tosser I was. But he was kind and friendly and amiable about me. I should think he was surprised at the subsequent fuss.'

The truth was that Patten faced an insoluble dilemma. He knew that it would be exceptionally difficult to parachute back into British politics, even if a seat could be found for him. In any case, he was not yet at all sure that he wanted to re-enter that insular and incestuous world, which, viewed from Hong Kong, sometimes seemed to be dominated by the vanities of a preposterous cast of also-rans. He had already been approached directly by the local leaders of two safe Tory constituencies, who asked him if he would become their prospective parliamentary candidate in the forthcoming general election. One offered a new constituency in East Anglia, close to Major's Huntingdon stronghold; the other was – yet again – from Kensington and Chelsea, where, he was told, Nick Scott would either stand down voluntarily or be deselected to make way for him. Patten declined both invitations, repeating that since he still intended to remain in Hong Kong until the handover, it would be impossible for him to consider either of them: the election, as they all knew, would have to be held before the middle of May 1997 at the latest.

In April 1996, Patten confided that he thought the option remained 'live, but difficult', adding, oddly, 'not least because I don't have any roots in British politics'. He reiterated that, although there would be 'all sorts of hurdles to clear', if he did decide to re-enter the fray, he did not intend turning his back on political issues. 'I hope I can find another job in public service, but whether I want to go back into the House of Commons, or whether a constituency would have me, are both issues to resolve in the future.' Even though he had little appetite for the prospect of leading of a broken opposition party at war with itself over Europe, he did sometimes indulge in prime-ministerial reflections. With characteristic but not entirely convincing self-deprecation, he adopted a sporting metaphor to explain:

If you are a club cricketer, I guess there are times in a hot bath after a game when you imagine yourself walking down the steps at Lord's. So when I go back to see John at Number Ten, I do think about what it would be like to live there myself. But if you ask me as a sentient, rational human being whether I think I will ever be prime minister of Great Britain and Northern Ireland, the answer is, no, I don't.

Two years earlier he had described the prospect of a return to British politics as remote. Now, a year away from the handover?

'Distant.' It gave him a moment of amused satisfaction to receive a letter from All Souls, Oxford at the height of this dramatic sideshow inviting him to become the next warden. In truth, he did not spend a great deal of time thinking about what he would do in the future: there were too many imponderables and there was too much uncertainty. Moreover, there was still much to be done in Hong Kong.

Immediately after the prime minister's departure, the Chinese government reiterated that it would dismantle the Legislative Council and replace it with a provisional body that would be 'elected' later in the year, confounding Patten's earlier confidence that, in the end, Beijing would hold back from such drastic action. Soon afterwards, the members of the Beijing-appointed Preparatory Committee voted by 148 to 1 to endorse the Chinese threat. The only member to vote against the establishment of the provisional legislature, Frederick Fung, was not only reprimanded by the director of the Hong Kong and Macau Affairs Office but removed from the committee and told that he would not be permitted to play any further part in Hong Kong's future governance unless he was ready to recant. In private Patten responded to what he described as a 'nasty, bullying bit of old-fashioned Leninism' with suppressed anger, noting that Beijing's 'decapitation' of Fung would send 'some pretty nasty messages around the world'.

Paradoxically, this latest example of intimidation, which happened to coincide with another crackdown on 'dissidents' in China, offered Patten some respite from the charge that his approach had been overly confrontational. His persistent refusal to acknowledge the validity of what was now widely regarded as a puppet body began to seem far less obstinate than his critics had sought to establish. In public, he was seen to occupy the high ground; in private he rejoiced that the heat was now on China.

Nobody can now seriously believe that the argument has been about whether or not we somehow broke the Joint Declaration or the Basic Law or the understandings or agreements between the two sides . . . The Joint Declaration is about establishing democracy in Hong Kong, the sort of

democracy they have in Taiwan, Korea, Japan and – it has to
be said – the same sort of democracy that we have in the
United Kingdom. That's what China signed up to – the
development of representative government. So don't let's have
any more pretence that somehow the argument has been
about the 'triple violations'. The only violations there may be
will be from the Chinese side . . . They're in the throes of
defining words in the Joint Declaration in their own terms.

In support of this contention he quoted China's foreign minister,
Qian Qichen, who had recently declared in a disconcerting blend
of neo-populist and sub-Marxist jargon: 'To mechanically ape
the Western democratic model does not accord with Hong
Kong's actual conditions.'
    In his contempt for Beijing, Patten sometimes allowed himself
to invest the Joint Declaration with a far less equivocal commitment to 'Westminster' democracy than the wording of the treaty
itself, with its opaque references to elections, could sustain.
Nonetheless, his essential point was valid: China had wrenched
the treaty's ambiguities out of context in order to justify the sup-
pression of democracy in Hong Kong. Patten foresaw a long
battle ahead after the handover. He noted privately in April:

I dare say we'll spend the next five or ten years arguing with
China, and with some apologists for China, about whether
democracy really means choosing your representative institution, or having it chosen by the people of Hong Kong;
about whether protecting human rights really means closing
down newspapers and locking up editors, or whether it
means allowing freedom of speech.

Patten could not speak in public about his fear of China's repressive intentions without risk of precipitating an onrush of panic in
the population, but in private he was more scathing than ever
about his critics, and in particular the sinologists in London.
Unmoved by their case, he commented for the future record:

Stripped of its sinuous charms, the argument amounts to

this. You should have ratted, in practice if not in rhetoric, on the undertakings given to people in the Joint Declaration. You should have risked Britain leaving Hong Kong with maximum obloquy after years of fighting Martin Lee and the Democrats, after years of fighting internal opinion. And you should have accepted the undertaking to do China's dirty work for it, and to try to chloroform Hong Kong and international opinion as Hong Kong was frog-marched into the future. I think that would have been appalling.

It was the fiercest defence of his own approach he had yet essayed, and it was underpinned by the confidence that the roots of democracy in Hong Kong had grown much deeper since his arrival. Every significant poll showed that at least 60 per cent of the public continued to support the Democrats, despite the 'subversive' tag Beijing had placed so ostentatiously around the neck of Martin Lee:

Nobody now doesn't know that there is a Hong Kong, and what is happening in Hong Kong, and I think that there is in Hong Kong enough momentum behind the development of representative government and civil society to make those things in the long term unstoppable. You can wind up the Legislative Council, but you can't actually wind up the sixty to seventy per cent of the population which still supports the Democratic party.

But you could, surely, crush that expression of support? 'Maybe for a bit . . . I don't believe that 30 June represents the end of democracy and pluralism in Hong Kong. I think those things may have been turned into papier mâché if one had followed some of the sinologists' advice.'

If he was right, the prospects for a confrontation between China and Hong Kong were greater, and more alarming, than he seemed able to recognise. Nevertheless, he took heart from his belief that, in the cliché so often deployed by optimists, China would not wittingly destroy the goose that laid the golden egg.

What the Chinese are trying to do at the moment is to
bludgeon public opinion into submission . . . What I think
it all tells one is that they are very anxious about political
control; that they are very sensitive about the extent to
which civil society and democracyhave developed in Hong
Kong. And I fear that nervousness means they are handling
these matters with a very shaky hand. It was very ham-
fisted, very maladroit.

Patten's view that, on the one hand, China was not willing to tolerate dissent from a community which had become irreversibly
pluralistic, while on the other, Beijing would contrive to avoid
open confrontation with the people of Hong Kong after the
handover, was contradictory. It was a flaw in his reasoning that he
skirted for the time being by boasting that China's belligerence
did not make it any more difficult for him to govern Hong Kong
because 'it is such a clumsy piece of authoritarian artifice'.

Three days after Major's departure from Hong Kong, China
started a nine-day missile test off the coast of Taiwan to 'preserve
the territorial integrity' of the People's Republic. US naval forces
were diverted into the area. Deng Xiaoping was reported to be
'very concerned' about this show of strength, and a Chinese
source held that Beijing's policy had shifted from 'peaceful reunification' to 'defending reunification by force'. An official from the
Foreign Ministry in Beijing said that the people of Hong Kong
should not be worried but 'pleased with the strengthening of the
power of defence of their own country'. Partly as a result of the
tension over Taiwan, and partly because of a sharp fall in the US
stock markets, the Hang Seng Index plunged by 820.34 points, or
7.3 per cent, to 10,397.45, the largest reverse recorded in the
Asia–Pacific region. The financial secretary, Donald Tsang,
claimed that there was no cause for alarm. In a telephone survey
conducted by the *Apple Daily*, 50 per cent of respondents agreed
that the live-ammunition exercise in Taiwan had undermined
their confidence in China's commitment to the idea of 'one
country, two systems', which had originally been applied by
Deng to Taiwan and only later to Hong Kong.

At the end of March, the Royal Hong Kong Police had to

move in with batons to quell a scuffle that almost became a riot after tens of thousands of people arrived en masse at the Wanchai Sports Stadium to register their applications for BNO passports twenty-four hours before the closing deadline. Although hundreds of extra staff had been drafted in to cope with the last-minute rush of applicants, emotions were running high. This stampede for BNO passports, coming as it did only three weeks after the British prime minister had assured the Hong Kong citizenry that SAR passports, for which all of those in the stadium would be eligible, would enjoy visa-free access to Britain, was an eloquent illustration of the tensions which ran only just below the placid surface of the colony. As one correspondent to the *South China Morning Post* wrote:

> I am ethnic Chinese and was born and bred in Hong Kong . . . the silent majority feel helpless. But they do not bother to take their discontent to the street, or make their voices heard through any channel. Their feelings will only be expressed in incidents like a scuffle in a crowd . . . I am glad I obtained my BNO passport long before the deadline for applications and did not need to join the queue the other day, otherwise I could have been involved in a scuffle too . . . I would rather be a third-class national of Britain than a 'loyal' and 'patriotic' Chinese puppet.

In one of Beijing's crasser attempts to secure the allegiance of Hong Kong, the civil service came under increasing pressure to demonstrate its 'patriotism'. Soon after the 'decision' by the Preparatory Committee to set up a 'provisional' legco, officials in Beijing issued a statement in which they tried to coerce Hong Kong's civil servants into showing their loyalty to the future sovereign power. Civil servants should offer to co-operate with the provisional legco, even at the expense of violating their obligations to the present sovereign, a spokesman cautioned; otherwise, they would not be able to 'transit' into senior posts after the handover. This caused such a spasm of alarm that Beijing half withdrew the threat, though not before its significance had hit home. Such pressure on the civil service had become a source of growing anxiety at Government House. Nine months earlier, one of Patten's most senior advisers had identified the threat to Hong Kong's civil servants as coming from a disparate combination of Chinese officials (both within Hong Kong and on the mainland), the Bank of China and the People's Liberation Army, 'each thinking that 1997 would tip the balance in their favour', albeit against one another. The aide argued then:

> There will be no institutional defence against Peking if they decide, damn it, we're going to crush Hong Kong. That is a possibility. But if Peking sobers up, then it is a matter of the Hong Kong system being strong enough to resist encroachments from the Public Security Bureau telephoning the police and saying, 'That bloke you arrested the other day is actually a friend of mine. Could you please just deliver him to the border and not put him on trial?' Or a Chinese company leaning on someone in the Legislative Council, or someone on the Central Tendering Board saying, 'If you know what is good for you, deal us into this consortium.' It is that we have to guard against, and that all depends on the individuals in the system.

At that time, Patten's advisers believed that Hong Kong's protection in this sense hung, by a thread, on a handful of the colony's most senior public servants, including the chief secretary, Anson Chan; the financial secretary Donald Tsang; Michael Sze, now head of the Hong Kong Trade and Development Corporation; and the constitutional secretary, Nicholas Ng. The pivotal figure was Anson Chan: were she to resign or to retire before the handover, Hong Kong's self-confidence would be irreparably damaged. 'I don't think there is anyone who matters as much as she does,' Patten noted. 'If she stays, if she is part of the system, then a lot of other decent people will stay as well . . . If she goes, it will be a very bad blow. For other, very good, civil servants, I think, she is the determining factor in whether they stay in public service.' Although the civil service was blessed with a wealth of talent at first-secretary level (individuals who might expect to inherit the top jobs within a decade or so), they did not yet have the experience or authority to take over. If Anson Chan and her most senior colleagues were unable to sustain the pressure from China, Hong Kong, in the view of a Patten adviser, would soon be left with a 'flabby, Third World bureaucracy' which would rapidly succumb to the predators from the mainland. Patten and his aides were keenly aware that an exodus from the civil service could easily be triggered by Beijing's bullying ineptitude. In the words of one senior official:

> You can't underestimate the extent to which these people have options . . . They've all enjoyed tremendous asset infla-tion over the last few years . . . Anyone who took out a loan immediately after Tiananmen is sitting on several million dollars of profit. So you can sell your three-bedroomed apartment here, buy a six-bedroomed ranch in Vancouver and still have several million in the bank. It is pretty tempt-ing when you compare that with the prospect of having to deal with Lu Ping's emotional outbursts, and the creeps from the NCNA trotting around poking their noses in your files.

Now, in the spring of 1996, the focus of media attention began to switch from Patten to Anson Chan. In the two and a half years since her appointment as chief secretary she had become a very public figure. Her dress sense was closely observed while her pen-chant for ballroom dancing had rejuvenated the foxtrot and the quickstep at every fashionable party she attended. The public was by now familiar with her potted life story: how she had been born in Shanghai in 1940, the daughter of a famous painter and the granddaughter of a Chinese general who fought with great gal-lantry in three separate wars, only to be assassinated in the year after her birth; how her parents had fled to Hong Kong, and how the star pupil had joined the civil service in 1962 and risen steadily through the ranks to become Hong Kong's first high-flying female public official; how her uncle, Harry Fang, a distinguished doctor, maintained a close relationship with the family of Deng Xiaoping because he had attended the Chinese leader's disabled son; and how, over the years, she had demonstrated great administrative flair but developed an ill-concealed animosity towards the media. It was well known that this hostility originated from an incident in 1986, when, as director of the Social Welfare Department, Chan had presided over an over-enthusiastic posse of social workers who had taken it upon themselves to storm the apartment of a mentally ill client to rescue her child. Her defence of the individuals involved had been high-handed and self-righteous; murmurs in the media that she was unsuited for so sensitive a post grew to a noisy crescendo before fading soon afterwards from almost every memory – except hers. Years later, Anson Chan still bridled at the memory of the 'persecution' she had had to endure from the media. 'I have no hang-ups about the press,' she insisted, while demonstrating quite the reverse, 'but some seem to think that if you're in public office, you're supposed to take all that flak. I can take plenty, but there is a limit to what one can bear.' Some feared that this antipathy, combined with a well-honed streak of arrogance, would make her a less enthusiastic defender of Hong Kong's rights and freedoms than Patten had allowed himself to believe.

Yet as chief secretary Chan had rapidly developed an astute sense of public relations. The dour, unsmiling persona with which she had been invested by her critics before she came to prominence was replaced by a stylish image in which an air of easy authority blended with an apparently warm smile. In July 1995, she had accomplished a secret mission to Beijing to meet Qian Qichen and Lu Ping and had demonstrated a flair for diplomacy. At the same time she had been able to reassure the Legislative Council that her trip had been a 'get-to-know-you' exercise and that there had been no secret deals. Although the governor and his entourage had been dismayed by her ill-judged attempt in September 1995 to nobble the right of Hong Kong's newly elected politicians to introduce private members' bills, and by an earlier incident in which she had ordered a government bill to be withdrawn after it had been amended by LegCo (when she confided none too discreetly that her dubious decision had been taken to 'teach the Democrats a lesson'), she had otherwise demonstrated a refreshing fervour for the Patten project. In March 1996, she won herself plaudits from a suspicious media for expressing her regret at China's decision to establish the provisional legislature. 'I hope that the Chinese side would explain clearly to the Hong Kong people the reason behind that,' she said. 'In any case, we will not undermine the authority and credibility of the existing legislature.'

In the face of Beijing's threat to disown civil servants who failed to support the provisional legislature, she remained defiant – China's decision was 'bound to cause confusion and uncertainty', she declared. The mood of the moment was well caught in a leading article in the *Eastern Express*, which praised her bravery and dignity under the headline 'COURAGE IN THE ABYSS OF DESPAIR'. On 30 March 1996, on the advice of Patten's political advisers, she took the diplomatic initiative, inviting Lu Ping to meet her on his next visit to Hong Kong so that they could discuss the issue of 'loyalty' and 'other transitional issues'. A week later, the director of the NCNA, Zhou Nan, announced that he would be hosting a dinner for Lu Ping and the chief secretary on 18 April, when – conveniently – the governor would be away in London. Sixty per cent of the respondents to an opinion poll criticised the director of the Hong Kong and Macau Affairs Office for refusing, yet again, to meet Patten.

Lu Ping arrived in Hong Kong on 12 April to be confronted by a small but angry group of demonstrators protesting against the continued imprisonment in China of Xi Yang, the *Ming Pao* journalist. In the governor's absence, Anson Chan showed herself to be a doughty defender of Hong Kong's rights and freedoms, and a fortnight later, in response to an invitation from Lu Ping, she flew to Beijing to discuss the transition. Patten not only welcomed her growing assurance but encouraged her to step into his limelight, recognising that, for Hong Kong's sake, she had to walk a tightrope between loyalty and independence.

He was perturbed, therefore, to discover, in May 1996, that his trusted lieutenant was planning to deliver a series of speeches in the United States in which she would appear to be signalling her readiness to soften her opposition to the provisional legco. Any suggestion that he and Anson Chan were at odds on this matter would severely damage both his own credibility and public confidence. Halfway through her visit, Patten sent an urgent message to New York asking her to amend her speeches to bring them back into line with government policy. He followed this up by speaking to her directly. Appreciating that her remarks were open to damaging misinterpretation, she agreed to redraft the speeches to take account of his anxieties. It was a potentially uncomfortable moment in an otherwise increasingly harmonious relationship, and it demonstrated the extreme delicacy of their joint predicament in the countdown to the handover.

Patten had himself just returned from a fourteen-day trip to the United States and Canada, where he had made eleven speeches, given thirteen press briefings and held several dozen meetings with government officials and politicians, including President Clinton. By this time, the media had started to run 'Patten's last year' articles summarising his achievements and his troubles. One of these, a cover piece in the American magazine *Newsweek* of 13 May, headlined 'THE BETRAYAL OF HONG KONG', greeted him on his return. Above a picture of a symbolic Chinese 'prisoner' with the number 97 stamped on his forehead, the magazine asked, 'With a year to go, who speaks for his future?' In combative style, the writer, Dorinda Elliott, noted how easily China had 'recruited so many of Hong Kong's tycoons' and speculated that 'this tiny elite may go down in history as the class that betrayed Hong Kong'. With the exception of T.T. Tsui, a tycoon with close links to the Beijing leadership, who told his interviewer that Hong Kong was like a 'family company; you don't have your arguments in the open', the objects of Elliott's scorn preferred, as usual, to conceal their animosity towards the governor.

Alongside its main article, *Newsweek* carried an interview with Patten. In answer to the query, 'What motivates the rich people to do Beijing's bidding?' he posed his own question: 'Why is it that privileged people sign up to arrangements whose sole intention is to choke off the voice of those who by every measure represent the majority of public opinion? Well, I'll say this: they wouldn't be doing it if most of them didn't have foreign passports in their back pockets.' Patten's long-concealed contempt for the spinelessness and hypocrisy of the business community had, at last, broken through the surface. His remarks ricocheted around

Hong Kong, finally exposing the wound between the governor and the business elite which had festered for so long. Interpreting his incautious comments as an endorsement of the 'betrayal' headline, the leaders of Hong Kong's commercial sector were swift to indulge a spasm of self-righteous indignation.

At the instigation of Beijing, a Hong Kong executive called Nellie Fong (nicknamed Snow White at Government House), who was known to be exceptionally close to one or two members of the Chinese leadership, orchestrated the response of an apparently apoplectic business elite. She drafted a letter denouncing Patten for the leaders of seven Chambers of Commerce (whom the governor called the Seven Dwarfs) to send to the prime minister in London. Her protest was couched in language of such incontinent ferocity that even China's most fervent apologists felt obliged to modify its tone before dispatching it to London on 18 May. The letter stopped short of demanding Patten's recall, but expressed 'profound disappointment' at the remarks quoted in *Newsweek*, which, tycoons complained, showed that the governor had failed to recognise the scale and quality of their contribution to the wellbeing of Hong Kong. 'Mr Patten,' they declared, 'has, through his unjustified attacks on the business community, ended up doing Hong Kong a great disservice.' On 21 May 1996, they wrote to Patten expressing:

the concern of the business community on the Hong Kong government's position on the future provisional legislature, and, in particular, about the adverse effect which non-co-operation will have on the smooth transfer of sovereignty. We wish you to know of our sincere belief that the interests of Hong Kong will be better served by accepting the reality that a provisional legislature will be established.

Patten's response was to the point: 'Come off it.' The Chambers of Commerce received an equally dusty answer from the prime minister. Describing Patten's visit to America as a 'formidable success', during which he had 'vigorously defended and promoted Hong Kong's interests – not least the interests of the business community which you represent,' Major commented on their failure to give any public support to the judiciary, the civil service or the elected Legislative Council, adding tartly:

> It would be helpful . . . if the leadership of your chambers could make its voice heard on these issues too – just as you have to me about remarks inaccurately attributed to the governor. The governor has always been an admirer and energetic advocate of the great contribution which the business community has made to Hong Kong's spectacular economic success. I suggest you rather owe him gratitude for working so hard to make your case.

In America Patten had been on the receiving end of what he described to the press on his return as a 'massive and growing scepticism about Hong Kong's prospects'. Many of those he had met in the States, he reported, had told him that they had been briefed by Hong Kong business visitors who had struck them as defenders of Chinese policies rather than advocates of Hong Kong. This in itself had raised questions in people's minds about 'one country, two systems'. 'Does it matter that our American and Canadian friends are sceptical about the future for Hong Kong? I think it matters a great deal . . . We cannot afford to lose their confidence. But we must recognise that their confidence has been damaged by recent actions and decisions by China.'

Off the record, Patten was even less repentant. Some of his detractors, he noted, had simply been driven into saying things publicly which they were saying privately anyway – 'I think, more for Peking's benefit . . . to demonstrate their credentials.' Those who had lined up against him in the Chambers of Commerce, who included the chairman, James Tien, had now taken the 'dangerous' step of joining the united front 'in the trenches against anybody who believes in democracy or protecting civil liberties in Hong Kong'. They had allowed themselves to become, collectively, a 'megaphone for Peking . . . I think they've let Hong Kong down'.

Exhausted by the American trip and somewhat deflated by the row with the business community – especially given that, in the States, he had managed to sound 'wearily bullish' about Hong

Kong's future and the remarkable achievements of the colony's entrepreneurs – Patten was consoled by a comment by the *Asian Wall Street Journal*. Quoting from memory, he recalled that the newspaper had observed: 'This is a controversy about something which the governor didn't say, which, if he had said it, would have been regarded by the man in the street as being completely uncontroversial.' He believed that the 'international card' was a very important element in the 'survival of decency' in this very international city.

> If I belted up it would be so much more difficult for anyone else to speak up about those things which are important and of lasting value in Hong Kong. I've got to go on making sure that not only is Hong Kong not chloroformed into the future, but that the rest of the world notices what is happening.

However heavy-going the effort now seemed, Patten remained convinced that he had no choice but to carry the fight for democracy and freedom to his adversaries.

I9

'THE HEADBANGER IN HONG KONG'

China Maintains the Pressure

In the midst of the governor's conflict with the 'Seven Dwarfs', Michael Heseltine swept into Government House for a twenty-four-hour stopover on his way back to London from another triumphant mission to China. To his evident satisfaction, he had once again been fêted by the leadership in Beijing; as on his trip a year earlier, he had been accorded the privilege of a tête-à-tête with the premier, Li Peng, and the president, Jiang Zemin, which, he reported, had been most productive. 'The truth is,' the British deputy prime minister said at a press conference in the Chinese capital, 'that our interest and the Chinese interest in Hong Kong are identical, and that we have got to bring about the transfer of Hong Kong in the condition of prosperity and stability. That is what we are totally committed to, and I believe that this is what will happen.' Echoing Heseltine's tone, a spokesman for the Chinese Foreign Ministry added that, during the deputy prime minister's visit, 'both the Chinese and British side have expressed their full confidence with regard to China's re-exercise of sovereignty over Hong Kong in 1997'.

At Government House there was no such confidence. Heseltine's failure to caution China publicly, and his evident eagerness to trust Beijing's good faith, stood in stark contrast to the stance taken by the governor. Patten admired Heseltine, but disagreed deeply with his judgement. He observed that on this occasion the deputy prime minister had been the only Western politician of note who had managed to complete a visit to China in recent years without making one mention of human rights, even in private conversation with the Beijing leadership.

At a private dinner at Government House, Heseltine caused resentment by informing the guests – who included leading members of the civil service, the judiciary and LegCo, as well as a number of Patten's senior advisers – that they had 'nothing to fear' from China. On the basis of his meetings in Beijing, he declared, he could assure them that China would honour the Joint Declaration and the Basic Law and that, 'from the president downwards', the leadership was committed to the future stability and prosperity of Hong Kong. For such an accomplished states-man, it was – even in the eyes of his admirers – a lamentable homily: complacent, jejune and ill informed. His failure to rise to the moment was symbolised, for his critics, by an unaccountable lapse of either knowledge or memory: he rephrased Deng Xiaoping's famous dictum as 'one nation, two states'. If he could not even be bothered to find the term that was supposed to define his rosy vision of the future, they wondered aloud, how could anything he said about China or Hong Kong be taken seriously – except as an apologia for Beijing on behalf of the Foreign Office and the Department of Trade and Industry?

The following day, Heseltine's performance at a press confer-ence confirmed the widespread impression in Hong Kong that the deputy prime minister cared less for freedom and democracy in the future SAR than he did about British trade with the People's Republic. With the governor beside him, looking glumly embarrassed, he delivered himself of some vague general-isations about China and the injunction that, in effect, the media had a responsibility to look positively towards the day when Hong Kong would once again be part of China according to the guid-ing principle of what he referred to this time as 'one nation, two regimes'. He made no significant mention of the mood in Hong Kong and his apparent ignorance of the fundamental issues at stake incensed many of his listeners, who went away convinced that his insouciance reflected the British establishment's indiffer-ence to their fate.

It was an uncharacteristically inept display. Using one of the governor's favoured words, Patten's press secretary, Kerry McGlynn, professed himself 'gobsmacked'. The media, he said, were bound to conclude that 'there is not just a cigarette paper between the governor and Mr Heseltine, but a whole packet of cigarettes'. Patten's aides did their best to explain away Heseltine's performance, and, as it happened, McGlynn managed to 'spin' a way out of the situation the deputy prime minister had created. But neither McGlynn nor Patten was in any doubt that Beijing would have been delighted by this indication, however unwittingly made, that the support from London enjoyed by the governor was not as wholehearted as he liked to claim.

The governor was worried that Heseltine's high-handedness might undo some of the good done by the prime minister's visit in convincing the public that Britain was committed in the long term to Hong Kong. Stressing that the deputy prime minister had 'never done anything, or acted in a way, which was remotely disloyal', Patten explained that Heseltine was, and always had been, 'sceptical about the idea that we really can do anything in Hong Kong which the Chinese don't care for to safeguard its liberties . . . And he's very trusting of the economic opening up of China – safeguarding Hong Kong without having to bother about "all that stuff in the Joint Declaration".' Patten felt that, in his keenness to open up trade with China, Heseltine was overly susceptible to Beijing's blandishments. 'I think he takes the assurances that he is given and the welcome he gets at sort of face value – I think sometimes to the surprise even of those who are themselves enthusiasts for, or apologists for, China. I mean, he can go over the top on this.' Patten's sensitivity here was acute. After Heseltine's previous trip to Beijing, the British ambassador, Sir Len Appleyard, had claimed that the agreement on the Court of Final Appeal, which came soon afterwards, 'was all because of the "warm afterglow" from Michael's visit'. Patten did not believe this, although he conceded that it was important that 'it looks as though Sino–British relations are better – it is no help to us if people think they are still in the refrigerator'. Nonetheless, he worried perpetually that the 'warm afterglow' argument would acquire enough momentum to suffocate his reform programme, which was not yet complete. 'The Chinese, of course, use these things to try to isolate me from the British government,' he complained.

> You know, 'We'd have this wonderful relationship with you if only it wasn't for the headbanger in Hong Kong.' The danger is that they think these things are just sort of pro formas; that I, for some eccentric British reason, have been given Hong Kong to play with, but the broader strategic question of Sino–British relations is in good and more experienced hands.

If Patten's amour propre was pricked a little by Heseltine's failure publicly to endorse his stance, the issue between them nevertheless went to the heart of British policy. Aware that it was important for him 'not to turn into the all-time party-pooper', the governor believed with a passion that, for the foreseeable future, Anglo–Chinese relations were bound to be focused principally on how China behaved over Hong Kong. 'I suppose that really is the disagreement – the extremely civilised disagreement – between Michael and myself,' he said. 'I think Michael is hugely right about some things – inner-city deprivation and Europe – and wrong about one or two others. And I think China is an example.' The deputy prime minister had not made his role in Hong Kong any easier. 'I find myself living between those who think that Hong Kong *is* being sold out for British trade, and those who think Hong Kong *should* be sold out for British trade.'

Soon after Heseltine's departure, Patten sent him a genial note enclosing a pile of press cuttings, notably from the *Asian Wall Street Journal*, about 'what I call showbusiness – that is, the extent to which these trips by trade ministers and politicians are mostly show rather than real business'. The grandee of the Tory party did not feel this gesture of lese-majesty required a response.

Despite the proclaimed success of Heseltine's second visit to China, its tangible fruits were not easy to discern. In particular, it soon became clear that his rapport with the Chinese leadership had failed to unblock the negotiations between the two sides in the Joint Liaison Group over the arrangements for the handover ceremony, which was now only a year away, and to which both states attached great importance. The discussions had spluttered on to the JLG agenda in the previous autumn, when the Chinese foreign minister and Malcolm Rifkind had agreed in principle during Qian Qichen's visit to London that the ceremony marking the transfer of sovereignty should be, in Patten's translation of the Chinese, 'grand, solemn and decent'. Some months before this, early in 1995, the British had unilaterally decided to resist the temptation to leave the colony with any overt display of triumphalism. For this reason, although a British task force was due in the area in 1997, Patten advised that it would send the wrong message to have an aircraft-carrier on show. It seemed important to exploit what was bound to be a great media occasion to best advantage; 'to show', as Patten foresaw the historic moment, 'that China and the United Kingdom, members of the Security Council, had resolved their problems relatively peacefully . . . and that they had created together a government which was going to continue to give one of the greatest cities in the world the prospect of even greater prosperity in the future'.

On this basis, Britain proposed a day of celebration on 30 June, followed by a formal handover ceremony in full gaze of the peopleof Hong Kong which might also be etched on the televisual retina of the international community. The Chinese response was frosty. As characterised by Patten:

They wanted to have a ceremony in the City Hall, which will take about a thousand people and is a pretty grotty little building, at which we would, as it were, sign a piece of paper saying, 'Here's Hong Kong – we're sorry we've been here.' There'd be a glass of warm Asti Spumante and that would be that. There would then be a separate military ceremony behind the closed walls of the Tamar Barracks, at which a flag would go up and a flag would go down. I mean, the whole thing is preposterous. Here we are being told that there are likely to be six thousand journalists from all over the world; that there are likely to be up to a hundred television companies wanting to broadcast live – and we are told this is the way the SAR intends to start life.

By the spring of 1996, Patten thought the situation had become 'absolutely crazy'. He appreciated that the Chinese were inevitably worried about security, and in particular about the risk of hostile demonstrations – 'We'd proposed a ceremony at which members of the public would be present, and I suppose they might wear T-shirts or hold up banners' – but he and his advisers sensed that the underlying reason for China's reluctance to discuss the handover was Beijing's refusal ('which one understands in historical terms') to accept that there was any question of a change of sovereignty. The stand-off over what Government House had hoped would be a relatively simple negotiation became increasingly bizarre and fraught. At one point the Chinese side in the JLG informed their British counterparts, according to Patten, that 'they didn't understand why any foreign visitors were being invited. This was merely something that had to be resolved between Britain and China.' At the same meeting they proposed 'joint vetting' of all journalists who applied to cover the ceremony. 'What,' Patten wondered, 'is "joint vetting" a euphemism for?' Memories of the heavy-handed treatment of the media at the International Women's Conference in Beijing the previous summer were not a source of encouragement that 'joint vetting' would serve the interests of either Hong Kong or a free press.

By May, Patten had resolved to avoid spending the next six months arguing with the Chinese about the nature of the cere-mony. 'If, at the end of the day, we have to have a departure ceremony rather than a handover ceremony, so be it . . . But I'm not going to connive at us leaving Hong Kong with our tail between our legs in a sort of hole-in-the-corner way.' As it had already been agreed that the Prince of Wales would be on hand, and that both he and the Pattens would depart Britain's last sig-nificant colony aboard the royal yacht, making her final voyage, it seemed unlikely, in this respect at least, that the last governor would have any difficulty in accomplishing this modest purpose.

On 2 October 1996, the governor delivered his fifth and final policy address to LegCo. It was a long speech, lasting ninety minutes, carefully crafted and rehearsed to set the seal on his own accomplishments and to lay down no fewer than sixteen 'clear benchmarks' by which, he proposed, the world should judge Hong Kong after 1 July 1997. It was both an unsurprising and an uncompromising speech, delivered, by convention, to a silent and impassive chamber. He began by promising that he would speak in more personal terms than was customary on such occasions, although he invited his audience to accept that this did not mean that 'the government is closing down or going into hibernation for nine months . . . We still have plenty to do'.

Patten was addressing his audience in his role as the quasi-mayor of Hong Kong, the head of a mini-state in which he had over-arching responsibility for every area of public life. Reminding the legislators that when he arrived he had promised a more open and accountable government, he recited the list of performance pledges by which this objective was being achieved. 'I doubt whether there are many, if any, governments anywhere which try to be as frank about their failures as their successes,' he boasted. Yet, because of the diplomatic crisis with China, his achievements had received less attention than he, and his admirers in Hong Kong, felt they merited. As one of those politicians who enjoyed the practice of administration, he had, as it happened, derived greater satisfaction from his role as a social reformer in Hong Kong than from his reputation as a 'head-banging' adversary of the People's Republic.

With the assistance of a dedicated civil service, he had delivered virtually all the policy commitments he had made on his arrival: schoolchildren, students, the disabled, the disadvantaged, the sick and those in need of homes had all benefited. A surge in public spending had brought more teachers per pupil, more nurses and doctors, more hospital beds and a cut in waiting times for outpatients from one hour to thirty minutes. There were thirteen new clinics, a new Comprehensive Social Security Assistance Scheme (the first in Hong Kong's history), more than 5,000 'care and attention' beds for the elderly (another first), a Disability Discrimination Ordinance and greatly improved access to buses and trains for the disabled – a project which the governor had overseen personally. More than 100 new flats were being built every day and the numbers living in slum-like 'temporary

housing' had been reduced from more than 65,000 people to
fewer than 18,000, despite the influx of new arrivals from China
at the rate of 150 a day. Since the start of Patten's governorship in
1992, the deployment of 1,500 more police officers on the 'front
line' had helped to cut the overall crime rate by 9 per cent and
violent crime by 23 per cent. The crime rate in Hong Kong was
now on a par with that of Singapore, and, as Patten observed,
much, much lower than those in London, New York, Tokyo
and Toronto. Even the environment had been improved: pollution in rivers and streams in the New Territories was down by 70
per cent; most cars now used catalytic converters and ran on
unleaded petrol; the government at last had put in place, though
not yet implemented, a proper strategy to dispose of Hong Kong's
ever-growing mountain of waste, the cause of appalling marine
pollution.

Patten's record of social reform and welfare expenditure still
left Hong Kong languishing behind any advanced Western country: unemployment benefits and a universal pension scheme, for
example, were still conspicuous by their absence. Nonetheless, he
had overseen a leap forward in public spending targeted at needy
individuals and the community which obliged even his bitterest
adversaries to concede the seriousness of his intent and the competence of his administration. Nor could the business community
complain unduly: despite Britain's row with China, Beijing had,
under pressure from Hong Kong's tycoons, eventually allowed the
major construction projects to proceed. The first phase of the
new airport would be finished, complete with roads, bridges and
metro system linking it to the city centre, in 1998 – only nine
months behind the original schedule. Work was about to start on
Container Terminal 9, and plans for a further two container terminals were already underway. Hong Kong had also embarked on
what Patten described as 'one of the most advanced and competitive telecommunications systems in the world', complete with
four alternative fixed-telecommunications network services operators, four cellular-phone operators, six personal-communications
service operators and thirty-one paging operators.

The government had abolished or reduced a range of charges
and taxes, notably cutting the corporate profit tax to 16.5 per cent

from an 'already low' 17.5 per cent. Even so, the administration had begun work on a multibillion-dollar extension to the Convention Centre to ensure that Hong Kong remained the 'best conference venue of south-east Asia', a HK$50 million new technology training scheme, a HK$300 million investment in the Employees Retraining Board and numerous other grants designed to keep the territory at the forefront of Asia's tiger economies. Despite the cost of this programme of public expenditure, since 1992 the government had also contrived to increase the basic tax allowance, the married person's allowance and the single-parent allowance by 44 per cent, the first-child allowance by 16 per cent and the second-child allowance by 56 per cent. As a result, 60 per cent of the working population now paid no tax at all and only 2 per cent paid the top rate of 15 per cent. The virtuous circle which allowed the governor to reap the political benefit of tax cuts while increasing public spending was a reflection not only of Hong Kong's work ethic and entrepreneurial verve, but also of the territory's geographical location at the gateway to China. 'We all recognise that our economic success is part of a region-wide story,' Patten said. 'When the tide comes in, all the boats rise . . . China's success is Hong Kong's opportunity. That is the case today. It will be even more so as Hong Kong takes its place as the richest, most outward-looking and most modern city in China.'

In his recital of the colony's achievements under his guiding hand he was able to record that, on a per-capita basis, Hong Kong, with an average income of US$23,200, enjoyed a higher standard of living than Australia, Canada, 'and – I whisper it quietly – the United Kingdom'. As the eighth-largest trading community in the world, Hong Kong already had the world's busiest container port and would soon have the second-busiest airport. Since Patten's arrival – although, as he was quick to point out, not because he arrived – Hong Kong's gross domestic product had grown by almost a quarter, exports by almost two thirds and investment by over 40 per cent. 'We have been through some stormy seas during that time; stormier than any of us would have liked,' he declared, 'but we stayed true to our course, true to ourselves. Hong Kong has weathered the storms.'

A later passage of his speech was a stinging riposte to those who had sniped at his welfare programme.

> It seems to me to be preposterous to claim, as some do, that to respond to the community's desire for a little more compassion is to strike at the heart of the Hong Kong success story; that to channel a little of our new wealth to help the elderly, the sick, the disabled and the disadvantaged is to undermine our public finances and our system of government. This is propaganda dressed up as prudence, cant disguised as conviction.

Then, less like a retiring governor than a party leader seeking a second term of office, he highlighted five areas in which his administration had made no fewer than twenty-seven new 'policy commitments', almost all of which were designed to improve the territory's infrastructure, services, openness and accountability, or to make Hong Kong a better place in which to live and work. 'Our economic and social accomplishments here will give the new government of the special administrative region the best possible start in life,' he said in a sideswipe at those Beijing officials who had suspected that the last governor would take Hong Kong's family silver with him on the royal yacht. He pointed to fiscal reserves in the region of HK$320 billion, equivalent to seven times the government's annual capital spending programme, which, he said, constituted a 'serious downpayment on the future'.

Next he turned to the political relationship between Britain, China and Hong Kong, echoing the prime minister's pledge: 'Britain's moral and political commitment to Hong Kong will remain, inscribed in a binding international treaty spanning the next fifty years.' Reflecting on the ties of history and family which bound Britain and Hong Kong together in a mutually supportive embrace, he expressed the hope that these bonds would continue to flourish. In 1992, before his departure for Hong Kong, he had spoken of a smooth handover to China as an imperative. Now he declared: 'A community is a living thing which grows and changes . . . A "smooth transition" is certainly not an end in itself. What we want is a successful transition, which we would also like to be as smooth as possible. But reaching the right destination is more important than the occasional bump on the way.'

He was also at pains to point out, in language which scarcely disguised his personal resentment, that those who liked to divide the period after the Joint Declaration neatly into two phases – a period of 'fruitful and harmonious co-operation' up to 1992, followed by 'relentless and largely profitless hard pounding since' – were guilty of a 'travesty of history, in which some of the participants appear to have rewritten their own parts'. In support of this personal apologia he claimed, with some justification, that it had been 'tough going' from the start, and even more difficult since 1989. The prolonged argument with China over the Bill of Rights and the airport, for example, had long preceded his arrival. 'We have also sometimes suffered from the pretence that things are other than they are, and that words mean other than what the dictionary has always told us they mean,' he continued in a criticism aimed at sinologists in London and business leaders in London and Hong Kong as well as at his adversaries in Beijing. 'Freedom of speech, the obligations under international covenants, the political neutrality of the civil service, elections, co-operation. All those things should be clear, but they have provoked storms of debate.'

Then, in a trenchant defence of his democratic reforms, Patten warned against those who would 'snuff out legitimate aspirations and shut out those politicians who can most authoritatively claim to hold a popular mandate'. But he reserved his full firepower for an onslaught on the provisional legislature which China was proposing to establish as a rival parliamentary forum to the Legislative Council elected in 1995. The governor had been under great pressure from Martin Lee and the Democrats to charge China with a violation of the Joint Declaration. Privately, he believed that such a challenge would be profitless; that if pressed as a legal challenge, it would take many years to prosecute and be difficult to prove. He regarded China's repudiation of the terms and spirit of the treaty as a matter of urgent political significance, the character of which could easily be distorted or lost if the matter were taken either to the United Nations or to the International Court of Justice in the Hague. For this reason he chose to focus the attention of his audience on some of the threats that sprang from China's decision.

> The role of this institution, its credibility and legitimacy, lies at the heart of wider doubts about the future of pluralism and freedom in Hong Kong. How can you have complete faith in the future of the rule of law if you worry about the integrity of the institution which makes the laws? How can you have complete faith in the future of free speech if this assembly only allows it for some? How can you have complete faith in the future probity of government if openness and accountability are to be limited by what is deemed to be politically convenient?

In response to those who thought that he should accommodate China's prospective fait accompli by allowing the civil service to co-operate with the provisional legco, he was unequivocal: 'It is unnecessary as well as provocative, and we will have nothing to do with it. We will not assist a provisional legislature's establishment, its operation or its ability to withstand legal challenge.' And defying Beijing's threat to reverse his decision to bring Hong Kong's laws into line with the Bill of Rights, he said, 'We have done about eighty per cent of the work and we will invite this council to help us finish the job.'

In the final part of his speech Patten identified his sixteen 'benchmarks', the criteria by which he believed the international community would judge Hong Kong in the future. They merit restating.

> Is Hong Kong's civil service still professional and meritocratic? Are its key positions filled by individuals who command the confidence of their colleagues and the community and owe their appointments only to their own ability?
>
> Is the SAR government writing its own budget on the basis of its own policies, or is it under pressure to respond to directives dictated by Beijing?

Is the Hong Kong Monetary Authority managing Hong Kong's exchange fund without outside interference?

Is Hong Kong behaving in a truly autonomous way in international economic organisations?

Is the Hong Kong legislature passing laws in response to the aspirations of the Hong Kong community and the policies of the SAR government, or is it legislating under pressure from Beijing?

Are Hong Kong's courts continuing to operate without interference?

Is the Independent Commission Against Corruption continuing to act vigorously against all forms of corruption, including cases in which China's interests may be involved?

Is Hong Kong continuing to maintain its own network of international law-enforcement liaison relationships?

Is the integrity of the Hong Kong–Guangdong border being maintained, including the separate border controls operated by the Hong Kong Immigration Department?

Is the Hong Kong press still free, with uninhibited coverage of China and of issues on which China has strong views?

Are new constraints being imposed on freedom of assembly? Are the annual commemorations and vigils of recent years still being allowed?

Are foreign journalists and media organisations in Hong Kong still free to operate without controls?

Is anybody being prosecuted or harassed for the peaceful expression of political, social or religious views?

Are Hong Kong's legislators, at successive stages of transition, fairly and openly elected, and truly representative of the community?

Are democratic politicians continuing to play an active role in Hong Kong's politics, or are they being excluded or marginalised by external pressure?

Is the chief executive exercising genuine autonomy in the areas provided for in the Joint Declaration and Basic Law?

It was a blunt set of questions which identified with clarity precisely those concerns agitating the chanceries of the West, not to mention the incumbent leader of Hong Kong. Patten concluded his speech by offering the cold comfort that Hong Kong's autonomy need not be destroyed by China. Instead, those who had most power and influence in the territory – businessmen, politicians, journalists, academics and other community leaders – should resist the temptation to sell Hong Kong short to further their own interests as some of their number had already done. As if shaking himself free of such a morbid prospect, he ended the last policy address of the last British governor with the statement: 'I hope that Hong Kong will take tomorrow by storm. And when it does, history will stand and cheer.' It was made with more faith than certainty.

The audience remained silent in their seats: there was not a murmur of approbation or dissent, no applause, no smiles, no frowns. The legislators who had in so many ways imbibed the virtues of the democratic process on this occasion obeyed the dictates of convention: their governor had descended among them, he had delivered himself of his final formal testimony, and he would depart as he had arrived, without fanfare or gratitude.

As soon as Patten left the chamber, the legislators rose from their places and made for the exits to be met by probing cameras in search of soundbites. Apologists for Beijing used the freedom they still enjoyed – and which the governor had so assiduously promoted on their behalf – to demonstrate their unswerving loyalty to their political masters. From the right, Allen Lee complained that the governor had failed to make good his promise to increase co-operation with China; from the left, the DAB representative on LegCo, Ip Kwok Him, accused him of 'dividing Hong Kong's people and spreading pessimism in their midst'. Emily Lau, who rarely allowed her hatred of Beijing to diminish her hostility towards British colonialism, dismissed the governor's attempts to 'get Britain off the hook' of history and thundered that the Hong Kong authorities were doing 'sweet nothing' to ensure that China implemented the Joint Declaration.

More surprisingly, Margaret Ng, the most thoughtful of commentators, was infuriated by a passage of Patten's speech in which he had reminded his audience that, at the end of the Second World War, when the population of Hong Kong was no more than 600,000, the colony had been 'devastated by conflict, occupation and pillage', and yet over the next three decades, 'wave after wave of refugees swam, walked, ran and climbed over barbed wire to find a new life in this city. Why did they come and what did they find? The peace and safety guaranteed by the rule of law. Not rules, not laws, but the rule of law, that vital protection against arbitrary government.' As Ng explained later, it was not so much the values implicit in Patten's words which provoked her wrath, but the assumption of colonial virtue by which they were underpinned. Interpreting his litany of Hong Kong's qualities under colonial rule as a self-regarding apologia on Britain's behalf, she protested: 'We are the people who climbed the barbed wire.'

Ng's complaint went to the heart of a disconcerting ambiguity in the relationship between a colonial administration, however enlightened, and its subject people, however liberated. 'I was very upset. I felt very alienated. I had to exercise a good deal of self-control not to walk out of that chamber.' The governor had been 'condescending'; he had talked of Hong Kong as a 'British possession', and of 'how much Britain had done for Hong Kong. We were back to a hundred and fifty years ago. I don't think it is even a matter of colonialism. It's a matter of cultural superiority, which, let's face it, plagues the British as much as it plagues the Chinese.' Although the governor was taken aback by this reaction, it struck a chord with him. Margaret Ng, he reflected, saw Britain's colonial record 'through the prism of a thousand little humiliations and acts of discrimination' and the failure to begin the process of democratisation and protection of civil liberties early enough. As far as she was concerned, he concluded, there would never be a positive case to be put for Britain's administration. 'I respect her because I know that much of what she is saying about past discrimination is correct.' However, he maintained that in all fairness she should have conceded that it was indeed a British creation which attracted those waves of refugees, and that the institution of liberal values in Hong Kong had been a product of British administration. Yet at the same time the ferocity with which Margaret Ng launched her criticism encouraged him: she represented, he judged, the 'best and most constructive sort of intellectual awkward squad', the kind of person Hong Kong could ill afford to lose. He was also relieved that, even though so many legislators felt obliged to find fault with his final address, some of the Democrats, at least, had gone out of their way to tell him privately how pleased they were with the focus of his speech. The international response, too, was favourable, and the local polls showed him to be as popular as ever with the ordinary people of Hong Kong. His personal-approval rating rose in the days after his address from 65 to almost 69 per cent.

The pressure on Hong Kong from China was relentless. On 16 October, the *Wall Street Journal* carried an interview with Qian Qichen, in which, as if delivering a direct rebuke to Patten, he gave an ominous warning against the overt manifestation of dissent in Hong Kong after the handover. 'In the future,' he told his interviewer, 'Hong Kong should not hold political activities which directly interfere in the affairs of the mainland.' For good measure he added that, after 1997, the Hong Kong media would be free to 'put forward criticism, but not lies; nor can they put forward personal attacks on Chinese leaders, for that would not live up to the morality of their occupation . . . and is not compatible with personal moral ethics.' This prerequisite, coming from such a senior figure in Beijing's ruling elite, provoked a roar of dismay from those at whom it was aimed: the organisers of the annual vigil to commemorate Tiananmen Square retorted that they would go ahead regardless after 1997. Newspaper editors joined forces with lawyers to insist that the Chinese authorities had no legal right to threaten the free expression of opinion – a fact which, no less ominously, Qian Qichen had himself acknowledged in his interview. 'I don't believe that [future] laws will make such stipulations,' he had said, as if to indicate that, under pressure from China, the future executive of the SAR would intervene to enforce 'personal moral ethics' regardless of the law, in much the way as the Chinese authorities did on the mainland. So much for at least half a dozen of Patten's 'benchmarks'. Although a spokesman for the Chinese Ministry of Foreign Affairs later backtracked, claiming that Qian Qichen's

comments had been misinterpreted, the Chinese leader of the
JLG was quoted as saying that 'spreading rumours and lies is a different matter from press freedom'.

In London, the foreign secretary issued a statement expressing
the British government's concern. 'The Chinese should make
clear that they have no intention to depart from "two systems,
one country" and from the provisions of the Joint Declaration.'
Chris Patten, who was in London to see the prime minister and
other members of the Cabinet, remarked privately: 'My biggest
worry was that it showed a complete lack of understanding by
senior Chinese leaders about how Hong Kong works . . . Plainly
Mr Qian doesn't understand the difference between the rule of
law and the rule of man. But maybe the fact that he's a senior
Chinese cadre makes that inevitable.' Nor was he optimistic that
the Chinese could be brought to a more sensible view. Qian
Qichen's words, according to Patten, reflected the 'implacable
political will of the Communist party in Peking. And what is
always a worry is that there will be people in Hong Kong who
will say, "Oh, this is terrible, but I suppose we've got to be understanding and go along with it."' Although he had a residual faith
in the local media, the rule of law, the democratically elected
legislators and the source of their support, the citizenry itself, he
was painfully aware that Hong Kong's ability to resist Beijing's
'implacable will' lay principally with whoever was selected to
replace him as the SAR's first chief executive. 'We've got to
hope,' he confided in the middle of October, 'that a chief executive of Hong Kong will encourage Chinese officials to keep
their fingers off.' The auguries were not encouraging.

The main contenders for the post of chief executive had recently
emerged from relative obscurity, blinking in the glare of local and
international publicity. There were to be four candidates of note:
a retired justice of appeal, Simon Li; the former chief justice Ti
Liang Yang; the business tycoon Peter Woo and, in spite of his
previously professed reluctance, the shipping magnate C.H. Tung.
There was much speculation about the likely victor, although it
was generally presumed that C.H. was China's preferred choice.
In January 1996, the president of the People's Republic, Jiang

Zemin, had been steered across a gathering of Hong Kong 'patriots' to shake him warmly by the hand, a mark of distinction which did not go unnoticed in Hong Kong.

All four candidates had remained conspicuously silent about the threats made so lately by the Chinese foreign minister. Patten was depressed by this reticence, but not surprised.

> They ran for cover, and, I think, were very reluctant to say anything which suggested that they were prepared to stand up for the things which are guaranteed in the Joint Declaration and which Qian Qichen was specifically attacking. I don't think they will want to do anything at this stage which might annoy China, because we all know that the main ingredient in the selection is who gets China's blessing . . . I hope it will be different after a chief executive has finally emerged.

Under the terms of the Basic Law, the chief executive was to be chosen by a selection committee of 400 people, ostensibly elected by the Preparatory Committee, but in practice appointed by China. Nevertheless, for six weeks from the end of October 1996, the four candidates engaged in a semblance of an election campaign, producing personal manifestos, staging press conferences and walkabouts, giving interviews on radio and television and canvassing support among those who might have some influence with the Selection Committee. As the outcome had been preordained, this exercise in democratic accountability was a charade. Nonetheless it was not entirely unimpressive: all four candidates set about their self-imposed task with sub-Pattenite prowess, deploying some of the populist techniques the last governor had introduced to Hong Kong: they kissed babies, travelled on the MTR underground rail network and beamed delightedly amid a populace from which their power, influence or wealth had hitherto protected them. For democrats, this shadow contest was a bittersweet illustration of Hong Kong's thwarted potential. It offered a glimpse of what might have been – a genuine campaign for popular support from which one or other of the candidates would have surfaced legitimately triumphant – but the skill and sincerity with which the ritual was enacted mocked the very purpose it appeared to serve.

Pundits wondered what had prompted the other three contenders to enter a race that C.H. Tung had already won. Was it vanity, self-delusion or a bid for a place at the top table after the campaign? Certainly, the two lawyers, whatever their other virtues, were regarded as political lightweights without significant administrative experience. Peter Woo, though an able entrepreneur, had persistently denied any aspiration to lead Hong Kong, and most observers had thought that his apparent reluctance to succeed Patten showed sound self-judgement on his part. He lacked any significant base of support in China, and was intensely disliked by many of his peers in Hong Kong, some of whom were only too ready to recall the occasions on which they had been worsted, slighted or cold-shouldered by an arrogant competitor. As a result, he had too many enemies in and around the Selection Committee to be confident of more than a derisory vote, even in a rigged election where the votes would be carefully distributed to preserve the illusion of a genuine contest. His peers believed either that he was too thick-skinned to appreciate their disaffection for him, or that he was driven, forlornly, by a longstanding and bitter rivalry with the far more influential Tung, the preferred candidate even of those who did not vote for him.

Patten, who had long expected C.H. Tung to win, privately believed that the combination of the shipping tycoon as chief executive and Anson Chan as chief secretary was as near to a 'dream ticket' as Hong Kong could expect. C.H.'s contribution to ExCo's deliberations had left Patten with few doubts about his lack of enthusiasm for democracy or freedom; moreover, the governor felt that, as a deeply conservative and traditional figure, C.H. would find it very difficult to stand up for such issues. Nevertheless he had half hoped that C.H. would be prevailed upon by Beijing to stand for the leadership. As a decent and honest individual, he was more likely than any of his rivals to secure the confidence of the international community without betraying his loyalty to China.

Born in Shanghai in 1937, C.H. was the son of a prosperous merchant. In 1949 the family fled to Hong Kong, where his father built up one of the world's largest shipping fleets, Orient Overseas. C.H. was educated locally and then in Britain at Liverpool University. Later, he worked for General Electric in the United States before returning to Hong Kong to join the family business, which, by 1980, owned a fleet of 150 container ships. Yet by the time of his father's death in 1982, Orient Overseas was facing an acute financial crisis. Despite a deep recession in shipping, exacerbated by the war of attrition between Iran and Iraq, C.H.'s father had ignored all advice to the contrary and continued to expand his fleet. C.H.'s inheritance, therefore, was a growing mountain of debt which, by 1985, had reached US$2.6 billion. On the brink of bankruptcy, he had to placate some 200 bankers, a handful of whom could easily have co-operated to destroy his late father's empire overnight. At a meeting in Tokyo he faced his creditors, taking personal responsibility for his father's errors and promising to repay all his debts if they would stand by him. According to impartial observers, his sincerity and dignity won them over within fifteen minutes.

A consortium of American banks undertook to take on some of his debts, but the decisive factor was a loan of US$120 million from China, a rescue operation co-ordinated by a Hong Kong tycoon and Beijing apologist called Henry Fok. Thanks to China's munificence, Orient Overseas' fortunes were gradually restored until, a decade later, in 1995, the company was able to report a profit of US$60 million. C.H. Tung had much for which to be grateful, and, although no one suggested any malfeasance on his part, it was widely presumed that, as an honourable man, he would not regard his debt to the People's Republic to have been discharged merely by the repayment of the outstanding loan.

As soon as he had received President Jiang Zemin's 'blessing', C.H.'s aptitude for the post of chief executive came under close scrutiny. His tenacity in adversity was noted with approval; likewise his links with the international community and his close acquaintance with luminaries in Washington and New York. No one doubted that he had the capacity to represent Hong Kong with decorum and dignity. The question was whether he would be able or willing to stand up for Hong Kong's 'autonomy';

indeed, whether he even valued the crucial distinctions embodied in the concept of 'one country, two systems'. After much
speculation, amid which C.H. let it be known that he felt he was
too old for the post, and that, in any case, he preferred a quiet
family life to the vicissitudes of public responsibility, he had finally
announced his candidature in September 1996. To the governor's private consternation, he soon made it clear where his
instincts and his loyalties lay.

On 28 October, using terminology that could have been dictated from Beijing, he warned the people of Hong Kong to be
alert to the threat of 'international forces' seeking to use the territory in a campaign to isolate China. He volunteered that it
would not be easy to balance the need to guard against such
external threats with protecting freedom of expression in the
future SAR. Although he promised that the 4 June commemo-
rative activities would still be permitted as long as they were
'peaceful' and 'lawful', he used a series of subsequent public statements to distance himself from Patten's reforms and criticised the
governor obliquely for initiating them without Beijing's prior
approval. Moreover, far from condemning China's decision to
establish a provisional legislature, he made it clear that he thought
the administration should co-operate with the new body, and that
it should be given quasi-legislative responsibilities even before
the handover. In particular he argued that the provisional legislature should draw up a law on 'subversion' in line with Article 23
of the Basic Law, which stipulated: 'The HKSAR shall enact
laws on its own to prohibit any act of treason, secession, sedition,
subversion against the central People's Government.' He did not
say – he did not need to – that, after the handover, this self-same
law might be used to determine whether the Tiananmen Square
commemorations which so offended China would be 'lawful' or
not. Criticising Martin Lee's Democrats for their 'confrontational' stance towards China, he called on them to be more
'constructive' by agreeing to stand for the provisional legislature
rather than attempting to mount a legal challenge to its creation.

No one doubted that he spoke sincerely, an assumption that
made his remarks even more disconcerting. One or two of
Patten's advisers were perplexed. In private, C.H. had often

spoken with admiration of what one of Government House's most assiduous China-watchers described as the 'lobotomocracy' of Singapore and expressed his fear that Hong Kong was losing 'its Chinese values' – 'Whatever they might be,' added one of Patten's aides cynically. From his public pronouncements, it was not clear to Government House whether C.H. hoped to preserve Hong Kong's status quo; whether he would encourage the police to behave differently under Chinese sovereignty, regardless of the law; or, even more alarmingly, whether he would listen obediently to what Beijing might whisper in his ear and order the Hong Kong Police to behave accordingly.

Fears about what Beijing might require of them, and about their own security after the handover, had been rife among members of the police force itself. When Patten had first arrived in Hong Kong, the chief superintendent commanding Wanchai, a commercial district by day and the centre of the colony's nightlife in the small hours, was Dick Lee. Born in 1950, he was one of six children brought up and educated in Hong Kong. After graduating in history from the Chinese University, he joined the Royal Hong Kong Police Force in 1972. Identified as a 'local' with high-flying potential, he rose steadily towards the top via the Metropolitan Police Training School at Hendon on the outskirts of London, a public-administration course at Oxford University and secondment as an instructor to the Police Staff College at Bramshill in Hampshire.

In 1992 Dick Lee had been responsible for two divisions and 700 officers policing a citizenry of just over a million people. His officers confronted the usual catalogue of burglaries and street crime, though on a far smaller scale than in any European city. Apart from routine raids on brothels masquerading as nightclubs, and attempts to penetrate and combat the protection rackets run by the triads, Lee's team concentrated their operational efforts on the surge of firearms, including AK47s and grenades, smuggled across the border with China for armed robberies, and to an even greater extent on the crime syndicates who controlled the booming trade in cars stolen from Hong Kong and ferried in specially modified speedboats to secret destinations on the mainland at a rate, on average, of more than one a day. This illegal trade had reached such a level of sophistication that the triad bosses in southern China had begun to specify precisely the make, model and colour of vehicle required by their clients, many of whom held senior positions in the Communist party. The gangs operated with such speed and precision that it was almost impossible to apprehend them. Once afloat, the Chinese speedboats, travelling at upwards of 40 knots, could easily elude all but the fastest patrol boats.

Dick Lee was an impeccable public servant with the traditional virtues of his profession. In the early days of the governor's conflict with China, he had for the first time begun to focus on the post-handover uncertainties. He had been privately dismayed by the deteriorating morale of the men under his command. A tall man, erect in a neatly pressed uniform, he spoke slowly and with dignity, but without pomposity. The question which was uppermost in every mind, he said, was what would happen to them after 1997.

> Before Chris Patten's proposals, before the argument, we believed that the Chinese side was genuinely supporting the police service in Hong Kong, and that we would continue to receive the same conditions of service, the same salary, the same standard of living that we are getting from the current government. But what we now see is a different side of the Chinese government: they do not want to accept any proposals from the Hong Kong government. They say that if the attitude of the governor remains unchanged they will do things their own way after 1997. So there is uncertainty: what will the Chinese do with the police after 1997?

Some of the officers trained in the traditions of the British police were even more anxious about what the Chinese might expect of them. 'If you look at the policing methods and the legal system in China, it is very, very different from what we have here,' Dick Lee had explained.

> Our fear is that after 1997 we police officers will be directed

to perform in the same way as Chinese police officers do. Say, in a crowd-control situation. What we are doing now is maintaining law and order, but perhaps after 1997 we'll be asked to exercise force on the crowds when that is unnecessary. Put simply, we are afraid that we will be ordered to do things that we don't want to do.

And how would he respond to such an order? In late 1992, Lee had been unequivocal. 'As a professional officer trained in Hong Kong, I have to stand up and say no.' He would refuse to obey orders? 'I would, if I am asked to do things that, in my opinion, are immoral and incorrect.' His answer was given deliberately and without bravado; a line drawn in the sand.

Dick Lee's abilities had led to swift promotion. By 1996, he was a deputy commissioner responsible for security affairs. His viewpoint had changed as well. A study visit to China had reassured him about Beijing's intentions, and now he saw his task as 'enforcing the laws of Hong Kong. Whatever the law says, we carry it out.' Even if the law is unjust? 'If the new government changes the law, then the police have to enforce it.' It was a small shift in attitude, perhaps, but coming from such an eminently reasonable and honourable police officer it was a worrying augury, not least because Dick Lee himself seemed quite unconscious of the implications of his words.

20

'WE ARE NOT SIMPLY LIMP VICTIMS'

The Governor's Authority Begins to Crumble

The dismay caused by Qian Qichen's threats and C.H. Tung's authoritarian utterances was compounded by renewed evidence of China's indifference to international opinion about human rights. The most spectacular example of Beijing's insouciance was the case of Wang Dan, who was charged on 17 October 1996 with 'instigating turmoil' and 'creating public opinions' with the intention of 'overthrowing the state power and socialism'. The main indictment against him – conspiracy to overthrow the government – related to thirty articles the twenty-seven-year-old dissident had written for newspapers in Hong Kong and Taiwan since his release on bail, pending subversion charges, almost four years earlier. If found guilty he would face a minimum sentence of ten-years' imprisonment. Thirteen days later, on 30 October, after a hearing lasting three hours, Wang Dan was sentenced to eleven years in jail. The governor was swift to state that Wang Dan's activities would be regarded as quite legal in Hong Kong. Martin Lee warned: 'What happened to Wang Dan may happen to us after 1997.' His colleague Szeto Wah added: Wang Dan's case shows there is no judicial independence in China. The function of China's judiciary is to attack citizens and to prosecute opponents.' Even Allen Lee, on behalf of the Liberal party, said, 'It's a severe sentence for a young person like Wang Dan,' but he continued, reassuringly, 'We should not be so disappointed, as there is an appeal system in China.' Of the four candidates for the leadership of Hong Kong, the two lawyers declined to comment; Peter Woo advised: 'We should keep a mutual respect and attitude towards China's system, and not intervene,' and C.H. Tung said: 'China has China's law, and Hong Kong has Hong Kong's law; the two laws are different, and I think we should understand this point.' Two weeks later, the Beijing Higher People's Court took ten minutes to uphold the sentence. Wang Dan was refused leave to address the judges. His mother told reporters, 'The verdict was all prepared in advance. It was very unfair.'

In London at the end of October, Patten met both the prime minister and the foreign secretary to discuss the implications of the threats made by the Chinese foreign minister and the arrest of Wang Dan. He argued that these incidents made it an urgent imperative to put the revised Crimes Ordinance (covering sedition, treason, subversion and secession) before the Legislative Council. The governor was well aware that to introduce legislation covering these so-called Basic Law Article 23 offences, which China had already insisted would be for the future government of the SAR to determine, would be likely to cause yet another conflict with Beijing, but he advised the foreign secretary that if he failed to act, 'people would think we'd piked out of trying to complete our work on civil liberties and human rights'.

Not for the first time, Patten found himself up against senior officials in the Foreign Office, who had carefully briefed Malcolm Rifkind against him. The foreign secretary, whom Patten described as a formidable analyst, was in his most forensic mood. 'You do feel as though you've been gone over by George Carman [Britain's most famous libel lawyer] in the witness box . . . a two-hour meeting with a very well-informed Malcolm Rifkind, who's very anxious to find out exactly what one's objectives are, is itself pretty punishing.' But the governor stood his ground, asserting that 'we have to finish the job we have started'. According to Patten, one or two of Rifkind's officials were 'anxious to egg him on to come down against the governor', which made the process even more exhausting. His most difficult moment came when the foreign secretary asked if he could guarantee that the appropriate legislation would be passed by LegCo.

Patten's answer had to be no. He explained that he found himself 'in the usual Hong Kong position, in which some of those who criticise us if we go ahead with the legislation would criticise us on the other flank if we didn't; some of those who press us to go ahead won't actually vote for us if we put it forward'.

Rifkind's officials, led by the head of the Hong Kong Department, Sherard Cowper-Coles, intervened at this point to provide the foreign secretary with a list of names designed to show that Patten was bound to lose the vote in LegCo. The team from Government House speedily demolished Cowper-Coles' argument by demonstrating that his statistics were fundamentally flawed. One of them commented, 'You could see the foreign secretary shift ground at once.' Patten himself confided: 'It has to be said that the foreign secretary – after quite properly quizzing me on every option, on every angle – was prepared to accept my political judgement.' In return, the governor agreed to postpone publication of the bill for a fortnight so that it would not coincide with the visit to London of a group of senior diplomats from Beijing. With that, Patten left the foreign secretary's office, convinced that, as far as Rifkind was concerned, the issue had been settled in his favour.

However, immediately afterwards, Cowper-Coles continued the argument with Patten's advisers, telling them that the matter should not be finally resolved until the next meeting of the Cabinet subcommittee. According to one of those present, the departing Patten overheard this, turned on the official and informed him that the matter was closed. Cowper-Coles, who had a reputation for stubbornness and who, one of Patten's aides reported, was 'pathological' on this issue, evidently detected the menace in the governor's voice and made no further comment.

It was not the end of the matter. Within days Government House received the first in a deluge of telegrams from the Foreign Office, in which, according to Patten, 'Those officials who weren't hugely delighted by the decision which the foreign secretary had come to . . . spent two or three weeks trying to unpick the agreement.' This campaign achieved the desired effect: according to one of the governor's advisers, Rifkind was eventually 'ventriloquised' by Cowper-Coles into reopening the issue as if nothing had been agreed. Patten confirmed that, three weeks after his meeting with Rifkind, 'we fetched up with it looking as though the foreign secretary was going to reverse the decision and to propose that we should spend more time trying to reach an agreement with the Chinese'.

It was quite apparent to the British negotiators in the JLG that no such agreement was in the offing. The Chinese had made it clear in early October that they would oppose any attempt by the British to adapt the relevant Hong Kong legislation, and in early November they indicated that they would not discuss the matter any further. Patten maintained that it was vital to publish the revised bill before the selection of C.H. Tung as chief executive designate – if only to diminish the risk of an open breach with his appointed successor over whether or not he should press ahead with legislation to which Beijing was so resolutely hostile. After a strenuous effort, Patten finally prevailed, and the Crimes (Amendment)(No. 2) Bill 1996 was duly published in the last week of November.

The Chinese had already indicated in 1995 that they would reinstate the six laws relating to the right of assembly and free speech which had been amended to bring them into line with the 1991 Bill of Rights. It was no surprise, therefore, when Beijing reacted adversely to the publication of the new Crimes Bill, which so amended the concept of 'subversion' to ensure that no individual could be convicted of subversive behaviour unless that person's 'intention of overthrowing the government' involved the use of force. It would thus be virtually impossible to use the Crimes Ordinance to prosecute individuals in Hong Kong for the kind of 'dissident' activities for which Wang Dan and many others had been jailed in China. To Patten's surprise, Beijing's response to what the Chinese described as 'further provocation' was unexpectedly imprecise and muted. This did not prevent the hapless British ambassador in Beijing, Sir Len Appleyard, from dispatching an alarmist telegram to London which claimed, yet again, that the Crimes Bill would 'affect co-operation across the board'. One of Patten's advisers dismissed Appleyard's warnings that the 'roof would fall in' and that the bill would be the 'end of civilisation as we know it' as 'cobblers, and demonstrably cobblers'.

The gulf of perspective between the Foreign Office and Government House was growing ever more difficult to bridge. Patten's closest aides admitted that the 'realists' in the Foreign Office, represented by Cowper-Coles, were even more intransigent than the 'sinologists', the most significant of whom had, by now, either retired or been promoted into other departments. Patten himself thought that over the previous few months the 'realists' had 'persuaded themselves that this great big beautiful thing – the Sino–British relationship – is starting to show signs of life again and that it needs more pampering and more encouragement, and that we should avoid argument at all costs . . . That is complete nonsense, but there it is.' He was becoming increasingly concerned about the impact the conflict was likely to have on his senior civil servants in Hong Kong – and especially on Anson Chan. It was all very well for him, he argued, to insist that Britain had a moral responsibility for Hong Kong, 'enshrined in an international treaty' that would last for fifty years after the handover, but what store would Chan and her colleagues set by such rhetoric against the evidence from the Foreign Office? 'I think they must ask themselves the obvious question,' Patten noted. 'If British officials – or some British officials – are like this now, what are they going to be like afterwards?'

On Wednesday 11 December, C.H. Tung was duly anointed as the first chief executive of the Hong Kong special administrative region. The 400 members of the Selection Committee were required to cast their votes in public in an elaborate ritual conducted at the Convention Centre. Mimicking the formalities of Western democracy, Qian Qichen presided over the proceedings as if to give them his seal of approval. In an earlier round, the four leading candidates had been reduced to three: C.H. Tung, Peter Woo and Ti Liang Yang. While they waited for the verdict, a large ballot box was placed in the centre of the floor in front of the Selection Committee and a battery of camera crews and photographers. For the benefit of the press, an official inspected the ballot box, turning it this way and that to show that it was quite empty with all the showmanship of a children's conjurer. Evidently satisfied that the ballot could not be rigged, the organisers gave the instruction for the votes to be cast. One by one Beijing's appointees filed to the dais, smiled for the cameras and deposited their voting slips in the box. At Government House, Patten's officials failed to suppress their mirth at these televised proceedings. Patten himself declined to watch, claiming the pressure of other work.

In an attempt to inject further drama into the occasion, the organisers had rigged up an electronic scoreboard on which the 'results' could be displayed as each vote was counted. The votes were called individually and, digit by digit, the board duly illuminated the scores of the candidates. It was an excruciating process, aggravated by the knowledge that all involved were participating in a humiliating legerdemain. When the verdict was announced – C.H. Tung: 320; Ti Liang Yang: 42; Peter Woo: 36 – there was a polite murmur of applause before the Selection Committee hurried away to go about their normal business. In a chamber now deserted except by the media, the chief executive (designate) read from a prepared statement, expressing his gratitude for the 'highest honour of my life', and his undertaking 'to do my very best to create a better future for Hong Kong'. He also declared: 'Our society has become too politicised in recent years,' and, reiterating a theme of his campaign, urged the people of Hong Kong to 'try their very best to strike a balance between rights and obligations' now that 'we are finally masters in our own house'.

Although Chris Patten was by now far less confident than he had been even a month earlier that C.H. Tung would exercise his authority to protect Hong Kong's freedoms against China, he joined the foreign secretary and other international leaders in offering his congratulations. He made no comment about the 'election' itself, but was careful to remind C.H.:

The community will be looking to the chief executive to provide strong leadership with vision, integrity and determination; to defend Hong Kong's interests . . . and to preserve the cornerstone of Hong Kong's success – the rule of law, a level playing field for business, the protection of individual rights and freedoms in an open and accountable society.

Privately he observed, 'I think it would have been as surprising to the politburo in Peking if C.H. hadn't been elected as it would have been for the Cabinet to discover in June 1992 that I wasn't going to be the next governor of Hong Kong.'

Simultaneously, an equally bizarre 'election' process for the provisional legislature was now reaching its final stage. On 13 December, the presidium of the National People's Congress in Beijing had approved a shortlist of 130 approved candidates from which the sixty-seat 'shadow' legco would be chosen by the Selection Committee. The ubiquitous Qian Qichen announced that he would like to see as many incumbent or former legislators as possible taking their places in the new body. As Martin Lee's Democrats and a number of independents had long since decided to boycott what they regarded as an illegitimate exercise, only thirty-four official LegCo members, including Allen Lee, had put their names forward. Patten was optimistic that at least some of these 'pusillanimous and pathetic' politicians would end up losing all credibility. 'It is not quite so easy for mainland officials to control the way four hundred people vote for sixty candidates as it was to stage-manage the way four hundred behaved over three,' he surmised. But not for the first time, he had allowed himself to underestimate Beijing's corrosive will. On Saturday 21 December, the results of the 'election' were announced. Of the thirty-four 'pathetic' aspirants for 'shadow' power, thirty-three were duly chosen. The remaining twenty-seven seats were taken by a small army of obedient 'patriots', notable among whom were a handful of former legislators like Peggy Lam, Elsie Tu and Tsang Yok Sing – all of whom had been rejected by the voters in 1995. So much for democracy.

Any remnants of optimism Patten still harboured about C.H. Tung quickly evaporated. A week after his appointment, the new chief executive (whose office lost no time in dropping the 'designate' appendage from his official title) hastened to Beijing to be sworn in. Before leaving Hong Kong, he used a press conference to attack the governor, declaring that it was wrong to 'ignore the reality' of the provisional assembly, which, he claimed, would have a useful role to fulfil now that the 'through train' had been derailed by Britain's failure to abide by the Basic Law. Some of

Patten's advisers had hoped that C.H. would use his newly acquired authority to demonstrate his independence from Beijing; instead, he was sounding ever more like his masters' voice. At a reception in the Great Hall of the People in Beijing, the president, Jiang Zemin, echoing the words of Deng Xiaoping almost seventeen years earlier, reassured his guest that he should put his 'mind at ease', because, 'from now on, we shall strictly abide by the Basic Law when handling the issues of Hong Kong. We will definitely not interfere with matters that are within the high degree of autonomy promised for the SAR.' It was a statement which, of course, begged every important question now facing the British colony. C.H. Tung responded by promising his host that he would do his best to contribute to the wellbeing of both the SAR and China.

Precisely what this might mean for Hong Kong after 1997 was unlikely to emerge for some months, but it became increasingly clear that there was small chance of the new chief executive deviating from China's own sense of Hong Kong's priorities. During an eighty-five-minute meeting with the governor on 23 December, he restated his support for the provisional legislature: it was, he said, 'the wish of Hong Kong's entire six million people that we have a smooth transition', and it was therefore very important that there should be 'co-operation' between the Hong Kong government and the 'SAR government'. Patten's press secretary Kerry McGlynn reported bluntly that the pair had 'agreed to disagree'.

On 31 December, the new chief executive had an informal lunch with forty-eight members of the provisional legislature. Congratulating them on their success, he told them that although they would not be called upon to pass any legislation before the handover, they would have an important role in the months ahead. They would sit across the border in Shenzhen and prepare laws that would be enacted as soon as power had been ceded formally by the British, and his office would give them as much administrative support as possible. Soon afterwards he announced the appointment of his Executive Council: as Government House had feared, its balance was tipped heavily in favour of Beijing. Only one of its fifteen members had been heard to speak openly in support of freedom or democracy. The rest, led by the seventy-nine-year-old Sir S.Y. Chung (once staunchly pro-British) had shown themselves to be conspicuously hostile to Patten's reforms. Responding to criticisms that the post-1997 ExCo would be dominated by the anti-Patten business community, Sir S.Y. commented: 'We can only talk about social welfare and civil rights after we have made money.' It was the authentic voice of Hong Kong's elite.

There was worse to come. After a meeting on 17 January 1997, the so-called legal subgroup of the Preparatory Committee published proposals for abolishing or amending the civil-liberties legislation which, under Patten's instructions, had been revised to eliminate from the statute book those colonial measures which infringed the 1991 Bill of Rights. This threat to reimpose controls that would inhibit rights to assembly, free speech and free association sent a shiver of horror down the spine of Hong Kong. Patten described the proposals as 'legal nonsense', and, a few days later, used his monthly question-and-answer session to express his scorn for those present and former members of LegCo and ExCo who had once endorsed the very Bill of Rights which, at China's behest, they now seemed eager to repudiate. Several hundred members of the Democratic party and Emily Lau's new Frontier party picketed the NCNA's office in protest. Even the usually discreet financial secretary, Donald Tsang, felt moved to warn that international investment might flow out of Hong Kong if the rights of free speech and free assembly were withdrawn from its citizens.

Initially, C.H. Tung refused to comment, but on 23 January, at a dinner where he was honoured as 'leader of the year' by one of the territory's most fervently pro-Beijing newspapers, he asserted that the legislation proposed by the Preparatory Committee was indeed 'consistent with the Basic Law'. Later he was besieged by reporters outside the hotel where the dinner was held. In response to their questions, he snapped, 'We will find a way forward.' He paused before adding angrily, 'But it may not be the way you like.' Hong Kong had not heard such harsh words from this apparently mild elder statesman before, and, in the current febrile atmosphere, they set alarm bells ringing. According to a poll conducted by the Hong Kong University, his popularity plummeted overnight by 15 points.

No one was more disconcerted by C.H. Tung's apparent submission to Beijing than Anson Chan. At a breakfast meeting on 28 December, C.H. had asked her to remain in her post after the handover and, after careful thought, she had agreed. Patten knew that she would find it hard to serve two masters, and he was prepared for her to drift away from him in the months ahead, but he had not expected her to be caught quite so early in what she now described publicly as a 'very delicate situation'. Acknowledging her disquiet, she tried to skirt around the clash of loyalties she now faced by refusing to echo Patten's condemnation of the provisional legco. Instead she expressed the hope that the provisional body would not try to legislate in parallel or in competition with the existing, elected legislature. Within days observers had begun to speculate about how long she would manage to straddle the divide. At Government House, where her colleagues viewed her situation with sympathy, one or two people started to wonder whether she would be able to survive as chief secretary after the handover.

The governor's own troubles had been compounded by a visit to Hong Kong by the former foreign secretary Lord Howe at the beginning of January. In a speech at a joint gathering of the British and Australian Chambers of Commerce, he took it upon himself to caution the democrats that 'Hong Kong is not entitled to regard itself – would be very unwise to regard itself – as a bridgehead for revolution within the People's Republic.' Howe's appreciation of Beijing's concerns had recently been enhanced by his appointment as a consultant to the board of Cable and Wireless, which was increasingly active in China. He told his audience: 'Hong Kong cannot and should not expect to transform China. Trying to do so could risk destroying Hong Kong itself.' As one or two of Patten's aides observed, this warning could easily have issued from a spokesman for the Chinese politburo. Warming to his theme, the former foreign secretary urged the local media to exercise caution and restraint in its coverage of China, reassuring them that developments in the SAR and China would be under the careful scrutiny of their colleagues around the world. One or two of Howe's friends believed that the former foreign secretary had himself coveted the governorship of Hong Kong. Certainly he did little to dispel the suspicion that he considered his own ultra-emollient approach to be more suited to the conduct of relations with China than Patten's less equivocal stance.

Martin Lee denounced Howe's comments as 'shameless', adding that the former foreign secretary was simply trying to prove that the 'kowtow' policy of which he had been a principal agent had been correct. Patten himself was frustrated, although he did not realise the depth of Howe's aversion to his stewardship, or that, for the future record, Howe would volunteer the opinion: 'It would have been so much better if Hong Kong had got in place a governor who would have played that crucial part of managing the process of transition right up till the last minute.' Had Patten known of Howe's disdain, it is conceivable that he might have taken the opportunity to repudiate his views; as it was he grumbled in private but kept his counsel.

On 23 January the provisional legislature held its first meeting, electing one of Beijing's most unremitting apologists, Rita Fan, as its president. In his regular *Letter to Hong Kong*, broadcast by RTHK the following day, Patten declared, 'We are not simply limp victims of other people's decisions . . . Those who have agreed to help close down Hong Kong's elected legislature' – the 'honourable members' who had decamped to Shenzhen the previous day – 'can at least prevent the trashing of Hong Kong's civil liberties. Many of them actually voted for our Bill of Rights.' He signed off with a question: 'Is Hong Kong going to have the same freedoms after 1997? Yes or no?' His words were intended as a challenge, but they betrayed his growing despair.

On 29 January the re-elected president of the United States warned China to honour the commitment to 'one country, two systems'. Bill Clinton said that he was not sure Hong Kong could 'exist, with all its potential to help China modernise its own economy and open opportunities for its own people, if the civil liberties of the people are crushed'. C.H. Tung, who was in Beijing for a plenary session of the Preparatory Committee, responded that certain sectors of people around the world were being misled. 'They should spend more time to understand what is going on in Hong Kong.' He was immediately contradicted by the governor, who said that Clinton was concerned because these issues were not 'marginal issues . . . he is not misinformed about what is going on in Hong Kong'.

On 1 February, the Chinese foreign secretary opened the two-day plenum of the Preparatory Committee with the formal announcement that Government House had long feared and Chris Patten had once thought would never be heard. Qian Qichen told his audience that members of the provisional legislature would be free to scrutinise and approve legislation before 30 June, although it would not be enacted until after 1 July. The timing and scope of their work would be based on rulings by the Preparatory Committee and the National People's Congress.

As the 134 members of the Preparatory Committee readied themselves to cast their votes in favour of the 'recommendation' to repeal the civil-rights legislation put in place under Patten's administration, a storm of debate erupted in Hong Kong. Scholars, lawyers and politicians united to denounce the proposal to abolish or amend these crucial safeguards. Even Allen Lee was perturbed. 'I have read the Basic Law again, but I cannot see how it is infringed,' he told the *South China Morning Post*. 'I and my colleagues believe the ordinances have not damaged public order.' Declaring, 'There is no way I will change my view on this subject,' he vowed to oppose any attempt to repeal the Public Order Amendment and Societies Ordinances. On 2 February, 124 members of the Preparatory Committee voted in favour of dismantling the legislation after the handover. Ten members abstained. Only the indomitable Frederick Fung registered his dismay with a 'no' vote. The provisional legislature was thus authorised to act as China's Trojan horse for Hong Kong. Empowered by the National People's Congress to draw up a set of laws to inhibit human rights and civil liberties, they would also be given the task of drafting new legislation on subversion, secession, treason and sedition to replace the Crimes Ordinance which had by now been negotiated through a second reading in LegCo.

Now, somewhat later than he had originally anticipated, the

governor's authority began to crumble. Although he remained astonishingly popular in the community, winning just under 60 per cent support in the most recent polls, his power was ebbing away, and everyone knew it. He had slipped from the centre of attention; increasingly, he became a spectator, if not a spectre, at an unpalatable feast. His hopes for Hong Kong, expressed with undiminished energy and eloquence in speeches and interviews on radio and television, were more frequently at odds with the presumed certainties of his listeners. His words therefore hung in the air, forlorn echoes of what might have been, no longer carrying conviction.

By the beginning of 1997, Hong Kong's psyche seemed to have been gripped by a combination of resignation and suppressed panic. This contradictory mix was expressed most emblematically in popular ambivalence towards Britain. On one hand, it was becoming de rigueur to display a patriotic conviction that Hong Kong's return to the 'motherland' was a matter for unbridled celebration; on the other, any suggestion that the British might not honour their post-handover obligations under the Joint Declaration prompted intense indignation. This latent schizophrenia reached into the upper echelons of Hong Kong and was most evident in relation to the passports issue. Those who had been selected for one of the 50,000 United Kingdom passports granted under the 1990 British Nationality Scheme guarded their secret acquisitions jealously. Hong Kong's sensitivity on this subject was dramatically, if inadvertently, exposed by Britain's senior trade commissioner in Hong Kong, Francis Cornish, who was due to become Britain's first consul general after the handover. Showing reporters around the new British post-1997 consulate – a confident if fortress-like edifice designed by the British architect Terry Farrell – Cornish mentioned that holders of British passports granted under the Nationality Scheme could not be guaranteed consular protection after 1997 as the Chinese had refused to recognise the validity of the passports. As a result, he said, 'you end up with the situation of dual citizenship, dual nationality'.

Cornish's remarks caused an immediate outcry. Every news bulletin in Hong Kong and almost every front-page headline carried his chill warning: 'NO CONSULAR SHIELD FOR UK SCHEME PASSPORTS'; 'BRITAIN BLASTED FOR DENYING PROTECTION'. Politicians and civil servants, many of whom had placed their faith in the future in the protection apparently offered by these passports, rounded on the British authorities, accusing them of bad faith and treachery. 'The British passport,' a senior civil servant complained, 'will become a blank paper with no purpose at all . . . I am supposed to be a real British citizen, so how can Britain treat us differently?' Furious at what he regarded as Cornish's clumsy comments and alarmed by the sudden panic they had triggered, Patten summoned him for an explanation. Cornish was unrepentant. He reminded the governor about the limits of Britain's authority. Regardless of the fact that passports granted under the British Nationality Scheme were full UK passports, there was nothing to stop the Chinese asserting that any individual who held a Hong Kong identity card or an SAR passport would be treated as a Chinese citizen even if he or she were suddenly to produce a BNS passport to prove UK citizenship. As Cornish put it later, 'This group of people, to the Chinese, are Chinese nationals. China doesn't recognise dual nationality. To the British, they are British, and there is a full British passport to prove it.' In these circumstances, Cornish believed it would be virtually impossible for the British consul in Hong Kong (or, indeed, China) to guarantee this group of British citizens the usual degree of protection. In spite of the furore he had caused, he thought he had been right to explain the facts as he saw them.

> This is an excitable place and this is a neuralgic issue . . . but I think it is very important not to give any impression that you can do more than, in the real world, you can – which is not quite the same thing as saying you won't try. What it boils down to is that we are the absolute authority on who is British, but we cannot set ourselves up as any kind of absolute authority on who the Chinese regard as Chinese.

Patten was well aware that what Cornish had said was true, but he blamed the British official for expressing himself in terms which were bound to excite rather than to allay Hong Kong's anxieties.

After a flurry of telephone conversations between Government House and London, he persuaded the foreign secretary to issue a statement in the hope of limiting the damage. Rifkind duly announced: 'We would not regard any claim by the local authorities that a British passport obtained under the local British Nationality Scheme was acceptable evidence of dual nationality.' This attempt at reassurance made little impact. Patten was anxious about the gulf afflicting the colony 'between what people say, the confidence they claim, and the boiling emotions there are under the surface, particularly the nervousness about what life is really going to be like after 1997, whether the communist cadres have really changed their spots or not'. He also feared that the headlines would lead the public to believe that 'this was just the British ratting again: that we'd given these passports, that they were really worthless, that we weren't going to make even modest sacrifices for anybody in Hong Kong'. He was no less concerned that, if Hong Kong's civil servants started to believe that Britain 'would not lift a finger for people after 1997', they would start to wonder what point there was in remaining loyal to Britain and British political values.

In an effort to dispel these fears, Patten took the unusual step of inviting himself to LegCo, where, in what even his critics conceded to be a bravura performance, he insisted that Britain would not discriminate between a UK passport obtained under the BNS scheme or by any other legitimate means. Nor would a British government accept that 'the way in which a British citizen obtained his or her passport would be of itself evidence of dual nationality'. And he promised that even in cases of dual nationality, 'Britain will not stand idly by if British nationals are in trouble'.

He was brought up short, however, by Margaret Ng. She did not question his good faith, but asked for reassurance that the Chinese authorities would have no way of establishing how or where a British passport had been obtained. He answered with care. 'I do not believe that there is any way in which Chinese authorities will know how somebody acquired a British passport.' He then drew attention to what he described as a 'chilling' statement by an NCNA official, who was reported to have told the *Hong Kong Standard* that identified BNS passport-holders would be regarded as Chinese nationals even if they had lived in Britain and returned to Hong Kong as British citizens, and that China would be able to trace such people even though their files were kept by Britain. Patten then asked with barely suppressed fury, 'What is it, what state of mind is it, that brings people to make statements like that when all we are attempting to do is to give people in Hong Kong reassurances about their future, about their future stability and their future freedoms?'

Margaret Ng persisted, asking what had happened to the files containing the details of those who had applied for British passports under the British Nationality Scheme. Patten replied that, as far as he knew, the information was held by the Immigration Department and would be sent back to London through the consulate general before the handover. He added, 'I want to assure everybody in Hong Kong that we do everything humanly possible, technologically possible, to keep the material secure and to keep that material confidential.'

Emily Lau returned to the issue a little later, raising the suspicion that the Chinese government might already have access to the list of people who had been granted BNS passports. Patten retorted sharply:

I don't know how, if one's veracity is suspected, one can put the point more strongly than I am going to do: I know of no evidence, have no evidence, that Chinese officials have lists of those people who are beneficiaries under the British Nationality Scheme. I have no evidence whatsoever of that. I am not surprised, when things like this are said, that people worry. I can understand it – I would worry myself . . . I would not, I hope, even if I was a liar, put the point as explicitly, as comprehensively, as I have just done.

Emily Lau had perhaps touched on the most sensitive aspect of this tortuous and delicate issue. Six months earlier, the director of the Immigration Department, Laurence Leung, had suddenly resigned, on 'personal' grounds. Rumours soon began to spread that he had been forced to hand in his notice, and that the Hong

Kong government, led by Patten, was engaged in a cover-up of Watergate-type proportions of Laurence Leung's activities. One of these whispers had it that the Hong Kong official had managed to acquire the list of BNS passport-holders and had handed it over to Beijing. This story, among others, soon became a subject of open conjecture and rapidly acquired the status of a revealed truth. Patten's attempt to quash the rumours in LegCo was soon to be undermined by Laurence Leung himself.

On 10 January, the former director of immigration had been summoned to LegCo, where a committee had been set up to inquire into the circumstances surrounding his sudden departure. He told the legislators that, far from offering his resignation, he had been forced to resign on the instructions of the governor and the chief secretary. He went on to relate that in 1995 he had been the subject of an official investigation by the Independent Commission Against Corruption (ICAC), which had been unable to establish that he had acquired his wealth by improper means. The government was forced to concede that Laurence Leung had been under sustained investigation, but that the facts which had been uncovered about his activities were not adequate to justify his dismissal. Despite the agitation of a feverish media, the authorities had little more to say, except that, in the circumstances, it had been agreed that Laurence Leung would be allowed to depart from office with his honour, officially, intact.

The integrity of the Immigration Department was also crucial to Britain's efforts to establish the SAR passport as a valid international document which could not be faked. Worried officials from more than one country who were considering whether or not to grant visa-free access to SAR passport-holders now hurried to seek reassurance from the Hong Kong authorities. What if, as a result of lax security or internal corruption, the Chinese had acquired enough information to issue SAR passports illicitly either on the mainland or in any of their embassies around the world? The foreign consulates were particularly concerned about triad gangs or Chinese agents infiltrating their borders. On this question at least they were offered an unequivocal response. Even if any official had in the past enjoyed improper links with the mainland – and there was no evidence of this – the security features of the SAR passport, which had only recently been finalised, were intact: they had no cause for alarm.

The senior British officials most closely connected with immigration were convinced that Patten's uncompromising statement about the integrity of the British passports issued under the BNS scheme was justified. According to one of them, only one person had access to the list of people who had been given BNS passports, and none of this individual's colleagues had ever asked to see the list – which, as it happened, was due to be taken back to London before 1 July by the same official. So the list was safe. In any case, it was common knowledge at Government House that the fears which had led to the aborted investigation into Laurence Leung did not relate to the integrity of the Immigration Department, but to other matters, which – for good reason in an open society replete with libel laws – it was not possible to air publicly.

Patten himself was intensely irritated by what he regarded as the contemptible efforts of over-excited conspiracy theorists in the media who refused to accept his word on the subject. Privately he dismissed them as a 'relatively small group of expatriate journalists', and 'one or two people with axes to grind in the Legislative Council' – individuals who, he complained, 'think that Anson Chan and I are not only telling lies but are political innocents out of the kindergarten'. The issue soon faded from the headlines but the anxieties which it had brought to the surface were not erased.

In all these matters the honour and reputation of Britain was at stake. Patten had given as much reassurance as he could to British passport-holders. After a long battle, he had finally persuaded the home secretary to grant British passports to the war widows and to grant the same rights to those with SAR passports as those enjoyed by holders of BNO passports. As a result, almost every citizen of Hong Kong would have the right to enter the United Kingdom without a visa after 1997. Only the ethnic minorities were still without that security. On his visit to London the previous October he had tried unsuccessfully to persuade the home secretary to relent. In December, he returned to the issue again, reminding Michael Howard that the Labour party had committed itself to offering these soon-to-be stateless British subjects right of abode in Britain with the opportunity to acquire full British citizenship after five years of continuous settlement in the United Kingdom. He pointed out that as a result the government 'would not be in any political difficulties if it took what would be regarded as a generous-minded approach'. As he had expected, Howard was unwilling to give any more ground. Enough had been done already, the home secretary told him, and nothing had changed to warrant a shift by the government. Even though this was a special case, it was not special enough to justify offering British citizenship to more than 5,000 people from the Indian subcontinent who would, he claimed, still retain the right to stay in Hong Kong after 1997. 'I got nowhere,' said Patten after their meeting.

He was not willing to leave it there. 'I think it is inconceivable that we can be in that position come 30 June 1997,' he said flatly just before his last Christmas in Hong Kong. 'I think the story of Britain's departure from Hong Kong will be told at least partly through the experience of four or five thousand South Asians who think they're being abandoned. I think it would be regarded by a lot of people around the world as pretty shameful.' Acknowledging that he personally would also feel ashamed, he admitted, 'I think it will be something of a failure on my part if I don't get a better deal for them.'

'WE ALL KNOW THE END OF THE PLOT'

Wrangling About the Handover

The leaders of the Indian community in Hong Kong now saw that time was rapidly running out for them. The sense of despair in Hari Harilela's household was pervasive and overt. What would happen, one of his family asked, if they were in trouble with the authorities after 1997? 'I don't have a passport. I am in jail. How can the British get me out? What is this "guarantee"? We have no protection. If we have a British passport then we have protection. All China can do then is to say, "OK, we will deport you." As it stands, they can still deport us but we have nowhere to go.' Hari Harilela estimated that a third of his relatives had been granted passports under the BNS scheme; the rest would be stateless. His son was still without a passport. 'He has his PhD from England. He has lived there for thirteen years of his life,' Harilela entreated. 'They have promised me. In September, October, November, December, I call them. They say, "Yes, yes, yes," but so far, nothing. Strange. I don't understand.' As a last resort he went to see the chief secretary, Anson Chan, who was clearly embarrassed. It was not her responsibility, she explained; it was British law, and not in the hands of the governor. Hari Harilela concluded: 'I think the Home Office is behind it. But I don't know why. I just don't understand.'

At the Harilela family's weekly get-together one of his sisters said, 'I am very uncomfortable about what might happen in the next two years. Maybe it will be smooth to start with, but after that . . .' She spoke softly and her voice trailed away. Then she added, 'We've been abandoned.' Another relative explained, 'My father was a British subject. I am second generation. I was born and bred in Hong Kong. You ask what I think? The initial emotion is anger; then the anger subsides, and it becomes sorrow.' A cousin had an even more complicated problem. 'My situation is OK – I have a British passport; my wife has a passport. My daughter has a passport, but my two sons do not. I mean, how are we to stay together if we have to move out of this place?'

'Of course, I understand the "floodgates" argument, that the British can't let everyone in,' said Hari's stateless son in a voice tinged with sarcasm. 'But in the face of statelessness it feels different.' He outlined a depressing potential post-1997 scenario.

> In the case of my parents and myself, we will walk up to Immigration as a family, but they will look at our passports and see that they are different, and then they will question us. 'Are you really a family? Explain, how come you have different passports?' I get a lot of hassle at Heathrow. I have an identity card, I have a student visa, but I don't have a British passport. Or maybe it is because I am not British by race or origin. My parents go straight through . . . We fear being separated in the future. In our culture we live as a family, together, until we are married. We are one family, but the British government does not acknowledge that.

His father interrupted. 'You know, we feel proud because we've grown up in this colony and we have lived with the British. And then all of a sudden, they deny us. That is what hurts.'

His youngest sister added, in a hesitant whisper as if ashamed to utter the thought, 'When the Falklands were invaded, Britain ran down there immediately. And there were just a handful of people stranded. It makes me feel that probably it is because we are not white. That is why we are stranded.'

When Chris Patten heard about these remarks, he said bleakly, 'She is trapped between the explicitly racist nature of Chinese nationality policy and the British Home Office. And precisely how you describe the British Home Office's attitude on these matters, and precisely how you compare it with Chinese nationality law, I leave to you.' And where did that leave Michael Howard? According to the governor, weighing his words with care, 'The home secretary has a political agenda which is different from mine. I think the home secretary believes that he should be seen as a tough home secretary, not just tough on crime, but also tough on the number of immigrants coming into the country.'

Howard's tenacity, however, was matched by Patten's. And the governor had an advantage: he knew that the foreign secretary shared his view, and he was confident that Michael Heseltine could be brought on side. The prime minister had always been sympathetic – he had already told one of his private secretaries that the present position was 'morally untenable' – and although he was not willing to confront Howard at this stage, Patten felt confident that, if it came to a Cabinet showdown, the home secretary would be overruled. Howard clearly thought otherwise; he made it clear to his friends that he would fight until the bitter end to maintain the status quo. According to his critics he even persuaded the chief whip, Alastair Goodlad, one of Patten's close friends, to tell the prime minister that the Tory backbenchers 'wouldn't wear' any further concessions.

On 19 December 1996, Malcolm Rifkind, who believed that this was the last piece of important unfinished business to be resolved, had had a meeting with Howard at the Home Office. He suggested that the home secretary should at least shift to the position already adopted by the Labour party. At first Howard resisted, but under sustained pressure from the foreign secretary he eventually agreed to look at the situation again to see whether there was a case for strengthening the prime minister's March 'guarantee'. He insisted, however, that he would not agree to make any change at all unless it was discussed and agreed by the full Cabinet. Rifkind's officials were pessimistic about the prospects of winning Howard over, but the foreign secretary interpreted his reference to a Cabinet meeting as a concession in itself.

In January, the Foreign Office and Government House joined

forces for a further assault on the Home Office, making it clear
that it would not be good enough 'merely to tinker with the
wording' of the commitment to the ethnic minorities. With the
full backing of the foreign secretary, Patten had another meeting
with Michael Howard at which he challenged the home secretary
directly, asserting that it was specious to claim that the issue had
been resolved by the 1990 Nationalities Bill. At that point, the
exceptional predicament of the ethnic minorities had not even
been identified, let alone debated by Parliament. The ethnic
minorities had been sidelined in 1990, and it was most unfair to
suggest otherwise. At the end of their session, Howard, courteous
as ever, said, 'You've set out the arguments more eloquently than
ever before,' but he made it obvious that he had not changed his
mind. This time, however, the Government House team came
away with the impression – if only from his body language – that
the home secretary was not quite as unmovable as he might have
wished them to believe. They also detected that Howard's officials, who had come under persistent pressure from the Foreign
Office and from Government House, had begun to distance
themselves from their political master. Even his political advisers
now intimated that they thought Howard would be unable to
stand fast.

At this point the home secretary's fortress began rapidly to
crumble. On 30 January, a House of Lords bill to grant full British
passports to Hong Kong's ethnic minorities reached its third reading stage. The bill's author, Lord Willoughby de Broke, who had
campaigned tirelessly for many months, secured the support of
many Conservative peers, two previous governors, Lords
MacLehose and Wilson, and Lord Bramall, a former commander
of the Hong Kong garrison, who accused the government of a
'cruel and heartless' approach. Baroness Blatch, for the Home
Office, tried in vain to defend Howard's position. She emerged
from her drubbing with the words, 'This is an untenable policy' –
a judgement Chris Patten was careful to pass on to the prime
minister at a private lunch a few days later.

Approved by the Lords, the Willoughby de Broke bill went
straight to the Commons, to be introduced there by an elder
statesman of the Tory backbenches, Sir Patrick Cormick. He

told the house: 'This small group of people should be granted the security their loyalty to the crown merits.' It was by now doubtful that the government would be able to hold the line. Four days later, on 3 February, the home secretary, finally recognising how isolated he had become, asked to see the prime minister at 10 Downing Street. 'I've changed my mind,' he told John Major. The next day, in the House of Commons, Howard announced his surrender in a written reply.

> I have carefully reviewed the position of the solely British ethnic minorities in Hong Kong, in the light of expressions of concern in both Houses of Parliament here and in Hong Kong . . . It is clear that the assurances which they have been given over a number of years have not allayed this concern. I therefore intend to make provision enabling them to apply for registration as British citizens, giving them right of abode in the United Kingdom.

Jubilant at Howard's volte-face, Patten said: 'The case has been put with dignity and vigour, and today the right decision has been made.' Privately he added dryly, 'It shows how open-minded the home secretary is.' It was the first piece of good news he had received for many months. It was likely to be the last.

With six months to go before the handover, the Pattens were counting the days. 'Since we all know the end of the plot, the sooner we get to the last page, the better,' the governor commented cryptically. 'I'd now like to get on with the packing and get things over and done with.' In truth there was little left for him to do except to fulfil his official duties, to preside over the mundane task of finalising the details of the handover ceremony and to continue to stand up for the principles which had animated his governorship. The pleasures of Hong Kong had begun to pall many months before, and he looked forward to returning home. In January he and Lavender began to search in earnest for a house in London. Their friends speculated about his future. Would he return by some means to British politics after the general election, which it was presumed the Conservatives would lose? Would he succeed Sir Leon Brittan as European commissioner – a role it was widely thought would be available to him if Tony Blair were to form the next government? Would he be offered a senior posting at the United Nations? Would he accept an invitation to run an Oxford or Cambridge college? Would he take to the lucrative international lecture circuit? Or would he simply bide his time?

Patten had already made up his mind to stay away from Britain for at least six months. His intention was to live at the house he and Lavender had bought in France, at least until the spring of 1998, and to write the first of three planned books about his experiences of Hong Kong and the Far East. In this first book he would lay out his ideas about the success of the Asian economies and its implication for Britain and Europe. In the process he would almost certainly define his reformulated attitudes towards the European Union and Britain's part in it, his scepticism towards the European currency, his enthusiasm for otherwise widening and deepening the union and his conviction that the 'democratic deficit' should be made good through a strengthened European Parliament. By keeping away from Westminster, he hoped to escape the insistent speculation over his political future, about which he was himself entirely uncertain in any case. He had not completely written off a Westminster comeback, although he was not sure either how this might be achieved, or even that he really wanted to return to what seemed to him – in some moods – a tawdry and parochial stage. He certainly had little appetite for conscripting himself into the trenches for what he feared would be a vicious civil war in his party over Europe; nor was he tempted to pick up the clutch of company directorships that would doubtless be available to him on his return. However, at the age of fifty-three, he needed to earn a living and wanted to have a purpose worthy of his talents.

Some observers wondered if the Pattens would find it difficult to wean themselves off the grandeur of their Hong Kong status: the secretaries, chauffeurs, footmen, butlers, cooks, cleaners, gardeners and bodyguards. Would they miss the Rolls-Royce, the yacht, the official mansion and the grace-and-favour country house, and the deference with which, in public at least, they were treated? Would the governor find it hard to adjust to a world in which he did not have automatic access to presidents and premiers? The truth, as their friends knew, was that they would find it a relief to be free of the formalities by which their lives had been bounded for the previous four and a half years. Although Lavender Patten had developed the poise and style of a first lady, she had never allowed herself the indulgence of presuming that this elevation was anything other than accidental and short-lived. She had enjoyed the tennis and the golf and the walks which characterised the days of so many fellow expatriates. She had made friends in the Chinese community, although she was perplexed, if not resentful, when the wives of prominent local figures began to distance themselves from her as the relationship with China deteriorated. As the patron of more than fifty charities, she had attended luncheons, made speeches, and, with evident conviction, visited the sick and the needy. She had emerged from this experience confident but without vainglory.

The governor kept up the momentum of work without the illusion of power. By January his diary was crammed for the following months with routine business and official farewells. During his governorship he had made sixteen overseas trips (excluding his eighteen visits to London on Hong Kong business) and had been granted audiences with one emperor, three presidents and eight prime ministers. There had been innumerable formal speeches, ceremonial functions, district visits, political events; meetings with business and community leaders; charitable, academic, professional and sporting receptions. He had opened exhibitions and other cultural events, and together the Pattens had hosted 320 official dinners, 243 official lunches, and 175 official receptions at Government House, wining and dining for Britain with a dutiful vengeance. More than 500 visiting guests had stayed at Government House, some of them on several occasions – among their number four members of the royal family, Cabinet ministers, politicians, ambassadors, Lady Thatcher, Sir Edward Heath and the archbishop of Canterbury. It had been demanding, stimulating and frequently enjoyable. But neither the governor nor his wife regretted for a moment that it would soon be all over.

The removal men had already been booked. The Chinese chests, sideboards, chairs and tables, antique pots, vases, boxes and sculptures Patten had accumulated in his frequent forays to the shops in Hollywood Road were to be packed and shipped in the spring along with their books and the other modest possessions they had brought with them to Hong Kong. All that would remain on the day of their departure aboard the royal yacht would be a suitcase or two. The future of Government House itself was still uncertain. It seemed unlikely that C.H. Tung would consider it appropriate to take up residence in what, psychologically, would have become be a colonial relic. Some thought the house should become a museum, with its grounds open to the public and available for concerts; others that it could be used as a government guest house in the Chinese tradition. Some suggested pulling it down to make way for a commercial redevelopment. When the governor discussed the options with his successor, C.H. indicated that he was worried about the 'bad *feng shui*' of Government House. Although some years earlier a tree had been planted strategically in the garden to offset the adverse effects of the Bank of China's sharp-edged profile, which pierced the very heart of Government House, the incoming chief executive was evidently concerned about the Japanese tower at the eastern end of the building: the *feng-shui* man had told him that it would need to be redesigned in the shape of a dome and painted gold to create the good *feng shui* without which, C.H. was warned, he would be ill advised to take up residence therein. Patten, a devout Catholic who understood the pull of mysticism, nevertheless found it quite impossible to fathom such superstition. Although Betty Tung, Hong Kong's future first lady, had indicated to Lavender that she relished the prospect of inheriting Government House, she had intimated that her husband was strongly against the proposal. At the end of May, C.H. Tung confirmed that they would not be moving in when the Pattens left.

Whatever became of Government House, there was no question that Britain's colonial footprints would soon disappear from this most unsentimental of societies. Symbolically, the Royal Hong Kong Golf Club, the Royal Hong Kong Jockey Club and the Royal Society for the Prevention of Cruelty for Animals

(HK) had already discarded their emblematic relationship with the crown. In May 1996 the Royal Hong Kong Yacht Club voted narrowly to retain their link. Nevertheless, in early 1997 members decided to ask the Chinese president, Jiang Zemin, to replace the Queen as their patron and C.H. Tung to take over from the governor as vice-patron. It was doubtful, however, whether either would accept while the colonial stain remained on the crested notepaper. The 'Royal' was also due to be removed from the Royal Observatory, and, inevitably, from the Royal Hong Kong Police Force. In common with fourteen other public services, the police were to replace the crown on their insignia with a representation of the five-petalled bauhinia flower after 1997. But the stylised view of the Hong Kong waterfront which was to succeed the nineteenth-century trading schooners at the centre of the police badge had been carefully designed to exclude the headquarters of Jardine Matheson, Jardine House, one of the colony's most prominent waterside landmarks. The head of public relations for the Royal Hong Kong Police said, 'It's our badge, so we can do what we want with it.' He did not mention that the final design had required the approval of the new chief executive and the Chinese authorities. On Jardine's behalf, an emollient Martin Barrow retorted, 'Neither I nor anybody else is overreacting. We are here to stay. If anybody chooses to do anything of this sort, then fine, but I don't think one can read too much into it.' Traditionalists, sentimentalists and historians were relieved that there were no plans to erase British links with scores of streets, roads and drives, or Victoria Park and the Prince of Wales building on the waterfront in Central.

In February, a firm in the Chinese city of Guangzhou completed the first batch of 1,200 Chinese national and Hong Kong SAR flags ordered by the colony's pro-Beijing Federation of Education Workers. All were snapped up at once by schools throughout the colony, who were uncertain which of the two flags they would be required to fly after 1 July. The handover logo (featured on a selection of forty souvenirs), a smiling pink dolphin designed to highlight the threat to this endangered species, found itself in the troubled waters of cultural misunderstanding. The deal between an American company, CYRK, and the

'Association for the Celebration of Reunification of Hong Kong and China' gave CYRK a monopoly of official memorabilia. However, one of the colony's leading fashion designers, Mickey Li Honming, criticised the graphic and the colours selected by the Americans.

The pink dolphin could usefully have served as a symbol of the way in which the future of Hong Kong continued to thwart efforts by Foreign Office officials to 'warm up' the relationship with China. Politicians and diplomats on both sides continued to smile and shake hands for the cameras, but still they could find no common ground on democracy or human rights. As the handover approached, the language of diplomacy grew sterner. In Singapore for a joint meeting of ASEAN and European Union foreign ministers, Malcolm Rifkind had yet another fruitless conversation with Qian Qichen, the last scheduled under the current regime. Afterwards, the British foreign minister conceded that it would be naive and unrealistic to expect the Chinese to reverse their policy towards the provisional legislative council or human rights in Hong Kong. Some days earlier, in a characteristically quixotic gesture, Beijing announced that the Hong Kong journalist Xi Yang, sentenced to twelve years in prison in 1993 for 'stealing state secrets', was to be released. The crass cynicism of this arbitrary show of lenience did little to soothe the ever-deepening anxiety about the future of human rights in Hong Kong. Likewise, the promulgation of a directive instructing China's journalists how to report the world about them – which explicitly reminded them of their duty to 'promote patriotism, collectivism and socialism' and enjoined them to 'uphold the truth in news' – sent another chill wind through those parts of the media which had not yet succumbed to the inevitable. A few days later, a spokesman for the Hong Kong and Macau Affairs Office in Beijing gave a briefing for Hong Kong reporters to remind them that there was 'no such thing as absolute rights and freedoms'.

The feeling that Britain was on the back foot in Hong Kong was compounded when the *South China Morning Post* gave prominence to Singapore's senior minister Lee Kuan Yew's optimistic assessment of the territory's future. Echoing the thoughts expressed earlier by Lord Howe, the architect of Asia's model state (who was greatly admired by Hong Kong's future chief executive), Lee Kuan Yew wrote:

> Hong Kong looks set to prosper for many more years, provided its people mind Hong Kong's business, and do not meddle in China's politics. Hong Kong's people have to make up their minds whether they want to prosper under 'one country, two systems', or to engage China on human rights and democracy as the Hong Kong 'democrats' have been doing, encouraged by American human-rights groups, the US media and by Governor Chris Patten and his policies. No human-rights and democracy hero can reverse the inevitable – that over time Hong Kong will become more of a Chinese city, if nothing else than by osmosis.

Such sentiments could as easily have been expressed by C.H. Tung or by a host of other luminaries, including the chairman of the Hongkong and Shanghai Bank, Sir William Purves; almost any member of the Chinese or British Chambers of Commerce in Hong Kong; a significant proportion of the British Foreign Office; the British ambassador to Beijing, Sir Len Appleyard; two former governors, Lords MacLehose and Wilson; Sir Percy Cradock and a sprinkling of superannuated Cabinet ministers, led by Lords Howe, Prior and Young. This knowledge aggrieved and offended Britain's last governor almost more than anything else.

In Europe on a month-long tour, Martin Lee continued to pursue his case for genuine autonomy, warning Beijing not to 'meddle' in Hong Kong's affairs. C.H. Tung retaliated by castigating Martin Lee for 'bad-mouthing' Hong Kong overseas, declaring angrily that he had 'blackened the reputation of Hong Kong . . . giving the impression that Hong Kong is collapsing'. One of Martin Lee's colleagues, Dr Yeung Sum, responded sarcastically, accusing the future chief executive of being a 'megaphone for China' and adding, 'I want to ask Mr Tung whether, from now on, people who intend to make visits abroad have to seek his permission. I think Mr Tung is more interested in policing what people say both inside and outside Hong

Kong . . . than [in] trying to reflect people's anxieties.'

The gulf between the chief executive and the leader of the most widely supported political party in Hong Kong was proving ominously difficult to bridge. By the day it became clearer that C.H. Tung was fiercely committed to the authoritarian assumptions of Beijing. 'We should sit down and talk about our family matters in our home . . . Do we have to ask foreigners to tell us what to do? Why can't we decide our own fate and future?' he said in the course of an attack on Martin Lee for an article denouncing China in the *Asian Wall Street Journal*. The question on the minds of commentators was whether Martin Lee would be allowed to play any public role in Hong Kong after the handover, given that his 'patriotism' was already under such hostile scrutiny. The pro-Beijing *Wen Wei Po* remarked approvingly that C.H. Tung wanted to make the point that 'Hong Kong people should respect their own race and respect the dignity of the SAR government when he says that people should love the country and love Hong Kong'.

It seemed increasingly likely that the Democratic party would be obstructed after the handover. Not content with reintroducing the most repressive clauses of the Societies Ordinance and the Public Order Ordinance, Beijing now indicated through the Preparatory Committee that the provisional legislature would be invited to reinstate the system of appointments to the Municipal Councils and District Boards which, under Patten's reforms, had been replaced by elections. The prospect that Beijing was bound to vet such appointments exacerbated fears that the authorities in China would leave no aspect of Hong Kong's political life alone. There were even deeper anxieties. Margaret Ng was not alone in suggesting that C.H. Tung would use his executive authority to exclude the Democrats from any future electoral process that China might put in place for Hong Kong. Her reasoning was precise and chilling: to allow the Democratic party to compete in elections once China's proposed restrictions on political freedom and dissent had been put in place would be to hand Martin Lee a landslide victory on a silver platter – an outcome which both C.H. Tung and Beijing would find unacceptable.

The most effective way of achieving the exclusion of Lee and his cohorts, Ng argued, would be to reinstitute the kind of 'loyalty test' that China had apparently been willing to discard seven years earlier. The future chief executive had already asserted on more than one occasion that public figures should be seen to 'love Hong Kong, love China and uphold the Basic Law'. It would not be difficult, Ng predicted, to revive the subjective concept of love as a test of any candidate's willingness to 'uphold' the Basic Law and his or her 'allegiance' to the Hong Kong SAR, as required by the 1990 decision of the National People's Congress. Writing in the *South China Morning Post*, she commented:

> Once 'love' is revived, vetting by some kind of nomination committee is the next easy step, and it would not matter how many people have the vote, or how many voters want to vote for democrats – democrats will never even be allowed to stand as candidates. However, once this path is chosen, there will be nothing left of the credibility of Mr Tung's government at home or abroad.

Perhaps Margaret Ng was overly pessimistic, but no one was confident enough to mock her grim scenario.

In an interview with the *Australian* on 6 March, Chris Patten forecast that even if Martin Lee was not outlawed by any 'loyalty' test, the Democrats would be sidelined in any future election by the introduction of proportional representation for LegCo's twenty directly elected seats, in which they had almost swept the board in 1995. 'I'll tell you what will happen,' he prophesied gloomily. 'The Chinese officials will propose, for example, that instead of having twenty single-member constituencies, we should have ten two-member constituencies – thus, at a stroke, halving the number of Democrats who can get elected . . . That is what will happen, I can tell you now. Watch this space.' If so, instead of winning at least seventeen of these seats, the Democrats would be confined to ten at most. Patten was proved right. By restoring the gerrymandered character of the other forty seats in LegCo, Beijing, acting through the provisional legco, could easily ensure that Martin Lee and his allies would become an impotent rump in any future official LegCo.

As the provisional legislature began to flex its muscles in Shenzhen, across the increasingly nominal border with Hong Kong, doubts about the future independence of the judiciary began to surface once again. Under the Basic Law, the Legislative Council was required to endorse the appointment to and removal of judges from the Court of Final Appeal. So, on 11 February, Rita Fan, the president of the provisional legislature, suggested that she and her colleagues should be given responsibility for vetting candidates for these senior posts. A fellow member of the provisional legislature, Ambrose Lau Hon Chuen, the influential leader of the Hong Kong Progressive Alliance, was enthusiastic. Using as yardsticks 'personal integrity' and 'professional standing', his colleagues should, he said, be free to 'nosy around' to familiarise themselves with the judges under consideration for the Court of Final Appeal. Members should, if they so wished, have 'some direct access to the individual, but not in the form of a hearing – I would prefer a private meeting', he told the *South China Morning Post*. The DAB leader, Tsang Yok Sing, was more cautious. His party did not yet have a policy, he said, but he would not wish the provisional legco merely to rubber-stamp appointments to the Court of Final Appeal.

Once again Margaret Ng was the first of her colleagues to denounce this prospect as unacceptable, while Raymond Wacks, professor of law at Hong Kong University, warned that any such proposal would 'strike at the core of our system'. The vice-chairman of the Bar Council, Lawrence Lok Ying Kam, argued that the role of the provisional legislature should be severely circumscribed. 'Why should a body that is not fully recognised as lawful be given the power to veto judges?' he asked. His question went unanswered as the conviction grew that the provisional legislature would not only curtail the community's human rights but impose on it, at the highest level, a biddable, if not suborned, judiciary. Even the *South China Morning Post*, which had recently demonstrated a growing commitment to 'patriotism', was moved to comment anxiously: 'Of all the issues surrounding the handover, few are more crucial than the independence of the judiciary.' Pointing out that the judiciary was facing far-reaching change, not least in the matter of finding fifteen lawyers of equal talent and inclination to fill the places left by those retiring or leaving before 1 July, an editorial warned of the danger of nominated judges being cross-examined about their views on the Bill of Rights or the legitimacy of the legislature. 'If the independence of the judiciary is compromised, the common law system will face serious damage . . . In these times when everything is coming under the microscope, Hong Kong needs to have the fullest assurance that the rule of law is being maintained by a free and unfettered judiciary.' No such assurance was forthcoming.

Britain's foreign secretary arrived in Hong Kong from Singapore on 15 February 1997 on his second, and last, visit to the colony. Asked whether he thought that C.H. Tung was a puppet of Beijing, he responded ambivalently. The future chief executive, Malcolm Rifkind noted, had been very emphatic that he was not under the direction of the Chinese government. Nonetheless the foreign secretary appreciated the unease in Hong Kong generated by the fact that C.H. Tung's 'opinions on some very controversial matters have been very similar to the views of the Chinese government'. While he praised the governor for showing 'huge courage and conviction' in standing up for Hong Kong at times and in places where others had been reluctant to do so, Rifkind was unable to conceal the fact that Britain had lost the argument with Beijing over the provisional legco and human rights. When pressed about the impotence of the British government he became tetchy. A headline in the *South China Morning Post* on 17 February, 'RIFKIND CONCEDES DEFEAT', which prefaced a report on an uncomfortable session with the handful of LegCo members who bothered to turn up for a meeting with him at Government House, provoked him to an uncharacteristic display of public discourtesy. The newspaper 'should be ashamed of itself', Rifkind said dismissively on the *Hong Kong Today* programme, going on to tell his mild-mannered interviewer to stop asking such 'stupid questions' about the future: of course Her Majesty's government would not walk away from its responsibilities to Hong Kong after the handover. Patten thought that the foreign secretary had given an impressive performance, but Rifkind's assertive demeanour left a poor impression on a jittery colony. This mood was aggravated by his premature departure for

London to vote in a Commons debate about Britain's BSE crisis in which the government's majority of one was under threat. 'Britain may be anxious to leave Hong Kong "with honour",' the *South China Sunday Post* commented sourly, 'but its words now sound so hollow that one understands why some politicians here accuse London of simply playing games in the last months of its rule.' The headline over this editorial reflected a widespread resentment: 'WHEN MAD COWS MATTER MORE THAN HONG KONG'.

22

'HONG KONG CAN'T BE
LOBOTOMISED'

Patten Runs Out of Time

In the last few months of British rule a note of self-justifying cynicism could be heard in Hong Kong. It was as if Britain's failure to secure the eternal verities of Western liberalism in perpetuity for its last significant colony might serve as a convenient excuse for those in the civil service, the media, the law and business who had already resolved to adapt to future diktats from Beijing without a murmur. It had become unfashionable to express any nostalgia for the departing power, or to allow any sense of regret to seep into public discourse. Yet not everyone was indifferent or hostile to the recent history of the colonial authorities. On 14 December 1996, Captain Albert Lam, one of the last 'local' officers in the British Army to be demobilised, was on duty at the disbandment parade of the Hong Kong Military Service Corps on Stonecutter's Island, where the Royal Navy still maintained three patrol craft to fly the flag and to combat smuggling.

Captain Lam's father had been a soldier, and although he had himself originally trained as a tailor, a better-paid trade, he had soon followed his father into the ranks. He had now been a soldier for twenty-four years. 'Today,' he said quietly, 'I am very, very sad.' He watched as the column of men filed on to the parade ground – mechanics, carpenters, dog-handlers, chefs and chauffeurs, for whom square-bashing was not a regular routine – marching with precision under the proud gaze of families with clicking cameras. The Band of the Royal Hong Kong Police strutted back and forth playing those military airs which bring a lump to patriotic throats. The Union Jack hung limply from a flagpole, stirred occasionally by an idle breeze. Sergeant-majors bellowed. In charge was a brigadier, dressed in tropical kit, his sword vertical in his right hand. The parade fell silent. After a few moments the governor arrived with his wife in the back of the colonial Rolls–Royce. A retired colonel in the VIPs' stand muttered tetchily, 'He could at least have worn his uniform and his hat. It's not right.' Women and children waved as Patten approached the dais, took the last salute and then inspected each detachment, stopping frequently to show that he cared. An army chaplain said prayers in English and a Buddhist monk chanted from the holy writ. The regimental flag was carried solemnly to a table in front of the troops, furled carefully for the last time and then blessed. There was a dragon dance, the band played 'The Last Post' and the Hong Kong Military Service Corps passed from existence into memory.

Afterwards, there was a buffet lunch in the outdoor shooting range which was soon to be handed over to the People's Liberation Army. Hamburgers sizzled on a charcoal griddle, wafting smoke through the assembled multitude of retired comrades, heavily laden with medals, who reminisced over pints of beer. The wives stood in clusters together as home-counties officers and squaddies from Newcastle, separated by rank but not by emotion, exchanged awkward condolences. Captain Lam spoke of his pride and sorrow. 'The parade was really impressive, but now we go our own ways. And, sadly, we may not see one another again. I have been British for a long time.' Each local regiment had been allocated British passports by quota. 'We have done quite well – one in six.' Which meant than five out of six did not receive British passports? 'That's right.' And did that matter? Captain Lam was hesitant, apologetic. 'If you ask me – because we really served the British army, we served the Queen, we gave everything to the Queen when we joined the service – I think everybody should have a passport.' It was not a subject on which he wished to dwell.

This was Captain Lam's second disbandment parade. In September 1995, he had also been on duty at the closing ceremony for the Royal Hong Regiment, the volunteers, founded in 1854. In the battle for Hong Kong against the Japanese in 1941, 10 per cent of the regiment had been killed or reported missing in action. 'I actually saw people in tears at the last parade. When the men marched by for the last time, one of our honorary colonels, who is now in his seventies, could not stop crying. And loudly. And I absolutely understand his feelings. I think, today as well, everyone has the same feeling.' Captain Lam paused as his own tears welled up. 'I have had a long service in the army, and I have never regretted joining the British army,' he continued after a moment. 'But unfortunately I can't serve any longer. I have a terrible pain inside.' He pointed to his heart and the tears flowed freely.

The commander, British Forces, Major-General Bryan Dutton, preferred to look on the bright side. However, like Albert Lam, he was troubled by Britain's failure to pay its debt of honour to those members of the Hong Kong Military Service Corps who had been denied British citizenship.

> They are loyal, hard-working and amazingly gentle and courteous. They will need to find another job, another life, in a situation which will be very different for them. We have set them up as well as we could. There is generous financial provision; we are generous with retraining. We are setting up an ex-servicemen's association with the British Legion, I hope with a clubhouse. Yet, at the end, we've been rather mean-spirited in not giving them unequivocally a passport in recognition of their service. I think that is a great shame.

The general was responsible for the final stage of the run-down of British forces in Hong Kong. Appointed commander in July 1994, when the British garrison numbered almost 10,000 personnel, he had 'drawn down' 5,000 military personnel by the end of 1995. Two years later, the garrison had a symbolic complement of fewer than 2,500 men and women from the three services, all of whom would have to depart before midnight on 30 June. At the twenty-ninth meeting of the Joint Liaison Group in June

1994, immediately after Chris Patten had secured a one-vote victory in LegCo for his electoral reform package, the two sides had agreed the terms under which fourteen military sites – the 'defence lands' – would be handed over to the Chinese authorities in 1997. Since then the British had evacuated most of these bases, and by early 1997, aside from the garrison headquarters in the Prince of Wales Barracks in Central, they maintained a skeletal presence on Stonecutter's Island, in Kowloon and at Kai Tak Airport only.

The prospect of their replacement by 10,000 men of the People's Liberation Army was not calculated to enthuse the citizens of Hong Kong. General Dutton, a bluff soldier with an eye for public relations and a uniform which had started to bulge at the seams, had had the task of introducing his successor, Major-General Liu Zhenwu, to his forthcoming command. The Chinese general made two visits to the British colony in 1996 to visit all the 'defence lands' he was about to inherit. He was briefed on all aspects of the garrison's responsibilities; everything, according to General Dutton, 'from how we live, how we feed the troops, how we train, how we liaise with the police, how we interface with the law – the list is endless. We covered every facet of life for a garrison of 10,000 men.'

It had been obvious to Dutton and his colleagues that the Chinese team had no experience of any similar operation, but that they were keen to make it work. At one point one of them asked for clarification about the garrison's padre, whom they evidently equated with a PLA commissar. 'They wanted to know what control he had over me,' Dutton recalled a few days later. The general was anxious for it to be known that while the two armies were 'very different', he did not wish to make any criticism of the PLA. He explained:

> We are a small, regular, highly professional force, volunteers . . . We are used to being deployed to carry out quasi-diplomatic missions as much as straightforward military commissions . . . They are a conscript force of three million. They have been living in Chinese garrison towns in central China, doing things the Chinese way with very

heavy Communist party control. Their conscripts are pressed men. They are paid as conscripts. They live in very harsh conditions compared with us. The whole ethos of the two forces is totally different.

It will be a totally new world for General Liu's soldiers. For instance, his privates are paid enough to buy one beer a month in Wanchai – forty yuan . . . They will have a hard life here, only allowed out on controlled visits, for sporting occasions or cultural trips, usually in organised groups. But it is very important that they do establish contact with the community. One of the greatest dangers to the future would be to have a PLA garrison here which was isolated from the community, from the realities of life here.

Dutton reported that General Liu was likeable and responsive. According to the British commander, when he explained that it was of great concern to the people of Hong Kong that the PLA should not be above the law, General Liu and his colleagues responded eagerly. 'We understand that,' they told Dutton. 'We want to use Hong Kong as a window on the world.'

'You've heard of Tiananmen?' General Liu asked the British commander. 'We want to leave that image of the PLA behind us. We want to use Hong Kong as a means of rehabilitating the world's image of the PLA and show them that we are now a mature, modern armed force.' For a Chinese general to share such a confidence – when, according to the official version of the events of 4 June 1989, the PLA, insofar as it had been involved at all, had operated with restraint merely to assist in the maintenance of law and order – was a remarkable lapse of military discretion. Dutton was encouraged. However, it would not be easy for the PLA to adapt. 'The law in China is an instrument of government and is not about the rights of individuals,' he said. 'Military personnel are only liable to the military law. They are not liable to civil law at all.' For the benefit of his Chinese counterparts, Dutton had identified a variety of legal predicaments they might face in Hong Kong: 'What would happen when a Chinese military truck with a drunken driver knocks over a Chinese granny in Wanchai at a pedestrian crossing and kills her? Could he be breathalysed? Could he go to jail? Which court would he go to? Could he be arrested? Whom do the family sue for compensation? Which court do they sue in?' General Dutton had more questions than General Liu had answers.

The rapport between the two generals was not reflected in the negotiations between their respective governments on the role of the PLA before the handover. With less than 100 days to go, the two sides were still wrangling in the JLG over the number of PLA troops to be deployed in Hong Kong before the transfer of sovereignty, the date of their arrival, and whether they should enjoy diplomatic immunity or be allowed to carry weapons. The British argued that a small advance guard of unarmed PLA troops would be quite sufficient to meet China's needs; Beijing countered that at least 250 troops should be deployed, and that they should be free to cross the border without inspection. The British side realised that the Chinese team was coming under growing pressure from the PLA, which had originally demanded a presence in Hong Kong from January.

By mid-March 1997 Patten had authorised his negotiators to turn up the heat on the Chinese by linking any agreement on the PLA troops to another issue on which Beijing's JLG negotiators had long been stalling, even though there was no real disagreement between the two sides: the right of abode. Although all Hong Kong Chinese resident in the territory knew that they would continue to enjoy right of abode after the handover, the JLG negotiators had refused to finalise an agreement on the status of either foreigners resident in Hong Kong, or the million or more Hong Kong citizens who had emigrated to America, Canada, Australia and elsewhere. From the British standpoint, these emigrés retained their right of abode in Hong Kong, but the Chinese had refused to confirm this formally. This apparent impasse was the cause of significant public anxiety. Would they all be required to return to the territory before 1 July to qualify? And would the children of Hong Kong residents away at school in Britain and elsewhere also have to come back before the handover? The Chinese had been procrastinating with the evident objective of preventing the administration from putting the agreed legislation before the Legislative Council for approval.

The ulterior motive was not hard to fathom: if the legislation had to be in place before 1 July, and if, as the Chinese maintained, it could not be enacted by the British, then as far as they were concerned any agreement between Britain and China should be put before the provisional legislature. As one of Patten's team complained wearily in mid-March, it was 'transparently an attempt to create an argument for the provisional legislature to exist at all'.

In an effort to reach a compromise the British now suggested that the two sides should announce that they had reached an understanding on the key issues, and that appropriate legislation would be enacted formally after 1 July. If they had a written agreement on the substance, issued by the JLG, which could then be sent to the four corners of the earth, that would be fine. The Chinese response to this proposal came from Lu Ping, who told the British ambassador that Beijing would agree, but only if the British were willing to concede that it should at least be endorsed by the provisional legislature, on 1 June, a month before the handover. To the irritation of Government House, Sir Len Appleyard appeared to believe that Lu Ping's suggestion constituted a step forward. From Patten's perspective, it offered nothing of the kind. To concede Lu Ping's case would be tantamount to recognising the provisional legislature, the legality of which, Patten had already suggested, was a matter for determination by the International Court of Justice in the Hague (even though he did not think it worthwhile to seek a judgement there, not least because a settlement of the question would require the co-operation of the People's Republic). One of the governor's team commented: 'I don't want to be unfair to Appleyard and suggest that he is deliberately working against us. He just isn't quite on track.'

Although it was a tactic which they had themselves frequently deployed in the past, Beijing's negotiators affected to be furious at Britain's decision to contrive a link between agreement over the PLA's role and status in Hong Kong before the handover and the resolution of the right-of-abode issue. One of their number castigated the leader of the British side, Alan Paul: 'The man who thought that this was a good idea should know that he is in danger of torpedoing the "dignified" handover.'

Meanwhile, the man in question was locked in yet another bout of internal diplomacy with the Foreign Office, this time over the handover itself. The head of the Hong Kong Department, Sherard Cowper-Coles, had been charged with the task of drawing up the list of those who should be invited to join the Prince of Wales and the foreign secretary in the official British party at the handover ceremony. When the draft list was sent to Government House for approval, Patten was astonished to discover that the name of Sir Percy Cradock had been included. An explanation from Cowper-Coles, to the effect that Sir Percy had not only been the architect of Sino–British relations for more than a decade, but for some of that time Her Majesty's ambassador in Beijing, failed to placate the governor. He was particularly irritated that, clumsily if unwittingly, the Foreign Office official had placed him in the demeaning position of having to either allow Cradock to join the official party or exercise his gubernatorial veto, which was bound to be interpreted by Cradock's acolytes as pique on his part.

He could not understand why Cowper-Coles seemed so insensitive to the message that Cradock's presence at the top table would send to Beijing. Giving the Chinese the opportunity to fête a bitter foe of British policy so blatantly was bound to encourage them in the hope that, once the troublesome governor was out of the way, appeasement would once more be in the offing: that the hegemony of the diplomats would be restored; that the British did not intend to be unduly officious in their role as guardians of the Joint Declaration; and that a transgression by Beijing in Hong Kong would not be permitted to ruffle the restoration of good relations with the leaders of the People's Republic.

As it happened, Patten was spared further embarrassment. One of his aides proposed a neat diplomatic manoeuvre which would exclude Cradock without denying the former diplomat the chance to attend the historic occasion: instead of inviting all former ambassadors to join the Prince of Wales, he suggested, why not rule that only the present incumbent, Sir Len Appleyard, and his immediate predecessor, Sir Robin McLaren, should be among the official party? Cradock, along with a clutch of other diplomats and ministers of state, could be invited instead to join the much larger group 'accompanying' the official party. As guests of the British government at the farewell parade, the banquet and the handover ceremony, this group would be observers, not participants. They would also be required to pay for their own travel and accommodation. In the event, Cradock declined to attend.

Fortuitously for Cowper-Coles, Patten had not yet read Cradock's most recent onslaught on his 'incompetent' handling of the relationship with China. Had he done so, he would have had even greater cause to be aggrieved by the official's proposal. In an article for the April 1997 edition of the influential monthly magazine *Prospect*, Cradock cast aside all restraint. In characteristically precise but waspish prose, he charged Patten with taking 'at best a wild gamble with the future of over six million people' who had been encouraged by him to have 'unreal expectations' about the future and would now be left to 'face the consequences of a confrontation they never wanted'. Noting proudly that until 1992, British policy towards China had been guided by officials, and that recommendations by sinologists in the Foreign Office and Number 10 were usually accepted by ministers, Cradock observed disparagingly that thereafter, 'politics was in command. Officials were told to stand back.' Rehearsing his familiar argument in favour of 'co-operation', he accused the governor of abusing his role for his own selfish political ends. 'As a rising politician, he had his name to make. A tough rearguard action, without glory, was not an attractive option. He made instant democracy his slogan.'

It was the naivety as much as the venom of this allegation that lent credence to the view long held by Patten's allies in Hong Kong and at Westminster that Cradock was obsessed with the urge to wipe the stain of 'appeasement' from his own reputation, and that this had thoroughly distorted, if not unhinged, the judgement of this eminent diplomat.

A side-effect of the diplomatic hostilities for which Cradock blamed Patten was that the Chinese government dragged their heels over agreeing the international guest list for the handover. As late as March, embarrassed British officials were confiding to their counterparts in other capitals why it was not yet possible for

London to issue formal invitations to attend the ceremony. The foreign secretary personally contacted his peers to ask them to ring the date in their diaries for what both sides had agreed eighteen months earlier should be a 'solemn and dignified' occasion. A spokesman for Malcolm Rifkind was quoted as saying: 'It's not yet at the stage of an international incident, but we do want to get things moving. No one wants it to be a hasty affair, after all.'

This ludicrous diplomatic impasse was rivalled in Hong Kong itself by a local wrangle over a concert by Elton John planned for the run-up to the handover. A group of urban councillors exercised their powers to stipulate that the singer should be seen but not heard. They declared that the 40,000 fans expected to attend the performance should be required to listen to the music through individual headsets so that local people would not be disturbed by any untoward noise. The concert promoter pronounced the idea 'tragic' and an editorial in the *South China Morning Post* tried to mock the local worthies into reconsidering their proposal, suggesting that to ensure the success of the scheme, fans should also be issued with gags and gloves in case they felt tempted to sing along to the music on their headsets or clap to the rhythm. It was to no avail. When news of the edict reached Elton John, he decided to cancel his appearance. It was both a severe disappointment to the governor personally and a microcosmic illustration of his waning authority. In the hope of having the councillors' decision reversed, Government House hurriedly canvassed members of the Legislative Council, only to discover that none of them was prepared to rally to the support of either Patten or the singer. Kerry McGlynn said morosely: 'It didn't look as though we would get a single vote. It's very surprising and very sad. We thought an Elton John concert at that particular time would have been quite an event. It will be difficult to explain to the rest of the world.' In truth, the rest of the world was indifferent. Britain might have retained the vestiges of power, the symbols of constitutional authority, but the focus of attention was now almost exclusively on the incoming rulers.

Virtually every element of the prospective SAR was now in place. C.H. Tung had selected his new Executive Council, and the provisional legislature was already at work debating the 'reform' of Hong Kong's Bill of Rights and the proposed amendments to the territory's civil-rights legislation. The budget for 1997–8 had been agreed between the two sovereign powers, and, despite earlier threats to the contrary, the heads of the main civil-service departments had been reassured that they, at least, would be free to travel on the 'through train' from 30 June to 1 July. On the surface Hong Kong was calm. The exodus, either of people or capital, which Patten had once feared had not taken place, or not yet, anyway. The stock exchange was steady and the property boom was reaching new heights. On the surface the overwhelming majority of the population appeared to have come to terms with the inevitable.

In March the authors of the Hong Kong Transition Project, the most reliable statistical analysis of public opinion in the territory, published their most recent findings, based on a detailed study of a randomly selected 'focus group' of more than 500 respondents. The project's researchers, who had monitored shifts in public opinion from soon after Patten's arrival, produced an illuminating explanation for the apparent insouciance of the community during the intractable stand-off between Britain and China. On the face of it, optimists about the future outnumbered pessimists by ten to one, but when the researchers distinguished between economic and political optimism, the results differed dramatically.

While 60 per cent of the sample claimed to be optimistic about Hong Kong's economic future, only 40 per cent had a similar degree of political optimism. In this context, exactly half the respondents expressed anxiety about personal freedoms after 1997. The same number feared for the political stability of Hong Kong, and a higher proportion of the entire sample were more concerned about these two issues than any other. Intriguingly, a third of the sample, given the hypothetical choice, said that they would prefer Hong Kong to remain a British colony or to become independent (perhaps as a member of the commonwealth) than to be absorbed into the People's Republic. For the first time since the survey was initiated, however, a clear majority (62 per cent) expressed a preference for Chinese sovereignty over any other alternative. An overwhelming proportion (90 per cent, the highest figure ever recorded) declared that they were content with their lives under British rule, while Patten continued to enjoy the support of over 60 per cent of respondents, as opposed to 52 per cent for his successor, C.H. Tung. The authors concluded:

> As the sun sets on British administration in Hong Kong, many aspects of life under [British] rule seem suffused with a 'golden haze'. The burden remains, rightly or wrongly, on the Chinese government and SAR government to establish their own competence and good faith in maintaining a way of life and opportunity that the vast majority of the Hong Kong people support. On 1 July 1997 the transition does not end; the most difficult aspects of transition actually begin.

At Government House, the unease about that transition was palpable. The principal focus of anxiety was C.H. Tung himself. Patten did not directly criticise his successor in public, but for the post-handover record he conceded that he was dismayed by the chief executive's performance in the three months since his appointment. 'I think the charitable view is that Mr Tung has to deal with bombs rather casually left around by Chinese policy. Others would argue that he seems to share and endorse some of the Chinese views on democratic development and civil liberties. Time will tell whether his view of Hong Kong is right, or whether my view of Hong Kong is right.'

The chief executive's impatience with journalists was evident in the abruptness and ineptitude with which he handled awkward questions at press conferences. The contrast with the performances of the governor, who could be fierce and direct or oblique and obfuscatory as the situation demanded, was starkly apparent. If C.H. Tung was grateful to Patten for elevating this means of communication to the forefront of Hong Kong's public life, he showed little sign of benefiting from it. He rapidly developed an aversion to foreign correspondents. Those seeking interviews with him were required by his office to provide examples of their previous work on China or Hong Kong. They were also required to submit in writing a list of the questions that they wished to ask. More than one correspondent was reminded of the pre-censorship demanded by insecure dictators in third-world countries. It was a retrograde step, and a worrying indication of C.H. Tung's insensitivity to international opinion.

Hong Kong seemed increasingly benumbed. On 10 March, the Chinese foreign minister informed the Chinese People's Congress that a revision of Hong Kong's textbooks would be required after the handover. In the jargon favoured by communist apparatchiks, he advised his audience that the 'contents of some textbooks currently used in Hong Kong do not accord with history or reality, contradict the spirit of "one country, two systems" and the Basic Law, and must be revised.' The governor was quick to confute Qian Qichen. 'The Joint Declaration and the Basic Law are clear that educational policies are to be set by the post-handover government, and not to be vetted for political correctness,' he said. 'In a free society, teachers are not told what facts they can teach and what facts it is politically wrong for them to teach.' At a press conference the following day, C.H. Tung stood firm. 'Obviously textbooks need to be rewritten, especially those relating to the colonial past,' he declared. Asked whether the events of June 1989 would have to be rewritten too, he avoided the question, merely commenting, 'You may be interested to read what is written about the Opium Wars.' When a Hong Kong government official had suggested a year earlier that some textbooks might have to be rewritten, there had been an outcry in the press. It was a measure of the altered times that now the media scarcely bothered to report this exchange, except in the margins.

At the same press conference, a foreign correspondent asked the new chief executive whether he had ever said no to Beijing. Clearly angered, C.H. Tung pointed at his interrogator and said, 'Let me ask you, during the hundred and fifty years of British rule, have you ever seen a British governor talking back to the prime minister so openly?' Patten was outraged. Not only was C.H. Tung apparently content to underwrite China's decision to remove the protection of law promised to Hong Kong under international covenants; not only was he 'setting up a Mickey

Mouse legislature'; but now he seemed willing to rewrite Hong Kong's history as a defence against journalists' questions about his attitude to Beijing. 'Nobody has ever suggested for one moment that we don't make our own decisions here in Hong Kong – of course, with the authority of the Foreign Office and the foreign secretary and the prime minister – but nobody thinks of me or my administration as a sort of transmission mechanism for decisions made in London,' he said.

C.H. Tung's appointment of Elsie Leung as secretary of justice (designate) did not reassure the sceptics. Although she was considered a kind-hearted lawyer, and had a reputation for protecting the interests of the elderly and impecunious, her loyalty to Beijing as a representative of Hong Kong in the National People's Congress sent a ripple of anxiety through the legal profession. Within days of her appointment, she delivered her first public statement of significance, volunteering that after the handover it would be illegal to shout slogans like 'Down with Li Peng'. In an evident misunderstanding of the Crimes Ordinance, she justified her stance by claiming, incorrectly, that chants such as 'Down with the Queen' were already prohibited in Hong Kong under the British common law. This bizarre intervention embarrassed some of Beijing's allies in Hong Kong. The editor of *Ta Kung Pao*, Tsang Yok Sing's brother Tsang Tak Sing, attempted to soothe his journalistic colleagues by saying he thought it most unlikely that the prospective secretary for justice would in reality press charges against a newspaper 'just for being critical' of the Chinese authorities or the SAR government. 'I doubt if anyone will be arrested for saying "Down with Li Peng".'

In view of the warnings already given by Qian Qichen, Lu Ping and C.H. Tung – who was careful not to contradict Elsie Leung – Tsang Tak Sing's assurances did not carry great weight. It was not so much the specific threat to freedom that alarmed human-rights activists as the repressive attitudes Elsie Leung's statement appeared to reflect. In private, the governor wondered, 'How can you try to inflict on this incredibly sophisticated city those sort of attitudes through the statute book? What is it going to lead to? Hong Kong can't be lobotomised.'

Once again Margaret Ng was the first commentator to identify with precision this new threat to Hong Kong's legal autonomy. 'If Beijing insists on asserting its own ways of thinking, Ms Leung will soon find herself the wrecker of the law to which she has dedicated all her life,' she declared.

'I think that people tend to underestimate the extent to which Hong Kong people value their freedoms,' one of Patten's advisers disclosed, looking ahead to the possibility of serious confrontation after the handover, and even on the day itself.

> If they have a law on 1 July which requires people to seek permission to demonstrate at forty-eight hours' notice, then people are going to disobey that, because they will definitely want to demonstrate on 1 July, with six thousand press and forty foreign ministers and Li Peng and whoever else is there . . . So they will deliberately test the law. And then the police have to decide whether they arrest people . . . The police will have the task of enforcing it and beginning a completely new relationship between themselves and the community. It will be a new method of policing, a new situation in which the police commissioner has no discretion as to how far to go or how literally to interpret the law.

The same danger was likely to arise in the case of the ban on flying the Taiwanese flag. Under the existing law the police were free to exercise discretion, and did so by refusing to countenance any attempt to hoist the nationalist symbol on any public building while ignoring those which fluttered all year round in villages where loyalty to the nationalist cause remained strong. Government House wondered whether this flexibility would survive the handover; if not, trouble was inevitable.

The apprehension of Patten and his advisers was sharpened by C.H. Tung's treatment of Anson Chan. Despite their deep divisions on other issues, the community was of one mind about the chief secretary: she was Hong Kong's lynchpin, the guarantor that the civil service would remain genuinely autonomous and incorruptible, that the administration would be efficient and dispassionate, and therefore that the high standards of public life would prevail against any incursion from the mainland. For this reason, C.H. Tung had been widely applauded for persuading the governor's appointee to stay in her post after the handover. It may be that a nervous community invested too much faith in the potential of a single individual, but the prospect that Chan would remain at the apex of the SAR administration was a source of undisguised relief.

Government House was therefore perturbed when Chan intimated privately that her relationship with C.H. Tung was in serious difficulty. Her senior colleagues knew her to be resilient and discreet, and consequently the fact that she felt obliged even to hint that C.H. appeared unwilling to consult her on any issue of substance immediately alarmed Patten's senior advisers. Anson Chan had known C.H. for many years, and it had been widely supposed that the two partners on the erstwhile 'dream ticket' would easily develop the professional rapport without which a working relationship cannot prosper. The mutual regard between Chris Patten and Anson Chan had been a critical factor during the transition: the two met frequently and informally; they spoke on the phone on a daily basis; and, as Patten had freely acknowledged, he would never have made a significant decision without the support of his chief secretary. Now Chan found herself excluded from Tung's inner counsels, her advice ignored. In the early weeks of 1997, she had taken the view that he was still adjusting to his new role and had not yet discovered the crucial importance of identifying priorities and devloping strategies in close consultation with the head of the civil service. She was patient, if frustrated and anxious.

By March the formal meetings between the two of them had become even more cursory, the telephone conversations inconsequential. As one of her friends put it, 'Most of what he says or decides, she reads about in the papers first.' Tung's manner towards her, though courteous, tended increasingly to the Olympian and sometimes bordered on the peremptory. Instead of reading and digesting the papers she put before him, he appeared instead to spend most of his time either glad-handing senior Chinese officials at the NCNA or closeted with his personal advisers. These 'self-appointed misfits', as a member of Patten's team described the clique which now surrounded C.H., seemed to have acquired an extraordinary degree of influence. Of these, Nellie Fong, who was credited by some with the attributes of a latterday Mata Hari, and Paul Yip, a shadowy individual around whose past activities rumour clung with fetid persistence, were the two most prominent acolytes. Both were known to have exceptionally close links with Beijing and to be fervently antipathetic to Britain. It was no secret in the civil service that Anson Chan regarded their talents with distaste. The fact that C.H. Tung had clasped them to his bosom was dispiriting but illuminating.

Drawn ineluctably to the conclusion that she was being side-lined by these parvenus, the fears of the chief secretary – not for own future, about which she had long been quite sanguine, but for that of Hong Kong – began to coalesce. In public there was always a smile on her face; behind the scenes, her friends soon realised that the doughtiest and most able woman in Hong Kong was under intense strain. 'She thought it was going to be a part-nership, but she is one item in his weekly diary,' one of her colleagues revealed of her relationship with Tung. 'I think she is beginning to wonder whether she really knows the man, whether she really has known him over all these years. I don't think she can put it right. The question is whether she is prepared to carry on at all – and that still hangs in the balance. She is in a terrible state.'

On 11 March, Anson Chan agreed to be interviewed by the BBC. Probed gently by their correspondent, James Miles, about some of C.H. Tung's inauspicious public comments and the diffi-culties they might pose for their relationship, she suddenly snapped. Cutting off the interview, she leaped up, saying, 'You are impugn-ing my integrity!' and stalked from the room. The BBC team assumed that this sudden petulance sprang merely from the streak of irritable authoritarianism with which her relationship with the media had long been afflicted. They did not appreciate quite how painfully they had brushed the exposed nerve-endings of a deeply unhappy chief secretary. Patten was appalled when he heard later what had happened. Knowing that she was bound to face much more of the same in the run-up to the handover, and conceivably beyond, he was concerned that a repetition of that outburst would inevitably expose the fragility of the most important professional relationship in Hong Kong. If it became known that Hong Kong's 'dream ticket' was not beating with one heart, it could do untold damage to confidence, both locally and internationally.

It was also rumoured in the Hong Kong establishment that the days of the financial secretary, the widely respected Donald Tsang, were numbered; that – apparently at the behest of Lu Ping, who could not abide Hong Kong's second most senior civil servant – he would be ditched by Tung soon after the handover in favour of a more malleable candidate. This was bad enough. The thought that Anson Chan might also depart prematurely was inconceivable. Her dilemma was neatly summed up by a senior British official. 'It would be a catastrophe if she went now, but it would also be a recognition of a catastrophe to come. If things are so bad that she gives up, then she couldn't actually keep things on track for very long by staying. She'd simply be providing cover.' In any event, the odds that Chan would remain in office for long after the handover had shortened dramatically. 'If you want my bet,' said one of her colleagues, 'I think she'll be living in Pinner by the end of the year.'

Government House strove assiduously to disguise this situation, but it tempted some expatriate analysts towards an extremely gloomy prognosis. They foresaw that C.H. Tung would become the unwitting victim of a Chinese pincer movement in which the concept of 'one country, two systems' would lose all significance, except as a slogan. The NCNA would still be in place as the unofficial representative of the Chinese Communist party, exerting ever greater control. In addition, the headquarters of the new Ministry of Foreign Affairs Liaison Office was already near completion on the hillside looking down over the British Consulate, and would soon be occupied by a staff of perhaps 300 Chinese officials under the direction of the senior diplomat Jiang Enzhu. Both institutions would become alternative, if rival, centres of power, and C.H. Tung's only way of containing their influence would be to preserve his own channels to the very top layer of authority in Beijing. 'If he allows himself to be dragged down into the Chinese bureaucracy,' said one British official, 'if he is docking with China at the same level as Jiang Enzhu and whoever replaces Zhou Nan at the NCNA, then both of them will have him for breakfast, because they know their way around the system.' (As it turned out, Jiang would follow Zhou, to be himself replaced by former ambassador to Britain Ma Yuzhen.)

At Government House, Patten's feelings were mixed. He was delighted to be close to the end of his mission but increasingly worried about the 'rotten international press' to which Hong Kong had been subjected since the appointment of C.H. Tung.

> I think events in the last couple of months have made people seriously question whether Hong Kong is really going to enjoy its autonomy after 1997. All the rhetoric seems to have been about one country, and there doesn't seem to have been much about two systems. And I think there are worries about the way China and the SAR government will handle the whole range of political issues after 1997, which if mishandled, could go badly wrong . . . At the moment Peking seems to be getting its own way in Hong Kong.

British officials were dispatched to America to attempt to shore up support in the media and in Congress, where a growing number of Republican representatives were agitating for the chance to use the situation in Hong Kong against China. Their message was that reports of Hong Kong's death were premature. As long as Anson Chan and Donald Tsang were still in place, they maintained, the game was still worth playing. They urged the Americans:

> Don't use Hong Kong as a stick with which to bash China. Keep boosting your bilateral relationship with Hong Kong. Keep the focus on Hong Kong. Deal with the people here as international partners. Then you bolster their morale and their determination to keep operating as they do now. In the process you will also raise the political threshold for China. The moment you start to treat Hong Kong as part of China, then China is more likely to treat Hong Kong as part of China.

One of these emissaries, who was far more pessimistic about the future than he had revealed to his American audiences, said, 'I can just about square my conscience with that theme.' Patten tried to spread a similar gospel. 'Frankly, there is not much reassurance I can give about the future. I find myself giving endless interviews in which I'm asked what I think is going to happen in Hong Kong, and I find myself repeating, parrot-like, the same formula. So I shall be pleased when it is the end of June.'

Deng Xiaoping's death at the age of ninety-two had been so long foretold that the announcement of the event itself, in February 1997, was almost an anticlimax. The eulogies that poured forth from official scribes in the Chinese capital, written months or conceivably years earlier, reminded the Chinese people of the remarkable achievements of the last significant survivor of Mao's Long March. A close confidant of the 'great helmsman', he had been at Mao's side throughout the first tumultuous years of communist rule. He had been purged in the frenzy of the Cultural Revolution, and 'rehabilitated' in time to be purged again by the 'gang of four' in 1976. He had re-emerged to take power as Mao's successor in 1980. Restoring a semblance of order to a chaotic society, he began to lead China away from the ortho-doxies of state ownership and collectivism towards the free market. The public was encouraged to regard individual salvation in the form of personal wealth as a desirable objective. Extolling his extraordinary achievements as a great reformer, the official media in Beijing contrived to ignore the events of 4 June 1989. Nor did they make any reference to the repressive structure of political control over which Deng, and those who now jostled to succeed him, had presided with evident equanimity.

In Beijing the official mourning lasted for twelve days. In Hong Kong, the governor felt bound by convention to join the throng who attended the offices of the NCNA to pay their respects. Like them, Patten bowed his head three times before a black-bordered photograph of the man to whom he had once referred sardonically as 'one of the great immortals'. Deng's demise had no immediate impact in either China or Hong Kong. The caretaker administration of Li Peng had been in day-to-day control of the People's Republic for at least three years. Beijing's ritual denunciations of Patten and his works had certainly not been crafted by Deng himself, although it was rumoured that he had occasionally murmured in the ear of his daughter, who had long been the only link between the 'paramount leader' and the mortals who interpreted his will. It was the future that worried Hong Kong. Which faction would emerge from the inevitable struggle for power to succeed him? Would a 'modernist' or a 'traditionalist' triumph? Would the contest be peaceful, or, as in the past, accompanied by bloodletting and repression? And would the consequences, whatever they were, spill over into Hong Kong?

No outsider could penetrate the secret society of oligarchs who ran China. Rumours, based on conjecture for which there was no evidence, held sway: Jiang Zemin had enough backing from the military to consolidate his power base as president; Jiang Zemin, an ineffectual and backward-looking figure, would be removed. The stolid but crafty Li Peng would take the helm; Li Peng would be ousted. While no one, perhaps least of all the candidates themselves, could predict the outcome, it was generally assumed that momentous changes were afoot and that the mists would clear at or around the Party Congress in October 1977. In the meantime, Hong Kong had other worries.

Although it seemed insensitive to make the point, Deng's death had at least lifted one uncertainty about the handover. Until then, it had been widely presumed that a cortege would bear the ailing leader from Beijing to Hong Kong, allowing him to 'reclaim' the stolen territory in person on behalf of the People's Republic. If the citizens of Hong Kong grieved that fate had intervened to prevent this symbolic démarche, they managed to contain their emotion.

Aside from the continuing wrangle over the international guest list, the preparations for the day of departure were now in place. The choreography of Britain's valediction was in the hands of a production company reporting directly to the governor. Patten knew what he wanted: 'We will have a ceremony at dusk with bands and colour and light and spectacle at which we will say farewell, but I hope in a way which indicates that we are not just sugaring off and leaving Hong Kong to its own devices.' There was still a minor wrinkle in the plans for a squadron of Harrier jump jets to hover in final salute over the royal yacht, *HMS Britannia*, which was to be moored alongside the parade ground in front of the Convention Centre. The presence of a British air-craft carrier in Hong Kong's waters might be interpreted by China as a provocation, but without such a vessel, the Harriers could not fly. Eventually, the navy suggested that the ship could be stationed outside but just close enough to China's territorial waters to allow the Harriers to complete the round trip to Hong Kong. The diplomatic question was when to advise Beijing of the plan: to give no warning might easily provoke the Chinese mili-tary to scramble their own warplanes to 'intercept' the unknown intruders; to give too much notice might well lead to an incon-clusive contretemps with Beijing about whether the presence of the Harriers was conducive to good diplomatic relations. It was, Government House allowed wryly, a delicate matter of judge-ment which would require careful finessing.

After this ceremony – with or without the Harriers – there was to be a gigantic firework display of the kind at which Asia excels. Then the British party, led by the Prince of Wales and the new prime minister, Tony Blair, was to file into the Convention Centre for a banquet for some 4,000 guests. (Blair had rejected Patten's advice, given even-handedly to John Major and himself before the general election, against attending in person.) Just before midnight, under the eyes of a watching world, the British flag would be lowered for the last time and the SAR flag would be raised in its place. It would be a confusingly emotional moment: tears of nostalgia and regret would mingle with genuine feelings of liberation and hope. A footnote in the history of the world, the ceremony would be a defining moment in the story of the twentieth century. Careful to contain his own mixed feelings, Patten liked to describe his vision of the closing moments of Britain's colonial rule with calculated schadenfreude: 'Bands will play, and the Prince of Wales and the governor and family – minus dogs – will get on *Britannia* and sail off down the harbour.'

EPILOGUE

I n the final weeks before the handover, Hong Kong was shrouded in fatalism. The absence of any 'end-of-empire' elation about the future was matched by a lack of sentimentality about the past. By now every argument had been played out. As if numbed by what had become a ritualistic conflict over freedom and democracy, the citizens of what was about to become an SAR of the People's Republic of China awaited the transfer of power with stoicism: the optimists clung to their faith that Beijing would tread with care, while the pessimists prepared for the worst.

The portents were not encouraging. Late in April C.H. Tung published a set of proposals for 'public consultation' which were designed to curtail precisely those freedoms his apologists in Hong Kong liked to believe the new chief executive would seek to protect. Under a variety of proposed amendments to the Societies and Public Order ordinances, it would be forbidden to form any organisation without first registering it with the police, and permission to proceed could be withheld 'in the interests of national security'. Political groups would not be able to accept funding from abroad, and, for the sake of 'public order', no demonstration of more than thirty people would be permitted in the absence of a formal 'notice of no objection' from the police at least seven days in advance.

These proposals provoked an angry reaction from a wide cross-section of the community, led by Government House. Evidently taken aback, the chief executive retreated. At the end of a three-week consultation period, on 15 May 1997, C.H. Tung's office released a statement modifying the proposals: political organisations would, after all, be able to accept donations from abroad, but only from individuals, not from 'foreign forces'; and, although the police would retain extensive powers to ban public gatherings, it would not be necessary for protesters to secure a 'notice of no objection' before staging a demonstration. Nevertheless, the chief executive would retain the authority to curtail a wide range of freedoms 'in the interests of national security'.

C.H. Tung invited the community to accept that he had thereby struck a 'proper balance between civil liberties and social order'. He had indeed shown that he was not entirely deaf to public opinion but the emphasis – and the drift – of Beijing's legislative priorities was depressingly obvious. As if a further illustration of this were needed, the provisional legislature chose this moment to publish the text of a bill which would make it a criminal offence to 'defile' the new SAR flag. From 1 July, any individual found guilty of this crime would be subject to a fine of $HK50,000.

C.H. Tung's subservience to Beijing's diktat did not go unnoticed abroad. In the early spring, the chief executive had made plans for a visit to the United States, where he hoped to meet Bill Clinton and leading members of Congress. However, his advisers soon realised that he would be given an extremely critical reception. Nor were they at all sure that he would be able to handle the hostility of the American media. In May, rather than risk a public-relations fiasco, they quietly cancelled the visit on the grounds that the chief executive was too busy in the run-up to the handover.

In a symbolic rebuke to C.H., on 4 June, some 60,000 people attended the vigil on the eighth anniversary of the massacre in Beijing. The new chief executive, who had persistently warned against the threat of subversion against China, had urged Hong Kong to 'put the baggage of Tiananmen behind you'. In the centre of the demonstrators, who carried candles in memory of the dead, was a huge stone statue, the Pillar of Shame. A large sign lit up the sky with the words: 'Fight to the End'. The question in everybody's mind was whether the commemoration of this anniversary would be permitted in 1998.

In the last few weeks of his governorship, Patten was once again in conflict with London and, for first time in five years, found himself on the losing side. His position was weakened by the outcome of the general election – not so much because Robin Cook replaced Malcolm Rifkind at the Foreign Office, but because officials there seized the moment to advise their new masters, without reference to Government House, on some of the most sensitive issues relating to Hong Kong. This sleight of hand resurrected all Patten's fears about Britain's likely attitude towards its former colony after the handover.

His anxiety was sharpened when Government House discovered that the new foreign secretary had been advised that it would be an act of statesmanship for him to meet key members of the provisional LegCo for lunch a couple of days before the handover. Patten was furious. At his behest, Britain had all but condemned China's 'rubber-stamp' creation as a violation of the Joint Declaration. He had refused to have any formal contact with its members or to co-operate with its work in any way. And now, as if to subvert his position, the Foreign Office was seeking to ensnare Cook into appeasing Beijing at precisely the moment when Hong Kong needed to know that the British government intended to stand up for freedom and democracy in the future. Patten contacted Cook's office to express his concern. The new foreign secretary took the point at once and the proposed lunch never took place. Although Patten won that argument, it was soon to seem a Pyrrhic victory.

On 9 May, the Chinese informed Sir Len Appleyard, the British ambassador in Beijing, that they wished to deploy 3,000 PLA troops in Hong Kong on the day before the handover and of their intention to dispatch them in armoured personnel-carriers. Patten's immediate reaction was to reject the proposal out of hand. Anson Chan and Donald Tsang took the same view. All three of them were appalled, therefore, to learn that the message from the Foreign Office was 'Let's negotiate.' Reminding the Foreign Office that China already had an advance party of PLA soldiers in Hong Kong, and that 'this boulder has been tossed into the water at the very last moment', Patten argued against accommodating such an intimidating gesture. 'If we simply roll over it will send a pretty bad signal,' he reasoned. The Hong Kong people would not be disconcerted, but they would judge Britain's promises to support Hong Kong after the handover as so many empty words. He also thought that 'quite apart from the outrage itself', it would be the worst possible way for the new relationship between the government of Hong Kong and Beijing to begin.

A few days later, at a marathon session of the JLG, the Chinese harangued Hugh Davies, the leader of the British side, in the most offensive terms they had yet used. According to his colleagues, Davies held his ground with dignity and aplomb. The insults gave way to threats. If the British refused to yield, he was told, the government of the People's Republic would have to consider 'other measures'. In the ugliest display of apparent anger that any of those present had yet endured, the Chinese made it clear that the PLA would be instructed to cross the border whatever stance Britain took. The reason why the Chinese negotiators were so agitated soon emerged. Intelligence sources indicated that President Jiang Zemin himself was the instigator of the proposed démarche in what seemed like a bid to shore up his credibility with the generals. Patten's advisers were inclined to discount the threat of invasion; not even the Chinese, they argued, would display such crude indifference to local and world opinion on the eve of Hong Kong's return to the 'motherland'. Patten, meanwhile, accepted that the Chinese might disrupt the handover ceremony.

But Patten's inclination to reject China's demand out of hand was overruled when the new foreign secretary instructed the British to attempt a negotiated solution. Patten is swift to say that he does not 'for a moment' think either Tony Blair or Robin Cook believed they could 'simply discount Hong Kong's interests because of the importance of building a wider relationship with China'. However, he thought Cook had been badly advised and that his decision was a mistake. Patten's concern was the pervasive inclination among officials to 'slip away into the night from human-rights resolutions, cosy up with lots of "bilaterals" and allegedly – though there is no basis in fact for this – win boodles of business as a result'.

As it happened, the intensive round of negotiations that followed Cook's decision produced an agreement which, Patten conceded, was 'far better than it might have been, although it was a pretty rum last round of cards to have to play'. The Chinese were persuaded to reduce the size of their 'invasion' force to a maximum of 500 soldiers, who would arrive in trucks and not in APCs. If this was a triumph of diplomacy, Patten's team was unimpressed: 'It was,' said one of them, 'an act of prostration.' The governor merely observed: 'I think if you say no at the outset and then say, "Well, maybe yes, a bit," it perhaps sends the wrong messages about future negotiating.'

According to Patten's advisers, Foreign Office officials had argued that the concessions granted by Britain would induce a more conciliatory and sensitive attitude in Beijing. Patten retorted: 'None of us should kid ourselves that doing a deal like this with the Chinese will alter one iota how they arrive after midnight. The PLA will do exactly what it wants.' He was right. On the eve of the handover, Beijing announced that a further 4,000 PLA troops would be deployed in Hong Kong at dawn the next morning and that they would cross the border in four armoured columns, led by the APCs. Confidence in the new Labour government's readiness to stand up for Hong Kong was immediately put to the test when Patten heard reports that, on the plane out to Hong Kong for the handover ceremony, the prime minister's press secretary had briefed the press to the effect that with the departure of the last governor, Britain could look forward to a much warmer relationship with China. Moreover, he was told that the foreign secretary himself had expressed to journalists the view that Patten had been wrong to voice his outrage at Beijing's decision to send in such a massive force on the very day that sovereignty over Hong Kong was restored to China. In what seemed like a last public plea on behalf of the former colony, Patten said: 'I'm absolutely convinced that ministers are wholly sincere in what they say about Hong Kong being the most important part of their relationship with China . . . What I very much hope is that the experiences we've had and the points we have proved won't simply be forgotten, that the waters won't just close over the last five years within nanoseconds of our departure.'

It was in an atmosphere of uncertainty and foreboding that Hong Kong prepared for the arrival of 4,000 dignitaries and even larger numbers of the world's media to witness Britain's departure from Hong Kong. As the Pattens packed their remaining personal belongings and prepared to leave Government House for the last time, they drew comfort from the genuine friendships each of them had formed and from the goodwill, or perhaps the absence of ill will, of the community.

Certainly the Ng family bore the governor no ill will. Their prospects had changed little. Mr Ng still worked for the refuse company, but he had been promoted to foreman. The family's income had risen a little above the level of inflation, but he and his wife were still concerned about employment and the future stability of Hong Kong. Like so many ordinary citizens of the future SAR, the Ngs did not wish to say more than 'Life will go on.' It was, they believed, wise to speak cautiously.

The schoolgirl Norris Lam who had organised the school trip to China to exchange views about democracy was now twenty-one years old. A graduate of the Chinese University, she had studied for a year in the United States, where she considered her fellow students inclined to idleness. As an 'outstanding student' of her generation, she had not only met the governor (an encounter which confirmed her first impression that he was a 'real star'), but had also become a 'youth representative' on a government task force chaired by the chief secretary, Anson Chan. In the spring of 1997, Norris joined the Hongkong and Shanghai Bank at the start of what all who knew her presumed would be a high-flying career. She remained an optimist about China. 'Yes, we have differences. Maybe we want to go faster towards democracy and they want to go slower. But we share the same culture.' If Hong Kong lost its freedoms, then she would leave and start again somewhere else. But that, she was confident, would not happen.

Grace Wu, the antiques-dealer, was less sanguine. Although she did not intend to sell her apartment in Hong Kong, she expected to move most of her business abroad, to Europe or the United States. 'For the moment I have decided that this is my home, but it will depend on whether I can work here or not.' She had already sent many of her possessions abroad, fearful that she would be forbidden to export them after the handover. 'I am not a communist, but this is my country. It is a dilemma for me.' In

the past she had worried about her rights to move freely, to talk
freely and to read freely. 'They still matter to me, and I believe
that is true for many people in Hong Kong. Many people. Yes,
many . . .' Her voice tailed away. And if those rights were curtailed? Her dilemma would be resolved at once: 'I will leave.'

Hari Harilela and his family, now secure in the knowledge that
they could leave, intended to stay. 'I am really proud of Chris
Patten,' Harilela said. 'I knew he would do it. He is just one those
people who succeeds.' The 'ethnic minorities' were grateful for
their passports and Britain had finally fulfilled a 'legal and moral
duty'. In the words of another relative, the family was now 'so
happy' that a British government 'had not determined a policy on
the basis of racism'. Hari interrupted: 'The credit, if you don't
mind my saying so, goes to Chris Patten. He worked very, very
hard. Very sincerely.'

Then there was Jimmy Lai, the penniless immigrant who
became a multimillionaire publisher.

> Chris Patten gave people the sense of choice, the sense of
> what is right. He has raised their aspirations. And those the
> Chinese government will have to take into account if they
> want Hong Kong to be stable. After 1997, Hong Kong will
> not just be China's window on the world – it will be China's
> face to the world . . . I want to say one more thing. It is a
> shame to have your country colonised, but I have never had
> this sense of shame, because I have been a free man living in
> this colony. I have been blessed with a wonderful life.

He paused. His eyes filled with tears, and then he added: 'So
long, the British. May God bless you.' Occasionally what was said
behind the governor's back was worth hearing.

For the previous five years, Allen Lee had been a political
weathervane in LegCo for Hong Kong's most powerful tycoons.
Since 1995 he had also been an elected representative of the
people. Despite his failure ever to offer a significant criticism of
China, even he was disconcerted by C.H. Tung's apparent readiness to dismember the Bill of Rights and to curtail the rights of
assembly and demonstration on Beijing's behalf. Earlier in the

year Lee had raised the issue with the chief executive in person. C.H. had told him that his 'reforms' were not intended to take away the civil liberties currently enjoyed by the people of Hong Kong. Was the chief executive right or wrong? 'I won't use the words right or wrong,' said Lee. 'It is simply that he and I had a difference of opinion. I won't say whether he is right or wrong because on this kind of issue there is no clear-cut right or wrong.'

Such equivocation immediately before the handover testified to the genuflectory mood of the political old guard. Yet Allen Lee, like several of his peers, reacted with genuine dismay to the charge that he would soon be seen as a mere messenger for C.H. Tung. 'He is a very close friend of mine, but I do not agree with everything he does.' So would he resist any attempt by the new chief executive to stifle Hong Kong's freedom of expression? 'The Basic Law states very clearly that we have freedom of the press. It is up to the media people. They must not exercise self-censorship. If they do so in fear of Beijing's interference, then I do not think they should be in that profession.' So would he speak out against legislation banning media attacks on the Chinese leadership, which some of C.H. Tung's appointees seemed keen to accomplish? Allen Lee hesitated. 'Well, it depends on the issue. If we are simply talking about a slogan, then I would certainly not agree. I would say that that would contradict the Basic Law . . . If anybody tries to tinker with the Basic Law as far as these free-doms are concerned, I would not only oppose them, I would raise hell. If our chief executive thinks he has to make laws lim-iting the freedom of speech . . . he will embark on a very slippery slope, and I think support for him will slip.' But Allen Lee's con-fidence in C.H. Tung was, in his own words, 'absolute . . . I think he has no intention of making laws limiting the freedom of Hong Kong people . . . I don't think he is that kind of person.'

Like Allen Lee, Tsang Yok Sing had been disconcerted, or, as he put it, 'surprised' by C.H. Tung's eagerness to curtail individ-ual freedoms in the interests of public order. But, he said, he was even more surprised by the fact that 'the media and all those crit-ics who have never been slow to point out the mistakes of the Chinese government or those of us in the "pro–China" camp in

Hong Kong, were very, very kind to C.H. Tung'. He also declared himself surprised by C.H.'s accusation that Martin Lee and the Democratic party were hostile to China: 'Before that he didn't appear to be a really tough person, or high-handed.' The leader of the DAB party hoped that the new chief executive's 'tough line' was part of a strategy that would allow him to adopt a 'more moderate and conciliatory' tone after the handover. But if that was not his strategy; if he persisted on the present course? 'Well, we have our position. We have our principles. And if we believe he is doing something wrong, then we will speak up and try to stop it.'

Tsang Yok Sing's political adversary Martin Lee had already lost faith in C.H. Tung. According to the leader of the colony's most popular party, Hong Kong's future after the handover looked bleak. 'Big brother is already here and in control . . . If they press one button they can get one thing done; if they press another, another thing is done,' he noted. Resigned to the fact that C.H. Tung – 'a good man forced to do evil' – would seek to marginalise his influence, Martin Lee assumed that any future electoral system would be rigged to exclude the Democrats from effective power. He believed, too, that a cowed media would take their cue from Beijing and suppress coverage of him and his allies in the hope that they would thereby become 'non-persons'. He did not, however, intend to acquiesce in this plan.

> I cannot believe that, in the long term, the leaders of China can for ever stand in the way of democracy. The whole world is marching towards democracy, human rights and the rule of law – except Hong Kong, which is going in the opposite direction. But we don't have to worry: as long as we keep on fighting, the tide is in our favour, and one day democracy and human rights will come to China and return to Hong Kong.

In the meantime, he was prepared for trouble. 'I still don't think the chances of my being thrown into prison are high, though I can't rule that out altogether. We are prepared for the worst but hoping for the best,' he said. 'Of course my wife and son are worried. But there are times when people must make a choice between the community and their own families. The Hong Kong people need a voice, and we will be that voice.' He anticipated that the new chief executive would be unable to stifle free expression and protest.

> When you see people now demonstrating outside the New China News Agency, they chant slogans to give vent to very strong feelings. Then they go home and watch television or play mah-jong. If you don't allow them to express a very strong grievance, it might explode. So what Mr Tung is proposing to achieve by limiting the right to demonstrate will have the opposite effect. He will find out that you can suppress some people but you can't suppress all the people. And they will burst like a volcano.

The persistent failure of C.H. Tung to resist the blandishments of Beijing left Margaret Ng feeling 'desperate' about the future. At midnight on 30 June, her role as an elected representative of the legal profession in the Legislative Council would be abruptly terminated, and her place would be taken by a member of the provisional LegCo selected by China's appointees. 'What will I do? I imagine I will spend more time on my practice as a barrister,' she mused. 'But I will give some of my time to public issues. If I can still publish a column, I will publish a column. If I can still lobby, I will lobby. If there is a demonstration to join, I will join that.' Only two years earlier she had been ready to leave Hong Kong for London rather than endure life under China, but her unexpected electoral triumph in 1995 had made that option impossible, notwithstanding her impending removal from LegCo. 'My constituents elected me to a term of four years, and my obligation is still to them. I have to stay around. One of my duties to them must be to press for the early return of democratic elections.'

Margaret Ng predicted a collision between China and Hong Kong, but what she could not foresee was the scale of it or the character it would take. Invisible but fundamental, the replacement of one sovereign by another, she thought, could quickly change the political culture and, with that, the public sense of what constituted appropriate behaviour.

> I don't think that C.H. Tung knows at this point how strong the opposition is to him. I think he is a very sheltered man. I think he believes he has very wide support when he says we should have less politics . . . I think when he sees how naked the opposition against him is, he will be very angry. I don't think he will stay his hand. So I see confrontation.
>
> If you ask me what is best for Hong Kong, I would say the only viable future is to fight for autonomy, for democracy and for the rule of law, because otherwise we sink into darkness. But because I was brought up in the kind of society Hong Kong is, it is difficult for me to want that confrontation . . . We may have to pay a very severe price. It may bring on a great deal of very strong suppression from China. It may cost lives. So it is daunting for me to think of that price now.

At the same time Ng was encouraged by the resilience she found in the community. Although people who talked to her 'in the streets or in taxis' usually told her that it was 'unrealistic' to oppose the imposition of the provisional legislature by China, they invariably dissented when she countered, 'Would you then rather I shut up?' 'No, no, no, no,' they would say. 'It is all very well for us to keep quiet, but we want you to speak out.' She had no doubt that the underlying support for democracy and human rights was deeply felt.

> Perhaps a majority would not stand up – particularly if it means confrontation – but I think there may still be quite a lot of people who would be prepared to do that. I understand the fear and hesitation in their hearts. But even those who are not going to join demonstrations and express their views publicly want us to do it for them, and they will support us in spirit. And we – and this is not just those in LegCo who believe in democracy, but other bodies as well, like the legal profession – will not stand by and remain silent

when the rule of law is being undermined. And the future administration under C.H. Tung is going to be very intolerant. It will not admit that we may be right and he may be wrong.

Christine Loh, who had also found herself catapulted into public life by her own commitment to human rights and the impact of Patten's electoral reforms, spoke in less apocalyptic language but she shared Margaret Ng's foreboding. The outgoing governor, she believed, had opened up the political process.

I think politics is no longer for the elite few, and I am very concerned that the new administration will want to put it back the way it was. But how much of this genie can you put back into the bottle when Hong Kong people are now so used to all kinds of political pressure? It is now normal to have a demonstration. We have demonstrations about all sorts of things every day. That is now taken as very much the political culture here, and it is very good and dynamic compared to the rest of Asia. We are very, very different.

Although Loh knew that she was about to enter the 'political wilderness' she was not proposing to give up and tried to maintain her optimism. 'I hope I won't get snuffed out one way or another,' she said. Like Margaret Ng and Martin Lee, she was optimistic about the long term. In May 1997, she had founded a new political party, the Citizens Party, to focus on issues like the environment, equal opportunities and a range of other 'domestic' concerns sometimes overlooked by those democrats, like Martin Lee, for whom the relationship with China had been of pre-eminent if not all-consuming importance. 'I am going to have times, I am sure, when I will wish I was not doing this,' she admitted. 'I constantly get asked by members of my family, "Why are you doing this?" But I also feel a certain excitement that, in the historical sense, this really is a great step forward for China as a nation.'

Christine Loh, Margaret Ng and Martin Lee had not been uncritical of Patten's governorship. Ever suspicious of Britain's motives, they had been inclined to see a prospective sell-out to China in any of his public statements which failed their ambiguity test: the merest hint of equivocation had been enough to send them reaching into their extensive armoury of verbal grapeshot. Yet they admired the last governor. He had, said Martin Lee, 'stood up for Hong Kong whenever threats were made from Beijing, and he would respond immediately. That is something his predecessors would never have dared to do.' But more than this, all three of them agreed, he had transformed Hong Kong's 'political culture'. True, it was too late to make up for the time lost in the seventies and eighties by his ineffectual predecessors, but, at the very last moment, he had at least helped the people of Hong Kong to find their 'political identity' and potential, which, they believed, would be of lasting benefit. 'We now have open debate,' said Margaret Ng, 'more straightforward expressions of our differences of opinion. You can now criticise the government and the government can answer back. I think that has been very important for Hong Kong.' 'He has been good for Hong Kong,' Martin Lee concluded.

A few weeks before Patten's departure, Martin Lee and his colleagues had given him a farewell dinner at which Szeto Wah, the most radical of the Democrats, presented the governor with a piece of calligraphy he had painted himself. Punning with the symbols used to depict Beijing's denunciation of Patten as 'a criminal for a thousand years', Szeto Wah had transformed an abusive slogan into an affectionate tribute to a governor whose character and beliefs would 'charm and intoxicate for a thousand years'. Patten was greatly touched.

Tsang Yok Sing, the colony's most prominent ally of Chinese communism, did not entirely dismiss Patten's term of office, either. Inevitably, he condemned the last governor's role in the 'confrontation' with Beijing, judging him to have been a 'divisive' force who had polarised debate in Hong Kong. Discussions had too often been conducted 'in terms of black and white', he explained, a 'Western practice' which had not been good for 'our' community. But, echoing the words of his democratic counterparts, Tsang Yok Sing also volunteered approvingly that Patten had brought a 'new political culture' to Hong Kong.

'Nobody in Hong Kong has ever before seen such an eloquent politician,' he said thoughtfully. 'He has made the government more open and accountable. C.H. has a lot to learn from him.'

Allen Lee was less forgiving. In his valedictory assessment of the man who had removed him from the Executive Council almost five years earlier, Hong Kong's longest-serving politician commented:

> Mr Patten's tenure has been very, very unfortunate. He said when he arrived that he wanted to establish trust with the Chinese, and he failed to understand why, on his terms, that would be impossible. He has succeeded in establishing himself as a China-fighter, but that has certainly not been conducive to a smooth transition. We will long suffer what he has done for Hong Kong. He was a China-fighter, that's all. He has no other achievements.

Those sentiments were almost universally shared by members of the local and expatriate business community, whose leaders – with the exception of the Patten loyalist Simon Murray – had always managed to identify their individual and collective avarice with the presumed needs of the wider community which they affected to represent. In his quiet but insistent way – and, as ever, more in sorrow than in anger – Vincent Lo summed up the view of his fellow tycoons. 'I look forward to a new era for Hong Kong when we can do away with all this politics for a change, really start a new chapter and get on with life again.'

Despite – or perhaps because of – 'all this politics', Patten remained remarkably popular in Hong Kong. Within weeks of his departure, his favourable ratings in the polls, which still hovered around the 60 per cent mark – testified at least to a rare political talent. But on its own, as he would himself concede, public support for his leadership was not a sound basis on which to make even an interim assessment of his governorship. His critics claimed that this very support pointed to a cruel and deplorable lack of judgement on his part. By encouraging the illusion that political freedom and democracy on the Western model was a universal right from which no member of the community should be excluded, he had, they claimed, indulged himself at the expense of the Hong Kong people. China's probable retaliation, springing from an atavistic fear of subversion from the West, was likely to be severe, and certainly harsher than it would have been if the governor had made it his business to reconcile the community to the realities of Chinese sovereignty. Instead of surrendering to the demands of Martin Lee and the Democrats, he should have faced them down, regardless of how unpopular it made him.

This line of argument was based on a dubious premise: that in the post-Tiananmen Square era it would have been possible to govern Hong Kong as if popular opinion could be ignored. From the viewpoint of Government House, the implicit assumption that Patten could have overridden the electoral mandate secured by Martin Lee and his allies before his arrival was inherently implausible. To assume that the forces of democracy would have submitted to Beijing's 'bottom line' without a sustained struggle appeared preposterous. It seemed more likely by far that the 'debate' would have spilled on to the streets, which would have had an incalculable impact on Hong Kong's political and economic stability.

As we have seen, throughout his governorship, Patten's fiercest antagonist was Sir Percy Cradock. The way this former diplomat chose to deliver his judgement on Patten – through a battery of media interviews and articles – sharply diminished his reputation among those of his peers who felt that the former civil servant should have resisted the temptation to 'go public' so damagingly during such a delicate period. However, his views had a seductive clarity which lent them a carapace of intellectual rigour beneath which others of a more primitive cast of mind were able to shelter. According to Cradock, the governor's 'incompetence' sprang from a deplorable failure to engage in 'co-operative' dialogue with China and the pursuance instead of a self-promoting and destructive path of 'confrontation'. Cradock's corrosive judgement hung on twin assumptions that were rarely questioned by his acolytes: first, that Patten had chosen 'confrontation', and secondly, that 'co-operation' would have secured an acceptable agreement with Beijing.

The evidence for the first assumption was at best tenuous. Certainly the governor failed to 'consult' Beijing before announcing his electoral proposals, and Beijing did react with fury. But had his approach been 'confrontational'? Patten had made it clear in advance that his blueprint for electoral reform was negotiable and that he was anxious to discuss the entire package with China accordingly. Indeed, lengthy – though fruitless – negotiations eventually took place. To the detached observer, if not to Cradock, the word 'consultation' had clearly acquired a quite different meaning in China's diplomatic lexicon from that which usually described this form of dialogue between sovereign states. As understood by Beijing – and apparently by Cradock as well – the process of 'consultation' presupposed an acknowledgement that China had a right of veto. To consult, in this context, meant to secure prior consent, in the absence of which, the supplicant (in this case Britain) would be unable to proceed. In short, though the term 'consultation' had a sinuous charm, the process it described was, a priori, a sham. If refusing to participate in such a charade constituted 'confrontation', then Patten would be obliged to plead guilty.

In any event, the second of Cradock's underlying assumptions, that 'co-operation' – his neatly alliterative alternative to 'confrontation' – would better have protected Hong Kong's 'way of life', is no less fragile than the first. That 'co-operation' on the terms accepted by Cradock would have secured a settlement with China is hardly in doubt. It would have delivered an electoral system to Beijing's liking, a Bill of Rights similarly amended to limit Hong Kong's pre-existing freedoms and an agreement not to dismantle any of the draconian measures that were incompatible with the Bill of Rights. A 'co-operative' governor would have stayed silent in the face of threats to curtail the freedom of expression in Hong Kong; silent about the gerrymandered procedures for the selection of the chief executive and at the hint of an impasse on any other issue. He would have crumbled before the Chinese threat to forbid the major construction projects, and he would have made no allusion at any time to the character of the Chinese regime. But what would he thereby have achieved for Hong Kong that would not have been achieved in any case?

To put the matter the other way round: if, as all the evidence suggests, China was not willing to interpret the concept of 'one country, two systems' in such a way as to allow Hong Kong to preserve and develop its existing rights, freedoms and aspirations, what would 'co-operation' have delivered that 'confrontation' failed to provide? This question acquired an ever sharper edge as the noose of the future tightened around Hong Kong, and Britain's critics there inveighed anew against past 'betrayals' which had left them deprived of their democratic rights and dangerously exposed to the vagaries of the volatile Chinese regime. The case against Britain focused once more, but with growing resentment, on the period (covered in Chapter 6) between the signing of the Joint Declaration in 1984 and the decision by the British government in late 1987 not to introduce direct elections the following year. Allegations made at the time by Martin Lee, and later by an American journalist, Mark Roberti – that Britain had 'betrayed' the colony by colluding with the Chinese government in 1987 to thwart the expressed will of the Hong Kong people – were given renewed currency in a *Dispatches* documentary for Channel 4, 'A Very British Betrayal', broadcast in the spring of 1997.

At this last-ditch point in Britain's colonial history, it is clearly important to establish whether or not this charge is valid. If it is true, then Britain's reputation, not least in Hong Kong, is likely to be permanently tarnished. If it is false, then a festering sore can be healed, those who are innocent will have the cloud of suspicion removed from them and Britain's honour will be redeemed. In the absence of official documents it is impossible to establish, beyond peradventure, what happened and why, or who said what to whom and when, not least because the relevant British diplomats have been remarkably reticent about this crucial period. For example, the self-confessed overlord of Sino–British relations at this time, Sir Percy Cradock (who has written extensively about his 'secret' missions to Beijing in 1990), does not offer any explanation for Britain's postponement of the introduction of direct elections in 1988, after they had been proposed in the 1984 White Paper and enthusiastically endorsed by ministers at that time. In *Experiences of China*, he refers obliquely to the fact that there was a 'further review of the situation in 1987', and to a 'Sino–Soviet understanding' about the British decision to introduce 'ten directly elected legislature seats in 1991'. And that is all.

However, in the closing weeks of British rule, a final attempt to penetrate this protective shell has made it possible – at least in outline – to piece together some of the key elements of what happened before and after the 'consultation' of the Hong Kong people about direct elections which took place in the late summer of 1987. The available facts provide compelling, if not conclusive, evidence that the charge of 'betrayal', though emotive, is by no means ill founded.

The process seems to have begun at the second meeting of the Joint Liaison Group, in November 1985. The Chinese were in suspicious mood. In response to their warning that the People's Republic would not tolerate the establishment of direct elections in 1988, the British side reassured the Chinese that the 1984 White Paper proposal to that effect should not be interpreted as a commitment. On the contrary, the government would decide how to proceed only after soliciting the views of the Hong Kong people and taking into account other relevant factors. No deal was struck at this meeting, but it is clear that the two sides reached an understanding of each other's position which was to have a significant impact on Britain's strategy thereafter.

Fourteen months later, in March 1987, Sir Robin McLaren, the senior negotiator in the JLG, reiterated the 1985 stance and, for good measure, informed his opposite number, Ke Zaishuo, that the British government would, in any case, move towards direct elections only with extreme caution. Thus encouraged, China maintained the pressure. In the following months, they used every formal and informal channel to insist repeatedly that the introduction of direct elections in 1988 – even for a small minority of the LegCo seats – would constitute an unacceptable violation of the principle of 'convergence' to which the British negotiators had keenly assented after the Joint Declaration. In response, McLaren and other Foreign Office officials – including the governor, Sir David Wilson – not only confirmed Britain's commitment to 'convergence' but volunteered that the British side had no preconceived views about the desirability of direct elections in 1988, or indeed at any time before the handover. And they went a stage further, promising that, although the decision would be influenced by the outcome of the public consultation process, it would by no means be bound by it.

As the negotiations continued into the summer, the foreign secretary, Sir Geoffrey Howe, intervened. He suggested to the Chinese foreign minister, Wu Xueqian, that Beijing might care to indicate that the Chinese had no objection in principle to the creation of direct elections at some point after the promulgation of the Basic Law, which was scheduled for 1990. This, Howe intimated, would go a long way towards dampening down Hong Kong's impatient demand for more democracy in 1988. At this stage, there was no specific commitment from either side, but the seeds of a secret deal, nurtured by nods and winks, were starting to sprout.

Before long this Sino–British understanding became explicit. The Chinese implied that they would indeed be willing to make a pronouncement in favour of direct elections at a later date, but only if the British could undertake not to introduce such measures in 1988. As both sides now acknowledged, the only obstacle to this agreeable outcome was the will of the Hong Kong people – who, of course, had no idea that such talks were taking place.

The formal process of public 'consultation' began in July 1987 and was due to end three months later. It soon emerged that there was a groundswell in favour of direct elections in general and, specifically, of the 1988 start date. Informed of this not only by their own sources in Hong Kong but directly by British officials, the Chinese became increasingly agitated. Through the JLG and in private meetings, they began to press the British on how the authorities in Hong Kong would respond if – as now seemed possible – it were to emerge that a majority did indeed favour the establishment of direct elections in 1988. At a JLG meeting in London, Robin McLaren used stronger language than ever to make it clear that, while the British could not guarantee to veto this prospect, they shared China's antipathy to it. And, on Britain's behalf, he made yet another move towards Beijing by reassuring his opposite number in the JLG that, regardless of the result of the survey, the British government would not even consider introducing direct elections in 1988 without first consulting the Chinese.

As the consultation process intensified, the British, too, became increasingly concerned about the strength of opinion in Hong Kong. The foreign secretary had made it clear that the survey had to be genuine and open, but this did not prevent other British officials from encouraging Beijing to urge their allies in Hong Kong to make their own views known on an 'individual' rather than a collective basis. As we have seen (pages 107–8), those 'individual' submissions, in the form of preprinted letters distributed by these self-same allies, were to play a decisive part in the distortion of evidence eventually engineered by the Hong Kong government.

In late September, a few days before the end of the consultation period, Sir David Wilson made an official visit to Beijing, where he met leading members of the Chinese government. In a meeting with Zhou Nan, he discussed the Survey Office report in some detail. Although he indicated that the preliminary results did indeed show a majority in favour of democracy in 1988, albeit not a substantial one, he explored the implications of this in terms which led the Chinese to conclude that the British government would nonetheless not feel obliged to abide by this verdict. Zhou Nan's impression that the two sides had now reached a private understanding to this effect was doubtless reinforced when Wilson ventured that, in this case, a significant section of the community – the influential middle classes – would be gravely disappointed. It was, the governor intimated, a situation which would have to be handled with extreme delicacy.

Wilson stressed that the terms of his understanding with Zhou Nan were both preliminary and conditional, but they turned out to be final, if not entirely unconditional. In November, as the Hong Kong government considered the evidence, McLaren followed Wilson to Beijing. At a meeting with Ke Zaishuo, he reported that the full survey report had confirmed the governor's initial assessment in September. A majority of the 135,000 'individual' submissions expressed opposition to the direct elections in 1988, but more than 230,000 individuals had signed petitions advocating them. McLaren did not feel obliged to point out the self-evident truth that the survey had produced an embarrassingly large majority in favour of the 1984 White Paper proposal. However, echoing Wilson, he did voice concern that a significant number of those who endorsed the 1988 option came from the middle and managerial classes, on whose commitment to stay in the territory Hong Kong's future was so dependent.

Early in December 1987, Wilson returned to Beijing. Arguing now that the final statistics had failed to show a clear majority, he nonetheless reminded his Chinese hosts that every independent opinion poll had done so, and confessed that he had not anticipated that the signature campaign would deliver quite such a huge number of supporters of the proposal. In an oblique reference to his own administration's decision to turn the statistics upside down, he reported ruefully that some individuals had accused the Hong Kong government of rigging the figures in order to achieve the result the Chinese wanted.

Wilson then confirmed the secret deal the two sides had struck a few months earlier. As the British had already half promised, the White Paper on democratic development which was due to be published in February 1988 would defer the introduction of direct elections as long as the Basic Law included such a commitment for after 1997. Wilson intimated that the Hong Kong government would hope to isolate its more vociferous critics by promising a limited number of directly elected seats for the 1991 LegCo elections without violating the principle of 'convergence'. It was very neat, and precisely what Zhou Nan must have been hoping to hear. He responded sympathetically. It was, he did not need to say, the final triumph of 'co-operation'.

With the benefit of hindsight, it is hard to exaggerate the implications of this outcome. A 'virtual' historian might judge that if direct elections had been introduced in 1988, the prospects for the survival of democracy after 1997 would have been immeasurably enhanced. With what would by now have been the experience of three 'direct' elections and almost ten years in which to bed down this novel form of accountability, even the most antagonistic tycoon and the most dubious civil servant might have discovered that democracy was not incompatible with economic prosperity or executive efficiency. Moreover, the establishment of direct elections would have been accomplished before Tiananmen Square, at a point when the Chinese, though suspicious, were far less paranoid about 'subversion' than they subsequently became. In any case, it is almost inconceivable that even the Chinese would have been willing to defy the world by openly dismembering a democratic process which self-evidently enjoyed widespread support in the community.

Almost inconceivable, but not entirely so. Doubtless Lord Howe, Sir Percy Cradock, Lord Wilson and Sir Robin McLaren will in due course provide their own explanation for the 'betrayal' of which they stand accused by liberal opinion in Hong Kong. It may be that they will claim a victory; that the trade-off with China secured Beijing's commitment in the Basic Law to the introduction of direct elections after the restoration of Chinese sovereignty. They might indeed argue that this could not have been achieved in any other way and that the price of their success was having to conceal these realities from the people of Hong Kong.

It is too early to judge whether some such justification – or any other – will find general favour. In the meantime, when pressed for a reaction, officials in Hong Kong were unwilling to discount the plausibility of the above account of what happened in 1987. In the absence of any better explanation, the former foreign secretary and the officials then under his authority will find themselves open to the charge that the consultation exercise over which they presided was indeed the sham their detractors have alleged it to have been. They will be accused variously of arrogance, cynicism and dishonourable conduct. The bitterness in Hong Kong will fester and Britain's reputation there will be indelibly stained by the mark of appeasement.

Against this background, any judgement of the last governor must take into account not only what he set out to achieve, but what it was possible to achieve. In 1992, Patten had hoped to accomplish a delicate manoeuvre: first, to engineer the smooth transfer of sovereignty from Britain to China according to the principles laid out in the Joint Declaration and the Basic Law; secondly, to prepare the people of Hong Kong for that future; and thirdly, to extricate Britain from its last significant colony in a dignified and honourable fashion. On the first count, he failed. The 'through train' hit the buffers, and on 1 July 1997 the provisional legislature will replace the Legislative Council which was elected in September 1995 under the Patten 'rules'. The provisional legislature lacks credibility in Hong Kong and abroad (to the extent that, when C.H. Tung indicated in May that its formal inauguration would form part of the handover celebrations in the early hours of 1 July, he was notified that the American secretary of state, Madeleine Albright, would in that case not attend the proceedings). Nonetheless the new body will be charged to rubber-stamp proposals for its own replacement with a gerrymandered Legislative Council which will be structured to ensure that its deliberations will not prove 'subversive'. However, in the face of China's obduracy, Patten's failure was effectively preordained. To have been 'co-operative' might have secured a 'smooth transfer' (though even that is open to question); it would most certainly have required Britain to surrender to China's perverted notion of the concept of 'one country, two systems'.

As it was, no one was able to identify any tangible benefits that would have accrued either to Hong Kong or to Britain if Patten had succumbed to the policy of 'co-operation'. In economic terms, the 'golden goose' was as fecund as ever. Growth was steady. The property market was booming. All the construction projects which Beijing had threatened to veto were on course, albeit marginally delayed. Nor was there any evidence that Britain's direct or indirect trade with China had suffered as a consequence of the Triple Violator's sundry impertinences. Patten had certainly underestimated the intensity of Beijing's animus against him, and to this limited extent, he overplayed his hand. Ironically, however, the only economic 'punishment' inflicted on Britain by China bore no relation to Hong Kong at all. In the second week of May 1997, China cancelled a trade mission from the United Kingdom scheduled for the end of the month. Officially described by Beijing officials as a 'postponement to a more opportune moment', the decision was made in retaliation to Britain's endorsement of a UN resolution in April criticising China's record on human rights.

So what of the second criterion by which Patten might expect to be judged? How well prepared were the people of Hong Kong for what they were to face once Chinese sovereignty took effect? Certainly they had been steeled by the conflict between their governor and his adversaries, not only within the colony itself but in London and Beijing. As a result of his commitment to 'open' government, they were sharply aware of the issues which were supposed to underpin the concept of 'one country, two systems'. The transparency with which, for the first time in their history, a governor had conducted diplomacy on their behalf, had both exposed them to the arguments and included them in the dialogue. Again and again they had endorsed his stance, despite the verbal abuse Beijing had rained upon his head. By no stretch of a patronising imagination could they now be thought to be 'sleepwalking' into the unknown. Yet there was no evidence of panic; no rush for the boats. By the same token, romantic delusions were notable by their absence: to depict Patten as a latterday Robespierre urging the mob to self-immolation at the barricades in the name of 'direct elections' would not convince. Late in the day – unforgivably late – Britain, under Patten's 'reign', had encouraged the people of Hong Kong to participate in the political process on similar terms to those enjoyed by their counterparts in civilised societies. Could it possibly be argued – except by anti-democrats or communist cadres or purblind tycoons – that this either ran against the interests of the people or, in some unspecified way, threatened their prospects after the handover?

The third criterion was Britain's credibility in the world. In the United States, the European Union and south-east Asia, the last governor had been under close scrutiny – often closer, indeed, than at Westminster or in the British media. In most eyes Patten had come to be regarded as a belated advocate of important principles and values. In America, in particular, where anti-colonial sentiment and moral certainty formed a potent alliance, Patten's public declaration in support of democracy and human rights, combined with his readiness to 'confront' China on matters of principle, confirmed the impression that Britain was, in the end, mindful of past obligations and future duties. The passports issue was a case in point. As Patten entered the final days of his governorship, he could be confident that the international community would judge his tenure of office with favour and thus with benefit to Britain's reputation and interests, especially in the emerging democracies of south-east Asia.

Patten's critics, notably Sir Percy Cradock, had claimed or implied that his strategy had been driven by arrogance or by the frustrated ambition of an aspiring prime minister. According to this thesis, Patten used his time in Hong Kong to parade his admittedly formidable talents before an admiring audience in Britain which would, as a result, welcome him home as the nation's future saviour. This argument was not only vindictive but jejune, revealing more about the judges than the judged. Patten did not lack ambition, but he was never in its thrall. As a pragmatic politician, he was uncomfortable deploying the language of morality except in relation to personal behaviour; he preferred to talk of decency or, occasionally, of honour. Yet he did believe that politics had a moral dimension, and he felt that strongly in relation to Hong Kong. The evidence makes it preposterous to suggest that he conducted himself as the governor of Hong Kong with an eye on the main chance at Westminster.

In the wake of the humiliating and historic defeat of his party in the general election on 1 May 1997, Patten's allies in politics and many Conservatives throughout the country bemoaned his absence from the contest to succeed John Major as leader. Patten did not allow himself to indulge in the 'what if' school of contemporary history. From the moment of his own defeat in Bath in the 1992 election he had refused to participate in any of the schemes cooked up for him by his supporters for a return to Westminster. Adamant that he would remain in Hong Kong for the duration, he was well aware that the longer he was away from London, the less likely it would be that he could successfully rejoin British politics. In the absence of any self-delusion about his prospects of re-entry, he had been liberated from the constraints and disappointments that such ambition might otherwise have imposed. Although he did not entirely rule out a return to the British political stage, the result of the election served merely to confirm his judgement. Eighteen months earlier, he had confided to friends his intention to stay away from London after the handover and to spend the rest of 1997 writing in the seclusion of his home in France. Two weeks after the election (when he was in London to meet Tony Blair) he confirmed that intention. Despite the entreaties of some former colleagues, who chose to believe that he alone could save the party from itself, he reiterated that for the foreseeable future he would stay well away from Westminster.

Chris Patten had fought a sustained public and private battle to carry through his project for Hong Kong: publicly against the Chinese and a powerful minority in Hong Kong; privately against an influential number of politicians, diplomats and officials in London. It had been a gruelling and often lonely five years. The scale of his purpose and the character of his responsibility had required rare qualities of leadership: a clear vision, an abnormal resolve and a profound sense of public duty. The last governor of Hong Kong had arrived in the colony as a politician, hopeful of success. He would depart as a statesman, knowing failure as well as victory, but in dignity and with honour.

Sources and
Further Reading

U nless otherwise attributed, the quotations in *The Last Governor* are taken from conversations with the author. Almost all of these interviews, amounting to several hundred hours and more than a million words, were recorded on tape. A handful of my interviewees wished to protect their anonymity. With this exception, the transcripts of all interviews (which were conducted in parallel for this book and for the BBC series *The Last Governor*) are to be lodged in the William Mong Collection at the University of Hong Kong, where they will be available to researchers.

For background material, I have also drawn on a range of second-hand but authoritative sources, of which the following have been the most instructive. For my account of nineteenth- and early twentieth-century Hong Kong, I am indebted to Frank Welsh's *History of Hong Kong* (HarperCollins, 1993). As a scholarly, perceptive and entertaining guide through the thickets of that period, Welsh has no peer. Robert Cottrell's meticulous and balanced account of what he refers to as the 'secret diplomacy of imperial retreat' in *The End of Hong Kong* (John Murray, 1993) will be invaluable to those who seek to understand the crucial events leading up to the Joint Declaration and its consequences. Percy Cradock's *Experiences of China* (John Murray, 1994) is a vivid and elegant autobiographical portrait of a dramatic period in Sino–British relations, when, as the chief architect of British policy, Cradock was perpetually in the eye of the storm. Steve Tsang's *Democracy Shelved* (OUP, 1988) is a detailed examination of postwar British policy towards Hong Kong. His view of

Britain's alleged perfidy is cautiously phrased but leans towards the trenchant certainties of Mark Roberti's *The Fall of Hong Kong*, which is subtitled 'China's Triumph and Britain's Betrayal' (John Wiley, 1994). Roberti draws on his own experience as an American correspondent in Hong Kong and readers may detect an anti-British as well as an anti-colonial bias in his analysis. However, at least in the case of Britain's failure to advance the cause of democratic reform in the late 1980s, his conclusions bear close examination. In this respect, as I argue in the Epilogue to *The Last Governor*, the evidence appears to be on Roberti's side.

The media summaries produced by the Hong Kong Government Information Service have provided a useful digest of news and views culled from the principal English-language and Chinese-language daily press, and the Hong Kong Yearbooks published by the Hong Kong government supplied exhaustive annual facts and figures.

The reports produced by Amnesty International and AsiaWatch, who monitor human-rights violations in China (and Hong Kong) with diligence, are sources of vital knowledge.

I have also quoted briefly from David Owen's *Time to Declare* (Michael Joseph, 1991), *Excellency, Your Gap is Growing* by John Walden (Hong Kong, 1987), Ian Fleming's *Thrilling Cities* (1963), John le Carré's *The Honourable Schoolboy* (Random House, 1977) and Jan Morris's *Among the Cities* (Penguin Books, 1985).

INDEX